DUCKS, NEWBURYPORT

Lucy Ellmann

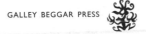
GALLEY BEGGAR PRESS

First published in 2019
By Galley Beggar Press Limited
37 Dover Street
Norwich NR2 3LG

Text design and typesetting by Tetragon, London
Printed in the UK by TJ International Ltd, Padstow, Cornwall

A CIP record for this book is available from the British Library

ISBN paperback 9781910296967
ISBN limited edition 9781910296974

For

Bathsheba

and

Pepito

No country perhaps in the world is better watered with limpid streams and navigable rivers than the United States of America, and no people better deserve those advantages, or are calculated to make a proper use of them than her industrious and adventurous citizens.

ZADOK CRAMER

I represent a field you are passing between Grover's Corners, Ohio, and Parkersburg, Ohio. In this field there are 51 gophers, 206 field mice, 6 snakes and millions of bugs, insects, ants, and spiders. All in their winter sleep.

THORNTON WILDER

When you are all sinew, struggle and solitude, your young – being soft, plump, vulnerable – may remind you of prey.

To be woken, biffed in the face by the paw of a sleeping kitten. The damp furry closeness in the crowded den sometimes gave her an over-warm sensation akin to nausea, or boredom. Snaking her long limbs as far as space permitted, she longed to be out on her winding path, ranging wide in search of deer. In her dreams she slaughtered whole herds. She sought that first firm clasp on a stag's neck, the swift parting of its hide, her mouth filling at last with what was hot and wet and necessary.

For all of life is really recoil and leap, leap and recoil.

Alertness was her new mode, but the cubs' easy slumber was contagious. She was always briefly astounded, on waking, by their continued presence. They troubled her, they were so needy: if she died, they would die too, and soon. And she would forget them. But for now, she belonged to them. They were not so much a conscious concern as the whole purpose of her being – lives engendered by her body, created inside her and released through pain and panting upon the world. She had borne them, and now she fed them with her milk. They were part of her still.

For the first week they were sprawling, crawling mush to her, demanding gentleness, forbearance, cleanups. The air shook with the vibrations of her purr. She learnt to maneuver her way round their wriggling forms with new steps. The more they squirmed, the more adroitly she had to dodge them.

She never left them for more than half an hour. The mere thought of the kittens bleating and scrabbling around back in the den diminished her resolve, made her less surefooted, ruined her joy in the kill.

She went hungry, even sank to eating the snowshoe hares that ventured near the den. And, once, a disappointing merganser, all feather, feet, beak and bone.

Her infant cubs, drifting back to sleep midway across each other's backs, never knew how long she was gone, or how far from them she roamed. She might still be inside the den somewhere, just an inch out of reach. In hope, they dragged themselves over to the wall like legless seal pups, their short stubby tails nothing like the muscly ropes they would later become. They toured the den in slow circles, chirping enticingly, feeling out for any sign of her, just the tip of her giant paw or long whiskers. Longing for her warmth, her tongue, her strong sleek rump, they sought her with determination, for they too were hunters, blind and strong and unafraid. Too brave to despair.

. . . .

The fact that the raccoons are now banging an empty yogurt carton around on the driveway, the fact that in the early morning stillness it sounds like gunshots, the fact that, even in fog, with *ice* on the road and snow banks blocking their vision, people are already zooming around our corner, the site of many a minor accident, the fact that a guy in a pickup once accidentally skidded into our *garage*, and next time it could be our *house*, or a *child*, Wake Up Picture Day, dicamba, Kleenex, the fact that a pickup truck killed Dilly, the fact that she'd successfully dodged cars for three whole years, the fact that she knew all about cars, but during that time the traffic grew, the fact that it's crazee now, the fact that after Dilly got killed, the kids painted a big warning sign with a big black cat on it and stuck it right by the fence, but nobody notices it, the fact that they're all going too fast to *see* it, ♫ *When the cat died we had catnip tea* ♫, the fact that failure to yield causes one in five accidents in Ohio, the fact that car crashes are up twenty percent since 2009, haw tree, buckeye, black walnut, hickory, butternut, the fact that Stacy's old enough to handle the road but the other kids aren't, the fact that a little boy was killed in his bed just the other day by a skidding car crashing into his house, Ben asleep, the fact that there are two cardinals right now in the lilac tree, brown sugar, the fact that eleven percent of Americans carry on driving when the fuel-tank-empty light comes on, the fact that, boy, you'd think it'd be more like eighty percent, Ronny, chicken feed, the fact that there are macrophages, the fact that I dreamt I flew all the way to India to get a teaspoon of cinnamon but when I got home I realized I needed flaked almonds too, security, holding pattern, go figure, not in my back yard, the fact that we have to do our taxes and try to remember every little bit of income and expenditure, the fact that there was more of the latter than the former, Family Dollar, Zyker's, password, user-name, "Your card is now active and ready to use," the fact that not only do we have to calculate our income and expenditure but we gotta figure out how to get *more* money, and keep on getting money till we're dead, Medicare For All, M4A, the fact that by the time Leo's old enough to get Social Security it probably won't even cover the price of a ham sandwich, much less a bottle of wine, the fact that we're in for a wineless old age, oi veh, OJ, the fact that Leo has to go to Philly tomorrow and I'm not so good on my own, the fact that Ben knows so much for such a little kid, maybe *too* much, the fact that he says drugs work on a molecular level that can be assessed using logarithms and Schild curves, but I just pop 'em and leave the rest to chance, break-fast, alarm clock, laundry, Spinbrush, the fact that we have to have a cocktail party and I don't know what to wear, the fact that the only fun part is deciding on the canapés, cocktails, cock-a-doodle-do, cock, oh my word, the fact that words just pop into my head like that, dear me, the fact that I've got to get the dough going for the cinnamon rolls, the fact that at least we're not having any more dinner parties, the fact that I put my foot down there, ♫ *Your feet's too big* ♫, feat of strength, footloose and fancy-free, the fact that our parties are always a big flop anyway because the kids come down in the middle in their onesies and kill all conversation with cuteness, the fact that they look like polar bear cubs and they know it, the fact that sometimes they end up serv-ing the drinks too, the fact that I don't know what Prof. Pranump would make of that, especially since she's teetotal, tea, Triscuits, Ritz crackers, Saltines, Fritos, Doritos, Frito-Lay, Planters peanuts, Blue Diamond smoked almonds, Prohibition, *Some Like It Hot*, the fact that soon polar bears and walruses will have nowhere to go, because the polar ice is melting, cheese and pineapple on sticks, cheddar cheese logs, school bus, ground cardamom, dried cherries, zest, the fact that walruses can swim for four hundred miles, sure, but not *forever*, for Pete's sake, the fact that animals don't pride themselves on irrationality the way we do, the fact that, according to Ben, half the mammals on the planet will disappear by 2050, two hundred species a day or something like that, the fact that Ben says everybody on earth will soon be starving or suffocating or dying of SARS or Ebola or H5N1, the fact that H5N1 only has to mutate a few more times and we're all goners, so maybe it was all for nothing, human achievement, but before that happens, we still have to do our taxes, and Leo needs to fix the garage door, the fact that it keeps sticking, missing button, bathroom grouting, the fact that Stacy would probably *approve* of a global pandemic, as long as it included *us*, her nearest and dearest, the fact that I don't know why we released our poor little terrapins into the pond at Northwestern, the fact that we thought they'd be happy there, free, the fact that nobody ever told us they were *tropical* terrapins, the fact that we actually thought they'd like swimming free, in that freezing cold pond, the fact that I saw a dead dog with rabies there once, near the pond, so theoretically our turtles could have gotten rabies first, before they froze to death, the fact that maybe we weren't much good as pet owners, the bumblebee at Bread Loaf, the fact that what we liked best was going to the Big Building, where Daddy worked, because sometimes you got a free pencil, the fact that we loved climbing on the big painted rock outside, the fact that there was this great big boulder right in front of the building, the fact that I don't know if somebody dragged the thing there or it was just there when they built the university and they couldn't get rid of it, the fact that the paint was interestingly chipped and you could see how many layers it had, blue, red, white, yellow, green, Chris Rock, the fact that I think they painted it a new color every year or so, Wolfgang Amadeus Mozart, the fact that Mozart had a starling, the fact that female starlings sing too, not just male starlings, murmurations, Ohio Blue Tip matches, phone call, a big ask, the fact that I don't know where my cell phone is, the fact that I *never* know where it is, the fact that cell phones are always trying to escape their owners, the fact that there are earthquakes and tornadoes and tsunamis and volcanic eruptions, the fact that where did I see that red velvet cushion with gold trim, Gillian's tall bird with sequins, felt and sequins, Christmastime, alone with Mommy in their bedroom at twilight, twi-night double header, sidewinder, sidecar, sidelines, left field, the fact that Stacy never mentions Frank, well, not to me anyway, Rex the Walkie-Talkie Robot Man, the fact that I don't think she misses him at all, *Reader's Digest*, Hardee's on 2nd Street, Arby's, Hy-Vee, Mommy and Daddy's bedroom in the late afternoon, the fact that I always liked sequins on felt, the fact that I don't think Stacy minds having a stepdad at all, the fact that these days most kids have half brothers and sisters, so they must be pretty used to it, the fact that all in all we're really just a normal Joy, Pledge, Crest, Tide, Dove, Woolite, Palmolive, Clorox, Rolaids, Pepto-Bismol, Alka-Seltzer, Desitin, Advil, Aleve, Tylenol, Anacin, Bayer, Excedrin, Vitamin C, Kleenex, Kotex, Tampax, Altoid, Barbazol, Almay, Revlon, Cetaphil, Right Guard, Old Spice, Gillette, Q-Tip, Johnson & Johnson, Vaseline, Listerine, Head 'n' Shoulders, Safe Owl, Eagle Brand, Jolly Green Giant, Land O'Lakes, Lucerne, Sealtest, Clover, Blue Bonnet, Half & Half, Snyder, VanCamp, Wish-Bone, French's, Skyline, Empress, Gerber, Nabisco, Heinz, Kraft, Quaker Oats, Sunkist, Purina, Vlasic, Oreo, Shredded Wheat, Arm & Hammer, Jell-O, Pez, Sara Lee, Chock Full o' Nuts, Libby's, Pepperidge Farm, Fleischmann's, Morton, General Mills, King Arthur, Bell's, Reese's Pieces kind of household like everybody else, "Houston, we got a problem," even *with* all these macrophages and tardigrades sneaking around, whatever they are, the fact that it's kind of lonely getting up in the early hours with all the macrophages and tardigrades, "Buck up," the fact that if you get two Land O'Lakes packets and cut them and fold them just right, it looks like the milk-maid's knees are her, well, like she's got great big, great big, the fact that I don't know why I'm thinking about *that*, for heaven's sake, the fact that there's a tiny lake called Lake Yueyaquan in the middle of the Chinese desert, the fact that why do I even know that, walruses swimming, the fact that they found a penguin fossil of a five-foot-tall penguin, the fact that it was *gigantic*, and all the paleontologist could say was "Cool," my missing earring, Ben's water project, Ben asleep, Gillian asleep, the fact that I'm surprised Jake isn't clomping down the stairs yet, sucking on his baby blanket, my Little Pillow, Mount Rushmore, President Taft, the fact that the best thing about having four kids is that other people leave you in peace, the fact that I hide behind the kids too much probably, more than is strictly necessary, soccer moms, Tiger Moms, baseball, Magic 8 Ball, the fact that nobody really wants to see you if you've got kids, even your best friends, Nanya, Anat, Jess, the fact that they all just assume I'm so preoccupied with the kids I can't think straight, and they're right, pretty much, most of the time, fireflies, damselflies, hoverflies, fruit flies, FOOSH injury, the fact that I don't even know Jess's address anymore, the fact that the problem is you drop all these people, all your old friends, and then the kids leave home and then where'll you be, bumblebees, hummingbirds, red-winged blackbirds, loons, the fact that Ben says there are at least sixty billion earthlike planets, just in the Milky Way alone, and I wonder if motherhood exists on all of them, the fact that I wonder if Land O'Lakes exists on them, polar bears, iceberg, lettuce, the Titanic, the fact that the Bourgogne disaster was maybe worse than the Titanic, though more people died in the Titanic disaster, the fact that the Titanic only had enough lifeboats for a third of its passengers, and nobody knew how to lower them or anything, the fact that that's just silly, the fact that the wreck of the Titanic still lies three and a half miles deep, the fact that it's way down there, nervous wreck, the fact that I like Lucerne butter better than Land O'Lakes, AEP, ATM, AA, AAA, A-AAAABA Locksmiths, IBM, ICBM, BMs, the fact that we eat too much meat, though Leo says we eat too many *carbs*, the fact that every few years they decide noodles are fatal, but I don't buy that, the fact that noodles seem pretty innocent to me, overall, and handy with kids, the fact that they never mention the dangers of Krispy Kremes and hog roasts, stranger danger, hydrangea, the fact that you wouldn't think you'd need the word "hydrangea" all that much but it's good to have it in your arsenal, the fact that it's the sort of word that's really pretty embarrassing not to have on the tip of your tongue when you need it, the fact that it's kind of like forgetting the name Hamlet, or Cher or Miley Cyrus or something, the fact that the Irish are "drunk on remembrance," the fact that folks just *expect* you to know certain things like the word hydrangea, they do, or some people do anyway, hydrangea, *hydrangea*, and if you don't they think you're weird, the fact that I should just write the darn thing down somewhere so I don't forget it again, but then I'll forget where I wrote it, and anyway I don't think I will forget "hydrangea" again, the fact that I've learnt my lesson on that one, apples, the apple-peeler, the fact that I could put it on the fridge, the piece of paper, not the peeler, the fact that nobody will notice it there amongst all the magnets and junk, and even if they do they'll never guess why I put it there, the fact that I forgot *Casanova's* name once and I had to hide that too, the fact that I forget how it came up but it did, the fact that I guess he just does now and then, the fact that I gotta go to the powder room, john, John-John, your johnson, the fact that sometimes I leave it almost too late, turn on the light, light switch, *For this relief, much thanks*, the fact that we all have to go to the bathroom all the time and it's a big, big bore, full moon, soap, the fact that now there's something in my eye, *They say the hen can lay*, Vaseline, Q-Tip, the fact that I'm sure we've got some Vaseline in the kids' bathroom, DON'T USE, the fact that I get sciatica every time I use the kids' bathroom, well, a twinge anyway, the fact that I don't like bending over, and the seat's too low, the fact that I get sciatica whenever I get tense, the fact that that's why I don't dare vacuum at the moment, or pick up heavy items, or wash the kitchen floor, or use the kids' sink, which is just way too low for me, orecchiette, origami, ocakbasi, mush, cornmeal mush, cornmeal mush pie, much too much, mush to mush, dust to dust, ♫ *What makes the muskrat guard his musk? Courage!* ♫, coffee and donuts, coffee and a cruller, dollars to donuts, heart scar, heart operation, Eight Killed In Crash Horror, the fact that I gotta do the dishes before everybody's up, I gotta, the fact that I'm a slob, slob, slut, tramp, cock, brontosaurus, pterodactyl, raptors, T-Rex, shrunken heads, yellow toy tractor, the fact that it really doesn't take all that long to do a few dishes, ten minutes tops, big deal, so why all the resistance, the fact that every day I have to force myself, like ten *times* a day, the fact that I don't exult in housework somehow, but dirty dishes are depressing, Anat always said, and I don't want the *kids* to be depressed by them, or Leo either, or me, the fact that Leo really has no idea what goes on here all day, the fact that he'd probably flip out if he ever found out what's really involved in feeding, clothing, housing and shepherding four whole kids, *kidherding*, the fact that my entire life is now spent catering to their needs and demands, cleaning toilets, filling lunchboxes, labeling all their personal property, shampooing and brushing hair, discussing everything, searching for lost stuff, baking fanouropita cakes to help find it, walking the plank, Fanourios, "Ahoy, my hearties!", KP, Officers' Mess, grist to the mill, the saint of lost things, and lost causes too, the fact that I am a lost cause, saints, Catholics, Greek Orthodox, San Martín, the fact that I like that San Martín, the fact that they make a special croissant for him in Poland, the fact that he really liked to help the poor, and *we're* poor, bail-out, buy-out, cook-out, clean-out, freak-out, cock fight, Fright Night, Friday night, the fact that then there's all the dusting, sweeping, ironing, making beds, washing sheets, towels and clothes, itch, sore eye, ironing pile, tending the chickens, feeding the goldfish, washing the windows, valeting the car, and myself, hunting down dust bunnies like Elmer Fudd on the Glorious Twelfth, the fact that Mommy and Daddy got *married* on the Glorious Twelfth, the fact that none of my kids probably even know that, nor can they say "twelfth," and it's catching, the fact that I'm forgetting how to say things too, the fact that I spend too much time with youngsters,

"Feburry," "li-bry," "twelth," the fact that it seems to take *years* to get that F in there, Twelfth Night, the fact that you're supposed to keep your Christmas tree up until Twelfth Night but nobody does anymore, the fact that it's icky when pine tree corpses line the street, the fact that I don't know when Twelfth Night is but I guess it must've passed by now, the fact that "twelve alive" is diner talk for a dozen raw oysters, baker's dozen, Celebs Who Had Normal Jobs Before, the fact that there's also the vacuuming, and holding the fort, and fielding the phone calls, planning the meals, settling the disputes, trying to keep track of everybody's cell instead of my own, *Rebel Without a Cause*, mending, sewing, making handmade pencil cases for everybody, just because I made one for Stacy years ago, and then of course, in my spare time, baking a million pies, the fact that, seriously, my life's all shopping, chopping, slicing, splicing, spilling, frilling, fooling, cooling, heating, boiling, broiling, frying, and macrophages, Tuesday, dentist, trash, mush, the fact that if I'd known what I was in for, like all the work involved, the endless chaos, before I had them, well, Walter Matthau, Harry Belafonte, helping them with their homework, and having to listen to all their groans, and screams, and sighs, and their Gameboys, and dance numbers, and all the unexplained bangs and crashes, *On the Waterfront*, or letting the cats in and out, out and in, in and out, out and in, and tending the chickens some more, *Sense and Sensibility*, *Persuasion*, *Pride and Prejudice*, the fact that I'm not used to having a moment to myself anymore really, uno momento, no problemo, like, just to read a *book* or something, Real-Life Revenge Stories, How Protein Helps You, ♫ *Figaro, Figaro, Figaro!* ♫, the fact that I sound like the factotum, ♫ *per carità* ♫, the fact that if I try to read anything these days, Jake immediately sits on my lap and makes me read him one of *his* books, baby of the family, the fact that I was the baby of the family too once, Reasons You Can't Stay Focused, the fact that I gave up trying to get Leo to share the housework way back, the fact that there's no point in *two* senses of defeat, Bedtime Rituals Of Happy Couples, the swordie, the fact that I tried to play a little trick on him once, when he came in the kitchen and asked what my nice, square wooden spatula's for, and I said, "Spatula? That's a swordie!" and he said "A what?" and I said "A swordie! They're an ancient Scottish kitchen utensil, used only for certain tasks," the fact that the whole thing was supposed to build and build, but it all flopped because Leo never asked *which* tasks, the fact that he just wandered off back to his study, so *that* was kind of disappointing, the fact that I was about to say a swordie's for whacking Scottish husbands on the sit-me-down-upon, and then I was planning to chase him around the kitchen with it, before someday admitting to him that it's really just a small square spatula and I don't even remember where I got it, but certainly not Scotland, where I have never been, the fact that I still call it the swordie though, and any day now I'm going to push on with the joke, if I ever get the chance, "I'm sticking with 'jerk store,'" Tetra Brik, bird of paradise, the King's Ransome, slumber parties, Playboy Bunnies, nurse's uniform, dolls' clothes, French maid, Japanese school-girls, apron, housecoat, the fact that I've never wanted to buy a proper housecoat because owning a housecoat implies you're going to do grimy tasks, so now I end up doing the grimy tasks anyway, just with-out the protective gear, *And that has made all the difference*, the fact that I don't like being *seen* doing housework, for some reason, the fact that it makes me self-conscious, the fact that somehow I don't want to be watched scrubbing and sweating and lugging and grouting and tearing at things and such, the fact that maybe that shows I don't take enough *pride* in my housework, the fact that I don't take *any* pride in housework, as far as I know, which isn't very Amish of me, house-proud Hausfrau, housewife, homemaker, the fact that I come from a long line of people who took no pride in housekeeping, except for Abby of course, the fact that she really did get something out of it, or I sure hope so, the fact that I think it gave her satisfaction, the fact that she liked her system anyway, her routine, and getting it all done right, every day, Polish croissants, the fact that Daddy was so terrible at making beds, the fact that he was just *awful* at it, the fact that bed-making clearly held no interest for him, the fact that I used to tell the kids to make their own beds, but it's easier if I just do it, the fact that

I take pride in my *baking*, at least now and again, but that's about it, and when I do, I do it in private, because Mommy taught us never to be proud, the fact that some moms teach their kids the opposite nowadays, bolstering 'em up nonstop like little gods, telling them how great they are at practically everything, E-G-O, E = mc², the fact that maybe *Einstein* had a right to be proud, the fact that you can be *positive*, without being overly proud, positive–negative, negatives, electrical circuits, the fact that maybe we should get an electric car, or a hybrid, the fact that electric cars are *worse* though, Leo says, because they're coal-fired, originally, instead of using gas, the fact that computers somehow use up all the energy in the world, the fact that nothing you do seems innocent anymore, the fact that even baking a pie has many ramifications, the fact that the more you bake the more you brood, Crooked Creek, the fact that what was that game where you had to decide on some moral dilemma, stay-at-home moms, the fact that when I vacuum I wonder if movie stars ever vacuum, or aliens on other planets, the fact that it's pretty unlikely we're the only creatures in the universe bothered by dust after all, the fact that aliens probably think we're real slobs not to Swiffer our moon more, the fact that it probably drives them bananas having to stare at our dusty old pockmarked little moon for millions and billions of years, ♫ *Drink to me only* ♫, to thine own self be true, the fact that I don't know if sci-fi books ever get into how to clean up on other planets but I bet microfiber cloths would come in handy, out there in the cosmos, mean dogs, ♫ *Mad dogs and Englishmen* ♫, homemakers, heartbreakers, working moms, young marrieds, Diseases You Never Heard Of, the fact that I don't know why you'd wear a white dress unless you absolutely had to, the fact that poor kids do better at school if you give them glasses, well, the ones that *need* glasses, the fact that maybe I needed glasses sooner than I got them, come to think of it, the fact that I sort of stopped looking at the blackboard around fourth grade, the fact that I thought I must be a dummy but maybe I was just nearsighted, or maybe both, the fact that I wore a silvery-gray dress for my first wedding, and a nice summery blue-and-white cotton dress for the second one, never *white*, the fact that who wants white, dirt, stains, stain remover, bleach, starch, the fact that I know I should teach the kids to do their fair share of housework like kids in olden times, the fact that Laura Ingalls Wilder always had chores, and she had even more chores after Mary went blind, Passengers Freak Out Over Pilot's Warning, penguin fossil, "Cool," the fact that the Ingallses' life is really essentially *Amish*, and they seem pretty happy too, even though they're poor, hair collector, the fact that Laura Ingalls Wilder glossed over stuff though, like that dead brother and all the times they lost their land, and their homesteads, and their horse team, even their dog, whatshisname, Jack, the fact that they all nearly *starved* during the hard winter, the fact that I think her publisher made her change it to the "long winter," the fact that "hard" winters are less attractive, I guess, a tough sell or something, cell, the fact that in one of the later books, Laura and Almanzo find an Indian mound when they're out courting in the buggy, near Silver Lake, the fact that in real life they both got diphtheria when Rose was just a baby, and she had to stay with Ma and Pa, Charles and Caroline, the fact that kids used to have to spend years in bed if they got diphtheria, the fact that Almanzo was really sick, and went back to working on the farm too soon and had a relapse, the fact that he always had a limp from then on, Chartier guys, celeriac, choke cherries, limp, cane, jalopy, toaster, Van Allen belt, tipping point, the fact that Pa seems kind of Amish, especially with his beard and all, the fact that the only thing *un*Amish about them all is Laura's interest in dresses and hats when she gets older, Mary's too, the fact that their clothes get less and less "plain and simple," the fact that Laura insists on cutting her bangs one day, which I guess the Amish would consider vain of her, the fact that Kelly McGillis laughs at Harrison Ford because the pants she gave him are too short, even for the Amish, chores, milking the cows, carpentry, the fact that kids used to have chores, then they had allowances, and now they just have devices, and snacks, the fact that Laura Ingalls Wilder always wanted blond hair like Mary's, but later she's proud of how long her hair is, and of her bangs, the fact that Ma disapproved of the bangs but Laura did it anyway, the fact that Stacy wouldn't dream of asking my permission about her hair, the fact that she'll probably dye it green next, hoop skirt, Carrie, Cap Garland, the fact that hoop skirts are dangerous in a blizzard, the fact that all through her childhood Laura feels envious of Mary's blond hair, the fact that I still don't really know the difference between envy and jealousy, the fact that sometimes I can see the difference but then I lose track of it again, the fact that they seem pretty much the same to me, envy, jealousy, envy, the fact that Laura might have been happier if she *was* Amish and not burdened with her hair worries and all the fancy sewing projects, the fact that the dresses they make sound so *complicated*, the fact that Mary's dress for college with the flared sleeves is such a tight fit that at first she can't get it *on*, which alarms everybody, but they get her into it in the end, I forget how, the fact that I think they had to tie her corset tighter, the fact that pages and pages are spent on Mary's clothes for college, the fact that it's pretty amazing they all fit in the trunk, let alone on Mary, but they do, the fact that there are even gaps, which Ma stuffs with newspaper, gaps in the *trunk*, not the dresses, the fact that those wide, flared sleeves with loose lacy cuffs, tight at the top but all loose at the bottom, don't sound all that nice to me, but they were probably all the rage then, Leghorn chickens, brown dress, housework, chores, hair, the fact that by eleven or so, Anne of Green Gables knows how to organize a whole tea party for company, "blacksberries pie," Bugs Bunny, the fact that she could get Matthew's supper for him and even cure croup with Ipecac, ibex, Prudential, Anne Shirley, Chuck Schumer, Chuck, the fact that at Mo's they called eggs "cackleberries," or Adam and Eve on a raft, Adam and Eve on a log, two dots and a dash, or wrecked and crying and let the sun shine, where the sun don't shine, the fact that I couldn't keep up with it all, Mo's Deli and Diner, klutz, the fact that I was so nervous I dropped a whole tray of dirty plates once, just like Mommy did with the glasses at her first job, the fact that she had a job at the country club, the fact that she didn't last long as a waitress and neither did I, dropkick, the fact that real waitresses make it look easy but it's really a very responsible job, and kind of tricky, the fact that now I'm back in the catering profession, "Jumbo Jockey," straw purchase, eggs over easy, sunny side up, scrambled eggs, skunk eggs, eggs Benedict, Washington Square Diner, pinball, give it shoes, hockey puck, hold the grass, mama on a raft, the fact that pride goes before a fall, mushroom omelet with a side of slaw, the fact that Ethan played a lot of pinball in college, the fact that I think he got pretty good at it, the fact that he should get himself a pinball machine for his den, Paterson Falls, the fact that a New Jersey Transit train derailed at Penn Station, or was it Hoboken, "hunted to the point of distinction," Montclair, NJ, 9/11, schnitz pie, Mo's, the fact that Stacy wouldn't be caught dead treating anybody with Ipecac, the fact that I used to think eventually the kids'll develop a liking for nicely made beds and start making their own beds but it hasn't happened yet, the fact that that was pretty dumb, the fact that once I start paying Stace to babysit, they'll all start wanting to be paid, just to do a few things for me around the house, and I don't believe in paying family members to help out with the dishes, the fact that they're not *guests*, but they're not *slaves* either, as Stacy's always reminding me, oh dear, the fact that if we can't afford a cleaner, how the heck can I afford to pay a staff of four greedy, grouchy, unmanageable kids, "the servantless cook," the fact that I have struggled to get even a dishwashing rota going around here, though it should be possible for anyone over eight to handle a dishwasher, the fact that it's not like I'm asking them to do the dishes by *hand* or anything, members, wombats, the fact that I am at the mercy of four little American brats, the Trapp Family Singers, the fact that Jake and Gillian do set the table, when I ask them, but I don't know how long that will last, *House Calls and Hitching Posts*, the fact that I still have that book somewhere, the fact that Elto Lehman sounds a nice man, the fact that he set up a birthing clinic just for Amish women, the fact that they're growing up and losing the urge to help me out, ketchup, mustard, BBQ sauce, the fact that ketchup stops rust on cast iron, but I don't have any cast iron, the fact that kids are much nicer before the age of reason, the fact that the best age is two, the fact that two-year-olds have a sort of politeness to them, when they're not having tantrums and things, and I like their plump smooth skin and the four dimples on their hands, and toddlers don't criticize you so much, or at least not as artfully or *hurtfully* as teenagers do, the fact that toddlers show a little mercy, they really do, or maybe I've just forgotten what two-years-olds are like, the fact that I missed Jake's best years, being busy "embracing change," otherwise known as having chemotherapy, toothpicks, the fact that my oncologist told me to embrace change, maybe because she *cost* a chunk o' change, the fact that what was that medicine they gave me for nausea, Bupadell or Budpell or something, Budapest, Buskydell, Buscopan, the fact that Leo took care of everything at home, and he did a great job, as far as I know, so I guess he does know what goes on here, the fact that you should never underestimate Leo, though Jake did start eating cat kibble, and once we found him hiding in the cupboard under the stairs, Jakey, not Leo, crying and all, which wasn't very nice, painkillers, nausea, the fact that we cured the poor kid of his cat kibble addiction by giving him little boxes of raisins and Cracker Jack instead, the fact that what he liked was pulling snacks out of a box, and it didn't matter what, hip, sip, more coffee, "Suck in your gut," coffee flip, rum flip, caramelized popcorn, oatmeal raisin drop cookies, the fact that I lugged all those pink dishes of Grandma's up from the basement to give the kids a little dishwashing *practice*, the fact that they're pretty ugly, so ugly I didn't care if a few got dropped, bright pink with gold filigree, just the kind of thing she went for, the fact that Grandma liked gold trimming on everything, lamps, chair legs with lions' feet, no-see-ems, bobbly glasses, the fact that she sure amassed a lot of icky stuff, the fact that Ethan inherited the lamps, and Phoebe and I painted them for him, to get rid of some of the gold, the fact that I got all her costume jewelry, and a few matronly chiffon creations that fell apart long before I could figure out how to take them in, *Good Housekeeping*, Home Ec, *Freaky Friday*, the fact that Phoebe got the spoon collection, which she'd asked for since she was six, the fact that Stacy really sabotaged my whole dishwashing scheme, by saying I was turning everybody into slaves, the fact that she hasn't been the same since she studied the Underground Railway, the fact that to her *everybody's* a slave, the fact that I'm a slave, Leo's a slave, the orphans on Prince Edward Island were all slaves, the fact that she says the orphans in *Anne of Green Gables* were all being used as unpaid farm laborers, and it's just by chance that Marilla and Matthew happened to *like* Anne so they didn't turn her into a slave, the fact that they brought her up more like their own child, though she still has a lot of *chores*, as I pointed out, unpaid chores, but that whole discussion kind of floored me and I abandoned my whole help-with-the-housework drive, boy, what a chump, camel hump, the fact that nobody around here wants to treat kids as *slaves*, my word, so now *I* slave for them instead, the fact that I've more or less given up asking Stacy to do *anything*, for fear of her sulks and freak-outs, "Speak, voice of young America," EZ Squirt, Philly Dip, ETHS, the fact that it would make my day if Stacy would just put her clothes in the hamper once in a while, in that lion's den of a bedroom of hers, the fact that she hates me going in there, but sometimes I have to, the fact that pigs are cleaner than people any day, boarlets, the fact that hogs make their own beds, though I'm not sure if they do it every morning, the fact that they're cleaner and smarter than anybody realizes, and don't deserve to be made into bacon, but everybody likes bacon so much, so it's a conundrum, it surely is, the fact that I used to think nasturtiums were nasty but now I think they're nice, and I want to grow some this year, the fact that you have to plant them out in May, the fact that I'll probably forget, the fact that when Almanzo Wilder was a boy he'd come home from school and do all the milking and clear out the horse stalls, unharness the team, Teamsters Union, the fact that *Farmer Boy* was Laura Ingalls Wilder's second book, the fact that I have led a lonely bereft life since Mommy died, but I do have Leo on my side, my "life partner," ow, the fact that now I've got a pain in my *side*, the fact that Leo has ankle pain and knee pain and thumb pain and his back itches and he won't go to the doctor, the fact that I don't know if it's to save money or because he just hates going to the doctor, or maybe he had some bad experience with a doctor once that put him off for life, or what, the fact that they say all men hate going to the doctor, *They say the hen can lay*, Obamacare, co-pays, flu shots, the fact that Jake has a constant cold, possibly because he eats only SpaghettiOs, or raisins and donuts and bagels and Cracker Jack, boxes, nurdles, the fact that I've tried to get him to try new things like canned ravioli, "ravololi," or franks 'n' beans, but he won't even taste them, the fact that Trump wants to take cover away from 630,000 Ohioans who took up Obamacare last year, and if he gets away with it, some of those poor souls are possibly going to *die*, the fact that I'm glad we're not on Obamacare, genocide, femicide, the fact that I will never see Mommy again, or Abby, or Bathsheba, or Pepito, and these are permanent sadnesses, the fact that I never liked the idea of anything being permanent, scars and wounds and such, chipped tooth, "never since the loss of her dear mother," Anne Elliott, Do The Macarena, doing the dab, "A little dab'll do ya," the fact that Anne Elliott thinks about her mom every time she plays the piano, and that's how *I* feel, I mean without the piano, the fact that it's how I feel *all the time*, the fact that I haven't felt loved since Mommy got sick, well, apart from Leo, that is, and Abby, and maybe Phoebe and Ethan, but they're far away, and Daddy, and Chuck maybe, and Nanya, I suppose, or Anat sometimes, and the chickens, the fact that at least the chickens really do love me, the fact that we kill fifty or sixty billion chickens a year, not *me*, other people, the fact that Mommy's illness wrecked my life, the fact that it broke me, the fact that I am *broken*, heartbroken, heart operation, heart scar, broke, Yueyaquan, Leo, the fact that that mean doctor gave me antibiotics for bronchitis, but so reluctantly, the fact that he seemed to *hate* me, and I never knew why, but that was years ago, the fact that I sure can hold a grudge, the fact that once in a while I remember *too* much maybe, *Persuasion*, plainsong, Schubert part songs, Pleasantville, Plainfield VT, taking the rap, the fact that the best way to tackle grouting is to apply all your frustrations to the task, all your humiliations too, all your flops and failures, flop sweat, slap happy, force, fork, torque, work, energy, statics, dynamics, stress analysis, the fact that statics is the study of bodies in equilibrium, civil engineering, civil

27

rights, civic duty, "Buck up," the fact that I *hate* it, the fact that I just slump when Leo's not here, but there are boarlets, the fact that boarlets exist, the fact that even now, somewhere on earth, there must be some boarlets, sweet boarlets with horizontal stripes in black and brown and white, and tiny, little, miniature-sized trotters, the fact that I just think those horizontal stripes of theirs make life worth living, the fact that my mouth is dry and I'm getting a pimple on my chin, the fact that I still get *zits*, at my age, the fact that we still have about thirty sealed packing crates in the attic and I have no idea what's in them, the fact that Stace and I moved in here ten years ago, but I'm too scared of hurting my back lugging all that stuff around, and I'm too busy, the fact that I couldn't do it when I was pregnant, the fact that I can't make Leo do it, move *crates* I mean, not get pregnant, the fact that he's always got so many papers to mark, or articles to write, Daddy making beds, the fact that now he's working on the dynamics of wiggling, of all things, in relation to bridges, with reference to hair ringlets, tutus, belly dancers, Jell-O, jellyfish, Giant Viper's Buglosses, sea foam, and the wagging of dogs' tails, so I don't feel I can ask him to spend his weekends sorting through old boxes in the attic, for pity's sake, pity, Pete's sake, fake, the fact that somehow building bridges seems a bit more important, Martin Luther King, Jr, SEABEEs, the fact that "a coward dies a thousand times before his death, but the valiant taste of death but once," but who said that, the fact that liquids do not expand to fill a space, the fact that when I told Leo I don't understand a thing he tells me about engineering, he laughed and said "Newton's Third Law is Let Sleeping Dogs Lie," and I said I always thought Newton's Third Law was that if you drop some toast, it'll land on the buttered side, but Leo said that's just aerodynamics, the fact that he once told me electromagnetic particles repel and attract each other all the time like one great big speed-dating jamboree, but that's okay with me, since it's thanks to civil engineering that I'm even here, the fact that without Leo's health benefits we'd be finished, finished, broke, broken, extruded polymer solutions, the fact that I hate the word "extrude," it's so ugly, *Marnie*, equal channel angular extrusion, brittle fractures, tumbling and vibratory finishing, electric cars, elastic, plastic, the fact that there's some other word I hate, something starting with F maybe, fortitude, or no, a verb, fumigate, something long, not fornicate, surely, my my, no, it's more like fructify, or refurbishment, fluctuate, fluctuation, furbelow, fermentation, fulminating, that sort of word, oh I don't know anymore, the fact that actually I think it might be pulchritudinous, not an F word at all, the fact that pulchritudinous sounds like completely the opposite of what it is, the fact that it sounds like barf really, Let Sleeping Dogs Lie, let lying dogs sleep, lying down dogs, letting down, Jakey asleep, the fact that maybe all parents like to see their children sleeping, partly because it means the parents can take a break, a coffee break, recess, recuse, breakdance, beatboxer, gravity benders, the fact that that dog on YouTube playing the piano and howling really seemed to be enjoying himself, freeze-frame, "It's a wrap," be kind, rewind, the fact that I don't know if it's just that "extrude" is an ugly word, or if it's the extruding *process* I don't like, the fact that noodles are extruded though, and that's fine with me, but I don't like extruded potato chips quite as much, the fact that *in*truding doesn't sound half as bad as *ex*truding, not at all, though Stacy doesn't like me to intrude of course, the fact that I always forget how to spell tutu, muumuu, tipi, peepee, the fact that *hoop skirts* wiggle, or any wide skirt really, depending on how you walk, the fact that I should tell Leo, the fact that hoop skirts are akin to jellyfish really, jiggle, Mrs. Piggle-Wiggle, shake a leg, but he probably knows all that, moo-moo, mo-fo, slo-mo, the get-go, googoo gaga, caca, mama, papa, Scarlett O'Hara, 7:13, the fact that most people our age get bad backs working on their *yards*, not their attics, the fact that moving pot plants around is a killer, and turf and stuff, agonist, antagonist, toprock, downrock, B-boy, or also hoeing or trimming or scything or weeding or pruning or carrying heavy watering cans or something, or lifting wheelbarrows in and out of ditches, or repositioning ride-on mowers, the fact that the human back simply wasn't made for gardening, ♫ *with thine eyes* ♫, plain and simple, fair and square, *Mary, Mary, quite contrary,* Holmes County, barn-raisings, do-si-do, the ivy patch in our back yard in New Haven, guinea pigs, hummingbirds, hurricanes, passenger planes, the fact that about three-quarters of the way through *It's Complicated*, Meryl Streep suddenly appears outside her house, picking big ripe tomatoes in her perfectly manicured vegetable garden, which you never even saw before, the fact that there's no sign of a gardener, the fact that are we supposed to believe she's solely responsible for that immaculate vegetable garden, while running some busy, trendy bakery in the center of town as well, unh-unh, the fact that she wouldn't even have time to do the *weeding*, let alone the planting and watering and harvesting and whatnot, the fact that Leo and I never get why she needs a new kitchen in the first place, the fact that she has to hire Steve Martin as her architect, the fact that Alec Baldwin seems a lot more fun, take it outside, get a room, "Bring. It. On," the fact that our success with vegetables is pretty minimal, I must say, zucchini, carrots, mush, hash, hash browns, pasta al forno, the fact that I like *lady's slippers*, Pueblos especially, and moccasin flowers, the fact that I guess I just want flowers that are like shoes, the fact that I'm no good with *any* flowers, the fact that my roses are all thorns, hardly a rose in sight, and they lost their smell, ♫ *She wheels a wheelbarrow* ♫, the fact that she really should've stuck with Alec Baldwin, it's never really going to work out with Steve Martin, the fact that he seems so, so *passionless*, the fact that who needs that, the fact that they found the smallest begonia in the world in Peru, the smallest begonia ever, and now they've built a *path* to it so everybody can go trample all over it, the fact that, I mean, really, what is *wrong* with people, the one and only *tiny begonia*, the fact that why they think that's a good idea, the fact that Trump wants to get mining and oil drilling going in all the National Parks, MAGA, MSM, the fact that next he'll get somebody to shave off Abe Lincoln's beard at Mount Rushmore, the fact that I always thought Mount Rushmore just came like that, when I was a kid, the fact that I thought it was a natural phenomenon, the fact that I was a pretty dumb kid, the fact that it really took me a long time to figure that out, Santa too, but finally I got it all straight, or I think so, somewhat straight, Gutzon Borglum, the fact that there is no Santa and geology didn't *come* with portraits of our presidents, the fact that it had help, "Rapid Sssitty, Sssouth Dakota," James Mason, Trump Tower, beauty pageants, sexual harassment, "ssssexual harassssment," George Washington, the fact that Roger Ailes was born in Warren, Ohio, Teddy Roosevelt, Thomas Jefferson, Roger Ailes, but other people come from there too, the fact that I like the way people gesticulate when they're giving directions, I just love it, Self-Taught Two-Year-Old Drummer, the fact that in my opinion, if you haven't gesticulated you haven't really *given* directions, the fact that the girls in Stacy's Morning Routine videos gesticulate an awful lot, but they're just out of control, the fact that I don't like "exuberant," or "exude" either, the fact that they're almost as bad as "extrude," excruciating, the fact that Daddy once asked this guy Gavin how school was, and Gavin said "excruciating," which embarrassed me but Daddy loved it, the fact that I bet Daddy wished I had a vocabulary like Gavin's and could say things like "excruciating," the fact that Gavin was a new boy, the fact that I hardly even knew him so it was kind of galling that Daddy took such a shine to him, the fact that finding dead leaves where you didn't expect them to be, like in our vestibule, sundogs, dogwhistles, whistleblowers, gesticulate, reticule, vestibule, residue, fibula, investiture, the fact that what *I* call the vestibule, I think Leo just calls the inner door, or hall door, the fact that I can't actually remember what he calls it, the fact that there are some things on which couples just can never agree, the fact that it depends on the way you were brought up, the fact that does that mean incestuous brother-and-sister or sister-and-sister or brother-and-brother couples agree on more stuff, since they were brought up the same way, the fact that if you have a son by your dad, your son is also your *brother*, the fact that he'd be both your dad's son and his grandson, weird, the fact that nobody ever talks about these things, but this stuff probably goes on all the time and there's nothing anybody can do about it, exude, extrude, excunt, exit, pursued by a bear, lychgate, the fact that Leo doesn't think our vestibule is big enough to deserve the word "vestibule," the fact that he thinks a vestibule is like the porch of a church, but *not* the lychgate, where they rest the coffin, just the covered doorway at the entrance, the fact that in a house, he thinks a vestibule's somewhere you leave your coat and shoes and baseball bat and the dog's leash, and all your rain gear, rainwear, Revere Ware, the fact that maybe you even sit down in there for a while, on a bench or something, if you're tired when you reach home and wanna take a load off, hang, or get your muddy boots off, the fact that he means something like an enclosed porch maybe, and I think having a place like that's a great idea, but who's got one, the fact that in my family we just always called the area between our outer door and an inner door a vestibule, and that was that, the fact that I thought it was just there to keep out the drafts, when people come and go, not to house any equipment or anything, skis and umbrellas and canes and snow shovels and sweaters and marshmallows and picnic baskets and such, *a-tisket a-tasket, a green and yellow basket,* the fact that that rhyme always depressed me, I'm not sure why, Waterlow Park on a damp day, Mommy by my side, the fact that Leo got me this stool so I can rest my aching feet when I'm cooking, but unfortunately it gives me a bad back, so now it's mainly just for Jake to fall off of, the fact that it's way too high for me too, the fact that Jakey likes to perch up there watching me cook, or when he's waiting for me to tie his shoes, the fact that I give him a spin whenever I pass by, the fact that you have to keep children entertained, straight, brittle plastic hinges, the fact that sometimes he does some coloring, sitting up at the counter, truck coloring book, the fact that he colors all the trucks yellow, occasionally red, the fact that he likes a good solid color, that boy, the fact that it's never red with yellow trimming or yellow with red trimming, the fact that he just likes the pure color, pure yellow, pure red, maybe sometimes black, the fact that there have been tears, Kleenex, when the other kids add some other color, the fact that we keep having to get whole new packs of crayons, just for the yellow ones, the fact that I always found those metallic crayons so disappointing, the fact that, come on, that gold doesn't look like gold *at all*, the fact that Jake likes the stool better than the high chair because it swivels, swivel hips, swizzel sticks, Pick-Up

Sticks, the fact that I always hated Pick-Up Sticks, and still do, the fact that they just make you feel clumsy, and who needs that, mensch, meshuggenah, the fact that I feel enough of a klutz already, precast segmented superstructure, epoxy jointed or dry jointed, underslung assembly truss, draw bridge, bascule bridge, vertical lift bridge, skew or curved bridge beams, ouch, the fact that now I've got a charley-horse, and goosebumps and pins and needles, funny bone, the fact that *The Long Winter* is the best one, the fact that *The Long Kvetch* is what it is, the fact that whenever it snows a lot out, I think of Laura waking up with ice on all the nails in the ceiling, and Pa going off to the claim with the team to get straw to make straw sticks to keep the fire going in the stove so they could keep warm enough to survive, and so that Ma could cook a little, the fact that the horses keep falling into deep snow holes in the Big Slough, because the snow is just held up on grasses, the fact that the Ingallses don't have much to eat either because the train's been held up and all, the fact that it can't get through for months, the fact that making straw into sticks really sounds laborious, the fact that Laura and Pa have to twist it into sticks some-how, the fact that the house had no insulation, so ice formed indoors like in *Dr. Zhivago*, the Lara poems, Julie Christie, Omar Sharif, the fact that Laura and Pa get so cold and blistered twisting the straw, they have to keep coming in to warm up by the stove, the fact that they can barely keep up with the needs of the fire, and the whole bunch of them can barely grind enough wheat in the coffee grinder to make one loaf a day, for the whole family, even by taking turns grind-ing, the fact that in real life they had some hangers-on as well to feed, some greedy people who didn't do their fair share of chores, just like *my kids*, the fact that I'm glad she left them out of her book, the fact that Mike Pence can't be alone with a woman in case he's tempted to sin with her, RFRA, whatshisname, Roe v Wade, the fact that some pro-lifers want women to get the *death penalty* for having *abortions*, which doesn't make a lot of sense, the fact that, thanks to Laura Ingalls Wilder, I now sort of know what to do if we ever had no heat, as long as we had access to a lot of straw, that is, the fact that I suppose if we didn't have any straw I could start twisting up all our paperwork, documents, coloring books, Lara poems, the fact that we have plenty of pieces of paper, more than anyone I know, except maybe that poor Julie Shriver at Peolia College, the fact that she was almost buried under the piles of paper on her desk once, the fact that a pile tipped over and she disappeared under it all for a little while one day and had to be rescued, or so the story went, the fact that she did a declutter number on it after that, but nobody dares go near her desk even now, for fear of scattering thousands of unmarked student papers across the room, the fact that I never get around to sorting through *our* stuff, that's for sure, just like Mommy and Daddy, the fact that I grew up in a house full of messy papers, and it looks like my kids will too, the fact that I don't *really* know how they made those straw sticks, because Laura Ingalls Wilder never explains things all that well, or anyway I can never follow her explanations, the fact that her description of making a whatnot is totally incomprehensible, the fact that whenever she tries to describe how to make stuff, like a bobsled or a bullet, or a whole front door with hinges and a latch, or a milk churn or something, you're really none the wiser after, though it's good of her to try and all, the fact that I think the kids just skim over those bits, the fact that they're pretty incurious kids all in all, and would probably be no help *whatsoever* in a hard winter, the fact that they'd just be playing Pick-Up Sticks, not twisting straw sticks, the fact that I don't know the difference between straw and hay myself, except that horses like one or the other better, I'm not sure which, man of straw, the Tin Man, the Cowardly Lion, ♫ *Courage!* ♫, Toto, Tintin, the fact that I'm a grown woman and I don't know the difference between hay and straw, or linen and cotton, or calico or flax or muslin, or porcelain and china, and all kinds of other stuff I can't even remember right now, well, *actors*, the fact that I get Yul Brynner and Charles Boyer mixed up all the time, and Warren Beatty and Burt Reynolds, Charlton Heston and Burt Lancaster, the fact that I get just about everything mixed up, the fact that I have to guess at everything, bluff my way through life, Hollywood Heartthrobs, the fact that horses prefer *hay*, it turns out, but they can eat straw in a pinch, a pinch of straw, salt, a lick and a promise, sack, bushel, barrel, ♫ *a bushel and a peck* ♫, an acre or two, hectare, leagues, my liege, the fact that Almanzo and that other guy, whatshisname, Cap Garnett, drove forty miles, twenty there and back, through snow and snow holes, in minus twenty or thirty degree weather, to get seed wheat so everybody in De Smet wouldn't starve, the fact that that's a true story, and they went off not knowing if a blizzard would hit, or if the seed wheat was even out there, the fact that there was just some rumor that some guy was wintering out on his claim with a lot of wheat, the fact that they had no idea where exactly, or if he'd even sell it to them, and it was hard enough just to try to see which way was *south*, the fact that they were so brave about it, the fact that maybe it's not the most dramatic story of heroism but they risked their necks, and their horses, and they almost didn't find the place in time, but then they saw a little wisp of smoke coming right out of the snow and it was the guy's sod house, the fact that it was so covered in snow it was almost invisible, apart from the little plume of smoke from the chimney, the fact that he didn't even have a very big fire going in there, he was all snug as a bug in a rug because of the blanket of snow on top, moth balls, the fact that he drove a tough bargain but they settled with him and poured the wheat into the sacks they'd brought along, the fact that he urged them to stay the night but they decided to risk the trip back to town, and the horses could barely walk and kept falling into snow holes, but they made it just in time before another three-day blizzard struck, the fact that they were lucky to make it home alive at all, and the *town* was lucky they made it too, because if they hadn't, the Ingallses and everyone else in town would've starved, the fact that then there'd be no *Little House on the Prairie* books, the fact that the train didn't get through to De Smet till June, the fact that there is some trouble though, when the grocer guy acts up and tries to make a big profit on the wheat they brought back, the fact that he was trying to profit off starving townsfolk, the fact that that makes Cap Garnet angry, the fact that Cap Garland rarely got angry, but this gets him going, because he and Almanzo had risked their necks to go get the wheat and they weren't taking a penny for that, the fact that *everybody* got angry with the grocer guy, and the townsfolk threatened to tear him limb from limb, or else snatch the wheat for free, or at least not patronize his store in future, the fact that Pa placated everyone, or that's the way Laura Ingalls Wilder tells it, the fact that Pa persuaded the grocer to sell it just for what he'd paid for it, and also got them all to share the wheat out fairly, according to each family's needs, the fact that I always like that bit, the fact that sometimes people really go all out for each other, like, for the public good, common weal, commune, Pepito, the fact that sometimes it's not just each man for himself, boarlets, Christmas candy, ginseng hunting, Mommy, the fact that the Ingalls girls give their mom a *hair collector* one Christmas, the fact that I don't like the sound of that much, the fact that I hope nobody ever gives me one, knitting, cutie marks, the fact that what beats me is what they wanted to keep all their lost hairs *for*, to make a creepy pin cushion or something, the fact that sometimes it's called a hair receiver, but it's still creepy, the fact that Leo knew some guy in Newcomerstown who got a whole suit made out of his poodle's fur, collected from several visits to the poodle parlor, the fact that the dog was a nice peach-colored poodle, but dogs would chase that guy all over town whenever he wore his poodle suit, the fact that I'm not sure Laura Ingalls Wilder ever mentions birthdays, just Christmas, 1 cakes, the fact that De Smet's a funny name for a place, De Smet, smegma, smug, Smeg, smog, smug, the fact that there are three or four De Smets, one in Montana and one in Idaho, I think, but the one where Laura Ingalls Wilder lived is in South Dakota, the fact that I don't know what kind of birthday cake to make Gillian this time, maybe just an 8, the fact that she's maybe too old for another My Little Pony creation, Kleenex, goat's milk, the fact that she's such a *Little House* fan, I should try to make her a log cabin cake, the fact that what I need is a Kleenex, and maybe breakfast, the fact that all I've had is one little cup of coffee, too busy kneading and caramelizing, compromising, comprising, the fact that, my gosh, I'm as hungry as a *De Smetter*, but if you eat, you have to go to the bathroom, well, eventually you do, and I'm sick of going to the bathroom, the fact that it's always bored me so much, the fact that I always needed to go to the bathroom at the movies when I was a kid, PAY TOILET 5¢ PERSONS CAUGHT CRAWLING UNDER THE DOOR WILL BE PROSECUTED TO THE FULLEST EXTENT OF THE LAW, the fact that Laura Ingalls Wilder doesn't ever mention going to the bathroom, the fact that how they handled that in a blizzard, the fact that we're about due for another blizzard ourselves, gizzard, wizard, buzzard, zigzag, ziggurat, mosque, piecemeal, peacetime, four-foot sword, the fact that I found an index card with Abby's BBQ sauce recipe yesterday, in her own handwriting, and it fills me with, with, Yul Brynner, seed wheat, the fact that she says you need 1 lge. onion, 2 tbsp. butter, ¼ cup lemon juice, 2 tbsp. vinegar, 1 tbsp. Worcestershire, 2 tbsp. brown sugar, ½ cup water, 1 jar chili sauce, salt & pepper, the fact that maybe I'll use it on some drumsticks today, freezer, animal-shaped ice cubes, water samples, urine sample, PCBs, the fact that wild killer whales have PCBs in them, and pregnant whales transmit the PCBs to the fetus, the fact that I haven't got any chili sauce like Abby means, but I could use some Hunt's and add a little chili powder or paprika, the fact that the kids won't want it too hot anyway, the fact that you brown the onion in butter, then add the rest of the stuff and cook it all slowly for twenty minutes till it thickens, and that's it, and it lasts quite a while in the fridge, or so she says, a couple of weeks anyway, the fact that she says to use it on "ribs, chicken, p. chops, hamburgers, and hot dogs," the fact that it always made me happy, sitting at Abby's kitchen table, the fact that I loved her warm kitchen and the imitation-brick wallpaper and the old-fashioned copper ceiling lamp that could be raised or lowered over the table, and the little cast iron toys on their own little wooden shelf, and her fridge with all the fridge magnets, a lot tidier than ours, and inside it, every kind of condiment you could think of for sandwiches, the fact that the freezer compartment was full of Abby's favorite ice cream, choc-choc-chip, the fact that sometimes I misspell "refrigerator," which is embarrassing, also "affect" and "effect"

are a big problem for me, the United Way, the fact that "fridge" has a
D in it, but "refrigerator" doesn't, affect and effect, cotton and linen,
nasturtiums, the fact that I will never tell the kids how much trouble
I have with affect and effect and just hope they don't have the same
problem and come running to me for help, effective, affective, affection, interactive, the fact that OoJ stands for obstruction of justice,
which is something Trump gets up to all the time, fiddlehead ferns,
podding peas, home-canning, the fact that somebody should really do
something about that whole problem, sort it out once and for all, I
mean "affect" and "effect," not OoJ, the fact that it's okay when you're
just talking, because nobody can tell you don't know how to spell
them, spelling bee, quilting bee, crochet bee, family tree, Mommy,
♫ *sassy as can be* ♫, the fact that the Senate could just declare that it's
always going to be "effect" from now on, and *never* "affect," and just
dump affect entirely, and that would be the end of it, *Imitation of Life*,
Lifting As We Climb, the fact that Abby was a *queen* of housekeeping,
whereas I'm a slob, a slugabed, "Divorced, broke and sloppy," the fact
that she was so punctilious that even her attic and her basement were
orderly, which seems sort of unnatural to me, but nice and all, of
course, the fact that I loved the smell of old pine in her attic, tsunami,
tater tots, deep-fried cheese curds, straight line winds, cyclone, the
fact that she'd be horrified by our attic, Alec Baldwin, but I don't
know, attics and basements kind of cry out for anarchy, I think, and
maybe it's not right to thwart them, old junk, old papers, papers, the
fact that an attic's better for jelly bean hunts if it's all messy, the fact
that Abby ran a tight ship, that's for sure, sore hip, flip, bug, fly, itch,
pimple, dear Abby, "Dear Abby," Skippy Peanut Butter, ♫ *Skip to my
Lou, my darlin'* ♫, humpback trunks, humpback whales, those poor
little terrapins, the fact that our attic's still full of Aunt Sophia's junk,
that she left to Leo's parents, the fact that I shouldn't call it junk, the
fact that they're heirlooms, "expelled heir from vagina," now how did
I, why did I, dear me, back, sac and crack, for Pete's sake, what is *with*
me today, the fact that we ended up with it all, the heirlooms, Family
Owned Since 1946, like Aunt Sophia's cherry corner cupboard, the

press back rocker, the banjo clock, the Shaker chair with the nice drawers on the side, the wicker high chair Jake's grown out of now, all that Bavarian china, the rag rugs that aren't half as nice as Abby's, the guns, bullet molds, candle molds, the moose head that scares kids at Hallowe'en, Aunt Sophia's old butter churn, an ornate cream skimmer, the fact that I think there are some old, old Amish toys in one of the trunks, pretty fragile now, and then there's the ox yoke, the fact that we've got Aunt Sophia's parents in our room, the framed photo, not the parents, and the locket with the pressed four-leaf clover, the fact that that's in my jewelry box along with Aunt Sophia's hard-earned watch pendant, commemorating forty years of playing bridge at her bridge club, the fact that it has a weird, thick, square gold chain, the fact that the only things we got rid of immediately were the guns, the fact that Aunt Sophia had a rifle and a shotgun, and bullet molds, but even if they were antiques we didn't want them in the house, even if somebody decommissioned them or whatever it is they do with antique guns so you can't use them anymore, the fact that I think they fill the barrel with cement or something, Perpetrator Was Heavily Armed, the fact that the kids were bound to find them and play with them someday, the fact that they sometimes try to play with the ox yoke but that's okay, the fact that if they want to pretend they're oxen, that's up to them, but no cowboys and Indians with real antique guns please, the fact that Abby did all her housework every morning in a set order, the fact that she had each task timed out so she knew exactly what she was doing and when, and that's partly why it was so nice to be there, the fact that she'd get all the morning tasks done, then we'd have a sandwich and do the dishes, and then she'd get the supper all sorted out, ready to go for when Hoag got home, and then there always seemed to be plenty of time to sit and talk some more, until 5:00, which was drink time, the fact that then we'd have a drink and talk some more, the fact that we usually drank Canadian Club and ginger ale, carefully measured in the jigger by Abby, less carefully by me, or else Scotch and soda, the fact that I first learned to drink Scotch and soda on a visit to Abby when I was nineteen or so, the fact that they called seltzer "balloon juice" at Mo's, the fact that Abby never felt very adept with liquor, the fact that she preferred it if I made the drinks, the fact that she and Hoag enjoyed a drink once in a while, like a screwdriver on Labor Day maybe, but they didn't usually bother with cocktail time except for company, so those great big jugs of liquor used to just sit in her little mahogany washstand undisturbed for months on end, from one visit to the next, ♫ *Drink to me only* ♫, the fact that Mommy and Daddy always had a drink every evening, and why ever not, I'd like to know, the fact that their cocktail hour was 5:30, not 5:00, the fact that Daddy liked cheese and crackers with it, or olives, or dips, the fact that Mommy liked a little bowl of potato chips, the fact that Leo's not usually back in time for a pre-dinner drink with me, so I usually skip it, ♫ *And I'll not ask for wine* ♫, the fact that Mommy and Daddy always used to sing "Drink to Me Only with Thine Eyes" to us as a bedtime song, "p. chops," the fact that now people would probably freak out and say it's not right to mention drinking in front of kids, even though the song's really about pledging to do *without* it, the fact that they also sang us "Show me the way to go home" a lot, but Mommy always changed the "had a little drink 'bout an hour ago" part to "had a cup of coffee 'bout an hour ago," ♫ *And it went right to my head* ♫, so they *were* very responsible parents really, the fact that that guy Anthony always used to change it to ♫ *Indicate the way to my abode, I'm fatigued and wish to retire* ♫, the fact that I still sing those same songs to my kids in the car, the fact that sometimes you just have to obey your own judgment and do things the way your mom and pop did them, Coco Pops, Three Simple Steps To, the fact that somebody once called Mommy an alcoholic because she had whiskey and soda every night, which was just so silly, the fact that Mommy was always very abstemious, the fact that she was the essence of abstemiosity, one whiskey and soda every night and that was it, never excess, the fact that it was her *dad* who was the alcoholic, not Mommy, abstemiosity, abstemiosis, fossiliferous, the fact that that sounds like a disease, like some kind of halitosis, symbiosis, osmosis, hostess with the mostest, the fact that Mommy was never addicted to *anything*, except maybe playing solitaire, but that's not going to damage your health or anybody else's, if they'd just have left her in peace about it, and okay, *smoking*, the fact that that was maybe her one big indulgence, and even after she got sick she still smoked, the fact that she smoked to her dying day, the fact that they both died too young, ready, aim, fire, Light the Night, Mohawk Valley 4-H Club, the fact that I should be thinking about my *canapés*, Irma Rombauer, the fact that she has some pretty good ideas sometimes, the fact that somehow I don't think shrimp sticks with a little bit of *cucumber* on the end are going to cut it, not for Leo's colleagues, even in Newcomerstown where they can't be expecting much, haute cuisine, full orchestra, standing ovation, the fact that the artichoke leaves holding a dab of mayo and a shrimp sound a bit better, but I don't much want artichoke leaves ground into the rug, the fact that Irma Rombauer was from Cincinnati, the fact that one canapé idea of hers is you boil baby celery stalks in chicken stock and then you place them on pieces of braised lettuce, and then, well I forget what but it sure would make a slippery handful at a party, the fact that she seems to think as long as you decorate everything with a dab of mayonnaise everything will be okay, the fact that she put a lot of faith in mayo, the fact that mayo removes *glue*, the fact that now I've found it, her shrimp recipe, and she wants you to put six or eight chilled shrimp on the celery stalks, 6 or 8, Deviled Eggs in Aspic, buffalo wings, taramasalata, What Happens To Your Body When You Eat Eggs, the fact that I couldn't find any good recipes *online* either, the fact that there it's all Jarlsberg and ham pinwheels, pumpkin ricotta dip, Romano and orange crostini, cheesy spiders, salad-on-a-stick, and chocolate-covered Chex Muddy Bunnies, Muddy Bunnies, the fact that Muddy Bunnies are for *kids*, the fact that the best thing about cocktail parties is when they're over and you get to sit down and relax, "let go," the fact that I always hide behind the hors d'oeuvres at our parties, or the drinks, the fact that if you bustle around enough like that you don't have to talk to people, and it saves you getting cornered, the fact that Leo *likes* talking to people, the fact that now where did this little pink flamingo in blue boots come from, maybe a Cracker Jack toy, hors d'oeuvres, canapés, the fact that all alcohol is bad for you, even a little glass of wine, but chocolate's okay, as I remind my customers, hornets, yellow jackets, yellow trucks, the fact that most people you meet are addicted to chocolate, the fact that it's probably worse than the opioid epidemic, but not so dangerous, hydrangea, the fact that chocolate has caffeine in it, the fact that I only just found that out, Waitress Gets Tipped $1,000 For Believing In God, the fact that sometimes you get a tip, sometimes you get shot, the fact that *I'm* addicted to online jigsaw puzzles and I wish I was doing one right now instead of making a hundred cinnamon rolls, the fact that people have no idea how much work goes into making a cinnamon roll, and I couldn't do it without my Candy-Apple Red, 7-quart kneading machine, the fact that where would I be without it, *where*, the fact that maybe I could make do with a different *color* 7-quart kneading machine, but I sure couldn't make all this cinnamon roll dough without *some* kind of kneading machine, and it wouldn't be as much fun if it wasn't Candy-Apple Red, the fact that just the sight of it cheers me up sometimes, the fact that I bet that mixer's paid for itself by now, or I sure hope so anyway, the fact that these things are so expensive, the fact that some cost thousands, the fact that even floor lamps cost thousands these days, Tastee Apples, the fact that everybody seems to earn six-figure salaries and they all want to spend thousands on a floor lamp but I don't, the fact that I was on minimum wage when I worked at Mo's, but now even wait-resses earn six-figure salaries, in New York anyway, and that's before the thousand-dollar tips, tax cuts, the fact that I hope those guys at the Washington Square Diner are making the big bucks too, the fact that that's our place, the fact that Washington Square's romantic in the snow, the fact that it's about time I opened the coop, the fact that the greatest thing about online jigsaw puzzles is that every piece is shown the right way up, right from the start, so it's easier to figure out where they go, and also you never end up with a missing piece at the end, which is such a killer, no way José, Child Star Set To Make A Comeback, child star, blue-and-white cloud puzzle, the fact that the first time I had fondue was at a friend's house, the fact that they lived somewhere in downtown Evanston, the fact that maybe they were rich, but anyway, after that fondue, I always thought those people really knew how to live, the fact that it was a different family that taught me to eat avocados, the fact that they weren't rich at all but they too knew how to live, I thought, the fact that I used to sleep over there a lot, Melanie, the fact that that does drive me crazee, a missing piece in the jigsaw I mean, the fact that I really liked that fondue, but I never got a good one again, the fact that most fondues are *cheese* but that one was a sort of a clear dark wine sauce or something, nice, for dipping little pieces of meat into, the fact that I should give the *kids* fondue sometime, 'cause it's fun cooking your own stuff, unless you cook all day long, that is, the fact that some restaurants make you cook the whole meal yourself at the table, or put your own sandwich together, the fact that it seems to me you might as well stay home, potato cheese puffs, cheese tray, Down East Clam Dunk, Philly Dip, Irma Rombauer, oatmeal and raisin cookies, toothpick meatballs, mini hot dogs, the fact that an eighty-eight-year-old woman was attacked in her bed, and she had to *crawl* to her neighbor's to get help, terrapins, the fact that crawfish have invaded a park in Berlin, but how is this my business, the fact that *two* of our faucets now need a new washer, the fact that the one in the upstairs bathroom has been off limits for a while, DON'T USE, the fact that Jake can't read the sign but luckily he's too small to use that sink anyway, the fact that Arnie Tulip's never going to come over for such a tiny job, the fact that the same goes for the window guy, Mike or whatever his name is, whatevs, the fact that he's more of a carpenter than strictly a window guy, ♬ *There's no business like show business like no business I know* ♬, the fact that I tried to entice Arnie over by saying he could check our *drains* as well, and the chickens' faucet, but that didn't seem to sweeten the deal, no dice, Mr Muscle, Jolly Green Giant, the fact that Leo could probably change a washer if he had *time*, Heart-Melting Moments, but he doesn't, so for weeks he's had to shave in the *kids'* bathroom, where the hot water works fine but the sink's so tiny and low down, bib 'n' tucker, one-arm and two-arm draw bridges, the one-armed man Harrison Ford's chasing, Eye Bag Treatment, sparrows, starlings, rag rugs, Abby's toaster oven, KSC, DCCC, CC&G, Shockwave Quick Detach, Highway 1, the B train, the fact that our windowsills rotted, got rotten, gotten rotten, gone fishin', plum furgot, tweren't me, the fact that I think the kitchen ones might even fall *out* in a high wind, especially this one, ouch, touch wood, cross fingers, rub thumbs, the fact that it never shuts properly anymore, rabbit's foot keyrings, that kid in an air-powered wheelchair, 750 sq. feet, 35 acres, Woman Jailed For Ten Years, the fact that any burglar could just pry the whole thing out of its socket and climb right in here in a second, but luckily you can't tell from outside, and they probably wouldn't try in the middle of winter, the fact that it's probably no fun at all being a burglar in wintertime, not-for-profit, iFlip4, the fact that some people live in houses with no heating at all, right here in Ohio, sick people with kids and all, the fact that that Black Lives Matter campaigner was beaten up by her boyfriend, the fact that she was pregnant and he beat her up so she'd lose the baby, the fact that first he made her swallow laxatives, telling her it was *acid*, the fact that the stuff people think up to do to each other, Thieves oil lozenges, bubonic plague, leprosy, lounge lizard, whiz kid, quiz, swizzle stick, Swiss on rye, Swiss Miss, cuckoo clock, banjo clock, grandfather clock, grandmother clock, Grandma, the fact that replacing a whole window will cost about a thousand bucks, and we don't *have* an extra thou just knocking around, fore-closure, executive lounge, chaise longue, Charles River, rowboat, twisted sticks of straw, the fact that we're broke because I had cancer, the fact that that broke us, it broke us, the fact that I shouldn't say that, because here we are, still kicking, and I am still producing cin-namon rolls by the ton but, sciatica, hip, Advil, painkillers, Leo's health plan, the fact that Phoebe helped us out and we'll never be able to pay her back, and Jake was at the height of his cute stage and I *missed* it, "You missed it, Oscar, you missed it!", and that hurts, Land O'Lakes, Sealtest, zip and zest, Jake's cat-kibble habit, Sun-Maid raisins, alphabet noodles, diapers, donuts, diapers for donuts, the fact that there was some kind of kibble from China that killed a whole lot of dogs and cats all over America a while back, but that was over long before *Jake* got interested in cat kibble, luckily, the fact that only last week though, they had to recall some Chinese *dog chews*, snowstorm, the fact that they weren't *lethal*, or fatal or anything, fake, sheik, imam, pharaoh, Cleopatra, the Sphinx, Sphinxy, the fact that they just made some dogs sick, the fact that a dog shouldn't *pass away* from eating a dog chew of all things, that's for darn certain, or from eating kibble either, dog kibble, dribble, drizzle, lemon drizzle cake, the fact that that just doesn't seem fair, "You're darn tootin'," insurance, retreat, endearing, enduring, BLM, the fact that the kids are always saying things aren't fair, the fact that that's their motto, their mantra, fondue, the fact that you never know what's *in* kibble, you're just supposed to trust the manufacturers, the fact that kibble factories must have quite an odor, I bet, *Bubble, bubble, toil and trouble*, Iago, the fact that Leo says he never thinks about Shakespeare, the fact that Shakespeare never comes into his head, the fact that the cat kibble we've got is *American*, but anyway Jake now eats nothing but SpaghettiOs, "Damsons you have to leave unstoned," and I don't know what to do about it, this SpaghettiO fixation of his, the fact that I have not read all the books I want to read, not even half, the fact that it doesn't take all *that* long to read a book so I don't know why I don't, except that the kids always interrupt if I try to read anything, the fact that even the cats interrupt, the fact that the last thing I read was about how noble all the Amish were about the Nickel Mines massacre, the fact that that horror really *was* "unfair," the fact that those children were not just maimed and killed but frightened out of their wits, the fact that Aunt Sophia's husband Fred never liked the Amish because of their pacifism during the First World War, the fact that he'd been gassed and it put him off pacifism completely, the fact that you'd think being in a war would have the *opposite* effect, affect, effect, the fact that he lived another twenty-five years after the gassing but the side effects, affects, did kill him in the end, and he passed on from some nerve-gas-related disease, the fact that after his passing the Amish neighbors couldn't do *enough* for Aunt Sophia, the fact that they brought her food, did her storm windows, helped her in the garden all the time, mowed her lawn, Amish, famish, famine, fantasy, fandango, phantasmagorical, the fact that that's what Leo's mom always said anyway, that the Amish just couldn't do enough for Aunt Sophia, and that thanks to them Aunt Sophia managed to stay in her own home right to the end, and whenever her washing machine went on the blink, they'd come *running* to help her with it, running across the fields, the fact that they could fix any kind of machine, even though they never used machines themselves, the fact that Aunt Sophia was okay on her own, for years, until the day her hair caught fire, *liar, liar, pants on fire*, the fact that it's just so terrible, the fact that she was trying to light the wood stove, as she did every morning, but she'd forgotten to put her hair up yet, and it caught alight from the embers and in seconds she was all ablaze, the fact that she ran out on the porch and called out, but it was already too late and nobody could save her, the fact that she died that very same day, just like Longfellow's wife, Canal Queen contest, quarterly meeting, Croc Blocks Road, Equestria, Fluttershy, Sugar Belle, that book about the Amish doctor, the fact that now that Jake's at his playgroup half the day I probably could read more, except I'm always playing catchup, ketchup, mustard, mayonnaise, coleslaw, BBQ sauce, making pies, promoting pies, delivering pies, the fact that a woman who seemed to have Crohn's disease for six years turned out to have a Heinz ketchup packet inside her somewhere, the fact that somebody else had a piece of glitter in her eye for six months, that had blown off a Christmas card when she was opening it, Loveless Monkey Adopts Chicken, the fact that I must attack the mound, Miamisburg Mound, Serpent Mound, the fact that this mound of shirts, sheets, and towels is always appearing in the corner of my eye, when I'm in the middle of baking, and it makes me feel bad, but what can you do about *ironing* in the middle of kneading or caramelizing or flipping, Grave Mound, the fact that I guess I could at least *fold* them, the fact that people frown on untidiness, the fact that Nanya's frown was the first thing I liked about her, the fact that she has a beautiful way of frowning, the fact that I tried copying it for a while but I think I scared people so I stopped, the fact that I gave Leo two books for his birthday and he read them both in a week, the fact that one was about that ship, the Bourgogne, where the crew kicked and stabbed the passengers so they could get on the lifeboats, the fact that three hundred women drowned, and only one survived, the fact that De Scott Evans was on board with his three daughters, and they all died too, the fact that De Scott Evans did trompe l'oeil still lifes, before all that happened, Trump l'oeil, Trump lies, the fact that he did a great picture of a cat stuck in a traveling crate, De Scott Evans, not Trump, the fact that no children survived that shipwreck at all, whereas many did survive the Titanic, which was just a few years later, the fact that I think the crew on the Titanic behaved a bit better, the fact that the Bourgogne crew turned into *monsters*, the fact that some crew member who helped women and children into lifeboats on the Titanic later took part in the Dunkirk evacuation, the fact that he saved a whole lot of people with his own little boat, and earlier in life he'd been a cowboy and then a hobo, riding the rails in America, unstoned damsons, damsels in distress, "I have struggled in vain," the fact that when Elizabeth tells her mom she's going to marry Darcy, Mrs. Bennet is struck *dumb*, for once in her life, stunned into silence, and it's funny, the fact that maybe some mini croque monsieur might do, and croque madame, or toasty Gouda nibblers, or we could just have shrimps with spicy cocktail sauce and be done with it, with horseradish, the fact that everybody likes that, the fact that once I made some homemade sushi that blew people's heads off, the fact that I'm not sure if that was good or bad, a success or a failure, the fact that I think I used too much wasabi, the fact that how *could* Grandpa have said that to Mommy, when she published her first and only book, "This book will either be a success or a failure," six years and six months, the fact that that's how long that woman had to live with a ketchup packet in her gut, six years, keyhole surgery, the fact that fried wonton would be way too much trouble, I mean as a canapé, not in keyhole surgery, the fact that keyhole surgeons probably deal with fried wonton all the time, easy-peasy, navel, naval, the Navy, What Scientists Found Deep In The Ocean, the fact that I think we should keep things simple, the fact that I don't have to show off every canapé I'm *capable* of, just give 'em a good time, the fact that we could have chicken liver biscuits and potato pancakes, no, blinis maybe, and mini corndog muffins, Compare Prices, Open House, gun groups, Chilling Last Social Media Post, the fact that parties are exhausting, pollution in Gaza, Tragic Mom Who Never Had A Passport, the fact that it's snowing again, and Jake missed out on the yellow gritter, the fact that we just dug ourselves out of the last snow storm and now here's another one, the fact that Fanny Trollope says everything's "colossal" in America, everything's "*fortissimo*," and I am beginning to think she's right, the fact that we get much colder winters now, and hotter sum-mers too, with a lot more, yeEEEOw, bugs, more bugs, the fact that, gosh darn it, that little yellow pickup truck just got me again, *ow*, limp, gimp, shrimp, pimp, oh no, dear me, why the, say "Djibouti" instead, the fact that I was thinking how much Jake would've liked to see that yellow gritter when I stepped on his little yellow backhoe truck, so the joke's on me, flashing orange lights, snowstorm, tornado, 2012, san-dals, sand, sand dunes, *boy* did that hurt, gosh darn it, right through my *slipper*, the fact that Jake just loves yellow trucks with flashing orange lights, well, all kids like flashing lights, whether it's fireworks and sparklers or Christmas lights and night lights, or just computer screens, addicts, opioid epidemic, light the night, computer games, the fact that dogs all seem to have lights on their collars now, and I like watching them running around at night, the fact that all you can see is the little light going up and down in the darkness, the fact that I don't know if the Northern Lights are so interesting for kids, or the Perseid meteor shower, the fact that it's a real pity he missed it though, the gritter, not the meteor shower, the fact that there *is* no meteor shower, as far as I know, and we wouldn't be able to see one anyway through the snow, the fact that what Jake really likes are lattice boom crawler cranes, the fact that he's in heaven when he gets a gander at one of those, the fact that it's time to get them up, *past* time in fact, pastime, but it's so peaceful without them running around under my feet, the fact that he was gassed in the war, Fred that is, the fact that, good grief, your heart must sink when you find out you've been gassed, tear gas, the fact that there goes Stacy's alarm so they'll be down soon, the fact that I should've hauled the trash cans out last night, down the driveway, but I didn't because of my bad back, the fact that, oh well, they probably won't come today because of *their* bad backs, or because of the snow, *They say the hen can lay, I don't know but they know*, the fact that I'm a reluctant shoveler and the mailman isn't always too pleased with my efforts, the fact that I can't blame him, the fact that I'm not all that pleased with them either, the fact that for more than two feet you really need snow-blowers, the fact that now we have a snow service, but *they're* reluctant too, the fact that those fellers never turn up when you want them, snow tunnels, the fact that I'm always scared Leo will have a heart attack shoveling snow some-day, as all good-hearted American men seem to, the fact that after Hoag died Abby's neighbor took over the shoveling, until he had a heart attack trying to shovel out his own sidewalk after a snowfall, the fact that he survived, but he gave up the shoveling, fall forward, the fact that every time there's a time change, heart attacks and car crashes briefly increase in number, ST, DST, the fact that I just don't think it's good for people. Dog Rescued From Frozen River, lake-effect snow, the fact that three hundred women drowned and only one was saved, the Bourgogne, the fact that I wonder what happened to *her*, after, the one woman that got saved, the fact that the snow people abandoned us for weeks last year and I had to do it all, three feet of snow, the fact that the Bourgogne wasn't all that far from Sable Island but that didn't help them, the fact that the wreck is somewhere near the Grand Banks, *The Perfect Storm*, the fact that it wasn't a storm, it was another boat that rammed into them in heavy fog, front, hunt, Project Grinch Dust, crescent rolls, hazelnut pudding, hazel, witch hazel, witch hunt, nutcracker, nutmeg, the fact that Jeff Bridges orders hazelnut pudding in *The Contender*, Captain Wentworth, bridges, the fact that he's always trying to catch the White House kitchen out but they have everything he orders, even shark sandwiches, the fact that in the end they don't have Muenster cheese, the fact that the trouble was everybody needed their sidewalk cleared at the same time, but you'd think they'd have planned for that and hired more people, the fact that at least we got our money back, but we'd rather have our *snow* cleared, for goodness sake, the fact that there used to be neighborhood kids who'd shovel the snow for you, or rake leaves, to make a little spare cash, Coming Soon, a step backward, How Nude Yoga Has Helped Me, local bounty update, anchor rods, eardrum, the fact that if teenagers need money these days they just go work at KFC or Hardees or Pizza Hut or Dunkin' Donuts, where they can stay warm and talk to their friends all night, even if it *is* slave labor, the fact that you don't get beaten up at least, working a snowplow, Louisa May Alcott, pink cheeks, the fact that a baby elephant was born in a zoo on Christmas day, pinto pony, piebald, gelding, My Little Pony, Night Glider, Double Diamond, riding in a howdah, Gillian's elephant act, Miley Cyrus Forbids, the fact that teenagers don't deliver the paper anymore either, the fact that they let seniors do it, by car, inhaler, amniotic sac, fluid, doulas, ♬ *I'm no chump, I just bit off a camel's hump* ♬, Gekelmukpechunk, Coshochgunk, the fact that maybe I'm all wrong about that though, and the old guys are really just overgrown paper boys who could never find another job and never asked for promotion either, the fact that they just stuck with the paper route for seventy or eighty years, Interstate 70, the fact that it's so sad when old folks have to keep working till they drop, but they probably need to supplement their Medicare, the fact that you never know, maybe they *enjoy* the work, the fact that a lot of young people can't afford to buy a house anymore, or even pay the rent, the fact that they live in their *cars* but what do they do when they have to, to, go to the bathroom, ah, activity, the fact that now I hear door-slamming, oh here they come, all talking to me at once, talking *back* to me at once, the fact that every morning we have to go through this chaos, *Mr. Blandings Builds His Dream House*, the fact that Cary Grant and Myrna Loy are "modern cliff-dwellers," because they live in an apartment in

Manhattan, the fact that that makes them sound like puffins or something, living in canyons, the fact that Gillian's lost her homework, *again*, the fact that they treat me like Rex the Walkie-Talkie Robot Man, the fact that they have no respect, the fact that this whole household is outta control, ouch, and now Stacy's frowning at me, the fact that I don't know what I've done wrong this time, the fact that she's riled by my *sweat pants*, of all things, the fact that I never know what to wear and Stacy gets so steamed up about it, the fact that she's probably right but, gee, I'm just trying to be practical here, the fact that there's no point in dressing up just to caramelize apples, the fact that I dress down instead, the fact that I'm lazy about it, my look, the fact that I'm torn between being comfortable and being presentable, very torn, the fact that half my clothes are torn too, come to think of it, but I still like them, the fact that whatever happened to that Greek or Mexican shirt, the one with all the embroidery, the fact that it was red and white mostly, slot car racing track, the fact that I only got to go to that slot car place once, and that was with a friend's dad, the fact that Daddy would never take us, the fact that that shirt was nice, the fact that it was just a loose, simple garment, embroidered all over, varmint, and really comfortable, the fact that it was just two squares of cloth sewn together really, with arm holes out the sides and a hole for your head to get through, Miley, smiley, pile on, "Let's all pile on Mom," dressing up, fessing up, Twister, *Friends*, the fact that I guess it was sort of like a poncho, but better because it had sleeves, sort of, the fact that she says I can wear my loose sweaters if I wear tight jeans with them, but I don't want to wear skintight jeans all day, the fact that I really liked that thing, though I haven't thought about it in years, the fact that it wasn't just shapeless and floppy or anything, the fact that I thought it looked okay on, the fact that I wonder if it's in the attic, the fact that if it is, I'll never find it, the fact that it's more likely Stacy caught sight of it in my closet one day and threw it in the trash, the fact that that's the kind of thing she would do, the fact that she probably does it more than I know, because my clothes are always disappearing for no reason, The Truth About Alcohol, triumph over

adversity, the fact that now she wants me to get a *makeover*, the fact
that I think she thinks that all middle-aged women do is just sit around
having makeovers and plastic surgery all the time like on TV, but I'm
no glamorpuss, Miss America, misanthropy, missed opportunity, the
fact that makeovers are the new normal, prankster, the Fool, the fact
that Trump called Melania a "monster" when she was pregnant, and
maybe she is a monster, but he's one to talk, big fat bully, "grab 'em
by the ——," the fact that the idea of a makeover scares the heck out
of me, the fact that I'm too shy for that kind of thing, the fact that the
same goes for manicures, or personal shoppers, the fact that the first
time I even heard of personal shoppers I was horrified, the fact that I
can't imagine anything *worse* than being told what to wear by a
stranger, hijab, the fact that some manicurist got run over by a customer who refused to pay, the fact that I don't know how you can
enjoy your nails after you killed your manicurist, the fact that what
Stace doesn't get is that I'm just a manual laborer, and the one good
thing about being a manual laborer is that it's not practical to get all
dolled up to go to work, the fact that I hope Stacy never has to find
this out the hard way, glamorpuss, closure, zip code, 43832,
NASCAR racing, doily, dolly, Dilly, willy-nilly, folkloric, the fact
that a female police officer led a double life for nine years, Horror
Movie Hotel, the fact that nobody knows exactly what she got up to,
but don't all police officers lead a double life, like when they're off-
duty, Good Cop, Bad Cop, cancer cluster, the fact that how do you
bear it if your kid dies from cancer because your town's polluted, the
fact that that Nickel Mines book talked like the Amish are all just
supposed to accept that their kids might get killed at school any day
of the week, but no mother can accept that, nobody can, the fact that
they must be crazee, the fact that I don't care how religious a woman
may be, the fact that you don't just *get over* that sort of thing, the fact
that it's not just my outfits that bug Stace though, the fact that it's
everything I do, or don't do, the fact that, boy, she keeps a beady eye
on me, the fact that it starts to feel like she's been glaring at you all day
long, from dawn to dusk, creepy, crepuscular, muscular, muscle man,

the fact that she really seems to watch my every move, waiting for me to do something she can *get* me for, or maybe just so she can feel even more disgusted with me, the fact that she makes me so nervous, the fact that she's got me so spooked and frazzled I'm scared of *all* young women now, because when I look at them I see another potential mother-hater, the fact that I always wonder now how they treat their own moms, the fact that I avoid young women whenever possible, the fact that they frighten me, they do, *Nobody knows how cold my toes, How cold my toes are growing*, the fact that last fall when I used the old scooter, so I could pull Jakey along on his, Stacy gave us the evil eye, the fact that at times like that I tend to giggle, which doesn't help anything, purple martin houses, purple martin condos, purple martin apartment complexes, purple martin monasteries, the fact that I want purple martins, Dean Martin, ♫ *That's amore* ♫, marlin, Hemingway's cats, the fact that to attract purple martins you need a special kind of bird house with a lot of separate compartments that are deep enough so owls can't get at the martin babies, berries, berets, and you have to have small semicircular entrance holes to keep the starlings and sparrows out, because they eat the purple martin eggs, Florida Keys, Iguana Found Swimming Four Miles Out In Ocean, the fact that the guy that saves the iguana keeps calling him dude, "Dude, where ya goin'? Whatcha doin', dude?", the fact that, come to think of it, I need a purple martin house like a hole in the head, the fact that you have to check the compartments every week, and get rid of parasites and sparrows' nests and I don't know what, mites and ticks and stuff, the fact that, no thanks, count me out, worms, ring-fence, floozies, scarlet, Scarlatti, Scarlett O'Hara, Tara, O'Hara, terroir, terror, terrorism, terabyte, tetrabyte, pterodactyl, fractals, fractions, the fact that do they start fractions in second or third grade, I forget, the fact that I've got all these kids and chickens to look after, the fact that I don't need martin mites on top of that, the fact that I haven't got time to keep cranking a little purple martin apartment block up and down all the time, the fact that I just like how those houses look in people's back yards, the fact that a martin house wouldn't suit our plot either, the fact that we've got too many trees, the fact that martin houses have to be in a wide, exposed clearing, and they're supposed to be about fifteen feet off the ground, with no trees nearby, the fact that martins fly up here from Brazil, moss, so they really deserve the right kind of house, aquarium plants, the fact that I don't even have time to grow carrots, so how am I going to take care of a caravan of migrant martin families, *Give me your tired, your poor,* the fact that Ingres and Liszt knew each other, the fact that Liszt sounds awfully ambitious, a bit of a showoff really, the fact that you can tell by the music, whack job, rinky-dink, *your teeming shore,* zanahoria, the fact that I'd probably hurt my back the first time I tried to crank my martin house up and down, damsons, bread and cheese, quince, pear and cinnamon, the fact that I never checked if *Amish* martin houses are adjustable, but they probably are, the fact that I'd like having a martin house better if you could just leave the martins to get on with things by themselves, the fact that as a mom you learn the hands-off approach, arm's length, stay-put, stagnation vacation, the fact that things are never that easy, the fact that a bird in the hand is worth two in the bush, the fact that it takes two to tango, turnstile, turn the tables, the Tiny House movement, the fact that martins used to nest in hollow trees but now that we've cleared all the forests, they really do seem to need manmade martin houses, the fact that we sort of owe it to them to provide alternative accommodation, "Four more years!", refugees, detainees, Japanese internment camps, Manus Island, the fact that birds have it made, the fact that sometimes you can't believe how simple life is for them, the fact that they get up, look around for some food, no cooking involved, squabble a bit, or bill and coo and fly around, in packs or on their own, flocks I mean, not *packs,* and then the day is done and they go roost again, the fact that they don't seem to mind the cold either, the fact that it must be hard for caged birds to watch free birds flying around outside, the fact that Gillian illustrated her seagull report so well, the fact that where did that thing go now, gulls, sea eagles, the fact that we can't have lost it, Gullah, purloo, civil engineering, Freshwater Geechees and Saltwater Geechees, the fact that the

Saltwater Geechees talk faster than the Freshwater Geechees, the fact that they kind of look *down* on the Freshwater Geechees, the fact that that Saltwater Geechee woman said "Can't they talk any faster than that? People don't have all day," the fact that not only do they get to fly, but they never have to pay *taxes*, birds, that is, not Geechees, the fact that Geechees do have to pay taxes, more and *more* taxes, Sapelo Island, the fact that my first car was a, was a, the fact that people make such a big thing about their car and all the different car brands, when they all look the same to me, asthma deaths, the fact that birds are flying reptiles, cold-blooded, killer, the fact that chickens don't fly but they're okay because they have a warm coop, the fact that chickens are the closest thing to dinosaurs, the fact that, bad back or no bad back, taxes or no taxes, snow or no snow, success or failure, I've got to get there pies to their destinations today, the fact that I'd rather stay here, nice and snug, staring out the window at the snow on the Kinkels' roof, the fact that the snow's really blue right now, and twinkling, the fact that they have a new marble bathroom, and a shabby chic cupboard in the downstairs hall, Marie Kondo, taekwondo, working mom, Dutch baby, the fact that I think *I* invented shabby chic, but I wouldn't tell Doreen that, the fact that I wouldn't want to spoil her pride in her new cupboard, the fact that I bet it cost a lot, the fact that she got it professionally spoiled, Mommy, peaches in cream, ivy patch, Abby's exact portions per person, and one extra for Leftover Night, Why Your Dog Hates Your Cell Phone, medical marijuana, gummies, the fact that wasn't there a movie called *Reefer* or, no, *Reefer Madness*, hummingbirds, Leo, Dare To Take Our Personality Test, the fact that the best way to get through stuff you don't want to do, I've decided, is to pretend it's not really *you* doing it, like you're just temporarily inside somebody else's body that this is all happening to, stable unless exposed to fire, Killer Of Widow Gets Life, water somersault, belly flop, synchronized swimming, PERSONS CAUGHT CRAWLING, the fact that people are always trying to think about what they *want* to think about, steer your thoughts, steerage, peerage, the fact that some people have more of a fondness for the past than I do, the fact that

Elizabeth Bennet recommends only remembering things that please you, but that's not so easy, the fact that I don't remember much, and everything I do remember makes me sad, Resurfacing Announced, mindfulness, the fact that my memory is so intermittent that sometimes I just tell people I'm living in the Now, man, but they don't always fall for it, the fact that I don't know what mindfulness *is*, the fact that if you have no memory, you get bulldozed by people with better memories than you, like my whole entire family for instance, *Remember remember the Fifth of November*, makeovers, Stacy, TV, the fact that they know I can't remember a gosh darn thing and love teasing me about it, out-remembering me whenever they feel like it, the fact that sometimes I kind of wonder if they're faking it, to beat me on the memory front, the fact that it sure seems to come in awful handy sometimes, the fact that the kids love to torment me about the past, when there's nothing else to do in the car, say, or the store, or in front of our friends, the fact that they're all hey, let's mock Mom, the fact that Leo says *he* can't remember anything either and it must be something in the water, and it's true, there *is* something in the water, a whole lot of things, like nitrates, lead, mercury, sewage, PFOA and PFCs and PFAS, and peas, probably *pee*, from Parkersburg, ♫ *On the banks of the Ohio* ♫, but Leo's just being nice, because I had a bad memory long before I ever drank Tuscarawas water, long before I even met him, though maybe Evanston and New Haven water wasn't that great either, H_2O, the fact that sometimes there were dead fish on the shore of Lake Michigan, our poor terrapins, Cemetery Mound, Circleville, ducks, the fact that secretly I think the real reason I have no memory is I find the past unbearable so I kind of *blot it out*, the fact that maybe everybody does, babies' dimples, ♫ *count your blessings instead of sheep* ♫, boarlets, the fact that my past's probably not as bad as lots and lots of people's, but I just can't seem to think about it without getting upset, so I try not to think about it, the fact that that's the only solution I've so far come up with, the fact that I have all those photos rotting up there in the attic, the fact that everybody else digitizes all their photos, or deletes them, spotted skunk, Doreen and

Jerry's Giant Viper's Bugloss, Scioto River, but going through photos just makes me paralytically sad, and I don't really have time to get frozen to the spot, weeping over old photos, most days anyway, the fact that anyway I think you can *overdo* remembering stuff, you really can, Nickel Mines shooting, Bourgogne shipwreck, Sable island, the fact that, after all, the present is more relevant than the past, Now, the fact that it's more in-your-face anyway, PFOA, PTA, ACA, ACLU, DuPont, shaky bridges, ♫ *London Bridge is falling down* ♫, Abby's old, yellowed, BBQ sauce recipe index card, the fact that I remember Declan Kiberd's talk at Notre Dame, the fact that that I do remember, and he said people *fetishize* the past, in Ireland, the fact that he said the Irish were drunk on remembrance, like Hamlet and the ghost, the fact that I can't understand people who want to go over and over old times, getting all nostalgic and stuff, the fact that I'm *scared* of old times, the fact that old times are soggy, saggy cradles of regret, about Mommy or Pepito, or even Pierre, or Dilly, or my bird costume, Phoebe's Marlboro cigarette packet, going to the movies with Chuck, the fact that I don't really see why I blot it all out, since it's not all *bad* or anything, the fact that nobody ever clunked me over the head with a frying pan, or shot me in the abdomen, or force-fed me laxatives or acid or left me in a burning building or dropped me from a plane, with or without a parachute, or stole my husband, not yet anyway, the fact that it's just that it's *past*, that's all, and there's nothing I can *do* about any of it anymore, so why go there, Revere Ware, Teflon, Ohio River, Mississippi, the fact that I was never in an avalanche or a war either, though I *was* in a bus accident, on Lake Shore Drive, snow banks, Lynn's broken femur, but I didn't get hurt, the fact that I've never been raped either, except almost, and when I had cancer they cured it, as far as I can tell, so all in all I don't have much to regret or kvetch about, Project Ketch, the fact that, still, just about every memory somehow takes me back to something I don't much want to think about, Fukushima, the fact that Chuck and I only went to the movies once, nuclear waste, Nagasaki, the fact that Mommy was so sick, the fact that I had to run the industrial-size dishwasher at Mo's and clean the bathroom, the Ohio, the Monongahela, the Cuyahoga, Potomac, the fact that even sea turtles now have PFOA in them, beluga whales, meerkats, dinner pail, the fact that the Ohio River was important to the Underground Railway, and so was Ohio, the fact that sometimes I forget the *nice* things, not just the bad stuff, and that gets other people down, like Leo, but I can't help it, catastrophe, enormity, disaster at sea, candy love hearts, Candy-Apple Red mixer, singles mixer, candy corn, camera, Opal and Frederick, the fact that I instantly forget all the stuff we've done together as a family, family trips to the zoo or all the fun fairs, slub silk, slug, or the Taft Museum or our visit to the McKinley Mausoleum, oh, those steps, the fact that I remember them all right, wow, the fact that there were over a hundred, with all kinds of people puffing up and down them, the fact that I was scared some-body would have a heart attack climbing up there, and it might have been *me*, the fact that it's hard to believe McKinley really wanted a sword-shaped stairway, or even a waterfall, jack-o'-lanterns, jigsaws, Jack and the Beanstalk, "Bienstock, I oughtta fire you!", Chicago Zoo, the Planetarium, Science Museum, the Art Institute, the fact that I think we'd just been to the Science Museum the day we had the bus crash, probably the Science Museum, with all the buttons to press, the fact that McKinley and Garfield were both shot in office, USB stick, styptic stick, scabbard, haggard, hassled, the fact that eight different presidents came from Ohio, McKinley, Garfield, Taft, Ulysses S. Grant and I forget the rest, Harding, the fact that because McKinley was assassinated, poor man, I had to drag myself up a hundred steps on a really hot day, Denali, denial, #resist, the fact that it was like Laurel and Hardy with the piano, the fact that we should've walked *down* the steps, not *up*, heave-ho, the fact that I also don't remember the jazz recordings Leo played me on our wedding eve, and that really upsets him, the fact that I can't remember much about the hotel we stayed at in Amherst either, when he proposed, though I know I broke a glass, out of sheer happiness, the fact that we bought Stacy a minia-ture piano at a junk shop the next day, the fact that that I remember, ♫ *love's old sweet song* ♫, euphoria, nap, Mommy, the fact that I don't remember much about the motel we stayed at near the Chillicothe mounds either, and it was all *my* idea to go there too, single-serve containers, seasonal fare, the fact that every year I forget how to cook asparagus and have to look it up, and artichokes, Leftover Night, the fact that things taste so much better once you've forgotten the effort of cooking them, the fact that it's like forgetting labor pains, or the effort involved in painting a room, the fact that wallpapering's worse, the fact that with wallpaper you really need a professional, the fact that you don't want all those bubbles and wrinkles all over the place, bumps, blotches, the fact that I would probably wallpaper myself to the wall, the fact that now I've forgotten what I came in the pantry for, the fact that I should finish filling the dishwasher first, the fact that the taste of lukewarm milk, and the smell of burnt toast, always remind me of our year in London, I don't know why, the fact that of course everybody remembers different things from childhood, the fact that that's why you need siblings, to tell you what you forgot, or tell you what happened from *their* point of view, but I really seem to remember the least of any of us, "baby of the family," so I'm no help at all, the fact that Jake remembers plenty, even though he's the youngest, the fact that he's good at remembering his dreams too, like the one he had about pancakes in a forest, "Why were they wearing helmets?", horse-hair worm, scooter, Leo kissing me on Orange Street, the fact that when people question me about the past, I often have to either fudge it, fudge brownies, hot fudge sundaes at Macy's, or change the subject, or just admit I don't remember what everybody else remembers perfectly well, burnt toast, rusks, Pepito, the fact that with four kids there are only so many poignant moments a mom can keep track of, ♫ *Soaky soaks you clean* ♫, fit to be tied, Central Street dime store, the fact that I remember the big sour pickles we used to buy at the store on hot days, sitting cross-legged, Hawaiian Punch, the ol' one-two, banana splits, cheerleaders in agony, group hug, live and let live, a bird in the hand, the fact that at Peolia I couldn't even remember the stuff I was supposed to *teach* unless I boned up on it the night before, swatting up Ulysses S. Grant, the Lincoln assassination, Quantrill's Raiders, Ohio canals, Netawatwes, Heckewelder, McKinley, Serpent Mound and Alligator Mound, the fact that all they really wanted to hear about was the Civil War, and how Ohio played a big role in it, venomous Australian sea snakes, the fact that they were a lot less interested in Indian mounds, the fact that Indian mounds were a real uphill struggle, like McKinley's hundred steps, the fact that thirty-five thousand Ohioans died in the Civil War, CBS, CNN, MSNBC, the fact that alligators aren't scared of sharks, the fact that Stacy attended one of my classes, and I really didn't remember that either, until she mentioned it, the fact that she must have been sick that day or something, and it was too late to cancel the class, the fact that that must have been in my first year, the fact that she must have been seven or so, the fact that all I know is I hope she wasn't there for the class on Hopewell burial customs, with me going on about extended burials, flexed burials, bundled burials and grave goods, cremated, decomposed, bad dreams, ♫ *I'm just wild about animal crackers, animal crackers* ♫, the fact that I just remembered *my* dream last night, the fact that I was at a pool complex but I left and got on a miniature train, the fact that there was a big wedding celebration going on right in the middle of the town and I passed right by it on the miniature train, the fact that we lived somewhere else but I wanted to find a more central spot, flexed, the fact that teaching really took it out of me, bundled, the fact that I always ended up staying up half the night prepping and then being dog-tired all through my classes, burial mounds, Hero Sheepdogs, Winning Jackpot Numbers, safari jacket, quinine, seltzer, Cute Pandas Share A Piece Of Bamboo, extended, the fact that I can remember buying the pants I'm wearing right now, the fact that it was about eight years ago, and I remember hesitating, because they're pretty awful, as Stace just pointed out, but they've actually turned out to be useful, dodo, do-si-do, do re mi fa so la ti do, the fact that women on the pill are twenty percent more in danger of getting breast cancer, the fact that Sally-Ann's mom told me, the fact that Jake's first word was "dangerous," the fact that maybe I laid the warnings on a bit thick, about stairs and sockets and steak knives, either that or maybe he was

60

just trying to say "hydrangea," hydrangea danger, the fact that Jakey's often in his own world, a world filled to the brim with nurdles, yellow backhoe trucks, raisins, excelsior, the fact that when Leo asked him how playgroup went, Jake said, "Rrrreally good!", with a *growl* on the "really" that was worthy of the tiger from the Frosties ad, whatshisname, baby bath, bassinet, brocade, brochettes, bruschetta, the fact that now I've forgotten the tiger's name, "Grrrrreat!", Frostie maybe, no, Tony, Tony the Tiger, the fact that nobody uses the word "enormity" right, the fact that Mommy was very bugged by that, but what can you do, the fact that there's always another person coming along who uses it all wrong, the fact that people think it's got something to do with magnitude, enormousness, something humongous, bigly, but it's not that at all, the fact that it's a *catastrophe*, not largesse, the fact that I was trying to explain this to Ben when Stacy piped up and said I was talking *down* to him, but I didn't mean to, the fact that she hates it when I adjust what I'm saying to the kids' level, the fact that she says you should talk to your kids just like you talk to anybody else, but I thought I *did*, do, flexed burial, fluctuation, fructify, fruity, zoot suit, lawsuit, three-piece suit, waistcoat, vest, the fact that now she's made me all self-conscious, the fact that I didn't know I was talking down to them, the fact that just because you speak *slowly* and *clearly* maybe to a child sometimes doesn't necessarily mean you're being condescending, the fact that "existential" is another one that nobody understands anymore, the fact that they all seem to think it just means you *exist*, the fact that they use it to mean something's *sustainable* or something, nothing to do with Sartre and feeling alienated and drinking a lot of wine at Café Flore, ecology, but what do I know, the fact that I don't know anything about French philosophy for a start, the fact that that stuff goes right over my head, in one ear and out the other, shutting the stable door after the horse has bolted, the fact that people used to bring live animals on ocean voyages, and slaughter them along the way for food, the fact that maybe they still do, the fact that the poor animal must think he's going on a trip somewhere, "Not so fast, Goldberg!", the fact that Gillian had her own existential crisis the other night, crying into her pillow, the fact that when I asked her what was up, she said she was worried about the *meaning of life*, the meaning of life, the fact that I just didn't know what to say, the fact that you can't tell a little kid that it's quite possible life has *no* meaning, the fact that what kid wants to hear *that*, the fact that it might push her too far and turn her into a Moonie or something, the fact that everybody means something *different* anyway when they talk about "the meaning of life," the fact that for some it's goodness or something, and other people think ice cream and popcorn and soap operas give their lives meaning, Gillian's honey bear collection, the fact that what do *I* know, the fact that just because you're a mom doesn't mean you've got all the answers, the fact that I said she shouldn't worry about it, cop-out, Hopalong Cassidy, fossils, flossing, fear of failure, Facts of Life, the birds and the bees, the bumble bee at Bread Loaf, the fact that it sometimes feels like my memory has very, very ancient times in it, like the dark ages, stuff from long ago that's pretty dim, and then come the *medieval* times that aren't quite as impenetrable but still pretty blurry, snow flurry, furry, curry in a hurry, and then there's the Renaissance, which is the more recoverable stuff, and then there's recent stuff that's clear and *vivid*, like Gillian crying about the meaning of life, the fact that I wish I could forget just about all of it, and live in a fog, merciful fog, prehistoric, petrified forest, water bears, microwave packets, mascara, Mr. Schaeffer, the fact that there are all the people I should have kept in touch with and now I can't even remember their names, teachers and people like that, or Mommy and Daddy's friends, the fact that *they* seem like ancient history but they're probably all still around and living about ten miles away, for all I know, somewhere anyway, and they eat and sleep and get up and go to the bathroom in the middle of the night just like everybody else, the fact that just because I neglected them, doesn't mean they don't exist, the fact that maybe they think about the meaning of life too, and drink coffee every morning and work and socialize and love people or quarrel with them and change gender even, and *I'm* ancient history to *them*, no ill will or anything, the fact that you dig up occasional relics of the past, memories or associations, but they're so cloudy you can't decipher their meaning, the fact that I keep remembering the warm draft from that window in Michigan, or the bee at Bread Loaf, and where does it get me, spelling bees, Bee Gives Man A High Five, Bee Chemical, Dow Chemical, Dow Jones National Average, snare drums, the fact that Stacy tried to comfort me about my bad memory once at dinner, the fact that I'd just admitted I couldn't remember something or other, I can't remember what, and she said "The past should be forgotten, the future should not be foreseen, and the present should be borne proudly," the fact that I don't know where that came from but it sounded *good*, the fact that nobody knew what to say, but maybe a family that gets confused together stays together, Girl With 2 Dads, triangle, poitrine, enceinte, toilette, eau de toilette, toilet water, chickens' water bowl, *Samson et Dalila*, Matted Dog Found In Barn, the fact that the kids really want a dog, the fact that the things we've done to animals, Bayer, 3M, DuPont, chemical plants, aquarium gardens, the fact that Ben knows about lots of stuff, yet all he really *wants* to think about is the Abominable Snowman, Yeti, Sasquatch, Big Foot, Skookum, the Loch Ness Monster, and the Mothman, cryptids, the fact that I liked it when all he talked about was *pirates*, the fact that he keeps seeing Abominable Snowmen in the back yard, the fact that we live in the Sasquatch Triangle, which may explain the way *I* feel most of the time, squamous, squeamish, squelchy, squishy, Princess Di, FLORENCE Y'ALL, the fact that he just stole Gillian's toast, y'all, rusks, the fact that we ate rusks at Channing, and I didn't know what they were, the fact that I still don't know what rusks are to this day, but they were okay washed down with lukewarm milk, rusks and milk, the fact that it's like feeding an *army* around here, "An army marches on its stomach," belly button, inny, outy, eggs over easy, queasy, sneezy, Dopey, Happy, Sleepy, bad eggs, Budington, the fact that Gary Cooper's trying to find a rhyme for Budington all through *Mr. Deeds Goes to Town*, but he never does, the fact that I think they forgot all about it, the fact that what rhymes with Budington, jutting gun, rubbing son, loving one, the fact that Clarence Budington Kelland wrote the original story that *Mr. Deeds Goes to Town* was based on, the fact that he was called Bud for short, the fact that I don't know now about having string beans tonight after all, the fact that I think maybe it better be butter beans, and some Harvard Beets, but butter beans might be too much with porcupine meatballs, Betty Boughter, Anthony Weiner, wieners, Lawrence Weiler, hot dogs, cheese croquettes, chicken à la king, Irish stew, creamed corn casserole, sheet cake, Australian sea snakes, the fact that maybe that's what I should make for the cocktail party, mini porcupine meatballs on toothpicks, stick shift, gearshift, styptic stick, cock, boner, stiffy, dear me, what's gotten into me, the fact that earthquake cakes always seem kind of tactless to me, the fact that they have all that shifting chocolate sludge on the top, like tectonic plates colliding and dissolving into mush, and the M&Ms float on top like rubble, the fact that it's really like the scene of a disaster, in miniature, the fact that even snakes get killed in earthquakes, because their tunnels cave in on them, the fact that you always think animals will get away but snakes can't, the fact that birds and butterflies can, and other bugs, and people in airplanes and helicopters are in luck, looking down at the cracking bridges and highways and all, the fact that animals often know an earthquake's coming, goldfish, TetraFin flakes, hamballs, the fact that dogs can be trained to predict their owners' epileptic fits, but not the other way around, the fact that Mommy used to make porcupine meatballs a *lot*, I don't know why, the fact that I sort of liked them but I was always a little thrown by the name, the fact that maybe I thought she'd somehow rustled up some porcupine meat from the A&P, or from some hillbilly, the fact that maybe she didn't make them exactly right, porcupines, hedgehogs, the fact that sometimes the rice wasn't cooked enough, the fact that it's terrible of me to wonder about that *now*, the fact that I'm sure she did her best, the fact that I think you're supposed to use cooked rice though, and maybe she forgot, the fact that recipes change all the time through forgetfulness, evolving, revolving, Chicago World's Fair, Thorne Miniature Rooms, jutting gun, muddied son, son of a gun, stepping stones, *It pays to advertise*, the fact that, no, you *are* supposed to put the rice in *raw*, and it's all just supposed to cook while the meatballs are frying, and the balls are supposed to look like little porcupines because of the rice sticking out all over them like quills, but the rice is bound to still be *hard*, the fact that maybe that's why they're not all that great, but it's just fun to say "meatball," I mean "*porcupine*," the fact that who wants to say "meatball," the fact that you hardly *ever* get a chance to say "porcupine," the fact that I should ask Phoebe and Ethan if *they* liked Mommy's porcupine meatballs, How Largemouth Bass Suck In Their Prey, the fact that I wonder if Bigfoot ever put his big foot in it the way *I* do, the fact that I dreamt somebody was driving me in her SUV, the fact that I don't know who it was but she was driving so fast I couldn't get my seatbelt on, on account of the G-force, and I couldn't imagine why anyone needed to go that fast, the fact that I was thinking of saying something but I restrained myself, possum stew, enormity, the fact that eventually she did slow down a little, extinction, roadkill, dead deer, The Lady Who Loves Lobsters, the fact that I didn't like that VR place at all, the fact that the underwater program was *scary*, the fact that they said it was just going to be *pretty*, but actually I felt kind of dizzy and over-whelmed, by *jellyfish*, they all kept coming at me and swimming right over my head, getting bigger and bigger and closer and closer, the fact that you could kind of waft them away with your hands but it was a big job keeping track of them all and I really didn't know what would happen if I missed one and it bumped into me, the fact that I half-believed it might sting me, the fact that VR makes you feel so silly, the fact that I felt like I was about to fall over any minute too, right in front of Brad and Ben, and what a dope I'd look, sprawled across the floor of the VR center in my baggy sweater, shooing jellyfish away, the fact that you never want to give nine-year-olds an excuse to laugh at you if you can help it, Marlon Brando on a motorcycle, I'm 74 And I Love Boxing, the fact that the oldest man in the world just passed on, the fact that he was an Auschwitz survivor, the fact that Stacy got this out of her Citizenship class, the fact that jellyfish are sort of like *weeds*, and their numbers are growing fast, the fact that they like

moving around in huge gangs, so I guess they're friendly enough to
each other at least, not so much to anybody else, the fact that a big
swarm of poisonous jellyfish got tangled up in that salmon farm and
56,000 salmon died in *agony*, in about half an hour, The Real Source
Of Your Fatigue, Kim Jong Un's brother's death, VR, VX, red tide,
the fact that jellyfish are five hundred and sixty million years old, and
there are five hundred and sixty million of them wiggling through the
world, give or take a few, the fact that that's a heck of a lot of jellyfish,
though nowhere near the human population, but still, the fact that it's
a bit of a weird coincidence, five hundred and sixty million years and
five hundred and sixty million jellyfish, one year per jellyfish, the fact
that maybe some scientist got all his numbers mixed up, the fact that
somebody said dried jellyfish could be the potato chips of the twenty-
second century, bleccchh, the fact that I'm sure jellyfish don't want
to become the next potato chips, the fact that fish feel pain, the fact
that they used to deny it, the scientists I mean, not the fish, the fact
that what's that movie where Marlon Brando's on a motorcycle heading for a town full of *squares*, town squares, pain, James Mason, James
Dean, *Some Like it Hot*, blunt force, the fact that there's probably a
movie called *Blunt Force*, the fact that Alec Guinness warned James
Dean not to get in that car, the fact that he said James Dean would be
dead in a week if he rode in that thing, but James Dean took off
anyway and crashed the very same *day*, he didn't even last a week,
the fact that I wonder if Hollywood stars have more road accidents
than everybody else, the fact that it sure seems like it, but maybe it's
no more than the national average, the fact that we're a nation of
daredevils, the fact that eleven percent of drivers keep driving when
the gas tank's empty, wishful thinking, the fact that maybe we should
have shepherd's pie tonight, "Sheppards Pie," the fact that I almost
tripped on Gillian's *snow globe* just then, the fact that the Great Barrier
Reef is dying, the fact that it can only exist if the ocean stays a certain
temperature, which it probably *won't*, and there's also some kind of
thorny star fish eating up all the coral, the globe, the fact that Triton
snails are the starfish's only natural predator, but the Triton snails are

all getting sold as tourist souvenirs, so they're not eating the thorny starfish anymore, the fact that it can't be easy eating a thorny starfish, the fact that nobody else wants to do it, Graham crackers, Girl Scout cookies, Gloria Grahame, the fact that Graham crackers are getting sweeter, but Leo still likes them, needs over wants, Production For Use, the fact that he doesn't go for s'mores though, the fact that turtles get stuck in those six-pack rings, with the plastic biting into their shells for *years*, until the turtle's all *deformed*, Chickens Wearing Pants, the fact that one turtle looked like a woman in a tight corset, like Vivien Leigh in *Gone with the Wind*, the fact that a turtle's not supposed to have an hourglass figure, figure eight, infinity sign, Gillian's next birthday cake, skating in Ackerman Park, the fact that these turtles suffer for life, so that we can briefly carry Coke in bulk, the fact that I don't know where all the plastic trash in the world should go, but not on a turtle, Northwestern University pond, the fact that Leo's new notebook's made out of *stone*, or stone dust, and it was supposed to be ecological, the fact that that's why he bought it, but then he realized this stone paper has a tiny amount of plastic all through it, which makes it *non-recyclable*, "Goodbye, Charlie," the fact that Spanish flu killed more people all over the globe than the First World War, the fact that if you have Spanish flu you feel like you're drowning and that's because you *are* drowning, oh dear, the fact that the Yale Co-op isn't what it used to be, Harvard Coop, Ford coupe, chicken coop, chicken poop, "Stay away from the Ivy League," the fact that I really should lighten up or it'll affect my cinnamon rolls, rolling pin with heart shapes on each rim, the fact that I oughtta roll with the punches more, don't sweat the small stuff, Half Moon Bay, waxing, waning, the fact that I better *eat* something is all, but if you eat too much you don't feel like baking, and I can't afford to slow down here, the fact that I have a lot of pies to bake today, Easter Island, the fact that I couldn't if I tried, with all these timers about to go off, the fact that the average teen checks their phone *two thousand times* a day, the fact that I don't believe that, two thousand times, the fact that the mainstream media are craphounds, gee, the fact that I don't think I've ever *used* the word "craphounds" before in my whole entire life, the fact that I've been corrupted by the internet, Katie's Divorce Gets Nasty, buckeyes, Sikhs, the fact that "Sikh" should be pronounced *sik*, Leo says, not *seek*, *I don't know but they know*, polluting the water table, the fact that Frederick's miaowing, *For he is of the tribe of Tiger*, the fact that I bet Ben's the only kid in school who actually takes in those movies they show in Earth Science classes, about the millions of people who died of Spanish flu, the fact that "curriculum" is an ugly word, *so* ugly, but it's not the one I was trying to think of before, the fact that the school motto is Build Body, Build Mind, Build Freedom, the fact that freedom's the *last* item on the list, the fact that schools aren't hot on freedom, usually, really, the fact that this place has all sorts of rules and regulations, the fact that the kids aren't supposed to eat candy or drink pop on the school bus, or wear any clothing that has drawings or sayings on it that refer to sex, drugs, alcohol, violence, death or hate, and you can't fix tears in your clothes with masking tape, though who would do that, or expose your midriff, or wear Spandex or pajamas, but you *can* get a day off to go deer-hunting, the fact that Ben's a good student, mostly, and he likes science stuff, but he hates *math*, the fact that he got the *police* to help him once, the fact that I was no help, the fact that as soon as I see numbers in parentheses I kind of freeze up, parenthesis, parenthetical, parental, the fact that Leo wasn't home, so Ben walked right on over to the phone and called the cops, martin houses, using algae for fuel, the fact that they said to send the problem over on Facebook, and it turned into a sort of fun thing, the fact that some police officer wrote right back to him and gave him the answer, the fact that it wasn't exactly the right answer but it was close, and his math teacher thought the whole thing was hilarious, the fact that she's always so cheerful, not like some math teachers, big mouth, the fact that she has a big laugh too, Mrs. M., the fact that she starts every class with a class yell, the fact that I had a Mr. T., when I was at school, Serpent Mound, Holmes County, Tuscarawas, Coshocton, caramel pretzel crunch ice cream, taco soup, Haiti, the fact that Haiti's a free country now, but it took a long while, the fact that that's the first place Columbus got to, Columbo, column, calumny, Worst Celebrity Splits, cheerleaders forced to do the splits, Harrowing Footage, the fact that the banana split was invented in 1904, the fact that someone actually had to invent it, the banana split, the fact that banana splits don't just happen like torn ligaments, the fact that there's a lot of planning that goes into a banana split, house-boat, Sophia Loren, the fact that in 2004, people marked the cente-nary of the splitting of the banana, the fact that there were all sorts of parades and festivities, I forget where, maybe in Latrobe, the fact that that's where the banana split was invented, in a pharmacy in Latrobe, Pennsylvania, or maybe a luncheonette, not a pharmacy, soda foun tain, franchise, galoshes, carhops, banana split eating contests, the Miss Banana Split contest, Little Miss Banana Split contest, Frank, Chuck, pinch pie, rice pudding pie, the fact that there's such a thing as *rice puddingpie*, the fact that I hope I'm never asked to make one, the fact that Cathy would never make me do that, the fact that first you make a pot of rice pudding and then you put meringue all over it, the fact that to eat a thing like that, the fact that it must really make you nau-seous just cooking it, never mind *eating* it, the fact that thankfully nobody here will ever ask for one, that's for sure, because nobody in this family's prepared to eat rice pudding in any form, even in a pie, the fact that they'd rather eat funnel cake, chimney cake, Earthquake Cake, the fact that Mommy liked rice pudding, and Daddy did too, but I associate it more with Mommy, the fact that maybe she would've liked a nice big rice pudding pie, steaming hot, or maybe it's better chilled, "shaken, not stirred," but I doubt it, the fact that her kind was baked with milk, butter, brown sugar and nutmeg, like Amish Baked Oatmeal, but not so thick, solid, Edgar Rice Burroughs, Tarzan, Tarzana, the fact that the Amish are just *gone* on sugar, the fact that Daddy liked semolina too, and all that kind of stuff, reflux, reflex, Latrobe, lactose, the Silver Bridg collapse, stress corrosion cracking, acceleration, inertia, momentum, spinal fluid, the fact that once that bridge started cracking, the whole thing came down in about a *minute*, right at rush hour, with lots of people crossing the bridge, the fact that

that *was* an enormity, the fact that Leo said they hadn't inspected it enough, Gallipolis, the Mothman, flying humanoids, meringue, the fact that after Mommy passed away we made Abby the official matriarch of the family and she thought we said "meringue of the family," which sort of suited her even better, the fact that I wish she was here right now, the fact that we'd have a great time, the fact that I probably wish this a dozen times a day, without even noticing, the fact that her German Potato Salad recipe uses salad potatoes, dill, and toasted caraway seeds, in a vinaigrette sauce, the fact that you fry half an onion, roughly chopped, till it's translucent, the fact that some people add some German sausage at the end but Abby didn't, Diet Now Pay Later, the fact that the main thing is the dill and the vinegar and the toasted caraway seeds, Ingredients Everyone Uses But Shouldn't, the fact that I often long to be back in Abby's neat, tidy house, with snow outside and ice cream inside, the fact that she was proud of all her colonial-style furniture and kept it well polished, polish wipes, Abby with her Swiffer, the fact that that was the first Swiffer I ever saw, and now everybody's got one, the fact that Abby was way ahead of her time, the fact that I loved her rag rugs, the fact that she braided and braided those rags and then sewed the braids together into a flat disk, the fact that she made one rag rug after another, right after she got married, the fact that I don't know if she used real rags or she bought the cloth somewhere, but they were pretty, and *useful*, the fact that they lasted her a lifetime, whiskey-and-gingers, the fact that I wish I was there right now, and *how*, just her and me and it's five o'clock, drink time, the fact that instead I'm in Newcomerstown, and it's 7:36 in the morning, the fact that I've been up for hours, more coffee, the fact that she was so house-proud she used to get a new roof put on every ten years, whether it needed it or not, the fact that Mommy thought that was way too extravagant, the fact that Abby got the whole exterior repainted every five years too, all spic and span, and always the same two shades, that tan color, and a muddy brown for the shutters, or no, once the *main* part was light brown, with beigey-yellow shutters, the fact that it looked good though, either way, the fact that I knitted a whole baby blanket there in Abby's house when I was pregnant with Stace, the fact that Abby taught me, the fact that it was terrible that time Abby wrote us she'd thrown out all of Mommy's letters, the fact that, boy, was Daddy mad, the fact that our whole *history* was in those letters, he said, the fact that she did keep the *photographs*, but that made him even madder, the fact that he didn't care about the photographs, the fact that Daddy never told Abby how he felt though, because it was already too late, but he told *me* he would've done *anything* to have all those letters, the fact that Mommy wrote great letters, and she wrote Abby about once a week, so there must've been a lot to throw out, the fact that he said "Our whole history was in those letters," the fact that some folks are just allergic to paper, the fact that Abby was always throwing stuff out, the fact that she prided herself on her neatness, the fact that their house was never full of papers like ours was, the fact that Abby's house was full of balls of wool instead, carefully stacked, of course, and eagle ornaments, and maybe ice cream, rag rugs, and that was about it, the fact that a teenager killed his dad's girlfriend on Christmas day, the fact that she was trying to protect her daughter, the fact that he stabbed the daughter too but she survived and now she's vowed to see him sent to jail if it's the last thing she does, the fact that the things people do, the fact that why do a thing like that, and at Christmas of all times, fluorescent bulb, Mommy, rice pudding, serum, mastectomy, black shoes, the fact that it wasn't enough for Mommy to be paralyzed for life, the fact that she had to get breast cancer as well, the fact that I cried with Daddy in the kitchen when we found out, bright fluorescent white strip bulb, blackness outside, snow, crown die-back, tiny ivory Inuit duck for using in a board game, Monopoly, two big wide Inuit snow shoes in a museum, the fact that I don't know how the Inuits ever walked in those things, the fact that it would be like walking on two great big laundry basket lids or something, the fact that I dreamt Phoebe gave me a pair of foot-high, foot-wide wedge shoes, the same as a pair *she* had in the dream, and they were surprisingly comfortable, the fact that it was like walking on great big cuboid cushions, and kind of nice, the fact that I wish I could see that Inuit duck again, rare spotted skunk, skunk eggs, skunk-skin loin cloths, Mommy, Ma Ingalls's corn bread with the imprint of her hand on top, the fact that Laura Ingalls Wilder's mom always pressed her hand on the top of the cornbread before she baked it, and Pa said that was all he needed, Ma's cornbread with her handprint on it, bundt cake, bumf, Drumpf, maker's mark, Do Your Kids Know The Value Of Money?, 7:59, the fact that I just can't believe now that I ever even used to teach at Peolia, the fact that teaching's a strange thing for *me* to do, the fact that teaching's for the spry, not the shy, the fact that I thought I'd get used to it or something, or at least get away with it, FOOSH, ♫ *The man who broke the bank at Monte Carlo* ♫, $24,000 for a broken arm, $100,000 for a leg, the fact that I never sued Peolia when I broke my wrist on their property, the fact that my reluctance to sue had nothing to do with any remaining loyalty to Peolia, far from it, the fact that I never *had* any loyalty to Peolia, the fact that I always felt nothing but *contempt* for Peolia College and still do, the fact that the only reason I didn't sue was because of the *way* I broke my wrist, tripping on one of those nice tree roots, the fact that they do have beautiful trees there, red oak, white ash, hemlock, hickory, and huge buckeyes, and their roots trail down like arteries, all the way down the hill, the fact that I was scared if I mentioned the tree root to Moira, that tree would be a goner, the fact that it would be just like Peolia College to cut the whole tree down in revenge, just to satisfy the insurance man, or maybe even the whole forest, why not, along with a bunch of unsuspecting backwoodsmen eating pancakes and bacon in some clearing, lumberjacks, OSH, OshKosh B'gosh, "My stew can stand on its own two feet," the fact that, nope, I wouldn't put it past Peolia College to bear a grudge against an old tree, Campus Security, safety, safety pins, the fact that they'd do anything to avoid a lawsuit, diapers, hot water bottle, colostomy bags, the fact that we aren't litigious types, but they didn't know that, the fact that maybe that's why Moira asked me so particularly what happened, just in case I had a case, litigate, ligature, legitimate, illegitimate, children, orphans, just in case there was some tree they could melodramatically cut down in my honor, the fact that she didn't care about my wrist, the fact that I never even realized I could've gotten some time off for it, paid sick leave, ick leave, the fact that I wasted my whole vacation recuperating, the fact that I'd just finished my last class for the semester when I broke it, the fact that I was all tuckered out, and excited all my classes were over, and just didn't look where I was going, foolish, FOOSH injury, Falling On Out-Stretched Hands, the fact that that was a mean impatient guy, that one who put on the temporary splint, the fact that he wrecked my favorite dress, the fact that all he had to do was put a towel over my lap to protect it but he couldn't be bothered, the fact that I was kind of in shock, and in pain, and he was rough with me, which is kind of mean, the fact that a kind student got me to the sick-bay though, the fact that I never knew who that was or I would've thanked her later, the fact that I never broke a bone before, the fact that I was so scared of what it was all going to cost, $5,000 or $10,000, plus the ambulance charges, the fact that she was just a young girl but she was so kind to me, ♫ *blessings instead of sheep* ♫, the fact that I phoned Leo from the ambulance, and all I could say was "I'm sorry," for screwing up, vestibule, reticule, pagoda, gazebo, hydrangea, signage, and it was all so *embarrassing*, the fact that I hate drawing attention to myself, telegraph office, mailbox, the fact that my life is just one continual embarrassment to me, *and* to my family, the fact that I can never really *relax*, because I never know what darn foolishness I'm going to get myself into next, the fact that maybe everybody feels the same, the fact that relaxation does seem to be a thing of the past, at least for MOMS, "hand-wringing neurotic," Philip Seymour Hoffman, Dustin Hoffman, *The Tales of Hoffmann*, the fact that I like that singing mechanical doll that flops over all the time, the fact that now everybody's got their own robot, Food for the Convalescent, the fact that you're practically crippled with one hand in a cast, the fact that Leo had to help me get *dressed* and stuff, the fact that there's a lot you can't do if you're one-handed, the fact that I couldn't get my cast wet in the shower either, the fact that I had to wear a plastic bag over it every time, JFK's Swim Trunks For Sale, the fact that how do you shower with a broken *foot* or something, the fact that Fukushima releases three hundred tons of radioactive waste a *day* into the Pacific ocean, and the Amazon's all polluted too, Amazon, drones, Jeff Bezos, "the Dahlberg repercussions," the fact that Peolia pays everyone so poorly, oh, they're terrible, and no health benefits, well, not for me anyway because I was part-time, the fact that just because you work part-time doesn't mean you have a *body* part-time, the fact that it doesn't mean you can arrive for work part-well, though come to think of it, that *was* how most people arrived for work at Peolia, the fact that everybody's tired at Peolia College, the fact that they got so nervous about giving me three months off for cancer treatment too, even though they didn't have to pay a cent for it, "Hoits you?", as the tough kid in the supermarket says, in response to the suggestion he needs to be weaned, weaning, the fact that they made such a big deal of it, meds, co-pays, closure, chaos, hoopla, Hula-Hoop, snafu, the fact that what was my Peolia password, I've forgotten, the fact that it was some-thing like L7PS33YD4T, so not too memorable, the fact that they *gave* it to me, and I never knew if I was supposed to change it or not, the fact that poor Julie's desk, with its stacks of paper, handouts and exams and dissertations and lord knows what, the fact that she had so little space to work, she had to hot-desk if she needed to get something done, Julie Shriver, the fact that she still owes me money, *Moira*, not Julie, horehound candy, pension, The Terrifying Symptoms Of Sleep Paralysis, Tuesday, the fact that they begrudge it, even though they have oodles of dough, grudge, drudge, pudge, fudge, nudge, hedge funds, ick, the fact that most of it came from *one guy*, Alfred Peolia, who'd probably flip in his grave if he knew what they'd done with it, like the amount they spend on signage for instance, the fact that you can't see the *buildings* at Peolia sometimes for all the signs telling you where they are, like the Chemistry Laboratories, Law School, Alfred's Pantry, Swimming Pool, Virtual Library, but there sure weren't any signs warning about *tree roots*, like BEWARE WURZELWEG or something, the fact that it's pretty amazing they got Paul Violi to do a reading, "Catalogue of the New Wonderment," the fact that for once they had an event that wasn't an alumni fund-raiser, the fact that Peolia College *stinks*, both as an employer and as an educational institution, Alfred, "Stay away from the Ivy League," the fact that Ivy League it ain't, the fact that the students don't seem to notice how lousy it is, or most don't anyway, the fact that they're too busy with their fraternities and sororities and loans and tailgate parties, and switching their majors, switching yards, anhydrous ammonia, the fact that the football team stinks too, the Possums, otherwise known as "the Possum pussies," Body Hair Taboos, the fact that Leo can't cook noodles, the fact that he obeys the cooking time on the pack, and then starts screaming if the noodles aren't done by then, the fact that it's better if I just cook all the noodles around here, gum disease, bubblegum, the fact that I really liked bubblegum ice cream when I was a kid, because it gave you something to chew on after all the ice cream was gone, the fact that I was never any good at teaching, the fact that I never really got the hang of it, never loosened up, the fact that I had stage fright before every class, ♬ *Whatta they got that I ain't got? Courage!* ♬, and always felt like an *impostor*, I mean, like teaching Local History to local people, who were all practically *born* here, the fact that what do *I* know about the Appalachian plateaus, Zadok Cramer, and the Wright brothers, and Gnadenhutten and all, Schoenbrunn Village, and Amish customs, and the last of the Wyandots, the fact that the Ohio history I taught is all water under the bridge now, Silver Bridge, "Bridge over Troubled Waters," the fact that nobody's buying expensive sneakers anymore, *trainers* I mean, the fact that the best thing about history is it's written down, so even I can't totally forget it, the fact that you can still distort it of course, Fox News, fake news, DON'T USE, the fact that libraries don't have any books in them anymore, the fact that Peolia was probably the first school to put all the books in storage somewhere, the fact that the students stare at screens all day, then get jobs for life where they stare at screens all day some more, the fact that Leo's a fantastic teacher and all his students and colleagues *love* him, the fact that that woman still sends us a fruitcake for Christmas, the fact that whatsher-name, Carole Forge, the fact that Monty gives him peanut brittle all year round, and Bettina knitted him that mouse, the fact that I'm sure *she* had a crush on him, maybe still does, the fact that I think he gave that mouse to Gillian, laundry pile, madeleines, Collin Street Bakery, cinnamon-roll dough, "Blue Tail Fly," crianza, the fact that my red kneading machine is kneading away in the corner, the fact that that Indonesian student of Leo's last year gave him lots of presents, like two carved wooden key rings, a replica of a temple near her home, and a sort of Indonesian puppet silhouette made out of balsa wood or some-thing, and the next time she gave him a bookmark inside a pretty little foam-lined bag, batik or something, and a teeny-weeny coin purse, which Leo said was just the right size for his salary, the fact that I took the coin purse, the fact that he went to hear her play the gamelan once in Philly, Bali, sunset, buffet, the fact that the women of Bali are the most beautiful on earth, or so they say, the fact that it really makes me *sick* my students didn't love me, but it made me even sicker to have to teach them, so all's fair in love and war, fair and square, Are Smart Guns Actually Smart?, "the luxurious handfeel of leather," the fact that teaching really did make me sick, the fact that it gave me colds, maybe even cancer, the fact that I was just so scared of those kids the whole time, the fact that they weren't even kids, the fact that some of them were older than me, "(picnic, lightning)," but even so, the fact that the *teaching* was the best part of the job though, the fact that it was a breeze compared to the admin and emailing and admissions, and committees, and meetings, and all the unpaid overtime you're sup-posed to put in just for love of the job, but really it's to hang on to the job, the fact that those overtime claim forms never resulted in any-thing, the fact that I spent a fortune on clothes too, because you have to look professional, the fact that no wonder I tripped over that *tree root*, the fact that, boy, that job must've aged me twenty years, the fact that my face literally started falling apart, Stacy to the rescue, cavalry, bugle, lynch mob, Botox, scalpel, the fact that she's got big plastic surgery plans for us *both*, the fact that I bet she'd make me do it too if we had the money, the fact that she says you're supposed to have your first facelift at forty-five, which means I'd better snap to it pretty soon, the fact that she says even Marilyn Monroe had her chin done, the fact that I think that's just sad, the fact that Marilyn Monroe of all people, having plastic surgery, "I have one word for you, Ben," microplastics, the fact that now *there's* a girl who never ever got to relax, "Let me get upstairs to my own bed where I can let go," the fact that Marilyn Monroe wore a bra *day and night*, because her breasts were her livelihood, fiddlehead ferns, fiddlesticks, goose grease, applejack, microfiber cloths, microfiche, Go Fish, Illnesses You Never Heard Of Before, FLORENCE Y'ALL, popcorn balls, cotton, plantations, slaves, Chappaquiddick, Chuck, the Ohio–Kentucky–Indiana crotch, crux, tripoint, Purple People Bridge, the fact that a teenager just shot and killed three kids in a high school cafeteria, the fact that a factory blew up in West Columbus, the fact that football players dragged an unconscious girl around naked in Steubenville, peeing on her, the fact that three teenage girls were held captive in Cleveland for a *decade*, the fact that for fifty plus years, hundreds of thousands of pounds of PFOA were dumped in the Ohio River, even though everybody knew it was harmful from the start, and two and a half million pounds of C-8, the fact that that farmer, whose land they wrecked, said "This cow's done a lot of suffering," water table, toxic waste, Ohio history, the fact that they put PFOA in dental floss, the fact that it's in all kinds of things, LBJ, IME, IGA, IBM, the fact that these people, the fact that sometimes I wonder how they sleep at night, the fact that DuPont helped build the atom bombs dropped on Hiroshima and Nagasaki, the fact that that twenty-foot inflatable rooster outside the White House really does look like Trump, Aardvark And Meerkats Killed In Fire At London Zoo, prisons, Death Penalty, the fact that they're always trying to decide whether to try children as a "juvenile" or an "adult," the fact that why is that always so up in the air, the fact that I don't get it, because juveniles are not adults, they're juveniles, "my mother's damn juveniles," the fact that even if it's a twelve-year-old psycho who dissolved his dad in an acid bath, he's still a *kid*, the fact that Cincinnati Zoo shot their gorilla, Harambe, Cincy, Sin City, for no reason, the fact that Ronny thinks everybody should be in jail, or else executed, well, practically everybody, the fact that one of the few people I actually have to speak to outside the family these days is Ronny, because he's always "dropping on by," even if I haven't ordered any feed, Hamburger Heaven, grated parmesan, boysenberry yogurt, aardvark, meerkats, easy target, deer hunting season, the Glorious Twelfth, Winchester, Luger, Remington, Browning, the fact that it's getting to the point where, because of all his unscheduled visits, I now have to try to be presentable at all times, just for *Ronny*, a guy I hardly even know, for Pete's sake, and he's always remarking on how I look, which makes me so *self-conscious*, it's like *Candid Camera* or something, the fact that *Candid Camera* wrecked all our lives, because you can't even pick up a dime on the street now without wondering if it's been glued onto the sidewalk and any minute you'll be on national TV looking like a dope, the fact that I always pick coins up anyway though, if I see one, the fact that we *need the money*, the fact that somebody did an experiment to see how many people would help a dog trapped in a car on a hot day and hardly *anybody* would, well, very few, the fact that they filmed a whole lot of people just peering in at him and then walking off, leaving him there to suffer, even die maybe, the fact that I hope I'd have the guts to help a suffo- cating dog but I can't trust myself because I'm such a coward about confrontations, and I'm always trying to be so polite, the fact that maybe I'm even too *shy* to help a dog, Cowardly Lion, because I don't really know what I'd do if it meant having to talk to people, the fact that Mommy thought it was rude to comment on people's appearance, but Trump does it *all day*, "Sad," the fact that everybody's *obsessed* with other people's appearances nowadays, *Poor Jeoffry! Poor Jeoffry!*, completely obsessed, with their *own* appearance too, the fact that I bet if everybody suddenly stopped talking about people's appearance for a minute, the conversation would just fall *flat*, but it'll never happen anyway because people would just laugh if you asked them to stop talking about how everybody looks, the fact that they just wouldn't get it, .38-caliber revolver, muzzle, barrel, eyelash curler, the fact that why's there an eyelash curler in the silverware drawer, I'd like to know, eyeliner, styptic pencil, moisturizer, hand cream, the fact that I hate it when people say I look well, the fact that it just makes you wonder how messed up you must've looked the last time, the fact that I never even notice if people look well or not, the fact that what business is it of mine, the fact that I just ask them, the fact that now we're all supposed to be skilled diagnosticians, the fact that I never clock what other people are *wearing* either, especially men, but everybody else is always checking out what everybody's wearing, the fact that they never seem to get enough of it, people-watching, itchy ankle, the fact that people sometimes tell me I look tired at PTA meetings, but who *wouldn't* be tired at a PTA meeting, and then you feel even more tired, Mamie Hazleton, the fact that I think she's just jealous because I'm skinny, the fact that she's always singling me out and telling me how drained I look, sallow, pale, frail, weary, waiflike, the fact that what does she expect me to do, just go straight home, put my feet up and drink a daiquiri, the fact that maybe they think they're being helpful in some way, warning you you need a break, vacation, broken wrist, broken, broke, the fact that I'd have to make my *own* daiquiri and nobody around here would let me drink it in peace anyway, hummingbirds, Old Lyme, oasis, Leo, the fact that I like to think of that secret overgrown garden with all the roses, and the tame birds walking around on the grass, not even noticing us kissing, the fact that we kissed on Orange Street too, 30 Tons Detonated, Half & Half, Sweet'N Low, the fact that there was a fish pond in Old Lyme that had lily pads but no fish, Leo, cell phone, but it was beautiful, *They say the hen can lay*, the fact that actually I think I spend almost as much time worrying about my *mood* as I do about my *looks*, the fact that really all I do all day is try my darnedest to remain *equable*, the fact that equability's my A1 priority, the fact that maybe it seems a pretty modest aim, as aims go, but it turns out to be quite a challenge, the fact that it really gets a bit like *Island of the Blue Dolphins* around here sometimes, the fact that she's stuck on an island fending for herself for *twenty years*, all alone, making necklaces for herself that nobody'll ever see, and making friends with wild dogs, the fact that I wish looks weren't so important but they are, the fact that Mommy said she didn't compliment us on our appearance because she didn't want us to get big-headed, but I could really have done with maybe just an approving comment from her now and then, like even once, though she did enter me in the baby contest, the fact that she must have liked my curls, Honorable Mention, baby of the family, the fact that *Leo* compliments me and it doesn't make me too big-headed, the fact that he tells me I'm pretty, and calls me sweetheart, and says he likes my eyes, the fact that I give the kids the occasional compliment but I don't make a big deal about it or anything, the fact that I don't want them to have no confidence at all, while I don't want them to boast either, or get vain and obsessed, or feel pressured, or start competing with their friends over who's the best-looking, the fact that they probably do that plenty as it is, bullying, Morning Routine girls, Beauty Pageant Queen Resigns, the fact that some mothers *make* their daughters wear makeup, the fact that I just can't imagine doing that, the fact that I just want my kids to be socially confident, unlike me, the fact that I seem to have loused this up good with Stacy, who is not confident socially and worries nonstop about her looks, and Ben, who's not confident socially and has one phobia after another, and Gillian, who's not confident socially and worries about the meaning of life and all manner of minor stuff, the fact that, dear me, Jake may be the only sane one of the bunch, even with his SpaghettiO fixation, the fact that I'm sure it's all my fault, the fact that insecurity's catching, security blanket, the fact that I'm the one who's always around, their role model, Lurch, Thing, the fact that *that's* no start in life, the fact that I wish they were more like Leo, Appalachia, bluegrass, banjo, Beethoven, the fact that the school's kind of obsessed with appearance too, with all their rules about pajamas and torn jeans and snagged tights, the fact that Stacy's addicted to those Morning Routine videos of hers, the fact that she's just glued to these things, day in, day out, the fact that all those teenage girls talk about is their makeup, and their pets, the fact that they all seem to have pet rabbits or miniature dogs, and cars and smartphones, and they start the day by drinking big cups of Starbucks coffee, the fact that I don't know how they get hold of those drinks though, since they never seem to leave the house, the fact that they just seem to stay home all day and film themselves packing an adobe wall of makeup onto their faces, the fact that they're completely gone on makeup, the fact that they all have whole suitcases full of it, and they're experts in applying it, the fact that they make hiding your pimples look like a *joy*, the fact that they brush and brush and brush their cheeks with those blusher brushes, the fact that it must feel good, kind of like pressing your face into your pet rabbit's pink fur, the fact that I've never owned a blusher brush in my life, the fact that they'd probably faint if they heard that, the fact that when I was their age I was wandering gloomily around New Haven not knowing what to do, while they're all videotaping themselves perfecting how to do smoky eyes, and transmitting the results to hundreds of thousands of fans, the fact that they like moisturizer too, as if teenage kids had any dry skin to moisturize, the fact that sometimes I wonder if maybe they're getting paid by the big cosmetics companies, the fact that who knows, the fact that those girls talk about love like they're talking sardines or shoe polish, except that most of them have probably never fallen in love, or even heard of a sardine, the fact that they're too busy doing their smoky eyes, and handing out advice like "friendship is a two-way thing," and "everybody has their sucky days," the fact that some girl in Pennsylvania actually said "you can never reach happiness if you're constantly sad," and got 2,478 views, the fact that even Stace admits they're pretty phony sometimes, though they try to be kind, sort of superior but kind, to all their viewers, Beethoven's last sonatas, Spandex, pink bedspread, pink pajamas, pajamas are not permitted, pinkness, pink-nosed rabbit, pink poodle, in the pink, the fact that Stace watches a whole bunch of these videos in a row and then she crashes, and gets real depressed, and who could blame her, the fact that she looks like *me* after I've done too many online jigsaw puzzles, Rocky Mountains, Glacier Lake, Salt Mountain, Montana, Rocky

Ridge Farm, River Roost, the fact that we named our house River Roost, but we still have to tell everybody the street number, so what's the point in naming it yourself, Smell-O-Rama, pumpkin patch, pink, orange, white, blue and green jigsaw pieces, dill, caraway, tear-away, Feliway, card-carrying, playing the woman card, the fact that Double Jumbo meant a two-quarter tip, and Jumbo Jockey was a buck, the fact that we all pooled the tips at Mo's, nickel and two dimes, clean counter, and four pennies, the fact that it's time to get rolling, with the rolling pin, I mean, the fact that I used to have a rolling pin with heart shapes sticking out all around the rims at both ends, and those heart shapes got on my nerves, I finally realized, because they made heart-shaped indentations in the dough, which then had to be rolled some more to get the heart shapes *out*, the fact that who needs heart shapes getting in the way all the time, Chagrin Falls, Ohio, the fact that you just can't get that kid to stop watching Morning Routine videos, just like I can't quit with the jigsaws, the fact that once you're hooked, you're hooked, drug mule, top-knot, top notch, Gender Reveal party, slumber party, the fact that I feel sorry for those girls though, I do, because they really are devoting their whole lives to putting makeup on and taking it off, the fact that they spend at least two hours putting it on in the morning, and almost as long taking it off at night, the fact that that's four hours out of every day minimum, the fact that most women don't have *time* for that, surely, Shirley, the fact that they film the nighttime routines too, but somehow those videos aren't as popu-lar, the fact that it's not as important, I guess, how you look when you go to bed, the fact that only the lap dogs will see, fake news, Best Price Compensation, condensation, cookie-cutter women, jigsaw pieces, Starbucks, the fact that these girls should be doing their *homework*, as Daddy would say, the fact that it might not be so bad if they didn't encourage other girls to do the same, by making all these videos, but Stacy avidly watches it all and tries to copy all their procedures, the fact that she doesn't spend two hours on her own makeup every morn-ing, but she makes up for it by spending hours watching these other girls do it, the fact that, all in all, she must be thinking about makeup almost all the time, and spending all her money on it too, the fact that Phoebe used to get up early to do her makeup in high school, but not two hours early, the fact that I used to watch her, but it didn't make *me* want to do it, the fact that I waited for the urge to come over me but it never did, the fact that I suppose I'm just not much of a glamorpuss, lipstick, whales, blubber, Heaviside Layer, Beauty Pageant Winner Told She's Too Fat, Mamie Hazleton, the fact that I'd rather think about German Potato Salad, get dill, cider vinegar, caraway seeds, Debbie Stabishen, dill, cider vinegar, caraway seeds, the fact that Debbie can just throw on a skimpy sundress without even looking at herself in the mirror, the fact that she's all ponytail and spaghetti straps, and then she just yanks off her hairband and shakes all that long straight hair loose and flies down her front steps like somebody in a shampoo ad, and I know Stacy's in awe of her, the fact that looking great just comes easy for some people, and for everybody else it's a killer, the fact that I'm sure Debbie Stabishen has her own problems, the fact that her dad's nice though, Cancer, Leo, Detroit Lions, the lion's share, the fact that I used to go on all those crash diets, the fact that I don't know why, the fact that you think you're accomplishing something, the fact that for a month I ate only bananas, but after you have all these kids you don't have time for that anymore, the fact that I don't check how I look two thousand times a day either, the fact that a man really doesn't know a woman until he understands how long it takes her to get ready to go out, the fact that they think we're all looking in the mirror to admire ourselves but we're not, the fact that we're just trying to make sure we're fit to be seen, the fact that now boys are buying cosmetics too, like in the eighteenth century, the fact that I wonder how many kids *would* wear their PJs to school if they could, the fact that, come to think of it, that's what I more or less did after Mommy got sick, but in reverse, the fact that I just never got *out* of my school clothes, the fact that I slept in them so I wouldn't have to bother getting dressed in the morning, the fact that how's *that* for a morning routine, the fact that Gillian says *she'd* like to wear her PJs to school, but only if everybody else did, like at one of those slumber parties they have in museums, the fact that some people eat *string*, to clean out their, well, I hate to think, the fact that, compared to that, what harm would it do if everybody wore their PJs to school, the fact that Claude Rains is good as the corrupt politician in *Mr. Smith Goes to Washington*, the fact that I still think he's attractive, "There's a quality," the fact that that Claude I met at the Strand was so *hand-some*, but you shouldn't think about people's appearance, Debbie Stabishen, the fact that I wonder if she practices that nonchalant air, the fact that Claude gave me a CD of Vivaldi's *Four Seasons*, and said he loved me and then I never heard from him again, the fact that it's like he went to the moon, the fact that if he did, he's probably the best-looking guy up there, the fact that maybe he was embarrassed about giving me the *Four Seasons*, the fact that why do people say they love you when they don't, the fact that I like it when Claude Rains calls Bette Davis his ewe lamb, black sheep, tie-dyed sheep, *Deception*, the fact that some artists get rich quick while Nanya's struggling to *survive*, and weeps whenever she hears about dead children on the news, mush, the numbness of muted beings, the fact that some artists have all the breaks while Nanya's beautiful painting of roses and tea packets languishes in our semi-rural Tuscarawas County kitchen, instead of the Venice Biennale, gondolas, gnocchi, Mandela, Gargantua, ocarina, the fact that her pink and yellow tea packets look like they're *blossoming*, like the roses, the fact that Nanya always wears nice clothes, the fact that she can wear red shoes with an ochre dress and forest-green leggings, and she looks great, along with her frown, the fact that her dad had a farm somewhere for a while but I'm not sure it worked out, yellow rose, yellow plastic truck, the fact that Claude was an artist too, the fact that he was from Puerto Rico, banana split, the fact that Nanya never comes to see me, the fact that I'm always inviting her down but who wants to stay in a house full of kids, the fact that she's too busy and I'm too busy too, what with the pies and cakes, and the chickens, the fact that *now* where is the cardamom, the fact that I am wallowing in domesticity here and I know it's stupid, hand-knitted baby blanket, toaster oven, Abby's rag rugs, Mommy,

Vacuum Cleaner Sales Rush, Eid cookies, the fact that I don't know how I got myself into all this, the fact that I can't remember, the fact that I always knew I wouldn't make much of a mother, but I like babies so much, or pre-K anyway, toddlers, man the decks, safe as houses, repel all boarders, OrthoAdvice, the fact that I like it when they can walk and talk, but not too well, and their legs are still chubby, the fact that they all have the same snub nose, the fact that is there anything better than a two-year-old's blue jeans hanging on the line, the fact that a toddler *can* be kind of squirmy of course, when all you want to do is hold them on your lap and rub your cheek against theirs and smell their soft hair, blusher brushes, pink rabbit fur, Claude Rains, monsoon rains, meringue of the family, gum balls, canallers, canal boats, horses, the fact that, on the down side, toddlers sometimes eat cats' kibble, the fact that Gillian got a star sticker from Mrs. Bethnel for her picture of canallers, PJs, honey bees, the bee at Bread Loaf, the fact that she spent hours just on one beer glass, the fact that nobody else in this family ever got a star off Mrs. Bethnel before, the fact that I think Gillian was inspired by our canal ride last September, the *Monticello III*, bright yellow leaves on black, green water, slack water, KEEP OUT, ♫ *I've got a mule, her name is Sal* ♫, raisins, Kleenex, Open Carry guy, DON'T USE, scrappage scheme, swatting hoax, the fact that one of the guys on our boat had a gun with him, the fact that everybody's got a gun now, even guys out for a canal ride, which should be a peaceful thing, "Get ready!", the fact that in *Mr. Deeds Goes to Town*, Gary Cooper's a pacifist, and in *High Noon* he's a reluctant defender of the whole lousy town, but then in *Friendly Persuasion* he's got a gun, even though he's a Quaker, which is kind of strange, *Persuasion*, the fact that it's like Anne Elliott shooting Captain Wentworth, which *these* days is probably what would happen, when he parades around in front of her with the Musgrove girls, acting so cold and distant, dancing, praising nuts, the fact that Grace Kelly lets him down in *High Noon*, Gary Cooper, not Captain Wentworth, the fact that I never liked that part, the fact that she's a quitter, the fact that "Gentleman will take a chance" means you got an order for chipped beef hash, chipped thumb nail, the fact that those Open Carry guys traipse all over Coshocton the first Friday of every month just to frighten everybody and there's not a thing the police or anybody else can do about it, the fact that people are always saying this isn't "who we are as a nation," but, well, it kind of *is* who we are, if you think about it, which I try not to, the fact that those Open Carry guys are given a free pass, while a weary, wan-looking, waiflike mom dragging four kids around is frowned upon, the fact that as a newcomer in Newcomerstown I've never really felt all that welcome, the fact that I'm only here for Leo, cheechako, and maybe the pickled beans, home-canning, canalling, canoeing, Professor Newcomer, deep-seated, deep-seeded, seed wheat, the fact that "cheechako" means newcomer or foreigner in Chinook Wawa, watermelon pickle, mid-winter garlic pickle, bottled tomatoes, beets, cucumbers, *Jaws*, the fact that there are alligators in Miami's canals, purple martins, hushpup-pies, wine slushies, the fact that some people get to live in *Paris*, for Pete's sake, the fact that quite a *lot* of people get to live in Paris, mainly because they're *Parisians*, and here we are in Newcomerstown, the fact that there are too many Americans in Paris already, the fact that it's kind of embarrassing, the fact that Parisians probably hate us, the fact that nobody bothered Leo and me much on our honeymoon, miel, ciel, except the two guys at Chartier, the fact that we had to sit at the same table with them for lunch and they openly mocked us in French throughout the meal, the fact that we couldn't catch exactly what they were saying, but you can tell if you're being laughed at, even if it's in French, the fact that we caught their drift, the fact that it wasn't hard, since they burst out laughing every time we did or said anything, the fact that there wasn't a thing we could do about it, the fact that one of them giggled so much his glasses fell off and broke on the floor, the fact that that did shut them up, the fact that glasses can only take so much giggling, jiggling, wiggle-room, Double Jumbo, the fact that that sure wasn't the most romantic lunch we ever had, but the waiter was nice to us, the fact that *he* was probably pretty sick of those two clowns too, the fact that I bet they ate there every day and mocked *him*, the fact that Chartier had good celeriac, the fact that I dreamt I had to take a course on the Paterson Falls but I missed the field trip, so my homework had to be all theoretical, based on watching our *bathtub* fill up with water, which really isn't the same as going to Paterson Falls, Campfire Girls, Wo-He-Lo, WOC, Nawat Itsaragrisil, the fact that Leo and I went to Paterson Falls once in the dead of winter and it was all iced up and very slippery, the fact that you could fall in and be carried deep down under the surface, black water, white foam, black rocks, white snow, the fact that it seemed impossible there could be that much water on the move all at once, gallons and gallons of water a second, the fact that I wonder if Parisians associate street-cleaning with croissants, because they're always cleaning the streets when you go out for your croissants in the morning, the fact that maybe they all start salivating when they see the water swishing around, chocolat, café au lait, the fact that every city should hose down the streets every morning like that, problem child, Preakness, half moon, quarter moon, quarter horse, the fact that all I did on our honeymoon was lie in bed, not because of too much, well, let's not go *there*, but because of the sore neck I got, dragging my luggage from the Gare du Nord, the fact that we really should have gotten a taxi from the station but the hotel looked so close on the map, the fact that it was my fault, the fact that I miscalculated, the fact that I *liked* lying there though, listening to the sounds of Paris, the fact that my neck is sore again *now*, from watching pan after pan of sugar and butter caramelize yesterday, the fact that the first tarte tatin I ever tried was at André Allard in rue de l'Éperon in St. Germain, with its mustard-colored walls and ducks everywhere, duck, duck, duck, black water, slack water, duck with olives, the fact that maybe second marriages are always better than the first, but nobody tells you, the fact that it's a well-kept secret, my sore hip, the fact that Cathy's on her second too, although they're not exactly married, the fact that Anat's on her second *hip*, the fact that she wore right through the first one, the fact that replacement hips only last about twenty years, don't they, the fact that it started at Zyker's, *my* sore hip, when I was lifting up that whole tray of SpaghettiOs, that

Jake, the fact that he'll be the death of me yet, yogurt, nurdles, the fact that it's not *always* good though, second marriages, the fact that Bree's second husband was crazee, and when she kicked him out he wrote letters to all her relatives, including her mean sister, accusing Bree of running a brothel in the marital home, the fact that nobody ever knew why he did that, O. J. Simpson's car chase, the fact that now he lives in a trailer someplace, the fact that that man really seemed to have the smelliest feet in the world, the fact that it wasn't his fault of course, or maybe it was, the fact that he was just *awful* to Bree, the fact that the mother of the little girl who got abducted and killed last month has now committed suicide, the fact that that's so sad, the fact that if one of my kids got abducted and killed I'd have to commit suicide too, and poor Leo would be left to bring up all our other kids, knock on wood, Ronny's gun beside him on the front seat, Browning Recoilless, famous last words, the pile of dirty towels in the bathroom, the ironing pile, Cathy smiling, Abby's steep basement stairs, the fact that Abby had a great way of just flinging the laundry down those stairs to the cellar, the fact that she had her rebellious side, the fact that in the end she fell down those same cellar steps, probably on her way to do a load of laundry, the fact that if I'd only lived closer, the fact that I would've realized something was wrong and I could've helped her, the fact that I wish I'd seen her more but it was like I was just paralyzed or some-thing, by having all these *kids*, working mom, the fact that I was no help to Abby, the fact that she was so understanding about it, the fact that she'd always wanted a big load of kids herself, the fact that after lifting the SpaghettiOs into my cart, I then had to lift the whole tray *out* again for the cashier, so she could scan every single can, for crying out loud, and somewhere along the line there, I think I really hurt my back, and now the pain's moved into my hip, the fact that next I'll get it in my knee and then my foot, and then I'm in for it, "keep the lor-dosis," the S curve, the fact that I should do the exercises right now, but I don't have time, the fact that they cure it every time, and they're not hard, the fact that they're just stretching exercises really, McKenzie, Robin McKenzie, great guy, the fact that he must've helped *so* many people, the fact that I have stomach trouble every day now and I don't know why, the fact that I practically overdose on Pepto-Bismol, the fact that I am completely falling apart, cinnamon, the fact that I dreamt we were going to be bombed at 10:30 p.m. and we all knew it, the fact that Mommy and Daddy were there, and Leo, and maybe the kids, check the rolls, the fact that we'd all gathered in the kitchen and I was kind of wishing we had a basement we could hide in, but then I thought maybe that would be worse because you might get the whole weight of the house crumbling on top of you, the fact that we were all just sitting around looking at each other, and I was thinking, so this is what it's like to be bombed, the fact that you just sit there hoping it'll happen to somebody *else* at the other end of town and your house will be spared, the fact that I had a bad dream about Trump last night too, the fact that he admitted to me he couldn't cope with the job, DSA, the fact that Bathsheba is gone and I still miss her all the time, her soft black fur, yellow eyes looking at me, Bathsheba curled up against my neck when she was a kitten, the fact that Laura Ingalls Wilder says that big ears and a long tail are the sure sign of a good mouser, the fact that Bathsheba didn't have big ears but she was good at anything she wanted to do, the fact that her ears were just right, and so was her tail, the fact that I'm sure she was a good mouser, though I can't actually remember now if she was, the fact that fennec foxes have *huge* ears, not just for hearing purposes but to help them cool down in the desert, the fact that they live in Africa and eat up lots of insects, and they mate for life, the fact that narwhals have two front teeth, and one grows into the sharp pointy tusk, like a unicorn's horn, the fact that people killed them for their tusks, the fact that Opal's a good mouser, and her ears aren't big either, the fact that she gets birds too, but it's mainly mice, the fact that she lays all the organs out in a row by the back door, better safe than sorry, better sorry than safe, "Things went south," by the seat of your pants, the fact that Bathsheba was dear to me, *dear*, check the cinnamon rolls, the fact that Ivo Pogorelic is playing Beethoven, the fact that you can have any music you want now, the fact that we all live like kings, the fact that you just clap your hands, or click your mouse, "good mouser," and whole orchestras start up for you, the fact that Pogorelic married his teacher, who was a lot older than him, the fact that all athletes take performance-enhancing drugs now, *all*, the fact that they must spend half their lives taking urine tests, the fact that I wouldn't like that, the fact that I'm shy enough already without having to hand over urine samples all the time, Jake's baby potty, Howard Hughes's milk bottles of pee, opioid crisis, red tide, the fact that in New York last time, we saw a man with a big hole in his nose, like a third nostril, and Leo said it was from cocaine, the fact that I thought it was acne, the fact that Katharine Hepburn was very spotty, not spotty, very *sporty* all her life, the fact that she golfed and played tennis and swam, the fact that they got her to play golf and tennis and swim in the movies too, ♪ *The Stars and Stripes Forever* ♪, the fact that *we* don't much care for sports, the fact that, oh, we watch baseball and tennis now and then, "Yankees win!", and slalom skiing maybe, but no football, and I don't like ski *jumping* much, Salzburg, the fact that it's all the same, the fact that I would never ski myself, why would you want to break a leg, the fact that anyway I'm too prone to ankle sprains, the fact that I have weak ankles, the fact that we pretend to be interested in soccer, for the kids' sake, but it's a real strain, sprain, the fact that all the other soccer moms and dads get so *excited*, while I just stand there getting cold, frozen, frozen out by the other *moms* as well, the fact that they always ask where Leo is, as if neither of us has anything better to do than watch little kids kick a ball around, the fact that the other moms and dads yell and cheer till they're hoarse, the fact that it isn't right, I don't think, to make kids so competitive about things, the fact that we think the other parents are too involved, but they probably think we aren't involved enough, white supremacists, "She's just about to close up the library!", mush, wilted lettuce, the fact that that woman in Erie just got killed by her boyfriend, leaving five children motherless and her twin sister twinless, twin set and pearls, the fact that all these terrible things happen, but *still* we have to do our taxes and get our windows fixed, fixture, in a fix, the fact that we should have had them painted last year, the fact that I really should do the grouting too, oh dear, the fact that what with my jigsaws and my sciatica and my Pepto-Bismol and Alka-Seltzer and my chipped thumbnail, I don't do anything right, procrastination, the fact that two little girls died in their beds in Texas because of an explosion at a chemical plant, the fact that it seems like nobody regulates chemical plants enough, the fact that they aren't inspected and they build them in the middle of residential areas and never ask how toxic or flammable the substances inside are, the fact that that plant was built of *wood* and was full of flammable chemicals in open bins, the fact that fertilizer grade ammonium nitrate is stable only as long as it isn't exposed to fire, but when a fire started and ashes fell on the fertilizer grade ammonium nitrate, the whole thing took off, and a whole lot of firefighters got killed too, the fact that they were volunteer firemen and weren't even trained to know how to deal with that kind of thing, because nobody from the chemical plant had ever told them what was *in* there, the fact that I don't know why everything doesn't stop dead until everybody gets together and sorts things out so no little girls ever die like that in their beds again, I really don't, nor the firefighters, but nobody fixes anything, not faucets, not window frames, not the Ohio River, the fact that sea salt now contains microplastics, the fact that coelacanths die now from eating plastic potato chip bags at the bottom of the ocean, the fact that sometimes I think that people today must be the saddest people ever, because we know we ruined *everything*, even geraniums probably, the fact that, heavens to Betsy, I'm sure people haven't always lived in such a constant state of alarm,

. . . .

What we prize in poets, the lioness already had: every muscle toned to tread precisely, every sense alive to wind and moonshine and other creatures, whether rivals or prey.

For her, movement was all. She could see, taste, smell it. She reacted faster than she could hear. A mountain lion needs to know how every flower behaves, so as not to mistake it for a glint of bare rock, or a doe's snout. She knew the difference between a tiny falling clump of snow and the kick of a vanishing rodent. She took it all in, from a beaver paddling through the stream way below, to the flick of a bare branch above, followed by the drip of an icicle.

She knew fish lived in water and birds in air and everybody else was either on the ground or up a tree. She knew rain, fire, snow, hail, thunder, lightning, gales. She knew the seasons, and how to plan for them. She knew light and dark, warmth and cold, peace, danger, leap and recoil, recoil and leap.

Nothing hurt her on her narrow path, the path she had always trodden, the path only she remembered because she had created it. The path accompanied a gently ambling creek that rolled, sneaking, snaking, along its own allotted groove. The river had a purr too, as water rhythmically rubbed, plopped, gulped, cracked, spat, splashed and flashed against stones.

At a certain point, the stream circled back on itself to form a serpentine double-helix of two interlocking peninsulas – nature's little joke on the water-shy. Land too can recoil and leap. Unfazed, the lioness swam one elbow of the stream, padded across the grassy outcrop of land between, swam again, and rejoined her path on the other side.

She avoided the lake now. Once she had swum right to the island in the middle, hot in pursuit of an eagle she'd seen paddling clumsily through the water, seemingly injured. This proved a mistake. The eagle was not hurt, not drowning. It was merely lugging its own catch – a fish almost as big as the bird itself – using its wings as oars. The eagle reached the island and dragged the fish with it. The wearied lioness swam closer, still half-expecting a chance to eat them both, but when she finally touched stone underfoot near the shore, the eagle rose heavily off the ground and perched in a tree-top to tear at its fish in comfort.

The lioness liked the island at first. It was large, with no other lions to bother her. She stayed, ruling over the place until every animal capable of flying or swimming to safety had left. Then she began to starve. She was annoyed by red-winged blackbirds, who kept darting at her out of nowhere, fearing the loss of their well-hidden chicks. She had no interest in chicks! All she ever wanted was a restful life. It was those blackbirds that had finally driven her back to the mainland.

Tonight, her secret path took her past a white colt with a black line down his nose. He didn't shy, too innocent to understand what he was seeing. She studied him – her right to eat whatever she wanted. But the mare was too close and might kick, a risk not to be taken with infants back in the den.

On and on she went along the sheltered path. Passing behind a waterfall, she lapped at the blue, green and white sheet of water that momentarily blocked the world from view.

In a clearing, she sensed a deer herd ahead, by the silence they carry with them – the silence of flighty animals on the look-out for trouble, in between hasty, tremulous nibblings.

A careful approach, sudden acceleration, crouch, recoil, leap.

She ate the innards and stowed the rest, scratching a perfunctory shallow cleft in the frozen earth. A few twigs on top completed the symbolic burial. Other creatures would mess with this carrion at their peril. For it was hers, and she was queen.

Heading home, milk-ripe, she was momentarily disconcerted by the brightness of the sky. Had she left her cubs so long? But it was only moonlit clouds glinting through low trees. The sky beyond was still midnight-blue.

A soft fog dwelt low in bushes. Wide, white, snow-caked horizontals of branches shone out against the darkness underfoot as she trotted swiftly back to her kits.

.   .   .   .

the fact that a bridegroom crashed right into the side of a house, injuring four people inside, the fact that he was probably partying all night or something, ♫ *just get me to the church on time* ♫, the flat beige plane of the countertop, Bearded Dragon Goes Crazy For Blueberries, blueberry muffins, ♫ *Pigeon, please do not fall on my blueberries* ♫, DUI, DNR, wood pigeons, ginseng, banjo clock, cream skimmer, spurtle, swordie, moose head, the fact that Aunt Sophia's buried in the East State Street cemetery along with all of Leo's other relatives and we'll probably end up there too, the fact that most people live and die where they were born, or they leave home and live somewhere else for decades but come back to pass away, like migrating birds, the fact that birds return to the same places year after year, or they get their ashes sent back home after they pass away, *people* I mean, not birds, the fact that Abby died not too far from where she was born, well, fifty miles or so, but it was still Massachusetts, the fact that most people live wherever they happen to find themselves, animals too, unless something really bad happens that drives them away, the fact that Recy Taylor left Abbeville, Alabama, but had to move back there when she got old, the fact that she probably hated that, the fact that I don't want to be buried in Evanston or New Haven or, well, *anywhere*, the fact that I don't want to *die*, I mean pass away, old news, AOL news, M4BL, not with four kids to bring up, the fact that moms are *important*, even if nobody else thinks so, possum mom waddling along under the weight of eleven big possum babies clinging to her back, the fact that mackerels migrate too, and whales, Rachel Carson, the fact that elephants have a place they go to when they're ready to pass on, World's Worst Parker, no man is an island, Newburyport, ducks, the fact that Lincoln's family got him moved back to Springfield, and McKinley got his mausoleum in Canton, *Spoon River Anthology*, the fact that I don't think people should smoke in the playground, *or* vape, not around kids, but you can't say anything in case they pull a gun on you, the fact that there's no telling what people have in their pockets these days, Barry, quilt, the fact that I dreamt I was gleefully prancing around an old hotel lounge somewhere, in my *underpants*, the fact that it was sort of a big tea room, the fact that they weren't pretty panties either, the fact that they were the heavy-duty, practical kind, and I was zipping around the tables looking for the tiny elevators I remembered from long ago, the fact that the elevators took you down to the train station below the hotel, the fact that it was like an old familiar place to me, maybe in Ireland or someplace, the fact that it seemed totally familiar and a place I'd known for years, the fact that I knew all about it, and even felt comfortable in my *underpants* in there, but it's not a real place, which is just as well, the fact that the last time I ever felt comfortable running around in nothing but my underpants was when I was about five, though with Leo it's okay of course, the fact that everybody in the hotel was really nice about my nakedness, so I was only half-embarrassed about it, and all in all it was a pretty happy dream, but I feel embarrassed about the underpants now, the fact that that dream sure came from left field, low strip of lilac-gray cloud, winding stone path, Cathy smiling, the fact that the Country Shoppe is doing so well Leo says it should be in *Buysville*, not Byesville, the fact that they sell all those jams, and ham 'n' cheese lasagna, the fact that Cathy claims they only sell American products and local stuff, but she can make an exception for my tartes tatin because *I'm* American at least, even if the recipe's French, the fact that I was born in Illinois probably helps too, the fact that everybody thinks I'm a New Englander but I'm not, the fact that Cathy's got some nine-year-old somewhere nearby making all the jewelry, the fact that that kid's good with beads, sip of coffee, the fact that many children get beaten by their parents, the fact that it's about a thirty-mile round-trip to drop the pies off there and all the other places I've got to hit today, in the snow and ice, the fact that I wish there was an easier way, like some way of slinging the pies out the window as I pass, the fact that it would be nice if they could just roll gently down an icy pie slide, slanted just right so they don't gain too much momentum, because you don't want them to crash, pie fight, the fact that I just want them to glide down into the welcoming arms of the store owners or a waitress, without me having to get out of my warm car and talk to anybody, the fact that I could just do a jaunty wave from the car and be on my way, the fact that, boy, am I shy, the fact that I'm even shy talking to Cathy half the time, and she's now my BFF, well, at least around here, Nanya, Mandy, Anat, the fact that that bridegroom's car got right inside the house, the fact that the earring I found in the washer yesterday is missing the bit that goes in your ear, the little loop of silver, the fact that maybe I should send it out to Cathy's nine-year-old for repair, my long-lost sky-blue earrings, Frank, the fact that Frank was always eating ice cream in bed, watching TV, and while he did that I lost my favorite earrings down the back of the bed and I never did find them, the fact that your favorite earrings always disappear down the crack between the bed and the wall, the fact that it wasn't Frank's fault, I guess, but I still associate it with him and his messy place, *and* his ice cream, mint choc chip, the fact that that was right when we first got together, bad omen, the fact that earrings get lost so easily, so you wear your less favorite earrings most of the time, the ones you think you won't mind losing so much, but then you lose *them* and you miss them too, because without the standbys you're gonna have to wear your favorite ones after all, the fact that I've had fake pearls as standbys, or seashells, and just gold studs and such, the fact that I miss those silver seashells a bit now, plutonium isotopes, platinum, beads, felt and sequins, our cocktail party, the fact that I don't know what in creation I'll wear for it, the fact that I've got nothing fancy anymore, the fact that I haven't bought any clothes since, since I had cancer probably, Target, down the hatch, drop in the ocean, tip of the iceberg, the ol' one-two, one-to-ones, one on one, threesome, the fact that I put the same outfit on every day, because it's my cooking outfit, just leggings or sweatpants and long T-shirts that give my sit-me-down-upon some camouflage, bread and butter, the fact that ever since my cancer I've been over-sensitive about my sit-me-down-upon, the fact that I just feel I've shown it to enough strangers for a lifetime, the fact that I don't really get why everybody's derrière has to be in your face all the time anyway, running around in my underpants, twisting between the tables, thong panty liners, the fact that all those young nurses in radiotherapy were maybe used to seeing such things but *I* wasn't used to baring my backside and having it positioned this way and that on a table by cold fingers, and then zapped, "Mrs. Robinson, you're trying to," the fact that nobody ever showed that much interest in my sit-me-down-upon before, and it's never been much to speak of, flat chest, flat butt, but *Leo* likes me, the fact that Leo *loves* me and that makes life possible, the fact that what is that song, the fact that maybe what I need is a *muumuu*, the fact that they're probably available on eBay, the fact that I don't even know most of the guests that are coming, the fact that they're all Leo's colleagues, and I hate parties, as guest or host, cocktail umbrellas, pointy paper hats, Groucho Marx, high heels, olives, guacamole, the fact that I don't know why anybody likes them, the fact that it's hard to believe they truly do, but somebody must or there wouldn't be any parties, which would suit me fine, cinnamon rolls, SAT scores, USA, PFOA, NBC, ABC, CBS, Fox News, snow foxes, boxes, possums, sand dabs, sand dollars, silver dollar piece, fifty-cent coin, the fact that I always end up cornered by someone I don't especially want to talk to, Pittsburgh, Bettina, Susan B. Anthony, edelweiss, the fact that Mommy and Daddy did seem to like having cocktail parties, even though Mommy was shy, the fact that Daddy was shy in certain ways too but he was also pretty gregarious, the fact that he was good at being congenial, congenital, cogent, consent, Dido, Ruth M. Arthur, *Death of a Salesman*, the fact that they'd get nervous before a party though, the fact that they were so tense beforehand about their parties that Phoebe and I decided never to host parties when we grew up, the fact that I think Phoebe changed her mind later but I never did, the fact that maybe I could get a tarte tatin horn fixed to the roof of the car, to squeeze when I'm approaching the pie slide, "A-HOO-GA!", to alert the store owner that pies are arriving, or maybe a little bell or siren, though there are enough of *those* around here already, car alarms too, the fact that a pie siren might give those Open Carry guys a jolt, which would be a good thing unless they reacted instinctively and shot me, reflex, the fact that I shouldn't think like that, dear me, live and let live why dontcha, a stitch in time, bird in the hand, the fact that a siren might be overkill anyway because my pies aren't really an emergency, they're just pie, pie slide, the fact that I'd settle for somebody just coming out to the car and collecting the pies, the fact that, boy, would that be a help, and it'd be too cold for them to stay and talk too, the fact that I guess I don't like pie deliveries much but the thing is I get so stiff after standing at the stove all day making the pies, that sometimes I really don't think I can drag myself out of the car, the fact that I guess I'm getting old, the fact that I should do yoga or something, Pilates, aquarobics, or eat more kale and broccoli or something, the fact that I need to get me some antioxidants quick, seaweed, the fact that I used to be agile, the fact that I used to have such limber hip joints that that doctor told me I was really flexible, the fact that yoga mats are so depressing, the fact that I can't believe you're supposed to carry one of those things around with you and bring it to the yoga class and unroll it and *lie* on it, the fact that how can that be comfortable, the fact that you must have to really hate yourself to do that, the fact that you must have to hate yourself to beat up on a *kid* too, Toto in the basket, Dorothy, the Munchkins, the fact that I was always really scared of the Munchkins, the fact that I just couldn't figure them out, the fact that the aardvark magnet on the fridge has a moving head and tail, the fact that Stacy gave it to me when I was in the hospital, the fact that I was scared of the Tin Man, the Scarecrow, the Cowardly Lion, *and* the Wizard of Oz, also the mean lady who takes Toto away in her bicycle basket, and the witch, L. Frank Baum, the fact that the whole bunch of them scared me but I hid it because everybody else seemed to think that movie was so marvelous, the fact that that really is one heck of a scary movie, the fact that it was always shown at Christmastime, like it was a big family event or something, like it was the *law*, and we eagerly watched it every year, discos, dance moves, the fact that I was scared of discos too, though that's got nothing to do with L. Frank Baum, aardvark magnet, genocide, the fact that I've always hated musicals in general, coffee, the fact that the aardvark's tail is all bent and hanging by a thread and I've got to fix it *right now* before it comes off altogether, Nickel Mines Massacre, pangolins, the fact that having had cancer once doesn't mean you're immune to getting it again, far from it, the fact that I keep thinking I've got a new kind and I won't live to see my kids grow up, the fact that luckily I've blanked out most of my cancer treatment though, "she passed away," death and taxes, Tuesday, dentist, passports, passport renewal, credit card bill, dirty towel pile, rotten windows, leaky faucet, the fact that they cured me and I'm grateful and Leo's grateful and I'm grateful to Leo and I'm grateful to the doctors and I'm *very* grateful that the kids barely noticed what was going on, at least as far as I could tell, except maybe Stace, Kaiser, HMOs, the nice nurse in the Oncology Department waiting room, health insurance premiums, deductibles, co-pays, the fact that I've recovered and all, but I don't know if I ever really recovered my state of mind, my equilibrium, my *equability*, equator, equation, equine statue, the fact that on some level I still think I'm dying all the time, Own The Journey, the fact that of course I had to get the most embarrassing kind of cancer going, the fact that most of life is just a great big embarrassment to me, the fact that all my life I have made such a darn fool of myself, and it does make you wonder what's coming next, like apoplexy maybe, or gangrene, or a great big swollen ear like Ben got after the bee sting, the fact that for a while it was so big he could *see* it, see his own ear, poor kid, the fact that that is never supposed to happen, the fact that things like this just shouldn't happen to you in America, aardvark, but accidents do happen, "It's not who we are," the fact that I even talk to *myself* in clichés, the fact that Gillian likes to sing lullabies to the cats in a voice so high, the fact that a little louder and she'd break chandeliers and stuff, if we had any, the fact that a male flight attendant yelled at a woman with baby twins, and somebody on Twitter said he hoped the flight attendant would die of anal cancer, which wasn't a very nice thing to say, even about a flight attendant, my lost sky-blue earrings, Phoebe and me hiding behind the couch in Evanston, John Evans, Evanston, vacuum cleaner, baby goats jumping up on a picnic table, goat yoga, the fact that goats always want to get up high, the fact that they all want to be *mountain* goats, the fact that I can't imagine wanting to climb mountains, the fact that I hate hills, the fact that the blue haze on the Blue Ridge Mountains is caused by terpenes, the fact that a third of all people get cancer, but many kinds can be cured now, or controlled, the fact that skin cancer usually can, or *some* kinds anyway, pink breast cancer ribbons, leprosy, Ebola, measles, Band-Aids, eggs Benedict, neighborhood block party, Bad Sweater party, towel pile party, Arvo Pärt, "Spiegel im Spiegel," the fact that Leo and I were talking about Stacy and how she's down on everything except vegans, but I said she has to sift through the world and decide for herself what's good about it and what's bad, the fact that so far she's better at deciding on the bad stuff, the fact that I said it's "a process of acceptance and reject-ance," the fact that I don't know how *that* came out but Leo liked it, the fact that I don't know if it's English but it's true, the fact that adolescence *is* a process of acceptance and rejectance, the fact that I dreamt Leo won a nice encyclopedia set, old, in dark blue bindings, and it was all about Germany, the fact that there were many volumes of it, the fact that it had been published in the thirties, and Leo'd won it for some ad slogan he wrote in high school, the fact that I wish I could remember what the slogan was, but I don't think that came up in the dream, the fact that I wish I'd dreamt up the *slogan* instead of the dark blue encyclopedia, the fact that meanwhile Leo dreamt our whole family had new blue shoes and he had to testify to Congress about them, the fact that that was quite a coincidence, the blue shoes and the blue encyclopedia, the fact that did we eat blue cheese for supper or something, or were we just feeling blue, the fact that those three young radiography nurses had to see me in my me-oh-mys, actually *without* even my me-oh-mys, the fact that they were always hovering over my posterior, the fact that my oncologist only visited me once when I was in the hospital, embrace change, the fact that it's good that she didn't visit more though or it would've *cost* even more, bright white lights, black windows, the fact that I hated being sick in public, in a public ward, just lying there feeling sick, the fact that it kind of drove me crazee, the fact that I had to get a nurse to help me take a bath every day, the fact that I couldn't handle it alone, the fact that they were pretty good about it but it was humiliating, dingy bathroom, metal handles, because she had to lower me in, the fact that then she'd leave me there a while, the fact that I remember trying to get out of the bathtub by myself but I wasn't strong enough and had to wait for her to come back, the fact that why am I thinking about this, "About turn!", the fact that I couldn't stomach the hospital food so Leo brought me chicken stock from home, in a thermos, my own homemade chicken stock, but I must have forgotten to salt it before I froze it, the fact that to this day unsalted chicken stock makes me feel a little nauseous, the fact that cancer patients are always being told to make memories, so these are my memories, the pretty young radiology nurses tending my rear end, and me trying to drink unsalted chicken stock, the fact that when I first found out I had cancer, I tried to be chipper, the fact that at first you don't *believe* it, the fact that that night, after we'd met with the oncologist, I went into the kitchen to get my car keys, the fact that I just wanted to drive, just about anywhere, and never come back, and save everybody a lot of trouble, my family and all the doctors, and the nurses and the radiologists and everybody else, the fact that I even felt sorry for our *HMO*, and that's not easy, pitying an HMO, Laura Ingalls Wilder, Mrs. Brewster, the fact that Laura has such a tough time teaching at the little Brewster School, teacher's certificate, dinner pail, but Almanzo comes and gets her in the cutter, the fact that a cutter's some sort of big sled, the fact that once we used the sled to get groceries, when the car was on the blink, and it was kind of fun, the fact that there was something very wrong with Mrs. Brewster, I think, wielding that knife, the fact that everybody was trying to be nice to me and all, but I just assumed I was going to pass away soon anyway, so it wasn't worth the money we'd spend trying to fight it, the fact that the oncologist had also made it sound like such a lot of work, for everybody involved, a three-week course of this, two weeks of that, three months bed rest, the fact that she wanted to zap me and poison me and somehow put me back together afterwards and it all sounded *impossible*, the fact that I guess I just got scared, Cowardly Lion, the fact that Leo suspected something was up though, and he followed me into the kitchen and sat me down and talked to me, the fact that he talked me out of running away, because he said he didn't want to lose me, black windows, bright white kitchen light, trees silhouetted against blue snow, the fact that he kept saying we would survive this, blue shoes, blue encyclopedia set, and we did, the fact that *he* got me through it, the fact that he did everything, the cooking, the cleaning, even got me books from the library and DVDs when I was stuck on the couch for months too weak to move, eating M&Ms, the fact that I think we *all* ate a lot of M&Ms, Mommy after her operation, Pepito by her bed, the fact that I think what they really mean about "making memories" is something more like going to the beach with your kids, or taking your daughter to a Celine Dion concert, not just sitting around feeling queasy and eating M&Ms together, Medicare & Medicaid, Frank, xiroscapes, the fact that not all xerophytes are succulents, but all hens are chickens, Zyker's, the fact that Zyker's owns a lot of hardware stores as well, buffalo wings, the fact that in Evanston it only seemed to snow out front, the fact that I can remember standing there in the living room, staring out through our diamond-paned windows, watching it snow, the fact that the back yard was always sun-dappled with buttercups, or that's how it seems now, the window seat in the dining room, Pepito barking, snapdragons, mulberries, the fact that when I woke up I'd look out of my bedroom window to see if Pepito was out there, Phoebe doing her makeup, the fact that there was a swing under the mulberry tree, kitchen nook, the fact that Mommy grew lilies of the valley and snapdragons which Pepito trampled, the fact that I was always a little leery of those snapdragons, the fact that maybe I associated them with *Mommy's* snappishness, which was rare but scary, the window seat, the fact that she was a very good-tempered mother, step on a crack, the fact that maybe every family should have a dog, the fact that we only have cats, the fact that I dreamt we got a tall, thin, curly-haired dog, the fact that he was pale apricot-colored, the fact that I think it was some breed that doesn't really exist, the fact that maybe we'd be more like a real family if we had a dog, but *we* could never get a dog as sweet as Pepito, the fact that he was like my little brother, a real member of the family, Leo, cranberries, the big numbers in my second

grade arithmetic book, the fact that Phoebe had guinea pigs, Ethan
had hamsters, and I had mice, Edward, my mouse Edward, the fact
that when Stace decided to be an actress, Leo and I read the whole of
King Lear with her, the fact that it took us three nights, sharing out
the different parts, depending on which characters were in the scene,
and it was fun, and then she went completely off the idea of being an
actress, the fact that I can't believe we even did that now, the fact that
she can barely be in the same room with me these days, Victim Relives
Attack, Your Views On North Korea, the fact that a teen shot his
whole family dead, right after his older sister bought herself a new
Hyundai, but I don't think that was the motive or anything, the fact
that parricide is on the rise, family annihilation, the fact that the man
who stabbed and strangled his wife complained about having to be in
jail on his *birthday*, the fact that the dishwasher has a collapsible
bottom rack, which often collapses, the fact that I don't understand
why it has to have that, the fact that maybe it's for washing pots, but
I would never put my Revere Ware pots in there, the fact that they're
too good to go in the dishwasher, the fact that Mommy had Revere
Ware pots, and Abby had Revere Ware pots, and I have a *few* Revere
Ware pots, inherited from Mommy, but not enough to share out
between four kids, the fact that they'll have to buy their own Revere
Ware someday, the fact that Abby had a nice little mini Revere Ware
saucepan that I so wish I had, well actually I wish I'd inherited all of
Abby's Revere Ware, the fact that I'm sure Barry didn't want his
mom's old pots and pans, any more than he wanted her rag rugs and
plants and the quilt she left to me that he never sent me, lobster rolls,
potato chips, CC&G, the fact that I wish I had that patchwork quilt,
the fact that Abby made it herself, the fact that I bet he threw it
straight out, along with all the pots, and couldn't bring himself to tell
me, the fact that he's quite a gourmand, so Revere Ware probably
wouldn't be good enough for him, the fact that he and his first wife
liked the Boston Pops, but what was her name, the fact that they had
to give away their English sheepdog when they had Bruce, because
Bruce was allergic to dogs, the fact that that whole family was kind of

good at getting rid of stuff, now I think about it, Mommy's letters, the dog, the pots, the fact that Barry's a big thrower-outer, just like his mom, I guess, the fact that eventually he threw out Abby's whole house and moved to Missouri, and that's the last I heard of him, and I guess he's thrown *me* out too, the fact that I wish *we* lived there, in Abby's house, I mean, not in Missouri, the fact that Laura Ingalls Wilder ended up in Missouri, the fact that I always think of Barry's new wife, whatshername, as "new," but they must have been married fifteen years by now, the fact that she always seemed nice, the few times I met her, and Abby liked her too, I think, even though she was so attached to his first wife, whatshername, basement stairs, laundry, ducks, Newburyport, the fact that Revere Ware pots have that nice copper bottom, which keeps stuff from burning or something, the fact that anyway it serves some important purpose, the fact that Barry probably has *pure* copper pans by now, the fact that the Indians mined copper for thousands of years all over Ohio, the fact that I don't like mines and quarries, the fact that in England they had pit ponies who were hardly ever allowed up to the surface, the fact that they spent their whole lives down mine shafts, pulling coal around in the dark, the fact that how do you think up a system like that, making a horse work that hard, awfulous, the fact that what we've done to animals, Revere Ware, American lungs, TB, lost button, aardvark, the fact that I don't know why we have this old American Lung Association calendar on the fridge still, the fact that, according to the American Lung Association, two hundred thousand Americans die from air pollution every year, and seven million American schoolchildren have asthma, the fact that those seven million kids have to struggle through the smog like pit ponies and go to school to watch movies about people dying of Spanish flu, "I got a snootful of it and I'll never go back," the fact that the police shot a pregnant woman seven times, because she was acting crazy, the fact that pregnancy *can* make you emotional, with all the hormones and stuff, hormone-free cattle, the fact that Mary Todd Lincoln may have had a vitamin deficiency, anemia, chicken, the fact that people just can't stop eating chicken, Chick-Fil-A, the fact that sixty or seventy billion chickens die a year to make chicken and dumplings, chicken à la king, chicken gumbo, chicken Kiev, chicken Vesuvio, chicken Stroganoff, chicken tetrazzini, chicken cacciatore, chicken fettucine primavera, garden chicken with wild rice medley, chicken chilaquiles, grilled chicken pouches, stove-top one-dish chicken bake, blueberry chicken breasts, chicken and pickled pepper fajitas, chicken lo mein, chicken nuggets, chili powder chicken nuggets, Italian chicken packets, smothered chicken, chicken Boston, chicken spiedies, chicken biscuit bake, Cornell chicken, smoky buffalo wings, King Ranch chicken casserole, easy no-guilt chicken pot pie, chicken 'n' peaches picante, fire precautions, the fact that there's nothing for breakfast around here except raw cinnamon roll dough, the fact that I'm hungry but not that hungry, the fact that Gillian would eat any amount of raw cinnamon roll dough if I let her, no problem, eggs, pantry, diamond-paned windows, "pained" windows, the fact that cats can eat all kinds of stuff and not get salmonella, the fact that chicken cacciatore was one of Mommy's buffet party specialties, peaches and cream, beaches and cream, cardamom, cinnamon, Margaret Wise Brown, Laura Ingalls Wilder, Robert Louis Stevenson, Wolfgang Amadeus Mozart, shoofly pie, whoopie pie, chess pie, Chesapeake Bay, the fact that I could have an *egg*, I guess, but I need them for other things, the fact that despite having fourteen chickens out there in the yard, we still run out of eggs, *Silent Spring*, the life cycle of a mackerel, recycle, upcycle, observation-outpatient stays, bald eagles, the fact that on my way from Abby's to Fort Lauderdale one time, to visit Grandma, the bus stopped somewhere in Kentucky or Tennessee, and there in the bus station cafeteria I had the best scrambled eggs of my life, "let the sun shine," fried egg, sunny-side-up, "wrecked on a raft," scrambled eggs on toast, the fact that I've been trying to recreate those Kentucky or Tennessee eggs ever since whenever I make scrambled eggs, but you really need a great big short-order griddle plate, the fact that I can remember exactly how he did it, but it took about one second, none of this stirring and stirring, the fact that that's no good, the fact that it's gotta be really fast, just on and off, in a bus station in the middle of nowhere, and they came out just right, bus station restroom, wallet, nice lady, "shingle with a shimmy and a shake," the fact that that's what they called buttered toast and jam, the fact that jam's another example of *wiggling* for Leo, bridge collapse, St. Louis encephalitis, A Dad's Heart-Wrenching Moment, the dark green glass at the top of the bus windows, Greyhound, the fact that after eating my scrambled eggs I went to the restroom and left my wallet beside the sink, because I was rushing to get back to the bus and was scared they'd leave without me, the fact that some very nice lady ran after me with my wallet, the fact that I've always had a soft spot for that state ever since, whichever one it was, the fact that maybe it was Tennessee, the fact that Grandma liked to write terrible haiku about zoo animals, and longer poems too that went on and on about giraffes or pelicans or something, flamingos, the fact that we never told her how bad they were, and she probably passed away believing she was a great poet, well, where's the harm, the fact that she looks like Shirley Jackson, not *Grandma*, that official in Kentucky who doesn't like helping gay couples get married, but Shirley Jackson would never have stopped gay people getting married, the fact that Shirley Jackson never complained about anything much, including her husband, who did play around a bit, with his students, Bennington, adultery, *The Contender*, the fact that maybe Shirley Jackson was too busy writing books to notice his goings-on, *Harriet the Spy*, the fact that I liked that book a lot, the fact that I wanted to be a spy for a while, but I can't remember anything about it now, except that she liked tomato sandwiches, the Xenia ban, the fact that Leo works with all sorts of young women, students and colleagues, but I trust *him*, implicitly, the fact that he's not like Shirley Jackson's husband, Leo asleep in our bed, Leo in his office, Bettina, jigsaw puzzle, Stacy, clothes pile, the fact that I don't worry at all, Department of Engineering, though they're all so young and pretty there, the fact that these are the people coming for the cocktail party, with me in my muumuu, Silver Bridge collapse, the fact that people like Shirley Jackson have *tact*, and that's a rare thing these days, Dog

Sees Himself On TV And Freaks Out, the fact that she never made a scene, but she was often depressed, the fact that she didn't like his stinginess with money, and she mocked his style of book-reviewing, but I think she let the philandering go pretty much unchallenged, philander, pander, panther, Cute Pandas, cutie marks, the fact that Mommy had tact too, but I'm not sure I have any, "*Grace?!*", the fact that I probably wouldn't be too great about things if Leo *was* a philanderer, because I'm the jealous type, boy am I jealous, like even if he even has a glass of *wine* without me I'm jealous, but some men are honorable, the fact that they're not all Bill Clinton, or Trump, giving everybody French smackeroos on the mouth the first time they meet, the fact that Bill Clinton's always trying to bite women's *lips*, the fact that he couldn't take his eyes off Melania at the inauguration, even though she was wearing that blue straitjacket dress, the fact that I shouldn't be so judgmental, but I don't know if coat-dresses ever really work, dear me, what's the matter with me, the fact that being married to Bill Clinton's a whole different ball-game, that's for sure, campaign hat, hat campaign, scenario, "I did not have sex with that woman," the fact that Leo thinks Bill must've promised Hillary the presidency to make up for all his shenanigans, but then she didn't win, so *now* what, the fact that George Bailey offers Mary the moon in *It's a Wonderful Life*, the fact that they didn't have much money, Shirley Jackson and whatshisname, what with his teaching and bookreviewing and flirting and all, the fact that he sort of bullied her into writing, to help make ends meet, what *was* his name now, infidelities, the real deal, the fact that we've still got autumn leaves in the corners of the basement, the fact that Hillary must have known Bill was no picnic when they got married, the fact that I don't like her much but there was nobody else to vote for, free country, Hyman, the fact that Shirley Jackson's husband was called *Hyman*, hymen, silkworms, starfish, toilet paper, little pillow, the fact that Grandma would hardly let me out of her condo for *one minute*, even though I was nineteen or something, and she wouldn't even let me have a glass of beer, the fact that it was really hot out, and her fridge was well-stocked with beer,

but it was only for men, like repair men or Uncle Bud Bar, the fact that
I've never quite forgiven her for not giving me a beer, and that's silly,
the fact that am I going to go to my dying day worrying about that,
Grandma's dark, windowless kitchen, the fact that she held me practically a prisoner in her condo for what felt like a whole week, waiting
and waiting for her ninetieth birthday party to happen, red tide, the
fact that I guess she felt responsible for me or something, the fact that
she let me go swimming once a day but that was about it, except for
the time she took me to see Howard Keel, bobbly glass of water on the
side table by the couch, cinnamon roll dough, red kneading machine,
the fact that she had Grandpa's nice old glass-fronted bookshelves in
her room, full of poetry and law books, and her big souvenir spoon
collection inside the glass coffee table in the living room, the fact that
she really liked *glass*, glass plates and glass tables and a big old crystal
candy bowl, with those old-fashioned, twisted, striped sugar candies
in it, only for special occasions, the fact that Phoebe bagged the spoon
collection as an inheritance as soon as she could write her own name
on a piece of paper and slip it in the glass case, the fact that Phoebe
really went for those spoons, I don't know why, the fact that most of
them aren't really all that nice, just cheap souvenir spoons from every
place Grandma and Grandpa went in America on legal business or
other trips, the fact that one has Niagara Falls and another has the
whole Chicago World's Fair in its bowl, the fact that I wonder if
Phoebe polishes them ever, but they're not even silver, most of them,
maybe silver plate, the fact that Grandma must have spent half her
time buying those things, and polishing them, and polishing the glass
case they were in, so she could show them off, the fact that Phoebe
now has a glass dining-room table, the fact that I somehow wound up
with a few of the spoons with roses on them, the fact that Grandma
left glasses of water out at night to catch thirsty bugs, and I had to
remember all night not to take a sip in case it was full of bugs, but it
never was, the fact that it didn't work, the bugs weren't that thirsty,
the fact that Grandma really hoped she'd find a bug in each of those
glasses in the morning, the fact that a glass of water at Mo's was called

"one on the city," twelve alive, "Gentleman will take a chance," Hyman, ladies' man, Howard Keel, the fact that Grandma'd been knocking around on her own in that condo for so long she'd managed to fill the whole place with bobbly glasses of water, the fact that all her glasses had big round glass bumps on the bottom, an anti-condensation idea, anti-coagulation, cloaca, Coca-Cola, compensation, constipation, the fact that the glasses were always covered with condensation though, so the bobble design didn't do any good, the fact that you had to keep wiping them and checking on the coaster, which stuck to the glass and then fell off, making it look like you were destroying the place, the fact that I don't know why I'm so mean about Grandma except she was mean to *Mommy*, the fact that she could have dragged me to thirty Howard Keel concerts and I still wouldn't have liked her, and I don't like Howard Keel anyway, the fact that I associate him with Grandma, the fact that Grandma and Grandpa were mean to Mommy from the start, not just after Mommy got sick, the fact that I don't think Grandma liked *me* much either, nothing like how much she liked Howard Keel, the fact that she still had a crush on him, in her nineties, the fact that she taught me some useful recipes though while I was there, chicken stock, challah bread, yogurt, the fact that I remember all those things to this day, but I never make yogurt anymore, the fact that the kids only like the store-bought kind, the fact that Grandma's yogurt sometimes had coagulation problems, but it was still *good*, just old-fashioned, lighter than yogurt is now, and not all homogenized, the fact that for chicken stock you need chicken bones, celery, onion, carrot, potato, ginger, garlic, black peppercorns, a few cilantro seeds, a bay leaf, a pinch of sugar, a glass of white wine or vermouth, or half a glass of gin, the fact that I don't remember if Grandma put wine in hers, the fact that if she was so stingy with the beer I kind of doubt it, the fact that you bring it all to the boil, and then simmer it low for at least eight hours, or preferably twelve, if you want to bring out the *glucosamine*, the fact that the more gelatinous it is the better, gelatinous, viscous, viscose, the fact that if you cook it long enough it turns *golden*, Rayon, radon, nylon, Jell-O, nervous pudding, the dynamics of wiggling, colloidal silver, the fact that some people cook it for *twenty-four* hours, but that's maybe *too* much, the fact that then you cool it and strain it, and *salt* it, and get it into the freezer as soon as possible, the fact that I'd rather have the recipe for donuts though from Mommy's dad, tapioca, the fact that Daddy always liked it when Mommy made it for him, the fact that they called tapioca "fish eyes" at Mo's, the fact that it was always hot when I visited Grandma, in Florida *or* in Detroit, the fact that it was always *stifling* somehow, and boring, the fact that in Fort Lauderdale we had to wash all the dishes in the kitchen sink because the dishwasher was stuffed with empty plastic bags, which I never understood, the fact that now I wonder if maybe she'd had a bug problem in there or something, and it put her off ever using the dishwasher ever again, the fact that I dreamt about a big slug eating a smaller slug last night, *yecccch*, the fact that I really should try to be more understanding about Grandma, I mean, *so what* if she bossed me around and didn't use the dishwasher and wouldn't give me a beer, for goodness sake, the fact that that's just silly, to bear a grudge for so many years, Tangee lipstick, uptick in injuries, the fact that Grandma blamed her pot belly on drinking beer when she was pregnant, enormity, but it was doctor's orders, the fact that maybe the doc was right, because she had three healthy sons, opossum mom, the fact that so what if she was a cranky old lady, lots of people get a little cranky in their old age, the fact that it's not a crime, but they sent that telegram, "WE FORGIVE YOU," the fact that *that* was unforgivable, the fact that there were just two main rooms in the Florida place, so I had to sleep on the couch in the living-dining room, and Grandma had the bedroom, the fact that in Detroit they'd had a whole big family home, the fact that it had a kind of sideways view of the ocean, the Florida condo, not the Detroit house, the fact that she moved all the way from Detroit to Florida for a *sidelong view* of the ocean, the fact that you could see a bit more if you went out on the balcony, but it was always too hot to go out there, the fact that you're totally dependent on AC in a place like that, swimming with the pelicans, the fact that Grandma hardly ever went out herself, unless there was a Howard Keel concert on in the evening, the fact that she just kept talking about him *the whole time*, Howard Keel, Howard Keel, the fact that I didn't even know who Howard Keel *was*, or why she was so keen on him, or so excited about him turning up in Fort Lauderdale, the fact that now I feel kind of sorry for the poor guy, having to go to Fort Lauderdale to entertain my Grandma, the fact that whenever I hear his name all I can think about are those bobbly glasses of water dripping everywhere, and my wallet getting lost in the bus station, but quickly returned, and the scrambled eggs, and swimming with pelicans, the fact that it was like *95°* or *100°* every day, the fact that it must be even worse now, 110° or something, voodoo, the fact that maybe she was tired of all the other old folks in the building, the fact that it wasn't exactly a nursing home but it was kind of *like* a nursing home, full to the brim with old folks, 90th, 90° out, dishwasher, plastic bags, chicken soup, the fact that imagine being born a pelican, the fact that what that must be like, learning how to handle that big beak, narwhal, bobbly glass of water, crystal candy dish, fluffy guest towels, the fact that I had a plan to go to Haiti for a few days but she wouldn't hear of it, something about voodoo, muumuu, tutu, tattoo, Lisa Felt "Revolted" By Her Body, the fact that cats are disappearing in Key West and Mandy says it might be something to do with voodoo, the fact that her nice cat disappeared this year, the fact that when we were kids she had a Pekinese, Mommy, Beethoven, the fact that Phoebe said Grandma didn't like *women* very much, the fact that she just liked boys, her three sons, the big barn at Bread Loaf, swerving bee, the fact that Mommy was probably her kindest daughter-in-law, the fact that when Daddy and Mommy eloped, Grandma and Grandpa said they'd never speak to Daddy again, all because Mommy was a Catholic, the fact that it was only when Ethan was born two years later that they sent the telegram saying "WE FORGIVE YOU," but Mommy had just had an emergency cesarean and wasn't all that interested in being forgiven, *La traviata*, hospital corners, cinnamon, OJ, the fact that still, peace was made, and for years we had to visit them once a year in Detroit, the fact that the only good thing about it was the motel swimming pool, the fact that they came to Evanston now and then too, Fighting For His Life, the fact that Grandma came and helped out when Phoebe and I were born, though Mommy said later she was no help at all, the fact that Grandma sent us Chanukah presents every year, the fact that we kept the menorah up in the attic and brought it down to the dining room and lit the candles every night, the fact that most of the presents weren't all that great, but who doesn't like getting stuff to open eight nights in a row, even if it *was* just nylon nightgowns and cheap jewelry and more *poems*, the fact that she gave us an ugly book of fairy tales once, the fact that I don't remember what she sent for Ethan, the fact that maybe she raised the quality of the presents in honor of a boy, like a watch and a pen and stuff like that, the fact that a lion tried to attack a baby through a glass window at a zoo in Utah, the fact that the baby never noticed what was going on behind him, and the mom seemed to think it was all really funny, the fact that the lion looked awfully thin to me, and really serious about it, the fact that he was hungry, the fact that when Grandma had me all to herself in Fort Lauderdale she kept telling me how hard Mommy's illness was on *Daddy*, beer, cold beer, the fact that she acted like it was all Mommy's fault she'd gotten sick, the fact that after five days of this I was a complete nervous wreck, the fact that I was blubbing in the bathroom by the time Phoebe arrived and comforted me, the fact that Phoebe was at NYU then, the fact that she had to go all the way down to Florida for that birthday too, the fact that I was just starting at CCSU, the fact that I don't know to this day why we all turned up for the birthday, ♬ *I don't know why she swallowed a fly* ♬, meringue of the family, the fact that you always remember who comforted you though, the fact that Phoebe's great in an emergency, the fact that Grandma hadn't even noticed me blubbing in the bathroom, the fact that luckily she had two bathrooms, Gnadenhutten fireworks festival, the fact that a man shot his pregnant wife dead in Columbus but they managed to save the baby, more or less, the fact that a motherless baby's now fighting for his life, the fact that Grandma sent me a doll once that could talk, and

I did like that, but Mommy didn't and I never knew why, but *now* I do, the fact that I've had to listen to enough toys with electronic voices myself, and they ain't Howard Keel, the fact that the raccoons have given up raiding our trash for the day but traffic sounds have taken their place, and now the chickens are trying to outdo the car noise, the fact that they're always on the move, and always in such a tearing hurry, *people*, not chickens, though also chickens, the fact that where can they all be going, screeching around the corner like maniacs, why did the chicken cross the road, why did the *person* cross the road, the fact that I think people are just trying not to think about their *mothers*, the fact that I think that's all anybody's doing most of the time, all over the world, Mother Earth, the fact that everybody's either *thinking* about their mothers or trying *not* to think about their mothers, the fact that nobody ever talks about them, the fact that mothers never get mentioned at dinner parties, even though they probably cooked all the food, the fact that mothers probably *invented* dinner parties, and cock-tail parties, the fact that the world seems indifferent to mothers, yet when they die it's so *empty*, the fact that Mommy's illness broke me, broke me, the fact that now who left their snow boots right in front of the back door for me to trip over on my way out to the chickens,

.   .   .   .

When they were ready, she would take them outside the dark and narrow den. The land was their real home, the land, and the land was huge.

She would teach them the chill that comes before rain, and that rain has a smell, even before drops fall. Snow is not food, flowers are not goslings. Trees smell wrong after other lions have peed on them. Run from the pee of males. Mergansers are no good. Likewise, loons, frogs, pike. She would show them how the heron could unsettle the sleeping ducks by flying too low over their heads.

She would show her cubs how to hide themselves in stillness: in shadows, in fog, bright sun. She would show them the guiltless, guileless lives of herbivores, antler dangers, the cleanest of kills. She would teach them to thread their way silently through the forest, sink at the sight of a deer, determine the moment to recoil and leap.

She would teach them to care for their paws. Never step on precarious ground, or things that may collapse under you. Test the terrain for crunch or slide. Avoid sharp stones, jagged edges of loose rock, anything unexpectedly hot or cold or wet. You must not fall through ice. You must not fall at all. A lion is alone in the wilderness.

She knew the dangers of hunting. Mistaking a brown blur for a deer, she had leapt swiftly through bracken to find a bear in front of her, standing upright. In her surprise, the lioness jumped twelve feet in the air, and landed badly. The bear took a wild swipe at her and ran away.

One furious stag butted her into a gully. Snowshoe hares can bite you on the nose. Making an unplanned grab at a turkey on a precarious summit, she had overshot and rolled down the desiccated cliffside, bare of bushes to soften her fall. She nearly starved there at the bottom, waiting for her front legs to work again. Made forlorn by the ease of her own ruin, the lioness longed for her own mother, now dead, and knew she too might die soon, if not from this injury then another.

She limped for some time after.

·   ·   ·   ·

the fact that I bet Aunt Sophia would never have balked at a little old cocktail party, heavens to Betsy no, the fact that she served up big banquets for everybody four times a year, Thanksgiving, Christmas, Easter, and Fourth of July, with her special stars-and-stripes paper tablecloth, maybe Labor Day too, the fact that she always served at least six different types of pie, the fact that Leo remembers those feasts, the big spread and a dozen or more family members chowing down until they practically burst, the fact that I wonder what kind they were, the pies I mean, not the relatives, probably apple, cherry, blackberry, pumpkin, lemon meringue, maybe paw-paw, ♫ *way down yonder in the paw-paw patch* ♫, pumpkin patch, Pumpkin Patch kids, Cabbage Patch, the fact that I bet she could make blueberry too, blueberry crumb pie, raspberry, huckleberry, boysenberry, strawberry and rhubarb pie, persimmon, sour cherry pie, mock cherry pie, linzertorte, pear pie, apricot pie, Eskimo Pie, the fact that Eskimos never made Eskimo pie, I don't think, Inuit ivory duck, walrus, narwhal, the fact that Phoebe had an Eskimo doll, what was his name, the fact that she got him after she had her tonsils out, ice cream, "blacksberries" pie, Kentucky mince pie, angel pie, transparent pie, moon pie, half-moon pie, scooter pie, custard pie, berry custard pie, rice pudding pie, lemon meringue pie, lemon chiffon pie, rum chiffon pie, Key lime pie, Shaker lemon pie, Mississippi mud pie, Jefferson Davis pie, Washington cream pie, Bavarian cream pie, Boston cream pie, Durbin sugar cream pie, sour cream pie, sweet potato pie, pecan pie, bean pie, fudge pie, Eve with a lid on it, the fact that I happen to know Sophia made a very good peach pie, or peach cobbler maybe, in winter-time, with her own canned peaches, the fact that Mark Twain liked pie, everybody likes pie, bean pie, custard pie, Butterscotch pie, buttermilk pie, fudge pie, cookie cake pie, Run for the Roses pie, the fact that I really do need something for breakfast or I'm going to *faint*, the fact that it's silly to have nothing but coffee all morning, the fact that even Ben eats his cereal like a good boy, the fact that he's very sensible that way, the fact that he *knows* he'll be too hungry if he doesn't, the fact that I could have a frozen madeleine, I suppose, and dunk it in my coffee, or some frozen lemon drizzle cake, Safari Park Fire Kills 33 Patas Monkeys, but none of us can really face any more lemon drizzle cake, the fact that I got soooo upset when my lemon drizzle cakes fell, boy, the fact that Cathy couldn't see why, Cathy standing on the porch smiling, winding stone path, the fact that she said it didn't matter a bit and they'd still sell it, and it still tasted good, but I was mortified, the fact that all of life is an embarrassment, the fact that it was bad for my reputation and hers, the fact that I had to make sure that would never happen again, the fact that I must have made about thirty of the darn things before I was sure the recipe was foolproof, mixing bowls all over the kitchen, lemons, trays, oven pans, chaos, the enormity, the fact that it was just like Julia Child with her mound of chopped onions, Meryl Streep I mean, the fact that for *20,000 Leagues Under the Sea* they made Captain Nemo's secret reactor out of glass salad bowls, the fact that it was kind of obsessive maybe, my lemon drizzle cake experiments, I mean, not Captain Nemo's control room, the fact that Captain Nemo had other things to worry about besides lemon drizzle cake, like *the end of the world* for instance, the fact that actually, for me, having my lemon drizzle cakes fall *was* the end of the world, and I felt I had to get my lemon drizzle cake right, once and for all, the fact that that's a strange expression, "once and for all," like "once upon a time," upon a time, bento box, incense sticks, joss sticks, josser, equestrian acts, Patricia Highsmith, the fact that I hate to think of all the rolls and rolls of paper towels I must've used up, perfecting my lemon drizzle cake, the trees that *died* for my lemon drizzle cake, the fact that I wonder if the new trees dotted around the parking lot at Old Orchard are big by now, once and for all, once in a while, the fact that they needed those trees, the fact that there was no *shade* at Old Orchard, and the car seat would burn the back of your legs when you got back from shopping, not that we went to Old Orchard much, the fact that it's funny I still remember those poor little trees stuck in a parking lot, doing their duty, "standing guard over the old castle," growing as fast as they could, rhododendrons, Highgate, Channing, perfectionist, confection, convection, convention, the fact that most of those *trial* lemon drizzle cakes are still in our freezer, the fact that they're edible and all, they just don't look right, the fact that I slip a slice into the kids' lunch boxes whenever I can, but they probably just throw them away, crumbs of lemon drizzle cake decaying in the weeds by the school playground, birds investigating and spurning them, the old felt lion on the top of our Christmas tree, "like a Christmas tiger," plum wore out, the fact that last summer some woman on Facebook threw an ice cream sandwich out on the grass and noticed it was still there *three weeks later*, and it looked just the same, the fact that it hadn't melted or anything, and even dogs and bugs had avoided it, the fact that it just sat there for weeks making a yellow patch on the grass, the fact that that's sort of weird, like an ice cream sandwich from another planet or something, the fact that meteorites are full of iron but they found one that had some nickel in it too, wooden nickel, the fact that some guy had been using it as a doorstop for thirty years and now it's worth $100,000, the fact that who would want to buy that though, a big lump of iron and nickel, carrot salad, bike trips, the fact that Leo's dad always said there was no telling what people would spend their money on, what they wanted more than money, the fact that I like to put lemon juice in my carrot salad as well as mayo, tho fact that all the kids like it that way, the fact that my lemon drizzle cake's another matter though, because all these kids really care about is frosting, and lemon drizzle cakes don't *have* any frosting, they have drizzle, and who in their right mind really wants *drizzle*, the fact that most people probably need drizzle like a hole in the head, Phoebe's Eskimo doll, *Coldy*, the fact that that was his name, Coldy, and I always envied her for having him, with his felt fish and felt fishing spear, and his hooded coat that you could take off but we rarely did, the fact that he really did look cold without it, still clutching his fish and his spear, embarrassing, like a naked Raggedy Ann or Andy, the fact that it looks all wrong when they're naked, indecent, the fact that everybody looks pretty much the same with no clothes on, or so they say, nudists I mean, *They say the hen can lay, I don't know but they know*, nudist colony, *Playboy* magazine, Rex the Walkie-Talkie Robot Man, the fact that as soon as I get my four feet of cinnamon dough rolled out across the counter, Stacy comes in asking where her English homework is and Gillian and Ben start arguing about who gets to hold Frederick, the fact that I think these kids think I think about nothing but *them* all day, but actually I spend most of the day trying *not* to think about them because I've got all this other stuff I gotta do, Coldy, the fact that Mommy once described motherhood as opening cereal packets for ten years, cattle, the fact that cows and sheep eat grass, not just grain, Mommy smoking, the fact that she used to lie on a towel on the beach and read a book while we swam, book, sunglasses, and I thought she was so beautiful, Jane Austen, the fact that one summer she was reading *Cancer Ward*, a huge book, and there was a big picture of him on the back, Solzhenitsyn, and he had a sort of Amish beard, the fact that I don't know if he picked that up in Vermont or it's a Russian thing, "It's a Russia thing," the fact that you never see Solzhenitsyn smiling, the fact that the dough's shrunk to a three-foot-square slab now, instead of four feet, because I had to rescue Frederick, and the buns I already rolled are starting to relax and take over the pan, the fact that when they spread out too far, they get all flat and silly-looking and they just dry out when they're baking, the fact that they don't look right, the fact that cinnamon rolls need to be very tightly spiraled, and packed tight, the fact that these are getting outta control, the fact that I really have no time for a debate about Frederick when I'm right in the middle of spiraling, sheesh, Judgment of Solomon, the fact that why didn't they come bug me during the kneading, knives, plastic chopping board, the fact that nobody respects my work, spirals, the fact that I wish I had a big wooden chopping board but you can't get them anymore, Mommy, the fact that all I have left of Mommy are my Revere Ware pots, the old poffertje pan, two or three ashtrays, a greenish cloisonné enamel box, her sewing scissors, blunt but still usable, my nice silver bracelet that I never take off, some ancient opera LPs I can't play anymore because we don't have a record-player, and an incomplete Chapman edition of Jane Austen, the fact that *Pride and Prejudice* is gone, I don't know where, the fact that it went missing years ago, the fact that I must've left it in Hamden somehow, the fact that somehow it got separated from the rest, the fact that maybe it's in one of the boxes in the attic, now that I think about it, the fact that that never occurred to me, the fact that I like to think of Mommy cooking supper in the kitchen in New Haven with *Samson et Dalila* playing on the record player in the pantry, bright white light, blue floor, yellow kitchen, white fridge, black windows, black widow spiders, Coldy, lilies of the valley, the fact that you have to plant nasturtiums out in May, cloisonné, the fact that I've got a few old photos too, including a great picture of her smoking, and a little one of her as a kid about Ben's age, but she looks more like Gillian in it, the fact that it's got a cloth border that Mommy embroidered, the fact that it was a present for her mom, and you can tell Mommy did the embroidery, the fact that even at ten she had her own distinctive drawing style, the fact that it's still there in all the birthday cards she did later, her hand-painted birthday cards, the fact that she did one for Stace every year when Stace was little, blue lambs, "my ewe lamb," and she even did one for Bathsheba, with flowers and a big beaming black cat, the fact that I also have all the letters she wrote me in college, the fact that I never threw out a single one, the fact that they were always precious to me, the fact that I loved her handwriting, and the italic pen she always used, the fact that I wish I had nice handwriting, the fact that I also have a few of her favorite sweaters, but that's about it, besides the stuff she gave me, like some books and stuff, UPS, FedEx, Rolex, X-ray, and my old patchwork quilt that was always on my bed as a kid, the fact that it's really falling apart now, the fact that Jane Austen no longer exists and only ever existed briefly, not long enough to finish *Sanditon*, tragedy, enormity, Bronx cheer, Graduation Gowns, Choir Robes, paper towels, humdinger, Uber, Lyft, beige countertop, the fact that some people work for Uber *and* Lyft at the same time, the fact that people work so hard, the fact that Mommy liked *Persuasion* best, because it's mournful, regrets, remorse, egrets, dceaglecam, government shutdown, the fact that they found a see-through lobster in Maine, but it's not an albino, it's something else, the fact that I dreamt we ran some kind of sandwich company, making mini-sandwiches, the fact that I wondered for years what that little white cylindrical thing was in the bathroom in Evanston, that was usually tucked away in the medicine cabinet, the fact that sometimes it was left out and it was all wet and sudsy, with or without its little plastic cover, the fact that I was sort of frightened of it, the fact that I thought it must have some, well, some kind of intimate purpose I wasn't supposed to know about, the fact that I didn't *want* to know about it, spirals, Wayne County Amish,

Solzhenitsyn, Swartzentruber, Rumspringa, teens, Schoenbrunn Village, hydraulic parenting, pneumatic drill, the fact that I never had the courage to ask what it was, but then I finally noticed that *Leo* had something very like it, and I asked him what it was and it's a *styptic stick*, for *shaving*, for heaven's sake, mystery solved, the fact that it only took me about thirty-five years to figure it out, downstairs bathroom, shelf by the sink, terrapins, the bathroom under the stairs, the fact that that was where the side door used to be, but long before *we* moved in, the fact that I used to give my turtles some free swim time in the sink, while I cleaned their tank, but they should have had a *tropical* tank, the fact that I guess I'll have to go to my grave feeling guilty about those turtles, tartes, the fact that snapping turtles like tuna fish, the fact that it's not like you can form much of a relationship with a tiny terrapin, the fact that people can get attached to tortoises, but I don't know if the tortoise is attached to *them*, the fact that maybe he's just looking for a way out the whole time, the fact that Leo's tortoise ran away when he was a kid, or maybe it just got lost and couldn't find its way back, TDs, Pepito, buttercups, mulberry tree, swing, slide, Muslim man feeding crocodiles, the fact that crocodiles always look so happy, with that crooked smile they've got, crocodile coming down a slipway, the fact that Stacy has found her homework, but now Gillian's lost hers, the fact that my back and neck feel better, but my hip still hurts, seventy-five billion chickens, the fact that keeping chickens probably makes us first in line for bird flu, the fact that the golden lancehead snake is not truly arboreal, and its use of vegetation is "facultative," whatever the heck *that* is, the fact that there's a whole island covered with these snakes somewhere, Zika, Dengue, E. coli, meningitis, staphylococcus, MRSA, norovirus, West Nile virus, hepatitis, cholera, shigella, vibrio, the fact that there's a big black hole in the middle of the Milky Way, but we already knew that, the fact that astronomers found out some theory or other about black holes was wrong, but I forget what, the fact that a thirteen-year-old rape victim in India has been allowed to have an abortion, The Most Popular Shopping Chains, State by State, menstruation huts, the fact that you can use meat tenderizer to get rid of old blood stains, the fact that the police in Utah arrested a nurse because she wouldn't give them a blood sample from an unconscious patient who'd been in a car crash, the fact that she said they needed a warrant, so then they hand-cuffed her and arrested her and strong-armed her out of the building, right in the middle of her shift, body language expert, Jell-O, Sun-Maid, the fact that Leo never liked raisins because the Sun-Maid girl, maid, scared him, the fact that I don't mind the maid, the fact that she's just a cheerful-looking person in a loose white peasant blouse, the fact that it's not her fault I can't eat raisins anymore, the fact that nobody can tell whether Melania likes her husband or not, the fact that it's hard to believe she does but if she *doesn't*, what's she hanging around for, the fact that Leo thinks Trump's got her blackmailed somehow, the fact that sometimes it feels like this whole country's got Stockholm Syndrome, like we're all held prisoner, the fact that I wonder how many people dream about getting along with Trump, Democrats too, the fact that I've had dreams like that, handcuffs, strong-armed, the fact that the police use *plastic* handcuffs now, the fact that I think they look kind of funny, hanging off the officers' sit-me-down-upons, the fact that they look like some kind of *corsage* or something, the fact that they're white, the handcuffs, not necessarily the police, the fact that if the cuffs were black they wouldn't look so silly, ivy patch, Ivy League, "Stay away from the Ivy League," "Suck in your gut," forward pass, the fact that our New Haven house had white walls and fireplaces, and big low windows, wide dark floor-boards, the fact that it was really old, eighteenth century, built during the Revolutionary War, or right after anyway, revolution, #Resist, Jane Wyman's Wedgwood fragment, the fact that it was U-shaped, our house, not Jane Wyman's Wedgwood fragment, the fact that Mommy and Daddy's room led on to a sleeping porch, open on three sides, the fact that it was dreamy to sleep out there in the summertime, catching the breezes, the fact that there were plenty of bathrooms, the fact that there were *four* on the second floor, like Myrna Loy wants in *Mr. Blandings*, the fact that the house had its original antique

Chinese wallpaper in the dining room, and a pantry, and I'll never live in such a nice house again, the fact that there were actually two pantries, one on the way into the kitchen from the dining room, full of plates and stuff, where Mommy fell when she first got sick, and one off the other side of the kitchen, for keeping things cool, scullery, scullery maid, milkmaid, goose girl, flower girl, flower basket, Longaberger Homestead, bathrooms, Blandings, the fact that Daddy asked if he could buy that house but Yale wouldn't sell it, so we were just renting, and then after he died they made Mommy move out, and then they let the whole place fall to rack and ruin, that Revolutionary War house, the fact that I went to look at it once and the living room ceiling had caved in, "a gradual process, the consequence of neglect," Benjamin Franklin, "Stay away from the Ivy League," but that house was wasted on us anyway, the fact that we were so broken by Mommy's illness it didn't help to be living in a palace, well, maybe it helped a little, ♫ *instead of sheep* ♫, the fact that I liked our Evanston house just as much, even though it was nothing special, staircase, banister, buttercups, diamond window-panes, the fact that I often think about the New Haven house lately, I don't know why, the fact that I like to think about the ivy patch that Pepito liked to sniff around in sometimes, and the terraced rose garden, where Mommy and I used to have peaches in cream, and the baking smells coming from the Culinary Institute behind, the fact that I think they've moved somewhere else now, the fact that we've all moved somewhere else now, Coldy, Pepito, Bathsheba, Bartholomew, the fact that Phoebe's guinea pigs ran around outside sometimes in the laundry yard, but we had to make sure Pepito wasn't loose outside when the guinea pigs were out, because in Evanston he'd managed to get hold of one of them once when we were out somewhere, either Guppy or Piglet or Tiny Tim, the fact that Pepito chased Guppy or Piglet or Tiny Tim all around the dining room, the fact that he didn't *hurt* him but there were tufts of guinea pig hair under the table, and Guppy or Piglet or Tiny Tim, or whoever it was that got chased, was pretty scared, when we found him, but okay, just sort of traumatized, PTSD, ADHD, RNC,

Republican National Committee, GOP, the fact that I suppose most guinea pig PTSD must go untreated, resignation syndrome, the fact that Piglet was white and orange and black, the fact that Guppy and Tiny Tim both had nice chestnut-colored fur, but Tiny Tim had white fur as well, the fact that he was sort of tortoiseshell-colored, turtles, peaches in cream, the fact that we ate peaches all summer long, it seems like, just me and Mommy, for breakfast out on the back porch, looking at the rose bed, the fact that somebody from the Divinity School shot a bee-bee gun at the upstairs bathroom window once, and it nearly hit *Phoebe*, the fact that there was a tiny hole in the window from then on, Myrna Loy, hydrangeas, the fact that we took Pepito for lots of walks in the Divinity School grounds, but I remember it in the snow, steep hills deep in snow, and Pepito running around, just me and Daddy, the fact that I should go back for a visit some time, the fact that after Mommy had to move it was hard to get my feet to budge when I had to go over to her new place, dried leaves on the road, the big, dark basement, the fact that basements usually are scary, because you're down there by yourself and it's all shadowy and uncomfortable, the fact that Ben often gets up in the night, but you can't *force* a kid to sleep, the fact that *I* don't sleep so well when Leo's not here, the fact that I was the thumb-sucker in the family, Phoebe was the nail-biter, and Ethan used swear words on the beach when he was two, and we all swallowed something bad when we were babies, the fact that Ethan swallowed ink, Phoebe swallowed Ajax, and I swallowed a mattress button, the fact that I probably thought it was a little cookie, so I ate it, the fact that we all had to be taken to the hospital and have our stomachs pumped, and I thought this was *normal*, an automatic part of babyhood, but none of *my* kids ever swallowed anything that dangerous, touch wood, apart from the kibble maybe, the fact that if dogs eat grapes, you have to take them straight to the vet to get their stomach pumped and of course it costs a thousand bucks, the fact that the kids've had plenty of falls requiring stitches and such, thanks to soccer matches and slides and jungle gyms and tree-climbing, but the worst time was when Stacy's stroller got away from me, the fact that that was the worst thing that happened when she was little, the fact that the stroller just started to roll and I couldn't catch up in time and it flipped over at the curb and she cut her hand, the fact that I felt so guilty and still do, the fact that I just looked away for *one second* to put some groceries in the trunk, the fact that people always say that when something awful happens to their kids, "I just looked away for a moment," and he was run over, snatched, drowned, the fact that I looked around, and it was just like that scene in *Babar*, and then there she was, bleeding and crying, the fact that she couldn't stop crying for ages and that made me feel even more guilty, the fact that no normal person would let go of a stroller for a *second*, the fact that I must be the worst mom in the world, the fact that Leo says I'm a good mom, but what does *he* know, the fact that luckily he doesn't see me at my worst, I *hope*, the fact that without Leo I don't know how I'd keep going, the fact that he's the only person that even seems to like me, the fact that he *loves* me, and that makes everything bearable, the fact that Stacy had a worse injury actually with Frank, that time she hurt her chin, and once she burnt her hand at his house and he called me up because he couldn't figure out why she was crying and crying, but I could tell as soon as I saw her hand, the fact that when she fell on her chin she had a big gash and we had to take her to the Urgent Care place on Dixwell Avenue, the fact that she still has a little scar on the underside of her chin, the fact that he didn't even apologize, the fact that he always seemed mystified when anything went wrong, as if it had nothing to do with him, the fact that I guess he was mystified by our breakup too, same deal, nothing to do with him, a stitch in time saves nine, stomach pumped, the fact that I *didn't* get my stomach pumped when I swallowed that mattress button, the fact that they used some kind of *fork* to get it out, ughh, the fact that Jake sucks his thumb, and Ben sometimes wets the bed still, when he's over-tired, and Gillian obsesses over her honey bears, maniacally rearranging them, and Stace is obsessed with makeover videos, the fact that getting four whole human beings operational and up to speed, getting them to adulthood alive, is a big undertaking, big business, Big Mac, not to mention just getting them all off to school in the morning, motivational training, Kung Fu, Karate, bikes, glasses of milk, dogs' pee-holes in the snow, Howard Hughes's milk bottles full of pee, honey bears, UPS, GPS, the fact that if you choke when you're alone you're supposed to do the Heimlich maneuver on *yourself*, the fact that you just fall forward on your stomach and wind yourself, and it might save you, the fact that if I did that I'd get a FOOSH injury as well as choking to death, the fact that in *Babar* they just shake Flora upside down, but I don't know if that really works on a stuck mattress button that looked like a cookie, the fact that some guy just shot two Indian engineers in Kansas because he thought they were *Iranians*, the fact that the murderer didn't even know who he was shooting at, and one of them has died, the fact that he thinks he's gotta shoot every Iranian in the world or something, and they reminded him of Iranians, the fact that they were just having a beer after work and this guy comes in and shoots them, the fact that the one who survived was only shot in the leg and managed to crawl away, but the other guy was killed, point blank, pellet hole, bullet-proof glass, bullet-proof shot glasses, optics, the Beast, Obamacare, Michelle, the fact that the dead man's family in India is just heartbroken, the fact that all of India is heartbroken, the fact that they were both engineers who'd come over to work on GPS, the fact that I don't know what that man could have been thinking, Frank, *Monsoon Wedding*, mitti attar made with sandalwood oil, the smell of rain, terpenes, the fact that Ethan liked *Monsoon Wedding*, the fact that we don't always agree about movies, the fact that he likes sci-fi, Mandy, the fact that I have a tiny little wooden Indian elephant, painted pale green, with tiny yellow spots and red and white daisies on its sides, the fact that the whole thing's about half an inch tall and it's got a few thin, twisted wires on it, like it used to hang from something, the fact that maybe it's part of a mobile or, or *what*, the fact that I don't even know where I got it, the fact that it's just been hanging around for years and refuses to go away, just a little green elephant carved out of wood, the fact that even though it's crudely made, it's still very recognizably an elephant, a tiny pale green elephant, with a roughly carved trunk and tusks, the fact that somehow the essentials of being an elephant are all there, though it might not pass muster with a real elephant, the fact that elephants would probably be amazed if they knew how much we think about them, all the times we'd painted them and photographed them and dreamt about them, the fact that elephants are scared of mice, though I think it depends on the elephant, and maybe on the mouse, the fact that we had a poor old erratic mouse in the kitchen once, that wasn't acting normal, the fact that the poor thing kept going in circles, the fact that maybe the cats had brought him in and played with him and injured him, or maybe he was just a little crazee, and came in all by himself, the fact that he didn't act like *Edward*, the fact that Edward always behaved very sensibly, the fact that Edward was brave, and smart, the fact that an adult mouse can have a friendship with a human child, the fact that maybe he was cold and hungry, or thirsty, the crazy mouse, not Edward, and we should have given him some *refreshments*, the fact that really he acted like he needed to go to a mouse *nursing home*, or a mouse senior day care center, the fact that we were going to try to catch him but he disappeared and I don't know what happened to him, the fact that the cats probably gobbled him up in the night, the fact that I don't think he was the same wild mouse we had last summer, the fact that I'd like to own that netsuke mouse reclining on a shogi chess piece, the fact that where did we see that, the fact that I dreamt about a friendly gray kitten with white-and-yellow paws and a white chest, and big white floppy ears like a dog's ears, the fact that I saw it at a party in somebody's yard and later I realized the kitten had no owner, school friends, Patty, Lynn, Maika, Susan, so I decided to go back and get it, but instead I ended up outside some buildings where two Middle-Eastern families lived, *Iranian* maybe, the fact that they were all gathered on the front lawn waiting to be deported, and I got mad and cornered the female immigration officer nearby, which I would never ever do in real life, the fact that it felt pretty weird even to do it in a dream, but I told her, I told her this was like *Nazism*, and she seemed so offended, so I tried to walk back the remark and started mumbling that it wasn't *exactly* like the Nazis, because the Nazis were murderous from the start, but it was a little like the Nazis, but by then she'd drifted off into the crowd, ICE, ♬ *La donna è mobile* ♬, dear me, the fact that anger doesn't solve anything, let sleeping dogs lie, sleeping dogs, the fact that two wrongs don't make a right, right-hand turn, the fact that in my dreams I'm usually a coward but even more so in real life, the fact that it's so rude to criticize people to their *face*, the fact that that's just not me, not my style, the fact that I leave that kind of thing to big-mouths like Amelia, and Senate hearings on C-SPAN, jeepers, blue-footed Boobies, *And that has made all the difference*, the fact that blue-footed Boobies aren't monogamous, the fact that their feet are amazing, the fact that they're really blue, the fact that I never read poetry, the fact that the only poet I like is Paul Violi, ever since he read at Peolia, Chinese fireworks, the fact that what does a chick think when it looks at an egg, the fact that everybody was bowled over, not by *eggs*, by Paul Violi, the fact that his reading was the best thing that ever happened there, the fact that I still remember his ransom note haiku, no, *tanka*, *Bring fifty thousand in cash*, and the poem about Chinese fireworks, tree roots, clover patch, cigarette stubs, podium, the fact that it's hard to believe they could actually get a guy like Paul Violi to come to Peolia, *really* hard, *Minimum order: 1 dozen*, the fact that then, afterwards, everyone in the Humanities Department took him out for dinner, humanity, humane, human, and I wasn't even invited because I was part-time, Arvo Pärt, the fact that I couldn't have afforded to go anyway, the fact that they always made everybody *pay* for their own dinner when they took some guest of honor out, everybody except the guest, so the whole dinner would descend into this big dividing-up of the bill thing, according to who had what, the fact that it was "excruciating," as Gavin would say, the fact that they sometimes tried to *fudge* what they'd had too, or leave before the dessert and squirm out of paying, people with big salaries too, Heads of Department, bickering right in front of the guest of honor, "Bicker, bicker, bicker," Mound City, tea cup, egg cup, chicks and eggs, hen and chicks, checks and balances, the fact that Phoebe collected egg cups and Ethan collected stamps, the fact that he had a lot of Roman coins too, in an album, the fact that he had all his pennies arranged in a pyramid on top of his bureau, and kept adding to it, a penny piggy bank, the fact that I can't *remember* what I collected, except those little china animals, and trolls, the fact that I didn't like trolls all that much, but there was always a new one with some kind of different-colored hair, or a miniature one, the fact that the smaller ones were the best, *Bring fifty thousand in cash*, the fact that I like being read to, by Paul Violi or anybody else really, even Ben, the Preakness, Shirley Jackson, the fact that Leo reads to me sometimes while I make the pies, the fact that he really does have a beautiful voice, the fact that he used to be on the radio when he was in college, the fact that I don't read out loud too well, *Babar*, the fact that Stacy told me so, long ago, the fact that she *still* hates my reading voice, the fact that she leaves the room whenever I start reading *One Fish, Two Fish, Red Fish, Blue Fish* to Jake, and slams her door when I start reading to Gillian too, at bedtime, beds, laundry pile, cinnamon rolls, dentist, faucets, the fact that Mommy and Daddy always read to us in bed, so now I spend two hours a night reading to Jake and Gillian, no matter what Stacy says, the fact that I like to read them Laura Ingalls Wilder, the fact that Gillian can read it to herself but she likes it when I read to her, well, I *think* she does, the fact that Gillian's not much of a complainer, United Flight 93, the fact that Ben reads to *himself* at night, the fact that he never liked fairy tales, or Dr. Seuss, the fact that all Ben wants to read is science stuff and I don't know how he can *sleep* after that, the fact that he doesn't sleep too well, the fact that I couldn't sleep after Dr. Seuss when I was a kid, heart operation, ICU, DUI, Daddy, Gavin, *Madeline*, madeleines, the fact that Stace reads plenty, the fact that some of it's assigned, like *Winesburg, Ohio*, the fact that I don't know why every kid in Ohio has to read that book but they do, the fact that I think the teachers just like it because Ohio's in the title, the fact that it's all about shriveled apples, Brick NJ, Shanksville PA, Alligator Found In Living Room, applehead dolls, Havahart cages, the fact that she also had to read *Lord of the Flies* and *Of Mice and Men* and that *Absolutely True Diary of a Part Time* something or other, but for fun she likes YA books, the fact that her favorite one lately is about a girl detective who can't drive, skateboards to the crime scene and looks everything up online, the fact that I think *Harriet the Spy* was better, but she won't read anything I recommend, and maybe she's too old for it now anyway, the fact that some of her books are full of hoop skirts and stays, England and all, Mammy, *Gone with the Wind*, the fact that the idea of hoop skirts seem to be catching on again with girls who wouldn't be caught dead in anything but jeans and a T-shirt, the fact that maybe they're preparing themselves just in case uncomfortable clothing has a revival, the fact that I wonder what's become of that lace-up corset thing Leo got me, humpback chest, humpback whale, sperm whale, Leo, the fact that hoop skirts seem awfully inconvenient, like it's always kind of a business when Almanzo's plump mom has to come through a doorway, especially if her hands are full, because she has to allow time for the hoop skirt to squeeze through, the fact that it involves a little tug, the fact that she liked to zoom around all the time, doing this, doing that, so I bet the hoop skirt annoyed her no end, really slowed her down, the fact that I've never understood why you'd make clothes so big you can't get through the *door*, like bridal gowns and such, stays and panniers, the fact that it's like trying to get one of those double strollers through a doorway, tradwives, the fact that Stacy likes to read about hoop skirts and clever little English heiresses who rebel against their moms, the fact that in one of her recent books a rough and ready ship's cap'n accosts a pretty young lady and her mom at an inn, the fact that he comments on the soup they're eating, then disappears and they think nothing of it until some Baron or Lord or something tells them a little more about that swarthy ship's cap'n, like that he's got secret wealth and has never been "caught" by a woman, "Thrice burnt but the flames ne'er took," fire, sloop, turret ship, sail-cloth, rip tides, skull and crossbones, Ben's pirate costume, Hallowe'en, tween deck, hull cracks, rocker towers, the fact that the daughter in the story just smiles to herself and then quietly folds her fan and returns it to her reticule, vestibule, and in that moment the mom realizes the damage is done and the saucy young wench will have the ship's cap'n if'n she can git 'im and so it turns out of course, after a lot of to-ing and fro-ing, rocking and rolling, and brigands, and dark pointy rocks, perilous seas and a moonlit ship-wreck, but not before the daughter gets carried to shore in a devilish pirate's arms, the fact that I don't see what Stacy gets out of these things, the fact that she's barely even seen the ocean, except in Hollywood movies like *20,000 Leagues Under the Sea*, Sabatini, swash-buckling, *The Three Musketeers*, Mouseketeers, the fact that the Liberty ships were always breaking in half, engineering failure, brittle fractures, the fact that Stace had to write a book report and I suggested she could write it on the shipwreck book, and she wrote the whole thing and it was so good, the fact that then she got a D, because her essay lacked verifiable facts that could be rebutted or substantiated, the fact that, never in all my born days, of all the silly, the fact that I just don't get it, because they never said it had to be a factual book, no-brainer, the fact that there's PFOA in the waters of Mahoning County, Gallia County, Greene County, Montgomery County, and Allen County too, *Scaramouche*, cat-o'-nine-tails, Lucille Ball, the Myrtles, high five, home canning, iceberg, the fact that Stacy was right, the fact that it *is* kind of appalling how we were all going about our normal lives in the eighties and nineties, while all these chemical companies destroyed the world and we never even noticed it was *happening*, the fact that they were burying drums of toxic chemical waste right beside the Ohio River, for Pete's sake, or dumping them straight in the ocean, the fact that you usually assume people mean well, and Americans wouldn't hurt other Americans, the fact that you assume everyone's essentially kindly, and then you find out they hap-pily poisoned everybody for the sake of profits, a danger to life on earth, stranger danger, buckram bindings, the fact that I just don't get why anyone would *do* that, Pottersville, the fact that people in the food business could poison people too, every day, if they wanted to, but they hardly ever do, Grant township, the fact that some people in

Illinois declared rivers and streams have a right to exist, a right to *flourish*, but that's in Illinois, the fact that I doubt anybody's looking after the rights of water *here*, Ben's samples, the fact that we gotta try to be upbeat though about these things, for the kids' sake, goetta, the fact that officially Illinois, Michigan, Indiana, and Ohio make up the Midwest, just those four states, Michiana, the fact that "Michiana" is a combo of Michigan and Indiana, the fact that Ohio's shaped like a petal, the fact that it seems so *vast*, the fact that Cincinnati seems worlds away, like *Paris* or something, FLORENCE Y'ALL, so we hardly ever get any good chili or goetta, the fact that Flight 93 flew straight over here, or near us anyway, before it smashed near Johnstown, or New Baltimore, the fact that they found some of it near Indian Lake, fuselage, body parts, what a terrible terrible *terrible* thing, the fact that it broke us, as a nation, but you're not supposed to say so, the fact that why would you *do* a thing like that to other people, *I will do such things, – what they are, yet I know not; but they shall be the terror of the earth,* the fact that being "upbeat" is so different from being "beat-up," the fact that the two things don't go together at all, the fact that people probably get *beat up* for being upbeat, *or* downbeat, the fact that either sounds unfair, the fact that Mommy went through terrible troubles, the fact that she was in a wheelchair for years, getting sicker and sicker, the fact that we were always folding and unfolding that wheelchair, adjusting the foot rests, the fact that I used to shampoo Mommy's hair at the kitchen sink when the beauty parlor was shut, but I prefer to remember sitting with her at the dining room table, each with a book, Jane Austen, Sabatini, Hardy, Muriel Spark, Toni Morrison, and Scotch and soda, ship's cap'n, How To Dice Butternut Squash, 1 cup tomato paste, the fact that no dish in the *world* needs a whole cup of tomato paste, *I* don't think, shampooing Mommy's hair, the fact that prosecco rots your teeth, the fact that a Chinese woman once asked Mommy at a party, "Are you evil?", sampans at sunrise, round mountains, Ming Dynasty porcelain, Mao jackets, terracotta warriors, Great Wall, wontons, pot-stickers, and Mommy, shy, sick, and stuck in her wheelchair, was so surprised she was knocked completely *speechless*, little wooden elephant, Abby's toaster oven, brick wallpaper, Scotch and soda, the fact that then the Chinese woman asked her "If you're not evil, why do you smoke?", the fact that after that incident, Mommy jettisoned *all of China*, sampan boats at sunrise, round mountains, Ming Dynasty porcelain, Mao jackets, cheap toys and electrical goods, everything, though not pot-stickers, or crispy duck and pancakes and sweet and sour pork and fortune cookies, the fact that she never *ate* her fortune cookie though, just opened it to see her fortune, her fortune, the fact that Ben came home with a *joke* fortune cookie, and the message inside was "Help, I'm being held prisoner inside a fortune cookie factory!", the fact that I think Paul Violi could write good fortune cookie messages, *Bring fifty thousand in cash*, the fact that China's now one of the few places on earth where Mommy *could* smoke, if she were still alive, indoors and out, without being frowned on, unless that lady turned up again, sampans, pot-stickers, round mountains, Yueyaquan Crescent Lake, the fact that Mommy would probably have *moved* to China by now, just to be able to smoke, the fact that Mommy was a defiant smoker right to the end, the rights of water, Smoker Friendly, Phoebe's Marlboro packet Hallowe'en costume, the fact that I still don't know why Leo didn't take a cigar when those guys offered him one, the fact that there we were, sitting on a wall in the sun by the canal, and those middle-aged golf guys were all smoking cigars, but when they offered him one he wouldn't take it, which really surprised me, because later he said he would've liked one, and he regretted not accepting their offer, the fact that they were very good cigars, he said, and Leo loves a good cigar, the fact that I get sick if people smoke cigars too near me, so I was kind of relieved, though outdoors it's not so bad, the fact that indoors it can be *excruciating*, Ohio Blue Tip matches, Speed Limit 25, **25% OFF THIS WEEK ONLY**, 99 44/100 % pure, the fact that 12,000 people are shot to death every year, the fact that, oh, the butter's melting, the fact that besides the Chinese, Mommy hated physiotherapists, all except one, that nice lady from Ireland, Limerick, the fact that I wonder if Paul Violi ever wrote limericks, the fact that

James Joyce wrote limericks whenever he was mad about something, *When Titian was mixing rose madder*, the fact that I don't know why I thought of *that* right now, the fact that for some reason limericks tend to be dirty, the fact that I don't know why, the fact that I think Daddy liked the one about Titian, just because of that rare mention of rose madder, the fact that that intrigued him, the fact that it would make a good fortune cookie, "There is rose madder in your future," the fact that you don't tend to hear about rose madder every day, the fact that I think Daddy recited that limerick when I thought I was interested in art, I mean in being an *artist*, the fact that I'm still interested in *art*, well, I *think* I am, Nanya, Alice Neel, "Popeye loves ya, Olive," the fact that Leo says Popeye swings his arms like he's dancing the hornpipe, the fact that Mommy hated her physios because they were always accusing her of cheating on her exercises, the fact that why would you accuse a half paralyzed person of cheating on exercises, the fact that who would do that, Flight 93, the fact that there was only so much improvement she could make anyway, no matter *how* many exercises she dutifully did, so why *say* that, the fact that that neurosurgeon just couldn't resist operating on her, scalpel, the fact that he paralyzed her, the fact that surgeons love to slice people up, *There was a young doctor called Wayne, Whose patient complained of a pain*, the fact that she also hated anyone who accused her of cheating at *solitaire*, which a surprising amount of people did, the fact that it's a pretty silly suggestion since who're you cheating except *yourself*, *a young doctor called Payne*, which is kind of, you know, your *right*, MYOB, mob, solitaire, solitary confinement, the fact that some people seemed to think it was sort of funny to joke about her card-shuffling method, but Mommy sure didn't think so, the fact that that really steamed her up, the fact that I don't know why they couldn't keep their traps shut, though I shouldn't say that, live and let live, the fact that they were all very kind people who thought they were being nice in coming over to see a sick woman stuck in a wheelchair, the fact that that's another thing she hated, the duty call, the fact that she'd rather have been reading a *book*, in peace, with me, or her real friends,

the fact that her real friends were mostly in Evanston, grousing, grouting, the fact that my mom never cheated in her life, the fact that she
wasn't cheating, she just had her own method of shuffling cards in
between games, big deal, developed over many years of boredom, and
maybe also because her arms were weak, the fact that her right arm
had always been weak, the fact that her mom massaged that arm every
day for six months when Mommy was a baby, Honorable Mention,
cards, the fact that I wish I was sitting cozily with *Abby* right now,
playing Go-Go at her kitchen table, brass lamp, her little collection
of cast iron toys, Colonial style, the fact that so what if Mommy
invented her own way of shuffling, the fact that all she did was put
the cards in lots of little piles, like about eight of them, and then
methodically gather them up, the fact that it wasn't *cheating*, it was
just easier for her to handle, the fact that you'd have to be a *mathe-
matical genius* to actually get anything strategic out of shuffling that
way, the fact that you'd have to be a chess grandmaster or something,
the fact that she spent almost as much time on her shuffling as she did
on playing the actual games, and that was what led to all the suspicion,
but gee, there was really nothing to worry about, nothing *immoral*
going on, the fact that she just shuffled in her own way, in her own
good time, so what were they, dear dear, I really should be nicer about
them all, them and their mercy visits, messy visits, but still, the fact
that I really find it hard to believe some people felt it was worth their
while to tease Mommy about her shuffling habits, the fact that it's
best not to think about such things, the fact that I've gotta dump the
lifelong grudges, blessings, sheep, the fact that *Mommy* was better at
holding grudges than anybody, partly because she had a fine memory,
"Are you evil?", the fact that I try to bear grudges but in the end the
original reason for it drifts away and I'm left with just a sort of negative
feeling about someone, but no evidence, and I don't know whether
to carry on the grudge or not, *Cabin in the Cotton*, *The Little Foxes*, *A
Stolen Life*, prescription charge, Walgreens, Colt 45, B189, Abby's
house fire, Barry, the fact that he saved them *all*, the fact that most
domestic fires are caused by candles, but theirs was a smoldering

cigarette in the trash, the fact that in those days Abby still smoked, the fact that maybe she gave it up after the fire, the fact that I don't know what the capital of Sardinia is, the fact that what is with this constant monologue in my head, the fact that why am I telling myself all this stuff, since *I know it already*, the fact that I knew it all before I said it to myself, because I'M ME, Kraft Miracle Whip, Medi-Wise Pharmacy, the fact that it seems kind of unnecessary for everybody to be talking to themselves all day long, the fact that do Babar and Celeste talk to themselves all day, and snails, and sportscasters, and the Ku Klux Klan, the fact that Kurz-Kasch is a name that somehow sticks in your head, the fact that here I am again, reading *Babar* to Jake, the fact that Flora just swallowed her rattle by mistake, the fact that elephant moms are always rescuing their babies from scrapes, not just in *Babar*, in real life, the fact that elephant babies are always falling in the water at zoos or getting caught in something, and people film them being helped by their moms and aunts, the fact that elephants work really hard to keep their kids alive, my little green wooden elephant with the crude tusks and trunk, the fact that I wonder what it would be like having a trunk, proboscis monkey, tapir, elephant fish, narwhal, unicorn, the fact that manatees have a small proboscis, the fact that now Flora's turning pink, and she looks so good that way, it makes you kind of *want* her to swallow the rattle, though I don't usually like pink and gray together, the fact that what is *wrong* with me, delighting in a little baby elephant choking on her rattle, the fact that Jake likes that bit too, Pom, Alexander, Zephir, Arthur, the fact that he always had a good sense of humor, Jake, even as a baby, the fact that Jake was such a charmer, kicking his little legs and laughing all the time, the fact that we must all be born happy, then learn to be sadder, the fact that Leo announced the other day "Jake has *charisma*," the fact that we need to get *going* soon, "Go, Possums!", Go-Go, Boltaron, Zyker's, KKK, DPRK, the fact that I liked Abby's face, I *loved* her face, especially when she was concentrating hard, like on needlepoint or something, or knitting, with her mouth slightly open, the fact that I wish I could see her right now, the fact that sometimes the open-mouthed eaglets on dceaglecam remind me of her, and I love them for it, the fact that Abby never thought she was pretty, I don't think, but she *was*, the fact that maybe she wasn't pretty like *Mommy*, the fact that Mommy was beautiful, but Abby was still very attractive, and kinder than I ever even knew, I now realize, the fact that when Mommy stayed with her Abby would do *anything* to make her comfortable, anything except hang the toilet paper outwards, the fact that they were always arguing about that, whether it should hang down the back or come out the front, the fact that Abby thought it was more dainty if it came down the back, but Mommy found it hard to reach that way, the fact that they hardly argued about anything else, just toilet paper, FFTS, eaglets, the fact that we've got to get a move on here, the fact that Abby's routine ran like clockwork, *There was a young doctor called Shane*, Wayne, pain, the fact that now Arthur's let go of the *baby carriage*, just like me with Stacy in her stroller, her poor hurt hand, Mommy's weak arm, baby elephants stuck in trees, baby elephants drowning in mud, the fact that I wonder whatever happened to that crazee yellow dress I bought myself when I was eleven, with the winged sleeves, the fact that it's risky sending an eleven-year-old out to buy her own duds, the fact that I must've spent thirty bucks on that thing, the fact that Abby wasn't vain but I think she was proud of her nose, and it *was* a good straight nose, the fact that Mommy had a good nose too, and Phoebe got hers from maybe both of them, the fact that I got mine from *Grandma*, souvenir spoons, the fact that a giraffe is on its way, Abby concentrating, Flora choking, Penthouse Hotel Suites, the fact that I can barely bear to be seen, the fact that it's hard just to turn up at PTA meetings, much less do anything really social except talk to Cathy, JFK, My Little Pony, the fact that Rossini studied the cello in Bologna, the fact that he trained to become part, part, part of, Arvo Pärt, the fact that there are some names you remember indelibly but why, 12A, H-1B visas, the whole pie, fidget spinner, Zelda Fitzgerald, jackpot numbers, nurse shark, loveless monkey, "Smart Phone" Spotted In 80-Year-Old Painting, cutie marks, the fact that the first European settlers in Ohio had babies by the dozen, the fact that a family like ours would be nothing to *them*, the fact that Leo's ancestors had twenty kids *each*, the fact that it says so on the census, and if the first wife passed away they just got a new one and had a dozen more, ♫ *as high as an elephant's eye* ♫, the fact that Jane Austen had over thirty nieces and nephews, the fact that it takes real guts to give birth to a load of babies all by yourself in the wilderness, ♫ *Whatta they got that I ain't got? Courage!* ♫, the fact that Eskimo women give birth in igloos with polar bears roaming around outside, or they used to, oil lamps, iglerks, igloo interior, dried up old mukluks, smiling weatherworn faces in fur-lined hoods, raw fish, fishing hole, Coldy, that little ivory Inuit duck, the fact that now the Inuit probably all live in houses and depend on central heating and canned food and Starbucks, along with maternity wards, the fact that there are probably still polar bears outside though, a few anyway, the fact that for most of human history women just had babies, and the species survived, the fact that the whole hospital idea is pretty new, forceps delivery, cervix, mucus plug, backward womb, waters breaking, epidural, episiotomy stitches, caul, fetus, speculums, yolk sac, butterflies, the fact that some people want to go back to doing it all on their own, the fact that it's called "wild birthing," like wild swimming, where you swim somewhere you're not supposed to, the fact that it *would* be nice to get away from the doctors of course, and the student doctors, the fact that obstetricians always scared me, the fact that they *stare* at you so strangely, and they're always threatening you with horrible complications like placenta previa, placenta accreta, placental abruption, preeclampsia and then eclampsia, ectopic pregnancy and hypothyroidism, monochorionic twins, twin reversed arterial perfusion, TTTS, TOPS, DVT, PPCM and PGP, maternal sepsis, chorionic hematomas, feto-fetal transfusion syndrome, and whatnot, hyperemesis gravidarum, amniocentesis, the fact that you go limp at the knees when they come at you with the Latin stuff, bloodied paper underpants, meat tenderizer, and they *cost* so much too, the fact that each birth cost us *thousands*, thousands and thousands, HELLP, but I guess I still wouldn't have dared go it alone, netsuke, Bettina, allantoides, "compliant and non-compliant women," miscarriage rates, gynandromorphs, the fact that in some state or other the pro-lifers want to stop doctors helping to extract dead fetuses, even after a *miscarriage*, the fact that they say it should just sit there inside you, and get expelled naturally, exude, which can take weeks or *months*, the fact that giving birth is a kind of extruding, and also excruciating, exclude, protrude, prostrate, prostate, castrate, Tuesday, the fact that pro-lifers are so *angry* they scare me, blue babies, the fact that Flora turns pink, not blue, my pale pink and pale blue colored pencils, red, white and blue, "The Stars and Stripes Forever," the fact that I still have the baby-blue acrylic baby blanket Abby hand-knitted for Stace, the fact that she also made me a pale yellow one, the fact that acrylic yarn doesn't look all that great *but* they go in the washer, the fact that Abby was very practical about stuff like that, housework, the fact that she really was an expert knitter even though she didn't always have the best wool, the fact that she could knit *anything*, Go-Go, Abby's kitchen table, being pregnant with Stacy, the fact that I wonder what Abby really made of Frank, though she was always nice to him, the fact that I'm sure she *wanted* to like him, but he could be so distant and temperamental, the fact that he never seemed to get how great Abby was, the fact that I don't think many people could *afford* to have twenty babies anymore, which is probably just as well, the fact that maybe we could concentrate on taking care of all the orphans instead, and overpopulation, the fact that it's a little late to think of this now in *my* case of course, the fact that there *is* a thrill in making a person, the fact that there's no greater thrill maybe, the fact that nobody ever talks about it, but motherhood gives you a bit of a buzz, a boost, the fact that it gives you such a sense of *power*, though that part's all kind of temporary, the fact that it all starts to feel a bit different once you're singing to a feverish baby all night, and getting three other kids off to school the next morning, the fact that most of time I don't feel powerful at all, especially when Stacy puts a "Do Not Resuscitate" sticker on her door, DNR, to go with the "Please Go Away" sign, PGA, PTA, the Potomac, the fact that now there's the

PTO too, which I always thought meant Please Turn Over, apple turnover, popover, poptart, UGRR, orphans, *Anne of Green Gables*, the fact that in the past nobody had any *choice* about reproduction, the fact that if you were born, you bred, and you crumbled where you stood, the fact that some guy in Miamisburg shot his wife when she went into labor because he suddenly decided he didn't want kids, Why Are They Wearing Helmets?, the fact that some pro-lifers sneak into abortion clinics, have abortions, then sneak out and start *picketing* again, for criminy sakes, Labor Day, midwife, housewife, homemaker, stay-at-home mom, filiopietism, the fact that, my word, is that the time, the fact that the school bus will be here any *sec*, so where are Gillian's boots and the bird's nest, the fact that she needs her bird's nest today, Hopalong Cassidy, bird's nest pudding, Eve's pudding, Eve with a lid, *All About Eve*, *The Lady Eve*, Adam and Eve on a raft, the fact that I didn't have any *cravings* when I was pregnant, not a single one, and Leo was disappointed, the fact that he wanted to be sent out for crackers and pickles and ice cream in the middle of the night, dirt, enceinte, the fact that some pregnant women eat *dirt*, sore lip, Chapstick, the fact that when we were kids we used to buy those big sour pickles for a quarter from the scary guys in the dark little store, one great big sour pickle *each*, the fact that we thought that was a real treat on a hot day, better than candy, and it was fun going out to get them, the fact that it was important somehow, to get a pickle, the fact that I wish I had one right now, the fact that *now* I get the craving for a pickle, the fact that maybe I can get some Vlasic pickles at Zyker's next time, Vaseline, the fact that most pickles are much too sweet, but Vlasic's are pretty close to what a pickle should be, solitaire, Mommy shuffling, the fact that *okay*, here's the bird's nest, so tiny, and it's still got feathers in it, the fact that Stacy found it deep in the Christmas tree we got this year, way inside, the fact that baby eagles are born knowing how to do that projectile squirting, projectile vomiting, the big pickle barrel, the fact that I want a big pickle, the Big Apple, the Bible, the fact that Open Carry-type guys are always quoting from the Bible, and you get tired of hearing it all, the fact that can't they read something else once in a while, like *Babar* or something, or *Winesburg, Ohio*, maybe some Jane Austen, the fact that Jane Austen died two hundred years ago, and I'll be *fifty* some day, half a century, deck-stiffened arch bridge, cook, cock, pickle, the fact that there's the bus at last, the fact that I don't know why I always have to find everybody's hat and scarf for them, *run*, run, sheesh, doolally alley, doohickey, rinky-dink, the rights of nature, the fact that now they're gone we can get a little *peace* around here, cinnamon, untouchables, Dalit, Lebanon, Yemen, Illinois, ♫ *Polly Wolly Doodle all the day* ♫, sorghum, the fact that I've totally forgotten what I was doing, dear me, oh, the caramelization, the fact that it's time to do the chickens too, eighty billion chickens a year, the fact that Jakey's little jacket's so cute, the fact that I have to get Jake to his playgroup and make the tartes tatin, the fact that that was a sad end for Aunt Sophia, just trying to get the stove going in the morning and *whoosh*, the fact that nobody could save her, Asta the dog in *The Thin Man*, the fact that we think that's the same dog as in *Bringing Up Baby*, the one that runs off with the dinosaur bone, the intercostal clavicle, the fact that Aunt Sophia left us her commode, the fact that it's hexagonal, and made of nicely polished mahogany, and it's got a deep antique china bowl inside it but, still, it's a *commode*, the fact that we've got it up in the attic, the fact that we gave the guns and the bullet molds to Leo's colleague, that guy in Philly, whatshisname, Arthur something, the fact that it really surprised me he wanted them, and it surprised him we didn't, the fact that I could ever forget the word "hydrangea," the fact that I think his name was *Andy* actually, and he was so surprised we didn't want guns in the house, AK-47, Smith & Wesson, 12-gauge Winchester shotgun, gun display at Walmart, Walgreens, the fact that we don't spread that news around too much, the fact that half the folks around here would call us irresponsible parents for not owning an M-15 or M-16 or an AK-47 even, What Heater Do You Haul?, the Open Carry poster on the telephone pole in Coshocton, red wine, apron, aorta, Triumph Over Tragedy, bullet trajectory, gelatin experiments, gummy bears, the fact that everybody seems to have military-style weapons now, not just hunting rifles, the fact that they all want weapons designed to completely destroy you, not just maim you, the fact that these weapons are designed to kill people as fast as possible, in war, the fact that they explode inside and tear you apart, school shootings, Umpqua, oomph, the fact that ER surgeons are all complaining about the gun injuries they see now, because they're too hard to fix, the fact that it's the intercostal clavicle, and the dog buries it somewhere, the fact that it all gets a little less fun once they're in the country just searching for the bone all the time, and the leopard, "David, 's in the box?", the fact that Katharine Hepburn says "'s in the box?", Five Days of Unlimited Data, the fact that fourteen thousand people get shot in America every year, ninety-three a *day*, the fact that it must be thousands already *this year*, the fact that that really *is* an enormity, the fact that "Umpqua" is a good word, the fact that I just like saying it, "Umpqua," the fact that it sounds like something out of *Charlie and the Chocolate Factory*, Oompa Loompas, but it's ruined now, now that everybody associates it with a *massacre*, just like Newtown, Connecticut, is ruined, Newcomerstown, cup of coffee, Coshocton Coffee Connection, collection, protection, "Easy, big fella," the fact that four and a half million women a year are threatened with a gun in America, four and a half million, the fact that now they want to teach the teachers and kids how to handle weapons, to protect them, no way José, not my kids, the fact that it's bad enough that they have to have shooter *drills*, the fact that I'm not raising a bunch of Annie Oakleys that want to use every animal in the neighborhood as target practice, the fact that surely kids that know how to shoot are more likely to shoot, the fact that kids are always taking guns to school and shooting other kids these days, either accidentally or on purpose, well, not in Newcomerstown maybe, not yet anyway, deer hunting season, big bucks, darts, pool, snooker, *The Music Man*, the fact that in domestic violence cases, women are five times more likely to be killed if there's a gun on the premises, promises, the fact that fifty women a month are shot dead by their husbands and boyfriends, the fact that Annie Oakley was from Greenville, Umpqua, Umpqua, extrude, usufruct, adjudicator, abductor, Beth's mansion in Evanston, Curves Health Club, the fact that whenever one of the kids goes over to someone's house for the first time, I ask the parents what their gun situation is, the fact that I absolutely *hate* doing it but you have to, for what good it does, the fact that all you can do is ask if all the guns they own are kept secure, and they always say yes, and then you just have to trust that they're telling you the truth, the fact that I figure maybe it helps them remember to at least *check* once in a while, the fact that most people don't store their guns properly, the fact that they should all be locked up, the guns, I mean, not the *people*, or maybe both, the fact that the bullets should be kept someplace *else*, separate, the fact that, also, what other people think is "secure" might be different from what *we'd* like, Larry Gilmont's dark hallway in summertime, the fact that some folks might think keeping a loaded Kalashnikov on a hook over the front door is safe, but kids can climb, the fact that I've told my kids never to touch a gun if they find one, and they say they won't, but you never know if curiosity will get the better of them, the fact that a kid shouldn't have to pay with his life for being curious, the fact that things shouldn't be that dangerous, in your own home, the fact that it's not wild swimming or something, it's sitting around the *house*, the fact that it's hard to believe gun ownership and gun violence are on the *rise* after Sandy Hook, but they are, the fact that you'd think that whole tragedy might've put some people off but no, the whole country's awash in guns and Bibles, and seven new dead children every day, the fact that seventy-seven people have been shot dead in Columbus alone this year, and it's only February, candlelit vigils everywhere, candlelit dinners, the fact that everybody thinks Chicago's the worst city for gun crime but what about Killadelphia, where Leo has to *teach*, American "annuals" of crime, *Rebel Without A Cause*, the Adler Planetarium, Agness Adler, the Thorne Miniature Rooms at the Art Institute, the fact that the Auditorium Theater is just a wonder, with all its pretty lights and gold trim, the fact that somebody in North Carolina just shot nine people in his family dead, for no reason, except that he and his wife broke up three weeks ago,

"Picturesque" Family Massacred, the fact that he went over to discuss childcare and ended up shooting them all, the fact that he went to three different locations to kill people, including his own kids, the fact that, man, was he thorough, the fact that that's all we need, a thorough man with a gun, the fact that he spent eight hours on that massacre, "taking them out," and then he complained about the police not killing *him*, because he'd been planning on "suicide by police," the fact that they only shot him in the leg, the fact that eight people in seven hours, no, nine people in eight hours, the fact that that averages out at more than one death an hour, taking a life, giving birth, give and take, the fact that men sure hate paying child maintenance, the fact that Frank never paid a penny, Jake's playgroup, day care, orphans, the fact that Lenin and Stalin had the Romanovs killed out of pique, just like the North Carolina guy, the fact that they were just bored with the whole problem, picturesque, the fact that men are so *impatient* sometimes, Daddy, the fact that Trotsky wanted to wait on things, but they didn't listen to him, Trotsky, the fact that "Trotsky" is a much better name than Lenin or Stalin, the fact that those guys were such sourpusses, the fact that the soldiers sent to kill the Romanovs were armed with Colts, Mausers, Nagants and bayonets, which makes them sound like most American citizens *now* actually, the fact that the Romanov children wouldn't die at first and had to be stabbed and shot some more, the fact that how can people bring themselves to do these things, so much blood, Mommy, the fact that I'm broken, the fact that *Cathy* might have a gun, the fact that I never dared ask her, but she runs a store and most store owners have guns, the fact that even Ronny's armed, just to deliver garden compost and turf and chicken feed and seesaws and trampolines, for no reason, the fact that who does he think he's going to have to tackle in the course of a normal delivery day, I wonder, a few angry roosters maybe, highway robbers, Russians, socialists, bushrangers, bushwhackers, the fact that, considering Leo and I have no church and no guns, it's pretty surprising we're tolerated at all, the fact that *he* has a right to be here, because he was born here, but I'm an intruder, extruder, the fact that my hope is Ohioans like guns and *pie* about equally, so as long as I keep churning out the pies we'll be welcome, the fact that maybe my pies are even antidotes to gun violence, the fact that, on the other hand, come to think of it, they might be *fueling* gun crime, the fact that for all I know there may be perps getting *energized* by my pies, and comfort-eating them after they carry out their crimes, the fact that what if my cinnamon rolls have given some gunslinger the energy to, to shoot his wife or something, for no reason, the fact that that could be my new pie slogan, "The Family Annihilator's Reward," oh dear, for the love of Mike, the fact that I've got to think about something *else*, and fast, and not the Romanovs, MYOB, Joan Cusack, backpack, beeswax, bees, sheet cake, sugar highs, bullet wounds, turtle apples, Tastee Apple, the fact that I wonder how many criminals have committed crimes after eating a chocolate turtle apple, because, let's face it, it's not just *me* providing all the sugar highs around here, the fact that beeswax candles have a light that's closer to natural sunlight, the fact that they are the purest candles and they don't give off carcinogenic by-products, but we haven't got any beeswax candles, the fact that you can't have candles around kids, the fact that a friend of Leo's once sent him a pizza in the mail, all the way from John's, but he didn't use refrigerated transport or anything, so when the pizza arrived it was just a mess, the fact that he didn't mean it to be disgusting, the fact that he just knew Leo liked John's NY pizza so he threw one in a jiffy bag, stuck on a stamp and mailed it, U.S. Postal Service, the fact that I wish Tastee Apple would give me some of their *reject* apples, the fact that they only use very high-quality apples, hog maw, the fact that Sherwood Anderson makes this big thing about how delicious the wrinkly old apples are, the apples left to wither on the tree after all the perfect specimens have been picked, the fact that what's he talking about, the fact that I guess it's like eating those dried apple chips, the fact that they're okay, they're not *delicious*, Winesburg, Waynesburg, Millersburg, Strasburg, Fredericksburg, Frederick, the fact that it's all symbolic of something or other, I forget what, Sherwood Anderson's apples I mean, *The Master Builder*, the fact that we watched that with Stacy during her acting kick, the fact that that Wally Shawn is *good*, and he translated *The Master Builder* himself, and directed it and acted in it, the fact that most people make pies just to be nice, but I make them for money, Fort Knox, Las Vegas at night, main drag, dollar bills floating down from the sky, La Lutèce, Jake yanking at Zyker's gumball machine, foot-long subs, perps, perks, burps, gurgles, the fact that there are a lot of historical figures you can hate in the annuals of American history, Garbage Plate, and the guy *I* hate most is Quantrill, Trash Dish, but some people still treat him like a *pin-up*, the fact that I don't like his smirking face at all, Laurence, Kansas, the fact that he killed *two hundred* men, widowed a whole town in a day, abolitionists, the fact that how can people venerate that, Kraft Miracle Whip, flying saucers, Beth's mansion, the fact that I often get a little glimpse of Beth's mansion in my head and I never know why, but I like it, the fact that it was just a crummy old mansion, nothing special, and I was only there once, but it made a big impression on me, the fact that it was the mansioniest place I ever went, the fact that I remember the wide spaces and thick woodwork, and how everything about it was so big, the big circular driveway, the big hallway, big doorways, big furniture, and the great big winding staircase, the fact that Beth was kind of big too, and it all made *me* feel small, the fact that I barely knew Beth really, but I can still picture her, the fact that her place was nothing like Clermont Manor, the fact that that place is so beautiful it gives you a tingly feeling, the fact that it's old, and Beth's wasn't particularly, Gnadenhutten Massacre, the fact that Robert Livingston was nearly shipwrecked but survived, and then he ended up being a great help with the Revolution, so I guess he deserved that mansion, Margaretville, Woodstock, Saugerties, Tastee Apple, the fact that it was two floors originally, the fact that they added another floor later, with all the gables, the fact that Leo and I saw it one winter's day, the white house, white snow, black tree trunks, the fact that Florence Griswold's place in Old Lyme *isn't* a mansion, the fact that it was a boardinghouse, but it's a much nicer building than Beth's too, the fact that Beth's mansion was practically brand-new, I think, but at the time, I was pretty impressed, I guess, or I wouldn't still remember it, the fact that I'd been in a few rich kids' homes but hers was much more substantial, the fact that it seemed to be made out of huge blocks of red granite, the fact that could it be granite, the fact that I think I've based my idea of mansions on it ever since, that mansiony feeling, Munchkin, the fact that the only time I went there was for Beth's tenth or eleventh birthday party, and now and then I think back on it, for no reason, the fact that I think I think about a *lot* of things for no reason, the fact that I think about Peolia College every time I'm on the john and I don't know why, DNR, and I think about Jeremy Driscoll whenever I start a new jigsaw puzzle, the fact that he just comes to mind, for a moment, for no reason, pantry, eggs, the fact that I can't for the life of me figure that one out, the fact that what's Jeremy Driscoll to me, but for some reason his face crops up almost every time I start a jigsaw, the fact that it's not even that irritating, it's become kind of funny, the fact that he'd probably be flattered to *death* to think I ever think about him but it's not really thinking, it's just some kind of reflex, a mental tic or something, mattress ticking, curtain ticking, deer ticks, bedbug registry, the fact that some switch got wired wrong in my brain and it's connected Jeremy Driscoll with online jigsaws and there seems to be no way of changing it now, the fact that it seems to be a permanent malfunction, black holes, galaxies, or some unconscious association I can't do anything about, the fact that Jeremy Driscoll was kind of like that Ned Ryerson guy in *Groundhog Day*, the fact that I wonder where he is now, the fact that he just comes into my head sometimes for no reason, even if I try and think about something else, like about Beth's mansion maybe, the fact that I've tried to find that mansiony feeling elsewhere, like at the Barnes Collection, the fact that they've moved it into Philadelphia now, I think, so I don't think I'd like it anymore, the fact that I just liked going to Merion and looking around the neighborhood where it used to be, Toulouse-Lautrec, the fact that Robert Livingston was important to Pennsylvania in some way, the fact that people are always getting killed in Penn State fraternities, hazing, young men, the fact that I don't know why they do those things, the fact that Pennsylvania is purple on the electoral map, because it can't decide between Democrats and Republicans, snow, sneckdown, lockdown, Conesville Power Plant, the fact that calcium, magnesium, total dissolved solids, sulfate, iron, arsenic, cadmium, chromium, and selenium were found in the *water* over there in Conesville, and they shouldn't be, Mommy, the fact that ten out of every hundred thousand people die in Tuscarawas County from power plant emissions, and that just shouldn't be *happening*, the fact that I was probably a lot more fun before I started worrying about absolutely everything, but I just can't seem to *help* it, PAY TOILET 5¢, the fact that I dreamt Peolia changed all their restrooms around, the fact that they'd decided against having separate private booths, the fact that they'd decided that was an *outmoded concept*, the fact that I was furious about it but I spoke very calmly, and told them this decision would probably put people off applying to the college, the fact that in real life I'd never say anything about it of course, the fact that I'd be too shy, YOU ARE NOT PERMITTED TO SHARE OR CRAWL UNDER STALLS, Babar rescuing Alexander from drowning, the fact that I can finally box up the cinnamon rolls now, so we're in good shape here, made in the shade, homemade, pomade, parade, the fact that everything always seems to work out for Babar, and maybe it's true, maybe things *can* work out okay, sourpuss, sour pickles, my skirt with little mirrors in it, that store in New Haven where I bought it, the fact that where is my missing Guatemalan poncho-blouse, Melanie, Chuck, Jeremy Driscoll, avocados, the low-branched tree in the park where I found the damp, frayed porno mag when I was a kid, the fact that I don't feel free to wander around outside the way I did when I was a kid, the fact that we don't let the kids just wander either, the fact that I used to go wherever I wanted, and explore things, and discover stuff, squirrel, porno mag, broken glass in my foot, rose thorns, the fact that now I'm too busy, too self-conscious, the fact that Mommy and Daddy were pretty intrepid travelers really, lugging us all around Europe like that, a year here, year there, that summer in Ireland, jetsetters almost, "Eat now, pay later, Diner's Club!", though they seemed less like jetsetters than just about anybody, the fact that I remember Daddy driving us through long tunnels in the Alps, bed bugs, the fact that Mommy always joked that Daddy stayed in better hotels when he was traveling on his own, but maybe it was true, the fact that everybody used to be a lot more frugal, frugal, fungal, frugality, abstemiosity, extravagance, gun sprees, shopping sprees, taking a life, the fact that Daddy had a lot of skin ailments, styptic stick, the fact that the medicine cabinet was always full of little tubes of ointment, unguent, ruminant, pertinent, impertinent, salve, Porter's Liniment Salve, from Covington, Ohio, the fact that Daddy was no jetsetter really, the fact that he only ever traveled for work, not for fun, for no reason, the fact that we stayed in Rome for a year and then London for a year, that's all, PERSONS CAUGHT CRAWLING UNDER THE DOOR, the fact that we brought Pierre with us to Rome, the fact that we didn't take Pepito to London, because we didn't *get* him until we got back, and we couldn't have brought a dog to England because of the quarantine restrictions, the fact that Mommy took Pepito to a dog training class when he was a puppy, and all the other dogs sat in a big circle and Pepito just wanted to lie down, the fact that that there were wild turtles in our back yard in Rome, Tastee Apple turtle apple, the fact that a nice waiter taught me how to twirl my spaghetti, twirl, swirl, spiral, Billie twirling around in a circle to show off her dress to everybody in some restaurant in Chicago, Billie in a bathing suit at the beach, the fact that mostly I just ate pasta in brodo in Rome when we ate out, the fact that I was only four and pasta in brodo's easy to eat, easier than spaghetti, unless it's SpaghettiOs, the fact that I had pasta in brodo all over Italy, and now I make it for *my* kids, the fact that sometimes I add beans, so it's pasta e fagioli, or potato, pasta e patate, the fact that Phoebe always liked Campbell's chicken noodle soup, the fact that the Campbell clan were mean fighters in Scotland, always massacring people, the fact that I was only *three* when we got to Rome, Dr. DeBoer, SpaghettiOs, raisins, vacuuming, Tuesday, the fact that I bet he'd be surprised to know I still remember him, that waiter, the one who taught me how to eat spaghetti, I mean, not Dr. DeBoer, but maybe Dr. DeBoer could be surprised too, the fact that who forgets their heart surgeon though, even if you're a little kid, the fact that it's crazee what I do remember, the fact that to think I remember to this day how Billie looked in her bathing suit of all things, and how shocked I was by her, her, well, various womanly traits, the fact that I remember going to Waterlow Park with Mommy on Wednesday afternoons and having beans on toast in the café, the fact that that was when I must have been about six, six years old, younger than Gillian, the fact that I remember the rhododendron bushes across from our house on Hillway Avenue, in Highgate, but that's about it, the fact that that's all I got out of our whole year in London, and now I can't remember if we went to the café *first,* or after our walk through the park, the fact that I've forgotten just about everything that ever happened to me, the fact that it's all wasted on me, the fact that how can you ever know though, because it might all be in my unconscious somewhere, and maybe if I got myself hypnotized I could dredge up some more stuff, but otherwise it's all lost to me, gone, years and years of stuff, years of my life, gone, no trace, the fact that I should've had one of those police body cams on my head all my life so I could watch the footage now and see if it triggered anything, I mean stirred a memory or two, trigger-happy cops, stir, swirl, be kind, rewind, Billie in her bathing suit, the fact that the police themselves never seem to have their cameras on when they're supposed to, fly-over country, the fact that a woman got hand-cuffed and stuffed in the police car but she managed to get out of the handcuffs and drive off in the car, the fact that what was she *thinking,* the fact that people can get desperate in situations like that, the fact that people come to blows over a loaf of *bread* sometimes, if the stores are running low on stuff, *Betty Boughter bought some butter,* beans on toast, Channing School, the fact that I had a half day on Wednesdays, the fact that I remember *that,* and Phoebe didn't, because she was older, the fact that she still is older, the fact that she always will be older, *But, she said, the butter's bitter,* the fact that those Wednesday afternoons were one of those times when I got to be alone with

Mommy, the fact that the third child probably doesn't get half as much alone-time with Mom as the older kids had, though Jake has plenty of time alone with me when they're all at school, the fact that Mommy would come get me for our little weekly outing, our lunch out and a walk, dinner and a movie, date night, the fact that the Obamas were always having date nights in the White House, the fact that lots of people do that, the fact that I wish *we* could, but it's not practical, the fact that the kids aren't old enough to be left here by themselves yet, unless Stace is here, and we don't have money for babysitters, the fact that maybe Marcia would do it, the fact that Cathy says Marcia only dates guys with motorcycles now, the fact that she likes riding on the back, the fact that I hope she wears a helmet, the fact that Leo's got a student who only dates men from *South America*, basically because she wants to move there herself eventually, feijoada, the fact that she's got a Brazilian she's working on right now, but it isn't serious, and he's leaving for Canada soon, so it's back to the ol' drawing board, or the computer screen anyway, the fact that everybody does computer-dating now, the fact that we probably had the baked beans *first*, now I think about it, because kids are always hungry, and then we did the walk, the fact that it would be so much *work* to take all our kids to London for a year, the fact that I wouldn't know what to do with them, but Mommy seemed to know just how to handle it all, the fact that she found us schools and got us school uniforms, the fact that Sylvia Plath committed suicide in London, the fact that in China a woman in labor committed suicide because the contractions hurt too much and they wouldn't let her have a cesarean, because her family wouldn't give her permission, so she jumped out of the *window*, that poor woman, forty-one weeks, the fact that giving birth certainly isn't pleasant, the fact that suicide during labor is maybe more common than I thought, the fact that I don't know why I wanted to go through it *four times*, the fact that I guess instinct just takes over, hormones, perpetuation of the species, propagation, penetration, pronunciation, promulgate, sea urchins holding their eggs up between their spines, milt, the fact that at first we lived in an apartment in Knightsbridge for a couple weeks, which was nowhere near our schools, the fact that it was kind of grim there, so gray, gray walls, gray sky, the fact that I'd never seen so much gray in my life, milk, the fact that the walls were white really, I think, but for the first time I noticed how white walls look gray in dim light, and it got me down, the fact that it was in the living room there that Daddy tried to help me learn to read, crash course, because I was behind in my class, the fact that the book was really boring and too advanced for me, and while he got all annoyed and corrected me, I was noticing the gray shadows on the gray walls, the fact that everything about the place seemed dismal, and the milk tasted funny too, and the toast was burnt, the fact that we ate it with Rose's lime marmalade, which I didn't like much either, the fact that the Highgate house was nicer, because it had a back yard, and it was a lot closer to the schools, my pale pink and pale blue pencils, the fact that Ethan went to a *boys'* school and Phoebe and I went to Channing, the fact that I'd never *heard* of boys' schools and girls' schools before, the fact that we liked hiding in the dark rhododendron bushes in that little open park across from our house, black dirt, the fact that we went trick-or-treating at Hallowe'en, the fact that we got good costumes somewhere, but the English don't trick-or-treat right, the fact that rhododendrons kill everything beneath with them with the acidity of their fallen leaves, or something, so there were all these caves to explore underneath, all sheltered and hidden, like under the buckeyes at whatsthename of that park, the fact that when was that, the fact that it was like a few summers ago now, Edward, bare earth, the fact that Phoebe and I used to creep around under those rhododendrons for *hours*, popsicles, chickens, the fact that from the side a perfect buckeye tree should be like a dome, a thick, leafy semicircle, that classic tree shape, with the branches all coming down to about two feet off the ground, just enough space underneath for kids to play, summertime, but buckeyes are good all seasons of the year, fir tree, twofer, threefer, the fact that buckeye blossoms stick up so earnestly, blossom, buxom, bashful, the fact that I like it when buckeyes are dark underneath like rhododendrons, the fact that they can cast a dense, dark shadow, the fact that a good buckeye takes all the space it needs, the fact that it's nice to see a happy, healthy tree, but you can't always find one anymore, the fact that *our* buckeye out back is like a village unto itself, home to kids and birds and squirrels, Channing School, the Pet Club, Tiny Tim, the fact that the whole place smelled of English school soap, seeping from the bathrooms, I guess, and at break time, recess, we got given milk and tea cakes, or scones, and raisin buns, burnt toast, rusks, recess, Quiet Time, the fact that they didn't call it recess, they called it "elevenses," the fact that I wrote something about a hamster there, and my teacher wasn't sure how to spell "hamster," the fact that she thought there might be a "p" in it, like in "Hampstead," so she went off to consult the dictionary and other teachers, and Mommy never forgot that, the fact that she was very impressed, not that my teacher couldn't spell, but that she made the effort to check the word in the dictionary, the fact that *none* of the teachers were too sure how to spell "hamster," or there was some disagreement about it anyway, the nun who shook Mommy, "Ducky! Ducky!", Abby, the fact that I was always a little leery of Ethan's hamsters because some of them bit, but they looked cute when he made them ride in his train set, the fact that Ethan got bitten a few times, the fact that that boy Ben knows has chinchillas or degus or sugar gliders, something like that, something exotic, white birds of paradise seedpods, Gillian's honey bears, the fact that no, it's somebody *else* who has the degus, the fact that half Ben's friends seem to have flying squirrels, and in the *house* too, the fact that how can they fly indoors, the fact that maybe they leap more than fly, the fact that sugar gliders are marsupials, the fact that Ben wants a *doop*, but they're hard to take care of, the fact that if a doop catches a cold it can be fatal, droop, dew drop, the fact that fraternities are always hanging the new recruits upside down out in the cold and then they die of pneumonia, dropsy, doozy, the fact that Leo's third grade teacher was convinced octopuses have *six legs* and from then on Leo never trusted any of his teachers, though she was a nice teacher otherwise, he says, "Never skip a grade," a pregnant woman jumping out the window, the fact that at Channing School we had to wear big navy-blue flannel underpants *over* our real underpants, the fact that that was part of the school uniform, and neckties, diagonally striped, which we had to learn how to tie, and big brown shoes and a thick woolen tunic dress that was a sort of purplish *brown* color that I was never too sure about, the fact that I'd never worn anything brown before, the fact that that whole year for me was dominated by gray and that purple-brown, and also the black dirt and ducks and leaves at Waterlow Park, water low, tides, water table, countertop, wastebasket, house swap, flipping homes, the fact that it was always cloudy out, in London and outside too, the fact that it rained every time we had a car trip anywhere, the fact that somebody's invented kids' clothes that stretch out as the kid gets bigger, because they're *pleated*, all over, so they just gradually expand on the kid, I guess until the fabric's lying flat against the body, the fact that it might take a lifetime, the fact that I wonder if it can accommodate middle-age spread, the fact that Daddy taught me how to read, but *irritably*, the fact that *he* was irritable, not me, though reading did irritate me for a while, but I guess I got over it, the fact that I guess it could save people money, buying pleated clothes for kids, the fact that maybe this is the fabric of the future, the fact that it would be good for thin people who're getting fatter, or vice versa, the fact that I never saw any pleated clothing in a Sci-Fi movie, the fact that I should ask Ethan, the fact that he's up on all that stuff, the fact that Ethan had a whole different uniform from us, at the boys' school, the fact that he had to learn Latin, maybe Greek, the fact that his uniform was dark blue with shorts, and a blazer and tie and matching cap, the fact that I used to have that family photo from our year in London, the fact that I wonder where that is now, the fact that we looked hilarious in our school uniforms, while Mommy and Daddy sat in armchairs, with us standing between them, looking kind of silly with our ties on and all, the fact that I showed it to Leo once, Leo laughing, Bermuda shorts, Bermuda onion, and it was pretty funny, but now where's it gone, the fact that they put *Teflon* in school uniforms these days, I guess just to make sure everybody gets cancer as soon as possible, the fact that I wrote my first poem at Channing, *They say the hen can lay, I don't know but they know*, the fact that you have to emphasize the "they" at the end for it to sound right, *but* they *know*, the fact that sometimes Leo makes me recite it, but the kids aren't too interested in Mom's old poem, the fact that they only care about *their* poems, the fact that I don't know where that thing came from, the fact that I'd never seen a chicken in my life, except in books, *They say the hen can lay*, the fact that there's a lot about yourself you can't share with your kids because they just don't care all that much, the fact that it's sad but true, like Meryl Streep in *The Bridges of Madison County*, the fact that why do I always want to call it *The Madges of Bridge County* or something, mad, bad and dangerous to know, death and taxes, the fact that Jane and Rock decide to be together in *All That Heaven Allows*, no matter what her kids think, or anybody else, but then the kids make such a fuss, the fact that children can be selfish, especially adult children, the fact that some kids never let up, not about their *mothers* anyway, Empty Nest Syndrome, boomerang kids, the fact that more grown-up sons now live at home than daughters, Rumor Wins Big, the fact that there's a class issue too, because Jane's got the country club to consider, and Rock Hudson's only a gardener, the fact that she wavers for a while, wavers, weavers, rovers, the fact that Jane Wyman was married to Ronald Reagan for a while, the fact that in the end he has to fall off a cliff to get her attention, not Reagan, Rock, ♪ *schmaltzy film music* ♪, 5¢, 10¢, "Real schmaltz, I think they called it," chicken stock, Mary Wickes, the fact that why do people have to cheapen everything, £1.20, the fact that we still have some 50p coins from London somewhere, the fact that I had to master English money at Channing, the fact that the 50p coin is pentagonal, Pentagon, 9/11, Pennsylvania, Flight 93, the fact that Stacy wasn't even born yet when 9/11 happened, the fact that she's grown up in a post-9/11 world, the fact that my whole class played a sort of fun shopping game for math, or "maths" as they called it, common ground, ground cinnamon, hibiscus, the fact that we all went grocery-shopping with plastic fruits and vegetables, and some people got to run the store, the fact that you had to be good at math to run the store, better than I was, but I was okay at math in those days, the fact that I think I forgot it all when we got back to America, the fact that Ben's got real math trouble, which is not good if he wants to be a *scientist*, the fact that maybe we need to get him a math tutor, but how much will that cost, Tastee Apple, Inc, calcium, space debris, the fact that maybe it was a *heptagon* actually, quadruped, quart, pintsize, "little half pint of cider half drank up," the fact that Phoebe and Ethan got car sick all over Europe, but I didn't, so I always had to sit in the middle and they both got the window seats, the fact that there probably wasn't much to see in England anyway, just gray rain and gray clouds and the wipers going back and forth, the fact that I can still remember looking at the back of Mommy and Daddy's heads from the back seat, the fact that maybe Sylvia Plath wouldn't have killed herself if the weather was better, the fact that all that rain is kind of a shock to an American, the fact that the Brits don't see the sun for *months*, Clermont Manor, the fact that we ate semi-raw lamb at some restaurant in France once and afterwards Ethan threw up, green fields, sheep, stream, the fact that Daddy stopped the car just in time, and after that Ethan always had to be near the door so he could jump out and throw up, though I can't remember him ever doing it again, our flat tire on the way to the James Bond movie in Chicago, the fact that Phoebe sometimes felt car sick but I can't remember her actually throwing up, the fact that I hate feeling car sick, the fact that I feel car sick if I sit in the back seat now, or if I try to *read* anything in a car, especially if somebody's a bad driver, the fact that it can happen even with Leo driving, the fact that I have to admit his driving *is* sort of jerky, and he takes corners too fast, so you're thrown this way and that, but I would never tell him, the fact that looking at Google Street View makes me feel sick too, so maybe it's me, Mulberry Street Cam, morning sickness, the fact that I never used to get car sick but now I do, the fact that luckily the kids don't seem to, the fact that we had some nice picnics in Europe, the fact that Phoebe and I were in charge of looking for a nice picnic spot, with sheep and cows and donkeys, buttercups, tall green grass, sunny field, preferably by a stream, the fact that once in Italy or maybe Switzerland, Mommy, Phoebe and I had all to go to the bathroom in a damp, dark cave, the fact that I don't know why I remember that and the rhododendrons and being with Mommy on Wednesdays, but nothing much else, Waterlow Park, blackcurrant pastilles, Ribena, lime Jell-O, Rose's lime marmalade, bitter lemon, the London Underground, the fact that we went to Ireland a few times too, the fact that we stayed in some big hotel in Dublin where they had live trout in a tank near the dining room, the fact that Phoebe, Ethan and I had a room on our own, and I insisted on sleeping in a little *baby cot* that had been left in there by accident, and during the night it broke and I ended up on the floor and had to share Phoebe's bed for the rest of the night, Daily Carry, the fact that it would be really weird to share a bed with Phoebe *now*, the fact that I can't get to sleep when Leo's not here, the fact that the Brontë sisters all had to sleep in the same bed I think, or the same room anyway, all their lives, sharing diseases, monkey playing a fiddle, Council Bluffs, the fact that Lewis and Clark met the Otoe tribe on the bluff, Bluffs, bluffing, and later the Chippewa and the Ottawa were forced to live there too, after they'd been kicked out of Chicago, after the Chippewa and the Ottawa were kicked out, I mean, *not* Lewis and Clark, which is maybe the wrong way around, the fact that the Potawatomi were sent there too, until they got moved on again about ten years later, De Smet, the fact that all that happened less than two hundred years ago, which is only a little more than four times my lifetime, Evanston, Winnetka, the fact that Winnetka means Beautiful Place in Potawatomi, Daily Carry, *as we forgive those who trespass against us*, the fact that there are all these photos of Daily Carry items on the internet, things like watches, wallets, pens, multi-tools, keys, coin purses and guns, the fact that maybe an *Open* Carry guy would have a lot in common with a *Daily* Carry guy, the fact that the only difference is the Daily Carry guys want you to see *everything* they've got, and an Open Carry guy just wants you to see his gun, Daily Carry photo of two huge knives, a butcher's knife and a serrated bread knife, the fact that maybe the guy's a chef or something but still, that's kinda scary, the fact that all I've got in my Daily Carry, otherwise known as my purse, are my keys, my wallet, some Kleenex, barrettes, tampons, lipstick, my little blue mirror, aspirin, some folding scissors, a tiny sewing kit, gum drops, old Bazooka bubble gum wrappers, some Ticonderoga Beginners pencils, crumbs, raisins, lost buttons, my sunglasses, and a beat-up single-portion packet of Kool-Aid I picked up for free somewhere, the fact that Hillary Clinton claims she's always got *hot sauce* in her purse, the fact that Leo showed me this Daily Carry site and I'm hooked on it now, the fact that he's not hooked, the fact that he was only looking at it for the pictures of pens and notebooks, the fact that Leo's always been sophisticated, the fact that when he was a kid he carried a red, modernistic candlestick around with him, just because he thought it was cool, the fact that he was really proud when some friend of his dad's called it "jazzy," the fact that I don't know if he slept with the candlestick or not, the fact that I'd like to see that candlestick, the fact that the Daily Carry guy with all the knives also carries an *inhaler*, an epinephrine injector, and a microfiber cloth, a pocket saw, duct tape, a forever-spin top, a pill fob, a flashlight, cough drops, Altoids, an iPhone, a Moleskine notebook and pen, $1800 in a bill clip, $250 in Confederate currency, *what*, business cards, a pocket reference manual for plumbing and other handyman jobs, a WikiReader, a *metronome*, an anti-shark knife, and a glider pilot flight log, the fact that I wish it was a *sugar glider* flight log, the fact that what does he expect to happen anyway, that he'll crash his glider plane into shark-infested waters, or a beehive, and have to duct-tape some sort of dwelling together for himself, complete with working toilet and homemade piano, *while* having an allergic reaction, the fact that I don't know what he needs the Confederate money for either, unless he's planning to join the KKK or something any minute, the fact that it's not valid currency, or I sure hope not, the fact that it's weird how these Daily Carry types show you all the money they're carrying around, like Jason Bourne with his red bag, the fact that this other guy's more restrained, with a switch blade,

maps, passport, pistol, lip balm, buttons, and an old buckeye, and
that's it, the fact that there was one honest sort of guy who included
an old *Kleenex* in the picture, but some get so fancy, like this other
guy who's got an electronic fitness strap, emergency strobe light, mini
tripod, headphones, a cable manager thing, water purification tablets,
hand warmers, compass, walkie-talkie, mini-umbrella, sunglasses,
lighter, cigar, and a grenade, the fact that he says a branded lanyard
is highly recommended for "retrieval" purposes, during pocket carry,
the fact that I don't know what he's talking about, the fact that does
he mean it's easier to find something in your pocket if it's on a lanyard,
or what, the fact that why can't he just say so, the fact that these Daily
Carry pictures are like that memory-game at birthday parties, when
moms bring in a tray covered with little items, and show it to you for
one second and then disappear and you're supposed to write down all
the little items on your pad of paper, the fact that I always lost, the
fact that, really, I kind of dreaded that game, the fact that the mom
would come in with the tray and I was always hoping she was bringing
cupcakes or jelly beans or something, not a bunch of antiques and weird
stuff from the kitchen drawer, the fact that I can't remember my *whole
life*, so why would I remember a tray of coins, scissors, key chains,
Scotch tape, pine cones, gum balls, paperweights, and a pocket watch,
Peolia College, the fact that we all wanted to win, of course, to get
the *prize*, the fact that a prize is a prize, Tang, tanka, Sanka, ginger
ale, highlighter pen, grenade, titanium, the fact that I never knew how
to spell "scissors" so I was always dreading scissors being on the tray,
the fact that I should've just pretended I'd *forgotten* them, but I always
wanted the darn prize so bad, the fact that I'm sure I never won it,
but luckily I can't *remember* if I did or not, the fact that who's that
artist who's always arranging all kinds of objects in a frame, kind of
like one of those party trays, La Wilson, the fact that she did one of
just felt piano hammers, the fact that even I could've remembered a
whole party tray of piano hammers if I had to, the fact that there's
something nice about piano hammers, the fact that La Wilson used
to bike around Akron with her pet crow, the fact that she was called

La because her brother couldn't pronounce her real name, whatever it was, when she was a baby, the fact that I *wish* I had a better memory, the fact that having a good memory's better than knowing lots of foreign languages even, the fact that a good memory would also be a *help* in learning languages, the fact that people make such a to-do about rich people and people who know lots of languages, like they're geniuses or something, but being rich doesn't prove you're great, and *anybody* can learn a language, the fact that most everybody learns at least one, Mommy in Paris, the fact that she couldn't understand her own wedding vows because they were in French, Julia Child, Tiny Twin Pygmy Marmosets, time alone with Mommy, isolationists, the fact that I was alone with Mommy that time in the hospital when she seemed to be fading out, a few months before she actually passed away, the fact that I was so shocked to see how pale she looked, that I touched her hand, and I felt this electricity running down my arm and into her hand, and she came back to *life*, the fact that she really seemed to come back from the dead, and she was well enough to go home for a while after that, the fact that I wasn't there to do it the next time though, the next time, the fact that Mommy's hands were so beautiful, the fact that everybody thinks their mommy's beautiful, the fact that do my kids think I'm beautiful, the fact that maybe they do sometimes, beans on toast, black muddy paths, ducks, red double-decker buses, my cow painting, the fact that my cow painting got a prize at Channing, and Mommy and Daddy had it framed and hung it on their bedroom wall in Evanston for *years*, in New Haven too, the fact that maybe that's what made me think about doing art, the fact that I wonder where my cow picture is now, the fact that it was of two cows, maybe three, in a green field, with blue sky and a yellow sun, the fact that that was a pretty optimistic version of English weather, my pale pink and pale blue colored pencils, the fact that *now* where the heck is my picture, the fact that I have no idea, probably crushed under the old wagon wheel in the attic, or under the camp beds, black dirt, white clouds, gray shadows on chilly white walls, rhododendrons, learning to read with Daddy, the fact that Phoebe brought Tiny Tim to London, the fact that he *went* in a little cage but we got him a turquoise guinea pig carrier at Harrods while we were there, and that's what he traveled in from then on, the fact that it was wooden and shaped like a nice round-roofed barn, round-hoofed, round-heeled woman, hex signs, Pennsylvania Dutch, Prescott, hooves, rooves, the fact that is it "rooves" or "roofs," "boof bourguignon," the fact that I never know, dived, dove, Mary Ingalls's humpback trunk for blind college, the fact that she had to go to the Iowa Braille and Sight Saving School, the fact that Tiny Tim was a very well-traveled guinea pig, the fact that Edward didn't get to come, but Edward didn't *exist* yet, the fact that I think I got him later, the fact that how many people bring their guinea pig with them to London, and what does a guinea pig make of traveling to London and returning home in a nice blue guinea pig traveling case, the fact that he'd probably rather have been going to *South* America, lettuce scraps, guinea pig pellets, guinea pig poo, guinea pig feet, paws, paw-paw seeds, memorizing times tables, the fact that I still don't get why multiplication works, PERSONS CAUGHT CRAWLING, tomato-shaped ketchup bottles, bear-shaped honey bottles, torso-shaped perfume bottles, the fact that some woman spent thirty million at Harrods in London recently, dollars not pounds, the fact that it only took her two years to do it too, the fact that it was mostly on perfume and jewelry, and it was her money, the fact that I think she owes taxes or something and that's what got her into the news, the fact that Phoebe and I got lost at the airport on the way to England and Mommy got so *mad*, the fact that we just went to the bathroom and then we couldn't find our way back to the right check-in line, the fact that it was just impossible, the fact that you learn early on that when parents get worried they get angry, the fact that I don't think *I* do that, or do I, the fact that *we* were worried too, me and Phoebe, but we didn't get angry about it, the fact that we were just scared we'd miss the plane, the fact that I think we were less scared of missing the plane though than making Mommy mad, "(picnic, lightning)," the fact that Stacy got lost in Macy's once when she was two, the fact that why were we in Atlanta, the fact that it was only for a few minutes but, boy, was I a mess, the fact that I wasn't angry, just terrified, the fact that you can't get angry with a two-year-old, or you *try* not to anyway, the fact that *she* wasn't scared at all, she was just running around imitating the bell, "Ting-ting-ting," the fact that that's how I know it was Macy's, the fact that Tiny Tim instantly became a member of the Channing School Pet Club, and lived at school with all the other pets for most of the school year, the fact that I hope he liked it, the fact that maybe it was more interesting for him, I mean if you *have* to be a caged rodent, maybe it's better to be a caged rodent among other caged rodents, not just all on your own all day, the fact that all the girls would come and fuss over the animals whenever they could, especially during lunch break, the fact that Phoebe's always been a great networker, the fact that it would've taken me a whole year just to even find out there *was* a club, but she was right on it, the fact that from then on Tiny Tim only came home on weekends, and one weekend we brought somebody's rabbit home as well, the fact that we were so excited about getting to take care of that rabbit, because we'd never had a rabbit, but the rabbit liked to run in crazy circles most of the time, spraying white stuff at our legs, which we didn't much go for, Tiny Tim in his turquoise travelling case, guinea pig carrier, the fact that I hated it when Mommy got mad, airport, the fact that I get angry a lot but I try to hide it, the fact that sometimes I dream Mommy's angry at me about something and it still really hurts, even now, with a big family of my *own* to worry about, Davina Beebee's "hurts," the fact that Davina Beebee is always talking about her hurts, the fact that she talks about them so much, she makes herself sound like one big ball of pain, but these hurts of hers always turn out to be pretty minor, like some old friend didn't call her up, or Davina has to junk her favorite souvenir dream catcher because it's falling apart and not catching the dreams properly anymore, the fact that it hurts *me* to listen to Davina Beebee's hurts, "Hoits you?", the fact that we stayed in a country hotel in Connemara someplace right by the water, and they had donkeys to ride and a litter of puppies in the barn, the fact that the whole place smelled of wet, cut grass, sort of like tarragon, the fact that I always thought tarragon must be how *donkeys* smell but now I think it was just the grass, Dingle Bay, County Cork, County Kerry, Daily Carry, Mosse pottery, the fact that Pepito couldn't come with us to Ireland, just for a summer, so one of Daddy's students took him to a commune in Maine, the fact that it can't have been a very nice commune though, because when we got him home he used to cower by the back door as if he expected to be *hit* when he came in or went out, the fact that he got in trouble at the commune once, for eating some other dog's food, the fact that how's a dog supposed to know whose food is whose, when he wasn't used to living with other dogs, the fact that that's just crazee, the fact that what did Pepito know about commune life, the fact that the commune people were even thinking about *giving him away* before we got back, without even telling us, all because of the food incident, Family Services, church services, the fact that he must have been so lonely there without us, so lost, and then they treated him like that, poor Pepito, cowering on the stairs by the backdoor, the fact that it's just horrible to think what they must have done to him to make him act that way, Lost and Found Department, the fact that fanouropita cake helps you find things, the fact that it's different from spanakopita, the fact that he recovered though, and forgot all about those crazee commune people, but *we* never forgave them, and I never will, to my dying day, dog days, the fact that at least he had a good time running around loose all summer in that pack of dogs, commune, commie, the Communards, the fact that Phoebe was accused of being a commie at Junior High, just because she didn't like *Reagan*, the fact that that summer was the only chance of a love life he ever got, Pepito, not Reagan, pack of cards, packin' heat, Blue Tip, the fact that Phoebe always said Pepito lost his virginity that summer, the fact that I don't know how she knew that, unless he left behind a litter of half-poodle puppies, the fact that maybe she made it all up but I hope she's right, because at home he was always on a leash or stuck in our yard, with zero chance of romance, the fact that the fur on his back was all *reddish* when he came home from the commune, bleached by the sun, because he'd spent all his time outdoors, while we spent the summer trying to catch the donkeys so we could ride them, and rowing around in a rowboat on the little lake, the fact that *Pierre* used to roam free all over Evanston having love affairs, but Pepito was so bad about cars he had to stay in the back yard or be walked on a leash, the fact that he chased a car once when he was young and hurt one of his back legs, so that was that, the fact that he was okay running around loose in Maine though, with a pack of dogs, the fact that most people neuter their pets these days, the fact that that always seems kind of mean, the fact that stopping a fellow animal from reproducing is quite a step, the fact that you never know how happy pets really are, Almanzo, Ashtabula, born happy, ♫ *Born Free* ♫, the fact that Cathy's always taking in sick stray cats, the fact that she says they come to her saying "Take me to the doctor," the Candyland game, the fact that I don't know why I liked that game so much, the fact that it's not much of a board game, and it's not like real candy's involved or anything, our Christmas-tree lights in Evanston, the fact that I just can't *take* the situation with Stacy anymore, the fact that Oprah would say build a wall, a symbolic, see-through, self-protective wall, "a great big beautiful wall," but walls don't work, except the Great Wall of China maybe, the fact that that worked, for a few thousand years anyway, a few *hundred* I mean, ceramic army, sampans, "evil" woman, cherry blossoms, fireworks, Paul Violi, Mao Tse-tung, Ming Dynasty, the fact that Trump's wall will impact on *wildlife* on both sides, but I don't think he cares about things impacting on animals, the fact that there's a "disconnect," impactful, impacted wisdom tooth, a Victim Impact Statement, VIS, the wild turtles in our back yard in Rome, the fact that we used to lower a toy plastic turtle out of our third-floor window, well, I *hope* it was a fake turtle, UFOs, Rome, ambergris, Inuits, Zello walkie-talkie app, Walkie-Talkie Robot Man, gas up your car, let's do lunch, the fact that last night I dreamt Stacy was about five, the fact that she's always about five in my dreams, the fact that I was driving with her on my *lap*, and teaching her the alphabet at the same time, "S is for snow," and I knew I should pull over and get her into her car-seat but it was snowing out and there was a lot of traffic and it was so hard to find anywhere to stop, the fact that then we were in some antique store and Stacy was interested in these little china mice and it was getting late and I didn't like the mice much myself, but she did, the fact that then I dreamt I was on board a houseboat, and I was supposed to get some little kid home to his parents but I was delayed by buying an artisan sourdough, the fact that in *another* dream, one of Leo's students was having canoe problems on the river and I had to go help him and, because of that, I missed out on a Buddhist wedding where five questions were going to be asked and now I'll never know what the questions were, the fact that it's time to get moving, where's Jake gone, the fact that you can put *certain* herbs in when you're making chicken stock but not parsley, never parsley, because parsley gets bitter if it cooks too long, the fact that something else gets bitter too, spinach, lettuce, cloves, too many cloves, our Christmas pomanders, pomade, pomegranates, the fact that nothing compares to the pain of losing Mommy when I was thirteen, nothing, though I didn't exactly *lose* her, the fact that she lingered on for years, the fact that I watched my mom turn to mush in my arms, *mush*, the fact that the whole world's based on *mush*, like that soggy old lemon drizzle cake, dust to dust, mush to mush, much of a mushness, charm school, and that is why I don't like *remembering* things, the numbness of muted beings, Rare Tiger Captured On Film, edible bandages for bears with burnt paws, the fact that all life forms emerged from mush and will probably turn back into mush pretty soon, especially if everybody carries on voting Republican, Walmart, hurricanes, Abby's tidy basement, but chaos rules the universe, supernova, suppertime, Happy Hour, the fact that sometimes Abby's neighbor would come over, Marie, and we'd all play one Go-Go game after another, the fact that they were both totally addicted to Go-Go, the fact that it's the easiest card game in the world but sort of fun, and you can talk while you play, or they sure could, the fact that I'd always dreaded her getting some terrible health issue because of her smoking, the fact that I was scared she'd get lung cancer or have a heart attack or something, the fact that when I first heard she was sick, I ran around the house crying, collecting all the cigarettes, and burnt them in the fireplace, the fact that I was given a note in school, telling me my mom was in the hospital and I had to go home, the fact that that's what I did when I got home, burn her cigarettes, the fact that Pepito lay at the foot of her bed when she came back, for weeks and weeks, just lay there, the fact that while she was in the hospital she couldn't smoke but as soon as she got out she started again, the fact that smoking was one of her few comforts besides solitaire, the fact that dogs know when you're really sick, sampans, fortune cookies, pot stickers, wonton soup, Yueyaquan, "evil woman," rude lady, the fact that it was months before she could walk, and then only with a lot of help, and a walker, the fact that *I* should have lain by her bed, but you gotta go to school, the fact that Mommy and Daddy wouldn't have liked it if I hadn't gone to school, the fact that I didn't do very well at school, but I wasn't doing too well at home either, the fact that dogs have such sympathy, loyalty, the fact that Anne Elliot misses her mom, the fact that her mom passed away when she was fourteen, the fact that *everybody* needs a mom, the fact that I have Mommy's first copy of *Persuasion*, with her name in it, in her handwriting, the fact that that woman, Kelsey something, or was it something Kelsey, the fact that she reminds me of Mommy, the fact that I don't know why, maybe because she saved everybody, the fact that she stood up against Thalidomide, Kelsey, not Mommy, the fact that the drug company wanted FDA approval for the American market, even though they already *knew* Thalidomide could cause deformities in babies, and Kelsey was the person that stopped it, the fact that she's like some kind of national hero, heroine, Mommy in her sunglasses, the fact that she stood up to the manufacturers all alone, the fact that they already knew about the side effects but they pushed on, poisoning people for profit, profiting from poison, Rachel Carson, *Silent Spring*, a rocky shore in Maine, the fact that how people live with themselves, the fact that I can hardly live with myself and I never tried to *deform* anybody or pollute a whole ecosystem just to make a buck, the Me Generation, me, the fact that ME stands for

Maine, the fact that Maine is where Rachel Carson hung out, among other things, the fact that Pepito's commune was also in Maine, the fact that even after Thalidomide was exposed and banned, doctors were still giving pregnant women all kinds of other drugs without even thinking about it, and they probably still do, the fact that Mommy always blamed my heart defect on the mumps vaccine she was given while she was pregnant with me, third grade, tardigrades, heart operation, Hallowe'en, the fact that I often feel a little low after the kids go to school, separation anxiety, the fact that I'm plagued by vague regrets about all the nice things I could have done for them but forgot to do, or cunningly ducked out of doing, the fact that I'm an expert at dodging their demands, the fact that you have to be, or you'd never get a single thing done, my talking doll, Jumbotron, Dido, *A Candle in Her Room*, the fact that I probably seem kind of distant to them, distracted, bossy, grumpy, poor kids, the fact that I hate it when they leave the house though, the fact that I'm always scared they go off thinking I'm not very *nice*, oh dear, because I *am* distant, I think, and scatterbrained and all, and busy sometimes, scattered, multitasking, Superwoman, pride goes before a, but at least I'm not a *spoiling* mom like Jill Baynes, who can't do discipline at all and just pampers her kids, who don't even like her much, I don't think, and at least I'm not a *pushy* mom like Erica, though I like Erica when she's on her own when she can just be normal for a change, be herself, the fact that when her kids are there she's always trying to squeeze something educational for them out of every moment, interrupting the conversation to check her kids are taking it all in and benefiting from this learning opportunity in some way, the fact that it makes me so *self-conscious*, the fact that she makes you feel like you have to put on an act, because *she* is, the fact that she turns every get-together into a kind of *seminar* for them, and yes, they're smart, they're doing well and all, so I guess it's paying off, her obsessiveness, possessiveness, the fact that I think giving your kids a head start is all very well, but it doesn't mean you can't leave 'em be for a single solitary *second*, the fact that I think it drains them of curiosity and imagination, well, *I*

sure find it draining, and at least I'm not a *boasting* mom like Davina
Beebee, who thinks everybody wants to know every time one or the
other of her kids gets an A or shows musical, athletic, or STEM talent
or whatever, WhatsApp, cyber charter school, the fact that her kids
never need math help from the police, amniotic sac, Mommy, hens,
the fact that the way she talks about them, it's like she thinks her kids'
every illness matters more to you than your *own* kids' illnesses, the
fact that she can be a little out of it at times, but she probably has her
own problems, Paterson Falls, Facebook, the fact that now she wants
me to provide yellow and maroon gauze for the school play, the fact
that she really tires me out, that Davina Beebee, so many demands,
"my hurts," the fact that nobody seems to notice I have a *job* and it
actually takes up all my energy, the fact that she can be kind of critical
too, about how I do things, the fact that when I do bring the gauze,
she'll probably tell me there's something wrong with it, it's too much
or it's too late, or she didn't think I'd manage it so she made other
arrangements, the fact that she always makes everything sound like
it's your fault, no matter what you do, the fact that she's one of these
people who thinks her way's the only way, Amway, Amtrak, and she
thinks her kids are the only good kids and everybody else got stuck
with the duds, the runt of the litter, the fact that, boy, she's so full of
advice on childrearing, the fact that she can't understand that in a big
family like ours it's really each man for himself and the kids have to
battle some stuff out between them, and I think kids in big families
become resilient that way, "Please, sir, I want some more," ♫ *Whe-e-
e-e-ere is love?* ♫, Ma, Pa, De Smet, East Street Cemetery, the fact
that kids from big families get good at being *alone*, for one thing, as
well as being in a crowd, the fact that they're good at both, Dolphins
Consider Signing, the fact that I feel most alone in a crowd, the fact
that I feel *obliterated* by a crowd, the fact that crowds neglect individuals, but some people like them, or why would they go to plays and
movies and baseball games and *parties*, muumuu, or head for the hajj
in Mecca to get stepped on, the fact that I wouldn't go to the hajj in
Mecca if you paid me, the fact that I wouldn't go if you *killed* me, no

sir, the fact that I don't wanna be in a *stampede*, the fact that I hate running even at the best of times, always have, 9/11, white picket fence, falling off my bike into the rosebush, heart condition, the fact that I think I never really adjusted after my heart operation to not being weak anymore, the fact that Dr. DeBoer cured me of my heart defect, my *deformity*, but I still hate running, the fact that I was the baby of the family, and sickly, so I lapped up the attention, Honorable Mention, the fact that I won Honorable Mention in a baby contest, the fact that Mommy must have thought I was pretty cute to enter me in that baby photo competition, Utica Shale region, "a stratigraphical unit of Upper Ordovician age," the fact that it's not the kind of thing she usually did, the fact that we took Pepito and all our other pets to the school Pet Show every year, and they all won prizes, but everybody's pet probably got a prize for something, Appalachian Basin, Fun Day, the fact that some people even brought their goldfish, the fact that I think the bike contests were the same day, the fact that you had to swerve around lots of bollards to prove you were a good bike-rider, the fact that it was sort of a slalom, Did UFOs Really Cause Marilyn Monroe's Death?, the fact that it's a pity our kids don't get an annual pet show at school, the fact that all they get is displayed on the neon sign outside the school, the fact that it changes every now and then,

NO HOMEWORK NIGHT
BOOK CLUB WITH MARY
UNITY DAY
FALL FEST
MARCH OF THE PENGUINS
TRUMPET DAY
NO SCHOOL
GREAT BIG PLAY DATE
YOUNG BUILDERS AFTERSCHOOL CLASSES
HIRUKO POWER OR NOW KARATE
WAKE UP PICTURE DAY,

stuff like that, *Frances* Kelsey, the fact that it was Frances Kelsey that fought against Thalidomide, Vicodin, Aleve, true-ups, the fact that I get her mixed up with Rachel Carson sometimes, fish, mackerel, whales, 1960s, Barbie Doll Bomb, the fact that for Wake Up Picture Day you're supposed to draw a picture as soon as you wake up, based on your dreams, the fact that I think that's a great idea, but Ben hates it, the fact that he prefers building electrical circuitry, the Young Builders club, the fact that I'd like to draw the dream *I* just had about Leo using our maxed-out credit card to buy a Buick convertible for a *lot* of money, blue snow in the shadows, the fact that I love it when it turns blue at twilight, the best time of day there is, the dusky, in-between time, the fact that I like reflecting puddles and pools that flicker at you as you walk along, or when you're driving, and when sunlight comes through green leaves, the fact that it's better than a movie, the fact that I think you only need to see sunlight coming through green leaves to feel *okay* about everything, at least briefly, the fact that you don't really need TV or Morning Routine videos, the fact that no one likes slush though, mush, motorcycles, the fact that I like Cathy, and Marcia's such a nice girl, cheesy chicken enchilada soup, Caesar salad, but she eats too much, the fact that it must be hard not to nibble at stuff when you're cooking up those big pots of soup and stew all day, COOK WANTED, bobcat truck, wiffleball, jinglebells, Echo Pass, the fact that they sell all *kinds* of things at Cathy's, beef tips, manicotti stuffed with seafood, Italian Wedding Soup, jars of local honey, and homemade salsa, all sorts of things, the jewelry, American-made gardening gloves, candy corn at Hallowe'en, maple-flavored and original flavor, or salt and chocolate candy corn, and Freedom Corn for the Fourth of July, the fact that candy corn has seven calories per kernel, and nine billion pieces of candy corn are sold annually, annals, anal, oh no no no, the fact that they started making candy corn in Philadelphia but I don't know where they make it now, the fact that most people eat the whole kernel in one bite, but a lot of people like to nibble the narrow end first, the fact that I don't know how they found that out, and I hate to think, the fact that I like candy corn because it's supposed to look like chicken feed, the fact that Cathy makes snickerdoodles with a kernel of candy corn on top, the fact that the candy corn stays whole when you bake them, so it doesn't melt into the dough, the fact that candy corn's pretty indestructible, the fact that Brach's has been going since 1904, the fact that a Brach heiress mysteriously disappeared in the seventies and I don't think they ever found her, the fact that maybe she fell into a silo of candy corn, the fact that actually I think the chauffeur did it, Colonel Mustard in the Conservatory with a, a, the fact that that's not nice, I mean, to joke about stuff like that, that poor woman, the fact that just because she's an heiress doesn't mean she deserves to disappear like that, Davina Beebee, lead pipe, rope, revolver, the fact that I saw a whole *corncob* made of candy corn once, the fact that I don't know what was holding it together, the fact that it looked like Indian corn, sort of, the fact that maybe the middle was marshmallow, the fact that you can cover a candy apple with candy corn, like a pomander, the fact that kids used to just buy their costumes for Hallowe'en, but now they make their own more, I think, well, around here at least, the fact that last Hallowe'en we didn't just get ghosts and goblins and cowboys and Indians, the fact that we got bats, angels, cats in tutus, chainsaw-massacre boys, a kid wearing a suit backwards, a mini-Mozart, a Grecian goddess, Roman centurions, a dinosaur, a gorilla, a bear, fairy princesses, Darth Vader, the fact that trick-or-treaters don't come as much as they used to though, now that every-body's so scared of kidnappers and jihadists and razor blades in the apples, Tastee Apples, the fact that we only visit the houses that have jack-o'-lanterns outside, and we went really early last time, before it was dark, which isn't as much *fun*, the fact that Ben was a pirate, Jake was a milkman, and Gillian was a squirrel, the fact that her fuzzy tail was a big problem, because she couldn't hold it up and other kids kept stepping on it, the fact that Hallowe'en's just not as good as it used to be, the fact that it's not supposed to really be a dice with *death*, but now it is, Day of the Dead, the fact that when *we* were kids, we trick-or-treated on our own, not with our *moms*, the fact that the whole point was to be out at night for once on your own, just kids, the fact that we never had to actually trick anyone, that I can remember, the fact that they never gave us any trouble, the fact that they all just filled our bags until they were so full we went home, the fact that Leo went as Frankenstein once when he was a kid, the fact that he glued Parcheesi pieces on to his neck, the fact that I don't remember my best costume, the fact that in London I got to be a mouse, the fact that the costume I remember best is Phoebe's Marlboro box, the fact that that was a beauty, the fact that Ben wants to be a *Star Wars* stormtrooper next Hallowe'en, Captain Phasma, the fact that I don't think he realizes Captain Phasma's a *woman*, the fact that boys don't want to be girls, so we should probably warn him, but we don't want to wreck his plans either, lady slipper orchids, the fact that Cathy's one of those people who just never stops, the fact that she is indomitable, Indomitable Snowwoman, Big Foot, the fact that when she's not cooking she's selling, and when she's not selling she's buying, driving far and wide for supplies, and when she's not taking care of her dad she's taking care of some new cat or harvesting the potato patch, or hunting ginseng, the fact that she says she'll take me ginseng-hunting in the fall, the fact that you can only hunt it between September and January or something, and you can only take plants that are at least three years old, Jake, the fact that Jake is *older* than the ginseng, the fact that when you dig one up you have to plant some ginseng berries in the exact same spot, the fact that I don't know when we'll ever get the time to do it though until Jake's in Kindergarten, mom-shaming, the fact that *Mommy* was never a spoiling mom or a gloating mom or a doting mom, the fact that she was rarely even an angry mom, except that time at the airport, the fact that later on, in her last years, she could get a bit riled if supper wasn't ready on time, but that was about it, and sick people are like that, the fact that *she* never had dinner ready on the dot herself, in Evanston, the fact that Ethan used to fume about it, the fact that teenage boys need food, the kitchen at night, black windows, *Samson et Dalila*, *La traviata*, Piglet, Tiny Tim, the fact that after Mommy got sick, we just dwindled as a family, the fact that we didn't know what to do with ourselves, donkeys, Kelsey, Thalidomide, the fact that we didn't even know what to eat, the fact that neighbors would bring over casseroles and we'd shove them in the fridge and forget all about them, the casseroles, not the neighbors, well, maybe the neighbors too, the fact that casseroles are supposed to be the thing when somebody's sick, casseroles, casseroles, the fact that at first the casseroles mount up, but then they stop coming, the fact that they couldn't keep on bringing food for fifteen years, the fact that everybody felt sorry for *me* because I was the youngest, the fact that Ethan was already in college, and Phoebe was in high school, but what does it matter how old you are when your mother nearly passes away, the fact that we were all a mess, the fact that somebody once brought over an undercooked chicken and told me and Phoebe to "finish" cooking it ourselves at suppertime, or whenever, the fact that even *we* knew that was unsafe, the fact that the last thing a destroyed family needs is salmonella from under-cooked chicken, or E. coli or whatever, basic food hygiene, medical science, the fact that we may have seemed pathetic but we weren't idiots, 5,000 Salmon Escape, the fact that when somebody in the family's sick, you're at the mercy of the do-gooders, though I shouldn't say that, my, how ungrateful, the fact that sometimes people brought us frozen spaghetti sauce, the fact that there really seems to be no limit to the amount of spaghetti sauce an American family can get through, but somehow it's not the same with lemon drizzle cakes, the fact that Marcia makes a heck of a lot of spaghetti sauce every day for the Country Shoppe, the fact that apart from the neighbors' stuff, it was all up to Daddy to provide meals, and he was never much of a cook, the fact that he usually just bought something precooked or in a can and heated it up, or we got takeout, the fact that he prob-ably would've *loved* Cathy's place, homecooked meals in family packs, Man On Phone Falls Into Manhole, the fact that Daddy had two signature dishes, pot roast and ice cream, the fact that we appreciated his ice cream, even if it was lumpy, the fact that who doesn't want their father making homemade ice cream, the fact that sometimes we'd drive downtown for ravioli and tomato sauce and all we had to do was boil the ravioli for a few minutes and dump on the sauce, or he brought pizza, the fact that New Haven has much better pizza than Newcomerstown, the fact that Abby came and cried, I mean she *stayed*, the fact that she came and stayed with us for a while when Mommy first got sick, when things were really bad and we were all in shock, and *she* fed us well, but then she had to go home and take care of Hoag, the fact that for a while a graduate student came in the afternoons to help out, the fact that I liked her, but then she disappeared and a *nun* came who tried to take Mommy's place and we hated her, the fact that she acted like Mommy was deceased or something, when she was right *upstairs*, trying to recover, the fact that we always thought that nun had a bit of a thing for Daddy, whatever-hernamewas, Sister something, Miss Scarlet with Professor Plum in the Library, the fact that she definitely had some kind of crush on him or something, the fact that she was always trying to keep us from bothering him, the fact that still, she did teach Phoebe and me how to peel tomatoes, the fact that you either put them in boiling water for one minute, until the skin starts splitting open, or you plop them in just-boiled water and leave them sitting there for about *five* minutes, until the skin peels off easily, the fact that I usually do it the slower way, so they don't get overcooked, the fact that I think of that nun every time I peel a tomato, can't help it, Otis, the fact that there must be *some* good nuns around, but I never knew any, frozen spaghetti sauce, SpaghettiOs, the nun who shook Mommy when she was little, tartes tatin, hog maw, plumber's wrench, window sill, Beyond Dirty Fuels, Frances Kelsey, the fact that the trees outside are waving in the wind, the fact that most Americans only eat foreign food, the fact that most American food is really Italian, German, Dutch, English, Jewish, African, Creole, Indian, Mexican, Japanese and Chinese, the fact that Cathy says there *is* no real American cuisine, aside from turkey sandwiches, that is, and sarsaparilla, sorghum and grits, the fact that the Indians grew the Three Sisters, corn, squash and beans, the fact that why do I bother making madeleines, when all most people want to eat is French fries and ketchup, the fact that they used marigolds to keep off the bugs, three sisters, the Three Graces, the Brontës, *Hannah and her Sisters*, the fact that three *brothers* doesn't sound as goofy as three sisters somehow, I don't know why, the fact that even *seven* brothers doesn't seem as bad, "All the bros," Bernie bros, Bear Steals Sandwich, the fact that codfish balls *are* American, as far as I know, the fact that I never had a codfish ball and hope I never do, but they were a big treat for Laura Ingalls Wilder, the fact that apples'n'onions were Almanzo's favorite thing as a boy, the fact that I make that, the fact that it's a good way to use up the leftover apples, log cabin, the fact that first you caramelize the onions and then you add big chunks of apple, flavor it with cinnamon and cloves, and let it simmer a few more minutes, until the apples are soft but not mush, the fact that the kids like apples'n'onions, the fact that I'm just starting to like cloves again myself, the fact that I overdosed on cloves when we made those pomanders for Christmas, the fact that that was the Christmas right before Mommy got sick, the fact that ever since then the smell of cloves, the fact that we suddenly decided to make this whole load of pomanders as Christmas presents for people, the fact that Phoebe was always coming up with ambitious schemes like that, the fact that it took much longer than expected and we got sick to our stomachs from the smell of cloves, the fact that it hurt too, Davina Beebee's hurts, the fact that actually pomanders look better if you *don't* completely cover them but we didn't know that, so we covered every inch with cloves, the fact that we didn't leave one little spot empty on the whole orange, the fact that the whole orange was brown with cloves, and we really hurt our fingers doing it, pressing all those sharp cloves into the oranges, the fact that we should've used *thimbles* or something, or not done it at all, the fact that I feel a little nauseous just thinking about it, the fact that I wonder if Phoebe's gotten over it yet, the fact that I never asked her, big project, Mommy, the fact that I should get the kids to make pomanders next year, the fact that at least it would keep them busy for a few minutes or so, like if there's a blizzard, and they're nice things to have around, while they're still fresh, if you don't mind cloves too much, the fact that they usually dry out okay but sometimes they rot, and then you've wasted a whole lot of cloves for nothing, for no reason, the fact that where do cloves come from, the fact that anyway you don't want to waste them, McCormick, the fact that I wouldn't let them hurt themselves, the fact that you only need about thirty cloves per orange, I bet, not hundreds like Phoebe and I had, the fact that you know you've goofed when the fruit flies start to appear in the middle of *winter*, but with all these apple peelings everywhere, the fact that the way to get rid of fruit flies is you put some vinegar in a glass with maybe a piece of fruit or a bit of lemon peel, cover it with Saran wrap and make a teeny hole in the top, just big enough for fruit flies to climb in, the fact that once they get in they can never figure out how to get out, the fact that they don't want to leave anyway, since they like the vinegar so much, Grandma's bobbled glasses, bugs in the night, fried ants, the fact that Jake's just had his third bowl of Cheerios, the fact that it's time to get him dressed so we can take off when the pies are out, custody disputes, ravioli, "ravololi," Paul Violi, pot stickers, thick, chick, Tex-Mex, the fact that Jake's very interested in baby animals right now, maybe because *he's* one himself, Flora the baby elephant, the fact that I've promised him a baby chick in the spring, eighty-five billion chickens, the fact that American cuisine is really kind of limited if you think about it, the fact that it's all little trays of TV dinners, "Dinner comes in. On trays," little packets of airplane food, little pellets of space rocket meals, cans, family packs, jumbo servings, Frank-a-roni Dinners, salsify, scrapple, home fries, sweet potato fries, onion rings, spanakopita, sandwiches, club sandwiches, hoagies, subways, grilled cheese sandwiches, tuna fish sandwiches, whitefish sandwiches, egg salad sandwiches, chicken salad sandwiches, ham and swiss on rye, pastrami on pumpernickel with a pickle, Reubens, BLTs, pastrami sandwiches, hot browns, tostadas, Waynesboroughs, chicken spiedies, chicken fried steak sandwiches, BBQ chicken and cheddar sandwiches, or chicken and egg sandwiches, family reunion, tiptoe through Wisconsin, chipped, chopped ham sandwiches, prosperity sandwiches, peanut butter and jelly sandwiches, burritos, jibaritos, Cuban sandwiches, muffaletta sandwiches, muffaletta calzone sandwiches, jalapeño popper grilled cheese sandwiches, pizza grilled cheese sandwiches, the fact that I don't know if pizza counts as a sandwich, maybe an open sandwich, no, pizza is not a sandwich, but a *calzone* is a sort of sandwich, the fact that there are Philly cheesesteak sandwiches, which Leo likes, Denver saddlebag sandwiches, The Cowboy, oyster po' boy sandwiches, slow-cooker Italian beef sandwiches, meal-in-one sandwiches, meatloaf sandwiches, *tacos*, the fact that I don't know if they're really sandwiches either but, Baltimore pit beef sandwiches, BBQ beef sandwiches, open-faced Beef Wellington sandwiches, steak sandwiches, "sammiches," horseshoes, French dip sandwiches with French's mustard and French fries, the fact that hamburgers and sliders surely qualify as some kind of sandwich, hot dogs too, the fact that hamburgers were invented either in Akron or New Haven, "a hockey puck and make it cry," Sloppy Joes, *Smoky* Joes, ice cream sandwiches, ice cream bars, the fact that it's hard to believe they really kill whales just to make lipstick, cutting edge, Bonwit Teller, the fact that America *has* invented a lot of desserts, and adopted a million from elsewhere, apple brown betty, apple turnovers, apple popovers, tarte tatin, the fact that I don't even *like* tarte tatin anymore, I've had to taste too many, Danish and donuts, or "life preservers," malasadas dois, sopapillas, pecan kringle, cinnamon rolls, cinnamon rolls with buttermilk icing, griddlecakes, fritters, crepes Suzette, muffins, lollypops, chocolate eclairs, Jell-O, milky Jell-O, Jell-O jigglers, shingle with a shimmy and a shake, fruit cups, ice cream, sorbet, sherbet, sherbert, frozen yogurt, hot fudge sundaes, invented in Evanston, banana splits, invented in, somewhere, Latrobe, Pennsylvania, Bananas Foster, banana pudding, sour cream fluff, parfaits, Lady Finger custard, fudge, hot fudge sundaes, cherry cobbler, peach cobbler, peach and raspberry cobbler, blackberry cobbler, marshmallow fluff, Football Field dessert, Christmas logs, Good Humor man popsicles, the fact that we had a Good Humor man in Evanston, the fact that the company started up in Youngstown, Ohio, in 1910, rum baba, Montmorency cherries from Michigan, ground cherries, fox grapes, spiced peaches, crab apple jelly, watermelon, huckleberries, puddings, hot fudge sundaes, hot fudge pudding, bread pudding, butterscotch pudding, Indian pudding, Spanish pudding, Ozark pudding, floating island pudding, Mexican chocolate pudding, tomato pudding, Indiana persimmon pudding, corncrackers' pudding, fiesta corn pudding, rice pudding, tapioca pudding, fish eyes, the fact that Daddy liked tapioca pudding, snow pudding, Ohio pudding, sweet potato pudding, prune whip pudding, Nesselrode pudding, corn pudding squares, Amish baked oatmeal, flan, Dutch pancakes, sweet noodle kugel, bombes, mousses, chocolate fondue, Kahlua soufflé, blancmange, butterscotch brownies with chopped nuts, caramel fondant, parfaits, and candy, maple syrup and maple sugar candy, penny candy, toffee, molasses, gum drops, gum balls, bourbon balls, wine gums, peppermint creams, lollypops, cotton candy, butterscotch, toffee apples, candied apples, potato candy, hoarsbreath candy, Amish caramel corn, divinity fudge, sugared almonds, maple walnut creams, peanut brittle, jelly beans, saltwater taffy, bubble gum, Milky Ways, Hershey's Kisses, peppermint sticks, licorice, and candy corn, and to wash it all down, we've got iced tea, Mississippi ice tea, applejack, O.J., lemonade, malted milk, black cherry soda, balloon juice, root beer floats, Big Gulp drinks, Double Gulp drinks, ping-pong frappes, milkshakes, cream sodas, moonshine, mint juleps, Bloody Marys, Old Fashioneds, whiskey sours, Manhattans, martinis, margaritas, Tom Collinses, sidecars, stingers, daiquiris, Brandy Alexanders, Artillery punch, Hawaiian Punch, milk punch, claret cup, eggnog, sour mash, and beer, ♪ *the beer that pickled dear old dad* ♪, Grandma, one on the city, water in bobbly glasses, the fact that the American diet also includes xanthan gum, saleratus, monosodium glutamate, dextrose, sodium aluminosilicate, niacin, thiamine, thiamine mononitrate, beta-carotene, aspartame, tetracycline, calcium carbonate, calcium disodium ethylenediamine-tetraacetate, apramycin, nitrous oxide, potassium carbonate, stearoyl propylene glycol hydrogen succinate, lecithin, acetylated monoglycerides, monensin, agar, zoalene, zeranol, estradiol benzoate, fen-prostalene, halofuginone hydrobromide, hydrocholic acid, labdanum, caramel color, cochineal, the fact that there are six thousand artificial additives approved by the FDA, and plenty more down cellar in a teacup, but Jake won't touch any of it, unless it's contained in SpaghettiOs, Cheerios, bagels and donuts, the fact that Mommy loved Leftover Night at Abby's house, and so did I, the fact that I must need something, the fact that I can't stop thinking about food, ♫ *We are, we are, we are, we are, we are the engineers* ♫, the fact that, accord-ing to Leo, Indian mounds are a great engineering achievement, Serpent Mound, boa constrictor, Alligator Mound, the fact that now they say Native Americans had *slaves* and maybe the *slaves* built the mounds, the fact that archeologists still don't know much about the mounds, like even how old they are, but they know they took years to build, and were used for at least five hundred years, the fact that it's not clear for *what*, Shark Bites Paddleboard, protein overdose, the fact that they found a scorpion on a plane, on a nobler plane, the fact that that 12-ounce baby got to go home, the fact that a laughing woman fell off her balcony, the fact that maybe that's the way to go, I mean with a laugh, the fact that a lot of boys tell girls to kill them-selves, and it usually *works*, the fact that they keep shooting all the grizzlies in Yellowstone, the fact that they've been taken off the Endangered list, the fact that we won't be content until we've killed absolutely *everything*, including ourselves, but I shouldn't think that way, dear me, the fact that it's not good to be negative, PTA meeting, Tuesday, a lick and a promise, all shipshape, ship's cap'n, deck-stiffened, bold as brass, Pepto-Bismol, bring to book, the fact that I had a cold when we got to Naples, so Mommy missed out on Pompeii and Vesuvius because she had to stay with me in the hotel, the fact that I still feel guilty about it, ducks, Newburyport, even though I was only four, the fact that a few years later she missed out on seeing a donkey on stage in some opera, because I hogged the binoculars, and I hate myself for that too, but I didn't realize they were going to lead the donkey offstage so fast, the fact that he left much too soon, the fact that once you got a donkey there, you'd think you'd hang on to him for as long as possible, the fact that maybe they were scared the donkey would steal the show, the fact that I really do think she was a little mad at me for hogging those opera glasses, but maybe she didn't care at all, the fact that maybe she only vaguely wanted to see the donkey better, and forgot it in no time, but I'll never know, so I'll never be off the hook, the fact that even if she was still alive, there wouldn't be an easy way to bring a thing like that up, without her thinking I was crazee, but I think she did mind, at least briefly, the fact that maybe I say "crazee" too much, but Mommy started it, the fact that I think Frances Borshun likes her new dog better than she likes her first grandchild, the fact that she's nutty about that dog, the fact that Jake wants a kitten too now, not just a chick, but I told him Opal's mommy-cat days are over, the fact that Stacy would say I'm using baby-talk again, baby animals, the birds and the bees, fear of failure, lava, calamari, Shopping Mall Shooting Spree, Pet Show, opera donkey, chocolate sundaes, the fact that Rosalind Russell makes some crack about a pregnant cat when she's racing through the newspaper office, all happy because she's about to quit and marry an insurance guy from Poughkeepsie or someplace, Ralph Bellamy, the fact that somebody mentions that her cat got pregnant again and Rosalind Russell says "It's her own fault," the fact that she just seems so smart and sassy, that Rosalind Russell, black-and-white movies, the fact that Rosalind Russell was from a big family in New York State and got along well with her dad, the fact that her whole childhood sounds very *healthy*, the fact that she had all these sisters and brothers and they were all very active, the fact that her dad was a doctor, I think, and the whole family rode horses together, the fact that she was probably the healthiest woman in America, or Hollywood anyway, the fact that she sounds a lot of fun, the fact that I wish *I* could be fun like that, and get all the kids riding horses, but I'd be scared the whole time they'd break their necks, the fact that it would *kill* me worrying about that, the fact that I'm so lucky none of them wants to get on a horse, count your blessings, Mommy, boarlets, Abby, the sidewalk in sunlight, with tufts of green grass on the side, B & J's hot roast beef sandwich, the fact that Americans spend more on Mother's Day than Father's Day, the fact that here's a bunch of Stacy's pressed leaves inside a cookbook, so pretty, the fact that they must've been there since the fall *before* last, to be this brittle, the fact that I don't know how to save them, the fact that maybe you can varnish them or something, Mystery In The Alley, moose winter tick, Mike and Ike, the fact that making a tarte tatin is a delicate chemical process, the fact that I don't know how I got into this baking business, except that we needed the money, and we still do, working mom, the fact that tartes tatin don't really pay, pay their way, all work and no play, but people kept asking me why I wasn't selling them, so I finally got up the nerve to go to Schumaker Farms, the fact that we always get our pumpkins and Indian corn there for Hallowe'en, the fact that they were nice about it and all but they didn't need any pies, the fact that they only sell their own stuff, the fact that they've been selling only their own stuff since *1806*, the fact that then I asked Zara at the farmer's market, but she didn't have room left on her stand, because she always has about a million buckets of apples, all different kinds, some big, some tiny, and gallon bottles of apple cider on ice, the cloudy kind, and dried Michigan cherries and apricots, the fact that a whole lot of water dripped on us, I remember, while we talked, from the awning, and I was scared I'd get Legionnaires' disease, the fact that to top it off, I upset a Mount Fuji of Fuji apples, Johnny Appleseed, the fact that Johnny Appleseed planted all the orchards of Ohio, or a lot of them anyway, Longaberger apple basket, buckeye, redwinged blackbirds, the fact that blackbirds eat all the Ingallses' corn and oat crops, so in return the Ingallses eat blackbird pie, the fact that I'd prefer blacksberries pie, ♫ *four and twenty blackbirds, baked in a pie* ♫, the fact that Laura thinks they won't have the money now to send Mary away to blind school, because of the blackbirds eating all the crops, but Pa sells the heifer calf, so Mary's dress with the flared sleeves goes into the trunk after all, and off she goes on the train, apples'n'onions, the fact that Zara said I should try to sell the pies to restaurants and I'd make more money that way, the fact that I started sounding a few restaurants out about it, kind of reluctantly, and then got in with Andy, the fact that they now take two dozen a *week*, which take four days to make, the fact that it can take a whole day just to make six or eight, and now I've got all these other places too, the fact that the Coshocton County Fair's at the end of September, Muskingum Valley Scout Reservation, Minnie Mouse watch, Stacy's alarm clock, eggs, chicken coop, swimming with our cousins in that motel pool in Detroit, the fact that I can only make two batches of cinnamon rolls a day, even with my great kneading machine, the fact that there are usually about two hundred rolls per batch, the fact that it's a big investment, this baking business, the fact that I had to buy all the racks and trays to cool the stuff on, rack and ruin, and boxes to transport them, the fact that the dough has to rise twice for cinnamon rolls, first in the bowl then in the pan, ♫ *Beethoven's Fifth* ♫, the fact that you need a little salt in the dough or they taste wrong, but you really need a little salt in just about everything, even rice pudding, just a pinch, to make it the way Mommy liked it, cinnamon and nutmeg too, the fact that nothing sweet tastes really good without either a sour or salty aspect, aspic, the fact that you need that contrast, "When it rains, it pours," it never rains but it pours, Morton salt, Horton, the Grinch, skunk eggs, the fact that I think my pie crust is more salty than sweet, but it's still too sweet for a *ham and egg pie, for Pete's sake*, because I tried that out in an emergency once and it was just terrible, really peculiar, the fact that a savory pie crust doesn't need any sugar at all, the fact that that crust tasted much too sweet and nobody could eat it, the fact that culinary disasters are so embarrassing, iced tea, animal crackers, Pepperidge Farm goldfish, Cheddar Large, Tetra Pak, TetraFin, the fact that what is that again, the fact that aren't tetras some kind of *tropical* fish, not goldfish, the fact that Leo had guppies as a kid, and a tiger fish, a six-barred distichodus, Miocene, pleistocene, plasticine, distichodus sexfasciatus, concave head shape, the fact that tigerfish look substantial from the side but they're barely visible from the front, the fact that they are "laterally compressed," the fact that when they reach maturity they turn a dull matte gray, kind of like *us*, London, distichodus sexfasciatus, dick, *oh*, the fact that if I'd ever had a tropical tank I would've gotten one of those elephant fish with the long probosces, and some bright green moss, first fiddle, Bastille Day, Kleenex, a chick for Jake, the fact that where *is* Jake, hake, cake, bake, wake, make, fake, take, lake, lake effect snow, the Great Lakes, the great unwashed, why am I, the fact that, for Pete's sake, everybody, why are there so many wet towels on the bathroom floor, Stacy, Stacy at five, the fact that an abused dog named Pumpkin now has a home, lost button, the fact that I really gotta do the grouting, The Staggering Cost of Alzheimer Care, the fact that where could that button be from, the fact that people started wanting my cakes and pies and at first I wasn't even breaking even, the fact that I just wasn't charging enough, the fact that I was running a *charity* pie service there for a while, because I'd never considered the *actual* costs, dinosaurs, Silicon Valley, professional, entrepreneur, billionaire, like all the extra equipment, transport, that sort of thing, the fact that the cost of flour doesn't amount to much if you're just a home cook and you don't use it all that often, home-body, homemaker, but if you're baking stuff all week every day, it adds up, homely, homestead, the fact that powdered sugar's really *high* right now, the fact that there are also all the hidden costs, like gas and electricity and cleaning up, gas for the *car* as well, Tuscarawas, cotton balls, Q-Tips, Tin Pan Alley, flax, Ajax, the fact that delivering the pies takes up time too, the fact that Grandpa said "Time is money," the fact that I think a lot of people have said time is money actually, not just him, the fact that Grandpa didn't come up with that on his own, the fact that now I add in driving time, cooking time, admin and accounting time, emailing and advertising time, the fact that I should really add in indecision time and procrastination time, and freaking-out time, highly strung, the fact that maybe *I'm* highly strung, whatever that means, the fact that maybe I'm high maintenance, the fact that how do you find out, IRS, deductibles, automatic oven timer, automatic oven cleaning, time to clean the oven, the fact that there are also all the hours I've spent promoting the business on Twitter and Facebook or email, and on the phone, and talking to people, many many *people*, because I'm always having to try to figure out more pie outlets, in case I lose the ones I've already got, the fact that people are so fickle, and you never know when they're all just going to want brownies instead, powdered sugar, cotton candy, the fact that Cathy told me all about where to get ingredients, the wholesale places, ♫ *Row, row, row your boat, gently down the stream* ♫, push-pull, to and fro, trick-or-treat, now or never, the fact that they've got all the stuff for *half the price* of Zyker's, apart from the fruit of course, the fact that I still go to Zyker's for that, because it's close, which saves time, and time is money, the fact that tomatoes are a fruit, Abby's BBQ sauce, Katie's BBQ sauce, Carole's pecan fruitcake, Bettina, ripe bananas, the fact that Katie doesn't cook her BBQ sauce at all, the fact that she uses a lot of apricot jam in hers, the fact that apples are pretty much in season all year round now, since they just get them from Peru or someplace if there aren't any ripe enough in America, the fact that I don't know if Cathy would approve of me using non-American apples, but she's never asked, Peruvian gold mine, slave labor, medieval conditions, Dickensian, Zola, tourist destinations, Aruba, beach resorts, terrorists, terrorist destinations, the fact that Shirley MacLaine should never have taken that part in *Being There*, big mistake, but everybody's gotta eat, the fact that the pies now pay their way, I think, but nobody's going to be moving into a *mansion* any time soon on the strength of them, the fact that I still make big mistakes too, embarrassing, hair trigger, Kardashian Kids, the fact that I liked Abby's big houseplants in their little baskets, the fact that she had a real green thumb, verdigris, moss, the fact that Abby's furnace was in the basement, the fact that her basement was so incredibly clean, crazee clean almost, Frazeysburg, the fact that it took me like three months or something to notice that building being gutted down in Walhonding, to make a coffee shop, black interior, bright white sidewalk outside, fall leaves, and by then they already had a cake supplier all fixed up, the fact that then I dithered and hesitated until the place *opened*, Whispering Willow, the fact that I'm lucky they even considered my stuff, wallflower, wall-eyed, deformity, the fact that Whispering Willow really pays well, and they're prompt, the fact that it took me weeks but finally I went in and asked if they had all the pies they needed already and they said they were happy to give me a trial, the fact that that was great, but then I messed up the samples, the fact that it was all so rushed and sloppy, mush, poor presentation skills, the fact that I did it all in such a rush, for no reason, the fact that I think I've got a fear of success, the fact that what would Daddy have thought if he knew what a screw-up I am, Mommy's giant Marlboro cigarette packet, the fact that when I finally brought the samples in, the waitress didn't seem to know what to do with them, and that freaked me out, Mar-a-Lago, the fact that I left them with her and just went back to the car and *cried*, gas station, gym shoes, laundry pile, *They say*, Chuck, RV, Judge Judy, amenities, manicure, handcar, hell in a handcart, hardscrabble, Scrabble, the fact that nobody knows who invented the handcar, but I always wanted one, the fact that I never expected to hear from the Whispering Willow again, but they sent me an email as soon as I got home, saying both pies were "fantastic" and they wanted more pronto, time is money, the fact that that's how Italians answer the phone, "Pronto," the fact that Mommy never knew what to say when they said that, the fact that she struggled with Italian during that year in Rome, poor duck, the fact that once she memorized a whole spiel and managed to get it all out, over the phone, and the person at the other end answered with an equally long long spiel, and she was sunk, post-nap euphoria, Mommy in the kitchen, the fact that they said "We really want to work with you," the people at Whispering Willow, I mean, not the Italian *Mommy* was talking to, the fact that I sometimes forget this *is* "work," well, *real* work, our old kitchen in Evanston, yellow walls, big old stove, the fact that at first they only ordered four a week, but now they take twelve, depending on the season and other varia-bles, twelve tartes tatin, four lemon drizzles, plus the occasional birth-day cake, the fact that it still bugs me that that Frazeysburg place rejected me, but they were just disorganized, them and their Matisse cutouts, and pepper pot soup, the fact that Leo loves pepper pot soup and I don't make it, the fact that I don't know how, the fact that I don't really want to know, because it's got tripe in it, and pigs' tails too, the Barnes collection, the fact that if Leo thinks my chicken stock stinks up the place, wait till he smells a pot of tripe boiling all day, the fact that I don't think you can buy tripe too easily around here anyway, though I never actually tried, triped, tripod, the fact that I really don't think they sell tripe at Zyker's, but *maybe*, the fact that I wonder if hog maw has tripe in it, the fact that it sounds like something that might, the fact that I've always been sort of scared of hog maw, the fact that it's mysterious, like haggis, the fact that I think maybe that's the real reason Leo sticks with the Philly job, I mean for the pepper pot soup, the fact that he likes to go out and get pepper pot soup for lunch, the fact that what if he left me one day for somebody else who's more willing than me to make pepper pot soup, the fact that *then* I'd regret not learning how to make it, "If I die you'll be sorry," the fact that I was always thinking that as a kid, always thinking what if I died, and how everybody'd feel about it, how sorry they'd be, and ashamed, and regretful, the fact that I wonder if my kids think that every time anybody's mean to them, or angry with them, the fact that you angrily think to yourself, they'll feel bad if you die, but what if they don't feel too bad about it, and your death will all be for nothing, for no reason, died for nothing, nil by mouth, DNR, the fact that I wish Leo was here more, just to keep me calm, the fact that it's hard to be calm when ninety-three people get shot dead every day, and there are all these impatient coffee shop clients, and I have a daughter disgusted by my refusal to become vegan, and we got that guy in DC, the fact that I think he plans to just *bluff* his way through the whole presidency, the fact that he smells so good, *Leo*, not Trump, dear me, pollution, nuclear war, Nagasaki, sciatica, the fact that there was one poor man who witnessed both Hiroshima and Nagasaki, I mean both *bombs*, the fact that he was in Hiroshima when the *first* bomb hit, survived and stayed the night in a bomb shelter, then managed to get home to Nagasaki the next day just in time for the *second* bomb, and he survived that one too, the fact that, I mean, how *awful*, vow renewal ceremony, "You'd be sorry if I died," the fact that there are all these clubs now for people to "prepare" for the end of the world, Doomsday preppers, the fact that I don't know what they do there, just talk about how to light a fire with petroleum jelly or something, or make stone soup, the fact that they act like they'll just have to live in the woods for like six months or so and then everything will be a-okay and they can come out in the open again and start repopulating the place or something, as if the world will still be *habitable*, the fact that if it's the end of the world, bud, it's the end of the world, well, that's what I think anyway, the fact that I just don't think there'll be much point in surviving, the fact that these well-prepared types are just going to spend their remaining weeks or months or years shooting other people if they come anywhere near their survival gear, "You call this living?", the fact that they all seem to think plants and animals will be safe to eat somehow, and all they'll need to do is hunt and gather all day, and hide, and shoot marauders, and everything'll be hunky-dory, as Daddy used to say, the fact that if you asked him how he was he'd say "Hunky-dory!" or "Tip top!", until he got really sick, the fact that my only hope is that after the apocalypse people will still need *pie*, so I could still be of use, if I'm still alive, as long as the fruit's not too contaminated, the fact that I might not make a *living*, since the money system will probably be over, but I don't make a living *now*, land of the living, the fact that maybe I could swap my pies for other necessities like water and fire-wood, the fact that pie-making may truly be my only survival skill, self-defense book, the fact that that dog Pumpkin was starving and living with her puppy under a piece of corrugated iron somewhere until they rescued her, the fact that the puppy was too weak to be saved, the fact that Trump said Melania better lose all the baby weight within a week of giving birth, *or else*, Nixon, Haldeman, expletive deleted, *All the President's Men*, the fact that I spend so much time alone brooding, that sometimes I'm scared I might blurt out something gloomy or unpatriotic in one of the restaurants or something, and they'll all take against me, the fact that when I deliver my pies and rolls we all act so *happy*, well, pie *is* a happy thing, or should be, even if your feet ache from making them, twinge, hip, back, highchair, euphoria, Mommy, the fact that nobody likes a happy person though, if they're not happy themselves, so you never know, the fact that my happy act could be causing *resentment* without my realizing, the fact that I sometimes look at the waitresses and think, they can't just be thinking about *coffee* and ham on rye, the fact that they're probably worrying about a lousy fiancé or an ominous lump or if they'll make the mortgage repayment this month, but the last thing you ever know about Ohioans is how they really feel about things, the fact that even Ohio children seem kind of cagey to me, like that poor little Anjolie, the fact that *James's* silence is kind of unnerving sometimes, the fact that I never saw a kid play that quietly with Play-Doh before, "unnerving," the fact that Mommy liked that word, the fact that Mrs. Bennet's always complaining about her nerves in *Pride and Prejudice*, jungle gym, jambalaya, the fact that Leo calls Play-Doh an amorphous solid, which is kind of exactly how *I* feel after a whole day alone here, the fact that sometimes I long for a friend that's just a little bit indiscreet, I must admit, the fact that they're like gold dust around here, the fact that that guy, that restaurant manager in Gnadenhutten, Anjolie, Nanya, seemed friendly at first, but then one day right out of the blue he said "Waken up and smell the coffee," the fact that I took that kind of amiss, amidst, askance, "This cow's done a lot of suffering," the fact that I forget what we'd been talking about, something about how it's hard for me to keep up on politics, being a working mom and all, doing my usual happy act, like everybody else, and he ups and says "Waken up and smell the coffee," the fact that I've tried to avoid him since, the fact that this is another reason for a pie slide, mud pie, fat lip, Play-Doh, the fact that it just occurred to me, maybe he really meant the *coffee*, the fact that he just wanted me to smell the coffee that he'd just brewed, huh, the fact that is that possible, the fact that maybe he was trying out some new kind of *beans* or something, boy, the fact that I never thought, Bear Interrupts Golf Game, Steals Sandwich, the fact that they've got an old African mask over the door in there, a lion face with a scrunched-up nose and a wide open mouth like it's hissing at you as you leave, the fact that I never know if it's there to encourage people to stay or go, but I got out fast that day, the fact that I think that Inuit duck is at the Peabody, *Bringing Up Baby*, "Ducky! Ducky!", the fact that Maika's dad worked on New Guinea, in the Anthropology department, the fact that I'd never seen anything like some of that stuff he had, masks and, and *penis tubes*, the fact that maybe I worry too much whether all these restaurant people are happy or not, "Waken up and smell the coffee," wake-up call, the fact that the Barnes Collection moved, Mommy, pepper pot soup, Pepperidge Farm gold-fish, elephant fish, the fact that Jake has just lowered his sights from kittens and chicks to a goldfish, but it has to be a baby one, ♫ *March of the Penguins* ♫, the fact that that was my first piano piece, and I learnt to play it on a cardboard keyboard in a class of twenty, the fact that we had a piano at home, but at school we all had to take turns, all twenty of us, the fact that I don't see why Amish dollies can't have faces on them, the fact that it doesn't make any sense, the hutch, the fact that I dreamt I inherited a nice house in the country and when I went to see it I found a long-lost nephew on the gravel driveway out front, the fact that he needed a place to live, so I said we could just live in the new house, because it was mine now, and he said he didn't think we'd be allowed to since we were both so young, the fact that that made me smile, the fact that I told him I was older than I looked, the fact that then I had to convince Leo that we were all going to live in that house from now on, with my nephew, because he needed us, and Leo was fine with it, which is just like Leo, the fact that he's really a very easygoing type of guy, chickens, the fact that why are they making such a ruckus, ninety billion chickens, what *is* the matter, the fact that it sounds like it's time to go cope with the coop, boots, coat, hat, Jake's jacket, unexpected nephew, the fact that Leo's so humble and generous, and always helping everybody out, the fact that he reminds me sometimes of Walter Matthau, *oof*, the fact that it's *free-ee-eezing* out here, just like when Almanzo has to go ice-cutting on the pond when he's a kid, and the ice they have to saw through is twenty inches thick, thicc, chick, check, peck, the fact that our hens do peck each other sometimes, but they're mostly fine healthy happy hens, *really* happy, not fake happy, the fact that Laura Ingalls Wilder preferred Leghorns, the fact that Almanzo nearly falls in the pond, and the other ice-cutters have to pull him out with their ice forks, the fact that what some people don't get is my pies are like my kids, the fact that they're like a little piece of me that I leave behind in restaurants, though I try not to leave the *kids* behind in restaurants, the fact that I leave my pies, never knowing how good they really are, the fact that you can't taste every one to see if it's okay, the fact that people don't want to buy a pie with a *hole* in it, by-the-slice, Buy The Slice, the fact that I can never really know if it's a really good one or not, you just have to hope for the best, accept the mystery, trust you know what you're *doing*, the fact that there's always a little niggling worry, and I'm always curious, and it's aggravating not to know for sure, embarrassing, but you can't micromanage every little thing, the fact that all you can do is rely on customer feedback, and how well the pies continue to sell, the fact that I've hardly ever had any complaints, actually, except the guy who wanted a chocolate cream pie instead of apple, which was just silly, not my problem, not my kind of pie, Leghorns, longhorns, shoe horn, horehound candy, hornrimmed glasses, the fact that I've had my chocolate cream pie disasters too, the fact that I had to make, and taste, about a dozen chocolate cream pies before I was sure I'd gotten it right, and I don't even like chocolate cream pie, the fact that it probably shows, the fact that that's why I only make desserts I think are good myself, the fact that it doesn't do to be too curious about what each pie is like, capeesh, the fact that in 1913, Mrs. Vanderheude in Oakland tried to peek at her apple pie when it was in the oven and the pie exploded just at that moment, causing a small fire, and all her hair got burnt off, the fact that the firemen found her soaking her head in a bucket of water, with bits of apple pie all over the kitchen, but at least she wasn't killed, my word, killed by her own pie, turkey club wrap, Brillo pads, Flora choking, the fact that I make excellent banana bread, but that's usually just for us, the fact that for us I don't bother frosting it, but if I have enough to sell, I whip up some sour cream frosting, the fact that a good banana bread should really speak for itself, but some people won't even try a cake unless it's got frosting and plenty of it, the fact that there's a hamster that eats miniature burritos, two at a time, the fact that he bites off a few bits then shoves the rest in his mouth in one gulp, the fact that it's kind of fun to watch his eating style, the fact that it's a bit like Ben's, the fact that some-times Ben stuffs his cheeks like that, my sky-blue earrings, the fact that I like to watch him eat, the fact that my breakthrough with banana bread was when I started putting marmalade in, because you have to keep banana bread *moist* at all costs, the fact that the same goes for, oh, what does it matter, the fact that you can't really make a lot of banana bread at a time, on a commercial basis, or I can't seem to, because it's all about the ripeness of the bananas, cheerleaders, the fact that they need to be a little *over*-ripe, bananas not cheerlead-ers, and you can never predict how many over-ripe bananas you're going to have around at any one given time, so you can't promise anybody you can bring them four banana breads or something, the fact that I just make it when I feel like it, apocalypse, and some get sold and some we eat, and the rest, well, they get forgotten in the freezer, 43832, styptic stick, suicide-bomb belts, Mrs. Vanderheude, Woman's Body Found In Trash Can, January, February, March, the fact that none of the kids can pronounce February, I don't think, but maybe *nobody* can, the fact that the French roll their Rs, and Scottish people too, the fact that I just imagined a Frenchman rolling some Scottish people along the road, like rolling cinnamon rolls, *cobblestones*, the fact that it's hard to get the French R right, the fact that actually people all over Europe roll their Rs, the fact that I guess it really caught on, the fact that Washington *wasn't* born on February 22nd, he was born on February 12th, but practically everybody thinks it was the 22nd, the fact that Leo says banana bread has to have a certain rubbery quality, the fact that maybe banana bread's the *only* good "rubbery" food, apart from maybe octopus or calamari or seaweed, or jellyfish, the fact that we got a seaweed salad in Toledo once, with soy sauce and sesame seeds, and it was really *good*, the fact that the kids didn't like it, the fact that they'll eat any amount of calamari but they see a little seaweed and act like we're trying to poison them, the fact that I don't think they have any idea what they're eating most of the time, the fact that as long as it's approved by their friends, it's okay, the fact that actually I bet they think calamari's some kind of onion ring, Dover power plant, zinc, lead, aluminum, the fact that the kids may even believe they're vegetarians, like Stace, but without the effort, pig, cow, pork, beef, the all-important difference between chicken, and chickens, What Is B12?, the fact that I'm not sure what B12 is or if your kids are supposed to have it or not, "died serving his country," died serving pie and SpaghettiOs, the fact that they still don't know who all the victims were from the latest Navy SEALs raid, but they do know they were mostly *little children*, the fact that I don't even want to know what this thing is, the fact that is it maybe part of a pen, the fact that we have so much broken stuff around here we can't fix, banana split, cheerleaders, that banana peel standing straight up on the sidewalk in Coshocton, just waiting to be walked on, classic, the fact that it was all splayed out like a wedding train, and I nearly did step on it, the fact that maybe somebody put it there on purpose, like for "Candid Camera," you never know, the fact that cinnamon goes great in banana bread too, but it's the marmalade, a big dollop of dark marmalade, that's the real secret, also a little touch of lemon juice, and maybe some molasses, to keep it moist, marmalade cats, the fact that we get the marmalade from the farmer's market, local business, working mom, emails, artisan bread, the fact that pears go well with cinnamon too, like that pear and cinnamon jam we got in Paris, apricot jam, plum jam, the fact that plums need cardamom and pears need cinnamon, the fact that green cardamoms are for sweet foods, black ones for savory, those little iron salt and pepper shakers shaped like Amish figurines, the fact that 20,000 gallons of crude oil spilled from a damaged pipeline into the Great Miami River, for the third time in three years, the fact that I don't know *where* in the river, somewhere between Dayton and Cincy, I think, but these things happen all the time, pineapple upside-down cake, ice cream cake, the fact that that woman's ice cream sandwich must have been full of preservatives or MSG or something, B12, the fact that insects and other creatures never disturbed it, they gave it "a wide berth," walk the plank, decking, a whole pig, buried and roasted in a sand pit, the fact that you do expect an ice cream sandwich to melt, the fact that they usually melt too *fast*, the fact that I waver between wanting to be a reliable rustic, traditional, "natural," instinctive sort of cook, who just has an eye for what'll work, and worrying if I need to get more serious around here, more professional, and start measuring everything and knowing exactly how every single thing'll come out every time, like David Downie in his Roman cookery book, the fact that David Downie's really punctilious, like he'll tell you exactly how many teaspoons of olive oil to use, the fact that I don't think that's how most people in Rome cook, measuring out their olive oil by the teaspoon, Lazio, the fact that I like his recipes though, the fact that "if you make your stock with trash, it'll taste like trash," but not everyone can get hold of Barolo for their Bolognese, Anna del Conte, at least not around *here*, the fact that I wonder if Mommy and Daddy ate all that stuff when we were in Rome, like artichokes, guanciale, carbonara, and gnocchi on Thursdays, Mommy, Vesuvius, donkey, binoculars, peeing in the cave, the fact that pianists can play an awful lot of notes at once, an *awful* lot, too many sometimes, the fact that I never got that good, or maybe I did, you just couldn't tell on a cardboard keyboard, keys, the fact that sometimes it's astounding what pianists can do, the fact that it's kind of like they become their own little orchestra or something, peasant food, the fact that the last Barolo we got *stank*, and it cost a heck of a lot, the fact that Julia Child liked to get measurements just right, but I don't bother, the fact that I'm not teaching anybody how to cook, or writing a cookbook, so why worry, the fact that if I was going to pass my recipes down to the kids, I'd have to be more careful, but so far they're not interested in cooking anyway, so, *Julie & Julia*, cup measures, tablespoons, a pinch of salt, sifting the flour, the fact that I never sift my flour, the fact that I can't remember the last time I sifted flour, maybe when I was a kid, the fact that whatshisname, the guy who plays Paul, Stanley Tucci, the fact that I like him, the fact that you really can't believe he and Meryl *aren't* Paul and Julia Child, *Kramer vs. Kramer*, *The Graduate*, the fact that in my head *All the President's Men* is almost a sequel to *The Graduate*, the fact that I like to think Dustin Hoffman and Katharine Ross get married and then they move to Washington, where he gets a job on the *Washington Post*, but then where does *Kramer vs. Kramer* come in, the fact that Dustin Hoffman would have to ditch Katharine Ross and marry Meryl Streep and then *they* break up and she moves to Paris and marries Stanley Tucci, the *Washington Post*, Ben, "Ben," Ben Bradlee, eggs Benedict, the fact that I get movies mixed up together, the fact that Meryl Streep's kind of a funny name when you think about it, memorable though, like Myrna Loy or Gwyneth Paltrow or Blythe Danner, or Rooney Mara, the fact that we like *Julie & Julia*, only we just *hate* the *Julie* bits, the fact that why couldn't they have just made a movie about Julia Child, the fact that who cares about this Julie person and her dead-end job and her Julia Child obsession, the fact that I do like their cat, but you hardly ever get to see it, Julia Child's mound of chopped onions, the Williamson Mound in Cedarville up beyond the Massies Creek bridge, Olympia Dukakis, World Trade towers in flames, collapsing, Amy Adams, Trump, the fact that Amy Adams has to make a new dish every night from *Mastering the Art of French Cookery*, no, *Cooking*, the fact that she works all day in a 9/11 call center and at night she makes extremely rich French food for her husband who's got a big appetite but also chronic indigestion, the fact that if Leo had chronic indigestion I certainly wouldn't be whipping up a lot of foie gras and chocolate cream pies for him every night, but this never seems to occur to *Julie*, the fact that she shows no mercy, the fact that I don't think

Julia Child would keep on cooking rich sauces either, if they made Paul nauseous, the fact that you don't want to go down in cooking history for giving your husband an ulcer, heartburn, dyspepsia, the fact that Meryl Streep was in *Heartburn* too, which is set in Washington, the fact that she's married to Carl Bernstein, so maybe you could slot that in too somehow, to make one very long movie about Dustin Hoffman and Nora Ephron and Julia Child and Watergate, Bob Woodward, Ben Bradlee, *When Harry Met Sally*, so it all fits together, the fact that Leo and I watch *All the President's Men* all the time, I don't know why exactly, the fact that Leo finds it comforting, I think, watching a bad president get cornered, the fact that Jason Robards is great in it, the fact that he always has his feet up on the table, Jack Nicholson, flipping omelets, mound of onions, copper pots, Simca, Cordon Bleu, the fact that Julie calls it "boof bourguignon," *boof*, oof, hoof, roof, the fact that I used to make *boeuf* bourguignon for Leo for a while, after we got back from Paris, with tiny onions and tiny mushrooms, the fact that that was before all the kids came along, the fact that there was just Stacy, who liked boeuf bourguignon too, the fact that I'm sure the real Julie whateverhernameis meant well and all, but I don't know about turning Julia Child's cookbook into a cooking marathon, and a blog and whatnot, the fact that it seems a bit disrespectful, the fact that Leo says it's crass, cruel, gruel, the fact that Mr. Woodhouse likes gruel, wood louse, field mouse, the fact that Julie's sort of a *stalker* really, she's nuts about Julia, crush, old flame, totem pole, *Totem and Taboo*, *Civilization and Its Discontents*, the fact that Anna Freud analyzed Marilyn Monroe for a while, the fact that she even wears pearls, *Julie*, not Anna Freud or Marilyn Monroe, though they might have too, Massies Creek, the fact that Julie tries to imitate *everything* about Julia Child, the pearls, the blue shirtwaist dress with a Trois Gourmands badge on it, the fact that it's all pretty kooky when you think about it, the fact that some people just wanna be somebody else so *bad*, Julia Child's TV show, "Bon appetit!", the fact that Julie juggles the cooking marathon with her 9/11 call-center job, the fact that *nobody* eats aspics anymore, Amish salt and pepper shakers, cast iron frying pan, Stanley Tucci, Brouilly, Paris, Place Dauphine, the fact that Leo and I drank cold Brouilly together in the Place Dauphine, and watched men playing boules in the dry dirt, which is different from pétanque in some way, the fact that I hope the real Julie did more for 9/11 victims than Julie does in the movie, the fact that it seems like the 9/11 victims just get in the way of all her cooking plans, though the cooking annoys her too, the fact that she just argues with a few people at the office and then goes home and eats lobsters with her friends, in her blue shirtdress and pearls, the fact that I don't know why I'm so mean about Julie, gorgets, the fact that I just wish it was an old-fashioned Hollywood movie with Rosalind Russell and Cary Grant, and just about the *Childs*, though Rosalind Russell would've played it differently, and Meryl Streep is very good, the fact that Leo saw Meryl Streep in *The Taming of the Shrew*, long ago, and she brought the house down, he says, she was so funny, the fact that if only Julie had spent the year cooking French delicacies *for* the 9/11 victims, brought the house down, the fact that that might not have worked though, with all that "Freedom Fries" stuff going on at the time, "Waken up and smell the coffee," taken, waken, woke, the fact that I know I should be kinder, dear me, the fact that everybody has to make a living after all, the fact that so what if this Julie person got famous with her cooking blog, the fact that who am I to question it, the fact that live and let, but they live right over a *pizza parlor* in Queens and it just seems to me they'd have been a lot happier if they just ate pizza every night and went to bed and watched a movie, the fact that once you're a mom you start to notice how people waste their freedom, *waste* it, Stars With No Makeup On, the fact that that's all Jack Lemmon wants to do in *The Apartment*, go to bed and watch a movie but there's nothing on TV, the fact that it's all Westerns with horses falling head-first and punchouts in the saloon and otherwise it's all ads, and he can't take it so he gives up and in the end he has to eat his TV dinner *without* TV, which is kind of against the rules, the fact that you're supposed to sit there with your Cal-Dak tray in front of you, the fact that we took the TV dinner idea pretty literally when *we* were kids, the fact that we *insisted* on eating our TV dinners in front of the TV, minus the Cal-Dak trays, the fact that Cal-Dak trays weren't so popular by then, not like in Eisenhower's day, the fact that *Grandma* probably had some but I don't remember, the fact that the Eisenhowers used to sit in the White House eating off Cal-Dak trays while they watched the news, but they weren't eating actual TV dinners, I don't think, just eating dinner in front of the TV, maybe something fancy, the fact that Jack Lemmon's so alone, the fact that Leo never got a TV dinner as a kid, or if he did he probably had to eat it at the table, which is no fun, the fact that I hope our kids never have to eat one, with the one little drumstick, a crumpled pile of peas and a thin pad of mashed potato with a yellow spot in the middle, the fact that it's weird to think that pad of butter must have to sit there on that patch of mashed potato for months, maybe years, from factory to freezer, the fact that mashed potato doesn't last a *day* usually, much less a *year*, the fact that in another corner you got your dessert, like on an airplane, usually something you didn't want, or if you did, you snuck it *first* and then had nothing for dessert at the end, the fact that I don't remember what the desserts were, the fact that they arranged it all so compactly into its molded tin foil tray, the fact that even *I* thought it was skimpy, and I never had much appetite, the fact that Hungry-Man TV dinners are bigger, the fact that the tin foil tray the TV dinner comes in is so shallow, it's almost impossible not to lose stuff over the sides while you try to eat your triangular portions, the fact that I preferred a little chicken pot pie, pies, pies, pies, the fact that everything's about pie around here, the fact that Woody Allen doesn't even bother to heat his TV dinners up in *Play It Again, Sam*, just sucks them frozen, ♪ *Plop Plop, Fizz Fizz* ♫, the fact that maybe people should just eat their *TVs* instead, like that guy who ate the cake and the dish it was on and then the *fork*, the fact that Ike had a bad temper, the fact that I don't know if bad-tempered men should eat dinner off flimsy Cal-Dak trays, the fact that it sounds risky, the fact that I like the black Cal-Dak trays with flowers on them, the fact that they remind me of our old black rocking chair, but why, the fact that that rocking chair had gold stars on it, not flowers, and where is it now, I'd like to know, the fact that I think maybe Ethan has it, the fact that Daddy used to read to us sitting in the rocking chair, that book about the fox, the fact that I think we sat on his lap, the fact that I wonder whatever happened to that book, the fact that you lose everything in life, everything, and then you lose your life too, fanouropita cake, crown dieback, the fact that Ethan has deer in his yard, the fact that Phoebe doesn't, she's in a loft, the fact that all she's got in her neighborhood are millionaires, the fact that, come to think of it, I don't know that pizza would've been any better for Julie's husband, given his dyspepsia, the fact that maybe *I* have dyspepsia, Pepto-Bismol, Pepito, Luden's cherry cough lozenges, the fact that they let us have Luden's cherry lozenges in school so we all had them on us all the time, the fact that we were never without some Luden's cough lozenges, not because of coughs, just for fun, the fact that Luden's don't do the nice white boxes now though, the fact that you have to buy them in a bag, "In a bag!", as Meryl Streep says when she fails her Cordon Bleu exam, the fact that Meryl seems like the real deal at flipping omelets, the fact that I don't see how they could've faked that with a stunt-double or an omelet-flipping expert or anything, the fact that the one thing Julie and Julia do have in common is that they both think about food all day, like *me*, the fact that I'm always thinking about recipes and all, but I forget to eat, the fact that it's hard to *cook* if you're full, so I just got out of the habit, the fact that I'm getting to be like a scrawny chicken, "March of the Penguins," the fact that when actors have to play musicians, they usually get some real pianist in to do the hands, but Mary Astor seems to really know how to play in *The Great Lie*, and Bette Davis could play the piano too, but they didn't let her, the fact that when she plays the "Appassionata" in *Deception*, they *dubbed* it, and they used some real cellist to play the cello for Paul Henreid, the fact that the other guy's hands come out from behind and take over, but it's not noticeable, the fact that Paul Henreid's playing a Haydn cello concerto when Bette sees him for the first time since the war, when they got separated, the fact that he survived a Nazi concentration camp, and he's come to America to play music and look for Bette, fanouropita, black-and-white, the fact that it's raining out, and first you just see her shoes, then you see her from behind, going into the concert hall, "It's you!", *Green Card*, the fact that Bette Davis took lessons from somebody on how to walk, and I think it paid off, the fact that I should take lessons on how to walk, CGI, Nazi concentration camp, the fact that Hollenius breaks his champagne glass while Bette's playing the *Appassionata* at the wedding party, ♫ *the Appassionata* ♫, the fact that they're all drinking the champagne Hollenius gave her when they were still an item, the fact that *Julie* drinks martinis in imitation of Julia Child, vermouth, cold glass, olive, twist, the fact that I could do with a nice martini right now, instead of a drive through the slush, rush, mush, mukluks, the fact that Julia and Paul Child really love each other and can't wait to, well, jump into bed all the time, while Julie and *her* husband, whateverhisname is, hardly even seem to know each other, the fact that there's zero chemistry, the fact that they wouldn't even *notice* if somebody else's hands came out from behind them, the fact that I think they break up after the raw chicken falls on the floor, and Amy Adams drops down too, till she's lying spread-eagled on the dirty kitchen floor, sobbing her heart out, the fact that I can't keep the Julie bits straight because Leo's always skipping them to get to Julia bits, Julia in the French market, flirting with the oyster man, the fact that it just occurred to me maybe Julie's hitting the gin a little *too* much, which would explain dropping the chicken, and her aspic failures, the fact that the son in *All That Heaven Allows* makes martinis, "my famous martinis," vacuuming, drugstore, the fact that I hope I'm not as bad-tempered a cook as Julie is, LET THEM EAT CAKE, the fact that I used to only sell cakes, the fact that when was it we pinned up that sign on the PTA bulletin board, not expecting much of a response or anything, the fact that it was supposed to look like a cross-section of a layer cake sitting on a cake stand,

❖ ❖ ❖ ✳✳✳ ☀ ⚙ ✷ ∞ ♥♥ ∞ ✳ ✳ ✿ ✳✳✳ ❖ ❖ ❖

❝ LET THEM EAT CAKE ! ! ! ❞
Great cakes for great occasions!

✳

✳   ✳ ✳✳✳✳ ✳✳✳✳ ✳✳✳✳ ✳   ✳

✳ ✳ ✳ ✳ ✳ ✳ ✳ ✳ ✳ ✳ ✳ ✳ ✳ ✳ ✳ ✳

Birthday and Wedding Cakes ! Thanksgiving, Xmas, Valentine's and Easter Cakes !
Devil's Food Cake, Gingerbread Cake, Angel Food Cake, and Eight Layer Cake !
Pound Cake, Coffee Cake, Spice Cake, Applesauce Cake, and Lemon Drizzle Cake !
Strawberry Cheesecake, Paw-paw Cheesecake, and Pennsylvania Dutch Crumb Cake !
Pineapple Upside-Down Cake ! Madeleines ! Chocolate-dipped Madeleines ! Cupcakes !

✳✳✳✳✳✳ Fanouropita cakes ! (and sometimes Banana Bread) ✳✳✳✳✳✳

❖ ✿ ✿ ⭡ ⭡ ❖ ❖

❖ ❖ ❖

❖ ❖

❖ ❖ ❖ ❖

❖

☞   **FatMoreCake**   ☞

☎ (331) 605 2290

8morecake@mom.com

❖ ❖ ❖ ♥ ☾ ☀ ⚙ ✷ ∞ ✳ ✳♥♥✳ ✳ ∞ ✿ ✳ ✳ ✿ ♥ ❖ ❖ ❖

like a two-layered cake with frosting and a cherry on top, Robert E.
Lee, Robert Oppenheimer, Eisenhower, the fact that Gillian helped
me publicize it and, boy, did people lap up those cakes, the fact that
they were phoning day and night, the fact that it was exhausting, the
fact that everybody likes sugary things, I guess, except for a few noble
moms who try to protect their kids from sweet stuff as long as possible
with pretzels, carrot sticks, cucumber, rice cakes, big fat sour pickles
and stuff, Ulysses S. Grant, opioids, Guy Gets Hit With A Stuffed

Animal, the fact that emailing customers is much better but you almost always end up having to talk on the phone as well, when somebody's ordering a cake, just to clarify things, especially a birthday cake, the fact that Jolene Foster Pearson, or whatever her name was, oh brother, the fact that I think they were Scientologists, the fact that now it's Philip Glass on the radio, the fact that I wonder how many people in Ohio care about Philip Glass, the fact that most cakes are so *easy*, compared to pies, the fact that the cake process is sort of magic, wall-to-wall carpeting, zigzag, ziggurat, Tag, steak knives, pink flamingoes, clarinets, chorus, seventeen musicians, no, eighteen, the fact that Steve Reich is over eighty now, the fact that making a tarte tatin is not so magical as baking a cake, though caramelization *is* magical, and also kind of tricky, the fact that with cakes all you have to do is beat the ingredients together et voilà, pretty much, plus the frosting stage, the fact that wedding cakes are a hassle, with all the marzipan and tiers and columns, marbling, marble bathroom, Bill Cosby, damp leaves, our pine tree, festive treats, frenetic, fret, threat, construction site, sight for sore eyes, sight, site, cite, cider, sidecar, "cup of chili and a side-car," the fact that three-tiered wedding cakes involve engineering skills I just don't have, the fact that it's really Leo who should be making them, wedding cake collapse, the fact that once I had an avalanche of frosting and the little plastic couple somersaulted off the end like a couple of parkour buddies, the fact that for wedding cakes you have to get all the little doodads in place *and* construct a personalized, meaningful, romantic edifice, and then you gotta keep the thing safe and fresh somewhere for the special day, the fact that it helps to have a pantry, WEDDING CAKE – KEEP OUT, sliced bread, white bread, crackers, white pepper, white people, black-and-white movies, reasoning, seasoning, bereaved, Mommy, loss, embrace change, burnt out, black out, flake out, stake out, "my hurts," the fact that there was no room in the pantry for anything else though, when I had a wedding cake I was working on, the fact that if the cake doesn't look A1, people take it as an ill omen about the marriage, and it calls for lavish frosting skills too, the cake not the marriage, the fact that you can't just plop some sour cream frosting on top and call it quits, the fact that I have stayed up all night fiddling with little crystallized sugar chrysanthemums, Marilyn Frome's daughter, and that silicon mold was expensive, the fact that it only allowed me to make three chrysanthemums at a time, and I haven't used it since, high five, the fact that fist bumps and high fives spread less germs than shaking hands, dabs, the fact that, oh, what a relief, it's over, the fact that Philip Glass can get a little bit repetitive, the fact that I don't know why they play that sort of thing, PlayStation, staycation, bikini, microkini, skirtini, burkini, Burkina-Faso, the fact that I can do a great one-story wedding cake, no problem, "Rrrreally good!", bobcat, bobsled, skidsteer, Frito-Lay in Canton, Dalit drumming band, clapping music, ring shout songs, Gullah, the fact that *our* wedding cake was a no-nonsense, one-story, tubular affair, angel food, and made by me, the fact that angel food is the best cake ever invented but nobody seems to realize it, the fact that none of my wedding cake clients ever asked for one, the fact that they all think it's too plain, I suppose, and if they're superstitious they probably don't want a big *hole* in the middle of their wedding cake, party-poopers, Make Your Own Party Poppers, the fact that I haven't used any of my tubular cake pans for ages, burnt-on crumbs, my bouquet of spatulas, Spartacus, swordie, chickens, the fact that, according to Mandy, Key West is full of "gypsy" chickens that just roam wild, Falls of the Ohio, music, summertime, strawberries, park benches made of recycled plastic, the fact that everything's made of recycled something now, my Statue of Liberty cake fiasco, the fact that I went to so much trouble over that thing and then the torch drooped, Papuan penis tubes, Priapan, poppin', popinjay, the fact that it was kind of embarrassing, drone strikes in Yemen, the fact that women and children were killed, and one Navy SEAL, SEABEE, bridges, the Titanic, CONSTRUIMUS, BATUIMUS, the fact that a hundred and seventy Jewish gravestones were knocked over in Philly, a hundred and *seventy*, the fact that that must take about a hundred guys, to push over so many gravestones, the fact that Leo thinks it might have been an initiation rite for some branch of the KKK or something, hazing rituals, rites, rights, the fact that that could be a new math problem for Ben and the policeman, how many anti-Semites does it take to knock over a hundred and seventy gravestones in one night, Hiroshima, Nagasaki, Doomsday Clock, the fact that *another* black man was shot down by the police, taking a life, the fact that, boy, I made a lot of birthday cakes but in the end there were just too many birthdays going on in Tuscarawas County for me to handle, the fact that it was like practically every day oftentimes, nervedays, the fact that my little business led to trouble with friends too, because they all want discounts or even a whole free cake, which is kind of, well, unfair, working mom, the fact that I *had* to prioritize the paying customers over freebies for friends, and that didn't go down too well, the fact that I felt terrible about it but there are only so many millions of cakes a person can make, all on her own, the fact that it's not like I run an industrial kitchen, or a catering company, the fact that this is just a two-bit, one-horse operation we got going here, and I didn't like it when the requests started getting risqué either, "The whole thing got outta hand!", the fact that what about that time they wanted me to make a cake that looked like a woman's naked *derrière*, of all things, a sit-me-down-upon cake, the fact that that was for a boy's twenty-first, the fact that I just couldn't bring myself to do it, bare bottom cake, the fact that who wants to make a nice cake anyway for a bunch of drunk kids, the fact that they probably would have ended up chucking chunks of it at each other or something, the fact that that derrière would have been wasted on them, Paterson Falls all icy, black water, white snow, the fact that then everybody started wanting edible photographs on their cakes and I don't think they look very nice at all, the fact that they look just like photographs do on mugs, mug shots, the fact that at least with a *cake* you don't have to look at the thing for years, and worry about it in the dishwasher, the fact that I just flat out vetoed the whole idea anyway because I'd've had to get a frosting printer thing, the fact that you *can* do it with an inkjet printer, but you really need a separate printer, so the edible inks don't get mixed up with poisonous toner, or vice versa, or something, the fact that we don't have the money for a whole new, separate printer, butt-naked cake, "right in the middle of my daily duties," mod cons, the fact that you'd think cakes for one-year-olds would be comparatively *simple* but they've got their challenges too, enormities, hardships, cruise ships, battleship, Navy SEALs, gun metal gray, submarine, sandwich, taco, torpedo, Toledo, the fact that the *parents* are the real problem, the fact that they're all so touchy, and they've got all these preconceptions about how the cake will be, like they want it in the shape of a **1**, with pink frosting and a valance of pink frills, or blue ridges with a green cowboy on top, all sculpted by me, the fact that then the moms would send photos of their kid's favorite toys and I'd try to draw them on top of the cake, the toys, not the moms, using lots of store-bought frosting tubes, which never turned out all that well, the fact that Gillian's much better at drawing Tonka trucks or Frozen Anna girls, but even she couldn't do a Paddington, the fact that maybe *only* babies liked my **1** cakes, the fact that they make the best kind of customer because they've never seen a cake before, striped onesie, **1**, the fact that a one-year-old probably wouldn't notice if *Michelangelo* himself had drawn pictures all over his cake, though my efforts were more Salvador Dalí, the fact that I surprised one mom with my smeary penguins and teddy bears, the fact that the narrow shape of a **1** cake is no help to composition, the fact that Smores does all kinds of fancy cakes now anyway, so I just refer everybody to them, the fact that I really came to hate frosting, the fact that it's such a messy business, and a good cake shouldn't need frosting, the fact that that's what *my* kids hate though, cakes without frosting, the fact that an unfrosted *madeleine* is a perfect thing, great shape, great taste, and very simple to make, the fact that I sound like Betty Crocker or something, fall leaves, Jane Wyman, **1**, TV set, TV dinners, the fact that I made the mistake of dipping some madeleines in chocolate for the kids once, and now they won't eat them any other way, and they hate the old kind, the fact that now they want everything choc-dipped, ring-tipped, Coke can ring pulls, pop tabs, stay-on tabs, dabs, the fact that children kept swallowing pop can tabs, but they've finally started making them differently so they stay behind in the can, the *tabs* not the *children*, the fact that now babies try to swallow those little round *batteries* instead, and that's even worse for them, the fact that batteries just poison them and there's nothing a doctor can do, the fact that they probably think they're candy, like me and the mattress button, Ajax, ink, Clorox, rag rugs, Mommy, *If I put it in my batter, it will make my batter bitter*, Birmingham, Alabama, buckshot, buckwheat, buckram, the fact that Birmingham, Alabama was built by slaves, the older parts anyway, the fact that the sand on the beaches of Normandy is four percent shrapnel, jellyfish, the fact that that's sad, the fact that more than a hundred French women are killed by their partners every year, the fact that I had to go all the way to Cambridge for the 1-shaped cake mold, the fact that they rent out every kind of cake shape, numbers, letters, cats, butterflies, reindeer heads, airplanes, ships, snowflakes, all sorts of things, the fact that they probably have a pistol-shaped cake tin by now, but when I went to get the number 1 tin, they didn't *have* it, the fact that they'd rented it out to some other poor birthday cake-maker, so I had to buy one, for I forget how much, a lot, the fact that now it hangs on its own special hook in the pantry, pants, butt cake, the fact that I figure I can use it through the kids' teen years, if I can just figure out how to make the $2, 3, 4, 5, 6, 7, 8$, and 9 to go with it, the fact that I can rent them of course, the fact that who can afford a whole set of numbers, uh-oh, sneezing fit, Sneeze No. 5, Bed & Breakfast, Kentucky, gnocchi, the fact that mating really is a matter of life and death, the fact that we tend to forget that, the fact that just because it's a very common activity doesn't mean it isn't important, the fact that it really *matters* who you have children with, the fact that that's why Romeo and Juliet get so worked up about it, the fact that you don't want to wind up with the wrong person and just have to make the best of it, the fact that sopranos are always being forced to marry the wrong guy, and then they have to kill themselves to get out of it, or kill *him*, the bad guy, the fact that Stacy didn't want a cake at all last year, a 15 cake, *or* presents, just charitable donations, of all things, spoilsport, Greenpeace, Doctors Without Borders, the fact that the women at that Cake Supplies Depot all have *PhDs* or something in cake decoration, cake construction, cake history too probably, not just the saleswomen but the customers, the fact that some of those women are making purse-shaped cakes that open, the fact that they put cookies inside in the shape of money, keys and lipstick, the fact that mostly though they make a lot of magic fairy castle cakes, tractor cakes, space rocket cakes, cakes shaped like pipes with real smoke coming out, giraffe cakes or grizzly bear cakes that somehow stand straight up, the fact that they must use a little piece of dry ice or something, for the pipe smoke I mean, not the giraffes, the fact that I just don't know *how* they do the giraffes, the fact that they make baseball caps, MAGA hat cakes, whiskey bottle cakes, beer barrel cakes and beer mug cakes, Massive Powerball Jackpot cakes, reconstructive surgery cakes, gender-reveal cakes, you name it, yeow, jeez, Djibouti, *Djibouti*, Djibouti, the fact that I really have learnt to say "Djibouti" now when I step on something, the fact that this time it's the caboose from Jake's metal train, the fact that "ARUBA" works if it's even worse, the fact that Abby always wanted to go there, Aruba, not Djibouti, the fact that I'm not sure Abby'd even heard of Djibouti, and I don't know now why I latched on to it, but it saves on cursing so it'll do, the fact that we never took her to Aruba, Phoebe, Ethan and me, the fact that we were all set to buy the tickets, but we never could agree on the dates, the fact that Abby always wanted to be somewhere warm, warmer than Massachusetts, for her arthritis, the fact that she and Hoag considered moving to Arizona at one point, iguana, Leo, Sally, the fact that we could at least have taken her to Aruba, the fact that the plan grew in ambition, then peaked and died, and I can't remember why, flop, mush, and then we just sort of forgot all about going to Aruba, the fact that I don't know if Abby forgot, the fact that why would she, with her arthritis and all, the fact that she died before we could get it together to take her, the fact that it would have been so great to see Abby snorkeling, the fact that if I got hold of a **9** pan I could produce **9/11** cakes, but who'd want *that*, the fact that don't I have enough to do around here without thinking up my own cockamamie cake ideas, Open Carry guys, the fact that when they pull you over for a broken tail light now, they beat you up, or shoot you dead, the police, I mean, or that's what it begins to sound like, my word, the fact that, 9/11, where is Jakey, the fact that it's time he got his pants back on, spoon, spatulas, swordie, the fact that most of those cake ladies are only doing it for *fun*, the fact that they seemed like they had all the time in the world to browse those shelves, the fact that they'd probably be cross stitching if they weren't baking, crocheting, or ninepatch quilting, batiking, while I frantically run around just trying to get by, HMO, taxes, college funds, faucets, window frames, the fact that sometimes it just doesn't seem quite fair, but that's the way it goes in cake land, Candyland, one-year-olds, dark ivy bed, Mommy, Pepito, peaches in cream, guinea pigs in the back yard, the fact that I never offered *Mommy* any peaches in cream, after she got sick, another oversight, just like Aruba, the fact that for the last twenty years or so I've been missing our peaches and cream breakfasts in the back yard in New Haven, those sunny mornings when Mommy made me peaches in cream and we ate them in the back yard, but *I* could've given *her* peaches in cream, later on, after she got sick, the fact that it never occurred to me to give her peaches in cream until right this moment, the fact that even if we couldn't get the wheelchair out there, she might still have liked to have peaches in cream, like *indoors* for instance, BEACHES IN CREAM, the fact that sometimes you just want to *sock* yourself, suicide by police, ARUBA, Abby's houseplants under the window, the fact that I dreamt we were burgled in the night while we slept, the fact that they took all our best furniture and checkbooks and passports, also my purse, and I woke up with my heart pounding and had to check the whole house for missing furniture, a stitch in time, the Abominable Snowman, corn, beans, squash, marigolds, blue snow at twilight, the fact that there's a trick, no, two tricks to making a good tarte tatin, no, *three*, Kleenex, Sneeze No. 25, Heinz 57, fifty-two weeks in a year, fifty-two playing cards, fifty states, twenty-six letters in the alphabet, *Thirty days hath September*, Hellmann's Mayonnaise, the fact that the main thing is getting the caramelization right, carrots, giraffe, gyrate, the fact that even after making fifty thousand tartes tatin I'm *still* nervous about caramelization, which is silly, because I do know how to do it pretty precisely now, André Allard's Tarte Tatin in Paris, the fact that you cook the apples in the butter and sugar just long enough to burn off most of the liquid in the apples without burning the butter, the fact that it's easy to mistake smoke for steam though, the fact that that's a problem, dry ice, especially when you've got more than one pie frying at once, the fact that when you burn the butter the whole pie tastes burnt, though sometimes that's okay, the fact that sometimes you can get away with it, but you never *know* if it's going to be okay, or inedible, indelible, unintelligible, unspeakable in pursuit of the uneatable, *April, June and November*, and what you really don't want is to end up with hard, brown, burnt-tasting sugar candy at the end of it all, that you can't get a knife through, and the apples all dried out and shrinking away from each other like the shriveled little apples in *Winesburg, Ohio*, the fact that they should be all plump and nudging against each other, the fact that a mistake like burning the apples is really embarrassing in my "profession," the fact that I have to watch my step, as the only purveyor of tartes tatin in Tuscarawas County, the fact that messing up the caramelization is really like going skydiving and forgetting the parachutes, the fact that some husband in England purposely sabotaged his wife's parachute before a jump but she survived, the fact that she broke every bone in her body but she survived, *Remember remember the Fifth of November, gunpowder treason and plot*, the fact that Leo wants to ride on a *microlight*, the fact that I think it's dangerous but what I told him was I bet it's awfully noisy, because you can hear those motors from a mile away, so it must be even worse being right next to it, but maybe they give you noise-canceling headphones or something, the fact that I don't think that changed his mind, the fact that I'm sure not doing it with him, the fact that I have vertigo, and anyway, *somebody* has to survive to stay with the kids, police shooting a black teenager in Cleveland, the fact that it's so wasteful, if I overcook a tarte tatin, I mean, the fact that by now I think caramelization has pretty much made me a nervous wreck, the fact that it's probably aged me ten years, making these darn tartes tatin, and what for, for no reason, the fact that what use am I to my family or the community, the fact that I wanted to help *everybody* when I was younger, and now all I do is study smoke and steam coming out of apples, sole purveyor, sole provider, sophomore, s'mores, Smores Bakery, sorority, initiation rites, the fact that I'm only doing it to help my family, and yet, to make any profit on these pies, I have to *ignore* my poor family half the time, family unit, head of the family, head on a stick, pike, pie charts, the fact that baking really requires peace and quiet, and privacy, which is hard to achieve with four kids around, yesterday's meltdown, the fact that sometimes I think I take some of my caramelization worries out on the kids, felt and sequins, late afternoon light, or maybe I take my kid worries out on the *caramelization*, the fact that I should just go shake out a rug on the back porch or something, shake a leg, Shaker Seed Company, Shaker rocking chairs, or do the grouting, for Pete's sake, Aunt Sophia's Quaker chair with its worsted lace seat, worsted web chair back, peg board, a rocker with no arms, a chair with no rockers, Mount Lebanon, New York, extant villages, defunct villages, short-lived villages, Watervliet Shaker Village, the fact that Sabbathday Lake Shaker Village in Maine has one Shaker left, or maybe two, the fact that I think that there were two *last* month but one may have passed on, the last woman, so the last Shaker man's still there maybe, laundry pile, the fact that the Shakers' god is both male and female, Serpent Mound, *Romeo and Juliet*, purple martin house, the fact that if I had to have a religion, maybe that's a good one, except Shakers don't have kids, church and state, the fact that my kids get prayers and hymns in *school* now, Doomsday Clock, second grade, the fact that the other tricky thing about tartes tatin is the *flipping* stage, flipping the hot pie out of the pan, the fact that I used to flip out a lot over the flipping, the fact that you can't flip it until about five minutes after it comes out of the oven, but you never know exactly when to do it, the fact that the pie needs to cool a little first, but not *too* much or it solidifies and the apples get stuck to the pan, the fact that it's still burning hot when you flip it and I've been burnt plenty, the fact that I should get *danger* money for this job, high five, on the flip side, the fact that at least my hair's never caught on fire, and none of my pies have ever exploded, *so far*, touch wood, but I've dropped my fair share during the flipping maneuver and it ain't pretty, the fact that instead of a nice elegant tarte tatin all you've got is greasy stewed apples all over your "nice clean floor," and Frederick skedaddling for his life, the fact that it's lucky nobody's usually around to see what goes on here, oh my, the fact that I do get tense sometimes, certainly about the caramelization but also about the flipping, the fact that I gotta put Jake and the pies in the car and drive places *now*, the fact that the young female rhino swept up in the floods has been returned to India from Nepal, no, the other way around, the fact that she was swept into *India*, I think, by the floods, and now she's been sent back to Nepal, the fact that she's just two years old, the fact that it took forty men to get her wherever they took her, and a tranquilizer dart, the fact that another two-year-old rhino *drowned* in the floods but this one sur-vived, monsoons, El Niño, the fact that she must have been so fright-ened, poor little rhino, first the floods and then being manhandled, Shakers, peaches in cream, the fact that I still get hippos and rhinos mixed up, the fact that I always have to stop and think which animal it *is*, the fact that hippos are cuddlier, but not exactly cuddly, and rhinos are hornier, the fact that *that's* not what I, the fact that I mean they have *horns*, the fact that rhinoceros beetles do too, pig in a poke, slow poke, ox yoke, egg yolk, yolk sac, the fact that one of my students wrote about "the yolk of our oppression," annuals of crime, the fact that after a lot of flipping I need some recovery time on the couch, a few pages of *Persuasion* or Fanny Trollope, "You have no compassion for my poor nerves," the fact that sometimes the apples don't come out of the pan because I overdid the caramelization or underdid the apples during the frying stage, or I used the wrong kind of apple, or the wrong kind of sugar or butter, or had the heat too high, too low, or because I delayed the flipping too long because I forgot about the pie for some reason, "Too tight, Toulouse?", as Toulouse-Lautrec's tailor said, fitting him for new pants, Tuscaloosa, the fact that what was that thing about Tuscaloosa, that Groucho Marx line, about how in Africa the elephant tusks are hard to remove but in Alabama the Tuscaloosa, Tuscarawas, Tallahassee, Anabaptists, the fact that, now that I've gotten the hang of it more or less, my tartes tatin usually come out all moist and dark, with the crust curling nicely around the Pink Lady apples, the fact that they should all be nestling together like plump pink ladies jam-packed into a Jacuzzi, the fact that Abby used to like the Jacuzzi at the King's Ransome, the fact that you need sweet eating apples for a tarte tatin, not cooking apples, and they have to not be too wet or wrinkled and dried out, the fact that I liked that other London park too, not just Waterlow, but I don't know where it was now, or what it was called, the fact that I can't ask *Mommy*, the turtles in Rome, the fact that at first my tartes tatin always turned out too wet, but now I'm much better at getting the right apples *and* handling the caramelization, even flipping, *Calooh! Callay!* euphoria, nap, Mommy, the fact that Jake is *not* putting his pants on, the fact that it's time for a sip from "Suck in your gut," the fact that this one's the biggest mug we own, the fact that the other two mugs say "Never skip a grade" and "Stay away from the Ivy League," good advice, the fact that it's amazing we've still got the full set, the fact that "Suck in your gut" has a slight crack but it's still good, the fact that her *mom* came up with these tips, and Breanna remembered them and got mugs made for herself, and then me, and now Cathy sells them, the fact that Breanna should get a cut but she doesn't care, the fact that she's just happy her potter friend is making some money, cinnamon rolls, the fact that Breanna really knows how to live, the fact that once in the park she got all the kids hugging everybody, and people were *crying* they were so happy to be hugged by all these little kids, that fact that Jake's pants are *on*, and we're outta here, check stove, lights, keys, rolls, pies, okay, the fact that first stop, the dentist, to have Jake's teeth counted and mine cleaned, the fact that he got in the car without any trouble, probably because he's never been to the dentist before, the fact that it'll never be so easy again, pepper pot soup, starving Syrian children, the fact that we hardly ever eat out as a family, the fact that we hardly ever even have a picnic, the fact that if we do go out it's a chaotic business, either Italian, Chinese, Mexican or American, hot dogs, hamburgers, meatloaf, chili, fried chicken, fried clams, tuna salad, chicken salad, noodle salad, potato salad, coleslaw, French fries, barbecued spare ribs, chuckwagon beans, brownies, cheesecake, popsicles, hot fudge sundaes, milkshakes, root beer float, Mommy, solitaire, peaches in cream, ivy patch, the fact that when she got sick we didn't do it anymore, the wheelchair, ♫ *Hitch your wagon to a star* ♫, the upstairs bathroom in Hamden, the fact that I need a sweater, pharma giants, the fact that I give the *kids* peaches in cream in the summer sometimes, for breakfast, sitting outside on the steps, before it gets too hot out, or else they have bananas in cream, in Jake's case pineapple rings, "Never skip a grade," tomato popsicles, peppery noodles, Brave Man Cookies, the fact that you might as well eat fried chicken out, because it's hard to do it right at home, turkey in a trash can, the fact that in Key West they deep-fry Thanksgiving turkeys inside trash cans, Mandy's cat, Hemingway cats, Opal and Frederick, Crab Key, Key lime pie, the fact that people who work on airplanes inhale toxic fumes, either from the engine or the fuel tank, I don't know which but it's bad for you, bone-dry, bonnet, burrito, the fact that Mandy told me the guy deep-frying the turkey in a trash can last Thanksgiving was a drummer in a blues band, the fact that he tended the turkey in between sets, the fact that I dreamt I had a new baby boy and had to nurse him somewhere kind of public, but I guess my baby-making days are over now, my mommy-cat days, concussion, brain injury, the fact that it looks like more snow's on the way, and I have many deliveries to make, the fact that they've got a huge aquarium at the dentist's, but not many fish, the fact that the water's so clear, the fact that do fish floss, the fact that I wonder if the receptionist girl has to feed the fish, or is it the hygienist, the fact that you never know if the kids have fed our fish or not, the fact that we really should have a chart but they'd never remember to fill it in, well, *Ben* might, mermaid ornament, china napkin ring, fish tank, the fact that there goes a big dog, the fact that big dogs need a lot of exercise, the fact that we had that old mermaid ornament in the fish tank when I was a kid and now we're using it again, the fact that being underwater doesn't hurt it, and sometimes the fish do swim through it, though not often enough, the fact that some guy taught his dog to clean up all its toys, the fact that I don't know why *all* dogs aren't trained to help out like that, the fact that, gee, they could clean the whole house for you, and they like jobs to do and it would be good exercise for them too, instead of lying around indoors all day dying for a pee, 9 Things You Never Knew About Miley Cyrus, the fact that cod stocks are still falling despite fishing quotas, china napkin ring, Mommy, floods, barnacles, blowfish, baby goldfish, the fact that it's Jake first for the dentist chair, the fact that he even gets a little Jake-sized bib, the fact that I used to do a hot 'n' spicy tarte tatin with fresh chilies, black pepper and cinnamon, but that's more of a summer thing, not much call for it these days, the fact that the chili knocks your socks off, the fact that a true tarte tatin is a plain and simple thing, not fiery or jazzy or anything, an *Amish* thing, no cinnamon, no nutmeg, nothing, and just an egg-based crust, the fact that the thing sinks or swims on the quality of the apples and the pastry, and the caramelization, and the darn flipping, the fact that the more I think about it, the harder it seems to make a good one, the fact that, I mean, for ten years I have been trying to get my tartes tatin to look as dark as the one at André Allard, the fact that we loved those mustard-colored walls, of the *restaurant*, not their Tarte Tatin, the fact that André Allard's coq au vin was even darker than the Tarte Tatin, rooster, Leghorns, but the whole restaurant was really about duck, the fact that you passed the tiny kitchen on the way to the tables and the chefs were knee-deep in ducks in there, raw ducks getting plucked, roasted ducks, fried duck legs, ducks cooked six ways from Sunday, the fact that what about that dish they had where the duck was served in a *sea* of green olives, just a sea, like two hundred olives at least, *The Hunchback of Notre Dame*, wet-roasted, the fact that there was that lady with the dog, obviously a regular customer, who snuck bits of roast chicken to her dog all the time, under the tablecloth, the fact that the dog sometimes peeked out, Brouilly in the Place Dauphine, neck ache, the Rue de l'Éperon, ♫ *Allons enfants de la patri-i-i-e, le jour de gloire est arrivé* ♫, gloire, Loire, Waterlow Park, Highgate, Musée Cluny, picnics on the hotel bed, baguette, pâté, cheese, the little Schubert concert, "Ave Maria," the fact that maybe I *am* too tense about my baking and should lighten up some, but it's so nerve-racking, the fact that so is having your teeth cleaned, the fact that she's using a new device on me she's really proud of, the fact that it involves a lot of whooshing air and water, like having a hurricane right inside your mouth, with the storm surge blowing your teeth off and threatening to drown you, the fact that it's like Key West or something in there, or Guam, the fact that I really am going to drown, think about the rhino, the baby rhino, the drowning baby rhino, but they saved it, the fact that it took forty men, rhinoplasty, the fact that I really don't think I can stand much more of this, ouch, the fact that all dentistry is torture, Abu Ghraib, Bush, George W, human pyramid of prisoners, starving children, drowned hippos, yeow, sheesh, the fact that I've got to think about something *nice*, not hooded naked figures standing piled high to be laughed at, ow, Djibouti, standing on crates for hours and hours to amuse American soldiers, the fact that I don't like this new tooth-cleaning method *at all*, the fact that I'm a damsel in some distress, but the hygienist doesn't seem to notice, damn, dam, damsel, damsel-fly, damsons, damson pie, the fact that Jake, no, *Leo* doesn't like damson pie, because I put the damsons in, pits and all, the fact that where's Jake, the fact that I don't have *time* for this, the fact that *this* is the pits, man, *help*, ARUBA, the fact that he didn't like the pits, the fact that I think this hygienist has gone crazee, the fact that for damson pie, you don't have to take out the pits, or that's what Tamasin Day-Lewis said anyway, the fact that it was her recipe, but she was wrong, the fact that you *should* take out the pits, for Pete's sake, for pits' sake, or else everybody'll choke on your *pie*, like I'm about to choke right now, the fact that Leo calls her "D-d-d-d-damson D-d-d-d-day-Lewis," the fact that I don't think he'll ever *forgive* her for her d-d-d-d-damson pie, the fact that damsons are good for you in some way, just like going to the dentist, and when cooked they get this beautiful deep purple color, damsons not dentists, a country fence somewhere in Holmes County, the fact that, boy, I'd certainly never make *that* again, damson pie, well, not that way, not D-d-damson D-d-day-Lewis's way, the fact that it's not safe for children, a p-p-p-pie full of p-p-p-pits, now is it, the fact that it's a nutty idea altogether, and Leo wouldn't eat it and I certainly couldn't eat a whole d-d-dangerous d-d-damson pie by myself, the fact that the crust forms a dam against the reservoir of damson juice, spillway design errors, purple martins, purple-brown school uniform, purple Pennsylvania, perplex, Perspex, the fact that I just don't know what to *say* to the hygienist, if she ever does stop, the fact that you're supposed to think about sex while you're at the dentist but I can't think about that *now*, the fact that I sometimes add herbs to my chicken stock, after the initial boiling, the fact that I never cut up the vegetables, the fact that it was so funny when Leo tried to make some chicken stock for me once, and he peeled all the potatoes and sliced the carrots and chopped everything into little pieces, the fact that that must have been when I was recuperating on the couch and couldn't do anything, M&Ms, the fact that I just take off any bad bits, on the vegetables I mean, but I don't cut anything up, I just throw 'em in whole if there's room, the fact that sometimes the celery has to be broken in half to fit in the pot, but that's all, the fact that I really *hate* her now, this hygienist, I hate her, hate groups, incel, tradwives, the fact that I don't usually hate anybody, the fact that I just try to be nice, the fact that I spend so much of my time making sure everybody else is happy, I never seem to get a chance to think about what *I* want, like how to escape from this dentist chair for instance, the fact that how'd I land myself in this spot today, the fact that I'm too busy heading off everybody else's dissatisfactions just so they'll leave me alone, but it never even works, the fact that, oh, my word, oh, it seems to be over, it's over, it's *over*, wow, *O frabjous day!*, rhino, hippo, the fact that that was just *awful*, the fact that I'm speechless, I'm *shaking* all over, the fact that how can I drive, getaway car, mandatory evacuation, compulsory, the fact that I've never known the difference between "mandatory" and "compulsory" and I used to think they were opposites but they're not, the fact that they're practically the same thing, Grandma's bobble glasses, the fact that as I was stumbling out of the room the hygienist was boasting about what a nice fruit-flavor scouring substance they use in that tornado machine, the fact that it tasted awful to me, and who cares anyway what the twister going on inside your mouth *tastes* like, playing Twister, the fact that I've just got to sit here in the car and recover for a minute, the fact that I'm seeing stars, the fact that I can't believe I look normal, the fact that I think that treatment changed me forever in some fundamental way, the fact that I feel faint, the fact that I should put my head between my knees, but the steering wheel's in the way, and what would Jake make of it if his Mom crumpled into a ball right before his eyes, selfish, selfie, the fact that I'll feel better once we're on the highway, my way or the highway, but $50 plus $150, so $200 for *that*, the fact that it cost fifty bucks just to have Jake's teeth counted, and a hundred and fifty to have my teeth sandblasted to smithereens, the fact that I'm surprised I've still got any left, *teeth*, not dollars, your mouth or your money, the fact that I could've counted Jake's teeth myself, if they really must be counted, the fact that my math isn't great but I can do *that*, seaside walkway, dunes, the fact that I don't remember getting the *other* kids' teeth counted, the fact that maybe the dentist counted them without telling me, the fact that I never check the bill properly, the fact that what was the point of the sandblasting, blowing abrasive nanoparticles or tardigrades at my teeth with such force that I probably have no gums or fillings or enamel anymore, the fact that what were those biscuits we liked so much at camp, swimming in the waterfall, the fact that it's supposedly to clean them but who *knows* what it's doing to you, the *rest* of you, I mean, the fact that I think some went up my *nose*, the fact that it might be permanently lodged in my *lungs*, giving me silicosis or asbestosis or something, that miner's disease, pit ponies, the fact that I really don't *care* if she thinks it's the best flavor ever, the fact that it could be *champagne* flavor and it still wouldn't help, the fact that she didn't even give me a choice, the fact that she didn't say "Do you want cherry, mint, champagne or tropical?", the fact that she just did it without asking, nanoparticles, the fact that I was in shock when I got out of that dentist chair, shaking, Shaker chairs, the fact that Shakers are celibate, the fact that that's kind of a brave move for a religion really, saying *don't* be fruitful and multiply, the fact that I just sort of limped out of the dentist's office, the fact that I should have run for my life, but I never think of things like that at the time, the fact that I couldn't even speak, the fact that I've got to hide this from Jake because the whole point was to get him used to the idea of going to the dentist, and show him the dentist isn't anything to be afraid of, tooth-counting, acclimatizing the child, the fact that *I'm* the one who's too scared to go back now, dentist phobia, the fact that I feel like I've been put through waterboarding or something, and now my left *ear* doesn't work right, singed feet, nail extraction, the fact that she might as well have dragged some state secrets out of me while she was at it, the fact that I would've told her anything she wanted to know, two hundred bucks down the drain for that, twenty tartes tatin, a week's work, the fact that even if our HMO covered it I don't care if I ever see a hygienist again, the fact that, goodness, I'd rather lose all my teeth than be put through that sand storm again, the fact that I don't want abrasive particles swished all over my face and hair and ears and up my nose and everywhere, the fact that if I hadn't been wearing goggles she might've *blinded* me with that haboob she created, the fact that a hundred fifty bucks just to go blind, the fact that in engineering, every action has its equal and opposite reaction, and this is *my* reaction to having nanoparticles blown at me, the fact that I feel sick, moose winter tick, the fact that deer ticks are on the rise in Alaska, and there he goes, the fact that Jake's always so happy to get to his play group, or maybe he's just happy to get in somewhere out of the cold, the fact that he *raced* away from me, the fact that I'm sure I wasn't very good company in the car, not after my ordeal, the fact that my stomach hurts, the fact that let's get these deliveries done quick and get home, the fact that Aunt Nuala was a hygienist, and she made me suspicious of all hygienists, the fact that she got a real buzz out of her job, the fact that she couldn't ever talk about anything but teeth, the fact that if you went out to lunch with her, she'd just talk about teeth the whole time, and how we should floss more, while we ate our hot dogs and lobster rolls and potato chips, root beer float, the fact that Mommy couldn't stand her but Abby was used to it, the fact that she had to see Aunt Nuala all the time, flossing, the fact that flossing's been downgraded now, two hundred bucks down the drain, twenty tartes tatin, the fact that it seems such a pity to boil all your bottled vegetables for *twenty minutes* when you get them out of the jar, but you're supposed to, the fact that they surely aren't worth *eating* after that, but of course you don't want to die of botulism, the fact that there's a squirrel, the fact that he must be freezing out there, the poor thing, looking for a nut he buried someplace and, oh gee, what now, the fact that, the fact that I think I've got a *flat tire*, oh no, this is not my day, the fact that it's thirty below, or actually thirty above, but it *feels* like thirty below, the fact that I knew we should replace that old snow tire, Mommy's cigarettes, the fact that I think I hit a log or something back there on the road, and that did it, aw jeez, the fact that I am standing by my car like a dummy and nobody's ever going to stop, the fact that why should they, thirty-five thousand Ohioans, Civil War, Band-Aid, the fact that they all have places to go, things to do, just like me, the fact that naturally they don't want to get out and fix my flat tire for me in thirty-below weather, the fact that Harrison Ford punches the guy out in *Witness*, the guy who's harassing the Amish, the fact that Harrison Ford is good at "whacking," the fact that I think it's about to snow too, the fact that he'd always prefer a fist fight to speechifying, the fact that he jumps down that dam, the fact that I have *pies* to deliver here, for Pete's sake, "All that work!", *The Accidental Tourist*, the fact that what'm I gonna do now, the fact that I must not cry, don't cry, "Buck up," gold coins, treasure trove, "Rapunzel, Rapunzel, let down your golden hair!", the fact that Jack sells the family cow for a few beans, the fact that I agree with his mom on that, the fact that it doesn't sound a very good bargain to me either, Mrs. Bennet's nerves, the fact that

Laura Ingalls Wilder's dog was called Jack, the fact that I keep thinking I see the Abominable Snowman moving between those trees down there, a Bigfoot, just behind the *bushes*, gully, the fact that Ben would be thrilled, the fact that I should photograph it, but of course I don't have my phone, the fact that if I had my phone I wouldn't *be* in this mess, freezing to death in the wilderness, the fact that I'm always forgetting my cell, the fact that it's so silly not to have it with you at all times, the fact that the people on the planes in 9/11 made good use of their phones, the fact that I bet every American has carried their cell phone with them ever since 9/11, well, except me, tsunami, haboob, yapping dog somewhere, the fact that is it Sasquatch, the fact that *Ben's* the one who wants to meet the Abominable Snowman, not *me*, the fact that I could be eaten by a *bear* out here, if they weren't all hibernating, and none of these people driving by would see or care, Care Bear, "If I died you'd be sorry," SpongeBob, the fact that I don't think they even see me standing here, and even if they do they won't remember it later when they hear the sad tale on the news about a lone woman found frozen to death in a gully, where she'd been dragged by a listless half-hibernating bear, hobby horse, witch's broom, Toto, torpor, the fact that many moms are neglectful and easily distracted but it doesn't mean they're not loving, and even perfect moms have their sticking-points, like, say, about illness, or vomit, or untidiness or something, punch card, punch drunk, punchy, punk, the fact that some moms are bullies, and some are cold, and some are monsters, and some are undependable, or critical, and, compared to all those, I don't think I'm so bad, but Stacy does, the fact that she'll probably be *glad* if I get eaten by a hungry bear, one carnivore inside another, carnivore karma, the fact that it's horrible to be criticized by your own daughter who once looked up to you, but that's over, the fact that Stacy can hardly even look me in the eye these days, and it makes me feel like retreating from *her* which I know I'm not supposed to do, the fact that you're supposed to hang in there, whether you like it or not, because the kid still needs a mom, teenager, gangs, mall shooting, even though she never listens to a thing I say, ♫ *Mele Kalikimaka* ♫, Frank, the fact that a lot of men make trouble about money after a breakup, the fact that they act like having kids is something you can get out of whenever you feel like it, the fact that I never got a penny out of Frank, not one single solitary penny, the fact that he acted like he didn't owe me anything, the fact that at one point he said he'd only give me child support if I added up all my expenses for him, the fact that I didn't see what that had to do with it, the fact that how was that his business, the fact that did he think it costs nothing to bring up a kid and I was just making it up about the expense, the fact that there she was, our child, a flesh-and-blood child, and a child *obviously* needs stuff, like food and clothing and shelter and all, and he was supposed to *help* with that, as her father, the fact that the last time we met I even paid for his coffee, what a chump, camel's hump, the fact that if I remember rightly, I think he had a *donut* too, the fact that I dreamt our attic was full of *weeds* and it really was time to tackle them, and also all the wood up there was really rotten, the fact that it broke off in your hand, and looked all sort of charred, rotten eggs, rocker, off your rocker, the fact that somewhere near me right now there really could be a *bear*, a great big grumpy dormant bear, the fact that Leo was right by a bear once when he was out hiking, just twenty feet away, the fact that the bear was on the other side of the stream, and it *followed along beside* Leo for a while, but then disappeared into the forest, the fact that I'd never leave the house again if that had happened to *me*, the fact that bears can run so fast, and they're so strong, the fact that they're scarier even than nanoparticles, the fact that I can't *bear* to think about bears, the fact that bears are unbearable, live and let live, Leo, *dear* Leo, the fact that he wouldn't like to hear that I was out here all alone and nobody helped me, the fact that there's no point in crying though, the fact that I gotta get a grip, the fact that Leo would beat all these drivers up though, for not helping me, butt-naked, butt cake, penis tube, sheath, condoms, oh, the fact that there *is* some dark shape moving over there, the fact that I think I'd really much rather it was an Abominable Snowman than a bear, the fact that Abominable Snowmen never seem to hurt anybody, though they don't *help* anybody either, the fact that they just seem to hide most of the time, the fact that, you never know, maybe they're *not* all that "abominable," the fact that at least there's a chance of getting on an Abominable Snowman's *good* side, which there probably isn't with a bear, the fact that why do people always talk about the Abominable *Snowman*, as if there's only one of them in the whole world, who's lived for hundreds of years or something, the fact that that seems unlikely, given the tough life they must have, if they exist at all, awfully lonely too, being the only member of your species for *centuries*, Chinese softshell turtle, the fact that there's a very yappy dog somewhere over there, stuck outside, like *me*, the trees at Peolia, the fact that it's kind of unlikely there's only one Abominable Snowman, given the way biology usually works, and reproduction and all, the fact that after all there seem to be some Abominable Snowmen in *Tibet* too, the fact that if it's all one guy, he must be a real jetsetter, Abominable Jetsetter, Abominable love miles, rushing across the globe to visit his Abominable Snowwoman and Abominable Snowchildren, Abominable Snowpeople, Snowmom, the fact that nobody ever seems to see an Abominable Snowmom nursing an Abominable Snowbaby, the fact that I wonder if a litter of Abominable Snowchildren would be welcomed into our abominable school system, shooter drills, math class, the fact that I keep thinking about that Abominable Hygienist, the fact that you'd think there'd be some intermarriage by now, I mean between humans and Abominable Snowmen, not *hygienists*, the fact that my uncle married a dental hygienist but nobody ever knew why, the fact that Snowdad sounds too much like *crawdad*, the fact that Frank was kind of a crawdad, the fact that he wasn't quite a deadbeat dad, just a crawdad, or maybe he is a deadbeat dad, the fact that, yes, I think he *is*, the crawl space under our house, Daddy's attic in Evanston, books and papers, the fact that book lice eat starch, the fact that there's starch in book bindings, spine, hip, the fact that they like kitchens too, Mars rovers, Spirit, Opportunity, Laika, solar panels, lapels, double-breasted jacket, waistcoat, boatswain, peeing with Mommy and Phoebe in that dark cave in Switzerland, single-sex restrooms, the fact that nobody knows yet what nanoparticles can do to you but they're releasing them into the atmosphere anyway, all the time, and directly into *my mouth* now, the fact that, gosh, look at these people, all these people, just driving by, like they think I *want* to stand by the road in sub-zero temperatures, like I'm just standing here for fun, the fact that I can hardly even stand *up* anymore, thanks to the cold and the hygienist, the *trauma*, the fact that, yep, just drive on by why dontcha, the fact that maybe they somehow sense I'm not an *Ohioan*, though I don't see how they could tell that when I'm all wrapped up in my puffy jacket, the exact same kind everybody in Ohio wears, even Abominable Snowmen probably, the kind that makes you look like an amorphous solid, the fact that my face is almost completely smothered in my furry Eskimo hood, the fact that I bet I look like Coldy, but without the felt fish and spear, the fact that they're giving me the real Tuscarawas County Cold Shoulder, the fact that maybe they sense my negativity about the *hygienist*, the fact that nobody wants to be driving around with a woman who's all steamed up about getting her teeth sandblasted, the fact that it's not steam though, Mister, it's *vapor*, vapor from the cold, because, in case you haven't noticed, it's kind of *cold* out here, the fact that, according to Leo, nobody uses the word "steam" right, the fact that according to him it's almost always "vapor" they mean, when they say steam, the fact that he's always correcting *me* on it but I still don't really get the difference, the fact that nobody talks about *vapor*, nobody normal anyway, the fact that it would be like suddenly coming out with something like "mists and mellow fruitfulness" in the middle of a conversation about raking the leaves, vapor, fog, condensation, evaporation, cloud formation, the fact that I'm no engineer, far from it, cumulus clouds, cirrus, mackerel skies, the fact that Phoebe and I used to pretend we were smoking cigarettes in weather like this, using our *vapor* to imitate Mommy, the fact that I don't think I've ever seen *my* kids pretend to be blowing smoke out, the fact that maybe they do it in private, or maybe it just wouldn't occur to them because hardly anyone smokes anymore, the fact that the tide has turned on smoking, red tide, Mommy, the fact that velvet curtains always seem to be red, though

Scarlet O'Hara makes a dress out of *green* velvet curtains, the fact that wearing heavy velvet curtains in Georgia, in the summer, the fact that that's gotta be tough, "What do we need so much velvet?", cobble-stones, Paris, Velvet Revolution, the fact that I think *I* could use that velvet dress though, right *now*, the fact that I think I really may be freezing to death, the fact that it may have started, frostbite, gangrene, chilblains, bunions, Geauga County Democrats, the fact that I gotta keep wiggling my toes, the fact that I've got all those pies in the car, the fact that I can't even *feel* them anymore, my toes, not my pies, the fact that I might as well sell them by the side of the road, the fact that then, while people are dithering about which one to buy, I can jump into their car and zoom off like Cary Grant with the pickup truck in *North by Northwest*, the fact that how can I *think* such a thing, my gosh, the fact that it's always sort of funny though, that he's got that big fridge on the back, in the bed of the pickup, pickup line, the fact that maybe I should get back in the car for a bit, just to warm up, but then *nobody* will see or help me, the fact that my teeth are chattering, my newly sensitized teeth, the fact that I should j-j-just think about s-s-s-something warm, that green velvet dress maybe, or my oven, caramelization, a hot bath, smoke, steam, vapor, Frederick's tummy when he's sleeping by the radiator, patting Frederick on his tummy, the fact that I bet if I was younger and more *attractive* they'd fix my flat tire *easy*, velvet, the fact that I don't get how they can tell I'm *not* young in this getup, with only a tiny little bit of my f-f-frozen f-f-face showing, the fact that I could be a very well-wrapped Marilyn Monroe for all they know, or Amy Adams or whoever it is that's the current dreamboat, the fact that they probably don't even know I'm a *woman*, the fact that maybe they think I'm a small Abominable Snowman, who oughtta know how to fix his own dumb tire, "Fiddledeedee," the fact that there goes another, slinking away through the slush, slime, slushing, flushing, the numbness of muted beings, the fact that they can't actually zoom away as fast as they might want to, for fear of skidding, so they go by me so slowly I keep thinking they're going to *stop*, but they don't stop, the fact that there goes another one,

"Toodle-oo," the fact that they seem to be pretending I'm not here, all cozy in their cars, the meanies, slimeballs, but I shouldn't say that, *dear* me, the fact that Art once said middle-aged people are "vestigially sexy," which I suppose is better than nothing, Marilyn Monroe, Sophia Loren, the fact that Dickens never got over meeting his old flame again years later and seeing how she'd aged, the fact that that story sort of puts a chill into any aging woman, a chill, the fact that I'm chilly enough without that, hot bath, Frederick, summertime in Evanston, Dora, David Copperfield, Miss Havisham, Haversham, Twist, the fact that it's so cold out here, even that yappy dog seems to have given up and gone inside, lucky guy, the fact that maybe he froze solid, the fact that he'll yap again when he thaws in the spring, the fact that I think I'm going crazee from the cold, "hhhurricanes hhhardly ever hhhappen," hamster, Hampstead, Highgate, Hawkley Hurst, nanoparticles, the fact that I wish Leo and I had sex more, I do, the fact that I think our problem is neither of us is good at *initiating*, the fact that I've seen a UFO, once, but I can't really remember it, the fact that I was staying over at Patty Lomax's apartment in Chicago and we saw it out the kitchen window, the fact that we were convinced it was a UFO and we didn't know what to do so we called the police, but nothing happened, the fact that we kind of wrecked the whole experience by calling the police, the fact that we should've just kept watching the UFO, the fact that what did we expect the cops to do about it anyway, take to the sky with their batons, to do battle with the flying saucer or *what*, the fact that they didn't seem to have much money, Patty and her mom, in that dingy apartment, the fact that they had to share a bed, the fact that when I stayed over, *Patty* and I shared the bed and I don't know what her mom did, the fact that she must've camped out on a couch in the living room, the fact that she was out though when we saw the UFO, the fact that it felt like we were alone a lot there, either in the apartment or at the kind of barren playground near there, the fact that we liked that big piece of cement water pipe that was so big you could almost stand up in it, the fact that how'd that ever get there, the fact that I think her mom worked as a nurse,

Marilyn Monroe, Frederick's tummy, the fact that last time I saw Chuck we were in our twenties and he was cold to me, UFO, and I wasn't even middle-aged yet then, the fact that I think a lot of middle-aged women are wasted because men have all these grand ideas about what we should all look like, the fact that it's just like a habit or something, reflex, *Playboy*, the fact that it's almost a form of elder abuse, seniors, if you think about it, but you can't *make* people fall in love, the fact that you'd think not having to worry about pregnancy anymore, with an older woman, might be seen as a bonus, but then of course there are all the mood swings to deal with, the hot flashes too, and maybe plastic surgery, which is expensive, the fact that your fertility goes way down in your forties, but Holly Hunter had *twins*, Alex Baldwin, the fact that I begin to think these drivers wouldn't help *anybody*, even Marilyn Monroe, the fact that it's not very *neighborly* of them, Nachbar, the fact that here I am in the snow, a damsel in distress, completely dependent on the milk of human kindness, and there just *isn't* any, the fact that there's a go-slow in the milk-of-human-kindness milking parlor today, milk pail, milkmaid, mouse pad, Minnie Mouse, mini kindness, the fact that this here that I'm getting seems to be the *skimmed* milk of human kindness, ♫ *Mele Kalikimaka* ♫, the fact that I'm starting to ache and shake all over, frostbite, exposure, the fact that all I can think about are those three-day blizzards in *The Long Winter*, seven months of blizzards and frozen nails in the ceiling, and Pa hiding in a snow hole, the fact that my *teeth* hurt, but that's probably the hygienist, not the cold, the fact that she probably ruined me for *life* with that newfangled machine of hers, the fact that I don't think she knows how to work it right, and there goes another one, a car, not a hygienist, and it looked pretty comfortable too, the fact that I'm gonna *need* some comfort, if I ever get myself out of this mess, predicament, the fact that that's hard to say when your face is frozen, predicament, predicament, ♫ *Mele Kalikimaka* ♫, the fact that now I have a pain in my stomach, the fact that for all I know it might be the first symptom of really freezing to death, the fact that next I'll get lightheaded, maybe euphoric, and then forget who I am or where I am and wander off into the snow, stripping off my clothes like a crazee person, "I may be some time," ♬ *Mele Kalikimaka* ♬, "Hereabouts died a very gallant gentleman," the fact that I feel so silly standing here flaunting my flat tire, the fact that these guys only want to fix the flat tires of fertile women, the fact that, come to think of it, I *am* still fertile, a *little* anyway, I *think*, fertile, "vestigially sexy," barren, sterile, mobile, Calder, but how do I convey that in the limited time I have left before I freeze to death, the fact that do I have to write a *sign* or something, I AM NUBILE, I am klootchman, the fact that how is that their business, Meryl Streep, Oprah, bagel platter, the fact that, heavens to Betsy, I sure could use a hot flash *now*, the fact that, you know, guys, women past forty are still *women*, even if we're not all Miley Cyrus or Zsa Zsa Gabor, and I'd give you all a big smile if I *could*, but *my m-m-outh's all f-f-frozen*, the fact that the snow hides the Coke cans at least, the fact that it makes the world seem clean, Abominable Snowmen, bears lumbering through the woods, the fact that it's funny how men all seem to like the same women, depending on the fashion of the day, like it's agreed in an underground bunker somewhere, This Season's Women, right down to height, weight, hair color, skin texture, bust measurements, lip size, the G7 of male approval, the fact that they could call it the Lady Godiva Convention, the fact that I guess that's what Miss World is for, so they already *have* a gala beauty spree, "A gal a day's about all I can handle!", the fact that I shouldn't *think* such things, the fact that you don't want to become bitter, the fact that some men now *prefer* silicon breasts to real ones, silver dollars, jumbo stuffed shrimp, disco fries, the fact that the boys in Jake's playgroup are already all in agreement on what's pretty in a girl, the fact that they all have a crush on Tammy because they've decided her long blonde hair is the thing, the *Green Book*, Yellowstone super volcanoes, banner headlines, the fact that what's wrong with a little more variety, fellas, spread the love, the fact that every girl in that room's absolutely *adorable*, with their dimpled hands and curls and paper chains, fold-out chairs, Jake, the fact that I *have* to live through this emergency so I can see *Jake* again, the fact that somebody's gotta *help* me, the fact that men are such pests when you're young, staring at you all the time, phoning you, following you and, and whistling at you, making grabs, pressing up against you in the elevator, walking behind you down dark alleys, and then all of a sudden one day you're beyond the *pale*, pink breast cancer ribbon, eggs, chickens, dental hygienists, the fact that *men* age too, it's not just *us*, but they don't seem to think about that, *I don't know but they know*, oh dear, the fact that I really shouldn't generalize, the fact that it's unkind, but if only men knew how *hurtful* it is, the change from major to minor, Davina Beebee's hurts, *Heartburn*, the fact that Julia Child was *middle-aged* when she got married, hydrangea, the fact that that waiter in Venice almost raped me, and then he acted like nothing had happened, the fact that he just blanked it out, blancmange, the fact that I feel sleepy, the fact that I think people get sleepy when they're *freezing* to death, the fact that I gotta wake up, look for help, but I'm about to collapse, "I *love* collapsing," bridge failure, Leo, oh dear, the fact that there goes another, the fact that I don't *need* any reminders that I'm old, actually, y'all, the fact that it's already clear from all the aspirin and Vitamin C and echinacea and cod liver oil pills I have to take to combat all the colds the kids bring home, the fact that with four kids you just sometimes wish you had time to blow your own nose, you really do, the fact that I know I should use more moisturizers to stay young, but I'm always scared it'll affect the taste of the *pies*, the fact that you can't be oiling yourself up all day long, the fact that it makes it hard to get a good grip on door knobs, the fact that I guess men don't care if you can get doors open or not, as long as you look amazing, and have a great butt, booty, and wear six-inch heels, the fact that I should say sit-me-down-upon, the fact that I don't like "butt" *or* "booty," the fact that everybody says "boob" now, the fact that Trump is always assessing women and commenting on them like he's some great *expert* on beauty, the fact that, okay, I'm outta here, the fact that I've *gotta* get back in the car before I can't even make it over there, *sheesh*, frostbite, lost fingers, asylum seekers trudging to Canada through the snow, the fact that it would be a lot safer and warmer there, in the *car* I mean, not in Canada, the fact that Canada may be *safer*, but not warmer, the fact that Canada does seem a pretty safe place, the fact that everybody's always sailing, playing tennis, and taking tea, *and* they've got healthcare, the fact that if I'm in the car nobody will notice me except bears, the fact that bears can get into cars too, the fact that they get in fine but can't get out, so they tear the whole thing to shreds trying to figure out an exit route, the fact that they don't just destroy the upholstery but the seats and the *steering wheel* and everything, the fact that actually I can sort of sympathize with that right now, right at this particular moment, the fact that what if I *die* in here, the fact that I don't know what *else* to do except dig a snow hole and eat the Christmas candy like Pa to survive, except I don't *have* any Christmas candy, the fact that there might be half an old Oreo down the back of the seat, oh and the pies in the trunk, of course, which are probably frozen pies by now, the fact that Hoag was once stuck in a traffic jam during a blizzard on his way home from Boston, an epic traffic jam that lasted six hours, and he had to pee in a coffee cup, the fact that he couldn't get out of the car to pee, I guess, or everybody on the highway would've seen him, the fact that there's etiquette even in emergency situations, in Massachusetts anyway, the fact that I hope I won't need to *pee*, the fact that it's not safe to wander around in a blizzard, Leo, the fact that Leo will be worried if I disappear under a snowdrift, drift, drifting off to sleep, wake up, the fact that Leo is still taut and virile and dynamic and has all his hair, the fact that he looks like Walter Matthau, the fact that people would probably *line up* to fix Leo's flat tires, the fact that people still want to know Leo, the fact that strange men follow him on the street, the fact that men have to deal with that too, predatory types, the fact that at the beginning of *Bigger Than Life*, Walter Matthau turns up with a big pile of steaks and starts making healthy, nutritious yeast, yogurt and molasses shakes for poor old James Mason, weakling food for the recuperating invalid, convalescent, milk toast, Caspar Milquetoast, the fact that Walter Matthau's a bachelor gym teacher and eats steak every *night*, while James Mason's family probably can't afford steak ever, the fact that

Trump likes steak, the fact that we'd all be better off if he ate less of it, the fact that red meat makes people aggressive, and then they go on a gun rampage or press the nuclear button or something, for no reason, mall shooting, the fact that soon we'll have to dress our kids in flak jackets every day, just to dodge all the bullets, the fact that some kids have bulletproof backpacks, the fact that backpacks are supposed to improve kids' posture, though that must depend how doomed they feel, and how much they crouch over all the time, from fear of being gunned down, Pepito cowering by the backdoor, the fact that James Mason blows his top over the level of milk in the milk jug, the fact that maybe all men need a sidekick like Walter Matthau to punch them out when they go bananas, but of course it's not fair to generalize, the fact that most men are very nice, the fact that *Leo's* nice, the fact that Leo can't do enough for people, which is why all his colleagues adore him, the fact that I don't expect adoration anymore, the fact that just a smile from a stranger once in a while would be nice, the fact that Leo smiles at me, the fact that Leo loves me, the fact that married men live longer than single men, but married women live *less* long than single women, and *nuns* live the longest of anybody, because they all know how to peel a tomato, and shake little girls, the fact that isn't there some joke that married men *don't* really live longer than unmarried men, it just *feels* like it, tomato, avocado, potato, flamingo, volcano, tornado, the fact that nuns don't get cervical cancer, the fact that Mommy's illness broke me, the fact that there are benefits that come from being married, governmental benefits, but I don't know what they are exactly, Government Accountability Office, golden lance-head, thrusts, burpies, burpees, the Burpee Seed Company, Main Line Families, Philadelphia, dumplings, soy sauce, molasses, steak, the fact that should I put the heat on in here, but I shouldn't wear out the battery, watery grave, James Mason, Mommy, solitaire, the fact that Leo's an only child, the fact that that's a strange expression, "only child," the fact that I just remembered I dreamt we all went horseback riding, and Gillian's little friend Bobby was with us, the fact that over a high wall we could see black panthers in the forest, small ones, the fact that they were full-grown adult panthers, just smaller than you'd expect, and afterwards Bobby really wanted to go swimming in a pool at the riding stables and he was planning to jump into the pool from a *second-floor window*, Jane Austen in Bath, the fact that I was in the room with him and I said he'd break his leg if he jumped out like that, but he was squirming to get out the window so I grabbed him by his pants and pulled him back inside, the fact that it was lucky he had on sturdy pants, the fact that later I checked the depth of the pool with my hand and it was only about two-foot *deep*, so he definitely would've hurt himself, the fact that Bobby's such a sweet boy, sort of sad and playful, the fact that I think he and Gillian are still friends, chyron, chyron fact checker, tag-line, Main Line, pesto pasta, the fact that men are much more used to eating out, I think, than women, the fact that maybe *that's* why they live longer, or not, the fact that they don't live longer than women, it's just *married* men that live a little longer than *single* men, New York, Chicago, Philadelphia, pepper pot soup, Venice, gnocchi at closing time, the fact that that guy insisted on walking me back to my *pensione* and when we got there he asked me for another *date*, as if that's what had just happened, the fact that pushing me against the wall while I struggled to get away from him, the fact that that is not a date, no way, the fact that he should've been going to *jail*, not out on dates, but I didn't do anything, the fact that I called the police for a UFO when I was eleven, but I let the Venetian waiter go free, the fact that I don't think I ever even knew the guy's last name, and now I forget his first name, Paolo maybe, or Beppe, burpee, Giuseppe Verdi, gnocchi, cicchetti, a rocking motorbus on turquoise water, the fact that maybe I should've called the police, but I never even thought of it at the time, the fact that I couldn't speak Italian, for one thing, so I couldn't have explained things to them very well, the fact that maybe they could've gotten me an interpreter, schlemiel, the fact that they probably would've blamed *me* for the whole thing because I hung around with him for a couple hours, the fact that I thought he was *okay* at first, until he got me alone and started holding me against the wall against my will, the fact that I am absolutely frozen now, the fact that I probably *will* lose some toes, the fact that, ATTENTION, male drivers, the fact that many gorgeous blondes all over Eastern Central Ohio are going to go hungry today because I'm stuck here with the pies and cakes they crave, the fact that have you ever thought of *that*, the fact that I should've brought my phone, the fact that I'm always forgetting it, the fact that I never think I'll need it, the fact that Leo thinks I should always have it with me, and he's right, but I just forget it, so now all I can do is sit here and wait for people's pity, the fact that on the down side, a pilot got his cell phone all caught up in the steering wheel of the plane, the yoke or something, and the plane went into a *nosedive* for four thousand feet, the fact that I don't know how long it was before he got things back under control, but his co-pilot was a *mess* and had to take three months' leave, thirty below, four thousand feet, ♫ *Your feet's too big* ♫, the fact that my feet are *frozen*, the fact that can't anybody see my emergency lights blinking, the fact that I'm not asking for much, just a little help because I'm stuck here, and I *exist*, whether they like it or not, the fact that I'm sure they don't mean to be rude or unfriendly, the fact that *I* wouldn't stop for a stranger either, even in this weather, because it's just not safe, the fact that San Martín would stop, the fact that he took the poor and the sick ito his *bed*, for Pete's sake, not like the waiter in Venice though, the fact that San Martín did it out of *kindness*, the fact that he said compassion comes before hygiene, but I don't think his views caught on, purple martins, the fact that I'd never pick up a hitchhiker, the fact that you never know what trick somebody's going to pull, the fact that if they don't carjack you, they knife you, and if they don't knife you, they shoot you, for crying out loud, the fact that nobody's going to take the risk with *kids* in the car, the fact that I'd never ever pick up a stranger with the kids in the car, the fact that Stacy says we should get *rid* of the car, both cars, but I have to have a car because of the kids, the fact that she said that was a false argument because those same kids will have to inherit the lousy environment I'm ruining with my car-driving and meat-eating and sugar-eating and consumerism and I don't know *what* all, my kneading machine, I guess, and the freezer, the washer and dryer, and all the Teflon and computers and gas and electricity, and AC, of course, and let's not forget the nanoparticles, and, and palm oil, orangutans, the fact that practically *everything* has palm oil in it now, and orangutans are being kicked out of the forests to make room for more and more palm trees, the fact that thanks to that hygienist, I'm never going to like nanoparticles again either, I mean *tropical-flavored things*, the fact that I'm never going to buy tropical-flavored stuff anymore, except for Hawaiian Punch, the fact that I can smell it now, the fact that it must have seeped into my *skin*, or my nasal membranes, the fact that Stacy says your carbon footprint is multiplied by six, with each child you have, the fact that I said if your carbon footprint's that bad you should wash your feet, but she hates my jokes, the fact that Paul Henreid's wife hates his jokes in *Now, Voyager*, Fifi, amused, accused, mollify, mohel, Elaine, bris, roadside antique store, girl's hike, the Hamptons, the fact that Stacy said producing a pound of lamb has the same carbon footprint as taking a crosscountry plane trip, or maybe it's two pounds of lamb, and two crosscountry plane trips, I forget, continents, and she said the fashion industry causes as much greenhouse gas as airplanes and shipping combined, or something like that, the fact that to cheer her up I said that someday I'll take her to Paris, and she said one return trip to Paris costs the Arctic three square meters of ice, the fact that she has an answer for everything, *Chattanooga Choo-Choo*, the Charleston, Churchill, Winston, Woodrow Wilson, *La* Wilson, the fact that kids need meat though, cell phone, the fact that Stonewall Jackson and John Brown both came from around here, Ohio, West Virginia, thirty-five thousand Unionists, the fact that Stonewall Jackson taught a slave how to read, which was illegal, and he taught him so well, the slave read something about the Underground Railroad and took off for Canada, the fact that at least our *washer* is eco, which is something, the fact that that's pretty feeble, I know, in Stacy's opinion, the fact that the *washer's* not feeble at all, the fact that it's actually kind of ferocious and beats our clothes to a pulp, so then we have to buy new ones, adding to greenhouse gases, the fact that I think it's got its own private starch supply, the fact that the towels come out like *cardboard*, and that's why we need the dryer, the fact that without our dryer our towels would be useless, the fact that somebody still has their Christmas lights over there, dear me, in *February*, the fact that maybe they *died* and nobody noticed, the fact that I'm still seeing discarded Christmas trees around, the fact that people just dump them anywhere, and they always look sort of sad, the trees, not the dumpers, the fact that the dumpers look relieved to be free of this tree that gave them so much joy just a month or two ago, the fact that first they're worshipped and decorated and everybody circles around and you put your presents under it, and then it's just trash, except it doesn't fit in the trash too well, ♫ *Mele Kalikimaka* ♫, Mommy, solitaire, on your own recognizance, the fact that Stacy's got a thing about the dryer too, but we'd be lost without it, the fact that actually I got tired of using the washer's eco setting, but I'm not going to tell *her* that, the fact that nowadays I usually use the Quick wash instead, the fact that Stace would blow her top if she knew that, four-thousand-foot drop, the fact that Stonewall Jackson's sister's husband divorced her over her care for injured Unionists, Laura Jackson Arnold, the fact that she was a Unionist and nursed Northern soldiers, the fact that she and Stonewall were *close* when they were kids but in the end she didn't even mourn his passing, Parkersburg, WV, the fact that some people say Stonewall Jackson might have come around to the black cause but the Civil War intervened and polarized everybody, the fact that that's a bit far-fetched, the fact that there's some Christian cult in Virginia that kidnaps kids injured by American drone strikes and Navy SEALs raids, and rehabilitates them back in the US, missionaries, *Pride and Prejudice*, the fact that Stacy also said "If you *drive* a car, you *vote* for the car," but I don't vote for the car, I just use it to get my kids, and the pies and everything else around, except for right *now*, that is, the fact that, I mean, dear me, there's no public transport, and we can't *walk* every place and get mistaken for deer all the time by hunters, the fact that I'm not going to the supermarket by bike, on the *highway*, for Pete's sake, cycling, sailing, Mounties, recycling, spiraling, the fact that "vote for the car" is a pretty silly idea right now, when my car's sitting in two feet of snow with hibernating bears all around, the fact that how could you vote for cars, when they're so *ugly*, the fact that they were better-looking in the thirties and forties, even the fifties, with the running boards and gangsters, open-topped with milk pails on the back, the fact that I wish we still used horses like the Amish, but then I'd worry about the *horses*, the fact that I already worry enough about the Amish, the fact that anybody would, in Ohio, the fact that they seem so vulnerable, driving their buggies along the highway, squeezed between all the trucks, and some drivers yell at them, Hungry-Man, Swanson, EAT LIKE A MAN, rinse and repeat, the fact that the Amish have a good rule that you must not beat your horse, but not everybody's that considerate or restrained, the fact that you'd have to set up a great big horse welfare program *before* people gave up their cars, *Black Beauty*, horse manure, *The Long Winter*, Almanzo, the fact that you'd have to keep an eye on people, horse owners, somehow, but *how*, when people can't even save kids from being chained to their beds by their parents and starved to death, the fact that Almanzo was crazy about his horses and refused to buy a car for years, pacifism, Fred, Aunt Sophia, the fact that I really can't see what's wrong with pacifism, the fact that some Confederate general horsewhipped a black woman in front of a hundred soldiers, until her clothes fell in *tatters*, ♫ *Mele Kalikimaka* ♫, kakistocracy, the fact that I woke up this morning hearing that darn song and I can *still* hear it in the background, even when I get it out of the foreground, the fact that I have no idea why it's popped into my head this long after Christmas, or why today of all days, ♫ *the island greeting we send to you from the land where the palm trees sway* ♫, the fact that I could put the *radio* on to blot it out, but I shouldn't use up the battery, Blythe Danner, the fact that I'm thinking about Blythe Danner, but *why*, the fact that it's a name that eats right into you, but still, the fact that I dreamt about a woman who could walk on water, the fact that I was deep-sea fishing and I got to touch some little squids swimming around near the surface, the fact that they were salmony-white, the fact that then I dreamt I was at a meeting where you were supposed to bring in two things an animal said to you, and I was trying to remember if Pepito had ever said anything, like maybe when he hadn't liked some brand of dog food or something, but Pepito always *liked* his dinner, the fact that I couldn't remember anything he'd said and wasn't sure if this was going to be a problem or not, at the meeting, the fact that Pepito ate Alpo, Alps, cave, Chuck, the fact that the woman heading that meeting was a hefty Hispanic lady in a long black lacy dress sort of like cobwebs, the fact that lots of people claim to have no imagination but we've all got these uncontrollable imaginations when it comes to *dreams*, dodge a bullet, lucky escape, "Yvonne, I love you, but he pays me," the fact that it seems such a pity you think up all this stuff for your dreams, and then you just *forget* it, or most of it, immediately, or almost immediately, the fact that that seems kind of wasteful, wasteful of mental energy, compost, mold, manure, the fact that it's so hard to remember conversations too, the fact that I can't remember a single conversation ever, even if it *just happened*, the fact that reporters get better at it with practice, the fact that I remember most things *Leo* says, but that's because we're, spatulas, ♫ *Mele Kalikimaka* ♫, in love, the fact that maybe I *could* put the radio on, just for a sec, turn off the heat for a little while, oh, Rachmaninov, the fact that that music always reminds me of *Brief Encounter*, Trevor Howard, the fact that what is she called, the main woman, main squeeze, Sheila or something, *Helen*, no, the fact that *Brief Encounter* is one of the few movies besides *Julie & Julia* that's about middle-aged people falling in love, the fact that they're not really *old*, Trevor, Sheila, no, *Celia*, Celia Johnson, your johnson, but they're not *young* either, the fact that they've both got their own families already, kids, Celia, the fact that I think middle-aged women *aren't* completely alone in the world, because we look at *each other*, the fact that we check each other out, not from envy or competitiveness, from *empathy*, the fact that we look at each other kindly, just to see how we're all faring, or fading, the fact that I'm fading fast, especially now, even though the heat's still coming through a little, the fact

234

that I am like one of those shriveled little pruny Sherwood Anderson apples still hanging on the tree, or the highway, forgotten, downgraded, left to rot, spurned, spawned, bike spokes, the fact that she's called "Laura" in the movie, and I don't know what Trevor's called, Mark or something, Celia, hydrangea, the fact that how long have I been waiting by the side of this road hoping some passing driver will have a heart, the fact that they *haven't* got a heart, just like the Tin Man, the witch melting, the fact that I always mix *The Wizard of Oz* up with *The Sound of Music*, the fact that it should be called *The Sound of Muzak*, the fact that Trump gave some guy the job of US ambassador to Austria all because the guy's a fan of *The Sound of Music*, and Leo said "You'd think that would be a reason *not* to give a guy a job, *any* job," the fact that it's best not to know why Trump does the things he does, the fact that he's making everybody feel dizzy and nauseous, with all his decisions, and then he changes his mind, "Backward, forward and backward and forward they marched, back and forth, back and forth," icky minstrel show in *Little Town on the Prairie*, the Western Expansion, the fact that when Trump first heard about Frederick Douglass, he said "Hire that guy!", the fact that I wondered which position he had in mind for him, and Leo said it must have been ambassador to Nambia, the fact that I once dreamt about an Arab family who gave each son a new watch every year, or did I *hear* about that somewhere, I can't remember, Fred Astaire and Ginger Rogers, shoepeg corn, the fact that L. Frank Baum wanted to exterminate all the Indians, which kind of puts you off *The Wizard of Oz*, but I guess, just because you write children's books doesn't necessarily mean you're the nicest person in the world, ♫ *when a man's an empty kettle* ♫, the fact that, still, you'd think a children's writer might want to keep his love of mass murder to himself, if only for the sake of sales, the fact that I never liked it anyway, the *movie* I mean, the fact that I never read the book, the fact that Leo did, I think, the fact that the Cowardly Lion used to scare me, but now he's the *only* thing I like, and the tornado scene, the fact that it used to bother me that he's not much like a lion but now he seems a *dandy* lion, the fact that he's doing his best anyway, Bert Lahr, dandelion, lion hunting, trophy hunters, the fact that trophy hunters still kill elephants, not for their tuscaloosas, just for the fun of it, the fact that before the Civil War the U.S. government declared slavery *legal* in the Western territories, the fact that they actually did that, the fact that DuPont seems to have gotten away with infecting the water table and the Ohio, and that's just in the tristate area, the fact that they're responsible for that Hanford site too, in Washington State, the fact that they sure like messing things up for everybody, the fact that people won't be satisfied until they've destroyed simply everything, tristate residents, the fact that I really need to pick up Jakey soon or that new playgroup leader will be mad at me, the fact that I don't even know her name yet, the fact that they're always changing people around, the fact that I don't think Jake knows all their names either, the fact that maybe it doesn't even matter because at this rate I'm never going to see him again anyway, the fact that I'm just going to freeze in here, the fact that *more* snow's falling, the fact that eventually the car will be buried under huge drifts by the side of the road and they won't even notice it's *here*, and they won't find my corpse till spring, my *corpse*, when they come collect all the Christmas tree skeletons, and check on those weirdsmobiles over there with the Christmas lights, which will either be before or after all the bears wake up and eat me, or what's left of me, the fact that my rescue will either be a success or a failure, dear, dear, what's got into me, the fact that, the fact that I think it's impossible to imagine your own corpse, Corbit-Swiggert Cemetery, the Pearly Gates, ♫ *land where the palm trees sway* ♫, the fact that I really should have brought my cell, black trees, white hills, four-thousand-foot drop, sandblasting my teeth, stupid hygienist, "stoopid," kids crouched under the weight of their bulletproof backpacks, Pepito, the fact that Jake's play-leader seemed a little distracted when I dropped him off, the fact that is she *mad* at me because we were late, the fact that she knew we had to go to the dentist though, the fact that was it about me taking off his coat, the fact that I know he's supposed to do it by himself, but today he ran straight over to the roller coaster marble-run with all his winter gear on, snow boots and all, so I thought I better just remind him and now I bet I'm in trouble, the fact that I'm always getting into trouble there, the fact that she takes me to the side to discuss it and the other mothers all look at me funny, the fact that I'm not the worst criminal in the world, ma'am, the fact that there are guys out there who beat horses, the fact that there are guys who manhandle girls in Venice, guys who kill lions, guys who kill *their whole family* with tranquilizers and then arrange them prettily in their beds after, each kid clutching a favorite toy and the ex-wife holding a red rose, "estranged," the fact that it seems to me the wife is often "estranged" when these things happen, the fact that it should be called "estranger danger," hydrangea, the fact that men really don't seem to adjust well to breakups, the fact that I think the trouble is they just can't face going back to doing their own laundry and cooking and stuff, and paying for coffee, or crumb and gravel pie, or moon pie, blacksberries pie, and fried chicken, though most men *are* willing to fork out for fried chicken, the fact that men really go for fried chicken, the fact that our Kentucky Fried Chicken's full to the brim every time I go by, the fact that yep, if there's fried chicken to be had, men'll be there, ninety-five billion chickens a year, turkey in a trash can, trash plate, garbage ice cream, the guy with a missing finger in *The 39 Steps*, bigly, the fact that that guy at the Dallas Cowboys football watch party, who shot eight people dead, said he did it because he didn't want to get divorced, Weeping Mary, "ma'am," the fact that it always makes me laugh when men say "ma'am," the fact that it might sound okay if you're in *Texas* but it sounds kind of funny in Newcomerstown, it sounds just fake, the fact that Texas spends less on education per capita than any other state, the fact that I'm just relieved it's not *Ohio* that spends the least, PTA, the fact that I can't remember when the next PTA meeting is, the fact that an old man in Illinois got killed by a hailstone the size of a *baseball*, and freak winter tornados have just wrecked, wreaked, a whole lot of homes all over Arkansas and Missouri, wreak havoc, the fact that the sky is darkening ominously now, and my pies are decaying, and Teflon and DuPont are thriving, the fact that, come to think of it, I could live on those pies for months if I have to, not that I actually like pie very much, the fact that I really shouldn't complain, the fact that at least I'm not a refugee trudging through snow and ice to get to Canada for the sailing, tennis, and healthcare, the fact that when they reach the border they're met by Mounties with cups of *tea*, not machine guns, the fact that some aren't illegals or anything, the fact that they're just Americans running away from Trump, the fact that a few years ago I thought I might not see another winter because of cancer, and look at me now, freezing to death in this car, the fact that everybody in America now has PFOA in their blood, *everybody*, children too, and all the animals and butterflies and hummingbirds, the garden at Old Lyme, the fact that even the oceans have PFOA in them, every fish in the sea, the fact that PFOA will outlast the human race, it'll never go away, the fact that when we're all dead and gone PFOA will still be here, all so we can use non-stick pans and wear carcinogenic, easy-clean clothing, *school clothes* for kids to wear, "Have you no decency, sir?", the fact that haven't they got a heart, the fact that James Baldwin said America was immoral from the very start, the whole setup, cotton plantations, slaves, 100% cotton, the fact that we ate as many olives as we could at André Allard, but we hardly made a *dent*, oh, the fact that I guess I'm actually very hungry now, so hungry I could eat a horse, or a bear, what's that expression, hungry as a bear, the fact that I think they were mainly decorative, the olives, not bears, the fact that is that a black bear over there or did that tree suddenly get bigger, the fact that can't anybody see my blinkers blinking, "Agness Adler's husband!", the fact that Dorothy Parker got left for a younger woman, *Dorothy Parker*, the fact that that says something, something about *men*, the fact that these men are forgetting that some middle-aged women have other talents, like some are witty, and some can cook, and almost all of us are willing to do the dishes every night, in my experience, the fact that some of us can even make *pie*, a dying art, though I don't know if Dorothy Parker could, Dorothy Parker baking a pie, Dorothy Parker battling with latticing, pie exploding, the fact that I don't think so, the fact that Leo's love for me obviously exists in defiance of the natural order, the fact that shouldn't he really be *abandoning* me about now for someone younger, like Alec Baldwin abandoned Meryl Streep, or be playing a lot of golf just to avoid being with me, but instead he sticks with me, and kisses me and all that sort of stuff, the fact that he *loves* me, the fact that I really believe that, Leo loves me, and that comforts me, the fact that that is a constant source of comfort, even when I'm dying of hypo—, the fact that what's that word, hypo something, the fact that he says he misses me all the time too, when we're not together, the fact that his love exists in a world where nobody else gives a hoot about me, the fact that I'm broken, broken, the fact that when he's home he's always coming into the kitchen to talk to me or read to me, or watch movies, or just watch me cook, oh poor Leo, the fact that he's going to *miss* me when I freeze to death, "You'll be sorry when I'm gone," poor Leo, the fact that it makes me cry to think about it, the fact that I must not freeze to death here, crying, the fact that Leo *needs* me, the fact that what I love most is bedtime, when we get to finally go curl up together, the fact that I live for those moments, the fact that that was funny when he asked me if I spread out in the bed when he's away overnight, because I *don't*, the fact that I use his side as a storage area for books and pillows and stuff but I stay on *my* side, the fact that I never even think about "spreading out," me spread-eagled across our whole bed, the fact that if I took over the whole bed I'd just miss him even *more*, "No His and Hers sinks," and I wouldn't be able to sleep at all, the fact that maybe *he'd* like to spread out some more, the fact that maybe he's more comfortable in hotel rooms, the fact that our bed's way too small for someone Leo's size, the fact that his feet stick out the end like Julia Child's, the fact that his feet get cold and then he warms them against me, which can take your breath away sometimes, I must admit, the fact that it's a shock, the fact that I should be thinking of *warm* things, not Leo's feet, nanoparticles, ♫ *Mele Kalikimaka* ♫, the fact that it's warm in Alaska, I mean *Hawaii*, the fact that Leo's quite gangly, the fact that I wonder if Ben will be all tall and gangly soon, the fact that Jake still fits neatly into my lap, Celia, the fact that how does *that* help me warm up, thinking about Celia Johnson in the middle of all this, "But you don't understand my plight," the fact that my mind is wandering, the fact that maybe I'm delirious, the fact that I like peeling apples, the fact that they're so 3D, potatoes too, the fact that Leo really gets off on Messiaen, the fact that I'm not so gone on it, I gotta say, but I *try*, the fact that I prefer watching *The Odd Couple*, especially when I'm baking, the fact that it's the dialogue that counts, the fact that Walter Matthau always plays good guys, except in *Fail-Safe* where he's a bad guy who wants a nuclear holocaust, the fact that *The Apartment*'s good for baking purposes, but there's no Matthau, only Jack Lemmon, the fact that they gave Shirley MacLaine really embarrassing roles to play as she got older, the fact that Fran Kubelik is probably the best part she ever had, the fact that I hate *Being There*, the fact that I hate being *here*, the fact that Leo likes it, *Being There*, not being here, and I don't know why, the fact that Shelley Winters always had to play floozies, just because she got a little plump and "mature," the fact that it's freezing even inside the car, the fact that I'll put the heat back on for a spell, or else I'll have to rub my feet with *snow* like Almanzo, to get the blood flowing again, the fact that I hope it doesn't come to that, the fact that I don't want chilblains, or corns or ingrown toenails or *any* podiatry trouble, the fact that we can't afford it, the fact that you spend your whole life worrying about gangrene but most people never get gangrene, same with tetanus, the fact that who has not worried about tetanus and who actually ever gets it, the fact that tetanus seems sort of old-fashioned now, like dropsy or something, whoopsie, whooping cough, word for word, work to be done, *The 39 Steps*, the fact that Messiaen was a prisoner of war, and he wrote the "Quartet for the End of Time," the fact that the prison guard helped him get instruments to play it on and eventually even helped him escape, but years later Messiaen refused to meet up with him, the fact that maybe he still bore a grudge or something, about Nazism, the fact that tempers must run high in a prison camp, stalag, the fact that I'm f-f-frrrreeeeeezing, the fact that I've got to, ahhhh, ahhhhh, ahhhh, heat, ahh, okay, heat's on, it's coming, the fact that this is better already, though the window's so steamed up I can't see what's going on out there, the fact that that guy's got a big carload of kids, so of course he won't help me, the fact that more men participate in parenthood these days, the fact that Leo's always been involved, the fact that he can throw a little kid up in the air for hours, *and* get them safely across the street, the fact that who cares if he once put Jake's onesie on upside down, with his head coming out of the diaper hole, *Jake's* head, not Leo's, movie theater shooting rampage, the fact that it's getting so you're nervous to be in any public place now, in case there's a *shooter*, and that just doesn't seem right, the fact that half of all fatal shootings begin as domestic incidents, *half*, weird, the fact that with kids around we often end up with a lot of over-ripe bananas, and that's handy for banana bread, ivy patch, peaches in cream, Mommy, losing Mommy, buttercups, ♫ *I am little Buttercup, sweet little Buttercup* ♫, corns, swollen ankles, frostbite, lipstick, the fact that it's really microbes that rule the world, and they'll just read- just themselves if we nuke ourselves, I guess, my plight, plight my troth, the fact that, heavens to Betsy, I sure hope my current plight is not being repeated on sixty million other planets, the Milky Way, the fact that I can't get that "Mele Kalikimaka" out of my head, ♫ *Mele Kalikimaka is Hawaii's way* ♫,

. . .

She had seen him in the forest. He moved languidly through the trees. He hadn't seen her – she was careful to avoid notice. But she hoped he would be the one to come when she called.

He smelled her scat, took in her scratches on bark. In silence he approached one night, until she heard his breathing. He rubbed against her tentatively, purring. She hissed, unsure, unused to any contact but that of predator and prey. He, too, rarely touched another lion except to fight. He retreated, but continued to walk near her, within twenty paces, for the next few nights. Soon he was sleeping just out of reach of her claws. She could feel his breath and the warmth of his body.

They hunted together, side by side. There were no disputes over the meat, since he always let her eat first. As she tore at the choicest parts, the livers, hearts, he only purred more loudly.

One day, he nuzzled her and licked her thighs. Instead of a spit or a swat she sank to the ground and lay still. He went on licking, until her eyes closed in delight.

When he clasped her tight from behind, she twisted round in surprise, but she subdued an impulse to growl. She settled beneath him, bearing more and more of his weight as he mounted her. Soon she was yowling in ecstasy, filling the forest with her pleas. At her urging he clung to her until she was all fuck, and every point of connection between them made her come – his every purr, his every thrust.

They were entwined all day. Not like coyotes. Coyotes fuck on rocky mountainsides in a great hurry, they fuck wherever they find themselves, standing up. Somehow there is never anywhere for them to lie down. But lions own the earth, and can lie across it if they will.

He didn't leave her side for days. It was the closest companionship the lioness had known since babyhood. The previous year she had mated with a young lion who was nervy, easily distracted, clumsy and slow in lust. The encounter was awkward, painful and barren. But she grew used to her new lover's touch and felt herself drawn to rub and purr and butt her head into his side, murmuring.

But just as his presence became familiar, unthreatening, and without constraint, resistance crept in. The wish for release rose within her. His attentiveness was nauseating, suffocating. His possessiveness, his proximity, the very smell of him, now revolted her. She slept, and there he lay beside her. She woke, and there he sat. His purr made her feel hot, when she longed to be cool, alone, and free to roam. Recoil and leap, leap and recoil.

She missed her alone life, and demanded it back, with snarls and swipes of the claws. He bared his teeth and hissed in surprise. She slunk away. Three cubs conceived, and passion spent.

.   .   .   .

poffertjes and maple syrup, the fact that I already *knew* Stacy wouldn't have any bacon, the fact that she doesn't have to say it that way, the fact that she'll have the *poffertjes* though, I know that, the fact that no one can resist poffertjes, the fact that I can't make them fast enough to satisfy the demand, the fact that this is fun, our Saturday treat, the fact that it's nice when they all gather around like seals waiting to be thrown a fish, pufferfish, the fact that it's Jake who calls them puffers, instead of poffertjes, syrup, the fact that it gives you a great sense of power, dishing up dozens of poffertjes to your family as they wait with bated breath, whatever that means, *baited* breath, abate, debate, the fact that I can only make fifteen at a time, and they disappear pretty fast into this family, I eo too, the fact that I could get a nineteen-cake skillet, nineteen's the next size up, **19** cake, but *Mommy* bought this poffertje pan, puffers, more OJ, the fact that I like to think we're probably the only family for miles around having poffertjes for breakfast, the fact that I just don't know what the rest of Ohio's waiting for, except that they're all so scared of foreign stuff, the fact that I'm sure they'd like them if they tried them, the fact that all of Holland does, for a start, the fact that maybe I should spread the word that puffers are "Rrrreally good!," poffertjes, I mean, the fact that maybe I should be making poffertjes for all our neighbors, be neighborly, the fact that if it weren't for my *shyness*, I'd probably be the biggest Earth Mother going, the fact that I'd take in strays, hold cocktail parties, dinner parties, picnics, cookouts, the whole deal, with hampers and checked tablecloths and a portable barbecue and a whole load of fried chicken and potato salad, live band, Hallowe'en parties, match-making, baby showers, vow renewal parties, mass sleepovers, you name it, nurse the sick, chauffeur everybody else's kids to school, run a stall at the farmer's market, sell eggs door-to-door, make pies and poffertjes for everybody in sight, no middlemen, talk suicides down from precipices, grab toddlers out of harm's way when they wander lost on busy roads, the fact that I'd happily do just about anything for people, anything, even spend time with them, if they'd just stop hurting my feelings, ♫ *De pony bein' berry shy* ♫, more poffertjes, more, the fact that everybody wants more, "Please, sir," okay, okay, hold your horses, syrup, ouch, hurt, hurts, "non-bruising encounters," the fact that even with Cathy I still worry about what we'll say to each other, *every time we talk*, or if she'll even want to speak to me, and I'm so shy, sometimes I don't want to see her, just in case she's a little distant with me for some reason, even if it's nothing to do with me, which is kind of sad, since she's my best friend in Ohio, "my best friend in the district," Hannay, and the only person who seems to like me in this whole state, besides *Leo* I mean, and of course *Jesus*, who *saved* me, Jesus López Pérez, the fact that even though Cathy's never ever been unfriendly, I still have this dread of arriving at some not perfect time, or saying the wrong thing, the fact that I never want to be this unwelcome broad, bursting into the store with her kids and her cool bags, the fact that I never know if I'm staying too long, talking, outstay your welcome, the fact that guests are like fish, they stink after three days, the fact that I dread offending her in the slightest, all because *I'd* be so offended, like if she was even just a little distracted, or seemed indifferent, or anything, even if it was just that she had to break away to serve a customer or answer the phone, the fact that I can get so hurt it wrecks everything, the fact that these worries make me almost not want to see her at all, the fact that it really does scare me off, Nachbar, and I know I'm being silly, *more* puffers, okay, guys, the fact that look at that sunlight coming in, the fact that the trees seem to be winking at me, rag rugs, brick wallpaper, the fact that it's hard not to think everything's right with the world when you see sunlight glinting through leaves, but it might not be true, of course, the fact that things could go wrong and the sun might still glint, like the pink and blue sunrise the morning Daddy died, the fact that it's good to be indoors, warm and cozy, after my scary escapade, safe with my kids all around me, the fact that I dreamt I was a teenager staying with a family far from home, and I was supposed to go to school, but I could never remember the school's name or where it was, so I was always lost, the fact that sometimes you wonder why kids go along with the whole school thing, the fact that some teachers try to make it enjoyable, I know, the fact that then there was this big flood and everyone got out their kayaks to get around the place in, the fact that I didn't have a kayak because I didn't really belong, the fact that I took my shoes off because it seemed easier to climb the muddy hill barefoot, more poffertjes quick, butter, maple syrup, Abby's broom cupboard, the fact that I keep thinking about *Chuck* this morning, I don't know why, the fact that I was thinking about how we biked all over New Haven on his last day, trying to find a good place to lose our virginity, the fact that he was leaving for Washington and we knew we wouldn't see each other for months, the fact that it was all over by the time we did meet up again, despite the letters, my shoebox full of love letters, treasure trove, the fact that now I begin to wonder why we left it so late, our deflowering, I mean, the fact that maybe we didn't *really* want to do it, but felt we had to, to prove our love, the fact that we were awfully young, the fact that we got to the old asylum, all overgrown and deserted, the fact that you couldn't help wondering if there were still a few maniacs hanging around in the bushes, but still, it was as private a place as we were going to get, the fact that he didn't say so or act it but I bet Chuck was a little spooked too, too spooked to, well, the fact that I took down my jeans and lay down on a bed of pine needles, and he smiled down at me, but nothing happened, the fact that I wasn't too clear on what was even supposed to happen, the fact that that's how young we were, but we *were* in love, the fact that the *next* time we met, when he came back from Washington for a week, he didn't love me anymore, the fact that I was probably a burden to him, the fact that I was always despairing about our being separated and he was always having to comfort me, and he must have gotten sick of it, "loving longest," the fact that that's what Anne Elliot says, that women love the longest, when all hope is gone, the fact that I was lost without him, and Mommy was sick, the fact that to this day I don't feel too warmly towards Washington, Flight 93, though we like the *eaglecam*, the fact that Gillian's keeping an eye on the eagle chicks with me this year, the fact that they live way up there in the treetops while the politicians tie themselves in knots down below, puffers, more poffertjes, the fact that it took me several *more* years in the end to lose my virginity, the fact that I bet eagles don't have any trouble losing their virginity, Pepito at the commune, the fact that I *tried* to love Frank but that wasn't a love you could spread yourself out in, "Buck up," William Hurt, hurts, buckeye, buckskin, Davy Crockett, Daniel Boone, coonskin caps, the fact that Cathy always used to get Daniel Boone and Davy Crockett mixed up, Betty Crocker, the fact that I set her straight, Alamo, 5¢ stamp, 6¢ stamp, the fact that William Hurt's so *hurt* at the beginning, *The Accidental Tourist*, before Geena Davis cheers him up, "Muriel Pritchett," the fact that it's set in Baltimore, and Geena Davis works at a dog kennel, the fact that in real life Geena Davis is in Mensa and has the same IQ as George Washington, the fact that how'd they ever figure out George Washington's IQ, the fact that William Hurt and Kathleen Turner lost their son a year back, the fact that he got shot by a "holdup man" at twelve years old, Ben, so then Kathleen Turner leaves William Hurt and there he is, all alone, George Washington, knocking around in that big house with just a corgi for company, the fact that the dog belonged to his son originally, the fact that the dog's a mess too, and he's called Edward, like my mouse, Edward, the fact that not many dogs or cats are called Walter, *Sleepless in Seattle*, the fact that William Hurt's always trying to get Edward to come down in the basement but Edward has a phobia about it, the fact that one day Edward's barking at the top of the basement steps while William Hurt's down there doing the laundry, and he's coaxing Edward to come down and Edward's just about to try when the washer makes a terrible racket and Edward leaps into the air, landing right on William Hurt, who falls backwards and slips on the skateboard laundry basket and breaks his leg, the fact that you can't help laughing, even though William Hurt's hurt and everything, more poffertjes required, the fact that sometimes I tell myself the plots of movies when I'm cooking or I can't sleep, and I get them all mixed up, with Bette Davis falling in love with Trevor Howard instead of Celia Johnson, the fact that I only really like the *early* parts of *The Accidental Tourist*, when William Hurt's all sad about the son and the wife and the dog, the fact that

Edward had three babies, my mouse Edward, not Edward the corgi, the fact that after he breaks his leg, William Hurt and Edward have to go stay with his sister and two brothers, in another nice shady old Baltimore place, the fact that I like those old Baltimore homes, the fact that Anne Tyler herself probably lives in a house like that, sun glinting, syrup, the fact that William Hurt's house has a laundry chute and, if you ask me, *all* homes should have one, the fact that I think William Hurt beat up his girlfriend or something, in real life, but I try not to think about that, the fact that he's good in *Broadcast News*, but he hurts Holly Hunter's feelings when he tells her to forget about coming over after the Correspondents' Dinner, just when she's decided she's in love with him, which she isn't really, the fact that she's just sorely tempted, Milwaukee Student Punches Teacher, the fact that the tail ends of eggplants look like the blunt noses of killer whales, the fact that French women do twenty-five times as much housework as men, and Canadian women do five times as much, the fact that I don't know how much housework American women do, the fact that Hillary Clinton says she does all the *emotional* labor in their home, the fact that she said this involved organizing all their parties and family get-togethers and that sort of stuff, the fact that I'm really terrible, the fact that how the heck does Hillary have time to organize all those parties and I can't even get one little cocktail party off the ground, without flipping, flipping, but bringing up four crazee kids is more than enough emotional labor for me, Bill Clinton ogling Melania at the inauguration, the fact that I guess people think Melania's pretty attractive, the fact that she always seems to me to be squinting, but I guess that's what men like, in Washington, Chuck, the fact that I like the way Holly Hunter talks, the fact that it would be good if she suddenly turned up in *The Accidental Tourist* and told Geena Davis how mean William Hurt can be, the fact that she and William Hurt got along, professionally, when they were just working on TV news together, but they can never figure out how to be together in private, the fact that I think Geena might've been very interested to hear how he treated Holly Hunter, because he hurts Geena too, when he suddenly retreats and goes back to Kathleen Turner, the fact that he's always drawing himself *away*, that guy, just like Chuck, the fact that Baltimore isn't all that far from Washington, so she could make it, Holly Hunter I mean, the fact that, actually, she could go see *Chuck* too while she's at it, the fact that Hurt's very indecisive, Hunter, hunted, hurt, the fact that a hunter near Baltimore shot down a goose and it fell right on top of his hunting partner, who was knocked unconscious, Hunter Hurt, Davina Beebee, the fact that Daniel Boone shot a panther, and a lot of bears too, I think, and then some Indians, and for that he got on a 6¢ stamp, Wounded Knee, the overgrown grounds of the asylum, straitjacket, Cy Young, gun capital, butter, mozzarella, oranges, Play-Doh, printer ink, Chuck, ductile-brittle transition temperature, the fact that poor women are more than *twice* as likely to be raped, which is not a nice thing to think about, and cleaners in hotels too, the fact that they are *always* being molested by the guests, the fact that it's just not safe to send a woman into people's rooms like that, the fact that they should always go in pairs, the fact that somebody just shot dead four people in Cleveland, young marrieds with kids, the fact that the guy was angry because he'd been rejected by one of the women he killed, the fact that a friend of his said the guy's interests were "guns and guns and guns and shooting and beer," duck and cover, twist and shout, uptick, the fact that he was wearing a bulletproof vest but without the ballistics panels, *more* puffers, the fact that that Cleveland guy, who held the young women captive for ten years in his basement, now wants *visiting* rights, so he can see the kids he fathered, the kids he didn't *kill*, that is, because his usual policy was to cause a miscarriage by beating his prisoners up whenever he got them pregnant, the fact that that's a deadbeat dad to beat all deadbeat dads, deadheading, the fact that his only excuse for his behavior was "I like sex," Nina Turner, Rice Pops, diced onions, spaghettini, blood oranges, the fact that orange oil gets gummy labels off stuff, orthodontist, the fact that Nina Turner's been working on trying to stop men getting visiting rights to kids they conceived through rape, the fact that you wouldn't think you'd *need* a law to settle a question like that, the fact that a mixture

248

of pineapple and salt takes varnish off, no, *tarnish*, the fact that nobody wants to take varnish off, the fact that women in operas sometimes kill *themselves*, rather than leave it to other people, *Otello*, the fact that as soon as the tenor shows signs of jealousy, you know the soprano's doomed, William Hurt, Holly Hunter, ballistics, the fact that Jack Lemmon and Shirley MacLaine are both depressed in *The Apartment*, puffers, the fact that not many movies show people being depressed, the fact that Celia whatshername's depressed at the beginning of *Brief Encounter*, because she's just had to say her final goodbyes to Trevor Howard, Chuck, the fact that they've only known each other for a few weeks in total, grit in her eye, "Here's mud in yer eye," the fact that Shirley MacLaine's in her eighties now, the fact that Daniel Day-Lewis is good at acting depressed, the fact that he usually seems depressed about *something*, D-d-d-daniel D-d-d-day-Lewis, the fact that Cathy says she has no time for depressed people, the fact that she thinks they should just snap out of it, the fact that he went off to Italy to work as a cobbler for a while, Daniel Day-Lewis, the fact that I didn't know there still *were* any cobblers, the fact that it sounds kind of like a fairy tale, "Then he went to Italy and became a cobbler," the fact that I bet elves came in the night and made all the shoes for him, happily ever after, the fact that it's hard to believe that Daniel Day-Lewis has cobbled, fairy, snow fairies, prance, pounce, the fact that Almanzo's dad saved a calf hide every winter, so the cobbler could come make shoes for the family, the fact that he stayed for *two weeks* making all their shoes, the fact that it's a big family, the fact that I wouldn't want a cobbler living here for two weeks, the fact that what if your shoes wore out before the cobbler's visit, the fact that "boughten" shoes were probably too expensive, the fact that the cobbler told good stories, the fact that he was actually a real fun guy to have around, probably more fun than Daniel Day-Lewis would be if Daniel Day-Lewis turned up once a year to make all our shoes for us, D-d-d-daniel D-d-d-day, Tuesday, yard work, cafetorium, a mani-pedi, the fact that a cafetorium is a cafeteria *plus* an auditorium, vomitorium, and a kegerator's a little fridge just for beer, the fact that a lot of men seem to want a kegerator, the fact that you must be really rich if you think you need a *kegerator*, Bud, Bud Light, the fact that people who like beer get so mad if the fridge is too full of other stuff that a lot of them do need their own fridge, Jesus "Talk is Cheap" Christ, oh dear, the fact that people used to have to open beer cans with a can-opener, totes, the fact that Jesus saved me, the fact that Junipero Serra just got canonized, the fact that he started slavery in California, *and* the first winery, neophytes, the fact that Serra converted a lot of Indians and then made them all work as slaves in the mission, probably making the wine too, the Indian Indenture Act of 1850, "Christ dug the ditches at Auschwitz," the fact that I should think about the slow shallow waves in that little lake in Michigan, clear water, gently rippling waves, a canoe or two bobbing around, the fact that the blue flowers growing out of our garage wall are such brave, tiny things, the only colorful thing around now, the fact that they're blue like the snow at twilight, the fact that they're doomed but they grow anyway, angiosperms, the fact that all purple plants contain antioxidants, the fact that anthocy-anins don't sound good but they *are*, the fact that they're just pigments that make flowers red, blue and purple, purple martins, blueberries, black rice, eggplants, ripe olives, snapdragons, puffers, yoga pants, the fact that that's what turns leaves red in the fall, *anthocyanins* not yoga pants, the fact that I feel like a short-order cook over here, slaving away, but it was my own idea, the fact that I asked them if there was any bacon left for me and they all looked so sheepish, the fact that it was funny, the fact that Stacy was the most embarrassed, because she'd just snatched the last piece, the fact that I'm glad she got a little protein, the fact that my kids don't like *Farmer Boy*, but I do, ice-cutting scene, Almanzo, Alamo, Indian corn, candy corn, the fact that, goodness, that was a well-run farm the Wilders had, in the Hudson Valley, the fact that everything seems to run like clockwork and every-body in the family runs around too, all day long, like I don't know what, the fact that Almanzo's mom's as busy as his dad, making butter and dyeing wool and carding and spinning and weaving it and sewing three-piece suits for all the men in the family, the fact that her butter's the best butter in the state too, the fact that she sells it for $250 and it all gets sent down to New York City, the fact that there's just not one moment to spare in that household, between all the work they have to do and all the food they all have to eat, the fact that there's ham and eggs and pancakes and muffins and cookies and preserves, and that's just breakfast, the fact that their cellar's fully-stocked for the winter with thousands of carrots and onions, the fact that there's no danger of starving there, not like the Wilders, who live more day-to-day, even in good times, the fact that even Almanzo's giant pumpkin's well fed, the fact that he gives it milk so it'll win a prize at the fair in Malone, the fact that nobody's allowed to move all day long on Sundays, the fact that that's tough, especially on a country kid, the fact that I think Laura envied Almanzo for his well-fed and more prosperous child-hood, the fact that William Hurt's related to Gloria Vanderbilt or some other aristocrat, Chuck, my shoebox full of Chuck's letters in the attic, Malone, Molly Malone, the fact that the Ohio State Fair has *piglet* racing, piglet racing, Piglet, boarlets, a hundred billion chickens, Chiclets, "Buck up," the fact that after Chuck, I still believed in people getting together, but after Frank, not so much, the fact that Leo cured me, the fact that Leo makes me feel better about everything, Paris, hummingbirds, baguettes, symbiosis, osmosis, two-car garage, the fact that it takes guts to love somebody and I just lost my courage there for a while, panthers, pearl tea, bubble tea, the fact that *Stacy* used to like them when she was younger, tea bubbles, not panthers, the fact that we went to that place in New Haven, the fact that bubble tea only started in the nineties, the fact that she didn't take to Leo at first, boeuf bourguignon, "boof," the fact that she'd sit on my lap and try to monopolize the conversation, funette, the fact that I probably didn't handle things right, too shy, and too in love, the fact that my shyness is another reason not to have kids, because kids inherit it, mush, mud, tiptoeing through slushy puddles on my way to school on the first day of spring, *The Birds*, the fact that I got my shyness from Mommy, who probably got it from *her* mom, except Abby wasn't shy, I don't think, and they had the same mom, so maybe shyness isn't necessarily passed on to your kids, the fact that *Barry's* shy though, the fact that Abby really liked people, the fact that she had about a million friends, just like Ethan and Phoebe, the fact that maybe they have *some* shyness, but not crippling shyness like mine, the fact that now people think shyness has something going for it, but I can't for the life of me imagine what, the fact that there are *TED talks* on how great shyness is, but I forget why, the fact that I don't even know why there are TED talks, the fact that Daddy hated me being so shy, and was always trying to coax me out of it, force me to make friends, always telling me to talk more in class and all, but it didn't take, just like those ugly shoes he bought me once, and the raincoat I never wore, corgi at the top of the cellar stairs, the fact that what I think is that anybody who can give a TED talk on shyness can't really be all that shy, because if *I* had to do a TED talk I'd drop dead, corpse, homemade coffin, armchair, dog dream, Dam Protester Woman Dies, dams, damsel, damn, darn, doggone it, though, come to think of it, I gave my fair share of talks at Peolia, but I didn't *like* it, the fact that I couldn't get out of it, the fact that I don't think I could even do it now, the fact that I guess maybe my shyness is getting *worse*, the fact that I think I got PTSD from teaching, or maybe shyness does grow with age, instead of magically fading the way Daddy always hoped it might, the fact that I think he thought I didn't try hard enough, but I did, the fact that I must've really been a disappointment to him, but I remember sitting on his lap on the stairs once and feeling really happy, complete, "Buck up," the fact that I only took that job at Peolia because we needed the money, the fact that I assumed I could do it because Mommy and Daddy both taught, and Phoebe and Ethan teach too, the fact that I think Mommy found teaching hard too though, because she was shy, the fact that I just dreaded every single seminar I had to run, the fact that I don't think I ever looked forward to a single one, though sometimes they weren't *so* bad, once they got going, but of course you never knew how it would go, and I exhausted myself over-preparing in case the whole thing flopped and the students went silent on me, the Silent Treatment, the fact that that nice guy really cracked me up once, the fact that he was talking about something like the Louisiana Purchase or something, something he found out online, some trail he'd followed, something you wouldn't think could ever be funny, but he made it funny, and the whole class was laughing, not just me, the fact that I had *tears* in my eyes from laughing, which is embarrassing, tears, bubble tea, balloon water, semolina balls, the fact that they *like* teaching, Ethan and Phoebe I mean, not semolina balls, and I don't, the fact that they're good at it, like Leo is, and I'm not, blueberries, blacksberries, cranberries, cardamom, basil, dill, myrrh, Rosencrantz and Guildenstern, the fact that I hadn't thought of that student for years, the trees at Peolia, roots spreading out like arteries, broken wrist, the fact that I can't understand how actors remember their lines, the fact that the kids can memorize stuff easily, time capsule, making memories, the fact that I can hardly remember a thing, even the good times, the fact that people get so *nostalgic* about everything, but I do too sometimes, or why would I want to go back to *Peolia* to see the trees or walk down Quitting Lane, where I used to go whenever I was sore about the job, TURN THE HANDLE, "Pull the string," pullet, powder puff, the fact that because I'm shy I have hardly any friends, the fact that *psychopaths* hardly have any friends, "guns and guns and guns and shooting," hypothermia, hydrangea, Jesus, touch wood, James's mom, James Thurber, the fact that Thurber grew up in Columbus, Ohio man, measles outbreak, chicken pox, people carriers, Zika, Brazil, the fact that I'm even shy with my own kids sometimes, the fact that I don't know why I had them, the fact that I never planned to have a such a big brood, with over-population and all, Planned Parenthood, but I was so crazy about Leo, and babies are so sweet, WATCH CHILDREN, the fact that I wasn't thinking too straight, I know, Single-Payer Insanity, the fact that what you sow, you reap, leap, the fact that I've made my bed and have to sleep in it, the fact that I wish I *could* sleep in it a little more, but with all these kids around there's not a lot of time for that, a stitch in time saves nine, what you sew, you rip, what you rip, you sew, my favorite pair of sewing scissors, so-so, the fact that I just got to feeling *fertile*, I guess, from being in love, so now I have to face sulky Stace, pedantic Ben, obsessive Gillian, and pell-mell Jake, the fact that gee, I make them sound like the *March* family, each with their own particular character flaw, black and white cookies, black-and-white movies, *Mr. Smith Goes to Washington*, Trump's inauguration, Melania's sky-blue straitjacket, the fact that it was probably made out of Kevlar, helmets, the fact that they use Kevlar for bulletproof vests, the fact that the woman who invented it came from New Kensington outside Pittsburgh, New Ken, nukin', nuke 'em, Newcomerstown, DuPont, Stephanie Kwolek, Kevlar, "What do we need so much Kevlar?", "Drop dead. You wanna drop dead?", bulletproof jacket, bomber jacket, flak jacket, straitjacket, Teflon, the fact that sometimes I forget how many kids I've *got*, I just know that there's a whole bunch of 'em, the fact that sometimes I have to count them, the fact that I should put a sign up on the fridge in case I forget, **4**, the fact that the kids are playing the tin foil game now, the fact that they can play it for hours, the fact that I don't even understand it except it involves a lot of tin foil coupons and Stacy usually wins, and Jake cries if he doesn't get enough coupons, so they sling him a couple extra ones now and then, the fact that they call it Mallrat, the fact that there was a boy crying outside the diner the other day, the fact that he was even smaller than Jake, and he was obviously crying because he was so *cold*, the fact that some people really don't wrap their kids up enough, the fact that kids can't control their body temperatures all that well, which not everybody seems to understand, "Capeesh?", and lose heat rapidly, but you can't tell them, because that would be mom-shaming, Mommy, kitchen, euphoria, "Waken up and smell the coffee," spirals, rolling out the dough, cinnamon, cardamom, orange zest and OJ, the fact that a good cinnamon roll depends on the type of flour and yeast, and the kneading, and how it's handled, the risings, the rollings, the spirals, the fact that you have to roll it out very, *very* thin to get the spirals right, but the real secret of my success, I owe to *Leo*, because he hates raisins, the fact that I hate raisins too, the fact that I think a *lot* of people hate raisins, the fact that Jake *loves* them but only if they come in a tiny box, the fact that I use dried sour cherries, *And that has made all the difference*, though I do do some with raisins on request, shady parking lot somewhere, sitting in clear shallow water as a kid, tiny rippling waves, the fact that there were crawdads in that lake, Angie's summer house, the fact that sour cherries add a tartness you don't get from raisins, raisings, risings, uprisings, raising kids, *Raising Arizona*, the fact that Holly Hunter's in that, the fact that I really liked the Mabons' summer place, the beautiful clear water, crawdads, me in my two-piece bathing suit, pebbly sand under my feet, the fact that I wished *we* had a summer place in Michigan, the fact that I still wish that, the fact that Montmorency cherries come from Michigan, MI, ME, Sun-Maid, the fact that raisins are really bad for dogs, also chocolate, the fact that Pepito ate a whole box of Whitman's Samplers once and had to go to the vet, the fact that when we went to pick him up, a parrot piped up from the side room "She's bringing your dog up now," the fact that that parrot was really on the ball, the fact that cats shouldn't eat all this fancy stuff full of kale and carrots, the fact that all cats need is *meat*, vet, Bliss, spirals, the fact that when Opal's outside she goes into her own world sort of, the fact that she turns feral and does her own thing, but Frederick never completely forgets about people because he likes to be patted so much, PFE, Pacific Fruit Express, refrigerated transport, the fact that Leo had a toy train when he was a kid that had its own PFE car, Harry & David's pears, peaches, grapes, the fact that the real Pacific Fruit Express had to get East *fast* with all the Californian oranges, empress, emperor penguins, the Aidans' quiet living room, the fact that the Chinese built the railways, sampans, Hong Kong harbor, King Kong, Selznick, black and white, velvet, velvet, red velvet cushion, red, white and black, the fact that when we bought Ben's train at the Amish store, the lady in charge kept asking "Be you sure?", like she thought it cost too much, but it was only twenty bucks and it's beautiful and all *hand-carved*, the fact that she was amazed we wanted it, the fact that I guess she couldn't believe anybody would pay that much for a toy, the fact that I still remember that deep purple dress she had on, the fact that it was a really nice purple, not purple-brown, or some other ugly kind of purple, purple martins, swallows, Oliver Twist, the fact that it must have been sitting on that high shelf for years, and she just thought nobody would ever want it, "Be you sure?", Amish carpentry skills, fall colors, stone steps, $20, the fact that Amish quilts often have good strong, solid colors against black backgrounds, not boring pale flower fabrics like everybody else makes quilts with, the fact that it's Ingredients List time again, for all the food-intolerance customers, gluten-free cinnamon rolls for people who hate gluten, a nut-free kind for nut allergies, a vanilla-less kind for Muslims, muslin, poncho, the fact that I really hate gluten-free flour, the fact that it's just not the same at all, and really hard to use, the fact that normal vanilla essence has ethanol in it, and there aren't that many Muslims in Tuscarawas County, I don't think, but you never can tell so it's simpler to just use non-alcoholic vanilla essence in everything, the fact that I guess I could grind vanilla powder from a *pod*, but that leaves tiny black specks in the food and who wants tiny black specks in their food, nanoparticles, sandblasting, the fact that, also, time is money, the fact that when you're a kid you always want to taste the vanilla, because it *smells* so good, and then you lick some and you're appalled, the fact that I usually get goats milk, soya milk or rice milk instead, for lactose-intolerant cinnamon rolls, the fact that they imprison the bees to make almond milk, the bees that fertilize the almond groves, the fact that I don't know why they have to be imprisoned but that's what the almond farmers do, the fact that sometimes I make nutty cinnamon buns for people who *don't* have problems with nuts, which is almost nobody, the fact that they drive me nuts with all their nut stuff, the fact that soon they'll want me to make a sugar- and butter- and flour-free version for people on a diet, and an air-free version for people allergic to air, and a beef-liver-flavored version for pets, but at some point you just have to say *these are the cinnamon rolls that I make,* the fact that I told the kids Jesus saved me but nobody's interested, ♫ *Jimmy crack corn, I don't care* ♫, *more* puffers, the fact that I've only got enough for about three more, *OPEN 24 HOURS,* Glacier Lake, dugout on the prairie, buffalo wolves, content farms,

Pryor And Brando Were Lovers, the National Organization for Marriage, NOM, the Lincoln assassination, *Psycho*, the fact that I always include an Ingredients List but they always lose it, the Ingredients List, not their tempers, "Waken up and smell the coffee," the fact that actually it's *me* that loses it sometimes, I'm sorry to say, especially when I'm right in the middle of making more cinnamon rolls and they call up about the last batch, with some customer mumbling in the background or taking off without a word, brownies, carrot cake, Amish gazebos, the fact that Seward was sick in bed when he got stabbed, the fact that that's not a fair fight, to stab someone in his bed, kicking him when he's down, the fact that it's like punching somebody who wears glasses, or hitting a woman, the fact that there used to be rules about stuff like that, but they didn't help *Seward* much, the fact that Seward was attacked the same night Lincoln was shot, the fact that his whole family got stabbed, and his wife was so shocked by it, she was never the same, and passed away just a few months later, the fact that Mary Lincoln never liked William Seward, but a lot of people never liked Mary Lincoln either, the fact that Ulysses S. Grant had a narrow escape that night, the fact that the Lincolns had invited him to join them in their box but he had a previous engagement, the fact that Ulysses S. Grant was a big drinker, black and white, apples'n'onions, feet, the fact that that's why I more or less gave up on nuts, not because of the *Lincoln assassination*, because of all the *phone calls*, the fact that it's easier if you just keep things nut-free, I find, though I can't claim there are no nuts on the *premises*, far from it, the fact that I don't know if the customers care about free range eggs but *I* do, so I put that on the Ingredients Lists too, the fact that I try to stick with only our eggs but it's not always possible, Zyker's Foods, IGA, B & J's hot roast beef sandwich, Jake on the Rodeo Rider, the fact that that thing makes him so happy, and then it's off to the gum ball machine, Anne Shirley, Celia Johnson, hydrangea, CVS, Ace Hardware, Ronny, barn owl, the Interstate Voter Registration Crosscheck Program, the fact that Ohio has removed two million voters from its registers since 2011, Barbara Bush, Hurricane Katrina, the fact that that's not playing fair really, Jesus saved me, the fact that it tickles me to say that, so I keep saying it, if only to myself, the fact that only Leo gets the joke, the fact that I guess it's not all that funny but I like it, the fact that I told everybody my school dream, with the kayaks and the bare feet and all, and Gillian said she'd dreamt about a pasha living nearby who had mysterious comings and goings at his house, the fact that that really killed me, a pasha, the fact that where'd she ever hear of *pashas*, dachas, Putin, Russian meddling, the fact that maybe she's studying pashas at school, *The Thousand and One Nights*, Scheherazade, the fact that *we* never got to study pashas, the fact that Leo said he dreamt he was Barbara Bush, and he was scared to leave his pocketbook anywhere because it contained very important documents, the fact that Jake dreamt about an owl, the fact that he said "But it's not a pure owl, it's also a boy," the fact that everybody else has better dreams than *me*, the fact that everybody has their own dreaming style, just like their own thinking style, and walking and talking style, the fact that I usually just dream that the bill comes to $145 instead of $124 because I didn't allow for tax, or that there was a huge airplane hovering in the back yard, unable to land, and we were signaling sympathetically to the passengers, and then the plane finally managed to twist itself around but, in the process, cut our phone line, or that a pregnant woman's eating a suspect slice of cake and I happen to know it might cause birth defects, and the only solution I can think up to the problem is to *reverse time*, so she won't be given that particular piece of cake, the fact that if that scheme didn't work out, I was going to tell her privately "Pregnant women shouldn't eat this kind of cake," the fact that somehow it never occurred to me to just take the darn cake *away* and give her something else, the fact that I don't know if it was shyness that was stopping me telling her, but maybe, the fact that that's kind of worrying, to be too shy to save somebody's *life*, not to mention her unborn baby's life, the fact that that's pretty darn cowardly, especially in a professional caterer, even if it's only in a dream, pasha, dacha, owl-boy, the fact that I used to like Frank's style of talking, Slow Talkers of America, Frank, Funk, the fact that he looks like Ringo

Starr, Sir Ringo, the fact that what is it like to be Trump, walking through that golden apartment of his in Manhattan, thinking "I'm president," the fact that sixty-nine percent of Democratic men want a woman president, and most Republican men can't stomach the idea, the fact that I don't know what that proves, the fact that middle-aged white men are all committing suicide now, statistically, the fact that extreme weather disasters have quadrupled since 1970, the fact that domoic acid is killing birds and seals in Oxnard, Southern California, domoic, demonic, *Raising Demons,* mnemonic, the fact that ninety-eight percent of insect species in Puerto Rico have disappeared, in just a few years, plankton bloom, the fact that the good news is the Amish are increasing in numbers, Celebrities That Are Currently In Jail, pelicans, loons, the snooze button, the fact that most dreams aren't worth repeating but every so often you have a really beautiful one, where everything's lit by a golden light and something really good happens, like swimming underwater, or flying dreams, or Mommy's back, alive and well, and we have a great talk and I know can see her as much as I want from now on, the fact that sometimes I dream Stacy's with me and the sun is setting and we're swimming together in calm, shallow, pale blue water, the fact that she's little, the fact that she's always little in my dreams, lap size, the fact that I seem to like to dream about her sitting on my lap, safe, the fact that I *miss* holding her, the fact that it becomes such a habit, touching your kids, and then they wrench themselves away from you, and the honeymoon's over, the fact that Stacy didn't tell us *her* dreams of course, the fact that she's so cranky in the mornings, and Ben denied he'd had any, total solar eclipse, partial solar eclipse, half-moon cookies, the fact that Frank's slow speaking style got annoying though, after a while, and one day I noticed the way he talks is too "*punctilious*," and I never got over realizing that, the fact that I can never tell Stacy, the fact that mothers have to keep quiet about so much stuff, "a forty-foot dive into a tub of water," the fact that Jean Arthur's real name was Gladys, the fact that she was born in 1900 so she was fifty-three when she made *Shane,* the fact that she had a funny way of talking too, but I like it, the fact that she hardly gets to say a word in *Shane* though, the fact that in *Mr. Smith Goes to Washington* she's called Clarissa, the fact that I'm supposed to call Kim at the market, PFOA, Gore-Tex, Akron, MLK, John Brown's Subterranean Pass-Way, passed away, pastor, Frederick Douglass, "Follow the Drinking Gourd," the fact that a hundred thousand slaves escaped through the Underground Railway, but millions didn't, the fact that they were all just left to sink or swim in the South, pull themselves up by the bootstraps when they had no boots, the fact that people still go visit the plantations for *fun*, Tara, the fact that Baltimore's the HQ of the KKK, the fact that some white boys tried to *lynch* a little eight-year-old black boy the other day, the fact that Florida was covered in Indian mounds made of crushed shells, but they all got destroyed to make the roads and railways, sand mounds, the fact that the shape of Indian mounds makes me think of pregnant women, or bras in the fifties, Buster crab, soft shell crab, shells, the fact that DuPont helped make the first nuclear bombs, the fact that their Hanford site is the dirtiest place on earth, the fact that it covers five hundred square miles of Washington State and all the toxins and radioactivity leak into the land and sea, the fact that one third of Americans live within fifty miles of nuclear waste, five hundred square miles, the fact that does that mean it's ten miles across and fifty the other way, or ten miles by *five*, the fact that I never know, but it's big anyway, the fact that it's more of a help really when they tell you something's the space of fifty Olympic swimming pools, or two hundred thousand elephants standing in a line, airline, the failing airplane cutting our phone line, flatlining, the fact that they found a fatberg in the London sewer, the fact that it's Victorian, not the fatberg, the *sewer*, the fact that London sewers can't cope with fatbergs anymore, the fact that they're all clogged up, the fact that fatbergs are made up of, well, kitchen grease and wet wipes and all kinds of unmentionable things, Nipplegate, breastfeeding, breast cancer, swapping bras, "What you need is a brow lift," Superbowl Halftime Show, the fact that they said it was the weight of a whole bunch of double-decker buses, the *fatberg*, I mean, the fact that I can't remember how many buses it was the length of, the fact that Cathy's dad had a plugged-up sink and it turned out he'd been putting his *drinking* straws down there, of all things, and nobody knows how long he's been doing it for, the fact that Mickey's got a roborovski, the fact that I thought that was a made-up name but it isn't, and his roborovski has the biggest habitrail I ever *saw*, the fact that however long and complex their habitrail is though, hamsters never seem very happy, hurricanes hardly ever happen, but it's hard to tell with a hamster, hampster, "Buck up," the fact that I think they're nocturnal, Mommy, the fact that I miss her, the fact that I never got over her illness, the fact that it broke me, the fact that you gotta live in the here and now, the fact that the sun still rises every morning, and there is twilight, when the sky glows, the fact that it happens twice a day, the fact that there are boarlets, and Leo and I get to sleep together almost every night, and the kids are healthy, the fact that Bette Davis said never look back, the fact that you gotta forward march, the fact that still, it's not nice to think radioactive material has been leaching out of Hanford into the Pacific Ocean *since the 1940s*, leach, leech, with everybody getting cancer and all, cluster, Custer, neo-Nazis, the fact that it's kind of strange for a government to poison its own people, I mean, gosh, the fact that you'd think these are the people it's supposed to be *protecting*, defense spending, arms deals, Russian meddling, hurricanes, intense vapor releases, vaping, the fact that there are fang-toothed tusky snake eels, and if you hang around with *kids* all day, this is the sort of stuff you find yourself thinking about, saber-toothed sand eels, but it makes a change from dinosaurs, hot sunlit wall in Paris, the fact that you get used to seeing strange things too in a household like this, like a small elephant passing by your bedroom door, the fact that Gillian's in her element doing her elephant, that she learnt in gym, the fact that she throws a towel over her head for the flappy ears, and one arm comes out like a trunk, swishing along in front of her, and the other hand does the tail, flicking back and forth, coordination exercise, the fact that it's like patting your forehead and rubbing your stomach at the same time, or the other way around, but it sure is cute, sammich, the fact that she also likes to "tie her guts in a knot," the fact that she acts like she's tying a big ship's rope neatly across her tummy, very neatly, the fact that I don't know why she finds that so funny but she does, and she can also do bacon frying, the fact that she lies flat on the floor and starts twitching all over, just now and then, the fact that Stacy got a good video of it on her phone, the fact that the teacher calls it Playing With Your Body, the fact that that's a pastime that probably isn't much encouraged after you reach puberty, sixth grade, seventh grade, grade school, the fact that it's certainly better than just flopping on the couch, the fact that Ben flops but then he suddenly gets up to throw imaginary grenades, but that's not really exercise, Ruth Dardis's apartment in New Haven, the fact that it doesn't really take much strength, the fact that once I lay on the cement at the top of the hill behind Abby's house, on a nice sunny day, I guess when Abby was taking a nap, the fact that that was nice, the fact that I used to do things like that then, the fact that Ben just throws it *lightly* too, the imaginary grenade I mean, the fact that it's not like he's trying to throw it very far, fourteen-year-old dog, sedentary, Ben and Gillian, the fact that they were really stuck on those magic 3-D pictures, the fact that they didn't move a muscle for weeks, the fact that they just stared and stared for hours, the fact that it's quite a relief that particular craze seems to be over, especially since I could never figure out how to do it, the fact that Bette Davis's daughter wrote a horrible book about her, the fact that she got married at sixteen, Bette Davis's daughter, not Bette Davis, the fact that Stacy's almost that age now, the fact that people get married before they know anything, the fact that they get married before they can drink or even vote, the fact that the more I read about the orbit of the moon, the less I understand it, the fact that I wonder if anybody truly understands this stuff, but I suppose they do, *I don't know but they know*, no ifs or buts, don't mention it, I'm outta here, true-ups, mash-up, sampling, sapling, starling, the fact that it saddens people, I think, to find out you're dumb, so you try not to show it, the fact that I've been doing that all my life, but it gets *tiring* putting on a front, Daddy teaching me to read in London, the fact that Emily Dickinson never dared admit to her dad she didn't know how to tell the *time*, the fact that he'd explained it once to her and that was supposed to be enough, the fact that I wouldn't have dared tell *my* dad that either, the fact that the rest of my class was ahead of me when I got to Channing, milk and rusks at break time, school soap, Hampstead Heath, Daddy's remedial reading lessons, the fact that he seemed so angry with me, it scared me, and I was embarrassed I couldn't read, sheik, harem, purdah, pasha, the fact that I've spent my whole life being embarrassed, harem pants, the fact that I just saw a bee, the fact that what's a bee doing out in *February*, raccoons, tattoos, saloon, moonshine, whiskey, moonshine whiskey, *wh*iskey, *wh*, whh, the fact that that's another thing, the fact that I always forget to pronounce my *wh 's*, the fact that I never noticed everybody was pronouncing "wh" that way, until I was a grown woman, *wh*oman, and that's embarrassing too, lazy talker, the fact that a Dover woman was hit by a speeding car at 3:00 in the afternoon, a speeding hotrod car, and it killed her, crushed her, the fact that the guy was doing ninety-five in a thirty-five mile-per-hour zone, but he blamed it on the *woman*, for nosing her car out on the highway and getting in his way, what a heel, *wh*hat a hhheeel, snaggled-toothed sand eel, *wh*h, whiskey, *wh*hiskey, *wh*hich *wh*hittler is *wh*hittier and *wh*en, *wh*y, *wh*o, *wh*om, *wh*ale, the Princess of *Wh*ales, football *wh*atch parties, the fact that we, *wh*ee, need some more Saran wrap, the fact that I want to do a Saran wrap *ball* next time we have a kids' party, *wh*ich is *wh*en, the fact that I can't remember, the fact that Ben's next, then Gillian, the fact that some moms seem to give birth to all their kids on practically the same day of the month, however many years apart, which is handy if you want to double up on birthday parties and things, the fact that it kind of makes you wonder though how it could've happened, a Magritte street, salmon spawning, radioactive salmon, bald eagles, the fact that bald eagle eggs always hatch at the end of March, that clear shallow water at the edge of the lake, pebbles underwater, the fact that it isn't really fair to have to share your birthday party, the fact that why should you, individuality, lucked out, luck of the draw, the fact that some parents give all their children names starting with the same letter, like J or M or S or whatever, and make them wear matching outfits, the fact that you stick lots of little presents in the ball, in between layers of Saran wrap, the fact that each kid gets to unwrap it until they reach a gift, and then they pass it on to the next child, the fact that it probably wastes of heck of a lot of Saran wrap but it looks like fun, and I need a few party solutions around here, the fact that I never know what to do for their parties except bake stuff, birthday cake, Sausage and Potato Bake, Dollar General, the fact that I can get all the little trinkets to put in the Saran ball at Dollar General or Walgreens or CVS or someplace, candy corn, the fact that maybe I should do an *adult* version for our cocktail party, with cigars in it, and earrings and cufflinks and such, like an ice-breaker, arctic thaw, but I'd be too shy, the new normal, the fact that shooting your ex-wife seems to be the new normal, the fact that men can be so *touchy*, the fact that he was driving 95 mph in a 35 mph zone, the fact that that's just crazee, the fact that Winnie the Pooh made Dorothy Parker fwow up, *The House at Pooh Corner*, the fact that I didn't like those books at first either but I got to like them, the fact that Gillian likes Pooh and Piglet, and Jake's attached to his toy Eeyore, because he likes unbuttoning the tail, the fact that I spend half my life searching for that tail, maternal love, the fact that now Jake's wondering *wh*y I keep making all these blowing sounds to myself, *Blow wwwinds and crack your cheeks*, the fact that Trump is like King Lear with all his tantrums, the fact that he even has a favorite daughter, the fact that people are *lining up* to play the Fool, Sparkle Plenty doll, Swanson TV dinners, the fact that at least King Lear could form a *sentence*, the fact that soon we won't remember what it's like to have a president who can do that, the fact that it's lucky King Lear wasn't in charge of any nuclear codes, *Blow winds*, the fact that Leo made fun of me for not pronouncing "wh" word's right, so now I've got a hangup about it, the fact that with every "w" I say, I *wh*onder if it's wight, right, the fact that I've got to master it, or at least make a gesture, court jester, gesticulate, because it's embarrassing not to pronounce "wh" *wh*ords *wh*right, the fact that

I can't seem to help making a fool of myself all the time, the fact that it just seems to come completely naturally to me, like when I called that civil engineer "Mario" when his name's *Dario*, the fact that I'm always lousing things up that way, especially with Leo's colleagues, the fact that it's like a compulsion with me, the fact that I'm bound to do something wrong at the cocktail party, the fact that I really think I've been embarrassed more or less from birth, Mommy, Ethan, hamsters, the fact that Gillian's got to get going on her John Brown project soon, ♫ *John Brown's body lies a-moldering in the grave* ♫, the fact that John Brown's family had a tannery in Hudson, just north of Akron, ♫ *John Brown's body lies a-moldering in the grave* ♫, and he started another tannery in Pennsylvania, as a front for the Underground Railroad, ♫ *John Brown's body lies a-moldering in the grave* ♫, ear worm, the fact that nobody much talks about *tanneries* these days, in normal conversation, "I'll tan your hide, young man," the fact that we're all too busy talking about computers to talk about tanning and cobbling, the fact that John Brown *wasn't* on Snapchat, he was running the Underground Railway, the fact that he was an expert on sheep-breeding too, ♫ *His pet lambs will meet him on the way* ♫, the fact that Gillian figured that out, the fact that I don't know if she's told her group, the fact that everything's got to be done in a group these days, the fact that I did my school projects all by myself, the fact that I did one on mystical medieval animals, and one on gemstones, the fact that I drew a lot of pictures of rubies and emeralds for it, the fact that I think I did one on Minneapolis too, or Duluth anyway, and Stephen Foster, and Amerigo Vespucci was another one, the fact that Amerigo Vespucci came from Florence and had a beautiful cousin-in-law, the fact that Stephen Foster died at the age of thirty-seven, the fact that I didn't really get who he *was* when I did my project on him, the twin cities, yogic flying, the fact that I remember looking stuff up in the school library, maybe the public library too, the fact that the school library had wall-to-wall carpeting and a nice smell from the children's books, the fact that everybody we know is getting rid of their books, and we probably should too, paperlessness, sustainability, palm oil, the fact that my report was on *Duluth*, the fact that I can remember the map I had to do, the fact that I don't know how much geography they get at school anymore, Tom Hanks, the fact that they seem to get most of their understanding of American geography from tornado reports, the fact that Bill Murray makes a pretty good weather man in *Groundhog Day*, the fact that most of them aren't as good as he is, and I instantly forget what they've said and have to look it up again and again online, so there's hardly any point in watching the weathermen plow through it all, the fact that at school once, we all acted out the news and I think *I* was a weathergirl, the fact that I bet I wasn't as good as Bill Murray either, the fact that later John Brown moved back near Hudson, where Kent State University is, or close to it, Kent State Massacre, Zenas Kent, Franklin Mills, Mommy, Chuck, the fact that he was hanged in 1859 but he spurred on the whole abolitionist debate, black-and-white movies, the fact that things are getting polarized again right now, Ku Klux Klan, the fact that the Tea Party started in Texas, I think, but it could have been Ohio, the fact that they could have chosen Stephen Foster, I mean Gillian's group could've, for their *project*, the fact that she could have done Harriet Tubman, Frederick Douglass, Stonewall Jackson, William Henry Seward, Lysander Spooner, Nat Turner, Nina Turner, Ida B. Wells, James Baldwin, Elijah Lovejoy, Sojourner Truth, or somebody else, I can't remember who, *who*, *wwho*, the fact that maybe it was Leatherlips, I can't remember, or not, the fact that I think it was Elizabeth Freeman, Mumbet, but John Brown's a good choice, Prize Draw, Appalachia, the Blue Ridge Mountains, the Smokies, the Rockies, the Adirondacks, Adirondack chairs, the fact that I can't sit on Adirondack chairs anymore and Leo calls them "'Ow-da-ruin-yer-back chairs," Living Treasures Animal Park, Leatherlips, guilty land, field goal, the fact that everybody knows about the UGRR but not everybody knows it started in the late *1700s*, the fact that Ulysses S. Grant's father was an apprentice to John Brown's father, the fact that John Brown had twenty kids, so what's my four compared to that, "I, John Brown," the fact that I like it when Gillian stands on a chair to proclaim "I, John

Brown, am now quite certain that the crimes of this *guilty land*," the fact that she does the "guilty land" bit just right, the fact that now they think John Brown was an influence on John Wilkes Booth, the idea that one violent act can change history, the fact that John Wilkes Booth had an *obsession* with John Brown, and disguised himself as a soldier so he could watch the hanging, the fact that Quantrill thought hanging wasn't good enough for John Brown, Harpers Ferry WV, snake oil, Laurence Massacre, Hartford, CSCU, dirty dish water, the fact that it seems like American history is pretty violent, the fact that after Lincoln, assassinations were the new normal, Garfield, McKinley, Kennedy, the fact that almost every president since Andrew Jackson has had assassination *attempts* at the very least, Quantrill, quadrille, Cassini, the fact that there are river channels on one of Saturn's moons and Cassini took pictures of them, the fact that Leatherlips was executed with a tomahawk for talking to white settlers, Dublin, Ohio, the fact that some of the Wyandots lived in caves, Greenville Treaty, the fact that the Indians sold Ohio to the government for twenty thousand bucks, the fact that I'd have done Frances Seward if I were Gillian, because she was a great abolitionist and a mom, month, moon, queen, Top Cat, top hat, national anthem, the fact that Mumbet said "I'm not a dumb critter. Won't the law give me my freedom?", the fact that "The Star-Spangled Banner" is racist, the fact that Leo doesn't think it's much of a song anyway, songthaew, the fact that Ben's got to do a project on Francis Scott Key, the fact that he was opposed to abolition, Key, not Ben, the fact that Leatherlip's brother was called Roundhead and I get him mixed up with Colonel Broadhead, Colonel Daniel Broadhead, who launched the Broadhead Massacre, the fact that he and his three hundred men destroyed Coshocton and killed twenty Indians, the fact that it was an enormity, *Tosca*, *Rigoletto*, *Il trovatore*, high C, three hundred men, cowards, the fact that there's a crossbow blade called a broadhead, and I hope it's not named after the Broadhead Massacre, the fact that I *think* it's just because the head of the blade is broad, so as to do maximum damage, the fact that why would someone *need* a weapon like that, the fact that you can buy them in packs of three, three-blade cut head, three hundred men, Bloodrunner 2 blade, tomahawks, rear blades, arrows, entry and exit holes, wound channels, canals, Chestnut Street, the fact that there was a lecture on the Broadhead Massacre at the Johnson-Humrickhouse, the fact that there is something rotten in the state of, well, *many* states, the fact that sometimes it just seems like there's not much respect around for *human life*, Jell-O, belly-dancers, belly button, jelly beans, beanbag, sleeping bag, the mechanics of wiggling, the mailman, Abby's big jade plant, the fact that that thing lived for years and just got bigger and bigger, sitting on Abby's nice, sunny coffee table, the fact that she had a mailman she liked, the fact that I don't think we get mail delivered every day anymore, River Roost, 43832, the fact that it seems more and more sporadic, and we aren't even all that rural, not like some people who *know* they aren't going to get mail for weeks, or months, or *ever*, Cy, the fact that somebody on the radio just got all emotional and said free health care's a right, because if somebody's drowning you don't go asking him if he can pay you, you save him anyway, the fact that six hundred and thirty thousand people are on Obamacare in Ohio, but who knows what'll happen now, the fact that Single Payer might make things cheaper, and easier, but if there isn't the will, I guess it ain't gonna happen, the fact that who in Ohio's going to vote for Medicare For All, the fact that Harrison Ford treats *himself*, but that's in *The Fugitive*, where he's a doctor, so he knows what he's doing, the fact that in *Witness* he's a police inspector, the fact that when he gets shot he doesn't do anything about it, the fact that he just drives Kelly McGillis back to the farm, with the boy, and then Harrison Ford finally he conks out at the wheel and crashes straight into their big purple martin house, and Kelly McGillis has to nurse him back to health, the fact that some purple martin lovers go out and kill *starlings*, the fact that everybody hates starlings for some reason, but it's even worse with people who own martin houses, the fact that those people *really* hate starlings, also sparrows and blue jays, the fact that they call them all non-native species and run for their air rifles when they see one, the fact that I've seen blue jays my whole entire life, so how come they're not native, Native Americans, African Americans, Chinese Americans, visa lottery, the fact that Kent, Ohio, is now ninety-one percent white, the fact that I guess nobody's supposed to move around, you're just supposed to stay put, no foreigners allowed, Muslim ban, the fact that purple martins are *migrants* though themselves, so I don't get it, broadhead, broadband, *Pride and Prejudice*, the swallows of Capistrano, purple dish soap, the fact that maybe purple martins are endangered or something, the fact that it's hard to keep up with which birds are the nice ones and which are the bad ones, the fact that, according to Ben, a quarter of all the bird species we've got now will be extinct by 2100, or even sooner maybe, the fact that Pa Ingalls is always shooting hawks and blackbirds, because the blackbirds eat the corn, and the hawks eat other birds or their eggs or something, the fact that it doesn't make a whole lot of sense, the fact that maybe if he'd just left the hawks alone, they would've helped him out with the blackbirds, the fact that these campaigns to rid the world of some species or other of bug or bird or beast usually backfire somehow, ♫ *She swallowed a spider to eat the fly* ♫, blacksbirds pie, the fact that there used to be cougars in Ohio, and now they're thinking of allowing them *back* because there are too many deer, the fact that people keep crashing their cars into deer, the fact that originally they killed all the cougars off because they didn't want them eating the deer, but now they *want* them to, go figure, the fact that I guess it's too late now just to leave the ecosystem to fend for itself, since we've destroyed most of it, the fact that when they got scared about Zika they started building bat houses everywhere, because bats eat mosquitoes, but I bet once the Zika scare's over, it'll be bye-bye Battie, geraniums, nasturtiums, Corpse Flower, the fact that we should make another trip to de Monye's Greenhouse some time, where I got my hen and chicks, not *real* chicks, *succulent* chicks, oh, the fact that that sounds kind of racy, succulent chicks, the fact that hen and chicks is a much better name though than Beard of Jupiter, the fact that the whole point is the main plant gets surrounded by these cute smaller ones, like *chicks*, not like *beards*, the fact that sometimes I find myself talking to *myself* in baby talk, Djibouti, whhh, the fact that purple martins are welcome because they eat insects, but sharks eat people, so they're not, even though sharks are going extinct too, shark in a shed, the fact that there are almost no hawks left now because people decided against *them* long ago, to protect game or fish stocks for people, the fact that they polluted the Cuyahoga so much there weren't any fish anyway, but now the Cuyahoga's got some fish again and there are some bald eagles there now, "There, there now," the fact that maybe people will leave them alone this time, Marnie's hurt horse, the fact that Native Americans had martin houses from way back, made from hollow gourds, the fact that they must've wanted the feathers, the fact that maybe they're a help in some way around plants too, *martins* I mean, not Indians, although Indians helped the settlers grow all kinds of stuff, the fact that the Amish helped Aunt Sophia with her garden, the fact that they eat dragonflies and ward off crows, *martins* not the Amish, ancient times, Fort Ancient mounds, Leatherlips, full moon sand altars, Quanah Parker, tipis, Chuck, the fact that he gave me a sari once, which I kept for years but never wore, and finally I left it behind somewhere, the thought that counts, the fact that I never really liked the ochre color of it, but I liked being given a sari, impulse buy, the fact that we didn't have much money, the fact that we were just kids, so that was a big deal for him to buy me that, the fact that usually we gave each other things we made, like poems, drawings and stuff, the fact that Chuck liked to do intricate black-and-white line drawings of buildings, the fact that after we rode our bikes to the East Rock, we went back to his house and he gave me ginger beer at his house, which I'd never tried before, the fact that that was my first date and maybe my most successful one too, the fact that on every other date I've ever been on, I just made a big fool of myself, dropping things, stuttering, faux-pas, Dario, Mario, going Dutch, the fact that one guy called me "reticent" once and I didn't even know what it meant, the fact that I thought it must mean something *terrible*, so embarrassing, the fact that I don't think dating's all it's cracked up to be, the fact that computer-dating sounds even worse, but maybe a little less embarrassing, the fact that at least you're not making a fool of yourself face-to-face, the fact that Chuck and I never thought of being together as *dating*, we just went places to sit and talk, and never spent a cent, except that one time he took me to the movies, which seemed sort of strange, too normal, or formal maybe, grown-up, elephant tusks, the fact that I just liked sitting with him somewhere outside all afternoon, just hanging out, and kissing, the fact that that day in the church on Orange, the Yale Chemistry building on a weekend, when it was all deserted, puppy love, the fact that how I hated that expression, and I still do really, the fact that they just use it to devalue how young people feel, teenagers, the fact that I hope I'd never say that to any of my kids, that what they feel is just puppy love, Hush Puppies, the fact that I have a hushpuppy dough ball recipe, the fact that Mandy used to come along with me and Chuck on our walks sometimes, and she took that photo of us from behind, with Chuck's deep red hair and white T-shirt in the sun, blue sky, surrounded by green bushes, green blue red white, the shoebox full of letters, the fact that I had *hope* then, even though Mommy was sick, the fact that I still had hope, thanks to Chuck, but then I lost him too, the fact that it's so hard to find places to go when you're in love, if you're a kid, the fact that you wander around outdoors together because there's nowhere *indoors* you're allowed to go, except that church we found on Orange Street, the fact that once Chuck and I were kissing on the chaise longue in the study when Daddy came in and turned the light on, the fact that he was so *mad* at me, just like Jake's playgroup leader, the fact that after Chuck went home Daddy said I shouldn't be fooling around with Chuck with Mommy sick in bed upstairs, the fact that she *was* really sick and I felt so terrible about it, the fact that I don't think I've ever been the same since, and everything I do in life makes me feel worse, worser, worst, the fact that I know Mommy wouldn't have been angry about it if she'd known what was going on, or not *that* angry, but she never did know anything about me and Chuck, the fact that by the time she started getting better he'd left for Washington, the fact that much later Daddy told me he reacted that

271

way because he was scared I'd get *pregnant*, the fact that that was kind of jumping the gun, the fact that we were just kissing, the fact that we hadn't even thought of taking it that far yet, the fact that adults forget the early ways to be in love, the fact that it doesn't always have to be about going to bed together, red blue green white, the fact that when I did get pregnant with Stace, I was scared at first to tell Daddy, in case he got angry again, but he was great about it, pleased, and proud, and *happy*, even though he never liked Frank, the fact that it turned out he really liked *babies*, which I hadn't realized before, the fact that he was delighted by Stace, the fact that he even helped plan the wedding, the fact that they helped us get a washing machine, the fact that it's such a pity he passed away too soon for Stacy to get to know him, and then Mommy passed on too, Tidepod Challenge, half moon sand altar, Sand Creek, the fact that in Millersburg they have hitching posts with parking meters for the Amish, the fact that Mennonites drive cars, mnemonics, the fact that Harrison Ford fixes the broken martin house later on in the movie, the fact that it turns out he's good at carpentry, the fact that he makes the little boy a marble run, and does a lot of hammering when they raise a barn too, the fact that it seems like movies about the Amish always have a barn-raising scene, the fact that they must need a lot of barns, barn-raising, brainstorming, blue-sky thinking, blue green red white, the fact that in *Witness* the men climb around on the skeleton of a barn all day, and the little boys get to hammer some nails in at the bottom, while the women cook up a big feast and have a quilting bee, the fact that it seems to work, their division of labor, the fact that everybody knows their role, and they just get on with things, the fact that everybody just pulls together, and they pull a barn together too, get it up in one day, the fact that there are probably some finishing touches still to be done, anemone, the fact that Harrison Ford has a rival, the fact that he was a ballet dancer in real life, a ballet dancer, not a belly dancer, the fact that that would be weird, a male belly dancer playing an Amish man, "Suck in your gut," Quick Quiz, quoits, Umpqua, candelabra, the fact that Harrison Ford's still convalescing from his gunshot wound, the fact that they made him drink a lot of herbal tea, bone-knitter, gun license, candlelit bathing scene, self-defense, the fact that I don't know what *Amish* people made of that movie, the fact that most of them probably never saw it, and that's probably just as well, but they probably *heard* about it, the fact that they don't like photos of themselves, so why would they like movies, red blue green white, Chuck's letters, the fact that all these serene tasks, like sewing and knitting, are actually very hard to do, and stressful, the fact that I wonder if these crafts are making women anxious all over the world, the fact that the pressure is on, when you're trying to sew a dress, or make a presentable quilt, "Pressing, pressing," the fact that Amish women sewing may look calm but how can they be, Bing Crosby, the fact that Leo loves *White Christmas*, the fact that he likes it so much sometimes we watch it in the *summer*, though he worries that's a sacrilege, "Little Christmas," women beside themselves with worry, Weeping Mary, my cow painting, ♫ *If you're worried and you can't sleep* ♫, the fact that Bing's not a very common name, the fact that I could have joined the Peolia quilting club if I hadn't quit my job, but who has the time, the Peolia Choir yodeling their heads off, Mary Ingalls's nine-patch, that big red barn, all black inside, with white barn doors and a big white milk can in the open doorway, the fact that that was in Holmes County, the fact that quilting's kind of a communal effort anyway, and I'd be shy, the fact that the same goes for barn-raising, and being *Amish*, for Pete's sake, the fact that I'd be lousy at being Amish, though my clothes are plain enough, Almanzo and French Pierre grappling with the oxen, the apples on the farm, the fact that I'm such a fraidy-cat, Tastee Apple, Jakey, shyness factor, emotional toll, emotional labor, Jakey, yellow tractor, Fisher-Price, the fact that shyness interferes with things, no matter how I fight it, the fact that I can't handle those bossy cake-equipment store ladies, or over-friendly clients who want to gab on the phone, the fact that that doesn't include Cathy, the fact that she somehow makes me feel at ease, winding stone path, big buckeye, herbal tea, the fact that my shyness probably affects our income, the fact that it's sort of a *disability*, the fact that we would definitely be better off financially if I wasn't so shy, the fact that all my life it's been that way, the fact that I'll get like Miss Havisham if I don't watch it, shootings, beheadings, the fact that *Harrison Ford* isn't shy, exit wound, the fact that I just don't understand anal sex, oh dear, what made me think about *that*, my goodness, fracking, flooding, the fact that flash floods in Dayton have reached the roofs now, or is it "rooves," hoof, hooves, goose, geese, mongoose, Cow Came Down, the fact that in 2012 we had an actual *derecho*, in Ohio, the fact that that's when the cow fell off of Young's Jersey Dairy, troposphere, straight line winds, tuscweather.net, the fact that when I saw "Cow Came Down" in the *Dayton Daily News*, I thought there must've been a *tornado*, not just a derecho, and a cow had been swept right up in the air, *And the cow jumped over the moon*, but it was only the cow emblem on top of Young's Jersey Dairy that had broken off in the wind, the fact that they made a big jokey thing about it, charting the cow emblem's recovery and all, after her "accident," cancer, medical bills, André Allard, the fact that French parents are happier than French *non*-parents, but American parents aren't happy *at all*, according to something, some survey, the fact that the kids *love* Young's Jersey Dairy, but what town is it in, I forget, the fact that we should go there more often, we really should, the fact that we don't do enough fun stuff like that, the fact that they have peaches and cream ice cream there, and eggnog ice cream at Christmas, the fact that I always get the caramel crunch, salty caramel pretzel crunch, the fact that you wouldn't think kids would want ice cream in the winter, but they'd eat ice cream anytime, the fact that Ben goes for their cow patty ice cream or the one called Trash, the fact that they have goats there you can play with, a real petting zoo, and everybody likes *goats*, the fact that some goats in Morocco can climb trees, the fact that in goat yoga they get the goats to stand on you, yoga mat, hair jewelry, egg shells, the fact that I should take those old blankets in the attic to Goodwill, the new me, the new normal, succulents, the fact that they're probably just rotting up there, the fact that twenty-two people were killed in the derecho, which makes it worse than a lot of *hurricanes*, the fact

that there are serial derechos, and progressive derechos, the fact that
I don't know which kind ours was but I know it had a backwards C
formation, *I don't know but they know*, warm air advection, mesoscale
convective system, bow echo squall line, anal sex, oh dear, the fact
that what is the matter with me, the fact that let's not go there, the
fact that I'd rather think about almost anything else, the fact that some
women do enjoy anal sex, I think, or are they just pretending, the fact
that sex is sex, I guess, and it all has *some* value, but that's not for me,
that's just not for me, "I was into it!", gone native, the fact that there
were power cuts for days after the derecho, and the thing came on so
fast, the fact that one minute it was a calm, still day, and the next, there
were ninety-mile-an-hour *winds* and half the *trees* were down, the fact
that it was the costliest natural disaster in Ohio history, the fact that
it's always about money, the fact that they think that's the only thing
that interests people, the fact that they can't just talk about a violent
storm, they always have to translate the damage into cash terms, the
fact that today there's just snow and snow clouds, gray, the fact that
that cloud has a face and a, uh, oh-oh, that cloud is *male*, oh my word,
toadstools, phallic symbols, graffiti, the fact that it's *Yellow Springs*,
where Young's Jersey Dairy is, I mean, the fact that Leo saw a *lion*
cloud from the airplane last week, the fact that he photographed it,
but it was kind of hard to make it out, like those 3D pictures I just can't
do, Duck Family Rescued From Pool, the fact that the Ackroyds kept
finding dead field mice in their little pond, the fact that they came to
drink and fell in and couldn't get out, the fact that they should've put
in some little mouse *stairs*, or a ladder, Heimlich maneuver, cough,
the fact that the poffertje-maker needs more coffee, cough, cuff, puff,
Susquehana turkey, Dutch goose, the fact that a Dutch Baby is kind
of like a pancake, Baby Dumpling, puff cake, puffers, poffertjes, the
fact that I think a Dutch Baby's the American version of a Yorkshire
pudding, the fact that I don't know if the Dutch eat Dutch Babies,
reheated in a Dutch oven, the fact that the Japanese have a kind of
soufflé pancake, that puffs up, the fact that they're *an inch thick*, Cy,
Young's Dairy, going Dutch, the fact that it's good we have the Cy

Young park, and the pool, in the summer, the fact that Cy Young passed away in Peoli without a penny to his name, poor man, a real shame, the fact that the Amish around Peoli are all Swartzentruber, the fact that I never found out if Peolia College has anything to do with Peoli, but it must, the fact that there have been one and a half million gun deaths in America since 1968, the fact that the main ways to pass away in America, apart from being shot, are heart attack, pancreatic cancer, a car accident, fire, alcohol, drowning in a lake, river, ocean or a swimming pool, gas poisoning, falling off a ladder, a building, or some other structure, plane crash, heat exhaustion, bike crash, getting caught in agricultural machinery, accidental hanging or strangulation, electrocution, storms, electrical storms, being crushed by objects, or crushed *between* objects, the fact that "being crushed between objects" sounds like my life, "pressing, pressing," piggy in the middle, the fact that it's a zoo around here, the von Trapps, the fact that you're very unlikely to die in a train crash, and you're much more likely to break your neck getting in or out of the bathtub, the fact that I dreamt we were staying in a New York City hotel and I was really worried about what it was *costing* us, because Leo'd booked the room without checking what their rates were, and it seemed like an expensive place, the fact that then I heard it was only $72 a night, so then I wanted to book it for another *week*, the fact that I cannot for the life of me recall what those dark, hard-shelled, spiky, spherical underwater things are called, the fact that they're made sort of like an orange, with segments, the fact that I don't think they're plants *or* vegetables, something in between, like a platypus, the fact that they may be some kind of crustacean, the fact that they're not sea anemones, amenities, anomalies, enemies, anomie, entropy, the fact that as a kid, sometimes I just could barely put one leg in front of the other, the fact that I can remember dragging myself along the sidewalk when we had to go grocery-shopping with Mommy, and having to rest, sitting on a curb, the fact that she gave us a treat sometimes, to cheer us up, Hostess cupcake, the fact that sometimes I still feel like that, like I can't move another *inch*, strain hardening, deformation, fatigue, yield strength, the fact that I probably need more sleep, buckling, dislocations, and less orders for *pie*, the fact that after Mommy got sick I had to make my own lunches for school, in my little Tupperware tub, lonely, estranged, hydrangea, the fact that that dead pigeon on our porch last summer was such a beautiful deep gray color, the fact that I put it in the trash, the fact that maybe I should've buried it, the fact that it seemed awful to just throw that beautiful thing out, but I was worried about *contagion*, bird flu, mites, the fact that I didn't want anything infecting the chickens, chicken coop, Ronny, the fact that Mommy always told us never to touch a dead bird, and it still goes against the grain when I have to dispose of a dead chicken or anything, the fact that our chickens do die occasionally, but not too often, touch wood, happy chickens, Kentucky Fried Chicken, the fact that I dreamt Bathsheba was old and sick and I was supposed to take her to the vet to have her put down, but on the way over there I decided not to, the fact that I felt she didn't deserve to be treated that way, and we went home, all *happy*, the fact that I don't know why I dreamt such a thing, the fact that she died in my arms that Christmas, just after we moved here, the fact that I had another cat dream too, about a whole load of tiny gray kittens that were living under a pot plant too near the stove, the fact that I had to move the plant and find all the kittens, but there were so *many* of them, maybe eleven, all squirming around and going in different directions and trying to hide, Pierre, Tiny Tim, Edward and his babies, Bathsheba, Opal and Frederick, The name of your first pet, Mother's maiden name, Your first address, Favorite color, the fact that I still miss her, beautiful Bathsheba, cornmeal mush pie, the fact that I wonder if women have always remembered their dreams while they're cooking, the fact that Nanya taught me to make a fanouropita cake whenever we lose things, and it really *works*, the fact that you often remember where you put the thing, whatever it is, while you're making the cake, or else you remember it when you're eating the cake, or sometimes it just turns up soon after I make a fanouropita, the fact that it's a great solution, since even if you *don't* find the thing, at least you have a nice cake to comfort you, the fact that sometimes just the fanouropita smell helps me remember where I put something, the fact that you're supposed to sit the fanouropita on the windowsill while it cools, or near a window anyway, so Saint Fanourios can come and get some, and in return he helps you find the lost object, but I don't always remember, the fact that I guess the guy really liked cake, the fact that a fanouropita cake's got to have either seven or nine ingredients, because they're lucky numbers in Greece, the fact that my fanouropitas usually have seven, because I skip the nuts and raisins, but sometimes it's nine, because I like to add brandy and olives now, sliced up thinly, the fact that that was one of Leo's innovations, the olives, the fact that almost all sweet things need a salty element, apart from Snapple lemonade, the fact that you put almost a whole cup of lemon juice in fanouropitas, yet it's still very, very sweet, and sort of sludgy, the fact that it kind of gets caught on the roof of your mouth, rooves, the fact that I better not've lost my recipe, the fact that I don't want to have to bake a fanouropita cake to help me find my fanouropita recipe, the fact that I better make another copy, though you can always go online, I guess, but I might not find the same one, Olivia Newton John, Ariana Grande, Killbuck Creek, Wiles Hog Farm, the fact that what is that mollusk called, if it is a mollusk, Ben's pirate outfit, the fact that Ben used to wear it to the park, like me in my bird costume, the fact that how I loved him in his scarlet doublet and tricorn hat, and the black pants and the black cuffs with white lace trim, Mary Ingalls, Pa and the bear, doublet, singlet, triplets, the fact that Ben's hat wasn't a tricorn exactly, more sort of a crazy red sombrero with the front and back rims pinned up, but it looked good from a distance, Ben running down the hill to the bridge, a pirate walking the plank, bridge collapse, the fact that I like seeing my kids from a distance, the fact that maybe that's what drives soccer moms too, the fact that I wonder what happened to those things, not soccer moms, our Dutch dresses, little Dutch girl folk costumes, the fact that Phoebe and I each had a red and blue dress with vertical stripes, and a white apron, the fact that I forget if we ever had white bonnets too, the fact that I'm sure I kept them somewhere, the fact that Gillian could probably still fit into the bigger one if I could only find it, fanouropita, but they might have fallen completely apart by now, or maybe we wore them out, but I can't remember wearing them all that much really, though we *wanted* to, the fact that there was just no way the kids on our block were going to put up with us and our little Dutch girl act for long, or maybe we grew out of the dresses and just couldn't wear them anymore, nothing to do with the neighbor kids, the fact that we got the dresses in Holland, during that year in London, the fact that we brought a lot of Dutch stuff back to Evanston, the blue and white salt and pepper windmill set, with china sails that really turned, the poffertje pan, and the two dresses, but no wooden clogs, the fact that I don't know how people can walk in those things, but people walk in crocks, which are kind of similar, the fact that I think we paraded around in those little Dutch outfits when we got back home and everybody just laughed at us, but we couldn't help ourselves because the dresses were so nice, the fact that we really loved those dresses, and I got to wear Phoebe's after she grew out of it, the fact that being a younger sister has its perks, as I'm always telling Gillian, but she's not too interested in Stacy's old clothes, *Oliver!*, the dead wife lying in bed holding her single red rose, estranged wife, strange husband, the fact that Jake doesn't seem to mind using up Ben's old clothes, "close," the fact that Jake's not too fashion-conscious as yet, the fact that he actually started out in Gillian's old onesies and other baby duds but we'll never tell him, the fact that they went off to Goodwill after *he* had them, no more babies for me, the fact that there are "anti-natalists" who think birth's a negative thing, but I don't think there are many around *here*, famous last words, packing heat, grounds coverage, five-story crematoriums, crazee, Abby, Bathsheba, sleepy, the fact that I better have another cup of coffee, my wedding ring, countertop, old batteries, tray of objects, memory gaps, the stop lights by the Front Avenue Shell gas station, New Philly, chickens, playing solitaire on the grass in the Nelsons' back yard, sprinklers, grass stains, the fact that we rehearsed *Oliver!* all summer long, the fact that I don't remember the actual performance, just the rehearsals, the fact that they seemed *endless*, the fact that Hillary Clinton grew up in Illinois, a Republican, *The Musical*, the fact that she was a Republican until she left *college*, the fact that she went to Trump's wedding, or one of them anyway, Melania's squinty eyes, the fact that a girl did a school shooting in West Kentucky yesterday, the fact that she brought the gun to school thinking it was a toy, the fact that I don't know why she wanted to bring a toy gun to school, the fact that I fell into the big rose bush right next door to our house, when I was a kid, the fact that I fell off my bike as soon as I got on it, practically, and landed right in the middle of a very thorny rose bush, the fact that how do I do these things, the fact that I think I'm accident-prone, mattress button, heart defect, the fact that Mommy had to come and rescue me and then take all the thorns out of my leg, one by one, the fact that I was trying to teach myself how to ride a bike, the fact that I'd left it as late as possible, the fact that I'll be late to my own funeral, always playing catch-up, catchup, catsup, the fact that I didn't *want* to ride a bike, the fact that I liked my trike, but I couldn't keep up with the other kids anymore on a trike, the fact that trikes have no speed, velocity, veracity, the fact that everybody was taking long bike hikes without me, the fact that I had to teach myself roller skating too, and I fell on my back and got winded, the fact that that scared me, the fact that now everybody has to master the scooter and the skateboard, the Hula-Hoop, and parkouring, and pogo-sticking, stilts, tight-rope walking, hanging from silks, and cartwheels, *doing* cartwheels, not *hanging* from cartwheels, which would be pretty dangerous, the fact that I never tried stilts *or* silks, the fact that I was always too scared of getting hurt, or *exhausted*, the fact that cowards walk on stilts, people scared to get their feet dirty, the fact that my kids all seemed to grasp bike-riding pretty fast, but we helped them, the fact that you need a little hill to practice on, which we didn't have in Evanston, the fact that Jake's just starting to get the hang of it, the fact that I loved my orange and white trike, with the big front wheel, the fact that why can't you just go on riding your trike your whole life, why must you transition to a bike, the fact that can't they put gears on a tricycle, the fact that

Mommy and Daddy gave it away one day while I was at school, to some needy kid I didn't even know, and I never saw my trike again, industrial soap, the fact that I think they waited until I'd mastered my bike, but I'm not even certain of that, well, probably, the fact that it may have been down in the basement for years before they gave it away, the fact that I can't remember, the fact that I don't know why they had to give it away without telling me, the fact that I just would've liked to see it one last time, maybe ride it once more, say *goodbye*, the fact that I should bake a fanouropita to try to get my trike back, oh no, the fact that Ben doesn't feel well, the fact that it's probably too many poffertjes, the fact that he's sitting quietly, on the iPad, *using* it I mean, not *sitting* on it, the fact that *Oliver!* was all Jill Worth's older sister's idea, whatwashername, the fact that she seemed much older than us and I never liked her very much, the fact that she scared me, the fact that, when you think about it, putting on a whole outdoor neighborhood production of *Oliver!* was a pretty ambitious summer project for a teenager, the fact that she and her friends were really *gone* on *Oliver!*, so they forced us to act it out all summer, the fact that all *I* had to do was sit on the grass playing solitaire, the fact that I wonder what became of her, the fact that I can't even remember her name, the fact that she was sort of a Hillary Clinton type, Wella, was it Wella, or Bella, the fact that it might have been Bella, Bella Worth, Bertha, Bertha Wortha, the fact that I don't even know whatever became of *Jill* Worth, the fact that we were best friends for years, and we tried to keep in touch after the move to New Haven, but neither of us was much of a letter-writer, the fact that she was a year older than me, lemonade stand, "Let's blow this pop stand, sister," popgun, electric toy car, the fact that Bella or Wella or whatever she was called made me be an urchin in Scrooge's gang, sea urchins, I mean *Fagin's* gang, ♫ *Whe-e-e-e-ere is love?* ♫, and I had to sit on the grass playing solitaire, and I did the best I could, the fact that it was pretty boring, the fact that sometimes I completely forgot there was a rehearsal going on, because they went on so long, the fact that I think I zoned out sometimes and had to be reminded to play solitaire, the fact that solitaire was the only card game I knew, so that's what I did all summer, play cards on the lawn, the fact that I guess Bella or Wella decided pretty early on I had no natural acting or singing abilities, urchin, *sea* urchins, the fact that is *that* what those round spiny mollusk thingies are, the fact that our "stage" was the Nelsons' back yard, behind their tall white clapboard house, the Nelsons who always had peanut butter and jelly sandwiches, and also that kind of special-occasion stripy candy in a fancy glass urn, the fact that I've been looking for that candy ever since but I've never seen it anywhere else, the fact that maybe the Vermont Country Store would have it, the fact that they have a lot of old candy, the fact that the Nelsons were a big family and they had one of the biggest houses on the block, and Amanda had lots of Barbie dolls with all the trimmings, all the outfits and accessories, Ken too, the fact that I only ever had one Barbie, I think, and I never had Ken, the fact that their house always seemed like how a house should be, the fact that it was always in perfect shape, all clean and white, with all the right stuff in it, even though they had six kids, the fact that their place wasn't drowning in papers like ours, the fact that they were sort of perfect people, the way everybody's *supposed* to be, rich and clean and calm, all athletic and healthy and good-looking, the fact that Amanda Nelson was perfect-looking, but she could be mean, the fact that I wonder where she is now, the fact that did she marry someone nice or has life been tough, the fact that she could be something like Illinois Attorney General by now, for all I know, the fact that every year the Nelson kids went to some really fun, normal summer camp, not an educational one, the fact that Phoebe went to Interlochen, the fact that I only did daytime Summer Schools, around Evanston, the fact that I did a drama class one summer, oh, and that little music camp once, just for string instruments, but that was just for two or three weeks, not all summer like Interlochen, pine trees, cliff edge, the fact that we all shared rooms in that old house, three or four to a bedroom, the fact that we got care packages from home, the fact that one day we all ganged up on another girl and I still don't know *why*, the fact that my favorite teacher scolded us and I felt so terrible about it, the fact that we used to all have lunch in a big tent, salads and stuff, which I liked, because you never had to eat more than you wanted, and then I got a terrible cold but they let me swim anyway, in that long series of waterfalls, the fact that they took us there on the bus, the fact that the water was just strong enough, and deep enough, to make it sort of scary and really *fun*, "Rrrreally good!", the fact that that was about the most fun I ever had in my whole entire life, the fact that the rocks were big but rounded, and the water was just fast enough to push you over but not scare you too much, the fact that I wonder why the Nelson kids were *home* the summer we did *Oliver!*, the fact that maybe they'd had a month in camp already, and now they were home and needed something to do, the fact that we all had to sing the choruses, but the only song I can actually remember is the one Oliver sings all alone in the orphanage or the bottle factory or wherever he is, which seemed so poignant at the time, the fact that I think I wished *I* was the one singing that song, but it was probably Amanda, the fact that the Nelson kids got all the best parts, the fact that Amanda was always a show-off, the fact that, boy, we must've rehearsed that thing a million trillion times, stardom, torture, USA, Jesus López Pérez, the fact that it wasn't "Somewhere Over the Rainbow," because that's in *The Wizard of Oz*, Munchkins, ♫ *Courage* ♫, the fact that it was ♫ *Whe-e-e-e-ere is love?* ♫, I think, or something like that, *wh*here, the fact that I don't know if songwriters should let one syllable trail on for several notes like that, ♫ *Glo-o-o-o-oria eggshell-sis deo* ♫, the fact that a lot of hymns do that sort of thing and they are embarrassing to sing, the fact that if you actually ta-a-a-a-alked li-i-i-ike tha-a-a-a-at, it wouldn't be very practical, yellow bird costume, the fact that pe-e-e-eople wou-ou-ould be-e-e-eat you u-u-u-u-up, the fact that I liked my bird costume even more than my Dutch dress, the fact that I *loved* that bird costume, ♫ *Whe-e-e-e-ere is it?* ♫, the fact that I wish I was wearing it *right now*, the fact that it was all hand-sewn by my teachers in Rome, the fact that they made us *all* bird costumes, the whole class, the fact that they dressed us all up as little yellow birds and then got us to run round and round a little makeshift

283

straw hut in the classroom, chirping hysterically, the fact that that was about as much fun as I ever had, even better than the waterfall, the fact that I still remember the dress rehearsal and all of us yellow birds running and screaming, nursery school, yellow feathers, the fact that my costume was made up of millions of separate feathers, or hundreds anyway, each one lovingly sewn on, the fact that even as a four-year-old I was amazed by that, the care those teachers took, and all those individual feathers, the fact that it still amazes me, the fact that you don't see any teachers in Newcomerstown knuckling down to a big sewing job like that, the fact that if kids need a costume for a school play, *I* have to make it, ♫ *I'd do anything* ♫, or the kids might do it themselves, I guess, with old clothes in the attic, the fact that maybe *that's* what happened to my nice embroidered Guatemalan poncho shirt, the fact that how I hated that song "I'd do anything," ♫ *I'd do anything* ♫, maybe because Bella made us practice it so much, sing-along, ♫ *I'd do anything* ♫, How To Lose Your Baby Weight In Five Days, the fact that "I'd do anything" to *gain* a few pounds, but you can't say that or people just think you're boasting, the fact that how is looking like a scrawny chicken anything to *boast* about, the fact that that thin scruffy teacher was so poor he was living in his *car*, somebody told me, National Life, before he quit, the fact that teachers don't make much, the fact that maybe he can make a better living doing something else rather than teach, Throwaway Society, roll-over discount, the fact that the little hut was decorated with fake leaves and stuff, and we ran round and round it, squealing and cheeping as loud as we could, what funettes, the fact that we were all so pleased with ourselves, *and* our costumes, and excited to be told we could run around and make noise, the fact that *that* is how to make a four-year-old very happy, euphoria, the fact that I think we really began to believe we *were* birds for a second or two there, well *I* did, the fact that Italian works better for operas, spaghetti twirling, cinnamon rolls, orange zest, zester, my basting brush, 350°, the fact that if children had that good a time these days they'd all be put on Ritalin, my math workbook with the plastic pages, though now they've got some *new* method for calming hyperactive kids, the fact that they make them wear weighted vests, Marley, singlets, the fact that they might as well make them bulletproof while they're at it, the fact that it can't hurt, ballistics panels, the fact that the weighted vests are already so popular that all the other kids want them too, whether they're ADHD or not, the fact that it doesn't sound like such a treat to me, to wear a weighted vest, the fact that that's nothing like being invited to become a *bird* for a day, "Queen for a Day," the fact that when we got back to Evanston I wanted to wear my bird costume some more, the fact that this must've been a couple years before we tried wearing the Dutch dresses around the neighborhood, 1979, 1980, 1981, the fact that I think I really did wear my bird costume outside in Evanston a couple of times, because I remember hopping down our front steps in it, trying to fly, and being real upset when I grew out of it, the fact that I hadn't put it on for a while and one day I saw it in my closet and tried to get it on but I couldn't anymore, without tearing it, the fact that it was very delicate, donkey, opera glasses, yellow birds, Rome, spirals, the fact that maybe that's why I had so many flying dreams as a child, because of *my bird costume*, imprinted, Fiesole, Frascati, Tiepolo ceilings, the fact that my kids don't seem to have *any*, any flying dreams, not Tiepolo ceilings, ♫ *Whe-e-e-ere is love?* ♫, the fact that one of my flying dreams was so vivid I really believed for years afterward that I *could* fly if I really put my mind to it, the fact that I secretly believed this for a few years, but didn't tell anybody in case it popped the bubble, the fact that I thought it would be effortful and all, getting off the ground, but it just might work, as long as I believed I could, and flapped my arms a lot and pushed with my legs, like I was swimming up to the surface from deep underwater, like when you're about to run out of oxygen and you strive upwards with all your might, the fact that in my most memorable flying dream, I jumped off the top porch step and beat my arms and churned my legs in the air, and slowly, slowly I gained height until I reached the lower branches of the tree, the fact that it just took concentration and self-belief, buttercups, alley, attic, atoms squeezed together, the fact that we used to take turns being on

"TV" in the alley, radioactive waste, "Queen for a Day," the fact that we used an old empty TV set we'd found out there, just Phoebe, Kristen, Karen, and me, while Pepito policed the back yard in case any trash men appeared, crazy squirrel, Trastevere, Pierre, the fact that Pierre came with us to Rome and he passed away there, old age, the fact that he was ten years old, and the Catholic vet crossed himself before he put him down, the fact that Mommy never forgot that, the fact that it meant a lot to her, even though she was a lapsed Catholic, the fact that I don't think it was anything to do with religion, the fact that she just liked how respectful the vet was towards Pierre, fried artichokes, ghetto, *It's Complicated*, the fact that Mommy never forgot the Italian vet crossing himself, so *I'll* never forget it either, even though I was only four at the time, and I don't think I was even around when the vet came over, the fact that I was probably at nursery school, cheeping, running riot, or getting a crush on a little boy in my class named Andrew, because *Phoebe* had a crush on a boy named Andrew in *her* class, the fact that I have a talent for forgetting, but it's not a talent valued by anyone, as far as I know, the fact that sometimes I forget about my *parents*, and Pierre, and lots of other stuff, the fact that I have the worst memory of anyone I know, the fact that most of my life is wasted on me, the fact that as the historian of my own life, I'm just going on *hunches* most of the time, running on empty, stumbling over sand dunes, hunted to the point of distinction, Chuck, Pierre, sea turtles, Mommy, the fact that the dog with the dinosaur bone in *Bringing Up Baby*, whatshisname, not Snowy, intercostal clavicle, the fact that I really sometimes forget they ever existed, just because they don't exist *anymore*, which doesn't do them justice, Mommy and Daddy I mean, not dinosaurs, the fact that I forget how *real* Mommy and Daddy were, the fact that existence is a fact, even if it happened in the past, as any History major should *know*, the fact that their deaths were such a shock that now I can't seem to believe they were ever born, but they *were*, and *they* were children once, and grew up and went to college and fell in love and got married and had us and all that, the fact that they had three kids, they wiped our sit-me-down-upons, and washed our me-oh-mys, and cooked us meals and watched us grow up, pulling thorns out of my thigh when necessary, and glass out of my foot, the meaning of life, the fact that they took us to the hospital, saw me through my heart operation, the fact that they taught, and read books, and wrote books, the fact that they led full lives and had a history as real as mine, realer even, more *productive* anyway, the fact that they were real in a way I'll probably *never* be, nor my kids, or anything, and I don't like their history disappearing with them, cinnamon, blancmange, Italian balcony, villa, vanilla, atrium, Pompeii, the fact that even though I've forgotten Pierre, *he* had his own history too, the fact that he had a rich and full life, the fact that he was born in Chicago and lived in Evanston, where he ran free and had love affairs and in the end he became an old dog, and then he went to Rome with us, and passed away and got buried in an Italian dog cemetery, the fact that he was quite an adventurer, a jetsetter, in his way, "died serving his country," the fact that Mommy and Daddy were very, very fond of Pierre, the fact that they had had him before they started having us, so he was like their firstborn, and an only child for about a year, "only child," the fact that he was always kind of a *myth* to me, the heroic Pierre, because I was so young when he passed away, the fact that I think I only remember *other* people's memories of him, the fact that I was older when we got Pepito, and he was like a real member of the family, my dog brother, the fact that that's about all I remember of my whole childhood, my bird costume, the Dutch dresses, my flying dream, Pierre's passing, the Italian vet, turtles, twirling spaghetti, rhododendrons, peaches in cream, rehearsals for *Oliver!*, and that's it, though for some reason I also remember that bar at the train station in Hickory, North Carolina, the fact that Leo ordered a Scotch and soda for me and I got like a whole quart of whiskey and soda, the fact that the bartender was new on the job and didn't know how much to pour, the fact that I drank it all, Canadian Club and ginger, Abby, "CC 'n' ginger," lobster rolls, refugees with frostbite, Canadian flag, Italy, Texas, ma'am, the fact that there's a place in Texas called Italy, the fact that they had a school shooting there, apples'n'onions, the fact that Jesus saved me, and without him I'd still be out there by the side of the *road*, probably frozen *solid*, or getting gnawed on by a bear, TV dinner for a bear, the fact that it's nice to be cozy at home, even though I've got a hundred cinnamon rolls to make, with rights comes responsibility, the fact that I could be a bear lying in a stinky hole right now, trying to hibernate but waking up hungry several times a day and wondering what season it is by now outside, the fact that hibernation seems kind of a desperate move to me, and kind of boring and grungy, insomnia and the worst case of morning breath in the world, torpor, BO up the wazoo, whoa, and who knows, *incontinence* maybe, the fact that you couldn't even play Go-Go to get you through the day, because you're supposed to be asleep, "Go Bears," the fact that what does a bear think about, the fact that do gorillas talk to themselves all the time like we do, the fact that I don't know how animals think but *I* think in spirals, dizzying spirals, the fact that that WWF video of a deaf girl talking in sign language to an orangutan was completely *fake*, and I fell for it, the fact that, landsakes, orangutans don't campaign for the *rainforest*, the fact that the good news right now is that animals don't yet know we've wrecked the place, or they don't know *we* did it at least, or they'd come after us, red in tooth and claw, the fact that it's actually pretty lucky they don't blame us for it, not like in *The Birds*, the fact that I'm lucky I didn't freeze out there in the car, so lucky it makes me never want to go out *again*, or not till summer anyway, the fact that I don't want to push my luck, the fact that I wish I could just hibernate *here*, in my own bed, the fact that luckily some driver saw me standing like a chump by the side of the road and called Jesus of Nazareth, no, Jesus López Pérez of New Philadelphia, the fact that it's all thanks to them, the fact that he drove out to look for me in a *snow storm*, a stranger, so I guess it was wrong of me to call everybody on the road a stinker, the fact that I wasn't being very rational, the fact that I was just mad at *myself*, really, and scared, the fact that you're not at your best when you're scared, Yeti, the fact that that nice Jesus drove past my car, stopped his pickup, peered back at me for a sec, established I wasn't a Marilyn Monroe, and he helped me *anyway*, the fact that he didn't say much, well, it was too cold to talk, the fact that he just gestured at me to get in his truck and then he towed the car to the auto shop in Gnadenhutten, the fact that that's not *his* garage, the fact that he works in New Philadelphia, but I guess they're all pals in the car repair world, and going to Gnadenhutten was quicker and easier, mechanics, Macarena, the fact that Chick's Wrecker Service here in town might've come to get me, if I'd had my stupid phone, but then I'd never have met Jesus López Pérez, the fact that everything worked out fine, and he was so *fast*, the fact that he fixed the tire in the time it took me to drink half my cup of coffee in the little office, warming up, Gnadenhutten Massacre, Donner party, street party, block party, the fact that he was so gentlemanly about it too, the fact that he wouldn't take any money, the fact that he seemed to feel kind of sorry for me, even though I wasn't Marilyn Monroe, the fact that he was so efficient I wasn't even late getting to Jake, and Jake and I managed to get all the pies to their various destinations after all, except the one I gave Jesus for helping me, the fact that we were back home in time to meet the school bus, as if I hadn't lost three hours of my life in a blizzard, the fact that it's all kind of a *miracle* really, the fact that, considering what I went through, it seemed to me my pies weren't greeted with as much amazement as they deserved, but of course nobody *knew* what I'd been through because I didn't have time to explain, I was in such a hurry to get home for the kids, the fact that of course if we hadn't made it in time, they could've gone across to Molly's, but they wouldn't have liked tramping over to Molly's in the snow, not knowing where I was, blue snow at twilight, the fact that all the time I was freezing in the car, I was worrying about the school bus and the kids and the chickens, never mind the Abominable Snowmen and hibernating bears, and nobody on earth knew anything was wrong, not Leo or the kids, the fact that *Mommy* didn't know either, the fact that that seems such a lonely thing to contemplate, the fact that I don't like thinking about it, the fact that by the time I made it to the playgroup I was so het up it was almost a surprise to find Jake there, not stolen by some governmental agency because of my incompetence and neglect, the fact that I felt like I'd been gone for *years*, Rip Van Winkle stuff, the fact that I felt like I'd been to the *moon* or something, but, sort of to my surprise, the kids were fine, the fact that they survived, as did the chickens and the goldfish, and Leo, and even the pie dough in the fridge, the fact that the fish were on my mind when I was freezing to death, because I wasn't sure I'd fed them, the fact that at the back of my mind, the whole time I contemplated my end, I was worried nobody would remember to feed the fish for days, the chickens too, because they'd all be upset I died and they'd just forget, the fact that chickens need *more* food in cold weather, not less, the fact that they need their winter feed, the fact that I was glad to know they had their heat lamp, so I knew they'd be okay for a while, the fact that the lamp makes them lay more, the fact that chickens are supposed to lay best the first couple of years but our seven-year-olds are still laying, the fact that we get about five eggs a day unless it gets too cold or hot, *The Long Winter*, the horses sinking into snow holes in the Big Slough, Slough of Despond, the fact that nobody wants to sink into a slough ever, especially a Slough of Despond, the fact that if bird flu comes, I'll have to keep the chickens inside their coop all the time, because I don't want them to catch bird flu and give it to *us*, Jesus, the fact that when the kids got off the bus we all had hot chocolate, with little tiny pink and white mini-marshmallows on top, and I told them "Jesus saved me," the fact that I told the kids, not the mini-marshmallows, but they didn't *get* it, the fact that kids hardly ever know what you're talking about, and they couldn't care less too, or that's how it feels sometimes, the fact that I had to wait for Leo to get home before I could get a real rise out of anybody, but when I told Cathy, she got it, the fact that it's only funny to atheists, but getting your tire fixed by a guy called Jesus is just not something a person can keep bottled up for long, Bozo the Clown, Tiffany Trump, the fact that for a few days after, I couldn't remember what day it *was*, the fact that I kept having to check, the fact that I was sort of disoriented, the fact that maybe a bit of my brain froze, chillbrain, the fact that that's supposed to be *good* for your brain, the fact that if you've had a brain injury they chill your whole head to stop the swelling, the fact that that darned darning pile has been sitting there for a year, at least, the fact that I really need a professional declutterer, or at least a book on decluttering from the library, unless they've decluttered the library too and have no books anymore, the fact that darned socks often aren't as comfortable, and the holes come back anyway, so it's hardly worth darning them, the fact that we might as well buy new ones, the fact that it's probably a false saving, darning socks, the fact that you don't want blisters, the fact that I don't think many people darn socks anymore, the fact that we're about to have World War Three and I'm worried about saving on socks, the fact that actually, in a war, things like socks might become precious items, and everybody will value darning again, ration books, darning egg, the fact that maybe we could sell the darned socks on the black market, darned sweaters too, but those sweaters in the closet have really had it, the fact that let's face it, war or no war, I'm never going to darn those old things, even if I *could* get my *Mrs. Miniver* act together, the fact that I gave Jesus a nice plum pie for his troubles, one of my best, a really dark red plum pie, made from the plums we picked and froze last fall, well flavored with cardamom, plum wore out, the fact that they were *pitted* plums, not d-d-d-damsons, palm oil, gorillas, orangutans, the fact that the tiniest hippo is at risk, no, the tiniest rhino, because they're tearing down the rainforest in Sumatra, the fact that rhinos always look like somebody's drawn circles round and round their little eyes, the fact that they look so tired, even tireder than me, even their babies do, but don't tell 'em or they'll feel *more* tired, Frankie Makes Surprise Admission, plums, paw-paw, papaya, custard apple, the fact that going wild-picking in the woods is no fun anymore, now there are so many hunters lumbering around in there, the fact that when you see some guy with a shotgun coming towards you through the trees, you just never know whether to run or stand your ground, the fact that he might be a genuine, experienced hunter who can tell the difference between your kid and a deer from half a mile away, *or* he could be a trigger-happy amateur, who'll shoot

you thinking you're a deer, or he could be an escaped convict or terrorist, a home-schooling fundamentalist door-to-door salesman, with
a temper, a dangerous dog freak and shooting-spree maniac, or just
your average run-of-the-mill family-annihilator, the fact that it's
un-American, I know, to admit you're scared of all these screwballs
but I am, my fellow countrymen, the fact that sometimes I wonder if
I'm scareder than I even know, like *crazee* scared, scaredy-cat,
Cowardly Lion, World War Three, the fact that I know I'm scareder
than I *look*, the fact that maybe we all are, but life has to go on, the
numbness of muted beings, the fact that, I mean, you just never know
if you're about to be shot, accidentally or on purpose, you just never
know, and you never will know, the fact that you can never be *sure*,
the fact that your life isn't guaranteed, the fact that behind every door
there could be somebody sitting up all day and night, holding a gun,
ready to shoot you for crossing their lawn, or asking directions,
"Knock, knock," "Who's there?", the fact that people used to sit in
their rockers on the porch, whittling, ready to say *hello* as you walked
by, but now they're all hiding inside with a *machine gun*, the fact that
any minute now some guy with a crush on Stacy could come in here
and kill us all and take her away to some cabin in the woods, the fact
that a guy shot two people dead at that medical facility, all because he
couldn't get a *doctor's appointment* when he wanted one, the fact that
if you're gonna shoot people for that you'd shoot 'em for anything, the
fact that we could be bombed or irradiated or robbed or foreclosed, or
raped, or poisoned by acid rain and pesticides or "pre-emptive" antibiotics, that stuff they use on livestock, the fact that farmers will be
the death of us, like that chicken farmer guy, Anton Pohlmann, allegations, Miranda Rules, the fact that some law man, complaining
about anonymous allegations, said "the anonymous alligators must
come forward," the fact that they torture alligators and crocodiles to
make alligator purses, the fact that I don't know why but it takes two
whole alligators to make *one purse*, the fact that there are two alligators
in the radioactive pond at the Savannah River Nuclear Plant, the fact
that they're called Tritigator and Dioxinator, and they must be *totally*

radioactive, the fact that the pond belongs to a plant that sits on three hundred square miles of radioactive poisoned land, the fact that does that mean it's thirty miles by ten miles or three hundred miles across or what, those poor alligators, the fact that it's a Superfund site, so they're supposed to clean it up but *how*, the fact that I'm not sure they can, the fact that the whole place is covered with buried and half-buried nuclear waste, the fact that nobody ever knew what to do with it, and they still don't, the fact that that site won't be safe for two hundred and forty thousand years, the fact that that's about how long humans have existed, in their modern form anyway, the fact that they let all that radioactive waste leak into the Savannah River and the water table, and thousands of workers got cancer, the fact that it's an awfulous situation, as Gillian said when she dropped her ice cream cone, the fact that it kind of makes you feel better about old socks, the fact that they're not the *worst* thing in the world, the fact that at least my closet isn't a three hundred square mile nuclear waste dump, not yet anyway, the fact that if anybody should declutter, maybe it's DuPont, the fact that everything gets cancer, even trees, so alligators probably get it too, the fact that if any alligator's going to get cancer, Tritigator and Dioxinator must be first in line, the fact that are they reptiles or amphibians, anal cancer, the fact that I think *I* have rhino eyes, atom bomb, hydrogen bomb, thermonuclear blast, World War Three, the fact that Ben just looked it up for me and sea urchins are not crustaceans *or* mollusks, they're a whole nother kind of thing related to sand dollars, nothing to do with sea anemones either, ane-nomes, anemones, the fact that I just can't pronounce that word, the fact that I always get it wrong, like the kids do with "cinnamon," the fact that anenome's a word you try to avoid ever having to say out loud 'cause you know you're sure to flub it, the fact that when I was a kid I couldn't pronounce a single thing right, and I still can't really, especially when I'm nervous, the fact that I can remember having trouble with stuff like "railroad," and Sweet William, and fragrance, shenanigan, pandemonium, tongue twisters, and no amount of Speech Therapy helped, the fact that they just gave me *more* tongue twisters to practice, the fact that sea urchins come in all colors, the fact that maybe they're kind of a *cross* between a plant and an animal but nobody ever says so, the fact that some man somewhere or other started growing bark right out of his legs and arms, so maybe animal and vegetable elements can coexist more than we think, vegetal, the fact that I hate it when music sounds like my kitchen timer, the fact that it's very distracting, the fact that "friendly" wolf eels eat sea urchins, friendly wolf eels, the fact that a wolf eel can crunch through a crab, a clam, or a sea urchin, no problemo, the fact that wolf eels can be up to six or seven feet long, and they're "friendly" but sometimes *bite*, the fact that somehow, if a friendly seven-foot wolf eel sidled up to *me*, I think I'd think there was a catch somewhere, SF, Smoker Friendly, Mommy smoking, "Are you evil?", the fact that wolf eels have nice blue patterned bodies and kind of funny faces, the fact that they're definitely kind of funny-looking, the fact that how much wood could a woodchuck chuck if a woodchuck could chuck wood, the fact that I was going to look up sea urchins myself after Ben finished with the iPad but now I'm into wolf eels, the fact that they mate for life, which is probably just as well, "Promise me I'll never be out there again," the fact that Native Americans called wolf eels "doctor fish" and only the medicine men were allowed to eat them, bird costume, Dutch dress, Ben's pirate outfit, the fact that sea urchins are useful in *aquariums*, the fact that they keep the glass clean by eating the algae, like snails, the fact that we always had a few little black snails in our fish tank in Evanston, but not anymore, the fact that we, boy, scallops sure get around, the fact that just look at them scooting across the ocean floor, the fact that when you dry sea urchins their needles all fall off, the fact that slate-stick sea urchins have wider spines than other kinds, the fact that sea urchins never meet their mates, the fact that I guess they're all just too prickly, the fact that I'm kinda prickly myself sometimes, the fact that male and female sea urchins live on totally different planes, levels, the fact that female sea urchins stay down on the bottom, and the males live higher up, glass ceiling, spreading their milt far and wide on the currents, milt, milk, Almanzo's milk-fed pumpkin, the fact that romance is low on the sea urchin's list of priorities, but the females care about their *babies*, or about the eggs at least, the fact that female sea urchins protect their eggs by holding them between their *spines*, which must be a pretty tricky maneuver, like trying to smoke a cigarette with your toes, in the middle of a gale, "Zowie!", perfect storm, slate-stick sea urchins, the fact that that maternal devotion doesn't last long though, the fact that once a sea urchin egg is fertilized things happen *fast*, the fact that sea urchin larvae grow into adults in *an hour*, the fact that even fruit flies take longer than that, like a few days or something, I mean, to get from the caterpillar stage to the annoying fruit-fly stage, vinegar, rotting fruit, bucket lists, woodchuck, Chuck, wood, cock, woodcock, red green blue white, the fact that it would be quite a surprise if Jake went off to playschool in the morning and returned in the afternoon a fully formed orthopedic surgeon or something, and all on a diet of SpaghettiOs, go figure, closure, pantsuit, college football rapists, the fact that to some extent Ben *is* fully formed, the fact that he knows so much, CliffsNotes, the fact that I don't think Mommy would have approved of a kid learning a load of facts like this though, Mommy playing solitaire, Jesus of New Philadelphia, the fact that that kid has an encyclopedic memory, birthday present, pie rack, Empty Nest Syndrome, the fact that sea urchins live for *years*, the fact that life must be pretty peaceful for them, except for the occasional wolf eel passing by, the fact that a sea urchin can't see what's coming, so they probably live in a dreamy state without a care in the world, just sitting there waving their spines around, the fact that they're probably not even sure themselves if they're plants or animals, and they don't care, doctor fish, Dr. Fish, go figure, go fish, *One Fish, Two Fish, Red Fish, Blue Fish*, the fact that Frances McDormand and Holly Hunter were roommates in New York, *Fargo*, the fact that I'll just wash my face in the kids' bathroom, faucet, Farrah Fawcett Majors, the fact that I got my usual twinge from leaning over so low, the fact that I really shouldn't do that, the fact that I really should get a plumber in to fix the DON'T USE sink, the fact that Arnie doesn't like us anymore, the fact that we were too slow to send the *check* the last time, the fact that I didn't *mean* to be slow on it, the fact that his bill just got buried under papers and I forgot about it, *temporarily*, garage door salesman, the fact that he had to send us a reminder, the fact that he didn't *have* to but he did, two weeks later, the fact that it was all a little embarrassing, and now he doesn't respond to phone messages, so I guess we're in the doghouse, and he's the best plumber around, the fact that, also, I always liked his name, because you remember it, Arnie Tulip, ♫ *Tiptoe through the tulips* ♫, the fact that it should be "tiptoe *around* the Tulip," given Arnie's touchiness, Arnie, Arnold, *My Dog Tulip*, the fact that he has a brother called Jerry Tulip, who does carpentry, tulip trees, dceagle-cam, the fact that maybe what we need to look for is another plumber with a memorable name like that, the fact that surely there must be one, the fact that maybe they should study this at plumbing school, the fact that they shouldn't graduate without a good catchy name like Forget-Me-Not, Dogwood, Rose, rose madder, *While Titian was mixing rose madder*, the fact that the ASPE should insist on it, the fact that a kind man in Europe somewhere refused to leave the side of a bomb victim, during a terror attack, the fact that she was a complete stranger but he stayed there with her and comforted her, even though nobody knew if more bombs were about to explode any second, the fact that he says it's what *everyone* should do, the fact that we should all do something, he said, not just run away or take pictures, the fact that I don't know if I could do that, the fact that when other people start running, it's hard to resist joining them, even though I'm not much of a runner, the fact that it's probably instinctive, like shoals of fish or herds of buffalo, or reindeer, starlings, the fact that lots of people get injured when everybody starts to run, the fact that stampeding didn't help the buffalo, the fact that they went *extinct*, so not a great ad for the herd instinct, "The Day The Dam Broke," the fact that everybody ran the day the dam broke in Columbus, according to Thurber, Bond, James Bond, Follow My Leader, mass hypnosis, the fact that somehow I can't see myself hanging around and taking care of people though, when everybody else is rushing away, *Charlie Hebdo*, the fact that the woman he took care of passed away, and if he hadn't stayed with her she would've died alone, die, dye, Di, the fact that I would just be thinking about my kids, and how to get back to them, the fact that that's how moms are, the fact that you don't even think about it, the fact that I hope I'd try to save Leo too in an emergency, but the mom instinct might be stronger, "Come out, my love," the fact that they rescued three little boys in that Italian earthquake, or avalanche, and when the rescuers reached the boys they said "Come out, my love," the fact that they said "Come out, my love" as they pulled the boys free, and for some reason that made me cry, the kindness, Arnie Tulip, the fact that *unkindness* makes you cry too, the fact that I wouldn't even pick up a hitchhiker, so who am I to, to, "Come out, my love," the fact that now we've got to go to the grocery store, hats, coats, the fact that who's coming with me, the fact that if you woke up one day and found you were a sea urchin, you'd just make the best of it, I guess, like they do, but maybe sea urchins get a real *kick* out of being sea urchins, for all I know, the fact that it's kind of hard to tell, *Her position to Titian*, oh dear, not *that* again, Ringo, the fact that I don't know why I'm thinking about *him*, unless it's my dream, the fact that I dreamt Ringo Starr tried every drug and every car, the fact that he and Paul are the only ones left now, the fact that Ethan and Phoebe liked the Beatles, the fact that our snow service has let us down again, the fact that this stuff is knee-high in places, the fact that ever since the sandblasting, my teeth react to the cold and it hurts so much I have to keep my mouth tight shut while we trudge to the car, the fact that I still can't believe that hygienist, her and her tropical-flavored nanoparticles, the fact that I don't feel like going back to the dentist ever again, *any* dentist, tissues, Kleenex, the fact that I can still smell that stuff, or else the kids've got hold of some gum back there, the fact that in India people ride on top of the train, or some do anyway, the fact that we need to buy everybody underpants today, the fact that today's the day, the fact that kids' underpants wear out so fast, the fact that as soon as we were all in the car Gillian gave me this really serious look in the rearview mirror and said we're almost out of 7 Up, the fact that it made me want to giggle, that she finds that so big of a deal, boy, the fact that I wish all *I* had to worry about was 7 Up, the fact that it's best not to know what your kids are really thinking about, and they'd freak out if they knew what *I'm* thinking about, wolf eels, Beatlemania, Fagin, Titian, the fact that it's not about 7 Up, that's for darn sure, darning egg, nanoparticles, the fact that our house was always such a mess and nobody else's house was like that, not on our block or beyond, the fact that all the neighbor kids' houses seemed really tidy and roomy, with pink bedrooms with frilly curtains and valances and trunks full of Barbie dolls and Barbie-doll clothes, "close," and sunken living rooms and better sprinkler systems and taller more serious slides and lots of peanut butter and jelly sandwiches for lunch and barbecued spare ribs for dinner, well, maybe not the Newmans and the Wilsons, but everybody else, the fact that the smell of barbecued spare ribs would waft across the back yards all summer, the fact that it is *painful*, when you're a kid, smelling barbecued spare ribs from afar, the fact that *we* never had spare ribs, the fact that we rarely even had hot dogs, though we did have *onion soup*, my favorite thing, the fact that Mommy made it on special occasions, as a reward for something, or whenever I needed cheering up, because she knew how much I liked it, Irma Rombauer's recipe, Campbell's Beef Bouillon, the fact that Gillian calls it "Beef William," 7 Up, underpants, the fact that it takes a while to make and it's quite rich, the fact that you can't eat stuff like that every day, the fact that "French people eat French food," Madame Child, sole meunière, the fact that I don't think you could do it in this weather, travel on the roof of the train, I mean, the fact that you *could* make onion soup, the fact that it's actually a fine day for making onion soup today, and maybe I will, the fact that we had a lot of tunafish sandwiches, because Phoebe liked tunafish, the fact that I like tunafish sandwiches again now, "I do, I do," but as a kid I got really tired of them, the fact that I really reached my tuna limit for a while there, the fact that I bet tunas would *like* us all to reach our tuna limit, the fact that I was so embarrassed by all our books and papers and tuna fish sandwiches when friends came over, the fact that it all seemed so *uncool*, the fact that everybody else's mom seemed to be sunbathing all the time, while my parents were upstairs typing, Daddy in the attic and Mommy shut away in the bedroom, the fact that I resented Mommy's absence much more than Daddy's, but sometimes I went up and bothered him as well, diamond window panes, raccoon, Anne Frank, Frank, the fact that he found a raccoon up there once, the fact that we ate our lunch in the kitchen nook overlooking the back yard, buttercups, swing set, mulberry tree, snapdragons, watching him race along his well-worn paths, *Pepito*, not Daddy, chasing back and forth from one side of the garage to the other, barking at anyone in the alley, the fact that I think I was sort of a sad kid, the fact that, I mean, what kind of a favorite pastime was *that*, decorating the little triangular niches between tree roots with grass and acorns and trolls and stuff, or photographing trolls standing inside shoeboxes, the fact that I hardly gave them any furniture or anything, the fact that they just stood there, the fact that I'd write the name of the room backwards, and stick it on the back wall of the shoebox, because I thought photographs reversed everything, like mirrors, me and my disposable cameras, the fact that we went to the park a lot too, and once I lost a *tooth* ice-skating there, and another time I had to limp all the way home with broken glass in my foot, Mommy, Band-Aids, the little downstairs bathroom, styptic stick, terrapins swimming in the sink, the fact that there is nothing like being comforted by your mom when you got glass in your foot, the fact that you need that so you can face the rest of your *life*, the fact that there was a friendly squirrel once on our trash can who scared me, the fact that at first I liked him and I thought we were going to be great friends, the fact that I thought I was befriending a wild animal, and maybe he'd become my pet squirrel, but then I got suspicious about him, the fact that he was just *too* friendly, friendly wolf eel, the fact that he seemed so tame and didn't run away when I talked to him, the fact that I got scared he had rabies, so I edged away and never saw him again, dead pigeon, the fact that Pepito's main entertainments were barking at the mailman, or going crazee when Daddy got down on the floor with him, the fact that Pepito found that incredibly exciting, the fact that the thrill of standing *above* Daddy just knocked him out, the fact that he'd start barking and running around and around, the fact that I was always more attached to Pepito than I was to Pierre, which I felt guilty about for a long time, but I hardly *knew* Pierre, and Pepito I helped choose, the fact that I was home sick from school that day, with a cold or something, and we went to Chicago where the breeders lived in a cramped apartment with two black standard poodles and six puppies all scampering around, and there was Pepito, the only brown one, the fact that Pierre had been black and I thought it was time for a change, so I chose him, dear Pepito, the fact that we brought him home with us that day, the fact that it's strange to think my decision meant he spent his whole life with us and not somebody else, the fact that meanwhile I was so scared he'd pee on me I didn't dare hold him at all when he was a puppy, the fact that later I made him a snow-jacket out of an old sweater of Daddy's and he sank right in up to his shoulders in the snow and came home all covered in snow burrs that we had to pull off his legs or he would've dripped all over the house, the fact that he was very patient about it, and I think he really got to like his sweater too, the fact that he was too strong for me to walk him on the leash, the fact that they said I could walk him when I was twelve, so on my twelfth birthday I took Pepito for a walk, twelfth, "twelf," "twelth," Otis elevator guy, getting my first period on my thirteenth birthday, the fact that I got the kids doing a pronunciation quiz in the car, the fact that we already knew how they say "twelfth," and "February" so we tried fifth, sixth, library, crayon, mayonnaise, caramel, squirrel, mirror, and towel, the fact that Jake and Gillian got them all wrong, "fith," "sickth," "lie-berry," "cran," "mannaize," "carmul," "scwurl," "meer," "tal," the fact that Ben's better at it but a reluctant contributor today, the fact that I say "scwurl" too, one syllable, the fact that I don't know how you're *supposed* to say it, the fact that "squirrel" has to be one of the weirdest words, but a lot of rodent names are pretty strange, barsuk, aoudad, Adad, deadbeat dad, the fact that I don't know why I thought of that, the fact that Almanzo's horses keep suffocating on the ride home from

Brewster's, because it's so cold out, the fact that he has to keep getting off the sled to defrost their *noses* for them, the fact that Almanzo always sounds like he was kind of embarrassed about his name, "Almanzo," the fact that he was named after some Arab called El-Mansoor or something who'd saved one of the Wilder ancestors somewhere, generations back, the fact that the saved guy declared that from then on there would always be one son named Almanzo in the family, the fact that Almanzo and Laura didn't have a son to name "Almanzo," unless there was a stillbirth or something, I forget, the fact that her *mother* had a baby boy that died at about ten months, during their travels across the prairies, and they had to bury him in the middle of nowhere somewhere, the fact that maybe Ben or Jake should've been named *Leo*, the fact that it never occurred to me, "Leo Junior," the fact that that sort of stuff seems corny, but the Wilders had a good excuse for "Almanzo," the fact that that doesn't explain why they named his brother "Royal," the fact that she never goes into *that*, but maybe it's a form of "Leroy," LeRoy, le roi, Daddy's legs in the headlights, Copley Plaza, ancestors, the fact that it would make you jittery, I think, if you were a Wilder, in case you couldn't fulfil the family pledge, the Almanzo Pledge, the fact that it sounds like some Elk reunion thing, the fact that I guess if they were really worried about breaking the tradition, Laura and Almanzo could've named Rose "Almanza," the fact that once we were in the store it was time to buy that precious 7 Up, along with some Beef William, also jalapeño peppers, avocados, onions, potatoes, carrots, radishes, toms, cukes, celery, lettuce, eight dozen dessert apples, limes, lemons, Dr Pepper, Coke, Diet Coke, root beer, Hawaiian Punch, Kool-Aid, beer, seltzer, sour cream, cottage cheese, tortilla chips, rice crackers, Saltines, Graham crackers, Cracker Jack, Milky Ways, frozen OJ, Jell-O, bread, grape jelly, peanut butter, tuna fish, tsunami, pastrami, cheese slices, pickles, pickled beans, pickle relish, mustard, "mannaize," mole, chipotle, soy sauce, SpaghettiOs, Grape-Nuts, *The Grapes of Wrath*, chocolate milk, eggnog, paper towels, wax paper, paper straws, paper napkins, toilet paper, papers, papers, books and papers everywhere, not cool, a bottle of whiskey, wine, gin, Ziploc bags, XL *and* snack size, Vaseline, Band-Aids, "crans," coloring book, dish soap and liquid hand soap, the fact that they had icky plastic jungle plants on special, honey-do list, the motel pool in Detroit, the fact that it's always surprising seeing your cousins in their bathing suits, Mommy, gym shoes, perfume, the fact that Vaseline is made from gasoline, the fact that they can now roll out instant solar panels wherever you want but what are they *made* out of, the fact that they must use gasoline to make the plastic to make the solar panels, along with energy to manufacture the panels, the house that Jack built, but maybe they use recyclables for all of it, the fact that when I started looking at kids' underpants Ben ditched us, the fact that he said he'd wait up front, the fact that not even Gillian's interested in underpants, the fact that she ran off to the candy department, chickens, Stacy lost in Macy's, Pepito and his tags, the fact that Pepito lost his collar in the park one day, and he always liked his collar because of all the jangling rabies tags, the fact that he hated losing it, so I took him back to the park later and said "Go find your collar, Pepito, where's your collar, find your collar," and even though it was dark out, he went straight to the place, the fact that he knew exactly where he'd lost it, and there it was on the ground, behind a bench, dear doggie, the fact that dogs make a real effort to understand *our* languages, so why don't we reciprocate, the fact that you'd think we'd at least *try* to master dog language, the fact that I wonder if it varies a lot between regions, or countries, or between breeds, like can Ethiopian dogs communicate easily with Argentinian dogs, or is it a slightly different dialect, the fact that can a German Shepherd from Chicago perfectly understand a German Shepherd from Berlin, the fact that, heavens to Betsy, some dogs learn German or Russian or Arabic, and I can't even speak *Spanish*, and my kids can't say "twelfth" right, Twelfth Night, the fact that we were walking in Cy Young park once and a guy and his dog were coming towards us, and then a cyclist suddenly wove between us and the dog cowered out of the way, so I patted her and said what a good dog she was, and then her owner reached us and put his hand to his forehead, frowning, and scolded his dog, saying "You don't just walk straight into the path of a bicycle," as if she would understand every word, the fact that he probably used the subjunctive too, the fact that can a Taiwanese Pekinese speak with ease to a Sudanese Maltese, the fact that I once dreamt I asked the cats if they understood what an hour is, and Opal said it was a lot of *space*, and I had to tell her no, it's a lot of *time*, but she was sort of close, the fact that she knew it was sort of an abstract concept of some sort, the fact that I don't think cats do know what an hour is though, and dogs have brains the size of tangerines, but brain size isn't everything, or women would be dumber than men, the fact that Anatole France had an unusually small brain, but *he* wasn't dumb, the fact that how do I even know that, the fact that how does *anyone* know how big Anatole France's brain was, MYOB, mind your own brain, the fact that Jake wanted to sit on the conveyor belt, the fact that there was a little scuffle over that, but Gillian helped me, mainly because she didn't want her M&Ms stepped on, coupons, pleasantries, "Have a nice day," the fact that I'm trying, I'm *trying*, I mean to have a nice day, the fact that after we paid we finally found Ben all scrunched up, the fact that he was hemmed in by a big bunch of noisy moms and strollers, the fact that they were in their own world, chattering away, and didn't see how they'd kidnapped my son, squeezing him into a corner like that, kidnap, shepherd, goatherd, sheepfold, hoarlets, the fact that some strollers hold two or three babies, but you could hardly tell how many kids those women had, they'd piled so much stuff all over them, all sorts of bags hanging dangerously on the handles, accident waiting to happen, Stacy's injured hand, the fact that they were just gabbing away while my son was getting *crushed*, by them and their stuff, the fact that let's face it, moms only really care about their own children, or children very *similar* to their children, in age or size or looks, and gender and stuff, the fact that they act like the rest don't matter so much, the fact that Ben looked so forlorn standing there that my heart ached for him, and I started to feel sort of *enraged*, the fact that I really felt like telling one of those women to stop shoving my kid around but I didn't of course, the fact that I didn't dare, because it might cause ill-feeling in a store, the fact that I never can carry off stuff like that anyway, the fact that you're supposed to "channel your inner Bette," be firm but fair, but I'm no good at that, the fact that I just start to shake and stutter and then I sound pathetic and insane, hysterical, the fact that I get scared in case people will hate me, so I usually just try to keep my mouth shut, the fact that Ben probably thinks I'm a flop and that I never defend him, and I guess he's right, the poor kid, the fact that boys Ben's age are so sweet, so soft-cheeked, the fact that they're model citizens, and *most* of them don't carry weapons yet, the fact that then some woman squeezed ahead of me, just as we were trying to reach Ben, the fact that she wasn't one of the obnoxious moms, the fact that she was a whole *other* obnoxious person, yelling at someone on her cell phone, really personal stuff, like there was nobody else in the store, or maybe the *world*, just her and whoever it was she was so angry with at the other end of the phone, the fact that I don't get some people, I really don't, the fact that at least we got the 7 Up, underpants, and M&Ms, the fact that Ben somehow managed to squeeze out of his mom prison by himself and we were finally nearing the exit when I caught sight of the girl hanging around by the door, hanging back and sort of cringing, the fact that at first I thought maybe she must have a phobia about automatic doors or something, or a stomach ache, but then I caught sight of the big snarly dog outside, with the big snarly owner, the fact that the girl was too scared to go out past that dog, the fact that she looked about the same age as Stace so I wondered if Stacy might know her, but Stace doesn't think so, the fact that it really was a mean-looking dog, the muscly slobbery kind, with the big haunches, and a big thick neck and short hair, sort of bristling all over with tension, dying to bite somebody's head off, the fact that he was probably just born like that and he can't help it, but he did look ready to slaughter something, or at least take a chunk out of you, the fact that I don't know why people need pets like that, the fact that they must be so insecure, inferiority complex or something, the fact that this dog was so scary, I bet other *dogs* wouldn't try to walk past him either, or talk to him, in whatever dog language he speaks, or even smell his sit-me-down-upon, the fact that it was sort of like a Rottweiler, or a pit bull but much bigger, the fact that can Rottweilers talk to pit bulls, the fact that they probably don't bother, the fact that heaven knows how long that poor girl had been standing there, helpless, the fact that who knew going to the market could be so emotionally draining, the fact that nobody else seemed aware of the situation, so *I* decided to do something, yep, Superwoman, the fact that I got Ben and Gillian to stay with Jake, who was perched in the cart, and I boldly stepped outside and politely asked the dog man if he'd mind moving a little way away from the exit so this frightened girl could get out, the fact that I maybe said "I think she's scared of your dog," and that seemed to make him mad, the fact that he rounded on me and said "Go jump in a lake," and I was so shocked I couldn't even speak at first, the fact that my first instinct was to run back inside, but those noisy moms were now blocking the way back in, and peering out at *me*, *The Stepford Wives*, the fact that I was so ashamed by now, in case the kids had heard what that man had said to me, the fact that I knew I had to come up with some kind of *reply*, but of course I couldn't think of one in the heat of the minute, the moment, so all I said to him was "No, *you*," meaning *he* should go jump in a lake, and then I retreated back inside, terrapins, Northwestern pond, the Big Building, the fact that luckily I don't think the guy even heard it, because his dog was wheezing so loud, and slobbering and slavering, and baying for blood, with bated breath, bait, vultures, vampires, ghouls, wraiths, zombie movies, ululating, Hershey's Kisses, the fact that the kids always want me to buy them a bag of Hershey's Kisses, the fact that I'm just no good at rejoinders, repartee, ripostes, boarlets, *boarlets*, the fact that "god hates a coward," as Cap Garland said to Almanzo when Almanzo was hesitating about whether or not to make the long drive out to the Brewsters' in temperatures of 40 below, to bring Laura back to town, De Smet, the fact that Almanzo somehow senses she's desperate, so he goes and gets her, the fact that she almost freezes to death on the way home but it's still better than staying at the Brewsters' all weekend, with Mrs. Brewster running around the bedroom with that knife and everything, threatening to kill herself or somebody else, the fact that Laura can't sleep at all, huddled behind a thin curtain in the same room as them, thinking Mrs. Brewster might barge through the curtain any minute and stab her, the fact that Laura had to sleep on their sofa, mean-looking dog, the fact that it's so *kind* of Almanzo to go get her, Almanzo to the rescue, Jesus saved me, the fact that he had a MAGA cap on, not Almanzo or Jesus, the guy with the dog, waltzing Matilda, the fact that soon the two of them went off to pester people in some other doorway, broken, pearl barley, Mommy's illness, the fact that she was never the same again, though she regained the ability to speak and she could walk a bit, the fact that it broke me, the fact that it really shakes a kid up, I think, to know how easily that can happen to a person, how your life can be ruined, from one day to the next, one *minute*, the fact that the ground beef they had on sale today seemed to be from *three different countries*, so I didn't get it, the fact that I think ground beef should come from one animal, and *one* country, and probably not from America, where all the cattle's kept indoors now in big hangars, fed on "pre-emptive" antibiotics, ♪ *Just rope 'n' throw 'n' brand 'em* ♪, Howard Hughes's display of milk bottles, the fact that Katharine Hepburn was his girlfriend, the fact that she must've liked taking care of people, Gillian's multi-colored honey bears, ♪ *where the buffalo roam* ♪, the fact that I know I should just put up with it like everybody else, the *ground beef* that's on offer I mean, not bottles full of pee, the fact that it probably wouldn't hurt us, the meat I mean, the fact that we *could* go to the farm store and get us some fancy organic ground beef from outdoor-bred cattle, but even that's near a chemical plant, where they make alkylphenols, chlorinated paraffins, polymer additives, liquid and solid antioxidants, organophosphates, flame retardants, and drilling fluid additives, so it's hard to say if their cows are really a lot healthier than any other cows, "expanded use FDA clearance," Dollar General, ♪ *dollars for donuts* ♪, Superfund site, the fact that anyway it takes too long to get there and the kids don't want to go, the fact that I'm tired too, the fact that Jake just yanked his M&Ms away from Gillian, who was right in the middle of opening them for him, the fact that he said he wanted to open his own M&Ms, "I can do it I-self", *no man is an I-land*, the fact that then his packet started "raining," and he lost half his M&Ms on the floor, SpaghettiOs, Fancy Feast cat food, the fact that Ben has a new riddle book, and wants to entertain us all by reading out every single joke, "Why did the duck cross the road?", "To give the chicken a break," *Up a Road Slowly*, the fact that now Gillian's started Knock Knock jokes, to cheer Jake up, the fact that she's a good big sister, the fact that now Ben tells me bird flu only has to mutate a few more times to cause a global pandemic like Spanish flu and that, if that happens, civilization will grind to a halt *within a year*, the fact that I know it's terrible of me but I can't help hoping the guy with the scary dog will be one of the first to go,

．　　　　．　　　　．　　　　．

Hers was a life of resentments, suspicions and alarms. She had her satisfactions though: an opossum swinging upside down from a high branch, the whoop of an owl, indicating dusk and the time to hunt, the sight of a dead sheep's face, surrounded by tight woolen curls, a sip of clear crow water, nibble of grass, large white snowflakes disappearing into a black pond. And now, her infants asleep in the den.

Finding food was a struggle. She needed a lot of it. Mice, ever-present, weren't worth grabbing except as playthings for cubs. Even a raccoon seemed a meager meal, that she was too worn out to catch. Raccoons sometimes bit back.

She was surprised by her kittens' ears, so soft; their chirps and purrs. They grew, doubling in size in a matter of days. The sight of them soothed her, this lion who usually felt nothing but antipathy for other lions – apart from her mother, her sister and, briefly, her last lover. She had no desire to meet male lions in the woods now; if anything, she feared them. Her life was constrained by this new intimacy with her cubs. She had begun to recognize them by their spots and stripes. It helped too that one was darker than the other two. They were soft and vulnerable, but more powerful than they looked, as she discovered when transferring them to a new den.

Alarmed to find her lover's pee, his mark, nearby, she snuck off with the cubs that very night. She could carry one in her mouth, holding her head high to prevent the kitten from dragging in the snow. The other two followed, intermittently sinking out of sight as they leapt from one deep hole made by their mother's paws, to the next. The snow was a foot high in places. Recoil and leap, recoil and leap.

The lioness looked behind her now and then, which set the kitten she carried swinging in the air. She wasn't looking for the cubs – she knew they were right behind her. She was scanning the forest for any sign of her mate. In her dread of him she never paused except to eye the trees, and trade one cub for another in her jaws.

Baby lions have hidden strengths. Unquestioningly, they followed their anxious mother for three whole miles on hitherto untried legs. It didn't matter if they ached for the next few days: all they wanted was to be where she wanted them to be.

·   ·   ·   ·

the fact that after you try again and again to lean the Swiffer against the back wall of the closet and yet it *keeps* falling forward, you just want to say "You ever heard of gravity, huh, Swiffer, ever thought of that? And you can tell the broom too, while you're at it," the fact that Leo asked me at breakfast what I thought was going to happen today and I said "Haircut," and he said "No, photographs of Pluto are arriving from outer space," the fact that even I can see a haircut takes a back seat to the first close-ups of Pluto ever seen, second fiddle, barber's shop quartet, chenille, the fact that I've still got Mommy's old wooden pepper grinder, shaped like a little beer barrel, salt and pepper shakers, the Shakers, the fact that the New Horizons spacecraft is about the size of our *fridge* and it's covered in gold foil, the fact that it looks kind of homemade, like somebody came up with it in the garage over a couple of weekends, or in a man cave somewhere, with the aid of a crate of Bud Lites, the fact that "ghetto" now means homemade, the fact that it makes me sad to think of our fridge traveling alone through space, the fact that they only discovered Pluto in 1930, the year Daddy was born, Ides of March, the fact that an eleven-year-old English girl came up with the name "Pluto" and Ben's very envious of her, the fact that Pluto's now downgraded to a *planetoid mass*, not a planet, so we all feel bad for it, even though it's now in the limelight, getting photographed, the fact that who wants to be "planetoid," the fact that we all want to name it ourselves, the fact that I said it should be called "Almanzo," because I always feel kind of sorry for Almanzo, I don't know why, the fact that he had a hard life, getting sick and all, right after they got married, the fact that I think Laura Ingalls Wilder must have been quite a handful too, the fact that she was a toughie, the fact that money was tight until they were in their *sixties*, when the books started coming out, the fact that if Ben was going to name a planet, he says he'd name it Opal, so sweet, except that now all of a sudden the cats aren't enough for these kids and everybody wants a dog, the fact that all their friends have dogs, or so they say, and Gillian's sick of trying to walk Opal and Frederick on a leash, the fact that Opal squirms out of her collar and Frederick just rolls over and purrs and won't budge, the fact that it would be fun to have a dog, if he was like Pepito, not that rotten Rottweiler or whatever it was at the grocery store, the fact that no dog could be the same as Pepito though, the fact that I reminded them of the scary dog but Stacy said "We're not planning to get a *man-eater*," and then the others all chimed in with "C'mon, Mom," as if they really thought they were making headway and I was about to give in right then and there, *today*, and rush over to the pound or something, or start searching for puppies on Craigslist, the fact that I said brightly "Why don't we keep bees?", and that quelled them briefly, the fact that I did once think of keeping bees, long ago, but I never wanted to wear one of those spaceman suits, the fact that I don't want to handle a hive, I just like *honey*, the fact that raw honey's supposed to be good for you, but only once you're old enough, the fact that it's not good for people under two, or is it eighteen months, eighteen moons, Pluto, the fact that it's a useful alternative to sugar in many recipes, *honey* is, not Pluto, the fact that having to tend a couple thousand bees would actually probably send me into a tizzy, the fact that two cats, four kids, and an ever-changing number of hens, are really about enough for me to handle right now, the fact that I told them "We have some great chickens!" and it's true, ♫ *I'm a little teapot, short and stout* ♫, jug handle and clover leaf intersections, flow diagram, the fact that Laura Ingalls Wilder was sort of short and stout herself, not *fat*, just sturdy, sturdy as "a little French horse," the fact that maybe that's why Almanzo liked her so much, the fact that he was always keen on horses, the fact that I pointed out how nice our chickens are, the fact that some of them are brown and some are speckled black and white, black-and-white movies, Bette Davis, and you can make all kinds of things out of their feathers when they molt, ♫ *Cut-cut-cut-cudacket, Said the little hen* ♫, and their chicks are fun, the fact that maybe I lay it on a bit thick, the fact that having hens is worrisome at times, the fact that they've gotta be let out early in the morning or they kick up such a rumpus, the fact that our neighbors probably wish we had a dog instead, even a barky dog, lawns, sidewalk, scooter, the fact that Mother's Day was invented in Grafton, West Virginia, about a hundred years ago, WV, VW, Mom's Day, Moms Demand, the fact that they have to be checked midday too, the chickens, not moms, and locked back up in the coop at sundown, the fact that at least we don't have a rooster, the fact that people have been run out of town for having roosters, or the roosters have been run out of town at least, the fact that roosters are why coq au vin was invented, the fact that it's not just the crowing first thing in the morning, but roosters can be *mean*, the fact that if it wasn't so hard to sex chicks, nobody would keep the roosters, the fact that Nebuchadnezzar was an accident, and then I couldn't *resist* keeping him because he was so good-looking, but then he started attacking the chickens, the cats, and *me*, the fact that six months with a rooster is my record, the coq au vin at André Allard, sore neck, Gare du Nord, terrorist attacks, the fact that taking care of chickens is not nothing, the fact that they need tending even in a blizzard, and it's all up to me, the fact that not every-body realizes the pecking order involves actual pecking, the fact that people seem to think it's just a metaphor but it isn't, the fact that it may not be the most democratic-looking form of government but it seems to work, the fact that sometimes they all pick on one poor hen though and you have to separate them, pariah chicken, the fact that I hate it when they keep pecking at its sit-me-down-upon, the fact that I wish they wouldn't do that, the fact that Audrey's currently top hen, the fact that she's so nice and fat and she runs the whole show like a queen, *The Lucille Ball Show*, pecking everybody that gets in her way, the fact that she never pecks *us*, just her coopmates, the fact that she's very affectionate towards me now, chicken feed, Ronny, Tuesday, red barn and silo, hex signs, the fact that they're free range but not organic, because organic would mean really cramping their style, and mine, the fact that organic honey is made from bees who've had their wings clipped, or that's what somebody told me once in a delicatessen in Hartford, so I don't buy that anymore either, off-campus, flat tire, Jesus of New Philadelphia, the fact that you have to watch every single little thing the chickens eat if they're organic, and it's much more fun for them to run around all day and eat whatever they want, without supervision, the fact that chickens really get around, the fact that we've found eggs in all kinds of places, *The Grapes of Wrath*, the fact that fewer than ten percent of Americans now work in factories or on farms, the fact that only *chickens* work in factories now, the fact that we give ours sunflower seeds and beets and skimmed milk, and chicken feed, and they help themselves to "rejectamenta" scraps, the fact that where did I see that word, the fact that Laura Ingalls Wilder always gave her hens skimmed milk in the winter months, so I do too, the fact that she really knew a lot about chickens, the fact that she had it in for hawks though, just like her dad, Laura Ingalls Wilder's poultry column, giagaccini, *Groundhog Day*, the fact that she thought hawks attacked her chickens, the fact that a few of *our* chickens have disap-peared over the years, but I don't think it's hawks, because there aren't any around here, not that I've seen anyway, the fact that it could be coyotes or foxes or, or even bears, the fact that I'm sure bears like chickens, the fact that most predators are nocturnal though, and by nightfall our hens are safe in their coop, so it's probably not bears, the fact that they usually march right in without any trouble, the chickens not the bears, the fact that you know when they're sleeping because they have ways of letting you know if they're awake, the fact that they screech, the fact that they're not shy, the fact that I think our chickens are pretty happy, the fact that they get to live in a little gingerbread-style house, just like a fairytale cottage, Stacy's old playhouse that we brought all the way from Hamden, the fact that it's got ornate shutters with heart-shaped holes punched through them, and pretty filigreed doodads all along the edge of the roof, and it's painted dark red to match our house, the fact that the chickens go right in there to lay their eggs too, mostly, aside from a rogue egg or two in the garage or a flowerpot someplace, *They say the hen can lay*, chicken stock, the fact that once we found two eggs in Jake's old shoe, which worried him, the fact that Haydn kept his chickens in a big stone building with lots of stairs, a big fancy disused water tank, a folly, the fact that it made a very grand hen house, the fact that the hens must've loved that, the fact that I think chickens like to feel special, the fact that they like getting up high too, like goats, so they can get a good view of old Papa Haydn, funettes, the fact that why was he called that, "Papa Haydn," the fact that did he *want* to be called that or did he hate it but it just stuck, *Up, up, turn around, Sergeant Smith, down down,* the fact that I wish we had some *goats*, baby goats, kids, the fact that why don't my kids want kids, the fact that ideally, I'd have all kinds of pets, dogs and mice and donkeys and Indian Runner ducks, and an orchard for them all to spread out in, the fact that jobs in retail are down by half since 2001, all thanks to Amazon, slavery, the fact that baby goats have such slender legs and tiny feet, the fact that the average shop assistant salary is $12 a day, I mean an *hour*, and they sort of *bounce*, baby goats I mean, the fact that they look like they want as little contact with the ground as possible, the fact that they're anti-gravity, piñata, cackleberries, How To Survive A Shark Attack, the fact that

Stacy didn't seem to mind when we turned her playhouse into a chicken coop, the fact that she was growing out of it anyway, the fact that I wish I'd kept her rocking horse, but we left Hamden in such a hurry, the fact that the other kids might've made good use of that rocking horse, the fact that it should have been an heirloom, the fact that in the chaos of moving I got rid of everything, but maybe I was a bit too ruthless, the fact that I was just dizzy with love, and not thinking straight, the fact that I never even dared ask Stacy, the fact that it's worse than my parents getting rid of my *tricycle* without asking, oh dear, regrets, regrets, the fact that parents do some terrible things in the name of practicality or something, the fact that what we need is one of those little apartment blocks for purple martins, all white with black doorways, the fact that I just kind of like the look of them, the fact that they look like that big old white hotel we went to in the Blue Ridge Mountains, white and black, purple, purple-brown, reddish-brown, gray, Pepito's coloring, the fact that martins like to get together, congregate, just like starlings, the fact that I can get 20¢ or 25¢ an egg at the Stop & Shop over in Coshocton if we have a surplus, but we hardly ever do, the fact that Laura Ingalls Wilder wrote a poultry column for the local paper before she started writing her books, the fact that it was her daughter who made her write those "damn juveniles," just to make money, because they were broke, broken, Rose, kids' books, memoirs, family lore, the fact that Rose felt guilty because she'd invested all their money and lost it in the Wall Street crash, the fact that she was always trying to make up for that, and one idea of hers was bullying her mom to write children's books, the fact that Rose edited all the *Little House* books, and made her mom take out anything gloomy, the fact that everything had to be seen through Rose-tinted spectacles, except the bit when Jack gets left behind, the fact that Gillian always gets anxious when we come to that, the fact that they had to get the covered wagon across a swollen river, which is much deeper than Pa expected, or he would have taken Jack on board instead of forcing him to swim across on his own, the fact that Pa has to jump off the wagon himself in the middle of the river and swim the horses to shore or they'd all have drowned, the fact that an erection contractor said that once to Leo, "no changing horses mid-stream," slab-beam bridges, the fact that the Ingallses sure could have used a bridge, ♫ *Sur le pont d'Avignon* ♫, overload analysis, live load, dead load, longitudinal girders, culverts, pont, Ponzi scheme, Amway, the bridge between awake and asleep, asleep and awake, the fact that when they reach the other side, there's no sign of Jack anywhere, and for the rest of that day Laura's scared he was carried way downstream and drowned, and they'll never see him again, but later that night, Jack crawls slowly towards their camp fire, Campfire Girls, Wo-He-Lo, the fact that his eyes glow in the fire light and Pa almost *shoots* him, think-ing he's a coyote or something, but it's all okay in the end, the fact that Jack remained their faithful companion for years, following the log cabin, no, the covered wagon all the way from Wisconsin to Minnesota and Dakota, Silver Lake, Plum Creek, the fact that I never could see why they didn't take him across the river in the wagon in the first place, the fact that they could've carried him the *whole way*, brindle bulldog, but especially for that river-crossing, the fact that he was just a small dog, and couldn't have weighed much, the fact that his death later on in the book gets you every time, but in real life the Ingallses didn't have him all his life, the fact that he left when they sold some horses off, the fact that he wanted to go where the horses went, the fact that I don't know why Rose allowed Jack's death to stand, because it's not very upbeat, but I guess she knew some people like a good cry, Westminster Dog Show, the fact that when Rose got enough money together, she paid for a whole new house to be built on the Wilder property in Missouri and made her mom and dad move into it, while *she* took over the old farmhouse that Almanzo had lovingly built him-self with his own bare hands, the fact that he made everything just the right height for Laura, and made all the pantry drawers and shelves and things she needed, a little French horse, the fact that I bet they had a whatnot too, the fact that our eggs stay nice and cool in the pantry, Laura Ingalls Wilder's homemade noodle recipe, the fact that I think everybody should have chickens and a pantry, and homemade noodles, the fact that a pantry is the perfect place for eggs and pies and butter and apples and flour, but *not* cake flour or cake eggs, because they need to be room temperature, the fact that pie flour stays nice and cool in the pantry though, just right, Highgate, high five, Watergate, Nipplegate, Deflategate, the fact that eggs shouldn't be stone-cold when you're making a cake, because if you add refrigerator eggs to creamed butter, the butter *re-solidifies*, which you don't want, the fact that our pantry can get *too* cold sometimes, the fact that it all depends on the season, the fact that as soon as Rose left town, Laura and Almanzo moved straight back into their old house, and later sold the one Rose had built for them, the fact that in *The Long Winter*, an old Indian warns the town that bad weather's coming, seven months of snow, and he's absolutely right, the fact that the Native Americans knew all about this land and they just got ignored mostly, Frank Baum, *L.* Frank Baum, Hitler, the fact that during the Gold Rush whole tribes were slaughtered, the fact that the first governor of California pledged to exterminate them all, the fact that in just twenty years the Indian population of California was reduced by eighty or ninety percent, half of them outright murdered and the rest dead from untreated diseases, the fact that almost all the Yuki died, two thousand or so, leaving less than two *hundred* by the end of the Gold Rush, the Tolowa too, and the Yahi were just *gone*, Fugitive Mom Captured, demolition, the fact that Leo's wasp-killing tennis racket's called the Pulverizer, the fact that Laura Ingalls Wilder was a Republican, but I don't think she hated Indians, the fact that Pa gets along with Indians but Ma's scared of them and Jack *hates* them, the fact that Pepito hated the mailman, the fact that he just couldn't see why a stranger would come right up to our door uninvited, the fact that he regarded everybody as a tres- passer, the fact that an Osage Indian saved all the Ingallses' lives one night, the fact that he galloped in from far away to persuade all the other tribes not to go to war against the illegal settlers, the fact that it's a true story, I think, and he got there just in time, last-minute stuff, or there would've been no *Little House* books for me to read to Gillian, the fact that I just remembered I dreamt I gave birth to a baby on board a ship and had to leave it behind when I got off, but I went back for it at the end of the day, the fact that I was scared the authorities would give me trouble about having left it there all day, accuse me of abandoning it or something, but I didn't care what they said, the fact that I just wanted my baby, and I think I got it, but I'm not sure and I'll never know, because I woke up, ♫ *What puts the ape in apricot* ♫, Chopper5, Flying Tee, Quantrill, eighty widows, Raccoon Hitches Ride On Windshield, Dog Adopts Orphaned Piglet, the fact that Leo says you'd think that after a *few days* Columbus might have rethought calling everybody "Indians," since he must've known by then he wasn't in India, but the name stuck, the fact that Columbus was really not such a nice guy, the fact that people are starting to rethink Columbus Day, the fact that maybe raping women and cutting people's hands off for not bringing him enough gold, and driving thousands of people to suicide, doesn't seem so worth celebrating anymore, Richmond's slave market, Virginia, Missouri, misery, the fact that Oberlin got rid of Columbus Day and now they call it Indigenous Peoples' Day, Columbus, Ohio, Columbia College, Columbia Records, Columbia Pictures, Columbiana, columbarium, the Knights of Columbus, Columbine Massacre, Columbia sheep, ♫ *We are poor little lambs that have lost our way, baa, baa, baa!* ♫, the egg of Columbus, Humpty Dumpty, eggs Benedict, scrambled, pine trees, swimming pool, homemade lemonade, corn dogs, corn dodger, draft dodgers, buffalo wings, the fact that Mommy's dad was in the Knights of Columbus, the fact that I never knew what that outfit was for and I finally asked Leo, and he said "If there's a single men's club that isn't about drinking, it's news to me," the fact that I guess the Elks are about drinking too, the fact that the Elks used to be Caucasian Only, the fact that the Elks currently have eight hundred thousand members, the fact that they let women in, because they were going to lose their liquor license otherwise, bit the bullet, the fact that I think they have African American members now too but I'm not sure, the fact that what about the Shriners, the fact that the Shriners are connected to the Freemasons, ♫ *and the thigh bone's connected to the* ♫, Daughters of the Nile, "the Exhausted Ruler," the fact that there are some female frogs who decide on which frog to mate with, depending on the number of croaks he can do, the fact that they like the ones who croak the most, the fact that it's news to me that frogs can count, the fact that *Jake* can't, s'mores, Anadama bread, popsicles, apples, oranges, tea bags, olive oil, soda, dishwasher tabs, butter, the fact that there's some artist in New York who paints pictures on used tea bags and egg shells, Easter egg dye, walking on egg shells, the fact that a lot of American history is nothing to be proud of, the fact that it makes you pretty sick, but my students didn't want to hear any of that, the fact that they wanted everything to make a pretty picture, upbeat, feel-good, the fact that I *tried* to stay upbeat but it's not that easy when you're teaching history, the fact that "All there is is NOW" is not completely true, the fact that there's before, and what's next, the fact that the PTA says we should all be instilling patriotism, optimism and contentment in our kids the whole time, the fact that we're under *orders* not to worry them, like the way Daddy told us not to worry Mommy after she got sick, in case it caused another stroke or episode or whatever, the fact that from then on I had no mom, really, but of course I wouldn't want to worry my kids about their country, the fact that what's the point in that, the fact that I would never say *any* of this to the kids, the fact that, statistically, American kids are shaken up enough already, Bra Thief Shot By Store Manager, the fact that the PTA wants to give them worry dolls and silly putty, sixth mass extinction event, Wounded Knee, taking the knee, housemaid's knee, the fact that everybody's now on opioids, even kids, the fact that there's a lot you just have to *blank out* if you want to get through life, the fact that I do it all the time and it helps, Family Raises $22K For Sick Baby, the fact that I try not to remember *anything* if possible, until it comes time to do our taxes and the whole year floods back and upsets me, the fact that Laura Ingalls Wilder started writing her memoirs to preserve her memory before it was too late, but what I say is, let it slip, the fact that she sure remembered a lot, Nellie Oleson and the leeches, the Brewsters and all, the fact that if *I* started writing my memoirs I'd probably be finished by about three o'clock today, the fact that that Nellie Oleson was *hateful*, the fact that she's a classic hateful little girl, and Laura got her revenge on her with the leeches, the fact that Pa seems a nice guy, the fact that he sticks up for Indians, and plays the violin well, the fact that he doesn't seem to notice or care though how the settlers were backing the Indians into a corner, the fact that Ma's maybe a bit of a drip, and prickly at times, stern, the fact that Pa's a loner type, always wanting to move further West, the fact that all Pa cared about was the hunting, and once it's no good anymore because of too many settlers, he wants to move on, the fact that Leo thinks Pa was a *maniac*, dragging his family to and fro like that, risking all their lives with bears, wolves, panthers, blizzards, leeches and plagues of locusts, and whatnot, smallpox, scarlet fever, and disenchanted Indians, the fact that Leo's pretty suspicious of Pa, the fact that he's got a theory that the whole time Pa's supposed to have been holed up in that snow cave for three days, surviving on the Christmas candy, he was really at a saloon in town, or the, the house of ill repute, ♪ *they call the Rising Sun* ♪, the fact that Laura Ingalls Wilder fans would get into a real kerfuffle if they heard that, I bet, Why You Need A Pet In Your Life, $22K, the fact that Leo despises all the *Little House* books but still I find it touching when Laura eats her first whole orange at the age of fourteen, and when Jack dies, defrost OJ, hair collector, the fact that I don't even know what they're *for*, the fact that I guess I've been wasting loose hairs all my life, the fact that maybe it's in case you get yourself into some kind of Rapunzel predicament, and need to weave a rope ladder, the fact that Gillian likes the earlier books best, the fact that her bedside light is too bright, the fact that it needs a different bulb, the fact that that's probably why she doesn't sleep all that well these days, the meaning of life, the fact that she *won't* sleep without the light on, but then it wakes her up, so then she reads some more Laura Ingalls Wilder, tropical-flavored nanoparticles, the fact that I should go change that bulb right now, the fact that maybe she needs a *nicer* lamp in there, the fact that lighting is almost always ugly, the fact that you just can't find a nice lamp to buy these days, the fact

that how many lamps do I remember fondly, or cherish, the fact that
they're all so intrusive, either too bright or too dim, either shining in
your face or too faint to read by, the fact that only candles are nice,
really, but they're too dangerous around children, Chicago fire, the
fact that Christmas-tree lights are nice, but not as nice as they used to
be, the fact that I hate those new icy blue ones, the fact that I don't
like the blueish-white headlights on cars either, the fact that white
light is always grim, the fact that I've always hated fluorescent tubes,
Daddy in the kitchen in Evanston at night, dim, grim, the fact that
we're in the Dark Ages and all our lamps stink, flatulence, flagellants,
the fact that street lights annoy birds and other animals who just want
to get some shut-eye, the fact that Chaucer said birds sleep with their
eyes open, the fact that street lights must really bother them, though
Chaucer didn't mention that, nocturnal, I mean diurnal, birthday
presents, Tuesday, laundry pile, ironing pile, Ben's water samples,
soft-pedal, soft shoe shuffle, snow-shoveling service, the fact that Ben
keeps firing more facts about Pluto at me, the fact that I think there's
maybe too much emphasis on facts these days, or maybe there are just
too many facts, the fact that the Hungarian police fire tear gas at children, the fact that I liked that dream about the stick that moved, the
fact that it was just a branch off the tree but it could sort of flex its
muscles, the fact that it broke off from a bigger branch and was writhing around, wriggling anyway, a bit like a starfish, the fact that I
wanted the kids to come out and see my writhing stick, but they
wouldn't, so I brought it inside and put it in the middle of the table,
but everybody was being really slow arriving for dinner, and it was
frustrating, the fact that family meals are really like team meetings,
where you share your news, unless someone's doing the Silent Act,
the fact that I also dreamt I was pregnant again and didn't know what
to do about it, the fact that we were thinking it over, Leo and I, the
fact that I was scared there'd be something wrong with the baby
because I'm so old, but I knew I didn't want to abort it, the fact that
it would be very hard to abort Leo's child, even in a dream, the fact
that I was thinking about Stacy in the dream, and hoping I'd do things

better with the new baby, the fact that I was going to call it Abby, so I guess we knew it was a girl already, but then I lost my change purse, the fact that I was on a bus and had a whole half-eaten pie in my purse, and I was still thinking about the baby and the night feeds and all, and getting her to school and watching her excel at computers, and how old I'd be before she went to college, "Really, Jake!", Alec, Abby, the fact that then there was something about having to go back to work at Peolia again, the fact that somehow I'd already *agreed* to it, though very reluctantly, and now I was trying to figure out how to get out of it, the fact that then I had to get off the bus at a stop I didn't know, but it looked like a nice place, and *that's* when I lost my purse, snow-bound, the fact that it took the biggest rocket ever to get this fridge thing, New Horizons, launched and it took nine years for it to reach Pluto, nine years, the fact that the pictures it's sending back travel at the speed of light and take four and a half hours to reach Earth, the fact that the ship is three billion miles away and now it's heading further out, the fact that it didn't stop on Pluto or anything, the fact that it's like those tourist groups that see all of Europe in a week, the fact that Pluto has a row of dark spots on it, and another dark shape they call the whale's tail, the fact that it has a snakelike skin, and canyons *five miles deep*, the fact that that's pretty deep for a little planetoid mass, it seems to me, the fact that it looks a lot like a poffertje, but what do I know, flapcakes, griddlecakes, English muffins, waffles, Swiss steak, "Dribble with syrup if desired," the fact that Clyde Tombaugh discovered Pluto, the fact that I think Leo's at his wit's end with all this Pluto stuff, the fact that he doesn't much go for astronomy really, the fact that he just interrupted Ben's Pluto lecture to talk about mammoth bones instead, the fact that the first mammoth bones were found on the banks of the Ohio, *And that has made all the difference*, the fact that he says that find changed the thinking about evolution, because it proved animals could go extinct, or evolve into new species, the fact that elephants will soon be extinct because of the ivory trade, the fact that all those little ivory boxes Bette's carving in *Now, Voyager* seemed *innocent* then, therapeutic crafts, ivory trade, cigarette butts hidden under Kleenex, "My castle, Doctor," the fact that at first they thought mammoths were carnivores, on account of their sharp tusks, but later they realized the tusks were for digging and uprooting trees, just like elephant tusks, not for mauling flesh, the fact that they ate with their molars, these huge blocks like packing crates, or more like a whole lot of flattened cardboard boxes, glued tight together, great big rectangular cubes with serrated tops for grinding through wood, oh, no, I guess it's *mastodon* teeth, not mammoths, the fact that I wonder what the hygienist would do with *those*, the biggest molars you ever saw, the fact that there'd be nothing left when she got finished with them, tropical flavor, the fact that now Ben's busy with mastodons, the fact that all the rivers of Ohio are full of fossils, not just the Ohio River, and full of PCBs too, plutonium isotopes, and three hundred and ten gigatons of carbon dioxide, GM, Toledo, the fact that the Ohio's the most polluted waterway in America, or maybe anywhere, the fact that more raw sewage gets dumped into it every time it rains, and acid mines drain into it, acid mines, dear me, the fact that I can't imagine people digging for *acid*, sulfuric acid, citric acid, the fact that what do they want all that for, the fact that you'd think we could do with *less* acid around, not more, acid attacks on women, the fact that farms and industries deposit whatever they want in the Ohio, the fact that there are twenty-four million pounds of chemicals in that river, *pounds*, the fact that three million people have to get their drinking water from there, including *us*, the fact that in 2007 it had sixty-one pounds per something of mercury, and now, just ten years on, it's got three hundred and eighty pounds of mercury or more, Ohio freshwater mussels, freshwater corals, bald eagles, crab boil, the fact that dentists used to put mercury in fillings, the fact that they stuck mercury right inside your head, Flying Tee, but what do dentists care, nanoparticles, hygienist, "Are you evil?", the fact that everybody now thinks Jemma went crazee because of the mercury leaking out of her teeth, dear me, Pietro, the fact that she had to have all her fillings removed but I don't know if it helped or not, the fact that I'll have to ask Leo, the fact that we don't have much to do with that side of the family, the fact that just having my fillings removed would be enough to drive *me* over the edge, to the edge, on edge, the fact that the magnificent old Ohio is now full of mercury and PCBs and I don't know what all, maybe roadside stands and Longaberger's baskets and cow statues, and tray bakes, tartes tatin, aborted babies, the fact that hoverflies eat aphids, the fact that caterpillars like nasturtiums, Young's Jersey Dairy, the fact that you only have to look at the Tuscarawas River to see *it's* ruined too, the fact that at the time of the 1913 flood it wasn't ruined, the fact that the water was perfectly clear then, dam, Thurber, the fact that all this pollution has happened since then, in just a hundred years, the fact that we let Lake Erie *die*, for Pete's sake, a whole Great Lake, the fact that Lake Erie used to have whitefish, bass, trout and pickerel in it, bald eagles, eaglets, the science of pain, the fact that the Cuyahoga started catching fire in 1868, the fact that the Cuyahoga caught fire in 1868, 1883, 1887, 1912, 1922, 1936, 1941, 1948, 1952, and 1969 and nobody did anything about it, but now they've cleaned it up some, The World's Most Romantic Hotels, and it seems in better shape than a lot of the other rivers around here, 111-Year-Old Woman Reveals Her Secret, the fact that there are a few hogsuckers and spotfin shiners in there now, Ben's water samples, the fact that we have to collect more samples for Mr. Bowder this weekend, so we are going to pollute the air in order to study pollution in the water, the fact that Ben's already taken samples from the Tuscarawas, at both Nugent Bottom and Stark Patent Bottom, twice from the Ohio, before and after rainfall, when the sewage gets poured in, and from Wolf Creek, Buckhorn Creek, West Fork Buckhorn Creek, Lick Run, Blue Ridge Run, Rodney Run, Swigert Run, Hoffman Run, Davis Run, Evans Creek, Browning Run, Frocks Run, White Eyes Creek, East Fork White Eyes Creek, West Fork White Eyes Creek, Indiancamp Creek, Stone Creek, Center Creek, Wills Creek, Birds Run, Johnson Fork, Yellow Water Creek, Dunlap Creek, Rocky Fork, Clear Fork, Turkey Run, Atkinson Creek, Fallen Timber Creek, Phillips Fork, Watson Creek, Crooked Creek, Fry's Creek, Oldtown Creek, Mud Run, East Branch Fork Sugar Creek, Brush Run, Pleasant

Valley Creek, Troyer Valley Creek, South Fork Sugar Creek, Brandywine Creek, Broad Run, and Goose Creek, the fact that he and Mr. Bowder analyze the samples and make flowcharts, fishbone diagram, the fact that Ben's going to use that Izaak Walton quote I gave him in his introduction, "nature's storehouse," the fact that water is a storehouse where nature locks away its treasures, the fact that I don't think Izaak Walton meant mercury though, and lead and other metals, bacteria, pathogens, PCBs, and industrial waste, the fact that, when you think about it, Izaak Walton's about the only thing they *haven't* found in there, the fact that we will all die, the fact that it's terrible to die alone, the fact that Ben keeps all his samples in our freezer, which at first I wasn't too keen on, the fact that it didn't seem very wholesome to have all this polluted water with our food in the freezer, but then Leo pointed out that most of this is no different from the water we use for ice cubes, or the water we wash our hands in, so what's the big deal, the fact that in Flint, Michigan, they were drinking poisoned water for *years*, the fact that that's so terrible, the sick children, the fact that now Flint residents get free bottled water, I think, but they still have to pay *water bills*, which is kind of weird, if you ask me, the fact that you can't use bottled water to *shower* in, so they must have to shower in all these contaminants, toxins, the fact that maybe they have a last *rinse* with bottled water, which must be a pain in the neck, the fact that they'd be better off standing in the rain, when there is any, unless it's acid rain, Legionnaires' disease, McLaren Flint, the fact that that Michael Moore guy is always bringing up the water problem in Flint but I don't know why, since nobody listens, Ignorance and Want, Mass-Transit Authority, the fact that people are still allowed to fish the Ohio but they're not supposed to *eat* what they catch, mastodons, Ohio River Valley, the fact that the Ohio's still got smallmouth buffalo fish, sauger fish, white and black bass, carp and catfish, but none of them are safe to eat, the fact that *eagles* have to eat them, whether they're safe or not, the fact that eagles can't read the warnings, boarlets, the fact that an eagle can't just go out for chicken à la king and French fries whenever it feels like it, or binge on a wedge of shoofly pie à la mode, a lemon wedge of a moon, the fact that eagles only like raw flesh, fish or birds or rodents, the fact that bears eat salmon, the fact that David Albatross, I mean David *Attenborough*, says albatrosses fly for miles and miles and bring back food for their young, but sometimes what they bring home is *plastic*, because that's all that's in the oceans now, along with turtles with their waists squinched by plastic rings for holding six-packs, the fact that a turtle with a waist, the fact that I dreamt about a turtle who only had front legs, no back legs, and he couldn't get himself out of a deep sort of puddle by the road somewhere, and I was scared he was going to drown, the fact that you don't need a belly button if you come out of an egg, the fact that turtles have umbilical scars for a while, or remains of the umbilicus anyway, the fact that hatchlings have yolk sac scars, but they disappear, the fact that Flint is full of lead-damaged children and soon Ohio probably will be too, lead- and mercury-damaged children, the fact that the Ohio is full of toxic waste from chemical fertilizers, the fact that it sure takes the fun out of *fishing*, but luckily none of our kids want to fish, the fact that they just want to be obsessively tidy or rebelliously untidy, or stare at the internet all day, or start yelling and screaming and then get all gloomy all of a sudden, or deposit a million little plastic Japanese warrior figures all over the floor for me to step on, the fact that I think the cops should use these little warriors to stop car chases, chafing, the fact that the Ohio's the most polluted river in the country, the fact that the Mississippi's the *second* worst, the fact that the only good news is that the Ohio *in Ohio* is less polluted than it is by the time it gets to *Indiana*, where Hoosiers dump in even more crap, chemicals and fertilizers, the fact that all the states bordering the Ohio blame each other for how polluted the river is, because nobody wants to pay for the cleanup, so there *is* no cleanup, upkeep, makeup, fry-up, uptown, downtown, look-out, outlook, the fact that I dreamt about a mom with lots of kids, and they all had big chenille hats on, sort of loose berets, the fact that the mom had a thing about chenille, the fact that the kids were all from different fathers and they were all nice kids, the fact that the mom was poor but determined to provide them with a happy, chenille-filled home, cupcakes, nuptials, the fact that I think there was more to it than that but that's all I can remember, Francis Scott Key, Quantrill, the fact that the two meet at Louisville, I mean the Ohio River and the Mississippi, not Francis Scott Key and *Quantrill*, the fact that the Ohio's actually bigger than the Mississippi when they join at Louisville, the fact that the Ohio's a mile wide there, the fact that without the Ohio there'd *be* no Mississippi, ♪ *So beware, Be-ee-ee-ee-ware... Drink-ing, drinking-ing, dri-i-i-ι-ι-inking, D-R-I-N-K-I-N-G* ♪, the fact that both these polluted rivers join and head down to the Gulf, which now has a dead zone the size of Connecticut, ♪ *Plop, plop, Fizz, fizz, Oh what a relief it is!* ♪, nitrate compounds, algae blooms, acid mines, the chenille mom, nice hats, the fact that green sea turtles in the Great Barrier Reef in Australia are full of human drugs for heart problems and gout, and cleaning products, cosmetics, pesticides and herbicides, the fact that Ben knows all about it, the fact that he just showed me something on YouTube, teenagers on a motor boat on the Ohio last summer, the fact that they saw some big, unidentifiable creature swimming near the surface, the fact that it doesn't look like anything you ever saw, and *they* didn't know what it was, so they chased it for a good while, by boat, and when they got bored, they tried *ramming* it, the fact that they drove their boat right over the thing and maybe they killed it or injured it, the only one of its kind in the world maybe, so now we'll never know what the heck it was, the fact that what is the point of, of, the fact that that was all they could think of doing, and they even filmed themselves doing it, *laughing*, casual destruction, cheap thrills, banality of evil, the fact that that's what people would probably do if they ever found an Abominable Snowman too, just drive over him or shoot him and then head over to IHOP for some *pancakes*, the fact that every day they kill hundreds of pets at the pound, and every day hunters go out to shoot at some poor animal, and just laugh, the fact that they see a stork flying above them and all they want to do is bring it *down*, atom bombs, the fact that it's not like they need a stork for food or anything, ♪ *On the banks of the Ohio* ♪, the fact that Hillary

Clinton laughed about General Qadaffi's death, after he was torn limb from limb by a mob, the fact that nobody has any manners anymore, Hillary, Trump, mobs, the fact that mobs have no manners, the fact that Hillary often seems to laugh inappropriately, the fact that maybe she can't help it, the fact that she's friends with Kissinger, the fact that the girl in that song rejects some guy's offer of marriage, he drowns her in the Ohio, and off she floats, more debris, revenge, estranged, Olivia Newton John, the fact that sometimes male logic seems no better than the logic of dreams, but I wouldn't ever say so to Leo, because *that's* bad manners, and it might hurt his feelings, or emasculate him, the fact that emasculation seems to be the thing lately, the big issue, big tissue, the fact that it's everywhere, and the PTA says something's gotta be done about it because it's really easy to emasculate kids if you're not careful, the fact that the PTA says boys feel emasculated at school, because the girls are better at everything, even IT, the fact that we've got to bolster boys nonstop, to help them compete with the girls, growth, progress, chicken pot pie, pot luck tuna, mock turtle soup, bolster, holster, the fact that at the last meeting we had, they said emasculated boys feel like second-class citizens, the fact that Amelia Eberhardt piped up as usual, saying "Now they know how it feels," and it was so embarrassing, I didn't know where to look, the fact that no one did, but that's Amelia for you, the fact that Zadok Cramer's got a few more Ohio River tributaries for Ben, ♫ *Now the riverbank will make a mighty good road* ♫, 150 West 4th Street, corner of 6th Avenue, the fact that first we still have some Coshocton ones to do, then we'll go further West of there, the Western Expansion, to Spoon Creek maybe, Mill Creek, Little Mill Creek, Turkey Run, Doughty Creek, Laurel Creek, Bucklew Creek, Killbuck Creek, the Walhonding and Muskingum, and the Little Muskingum, which is completely different from the Muskingum, and Crooked Run, Morgan Run, Bacon Run, Rock Run, Robinson Run, Mill Fork, Moscow Brook, Sand Fork, Simmons Run, Dickinson Run, Little Wakatomika Creek, Flint Run, Fivemile Run, Symmes Creek, Prairie Fork, Beech Run, and then, if we can find them, we'll try Big Seweekly Creek,

Duck Run, Big Beaver Creek, Little Beaver Creek, Raccoon Creek, Mildew Creek, Little Yellow Creek, Big Yellow Creek, Crookston's Run, King's Creek, Will's Creek, Harman's Creek, Mingo Bottom Creek, Indian Cross Creek, McMahon's Creek, Big Grave Creek, Captina Creek, Fish Creek, Sunfish Creek, Opossum Creek, Proctor's run, Fishing Creek, Stoncy Creek, Bull Creek, Duck Creek, Little Kenhawa River, Great Hocking River, Lee's Creek, Devil's Hole, Shade River, Little Sandy Creek, Big Sandy Creek, Tanner's Run, tanning, cobbling, damson p-p-pits, Letart's Rapids, West Creek, Dunham's Run, Sliding Hill Creek, Nailor's Branch, Leading Creek, Ten Mile Creek, Campaign Creek, Great Kenhawa River, Meridian Crcck, Eightccn Mile Cieek, Swan Creek, Little Guyundat Creek, Green Bottom Ripple, Federal Creek, Nine Mile Crcck, Seven Mile Creek, Big Guyandot River, Buffalo Creek, Ten Pole Creek, Twelve Pole Creek, Tottery River, Hood's Creek, Ice Creek, Stoner's Creek, Little Sciota River, Tyger's Creek, Big Sciota River, Conoconneque Creek, Salt Creek, Quick's Run, Pond Run, Stout's Run, Sycamore Creek, Crooked Creek, Cabin Creek, William Brooke's Creek, Limestone Creek, Eagle Creek, Straight Creek, White Oak Creek, Bracken Creek, Bullskin Creek, Bear Creek, Big Indian Creek, Little Indian Creek, Cross Creek, Muddy Creek, Little Miami River, Crawfish Creek, Deer Creek, Licking River, kissing cousins, Great Miami River, Laughrey's Creek, Gunpowder Creek, Big Bone Lick Creek, Kentucky River, Little Kentucky River, Bear Grass Creek, Salt River, Otter Creek, Doe Run, Falling Spring, French Creek, Buck Creek, Wyandot Creek, Big Blue River, Helm's Creek, Little Yellow Bank Creek, Harden's Creek, Flint Island, Clover Creek, Anderson's River, Blackford Creek, Green River, Pidgeon Creek, Highland Creek, Wabash River, Saline River, Grand Pierre Creek, Cherokee River, and Cash River, the fact that that oughtta do for now, for crying out loud, the fact that I can't keep track of where we've already gone but Ben has it written down somewhere, the fact that he's so organizcd, the fact that I don't think *he* feels *emasculated*, the fact that my favorite river names are the Monongahela and the Younghiogheny, but those are both in Pennsylvania so they don't count, at least for Ben's pollution study, the fact that they probably feature in some *Pennsylvanian* child's pollution study, Flint, Michigan, Walhonding, the fact that the Ohio's usually twenty feet deep or so, but Zadok Cramer says parts of it could be *fifty* feet deep after rain, castles on the Rhine, chateaux on the Rhone, Geneva, Montreux, turret ships, skull and crossbones, Ben's pirate costume, black still water, pool of motor oil, strange river creature, white motor boat, the fact that the Ohio was really important once, to commerce and such, the fact that Zadok covers all that, the fact that I made my students read Zadok, the fact that he's so upbeat about everything, but he never had to think about pollution, not for one single solitary second, house painters, the fact that he says the Ohio offers nine hundred and sixty miles of slack-water navigation, the fact that "slack-water" doesn't sound too nice, and probably doesn't help with pollution much either, but it's good from a nautical point of view, Olivia Newton John, just like canals, the fact that canals are easy to navigate, and naturally sluggish, because they have no currents at all, I don't imagine, the fact that the Muskingum's sluggish too, the fact that it just meanders slowly to Marietta where it merges with the Ohio, the fact that maybe that's why the Muskingum was important in the Underground Railroad, because it was easy to navigate, I don't know, the fact that the Big Bottom Massacre happened on the shores of the Muskingum, the fact that that was in retaliation for the Moravian Indian massacre in Gnadenhutten, which was about the worst thing that ever happened around here, worst thing ever *period*, ninety-two Lenapes, all Lenapes, Ma's palm on the cornbread, the fact that a guy committed suicide over in Chilicothe about a week ago and his suicide note said "ONLY PITY," the fact that something about that made me cry, the fact that I was damaged by Mommy's illness, it broke me, stork, the fact that that was during the Revolutionary War, not the Civil War, the Gnadenhutten Massacre I mean, Hillary Clinton, Qadaffi, World War Three, World War *Four*, the fact that somebody said if there *is* a World War Three, it'll be the *last* war we ever have, because of all the firepower, the fact that the Moravian Indians at Gnadenhutten were *pro*-American but that didn't help them, the fact that the soldiers thought they were harboring pro-English Indians, or that's what they claimed later anyway, so they murdered them all, every single person in the village, the men, women, and the children, and I had to *teach* this, year after year, to those tired, bored, suspicious students who just wanted to earn their credits and move on with their lives, the fact that they're probably all working at McDonald's now, apple-peeler, defrost butter, GM, the fact that some Cincinnati high school students chanted racist comments because there were Asian and African Americans on the other team, the fact that that's so, the fact that there are an awful lot of people who use the N-word in Ohio, and I think it's getting worse, the fact that I was shocked by that when I first came, the fact that they could have taken the Moravian Indians prisoner, as POWs, the fact that Colonel Williamson let his men decide on that and the soldiers decided to kill them all, just like that, the fact that seventeen soldiers refused, seventeen out of a hundred, so they just had to stand there watching while the other ones carried out the massacre, the fact that all this happened just twelve miles from here, so close, the fact that the Moravian Indians were just "sitting ducks," the fact that they were all pacifists so they didn't put up a fight, the fact that the soldiers *informed* them the night before that they were all going to be killed the next day, and the Indians stayed up all night praying and singing, and then the next day the soldiers came and tied up all the men and boys in pairs, and stood them up against the wall and bludgeoned them to death, two-by-two, the fact that after Builderbeck had finished killing seven pairs of men and boys, he handed his mallet to another soldier, saying "My arm fails me, go on in the same way, I think I have done pretty well," the fact that just the thought of the wailing, the screaming of women and children, while this was going on, but it didn't change the soldiers' minds, so then they went to the women's slaughterhouse and did the same to them, the fact that one old woman begged for her life and they killed her first, the fact that they bludgeoned twenty-seven women, twenty-nine men, and thirty-six children, and after they killed them they *scalped* them, and looted the village and burnt it to the ground with all the dead, the fact that one boy survived, the fact that he was beaten and scalped and left in a pile of corpses, but he was alive, the fact that he hid under the other bodies and managed to escape just before the men's slaughter-house was set alight, the fact that people can turn the world into a slaughterhouse like that, when they want to, sugar, butter wouldn't melt in their mouths, the fact that the soldiers needed *eighty horses* just to carry all their loot back to Pittsburgh, everything the Moravian Indians had owned and made and grown and harvested, the three sisters, the fact that Stacy's boots are *always* in the way, the fact that eventually Builderbeck himself was cut up into tiny pieces, by the Lenape, in revenge for Gnadenhutten, the fact that they cut him up *slowly*, butter, sugar, madeleine pan, cake molds, the fact that they held Builderbeck's wife captive for a while too, but they let her go, and later she remarried and gave birth to "the first white child" born in Fairfield County, the fact that the textbooks can never resist saying that, "the first white child," as if there was some *virtue* in it, the fact that I guess they're just remarking on the oddity, since other children had been born in Fairfield County for thousands and thousands of years before Mrs. Builderbeck or whatever got here, the fact that I just dreaded those Peolia field trips every year, but they were *my* idea, the fact that I knew we should do it but I always felt awfully shy on the bus, the fact that seeing students outside the classroom's scary, the fact that one student thanked me for taking them afterwards, and said "The mysterious world we live in is very cool," the fact that I think he just meant he liked going to *historic sites* or something, not that *massacres* are cool, at least I hope so, the fact that some people are just amazed that anything ever happened anywhere, and field trips really get them thinking, the fact that our kids never get taken to Gnadenhutten on school trips, so Leo and I took them, but when we got there we fudged it, because you really don't want your kids having nightmares about slaughterhouses and scalping and everything, the fact that Stacy and Ben were old enough to read the plaque on their own, so that was okay, especially since it doesn't go into much detail, the fact that all it says is the soldiers showed no mercy, *I don't know but they know*, the fact that everybody goes to Gnadenhutten now for the Fireworks Festival, and the Pet Parade and Tomahawk Trot, the fact that then they elect the best baby of the year, the best *baby*, after so many babies were bludgeoned to death there, thirty-six children, the fact that it kind of makes you sick, but that's just me, the fact that nobody else ever thinks about it anymore, the fact that the Gnadenhutten Massacre seems long forgotten, along with the Sand Creek Massacre, a hundred and fifty Cheyenne killed, most of them women and children, scalped and mutilated, the fact that that time, the soldiers saved people's *genitals* as trophies, dear me, and John Evans was all for it, and my home town was named for him, the fact that Evanston was stolen from somebody called Ouilmette, Wilmette, Potawatomie land, and Lake Shore Drive was once an Indian trail, Indian mounds, Laura Ingalls Wilder, Almanzo's jalopy, the fact that Ouilmette was half-French, half-Indian, the fact that he was married to a woman called Archange, who was also half-French and half-Indian, and they had eight kids, eight half-French and half-Indian kids, the fact that the US government stole Chicago from the Potawatomie, Indian Removal Act of 1830, the fact that Evans was an *Ohioan*, born in Waynesville, the fact that he studied medicine at Cincinnati College, Cincy, and was friends with Chivington, the fact that Evans gave out the order that all Indians should be shot on sight, and Lincoln *approved* it, the fact that Evans later decorated Chivington for the Sand Creek Massacre, best baby, the first white baby in Fairfield County, the fact that Lincoln was from Illinois, and we went for picnics on weekends in the woods behind Lincolnwood School, Grosse Pointe, Tinkertoys, Skokie, Wilmette, Potawatomie, the fact that Chivington's men tore a fetus out of a woman's belly, killed it and scalped it, and Evans rewarded him for it, the fact that he wants hunters to go back to using lead bullets, *Trump*, not Chivington, the fact that all the Trumps like hunting, big game hunting, the fact that if an animal's shot with a lead bullet, but survives, it's slowly poisoned by the bullet, sportsmanship, golf, the fact that apparently Trump can't golf well at all, the fact that you'd think he would've rigged his golf courses by now to help him win, put magnets in the holes or something, the fact that surely even Ohioans wouldn't give that man a second term, but Leo says most sitting presidents get re-elected, the fact that presidents abide, *preside*, OJ, O.J. Simpson, Gnadenhutten, the fact that two chiefs at Sand Creek ran forward with white flags, but it didn't help, the fact that they were killed instantly, civilians, civility, manners, the fact that a few Indians in the Sand Creek Massacre survived by hiding in caves they dug quickly out of the sandy banks by the creek, but the soldiers found most of them, the fact that they chased the wounded on horseback, chased women and children, the fact that some women killed themselves and their children to escape worse deaths, just like the 9/11 jumpers, I suppose, the fact that the government kept breaking all its *treaties*, broken treaty quilts, Lincoln, Andrew Jackson, James Monroe, our national heroes, the fact that that left the Indians no peaceful way to defend themselves or their land, self-defense manual, my lectures at Peolia, tree roots weaving down the hill like arteries, the fact that the Sand Creek Massacre took six hours, the fact that Mocchi saw her mom killed by two soldiers right in front of her, and then they tried to rape her but she killed one and escaped, and became a woman warrior, the fact that I think she fought at the Battle of Julesburg, the fact that before it happened, Silas Soule told Chivington's men they were sons of b——, well, a bad thing, for their massacre plan, but they did it anyway, the fact that Soule tried to stop them, the fact that it's hard to believe but a lot of massacres have a planning stage, premeditated, the fact that it's not much more than a hundred years before Leo was born, how the West was won, the fact that Chivington was known ever after as the Butcher of Sand Creek but he never got arrested or put on trial or anything, the fact that Silas Soule was murdered on the street, in Denver, just months after testifying about the massacre, the fact that it was twelve days after Lincoln was shot, the fact that I used to make everybody read Silas Soule's letter, the fact that Stace says one of the first things Trump did in office was re-approve the Dakota Access Pipe Line, DAPL, Wet'suet'en, Unist-ot-en, the horses, the fact that the National Guard shot at Indian protestors with rubber bullets, and shot the horses too, PODR, buffalo extinction, extermination, tipi camps, the fact that you start to wonder if protesting and civil disobedience, the fact that, I mean, you wonder if it's really necessary, passive resistance, because it's dangerous to rile the authorities, the fact that they won't let you get away with it, the fact that people are always talking about the right to peaceful protest, but they just get arrested, spirals, caramelization, concentration, the fact that Stacy wants to put up a Greenpeace sticker right by our front door where everybody can see it, and I just don't know if that's a good idea, the fact that you don't want to antagonize anybody, like the neighbors, or people who just come to the door, strangers, estranged, Builderbeck, the fact that an awful lot of folks around here don't like the sound of environmental protection one little bit, and they get all upset if you even mention climate change, the fact that that's probably why they voted for Trump, the fact that they hoped they wouldn't have to hear about climate change for at least four years, the fact that everybody has their own agenda, the fact that, if there are all those arguments at the PTA just about SROs, what would they say about this Greenpeace sticker, the fact that Stacy pointed out that the *Kinkels* have an ACLU bumper sticker on their car, the fact that I hadn't noticed, the fact that I thought all the Kinkels cared about was plants, ACLU, the fact that if it's true, they must be the *only* people in Tuscarawas County with an ACLU bumper sticker, or the only people with a Giant Viper's Bugloss *and* an ACLU bumper sticker, I'll bet, the fact that plants have rights too, and water has rights, and nature, and everything, but do you wanna go to jail for it, or get *shot*, the fact that that's the question, the fact that I didn't even think they were *political*, the Kinkels, the fact that the Ambergers have a reenactment civil war cannon in their front yard but I'm not sure which side they're on, the fact that maybe *they're* not too sure either, and that's about as political as we usually get around here, the fact that thirty-five thousand Ohioans died in that war, Ambergers, *The Magnificent Ambersons*, Sand Creek, Sandy Hook, the fact that I've gotta put on some *music* or something, the fact that I'm working myself up into a state, spiraling, boarlets, the fact that I need some, some Schubert, here, the "Twout Quindit" as Jake called it, trout, perch, smallmouth buffalo fish, the fact that that's what Jake is, the fact that he's a smallmouth buffalo fish, buffalo, mammoth, mastodon, Moravians, the fact that I just hope Schubert never had to hear about the Moravian Massacre, but he could have, the fact that he was born fifteen years after the massacre, ♫ *Trout Quintet* ♪, January 31st, 1797, the fact that he passed away on the 19th of November, 1828, the fact that at least he didn't have to know about the *Sand Creek* Massacre as well, the fact that they're hoping he'll put plenty of heavy industry back into Ohio, Trump, not Schubert, never mind the environment or anything like that, the fact that we gotta keep polluting everything to survive, or that's what *they* seem to think, *I don't know but they know*, but heavy industry's over, "It's over for Bozo," arsenic, fracking, and old lace, forest fires, ten percent of Americans, emasculation, the fact that I think the Ohio climate's changed during the time I've *lived* here, what with the derecho and all, backwards C, the fact that there used to be deer mice and harvest mice around here, meadow jumping mice, Southern flying squirrels, all kinds of bats, big brown bats, little brown bats, Eastern red bats, hoary bats, and pipistrelles, and possums, the fact that Phoebe did a wonderful painting of possums hanging from a tree, when she was a kid, the fact that I hope she's still got it somewhere, the fact that I was so impressed, the fact that we hardly ever see a possum now, besides dead ones lying by the side of the road, dead possum lying on its back, the soft whitish gray fur of its underside, white flag of surrender, the fact that it looked kind of *human*, like a pot-bellied beer lover sleeping one off comfortably on the couch, Peolia Possums, the fact that they named the football team after their Latin motto, OMNES TENEBRAE VIDERE NON POSSUM, which was kind of a dumb thing to do, stop lights, parking meters, Amish hitching posts, "Don't beat your horse," the fact that there used to be shrews, moles, voles, woodchucks, chipmunks, striped skunks, and beaver here too, and muskrats, coyotes, red foxes, mink, weasels, and *least* weasels, the fact that, according to Ben, the least weasel is the smallest carnivore in the world, but now, now there's just *us*, practically, "just us chickens," and a few raccoons, and maybe some exotic animals that escaped from their owners, ready to pop out of the underbrush at you at any moment, like Sumatran tigers and pet tarantulas and cobras and crocodiles and those, what are they called, boa constrictors, the fact that a man got strangled by his own boa constrictor just last week, one he'd had since it was a baby, the fact that there was that farmer upstate somewhere who thought there was a tiger in his cow barn and called the cops, but it turned out to be a *toy* tiger, the fact that the cops shot it anyway, just in case, big game, the fact that they completely destroyed the toy tiger in their zeal, the fact that it looked a lot like Stacy's tiger, now Jake's, I mean before they shot it to smithereens, the fact that she did such a good picture of that tiger, and Jakey likes to lie down on top of it now, the tiger not Stacy's picture, the fact that in the picture the tiger looks so happy, surrounded by jungly stuff, black white green orange, and blue, the fact that he looks at you with just one eye, just like *her* tiger does, because fur covers one eye, veil, veil toss duties, coin toss, snap pass, hissing, the fact that she exactly replicated that lopsided expression in her picture, the fact that she went to that art class clasping her toy tiger, and she came home with that picture, which we have over the mantel, because I like to see it every day, the fact that I don't know why we've still got that Woodrow Wilson thing hanging there, the fact that that summer school was really worth the money, however much it cost, but that was in New Haven, the fact that I wish we had something like that now for the kids, the fact that I never know what to do with them in the summertime, the fact that they can only set up so many lemonade stands, or egg stands or paw-paw stands, the fact that I liked Stacy's art teacher there, the fact that he was a real artist, a ceramicist, the fact that Ben probably wouldn't even *go* if I found them a good art class here, the fact that there's Frederick, tiptoeing daintily through the snow, the fact that animals know just what they're doing, the fact that they really know how to live, guns, gum balls, while all we do is watch Morning Routine videos and eat devil's food cake, and donuts and onion rings, the fact that Native Americans achieved all these engineering feats and had time to play Chunky as well, the fact that the Hopewell people lived here for thirteen thousand years and didn't wreck a *thing*, the fact that they just left a few arrowheads and gorgets lying around, the fact that *they* didn't pollute the drinking water of millions of people, or leave radioactive waste that won't be safe for three hundred thousand years, the fact that the Europeans managed to just *trash* the place in a few hundred years, the fact that that is kind of embarrassing if you think about it, the fact that it's not much of a plan really, the fact that once you pollute everybody's drinking water, you could say you don't even really *have* a country anymore, or not a country worth having, despoiled, spoiled brats, coal mines, salt mines, Mound City, seven hundred, seven hundred Indian mounds in Ohio alone, the fact that Alligator Mound's kind of nice, but Serpent Mound's really something, the fact that the mounds at Chillicothe are like another *planet*, and there's Moundsville, West Virginia too, the fact that we gotta take the kids there some time, the fact that Grave Creek Mound is like *seventy feet high*, and Miamisburg's sixty-eight feet, and there's Story Mound and Infirmary Mound, and Adena Mound and Cemetery Mound and all the other ones, pregnant bellies, Mother Earth, Mocchi, the fact that after we went to Mound City we went to Cincinnati and had chili, served on spaghetti with cheese on top, the fact that just a little cup will do you, "a little dab'll do ya," the fact that until recently nobody took care of the mounds, the fact that they let cattle graze all over them and some mounds collapsed under the weight of the cows, cow patty ice cream, grass-fed, grain-fed, but some got left alone, the big ones, the fact that for a while Mound City was Camp Sherman, and they leveled all the mounds that got in their way, but they supposedly sort of restored them later, Woodrow Wilson, the fact that at Camp Sherman one day they had nothing better to do, so they did a crowd-formation portrait photo of Woodrow Wilson, the fact that it was made up of thousands and thousands of individual soldiers, 21,000 soldiers standing to attention, the fact that I wonder if they photographed it from a mound, the fact that it took 13,380 men just to form his hair, including the parting, and another 1,170 soldiers for the coat and collar, and 6,450 for the face and neck, the fact that we still have it in the dining room, the fact that I used to take it in to Peolia to show it to students, the fact that I should move it somewhere else, the fact that it's always catching the glare of the sun, so he glints at me all the time when I'm baking, La Wilson, the fact that a lot of students thought it was pretty cool, but I think it just looks like a black-and-white newspaper photo, like the one it was based on, and those soldiers might've been better off playing Chunky, or going into Cincinnati for chili, or doing something *useful*, Gekelmukpechunk, the fact that Leo had a whole bowlful, a bowlful of chili, not soldiers, and he had the spaghetti too, the fact that I got a cup of chili on its own, just straight chili, and the kids all had hot dogs, and then we drove home via Young's for ice cream, salty caramel pretzel crunch, the fact that they have good cones there too, the fact that they have all that hot food too but we don't usually get it, stuff like Amish beef and noodles and chicken 'n dumplings, the fact that they're always trying to sell you those Deep Fried Cheddar Cheese Curds, the fact that they put them on burgers even, the fact that, who knows, maybe they're nice, the fact that at school we were always told never to use the word "nice," but *everybody* uses it so I never knew what the teachers were talking about, the fact that I want to try their hot roast beef sandwich some time, because it might be like the ones we used to get at B & J's, the fact that they don't call it a hot roast beef sandwich at Young's though, the fact that they call it a Roast Beef Hot Shot, Gatling gun, Loaded Pork Chops, "MR. PRESIDENT HOW LONG MUST WOMEN WAIT FOR LIBERTY," the fact that Woodrow Wilson left Eugene V. Debs to rot in prison, Convict No. 9653, the fact that his speech in Canton led to his arrest in Cleveland, Debs's arrest, not Woodrow Wilson's, Miss Treat, the fact that it's silly to call it Alligator Mound, when there never were any alligators in Ohio, mammoths yes, but no alligators, the fact that why would Indians in Ohio be thinking about *alligators*, "the anonymous alligators must come forward," the fact that I keep going hot and cold, the fact that that guy tried to drive his pick-up truck all over Serpent Mound last summer, the fact that I bet he was drunk, the fact that he made big tire marks all around the outside but didn't manage to damage the mound itself, manage, damage, borage, the fact that Serpent Mound can actually be seen from *satellites*, Stranded Minke Whale Rescued, the fact that a cat was stranded at a train station in Japan somewhere, when the whole train station had to be automated and the station master had been fired, the fact that the cat got named Honorary Station Master, lunchbox, Lunchbox Menus, Mighty Cars, Hello Kitty, wolf eels, butterflies, *Madama Butterfly*, Mound City, OHCR, IHOP, poffertjes with butter and syrup, the fact that we saw a movie about the Tokyo fish market where they auction all the frozen tunas, the fact that the way they treat the live eels, OJ, the fact that you have to rinse out the OJ squeezer *immediately* or you're in trouble, the fact that Howard Hughes cured himself by drinking gallons of fresh orange juice, after he was in a terrible plane crash, but we usually have the frozen kind, the fact that he wouldn't approve of that, the fact that he also designed a new hospital bed which Ben says is still in use, Candyland game, the Brontës, the fact that I wonder if *they* ever got fresh orange juice, Jew's harp, the fact that I don't think they can grow oranges in England, mosquitoes, fireflies, dragonflies, daddy long legs, Laura Ingalls Wilder's first orange, OJ in a carton, Queen Victoria, Tetra Pak, Teflon, the fact that Queen Elizabeth likes Tupperware, the fact that the English Royal Family eats cereal out of Tupperware containers, and then they put on their rubber boots and drive around in their Land Rovers, the fact that I dreamt I saved a toddler from running into the street and then had to hand him back to his mom, which I wasn't too sure about because she was the one who'd let him run out into the street, the fact that she didn't seem a good mom, the fact that some kids are so painfully beautiful it just kills you sometimes, chicken stock, feed, Ronny, Jesus, Chuck, Mommy, check on the chickens, the fact that Woodrow Wilson was against female suffrage till the last possible moment, the fact that women picketed the White House for *years*, ****** ESTABLISH JUSTICE ****** the fact that I wonder why they do these things, the fact that I don't know how people have the energy, I really don't, and it only annoys everybody, the fact that I also dreamt I had a donkey that got away from me in a park and I couldn't find him, and I was scared he might get eaten by the lions and tigers in the zoo, the fact that when I woke up I still felt worried about the donkey, so I reached for Leo and we made love, the fact that I don't know how that happened, the fact that it seemed kind of a miracle, after all these months, but suddenly I couldn't resist him, and he smelled so good, the fact that all my feelings for him are still there, they're just dormant or something, doormat, dormouse, torpid, torrid, the fact that you can wake them up, my feelings, sweetheart, Sweethearts Candy Crisis, heart-shaped rolling-pin marks, Sugar Creek, sugar trees, maple sugar, the fact that Ben's now talking about the other aurora, *Steve*, the fact that Steve's a ribbon of gas and he's *5432 degrees Fahrenheit*, the fact that the caramelization's coming along, on my tartes, not Steve, gas planet, the fact that Steve's fifteen miles wide and moving westward at thirteen thousand miles an hour, 3.7 miles a second, the fact that I don't get where Steve *is*, a ribbon of gas, the fact that it's fine they found Steve, but I'm bored with the aurora borealis, the fact that maybe it's called *bore*-ealis for a reason, the fact that I've really tried to like it, for years, but I think I give up, the fact that sometimes you have to admit defeat, the fact that all my life I've been feigning an interest in the aurora borealis, hoping, waiting, to get interested in it, the fact that I didn't start out with a negative attitude or anything, far from it, the fact that I really expected to get into it someday, but I've finally realized that I just don't see what's so *great* about the aurora borealis, the fact that I get no kick out of the aurora borealis, and I don't think I ever will see the point of the aurora borealis, the fact that I can't tell Ben this, the fact that he'd be hurt, and surprised, because we've had so many discussions about the aurora borealis, and where it appears, in which hemisphere and stuff, and the spooky sounds it makes and everything, the fact that he's tried his darnedest to make it interesting, the fact that maybe the photos just don't do it justice, like photos of fireworks, the fact that the aurora borealis is just green with a little purple now and then, Little Miss Firecracker, the fact that it would help if it had more colors, the fact that I don't think green and purple go very well together at the best of times, the fact that purple almost never looks good on anything, unless it's a *flower*, or a purple martin, or maybe a gas ribbon, the fact that nature can get away with some pretty screwy color combos, like pink and yellow, the fact that Mommy didn't approve of people wearing blue and green together, but I think it looks fine, grass and sky, fields and water, the fact that I never actually agreed with her on the green and blue business, or even her pink and orange ban, the fact that orange and pink together is better than people think, but orange does *not* go with purple, or maybe it does, the fact that I don't like purple and yellow, but it depends what kind of purple or yellow, the fact that Mommy was funny when she got all adamant about something, the fact that I liked to hear her arguing with Abby about the toilet paper, the fact that I think they both got a kick out of rearranging it, every time they went to the bathroom, the fact that it was *war*, in a small way, the Charmin Offensive, Hillary, Qadaffi, Syria, North Korea, sisters, sororities, Elks, the Brontës, Phoebe and me, upside-down possums, the fact that I think in middle age you get to decide what you really like and don't like, so aurora borealis-wise, we're done here, and that goes for Steve too, the fact that auroras just don't float my boat, floating, bloating, the fact that the aurora borealis doesn't give a hoot about me so why should I care about the aurora borealis, cara-melization complete, roger and out, four down and two to go, next pie to the stove, NASCAR, zero tolerance, the fact that Stacy taught the little kids how to do the Macarena, and now they do it all the time, the fact that it's more fun than skipping rope, the fact that now Ben wants an electric unicycle, the fact that koala bears are in danger, the fact that I first heard of koala bears when I was in London when I was six and I still associate them with London and being six years old, the fact that then for a long period I forgot all about koala bears, until Gillian got a little plastic one that clings on to her pencil, the fact that for a while she transferred it to whichever pencil she was using, but then she forgot about it, the fact that I think she may have grown out of the koala bear stage, the fact that the koala bear stage comes at about six, so her pencil ornament may have reached the kitchen drawer stage, aurora borealis, the fact that I just gave Jakey a spoon for his Cheerios and he says it looks like Pluto, and he's *right*, the fact that our spoons all have stains and scratches and white patches on them, and they do look like Pluto, just without the five-mile-deep chasms, so far, Pluto, Saturn, the Plow, phases of the moon, periods, the Milky Way, least weasels, the fact that Ben tells me all these things first thing in the morning, so many things about Pluto, or least weasels, or the latest creature to go extinct, or Steve the gas ribbon, and then I don't know what to do with myself for the rest of the day, the fact that he tells me the oceans are acidifying or something and then goes off to school and thinks about something else, while I worry and worry about the oceans, or Steve, or least weasels, the fact that he finds it easy to just move on to some other fact, the fact that he *loves* facts, facts for facts' sake, the fact that I think this must be cup of coffee No. 4, and I seem to have dropped half my madeleine on myself, the fact that it's silly women feel silly when they drop crumbs on their chests or their laps, because where *else* is food going to go, and these are handy, horizontal surfaces, the fact that crumbs are subject to the force of gravity like the rest of us, the fact that I hate to think that women have probably been feeling silly brushing crumbs off their breasts for thousands of years, women in animal hides, women in grass skirts, women in classical robes and tunics, women in the Dark Ages, the fact that they're practicing for life on Mars in the desert of Oman, NASA I mean, not *women*, the fact that they seem to assume they'll be able to drive all kinds of vehicles around up there, just like here, business as usual, the fact that they probably want to trash the place, the fact that do all planets have gravity, gravitas, spoons, Hillary's pants suits, Jane Fonda's hallway, Donald Trump's fear of germs and stairs, germophobe, Glacier Lake, Chuck, red white green blue, purple, the fact that if Trump is so scared of stairs he must be totally dependent on the Otis elevator company, Mommy, snapdragons, buttercups, mulberry tree, Pepito barking at the trash men, the fact that Leo thinks the failure to elect Bernie Sanders as president was one of the worst collective mistakes in American history, or did he say tragedy, one of the worst collective *tragedies*, no, I think it was mistakes, because Bernie wanted to bring in universal healthcare, the fact that he said it when we were lying in bed this morning and it worried me, the fact that Cary Grant tells the taxi driver to take him to the United Nations, the fact that doesn't everybody want to say that some day, "Take me to the United Nations, and step on it," the fact that Republicans prefer respectful, obedient children to independent, curious, rebellious ones, the fact that on Saturday a bus driver in Dayton talked a woman out of jumping off a bridge into the Miami River, the fact that he was so kind to her, and he's only twenty-five years old, the fact that it wasn't his problem, but he acted so understanding, so sweet, and it worked, the fact that it was all caught on the bus's camera, the fact that he told her that he knew she must be very bothered by something right now but we've all got to stick around as long as we can, Paterson Falls in winter, black stones, white foaming water, the fact that maybe bus drivers have the best people skills, the fact that they develop them on the job, though there are some mean bus drivers, like the one in Paris when I didn't know how much money it cost to take the bus and he was so impatient with me, the fact that Parisians are impatient, Chartier, bouillon restaurant, the fact that Mommy didn't understand her own wedding ceremony because it was in French, Titusville, Pennsylvania, oil strike, Ida Tarbell, the fact that I heard somebody on the radio say she wants to live in the same zip code as her boyfriend, Poland, Ohio, the fact that I'd never heard of anyone finding zip codes romantic before, the fact that maybe I should mention ours to Leo more often, over a candlelit dinner, perfume, the fact that I could pour him a glass of wine, and murmur 43832 and see what happens, zip code, zipper, zipless, the fact that the woman didn't mention sharing an *area* code, which may not be so romantic but it sure saves money, on local calls anyway, the fact that that poor woman thinking of jumping into the Miami, the fact that there are plenty of rivers to jump into around here too, rivers that'd eat you alive with all their PCBs and other stuff, BP, Shell, Exxon, the fact that there'd be nothing left of you, like one of those hot geyser pools, where you just dissolve in a matter of seconds, the fact that suicide always seems such a pity, "ONLY PITY," the fact that, given the life span of the *universe*, it seems a mite precipitate to cut short your few paltry sixty, seventy or eighty years on earth, the fact that a human lifespan isn't all that long to bear, in *galactic* terms, though it's longer than a *bug's* of course, the fact that aphids can reproduce when they're about an hour old, so one single female aphid can have about five hundred billion descendants within *days* or something, aphid grandma, 111-Year-Old Woman, the fact that Gandhi said the Jews should have committed suicide before Hitler could exterminate them, but I don't see what for, unless it's to save the Nazis the effort, collective suicide, passive resistance, whiskey, killer whale fetus, the fact that I'm with the bus driver on this, that you might as well stick around, if you can, because if you're lucky you might live long enough to see close-ups of Pluto, and dust devils on Mars, and maybe even some exciting aurora borealises, as well as watching a few crackpot presidents come and go, the fact that I thought about it a lot when I was young, suicide, not presidents, before I had the kids, koala bears, the fact that I wonder if Stacy does too, no, I'm sure she doesn't, dear me, even though she gets depressed by all those Morning Routine girls bossing her around from afar from morning to night, cyber bullies, dictators, the fact that sometimes they hate on each other's lips or *eyebrows*, the fact that one girl got like 224,000 thumbs up for her eyebrows and 2,000 thumbs down, the fact that two thousand people had the time to express a negative opinion of that poor kid's eyebrows, the fact that they hated on another girl's *sit-me-down-upon*, though they didn't call it that, the fact that they called it her "butt" *and* worse things, and the majority were not in favor of it, this particular butt, mean girls in high school, junior high,

343

Judy, Melanie, and that Sue, lunatic asylum, bike rides with Chuck, the fact that Stacy has to weave her way through all this nonsense to become a *person*, the fact that *of course* she now worries nonstop about how she looks, the fact that it's sad to see, the fact that I tried telling her beauty's no good if you have to work at it, the fact that you have to cultivate a glamorous soul, the fact that you can starve your soul by obsessing about *pores* and *nail jewelry* all day, the fact that she won't listen to me though, the fact that anything I say just seems to drive her right back into the unloving arms of the Morning Routine girls, like "the cute twins," the fact that she *hates* the cute twins but she still watches them, the fact that they really are acutely cute, and they both have their own tips on life, the fact that first of all, everything is cute, they find everything cute, the fact that they wear cute stuff and do their hair the same cute way and then they go downstairs and make cute cupcakes out of cute ice cream cones, and cover them in cute marshmallows, and it's all just so cute, cute, *cute*, the fact that I don't know how kids put up with this, all these pressures, the fact that they're on call twenty-four hours a day, scrolling down their phones and stuff, the fact that they look like they're *scratching* at their phones actually, trying to get inside them somehow, the fact that it was enough for me to be ostracized at *school*, the fact that I didn't need it at night as well, discos, rock concerts, nanometers, nanoseconds, nanoparticles, the fact that I should really be very gentle with Stace, the fact that who knows what kind of problems she's having, and so what if she'd rather eat pineapple rings with Jake than do her chores, the fact that I haven't been much of a mom to Stacy, I don't think, what with Frank leaving us in the lurch like that, and Mommy and Daddy dying at practically the same time, and then I fell in love with Leo, and had all these other kids, the fact that by the time Stace was six she had a new dad and a new brother, the fact that I feel bad about neglecting her, the fact that I neglected Bathsheba too at that time, oh dear, the fact that luckily cats don't bear grudges, or I hope not, the fact that cats don't give you the Silent Treatment, well, no more than usual anyway, the fact that sometimes Stace can be a real cold fish, chestnut mare, foal, Longaberger Basket Building, but what if it's *me* that's cold, the fact that maybe I was, without meaning to be, the fact that I just get so easily distracted when I'm in love, Chuck, Mommy, euphoria, nap, back stairs, kitchen, the fact that I've probably been a much better mom with the other kids, the fact that maybe after a few kids you start to get the hang of it, just like with starter marriages, the fact that it's an awful thing to say, but maybe the first kid's practice, ♫ *the surrey with the fringe on top!* ♫, kerplop, the fact that girls now start dieting at five and some are *dead* by fifteen, encouraged by cute twins and anorexia sites, of all things, the fact that Stacy's going all vegan but I don't think she's anorexic, the fact that I'd never even heard of anorexia until I was around eleven and announced I was going to eat only bananas from now on, and Phoebe said I better not because I might become anorexic, and I *laughed*, thinking she'd just made that word up out of the blue, the fact that I thought she was just pulling my leg, the fact that now every kid knows about anorexia and bulimia, the fact that the PTA had that evening session on anorexia and social media and sexting, and we all came out sick to our stomachs, Dairy Queen, Hardees, Kentucky Fried Chicken, the fact that the next one was on childhood stress, the fact that Leo lucked out, he was out of town, but I had to go, the fact that they handed out stress-busting instruction sheets, the fact that children have record levels of anxiety now, but there's a solution, stress packs that cost sixty bucks each, $59.99, the fact that paying that much for a stress-buster is very stressful for the *parents*, I think, and all you get is a notepad and pen, silly putty, Guatemalan worry dolls, and a fidget cube, the fact that a lot of the parents said their kids already had fidget *spinners*, so did they need a fidget cube as well, the fact that then somebody else said those things have lead and mercury in them, lead and mercury in a *kid's toy*, for heaven's sake, the fact that it's probably just the glow-in-the-dark kind that has all the lead, but who knows, the fact that the fidget cube *is* kind of different, $59.99, the fact that we're supposed to get our kids to make worry lists in the notebooks, and do breathing exercises too, the fact that I think what would worry *my* kids is if I start stressing out about their stress levels, the fact that I'd rather they just come talk to me, but the woman at the meeting said kids have to tell their worries to their Guatemalan worry dolls because they *can't* talk to their parents or teachers, the fact that that's sad, the fact that they're supposed to tell the doll one worry and shove it under the pillow, and then get out another doll for the next worry, the fact that I guess each doll can only handle one worry, after all they're pretty tiny, the dolls, not the worries, the fact that I'm sure *my* kids feel free to talk to me, the fact that she said kids worry about money, global warming, and divorce and stuff, the fact that I worried about stuff as a kid, but I can't remember what, the fact that sometimes Mommy treated Daddy like he was an *ogre* or something, the fact that she probably got that way from having a drunken dad and a scared mom, the fact that Daddy really wasn't such a bad guy, the fact that once he asked me if he frightened me though, and I said yes, oh dear, poor Daddy, but he did, a bit, the fact that I must have been about ten, the fact that I didn't mean any *harm* by it, I just thought he wanted an honest answer, the fact that I bet he wished he'd never asked, the fact that he seemed a bit surprised and hurt, the fact that I thought he *knew* he frightened me so I didn't think it was a big deal to tell him, but I guess he didn't know, the fact that I was always a little scared of him, the fact that he died before I ever really relaxed with him, and now I realize he was really probably one of the kindest guys in the world, the fact that what can you do though, if somebody makes you nervous, the fact that I always thought he disapproved of me, the fact that it was such a shock when he passed away, the fact that he died *first*, even though Mommy had been sick for so long, the fact that she'd been sick half my life, the fact that before he passed away he asked me to take care of Mommy and I *tried*, but she died too, the fact that I was a real wreck, broken, the fact that after Mommy passed on I had trouble getting out of bed, the fact that I had to pull myself together for Stacy, somehow, hostas, lady slippers, lilies of the valley, Hummingbird quilt, Greek Revival architecture, ladybug, apple-paring bees, quilting bee, bee in your bonnet, by hook or by crook, JAKE, the fact that I caved and bought a worry pack for

Gillian, the fact that I knew Ben wouldn't want one, the fact that *my* biggest worry now is that one of the little Guatemalan worry dolls will get stuck in my nice new washer, or the kneading machine, embroidered Guatemalan square shirt, boxes in the attic, fake news, Fox News, Stacy, the fact that I still feel bad about that time in the kitchen, just the three of us, the fact that I was heating up vegan vegetable soup for Stace and she started talking about Frank, the fact that I don't know why she brought him up because she hardly ever does, the fact that she nearly broke down and I so wanted to hug her, but I was busy with the *soup*, and Leo just kept blasting her with more questions, the fact that I think the whole subject makes him nervous, stress-buster, the fact that I'm sure he meant to be helpful but it sort of became an *interrogation*, instead of a, well, conversation, the fact that it seemed to me he was trying too hard to get her to be more rational about Frank, as if anybody's ever rational about their dad, the fact that, I mean, give the girl a break, the fact that I wanted to give her time to say whatever she wanted to say, especially since she so rarely shares anything about Frank at all, but I couldn't get a word in edgewise, between the two of them, and the soup, the fact that I just hope Stacy knows I understand it's rough for her, the fact that it's tragic actually, the fact that it's just awful to lose your dad and never know where the heck he is, or why he disappeared, the fact that it's like she's just stuck in limbo, sitting duck, waiting for Frank's next move, his next urge to get in touch, next Stacy mood, the fact that we don't even know if he's in Connecticut, *Something is rotten*, the fact that somehow I don't think talking to a whole ton of Guatemalan worry dolls is going to solve this one, though it might inadvertently help the Guatemalan economy of course, which is *another* worry, the fact that I just realized that with this worry-doll industry, Guatemala's indirectly benefiting from stress levels all over the world, or even *directly* benefiting, the fact that that is one weird export, but it's kind of them, trade deals, Thoreau's cabin, the fact that somebody in the PTA's starting a knitting group to knit banners asking people to help fund the school, the fact that they think this is a cute way of fundraising for the school and we're all supposed to help out, but I don't knit or crochet or cross stitch, though Abby tried to teach me, and who has time for stuff like that anymore, leisure time, mod cons, the fact that Abby liked to do all those sorts of things but I don't have time to stitch a nine-patch or knit a big banner, the fact that all my fundraising efforts are directed at amassing my own kids' college funds, which is selfish I know but that's what we're reduced to, the fact that I'm going to try to do my best by my kids and that's about it, the fact that usually when they ask me to crochet something, I offer to make them a pie instead, the fact that anyway those banners may make trouble, the fact that some folks are tricky about stuff like that, ♫ *Gone with the Wind* ♫, the fact that people get mad so easily these days, and then they pull a gun on you, or a sword, without pausing for breath, without breaking a sweat, Eugene V. Debs, the fact that it's no joke, take a chill pill, Thorne miniature rooms, the fact that Eugene V. Debs ran for president five times, the last time from prison, Spiderman, the fact that Bowling Green University now has a Department of Popular Culture, where you can do a PhD on cartoons and comic strips and YouTube channels, the fact that maybe Stacy should go there some day to study Morning Routine girl videos, dear me, let's hope not, the fact that I don't know why I just thought of *Gone with the Wind*, the fact that they used to show it at Christmastime but I don't think they do anymore, the fact that a lot of people love it still, maybe because of the hooped skirts, *The Wizard of Oz*, the fact that Uranus has a layer of diamonds in its ocean, the fact that the Beatles came from Liverpool, the fact that it's got dozens of tiny moons, Uranus, not Liverpool, each with its own orbit, "your anus," the fact that Saturn has sixty-two moons, but no diamonds, and the biggest moon is Titan, the fact that Uranus's moons are very, very small, like about fifty miles wide, the fact that you could drive around one of those things in about an hour, depending on traffic, and gravity, and terrain, *Around the World in Eighty Days*, drunk drivers, the fact that the planets in our solar system really do exist, all these planets and planetoid spheres, the fact that they really are out there, spinning around, the fact that they aren't a fairy story, the fact that they're just as real as my aardvark magnet or Stacy's one-eyed tiger, or *The Stepford Wives*, but they don't *feel* real, the fact that you never think of the solar system that way, the fact that it's hard to feel very intimate with a solar system, Highgate, orbits, it's too intangible, but what I say is, if the universe is chaos, then why not my kitchen, dish soap, the fact that I don't know who that man is standing at the bottom of our driveway, the fact that if they could only invent a zero-gravity machine, we could all *fly*, the fact that I hope he isn't coming up here, the fact that there was a scary screech right outside the window last night when we were getting ready for bed, a hawk or an owl, but the chickens were safe in the coop, the fact that there's nothing nicer than a broody hen with her wings stretched out, sheltering a dozen chicks, the fact that it's always good to have chicks around, though they grow too fast, the fact that I don't think it's good for chicks to lose their mom too early, like those poor little guys that get sent around in cardboard boxes, just in the *normal mail*, the fact that they must be the most frightened thirsty little things in the world, or maybe the universe, the fact that there are no worry dolls or fidget cubes for *them*, poor little things, the fact that somebody tried to send a two-month-old tiger cub in the mail in Mexico, and he survived more or less okay but he was dehydrated, the fact that he has huge paws, paw-paw, pow wow, Wo-He-Lo, the fact that I dreamt I helped a cat by undoing a bird-shaped piece of cardboard tied to his back paw, the fact that I also dreamt I almost fell off a ladder but didn't, and then I went to a very busy restaurant in Japan, the fact that George W. Bush was seated prominently in front, Dubbya, hoping people would notice him, the fact that the restaurant only served minuscule food, really tiny, almost microscopic, and everybody was supposed to use these teeny-weeny tongs to get at it, like the tweezers in Leo's pocket knife, the fact that you had to make a note of your order with a tiny pencil, the fact that I liked the inch-tall mineral water bottles so much I pocketed one, but I didn't think they'd mind, the fact that Trump is always scared somebody's poisoning his food, and that's why he eats takeout all the time, and McDonald's cheeseburgers, because he thinks that can't have been tampered with, Roman emperors, the fact that who does he think is poisoning his food at the White House, the fact that is it Melania, the fact that that strange man seems to have gone now, the guy that was near our driveway, not *Trump*, trompe l'oeil, the fact that now it's Gillian's turn to tackle Robert Frost's fork-in-the-road, Jack Frost, the fact that it has taken me forty years to get a handle on that thing, the fact that elementary school teachers all seem to think it's *simple*, like math, four score and twenty years ago, the fact that it seemed like every year practically we had to write some explanation of "The Road Not Taken," and every year everybody else seemed to be getting it done better than me, the fact that I just got into a tizzy over it, fizzy, dizzy, fissiparous, the fact that I probably should've asked Mommy and Daddy, but I didn't want them to know how *dumb* I am, the fact that I still don't really, so I'm still glad I didn't ask them, *Two roads diverged in a yellow wood*, Canal Street, Snickers, sneakers, four score and *seven* years ago, not *twenty*, dear me, hydrangea, Obama's memoirs, the fact that once a year, teachers you thought were pretty sensible would suddenly get all over-excited and expect the whole class to join them in their Robert Frost fixation, "The love impulse in man," the fact that they think all they have to do is stand there and tell you some things are *symbolic* and somehow you'll get with the program, but I never got with the program, not on that poem, anyway, nor the other one, the snow one, the fact that, for the life of me, I still can't even tell them apart, the fact that it's like the aurora borealis, the fact that I just couldn't see what everybody else found so darned fascinating about it, the fact that okay, there's this guy on a horse, and there's a fork in the road and it's autumn and all that, Autumn Man, the fact that if only he'd left it at that and gone on his way, but no, you've got to find something *else* in there, hidden between the lines, some metaphor or analogy for something, Frost's horse, Frost's wood, Frost's fork, Frost's road, Frost's moons, Frost's planets, Frost's orbits, Frost's gravity, the fact that Frost is not Wordsworth, Woolworth's, a hundred and five billion chickens a year, the fact that it could just, you know, be a guy riding along a disused road and, well, he says it *himself*, that either fork would do, forks and knives, so what's the big deal, the fact that I never could care less which fork he took, it was all the same to *me*, just pick one, buddy, *the one less traveled by*, but Frost says it made *all the difference*, so who am I to, the fact I guess you have to take a man at his word on stuff like that, the fact that, I mean, *he* oughtta know, Gnadenhutten Massacre, the fact that the other problem is I always mix it up with the *snowy* one, though I'd never tell Gillian that or she'll start mixing them up too, and then blame me when she flunks the test, Chicago Art Institute, the fact that at my school we were all supposed to recite one or the other, and now my kids have to too, the fact that it's like *the* American poem that all American kids have to learn, whichever one it is, when they could be reading *Paul Violi*, the fact that maybe we wouldn't need these stress-buster packs if they didn't assign all this Frost, the fact that it wasn't until Gillian was crying about the two roads that I was finally able, I think, to try and explain it to her, enough to get her to calm down anyway, and now I think even I get that poem, but I could be all wrong about it, Neptune Society, bad man pushing me from behind, *a lonely wood*, the fact that I was looking at some stuff in the Art Institute shop once, and some guy pushed up behind me and pressed something hard into my spine, a bulge in his stomach, or that's what I thought it was then, the fact that he wouldn't move away and I had no idea what to do, the fact that I was only about ten, the fact that he was pressing against me, crushing me against the counter, and the store was crowded, the fact that it was so strange, but I wasn't scared exactly, the fact that Daddy was right nearby, and Phoebe was somewhere too, maybe the whole family, I can't remember, the fact that finally I managed to squirm away and I told Daddy about it and Daddy got amazingly mad, and started searching all over the store for the guy, but I hadn't seen the man's face so I couldn't tell Daddy who to look for, Thorne miniatures, the fact that it took me *years* to realize what it was that guy pressed against my back, the fact that I never would've guessed in a million years, at that age, the fact that who would ever *believe* how penises behave, until you *know*, the fact that you'd never expect them to do *that*, the fact that if anybody ever tried that on Gillian I'd kill him, the fact that Frost chose the road less traveled and that was okay for him, for Frost I mean, not the guy in the museum shop, the fact that the truth is you always wonder if you should've taken the other road, done things differently, the fact that in real life that sort of question is never really settled once and for all, though I know I was right to marry Leo, the fact that there are *some things* I don't regret, the fact that Mommy never made me a Hallowe'en costume as good as Phoebe's Marlboro cigarette pack but I didn't mind, the fact that we were all just so pleased with the Marlboro costume, the fact that I'm sure I had some other costume I liked, my rented mouse costume in London, the fact that Mommy made the Marlboro costume all by herself, stayed up all night painting a cardboard box to look just like a giant Marlboro pack, which were her favorite cigarettes at the time, the fact that it fit Phoebe perfectly too, the fact that Mommy really did a great job on that thing, the fact that you could probably be *arrested* for dressing your kid as a pack of cigarettes these days, but that Marlboro box was a real work of art, the fact that Claes Oldenburg would've liked it, the fact that Giacometti thought Picasso was full of, well, let's not go there, the fact that you always remember the costumes you wore, but Phoebe's was the best, the fact that that year in London, she was a witch and Annie was a devil, and I don't know what I was, the fact that one year I was a blob, when I was about twelve, the fact that I made that one myself, pillowcase, the fact that Ruth told me once that she and Mommy used to sit in the back row and giggle during our school plays and concerts and things, the fact that my feelings were really hurt by that, though I know it's silly, the fact that I just didn't much like to think of Mommy giggling while I sang my heart out in *Pinafore* or something, ♫ *Poor Little Buttercup, Sweet Little Buttercup I, Dear Little Buttercup* ♫, but maybe they didn't giggle *all* the time, Marlboros, *Oliver!*, SpaghettiOs, lipstick, opening cereal packets, the circles under my eyes, spirals, rhino eyes, the fact that of course, now that I've attended about four billion school plays myself, approximately one million billion per child, as well as four kids'

worth of concerts and contests and soccer games and scouts tourna-
ments, I totally get it, the fact that I wish *I* had somebody to giggle
with in the back row, the fact that Leo can't usually make it, because
of work, the fact that I tend to sob, if there's singing involved, the fact
that kids singing always gets me, "The dam has now broke!", the fact
that it's really a killer, the fact that I always have to bring Kleenex in
case they sing, the fact that listening to ten beginner trumpeters playing "Yankee Doodle" is a different kind of problem, the fact that the
same goes for a thirty-kid violin ensemble playing "Spiegel im Spiegel"
in a school gym, all squeezed together between the basketball boundary lines, the fact that you have to sit on those hard wooden benches,
trying to look appreciative, the fact that it's hard, the fact that even a
solo violin arrangement of "Spiegel im Spiegel" makes me anxious, the
fact that it's supposed to be all meditative, and calming, but it makes
me all of a jitter from worry in case one or the other musician goofs,
or even the page-turner, the fact that even when I've heard the same
particular recording of "Spiegel im Spiegel" before, and know what's
coming, it *still* makes me tense, because you can never stop thinking
about what trouble one falter of the bow would cause, the fact that all
would be lost, so that's not really all that relaxing, the fact that I just
feel sorry for the musicians the whole time, so sorry that I can't wait
for it to end, the fact that it sounds easy to play but it's not easy, not
easy to listen to either, especially when thirty children try sawing it
out, fretting fatigue cracks, the fact that Leo is annoyed the batteries
are always running out on our new keypad and mouse, the fact that
batteries are unecological, he says, but electricity is unecological too,
I say, Sand Creek, the fact that how is an electric mouse and keyboard
any better, but he's better on all this stuff than me, so I should shut up,
the fact that, also, he loves the dryer and that's not ecological, the fact
that I guess everybody has their environmental blind spots, the fact
that I think we should just dry stuff outside if it's a nice day, but Leo
insists it's not the same, the fact that he *hates* it when I dry his clothes
outside on a nice day, the fact that they don't come out as soft, the
fact that running your dryer's even worse than air conditioning or, or

something, according to Stacy, the fact that "This is a terrible time to be alive," as Julie Christie says to Omar Sharif when war's raging all around them and they're lying together under fur rugs in the ice-covered dacha, pasha, Papa, Pa, Ma, the fact that Mommy loved *Dr. Zhivago*, including the music, the fact that that music was guaranteed to get her swaying from side to side, the fact that I always thought there's something very involving about that movie, the fact that you feel like it all happened to *you*, but maybe that's because I saw it first when I was a little kid, the fact that Omar Sharif's Egyptian, not Russian, and he likes to play poker, casino, tuxedo, gazebo, Monte Carlo, no, no, the fact that it's *bridge* he plays, bridges, asleep and awake, flipping, stress cracks, fracture-critical, structurally deficient, the fact that he sort of gave up acting and just played bridge, Brooklyn Bridge, *The Bridge*, the fact that in *The Apartment* they play gin rummy, when Shirley MacLaine's getting over her suicide attempt, the fact that in *The Odd Couple* it's poker, peacock feathers, peahens, mice, the fact that poker games in Westerns always go on for hours, the fact that the only Westerns I like are *High Noon* and *Shane*, and the only one Leo likes is *Stagecoach*, I think, or *Red River*, the fact that he's keener on John Wayne than I am, the fact that most Westerns are just so boring and repetitive and predictable and gory and that's all there is to it, the fact that he hates *Shane*, "Shane! Shane!", the fact that while he and I argue about *Shane*, our mouse batteries run down, the fact that somebody, some government body, wants to stick radioactive waste in the Marianas Trench, so that it'll pollute the oceans for all eternity, the fact that Trump's son Eric spent fifty million taxpayers' dollars going to Uruguay to promote an apartment-building scheme, the fact that his son-in-law Jared Kushner just made a four hundred million private business deal with China, the fact that the whole family seems to see the presidency as just another business venture, arms deals, missile attacks, extremism, terrorism, 9/11, Saudis, Scotch and sodas, whiskey sours, Manhattans, the Manhattan Project, the fact that we're running low on Scotch, the fact that Mommy liked a Manhattan once in a while, the fact that they were planning to bury a whole lot of radioactive waste under prime Pennsylvania farmland for a while, Project Ketch, ketchup, *The Long Kvetch*, but I think they dumped that, the *plan* I mean, not the nuclear waste, dumpster, bump-stock, the fact that they probably want to dump it on *Pluto* now, or Uranus, but not in the sea of diamonds, because they probably have other plans for that, big, bigly plans, Big Bill Broonzy, the fact that NASA's now designing a robot Venus rover vehicle, so a Uranus diamond-scooper doesn't sound too farfetched to me, the fact that who's that woman who blogs about loving everybody and taking each day as it comes and never stressing out, hypnotherapy, Standard Life, barrel rib, recoil pad, cocking lever, cock, the fact that I've never used that word in my *life*, Claudia Cardinale, Gina Lollobrigida, Sophia Loren, Raquel Welch, Brigitte Bardot, Marilyn Monroe, the fact that the PTA's stress-busting instruction sheet also recommends getting your kids to bake cookies, but personally I don't find that baking reduces stress, far from it, the fact that cookies are easier though than cinnamon rolls, muzzle, cheat sheet, the fact that I'm off the hook about the cocktail party at least, it looks like, the fact that it's because of the weather and also it turns out none of his colleagues really wanted to come all the way here in the middle of winter just for a cocktail party, the fact that they all sounded pretty enthusiastic about it at first, but now they're getting nervous, the fact that I'm offended on Leo's behalf, but it's such a relief they're not coming, the fact that now I don't have to make tidbits in blankets, cheese and rice croquettes, cheese and bacon pin wheels, Hoosier corn queso dip, guacamole, salsa, corn chips, deviled eggs, cheese straws, spiced pumpkin seeds, shrimps with my famous cocktail sauce, or ham and cream cheese pinwheels, and I don't have to find, and wear, a *muumuu*, ♫ *Marietta's song* ♫, Leontyne Price, Scottie pinwheel, the fact that I think I'll make a no-bean chili for tonight but *mild*, the fact that I made it too hot last time, the fact that just a pinch of mild chili powder will do, and a little cayenne, unsweetened chocolate, cumin, cinnamon, sage and a bay leaf, and a pinch of ground cloves, the fact that we all like no-bean chili, with some chipotle beans on the side, not in, the fact that the cumin's crucial, the fact that Abby was so *relaxed* about cooking, or she sure seemed it, the fact that she had it all worked out and hardly ever even consulted a recipe, or not that I noticed, the fact that I think all her recipes were on index cards, probably alphabetically arranged, the fact that she always knew what she was doing, and always had the right ingredients, because she knew what she was cooking a week ahead and bought all the right ingredients on her trip to the market every Saturday, or was it every other Saturday, the fact that she always had it ready right on time, when Hoag got home, the fact that for years and years she produced those dinners but when Hoag passed on, all she ate was grilled cheese sandwiches, and that makes me sad, the fact that when Barry was a boy the schedule was strict, the fact that she put him to bed at 7:00, the fact that my kids would never stand for that, the fact that Barry must be one of the few kids who ever got enough sleep, the fact that she liked to take me to Rockport, where we always bought another little stained-glass ornament to put on her back door, to catch the evening sun, Motif #1, the fact that I've got to get cilantro, sour cream and chipotle, and tortillas, and more Hunt's, the fact that I've gotta hunt down the Hunt's, Hunt's tomato sauce, not chili sauce, the fact that that would be cheating, Mommy's card-shuffling method, the fact that I often dream Mommy and Daddy are still alive, computer mouse, a mouse in the house, the fact that *I* wasn't all stressed out as a kid because I had *Edward*, so sleek and white and funny, and so friendly, Edward hiding under the TV in the dining room, the fact that everybody should have a pet mouse, the fact that he always came back out from under the TV when I called, the fact that I found a wild mouse in our house once when I was a kid, a little brownish gray field mouse, and I tried to keep him alive but he passed away, the fact that it just occurred to me he was probably sick already, or what was he doing indoors and why was he so easy to catch, and he didn't put up much of a struggle when I caught him, the fact that we should've taken him to the vet and asked the parrot what was wrong with him, the fact that that parrot knew everything, the fact that, on the other hand, it might have eaten him, the fact that I don't even know if parrots are carnivorous, the fact that an owl would happily eat a field mouse, the fact that parrots like papaya, maybe paw-paw, the fact that our vet is called Bliss, which always seems sort of paradoxical when you see all the trembling dogs in there, the fact that Edward had three babies, one in the first litter and two in the next, which is pretty restrained for a mouse, the fact that Daddy was scared we'd be *inundated* with mouselings, once Edward started having babies, but we never were, the fact that Edward was very restrained, abstemious, abstemiosity, in extremis, estranged, exchange, the fact that once I tried to hatch grocery-store eggs as a kid, but nothin' doin', the fact that being a child is so frustrating, the fact that Gillian was so disappointed that she couldn't make scrambled eggs the first time she tried, shirred eggs, sunny side up, egg foo yong, Young's Jersey Dairy, the fact that people are so down on mice, the fact that they'll go to any length to buy a gerbil or degu, or a chipmunk or chinchilla or duprasi from a pet store, get it the right food, give it a running wheel and a habitrail and one of those water-drip things and sawdust and all the other stuff a rodent's supposed to want, and even take it to the vet if he looks sick, but if a poor little wild mouse comes into the house uninvited and makes off with a bread crumb, it's like a national emergency, exterminators, Terminix, Pulverizer, drone attacks, Yemeni children, the fact that Ronny was complaining about mice getting into *his* place, the fact that he was really freaked out about it, but field mice sometimes just need somewhere to go in the winter, the fact that you don't have to call the fire department about it, the fact that they did some experiment where they gave the participant a computer and told them to surf the net, but warned them each click would cause some unseen stranger excruciating pain, click, hair clip, TV clip, the fact that the experiment was just to see how tempted people would be by clickbait, the fact that it turned out most people wouldn't resist a bit of clickbait even to save their own mother's life, and they certainly didn't give a darn if total strangers were suffering every time they clicked on some dumb story, bargains, Pinterest, the Pentagon, pentagram, peonies, Opal, the Opelousas massacre, ♫ *Gone with the Wind* ♫, dahlia, the fact that I can't get that tune out of my head, the fact that I don't know where I heard it but it's fatal if you hear that thing, the fact that it sticks for days, just like "Lara's Song," Mommy, Lara, Tara, ♫ *Gone with the Wind* ♫, the fact that I really sort of hate computers but you can't have kids anymore without having a computer in the house, the fact that they need it for all their learning games and homework and their social lives and anorexia networks and stress-busting questionnaires, the fact that *we* need it too, so we can receive the PTA announcements and newsletters and Fun Day info, and notifications of school closures and snow reports, and the national news too, the fact that Leo needs access at home for all his university work, and to write lectures and articles as well, and do his PowerPoint slides and all, the fact that his portable typewriter's long gone, the fact that it disappeared into the attic way back, the fact that we got it out for the kids once for the kids to play with it and I think they broke it, the fact that it makes you feel so ancient when they look at something like that and can't believe anybody ever used one to write on, the fact that even I need a computer now, though I resisted as long as I could, but I need it for my HMO stuff, and pie orders and everything, and to source ingredients and get new recipes too, and order the chicken feed, and email other people too, the fact that I can't think *who* at this precise moment, but there are lots of people I do email, well, other moms, though I usually end up phoning them because they never answer their emails, the fact that I prefer emailing to phoning though, the fact that it seems much less stressful, and you don't have to worry about interrupting something, the fact that sometimes I have to email friends and neighbors and the restaurant managers if we have extra eggs to get rid of, because I really don't like to put up a sign on the curb and get strangers coming to the door, total strangers, the fact that we could have an HONESTY BOX and just hope they drop the right money in, but most people wouldn't know what to do with an HONESTY BOX except *steal* it, the fact that most conmen come from Indiana, con artists, persuasion, *Persuasion*, AIDA funnel, the fact that long ago Ethan urged me to get on email so he could write to me, but now I'm on it he's too *busy*, the fact that we both have these big families, the fact that the AIDA funnel sounds like something that you get sucked into, and it is, Awareness-Interest-Desire-Action, the fact that it's how advertisers get you to buy stuff, brand lifts, ad recall, desire metrics, affinity, infinity, buzzworthy, test drive, hot tub, clickbait, bait dog, bated breath, breadth, Amos and Andy, the fact that it's pretty hard to claim I'm making any money out of these chickens, or saving any, the fact that they eat up fifty-pound bags of feed in no time, but I am saving something on eggs, and if I have any surplus it's a good time to make a ham and egg pie for the kids, which they like, or we have Salade Lyonnaise, the fact that maybe we need *more* chickens, the fact that maybe fourteen chickens aren't enough, tiffins, dinner pail, haybox meals, wonderbox, HONESTY BOX, funnel, the fact that at least if they're your own eggs, you know they're free range and the hens didn't suffer, since you can see them not suffering right out the window, the fact that they did suffer that time the coyote came, or whatever it was, blood and feathers everywhere, fall colors, windy day, "This cow's done a lot of suffering," HONESTY BOX, the fact that the coop is much more predator-proof now, knock on wood, the fact that everybody should have mice and chickens and goldfish and I don't know why they don't, because they're no trouble, the fact that cats too are no trouble really, unless you live in an apartment, the fact that most people used to keep a few hens for their own needs, in the old days, and maybe a pig, the fact that Z is the best letter in the alphabet, because it comes at the end, and it's jazzy and buzzing and fizzy, the fact that zebras starts with Z, the fact that in English you use E the most, the fact that I don't know why kids have to learn the alphabet, Abby's recipes in alphabetical order, alphabet salad, the fact that alphabetical order has no meaning, it's just an agreed code for organizing stuff, I guess, that we all have to memorize, like Frost poems, the fact that I never knew why typewriters and computer keyboards aren't alphabetical, qwerty, the fact that it's to help touch typists or something, the fact that how did they all agree to do that, the fact that it's like getting the whole world to agree on turning the clocks back, or forward, the fact that who decided on the alphabet, I'd like to know, the fact that every kid has to learn to sing that alphabet song, but why, *I don't know but they know*, your pinky and your pointer finger, the fact that things don't *have* to be arranged in alphabetical order, the fact that you could arrange stuff thematically, or by size, or age, or color, or just about anything really, apple pie order, not just in libraries but everywhere, the fact that I don't get why the vowels are all dotted around the alphabet like that, the fact that they're all over the place, a e i o u, the fact that I think E should come *first*, the fact that wouldn't it be more practical to have one section just for vowels, and then another section for the consonants, physic garden, comfrey, the fact that if you changed the alphabet though, you'd nullify all those old samplers girls used to sew, and that would be a shame, the fact that most samplers were made by children under twelve, funettes, the fact that some girls started sewing samplers at *three*, the fact that boys often made samplers as well, boys going in to some trade that required sewing skills, A B C D E F G, elemenopee, the fact that I saw a whole times table in a sampler once, stitched by some nineteenth-century girl, the fact that I can't believe some of the things those kids managed to make, the fact that even a buttonhole takes so much skill, the fact that they had to master that and other tricky things before they were allowed to do a sampler, the fact that what is that terrible noise outside, somebody backing up, beeping away, the fact that trucks all talk to themselves now, the fact that they make all these inaudible remarks, the fact that when you get close enough so you can hear them, it's always a disappointment, like a talking doll, "This vehicle is turning left, This vehicle is turning left," the fact that I used to love walking home from school on a warm spring day when I was a kid, the fact that I liked it when the breeze blew into my room and I could look out on the tree outside my window and hear the lawn mowers and electric tree saws, the fact that they were always sawing down trees in our neighborhood, I don't know why, but I didn't mind it then, the fact that it just sounded like home, the fact that now I fret for every tree they trim, because just when are they going to realize we *need* the trees, the fact that in Mexico they're growing vertical gardens on the *highway*, like on the overpass bridges, the fact that Leo's keen on that idea, *more* beeps, and a faraway train whistle, the fact that I like train whistles, the fact that Daddy could pick plums from the tree outside his office at Yale, just by leaning out the window, or was it figs, the fact that he cried easily over operas and old movies, the fact that he was a real softy, the fact that we found it kind of embarrassing at times, the fact that kids are so mean, the fact that we didn't like the way his chin crumpled when he cried, or I didn't anyway, the fact that we didn't like the way he pronounced eggs either, "aigs," but, you know, it's really not such a bad thing, is it, the fact that, I mean, to blubber through a few movies, I don't know about the "aigs," the fact that why shouldn't he cry over *Casablanca* and *It's a Wonderful Life*, the fact that that's what those movies are for, the fact that *It's a Wonderful Life* could really pummel him, like when Jimmy Stewart tells Mr. Gower he won't tell on him about the poison capsules, or when, later on, Mr. Gower buys him a suitcase for his travels, the fact that Daddy's lips would start to quiver and he'd get those little crinkly indentations in his chin, and you knew he'd lost it, the fact that I was always scared of *my* chin looking like that but I've since noticed that lots of people's chins get that puckered look sometimes, so I shouldn't have let it bother me, but I didn't know that then, the fact that I thought it was only Daddy's and mine, complexion protection, the fact that Daddy would cry over the suitcase and then he'd cry some more when Jimmy Stewart sees Mary at the high school dance, and when he finds her standing in the broken down old house in the rain after they get married, the fact that Jimmy Stewart's been at the Savings and Loan place all day dealing with the run on the bank, instead of having a honeymoon, and he gets to the house and Mary's got the old phonograph cooking them a rotisserie chicken, the fact that actually we were *all* suckers for that movie, tearing up and finding it hard to swallow when the Martinis get their first house and it's brand new, and Jimmy Stewart and Mary give them their house-warming presents of wine, bread and salt, so life will always have flavor, the fact that the moment when Clarence says Harry's dead, the fact that when Harry turns up right at the end to save Jimmy Stewart from going to jail, ten-cent Jimmy, the fact that I can't remember the name of the family business, Business and Loan or something, Pottersville, the fact that Leo thinks the whole of America is getting like Pottersville now, the fact that St. Louis is now the gun crime capital, with the highest rate of shooting deaths in the country, the fact that our house in New Haven was so pleasant, Federal style, the beautiful wide, dark polished floorboards, the fact that Republicans like children to be respectful and obedient, the fact that that family of thirteen kids chained to their beds were pretty obedient, the fact that Ivory soap floats, maybe Dove too, Ivorydale, Ohio, styptic stick, "99 $^{44/100}$% pure – It floats," Nivea, the fact that I miss Mommy, the fact that if she were still alive I'd make sure everything was nice for her, the fact that she could live here with us, the fact that Daddy died before I really got to know him, the fact that I always thought I was an embarrassment to him, the fact that I dreamt Daddy was telling me to wear a fancier outfit than I had on, the fact that I'd dressed up for some occasion but he didn't think it was fancy enough, the fact that I almost bought a dark green feathery hat, just to please him, but it was too big for my head and it kept sinking lower and lower, the fact that plutonium was named after Pluto, and uranium after Uranus, and I don't know what cesium's named after but Russian gangsters love it, the fact that they're always selling it on the black market and soon ISIS will get hold of some and start making dirty bombs, the fact that the Russians interfered with the U.S. election, the fact that some Russian journalist was poisoned with radioactive tea at a hotel right in the heart of London, the fact that eight out of ten kids are abused, the fact that that can't be right, the fact that actually I think maybe it's *one in eight*, which is still too many of course, statistically, the fact that America has the highest rate of child mortality of any major rich country, from infant mortality to road deaths and school shootings, as American as apple pie, the fact that it's like it's getting unsafe to send your kids to *school*, the fact that some

362

girls spread a nerve agent on the North Korean leader's brother, Kim Jong Ill or something, and he died within twenty minutes, Mommy, Waterlow Park, white fog and black leaves, the cemetery, the ducks and geese, the fact that Highgate Cemetery's famous, the fact that Karl Marx and George Eliot are buried there, Anne Elliott, rhododendron dens, Tiny Tim's turquoise traveling case, Jimmy Stewart, Seward, beans on toast, the fact that it seemed like London was always foggy and drizzly, peanut butter, ♫ *Einaudi piano piece* ♫, cinnamon roll dough, black wet leaves on black wet soil, Edward under the TV set, Jake's bagel, the fact that it's Bailey Brothers Mortgage and, no, Building and Loan, Bailey Brothers Building and Loan, Mary, Mr. Gower, Lionel Barrymore, the fact that who's that other Barrymore, John Barrymore, Ethel Barrymore, the Taliban, al-Qaeda, ISIS and Boko Haram, the fact that climate change is a worse threat to life on earth than terrorism, Bernie Sanders says, and, apart from 9/11, the worst terrorist incidents in America are all committed by native-born American citizens, Oklahoma, the fact that there's no gun registration in Ohio, no background checks, no paper trail, no nothing, Open Carry guys, the fact that Trump wants even fewer restrictions on guns, the fact that he just wants everything to get just about as crazee as can be, stir crazy, trigger-happy, slap happy, fiddlehead ferns, spirals, the fact that Walmart's selling more and more heavy-duty military-style firearms, the fact that I just hate to see those Open Carry guys standing around on the street in Coshocton, talking to police officers, the fact that they're always quoting articles and codes and clauses, the Open Carry guys, not the cops, like Article 1, Section whatever, Code 9.68b of the Ohio Constitution, the fact that I saw some on Chestnut Street once, holding their Kalashnikovs up in the air and yacking away about this Article and that, the fact that they don't seem to realize how silly they look, though sinister too, arguing Codes when you can tell they just want to show off their toys, just like little boys, the fact that they love to hark back to the American Revolution, the Open Carry guys, not little boys, but, NEWS ALERT, there are no redcoats in Ohio anymore, the fact that after that terrible shooting in Scotland, they had a new handgun law in place in no time, Lockerbie, but it never seems to happen here, even after Sandy Hook, the fact that the children crouched down, all bunched together, the fact that I meant *Dunblane*, not Lockerbie, the fact that Lockerbie's where the plane came down, Libyan terrorists, the fact that people are always talking about mental checks and a three-day wait when you purchase a gun, but gosh, a *three-year* wait would be more like it, the fact that then people would get bored and probably forget the whole idea, but the gun industry wouldn't be happy, the fact that the NRA objects to mental illness checks, the fact that they don't think it's fair that having a history of just OCD or bulimia or something might prevent you owning a gun, but I don't know, the fact that some of those people with eating disorders have pretty bad mood swings, the fact that there's nothing we can do about it anyway, the fact that they've got the Second Amendment on their side, shooting drills in gym class, lockdown, ♬ *Lockdown, lockdown, lock the door* ♬, ten million AR-15 rifles, crouching children, the fact that a judge in Detroit was trying a case where a nine-year-old got hold of his mom's gun, which she kept in her purse, and the kid had shot himself in the hand, the fact that the mom was arrested, and the judge said nobody needs a gun, nobody, the fact that he said the Second Amendment dates back to the early days in the New World, before there was an official police force to handle things, the fact that he said guns only cause trouble, and he's eighty and he's never owned one, the fact that the mom got three years probation, along with the lecture, neglect, reckless endangerment, the fact that Judge *Roberson*, the fact that that was his name, the fact that I think it'd be great if the right to bear arms thing turned out to be about wearing short sleeves, the right to *bare* arms, or else maybe they meant heraldry, like the right to a family crest, the fact that you get to have a pennant with a lion rampant or dormant on it, armorial, armed conflict, Ben's book on heraldry, dormant, torpor, the fact that it would be really nice to see all these gun nuts just settle down and design their own coat of arms and get some plaques made, the fact that maybe they could have their own tartan too, get a whole Scottish thing going, a family clan, kilts, swordies, the fact that I wouldn't even mind bagpipes if they'd just quit talking about the 2A for a while, and stopped killing people too, all these estranged wives, the fact that where's that book on heraldry gone, the fact that here it is, with a postcard from Anat inside, passant, gardant, passant gardant, statant, salient, sejant, sejant erect, sejant dormant, the fact that those guys could have a lot of fun with all these unicorns and stuff, rampant, regardant, trident, leopard, coward, the fact that they could get together and drink beer and compare their *emblems*, instead of their Kalashnikovs, the fact that lion rampant means its tail goes between its legs and over the back, or does it mean rearing up, the fact that it's not "rampant" as in *gun* rampages, rampant passant, the fact that it symbolizes magnanimity, lion sejant erect, lion coward leopardé, salient, sejant, the fact that a lion passant gardant means it's walking and showing its face, full frontal, the fact that that lion looks so *friendly*, salient, sejant, sejant erect, sage, birds, dolphins, bears, lion coward, lion dormant, the lion's share, let sleeping dogs lie, leopard, cows, horses, unicorns, the fact that everything means something in heraldry, dormant, statant, statant gardant, coward, rampant regardant, hauriant, urinant, glissant, pascuant, the fact that pascuant means grazing, the fact that you have to be a cow or a rhinoceros to be pascuant, the fact that lions can't do it, rhino eyes, the fact that the Open Carry guys might really like this, because heraldic shields are made up of metals and azure and gules and purple and sable, along with fesses, chevrons, bends, birds, bears, reptiles and other very exact and symbolic things, the fact that it would keep them all busy for years, the fact that call me crazy but a concealed pennant sounds a lot safer than a concealed pistol, kids' samplers, Victory banner, shooting drills, the fact that Trump said everybody in the Orlando nightclub should've been armed, the fact that that's his answer to every mass shooting, but even the head of the NRA admits that guns and alcohol don't mix, the fact that my kids are so used to having to hide in school closets now, they're really blasé about it, the fact that I hate to think of the police officers who have to go up to those cockamamie Open Carry guys in Coshocton and talk to them about their guns and the Codes and Articles and all, but that's the job, the fact that it must be pretty scary though, the fact that they must have to steel themselves to approach one, screw up their courage, screw-up, the fact that some cop arrested a woman for drunk driving and told her to get her license out but she was too scared to move, because of all the reports of the police shooting everybody for no reason, the fact that she thought if she moved her hands she'd be a goner, the fact that the cop joked that didn't she know they only shoot *black* people, which wasn't very funny, the fact that I think he got fired, misfired, Dollar Tree, Klein bottle, #neveragain, #NoMore, #ShameOnYou, #MeToo, the right to *draw* arms, the fact that the Metropolitan had a little show about a little guy in the eighteenth century, I think, who liked to draw coats of arms, the fact that maybe he was alive in the *seventeenth* century actually, the fact that he had no hands or feet, the fact that he made little pictures with microscopic bits of writing in them that you can only read with a microscope, no, a *magnifying glass*, Matthias Buchinger, the fact that he was famous because he was born with no hands and no lower legs, but he could do all this *stuff*, not just the fine penmanship and the coats of arms and all the trompe l'oeil paintings, "Trump lies," but card tricks and magic tricks, the fact that he was also famous on the dulcimer, bagpipes and the trumpet, and he built ships in bottles, and somehow he even managed to dance the hornpipe, musician, magician, the fact that not only that but he had three, four, maybe eight wives, and seventy mistresses, and fourteen children or more, and died in obscurity, the fact that I don't get how you die in obscurity with that many children and mistresses, but anyway, the fact that Milton was blind, kitten, the card Anat sent me, the fact that it's a photo of a kitten sleeping on top of a pile of encyclopedia books, but the kitten actually looks kind of *dead*, or at least anesthetized, the fact that how else could they have gotten it to fall asleep like that, lying on its back on top of the books, rest in peace, RIP, the fact that Pluto sure looks peaceful compared to us, the fact that, come to think of it, one of those five-mile-deep chasms would make a fine home for some

Open Carry guys, and they can take their AK-47s with them, the fact that, dear me, that's not a very nice thing to say, even to myself, the fact that I sound like one of those clickbait clickers who don't care how many people they hurt, the fact that you have to try to see the good in everybody, you do, and I do, I mean I do *try*, I think, most of the time, the fact that you have to live and let live, the fact that everybody's so *aggressive* now, me too, #MeToo, the things we all come up with, the fact that Uranus is very blue, from all the hydrogen or the diamonds, the fact that it's sort of like the color of Tiny Tim's turquoise traveling case, Coldy, Hallowe'en candy, *Island of the Blue Dolphins*, the fact that I think Ohio looks sort of like a rose or daisy petal hanging off Lake Erie, the fact that many tribes were living here when the European settlers invaded, the Wyandots, the Lenape, the Shawnees, the Iroquois and Ottawas, and there are still a lot of Indian place names, like Tuscarawas, the fact that Newcomerstown used to be called Gekelemukpechunk, and Coshocton was Goschachgunk, but a lot of Indian names are gone now, the fact that Ohio settlers had other ideas, like Proctorville, Doctorsville, Painsville, Painesville-on-the-Lake, Pennsville, Pencilville, Pleasantville, Portersville, so why not *Pottersville*, and Perrysville, Perilousville, Perishville, Blainesville, Batesville, Byesville, Crysville, Diesville, Beallsville, Bellville, Bellevueville, Beamsville, Off-the-Beamsville, Barnesville, Braceville, Brecksville, Breakville, Brookville, Crookville, Bridgeville, Bettsville, Heavens-to-Betsyville, and Bangville, Banksville, Botherville, Bourneville, Bursville, Buckeyeville, Burysville, Blowville, Don't-Blow-Itville, Hellosville, Byebyesville, Wo-He-Loville, Camp-ville, Greenville, the fact that Annie Oakley came from Greenville, Ohio, the fact that Toni Morrison came from Lorain, the fact that then there's Queensville, Kingsville, Princeville, Sultanville, Pasha-ville, Dachaville, Kettlersville, Potsville, North Kingsville, Footville, Fayetteville, Vaughnsville, Gillespieville, Gunnerville, Gunher-downville, Gurneyville, Garrettsville, Gibsonville, Chesterville, Chandlersville, Cobblerville, Clobberville, Bulimiaville, Sherrodsville, Jeffersonville, Georgesville, Jacksonville, Jeromesville, Columbusville,

Washington-ville, Blueville, Redville, Yellowville, Purpleville, Ochreville, Oakleyville, Marshallville, McConnelsville, McCuneville, Mechanicsville, Hartville, Heartbreak-Hotelville, Hallsville, Hayesville, Holmesville, Homelessville, Stop-&-Shopville, Open-Carryville, Donutsville, Dunkin-Donutsville, Mohicanville, Mudsock, Knockemstiff, Knockemdead, Funk, Funk Bottoms, Fatburg and Businessburg, the fact that maybe men think if they just *name* every-thing, everything'll be okay, the fact that it's like dogs marking their territory, the fact that I really don't know why they didn't name Canton McKinleyville while they were at it, the fact that some people are still all bent out of shape about Mount McKinley being renamed Denali, but McKinley's already got a gazillion other things named after him, and not just in Canton, the McKinley Cement Plant, McKinley Pet Store, McKinley Gas Station, the William McKinley Mental Health Society, the fact that I better watch out or I'll be deported for disrespecting Ohio, the fact that at least the name Zoar sounds kind of a little bit *original*, though it's not as good as Funk, the fact that people are always stealing Funk's town signs to hang on their bedroom walls, the fact that some teens in Pennsylvania stole a big sculpture of a pig by André Harvey, but the police got it back, Transylvania, the fact that André Harvey himself suspected it was just a kids' prank, the fact that he does very realistic sculptures of animals in bronze, the fact that I don't go for bronze statues too much, like Käthe Kollwitz's "Tower of the Mothers," *yeow*, broken plastic giraffe, my ankle, what next, ouch, neon-blue yo-yo, Wo-He-Lo, Djibouti, aardvark, elephant, koala bear pencil ornament, Sarah Palin, the fact that McKinley never even went to Alaska his whole entire life, so why name that mountain after him, the fact that he might have *wanted* to go to Alaska but he never did, never set foot in the place, not once, the fact that he probably wouldn't even have wanted a sword-shaped mausoleum named after him either, and the motel and everything else, though who doesn't want something named after them, at least a park bench, or a drink, or a dance craze, or a rose, the "Mrs. Miniver" rose, the fact that how is there room for everybody who passes on to get their own park bench named for them though, when there are hardly even any parks anymore, well, maybe there's room in the state parks still, the fact that I hate to see a dried-up one, a dried up *fountain* I mean, Denali, denial, Holocaust deniers, the fact that it was probably *95°*, at *least*, but that's not McKinley's fault of course, weeping willows, McKinley assassination, Abe Lincoln, Kennedy, Martin Luther King, Jr, the fact that fountains are always going on the blink, the fact that McKinley sounds a good guy, fog, Funk, fig, the fact that there's not much to see in Funk, junk, trunk, Tuscaloosa, the fact that there's the Funk Bottoms Wildlife Area, where canoeists get stuck, mosquitoes, portage, the fact that Funk is on Muddy Fork, a winding stream of the Mohican River, and it's just barely navigable by canoe because of all the mud flats and mush and muck and mukluks and bunk and funk, the numbness of muted beings, the fact that we thought of going there once but didn't in the end, the fact that Stacy said if Trump wants to call Denali "Mount McKinley" again, Canton should rename itself "Denali," fair's fair, the fact that a tourist bus in Switzerland almost went over a cliff but one of the passengers near the front saw that the driver had conked out and put his foot on the brake pedal just in time, the fact that one whole corner of the bus was left hanging over the cliff edge, bus accident, Lake Shore Drive, Lyn's broken femur, the fact that I dreamt we were in a Swiss town and a whole bunch of people were heading off on foot to go hunt antelope, the fact that a herd had been spotted just outside town, just like in *The Long Winter* when one guy gets too excited and shoots before they're close enough and the whole herd disappears, along with Almanzo's best horse, "Ali Baba and the Forty Thieves," Al-Manzoor, the fact that forty thieves would be a pretty daunting prospect, the fact that you wouldn't want to meet forty thieves down a dark alley, tag along, Tagalog, the fact that Osama bin Laden's fifty followers *dreamt* about planes hitting buildings just before 9/11 happened, even though they hadn't been let in on the plan, the fact that the CIA knew about two of the pilots for a year and a half, but kept it from the FBI out of spite, CYA, the fact that the FBI and CIA are always squabbling ♫ *Goin' courtin', goin' courtin'* ♫, and I don't see how that helps the American people, the tax papers, *taxpayers* I mean, who pay their salaries, "Bicker, bicker, bicker," concertina wire, the fact that I also dreamt I saw this guy selling bread in varying stages of decomposition, really old bread, the fact that he'd arranged it all in a pyramid, with the worst loaves at the bottom, swarming with worms, and the less rotten bread at the top, with only a few little bugs on it, the fact that only the bread-seller himself seemed willing to eat this bread, since everybody could see all the bugs and worms, Ethan's pyramid of pennies, shut-eye, dead kitten on an encyclopedia, the fact that then I dreamt our cats could make doubles of themselves, but only when they were feeling particularly happy, and there was a man lying naked in a full bathtub in the middle of a *restaurant*, and I wondered how he managed to order more drinks from there, the fact that Leo and I were being urged to do the bathtub dining thing too, but we were resistant, the fact that all that urging just made me feel *old*, the fact that we are old, the fact that we're too old to enjoy our birthdays, the fact that Leo gets all het up about his now, and he's not even fifty yet, McKinley, Buchinger,

.   .   .   .

To her kittens, she was a great beauty. They admired her white muzzle and the long lovely white belly where milk was stored. The undulating landscape of those apricot flanks and lemon-yellow ridges became their first mountain range, with wide ledges, steep slippery slopes, and darker crannies below providing places to hide and leap out at each other unexpectedly. They climbed all over her, benefiting at the same time from her warmth, her heartbeat, and vigilance.

When she wasn't there, they slept side by side, entwined, purring to each other as a signal of camaraderie. Rejoining them in the den, their mother slept much more than she realized. So much dreaming going on! Paws flickered, whiskers twitched, and eyes beneath closed lids darted up, down and sideways, in response to invented excitements, conflicts, terrors, pleasures.

The mother's dreams were concrete and practical: quests; sudden face-to-face confrontations with varied species of prey; the vertiginous view from a tree; fateful falls; her pretty path; her own mother, lost and loved; the flex of a deer's white tail; flashes of white water curling around rocks in a river, or fast flowing between deep, bent ferns; to step with care, by starlight, through a rugged, gray creek that lies muddy and still.

The kittens' dreams ranged more freely. Details were blurry, since they had experienced nothing yet except small spats over teats, frustrating coordination problems, puzzlement about the unknown, their first tastes of meat, sightings of snow and melting ice, and the now nearly vanished memories of their strenuous three-mile trek. Their dreams were fanciful: the possibility that twigs can furiously swat or eat you; that trees might sink straight into the ground when you tried to climb them; that pebbles could leap and be chased for miles.

They dreamt up outlandish animals to kill; rode on their fast-moving mother's back like merganser chicks (little knowing her animosity towards mergansers); slipped perilously close to her huge front paws, big enough to flatten you in an instant. One kitten, dreaming she could fly, kicked so hard with her back legs that the kitten beneath her dreamt of burrowing deep into snow.

What kittens fear most is falling, drowning, being too small, getting crushed or buried alive – for kittenhood is about enclosure and escape. They bravely blunder forth in birth, then press on through one lucky turn after another, until life or death overtakes them. They dream of preparation and release: the release in them of untold power.

To leap and recoil, recoil and leap.

· · · ·

the fact that I dreamt I had to eat some dog do and when I woke up I could still *taste* it, the fact that I think I have a *phobia* about dog do, do-do, caca, the fact that all my kids have phobias and Leo has one about wasps, that darn fly, why don't you get outta here, the fact that you're supposed to tell flies to leave and then they will, sometimes, so *go*, wouldja, the fact that I'm not sure how politely you're supposed to tell them, doggie diapers, the fact that they've got diapers for everybody now, Peolia College, powder puff football game, the fact that I woke up this morning with a whole clump of hair sticking straight out at a right angle from my forehead, proving unicorns do exist, the fact that there are many Norwegian miniature bundt cake pans I crave, for making fancy cupcakes, because they're so beautiful, like the rose-shaped ones, or the snowflake ones, but I don't *need* them, I just *want* them, parent–teachers' meeting, the fact that for some reason none of my kids has a *gun* phobia, the fact that their phobias are all about slugs, snails, spiders, feathers, raisins, Hershey's Kisses, newspapers, balloon animals, dollar bills, and certain letters of the alphabet, for the love of Mike, the fact that Gillian doesn't like B or J, the fact that when I pointed out to her that no one in the Ingalls family has a phobia about anything, quick as a whip she said they can't stand *grasshoppers*, the fact that they do get pretty freaked out by grasshoppers, but that's natural enough, the fact that who wouldn't be thrown by seeing a long line of migrating grasshoppers march right across your *baby*, the fact that Ben's had the most, phobias, not grasshoppers, the fact that his are about everything, the fact that I can't remember if his Hershey's Kisses *ad* phobia came before his plain Hershey's Kisses phobia or after, bundt cupcakes, the fact that he had a phobia about *that* for a while too, I think, the word "bundt," the fact that in 1949 a guy called Howard Unruh threatened his mom with a wrench and then went on a rampage through the neighborhood, killing people at random mostly, and he killed so many people, the fact that he started with some neighbors he didn't like much, and a baby, and a six-year-old boy in a barber shop, and he was proud of it, killing twelve people, just like Builderbeck, the fact that he said "it looked like a pretty good score," the fact that that happened in Camden, New Jersey, the fact that *ow*, Djibouti, Djibouti, the fact that now how did that old buckeye get there, the fact that it could've *killed* me, or at least knocked me off my feet and sent me sliding headfirst right over to the stove, where the oven door could have jolted open, dumping a red-hot tarte tatin right on top of my head, "my poor nerves," nerveday, but it didn't happen, "Buck up," seeing stars, a plane pulling a banner ad along behind it beside the beach on Lake Michigan, sun cream, BEACHES IN CREAM, Sea & Ski Sunscreen, the fact that I think all these phobias of Ben's are the result of his choice of reading material, the fact that it's too factual, the fact that I think he's starving himself of *fantasy* with all these facts, the fact that he's not just weaning himself off childhood with science, he's weaning himself off *life*, the fact that his report cards are surprisingly poor, Young Builders, the fact that I think maybe his unconscious makes up for it with weird dreams and all these anxieties, the fact that, sure, a Hershey's Kiss phobia doesn't do you any real harm, as long as Gillian digs all the Kisses out of his candy bag for him at Hallowe'en, but for a while he had a horror of peas and tomatoes too, and that's not healthy, the fact that it's silly to worry though, silly putty, weeping willows, worry dolls, "bundt," the fact that children usually sort themselves out, the fact that I think maybe he thinks all his scientific knowledge will impress his dad, or get Leo's attention anyway, not realizing Leo couldn't care less about science, the fact that Leo now regrets all the time he's spent on science and wishes he'd studied something else besides engineering, the fact that he'd rather be listening to Messiaen or bird-watching, or eating pepper pot soup, or Venus de Milo soup, or a date-nut sammich, or even doing yard work, the fact that ornithology's a science too though, the fact that I sometimes wish I'd studied horticulture, the fact that Leo thinks topology's a big *joke*, the fact that I have no idea, the fact that I don't think Ben has a phobia about Messiaen yet, but I know he hates birding because you have to go outside to do it and Ben doesn't really do the outdoors if he can help it, the fact that I'm all wrong about things, because now he does want to go out and play in the tree house with Gillian, but I'm scared they'll break their necks on the icy ladder, or get speared by an icicle dropping off the roof, the fact that weekends can be a trial, keeping all these kids occupied, but even Jake seems to have sense enough to stay in today and play with Gillian's old doll's tea set and an Action Man, no, now the Action Man's getting a ride on a yellow tractor, SUV, HIV, MRSA, necrotizing fasciitis, plantar fasciitis, the fact that they fought for days over how that tree house should be built but Gillian won and, thanks to her, it has really pretty gables and curtains and a fake chimney, well, I sure hope it's fake, the fact that she had to give up on her original *log-cabin* idea because we didn't know where to buy the right kind of logs, and anyway they might've been too heavy for the tree, the fact that she wanted to make a door that hung on leather hinges like the one Pa makes in the claim shanty or somewhere, with the latch on a string that you can pull in to keep intruders out, but it never happened because nobody in this family knows how to do stuff like that, except maybe Leo, but he was busy, the fact that we'll have to wait until Ben's been at the Young Builders club a bit more, Cy Young, Young's Jersey Dairy, cow, Young's modulus, Wake Up Picture Day, donkey, ass, whip hand, the fact that Ben wants to join the 4-H club now too, more driving for me, but it's good he has some outside interests, the fact that now Stacy's teaching them all how to jump rope in the den, so they're safe for a while, *There's a place in France Where the alligators dance*, Your Recent Accident, *Up, up, turn around, Sergeant Smith, down down*, the fact that we watched *Annie Get Your Gun* yesterday, just me and the kids, the fact that Annie has to pretend she's a bad shot so Frank won't feel too bad about himself, Frank, the fact that otherwise he might feel emasculated, the fact that that's just not true though, *Time* magazine, IMO, the fact that the real Annie Oakley and Frank Butler started out as colleagues in a fairground act, and then became romantically involved, main squeeze, sweetheart, and they were *never* rivals, the fact that after they got married they carried on with the shooting act, but to get some drama into the musical, they make out that Frank resents Annie's shooting abilities and won't marry her if she keeps beating him at target-shooting, so she has to purposely lose a shooting match to win him, Rogers and Hammerstein, Irving Berlin, Howard Keel, coward heel, the fact that some of the numbers in that movie seem kind of out of place, the fact that what's "There's No Business

Like Show Business" doing there, or "Doin' What Comes Naturally," the fact that they've got nothing to do with *Annie Oakley*, the fact that it seems like Irving Berlin just had some old songs lying around and threw them all in, the fact that the "Yes I Can No You Can't" number is probably the only good song in the whole movie, ♫ *Anything you can do I can do better!* ♫, which isn't saying much, because it really isn't much of a song, and it isn't much of a movie, but who'm I to judge, the fact that I don't even like musicals, the fact that I've always tried to avoid them, the fact that it's kind of weird how many of them are about pioneer days and taking over the West, and the conflicts between cowboys and farmers, the fact that the best bit is when both admit they can't bake a *pie*, Annie and Frank I mean, not cowboys and farmers, Anne Frank, but cowboys and farmers probably couldn't bake pies either, the fact that maybe the farmers' *wives* could, the fact that I couldn't resist nudging Stacy with my elbow when they said that about pie-making, since she sees my pies as pointless, the fact that Stace's all wrong about that, the fact that pies do have a point, I'm just not sure what it is right this minute, flipside, ♫ *Tradition!* ♫, procrastination, *Fiddler on the Roof*, the fact that thousands of years ago we evolved to eat cooked stuff, and now people are trying to go back to eating *raw* food, and those are the types who won't eat pie, the fact that Stacy still eats cooked food at least, thankfully, the fact that I'm making an upside-down-leftover-vegetable pie for Stacy today, veg. tatin, zoom lens, Lassie, ritual sacrifice, self-sacrifice, self-satisfied, self-conscious, sage brush, tumbleweed, slumber parties, renegade, degenerate, oxygenate, WWTP, waste water treatment plant, *MY FIRST* TICONDEROGA, the fact that those beginner pencils seem too *big* for a little person, the fact that sfogliatelle look so fantastic, the fact that I wish I knew how to make them but I don't, the fact that they look really hard, I mean hard to make, the fact that I can't get over how pretty they are though, the fact that maybe I'll master them one day, the fact that cinnamon rolls seemed tough to make at first too, the fact that Meryl Streep suddenly makes chocolate croissants in the middle of the night with Steve Martin, pastry chef, Carmel, no, the fact that it's set in *Santa Barbara*, paternoster elevator, envelope, envelop, emptiness, loneliness, the fact that I dreamt I was the sun and Stacy was the earth, the fact that she looked almost my size, and she was getting too close to me, I thought, and I was scared she'd get singed or something, the fact that I was looking through some NASA photos of us in the dream, and it didn't look good, the fact that we were all out of proportion in relation to each other, related, elevated, hook and eye, JAKE, buckle, toggle, zipper, button, the fact that Leo says Fred Astaire was only good in the thirties, and any Fred Astaire movie after that is no good, Chuck, neck, flower power, pragmatic, champions, Chesapeake Bay, ♫ *Beethoven quartet* ♫, chanting, the fact that the police forcibly removed some disabled protesters inside some building in Washington, Congress, the fact that they were protesting against plans to abolish Obamacare, universal healthcare, Medicare, Medicaid, Kool-Aid, AIDS, Appalachian plateaus, the fact that Newcomerstown is on the cusp, geographically, geologically I mean, topographically, between the central lowland and the Appalachian plateaus, whitetail deer, doggy diapers, enclave, Snickers bars, Corn Flakes, Tony the Tiger, the fact that in another dream this sort of hippy guy told me to "hack the groovy," the fact that the real Annie Oakley *had* to learn to hunt and trap, to feed her family, the fact that the way they portray Indians in that movie, I mean, *really*, the fact that the Indians are all milking goats on the train, and washing their clothes and shooting arrows and cooking beans and cutting up the upholstery and trying to pitch a whole tipi village in the middle of the traincar, the fact that I don't know what Stacy made of all that, ♫ *There's nothing to be done* ♫, the fact that it really was kind of disgusting, even insulting, the fact that, I mean, how dare they suggest Native Americans weren't civilized or something, when the Clovis people were living here in 11,000 BCE, and using advanced engineering techniques too, long before Hollywood musicals were even dreamt of, the fact that the Iroquois Confederacy is the oldest democracy in the *world*, Circleville, Conesville, the fact that Frank never liked being called an Indian, or a Native American either, *my* Frank, not Frank

Butler, the fact that he wasn't interested, chicken feed, Ronny, the Queen of England, Tiny Tim, the fact that after *Annie Get Your Gun*, Stace wanted to watch some *Pride and Prejudice*, the fact that I wish she'd read the *book*, but maybe she has, I can't remember, the fact that she goes for that Colin Firth, but she only likes him in *Pride and Prejudice*, not in *The King's Speech*, because *I* like him in *The King's Speech*, the fact that Ronny looks a little like the speech therapist in that movie, Geoffrey Rush, *For I will consider my Cat Jeoffry*, the fact that I dread Ronny's visits more and more, but it's my own fault, the fact that I got myself into this, the fact that I just couldn't lug fifty-pound sacks around all by myself anymore, the fact that Leo, *dear* Leo, offered to help, but he's never here when I need to get the sacks out of the car, so now Ronny brings them and gets them on to the back porch for me, the fact that from there I can take it to the hens, a scoop at a time, the fact that Ronny doesn't even break a sweat carrying those sacks, the fact that some people get their chicken feed from China but ours comes from somewhere in Ohio, maybe Sandusky, or Gunnerville, Gunnerdownville, Gurneyville, I forget, the fact that we buy local, sometimes, Norwegian bundt cake pans, the fact that we try to buy American too, BA, air miles, the fact that Marilyn Monroe says she comes from Sandusky, in *Some Like It Hot*, Sugar Cane, Marilyn Monroe's chin, the fact that I never know what to say when Ronny turns up, especially when he's wearing that MAGA T-shirt of his, the fact that I think maybe he expects me to offer him a cup of coffee but if I did it once, I'd have to do it every time, and then I'd have to talk to him more and more and more, or listen to him rather, the fact that the guy's a big talker, the fact that in the end I'd just have to give up my whole pie-making business in order to listen to Ronny all day, or else I'd have to cancel the feed order and find some other way of getting it delivered, the fact that I really don't want to do that, so I think it's best if we keep the relationship as formal as possible, the fact that I give him a five-buck tip every time but he probably still thinks I'm a cold fish, stuck-up New Englander, or maybe an "idiot," the fact that Ronny calls just about *everybody* an idiot, brownies, cinnamon roll spirals, circles made by a drip falling on a puddle, just like his buddy Trump, the fact that everybody's an idiot except himself, *ne plus ultra*, *noli me tangere*, *e pluribus unum*, *pro bono*, boner, oh dear, the fact that I don't get why I'm supposed to drop everything to talk to a guy who thinks everybody's an idiot, the fact that, well, for heaven's sake, somehow I just don't really want to do that, the fact that Leo and I met at the Florence Griswold museum, very soon after Mommy's passing, the fact that I seem to fall in love during family crises, first Chuck, then Leo, the fact that Frank doesn't count, the fact that I tried to love him but we were just playing house really, and not with much enthusiasm either, the fact that there were hummingbirds, and poppies, and mountain laurel, in Old Lyme, not in Frank's apartment, hummingbirds, Hummingbird quilt, the fact that Leo never met Mommy, and that has always felt wrong to me, that they never met, the fact that Daddy would have liked Leo too, the fact that he would have called him "dynamic," high praise coming from Daddy, the fact that Leo's more dynamic than Colin Firth will ever be, the fact that he's kind of a cross between Stanley Tucci and Walter Matthau, Julia Child, *Bigger Than Life*, the fact that I still have a crush on Leo and it looks like lasting me for life, the fact that I like the way he *talks*, the fact that Colin Firth seems a nice man and everything, but not especially dynamic, the fact that I think Stacy's all wrong about him, the fact that women always hope there's *more* to silent types but there often isn't, Darcy, Frank, the fact that Florence Griswold's house was a boardinghouse for a while, boardinghouse reach, aspartame, Sweet'N Low, Splenda, Truvia, Equal, the fact that Mommy objected to me using artificial sweetener once, and I was so offended, the fact that now I think maybe she just meant I was getting too thin, but I don't know, the fact that it's way too late now to ask, Sweet'N Low, Wet'suet'en, the fact that Leo was married to someone before me, an iguana, the fact that she *had* an iguana, she wasn't an iguana herself, the fact that there were beautiful long bands of gray-pink cloud the day Frank and I broke up, the fact that I now remember those clouds better than I remember *Frank*, the fact that we went to

Tangier Island once, just for a weekend, just Leo and me, Saltwater
Geechees, taking a shower together, the fact that the house had that
big porch, the fact that I stared at Leo's bare chest, shaded by the
awning, the fact that striped light came in through the thick wooden
Venetian blinds every morning, red at first, then brighter and brighter,
falling across the bed, breaking the glass, broken, the fact that Tangier
Island is now threatened by rising sea levels, the fact that the Great
Barrier Reef is being cooked alive, the fact that it's eighty percent
bleached, El Niño, symbiosis, algae, coral animal, bellwether, the fact
that Ohio used to be a bellwether state but now it's not, I don't think,
so politicians don't come visit as much as they used to, sheep, Trump
steaks, Wally, Walter Matthau, the fact that in the end it's Walter
Matthau who saves the little boy in *Bigger Than Life*, not the mom,
the fact that she can't even slip the kid a glass of milk without James
Mason flying into a rage, the fact that Trump flies into rages too, but
many presidents do, Eisenhower, the fact that you'd think being voted
president would put you in a pretty good mood but no, the fact that I
guess these grumpy presidents just stick with their original behavior
pattern, the fact that men get so *angry* at times, school shootings, the
fact that Daddy blew his top sometimes, the fact that he was never
violent though, never in James Mason's league, the fact that Frank was
always getting mad, the fact that he was kind of volatile, the fact that
Leo isn't at all, the fact that at the worst, if he's *tired*, Leo can get sort
of glum, but he's always fair-minded, and pretty even-tempered, the
fact that I wish *he* was president, presidential, a judicial temperament,
"Roger, pay the two dollars," the fact that Daddy's temper frightened
me, ogre, Mommy, the fact that at the start of the movie, James Mason
and the water heater are both on the verge of collapse, the fact that
water heaters in movies are probably always a bad sign, the fact that
he's a teacher, so of course he's exhausted, the fact that I know the
feeling, the fact that he's actually a kind of mild-mannered guy, but
he's working two jobs, just to make ends meet, the fact that he's moon-
lighting as a dispatcher for the taxi company, the fact that he wears a
ratty old green cardigan when he's manning the phone in the taxi

office, just so you know how lousy his life is, and then he forgets the olives and his wife gets mad, and meanwhile he's having all these headaches and stomach aches, the fact that the son watches noisy cowboy shows, and on the walls of their home are all these posters of foreign places they never get to go to, the fact that even his old football's kind of deflated, sitting on the mantelpiece, the fact that Leo says James Mason always liked playing guys in pain, so this was the perfect movie for him, like when he holds his aching head or his belly, or grips the doorframe so hard he presses his own doorbell by accident and can't stop until the spasm's over, and the doorbell keeps ringing and ringing, the fact that he hurts his hand in *North by Northwest*, from punching Martin Landau, R-O-T, bolster pillow, holster, trigger, blanks, cartridge, Boris Karloff, the fact that once he gets to the hospital for tests, the doctors realize he's going to *die*, pass away, if he doesn't take cortisone *for the rest of his life*, the fact that cortisone won't cure it but it'll keep his symptoms in check, "Check!", so they send him home with a bottle of pills, which is kind of dumb, the fact that when he gets home from the hospital he's already sort of demanding, the fact that because the water heater's still on the blink, he gets his wife to fill the bathtub for him with hot water from the stove, and she gets so sick of his attitude and having to lug hot water upstairs, she slams the medicine cabinet shut and breaks the mirror, "It makes me look the way I feel," the fact that then he starts taking too much cortisone and gets all bigheaded, and suddenly he can't take domesticity anymore and decides their marriage is over, "In my mind I've already divorced you," just like Peter Strand, the fact that James Mason keeps packing his bag to leave, just like Peter, the fact that Pru never knows if Peter's coming or going, the fact that the suitcase just appears in the hall, then disappears again and she realizes the fever's past for now, the time being, the fact that cortisone makes you braver, but also angrier about stuff, the fact that most men surely don't need help getting *angry*, the fact that it seems to me they're already pretty good at it, if you listen to the news, I mean, the fact that somebody said the trouble with men is they're very *emotional*, much more emotional than women, which was a surprise, because people are always saying how emotional women are, canned corn, Beelzebub, the fact that James Mason starts to think he can change the world, but first he wants to tackle his *son*, teach him how to play ball and do math, the fact that he takes things out on his wife a bit too, Cary Grant trying to shave with the tiny razor in *North by Northwest*, Cary Grant trying to shave in *Mr. Blandings*, with the steamed-up mirror, the fact that men get so steamed about things, the fact that Cary Grant gets crabby about having to share a bathroom with *Myrna Loy*, His and Hers sinks, the fact that because of that they build a whole new house full of bathrooms, the fact that you'd *think* most men would gladly share a steamy bathroom with Myrna Loy, even if she does open the medicine cabinet when he's right in the middle of shaving, bridging the gap, bridge party, *Mrs Bridge*, drawbridge, vertical lift bridge, bascule bridge, fixed trunnion, single- or double-leafed, cantilever bridge, the fact that Walter Matthau's a gym teacher and eats enormous steaks all the time, just like Trump, the fact that the little boy seems so vulnerable, way, way upstairs in his bedroom, like how babies must feel, left alone for hours on end with nothing but an intercom for company, the fact that, okay, the parents know the monitor's on and the baby's okay, the fact that even the grandparents far away know the baby's okay, by watching their remote baby-cam via the internet, digital, web links, but the *baby* doesn't know he's okay, the fact that all babies know is they've been left all alone and babies don't like that, symbiosis, osmosis, the fact that babies like to be *part* of things, even if they don't have an awful lot to contribute, the fact that they're curious and entertained by everything, and most of them just like looking around, the fact that some babies have very good eyesight, the fact that how can a baby feel safe, left all alone like that, the fact that you're not supposed to keep the poor things in *solitary confinement* until they can walk and talk, Walkie-Talkie Robot, *There's Always Tomorrow*, Fred MacMurray, the fact that I bet grandparents with a baby cam argue nonstop with the parents about baby care, by phone or Skype, or Facebook, the fact that there's probably a sitcom about that by now, *Friends*, Edward, the fact that I can't imagine Mommy and Daddy using Facebook, the fact that it's time to melt the butter, sour cherries soaking, cinnamon, *The Lady Eve*, the fact that I'm always running out of ground cardamom, Barbara Stanwyck, Skype, the fact that all we do now is look at actors on screens, the fact that people have surely never spent so much time watching strangers do things, people we have nothing to do with and no influence over, the fact that they don't listen to *us*, the fact that we mean nothing to them, zilch, the fact that it really is one heck of a one-sided relationship, Colin Firth, Morning Routine videos, the fact that it's hard to remember you have a life of your *own* sometimes, away from all of these people on TV, the fact that you get to feeling all chummy with newscasters, looking at you from behind their big clean desks, the fact that they all look so uncomfortable *without* their desks it's better if they have one, the fact that it's really sort of embarrassing for everybody when you suddenly see their whole body, like if they're doing some special interview in an armchair or something, the fact that actors have the decency to talk amongst themselves, as if you aren't there, but newscasters tire me out pretending they're talking to us direct, the fact that if you met them in an elevator, they'd probably just trample all over you, the Marianas Trench, Amish horses, the fact that they all put on this big friendly act, the newscasters I mean, not Amish horses, and look you right in the eye, first thing in the morning, male and female newscasters like your new Mommy and Daddy, the fact that they must know we're all still in our PJs, but they don't mind, the fact that the nation is actually full of people like Ronny yelling at their plasma screens and not getting an answer, the fact that TV pundits are always offering advice you never even asked for, the kind of advice you'd only need if you'd been in *prison* for thirty years, like what shoes to wear, mules trimmed with fur or feathers, or how to cook an omelet, the fact that the Indians cured colds with chokecherry juice, facts and figures, polls, statistics, the latest school shooting, Russian collusion, Oprah, Matt Damon, Tom Ripley, the fact that I sometimes catch myself thinking Jason Bourne should just go back to Italy and be Tom Ripley instead, just be rich and take things easy, instead of getting into all these dangerous scrapes, Treadstone, car chases, hitmen, the fact that my Ripley solution doesn't make a whole lot of sense though, since Jason Bourne would have to be a time-traveler as well, to get back to Rome and be Tom Ripley after he's killed Jude Law and bought himself a bust and a piano and all, the fact that Tom Ripley being in the CIA would kind of make sense, the fact that a job like that would suit him well because he's sneaky, the fact that there was an FBI guy, John O'Neill, who was on to Osama bin Laden, but he had a very complicated private life, with a girlfriend in every city, a girlfriend or *two*, a wife in every port, the fact that I guess you never know what undercover agents get up to under the covers, the fact that instead of listening to what he had to say about Osama bin Laden, they kicked him out of the FBI and he got a new job as head of security at the World Trade Center, and ended up dying in 9/11, which is kind of ironic because if the FBI had just *listened* to him it might not have happened, *Funtastic Voyage*, the fact that I really think that on some level I believe *The Odd Couple*'s a sequel to *The Apartment*, though it would be a shame if Jack Lemmon and Shirley MacLaine had to break up, after twelve years of marriage, leaving Buddy Boy to go bunk with Walter Matthau, the Dahlberg repercussions, ouch, the little china tea cup from the dolls house, Djibouti, the fact that the *cup's* okay but I'm crippled for *life*, sheesh, Jesus saved me, San Andreas fault, Death Valley, Las Vegas casinos, the fact that I've always gotten *Rebecca of Sunnybrook Farm* mixed up with *Anne of Green Gables*, though I've never even read *Rebecca of Sunnybrook Farm*, "I do declare," Sunnybrook, Atticus Finch, deductibles and co-pays, the fact that Morning Routine girls never forget to brush their hair, the fact that they never read a book, though they all have *The Great Gatsby* or *Girl, Interrupted* on their bedside table, the girl in *Island of the Blue Dolphins* making herself necklaces, even though nobody will ever see her, the fact that I learnt nothing about life when I was a teenager except that I can't do things, and that I'm a disappointment, to myself and others, the fact that high school was like a four-year training camp in how to be disappointed in myself, kneading, stuffed shells, sfogliatelle, the fact that my whole life is a series of mistakes, large and small, the fact that how I wish I could save Stacy from some of this, the fact that anyway, she certainly doesn't need to worry about her *appearance*, though being good-looking means you have to try to *stay* good-looking and that's stressful, My Little Pony, fidget cube, the fact that now she's so interested in self-defense, she reads that old book of mine all the time, the fact that she *studies* it, the fact that she used to read it just to laugh at the seventies clothes and hairdos, because the men have long locks and beards and the women all have mop tops, Top Cat, popgun, but now she seems genuinely curious about all the horrifying scenarios, Adam's apple, the fact that that book can really give you the heebie-jeebies, the fact that it makes you think bad men are lurking in every bush, behind every door, with long hair, just waiting to molest you, Sean Spicer hiding in the bushes, rhododendrons, the fact that I need to buy apples, cinnamon, Thursday, the fact that I suppose there wouldn't be much point in a self-defense book that never mentions any actual occasions when you might need to defend yourself, the fact that I guess there's no point in pussy-footing around in a book like that, ♫ *Tiptoe through the tulips* ♫, the fact that it doesn't go into how *likely* these attacks are, but that's not its job, the fact that you really start to think it's *very* likely, just because they keep *talking* about it, the fact that if you're out all alone and you slip and land on your back, and *a man with long hair* appears out of nowhere and *jumps on top of you*, the fact that the book says don't panic, because not that much can happen as long as the long-haired assaulter guy's using both his hands to hold you down, the fact that for some reason I don't find that image too comforting, the fact that, for crying out loud, I don't want some strange man using both his hands to hold my daughter down, the fact that the thought of Stacy tripping over somewhere and immediately being leapt on, the fact that there was some woman in the news who reported a stalker to the police a hundred and twenty-five separate times but they didn't do anything and eventually the guy stabbed her, the fact that another woman was just driving by though and saw what was going on, and *saved* her, the fact that I hope I'd be brave enough to jump out of my car like that but I don't know, the fact that the police must be pretty embarrassed about that, the fact that they treated her like a Badge Betty, like she was just turning up at the police station to see *them*, the fact that how many women do that, the fact that if there's a mass shooting in America *every day*, there must be three hundred and sixty-five a year, the fact that if the man releases one of your arms, you're supposed to use the technique illustrated on page 38, the fact that the book's organized like a cookbook, "for shortcrust pastry, see recipe on p. 201," recipe for disaster, the fact that you go to page 38 and it tells you to hit him fast, on the *nose*, the fact that he's probably stronger, taller and heavier than you, so you can't wrestle with him, the fact that all you can do is start attacking his "vulnerable areas" like his nose, his mouth, the eyes, Adam's apple, and genitals, "whacking," the fact that Stace laughs and laughs about the photos of people in flared jeans grappling with each other, but underneath I think she's scared to death and that's why she reads it over and over again, hoping she'll get less scared with familiarity, the fact that she reads it out loud to us, the fact that familiarity isn't helping *me*, the fact that I *stay* scared, the fact that I'm sure it gives me nightmares, the fact that if you're attacked by *two* men, your natural reaction is to try to tackle the guy in front, but that way the girl *will always lose*, the fact that a girl always loses in a contest of strength between one girl and two men, one girl and two men, only child, the fact that I don't like the sound of that at all, Christopher Columbus, crematory columbariums, McKinley's mausoleum, the fact that I'm sort of hyperventilating just *thinking* about any of this stuff happening to Stace, the fact that the correct procedure, for a girl who's been *grabbed by two guys*, one in front, one behind, is you tackle the guy *behind* first, but for the life of me I can't remember *how* you tackle him, the fact that maybe *I* should be studying this book too, so I can help Stacy master all the moves and strategies, the fact that maybe we could do self-defense training together, a new mom-and-daughter bonding tool, the fact that for all I know, moms and daughters are bonding all over

America by learning the right way to shove keys up a man's nose, or knock him off his feet by pinching his inner thighs, the fact that they used to just knit together, moms and daughters I mean, not *thighs*, the fact that if you're attacked by a *woman*, on the other hand, "tigress-style," you're supposed to box her ears, claw at her collar bone, jab the tips of your fingers into the sides of her neck, punch her in the ribs, and flap your fingers at her eyes, oh dear me, bird costume, running around the hut flapping our arms, the fact that the book warns women against carrying a gun, because the chances are your assailant will snatch it from you and use it against you, the fact that they don't recommend carrying any weapons at all, the fact that I'm not sure if they talk about pepper spray, or mace or something, the fact that I think you can use *hairspray* if you have to, maybe *any* spray, perfume, deodorant, bug spray, Dr. Bronner hand sanitizer, mouth freshener, whatever's handy, the fact that maybe they didn't *have* pepper spray in 1970 when the book came out, the fact that pepper spray's illegal in a lot of countries, but it's okay in the US, OC, the fact that maybe Stacy should carry some in her backpack, and maybe one of those personal alarms, the fact that never mind basketball and school-shooter drills, for Pete's sake, the fact that they should be teaching everybody *self-defense* at school, the fact that that's one useful thing they could do in gym class, stalkers, hackers, hoaxers, mace, the fact that all the kids in Cleveland were sent home from school the other day because of another hoax email threat, the fact that all the schools in town shut, the fact that the hoaxer must have been thrilled with his power, like Chris Christie making all the school buses sit on the bridge, criss-cross, the fact that Leo thought that was just *criminal*, the fact that however good a bridge is you don't linger on it, and you certainly don't load it down with buses full of kids, the fact that you're just tempting fate, Jesus of New Philadelphia, the fact that Stace used to practice her self-defense moves on Ben, but he got sick of being poked and pinched, *Walden Pond*, Warren, Connecticut, the fact that I really don't want to hear about those young men who went to Thailand to abuse babies and toddlers, chiffon, satin, sateen, wild silk, the fact that Buddhists like *wild* silk because no silk worms have to die to make it, cruelty-free, additive-free, aspirin-free, caffeine-free, land of the free, Splenda, the fact that wild silk lacks luster but no worms die, because they just take the empty *cocoons* after the moths have abandoned them, and spin the broken fibers together into a rough kind of silk, choke hold, knee him in the groin, trip him with your foot, the fact that Leo wasn't sure about my velvet hat at first but now he says he likes it, the fact that the way they make velvet sort of blows your mind, the fact that it involves weaving two layers, then slicing them apart, the fact that velvet's created by warp, and velveteen by weft, and velour's something else again, the fact that velveteen's usually made with cotton, but other velvets use rayon, linen, raffia, silk, the fact that there's crushed velvet, hammered velvet, voided velvet, pile-on-pile velvet, stamped velvet, embossed velvet, "What do we need so much velvet?", ciselé, nacré, devoré, bouclé, lyons, Leo, the fact that lyons has a stiffer pile and is often used on hats, the fact that maybe my hat's made of that, woad, sprang, dying corals, diamonds, clouds, the fact that a Filipino maid was raped in Saudi Arabia and got pregnant, so then they arrested her for having *unmarried sex*, the fact that the police Taser pregnant women in America, which can lead to miscarriages and some of the babies are born prematurely and some have *fits*, what in the world, the fact that they started using all these Tasers on people before they knew what the effects would be, the fact that sometimes they do intimate *drug searches* by the side of the road, in public, the fact that sometimes they punch black girls, the fact that the police *punch girls* in order to restrain them, the fact that that doesn't seem very gentlemanly, self-defense techniques, the fact that soldiers are always hitting women too, the fact that they must get *taught* that, "Today's training exercise if about how to beat up a female protestor," the fact that a woman whose daughter was killed thought the daughter's husband probably had something to do with it, because he'd killed his *previous* wife the same way, but the police wouldn't *listen* to her, the fact that she had to have a *heart attack* before they listened to her, Tutankhamun, the fact that it took ten years, the fact that now he's in jail, I guess, but it sure took a while, pinkwashing, upskirting, chickens, Vikings, Visigoths, Riddle of the Ages Solved, fly agaric mushrooms, the fact that comets have rocks sitting on them and they have *snow storms*, the fact that you don't think of stuff like that going on on a comet, the fact that they seem too busy racing through space, the fact that I guess *we're* racing through space too, the fact that Pluto has an atmosphere, and shifting seas, so does that mean it gets *cloudy*, planetoid mass, cinnamon rolls, the fact that I don't want to be dug up like an Egyptian mummy after I'm dead, and displayed in a museum, the fact that everything was done so much better in the past, I mean not mummies but clothes and stuff, and there weren't all these gun rampages and dirty bombs, the fact that once in a while, some dad would walk to the schoolhouse and shoot the teacher dead for boxing his kid's ears the day before, bento box, but nobody was turning up with machine guns, hara-kiri, kamikaze, seppuku, the fact that maybe the *only* good thing about living now is we get to look at close-ups of Pluto and Mars and comets and the moon, from the front and the back, and Jupiter and Saturn, and see all those pictures of multicolored nebulae and whatnot, and micrographs of tardigrade eggs, but I don't know if it makes up for all the beheadings and men jumping out of the bushes on top of your daughter whenever she just happens to step outside, the fact that I often forget about tardigrades, water bears, moss piglets, boarlets, the fact that tardigrades continue to exist though, even if I forget about them sometimes, the fact that they even have a love life, which is very hard to believe, though why can't they, the fact that tardigrades are entitled to a love life just like me, the fact that I wonder how a *tardigrade* defends itself against men with long hair and seventies beards, Lone Ranger, stranger danger, hydrangea, the fact that my libido returned, but now it's deserted me again, shortcrust pastry, the fact that it's amazing I can think about anything at all, given the *noise* these kids make, the fact that sometimes I wonder how a bee can stand its own buzz, the fact that it would drive me crazee, the fact that it drives me nuts if there's just one little bee or fly in the house, and that's from a distance, the fact that it must be worse if you *are* that bee, the fact that I don't know how bees can stand *our* noise either, all our construction projects and cars and planes and road rage and all the yelling and screaming and raping and the punch-ups, and all our crying and laughing and whatnot, and trumpets and whistles, not to mention the hullaballoo our chickens make every morning, the fact that just the noise from one of those battery hen factories, along with the smell, the fact that it must be hard for a bee to pass a thing like that, but some bees must have to fly past there now and then, unless the stink keeps them far away, the fact that battery hen factories pour manure and liquid fertilizer straight into the creek, dead fish, the fact that even the sound of the toilet flushing seems deafening to me sometimes, the fact that every sound gets magnified in this flimsy house, the fact that most of the houses around here are just overheated boxes made out of glue and plywood, with a few pretend colonial columns out in front, pretentious, the fact that I think we should paint our house white sometime, the fact that I think the dark wood is kind of uninviting, but when will we ever have the money to get the house painted, the fact that it's amazing we can make it through the winters in these houses at all, Chinese ice festival, ice sculptures, Chinese workers crawling on the road because they didn't meet their production deadline, the fact that the flimsiness of our homes should make us feel more in touch with *nature*, but nobody feels in touch with nature, the fact that the Japanese are supposedly in touch with nature, in their paper houses, Frank Lloyd Wright, the fact that our *chickens* are in touch with nature, but we aren't, the fact that Ben says he envies animals for their "picnic lifestyle," the fact that at first I thought he said "piquant," piquillos, paprika, chorizo, patatas riojanas, Birrieria Zaragoza, the fact that I reminded him that he's never even been that keen on picnics, sweet and salty popcorn, peanut butter on celery sticks, the fact that he hates most insects and doesn't like dirt much either, unlike Gillian, the fact that I think his phobia about bees is over though, the fact that if not, it's going to hamper his enjoyment of most picnics, the fact that Gillian really wants to do the Indian Mud Run this summer, the fact that I don't like the name "Indian Mud Run," the fact that it sounds a little disrespectful to me, but what do I know, the fact that maybe it's just that I'd rather not have to watch a bunch of beer-bellied Open Carry guys lumber through an obstacle course, the fact that they should have to carry bows and arrows at least, for the day, instead of their guns, with arrows they made themselves, the fact that they should have to set up a wigwam and carve a totem pole, tipi, but I suppose that wouldn't be a mud run, the fact that I'm not too happy about Gillian climbing around and splashing across muddy leech-filled streams and getting her shins all cut up by thorns, the fact that I think it's for older kids really, falling off my bike, Coke, blisters, pancakes, glass in my foot, Ackerman Park, Yosemite, the fact that it just occurred to me that maybe *our kids* will become Open Carry dudes and dudettes someday, the fact that that could happen, the fact that they're Ohioans after all, the fact that you never know how your kids'll turn out, the fact that people take a *big risk* having kids, the fact that the parents of psychopaths are always really surprised, no matter what the rotten kid's gotten up to all his life, like no matter how many pets he eviscerated, or how many years he's spent holed up in his blackened bedroom with a stockpile of guns, looking at Columbine sites, sights, and flying into a rage all the time about girls or Big Government, computer, shooter, Krispy Kreme, Dunkin' Donuts, Isadora Duncan, "Are you evil?", incel, the fact that most parents just never expect their kids to do anything really bad, the fact that they expect the kid to be more or less what they *want* him to be, which is kind of a crazee idea, jiggery-pokery, jiggery, jaggery, jagged, jerk chicken, the fact that once the kid's finally flipped and gone on a rampage and shot two dozen people in the back, and maybe himself as well, the parents say they had no idea he was capable of harming anyone, computer, shooter, the fact that I guess they go into a state of denial, defensive posture, keys, Adam's apple, finger-flapping, flared jeans, the fact that whenever I see kids who don't say Please and Thank You, I wonder if they'll wind up being mass murderers, the fact that it's a terrible habit of mine, the fact that parents who are too scared to tell their kids to do what's right just should not be parents, the fact that actually *I'm* scared of telling my kids what to do, the fact that I'm terrible at discipline, the fact that I never even get them to write thank-you letters, the fact that I shouldn't have ever been a parent either, and don't I know it, crustaceans, cetacean, citation, train station, the fact that if you were an animal you'd just bat the kid around a little, give them a growl, and they'd soon learn to do what they're told, the fact that there's no monkeying around in the animal world, the fact that Ben used to head-butt men all the time when he was little, but Jake's never done that, the fact that if it was up to them, Jake and Ben would probably just sit around most of the time, peaceably playing with their Gameboys, the fact that thankfully they don't seem to want to *eviscerate* or *obliterate* anything, as far as I know, the fact that they're not really very rambunctious boys, the fact that if girls hit them at school they know not to hit back, the fact that it's Gillian who's always egging them on to race around in the mud, the fact that our biggest effort to be outdoorsy was that time we went out and tried to sap our maples, like Ohio pioneers, the fact that Zadok Cramer recommended it highly, the fact that where *is* that book, the fact that I'm not cut out to be a sugar farmer, I don't think, because I felt sorry for the *trees*, the fact that sapping them felt kind of like trying to eat them alive, the fact that it made me feel a little queasy, though maybe I should try it again, because it might save on sugar, grappling with a sapling, sapping maple trees, buttercups, snapdragons, Mommy, mulch, mush, the fact that it broke me, the fact that I'm broken, the fact that we only got a tiny bit of syrup, which wasn't worth boiling up, the fact that I think I'll stick to poultry farming, the fact that that was so terrible, what happened at the egg factory, the fact that the worst thing that could happen to a place like that is a tornado, and they had *two*, the fact that that was back in 2000, before I moved here, or I would've tried to help, the fact that we could've taken in a few chickens, the fact that I wonder how hard it is to rehabilitate a factory chicken, the fact that the kids could feed them watermelon rinds, the fact that I get a lot of innocent pleasure from watching my kids do almost anything, even Jake clobbering a madeleine on the kitchen floor right now with my favorite wooden rolling pin, the fact that on the phone I was listing to Leo all the things I had to do today and Jake added supportively "*And you have to half-hold the piano!*", whatever that meant, the fact that the name keeps changing, but not the practices, I don't think, at the egg factory I mean, the fact that the guy who started it all had already been convicted of animal cruelty in Germany and banned from having anything to do with livestock there, so he came over *here*, and nobody stopped him owning animals, the fact that Hugh Hefner says he loves animals, and the proof is he's got a zoo full of flamingoes and monkeys and a few tortoises, no bunnies, captivity, capsicum, the fact that I've seen the pictures of all those poor chickens, after the tornadoes, millions upon millions of white chickens, crammed into three-tiered "coops" that looked like Auschwitz, the fact that they had thousands on each tier, and there were *sixty-four* of those buildings and each one held 85,000 laying hens, the fact that treating farm animals like that just seems so *ungrateful*, Make America Grateful Again, as well as cruel and unsanitary and all, the fact that the arrogance of it, the fact that chickens willingly give up their eggs to us, or fairly willingly, and in return I don't think we should torture them, the fact that that doesn't seem quite fair, and it doesn't even make sense, the fact that it's well, just cruelty for cruelty's sake, "Are you evil?", the fact that there's a lot of death and disease and wastage caused by factory farming, and how healthy will *humans* be if they eat unhealthy animals or unhealthy eggs, the fact that after the tornadoes, the whole place looked like one of my wedding cake disasters, the fact that there were millions of dead and injured white chickens squashed between the crumpled tiers, the fact that half the birds were crushed, but not all of them were *dead*, the fact that millions of birds were in distress and the only solution the factory could come up with was to burn the whole place down, but they never got around to it, the fact that in the end they just left them all stuck in the tiers to rot and peck at each other until they all died of thirst and starvation and injuries, Money For Your Injuries, the fact that *that* was an evil thing to do, beyond criminal, the fact that chickens can live for some *weeks* without food and water, so a whole bunch of them, millions, lingered *on and on* in there, the fact that some nice people took maybe a thousand or so off to animal sanctuaries, but nobody could cope with the numbers, of both the living and the dead, the fact that this all happened so close to here, the fact that I think a National Emergency should have been declared, but what good would that do, "Just us chickens," the fact that I actually think it's criminal to have that kind of factory in the first place, the fact that I better think about something else, like the New Philadelphia Chalk Art Festival, or Good & Plenty, the fact that I don't like licorice, I just like the way Good & Plenty look, though sometimes they look like *microbes*, if you're not careful, which is none too appetizing, gosh, Goshen, New Philadelphia, the fact that the stink that came out of that chicken place was a scandal long before the tornadoes, chickens by the trillion, the fact that the whole idea of keeping animals in such numbers is disgusting, disgusting, the fact that there's something really sick about it, one hundred and ten billion chickens, zillion, trillion, trillium, Goldfinger, the goose that laid the golden egg, the fact that trillium's the state flower, frillium, brillium, fritillaries, *'twas brillig and the slithy toves*, trivium, trivia, the fact that Ohio is like a trillium petal hanging off Lake Erie, the fact that the chicken factory used slave labor too, undocumented, underage Guatemalans, *child slaves*, slave children, the fact that I feel like going over there right now and giving them a piece of my mind, speaking as a mom *and* a poultry farmer, but of course I'd never do it, the fact that I must be at a low point, to get so riled up like this about something that happened *years* ago, squelchy mud, squelch, Welch's grape juice, the fact that I dreamt about a secret watery garden hidden behind some buildings, the fact that it was all cool in there, with ivy and big trees, maybe watercress or something dark green and squelchy anyway that was nice to walk on barefoot, and the fact that then I dreamt I was with a big family in a big People Mover bus, and on the back seat with me was this teenage boy who said he had flu, which worried me though he didn't exactly look like he had flu, the fact that we dream all this stuff, and then just forget most of it between being asleep and awake, Playboy Bunnies,

Hooters, Costco, Chuck E. Cheese's, the fact that Emily Dickinson didn't know how to tell the time, aspirin, ground cardamom, the fact that Ben said an old lady passed away in Newcomerstown last week and when the family went in to try to sort her house out, they found twelve million plastic margarine tubs in the attic, all covered in cobwebs, the fact that I wonder why the spiders liked those margarine tubs so much, the fact that I guess there must've been lots of flies buzzing around them, or around the latest additions to the collection at least, and the spider colony just built up from there, house fly, flesh fly, bottle fly, cluster fly, cluster bomb, cancer cluster, the fact that the good news is she kept those tubs so long they can now be *recycled*, which maybe wouldn't have been possible when she first started collecting them, the fact that I think she should get a posthumous award or something, for saving so much plastic from the landfill, or the ocean, the fact that "posthumous" is a kind of scary word, the fact that it makes you think of exhuming, exuberant, exuberant exhumation, extruding, estranged, ex, humongous, humus, hummus, halloumi, the fact that what's also scary about it is that she *ate* that much *margarine*, the fact that I hope she had it on a cracker, the fact that we're a butter family, the fact that I'm with Julia Child on that issue, the fact that I wonder how old that old lady was when she passed on, the old lady with the tubs I mean, not *Julia Child*, old lady, the fact that I've got to try and forget about those "blankets" of cobwebs, the fact that Ben says they were really *thick* too, and the whole place just crawling with spiders, haunted house, the fact that we need spiders, I know, but maybe not that many, the fact that most homes have at least ten different kinds of spider in them, crab spiders and other kinds, the fact that, according to Ben, you are never more than four feet from a spider, the fact that before they tackle those tubs, why don't they put some animal in the attic that likes eating spiders, like a bird or something, or a mongoose, ♫ *There was an old lady who swallowed a fly* ♫, the fact that I bet he's going to have a spider phobia now, Ben, not the mongoose, the fact that I saw a YouTube video of a mongoose *screaming* at a pack of lions out on the plains of Africa or wherever, driving them away from the mongoose's underground lair, the fact that that was one brave mongoose, the fact that mongooses, mongeese, have long tails, the fact that the lions looked perplexed, the fact that they're used to running the show, ♫ *There was an old woman who lived in a shoe, She had so many children she didn't know what to do* ♫, the fact that Old Mother Hubbard rhymes with cupboard, the fact that she sounds a lot like *me*, so many children, the fact that I think we get more bugs in the summer at our house, because the cats keep the birds away, so it's bug heaven around here, the fact that we need more spiders, and a purple martin house, to cope with the bugs, the fact that the chickens do their bit, but they can only eat the bugs on the ground, the fact that some of our chickens are old ladies now, the fact that I dreamt Grandma was more fun than I thought, and pretty good on the computer, the fact that she also drove a horse-drawn truck for short errands, lilium, trillium, gazillium, the fact that Dorothy Parker said palm trees were the ugliest plant ever invented, but she probably hadn't seen a Giant Viper's Bugloss, nor a *lilium stinkium*, the fact that it's not called *that*, the fact that it's called an *amorphophallus titanium*, though that sounds even sillier, the fact that when we got to the grand unveiling of that thing at Ohio State we were so disappointed, because it hardly stunk at all, the fact that it was quite good-looking, from *below*, in a mammoth sort of way, enormity, but we waited and waited to smell something awful coming off of it and nothing happened, the fact that the stink is supposed to attract flies and sweat bees, a bit like a big bunch of old margarine tubs, the fact that I don't know what a sweat bee is and don't intend to find out, gravity benders, freeze tag, the fact that David Attenborough's plant series on TV had a Sumatran corpse flower in it, which is the same thing, I think, as an *amorphophallus lilium*, the fact that I like that David Attenborough, because he goes on TV with messy hair, and wades through mangrove swamps despite the leeches, Nellie Oleson, and he never harms a plant, except *once* maybe, just in a minor way, when he tricked a little desert plant into blooming by pouring some water on it, but that was no big deal, the fact that making a little plant prematurely flower doesn't seem all that mean or anything, the fact that I'm sure the plant didn't mind, the fact that it probably enjoyed its own personal rain shower, the fact that that's nothing, I think, compared to bumping people off with a bump stock down at the bowling alley, the fact that David Attenborough really seems to care about plants and animals, and he makes you feel like you're right there with him, the fact that Obama consulted David Attenborough about climate change, Flint, Bo on the White House lawn, Michelle's vegetable patch, Malia, Melania, Stacy, the fact that Michelle is really tall, the fact that she's about six feet, the fact that I wonder what'll happen to the White House vegetable patch *now*, the fact that the Trumps have probably trampled it, on purpose, or turned it into a miniature golf course, the fact that Melania doesn't seem much like the outdoorsy type, the fact that I can't see her with a trowel digging potatoes, unless it was some punishment Trump thought up, corpse flower, the fact that Leo can't *stand* David Attenborough and his plant show, and doesn't see why I bought the DVDs, but they were on sale, and they were great when I was sick, the fact that he may hate *Richard* Attenborough even more than he hates *David* Attenborough, the fact that I don't know why exactly, maybe because of *Gandhi*, the fact that he says Richard Attenborough is a feeb and David Attenborough doesn't know what he's talking about, the fact that Leo doesn't think David Attenborough knows a *thing* about plants, the fact that he just does what he's told by BBC TV, the fact that Leo thinks David Attenborough will cover plants or mammals or fish or insects or birds or tornadoes and whatever's leftover, if they tell him to, and that he's just in it for the money, the fact that Leo *rails* against David Attenborough, David Attenborough's show, David Attenborough's appearance, David Attenborough's ignor-ance, David Attenborough's manner, David Attenborough's hair, David Attenborough's voice, which is dubbed, Leo says, David Atten-borough's hypocrisy, David Attenborough's English accent, and just everything else about David Attenborough that he can think of, the fact that it's really reached the point where I try never to mention David Attenborough to Leo, *or* the plant show, or even *plants*, in case it riles him, the fact that Leo threw out all our radishes and celery the other day, from the fridge, and that riled *me*, because they were still okay, though past their date, Bettina, Moira, that Peolia student who helped me when I fell down, the fact that I sort of have to watch David Attenborough's plant show in *secret* now, and because of that I haven't seen it for a long time, the fact that I find it kind of comforting, I don't know why, the fact that lots of people get into botany in later life, or bonsai, the fact that plants don't move much, unless they speed up the film, so it's usually a pretty restful show to watch, like golf can be sometimes, if you *have* to watch it, amorphous phallus, the fact that bananas grow from a corm, and they're *radioactive*, just a little, the fact that Leo says it's because of the potassium, groundhogs, mongooses, anorexia, dust devils, tumbleweed, the fact that scientists sometimes measure radiation in relation to the amount of radiation there is in a banana, like one banana's worth of radiation, two bananas' worth, the fact that it doesn't sound very precise to me, because bananas vary in size, but what do I know, *I don't know but they know*, the fact that they call it the Banana Equivalent Dose, BED, the fact that I think it should stand for Banana Eating Danger, or Better not Eat Dat, JC Penney, Jo-Ann Craft Shop, slipping on a banana peel, *Candid Camera*, my kids eating banana bread, organs, tissues, the fact that NORM means Naturally Occurring Radioactive Material, and TENORM is a technologically enhanced NORM, the fact that brazil nuts have potassium and radium in them, and tobacco has thorium, polonium, and uranium, ingestion, inhalation, DAC, ALI, Cal-Dak trays, small intestine, upper large intestine, lower large intestine, REM, Roentgen equivalent man, rapid eye movement, the fact that it would be dangerous to approach that giant banana in *Sleeper*, the fact that you'd be better off in the Orgasmatron, giant celery stalk, flying pack, BED, the fact that BED begins to sounds pretty good right now, pillows, birdsong, the fact that I'd like to be back in that secret watery garden, the fact that I wish you could return to the dreams you like, like with lucid dreaming, where you're sort of half-awake and half-asleep, but I can't believe that stuff works, the fact that lots of people *die* in their beds, the fact that maybe bed is the most dangerous place to be, the fact that when I was waiting in line at the convenience store in Gnadenhutten, that man behind me called the customer at the counter a "b——," just because she was taking too long getting her stuff, in his opinion, the fact that I thought that was way outta line, but I didn't say anything, the fact that you never know when somebody's going to pull a *gun*, and anyway, there are worse people around than him in Ohio, the fact that there are police officers who call black girls "n——" and punch them in the stomach, the fact that what ever happened to the idea of, of being gentlemanly, gallant, "Men are queer hawks," the fact that who said that, the fact that somebody once said "if a man makes a nuisance of himself, kick his ankle," the fact that it's probably mentioned in the self-defense book, kick off, kickball, dodgeball, touchdown, safeties, halftime, end zone, the fact that I think they meant if some guy makes a pass at you in a *bar* or something, not if he's a police officer and he's punching you in the stomach, the fact that that was the same day I was delivering my cakes to the coffee shop in New Philadelphia, and that manager guy, Mark, accused me of changing my lemon drizzle cake recipe and said he liked them better *before*, the fact that I never felt so insulted, the fact that I left there almost in tears, the fact that I felt so mad he didn't like my lemon drizzle cakes anymore, ashamed, buckeye, the fact that I couldn't help it, the fact that my recipe let me down and I *had* to change it, lemon drizzle cake disaster, the fact that you can't please everybody, twenty-yard line, the fact that I guess I don't take criticism all that well, the fact that I was always scared of Mommy and Daddy being critical, the fact that Daddy could really lose it sometimes, the fact that it was harder to make Mommy angry, the fact that she was hardly ever harsh with me, but when she *was*, boy, it knocked you sideways, like that time with the artificial sweetener, right in front of Abby, Salem, Mass., asparagus, sparrow grass, marshmallow, milk thistle, Sarah Orne Jewett, witches, the fact that marshmallow flowers look a bit like marshmallow candy, with that faint pink tinge to them, pale pink pencil, pale blue pencil, the fact that I guess it's pretty easy really to throw me for a loop, burning witches at the stake, ASS, Mass., NORM, the fact that we never did see eye-to-eye on that issue, the artificial sweeteners I mean, not the Salem witches, the fact that aspartame does give you cancer, but sugar's a depressant, so they're both bad for you, the fact that I don't think Mommy was thinking about that though, the fact that she just thought I was being silly, which really hurt, twinge, lunge, lunch, hunch, hip, David Attenborough, Venus Fly Trap, Venus Fly von Trapp, Pepito, one hundred and one Dalmatians, one hundred and fifty billion chickens a year, the fact that, according to Oprah, you need *support* when receiving criticism, and I get mine from Leo, my support I mean, not my criticism, but when I think of that guy, Mark, beige décor, red booths, criticizing my new perfectly good lemon drizzle cakes, Active Shooter Situation, the fact that Leo wasn't there so I just fell apart, and when I got to the car I started to rethink my whole system, the fact that if I went back to my previous method of making lemon drizzle cakes though, just for the cakes I sell *Mark*, I'd be making two different types of lemon drizzle cake all the time, one for him and one for every-body else, and that would be confusing, and maybe a little bit irritat-ing, the fact that knowing me, I'd probably end up bringing Mark the wrong kind anyway, the fact that, now I think about it, maybe his comment was meant as a *compliment*, the fact that maybe he was just sort of speaking up for my previous lemon drizzle cake efforts, which I thought were a total failure but actually were usually fine, the fact that he said it in a slightly hostile way though, like why the heck did I change my recipe, the fact that there was an edge to it, the fact that, as a result, I internalized something negative about my drizzle cakes and that's what's stuck, the fact that negative stuff sticks much better than positive stuff, for some reason, and it's made me hate making lemon drizzle cakes, the new way *or* the old way, the fact that negative stuff *cloys*, like duct tape versus magic tape, or like peanut butter or fanouropita, the fact that maybe a peanut butter fanouropita cake would work, the fact that maybe Mark would like one of *those*, the fact that he'd never have to know *why* I made it, a negative energy cake, and at least it would keep him quiet for a while, because the roof of his mouth would be all clogged up, the fact that where's all this *aggression* coming from, dear me, the fact that unless you're upbeat enough, and immune to criticism, you're just a sitting duck if somebody makes a single untoward remark, the fact that Oprah's always saying how you shouldn't internalize stuff too much, or you never get *closure*, I'm not sure why, the fact that she wants everybody to expel whatever the bad thing is and then close up again like an airtight submarine, sphincter, because otherwise the internalized stuff eats away at you from the inside, ingested radiation dose, the fact that she makes internalizing sound much worse than just getting mad, and maybe medically unwise, the fact that it begins to seem positively *unAmerican* to internalize things, ♫ *Accentuate the positive!* ♫, Internal Revenue Service, but I think it's pretty impossible to get through life without internalizing a *few* things, flotsam and jetsam, fan-tails, toenails, foolhardy, Laurel and Hardy, marmalade, the fact that Oprah never recommends simply *forgetting* stuff, which is *my* basic tactic, and really pretty effective sometimes, the fact that it doesn't always work, like I remembered Mark just now, the fact that sometimes stuff does come back at me, against my will, the fact that some of the time people try to make me remember stuff I don't want to remember, and I feel like saying you know, I've got some good closure going on here, dude, so drop it, but they never do and they all make me remember stuff that makes me sad, ♫ *and the walls come a-tumblin' down* ♫, the fact that even if they think they're just talking about good stuff, not Mommy passing away and stuff like that, the fact that it can still get me thinking about all the bad stuff, the fact that it's better to just live in the present, like a shark, the fact that sharks aren't worried about the past, the fact that they aren't always getting together for group nostalgia sessions, the fact that a shark has to keep *moving*, moving, living in the now, embrace change, the fact that sharks are the biggest embracers of change there are, and they embrace it *fast*, the fact that in my dreams Mommy's alive, the fact that when she was dying in the Emergency Room, I put my hand on her arm and my touch revived her, the fact that it felt like an electric charge going down my arm and into her hand, and then she stirred and she got *better*, for a few months anyway, the fact that I wasn't there the next time it happened, or maybe I could've saved her again, broken, bridge closure, three tiers, dead and dying chickens, my Little Pillow, Pepito, the fact that this is exactly the sort of stuff I'm trying to forget, because if I don't forget it I can't think or do anything I gotta do, like make lemon drizzle cake, the fact that I had to grit my teeth this morning and sort through Mommy's old sewing box, but it wasn't so bad in the end, the fact that I put it off for years, because I'm just so darn terrified of remembering anything, but then I was really glad I'd done it when I found an old clay mouse Stacy made, Little Known Yoga Pose, the fact that I don't know if I was more scared of the sewing-box *memories* actually, or all the loose needles tangled up in there, the fact that it was a real mess, one great big porcupine ball of thread with needles stuck in it, fatberg, Pittsburgh, the fact that madeleines are like little memory sticks, but when you bite into one you get closure, the fact that I get the kids to help make them, so they'll have nice memories of making madeleines, the fact that I have plenty of madeleine pans so the kids can fool around with one while I keep up a steady use of the oven with the other pans, the fact that the kids are kind of slow to get their madeleine pan filled and into the oven, the fact that they drip batter a lot too, but that's okay, because I can keep going while they dither, dabble, squabble, diamonds, Rose Bowl, Super Bowl, CTE, Omalu, apple turnovers, the fact that some people don't like introverts, the fact that everybody's got to be an extrovert these days or they think you're a psycho or something, compost, decomposing, the fact that a madeleine has so much butter in it it's really like a tiny pound cake, or *ounce* cake, the fact that you have to use unsalted butter and caster sugar and the finest pastry flour you got, flower, flour, "00," OC, OS, cornstarch, confectioner's sugar, the fact that madeleines are maybe the second best kind of cake in the world, the fact that angel food's the best, the fact that I don't know why people still bother with bundt cakes, except mini ones, that is, mini bundt cakes, not mini *people*, the fact that most bundt cakes just aren't *moist* enough, the fact that red velvet cake *is* moist, the fact that red velvet cake is supposed to be made with beets but I don't think most of them have any beets in them anymore, ruta-baga cake, carrot cake, potato cake, the fact that madeleines have that nice shell shape, and okay, maybe they're not as amazing as sfoglia-telle, but they still look very sweet, not *cute*, sweet, teenage suicide, the fact that sfogliatelle are clam-shaped while madeleines are scal-loped but more elongated, the fact that Jake calls them spaceships, Overcome Your Fear Of Turbulence, sequins, felt, the fact that cup-cakes are cup-shaped because people used to make them in cups, not fancy silicon mini bundt-cake pans, but people forget that, the fact that I only recently found it out myself, a foul, fowl, the fact that the NFL makes ten billion dollars a year, the fact that my one real made-leine disaster wasn't my fault, the fact that the chickens weren't laying so well so I'd bought eggs from some store, Yoga Alternatives, and they were all *rotten*, the fact that I only realized that after I'd already cracked two of them into the bowl of sugar and melted butter, such a waste, the fact that those eggs were weird, the whole dozen of them, once I checked them out, the fact that they were all bad in one way or other, some foamy, others sort of liquefied, with membranes floating around loose inside, madeleine, Madeleine Carroll, Madeline, *Miss Clavel ran fast and faster, to the scene of the disaster*, Mr. Memory, the fact that Madeleine Carroll gets to be handcuffed to Robert Donat, which is quite a romantic prospect, whatevs, the fact that Stacy says "whatevs" all the time, the fact that the eggs didn't smell that bad or anything but there was something wrong about them, the fact that they probably came from that new chicken factory, the fact that "free range" doesn't mean a thing, ivy garden, New Haven, peaches in cream, Mommy, the fact that it's well known that some places sell six-month-old eggs as fresh, the fact that, whatevs, I had to throw all that batter out, like several dollars' worth of butter and sugar, because I'd been planning to make about sixty madeleines, some chocolate-tipped, some not, *It will make my batter bitter*, Strangers Fold Flowers, online jigsaw of an Amish farm, green and gold fields, clouds, dappled sunlight, *But if I buy some better butter, it will make my batter better*, DAPL, faceless Amish doll, Ohio like a petal, the fact that I didn't like to keep that rotten batter around, or have any rotten eggs in the house contaminating things, and I couldn't put melted butter down the sink, so I poured it all into coffee cans and out I went in 35-mile-an-hour winds, the fact that getting rotten eggs and several cans of buttery goo into the trash can in the dark, in the middle of a snow storm, didn't go too well, the fact that when I started pouring, the wind whipped the batter right up into the air and spread it across my face, and my nice new winter coat, great big dollops of it, the fact that I had to have a bath after, and the coat had to go to the cleaners, the fact that in the end, with the wasted sugar, butter and eggs, the hot water and the dry-cleaning costs, the whole incident must have set me back about $40 or $50, so *that* was memorable all right, the fact that I really should've sued somebody, Mr. Memory, Lilian Gish, and this is exactly why cooking makes me so jittery, because you never know when you're going to screw up big time, and waste a lot of ingredients, or electricity and all, or just waste time, and make a fool of yourself, the fact that I think this baking enterprise has basically made me a nervous wreck, aspartame, though it's better than an office job, if there *were* any office jobs around here, which I doubt, the fact that maybe I could be a secretary at that Kurz-Kasch place, but I think they shut down, the fact that if I was a *welder* I might get work somewhere, otherwise no deal, the fact that Alec Baldwin does a good Trump impression on SNL, but what good does that do, the fact that of course I never complained to the store where I bought the eggs, the fact that I'm not a complainer, six-month-old eggs, millions of chickens in one gigantic multistory coop, concentration camps, "Call this living?", *Witness*, martin house, the fact that some battery hen factory had to pay off all the neighbors, for the stink and the flies and a darkling beetle problem, the fact that the dead flies were inches thick on the ground, the fact that I think maybe they introduced the darkling beetles to kill the flies, but then the beetles became a problem too, ♫ *perhaps she'll die* ♫, the fact that Ben will get a phobia about darkling beetles if I'm not careful, and stink bugs, the fact that there's a stink bug epidemic now, the fact that $20 million it cost them, the class action lawsuit against the chicken factory, but they were still allowed to keep dumping manure into the creek, killing off all the fish for fifteen miles downstream, or was that from that dairy farm, where they were beating the cows, the fact that some EPA official came and inspected the place and said certain kinds of beatings are *okay*, but he drew the line at intentionally breaking calves' legs, bundt, brunt, palm trees, David Attenborough, the fact that that kid in Cincinnati just couldn't decide whether to do a school shooting or not, so he decided to flip a coin, flipping, flipping out, flipping tartes tatin, the fact that if it was heads, he'd carry out the rampage, and if it was tails, he'd give the whole thing a miss, Hobby Night, the fact that he went home to get his dad's guns, and found two coins on the floor, the fact that the quarter was heads up and there was a penny near it that was tails down, so he used another coin to cast the deciding vote, and that coin, the coin he threw himself, was heads up, so he went back to school and shot four kids and one died, the fact that he shot four people for no reason except that a coin was heads up, and he would've shot even more people if his guns hadn't jammed, the fact that two of the injured kids are back to school now and the whole place is full of therapy dogs, the fact that I don't know how they can bear to go back, the fact that every kid in that school must be scared to *death*, but they look cheerful in the pictures, as if they've all gotten over it and already forgotten the kid who passed away, or they're *trying* to forget it all, but how do you get over something like that that happened *for no reason*, just the flip of a coin, the fact that that poor dog got shot by the neighbor over in Coshocton, the fact that all he did was run near the neighbor's lot, and he got shot, the fact that the dog survived but now he's *scared* all the time, the fact that he used to be a good watch dog, the fact that now he just barks at everybody and prefers to stay upstairs in the bedroom all day, the fact that there was that black child too, just standing near a car at the gas station in North Carolina or somewhere, the fact that there was music coming from the car and some white guy took offense at this and shot the black kid *dead*, for no reason, just because of some *music*, and it wasn't even the boy's car, *Bringing Up Baby*, the fact that there are twenty threats of school shootings a week now, across the whole country, and hundreds or thousands of false alarms and lock-downs, and a million shooter drills, and now some schools have cops on hand all day long, and some have metal detectors and I don't know what, the fact that no wonder Gillian wants to know the meaning of life, the fact that the whole country's gone *crazee* almost, the fact that maybe I need a walk, Leo's shoes in the hall, David Attenborough, the fact that sometimes I freak out after spending too long all alone at home and think he's going to call me, *Leo*, not David Attenborough, and say he's in love with somebody else and he's not coming home, but so far that hasn't happened, knock on wood, the fact that I'm scared anything could happen, *anything*, from finding a rotten egg to us all being obliterated in one second by a nuclear holocaust, just reduced to soot silhouettes against the wall, but a walk helps, the fact that when the kids go stir-crazy, I sometimes take them on a walk, the fact that yesterday we went out in the wind and I got them all to pre-tend we were flying, the fact that they got kind of into it, Gillian especially, the fact that I warned her not to try doing it off the porch or anything, the fact that we don't need any parkour stuff around here, thanks, buildering, bouldering, extreme, Ben running down a hill in his pirate costume, the fact that Leo says some nut broke a thumb off a Chinese soldier at the Franklin Institute in Philly, and China's not happy about it, the fact that some people have no manners at all, the fact that I think we've dropped down a class, due to all my healthcare costs, Kaiser, Chronos, Single Payer, the fact that sometimes all these payments and co-payments and deductibles and whatnot make you feel like you're *buying your body*, section by section, and you'll only be able to own the whole thing if you're really really rich, the fact that Stacy and Gillian have invented some new names for lipsticks, Bruised Thumb, Busted Plum, Sugar Highs, and Snailburst, the fact that maybe children do their best stuff at home on the weekends, *not* at school, but what can you do, my cow painting, Phoebe's possum picture, our neighborhood newspaper, flip of a coin, shooter, pewter, cuter, suitor, scooter pie, Kinder Morgan pipeline, dancing the hornpipe,

.   .   .   .

Puddles favored by crows have a sweet, earthy taste. White fluff rises in summer like a blizzard, but is not snow. You can chase it for fun. It will soon settle, then disappear. Everything disappears eventually.

She would teach her kittens to stick to lion paths and overgrown dirt tracks, rather than rely on the wide straight gashes in the land, the highways that attracted all the cars and trucks that snarled and squealed and stank. Zooming balls of metal. Those paths were smooth, but covered in sticky black tar that could give under paws in hot weather.

Hide from the bare-faced men inside those cars. Listen out for their guns, metal sticks that pop and savage from afar.

Men are noisy, clumsy animals, unpredictable compared to bears: you never knew what they were going to do next. Most of the people she came across were male, though once she had come on a bunch of berrying women and children, quietly chattering as they tugged at branches and pulled down fruits. She slunk quickly away and they never knew she was there. It is best to keep your distance from mothers in search of food for their young.

She would teach her kittens that the wind is alive, likewise the sun, stars and moon, and that such forces can be exploited: the sun, to blind your quarry; the breeze, to cover your smell and the sound of your step. Stand against the light. Let shadows disguise your progress. Keep leeward of a deer.

Deer like high open ground and the edges of plains. In the middle of the day, they hide among trees; in storms, they seek shelter behind the windswept hills.

She had never fished a lake, but rivers, yes. With quick strides, a fine pink-fleshed fish could be caught. Fish are slippery. Hold them tight in your mouth while you pad out over uneven stones. The pain of a jagged rock can cause you to lose a fish. Eat the fish, bones and all, sliced by your teeth into four swallows. Never share.

There is a bone-filled cave where mountain lions have always camped. You need to know where it is. Nearby, a sheet of water hides you while you await the fish that jump. Never be spooked by sparkling things.

Respect bears, and wolves in packs (a lone wolf is not a threat). Ravens, buzzards and coyotes will dog you, but they only want your leftovers.

To kill is irresistible. Once, on finding a large wooden hut full of chickens, she had killed them all, every single one, driven to a frenzy by their flutterings. But it is rare to find a density like that, a wooden box jam-packed with captive prey.

What you see, you take – if you're quick enough. You can swipe a bird right out of the sky and eat it. At dusk, a bat. Survive. Take what you want from the earth. Live. Never let yourself tire to the point of despair.

Ignore carrion.

All mountain lions are one. You are just one example of a lion. Mountain-lionhood is strong and immense, and goes beyond the individual. Each lion is part of a continuum, and privy to everything good and bad that happens to other mountain lions. You tough things out on your own, but you're linked to the pleasures, pains, and drama, the leap and recoil and lonely deaths of others.

All living things are.

.   .   .   .

the fact that it's after Rock Hudson helps Jane on with her galoshes that they decide to get married, the fact that they bond over *galoshes*, of all things, the fact that that must be one of the big galoshes moments in the movies, the fact that naturally I didn't say anything about it to Stace, the fact that she probably doesn't even know what galoshes *are*, the fact that nobody does anymore, the fact that people used to call them rubbers, or overshoes, the fact that the only other galoshes in a movie I can think of right this minute is in *Holiday*, when the butler helps Cary Grant's old friend the professor off with his galoshes and takes off one of his *shoes* too, by accident, right in the middle of the big New Year's party, engagement party, the fact that the professor has to ask the butler for his shoe back, "We're ruined," the fact that somebody mentions them in *Mr. Smith Goes to Washington* too, galoshes I mean, "Leave your rubbers outside the door," the fact that Ralph Bellamy's wearing rubbers when he first meets Cary Grant in *His Girl Friday*, the fact that he's got an umbrella too, because there's a slight chance of rain, the fact that the galoshes movies could join the movies that feature shaving and bathroom medicine cabinets, the fact that Rosalind Russell says "I don't know from water buffaloes," the fact that Stace would never watch *Holiday* or *His Girl Friday*, because they're black-and-white, but she was willing to watch *All That Heaven Allows*, the fact that we both agreed Jane Wyman doesn't know what the heck she's doing, the fact that any normal person should be able to see that Rock Hudson's a catch, what with his twigs and leaves and baby trees and his big mill out in the country and the Wedgwood jug and all his down-to-earth friends and his ability to pull corks out of bottles with his teeth, the fact that Rock rocks, the fact that he always seems to be surrounded by fall colors too, the fact that the whole world turns red and yellow for this guy, *and* he has a green thumb, the fact that what's old Harvey got to compete with that, the fact that Stacy decorated her room last fall with dried leaves that she pressed inside Irma Rombauer, not Irma *herself*, inside her cookbook, and they're still pretty, though they've faded a bit now, the ancient forests of Tuscarawas County, Treat Rattle Snakes With Respect, the fact that Jane Wyman's kids are real spanners in the works, the fact that they want her to marry Harvey because he's dull and safe, the fact that they don't want Rock Hudson, because he's handsome and rugged and younger than their mom, and because he's only a gardener and they're snobs, rock garden, the fact that there's a deer that visits the mill all the time, the fact that people still shoot fawns, the fact that how can they bring themselves to do that, AR-15s, bullet wounds, the fact that AR-15s tear a path through body tissue like a cigarette boat in a narrow canal, lock, bridge, berm, North Pole, the fact that everything is so ugly now, the fact that cars are *ugly*, and buildings are *ugly*, the fact that kingfishers, dragonflies, damselflies, and deerflies are not ugly, but nobody seems to care about deerflies and damselflies, *or* about the North Pole, the fact that all they care about is the aurora borealis, and Walmart, the fact that they do really care about Walmart, wall, mart, martins, car, carpet, pet, petal, your pedal extremities, ♫ *Picking on a wishbone from the Frigidaire* ♫, orbital, the fact that Harvey's the local bore and hypochondriac, the fact that he's always going off for cures, Otis elevators, North Pole, Northern Lights, Trump Tower, *Towering Inferno*, diamond-cutter, Uranus's ocean of diamonds, the fact that Jane Wyman's son prides himself on his martini-making and he offers Harvey a second drink, but Harvey says one is his limit, the fact that he says so again and again, the fact that the son's worried Jane Wyman's red dress might scare Harvey off, but Harvey says it would take much more, or much less, to scare *him*, the fact that Harvey thinks he's being really risqué there, the fact that Jane Wyman was married to Ronald Reagan for a while, the fact that Ronald Reagan was always sleeping through the 3:00 a.m. phone calls, the fact that the walls of Trump's Manhattan apartment drip with gold, the fact that Mommy didn't like people with bad taste, the fact that Grandma had bad taste, the fact that *she* liked fake gold too, just like Trump, her lamps and things, ♫ *the walls come a-tumblin down* ♫, the fact that she left us a lot of awful costume jewelry that the kids now use for dressing up, Richville, Ridgeville, Ridgeville Corners, Billionairesville, Hankersville, Grudgeville, the fact that you just know Jane Wyman would have a terrible time if she wound up with Harvey, the fact that anyone can see it except the mean son, the fact that the daughter has her doubts about Harvey, but she completely freaks out about Rock Hudson, YOUR WEIGHT FREE, the fact that the kids force Jane to give Rock up, TOLEDO – NO SPRINGS, and then they forget all about it, the fact that they're busy with their own lives, whatevs, whichevs, whatnots, beans on toast, hit-and-run, the fact that sometimes you do have to wonder if children always have their parents' best interests at heart, the fact that parents have a moral obligation to make their kids happy, but kids don't have to make their parents happy, the fact that I think most parents are happy enough if the kid just survives, and doesn't commit too many crimes, the fact that depriving your mom of Rock Hudson kind of takes the cake, the fact that he's so patient and gentle and forgiving, almost too good to believe, saintly, and he's got a *deer*, the fact that it's not like the playboy type he plays in *Magnificent Obsession*, but even *that* guy becomes a greatly reformed character after making Jane Wyman go blind, the fact that Rock's heroic right from the start in *All That Heaven Allows*, a real nurturer, a plant-nurturer, like David Attenborough, aching to give Jane Wyman what she needs, the fact that he's crazy about trees *and* Jane, the fact that when she says she likes his broken Wedgwood jug, he fixes it for her, and then she breaks it *again* during one of their fights about whether or not to get married, the fact that she's scared of her kids and all the snobs and stinkers in her social set, the fact that even her friend Agnes Moorehead's a stinker, the fact that she's always turning up in her car coat with a station wagon full of china for Jane Wyman, buccaneers, the new normal, and she wants Jane to settle down with Harvey and get a TV, hook, line and sinker, *plus tax*, the fact that Jane gets a TV set for Christmas, but she never watches it, because all she can think about is *Rock*, cock, oh dear me, calm-down kit, color therapy, synesthesia, the fact that it was amazing Stacy stayed and watched the whole thing like that, the fact that, boy, I miss her company, now that she hates me all the time, the fact that we used to go on outings together, like to get clothes for school, or some afternoons we'd just take off on our own, leave Leo in charge, sneak off for milkshakes and a movie, just the two of us, the fact that what I miss most though is her sitting on my lap when she was little, the fact that, gosh, how she'd cringe if I ever told her that, the fact that she'd swat me right and left with galoshes if she had any, the fact that she hates practically everything I say and do now and can hardly bear to be *near* me, the fact that it breaks your heart, the fact that my heart is broken, I'm broken, the fact that we're all going to *pass away* some day, but she'd rather spend time with those Morning Routine girls than listen to a thing I have to say, the fact that I've got to nurture her like Rock Hudson would treat a delicate plant, the fact that people in movies never have kitchen tables covered with paperwork, apart from Erin Brockovich, but that's only because she has a big lawsuit on her hands, the fact that in real life there must be very few kitchen tables that *aren't* covered in paperwork, at least sometimes, but you'd never know it from Hollywood movies, the fact that Jane Wyman's house is so depressing, neat and barren, while Rock Hudson's so in tune with nature that his home is partly a greenhouse, the fact that he has his trees, and the barn, and a deer, *Because it was grassy and wanted wear*, the fact that Rock Hudson was always having to play the ideal leading man, the fact that maybe nobody else wanted those roles anymore, the fact that in *Imitation of Life* it's *not* Rock Hudson, the fact that somebody else plays the Rock Hudson part, a saintly guy who hangs around for years, waiting for Lana Turner to appreciate him, *Lana Turner has collapsed!*, our living room in Evanston, staying home from school sick, cheating with the thermometer, learning how to play solitaire, peaches in cream, fingering the wide corduroy ridges on the yellow chaise longue, the fact that I like doing latticed pies but I almost always louse up the *latticing*, when I'm weaving it in and out, the fact that it's kind of embarrassing, the fact that surely anybody can do *that*, the fact that it seems ridiculous I can't weave a simple crisscross basket pattern out of dough without getting myself in a pickle, big sour pick-les, but that's the way it is, the fact that there's no denying it, the fact that nobody would *believe* how hard I find this, the fact that there are all kinds of instructions online for doing latticing, videos too, but I can't follow them, the fact that you'd think that if you just stuck with the straight basket-weave design you couldn't go wrong, but I do, almost every time, the fact that so far nobody's noticed my latticing mistakes, or else they're too polite to mention it, the fact that latticing's getting awfully sophisticated now too, the fact that everybody's doing leaves and flowers and words now, or one big spiral of dough covering the whole pie, the fact that I really gotta make more of an effort or I'll be out-spiraled by some other local piemaker, the fact that I see these things online and start feeling so crummy about myself and my pies, criticism, fear of failure, fear of success, the fact that Trump's always talking about terrorism but maybe *he's* the terrorist, the fact that I gotta keep on my toes, car coat, china, *we love you get up*, "Buck up," the fact that Leo's been a great stepdad to Stacy, the fact that that pumpkin field we found last year had that gigantic inflatable bouncy Titanic and all the kids were climbing up and sliding down it, as if drowning in the Arctic in the middle of the night in 1912 is just a big joke, Kate Winslet, Leo DiCaprio, Haunted House, Mirror World, Leo, the fact that my nice fluted wooden pastry-cutter makes a good zigzagged edge, the fact that lattice pastry shouldn't be cut too wide or it looks clumsy, nor too thin, because it'll break when you try to weave with it, the fact that big wide strips, tightly woven, *can* be good on an apple pie, but not on berry pies, because you have to leave spaces for the juice and steam to come out, release liquid, tapioca disaster, galoshes, rubbers, overshoes, candlelit vigils, Jane Wyman, Reagan, the fact that *Imitation of Life* is almost too much to bear, especially the last half, and Lana Turner's so cold, at least in that movie, the fact that it's hard to like her, the fact that all she cares about is her dumb career, while everybody else is going nuts and her hangdog boyfriend acts like a lost, well, sheep, sheepdog, the fact that with berry pies you only half-cover the surface, the fact that there's latticing flexibility with a berry pie, too much maybe, the fact that bananas are a kind of berry, which is hard to believe, radioactive berries, the fact that I've never tried to bake a banana pie, the fact that some people like banana cream pie but that's different, the fact that I don't like those cherry pies with random holes bored into the top crust, like Inuit fishing holes or something, the fact that that seems a lazy latticing job to me, the fact that if the strips of woven dough are rolled too thin, they get dry and brittle when it bakes, which you don't want, oyster loaf, ouster loaf, the peacemaker, the fact that Leo says friction exists between surfaces, and smooth surfaces in contact have reactions that are normal to the surface, but rough surfaces produce reactions that slant to resist any tendency to move, or something like that, the fact that this principle affects bridges in some way or other, the fact that a cherry pie shouldn't get too brown, while a blueberry pie can be almost as brown as can be and it won't wreck it, the fact that blueberry pies are tricky though, because they can be too wet, tapioca, and lots of people don't seem to mind that but I do, the fact that I tried to cure it once using tapioca, because Irma Rombauer said to, and it was a *complete fiasco*, the fact that Sarah Jane sort of steals the movie, except when her mom gets the big funeral, which comes out of the blue, the fact that I like her mom, the fact that I like moms in movies in general, basket weave, the Longaberger Basket Building, our laundry basket, ironing, Wednesday, the fact that I have to make six latticed cherry pies today, whether I weave them right or not, and four tartes tatin, or Cathy won't be happy, the fact that this is actually my big chance, because *she* usually makes the cherry pies, but she's not feeling well, the fact that if she likes my cherry pies maybe she'll ask me to make them on a regular basis, the fact that we already agreed the best cherry pie is a sour cherry pie, the fact that she was all out of sour cherries herself, but I just happened to have a big load of sour cherries in the freezer, all pitted and ready to go, not d-d-d-damsons, and those cherries are now quietly defrosting in the pantry, the fact that I think that impressed her, the fact that it probably made me sound more efficient than I am, having all these sour cherries on hand at all times, success, failure, effective, effectual, Grandpa, "This book will either be a success or a failure," the fact that nobody wants to hear *that*, for Pete's sake, Pepito, lamps, bobbly glasses of water, the fact that I was really surprised by finding some sour cherries still hanging around at this time of year, the fact that that was a *real* lucky freezer find, the fact that some man got pummeled on the way to the drugstore, just here in Newcomerstown, and he still doesn't know who did it, the fact that if you don't have sour cherries you add more lemon juice, but it's much better to use sour cherries, the fact that Cathy makes and sells all kinds of pies, but most of hers are savory, the fact that she does a chicken and sweet potato pie, a chili con carne pie, a curry pie, spanakopita pie, zucchini pie, Ohio meat pie, grilled cheese pie, shepherd's pie, and a ham and egg pie, but I'm providing more and more of her fruit pies, the fact that she liked my plum and cinnamon and cardamom pies last summer, *success*, and the wild strawberry one, but that was just for her, the fact that you can't collect enough wild strawberries to make wild strawberry pies on a regular basis, bees, cake shaped like a purse, purse shaped like a cake, red lips, some animal, see-through school knapsacks, see-through purse, the fact that I wouldn't want everybody seeing what's in *my* purse, plums, paw-paws, "pummeled," berrying, picnic, the fact that I want a strawberry plant tower like Cathy had outside the store last summer, the fact that hers could've been six feet tall, with strawberries coming out of all its balconies, peering over the side like the people in *Network* who go to their windows and yell "I'm mad as hell and I'm not going to take this anymore!", cliff dwellers, the fact that in wintertime Cathy's kept busy making hog maw and Italian Wedding Soup, and Sloppy Joes, and other warming stuff, cannelloni and quesadillas and corned beef hash with homemade sauerkraut, the fact that it's sort of heavy food, but I guess they sell well, the fact that it's partly because nobody knows how to *cook* anymore, so when they want home-style food they go to Cathy, the fact that her sauerkraut's especially popular, Pennsylvania Dutch, German ancestry, the fact that some of her customers just can't do without their sauerkraut, the fact that some of her stuff's probably like old-fashioned school food, the smell of school spaghetti at Hamden Hall, milk and rusks at Channing, before they started serving sushi and tater tots and corn dogs and I don't know what, the fact that I make my kids' lunches, the fact that I'm not paying for that stuff they serve down there, not that the kids always eat what I give them but at least I try, the fact that sometimes they only have twelve *minutes* for lunch, or that's what Gillian tells me, the fact that maybe I'll make Sloppy Joes tonight, the fact that at first Cathy was selling stuff like Sloppy Joes in little takeout packets, doggy bags, but now she makes whole pots of stew for people, the fact that they put a deposit on the Tupperware, the fact that she tries to get them to order in advance but they don't always remember, the fact that with most people nowadays they just want something right now that they can stuff in the microwave at home, or at work, and then stuff in their mouths, the fact that they don't want to cook or use the stove, the fact that some people don't even *have* a stove anymore, I don't think, especially if they're living in their car, the fact that people sometimes hang on to the Tupperware containers she gives them, just out of laziness, but she's got plenty, the fact that she may have *too* many, like the old lady with the margarine tubs and all the spiders, the fact that Cathy sells an awful lot of cookies too, and brownies, the *enemies* of pie, the fact that it seems like nobody can get enough brownies these days, but I think they're missing out on fruit and Vitamin C, not to mention cardamom, the fact that I think the trouble is It's easier to eat a brownie while you're *driving*, than a piece of pie, the fact that you can just shove a brownie in your kid's lunchbox too, along with a whole bunch of other snack foods, the fact that I dread to think what most kids eat for lunch, the fact that brownies are getting more and more elaborate too, with chocolate-raspberry brownies and caramel-coconut brownies and Oreo brownies and Reese's Pieces brownies and all that, vegan brownies, the fact that I've been trying to counteract the brownie trend lately by making tartlets, "For people on the go," but they're not cost-effective, especially if I have to *lattice* them, the tartlets, not the people, the fact that latticing takes even *longer* on a tiny tart than it does on a big pie, compact desserts, powder compact, compass, the fact that anyway I don't want to have to use a magnifying glass to peer at my latticing work, like some kind of housebound Sherlock Holmes, the fact that Sherlock Holmes *was* sort of a shut-in, the fact that Cathy's cookies go like hot cakes, her snickerdoodles, candy corn snickerdoodles, hermits, apple crisps, Ohio toads and buckeye bars, and sometimes those Nanaimo bars, the fact that she's so good at buckeye bars, the fact that she seemed kind of hesitant about asking me to make the cherry pies, the fact that I don't know if it's because she takes a certain pride in her own cherry pie, or she didn't think I could do it right, the fact that if you make them too deep the cherries don't cook, which is why I simmer them ahead of time a little, the fact that that's my only secret, the fact that, also, there has to be just enough flour in the cherry juice to slightly thicken the mixture, without stiffening the whole thing into a gelatinous goo, like you get with inexpert blueberry pies in bad diners, bridges, latticing, modulus of elasticity, the fact that nobody likes chunks of solid pink goo in their cherry pie, or purple goo in their blueberry pie, blurberry pie, Burberry pie, the fact that some people use arrowroot, or tapioca, or cornflour, but I just use normal flour, *never* tapioca, not since that fiasco, the fact that I made that pie for the PTA, for heaven's sake, the fact that that was embarrassing, and I do blame Irma Rombauer, though I should've checked it myself before I served it, the fact that she just says use tapioca as a thickener but she doesn't tell you *how*, so the tapioca never dissolved, and there were little white *dots* all through the pie, the fact that I still don't get why, Anne Tyler novels, little white *balls*, photo portraits exhibition, the fact that everybody gathered around the card table at the end of the PTA meeting to get a piece of pie, the fact that I'm sure Frances Dent was looking down on me and my pie, just my luck, in front of the entire PTA, the fact that that is really one of the worst culinary blunders of all time, or the worst *I* ever made anyway, though maybe the most inedible thing I ever made in my whole entire life were those Brave Man Cookies for the school fair, ♫ *Courage!* ♫, Frederick at the pet show, bicycle relay race, the fact that I put too much ginger in, or something, the fact that I *couldn't* have put chili powder in by mistake, the fact that I don't know how it happened but those cookies were so bitter and peppery, and it was too late to rethink, because we had nothing else to bring, so we called them Brave Man Cookies and dared people at the fair to eat one, penny a time, the fact that in the end those cookies were a big hit, proving you never can tell with people, the fact that eating one became a badge of courage, an orange badge of courage, Tradersville, Deweyville, Dutyville, Decaturville, Dumontville,

Do-notville, Gov class, lemonade in junior-size single-shot cups, Raccoons Take Over Bank, masked bandits, armed robbery, AR-15s, the fact that *Anne* Brontë was the governess of the family, not Charlotte, the fact that they all wrote poetry too, the Three Sisters, the Three Sisters Bridge in Pittsburgh, Oroville Dam, emergency spillway, headward erosion, residual compressive stress, fretting wear, velocity of a mass, friction force, transfer of momentum, limit of proportionality, the fact that the one thing that worries Leo even more than bridges is dams, the fact that he calls them "damn dams," and thinks they always cause more problems than they're worth, "all the Taylors and Paines and machines and lies," the fact that dams wreck the river, destroy the fish, and release greenhouse gases, because of all the decomposition that happens in the reservoirs, manmade lakes, Griggs Dam, unknown unknowns, concrete weir, the fact that I don't mind a small weir or canal lock, but I don't like dams, the fact that the Oroville Dam's dam management manual was way outta date, but FERC approved it, the fact that Lake Oroville's the second-largest manmade lake in California, bypass valve, spillway chute, at risk list, the fact that I always found dams creepy myself, scary, and still do, but I never knew why, the fact that they're so big and ugly from below, stained by a trickle or two of water that's allowed to get out, the fact that you can never look at a dam without imagining it failing and tons of water suddenly bursting through, the fact that they're so unnatural, anti-nature, ant hill, swimming lessons, choking in the deep end, dark water, nine hundred feet deep, turbidity, torpidity, plunge pool, ♫ *The Stars and Stripes Forever* ♫, the fact that people used to go on *day trips* to admire dams, but I only go if Leo makes me, the fact that I don't mind visiting bridges, but who wants to go see a dam, Dover Dam, Wills Creek Dam, Mohawk Dam, O'Shaughnessy Dam, Willet Creek Dam, the fact that the Wills Creek Dam overflowed in 2005, the fact that Ohio has its own Hoover Dam too, the fact that the only dams I like are tampons, but I shouldn't say that, the fact that they're more sort of plugs, but a dam *is* a plug, the fact that I dreamt a big truck drove noisily past our house and I ran outside and chased it to tell the driver he was never going to get that thing around the corners further up, but somehow he didn't get stuck, and I kept running and never caught up with him, the fact that I followed him for so long I wasn't sure of the way home anymore, and then I went in a bookstore where the manager told me her husband yelled at her all the time, the fact that the store was full of her pretty, pink me-oh-mys hanging up to dry, and I asked how he could treat her like that when she had such nice underwear, the fact that then some other guy in the store defended the husband, saying Picasso treated women the same way, the fact that I wanted to buy something there, just to sort of help the woman out a bit, and I found an animated card with lions and tigers that sort of moved, kneading each other, and I really wanted to buy it, the fact that I just remembered that dream, the fact that the only antidote to reality is dreams, and vice versa, along with plenty of cups of coffee, holding pattern, Badge Bettys, bridges, me-oh-mys, the fact that the present is more relevant than the past, it just is, whatever historians may say, the fact that chickens are being tortured all over the state of Ohio *right now*, the fact that one person is shot dead in Ohio every eight hours, and there are crowds of Syrian refugees being smothered in trucks, and Hungarian police are shooting tear gas at children, and people in Detroit are getting their water cut off, the fact that guys come draw a blue chalk line on the curb outside the house to help them find the water pipe more quickly, when they come back to turn it off, time-servers, yes men, salaryman, the fact that people have to pay $200 a month for water in Flint, water they can't drink, the fact that bottled water is now the most drunk beverage in America, because of all the problems with local supplies, but the plastic bottles are clogging up the oceans, plug, $200 a month, the fact that what do *we* pay now, dear me, the fact that I can't remember, the fact that Nestlé is bottling water from some pure-water spring near Flint, and then selling it back to people in Flint, and Nestlé only has to pay $200 a *year* for the water rights, the fact that now I'm thirsty, from thinking about all this water, the fact that I used to enjoy a root beer float, but now I've grown out of them, the fact that it's getting cloudy out, the fact that Leo says spring is one giant annual party to which we're all automatically invited, block party, street party, the fact that I don't remember much but I remember everything Leo says, from *way* back, root beer, tear gas, bridge collapse, the fact that every February everybody in Bosu, Hungary, dresses up in sheep hides and masks with horns and they have a big parade in celebration of spring, and burn a coffin that's supposed to represent the winter, the fact that I like their sheep costumes, the fact that now they think Jane Austen went *blind*, before she passed away, the fact that there are things you just wish you didn't know, the fact that I'd really like to be reading *Persuasion* right now instead of latticing *pies*, the fact that I never seem to get past Anne's first reunion with Captain Wentworth lately, because Jake interrupts, the fact that all the older kids were the same, the fact that I have to hide out like Anne Frank almost, to read anything, the fact that I should have a little closet to go to, with a chair, a lamp, and a lock on the door, the fact that I guess it's called a bathroom, the fact that Anne Frank gave up hope and *wanted to die*, the fact that she was broken, the fact that people shut down when things get too bad, kids especially, the fact that Leo stays up late in his study to read if he wants to, but I'm too tired to read at night, the fact that Stacy used to read the L. M. Montgomery books but now she despises them, and maybe she's right, I don't know, the fact that the weird thing about L. M. Montgomery is she thinks you can solve any neighbor problem just by bringing over a cake, which I've never found to be true, no matter how many cakes I make, and I know how to make a cake, the fact that my cakes are only meant to solve *financial* problems, not neighbor problems, the fact that we don't really *have* any neighbor problems, the fact that we hardly know our neighbors, the fact that there's no borrowing cups of sugar around here, the fact that everybody keeps pretty much to themselves on our block, the fact that, also, people only seem to have to meet Anne Shirley, or Emily Byrd Starr, to *like* them, the fact that I don't think being liked is that easy, even if you bring cake, the fact that some people *act* nice, right from the start, but they may well be harboring reservations about you, the fact that there might be something about you that reminds them of somebody they never liked, and there's not a thing you can do to get past that, and you never will, and you'll never know why they never took to you, the fact that they could never explain it themselves, the fact that people just have their limits, the fact that some are more limited than others, the fact that somebody said the MAGA hats are the new KKK hood, the fact that I hope that's not true, because there are a lot of MAGA hats around, the fact that once in New Haven, that neighbor kid Zeck borrowed some eggs from us and Mommy was really mad because he never returned them, *Zeck*, the fact that it was short for Ezekiel, the fact that I wouldn't mind so much now, because we have plenty of *eggs* around, but it did kind of surprise us then, the fact that we didn't have that much food in the house once Mommy got sick, the fact that Daddy didn't mind buying groceries, but he didn't have much time to get to the market, so it was kind of a big thing for a neighbor to take away a whole dozen eggs like that and not return them, the fact that they were Jehovah's Witnesses or something, downward spiral, cinnamon, coffee, real life, Lucy Maude Montgomery, the fact that Stacy said *Anne's House of Dreams* is just terrible, the fact that Anne's all grown-up and she talks to her baby in baby-talk, which of course Stacy would hate, the fact that she says Anne Shirley's lost her spirit, the fact that there's a neighbor woman in it too, who's in even worse shape, the fact that she's been nursing her violent, amnesiac husband for *eleven years*, but he finally goes off to Montreal for a brain operation and afterwards he realizes he's *not* the woman's husband at all but his lookalike cousin, the fact that the two almost identical cousins had gone on a trip to Rome or someplace eleven years before and they were in some kind of accident and the husband was killed, and his cousin was mistaken for him and sent back to be unknowingly nursed by the dead guy's wife, because everybody, including the amnesiac cousin, thinks he's her husband, the fact that she's been nursing *the wrong guy* for eleven years, which must be some kind of record, John Chersky, jagging wheel, crimping wheel, lattices, egg yolk, sprinkle of sugar on top, caramelized, Picasso, Charles Laughton, the fact that now that the exhausted "wife" realizes she's actually a widow, she's free to marry some other guy who's been mooning over her for years and years, maybe the whole eleven years, or almost, a very long time anyway, the fact that it's a bit of a stretch to believe you could be fooled by an imposter-husband, I mean, enough to mistake your difficult husband's cousin for your difficult husband, for *eleven years*, the fact that L. M. Montgomery had a difficult husband herself, the fact that he was a hypochondriac and they were both depressed all the time, Harvey, but it was the Second World War that really finished her off, she just couldn't take it, sort of the way Hawthorne felt about the *Civil* War, so she killed herself one day, in the mid-afternoon, the fact that they found her upstairs on the bed, a bit like Shirley Jackson, Anne Shirley, the fact that Shirley Jackson had a difficult husband too but she *didn't* kill herself, or not exactly, the fact that having a difficult husband can surely wear you down though, "and stop calling me Shirley," the fact that I don't know precisely how old Shirley Jackson was when she passed away, but not all that old, the fact that Hawthorne was probably a difficult husband too, the fact that on his last birthday Ben ran around the house banging a pot, but not a Revere Ware one, the fact that he got so excited banging the pot he went out and banged it up and down the street, telling all the neighbors it was his ninth birthday, the fact that Gillian followed him, drumming on a plastic mixing bowl, the fact that I made him a **9** cake, using the number **1** pan and the smaller angel food cake pan, because I still don't have a **9** pan, a **9/11** pan, the fact that the thing he liked best was the planets I made out of marzipan, the fact that he gobbled Saturn right up, the fact that I like watching him eat, the fact that he doesn't quite close his mouth when he swallows, and there's something pleasing about it, even if it *is* bad manners, the fact that he likes marzipan, which is unusual in a kid, thank you letters, the fact that almond milk is pretty popular now, confetti, maraschino cherries, the fact that once I drank lemonade alone with Angie's parents on their quiet, shady porch, when I was about ten, but where was Angie, the fact that I think we were waiting for her to get home from somewhere, the fact that I can do him a **10** cake this year, easy, because I've got the **1** just hanging around, and I can do the **0** with the *bigger* tube pan, the fact that I think I'll make it two layers this time, the fact that I gotta do some more marzipan decorations, but what, water sample bottles, stink bugs, mammoth fossils, the fact that maybe I should start a cake pan rental service myself, with my **1** pan, the fact that that thing is burning a **1**-shaped hole in my *brain*, surfer riding a hurricane wave, H_2O, the fact that people who've been in accidents hardly ever remember the actual accident, the fact that John Chersky had a heart attack swimming in Florida and was in a coma down there for such a long time, in Florida, not underwater, the fact that then he got transferred back to Ohio, and he was in the rehab place for a few *months*, the fact that now apparently he doesn't remember a thing, from a few weeks before the swimming accident to finding himself in the rehab place, but he's fine otherwise, the fact that did he have a *heart transplant*, the fact that I think he did, the fact that it's awful how you forget other people's health problems, just like how you forget when they're getting home from vacation, and even where they went on it, the fact that I blanked out most of my cancer treatment, but the *present* is what matters, the present, birthday presents for Gillian and Ben, **10** cake, fretting zone, ductile overload, orange zest, "Ducky! Ducky!", the fact that Leo has to go to Philly tomorrow, the fact that I wish he'd give up on that old duffle-bag and get a suitcase with *wheels*, the fact that somebody just died who was a world-famous diamond-cutter, the fact that how do you become a world-famous diamond-cutter, and why, the fact that I worry about his sore knees, Leo's, not the diamond cutter's, because he has to carry so many books and papers back and forth to Philly and Atlanta, the fact that I think he thinks a suitcase with wheels is beneath his dignity, the fact that I keep telling him the wheel is a great feat of engineering so he should like it, feet, the fact that he says, when they start making remote-control suitcases that just follow you around like those golf bags, he'll get one, suitcase chasing after Leo through the airport, the fact that we eat 450 billion Oreos a year, well, not *us* personally, but somebody does, and who knows how much candy corn, the Three Sisters, Wyandottes, the fact that Leo is instinctively cool, hip, hip-hop, Pez dispenser, zoot suit, Zillow, pillow, pillars, "capable of abstract thought," the fact that Leo's work is all pie in the sky while mine's just pie, the fact that he's a professor married to a *manual laborer*, which must be sort of embarrassing for him, the fact that no wonder he didn't want the cocktail party, Jane Wyman and Rock Hudson, the fact that here I am, effortfully constructing pastry lattices and longing to buy expensive mini-bundt pans and cookie cutters online, while Leo's in his study writing an article on displacement, velocity, and acceleration, and the relevance of these actions to road-bridge construction, the fact that he started out working on microbiological uses of analytic ultra-centrifuges and amino acid analyzers and protein peptide sequencers and synthesizers, right after college, but bridges took over, and then he fell in love with Maillart, with Maillart's *bridges*, not the guy himself, sheesh, Zürich, Schiers, the fact that somebody said a housewife's salary would be about a hundred and fifty thousand bucks by now, if we were really paid for what we do, but it would still be manual labor, or some of it anyway, personal-assistant-type manual labor, PA, with 24-hour shifts, the fact that it's not just cooking and cleaning either, the fact that housewives do other stuff too, like accounting and secretarial stuff and "leadership roles" and what have you, the fact that somebody with a lot of time on her hands figured all that out, probably while eating bonbons in bed, bonbon-eating mamas, the fact that the cookie cutters I want are nice delicate little rectangular stamps with a silicone tablet mold, the fact that they're for Petit Beurre cookies, André Allard, Paris church bells, James Mason's posters of foreign destinations, and each stamp has a different little picture on it, with little pictures of cities like Paris, New York, Cairo, the fact that they're so cute, the fact that there are eight altogether, eight cities, the fact that the urge to splurge is just about overwhelming, oh dear, purge, regurgitate, Lurch, the fact that something's gone wrong with my lattice here, spinning, spanning, the fact that, oh, it'll be all right once I paint it with the egg yolks, chickens, chicken feed, phone Ronny, that bad Indian restaurant we went to in Brooklyn, the fact that Brooklyn Bridge has steel wire cables with a strength factor of six, or is that the Silver Bridge, the fact that no, the Silver Bridge used eyebars instead of cables, and that's what caused all the trouble, the fact that sixty-four people fell in the Ohio River, and forty-six of them died, the fact that Leo's going to the commemoration this year, in December, fifty years, the fact that I hope he doesn't have to cross too many bridges to *get* there, remote-controlled golf bag, because they're *all* unsafe, infrastructure, the fact that there are over six hundred thousand bridges in the United States and, according to Leo, twenty thousand of them are fracture-critical, the fact that they have the bridge version of *osteoporosis*, or the metal equivalent, the fact that sixty-five thousand are structurally deficient, and almost eight thousand US bridges are both fracture-critical *and* structurally deficient, triangulated girders, through-truss design, too-thin gusset plates, cross that bridge when we come to it, *The Bridges of Madison County*, the fact that the average score for an American bridge these days is C minus, Skagit River Bridge, the fact that most of them were built before metal fatigue was even known about, the fact that they were only meant to last fifty years or so, the fact that they're all past their demolish-by date, skulls, sculling, exhausting dreams, the fact that last night I dreamt our house was suddenly in just a *terrible* state of decay and the walls were all spotted with mold, and it had happened like *overnight* or something, and I was really scared about how much it would cost to fix, the fact that the dream felt a *little* like a dream, but I knew it wasn't a dream, the fact that I begged myself to wake up, even though I knew that couldn't happen, but then I did wake up, and we've got no mold problem after all, as far as I know, touch wood, "There, there now," the fact that I think of that a lot, Marnie's "There, there now," the fact that that line and "Buck up," "Waken up and smell the coffee," "blow this pop stand," and "hack the groovy," are my current least favorite ear worms, the fact that why are people always ordering you around, ordering me around, the fact that hundreds of racehorses get shot every year because of racing injuries, the "racing industry," the fact that making horses run in circles is an *industry*, the fact that why not mice too, or frogs or something, the frog-racing industry, the fact that there already *is* a dog-racing industry, and maybe ostrich races and piglet races, rubber duck races, and dog fights and cock fights and cricket fights and who knows what, the fact that Ben says frogs did well for two hundred and fifty million years, until *we* came along, and now two hundred species of frog have disappeared, just in the last fifty years, Silver Bridge, maybe even since *I* was born, but *I didn't do it*, I promise, well, not knowingly, the fact that I released tropical terrapins into an Evanston pond, but that's about it, the fact that I never destroyed a whole *species*, I don't think, *yet*, the fact that Stacy probably thinks it *is* all my fault, that I am personally responsible for the sixth mass extinction, the fact that when the moon is waxing, the dark side is on the *left*, the fact that that is something I will never remember, the fact that it's hard enough to remember which is "waxing" and which is "waning," the fact that I think I had them totally mixed up for a while, like compulsory and mandatory, and panegyric, the fact that there's no end to how little I know about the moon, yet there it is every night, just waiting to be understood, wanting to be understood, the fact that I really don't think it *was* my fault all those frogs disappeared, the fact that in my other dream we were in the New Haven house and a passenger plane landed in the back yard, so I jumped up and said "When a plane lands in your back yard, you *leave*," and they all seemed to agree with me but they were kind of slow to move, so I tried to set an example by jumping out the front window, the fact that luckily it was a low ranch house, the fact that then I waited for them all out front, but they were so *slow*, the fact that I was scared the plane's leftover fuel would explode any *minute*, the fact that Leo was the last one out, carrying Mommy who brought her walker with her, the fact that weirdly I felt we'd be safe just out front, which wasn't really all that far away if the plane did explode, but that's about as well-thought-out as my dreams get, the fact that then I woke up and everything was okay again, no rotten house, no exploding plane, the fact that I never dreamt about exploding planes before 9/11, the fact that one modern nuclear bomb will see us *all* off, Leo says, and there won't be any point in retaliation, the fact that Trump may not understand this, the fact that he still seems to think you can threaten people with nuclear weapons, and even let a few off now and then, whenever the mood strikes you, and it won't be the end of the world, fallout, Wyandottes, the fact that Leo thinks Trump *wants* a world war, the fact that I think he just wants to be alone in the world, with a few yes men and his millions, the money he cheated people out of, the fact that he'll probably keep his gold furniture and lion skins and a few Playboy models too, "grab 'em by the ———," the fact that if he kills all the young women in the world, he'll be sorry, our back yard in New Haven, guinea pigs, the fact that I wonder if the White House is full of piles and piles of paper like ours is, and mold, and rotten eggs, and old buckeyes to trip over all the time, the fact that the White House attic must be quite a sight, LBJ's old shoes and Reagan's tennis rackets and Clinton's stained cushions and the accumulated coffee pots of forty-five presidents, along with a lot of top-secret tax returns, Woodrow Wilson's bicycle, Jackie O's napkin sets and Eleanor Roosevelt's old bulletin board, cannibalism, nuclear winter, the fact that if the world ends, the fact that I shouldn't think such things, dear me, *cannibalism*, the fact that I don't know where that came from, the fact that it'll affect the pies, the fact that he has a very sulky face, Trump I mean, the fact that he's like a kid who breaks all his toys on Christmas day and then wishes he hadn't, the fact that Trump's toys are kind of dangerous though, the fact that I'm glad Mommy and Daddy didn't live to see as much of Trump's face as we have had to, the fact that they never had to watch the end of the world, but we might, ridge collapse, extinction, extinguish, Highgate Cemetery, the fact that in London we had that room-temperature milk at break time, that tasted kind of sweet, sweeter than cold milk tastes, but I liked it once I got used to it, and the "rusks," the fact that I was pretty perplexed by the rusks at first, but they somehow tasted okay if you ate them with the milk, the fact that nobody eats *rusks* anymore, do they, even in England, the fact that does anybody eat Spam still, the fact that the eight-billionth can of it was sold in 2012, the fact that I wish people would turn their appetites more towards pie, cargo plane, cargo cult, the fact that maybe we watch too many movies, the fact that Laura Ingalls Wilder used to read out loud to Almanzo and Rose while knitting at the same time, the fact that why isn't the past tense of knitting "knat," gnat, but it's not, knot, gnome, gnu, Ganesh, genough is genough, the fact that Stacy's little friend Chantelle would never eat anything I made for her, the fact that the poor little kid hated everybody's food except her mom's, but she wanted to play with Stace so she kept coming over, the fact that she came with her own food for a while, but she seemed embarrassed about eating it, and I'd often find it somewhere in the house after she'd gone, just peanut butter sandwiches with no crusts, and some little drink, the fact that I could've made her *that*, the fact that I think she was aware that it was a bit insulting to bring your own food to somebody's house, though I tried my darnedest not to seem defensive or anything, the fact that then we had a breakthrough, the day I made fried chicken for Stace, the fact that Chantelle liked fried chicken so much she tried some of Stacey's and from then on, every time she came, I made her some fried chicken, the fact that she asked me every time if there was going to be fried chicken and she ate up all the fried chicken I could make, the fact that I became her own personal KFC, poor kid, two hundred and sixty billion chickens a year, My Little Pony, the fact that she wasn't as annoying as Abigail, who was always hungry and ate absolutely everything you gave her, but it never *took*, the fact that she was still hungry, the fact that she must've had *worms*, that kid, the fact that she was skinny as a rake, stick thin, the fact that if you gave her all the food she wanted she often threw up, so it was kind of tricky getting it right, the fact that she acted like she was *starving*, always asking for something to eat or asking when dinner was, or asking me what time it was in case it was dinnertime at *home*, the fact that then she'd call her mom to come get her but then the two of them were always in the middle of something by the time her mom came, Barbies or Sylvanians or plastic ponies, so I'd have to talk to her not very nice mom for an hour, the fact that we've still got a suitcase full of those ponies in the attic, Eleanor Roosevelt, tax returns, the fact that Jake and Gillian never seemed that into My Little Pony, and Ben would *scream* if he ever had to touch one, the fact that Marcella Hazan says you should come to the table with an open heart like a child falling into its mother's arms, cooking with love, the fact that you're supposed to love the people you cook for, or that's what the chef at Lutèce said, the fact that I don't know if I love all the people I cook for but I *try*, the fact that I certainly try not to *poison* anybody at least, love, Leo, the fact that I like *Cathy*, the fact that I think I cook for her really, the fact that I don't know if I love her customers, because some seem like loudmouths, wet brains, deer hunters, Open Carry guys, the fact that that's terrible of me to say, I know, the fact that even if they aren't the sharpest pencils in the pack, they may be nice people, *Pride and Prejudice*, the fact that it's awful, I know, but the phrase "pearls before swine" sometimes does come to mind when I'm baking and delivering my stuff, not just at Cathy's, just about anywhere, the fact that I just don't know if everybody appreciates what goes into making a good tartes tatin, or even a cinnamon roll, the fact that I do kind of doubt it, but come on, they don't have to understand 'em, just pick and buy and bite 'em, the fact that Julie's husband in *Julie & Julia* guzzles all the chocolate cake until he gets heartburn, the fact that I've seen people swallow my cinnamon rolls in one bite, the fact that it's their way of showing appreciation, I guess, but it's no way to savor the flavors, the *finesse*, gulp, Gullah, gullet, guzzle, ne plus ultra, alpha-beta cheetah, the fact that when the New York Lutèce was sold, the owners opened a new one in Vegas of all places, the fact that you have to love the people you cook for, in *Vegas*, timeshare condos, crap games, the fact that what's that fake Venice hotel called there, the Venetian or something, Fenice, Venezia, the fact that they have a tiny bit of "canal" for gondolas to row around on, kind of like a Fred Astaire set, the fact that it's just a shallow pool really, and not too inviting, the fact that they should install an *Erie Canal* in the middle of Vegas, with canal boats, shooting, shooter, the fact that Katharine Hepburn got a permanent eye infection after falling backwards into a Venice canal, shooting some picture, movie theater, the fact that she always insisted on doing her own stunt work, because she was so athletic, the fact that she never had trouble crying in a movie after that, what with the permanent eye infection and all, the fact that she cries a *lot*, the fact that *You Can't Take It With You* has almost the same cast as *It's a Wonderful Life*, but *You Can't Take It With You* is too kooky or something, the fact that it was never a big hit, and Jean Arthur's in it but she doesn't have much of a part, the fact that she's not in *It's a Wonderful Life*, the fact that she's in *Mr. Smith Goes to Washington*, Jean Arthur and Jimmy Stewart and Claude Rains, who was English originally, the fact that if a chicken has a cold, you put asafetida and butter on her nostrils, or that's what Ronny says, the fact that I was scared he'd say colloidal silver, because a lot of people swear by that for *human* colds, the fact that I don't know but *they* know, chicken colds, bird flu, the fact that Ronny drops by *all the time* now, supposedly to bring me more chicken feed, but sometimes just if he's passing, passing by, Beethoven, the fact that I really don't much feel like asking him in when I'm all alone here, the fact that Laura Ingalls Wilder sends five Indians packing when they show up at the house and she's all alone, the fact that I don't *know* Ronny all that well, so I wish he'd stop pestering me, the fact that he interrupts the whole cinnamon roll operation a couple times a month now, the fact that he's like the person from Porlock, the fact that making cinnamon rolls is a delicate *process*, and I can't always stop in the middle for any old reason, the fact that the kiwi bird might be extinct in fifty years, and some other animal, I can't remember what, giraffes or elephants, and koalas, the fact that pandas are off the endangered list now, but their *habitat*'s still on it, the fact that some zoo set up a panda sanctuary but planted the wrong kind of bamboo and the pandas wouldn't touch it, trash pandas, the fact that Cathy likes visiting on the phone, "family visit," and giving me all the gossip and telling me her troubles, the fact that she's good on the Stacy situation, because she went through it all with Marcia already, barbecued spare ribs, the fact that she keeps telling me it'll all be okay in the end, which is a little hard to imagine when Stacy won't even talk to me, the fact that maybe we should do Family Therapy, the fact that I hope Cathy likes the pies, the fact that she says she wants to sell my fanouropita too, the fact that I wonder if it works if you buy one ready-made, I mean if it still helps you find stuff, the fact that we're going to call it found cake, as opposed to *pound* cake, lost dog in the pound cake, readymades, ready meals, the fact that Cathy's dad's the real problem, the fact that he refuses to stop driving, even though he's ninety-seven and can only see with one eye and has to stick his head out the window to make a left, the fact that he no longer notices pedestrians on crosswalks at all, she says, and he can't see a thing at night, the fact that he hasn't really driven safely for about ten years, the fact that she doesn't want him to wind up in the hospital, or in *court*, or find out he's hurt somebody else, the fact that an eighty-year-old driver killed a baby last week, in its stroller, at a crosswalk, Is Tai Chi Good For You?, taekwondo, jiujitsu, the fact that Cathy told him "Injured people sue you these days" but he won't listen, so now she's banned Marcia from riding with him because the last time he drove Cathy and Art home after work, he nearly drove right into a *parked car*, the fact that his night vision *stinks*, the fact that Art was in the front seat with him and, if he hadn't warned him, Cathy's dad probably would have had a smash and probably killed *Art*, because Art was in the death seat, the fact that I hardly ever know what to say when Cathy tells me this stuff, the fact that who am *I* to give advice, the fact that Mommy passed away in her sixties, and neither of them ever got *that* old, the fact that all I could think of saying was maybe her dad could donate his car to a radio station or something and get some money off his taxes for it, the fact that she really liked that idea, but she still doesn't know how to persuade him, the fact that of course it's not easy for an old guy to live without a car, though Art and Cathy already bring him all the food he needs, the fact that he gets anything he wants from the Country Shoppe, but they've been doing that for years, the fact that there certainly aren't a lot of buses if he wants to go someplace, but he doesn't really want to go anywhere, or that's what Cathy says, except maybe the pharmacy, and the barber's, the fact that Leo's mom and dad passed on a while back too, so I really don't know what it's like to have a ninety-seven-year-old to worry about, the fact that Cathy's dad's main interest outside the home is going to pick up his prescriptions but they could deliver, or there are taxis, Lyft, Uber, Up Hail, the fact that actually he could probably get *Ronny* to drive him around all the time if he wanted, the fact that Ronny's often at a loose end, the fact that Ronny could pick all kinds of stuff up for him if he asked, and save Cathy having to get his Coke and toilet paper all the time, the fact that I should tell her about Ronny, the fact that maybe he and her dad would get along well, the fact that maybe her dad would actually *like* a guy like Ronny turning up all the time, the fact that Daddy also used to cry when the maid sticks up for George's dad, in *It's a Wonderful Life*, and when George and Mary decide to get married, talking to old Hee-Haw on the old-fashioned phone, with Mary's mom eavesdropping on the extension at the top of the stairs, the fact that it's hard not to cry when everybody brings all the money they have to get George out of a jam, after he's almost committed suicide, jumping off a bridge, jumper, the fact that that kid jumped off the Golden Gate Bridge and *survived*, the fact that jumpers are another major factor in bridge design, because bridges always attract depressed people for some reason, the fact that I guess they stir the imagination, the fact that *It's a Wonderful Life* is kind of like a dream, especially when Clarence erases George's whole entire existence for a while, the fact that it's more like a nightmare, when George finally catches on that he's never been born, never existed, and because of that his brother Harry passed away as a little boy because George wasn't there to save him, so Harry never saved the troop ship in the war, the fact that it's creepy that George's widowed mom runs a boarding house and she doesn't recognize him, and his uncle's in the nut-house and Bailey Brothers Building & Loan is long gone and so is anything that was ever good about Bedford Falls, the fact that the blonde lady's become a prostitute, Ida, Ivy, I forget her name, and Mary's a spinster librarian, who wears *glasses*, "She's just about to close up the library!", the fact that

I wonder if Newcomerstown would be any different if *I'd* never been born, the fact that I don't think it would, the fact that as far as I know I haven't contributed much to this place, the fact that I haven't saved anybody's life, except maybe with my own kids now and then, as any mom would, without even noticing, the fact that I'd probably remember it if I had saved anybody *else*, no, the fact that I'm much too shy to save anybody's life, the fact that shy people really are a burden on humanity, if you think about it, the fact that their cowardice is no help to anybody, the fact that shyness interferes with compassion, I'm sure, TED talk, hip twinge, *Violet*, the fact that her name's Violet, purple martins, the fact that I'm afraid that if I'd never been born nobody would miss me one iota, ion, eon, Ithaca, Peolia, though there would be fewer tartes tatin around maybe, and there'd be no Sloppy Joes on the table tonight, "come to the table with an open heart," but there'd be no kids here to *eat* my Sloppy Joes, so that wouldn't bother anybody either, the fact that that thought makes *me* cry, Daddy crying, the fact that I don't want my kids never to have been *born*, or me either, p. chops with brandy and sour cream, madeleines, candied yams, marshmallow fluff, styptic stick, shoebill storks, the fact that I always liked Sloppy Joes but we never had them at home, only at school, the fact that Leo never got Sloppy Joes at home either, only hamburgers, the fact that in my family we had hamburgers without buns sometimes, which Leo thinks is *disgraceful*, the fact that I do too kind of, now, the fact that I always preferred grilled cheese sandwiches, the fact that they give kids tater tots at school, the fact that I don't know what's even in a tater tot and I hate to think, the fact that all I know is they sound like they're *extruded*, the tater tots, not the kids, the fact that Leo has a thing about cheeseburgers, the fact that he has to have a cheeseburger just about every week or he starts to feel funny, crumple, crinkle cut, cut and dried, cut to the chase, an open heart, open-heart surgery, the fact that *I* had open-heart surgery, the fact that *Leo's* very open-hearted, and never bad-tempered, the fact that I could be more adventurous, I mean about family dinners, since here I am all day, the fact that I just end up making the same old stuff again and again and

never try new things, the fact that I'm kind of stuck in a rut, but life
sure is easier that way, the fact that after cooking all day I don't always
feel all that interested in what we eat for dinner, doggone it, the fact
that I'm too busy to make oysters Rockefeller, oysters fried, stewed or
nude, "ersters," like in that book Leo got me, the fact that I hope it
wasn't a hint he wants *me* to make all that stuff, because, my word, I
ain't got time to make no soft-shell crabs and oyster loaves, deviled
crab, crab boil, crab cakes, catfish cakes, clambakes, clam dunks, fried
clams, clams casino, rice and shrimp bake, Bayou fried shrimp, creole
shrimp, broiled shrimp, crayfish, mudbugs, crawdads and scallops,
crawfish étouffé, stuffed flounder, deep-fried sand dabs, Lake Erie
perch chowder, but who'd want *that*, or Dijon crusted catfish, million
dollar mussels, cod ceviche, cioppino, brook trout, lake trout, lemon
garlic tilapia, codfish balls, tuna fish balls, tuna and potato chip loaf,
jellied tuna fish salad, tuna fish spread, pot luck tuna, tuna à la king,
tuna fish surprise, the fact that the surprise is it's got noodles, sardines
on toast, gefilte fish, mock turtle soup, Lobster Thermidor, Lobster
Newburg, Lobster de Yonghe, the wild turtles in the back yard in
Rome, the fact that Pierre passed away in Rome, when I was younger
than Ben, I mean Jake, and the Italian vet crossed himself, Swedish
meatballs, hog maw, timbales, maple syrup pork loin, pulled pork,
sausage squash bake, shish kebabs, cheese and veal birds, Wiener
schnitzel, veal cutlets, veal scaloppine, eggs Benedict, Easter eggs, egg
creams, shirred eggs, Adam and Eve on a raft, egg foo yung, Western
omelets, burgoo, knish, jibarito, bratwurst, the fact that it makes you
sick thinking about all this stuff, the fact that it's probably all really
bad for people, braunschweiger sausage, buckeye dumplings, dump-
erlings, quesadillas, jambalaya, mole poblano, habaneros, paprikash,
bologna and hot dogs, fricassee, kasha, couscous and quinoa, grits
cheese grits, cereal, honey glazed ham, ham balls, luau ribs, pork chops
with pepper jelly sauce, jellied pig's feet, baked Virginia ham, pork
chops, cabbage and apples, chow mein, chop suey, sukiyaki, spaetzle,
Rink Tum Diddy rarebit, the fact that Leo can't want that, surely,
Rink Tum Diddy, the fact that it sounds like Rip Van Winkle, Doreen

Van Kinkel, the fact that there's osso buco, which Leo might like, and Wiener schnitzel, veal saltimbocca, porcupine meatballs, ah, porcupine meatballs, Mommy, company pot roast, anything au gratin, mock paté de foie gras, liver and onions, mortadella, Irish stew, drop biscuits, cookies, blini, blintzes, flapjacks, Slapjack, cornmeal bread, cornmeal mush pie, or mush cakes, mush, the fact that that was George Washington's favorite breakfast, mush, the numbness of muted beings, make-ahead mash, hush puppies, the fact that alternatively we could have tidbits in blankets, cheese and rice croquettes, cheese and bacon pinwheels, not Scottie pinwheel, and Hoosier corn queso dip, California dip, corn chips, guacamole, salsa, deviled eggs, Kentucky biscuits, Arkansas sin, cheese straws, popcorn, spiced pumpkin seeds, and shrimps with cocktail sauce, cock, cook, butt, boob, chitterlings, pierogi, pizza, copycat gravy, poor man's steak and thrift stew, quick tomato aspic, *Emergency Aspic*, the fact that what *kind* of an emergency, I wonder, like is anybody about to starve or something if they don't get some aspic quick, Geauga maple pork loin roast, pig wings, scrapple, Amish haystacks, carne adorada, goetta, runzas, bierocks, slow-cooked Kielbasa sausage and beer, short ribs, maple glazed ribs, barbecued spare ribs wafting across the back yards, boiled hams, baked hams, roast beef, beef tips, the fact that I already have *Abby's* recipe for beef tips, *and* her BBQ sauce recipe, fried onions, Abby's basement, Abby's furnace, corned beef jerky, creamed chipped beef, corned beef and cabbage, beef brisket, braised beef and onions, chuck roast, Swiss steak, ground beef Stroganoff, Boston boiled dinners, Daddy's pot roast, meatloaf with eggs and green peppers in it, Abby's recipe, fake-brick wallpaper, Go-Go and chocolate chip ice cream for dessert, flank steak, minute steak, Brunswick stew, burgers au poivre, hash, squirrel gravy, possum stew, chili con carne, five-way chili, Cincinnati chili parlors, Skyline versus Empress, roast turkey and dressing with cranberry sauce, Chicago-style roast duck, turkey soup, turkey chili, deep-fried turkey in a trash can, chiles rellenos casserole, Bierock casserole, pizza spaghetti casserole, *Shipwreck* Casserole, the fact that you could follow it with Earthquake Cake, big bear stew,

Hungarian goulash, Hunghoulian gairlosh, hotchpotch, spaghetti Bolognese, garlicky spaghetti, Cajun spaghetti, home-style macaroni, macaroni and cheese, Amish church noodles, veal steak with noodles, tortellini, cannelloni, meatballs and noodles Monte Carlo, quiche Lorraine, Welsh Rabbit, Piglet, Eeyore, lasagne, baked manicotti putanesca, baked ziti, stuffed shells, the fact that I should think more about vegetable dishes, the fact that you're supposed to get your family to eat their greens, the fact that Stacy likes them, like steamed spaghetti squash, the fact that Abby introduced me to spaghetti squash, the fact that vegetables would be a relief after all that heavy stuff, baked Hubbard squash and acorn squash, collard greens, fiddlehead ferns, but vegetables can be heavy too, spinach ravioli, pumpkin ravioli, lima bean casserole, sweet potato casserole, Yankee beans, party beans, red beans and rice, Tex-Mex rice, caramelized carrots, copper pennies, fried okra, salsify, Texas caviar, corn pones, fried confetti corn, cowpeas, scalloped potatoes, deluxe scalloped potatoes, silver dollar scalloped potatoes, chive-whipped potatoes, potato kugel, potluck potatoes, hash browns, home fries, Delmonico potatoes, baked potatoes, Chantilly potatoes, Kentucky bourbon sweet potatoes, shoestring potatoes, parmesan truffle fries, more tater tots, succotash, sauerkraut, creamed cabbage, liberty cabbage, sweet and sour cabbage, purple cabbage and apples, sautéed angelica, coleslaw, baked stuffed tomatoes or peppers, fried green tomatoes, pickled green tomatoes, piccalilli, Ozark pickles, green tomato pickle, pickled beans, hot pickled beans, watermelon pickle, Indian relish, braised onions, pickled beets, oh, Harvard beets, the fact that I like those, the fact that there's always Company Cauliflower, the fact that asparagus au gratin's easy enough, but I don't like candied yams with marshmallows, the fact that I don't know how anybody eats that, but the kids like them, turnip greens stew, scrapple, maque choux, eggplant parmigiana like Mommy used to make, and why not a salad, saladsky, cuke, tzuke, zucchini, Waldorf salad, Caesar salad, Louisville rice salad, alligator pear salad, chef's salad, cobb salad, tuna salad, chicken salad, potato salad, noodle salad, cardinal salad, conch salad, zucchini salad, orange

Jell-O salad, seven-layer salad, cornbread panzanella salad, Michigan salad, blueberry and tortellini fruit salad, fruit salad molds, with blue cheese dressing, thousand island dressing, Paul Newman vinaigrette, schmeers of mayo and cream cheese, cottage cheese, potlatch and celery salt, Worcestershire sauce and Tabasco sauce, Avery Island, family meals, the Silent Act, the fact that I was like Gillian when I was a kid, the fact that nobody ever listened to me, the fact that I never had much of anything to say either, but Gillian does, the fact that in a big family it's hard to get heard, the fact that Mommy's best dish was fried pork chops with sour cream and brandy, the fact that we all felt really proud that she knew how to make that, and I think she was sort of proud of it too, the fact that it seemed very sophisticated to us because you pour on some brandy at the end and set *fire* to it, the fact that not everybody in Evanston was eating flambéed food in those days, the fact that after the brandy stage you add the sour cream, and cover it and cook for a few more minutes, and it really was delicious, the fact that I should do it for Leo, the fact that maybe even the kids would like it, the fact that I really should make that, the fact that I've still got her recipe around here somewhere, and the Revere Ware skillet she used to cook them in, with its lid, but I don't think the kids would go for it, the fact that the kids know what they want to eat, barnyard in Connemara, donkeys and puppies, pillows, the fact that American kids seem to be born knowing they've gotta have hamburg-ers and French fries, freedom fries, and Coke, though I never liked Coke, which is very unpatriotic of me, the fact that I always got root beer instead, the fact that come to think of it, I'm sure the kids would love it if I set fire to something on the stove, plane in the back yard, the fact that it would be fun just to see their faces, as I flipped the fiery pork chops with my swordie, the fact that I could get a flame-thrower or whatever you call it, like for crème brulée, trigger happy, trigger, Tigger, Piglet, Eeyore, the fact that the other day some dad shot his estranged wife and two daughters in Cincinnati, but one of the daugh-ters *survived*, and the dad didn't notice, the fact that he was too busy shooting *himself* by then, the fact that he left a note explaining he'd killed his wife because she left him, and he'd killed the kids so they wouldn't have to grow up in foster homes after he killed their mom and himself, dog pound, Lost and Found Cake, panda sanctuary, the fact that now that wounded child *will* have to live with foster parents, but at least she'll have a *life,* the fact that we should probably foster kids, and we *could* if we got bunk beds, but I don't have enough time for the kids I've got already, and one of them isn't even speaking to me anymore, so I probably wouldn't even be *allowed* to foster anybody else's kids, audition tape, Pottersville, the fact that I don't need more stress either, the fact that I'm almost the age Mommy was when she had the stroke, the fact that visiting her in the hospital was the worst thing that's ever happened to me, the sight of her like that, with tubes and things, her swollen head, the fact that it was so shocking, the fact that it broke me, the shock of it broke me, the fact that I changed overnight, the fact that I could never really love anybody again, or not as much anyway as I might have before, Clarence, because I could never risk going through that kind of loss again, the fact that my capacity for love was nipped in the bud, crippled, broken, the fact that I sure shouldn't *foster* anybody, the fact that what if they put it on the form at the fostering agency, "Were you ever emotionally damaged?", the fact that it would probably be multiple choice, like were you ever emotionally damaged 1, hardly at all, 2, just a smidgeon, 3, somewhat, 4, substantially, or 5, a cataclysmic amount, but that's silly, pain scale, the COMFORT scale, the handlebar in the bathroom, the booster seat on the toilet, Mommy's walker, her special leg brace, the foot rests on her wheelchair, the solitaire games, her bedside commode, her stair-climber machine, her lank hair that I washed for her sometimes in the sink, the fact that, dear me, I must hold the world record on grudges and gripes, the fact that it's not just Hungary that's bad about Syrian refugees, the fact that the US won't help the Syrian refugees either, that little boy Omran, the fact that I always get Susan Sontag mixed up with Doris Lessing, the fact that Susan Sontag was photographed by Annie Leibowitz, I don't know about Doris Lessing, the fact that maybe she was too, the fact that what do I care who photographed Susan Sontag, the fact that I associate Susan Sontag with Mommy, maybe because Mommy read her, the fact that Katharine Hepburn was good friends with Howard Hughes, the fact that they were a couple for a little while, Leo DiCaprio, Leo, the fact that I think Susan Sontag and Annie Liebowitz were a couple too, the fact that, according to Stephen Hawking the human world will end within a thousand years, but I think it could be a lot sooner, and my response to this is to make more *pies* and read *recipe books*, the fact that, I mean, gosh, talk about fiddling while Rome burns, Ohio Blue Tip matches, but ya gotta *eat*, the fact that every day we gotta eat, watch, fish, bread, butter, the fact that Leo says movies are never as good as the book they're based on, and no matter how good a movie is, it won't be good in the same *way*, the fact that, like, *Tess* is a pretty good movie but not the same as the book, strawberries, blackberries, iceberg lettuce, milk, cucumbers, shallots, flour, liquor store, plums, 12, a dozen, the fact that seventy-five percent of the women in American jails are *moms*, tornado, the fact that the roof caved in on a lady in Cincinnati, and the guy on TV said she was "an elderly female which was located in the kitchen part of the house," the fact that what is so hard about saying "an old woman died in her kitchen," the fact that it's so *shameful*, incarcerating moms I mean, the fact that Tabasco doesn't grow its peppers on Avery Island anymore, not since Katrina, the fact that eighty-three of the soldiers voted for the Gnadenhutten massacre, eighty-three, and only seventeen against, M-16, AR-15, the fact that hundreds of pilot whales have beached themselves off the California coast, because people let off bombs underwater, the fact that *why are they letting off bombs in the Pacific*, the fact that it could be the noise from the container ships that drives whales crazy, the fact that sulfur dioxide and sewage from container ships cause oceanic dead zones, dachshunds, Active Shooter Situation, the fact that whales will be *glad* when humans disappear in a thousand years, if they somehow outlast us, the fact that *this* is the world I give to my kids, *this*, whales, wails, *wh*, carrot salad, no raisins, the statue of Wilde lounging on a rock in Merrion Square, with quite a silly expression on his face, the fact that

Abby and Hoag went to Ireland once, Knox, the fact that they both
had Irish ancestry, the fact that Abby always knew the order in which
to do everything, like you dust first, *before* you vacuum, which I always
forget, *wh*ich I always forget, the fact that I never learnt that stuff, the
fact that nobody ever taught me, *wh*istle, *wh*ittle, *wh*ite, *wh*atnot,
*wh*atevs, the fact that *I* grew up like an *orphan*, a foster child, "Little
Orphan Annie," Anne Shirley, *Anne of Green Gables*, because Mommy
got sick, the fact that I suppose I could've learnt housekeeping from
Abby, but I just watched, I didn't really take it in, Hoosier poet, the
fact that container ships cause half the smog in LA too, all because it's
cheaper to ship stuff all around the world than pay workers at home,
sulfur dioxide, the fact that I kind of feel like beaching *myself* right now,
every time a motorcycle revs up outside the window, zither, Zimmer,
Ziploc, hemlock, xylophone, the fact that I wish people wouldn't
blame eagles for all their problems, "I'm not a dumb critter. Won't the
law give me my freedom?", the New Deal, prisons, bondmen,

·   ·   ·   ·

The approach of rain. She always knew when it was coming, she
smelled it in the stones. She knew if concentric rings on water were
caused by rain and not frogs, fish, leaves or bugs.

A porcupine wandered past. After many porcupine failures in the
past – sore nose, seeping paw – the lioness had no love of them or their
meat, but she couldn't risk quills piercing a curious kitten. She knew
how to flip a porcupine over on its back before the quills could come.

She leapt on the awkward creature before the cubs had even seen
it. They were soon chirruping in appreciation of the porcupine's soft
belly flesh, though the taste was new to them and it was hardly a snack
between three.

The previous day she had shared with them the intricate maneuver
of squeezing the dung out of a deer before you eat its tripe.

While the cubs gnawed at the quills and tugged in play at the empty
shell of the porcupine's hide, the lioness stood again atop her boulder,

sniffing as usual for her shunned lover's scent. Someday, the kittens would learn to stand still, to move so slowly and silently you can't be seen. Not everything is about scampering headlong. A lion is formed for the art of not moving at all.

The kittens eventually joined her on the boulder to suckle in the rain. Not sleepy, they bravely leapt on her tail, pretending it was a snake: it was long and wide and firm enough to be a rattler. They would kill it once and for all, or exhaust themselves trying. They got so involved that they fell back hissing, surprised and annoyed, when its black tip curled back up once again, immune.

.   .   .   .

the fact that I dreamt I went to return some stuff to the Kinkels but I forgot the *sliced cheese*, the fact that I kept thinking in the dream, boy, am I getting forgetful, the fact that I also forgot to put any *clothes* on, and was only wearing a short thin button-down shirt and nothing else, the fact that the Kinkels were both asleep when I got there so I had to wake them up and ask for clothes, the fact that it was all pretty embarrassing, especially when Doreen went and got me a sort of onesie pajama outfit to put on, and Jerry looked away until I got it on, the fact that I'd left our house at the same time as Nanya and Leo were leaving, and neither of them seemed to even notice I was practically naked, or they didn't say anything anyway, the fact that Nanya was going off to try and get an acting job, and Leo was just off to work, the fact that I don't know where any of that came from, the fact that I'm sure Nanya's never wanted to act, the fact that all she cares about is art, the fact that ever since *Annie Get Your Gun*, Stacy's been on a musicals kick and she's now watched, in stunned silence, *Oklahoma*, *Fiddler on the Roof*, *High Society*, *White Christmas*, *Singin' in the Rain*, *An American in Paris*, *State Fair*, *My Fair Lady*, and *The Sound of Music*, the fact that while she watches, she sometimes helps me peel apples, so I'm all for it, the fact that she's never shown any interest in musicals before, or singing and dancing, even when her friends bring over their guitars, and start strumming away down in the basement, the fact that we tried to get all the kids playing some instrument once but it didn't really work, the fact that we couldn't convince them to *practice*, Pineapple Upside-down Cake, the fact that we started Stace on the piano but she wanted to become an instant sensation, the fact that Stacy won't do anything unless she's stunning at it, the fact that I told her to try not to think about what music could do for her but what she could do for music, but no dice, the fact that they barely even touch their instruments now, but who can blame them, the fact that who wants to play the *recorder*, or squeak away on a violin, the fact that Gillian tried, thankfully, for only a couple weeks, the fact that Ethan played the bassoon and Phoebe played the flute and I played the cello for a short time, the fact that I still love the sound of a *bassoon* though, the fact that music isn't taught at school much anymore, unless you want to be in the JROTC marching band, the fact that Stacy only seems to like trance music or trap music or something, mitti attar, so her sudden liking for old-fashioned musicals is a real mystery, seismic shift, the fact that she likes the pure authentic old Hollywood technicolor kind, not black-and-white Fred Astaire movies, and nothing too recent either, like *Grease* or *Dirty Dancing,* or *Cats* or *Oliver!* or *Hamilton* or *Avenue Q*, the fact that she just likes the old classics, the goofier the better, the fact that it's hard to get Leo to watch musicals, really hard, the fact that he says he can't stand people jumping up on the furniture and belting out a song, arms akimbo, he just can't, the fact that he only likes *operas*, and maybe Gilbert and Sullivan once in a while, on a CD, opera, operetta, musical, musicale, the fact that I think it's a wonder Hollywood ever managed to get *anybody* to watch musicals, the fact that he says there's always a scene in a Rogers & Hammerstein musical when the women run around in their underwear, the fact that he thinks either Rogers or Hammerstein had a thing about antique underwear, or else the audience did, the fact that anyway, at some point in the picture, the actresses all have to strip down to their corsets and petticoats and bodices and shifts and hoop frames and stuff, like in *Oklahoma*, Katie's BBQ sauce recipe, where all the women are getting ready for the picnic or barn dance or whatever, the fact that there's too much ballet dancing in that one too, and far too much of that Aunt Ellen, and Laurey's dream, the fact that that dream goes *on and on*, the fact that I don't like *Oklahoma*, the fact that it's based on a book by Edna Ferber though, who wrote *Giant*, which was pretty good, the fact that the icky sister in *Giant* is a bit like Aunt Ellen in *Oklahoma*, a lonely, frustrated, bossy type, the fact that I hope *I'm* not like that, "She's just about to close up the library!", the fact that middle-aged women usually mean trouble, in the *movies* I mean, unless they stay quietly in the background, the fact that Rod Steiger is really *scary*, the fact that I think he's too scary, the fact that I don't know if Stace was scared exactly, but she didn't really take to *Oklahoma*, the fact that she said there was too much ballet-dancing, the fact that the thing about musicals is they're sort of out-of-this-world, but I think that's what people *like* about them, *Mary Poppins*, the fact that maybe if you watch enough people capering around caterwauling, you stop thinking about your own problems, for a minute, the fact that Stace says *The Music Man* is too surreal for her, too corny, "T rhymes with P and that stands for pool...," itch, "too surreal," the fact that everybody has their sticking points, I guess, the fact that I hope she doesn't think *State Fair* is "*real*," the fact that I got her to watch *The Sound of Music* next, just to see what she made of it, the fact that I don't like nun movies much, mush, the nun who shook Mommy, but I like that Christopher Plummer, the fact that he has such sad eyes, ♫ *Edelweiss, edelweiss* ♫, the fact that *The Sound of Music* must be the true test of a person's Hollywood musical kick, what with Julie Andrews twirling around in her dirndl, and all those chirpy kids in jodhpurs or whatever it is little Austrian boys wear, leghorns, shoe horn, no, *lederhosen*, lederhosen, the von Trapp family, Tschagenny, wool flower, 60cm, *Give me your tired, your poor, your huddled masses*, the fact that masses of stink bugs are arriving now, which is good news for chickens, not so good for homeowners, the fact that if you vacuum them up, the stink bugs, not the homeowners, your vacuum smells for *months*, the fact that purple sea urchins are on the rise too, the fact that they chomp through kelp forests, the fact that "vacuum" is a strange word, the fact that they've been eating up the whole Californian kelp forest, urchins not vacuum cleaners, and now they've started eating barnacles too, the fact that they've turned into omnivores, the fact that the Blob killed off a lot of kelp too, the fact that it drifted over to California a few years ago and they can't get rid of it, the fact that sunflower starfish used to eat the purple urchins but starfish got sea star wasting syndrome, which makes their two dozen legs start to fall off, the fact that purple loosestrife wrecks wetlands, the fact that rhinoceros beetles can fly, the fact that Julie Andrews doesn't care about kelp, the fact that all Julie Andrews cares about is the Alps, the fact that neither of us could stand all the nun stuff, so we fast-forwarded, the fact that I think maybe they used real nuns to play the nuns, because not one of them seemed to know how to act, Mommy as a little girl, her embroidered picture frame, the fact that Stacy got hooked on the movie though, and lapped it up, the fact that thanks to Stacy and *The Sound of Music*, I made six tartes tatin, the fact that just when things start getting romantic in the gazebo with Christopher Plummer, Julie Andrews starts *warbling*, the fact that you'd think she'd be *swooning*, or spooning, the fact that it's enough to put any man off his stride, the fact that there's no chemistry between the two of them whatsoever anyway, no way, no how, or am I just jealous, the fact that Stacy noticed in the credits that it says "with the partial use of ideas by Georg Hurdalek," the partial use, the fact that I guess his ideas as a whole sucked, so they could only use a few little bits, the fact that I bet Georg was sore about that, the fact that then we watched the extras, and not everything went right when they were making that movie, the fact that when they were filming the boat scene, Julie Andrews almost let one of the kids drown by accident, the fact that she knew the kid couldn't swim too well so she'd personally promised to keep an eye on her during the boating scene, but in the chaos of the boat turning over Julie Andrews forgot all about the kid, who was left to struggle out on her own, Olympic pool, ♫ *The Stars and Stripes Forever* ♫, the fact that this is another reason why every kid should

443

learn how to swim, just in case they're ever in a boat with Julie Andrews, the fact that she'll be too busy yodeling to save them, the fact that the words "Olympic pool" always fill me with dread, the fact that that kind of pool is always too deep and dark for me, Plummer, plumber, Tulip, ♫ *Tiptoe through the two lips* ♫, the fact that actually one of those nuns was a ghost singer, just like Debbie Reynolds in *Singin' in the Rain*, the fact that she did the singing for Deborah Kerr in *The King and I*, and for Audrey Hepburn in *My Fair Lady* and about a million other big stars who couldn't sing a note, the fact that Lauren Bacall can sing but you wish she wouldn't, the fact that this singer, whateverhernameis, got paid $400 per movie and was ordered to never reveal that she'd done all the singing for all these famous stars that everybody thinks could sing but they couldn't, the fact that you'd think they would've paid her a bit better than that for taking the back seat that way, and keeping it so secret, but they didn't, the fact that in the end she got sick of that whole setup and blabbed, the Blob, skinflints, penny-pinchers, the fact that those were big hit movies, Technicolor, North Korean nuclear missiles, Marni Nixon, the fact that she was called Marni Nixon and she just died last year, *Marnie*, the fact that Dennis Quaid sued somebody for telling him *Brokeback Mountain* was just going to be a little independent film, the fact that they tricked him into agreeing to taking a small fee, and then the movie grossed a whole lot of money, big hit, gross, and he felt he'd been misled, the fact that we never saw *Brokeback Mountain*, Chattanooga Choo Choo, Oscar Mayer, funnel cake, lederhosen, hydrangea, the fact that I just gave Jake a box of nurdles to play with, and look at him, totally absorbed, the fact that nun movies are usually about luring new novices *into* the order, but in *The Sound of Music* Julie Andrews deserts the order in favor of family life, nuclear family, nuke attack, nunnery, order, *Roger & Me*, Roger and out, Coast Guard, flinty voice, vocal fry, purple urchin, purple martin, the fact that they got almost every Austrian detail *wrong* in that movie, apparently, except that Austrians still drove on the left, before the war, left, right, left, right, the fact that Christopher Plummer plays the father, Captain von Trapp, the fact that he didn't like the "Edelweiss" song, the fact that he thought it was too schmaltzy, the fact that he drew the line at "*Edelweiss*," but the rest of the songs were *okay* with him, go figure, Texas tea, the fact that we had to sing "Edelweiss" at school, along with a lot of *Mary Poppins* songs, oh dear, the fact that Mary Poppins is a lot like Maria von Trapp, maybe because Julie Andrews did them both, the perfect nanny, the fact that Bella Worth knew all those musicals by heart, the fact that the guys making *The Sound of Music* really thought "Edelweiss" was going to be their "Marseillaise" moment, but somehow a bunch of stiff little kids performing "Edelweiss" on a stage somewhere in Austria never had the same impact Paul Henreid had singing "The Marseillaise" in the middle of Rick's Cafe in Casablanca, the café in Cambridge, Cambridge, *Ohio*, not Cambridge, Mass., opening cereal packets, the fact that "Edelweiss" just doesn't come close, no matter what Bella Worth might have said, the fact that Ingrid Bergman falls back in love with Paul Henreid because of that song, Paul Henreid lighting two cigarettes at once with Bette Davis, "The Marseillaise," "Edelweiss," "Liebestraum," the fact that Bette Davis gets drunk well, the fact that who else is good at that, Meryl Streep, the fact that you'd *think* the easiest way for an actor to act drunk would be to actually *be* drunk, but it doesn't work that way, the fact that usually Hollywood doesn't let adulteresses get away with anything, like Bette Davis finds herself in a real jam in *Deception*, and Barbara Stanwyck's doomed from the start in *Double Indemnity*, the fact that she's such a tease, the fact that only Ingrid Bergman gets away with it, loving two men, the fact that maybe she's just too beautiful for the audience to be mad at her for long, the fact that she comes off looking sort of innocent, just a woman torn in two by love, and her punishment is she loses Bogie, the fact that her excuse is she didn't *know* Paul Henreid was still alive when she fell in love with Humphrey Bogart, the fact that in real life, though, she got blacklisted or something for running off with Rossellini, the fact that everybody passes away in *Double Indemnity*, except maybe Edward G. Robinson, the fact that Fred MacMurray was not a very nice guy, in real life, the fact that he betrayed someone, I think it was Mitchell Leisen, the fact that Mitchell Leisen needed money bad and Fred MacMurray wouldn't give it to him, and he was mean about it too or something, the fact that I can't really remember anymore, the fact that Fred MacMurray plays a bad guy in *The Apartment*, and a guy who turns bad in *Double Indemnity*, but in that other one, *There's Always Tomorrow*, he's just a poor neglected husband, the fact that he ends up staying with his wife that time instead of running off with Barbara Stanwyck, Rex the Walkie-Talkie Robot Man, Hollywood Spats, Spats in *Some Like It Hot*, "Zowie!", "Goodbye, Charlie," the fact that *The Sound of Music* has such a gloomy undercurrent, I don't know why, the fact that, to me, Nazis seem a bit out of place in a light musical, but maybe that's just me, the fact that *America* has a pretty gloomy undercurrent these days, ♫ *I'm just wild about animal crackers!* ♫, Gnadenhutten, the broken Wedgwood pitcher, galoshes, PFOAs, Jason Bourne, the fact that a man just dropped a three-year-old girl from a bridge over the Tuscarawas, but she's going to be okay, "Edelweiss," Christopher Plummer, Molotov cocktail, the fact that her wrist was broken but she's all right otherwise, the fact that the *dad* jumped too, and he survived too, the fact that he's now under arrest for attempted murder, the fact that first he dangled the little girl over the bridge, while the police tried to talk him out of it, and then he let her fall, broken wrist, broken, the fact that, according to the self-defense book, if a man bothers you in a movie theater, you're supposed to try to talk him out of it, and if *that* fails, you just start pulling the hairs at his temple, his *temple*, chapel, nuns, the fact that if that fails, you pull one end of his tie tight, so it starts to *choke* him, the fact that I don't think that'll work, because most men in Ohio don't *wear* ties anymore, the fact that this is the trouble with a self-defense manual from the seventies, the fact that the clothes are all out of date, long hair, damp towel, countertop, long hair, the fact that some men have such a temple, I mean *temper*, the fact that Maria von Trapp had a temper too, the fact that she was famous for it, the fact that she was a bit of a toughie, apparently, plaster of Paris, the fact that I don't think Julie Andrews conveys Maria's dark side, the fact that she's too busy serenading the woods, Austrian-style, the fact that the woman who shot both her daughters in Texas was just in a "bad mood," nun shaking Mommy, PTA, the fact that you can also bash the long-haired guy's nose with the heel of your hand, but you have to do it hard, otherwise you might only "provoke a struggle," which you don't want, with a long-haired guy in a dark movie theater, bright yellow sou'wester, the fact that the von Trapps went completely broke when they got to America and had to run a ski resort in Vermont, the fact that you'd think they'd be in clover after *The Sound of Music*, but actually they were gypped out of millions by the movie-makers, just like Dennis Quaid, only worse maybe, the fact that I hate to think what happened the day Maria von Trapp realized they'd been tricked out of their cut of the dough, the fact that the hills of Vermont must've been alive to the sound of her blowing a gasket, the fact that Stace and I also watched *State Fair*, itch, the next day, but Stace didn't help much with the apple-peeling that time, not because *State Fair*'s that fascinating, but because she'd just done her nails, the fact that I didn't mind, and her nails *were* amazing, the fact that they were half orange and half green, with gold spangles, but they were elegant still, not crazee or anything, the fact that she has nice fingers, and that helps, the fact that she really should play the piano, the fact that you grind your foot into the long-haired man's shin, and then, when he bends over, you grab him by the collar, and pull his head down, and that somehow gets him in the Adam's apple, the fact that any attack on the Adam's apple is highly recommended, my Candy-Apple Red kneading machine, purple urchins, the fact that it's good she doesn't bite them, her *nails*, I mean, not molesters in movie theaters, ♫ *dollars to donuts* ♫, the fact that now I can't get that song out of my head, just that one line, "dollars to donuts," habit, habitrail, the fact that we don't have any nail-biters in this family but Jake still sucks his thumb, the fact that *I* was a thumb-sucker, and Phoebe was the nail-biter, and I don't think Ethan *had* any bad habit like that, the fact that I found it so hard to stop sucking my thumb, as hard as learning to ride a bike, or whistling, the fact that I've never mastered whistling, *wh*istling, the fact that I can't even say it right, the fact that I guess I found just about everything hard, the fact that I balked at every little kid hurdle, nurdle, and now every adult hurdle too, the fact that I finally gave up sucking my thumb though, because by ten it gets embarrassing having to explain it to your friends at slumber parties, the fact that still it seemed to take everything I had in me to stop myself sucking my thumb, and to learn to ride a bike too, and I think I used up all the willpower I had in me for *life* on those two tasks, the fact that I haven't tried that hard on anything since, except maybe my lemon drizzle cake, or making Butter Marshmallow Party Frosting, the fact that it's very compli- cated, "drool yet," the fact that Stacy got a big kick out of that, not my frosting problems, the way they rhymed "Juliet" with "drool yet," and also "in love" and "certain of," the fact that the girl who falls for Dana Andrews is so *innocent*, I guess because she's a country girl, the fact that I asked Leo how cutiepies like that last a *minute* in the world, but he said, "Cutiepies are safe in that world," the fact that I always worry about the romance between the prize pigs, the fact that there's a disconnect somewhere, it has no closure, the fact that all the *human* romances work out fine, and the pigs' courtship is just dropped, the fact that all they had to do was show some black and white piglets at the end, just to make things crystal clear, Hollywood-style, that every- thing worked out, but they didn't do it, boarlets, bee-bee guns, Bazooka Bubble Gum, Bazooka Joe, Superman, Ben as a pirate, the fact that I really can't get that "dollars to donuts" thing out of my head, pigs, "Pigs is pigs," the fact that I like keeping Stacy company, when she's nice to me, but I don't really like these musicals, the fact that sometimes I find myself longing for a tornado or something to interrupt the shenanigans, I mean a tornado in the *movie*, not in Newcomerstown, like especially when there's too much singing, ♫ *dollars to donuts* ♫, the fact that sometimes you just think these people need a little shakeup, like the tornado in *The Wizard of Oz*, hens, chicken feed, stink bugs, cat kibble, the fact that *we* always wanted to have a tornado in Evanston, me and Phoebe, or a flood, the fact that we really wanted to row around town in a boat, the fact that I could never understand why adults didn't see how much fun that would be, the fact that there seem to be *more* floods and earthquakes nowadays, hurricanes, tornadoes, forest fires, volcanic eruptions too, and Blobs, derechos, Lake Effect Snow, the fact that now I can't remember if the male pig is white with a black stripe, or black with a *white* stripe, the fact that I have the memory span of a *cat*, I really do, party tray of objects, grown-ups, adult children, ♫ *dollars to donuts* ♫, the fact that I wish I'd never thought of that *song*, Jake on the floor, the fact that Hungarians tear gas children, exhaust gases, conservation of energy, conservation of momentum, Killbuck Creek, the fact that some of our DVDs of musicals have a *singalong* feature but I would never suggest we sing along, the fact that Stacy would run a mile if I sprang anything like that on her, turkey soup, garlic bread, lasagne, ground beef, lemon drizzle cake, the fact that I need a new China pencil for labeling frozen foods, rue Mouffetard market scene, the fact that you get so addicted to moving the pieces around, near the end of a jigsaw, that your fingers are still twitching after it's all over, ready to move one more piece when there *are* no pieces to move, Jeremy Driscoll, and whatshername in Paris, Abby, the fact that I often think about Abby, the fact that at any point in the day I might think of her, the fact that I miss her so much sometimes it hurts, the fact that it's nice to see the kids out in the yard at last, but our seesaw needs oil, gee, 3-in-1 Oil, WD-40, the fact that all seesaws creak no matter what you do, Tuesday, Juliet, drool yet, the fact that I wonder how long seesaws have been around, the fact that they're still popular with kids, tall swing at the Annual Northwestern Faculty Summer Picnic, bascule bridge, rolling lift, lift-off, Tower Bridge, the fact that the kids don't go out to play as much anymore, the fact that kids don't even like toys anymore, the fact that all the toy shops are shutting down, the fact that children learn about democracy through play, justice, liberty, hopscotch, OF THE PEOPLE, by the people, for the people, February 22, the fact that Washington *wasn't* born on February 22nd, the fact that he was born on the 12th, jumping jacks, taw, C-SPAN, government shutdown, Hieronymus Bosch, the fact that last night I dreamt I went all

the way to New York by bus for an interview for some kind of receptionist job, attracted by the promise of a steady income, the fact that
the bus had to drive up almost vertical hills but we made it, and I got
to New York, and I was told I'd have to wear a really short leather
skirt, and in *their* opinion the skirt would not suit somebody my age,
which really kind of upset me, as I couldn't see what was such a big
deal about the skirt, though they were probably right, the fact that
maybe it was a little too short for my knobbly knees, the fact that
maybe the dream was a warning I shouldn't wear short leather skirts
anymore, not that I ever do, men's ties, the fact that the only leather
thing I ever wore was Mommy's nice old suede jacket, just for senti-
mental reasons, the fact that it hung on me like a sack but I still liked
it because I could almost remember her in it, the fact that I guess it's
up in the attic now, New York, the fact that I sometimes envy people
in steady office jobs, although I'd most likely go completely nuts if I
had to get dressed up and go to an office and talk to people every day,
the fact that I also dreamt I was in a hotel suite in Paris with Eldridge
Cleaver and he was real angry about something and punched the wall
until his hand bled, Cleveland, Main Avenue Bridge, but then he
calmed down and we went into the adjacent bedroom and he and I,
uh, hmmm, well, the fact that I guess we fooled around a bit on the
bed, just a bit, the fact that I told Leo about my Eldridge Cleaver
dream but left out the sexy part, the fact that Leo said Eldridge
Cleaver designed codpieces while he was living in Morocco, the fact
that I didn't know about the codpieces, cod, codfish balls, codfish
gravy, fishing stocks, ♫ *dollars to donuts* ♫, whales, Wales, the fact that
they sound kind of intriguing though, codpieces, not codfish balls,
rhododendrons, nasturtiums, hydrangeas, plant out in May, caterpillars, Cyrano de Bergerac, the fact that I just did such a clumsy repair
job on Stacy's old Mexican aardvark magnet, the fact that it's hand-
painted in red, yellow, blue and black, and losing its tail, the fact that
I think it's made out of a tiny gourd, the fact that the tail was about to
fall off so I tried putting some Scotch tape around it to keep it on, and
in the process managed to tear the tail *off*, the fact that my guilt about

my poor repair job will no doubt diminish over the coming hours, days and months, but that won't help the *aardvark*, the fact that the aardvark will remain in poor shape from now on, the fact that I should have let Stacy fix it, or Gillian, the fact that Gillian has great dexterity, the fact that the tail is an all-important feature because the head and tail both bob around, like those icky plastic dogs people put in the back window of their cars, bob, Blob, global warming, itch, BOB, Baby On Board, the fact that I can't bear to look at these videos of people driving away from forest fires on the highway, the fact that people seem to think nothing will hurt them as long as they're in their *cars*, but cars melt, and sometimes explode too, and break down, the fact that they're brave to trust their lives to a car, the fact that when she was about eight Stacy made a great little clay sculpture of Dilly nursing two kittens, the fact that it looks just *like* Dilly with her kittens, the fact that one of the kittens is striped just like the mom, but the other one's white with black spots, the fact that it's a very faithful depiction of that litter of Dilly's, the fact that the mom cat's front paws are so nicely crossed too, the fact that we gave all those kittens away, and it was a hard thing to do, but at least we have the *clay* version, *For he is of the tribe of Tiger... For he can creep*, the fact that Stacy made that at her special art class, the fact that I think Stacy's a born artist, but now all she wants to paint are her nails, or her face, the fact that she could get the thin hips of cats just right, the fact that cats have such bony hips, cows too, a lot like *mine*, so I'm not surprised they didn't want me to wear a leather skirt, the fact that I'm way too angular for that kind of thing now, the fact that leather skirts are for *fleshy* women, not people with jagged points sticking out everywhere, tormenting the leather, the fact that that skirt would probably have slipped right off me anyway, exposing my bony hips for all to see, as well as my knees, the fact that some aging guy said he's only attracted to women in their twenties and there's nothing he can do about it, the fact that he says middle-aged women just don't look good, the fact that I'm broken, the fact that Leo said cows are like suspension bridges, the way the body hangs between the shoulders and the hips, suspension of disbelief, the fact that I like how square cows' heads are, cows' hips, cowslips, the fact that cowslips are one of the prettiest flowers in the world, bees, Wiener schnitzel, lederhosen, little Dutch girl dresses, hinges, highchair, hipped roof, nipped in the bud, Eldridge Cleaver, codpieces, the fact that our high chair has swiveling hips, the fact that Aunt Sophia's highchair can't swivel, the fact that babies are born with naturally supple hips, and kids have agile hips, but their cranky old moms have creaky old hips, seesaws, hinge, twinge, the fact that it must be really terrifying to be old, not to know what'll go wrong with you next, the fact that all you know is that *something* will, leather skirt or no leather skirt, the fact that I have a headache starting, probably because of the aardvark, the fact that I'm actually still feeling hot from guilt about the aardvark, smarting over my not so smart repair job, the fact that I docked that poor aardvark's tail, but it's not the end of the world surely, the fact that I hope it's not a hot *flash*, dear me, the fact that it's illegal to dock dogs' tails now, which is good, but you're still allowed to clip them any way you want, poodle parlors, the fact that Pepito had already been docked when we got him, the fact that I don't know if sheep still get their tails cut or not, stink bugs, the fact that stink bugs eat absolutely everything, the fact that some farmer had his whole corn crop ruined, the fact that not a single ear was free of blemishes from stink bugs, and they affect the taste of wine too, the fact that you're allowed a certain number of stink bugs in the grapes, but eventually the wine tastes bad, the same with grape juice, the fact that you can drown them in soapy water, *For he can creep*, the fact that I don't want to be having hot flashes *yet*, the fact that I'm not old enough, or am I, itch, the fact that I have to go see the gynecologist about my itch next Tuesday, the fact that more and more girls are having plastic surgery done on their, well, their private parts, the fact that the stamen of the americophallus titanum was drooping a bit by the time we got to see it, Amerigo Vespucci, drool yet, Juliet, the fact that that could be a pop star's name, Drool-Yet Juliet, the fact that it was hard to detect the whiff of dead mouse you're supposed to get from the stinky plant, not the pop star, and the kids left but I hung around and I think I did smell it a bit, the fact that every botanical garden in the world now wants its own amorphophallus titanum because it draws crowds more than any other plant, but the kids had to wait in line too long, the fact that they got ice cream immediately after as their reward, itch, pap smear, gynecologist, Tuesday, the fact that do they have to call it that, a "*smear*," schmeer, smudge, fudge, fugue, the fact that it sounds so messy, like finger-painting, the fact that Gillian will eat raw pie dough until she barfs if I let her, the quiet back alley, the fact that the dandelions are just coming out, the fact that they look so small and compact that I didn't even recognize them as dandelions at first, the fact that they look good with their petals still clenched up like that, dandy lions, the fact that I think maybe brand-new, uptight dandelions are better-looking than the older, laidback dandelions, even better than *daffodils* maybe, or marigolds, the fact that many things are just starting to turn green now, the fact that the seasons still come and go despite climate change, floods, the fact that it's always a relief though, to see them come, the seasons, not the floods, the fact that on some level I think I still believe I can fly and might just take off in a high wind one fine day if the mood strikes me, the fact that today the sun was out and there was a nice breeze blowing and every red-winged blackbird was declaring his love, and it really seemed like I just might be able to fly, and then there was a big commotion, wild whooping sounds and laughter coming from behind me, and knew I was in for trouble, keys, Adam's apple, pinching temples, the fact that I tried to pay no attention, just keep walking, the fact that I was scared though, because I was all alone in the alley with whoever it was behind me, the fact that a police officer was shot dead in her own car, but that was in New York, the fact that I started really wishing I knew more self-defense tactics, the fact that I was trying to remember the stuff Stacy had read out, pulling the tie and all, and then this great big hulking teenage boy zoomed up behind me on a bike and when he got within half an inch of me he yelped right in my ear, and then zoomed off laughing, the fact that he had a sidekick with him who was planning to whoosh past me too, but something went wrong with the chain on his bike just as he came up beside me and the poor guy had to get off and try to fix it, pretending the whole time I wasn't there staring at him and waiting for an apology, the fact that it must've been pretty embarrassing for him, the fact that I'm sure he was a little ashamed of how his friend had behaved, the fact that I was trying hard to think of something really cutting to say about his *pal*, but in the end I didn't say anything and just walked on by, the fact that he looked scared enough already, the sidekick, not the bully, ♫ *Courage!* ♫, the fact that I don't know how to confront anybody, but I did hold my keys tight all the rest of the way, in case I had to jam them up somebody's nose at any moment, the fact that I don't like teenage boys, I never did, concrete dolosse, except for *Chuck*, I guess, and *Ethan* and his friends, because they were nice to me, the fact that I'm sure Ben and Jake won't be scary teenagers, the fact that I think those two might've been on drugs, or glue, not *Ben and Jake*, the guys on the path, the fact that they should be in *school*, the fact that if they'd tried to bother me on the way back with *Jake*, that would have been a different story, the fact that you don't interfere with a mother bear and her cub, the fact that I would have kicked him right over, bike and all, and then moved on to his pal, dandelions, thorns in my thigh, Mommy, the fact that luckily that didn't happen, the fact that I'm making something new for Cathy, cinnamon sand dollar cookies, the fact that it's time for a new freezer contents list,

TOP SHELF

hot dogs (4 packs)
pizza x 3
chicken wings (2 packs of 16)
drumsticks (4 packs of 8)
pretzels
butter
cinnamon rolls x 23
cinnamon roll dough x 2
cinnamon sand dollar cookies x 51
ham stock

beef tips x 8
spaghetti sauce x 5
Sloppy Joe sauce x 4
scalloped potatoes
parsley flakes
pie dough x 8
sour cherries
blueberries
stewed plums
paw-paw (raw pulp)
paw-paw (cooked)
ice cream
frozen yogurt
Stacy's choc choc chip cookies
green beans
corn
peas
spinach
lima beans
liverwurst
chicken pot pies x 10
fish cakes x 24
pesto
stollen bread
fish for cats
mushroom soup x 4
1 moth-eaten sweater
1 tablecloth with wax on it
Leo's wax-stained corduroys
2 candlesticks
1 Ziploc pot schmaltz
pretzels x 6
madeleines x 45
the last of Nebuchadnezzar (coq au vin)
choc chip cookies (big ones)
tomato popsicles
normal   ″   (orange, lemon, lime) x 10

LOWER Shelf

butter x 10
milk x 4
fish stock
chicken stock x 9
chicken soup with rice x 3
chicken noodle soup x 4
baba ganoush
chipotles (4 mini-pots)
apple chutney x 2
apples'n'onions
stewed rhubarb
cheddar cheese
1 bottle white wine
French fries (2 bags)
martini glasses
Ben's river water samples
lemon drizzle cake x 11
bacon (5 packs)
Hershey's Kisses (2 bags)
white bread (organic) x 4
brown bread x 3
lamb chops x 8
lasagne x 2
more fish for cats
catfish
O.J. x 8
apple cider x 3
ice,

the fact that there's never enough ice, Leo thinks, especially if he wants to make martinis, the fact that he uses just dozens of ice cubes to make martinis, the fact that the kids have never forgiven me for those savory tomato popsicles, but I was just trying it out, what a fuss, the fact that they still make vomiting sounds if the subject of tomato popsicles comes up, and then they bring up the Brave Man Cookie episode, just to tease me, but the chickens *like* my tomato popsicles, the fact that they fight over every shard, the fact that I haven't been forgiven for the pepper pasta incident either, the fact that I actually fed my poor kids spicy pasta for a whole week running without realizing it, the fact that I thought they were just *tomato* noodles, tomato-flavored, the fact that the kids kept telling me they were spicy but I *ignored* them, the fact that I thought they were just kidding around but, boy, was I wrong, and I freely admit this now whenever they bring the matter up, the fact that somehow men got away with the ATOM BOMB but I can't get away with one little culinary boo-boo, or two, Liberty Mutual, the fact that I need flaked almonds for the sand dollars, the fact that sea urchins are related to sand dollars, the fact that my hand hurts, now why is that, the fact that where are the flaked almonds, the fact that two whole jars of bay leaves is really like a *lifetime's supply*, the fact that I wonder if every household has too many bay leaves, the fact that the number of bay leaves you own can easily get out of hand, like kittens, or baby mice, or stink bugs, the fact that the Hong Kong–Macau Bridge is thirty-four miles long and includes two artificial islands and a tunnel, and dozens of workers have died making that bridge, the fact that there have been suspicious deaths of people higher up too, not higher up the *bridge*, higher up in the management side of things, rice-bowl job, the fact that the management people keep committing suicide all the time, but Leo says that's probably not what really happened, the fact that it is a cable-stayed bridge, the fact that I'm already getting requests from some places for plum, pear or strawberry tartes tatin, but that's a summer thing, like peaches in cream, the fact that it's no good using frozen strawberries, the fact that there are way too many kinds of cinnamon roll in the world, *bad* ones, like floppy ones, and raisiny ones, and ones with no cinnamon or hardly any, the fact that some are too dry or sparsely spiraled, a gyp, the fact that a good cinnamon roll should spiral as much as possible, "Let's roll," sfogliatelle, raw pie dough, ice cream, tomato popsicles, lollypops, the fact that we used to get a free lollypop when we went to the bank with Mommy on hot summer days, the fact that the bank was always so boring, you really needed a lollypop, but it was cool in there, the fact that banks don't do that anymore, the lollypop thing I mean, not the air-conditioning, the fact that they must have had too much trouble from parents who disagree with their kids eating candy, horehound, Indian Pudding, hot water crust, Sloppy Joes, BBQ ribs, lemon chiffon pie, corn chowder, dilled turkey chowder, hog maw, succotash, the fact that I just remembered I dreamt some guys were putting scaffolding up all over our house and I was worried about security, since there aren't any locks or anything on the upstairs windows, the fact that one of the workmen was talking to his girlfriend on *our phone*, the fact that it was a whole different house and a whole different life, really detailed, the fact that then I dreamt I went somewhere with Daddy in my nightgown, the fact that *I* was in a nightgown, not Daddy, and I had bare feet, so I said I'd wait for him in a park while he was at some meeting, the fact that then I was cooking dinner somewhere, the fact that I seem to think about food practically *all the time*, even in my dreams, occupational hazard, dear me, gug, the fact that Jake's taken to saying "gug" all the time now, and we don't know why, the fact that Leo wondered if he's trying to say "god," the fact that maybe he's receiving religious instruction at his playgroup or a friend's house or something, loaves and fishes, "Baby Jesus made topspin," the fact that these days, when children aren't finding loaded guns lying around their friends' houses, they're finding *god*, the fact that *I* had a Christian phase as a kid for about a week, the fact that I was just trying it out, the fact that I would pray secretly at night, *Now I lay me down to sleep*, the fact that then I got angry at Ethan one day and said a curse word, and that was the end of my Christianity, the fact that I felt I had to excommunicate myself, *If I should die before I wake, I pray the Lord my soul to take*, the fact that I don't think kids should worry about *dying* every night, the fact that they have enough bad dreams as it is, the fact that I once dreamt I had passed on, or maybe we all had, but it really wasn't too bad, and not so different from being alive, the fact that you did all the same sort of stuff but you had to *pretend* to need food and all, and we could pass right through each other, the fact that I need a new grocery list, milk, flaked almonds, celery, leeks, parsley, beef, chicken, sodas, lemons, cream, salad stuff, curry, butter, veg, stuffed vine leaves, potato chips, olives, cheese, falafel, the fact that *babies* only think about food too, starting with the breast, Sara Lee, Betty Crocker, Crocs, cocks, cocker spaniels, the fact that people are all trying to avoid desserts these days and it's driving away business, joggers, health freaks, the fact that there are plenty of healthy things about pie, if it's a fruit pie, I mean, and even cinnamon rolls have some goodness, because cinnamon's good for the heart, and there's nothing wrong with a bit of orange zest either, and what about the vitamin C in the dried cherries, the fact that they never think about the *psychological* benefits of eating something nice, the fact that it can improve your whole outlook on life, to eat something that makes you feel good, something flavorful and well-made, a professional product, the fact that, personally, I think celery sticks and rice cakes are indigestible, even if you spread peanut butter on them, "Spread 'em," the fact that those police officers stopped that young woman for going through a stop sign, and first they handcuffed her and then they threw her on the ground in a parking lot, stripped off her panties, put her ankles up over her head, spread her legs and, well, did a, a "cavity search," right there in the *parking lot*, for all to see, like they were *gynecologists* or something, and she was only twenty, the fact that the poor girl was running an errand for her sick mom, Mommy, the fact that just because they thought they smelled dope on her, they body-slammed her to the ground and, my word, the fact that, sure, it was a female officer who did the internal examination, but still, a twenty-year-old, and it was done in the *presence* of male officers, the fact that we pay our taxes for *this*, "I want another cup of coffee," the speakeasy guy in *Some Like It Hot*, the fact that Jake can play for hours by himself, he doesn't need toys, just a box of nurdles, gug, the fact that Christianity's the one religion with no hygiene rules, and that led to so many cholera epidemics in Christian societies, the fact that Christ didn't wash his hands before the Last Supper, *And that has made all the difference*, the fact that most Ohioans would probably *kill* me for saying it, but it's the god's own truth that Christians spread disease, cholera, polio, the fact that policemen now send out robots to kill suspects with bombs, which is execution without trial, according to some people, ACLU, nurdles, nasturtiums, May, lethal injections, the fact that dear me, the fact that I should eat something, the fact that if you're too hungry accidents happen, like dropping boiling-hot pies, the fact that you need to be just hungry enough, and cheerful, the fact that despair and dejection can make a cake fall flat, I'm sure, and exhaustion, the fact that I misread recipes when I'm low, blue, purple, the fact that I think you can always sort of tell a depressive's pie, Hong Kong–Macau Bridge suicides, the fact that most everybody in the food industry is fighting boredom and nausea most of the time, but some-how you have to convince yourself you're thrilled to feed people, the fact that if you don't you're bound to mess up the spices or get the measurements wrong, or the caramelization, the fact that it's hard though sometimes, because cooking all day can get kind of annoying, just like at Christmastime, basting the turkey, making mushroom gravy and cranberry sauce, and mashed potatoes, and caramelized yams, Phoebe's Christmas log, Ethan's eggnog, Daddy's marzipan fruits, the fact that in 1976 somebody made a 69,000-pound bicentenary cake in Baltimore, the fact that you've got to have some vim and vigor to make a cake that big, the fact that a little tiny spider's building a web in the window, the fact that it zigzags so gracefully, swinging itself rhythmically back and forth as it goes around and around, the fact that spiders don't have to worry about money or taxes or catching cholera or meeting Open Carry guys or being searched by the cops, or what makeup to wear, or who's President even, screen door, the fact that we need a new latch on the screen door, Laura Ingalls Wilder, chick-ens, skim milk, the fact that everybody thinks it's easy and I can just produce all these things like clockwork but, gee, gug, it's taken years of practice to learn the ropes, the fact that baking cakes and pies for profit is a lot trickier than it looks, the fact that you have to have steady production and consistency, and reliable products, the fact that what I've done is invent a job for myself out of nothing and it still feels precarious, the fact that if you're self-employed there aren't many perks except privacy, the fact that I am a failure, but Leo still loves me, Old Lyme, hummingbirds, Laura and Almanzo in their first house together before Rose was born, the lost $100 bill, the fact that the pies have to look right, taste right, cost a reasonable price, the fact that it's all about supply and demand, but you just have to guess at the demand, the fact that it's all a gamble, slot machines, pinball, the fact that you have to have the right hygiene standards, and deliver the pies on time, like *clockwork*, the fact that making food for people is actually a highly pressured, skilled, responsible job, just like motherhood, but nobody seems to notice, cooking *or* motherhood, the fact that they just take it for granted that we're going to keep our kids safe and make safe food, the fact that pies are light relief though actually, compared to *kids*, and at least there's some variety with pie-making, like once in a while I have a cup of coffee with a restaurant manager or a waitress, if I can't get out of it, that is, and usually they compliment me on my stuff, the fact that once I got written up in the paper, the fact that I had to talk to some woman over the phone and I felt so silly, but I thought I better do it because it might lead to more orders, the fact that most of the time I get my privacy though, except for when Ronny turns up, the fact that I'm a little vulnerable at home here, or if a bully boy accosts me down some deserted alley, desserted, spring sunshine, the fact that another plus of my job is I get to watch movies while I bake, or sometimes Leo reads to me, something from the paper, or a bit of what he's been working on, which I like even if I don't totally get it, the fact that it's hard to believe that all day Leo works with the derived units of velocity, momentum, acceleration, gravity, angles, forces, torques, energy, power, density, specific volume, pressure, stress, noise and frequency, but maybe I do too, the fact that gravity acts vertically downwards towards the center of the earth, and $E = IR$, itch, the fact that no wonder he's a wreck when he gets home, stress factors, cracks, eyebars, the fact that matter cannot be created or destroyed, but pies can, the fact that mass is a measure of how much material exists within a body, but I just measure how much cinnamon mixture I need for my dough, *Bigger Than Life*, the fact that my job is a *kind* of chemistry, a lowly kind, well, chemistry and driving, the fact that Leo came into the kitchen the other day and said it was weird that throughout evolution, everybody bought into the two eyes, two ears, two arms, two legs, two lungs, two kidneys idea, two tusks, two horns, two sides of the brain too, and I said "Bivalves didn't buy into it. Bivalves didn't buy into anything," and he said "They got two *valves*, don't they?", the fact that he won on the two thing, binary systems and all, but the weirder thing was that when he came into the room, I tensed up, like I was afraid he was going to *scold* me for sitting around, though I wasn't sitting around, the fact that I was caramelizing, or my sugar was anyway, not *me* personally, I hope not anyway, the fact that my tension made no sense though, since Leo has never once in his life scolded me for anything, the fact that he's usually *encouraging* me to sit around, like the Mona Lisa or something, Lake Minnetonka, the fact that he even bought me a stool to sit on, the fact that I don't use it enough, the fact that Leo actually likes me to take things easy, the fact that even before I got sick he was like that, the fact that it's *Daddy* who made me feel guilty about what I was doing or not doing every single minute of the day, every waking moment, clockwork, shot peening, mug shot, Mdewakanton, the fact that he was always checking up on me, and not really in a friendly way, more in a critical way, the fact that he was checking if I was being industrious enough, suspicious that I was wasting my time, watching TV, not doing my homework, and I internalized it, nasturtiums, laziness, mess, itch, "Do you expect me to clean up after you?", the fact that of course I *was* usually watching TV, which must've driven him nuts, the fact that I don't like it when *my* kids watch TV too much, or Morning Routine videos, the fact that Jane Wyman doesn't even want a TV in the *house*, the fact that after Mommy got sick I secretly slept in my school clothes every night, to save time getting dressed, the fact that, boy, was I depressed, while that nun peeled her tomatoes downstairs, the fact that what makes me feel guilty *now* is Stacy, and if I make a bad pie, because of all that wasted time, not wasted on Stacy, wasted on the pie, and all the wasted

462

ingredients as well, the Blob, the fact that I hate leaving some customer in the lurch, my clients, patrons, Spirit Knob, Tonka toys, Hasbro, the fact that I don't dare tell Leo how much money I've wasted on pastry mistakes, not that he'd be mad but it's just so embarrassing, the fact that luckily Leo doesn't go around tallying up my outgoings, the fact that Daddy wouldn't approve of me making pies in the first place, good *or* bad, the fact that he got so angry when he caught me kissing Chuck when Mommy was sick, *Blossom*, the fact that I used to try to justify my TV-watching, I forget how, the fact that I can remember telling him I was *learning* things from those TV shows, but Daddy didn't fall for it, and he was right, the fact that I really did watch too many dumb TV shows, just like our kids do, the fact that you *could* question whether checking up on me was a good use of *Daddy's* time, but maybe it was, the fact that I saw an episode of *Blossom* recently and it seemed kind of *coarse*, vulgar, all innuendos and double entendres no kid should have to say, The papers were full of innundo," the fact that Frank was kind of a bad influence on me, the fact that maybe that's why Daddy couldn't stand him, even though Frank was a fellow Yalie, the fact that Frank taught me all kinds of new ways of wasting time, the fact that he knew every laziness trick in the book, a master stagnator, couch potato, La-Z-Boy, which may be why he still doesn't have time to visit his own daughter, the fact that there was no sport on TV that he didn't watch, the fact that if it wasn't baseball season, it was football, or hockey, or skiing, or surfing, or horse racing, the fact that I think he watched golf just because it goes on so long, not because he really liked it, the fact that he never considered participating in a sport himself, unless you count checkers, the fact that he also had a lot of music to listen to every day, a *lot*, jazz and bluegrass and Sibelius symphonies, the fact that he listened to it all sitting in a darkened room, the fact that you don't actually *have* to listen to that much music, it's not the *law*, the fact that a lot of people don't seem to know that though, or there wouldn't be muzak playing in every store and restaurant and bank and doctor's waiting room in the country, the fact that they even play rock music at the farmer's market now, the fact that it wouldn't be so bad if they played nice barn-dance music, the fact that the strange thing, maybe his stroke of genius, was the way Frank made out that every form of laziness and procrastination he had devised was actually a very important activity in some way, the fact that he never once admitted he was wasting time, the fact that, on the contrary, he was always insisting *his* time was so precious it couldn't be interrupted for any reason, the fact that even stopping whatever he was doing to look after Stacy for a *half hour*, while I had a bath, was like a big deal, big ask, the fact that Leo *always* helps out if I ask him, no problem, but Leo's not an expert in relaxing like Frank was, the fact that still, it was Leo who got me watching movies all the time, and encouraged me to bake if that's what I felt like doing, which Daddy would never approve of, the fact that Leo's a big believer in doing what makes you happy, though engineering doesn't make *him* happy, the fact that I wonder what Daddy would have made of me becoming a chicken-farmer and self-employed catering person, in *Ohio* yet, concocting afternoon dainties for Republicans, the fact that I bet he would've considered it unworthy of a college grad, the fact that he would probably have wanted me to be a professor at Peolia by now, or maybe at Kenyon, or Antioch or some place like Oberlin, instead of the dropout I've become, the fact that I'm practically a *shut-in*, a drop-out and a shut-in, the fact that he would've been shocked by how they treated me at Peolia though, the way they ducked out of offering me a permanent contract, never mind *tenure*, the fact that, heavens to Betsy, they didn't even pay me back for the computer glasses *they* made me buy, which I've never used, the fact that Kenyon's just about as close as Peolia from here, and Gambier's just a short drive, so that's another failure of mine, that I don't teach at either of those places, the fact that I wish Leo worked at Kenyon, because all this traveling he does is *crazee*, but what can we do, the fact that Daddy would have hated all the movies I watch and re-watch too, the fact that Daddy would never understand that, watching things again and again, unless it was *Casablanca* or *The Quiet Man*, and I bet he'd disapprove of Leo for encouraging me to watch them, but now

I'm a *grown-up* and I get to make my own dumb decisions, like Laura and Almanzo in their new house, Trixy the pony, the fact that she called Almanzo "Manly" for short, the fact that Leo likes to watch movies and so do I, and it's not a crime, bump stocks, blizzard, the flood of 1985, the fact that, anyway, by combining two unworthy practices in one, baking pies *while* watching movies, I think I save time in the long run, I mean compared to if I baked and watched movies *separately*, the fact that I also make some money, though, I know, not a lot, the fact that then it occurred to me maybe all this guilt is really just a way of *missing my dad*, the fact that maybe I invent stuff he might scold me for, to make up for his absence, the fact that I would certainly prefer his criticism to all these years of utter silence, because at least it showed he cared, the fact that the dead don't care, the fact that once people have passed away they don't think about you anymore, the fact that it kind of feels like the *Silent Treatment*, poor Daddy, the fact that he can't *help* it, the fact that I'm sure he'd rather still be alive, even if it meant watching me do stuff he didn't like, the fact that if only we didn't pass away but went into *diapause* like stink bugs, just fumbled around for a few months and then *revived*, the fact that I'm sure he meant his criticisms kindly, the fact that he was actually a warm, genial, affable guy, much liked, and very forgiving, the fact that his friends and his students and colleagues and everybody liked him a lot, and I've forgotten all that now and just remember his critical side, and that's so mean of me, the fact that my memory isn't being fair on him, the fact that that's why you gotta stay *alive*, so you can correct all the mistakes other people make about you, what they think and say about you, the fact that, after all, how bad can a guy be who cries over *It's a Wonderful Life* and *Casablanca*, the fact that Daddy really liked a good pastrami sandwich too, or bagels with lox, the fact that I was just a stubborn, sulky, defensive adolescent, the fact that I wasted so much time telling myself he didn't like me, and now I wonder if maybe I got him all wrong, the fact that I wasted what little time we *had* together, self-defense, keys, Adam's apple, assailant, assault, tigress-like manner, Tiger moms, the fact that I defended myself right out of having a fun time with my dad, but he was always so *critical*, the fact that he brought me those beautiful gold filigree earrings from Mexico once, the fact that I need to get them fixed, the fact that he bought me those awful ugly shoes too, and the raincoat I never wore, but he *meant* well, the fact that the real truth is he cared about us all and didn't want to leave us, Mommy especially, the fact that he was always so loyal to Mommy, the fact that he probably would have had a lot more conversations with me if he could have, but he passed on, and it wasn't his fault or his intention, the fact that maybe it was *Daddy* who taught us how to love, not Mommy, euphoria, nap, afternoon, Mommy in the kitchen, the fact that he probably was the warmer of the two, the fact that Ethan and Phoebe are better at love than I am, the fact that Phoebe's very kind, the fact that when all our medical bills started piling up she just said "Tell me what you need" and she sent it, thousands, no questions asked, the fact that I don't know how we'll ever pay her back, the fact that selling eggs and pies sure ain't gonna do it, itch, the fact that she has a good salary but she didn't have to share it with us, the fact that the main thing is getting the kids to college, and she's offered to help us with that too, the fact that Leo should get a discount though, as long as he keeps working, the fact that I don't know why Phoebe's so nice to me, the fact that we quarreled for our first fifteen or twenty years, the fact that whenever we asked Daddy for money as kids he'd ask what for, but he always gave it to us, the fact that he helped me out after I had Stace too, the fact that he was charmed by her from the first, and put up with Frank for her sake, the fact that he even tried to get him a job but Frank didn't turn up for the interview, the fact that I remember all *this* but can't remember where I stayed the first time I went to New York on my own, some hotel Daddy booked for me, the fact that that's okay though because I wouldn't want to go back there, the fact that it was a bit of a fleabag-type place, the fact that I think people with kids automatically waste a lot of time, what with all the tending, the mending, the helping, the yelping, decluttering, opening cereal boxes, combing heads of hair and answering messages from the teachers, the fact that loving them takes up time, and I feel guilty about the time that takes *too*, the fact that I need a good shakeup, Shaker boxes, chores, Pillsbury Doughboy, Jolly Green Giant, Aunt Jemima, Sugar Creek, the Swartzentruber Amish, purple martins, martinis, Procter & Gamble, the fact that they're experts in contentment, the Amish, not Procter & Gamble, or so they seem to me, the fact that in many respects I really wouldn't mind being Amish too much, apart from the religious side, the fact that it's a hard life but at least they have self-respect, because they're all contributing to the success of their families and the rest of the Amish community, while I just try my darnedest to get faster and faster at making pies and cakes in order to make a buck, so this tiny chaotic household can keep going, and it's stressful, strain hardening, spiraling, the fact that if I get any more stressed out they'll have to Baker-Act me, baker act, mesocyclone, the fact that speeding up doesn't make my job more fun, or safer even, the fact that there aren't all that many shortcuts to peeling, coring, chopping, beating, kneading, mincing, mixing, grinding, pulverizing, frying, grilling and baking that don't risk injury, and our medical bills are already up the wazoo, Single Payer, Phoebe, chenille, chamois, sheep, chassis, carburetor, vibratory finishing, the fact that the Amish don't have to worry about crime all the time, I don't think, long-haired assailants jumping out at you from the bushes, "Ain't I a woman?", klootchman, nasturtiums, Donny, Ronny, Ronny's Trump T-shirt, the fact that if a man won't stop pawing at you when you're alone in a room with him, like if he's grabbing at your p—, I guess, and that sort of stuff, you're supposed to suddenly yank his pants up hard by the belt, the fact that it took me a long while to figure out how to use soft fruits in a tarte tatin, the fact that it *can* work, as long as you caramelize the butter and sugar *before* you add the fruit, not with the fruit, the fact that I learned that the hard way, the expensive way, the fact that when I tried frying the plums in butter and sugar, the same way I fry the apples, the fact that all I got was a plum jam fiasco, embarrassing, the fact that pears are even worse, the fact that they dissolve *immediately* and they lose their flavor, the fact that they're too delicate to be fried, the fact that they're okay if you poach them,

the fact that even if I never let anyone see my failures, and Daddy isn't
here to get exasperated with me, I fall in my *own* estimation, the fact
that my sit-me-down-upon really hurts now, *why*, the fact that it's
from sitting on this stool waiting for the cinnamon roll dough to rise,
the fact that, oh shoot, I probably didn't use enough yeast, the fact
that Leo says there's yeast in the air all around us but that won't help
with the cinnamon rolls, ears of corn, stink bugs, the fact that Leo said
last night he likes ears, human ears, animal ears, all kinds, but I'm not
so sure about them, like feet, the fact that I think they're awfully
funny-looking, the fact that he doesn't like it much when the tips of
people's ears stick out through their *hair*, the fact that that's no good,
he says, but otherwise he thinks ears are really interesting, the fact that
I think bats' ears are crazee, but dogs have the right idea, at least the
ones that cover their ears with a flap, so you don't have to look at all
the spirals, elephant ears flapping, Gillian doing her elephant imper-
sonation, the fact that I used to make sourdough bread but then Leo
decided not to eat bread anymore, so I just buy organic sliced bread
for the kids, the fact that they don't mind as long as there's enough
peanut butter and jelly on it, the fact that we should buy only organic
and local but we can't afford it, spinning gold, fairy tales, alchemy, the
fact that the nicest time I ever had with Daddy was when we went out
on our own with Pepito that night, and walked around in the Divinity
School grounds, the fact that there is nothing so good as tramping
through new snow on a clear, quiet night and feeling alone in the world
with your *dad*, the fact that I didn't usually know what to say to him
but that night there didn't seem to be a problem, the fact that the place
was all empty apart from us, and so beautiful, with the snow lighting
everything up, Pepito running up the steep white hills, black trees, up
hill and down dale, the fact that I dreamt George Clooney came over
for a drink and I'd forgotten he was coming, and he simply would not
make up his mind on if he wanted wine or a beer, the fact that when
he left I was quite relieved, the fact that I didn't like him anymore because he'd made such a fuss deciding between wine and beer
when I was in the middle of trying to rustle up a meal, the fact that

I've forgotten George Clooney's wife's name, the fact that George Clooney and his wife threw big parties for Hillary, the fact that it's all so much about money and influence now, the fact that that's not very democratic really, "Mankind should have been my business," DNC, ACLU, LTCF, CHP, ITMFA, the fact that if I spent $300,000 or even *$3,000* on a candidate I'd be so pissed if they didn't get elected, the fact that it's frustrating enough already without that, clone, drone, Six Robbers Flee Raid On One Motorcycle, the fact that Leo says George Clooney's acting is flat, the fact that there's some woman who helps people declutter, the fact that you have to hold every possession in your hands and decide if it gives you *joy*, the fact that if it does, you get to keep it, and if it doesn't, you dump it, the fact that everything you've got has to *deliver*, the fact that Scotch tape doesn't give me any joy, I don't think, but sometimes you *need* some, the fact that a book on *decluttering* might not give you joy either, but you might still *need* it, six months, the fact that what if you miss something you dumped and it's too late, because it's already landfill, six-pack wastefulness, plastic rings on turtle waistlines, the fact that that poor woman must be so *lost* when she needs to sew on a button or something and she got rid of all her needles and thread already because they didn't bring her joy, the buttons too, the fact that she must just wander around her apartment all day wishing she hadn't thrown this or that out, the fact that some things might come in handy some day in ways you never even thought of, the fact that she's rich though, so she can just go out and buy some more buttons or Scotch tape or whatever it is she needs, the fact that I hope she's hanging on to her tax returns, the fact that most people's clutter is there so they can hide the piles of past tax returns behind it, the fact that you have to keep most of this stuff for seven years, and some of it forever, papers, papers, the fact that Hillary Clinton didn't give me any joy so it was easy to let *her* go, Bill, Qadaffi, the fact that snipers and suicide bombers and American police officers are the real declutterers, the fact that they get rid of people at the drop of a hat, and, heavens, they probably get joy out of that, Taser, Terminix, jumping the gun, selling like hot cakes, corner hutch, cat o' nine tails, kolams, kelims, muumuus, murphy beds, the fact that this decluttering guru says a once-in-a-lifetime sort-out takes *six months*, the fact that you pile all your stuff up in the middle of the floor, all your clothes, books, papers and whatnot, rugs, cushions, knickknacks, tuna fish, raisins, tax returns, and then you hold each of these objects to your heart and do the joy business, hugging your tax returns to your heart, and deciding if you want to keep them or not, the fact that once it's done you're left with crisp, empty shelves, and a lot of carefully rolled-up clothing, standing up on end in your drawers, at least for a while, the fact that I think that's just wasteful, the fact that anyway whenever I clear some space around here, somebody immediately fills it with *their* stuff, so I don't see the point, Apple sign, Google doodle, cheat sheet, James Baldwin, Alec Baldwin, the fact that she is really into folding, or rather rolling, spiraling, cinnamon rolls, the fact that she's kind of *Amish* with her folding, the fact that there are videos of her just putting clothes away in drawers, the fact that everybody kind of likes a pile of folded stuff but she *really* likes it, the fact that she takes it a lot more seriously than most people, the fact that first you fold your sweater once, then you roll it, then you stand it upright in the drawer, the fact that I think this might lead to wrinkling, but I may be wrong, or maybe she doesn't *care* about wrinkles as long as everything's all safely spiraled, the fact that she's probably addicted to ironing too, the fact that there are some people like that, the fact that Jumpha never travels without a real iron, not a *travel* iron, the fact that what would Daddy have done if I spent all my time rolling up my clothes, and ironing, and holding pieces of paper to my heart, chickens, the fact that her book has sold a billion copies, the fact that I wish *my* obsessions paid off that well, the fact that every kid you meet thinks they're going to make a million bucks but very few people make a million bucks, "so you do the math," the fact that women in Asia draw these intricate, geometrical kolams with rice flour, so birds and ants will have something to eat, the fact that maybe art should always be edible, just in case, tarte tatin, the fact that that sprig of money plant I picked gives me joy, the fact that it is *so pretty*, the fact that its pods, or coins, are a deep fresh bluey-green, not white yet, the fact that you usually see them white and all dried up, but they look great either way, white *or* green, the fact that they're one of the greatest things, I think, like dandelions, the fact that what about souvenirs though, the fact that I'd remember even less if I didn't have any souvenirs, shoebox of love letters, the fact that I dreamt Chuck wrote me a letter and said our time together was beautiful and he wished he'd done more for me, the fact that in the dream it felt like he just gave me all the closure I'd always needed from him, validation, so that now I could finally *forget* about him, triangulated girders, souvenirs, the fact that the old rusty folding veggie-steamer is waving around in the wind, the fact that we hung it there to scare the deer away from the carrot patch, the fact that I don't think they care much about it, but it looks sort of pretty, twirling out there, ♫ *Gone with the Wind* ♫, Lyme disease, Christians, Colfax massacre, hygiene, decluttering, trepanning, the fact that I also dreamt about a guy who was living inside a *tree*, not up in a tree house but right inside the tree trunk, the fact that he had to stand up all the time, lollypops, trepanning, tomato popsicles, peppery pasta,

· · · ·

The kittens were boisterous and agile now, beyond the point when she might crush them beneath her paws. Their games were intense, so there was less time for suckling. Now that they were interested in meat, they came with her on the hunt. She was never alone.

Uneasily, she sniffed the air for any sign of a male nearby, or any hint that her mate had managed to locate her again. The wind and heavy rain interfered with small sounds and smells, and made her nervous. Their previous den had been on higher ground. This rocky shelter was too close to the river, which had widened over the last few days. When a river ran swift and muddy like that, there were no fish to be had. The deer wouldn't come either. After the hunt she would take the kittens somewhere higher, not back here.

Everything excited and surprised them. They had now seen snow, rain and sun, and were beginning to know the world. But the hurried excavations of blackbirds as they flipped leaves over, the rustle of paper, cardboard and plastic debris in the wind, fallen branches, moths and bees – to the kittens these things were confusingly alike, all part of a vast mysterious array beyond their mother land.

They were fascinated by water. They convulsively tried to bite its ripples and flashes of light, in the same way that they would pounce on a rat their mother brought them.

There were rocks beside the swollen river to spring up and slip down, cold black mud squishing between their toes. Beneath the gleaming hips of birches, beside the meandering stream made high by recent rains, they wrestled. Pushed too near the edge, the darkest kitten fell in the freezing river and was quickly carried off, further and further away from his siblings, who continued wrestling without him, spinning wildly on the bare muddy ground between boulders.

He tried to paddle his way out of the roiling creek but was flummoxed and quickly exhausted by the current that fought him. Down and down the rushing stream he floated, stunned, frozen.

His mother strode nonchalantly into water two-feet-deep and picked him up by the scruff. Listening again, alert to any interference, she stood a moment in the gushing stream with the kitten dangling from her mouth. Any disturbance in the forest might betoken a bewildered deer, frightened by the approach of another lion. But she heard nothing. On powerful legs she exited the creek and carried the helpless kitten the quarter of a mile back upstream. The other cubs broke from their game to sniff at this limp, wet, shiny thing, hoping at first that the lioness had brought them some new form of food.

Restored to his feet, but still freezing, the sodden cub stiffly shook himself, and at that the other kittens backed away, unsure. He licked his chilled, drenched body irritably, purring to himself. He felt a loss of dignity, division from his siblings, and he'd had a scare. It was only at the sound of his purr that the other two cubs recognized him as kin.

Their wrestling match resumed, and their mother was allowed a half-sleep on the boulder above.

.　　　.　　　.　　　.

the fact that hamsters can't ever be delighted to see *horses*, I don't think, even from a distance, the fact that elephants don't like mice, the fact that there's been a pause in executions by lethal injection in Ohio, but only because they can't get hold of the right drugs, right from wrong, the fact that there's one guy who's been on Death Row for thirty years, and that's just so cruel, the fact that it's illegal, in international law or something, the fact that it's torture, Sweet Fanny Adams, Anadama bread, Anabaptists, Alabama, the fact that he raped and beat and killed a little girl in Akron, the fact that why did he do such a thing, the fact that in all this time you'd think he could've explained himself, well, maybe he did, the fact that why torture him for thirty years, the fact that they could've just sent him to prison without parole, though some say that's torture too, the fact that it's terrible for the government to kill citizens, the fact that it doesn't set a very good example, the fact that rubber's still made in Akron, the fact that somebody's making such a *racket* out there, that new house they're building down by the bridge, the fact that I think human beings have built *enough* stuff by now, but there's no end to it, clunk clunk, chop chop, choc choc chip, the fact that there are people who rhapsodize about Chicago skyscrapers, *History of Tuscarawas County*, *Events of a Century in the Muskingum and Tuscarawas Valleys*, the fact that no one has time for nature anymore, the fact that wolves were an annoyance to the first settlers so they shot them all, but bears are back, the fact that there are a lot of bears in *New Jersey*, the fact that I know that because Mary Anne told me, deer ticks, the fact that she never stops talking about the Donner Party, the fact that some party *that* was, the fact that Stacy's doing an essay on Dorothy Counts, the fact that Stace is the same age as Dorothy Counts was when she had to walk to school all alone, and she did it day after day, and got jeered

at and spat at and everything, the fact that Bobby Kennedy was invited
to accompany her but he refused, the fact that they threw stones at
her too, just a young girl, like Stacy, the fact that in the end her family
had to move to *Philadelphia* because it was just impossible in North
Carolina, the fact that if anybody spat at Stacy, nun shaking Mommy,
the fact that James Baldwin said freedom's a myth white Americans
tell themselves, the fact that sometimes you do start to wonder if this
country was sort of doomed from the start, like Scratch says in *The
Devil and Daniel Webster*, but I shouldn't say that, the fact that I'm
sure the settlers meant well, or some did anyway, land grab, grab 'em
by the, broken treaties, gold-diggers, and things are much better now,
apart from when the police shoot black people, the fact that there are
many, many good people surely, plenty of them, "No, there aren't,
and stop calling me Shirley," the fact that you shouldn't judge the
barrel by all the rotten apples, or whatever the expression is, joy, Death
Penalty, death sentence, Dorothy Counts, Dorothy Parker, impending
doom, the fact that a black woman in labor asked for a cesarean
because she felt "a sense of impending doom," but they thought she
wouldn't be able to pay for it, the cesarean, not the sense of doom, so
they refused and she hemorrhaged, and in the end she had to have a
cesarean anyway, and then they left a piece of the *placenta* inside her,
the fact that she never even woke up from the operation, the fact that
she passed away, at just thirty years old, leaving behind a husband, a
son, and the new baby, Placentia, California, the fact that "placentia"
means peaceful, Lake Placid, *Holiday,* Cary Grant, Ned's bump on
the forehead, the fact that Katharine Hepburn calls Ned "my fine
buck-o," Spencer Tracy, the fact that I like the bit in *Desk Set* when
she takes him home in the rain and they both put on bathrobes, and
have that big mix-up over "galoshes" and "goulash," because they're
talking to each other from separate rooms and they can't hear that well,
the fact that that's *another* movie with galoshes, the fact that then he
puts his shoes in the oven to dry out, the fact that they have fried
chicken for dinner and lettuce in a towel, and floating island for dessert, *no man is an island*, the fact that they really seem to be having fun

together, and then the shoes start to stink up the apartment, the fact that Katharine Hepburn's boyfriend's a stinker too, the fact that he interrupts the whole cozy evening and gets all jealous about Spencer Tracy being there, Daddy in the Divinity School grounds, the fact that now I think about it, maybe the lettuce in the towel's in the *other* movie, the one where she's a lawyer, the fact that they're *both* lawyers, and she's defending a woman who's shot her husband, Adam's apple, the fact that it's easy to roll all Katharine Hepburn's movies into one somehow, *Holiday, On Golden Pond, Bringing Up Baby*, slugs, shabby chic, ironing pile, cinnamon dough, peeler, the fact that it's *Adam's Rib*, the one where they're lawyers and they get all messed up by the case they're on, the fact that she's defending and he's prosecuting, and eventually it's all slamming doors and the Silent Treatment and nobody's eating lettuce anymore, the fact that that *is* a good way to keep it fresh in the fridge, in a damp towel, the fact that we learnt that from that movie, the fact that Leo commented on it, and we started doing it too, the fact that I probably learnt most of my housekeeping methods from movies, the fact that Cathy and Art just went off and got *hitched*, itch, after *thirty years* together, the fact that maybe it's for legal reasons but it's still exciting, the fact that I thought they might not have bothered having a honeymoon, because of being together so long, but off they went to Hawaii, the fact that Cathy's always full of surprises, the fact that Marcia's looking after things at the Shoppe, the fact that she's a very efficient person, the fact that I could see them going to Niagara for a weekend, but Hawaii, wow, Maid of the Mist, Fruit of the Loom, the fact that I'm not going to make them a wedding cake, the fact that that's too corny, the fact that I'm going to make them a wedding pear tarte tatin instead, with cinnamon and carda-moms, unless of course I made them an *angel food* cake, the fact that I wonder which Art would prefer, frosting, the fact that Katharine Hepburn and Spencer Tracy never got married, Niagara Falls, Paterson Falls, black rocks, white snow and ice, white water, Jake's VW bus pillow, the fact that when the kids are all grown-up, Leo and I plan to buy us an Airstream and just take off, maybe with a calliope on the back to play old favorites, Kleenex, pear tarte tatin, the fact that everybody says Airstreams are much better than Winnebagos and that Winnebagos literally *stink*, because of the toilet pump system or something, motorhome, Yosemite, bears, whales, the fact that some Winnebagos can be huge and sort of luxurious, but the furniture's always so plasticky, deformed turtles, hourglass figures, the fact that they seem to be going for an Air Force One kind of look for the interior, 9/11, the fact that all Harrison Ford wants to do is relax and watch the ball game when he gets on Air Force One after his big speech, the fact that some aide immediately blurts out the final score as he climbs on board, but Harrison Ford's such a sport about it, he doesn't even get mad, the fact that I wish Harrison Ford was the President *now*, the fact that he'd be a lot better than the one we got, stink bug, even if he's just an actor, the fact that he looks sort of presidential, the fact that Jeff Bridges looks presidential too, in *The Contender*, the fact that maybe it's the way his hair is swept back, the fact that things sure have changed, pinch his neck, bang your head against his, the fact that Harrison Ford's devoted his whole life to making violent action movies, but even so he'd be better than Trump, pinch, headbutt, Mile High sexual assault, the fact that *Air Force One* is so violent I just can't watch it, the fact that at first it seems fun enough, but then it gets gorier and gorier, the fact that they shoot so many people it seems kind of impossible anyone could survive, like a Tom and Jerry cartoon, Donald Duck, the fact that once the Russian terrorists have got all the guns and taken all the passengers captive, and killed the President, or so everybody thinks, the fact that it all seems pretty hopeless, the fact that Glenn Close is in DC, and she's the VP, veep, VIP, all geared up to take over, but she loyally holds off, in the hope that Harrison Ford isn't dead, and he isn't, of course he isn't, the fact that Glenn Glose, *Close*, is absolutely right to wait on that, because Harrison Ford survives and single-handedly saves the day, or it wouldn't be a Harrison Ford movie, a Harrison Ford *vehicle*, the fact that it's not a *Glenn Close* vehicle, the fact that some people pronounce the H in vehicle, the fact that I was brought up to keep the H silent, the fact that Leo was brought up to pronounce both Cs in "flaccid," like *flak-sid*, but I wasn't, "ve-hicle," Harrison Ford hanging outside the plane, in midflight, the fact that in the end he is the last guy on board and almost goes down with the ship, the *plane* I mean, the fact that then he returns intact to the White House with his wife and teenage daughter, the fact that, according to Leo, there always has to be a teenage girl in action movies, the fact that she's like the girl tied to the tracks in silent movies, Silent Treatment, somebody for everybody to worry about, Stacy, the fact that girls aren't tied to the tracks anymore but they get a lot of guns put to their heads, forcing the hero to make difficult choices, the fact that he has to decide whether to save the humble girl or the nation, or that kind of thing, the fact that it always works out that, if you save the girl, the nation too will survive somehow, the fact that morality starts small or something, I guess, deep inside the hero, the fact that they're always to blame in horror movies too, teenage girls, not heroes, like if there's any shabby chic furniture flying around the room there's bound to be a teenage girl in the vicinity, the fact that the daughter in *Air Force One* acts sort of brave and defiant when Gary Oldman leers at her in an icky, child-molesterish way, the fact that she's only about twelve, Stacy, Gillian, my twelfth birthday, walking Pepito, the fact that maybe these movies aren't really about presidents at all, they're really about what it's like having *an adolescent girl in the house*, because they do cause havoc sometimes, Ronny, the Queen of England, the fact that they sure can hog the bathroom, teenage girls, not Ronny and the Queen, working on their de rigueur long straight hair and, dear me, I don't know what, the fact that Ronny loves action movies, the fact that he's always recommending the most violent trash, the fact that I don't know why he thinks I'd like it, the fact that occasionally we've taken his advice, out of curiosity, and we always regret it, the fact that you end up with something like *White House Down* or worse, the fact that in *White House Down*, the hero has to sacrifice everything to save his teenage daughter, but the president's got a teenage daughter too, so the hero saves them all, the fact that he's a failed bodyguard, this bodyguard will

477

either be a success or a failure, the fact that I forget who the actor is but somehow he survives a constant rain of bullets coming from all directions, just by sheer willpower, the fact that the whole movie just seemed like an excuse to go joyriding on the White House lawn, like that guy on Serpent Mound, the fact that I missed out on Jake's babyhood, the fact that I wonder if Mommy was sorry to have missed out on my adolescence, when *she* got sick, the fact that I kind of doubt it, the fact that I was just starting to get obstreperous when she collapsed, so I dropped the obstreperousness and just got depressed instead, sleeping in my clothes, "close," and eating bananas, jigsaw puzzle, carrot salad, pale pink, pale blue, the fact that women do twice as much housework as men, the fact that I know you're supposed to share it out but that's so much more work, the fact that I'd rather sit down with a glass of wine and watch a movie when Leo gets home, rather than discuss *cleaning rotas* and stuff, James Mason, the fact that Leo says he likes the way I move and how I stand, the fact that he likes to see my profile in the kitchen when he gets home, the fact that I dreamt about trying to rehabilitate six or eight mozzarella balls, the fact that they were alive and sort of *human*, but also kind of like deadbeat dads in some way, just a gang of mean mozzarella balls that we were trying to reintegrate into normal society, thirty years, Death Penalty, Niagara, *Niagara*, Marilyn Monroe, Maid of the Mist, the fact that I also dreamt I had a long talk with a Peolia student, and afterwards, because of our talk, she upped her game and got better marks, like she moved from Cs and Ds to an A minus or a B plus, and it was all thanks to *me* and my mentoring, the fact that that's not something ever likely to happen at Peolia in real life, "Go Possums!", since nobody has time to talk to students individually anymore, contact time, rotas, Purdue OWL, the fact that at least Stacy's not a juvenile delinquent, *Rebel Without a Cause*, the fact that she *is* a rebel without a cause though, the fact that I was always scared of becoming a juvenile delinquent, without really knowing what a juvenile delinquent even was, the fact that it sounds so dreadful, "juvenile delinquent," when you're a kid, "extrude," the fact that I don't want any juvenile delinquents in *this* family, touch wood, the fact that luckily the only crime spree Stacy's been on so far, well, as far as I *know*, was when she went tiptoeing with Annie, or was it Susan, through the forest of aisles at the dime store in Coshocton, when they were both about seven, and they danced around plucking plastic flowers out of the buckets, but they gave them all back, so big deal, the fact that they were just playing, but that awful manager guy made such a fuss we've never gone back to that store, the fact that there was also the time she and Annie wrote naughty words in chalk on the sidewalk, but they didn't even know what the words meant, the fact that I have to admit I thought it was *funny*, and it washed right off, so come on, people, pumpkin patch, yard sale, the fact that James Mason's just got home again now, to the water heater problem and the olive problem, the fact that in one dream I had, we were all on a plane eating chicken, and there was a wonderful big white woolly sheep we could have bought, and *should* have bought, cinnamon, brown sugar, zest, the fact that in *It's Complicated* Meryl Streep makes a whole lot of pies because she's having an affair, and when she has insomnia she makes ice cream, the fact that *I* don't feel like making pie after we make love, the fact that that's probably the one time I *stop* baking for a while, oh no, doorbell, the fact that I bet it's Ronny, the fact that he always seems to turn up when I'm all covered in dough and kneading something, all floury and sweaty and, oh darn it, the fact that here he is, peering at me as usual with that lonely hound-dog look he has, hang dog, hangnail, hobnail, bobtail, rabbit, "just passing by," Paterson Falls, Flight 93, stink bugs, the fact that how he loves talking about stink bugs, but that's my own fault, because I told him how much the chickens like them, the fact that I know I should invite him in and give him a cup of coffee or something, piece of pie, but they're not done yet, the fact that all I've got are some Oreos, the fact that how do I get out of it, the fact that I've got Ronny droning on at the door and James Mason groaning in the background, brain drain, venison stew, the fact that it's so hard to get a word in edgewise with this guy, the fact that he used to be beautiful but he's still very nice-looking, Alec Baldwin not Ronny, the fact that grousing all day about the government can really add some wrinkles, mobile drug factory, the fact that he thinks Obama's the *devil*, "Are you evil?", the fact that is that a deer back there, dark shape, the fact that I won't mention it, the fact that I'm sure he's got a million *deer* stories, the fact that, yep, here we go, the fact that he wants to tell me about brown marmorated stink bugs, the fact that they'll eat just about anything, the fact that I already knew that, the fact that my pies, my poor *pies*, the fact that I gotta save the pies, "All that work!", as William Hurt's sister says when everybody raises doubts about her Thanksgiving turkey, the fact that finally I have to tell him, Ronny not William Hurt, "I've got to get back to my pies," the fact that the kitchen timer rang just at the right moment, my faithful timer, the fact that, oh, what a *relief*, it's over, and it only took about ten minutes for him to get the hint this time, how merciful, the fact that, oh no, there's a sticker in my *hair*, for Pete's sake, the fact that now where the heck did that come from, the fact that I know I should've asked the poor guy in so he could talk to me for an hour about stink bugs and violent movies, but I couldn't face it, the fact that all I can think about the whole time is how to get *rid* of him, the fact that every atom of my body just works on that one plan, and he must sense it and think I'm horrible, but I just don't like talking to the guy very much, I just don't, so why should I, free country, the fact that the trouble is he never *listens*, and that gets really tiring, the fact that he just talks and talks and talks, jabbers, and you just want him to *stop it*, the fact that, sure enough, he commented on the smudges of flour on my face, which he always seems to find highly puzzling and amusing, and always comments on, the fact that he told me he doesn't mind them though, my smudges, the fact that I don't care if Ronny minds my smudges or not, "just passing by," the fact that he wants me to feel embarrassed about my smudges but *he's* the one who should feel embarrassed, barging in on a lone woman like this in the middle of the day, the fact that he didn't even bring any chicken feed, because he was "just passing by," the fact that Leo never mentions the smudges on my face, the fact that Leo wouldn't mind if I was covered in flour from top to toe, the fact that he'd still love me, the fact that it is simply not humanly possible to bake four cakes, six pies and eighty cinnamon rolls without getting a little flour on your face, but that doesn't explain the sticker, the fact that it was polite of Ronny not to mention the great big red sticker in my hair, those darned kids, the fact that it's shaped like a mustache, and I have no idea how long it's been there, the fact that maybe I picked it up from the couch, when I was reading Cathy's Amish book, the fact that I may even have nodded off there for a moment, the fact that it's not a great book, the fact that I don't know if Ronny even *wants* coffee, the fact that maybe he stares at *everybody* that way, from gas station attendants to red-winged blackbirds, the fact that the trouble with Ronny is he thinks the world owes him something, but *I* don't owe him anything, the fact that I always pay him for the feed straight up, COD, the fact that I can't *afford* to owe that guy anything, the fact that I have enough debts already, big ones, the fact that maybe I'm just being mean, skunk eggs, angels on horseback, but that guy really can talk to beat the band, and anything you say back just opens up a whole new can of worms, stink bugs, nematodes, the fact that it's all too easy to hand him more stuff to talk about, without even trying, the fact that I asked him how the roads were and he launched into a whole long story about that police officer and the mobile drug factory, the fact that the whole story was made up and the officer shot *himself*, the fact that *I* might try to commit suicide too if I had to confront Open Carry guys every day, or guys like Ronny, the fact that I don't think he parades *around* with his gun but he's got one on the front seat, the fact that I'm not even sure that's legal, the fact that then he got going on Obama, or O'Bummer, as he calls him, and fentanyl, and Interstate-95, I-95, the fact that I just don't feel comfortable asking Ronny in, the fact that he's very large, with that little head that looks like it's about to lose its balance and topple down his back, the fact that his face is like a little lopsided poffertje, but I shouldn't say that, the fact that it's not nice to comment on people's appearance, the fact that people can't help how they look, the fact that why am I so, so *hostile*, the fact that he doesn't mean any harm, the fact that it's silly to be so bugged by him, the fact that he's just a lonely guy who needs somebody to talk to, and maybe a nice piece of pie, the fact that I'm sure he'd never *try* anything, but still, I'm the only stay-at-home mom in the neighborhood so there's nowhere really to go if anything like that happened, the fact that I just don't like this new development, coming without the feed, the fact that he's just so sort of needy, greedy, ♫ *Big deal, big star, Cary Grant!* ♫, the fact that I'm not all that thrilled with that feed anymore, the fact that there aren't enough sunflower seeds in it, especially in winter, the fact that I always have to add more, the fact that I suppose I should ask the poor guy in for a cup of coffee some time, but I'm *working* here, the fact that I'm not just sitting around, the fact that I was busy doing stuff when he came, all kinds of stuff, even if I had James Mason on, to keep me company, a family call, multi-tasking, milk, the fact that just because I'm at home all day doesn't mean I don't have a family to feed and clothe and medicate and, well, eventually *educate*, I hope, the fact that I'm busy trying to save this here little nuclear family from *ruin*, the fact that just their four birthdays alone cost a chunk o' change, **10** cake, Christmas too, the fact that I can't just be giving every lonely guy out there pie and coffee all day, for free, the fact that I was wearing my big plasticized, window-pattern apron as well, the fact that I'm sure it makes me look like a morgue technician or something, forensics, goldfish, Katharine Hepburn, the fact that Schumann and Clara hated Düsseldorf but they couldn't move because they had six kids, *six*, von Trapps, the fact that I wonder whatever happened to all those Schumann kids, Trapp Family, bruxism, hirsutism, the fact that Schumann was no good as a music teacher *or* as a conductor, the fact that not everyone can teach, the fact that he was only good at composing, this will either be a failure, either be a failure, be a failure, a failure, the fact that Katharine Hepburn played Clara Schumann in the movie, the fact that I remember her with her sleeves rolled up, washing kids in a basin on the kitchen floor, while Schumann taught piano or something, the fact that Katharine Hepburn always liked getting wet, the fact that James Mason was battling with his disease in the background while Ronny went on and on about his plight, and slights, the fact that then he wanted to talk about President's Day, and Obama outstaying his legal time in office, the fact that even getting Trump into the White House doesn't stop Ronny dumping on Obama, the fact that he's *obsessed* with Obama, the fact that Ronny doesn't like FDR either, and FDR had more than two terms, the fact that he watches the History Channel all day and night so he thinks he knows everything, the fact that he says FDR was a communist, hotel swimming pool, horses, therapy dogs, tetras, terrapins, the fact that I just don't know what's *eating* him, I really don't, the fact that he seems to think I *agree* with all this stuff, the fact that I could argue with the guy but what's the point, the fact that he thinks Trump should bomb Chicago, because they all drive like "idiots," the fact that when I reminded him I'm from around there, he just changed the subject to how mailmen are all idiots too, because they don't shut the mailboxes properly, the fact that Ronny's out driving around all day and he's always seeing all these mailboxes left hanging open, the fact that the Street Department people in Smyrna told everybody to bag their leaves but then they didn't pick up the bags, the fact that they won't let you burn the leaves either, so *they're* nuts too, Smyrna's Street Department, not the leaves, the fact that leaves are *leaves*, not nuts, itch, the fact that Ronny thinks next fall everybody should dump their bags of leaves in front of the Street Department building, the fact that he lives in Smyrna, *Ohio*, not Smyrna, *Tennessee*, nor Smyrna, *Georgia*, nor Smyrna, *Delaware*, unincorporated, the fact that I kind of wish he lived in Smyrna, *Greece*, three-course dinner, three-piece suit, three-piece suite, avocado ensemble, three-finger salute, effed-up, BSA, MLB, the fact that what's kind of funny is how, the whole time Ronny was here, I was trying to talk to him over James Mason, hoping Ronny wouldn't notice *Bigger Than Life* was on, in case he thought I was just sitting around watching TV, or it led to a big discussion of Hollywood, and all his favorite actors and action movies, and anything else that occurred to him, pain, cortisone, Giant Viper's Buglosses, who knows, SJW cucks, cuckservatives, the fact that luckily there's no sign of the Kinkels' Viper's Bugloss yet, so we didn't have to talk about that, though that's one thing we *agree* on, that Giant Viper's Buglosses are kind of ugly, the fact that I was getting colder and *colder* standing by the open door, but every time I said I had to go back to my baking, Ronny started a whole nother subject related to local or national news or Trump's Twitter habit, the fact that he's really hoping Trump will make it to England for a state visit, the fact that for some reason this is important to him, to *Ronny*, I don't know about Trump, the fact that Ronny seems to have a thing for the Queen, the fact that once, when I mentioned that I lived in London for a year as a kid, he asked me if you can get there by *car*, from *here*, and if Paris and London are the same city, the fact that then he wanted to know if they *shared* the Queen, *I see London, I see France*, which sounds a very economical idea, the fact that then, weirdly, he started wondering out loud if the Queen eats stews or if they're beneath her, the fact that there's some kind of really rotten-sounding stew Ronny makes out of venison, the fact that he cooks it for days, the fact that I guess he's hoping to give the Queen of England some, if she ever happens by Smyrna on her way to Paris, the fact that that guy in the restaurant was talking to his wife about Cape Cod, and he insisted it was an *island*, and when she expressed some doubt about it, he started bellowing "*Everybody* knows Cape Cod is an island, woman," the fact that I didn't know *what* to say, I was just there to drop off some lemon drizzle cakes, the fact that the whole time Ronny was talking just now, I was searching the woods beyond him for something else to look at besides Ronny's big puffy face, and at one point I thought I saw a deer but I didn't say anything, for fear Ronny would either shoot it or talk it to death, the fact that he said himself he's going hunting this weekend and hoping to land a white-tailed doe, the fact that he specifically mentioned a doe, I don't know why, the fact that are they easier to catch or better to eat or what, or did he hope I'd flinch, reel, quail, from echoes of *Bambi* or something, but I never saw *Bambi*, venison stew, the fact that it's always such a relief to see that guy zoom away, with his gun on the seat beside him like some kind of lone bandit, Shane or something, the fact that I don't know if that's his hunting rifle or some other thing he likes to have in the car, the fact that how frightened does a guy have to be to keep a gun right out in plain view like that, the fact that I've seen it, you're *supposed* to, and if the Queen of England dropped by she'd see it too, until her bodyguards wrassled Ronny out of the vicinity, that is, the fact that this is a guy who doesn't even know that London and Paris are two different places, yet he's in charge of these lethal weapons, legal, lethal, in charge of life and death in Tuscarawas and all neighboring counties, Coshocton County, Holmes County, Harrison County, "Aw, shoot!", "shooting for around 3:05," shooting pool, shooting a movie, shooting a blowdart, shooting gallery, shooting range, shooting suspects, shooting victims, MAGA, KKK Konclave, laundry, Jackson Township, draining the swamp, Jesus of New Philadelphia, PF Chang's, the fact that Tangier Island is now half the size it used to be, I think, because of rising sea levels, the fact that there are only about seven hundred people there and some golf bags, golf carts, golf balls, ice, awnings, crab-fishing, jumbo lump crab sandwich, the fact that Tangier Island's in decline, but Trump says it'll all be okay, because he says so, the fact that he thinks as long as you can still play golf somewhere, everything's fine, hay box meal, hollow box girder, bending moment, beams, Maillart's lotus shaped arches, meeting Leo, the fact that I wonder if trees feel a tingling at the tips of all their budding branches every spring, the fact that it must tickle when there's been rain or dew, and every bud has a drop of water dangling from it, the fact that that *must* tickle a bit, the fact that there are huge blue forget-me-nots out back this year, or I *think* that's what they are, the fact that I've forgotten what *forget-me-nots* look like, for heaven's sake, Florence Griswold, Old Lyme, the fact that Fairfield Porter's family owns an island in Maine, Mary Cassatt, John Henry Twachtman, Childe Hassam, Philip Leslie Hale, the fact that William Penn had a beard, the fact that I don't suppose I'll ever see him again, *Jesus Lopéz Peréz* I mean, not William Penn, the fact that Jesus was a man of few words, unlike *some* I could mention, the fact that William Penn had two wives and sixteen children, the fact that it's raining now, and the chickens look wet, but they could do with a little rinse-off, the fact that now our drinking water's so polluted they're advising us to voluntarily filter it, boil it, or use bottled water, the fact that the lead level's up and other stuff, the fact that they say we can wash in it but we drink it or cook with it at our own risk, *I don't know but they know*, the fact that we already have a DuPont water filter in the fridge, Bed-Sty, UWS, LES, gem wit, the fact that I should probably get another of those filter things, the fact that first they poison you, I mean DuPont, and then they sell you the *antidote*, the fact that the kids hardly ever drink water though, the fact that it's always soda or seltzer or milk with them, bubble water, but I guess I shouldn't make *popsicles* out of it either anymore, or boil peppery noodles in it, pepper spray, OC, brain damage, sea turtles, oysters, the fact that you can get an expensive filter *installed* if you want, plumbed in, by a plumber, Tulip, but we can't afford *that*, the fact that we need that money to pay our water bills, the fact that some people are organizing some kind of protest about it, the fact that I bet Amelia's behind it all, as a *protester*, I mean, not a polluter, the fact that she loves a fight, the fact that I don't know why she does these things, *White House Down*, the fact that I'm too busy trying to protect my kids from *brain damage* to go to demos and protest about every darn issue that comes along, ♫ *Stuck a feather in his cap, and called it Macaroni* ♫, the fact that they protested about the new nuclear power stations, and where did that get them, Aynrandocrat, DAPL, the fact that Fukushima's still burning, and the Pacific Ocean's completely full of fallout, salt dome, sacred mounds, the fact that sea salt now contains microplastics, but what can you *do*, the fact that who knows what my kids were born with, in their systems, the fact that the placenta can't filter all this stuff out, but we probably should've known what was heading our way when they killed Lake Erie, NASCAR racing, the Super Bowl, *Miracle on 34th Street*, Colt 45, Winchester 12-gauge, Remington, Birmingham, Alabama, Montgomery, Alabama, SPLC, Peachtree Walk, Mohonk Lake, Mohawk, the fact that I do my bit, the fact that I don't kill *bugs* if I can help it, especially spiders, and I buy organic milk, because it's better for the cows and better for the kids, the fact that people who eat organic get less cancer, like *twenty-five percent* less, the fact that cancer costs money, the fact that, landsakes, Land O'Lakes, when you really come to think about it, *not* eating organic might be a false saving, budget, taxes, plumbers, the fact that that book of Cathy's doesn't tell you *much* about the Amish, the fact that this Sue Bender person just seems to want to talk about *herself* the whole time, Shakers, Quakers, the fact that the Amish were originally German Anabaptists, the fact that the Anabaptists always scared me, but it turns out they don't think you should get baptized until you're an adult, the fact that that seems a *good* idea, live and let live, ♬ *Let it be* ♬, Rumspringa, the fact that I think I've always confused nuns with the Amish and I really *shouldn't*, Laura Ingalls Wilder, Ingles, inglenook fireplace, Green Acres Amish Furniture, wraparound bed, the fact that for *Witness* they made all kinds of actresses audition for the mom character, but the director wanted somebody that looked *real*, and womanly, so he gave up on American actresses and was about to start auditioning *Italian* women to play the part, but then he saw Kelly McGillis in some play or something, and chose her, the fact that she was working as a waitress at the time, in New York somewhere, Greenwich Village maybe, the fact that the name "Amish" comes from Ammann, Jacob Ammann, the fact that he was a pacifist and didn't like *buttons*, Mount Eaton, Dr. Lehman, the fact that they use hooks and eyes instead of buttons, *Patty cake, patty cake, baker's man*, Baker Act, pious desire, Kelly McGillis undoing her blouse, to this day, nowadays, the fact that Sue Bender says Amish women use polyester fabrics in their quilts, the fact that I like the geometrical quilts best, because of the colors, the fact that the Amish really let themselves go in their quilts, the fact that luckily they don't seem to consider beautiful quilts vain, Calico Harvest Quilt Shop, the fact that the Amish always leave a *mistake* in their quilts, I think, to let the "spirit" in, the fact that Sue Bender talks too much about the spirit, IMO, and the heart and the soul and all, and your *journey*, the fact that she even sticks in a "wise Tibetan leader," which goes a bit far, mules, pumps, kitten heels, the fact that not in my back yard, the fact that I just want *hens* in my back yard, hens across the sea, the fact that the Amish love all kinds of plastic stuff, she says, like plastic buckets and Tupperware and cleaning equipment, PFOA, DuPont, Monsanto, bottled water, the fact that the Amish women Sue Bender stayed with washed their dishes in two plastic basins, Appalachian Basin, one with suds and one for rinsing, the fact that they had no running water or electricity, ivy garden, Pepito, the fact that I don't know why Cathy reads these kind of books, the fact that her reading habits are sort of unpredictable, the fact that maybe people with no time for reading just settle for anything, the fact that she's also a *fast* reader, so she's always just grabbing something, I think, without much caring what it is, the fact that she and Art have a cabin somewhere but they hardly ever have time to go, the fact that she probably picked the thing up in a supermarket someplace, the Bender book, not the cabin, the fact that the Amish get their Mennonite friends to take them places and make phone calls for them, the fact that the founder of Jim Beam was a Mennonite, bourbon, rye, the fact that bourbon on ice cream can be rrrreally good, ferrous material, force analysis, the fact that electromagnetic forces are the basis of all electric motors and actuators, *The Limits to Growth*, Club of Rome, the fact that it's always embarrassing to be lent books, in case you don't *like* them, the fact that if you pretend you liked it, the lender gives you *another* one, that's probably just as bad, and you have to read that one too, the fact that if it goes on and on, you never get to read what *you* want ever again, the fact that I wouldn't want to hurt Cathy's feelings though, the fact that at least she doesn't talk about her "heart's journey" all the time or her "spiritual advisors," the way Sue Bender does, the fact that I don't think Cathy *has* any spiritual advisors, nor the time for any, the fact that she's too busy making hog maw and buckeye candy, celery, bananas, lime, blank doll faces, the fact that Cathy sells those Amish dolls with no faces, the fact that I just don't get it, why the Amish consider it okay to make the doll's body, but not the *face*, the fact that they're allowed to sew a whole doll and give her arms and legs and a dress and an apron and a bonnet and hair and everything, but no facial features, the fact that you'd think that wouldn't be so out of line, and they sure would look better, the fact that they give the man-dolls *beards*, but still no nose or mouth or eyes, ENT, otorhinolaryngology, Mayo Clinic, tetanus booster, the fact that Sue Bender goes *bananas* over those spooky dolls, the fact that she's got a whole collection, and she made some nice Amish women make her a whole nother bunch of them, the fact that she has these things *in her home*, the fact that my family would freak out if I put a lot of faceless dolls all over the place, the Abominable Snowman, King Kong, the fact that we saw an Amish horse and carriage just the other day, Sue Bender's illegible to-do lists, the fact that before her heart's journey, Sue Bender was always making long to-do lists, and then she'd revise the to-do lists, and write to-do lists *about* the to-do lists, inserting "leftovers" from the to-do list from the day before, the rice salad in the fridge, the fact that it's time for the old heave-ho, the fact that you can't keep rice forever, the fact that Abby had Leftover Night, but she threw a lot of food straight out as well, stuff she didn't consider worthy or relevant for Leftover Night, the fact that she was a big thrower-outer, Go-Go, the fact that I don't have *time* to make to-do lists, I'm too busy doing the stuff I got to do, to do, to-do list, what a to-do, toodle-oo, cock-a-doodle-do, Yankee Doodle, doodlebug, ♫ *Sing Polly Wolly Doodle all the day* ♫, stink bug, stunning childrenswear, the fact that all I know is I have to get up, fill lunch boxes, make a million pies, and I don't know what else, the fact that Sue Bender complains a lot about their sugary diet, the Amish people she lives with, the fact that she feels they eat too much sugar and carbs, the fact that sugar *is* a carb, the fact that they're good farmers though, the fact that I think they're mostly organic too, but I'm not sure, pacifism, don't beat your horse, Ammann, the fact that they fired rubber bullets at the horses in North Dakota, the fact that to shoot at a horse, for no reason, the fact that the Amish rest the soil with alfalfa and clover, the fact that Sue Bender didn't go live with the Amish in order to study them, she says, she went to study *herself*, the fact that the whole last quarter of the book is just about what it was like for Sue Bender to *write* the book, which is kind of hard to care about, Leftover Night, since it isn't even a very good book, faceless dolls, the fact that I should be reading my Hopewell Archeology Newsletter instead, sinking into Seip Mound, Paint Creek, Portsmouth Mound Park, Adena burial mounds, Story Mound, Camden Park Mound, an old fun fair, the Hopewell graded way, fossils, adjacent picnic sites, the fact that Ohio's state fossil is a trilobite, nematodes, the fact that only ten percent of the original earthworks are visitable, the fact that we could have a picnic next time, by the Ohio somewhere, with a ham and egg pie maybe, mercury poisoning, sugary foods on plastic plates, with a polyester tablecloth, the fact that you have to do *something* to stop the kids going stir crazy, "They have only chaos to climb," the fact that we were thinking of going to Salt Fork State Park sometime, the fact that Leo *promised*, but we haven't done it yet, Man Drowns in Same River Wife Drowned In Two Years Ago, WATCH CHILDREN, National Hammered Dulcimer Championships, the fact that I'm probably a lot more Amish than Sue Bender will ever be, though my kitchen isn't spotless, and I'm not too good at bottling things, milk, cucumbers, relish, the fact that I don't get a kick out of oiling the furniture either, pot luck, At Home, the fact that there is no room in this world for a halfhearted pickler, the fact that picklers need to be bold, wad of bills, enormity, the fact that Mommy would really disapprove of Sue Bender's misuse of the word "enormity," the fact that I miss my mommy, the fact that Sue Bender mentions halfmoon pie and shoofly pie, but not moon pie, chess pie, crumb and gravel pie, or Shaker lemon pie, faceless dolls, Eskimo Pie, Phoebe's Eskimo doll, Coldy, hydrangea, pumpkin pie, Pumpkin Patch dolls, pear tarte tatin, "Little Girl in a Blue Armchair," the fact that Mary Cassatt uses such a beautiful *blue* for the armchair and the couch, cerulean maybe, cyan, CYA, something, the fact that it's almost the same blue as Tiny Tim's traveling case, the fact that the little girl looks so funny and fed up, the fact that you know, there aren't enough paintings of bored, sulky kids, the fact that kids actually look *great* when they're mad, though it would make them even madder if you told them so, O.J., Stacy's laundry pile by her bed, the fact that I wish I could go back in time and make it all up to Stacy, just take better care of her when she needed me to, eating disorders, makeup tutorials, Cassatt, Manet, Monet, makeup, shoutout, takeout, tank top, TeenSpot, Ben, the fact that Ben and Gillian just got back from swimming and a child in the wave pool almost *drowned*, the fact that he was saved by a keen-eyed female lifeguard, the fact that she instantly spotted him floundering, even though there was a huge crowd of kids in the pool, and she dived right in and rescued him, dove, dived, the fact that I'm sure women make the best lifeguards, the fact that we might not be the strongest, but we're always on the lookout for trouble, the fact that the thing is, now I never want *my* kids to go swimming again, even though it's *good* for them to learn how to swim so they *won't* drown someday, the fact that I knew something was wrong about today, the fact that I just had a feeling, I sensed it, "impending doom," the fact that I felt there was some danger looming but I didn't know what it was, the fact that I was beginning to think it was just my dread of Ronny, and now *this* happens, close call, tailgating, tailgate parties, the fact that do people think that if they tailgate you enough you'll stop the car and invite them to a *tailgate party*, the fact that I never liked my own Saturday morning swimming lessons, the fact that I liked swimming, just not the lessons, because they were always pushing you into the deep end before you were ready, or making you learn to dive and stuff, the fact that they were always trying to get me to do things I just didn't feel up to doing, like too many laps, or the butterfly stroke or the back stroke, the fact that they loved making you do anything that made you feel like you were drowning, the fact that nobody rescued *me*, the fact that I always felt out of my depth and I just couldn't seem to stay afloat, the fact that I got so tired, I was scared I couldn't stay up at the surface anymore, the fact that sometimes I really thought I wouldn't make it out alive or see my mom again, the fact that I don't think a swimming lesson should feel like a *dice with death*, the fact that at the time I just assumed *everybody* was coming up choking for air after every lap, and it was just something we all had to put up with, but maybe they were all having a great time, the fact that I was scared I was too skinny to float, too weak, too unathletic to be allowed in the pool, the fact that I was so ashamed and embarrassed the whole time, the fact that I never did learn to dive very well, dived, dove, the fact that the instructors were always shouting at you and advancing you to a higher swimming class before you'd mastered whatever it was, the fact that they shoved me into the deep end before I could cope, and I always got water up my nose, and I *still* hate the deep end, and deep water in general, the fact that I only like water I can stand up in, the fact that I like to be able to feel the bottom, in case some swimming instructor suddenly shoves my head under the water, the fact that I only do breast stroke, or side stroke, though they made us learn the crawl and the butterfly and the back stroke, ice-skating lessons, the fact that I hate the crawl but swimming teachers love it, *and* the butterfly, the fact that why do you need all those different strokes, unless you're going to be in the Olympics, the fact that the butterfly is just *impossible*, and kind of inelegant too, the fact that I don't know why anyone would ever want to swim that way unless you're trying to imitate a paddleboat on the Mississippi, the fact that they should make you carry a calliope on your back while you do it, "Little Girl in a Blue Armchair," the fact that I was happy as a clam with the dog paddle and still am, or the breast stroke, or just swimming underwater, but not diving, the fact that diving can go wrong so easily, the fact that I can do kind of a breast stroke on my *back*, the fact that it's fine as long as there aren't too many people in the pool, splashing water in your face, the fact that there's nothing I hate more than a crowded pool, where you keep getting bumped by the lap-swimmers zooming by, *crawling* by, I should say, or flapping by, the fact that as a kid I only liked swimming underwater, because of Jacques Cousteau, which was the one show I think Daddy let me watch without complaint, the fact that at our swimming lessons we only ever got *five minutes'* Free Play, right at the end, Free Play, and that's when I'd swim underwater, the fact that at the end, they played this horrible military music, "The Stars and Stripes Forever," which meant it was time for us all to get the heck out of the pool, the fact that they seemed to think all the kids would just march out of the pool area in time to the music like good little boys and girls, like von Trapp children or something, the fact that I still hate that tune, the fact that I associate it with almost drowning every Saturday, and the end of Free Play, the fact that I would very reluctantly stop my underwater swimming and stumble exhausted into the changing room, doldrums, Bordens, the fact that I like that tired leg feeling though after swimming, the fact that you haven't swum enough if you haven't reached the trembly-leg stage, Leonardo DiCaprio, Howard Hughes, bras, the fact that that is the tune I always hear in my head when I'm in a hurry, "The Stars and Stripes Forever," the fact that it must have gotten ingrained during those swimming lessons, and now I'm stuck with it forever, starred and striped with it, the fact that to appease my maternal instincts I gave Ben and Gillian a glass of milk and a fresh cinnamon roll, just the thing for kids who've witnessed a near-drowning, the fact that *I* need a cup of coffee and I wasn't even there, Maxwell House, the fact that coffee is good for the liver, or so they say, *They say*, liver, lover, the fact that this is when I tend to wonder why I had all these kids though, whenever I'm most worried about them, the fact that once kids are born you just cope with it somehow, barely noticing how *your* life has disappeared and how you're now totally consumed with *their* lives, just their basic survival, and you're going to be unable to think straight about anything for the next twenty or more years, the fact that it's a shock to have a baby, butterfly twisting on a pin, the butterfly stroke, the bee in the barn at Bread Loaf, the fact that I don't know why it comes back to me, that *bee*, the fact that all it did was get up off the windowsill, for Pete's sake, and slowly swerve in the air and then fly out the window, but for some reason I remember that, the fact that I can remember that *exactly* but not what Mommy's face looked like, the fact that her face comes to me vividly sometimes and I try to hang on to it but I can't, the fact that I don't even remember how I got to school, if I took a bus or what, but I remember that bee I saw when I was seven, slowly rising up off the sun-bleached wood, the bee, not me, the fact that Mommy almost drowned when she was *two*, the fact that she waded out into the pond, calling "Ducky! Ducky!", and she was soon out of her depth,

493

but Abby saved her, and Abby couldn't even swim so it was a brave thing to do, the fact that you can have lots of children, the fact that William Penn had *sixteen*, and the von Trapps had a dozen, but you only have one mom, signs of the Zodiac, unless you count adoptive mothers and surrogate mothers and stepmothers and mothers-in-law and mother *figures*, who are not always satisfactory substitutes, artificial sweeteners, aspartame, the fact that I was always seeking out mother figures after Mommy got sick, until I gave up and just had kids of my own, becoming my *own* mother figure, the fact that maybe I still look for people to mother me, like Cathy maybe, the fact that she's so warm and womanly and friendly, but maybe she's like that to everybody, the fact that I really was in love with Mommy as a child, and it wasn't "puppy love," the fact that it was more like *unrequited* love, the fact that I always worried I loved her more than she loved me, and I think I probably did, the fact that I still worry about it sometimes, the fact that the mother–child thing is a very unequal relationship, the fact that while my kids are downing their milk and cinnamon rolls and assuming I'm all bound up with them and their swimming class, I actually can't think about them for more than a minute, because, well, I don't know why but my mind moves on to other things, like the bee at Bread Loaf, the fact that my mind moves on to the *bee*, or on to Chuck, or Leo, or Mommy, or pies, or Ronny, the fact that I wish not Ronny but he does sometimes come to mind, leftovers, to-do lists, bottled water, the fact that you can never admit this to anybody, and certainly not to your kids, the fact that they'd be so hurt, false promises, fake facts, dandelions, Fox News, the fact that sometimes you just have to ignore everything and remember you're glad to be able to move and breathe, the fact that you're glad to be alive, the fact that sometimes I forget that, the fact that I think I lost out both ways, first by being too in love with Mommy, who had many other more important things to do besides be with me, bee at Bread Loaf, and now, by losing ground with *Stace*, who also has more important things to do than be with me, to-do lists, Tuesday, the fact that Mommy passed on when I was in my thirties, twelve years ago now, the fact that she left me, the fact that I can't bear to even think about all her health problems, the fact that it's best not to think about it, best to block them out like most other things, like my swimming classes, the fact that that is really all I do all day, the fact that instead of caring for my kids, or Leo, or myself, and loving my customers, all I do is go around in circles trying not to think about my *mom*, 6 Kinds Of Dizziness, the fact that maybe everybody does that, but look at me spinning around in circles to make my spiraling pastries while I myself spiral out of control like a whirling dervish or whatever, and at the center of the vortex is always Mommy, tornado, waterspout, dust devil, the fact that moms are at the center of everything of course, motherland, mother nature, mother tongue, Mother Goose, mother vinegar, Mommy, mama, so why should my mom be any different, belly buttons, the fact that Abe Lincoln, Edgar Allan Poe, George Washington and Harry Houdini *all* loved their moms, circles, dollars for donuts, the fact that, hey, I think I've finally cracked it, why Jake only likes SpaghettiOs and Cheerios and bagels and donuts and Life Savers and baked apples and angel food cake, and pineapple rings and slices of cucumber with the seeds scooped out, and cinnamon rolls that somebody's eaten the middle out of first, the fact that the kid eats anything *circular*, but particularly anything round with a *hole* in it, the fact that maybe it makes it easier to grab, long-haired man, topology, the fact that why didn't I notice this before, the fact that, ♬ *dollars to donuts* ♬, that must be it, the kid likes food that comes in circles, hollow circles, the fact that I'm going to use this new finding against him, and get him eating hamburgers and omelettes and bananas, just by cutting a hole in the middle, "Damsons you have to leave unstoned,"

·   ·   ·   ·

Mountain lions, being stealthy, see more people than people see lions. The lioness would not retreat in honor of a man, but nor did she seek them out. They were a threat and a nuisance merely, like fire or flood.

In search of a new den, she escorted her zigzagging cubs across a smooth black highway, the province of men and cars. A jeep roared towards them but she stared it down, with that wrinkle in the middle of her forehead that meant business. The car slowed, then came to a stop. She and her cubs proceeded into the woods on the other side at a leisurely pace, without a backward glance.

But men were all around them in the forest, trespassing continually on lion territories that had long been demarcated. Such invasions were an affront. They stole the deer too, or scared them away with their stink and their squawks and the snapping of their guns. They left behind them injured, poisoned animals, and long unnatural deaths.

Deep snow is the quietest time. Now and then the air rang with the noise of gunfire, the human clatter of clicks, rumbles and beeps, and the distracting blasts of men's voices and those of the callow dogs that shadow them wherever they go. Evidence of their incursions was everywhere, in all sorts of unburied human belongings – glass bottles, metal cans, shreds of paper and plastic – of no use to anyone but a jackdaw.

In a clearing, sounds muffled by rain, she unexpectedly encountered a man with a small dead doe draped across his shoulders. Unwilling to allow him a step closer to her cubs hidden in the underbrush, the lioness stood her ground, ready to pounce. But the deerkiller never even noticed her. He lurched away, panting, into the forest, leaving a trail of fawn blood behind him. Settling the kittens under a log for camouflage, the lioness followed that blood trail a mile or two, just to be sure that the fumbling man wouldn't circle back and harm her young.

She had warned them of men, gangly birds too heavy to fly. She had taught the cubs to listen out for the telltale rustling sounds from the loose extra flaps of skin in which people wrapped themselves, wrappings that made men's bodies swish as they smashed their way through ferns.

Through her own extreme caution, she conveyed to the cubs that men are more dangerous than they look. They killed with ease, and often didn't even eat their prey. They plundered, lay waste, then abruptly retreated to their cars. They were not true inhabitants of the forest, they were usurpers, dangerous visitors who roughly invaded the territory of others.

They did not respect lions.

The cubs saw the cars that zipped past on the highways, and the loud, ungainly helicopters that flew across the sky. One passed overhead once, shaking the trees with its whirling winds. A noise like that put the whole life of the woods temporarily on hold. But men's other machines, on the ground, were the more immediate enemy. Just as their mother detected the cries of many birds and animals, and tracked them, she knew if a distant truck or motorcycle was heading their way.

But even she was confused by the changeable stink of men, and hated the look of them. Where was the neck, the bit to grab if they came too close?

One night, she was out hunting while the kittens slept, and a car clumsily knocked over the stag she was just about to pounce on herself. Two large men stepped out on to the roadway and slowly walked over to examine the carcass. When they spotted the lioness, they froze. Having no intention of sharing prey with them, she slunk back into the underbrush. Loud clangs sounded and bullets rushed past her, splintering branches off the trees.

She knew that cars are not living things, and therefore not killable. Nonetheless she dreamt of subduing one, forcing it to the ground, squashing the life out of it under her own weight and parting its hard, smooth, shiny hide with tearing teeth.

．　　　．　　　．　　　．

the fact that I think convicts should wear those *striped* outfits like they used to, not those awful orange onesie jumpsuits they all have to wear now, that look like medical workers' scrubs, the fact that they don't look that nice on medical workers *either*, the fact that Harrison Ford's both a doctor *and* a criminal in *The Fugitive*, or a convict anyway, but he gets rid of the orange jumpsuit as soon as possible, the fact that he never stops doctoring people all through the movie, even though he's on the run, the fact that I think Nanya liked that movie too, Nanya, the fact that I am a very neglectful person, the fact that I neglect all my friends, the fact that I probably neglect my kids too, the fact that I should be arrested, child neglect, jail, orange jumpsuit, global dimming, Harrison Ford, the fact that I neglected *Mommy*, the most important person in the world, the person I need most to be in the world with me, the fact that why'd I *do* that, He Doesn't Care, The Worst Husband Ever, the fact that after Daddy passed on I could've moved in with Mommy and taken care of her, but I didn't, and I still don't know why, the fact that Ethan and Phoebe couldn't move to Hamden, they had real jobs, so it was up to *me* to do something, the fact that I *could've* done it, easily, I could've moved, the fact that Stacy was still little, the fact that so what if we had to change playgroups, the fact that you make so many crazee decisions in life and later you can't figure out why you did things the way you did, *And that has made all the difference*, the fact that I didn't know she was that *sick*, the fact that I was worried about her though, the last time I saw her, the fact that she was in the hospital again and I could only stay for an hour that day, and after I saw her I decided I *would* move in with her, but I never got the chance to tell her, before she passed on, that very night, passed away, the past, the fact that why'd they both have to die so young, the fact that you get no warning about the most important things in life, and she didn't know either, the fact that she was happy, the fact that we were laughing about something, the fact that everything stinks when it comes right down to it, the fact that we're all going to be nuked any day now and that'll be the end of it, but I *still* don't get why I neglected the person I now miss all the time, the fact that I'm probably neglecting *somebody else* right now that I'm going to miss like crazy after *they're* gone, the fact that I still miss Abby, the fact that I would have done anything Mommy or Abby asked me to do, but they never asked for anything, the fact that it's just terrible to think

about, the fact that I *shouldn't* think about it, the fact that I gotta buck
up, the fact that I have *kids* to think about, the fact that I don't want
the world to end, not while they exist, but such terrible things have
happened, such terrible, terrible things, the Gnadenhutten Massacre,
and lynchings, the March of Tears, Hiroshima and Nagasaki and the
Holocaust, Mao's famine, that bus rape in India, the fact that it's not
just guns or bombs or rapes or car crashes either, the fact that the
whole world's full of *PFOA*, the fact that there's PFOA in Teflon,
Scotchgard, Gore-Tex, dental floss, microwave packets, and mascara,
and there are turtles stuck in plastic six-pack rings, and bumble bees
get killed by pesticides, Roundup, and penguins can't reproduce, and
Stacy and all the other girls like her are wasting their lives watching
other girls like them put on makeup, and people get cancer, and
schools have shooting drills, and every twenty-year-old boy wants to
kill somebody, or else eat a birthday cake shaped like a woman's sit-
me-down-upon, the fact that why can't they just go snorkeling, or
something, deep-sea diving, surfing, or photograph birds or climb
mountains, if they need an outlet, I mean, the fact that tennis was a
good outlet for McEnroe, coffee, Kleenex, peeler, the fact that swear-
ing at an umpire's a lot better than getting physically *violent* or something, the fact that that KKK guy, that shot nine people dead in the
church, didn't even know why he *did* it, once it was all over, but it
was no accident, the fact that he joined their prayer meeting and sat
there for forty-five minutes debating with himself whether to shoot
them or not, and actually hesitated because they were so nice to him,
but then he decided to shoot them anyway, because they were black,
and he shot them all again and again, the fact that there was a five-
year-old girl who had to *watch* this and what'll become of *her*, the fact
that global dimming was noticed in *1961* but nobody did anything
about it, the fact that the whole world's ruined, and full of crackpot
despots, teapot, pot plant, Planet Hollywood tape, and what's more,
I can't stand to *look* at myself anymore, and it'll only get worse, the
older I am, the fact that nothing's going to improve, only get worse
and worse, but oh my, I can't let the *kids* find me like this when they

get up, or *Leo*, the fact that Leo doesn't deserve to find me like this, the fact that he actually thinks I'm *nice*, the fact that I thought all I had to do was take care of Stacy and go to my job, but Mommy needed me too, the fact that they were a bit of a trial when they were together actually, Mommy and Stace, the fact that there was a bit of a rivalry going on there, over *me*, the fact that they both wanted all my attention, the fact that they didn't like sharing me, the fact that I remember telling Jannis I just couldn't cope with both of them at the same time, the fact that that was why I always tried to get a babysitter when I was going to see Mommy, and that was maybe partly why I hesitated to move in, the fact that I can't *remember* why I didn't think of moving in with her sooner, the fact that their rivalry's a dumb reason if that's the reason, the fact that I think I wanted my freedom, but for what purpose, the fact that many an innocent person passes away, innocent person, Violetta, Verdi, Nicolai Gedda, but Mommy was the cat's pajamas, and *I neglected her*, the fact that I just can't live with that, but I do, I do live with it, the fact that my only strategy is never to think about it but it's the truth, the smell of rain, the fact that what right do I have to think about her all the time, when I neglected her while she was still around, the fact that I don't *deserve* to think about her, the fact that I don't deserve the few memories I have of her, lilies of the valley, neglected, negligence, chickens, geosmin, petrichor, Andy Schaeffner, Vermont, failure, fear of failure, either a failure, this geosmin will either be a success or a failure, the fact that I really do need coffee now, "sobbin' women," the fact that after I cry about Mommy I always need coffee, the fact that Mommy loved coffee, the fact that I bet Grandma liked *Seven Brides for Seven Brothers*, because it's got Howard Keel in it, her favorite guy, Grandma, plastic bags, blubbing in her bathroom, WE FORGIVE YOU, the fact that Bride No. 1, whateverhernameis, is like a big *mommy* to everybody, the fact that she has to take care of not just her husband and all his brothers but the abducted girls as well, and she does it all with a *smile*, the fact that I can't take care of *anybody*, and when do I ever smile, the fact that she keeps everybody fed and the abducted girls secluded, the fact that everything's prim and proper until they have their cat fight, in their me-oh-mys, the fact that Bride No. 1 sort of got *tricked* into marriage by Howard Keel, because he never told her about all his brothers back in the cabin, six full-grown men all waiting for waffles and urgent schooling in etiquette, the fact that she gets over the shock though and takes those six brothers in hand and pretty soon they're all spruced up and ready for courting, the fact that they seem to appreciate her a lot more than Howard Keel does, the fact that he just takes her for granted, and deserts her when she's *pregnant*, the fact that he's a deadbeat dad, but he comes around in the end, the fact that he *has* to, it's Hollywood, the fact that the brothers don't look alike at all, which always bothered me, but I think they look good at the barn dance in their colored shirts, the fact that it's depressing though when they mess up the barn they just helped build, the fact that it's a bit like an Amish barn-raising, apart from all the fighting, the fact that Leo says the *whole musical's* depressing, the fact that he says it's just about *rape*, prettied up with music, dancing, and an avalanche, and of course a corsetry scene, the fact that there are also far too many guys with their arms akimbo for Leo to bear, ♫ *Secretly they was overjoyed* ♫, the fact that I'd never say anything bad about it to Stacy though, for fear of wrecking her new musical kick, the fact that at least it brings her downstairs sometimes, away from those Morning Routine videos, the fact that she prefers to watch a musical on the big screen, the fact that *Madama Butterfly* is really about rape too, because Madama Butterfly's been tricked into a fake marriage, Jerry Hall, rape, abduction, Mick Jagger, Benjamin Franklin Pinkerton, the fact that I wonder why Puccini chose an *American* as the bad guy, the fact that there's an avalanche in *The Lady Vanishes* too, Mommy, ducks, Newburyport, the fact that Mommy grew up in Newburyport, Mass., white steeples, sailboats, lobster rolls, potato chips, Marblehead, Motif #1, the fact that they lived on just one floor of that white clapboard house on Coffins Court, the fact that why anybody would name a street *that*, and a dead-end street too, the fact that they never had much money, the fact that her father had all kinds of jobs but none lasted long,

Knights of Columbus, the fact that for a while he ran a bakery, the fact that that always interested me, but Mommy never said much about his bakery job, except that he gave all the stale bread away to the poor at the end of the day, so everybody stopped coming during the day and just tramped over at closing time for the free bread, the fact that, as a result, he soon went out of business, the fact that I'd love to know what his bread was like, the fact that he could make very good donuts too, the fact that Uncle Joe got out of night duty in the Navy by making those donuts, the fact that he wrote home from the ship to get the recipe, and everybody was so crazy about those donuts they gave Uncle Joe special privileges, KP, the mess, the fact that I *wish* I had that donut recipe, dollars for donuts, but it's lost forever now, the fact that I really need a rolling machine like Meryl Streep's got, that rolls the dough out flat for you, chocolate croissants, the fact that mostly, though, her dad was a drinker, Mommy's, not Meryl Streep's, the fact that her mom was always pouring his liquor down the kitchen sink, but she just couldn't compete with the booze in the end, the fact that to him the bottle was six feet tall, and his wife was only about *five* feet, the fact that Mommy and Abby were both around five feet too, the fact that Humphrey Bogart tells the Nazi guy "I'm a drunkard," when the Nazi asks him what his nationality is, the fact that Humphrey Bogart really was a drinker, in real life, the fact that Lauren Bacall later married Jason Robards, Jr, who was in a bad car crash, just before he did *All the President's Men*, Donald Trump, Jr, but he recovered, the fact that I like that Jason Robards, the fact that I like the way he puts his feet up on the table in the editorial meetings, the fact that I can never read *WaPo* articles online now because you have to subscribe, Mommy, the fact that in 1900 there were seven thousand varieties of apple in America, and now it's only *fifteen*, opodeldoc, Ipecac, Opelousas, the fact that maybe I *need* opodeldoc, Opal, Frederick, the fact that the only time I ever saw Mommy cry was when her mom passed away, the fact that I found her crying in her bedroom while she packed for the funeral, the fact that I must have been about five, the fact that now I realize I don't really know how Mommy felt about *life* after that, the fact that did something die in her forever like it did with me, when *she* passed away, the fact that life just doesn't mean as much without your mom around, well, unless you're Stacy, the fact that I bet she'd breathe a big sigh of relief, "Never skip a grade," the fact that, gee, that was a *two*-cups-of-coffee meltdown, downward spiral, dirty dishes, dollars for donuts, Kleenex, the fact that do other people cry all the time and then just buck up and you never know anything about it, the fact that do we all just plow on, pretending we feel all right, the fact that Mommy liked solitaire, potato chips, Jane Austen, lilies of the valley, sheep, parrots and Pepito, the fact that little did Pepito know how closely he resembled a sheep, the fact that she also liked cigarettes, fresh ravioli, and peaches in cream and *me*, the fact that *she liked me*, the fact that I can hardly remember her now, and I can't remember her mom at all, the fact that I think I only saw her mom once or twice when I was a baby, not like Daddy's mom, who hung around so long we all got to know her maybe too well, the fact that I even had to watch her keel over over Howard Keel, the fact that that sounds like a palindrome, keel over Keel, head over heels, except it would have to be "leek over revo Keel," which doesn't work at all, limericks, rose madder, "A man, a plan, a canal: Panama!", canal, jigsaw, the fact that palindromes are harder than they look, look hard, hard look, Keel was I ere I saw leek, take a leak, oh dear, con- densation, compensation, was it a cat I saw, the fact that I met Mommy's dad a couple times, the fact that he had an electronic device he used so he could talk, the poor man, the fact that he held it against his throat, the fact that he outlived her mom by a couple years, pre- decease, disease, deceive, *Deception*, the fact that her mom died of ovarian cancer, and he died of throat cancer, Bette Davis, buttercups, Uncle Joe, the fact that why do things like that have to happen to people, the fact that when Cathy took her dying mom to the hospital they made her wait all alone in an empty room for eight hours, and Cathy didn't know where she'd *gone*, and the next day she passed on, the fact that they lost all that time together, the fact that hospitals are always losing patients, and then somebody finds them dead in the basement, or a toilet, the fact that Daddy's father was born in Galatz in the nineteenth century, the fact that I have met somebody born in the *nineteenth century*, though I never knew him very well, the fact that he still had a slight accent, the fact that slavery only ended a little over a hundred years before Leo and I were *born*, but in some ways it's still going on, "Black tail fly," the fact that the Emancipation proclamation was signed in the middle of the Civil War, but the police are still shooting black people for no reason, as if they had the right, the fact that I think it's worse now than in the seventies and eighties, the fact that maybe Ohio never changed, the fact that once they had the UGRR and now it's all orange jumpsuits, the fact that Mommy was born with a weak arm, but the doctor told her mom to massage it, and she did, every day for six months, and after that the arm was pretty much *okay*, ducks, barnacle geese, pink-footed geese, a stitch in time saves nine, a bird in the bush is worth two in the hand, no, the other way around, a bird in the *hand*, the fact that I'm all at sixes and sevens today, raining cats and dogs, the fact that sometimes it rains *frogs*, but nobody believes that until they see it themselves, and not many people get to see it, peaches in cream, the fact that I don't think it ever rains peaches in cream, but it *could*, the fact that thanks to all those massages in babyhood, Mommy had no trouble with that right arm for the rest of her life, except that it was a little hard for her to raise it right over her head, but not so as anybody would notice, asafetida, sumac, the fact that Mommy was about two when she walked straight into the pond saying "Ducky! Ducky! Ducky!" and Abby rescued her, the fact that Abby was scared to *death* of water, but her devotion to Mommy outweighed her fear, so she waded right in and dragged her baby sister out, the fact that Abby always loved Mommy, and vice versa, ditto, "That goes for me, double!", the fact that Abby comforted me when Mommy got sick, the fact that we were sitting in the hospital corridor and Abby was crying and she turned to me and said, "But I should be comforting *you*," the fact that that was sweet of her, the fact that I never forgot that, the fact that I didn't cry when Mommy got sick, after the first day, the fact that I just felt numb, blank, but Abby comforted me, just by being there, the fact that maybe she even thawed me out a little, the fact that Abby always seemed to have such a quiet, orderly life, friendly and serene, tucked away like that in her nice snug house behind the pretty stand of trees, with nice neighbors and a nice husband, and embroidery and Leftover Night, but that wasn't the whole story, the fact that that was just the story I told myself, the fact that actually Abby had a *hard* life, the fact that they weren't too well off, especially when they first got married, the fact that she never got to go to college, because of money, the fact that I think she was kind of *lonely* most of her life, though she loved Hoag and all, the fact that he wasn't a great talker or anything, and Abby was, and those neighbors were actually kind of boring, most of them, boring for *her*, but she never said so, the fact that there was one who was a real hypochondriac, the worst one I ever met, the fact that she *looked* healthy but apparently just about everything was wrong with her, and she could talk about it for hours, the fact that Mommy always said it was just because she had nothing to do, the fact that she thought the whole crowd were going crazee just being housewives, the fact that she had a lot of illness too, Abby, not the hypochondriac, the fact that the hypochondriac woman would have *killed* to have Abby's real illnesses, the fact that Abby took too many aspirin over the years for her arthritis, so she got an ulcer, the fact that then she had to have scoliosis surgery and was bedridden for a year, the fact that I *hate* that all that happened to her, for no reason, the fact that she had so many health problems and it wasn't fair, the fact that what did she ever do to deserve it, the fact that it's nice they had a trip to Ireland, the fact that Abby saved Mommy's *life* in that duck pond, the fact that if she hadn't gotten Mommy out of the pond, or if their mom hadn't massaged Mommy's arm every day for six months when she was a baby, Mommy might not have survived and gotten married and *I* might never have been born, and then my poor kids wouldn't ever have existed and Leo would have had to shack up with *somebody else,* and I would never have known my *mom,* the fact that there might even have been a slight pie deficit in the Tuscarawas area, but probably not a noticeable one, Otis, owlets, boarlets, ducks, Newburyport, cinnamon mixture, spoon, brush, vanilla, the nun who shook Mommy, the fact that Mommy was always bored at school, because she was so smart, the fact that she was always getting in trouble for daydreaming, and one day she went to the bathroom and a nun found her in there daydreaming, and the nun gave her a terrible shaking, the fact that Mommy reported this to her mom when she got home, and her mom was so mad she marched straight back to the school and gave that nun a real talking-to, *Mother Goose Rhymes*, the fact that that nun probably never dared shake another child again after that, or even touch one, or I hope not anyway, the fact that I could shake that nun right now for shaking my mom, the fact that Mommy loved her mom for that, the fact that she *never* had a bad word to say about her mom, and neither do I about *my* mom, the fact that I come from a long line of mother-worshippers, but Stacy seems to be bucking the tradition, the fact that she wrote her PhD, Mommy, not Stacy, on *Tennyson's Ten Silent Years*, the Silent Treatment, the fact that I have led a long bereft life since Mommy passed away, ten silent years, or eleven, no, twelve, of *no Mommy*, no mulberry tree, no peaches in cream, no, *twelve*, though Leo makes up for a lot, Tennyson, tension, the fact that I don't appreciate him enough, Leo I mean, not Tennyson, though I'm sure I don't appreciate Tennyson enough either, the fact that I take Leo for granted sometimes, but not as much as I take Tennyson for granted, *Come into the garden, Maud*, last night's outburst, the fact that I really shouldn't drink, the fact that what was I freaking out about, the fact that was it just about the *PTA*, the fact that I don't even know how it started, the fact that I think I got annoyed when the kids didn't finish what was on their plates, because that always makes me mad, the fact that after they left the table Leo said I was acting nuts, and then I did go nuts, all because I didn't like him *saying* I was acting nuts, the fact that, well, nobody wants to be told they're *nuts*, but still, the fact that I don't know what got *into* me, I really don't, wine, Knights of Columbus, nuts of Columbus, nut allergies, allergens, Captain Wentworth and the chestnut, Scratch and Daniel Webster, Webster's, worry dolls, gluten, chicken, three hundred billion chickens a year, the fact that Stacy says if a girl goes to school wearing the same outfit two days in a row, everybody says she's nuts, and the same if you don't wash your hair every single day, or you don't wear makeup, or if you're not on social media all the time, the fact that the *boys* don't get called nuts unless they turn up in a trench coat carrying a machine gun, but by then it's too late, the fact that I think some of the *teachers* are nuts myself, nun, like that gym teacher yelling at that little kid last summer, calling the kid a "screw-up," nun shaking Mommy, the fact that it was a verbal *assault*, and it lasted a full five minutes, the fact that I was standing right outside the playground fence and I couldn't hear every word, but I got the gist, the fact that the guy was firing all these questions at the kid and he didn't give the kid a chance to *answer*, the fact that it was like a CIA interrogation, and he kept screaming "You're a screw up," the fact that I couldn't bear to listen, the fact that I was so shocked I even considered reporting that teacher to the principal, the fact that if it had been *my* kid, I'd have called the principal, heck, I'd have been calling my *lawyer*, if we had one, and could afford one, the fact that I don't think a gym class should be conducted like a boot camp for the *Marines* or something, nun shaking Mommy, the fact that that man sounded like a *maniac*, yelling at a child like that, a *child*, the fact that I don't care how bad the kid was at baseball or whatever it was, tennis, McEnroe, quoits, croquet, the fact that no sport training warrants that kind of scolding, the fact that Ben thinks the screamer was probably Mr. Glean, the fact that Ben hates Mr. Glean, Mr. Clean, Mr. Muscle, the fact that I always hated *my* gym teachers too, or I shouldn't say "hated," the fact that I just never liked gym all that much, my scary swimming lessons, the fact that they were always trying to tire you out and I didn't *like* being tired, the fact that I still don't, the fact that I resent being tired out by people, like at parties, the fact that for some reason my gym teacher used to tell us not to *pant*, the fact that he thought we should all breathe through our noses instead, but that's hard to do when you're out of breath, the fact that it seems kind of intrusive to tell a kid how to *breathe*, but okay, tell them to breathe through their noses if you have to, but don't tell a kid he's a *screw-up*, never ever, because that will cause stress and trauma and reduce self esteem, and we're all supposed to be making our kids feel *less* stressed, not more, and less emasculated, the fact that we go to all this trouble to try to boost a kid up and then the gym teacher does a thing like that, the fact that no amount of *silly putty* is going to make *that* kid feel better, the fact that it sets a bad example too, because "screw-up" is a cuss word, though everybody says it now, "get screwed," "screw you," oh my, the fact that I don't know how people can talk like that, B & J's hot roast beef sandwich, watching Leo shaving, his styptic stick, the fact that it's *Mr. Glean* that's the screw-up, if you ask me, the fact that I bet the principal wouldn't have done anything about it anyway, if I *had* complained, and Mr. Glean might have taken it out on *my* kids, in response, the fact that the guy needs Anger Management classes though, big time, the fact that maybe *I* need Anger Management classes too, after last night's scene, yelling at top of my lungs, the fact that it wasn't quite yelling, but it was bad, bold as brass, off my rocker, purple and green, laundry, ironing, chickens, goldfish, the latch on the screen door, the fact that you should never *ever* shake a child, the fact that it's very bad for them, the fact that it can kill them, the fact that deadbeat dads are always losing it and shaking the baby, Daddy's legs in the headlights, my mouse Edward, chicken eggs, the fact that Mommy and Daddy met on a blind date at the Copley Plaza in Boston, the fact that they were both PhD students when they met, the fact that Mommy was working on Tennyson and Daddy was teaching already, writing his PhD on the side, the fact that I was in Filene's Basement in Boston once and I bought myself a Minnie Mouse watch, the fact that the first time Mommy knew she loved Daddy was when they were out on a date and the car broke down somewhere, the fact that Daddy got out to look at the engine, and when she saw his legs lit up by the headlights of the car, she knew she loved him, the fact that getting out of the car that night to peer at the engine decided Daddy's whole future, the fact that I don't think Daddy knew much about cars, but he did have nice legs, the fact that he taught himself to drive when he was about six-teen, the fact that Leo's PhD was on Maillart and early reinforced concrete, and he went all over Europe for it, Switzerland, Bern, Zürich, Rorschach, the fact that Mommy helped him edit his PhD as they rowed around in a rowboat somewhere in Cambridge, *Daddy*, not *Leo*, the fact that Daddy rowed them around some lake, while Mommy read his latest chapter, or maybe it was the Charles River, no, probably some pond somewhere, Fresh Pond, Walden Pond, no, not that, Thoreau, the fact that the Charles is eighty miles long and it's fed by eighty streams, which sounds a bit of a coincidence, the fact that Boston is at the mouth of the Charles, Boston Tea Party, Red Sox, Bruins, pollution, the fact that they must have done a lot of rowing to get through a whole PhD, robocall, the fact that this was long after Mommy'd been dumped by the Otis elevator guy, not in the river, just romantically, thrown over, escalators, elevators, esca-pade, escape artist, con artist, "My wife'll buy anything marked down – last week she bought an escalator," Grandpa's donuts, baker's dozen, the fact that she really loved that guy and he was pretty keen on her too, but he decided to marry some Otis elevator heiress, the fact that it turned out he was just a gold-digger, gigolo, lounge lizard, the fact that their wedding was a surprise to Mommy, and she was terribly hurt, but then, a little while later, like maybe just a few weeks, he turned up again and suggested he and Mommy could carry on seeing each other, secretly, behind the scenes, the fact that I guess he must have regretted the marriage almost immediately, regretted losing Mommy, or maybe that was always his plan, the fact that Mommy didn't go for the whole idea though, the fact that she had no interest in a clandestine affair, especially with a guy who'd just thrown her over for an Otis elevator heiress, and that was that, the fact that *that* guy was a real "screw-up," a two-timing, money-grubbing snake in the grass, the fact that he really blew it with my mom, the fact that he broke her heart, broke her, broke her spirit, well, a bit anyway, "a bit," the fact that can you can have your spirit broken "a bit," the fact that Mommy was also briefly engaged to some *gay* guy, maybe on the rebound from the elevator guy, the fact that she never said much about the gay guy, except *she* thought they could be happy together, but he broke it off, the fact that the whole thing collapsed somehow, but amicably, and they remained friends, in a distant sort of way, the fact that I don't think she saw him many more times but she always thought kindly of him, cigarette, not like the Otis elevator guy, pen, peaches in cream, book, sunglasses, Lake Michigan, inner tube, the fact that I forgive the gay guy too but I'd like to wring that Otis elevator guy's neck, right after I finish shaking the nun, the fact that I know, I know, I shouldn't say such things, but I just think, how dare you *dump my mother*, the fact that it's lucky for me he did though, or I wouldn't be here and neither would my kids, and Leo would have shacked up with somebody else who'd get to look at him with no clothes on and watch him shave or read under his Anglepoise desk lamp, and *she'd* get to snuggle up to him at night, *Come into the garden*, and put his carefully rolled socks in his sock drawer the way he likes them, and *she'd* be Swiffering the dust bunnies under the kids' beds, but they wouldn't even be my kids, gosh, galoshes, socks, the fact that household dust contains toxic chemicals, the fact that Cary Grant has trouble finding his socks because Myrna Loy and the maid have put them all in a basket in the closet, the fact that I can't remember the maid's name, the fact that most actresses have the strangest names now, like Cate Blanchett, or Gwyneth Paltrow, or Mia Farrow, or Uma Thurman, the fact that they used to make you change your name in Hollywood to something more *ordinary*, or more elegant and romantic, but now you can't make a living unless you're called Meryl Streep or something, the fact that maybe it makes her more memorable, *Merylable*, the fact that Hollywood actresses used to be forced to have all their *molars* out too, to give them more concave cheeks, the fact that if I told Stacy this she'd probably want hers out, her molars, not her cheeks, and I know just the dentist to do it, or the hygienist anyway, the fact that she could just blow a person's molars to smithereens in a few minutes with that sandblaster of hers, the fact that I think I still have three at the back, molars, no thanks to dental hygienists, and all my wisdom teeth, but I still can't chew on one side of my mouth and my teeth are hyper-sensitive to cold drinks, cold air, hot things too, all thanks to that hygienist and her sandblaster, dental records, forensics, bones, grave robbers, forensics teams, the fact that there's something dismal about teeth, the fact that they last too darn long, sitting there in your jawbone for thousands of years after you pass away, until a few archeologists come along and take an interest in them, or not, Hallowe'en pumpkins, the fact that if archeologists do find my skull someday, I bet they'll immediately see my teeth were brutally sandblasted at some point during my lifetime, but will they be able to tell how much they *hurt* after they got sandblasted, the fact that now it's all about bust enlargements, Hollywood I mean, not *archeology*, well, as far as I *know*, Blandings, blandishments, molars, "You're a screw-up!", the fact that my four kids are like four limbs, and it feels like if I lost any of them I might die, the fact that you'd think that, with four kids, you could just *divide* your love up between them, in quarters, so if you lost one it wouldn't be so bad, safety in numbers, but instead the love gets *quadrupled*, leaving you with four times the anxiety, four times the sense of helplessness, four times the afterschool activities and all, the fact that people with no kids seem so *free* to me now, the fact that I half-envy them sometimes, though I know I shouldn't say so, the fact that, sure, it *looks* fun, the fact that most people are convinced they've *got* to have kids, fertility clinics, hard-boiled eggs, and nobody ever tells them they might be happier just the way they are, the fact that nobody ever tells them the terror of what could happen to your kids *cripples your life*, the fact that all mothers are going through this all the time, I think, but we never talk about it, the fact that I worry over every bruise, every blemish, the fact that you never know if you've given birth to a monster, or if they've got some fast-growing tumor or what, the fact that if every mom is worrying about every kid this much, that's an awful lot of fear and anxiety resonating through the world, echoing, skimming, skimming a stone across the water, the fact that I'm sure even *chickens* worry about stuff, eagles, foxes, the fact that hens pant and squawk while laying eggs, the fact that it's not *nothing*, laying an egg, the fact that they should breathe through their nostrils, according to my old gym teacher, the fact that it's a big effort for birds to lay eggs, but nobody ever thinks about that, nobody but poultry farmers anyway, and maybe vegans, the fact that I guess vegans really do think about it, eggs, the fact that you don't want to sound negative about motherhood or anything, the fact that that would be *depressing* for everybody, eaglets, dceaglecam, Hope and Glory, Mr. President and the First Lady eagle, the fact that now there are leaf buds on the tulip tree beside the eagles' nest, the fact that Mommy and Daddy had their worries too, the fact that we all had our dramatic childhood accidents, ink, Ajax, mattress button, the fact that I tugged it right out of the mattress and swallowed it, but it got stuck in my throat and I cried, just like Flora, the fact that babies will eat *anything*, you gotta watch them, kibble, Babar, Celeste, ma'am, the Queen of England, the fact that I wonder how bad Mommy felt each time we swallowed the wrong thing, like did she feel bad about it for *life*, or did she get over it fast, because life goes *on*, especially when you've got three kids, the fact that there's no time to pause for thought if you have a lot of kids to take care of, and if you did you'd be sad, because too much can go wrong, with *you*, not just with your kids, the fact that you could have a stroke at any moment or an ulcer, or lose the ability to hear or see or breathe or walk or get to the bathroom when you want to, the fact that there's terror in that, along with the terror of heart attacks and seizures and cancer, or getting a teeny-weeny facial twitch that might turn out to be the start of Bell's Palsy, the fact that you could be crushed in an elevator like Helen Gurley Brown's dad, the fact that there are hurricanes and tornadoes and volcanoes to engulf you, and floods that'll leave you sitting helplessly on your own roof, and avalanches and fires and bombs and explosions and train wrecks and collapses of all kinds, the fact that I could get a debilitating, life-narrowing, happiness-ruining hip or knee problem tomorrow or the next day, rheumatism, arthritis, tennis elbow or housemaid's knee, though I don't even play tennis and I certainly don't wash the floors on my knees, the fact that

I *couldn't*, it would wreck my *back*, the fact that then there's psoriasis, paralysis, peristalsis, dialysis, diabetes, T2D, Q fever, or plague, senility, servility, sycophancy, vigilantes, posses, pustules, poultice, practice makes perfect, the fact that, heavens to Betsy, just losing the ability to cut your own toenails, or pluck your own eyebrows, or brush your own blasted, sandblasted, teeth, would be tragic, or getting so thin your bones start breaking of their own accord, *North by Northwest*, or so *fat* First Responders have to come with a *crane* and crank you out of bed into their specially reinforced ambulance, the fact that there's the terror that all your *hair* will just suddenly turn white overnight, or fall out, and you find it all over your pillow, and you'll have to find a wig store the very next morning and explain your white or hairless head to your appalled kids, who will never love you as much again, because how *could* they, the fact that a hairless mom, the fact that I sometimes think I'll wake up one day and everyone will have suddenly changed their *minds* about me, or about moms in general, or pie, and I won't realize because nobody kept me in the loop, Chicago Loop, the fact that does everybody have all these fears, or is it just me, flea collars, dust mites, deer ticks, tape worms, because sometimes it makes me a bit crazee to have to contemplate all these disasters on my own, the fact that I think that's why people invented languages, so they wouldn't feel all alone with their terror, the fact that, I mean, we're all so terrified, who needs *terrorists*, the fact that the terror of being alone is enough to floor you, never mind the fear of mortality, fear of failure, the fact that, heck, just the medical bills have *me* cowed, without suicide bombers and school shooters muscling in, the fact that everybody's life is bound to go wrong *eventually*, because we all pass away, me, Leo, the kids, Mommy, Abby, ISIS terrorists, everybody, and that's the worst thing that could possibly happen, that you disappear off the face of the earth, the fact that the worst thing that can happen happens *every time*, eventually, to everybody, the fact that those ISIS people are just speeding things up a little really, 9/11, but there's no need for *that*, the fact that I don't believe *they* want to pass away either, the fact that they just don't know what they're talking about, because it's *awful* that most mothers pass away never knowing what'll happen to their kids, the fact that that's so sad, because you're supposed to *protect* them, not desert them, and no matter how old your kids get you'll still want to know how they are, you'll always want to know, ♫ *It won't be long until we're there with snow, snow, snow* ♫, the fact that maybe I should just, like, zone out and be Zen or something, meditate, levitate, contemplate nothingness, reach nirvana, communal crying, the fact that Ethan got me to promise him long ago that if I was ever really desperate, like suicidal or something, that I would tell him, which still really comforts me, the fact that I know he's there if I need him, the fact that I think he was kind of worried about me for a while, when I was a teenager, the fact that everybody should have that promise from somebody, a guaranteed listener if you're ever really losing it, the fact that I *would* call him too, if I ever had to, the fact that he's a sweet guy, a fun guy too, fungi, the kind of guy you're proud to know, the fact that these days we usually talk about Netflix, not suicide, the fact that he was so handsome when we were teenagers I liked to show him off around New Haven, if we went downtown or somewhere people from school might see us, in case they'd think we were a couple, the fact that it wasn't *incest*, the fact that I didn't want to *be* a couple, I was just proud of hanging around with such a handsome guy, bandwagon, chuckwagon beans, Chuck, *The Odd Couple*, the fact that I just realized that when this monologue in my head finally stops, I'll be *dead*, or at least totally unconscious, like a *vegetable* or something, the fact that there are seven and a half billion people in the world, so there must be seven and a half billion of these internal monologues going on, apart from all the unconscious people, the fact that that's seven and a half billion people worrying about their kids, or their moms, or both, as well as taxes and window sills and medical bills, shut-in, shutout, dugout, bullpen, the fact that that's not counting the multiple-personality people who must have *several* internal monologues going on at once, several each, *mom*ologs, Mommalabomala, Bubbela, blogs, vlogs, log cabins, Phoebe's Christmas logs, the fact that animals must have some kind of monologue going on in *their* heads, even if it's more visual than verbal maybe, the fact that bald eagles certainly always seem to be thinking about something when you watch them on the eaglecam, the fact that they're very alert, they're so alert it gets tiring to watch, the fact that they make me nervous, gripping a branch like that for hours on end and twisting their heads around all the time with those 350° turns, the fact that it's kind of disconcerting, the fact that they're not easily scared, I don't think, but they're very aware of danger, the fact that they keep everything in mind at all times, except when they're asleep, but then they're *dreaming*, and that's like a monologue too, in a way, the fact that sometimes you don't need the really long tin foil, I mean *wide*, the fact that sometimes it's too wide, the fact that I think a lot of people think all I think about is pie, when really it's my spinal brain doing most of the peeling and caramelizing and baking and flipping, while I just stand there spiraling into a panic about my mom and animal extinctions and the Second Amendment just like everybody else, twinge, back, the fact that Ohioans can talk the talk till the cows come home, but it's all show, the fact that really they're scared all the time, I bet, of being shot or foreclosed or fired or who knows what, nuclear war, the numbness of muted beings, ♫ *hot cross buns, hot cross buns, see how they run* ♫, the fact that nuclear war is probably imminent but nobody ever mentions it, the fact that it would be impolite to bring it up, ink, Ajax, mattress button, the fact that I like it when they give you a piece of cheese with your apple pie, the fact that an apple without the cheese is like a kiss without the squeeze, the fact that a kiss without the cheese is like an apple without the squeeze, community columbarium, lemons and limes, archeologists, Magna Carta, ♫ *London Bridge is falling down* ♫, the fact that life is so easily taken away, stolen, screwed up, jigsaw, the fact that a human lifespan isn't all that long, compared to planets or rocks or even trees, and I fill mine up with regrets and shyness, disappointments, embarrassments, success and failure, and yes, *pie*, and music, longings, evasions, neglect, driving, chicken feed, nostalgia, and then back to regret, the fact that I am always trying to *remember* stuff, *Remember, remember*, 7 Up,

Hawaiian Punch, Bo the dog, *treason and plot*, black leaves, white water, half-naked cousins in a motel pool, the fact that sometimes, in the middle of a long day, I look at a shadow and it seems like a little portion of *nighttime*, like envelopes of night that hang around in the day, and that comforts me somehow, because the time I like best is when the kids are asleep and Leo and I can go to bed, the fact that there's nighttime in *clothing* too, like pockets of darkness up a sleeve, or in your pants, or under your jacket, upskirting, secret nighttime, the fact that I dreamt it was night and I heard a strange crumpling sound, and in the dream I could fly, so I flew over to a dark hedge to see what was making the crumpling noise but I couldn't see anything except pure blackness, the fact that I kept peering into the blackness, hoping my eyes would adjust but they never did,

.   .   .   .

Roaming with the cubs by daylight, the lioness found the tracks of a female jogger. They soon came upon the woman, who was leaning up against a tree, panting heavily from running up the hill. The lioness watched her intently, assessing the risk to cubs. They lost interest and started to play, and their cheerful cheeping finally drew the woman's attention.

Running for her life now, she stumbled through ferns and poison ivy. The lioness followed steadily, and the cubs kept in step. The jogger slithered unadroitly halfway up a tree, tearing her pants and cutting her leg. She gained a low branch, and gripped it tightly, wide-eyed and crying.

The cubs gingerly approached the woman's backpack, that lay at the foot of the tree, as if they thought it might be alive. They sniffed and prodded it, taking in its unfamiliar scents of cloth and sweat and plastic. Then they started to tear at it, and bat it around between them. One cub stopped to scratch herself.

Their mother had never once taken her eyes off the woman in the tree. At first so still, she now crouched, tensed, and sprang twenty feet in the air, reaching a branch above the one the mewling, bleeding woman clung to. The cubs began to follow and, still unable to leap, they struggled to scratch their way up the trunk. The lioness stared down at the cowering woman, whose vulnerability had a smell. She knew now that this person was neither hunter nor prey. She could afford to leave her be.

The woman, barely breathing, lay there frozen, assuming she would soon be dead for having come between a mother cougar and her cubs. One of the cubs was now tottering on a branch below, getting fretful but still trying to balance. Roused by his distress call, the lioness couldn't linger. Slowly she ventured down to the woman's branch, offering a cautious purr. She came so close that for a second their noses touched.

The sweet, sorry smell of the sobbing woman was briefly intriguing. Then the lioness dropped, twisting in a circle mid-air to land on all fours, and swiftly wound her way through the underbrush, the cubs trotting after her. For them, it was all good tree-climbing practice.

.   .   .   .

the fact that after Leo read me one chapter of Sabatini, I dreamt I saved somebody from getting hanged, hung, me the big *hero*, like *Zorro* or something, fork, force, torque, *Running a Thousand Miles for Freedom*, Gillian's lost barrette, the fact that "swashbuckler" sounds to me kind of like blowing your nose, or a sneeze, the fact that maybe it would be a good name for Kleenex, "Gimme a swashbuckler please, I think I'm going to sneeze!", please, sneeze, *Blow, winds, and crack your cheeks!*, the fact that a dab is a dance move based on *hiding* a sneeze, or sort of *catching* one, with your *elbow*, when you're too busy to get a Kleenex, busy *dancing*, dance move, the fact that it might not've gone down so well during the Bubonic plague, the fact that I'm so tired of coughing, the fact that I *hate* to be a cougher, the fact that I'm always trying to avoid coughers myself, the fact that I'm scared *sick* of sick people, the fact that I'm no good when people are sick, or even if they're just old, the fact that ever since Mommy got sick I've been scared of sick people, the fact that I took care of *her*, or tried to anyway, but all *other* sick people worry me, the fact that I'm also scared of most men, and pretty scared of *women* too, such as other moms, and I'm not all that good with *kids* either, the fact that there are people like Jean Stabishen that are just maniacs for helping people, the fact that Jean would actually be bereft if she had nobody sick to take care of, whereas I'm too drained to do much for anybody, the fact that there are the useful and the useless, takes all kinds, platitudes, failure, the fact that then I dreamt I had a *striation* rash all across my chest and neck and had to cancel my get-together with Jean on Tuesday, tom. paste, Jell-O, the fact that it looked like something out of the book of childhood illnesses, the fact that maybe I secretly *want* to get out of our get-together, the fact that Jean is a bit much, especially when she gets going on that kid of hers, like that story she told me about Alicia with her best friend on the school bus, the fact that somebody said something racist to her friend, who's black, and Alicia asked her if she was okay, the fact that the other girl didn't say anything, so Alicia just scooted closer to her to make her feel better, and Jean thought this was just *marvelous*, and terribly perceptive and heroic and all of Alicia, the fact that I thought she did fine, but it's not exactly Zorro stuff, the fact that of course there's only so much a couple of little girls can do about racism on the bus, the fact that still, it's hard sometimes to find the right expression when somebody's boasting about their kid, the fact that when I woke up I checked and I *didn't* have any rash, so I guess I still have to see Jean, the fact that it was Daddy who used to have all the rashes in the family, the fact that his many skin ointments bothered me, unguent, liniment, styptic stick, the fact that what a squeamish little person I was, or *am*, the fact that it's hard enough to go to school without that happening to you though, racism on the bus, the fact that 32% of teens now have anxiety disorders, probably from all the *lockdowns* they've been through by that age, the fact that I think just going to school all day is bad enough, and pretty stressful, the fact that I should take the kids on a long walk when they get home, burn off their pent-up tension, "Zorro!", but instead they just sit around watching cartoons and playing on their Gameboys, while I carry on making pies, dredge with flour, drudge with flour, the fact that Stacy bakes cookies sometimes, just for fun, and because she won't eat *my* stuff anymore, and then she'll go upstairs to her Morning Routine girls for some more antagonism of an indirect sort, the fact that no wonder she's always in such a bad mood, living on a diet of sugar, criticism, and self-doubt, the fact that last week she had a tiny bit of trouble sifting the flour or locating the cookie-cutters or something and she just stomped off and barricaded herself in her room for *hours*, leaving me to clear up the mess, the fact that I think *Trump* watches too much TV too, news programs, the fact that maybe *golf* is the only thing keeping us out of nuclear warfare, the fact that at least he gets some fresh air, even if it's at the taxpayers' expense, shell noodles, orecchiette, little ears, the fact that he's no good at golf, apparently, "Are you evil?", hourglass dolphins, tortured turtles, the fact that what if teens really do look at their phones two thousand times a day, the fact that that's, like, about seventy times an *hour*, more than once a minute, the fact that I don't think that's possible, the fact that they must mean they scroll through two thousand *items* a day, the fact that that *is* possible, the fact that my feeling is they're just *pretending* to text people a lot of the time, the Dodgers, swash-buckling, the fact that how many friends can they really have, the fact that what do they have to *talk* about, except what they've found on the internet, the fact that I suppose it's all about *boys*, Swatch, Nike, the fact that aren't we a sorry bunch, blowing our noses and wrestling with our ukuleles and really just thinking about sex and food all day, the fact that I'm the worst, I mean about food, the fact that I get so angry if people don't eat my stuff, or leave half of it on the plate, dear me, the fact that what is *that* about, the fact that it's not just with the kids, the fact that I'm like that about my *customers* too, the fact that I've got to learn to take it easy more, take a chill pill, the fact that how is it my business what my customers do with pie, the fact that do I really care if some pies get wasted, the fact that what the heck does it matter to me if every scrap of my pies gets eaten, as long as they get *bought*, boughten clothes, close, the fact that most people would actually be a lot better off *without* my desserts inside them, healthwise, I mean, if you leave out the whole pleasure and wellbeing angle, the fact that I guess they haven't found a way to measure the health benefits of sensual pleasure yet, the pursuit of happiness, BED, Big Edible Delights, Bad Eating Developments, mounds of butter, Indian mounds, Twelve Killed in Horror Crash, the fact that people just don't know how to drive anymore, the fact that they crash all the time, the fact that they drive into walls, houses, bridges, and other people, and animals, the fact that I suppose it's just that there are more cars on the road all the time, Brad Pitt And Leonardo DiCaprio To Unite In Sharon Tate Movie, the fact that Frederick has arranged himself just like Alligator Mound, all four feet splayed out, the fact that he even has his tail curled around to the left just right, the fact that he must be hot, the fact that Alligator Mound looks more like a cougar than an alligator, the fact that it makes a lot more sense that they would build a *cougar* mound in Ohio, and leave alligator mounds to the Seminole, the fact that Florida still has cougars as well as alligators, the fact that it can't be easy to be a Florida cougar, stuck in the Everglades, feeling damp all day, unless it's one of those *underwater panthers*, the ones in charge of storms, waves, whirlpools, skookumchuck, waterfalls and white-water rapids, Mishipeshu, the fact that in *Little House in the Big Woods* Pa says a panther screams like a *woman*, like how Ma must've screamed when Pa dropped that log on her foot, when they were building the log cabin together, the fact that *Frederick* never screams, the fact that bald eagles have surprisingly high voices, much higher than you'd expect, but most birds do, I guess, so why am I so surprised about bald eagles, the fact that they now make sows have twice the normal number of piglets and they keep the moms in cages so small they can't lie down, the fact that what we've done to animals, the fact that we really shouldn't eat pork, I know, the fact that I don't even think I *like* meat anymore, the fact that I don't like *me* either, "I hate me," as Jack Lemmon says in *The Apartment*, no, it's in *The Odd Couple*, the fact that in *The Apartment* he doesn't hate himself as much, though he *ends up* hating himself for lending out his apartment to all the sleazy guys at the office, "a mensch...a human being," putz, Mr. Baxter, the fact that loving Shirley MacLaine changes him for the better, p. chops with sour cream and brandy, the fact that a thousand chickens are killed every *second* worldwide, four hundred billion a year, the poor things, Chick-fil-A, Thanksgiving turkeys, presidential pardon, the fact that they are so mistreated, and then we give thanks for them, thanks, ma'am, meat, the fact that livestock farming doesn't have to be this bad, the fact that we could do it all differently, if we *wanted* to, but not enough people want to, or if we *cared*, but not enough people care, Rachel Carson, Ray, the fact that they've even figured out how to overwork *bees* now, transporting them long distances to pollinate even more fields than they could reach on their own, the fact that bees are migrant workers, slaves, illegals, Green Card, detainees, deported, exploited, the fact that I must not think about any of *that*, the fact that I don't want to become a bitter person like Amelia, a *bitter person*, the fact that it sounds so terrible, the fact that in a farming community you really have to keep your thoughts to yourself anyway, the fact that nobody likes the way Amelia freaks out at the drugstore, the fact that I dreamt we were all born on the planet Alcrin or Balfour, something like that, the fact that Mommy didn't dream, or so she claimed, the fact that she never had dreams after she got sick, she said, the fact that she had sneezing fits instead, the fact that Mommy could sneeze seventeen times in a row, the fact that she could sneeze to beat the band, the fact that she was a world-class sneezer, the amplitude of the current, watts = amps × volts, light bulb, the fact that sneezing's no substitute for *dreaming* though, the fact that she missed out on that triple bill the rest of us get every night, with yourself in a starring role or at least a ringside seat, saving lives, falling off cliffs, mingling with royalty, or the president, searching for your checkbook, throwing out tea leaves, Strange Invention Selling Out Fast, the fact that I wish I didn't have to enter Stacy's room, but we're running out of *glassware* around here, the fact that, my word, what a mess, the fact that it looks like the bedroom of a depressed person, it really does, the fact that there's her framed picture of Darcy, I mean Colin Firth, Elizabeth Bennet, the fact that I could yell at her about this junk all over the floor, but what would be the point, the fact that I could probably win every argument with Stacy, but I don't want to deflate her, so I shut up, the fact that it doesn't make her any less angry with me, the fact that maybe she *wants* more discipline, more input from me, the fact that that never occurred to me, the fact that she'd never listen though, the fact that what did I even come in here for, glassware, glassware, oh my, the fact that what is *this* now, a Sex Education pamphlet, the fact that it's got a cartoony cover and, the fact that, dear me, this is not *biology*, Licking Country Fair, styptic stick, grab 'em by the styptic stick, the fact that it seems to be more *historical*, or cultural or something, sociology, sexology, the fact that it's got stuff on *Osiris*, and Ishtar and Isis, Caligula, Tiberius, Nero, Messalina and Dionysus, Boccaccio, and oh, just as I suspected, dear, dear, Casanova and the Marquis de *Sade*, Jezebel, Medea, and here's *Medusa*, of all things, potatoes at the farmer's market, the fact that here's a little chapter on *fetishes*, bondage and venereal disease, the fact that this is for *kids*, Orry-Kelly, the fact that what the, the, the, oh my word, the fact that they're on to *Priapus* now, shoppin, floppin, droppin, "plop, tap, swop," well, I never, the fact that what do you, the fact that *I* never knew Masters & Johnson were an item, the fact that they had an *affair*, the fact that talk about mixing business with pleasure, but maybe Masters was all business and Johnson was all pleasure, or the other way around, the fact that well, I guess it makes sense when you're working together all the time, pooling your sex research, fish pond, fish flakes, china napkin ring, glassware, Johnson & Johnson, J&J, JR, *Dallas*, the fact that, whoa, there seem to be a lot more hermaphrodites around than I ever imagined, the fact that it's hard to believe this gets handed out at school, not hermaphroditism, the *booklet*, the fact that this seems more college-level type stuff to me, though of course at fifteen I guess it's probably about time they learnt *something* about it all, besides watching nonstop porno videos, that is, the fact that I bet there'll be a big hullabaloo about it at the next PTA meeting, unless everybody's too embarrassed to even bring it up, tummy trouble, belly button, doily, D'Oyly Carte, *D'Oyly*, the fact that Amelia will probably stick up for the First Amendment or something, and all the other parents will invoke the Second Amendment, the fact that what in the world are "phallophores," the fact that the phallophores were a *cult* that wore masks of acanthus leaves and carried big stone *phalluses* around, the fact that the women crowned them with fruit and flowers, the phalluses not the phallophores, Borneo, no promo homo, bathroom laws, menstruation huts, up in arms, the fact that there's that sect in Newfoundland, PA, some offshoot of something or other, offshoot, shoot-off, shooting gallery, the fact that they literally worship guns and Trump, and wear bullet crowns and stuff, gun freaks, the fact that Pennsylvania's kind of welcoming to the gun crowd, very accommodating, and it scares me, tintinnabulum, skillet, puffers, "Buttermilk!", the fact that those gun nuts all got together and had some ceremony with big game animals that had been stuffed, the fact that the lion and jaguar were posed like they were in a big snarly cat fight over who got to eat the antelope, the fact that the Romans had tintinnabulums all over the house, *tintinnabula*, the fact that they were punished if they seemed too uxorious, Roman men, not the tintinnabulums, the fact that how would anyone punish a tintinnabulum, for heaven's sake, except by shaking it maybe, nun, the fact that Casanova wrote poems about rubbers, and seems to have had quite a collection of them, the fact that you gotta hand it to him, that was one busy guy, the fact that the kiss developed *two million years ago* but it says here it only hit Japan in the twentieth century, the fact that what slow pokes, poke on a slope, peas in a pod, Daddy's nun, the fact that it's pretty hard to believe actually, that there was two million years of kissing going on and the Japanese never even *noticed*, Eskimo kisses, the fact that maybe they just didn't want to do it, the fact that nobody should be *forced* to kiss anybody they don't want to, the fact that I hate it when little kids are dragged over to kiss some creepy old relative, the fact that I'd never make my kids do that, the fact that who you kiss is your own decision, except when Jane Wyman gets pawed by that guy in *All That Heaven Allows*, the fact that she hesitates even when Rock Hudson makes a pass, the fact that how do they even know a thing like that, about when the Japanese started kissing each other, the fact that I'm sure Madama Butterfly and Pinkerton kiss, though maybe Puccini got that wrong, the fact that *Trump* kisses complete strangers on the mouth all the time without asking, just like Bill Clinton, the fact that you'd think those two would catch colds all the time, cough, itch, lamb, foal, calve, whelp, sire, "I did not have sex with that woman," crown, crack, cock, stacked, cheek, jowl, Wookey Creek, the fact that, boy, I don't know but I really do think there's going to be one heck of a PTA meeting about this, the fact that I grew up with *Friends* and *Seinfeld* and all, but some people around here might be pretty surprised by some of this stuff, the fact that there's *nothing* about periods or pubic hair or secretions or anything, the fact that it's more G-strings and Babylonians and bonobo monkeys, and what Cleopatra got up to with her bodyguards, or Prince Albert with his, well, jewelry, *adornments*, the fact that Ancient Babylon of all places, credit-or-debit, butt cracks, the fact that this pamphlet thing really covers a lot of ground, chains, leather, stump, stalk, ream, Peolia, herpes simplex and complex, vaginismus, the fact that it's kind of like a sex guide written by *David Attenborough*, the fact that to get to the lilium phallowoppia, you nympho facto push past sprays of spermatozoa adorning banks of chastity beltia, culminating in a flopsweat jettison at the summit of the mons veneris in a naughty, nasty, nasturtiummy-worshippy georgium-porgium orgium of velvet chasms, breasts, chests, clefts, quests, primp, pimp, pump, plump, clump, enter, engender, copulate, populate, propagate, bajingo, vajay-jay, the meaning of life, and Amelia Earhart, the fact that a giraffe comes into the bar and says, "The highballs are on me," basketball, baseball, volleyball, oh my, the fact that I have got to get a *grip* here, the fact that Leo likes baseball better, the fact that Leo's so handsome, and his, no I won't even think such things, his, oh dear, the stuff that just pops into your head at random, the fact that I gave myself a real Aphrodite *frighty* there with that sex pamphlet, gee whiz, G-force, G-string, G-spot, "if you really crave cock," buzz, rearing horse, pudding, zest, toybox, "until she just can't take it anymore," the fact that I'm going doolally alley here, dear me, boy, the fact that if I'd taught history *that* way at Peolia, I'd have been a big-titted hit, "gonna get her tit caught in a big fat wringer," Katie Graham, oh my, the fact that I've got to, oh, Leo though, the fact that I just want to think about Leo, the fact that Leo's too handsome to have done his homework in high school, Leo, Leo, the fact that he was an only child, the fact that that's such a strange phrase, "only child," the fact that I'd like to give him a big smackeroo, cannelloni, lima beans, Mattel, Hasbro, Carnation Evaporated Milk, Azerbaijan, the fact that Leo's the best lover, but we just never seem to get the *chance* in this house crammed full of kids, the fact that it's really like *The Brady Bunch* around here, or *The Addams Family*, the March girls, the Bennets, the fact that once you have this many kids I think maybe your libido cuts out, the fact that it goes into hibernation, like a dormouse, the fact that it's dormant or moribund or something, no, not moribund I hope, just in diapause, diamanté, caterpillars, butterflies, nasturtiums, hummingbirds, the fact that maybe your reproductive system feels it's done its duty, and it just wants to take it easy now, retire, go take a hike, fly a kite, but lots of *men* just keep on having affairs and babies, without cease, Alec Baldwin, Leo, Jesus of Philadelphia, the fact that I've got this itch now too, which puts me off initiating things, and I get stomach aches sometimes, and my teeth hurt, and I'm just so *tired* all the time, the fact that I'm always hoping to be less tired when we go to bed, but then I conk right out, oncologist, embrace change, Ntozake Shange, the fact that "Shange" means a pride of lions, the fact that who is that actress, the fact that I couldn't *sleep* last night for worry about her and that daughter of hers, the fact that her daughter, some big Hollywood actress, the fact that what is her name, the fact that it'll come to me, the fact that I don't get what's gotten *into* daughters these days, the fact that they all seem to hate their moms so much, the fact that why is that, the fact that either moms suddenly got much worse, or daughters did, or else maybe it's something in the *water*, water daughter, the fact that it seems to me daughters have never been so down on their moms in the whole of human history, tintinnabula, tinnitus, yeast infection, uxorious, the fact that I'm nervous around *all* young women now, because of Stace, the fact that I think they're all about to yell at me, or hate me at least, *The Stepford Wives*, the fact that I'm glad men don't usually turn their wives into robots, though Melania's a bit, well, no, now that's not nice, the fact that Leo likes to watch *All the President's Men* all the time, the fact that he can watch it and watch it, vaginoplasty, the fact that we were barely *born* when Watergate was happening, but we still like it, just like *The Graduate*, the fact that Leo likes looking at all the old cars, the VW beetles and all, the fact that I like it too, but I like *The Graduate* better, the fact that Dustin Hoffman's in both, Katharine Ross, the fact that she's not in very many movies, the fact that she's married to Sam Elliott, the fact that we like *Broadcast News* too, though Dustin Hoffman's not in that one, the fact that I like that blue dress Holly Hunter wears at the party, just a plain shirtwaist dress but it's a really great color, nice sleeves, the fact that it's a daytime party, which is kind of unusual, the fact that then they all have to race back to the studio because of something that happened in Libya, so it was kind of lucky they were all at the same party, "I used to be *attracted* to you," the fact that I dreamt I had to wait for Stace to meet me in a hotel room and she was late, and then I was carrying all these Teflon pans home from somewhere, along with my other luggage, and I was so embarrassed, the fact that I had to explain the pots and pans to everybody on the bus, and then on the plane, the fact that I guess they were pretty good pans or I wouldn't have gotten myself into such a predicament, the fact that I find it hard to believe that people actually buy Teflon clothing for their *kids*, when everybody knows it's bad for you, the fact that people trust anything they find at Walmart or Target though, the fact that some people who work at Walmart have to get food stamps to survive, the fact that that's not making a living, making ends meet, ABC bridges, the fact that

that's like working for *Peolia*, the fact that then I dreamt we were flying to the Arctic at night and coming in to land, and I was looking down at these huge thick dockland ropes, and the deep dark water in the harbor, the fact that it was really dark blue, ultramarine, and scattered with icebergs or ice floes or something, the fact that I suddenly realized I probably didn't have enough *clothes* on, like I didn't even have socks, so I really didn't know if I was going to make it from the plane into the airport without freezing to death, but somehow I survived being out on the wet concrete, because the next minute I was inside the building, being introduced to gangs of female police officers, the fact that then I went to a coffee place to buy donuts for Jake, but they were all gone because some lady had bought them all to give to her dogs, penguin sanctuary, the fact that how greedy can a squirrel *get*, stealing chicken feed like that, the fact that he must've run out of buried buck eyes, rooting for the underdog, covering all the bases, innings, outings, innies and outies, stillborn babies, the fact that sometimes it seems like plants and animals live in an alternative universe from us, a whole different time frame, different planet almost, or they're all in a nature film or something, but actually they're right here *with* us, the fact that that squirrel is my *contemporary*, the fact that as a teenager I wondered how married couples could bear to stay together, but now I wonder how they can bear to *part*, the fact that there's something to be said for knowing each other well, bulldozers, paella, the fact that animals don't treat life like it's a nightmare, the fact that the demonstrators in North Dakota just wanted to protect their water supply, and their land, the National Guard, Army Corps of Engineers, tear gas, the fact that five people died in Athens, Ohio, when a guy arrived at a party going on in the back yard and started shooting, the fact that he got his ex-wife and four other people, hump back trunks, Spider Invasion Across America, the fact that some people like Abby are so organized about everything, their descendants have almost nothing to worry about, and then there are the old ladies with the seven hundred thousand margarine tubs and enough spiders to fill a football field, and somebody has to go sort it all out after they're gone, the fact that I'm not too organized, not like Abby was, the fact that most conmen come from Indiana, Queen of Heaven Cemetery, Chicago, Neptune Society, Columbus, Grant's Tomb, Ty Inc., Hoosier hutch, the fact that another black guy got shot by the police over a broken tail light, the fact that a guy with a broken tail light gets executed on the spot, but politicians get away with *genocide*, columbarium, community mausoleum, grouting, ginger, Kleenex, the fact that Cathy didn't seem to have any *idea* why I made her that pear tarte tatin, though I *told* her it was a wedding present, a late wedding present, the fact that maybe she didn't hear me, she was gobbling it so fast, the fact that she sure didn't say much, like thank you or anything, the fact that she just started *eating* it, right then and there, no sign of *Art*, though he's usually around, the fact that maybe he's come down with diabetes or something, so she knew he shouldn't have any, or else they'd had a *fight*, but I never heard of them fighting, the fact that you never really know what's going on with people, the fact that the thing was half-eaten, if not gone, before Art ever even saw it, Art and Cathy's pie, or is it *Art's* and Cathy's pie, and she never even thanked me, the fact that she just ate that huge great piece and took the rest into the back, and then started doing a million other things, the fact that this is when you realize that giving a gift is *not* selfless, the fact that you do expect a little gratitude, not just acceptance, emolument, embrocation, the fact that I know that's selfish, and that's no good but, heavens to Betsy, it really would be hard to imagine any gift being received less graciously than my wedding pear tarte tatin was, the fact that the only thing worse would have been if Cathy had actually used it to start a pie fight and threw the nuptial pear pie right back in my face, cat fight, eating humble pie, pear, pair, couples, Masters and Johnson, the fact that I know she said she didn't want wedding presents but well, this kind of takes the cake, the fact that she didn't just nibble at it but pretty much demolished her own wedding present right before my very eyes, the fact that it does make me a bit, well, *sore* at her, though I know I shouldn't be of course, the fact that it was *her pie*, the fact that I just don't get people at times, Parabens: What You Should

Know, the fact that she seemed to like it well enough but, well, who *doesn't* like a nice pear tarte tatin, the fact that that pie was based on years of practice, though she should've had it with crème fraiche, the fact that maybe she thought it was a *sample*, for the *store*, the fact that that's a possibility that I never thought of, but why would I do that *unasked*, when she's already tried all my pies already anyway and *knows* which ones she wants me to make, the fact that she really loves my sour cherry, so maybe I should've made her one of those instead, the fact that maybe she's not all that into tartes tatin herself, the fact that it's kind of weird, but I know I should just try to get over it already, the fact that maybe an angel food cake would have been a better idea after all, a clearer statement, more like a real wedding cake, and I could've written something on it too, just to make things *crystal-clear*, like if I'd put **Congratulations Art & Cathy!!!** on top, the fact that she wouldn't have *dared* eat it all on her own then, the fact that I could have added around the side, for extra emphasis, **CAUTION: do not eat this whole dang cake yourself,** but she's been saying all along she didn't *want* a wedding cake, so I didn't make her one, Chuck, Gilbert Blythe, the fact that I dreamt Leo and I wanted to remarry each other but we couldn't because that would be bigamy, but I couldn't remember the word "bigamy" in the dream, the fact that then I dreamt I was visiting a family in a little house on a cliff top and they'd had twins, the fact that they'd given one of the twins away to relatives in Italy, which I thought was a real pity, the fact that as I was leaving, I had a big coughing fit and needed water, and then I woke up coughing and really did need water, the fact that this is the worst cold I ever had, a real doozy, **Congratulations Art & Cathy!!!**, the fact that I seem to have reached the age when you gotta take colds seriously, the fact that I have to take to my bed when I get a cold, the fact that maybe I should have thought of that *before* having four kids who bring me their colds, chickens, feathers, sunflower seeds, infielder, outfielder, the fact that the kids all seem to have constant colds but they *enjoy* their colds because they get days off school to loll around the house and hang out with Mom and slurp down whole potfuls of homemade chicken noodle soup, with either tubular or donut-shaped noodles if it's Jake that's sick, the fact that Ben likes dilled turkey chowder when he's got a cold, the fact that he's bored with good old plain chicken noodle, the fact that what he never needs to know is how much chicken broth goes into his dilled turkey chowder, the fact that I also have to provide a constant supply of freshly squeezed OJ, O. J. Simpson, Howard Hughes, Howard Keel, the fact that nobody brings *me* fresh OJ, or checks on me every few minutes and gives me a whole extra day off, just to make sure the fever's gone, the fact that once when I was home sick, I lay on the yellow corduroy chaise longue in Mommy and Daddy's bedroom, Mommy's and Daddy's bedroom, mommies and daddies, and Mommy taught me how to play solitaire, the fact that she was so nice to me when I was sick, afternoon nap, euphoria, the fact that I try to be nice to my kids too, and in return they give me their colds and I am much sicker than they ever were, and nobody makes me chicken noodle soup, the fact that here I was, all alone in the house and sick as a dog and *longing* for chicken broth, the fact that when I'm sick as a dog I still have to make my own chicken broth, from scratch, though sometimes I use the store kind, "100% NATURAL," the fact that we always seem to be out of chicken stock by the time I get sick, so there I am, gathering old chicken bones and the onion, carrots, celery, and potato all by myself, plus the peppercorns, coriander seeds, ginger, garlic, pinch of sugar, glass of white wine, poor me, and the gallons of water, and then I have to wait a whole day while it simmers, and strain myself straining it after, and all the while, I'm getting sicker and sicker because I don't have any good chicken broth yet, the fact that making chicken stock is a lonely job, and Leo hates the smell of it, the fact that then I have to find a whole lot of matching Tupperware things to freeze it in, and our Tupperware's a mess, the fact that a better organized cook like Abby would have all the Tupperware containers she needed, ready and waiting, with their lids, beforehand, the fact that Abby was really into doing things *beforehand*, corm, Rose Wilder Lane, those Berta and Elmer Hader books for kids, paper dolls, the fact that I guess I could've asked Stace to make the chicken stock, and it would be good for her to learn how, like Grandma taught me, but she hates cooking and hates my guts and I don't want to provoke her, the fact that anyway she already does a lot of babysitting, especially if I'm sick, the fact that I couldn't ask Leo either, the fact that he's busy trying to juggle all the stuff *he* has to do when I'm out of action, like shepherding all the kids around and stuff like that, chauffeuring too, and last week he had to be in Pittsburgh for some reason, the fact that I just always catch whatever's going, that's the way it is, the fact that I used to catch all *Phoebe's* illnesses too, even if she was hundreds of miles away and I only heard about them over the *phone*, the fact that it seems to me I caught some of her old boyfriends that way too, *Hannah and Her Sisters*, the Three Sisters, corn, squash and beans, four sisters, five, 1787 North-West Ordinance, Three Sisters Bridge, marigolds, itch, the fact that I was reduced to watching action movies in my sickbed, *Die Hard I*, *Die Hard II*, *The Fugitive*, *The Bourne Identity* and *Witness* and, well, I don't know what, the fact that I couldn't *find* the David Attenborough DVDs, unfortunately, which probably delayed my recovery, the fact that it took me so long to get over this cold I sank to going to Medi-Wisc and bought the strongest cold medicine I could find, a "mucus reducer," mucus preventer, annihilator, dam-buster, WHAM-BAM THANK YOU MA'AM, and, for crying out loud, that medicine darn nearly annihilated *me*, the fact that those tablets really should be taken off the market, the fact that I was so impressed at first by the packet, touched even, by all their proud boasts and the promises of "mucus reduction" and "mucus relief," the fact that I was so desperate I innocently forked out for the stuff, feeling it was my duty to speed up my recovery, the fact that I hate taking strong medications usually, even ibuprofen, the fact that you try to avoid it if you can, though I think Christian Scientists go too far, just praying over their sick kids, the fact that so I took this heavy-duty medicine for my heavy cold and proceeded to come down with almost every known side effect listed on the accompanying leaflet, *every* side effect, I think, apart from "*Death*," the fact that these people openly admit their *cold remedy* can cause *death*, the fact that do they really think people want to risk death just to get over a cold, the fact that I didn't get that particular side effect, *yet*, but I did get the "Throat Ulcerations," which made my already sore throat *unbearably* sore, and the rarely cited "Rash" under my rarely sighted boobs, all the way from my boobs to my groin, *breasts*, I should say, majumbas, mounds, my wah-wahs, boob chicka wah wah, and I got the "Palpitations" *and* the "Nausea," and I don't know what else, but at one point I really thought I was about to kick the bucket, the fact that I was sick and faint and dizzy, and then I got palpitations on top of that, and I really thought I wasn't going to make it, the fact that *that* was when I read the list of side effects and got even more scared, so I grabbed my cell in case this was going to be my last chance to make a goodbye call to Leo, like everybody did in the 9/11 planes, the plunging skyscrapers, pulverized, boxcutters, the fact that the cellphone companies must've had a big sales boost after 9/11, a real bonanza, the flag factories too, the fact that in the end though, I resisted, not resisted *passing away*, resisted calling *Leo*, because I started to feel a little better, though I still felt trembly and panicky, the fact that it wasn't until the next day that I had the sense to make selfies of my stomach rash for future lawsuit purposes, the fact that I really do feel like suing their mucus-reducing sit-me-down-upons, and I have the photographic proof, proving the complete uselessness of their product, the enormity, but then I had another look at my selfies, in a calmer moment, and I knew I was licked, mucus remedy, the fact that I knew then I was never taking any pharma giant to court, the fact that even if their stupid pills had *killed* me, the fact that vanity outweighs justice, and I wasn't going to have a bunch of young whippersnappers, lawyers, and members of the board sniggering over those snapshots of my stretch-marked stomach and paltry bazungas, not if I could help it anyway, the fact that when your flag's too old to fly anymore, you're supposed to give it a retirement ceremony, the fact that my snaps were convincingly medical-looking and all, and pretty alarming really, but I hadn't *posed* right, the fact that with my last breath I would've ordered my family to destroy those photos, if I wasn't able to crawl from my deathbed to do it myself, and if, by some misunderstanding, the pics *survived* my passing and my poor bereft family tried to use them somehow to avenge my untimely demise, either with a lawsuit or maybe by leaking them to the mainstream media, or just posting them on social media, pic-sharing, revenge porn, I'd turn in my mucussy hummusy grave thinking about everybody seeing my tummy at its worst, ribcage, belly button, blue blanket, the fact that no in or out of court settlement could make up for that humiliation, even if I was already deceased, the fact that anyway the rash was already a bit less severe, the fact that most medical photos *are* pretty icky of course, at the best of times, the fact that our book on childhood illnesses wasn't photos though, it was color illustrations which were frightening but not revolting, the fact that they were just little *paintings* to help you identify hives and chicken pox and prickly heat and pinkeye and acne or anything else you thought your kid had, the fact that a couple pictures of kids' tongues, with various kinds of white or yellow spots on them, have stuck with me, "Stick out your tongue," the fact that that book may have calmed Mommy and Daddy down but it gave me the *heebie-jeebies*, the fact that I was always staring at those pictures and wondering how long I had before I got something terminal, fatal, like postulating, epidermal ulcers erupting all over me, I mean pustulating, the fact that even diaper rash and sunburn looked pretty bad, the fact that imagine having to paint all those pictures for the book, the fact that when do you face the fact you're never going to make it as an artist and you're going to have to paint pictures of strep throat and scabies for the rest of your life instead, the fact that that mucus-exploiting pharma company shouldn't get away with it though, the fact that I actually feel like writing them a sharp letter and telling them I'm going to warn everyone I know about this mucus eradicator, or obliterator, pulverizer, postulator, pustulator, liquidator, the fact that it's lucky I never gave that medication to the *kids*, wow, the fact that I never thought of that till now, the fact that what I don't get is why they keep *manufacturing* a cold cure that they know makes you sicker than you were before you took it, because it can't be a big seller, the fact that once you kill all your customers, or anyway make them hate your guts, you no longer have a shiftable product on your hands, "What do we need so much velvet?", the fact that, I mean, what is the point, like who *benefits* from that, the fact that I know I don't know much about people, *I don't know but they know*, but still it sure seems weird that this is an established and I guess maybe popular over-the-counter product, the fact that, well, I hope somebody in that company reconsiders someday, ivy garden in New Haven, the fact that it's not like you're signing up for *chemo*, or something you know your life depends on so you're willing to put up with a few unpleasant side effects, the fact that this was just a cold remedy, and a cold is just a cold, a temporary pain in the sit-me-down-upon, but not a danger to life and limb, limp, swashbuckling, awash, the fact that okay, you get real tired of blowing your nose nonstop, but that doesn't mean you're ready to *kill* yourself to get rid of it, the fact that I'm much sicker, since taking it, the fact that it's like those Thalidomide manufacturers who *knew* about birth defects in Europe caused by Thalidomide, and still begged the U.S. government, *begged* them, to license it *here*, monsters, oh dear, *sticks and stones*, but really, "All for a little bit of money," pharma giants, the fact that "pharma giants" sounds weird, like they're these huge people traipsing across the country in hobnailed boots, covering a hundred miles with each step, and crushing everything in their way with bottles of mucus relief pills, "Jack and the Beanstalk," bean stock, "Bienstock, I oughtta fire you!", the fact that I don't know how such people manage to *sleep* at night, but maybe they don't, or not without the help of some *other* dubious drug, frug, frog, fugue, fluke, *The Fugitive*, the fact that there are some evil doctors in *The Fugitive*, trying to get some evil drug approved, "Are you evil?", even though they know it doesn't work and it's dangerous, the fact that they fake the test results and even try to murder Harrison Ford, just so they can make a lot of money, the fact that Harrison Ford's *wife* has to die, so they can make money, the fact that the one-armed man kills her, and Harrison Ford gets unjustly accused of the murder and nearly gets *executed* for it, and he's the *president*, well, in other movies he's the president, Death Penalty, the fact that the Death Penalty's a "blot," a blot on America, plot, plotz, able was I ere I saw Elba, an eye for an eye, ashes to ashes, lethal injections, legal, pustules, the fact that they tried to execute a man with *cancer* the other day, the fact that he's dying *already* but the execution still went ahead, but they couldn't find a vein to give him the lethal injection so they ended up puncturing his *bladder* and all kinds of terrible things, and finally, after putting him through all that, they had to give up, the fact that that is maybe the most disgusting thing I think I've ever heard, apart from, well, the Gnadenhutten Massacre, and school shootings, and lynchings and beheadings and genocide and all, Rwanda, Nazis, *Shadow of a Doubt*, the fact that reporters and newscasters rush to tell you that the victims of shootings were somebody's wife or daughter or brother or granddad, as if otherwise you might not realize that those people had any connections with other people at all, the fact that do they think we think they all came out of eggs just in time to get shot, like lizards or something with no friends or relations, the fact that even lizards have friends, the fact that don't they live in colonies, the fact that the same kind of thing happens in *The Third Man*, making money out of drugs, diluted penicillin, Harry Lime, the fact that diabetics with no insurance dilute their *insulin* to make it go farther, black market, staff infection, the fact that once, when the whole office came down with something and all went on sick leave at the same time, Leo's dad told his boss "They must have a staff infection," and his boss sent it into the newspaper, Joseph Cotten, cotton boll weevil, the fact that the word "weevil" always sends a shiver down your spine, the fact that at first Joseph Cotten's not convinced it's such a terrible thing to do, giving children diluted penicillin, but then Trevor Howard shows him around the children's hospital, and he sees all the mangled kids, the fact that what's the name of the guy that plays Harry Lime, the fact that it'll drive me crazy until I remember, Orson, Orson Welles, the fact that I like Joseph Cotton's niece in *Shadow of a Doubt*, because she reminds me of Mommy, but I can never remember her name, the fact that she's in *The Best Years of Our Lives* too, and *Mrs. Miniver*, all the movies the kids won't watch because they're black-and-white, the fact that I get tired of Greer Garson myself, Teresa Wright, the fact that that's who it is, the fact that she doesn't play Mrs. Miniver, the fact that she's the son's girl-friend, the fact that Greer Garson plays Mrs. Miniver, the fact that Greer Garson is the perfect person to *say* "Mrs. Miniver," because of the sort of mincing way she talks, "Missusss Miniva," the fact that I didn't even *have* a cough before I took that medication and now I've got a really bad one, and there's *still* something wrong with my throat, the fact that it hurts all the time, and there are lots of odd spots on my tummy that weren't there before, the remains of the rash, but at least I haven't had any more palpitations, and I didn't go to the doctor, even when I seemed to be getting conjunctivitis as well, because I knew he'd only tell me there's nothing he could do for me, the fact that how annoying it is when people give you advice on how to treat a cold, the fact that I know they're just trying to be nice, but it's kind of unnecessary to tell a full-grown woman with a cold that she needs chicken soup, honey and lemon, steam, *vapor*, aspirin, hot liquids, OJ, keeping warm, Vitamin C, throat lozenges, and menthol inhalers, as if they think you never had a cold in your life, the fact that Thieves oil lozenges are another matter, because not everybody knows about them, the fact that they're too expensive though, the fact that people tell me to do steam baths, but I've been doing steam baths for *days* and my left ear's still deaf and my eustachian tube's still blocked, the fact that I must have drunk gallons of chicken broth, schmaltz, Grandma, thermometer, Teresa Wright, the fact that anyway, the logistics of going to see the doctor probably would've finished me off, because I'd have had to get one mom to pick one kid up from here and another mom to pick one up from there, the fact that I thought of calling Carol Stalwart or Carol Stewart or whateverhernameis, Carole *Lombard* for all I know, the one who's always trying to get me to take up aerial silks and break my neck, the fact that Leo had to stay home a whole week, because of Jake, the fact that Stace can't stay home from school to babysit, even if she wanted to, the fact that Leo made Jake some mashed potatoes one day, the fact that it was the first time he'd ever mashed a potato, the fact that he confessed that to me in *private*, the fact that he didn't want Jake to know, but he did a great job for a first-timer, the fact that it was a bit wet but solid enough to make the all-important hole in the middle, which is all that counts, the fact that they went down a treat, the fact that mashed potatoes vary a lot, the fact that some people *like* them wet, liquefaction, the fact that Cathy doesn't *have* an internist, a GP, MD, the fact that she just goes straight to specialists, but mainly she just doesn't go at all, the fact that I think it's some insurance problem, the fact that Teresa Wright's eyes always get me, the fact that I really should "sue their a—," CYA, the fact that I was so hyped on Leo and so thrilled to have his kids, the fact that I missed Jake's best years, the fact that you have all these kids as an expression of love, and then the kids start *killing* your love with all their needs, all the diapers and arguments and blocked eustachian tubes, and busting in on your love life every chance they get, just for a glass of milk and more chocolate chip cookies, the fact that cookies are the real passion-killer, Plutonium isotopes, Gameboys, the fact that maybe there's a biological purpose to it, the fact that maybe the current kids have an instinct to prevent more kids being born, like eaglets or something, or cuckoos in the nest, cowbirds, the fact that eaglets *don't* push each other out of the nest though, the fact that they kind of resignedly cohabit, and even politely take turns eating, the fact that it breaks your heart because it always looks like one of them isn't getting any, but it all seems to work out, the fact that they both always seem to thrive, and all on raw fish torn to shreds for them by their devoted parents, no cookies and milk or choc-dipped madeleines or Sloppy Joes, just pink-fleshed fish and bones, the fact that when I was all gunked up I wondered if these kids of mine would even notice if I dissolved in a pool of goo and disappeared, the fact I'm not sure it would register with them until my absence began to affect their extracurricular activities, like dancing class and meals and laundry, the fact that kids grow, while their parents gradually subside and disintegrate, subsidence, the fact that it can be a little cannibalistic if you ask me, vampires, the fact that I shouldn't say that, but they eat you out of house and home and then they become Open Carry guys and shoot you one day when you're sick in bed from a cold *they* gave you, How Kids Learn From Play, the fact that I don't know where all this *hostility's* coming from, gosh, and I was thinking of the kids so *tenderly* from my sickbed, the fact that I longed to survive and be reinstated as their mom, their mild, undemanding mom, Moms Demand Action, the fact that I can't bear to think that my kids must die, not now but *some day*, the fact that no, that is not going to happen, not on my watch, no sirree bob, Bob, Bobby Kennedy, Bobby-Sue from my class, the fact that suddenly I felt really sorry for Stace too, that her dad hasn't come see her in six years, and even before that it was pretty intermittent, the fact that that's a tough thing for a kid to have to go through, and there's nothing I can do about it, the fact that the best thing I could do was provide her with a nice stepdad to make up for it, and I did that, the fact that he can't help it if he's not Frank, the fact that he always tried to get along with Frank, the fact that he was always nice to him even though he doesn't like him, well, *nobody* likes Frank, nobody I know anyway, the fact that Leo even started handling the phone calls for me because I just couldn't take it anymore, the fact that I wonder if Frank's indifference eats away at her though, the fact that she never mentions it, and I don't know how to bring the matter up, the fact that I never bring Frank up voluntarily, I just can't, the fact that he let her down like that just makes me sick sometimes, but I try not to show it, in case that makes everything worse, the fact that he never paid me a cent of alimony or child maintenance, but Leo and I don't want his darned money, ♫ *dollars to donuts* ♫, parabens, pharma giants, the fact that Stacy took to Leo right away, and when she was little they got along great, the fact that she was only a little older than Jake is *now* when they met, the fact that she was so friendly and outgoing then, the fact that Jake's friendly too but he hardly notices anything going on as long as he's got his VW bus or a wooden spoon to hold, the fact that Frank's never even met

Jake, the fact that his visits were painful for everybody, especially Stace, the fact that everybody always says dads are important, but why can't it be the *stepdad* that's important, the fact that we need a Stepfather's Day, the fact that a *Stepmother's* Day might take more expert PR work, the fact that stepmothers have a bad press, "Are you evil?", the fact that Rachel Carson said the sea is the mother of every- thing, the fact that she loved the shoreline, the fact that she never learned to swim, the fact that they're thinking of having a Grandparents' Day now, but our kids don't have a single grandparent left, which is a pity, four grandparentless children, unless Frank's *mom's* still around, which I don't even know, the fact that he never had anything to do with *her* either, the fact that he hated going to the reservation, except to get his teeth done, the fact that poor Stace forgot all about Frank in between visits, or she seemed to anyway, and then he'd suddenly turn up and bother her again, demanding his quality time with her, Ivanka Trump, Princess Di, CIA, FBI, molester on the farm path, the fact that Frank could be a bit cloying, when he felt like it, but mostly just cold, and he was such a hypochondriac, the fact that Stacy had to be *pushed* to spend time with the guy, the fact that she faked illnesses to get out of it, the poor little kid, and I just hated making her go, but everybody's always saying how "a kid needs their dad" and all, the fact that it seemed to mean a lot more to Frank than it did to her, and it didn't mean all that much to *him* either, but he still insisted, the fact that I'm not sure everybody needs a dad, but I know you can't say so, *I don't know but they know*, the fact that secretly I sometimes think they just need a mom, KEEP OFF PRIVATE PROPERTY AND YOU WONT GET SHOT, the fact that I have lived a lonely bereft life since Mommy died, the fact that being sick is no fun once your mom isn't there to bring you chicken noodle soup, or teach you to play solitaire, sneakers, party tray of objects, Mystery Train, swordie, the fact that having a birthday isn't any fun either without your mom to make a big deal of it, and give you books you'll feel guilty about not reading to your dying day, the fact that Mommy gave me some book about a mouse and I never read it because it seemed too serious, the fact that I thought a story about a mouse was too *serious*, the fact that I always felt so *bad* about not reading it, but I still never could, the fact that she probably didn't care if I read it or not, Evanston kitchen at night, icky fluorescent ceiling light, the fact that she must've minded a *little* though, the fact that, I mean, you go out of your way to get to a bookstore and select this book for your kid, and you bring it home and wrap it up and ceremoniously hand it over to her on her birthday and then this ungrateful child never reads it, sea urchin, the fact that what a jerkosaurus, the fact that that just seems awful to me now, purple urchins, though *I* probably wouldn't be hurt if my kids didn't read some book I gave them, the fact that they hardly ever do *anything* I tell them, so I have pretty low expectations, and a very sore *throat*, the fact that I was a pretty unadventurous reader, very cautious, the fact that I was always a slow reader, despite Daddy's efforts, and it was always a battle to get into a book, so I resisted a lot of books in the hope of only reading ones I really liked, the fact that I wasn't like Leo, who read everything he could lay his hands on as a kid, really *anything*, the fact that he tried the whole world out for himself, the fact that I definitely read *some* books Mommy gave me, like I read *Up a Road Slowly*, though I didn't really get it and I still don't, the fact that that's another orphan book, Julie, and that was what I liked about it, the fact that just put an orphan in and kids'll read it, the fact that once you realize your parents are fallible, the idea of being an orphan gives you an out, or something like that, Freud, but I can't remember what *age* kids are when they realize you're fallible, the fact that I guess I could look it up, the fact that I think I liked orphan stories from the *start*, because you instantly feel for a kid who's got nothing, all alone in the world, the fact that after her mother passes away, Julie has to live with Aunt Cordelia and she's only about seven, Gillian, Stace, the fact that I tried to give *Up a Road Slowly* to Stacy, but she rejected it, gave up, the fact that she said the language was too antiquated, the fact that I think it was maybe when she got to the word "propitiated," the fact that I did get her to read *Island of the Blue Dolphins* though, and *A Candle in Her Room*, and she liked them, the fact that in return she made me read *Marianne Dreams*, which was sort of scary, but good, the fact that there are some big boulders in it that come alive, the fact that maybe all children's books have a dark side, especially with all the orphans they have to handle, the fact that Anne of Green Gables is so alone in the world, and has so many chores to do, the fact that she's so cheerful about it all, you feel even more sorry for her, the fact that nobody likes a *sulky* kid, except maybe Mary Cassatt, but that's a sulky kid set off against a blue armchair, the fact that people care about Oliver Twist because he's an orphan, though that's not a book for kids, the fact that the *musical* might be, not the book, not with whatshername, Nancy, getting killed and all, *Christmas Carol* jigsaw, the fact that Jane and Elizabeth Bennet might've been better off if they *were* orphans, or motherless anyway, "my poor nerves," the fact that Stacy says *I'm* like Mrs. Bennet, because I always chatter when I'm nervous, the fact that I hope she's wrong, dear me, David Copperfield, Oliver Twist, Esther in *Bleak House*, Dedlock, wedlock, Anne and Captain Wentworth, went forth, the fact that I always wanted to be an orphan, but now I am one and it's not so great, the fact that I know Stacy's often hoped she was adopted, the fact that she *says* so often enough, "family romance," the fact that Anne Elliot's mother died when she was fourteen and she's still missing her when the book begins, the fact that she's really sad and alone, the fact that bald eagles only catch one in twenty fish successfully, a success or a failure, "All that work!", but they keep on trying, and they get a fish back to the eaglets every day, sometimes two fish, *One fish, two fish, red fish, blue fish*, usually pink, the fact that Laura Ingalls Wilder censored the more alarming stuff but she doesn't gloss over all the hardships, the fact that her books are really one long survival story, because her family was pretty hard up, living close to the edge, preppers, the fact that once they had to eat a green pumpkin mock-apple pie, the fact that maybe it's *good*, the fact that I should try it some time, the fact that it might be good for the kids in some nutritional way, the fact that it sounds *sour* but I'm sure it doesn't have to be, the fact that a little honey would correct that, the fact that they almost *starve*, the

Ingallses, not my kids, *The Long Winter*, the fact that in *Plum Creek* Pa has to sleep in a snow hole and they don't know for days if he's dead or alive, the fact that if he'd died they might *all* have died, though I guess Ma would've tried her best, gone back East to her family, or remarried, the fact that then they'd have had to endure a stepdad situation, Stepfather's Day, the fact that anyway Ma loves *Charles*, the fact that she doesn't want to have to get *remarried*, the fact that Gillian's reading the *Little House* books to Jake now, and I'm scared someday she'll notice I'm not the paragon of motherhood Ma Ingalls was, the fact that Pa has to sell the heifer calf to send Mary to college, because of the poor harvest and the blackbirds and all, falli-bility, wing sleeves, lace, Pa eating the Christmas candy, the Big Slough, "Drain the swamp," the fact that we're running low on dried cherries, the fact that in the first book, about Wisconsin, Laura Ingalls Wilder writes as if there were no other people for miles around, but actually there were Ojibwe, Potawatomi, Winnebago and Ottawa living there still, the fact that she doesn't even mention it, the fact that they probably didn't see Indians as neighbors, or even as *people* exactly, Republican, Hochungra, Ho-Chunk Nation, Anishinaabe, Amish, the fact that Stace shows no interest in her Indian heritage, like Frank, the fact that I was a lot more curious about it than he was, because I'd *studied* this stuff, Cheyenne Diner, Skyline, Empress, Whitman's Sampler, Christmas candy, the fact that the Ingallses ate tomatoes in *cream* sometimes, for *dessert*, as a special treat, the fact that they ate them with a little sugar, so maybe it was *sort* of like peaches in cream, tomatoes in cream, the fact that I'm gonna try that this summer, right after I make the green pumpkin pie, or before, the fact that Gillian would love that, if I made all the food from the *Little House* books, the fact that Stacy would probably get mad but I don't see why, sour grapes, sour cherries, the fact that we need sour cherries, butter, whiskey, steak, ham, onions, potatoes, coleslaw, the fact that while I was sick I dreamt I had to drive my car out of a maze-like car repair place, labyrinthine, the fact that "labyrinth" is a Babylonian word, no, *Minoan*, or Lydian, the fact that the garage was built on many levels like a multistory parking lot, and in order to be allowed out of the place I had to divorce *Frank* again, and to accomplish this I had to provide the court of car mechanics with three pages of Frank's handwriting, the fact that I wasn't sure I still had any examples of his handwriting at all, so I was going to have to ask Stacy if she still had any of his old letters that I could use, and even in the dream I didn't want to ask her, because I don't like reminding Stacy about Frank, the fact that I don't know how it all turned out, in the dream, I mean, the fact that we always *tried* to be welcoming when Frank deigned to visit, but it's hard to pretend you like someone when you don't, the fact that that's a silly thing to say though, because most people spend their whole entire lives pretending to like people they don't like, and I do too, the fact that Frank said that I once sort of sat up in bed in my sleep and said "A dollar?!" in this really incredulous way, like I was *bargaining* with somebody in my dream, and then I lay back down, sound asleep, slow reader, Ticonderoga, the fact that after Mommy got sick, I read the *phonebook*, just to feel even more alienated, chili powder, mayo, get two, the fact that I *tried* making my own mayo once and that was enough, though it did taste good, vinegar, the fact that I dreamt Bathsheba wanted to sit in my lap but there was a funny-looking dog outside, and then I was in my nightgown shopping, and cars were flipping off cliffs in high winds, so we rode our horses away at a gallop, the fact that I never could ride a horse but always wanted to, the fact that people make it look easy but it's not, the fact that I'm glad none of our kids want to ride horses and break their backs all the time, the fact that my back's never been the same since *my* fall, but it was my own fault of course, ♫ *of course, of course* ♫, the fact that I think I'm a little accident-prone, the fact that I was supposed to be breaking *him* in, not the other way around, the fact that besides the fall on my coccyx, I had a huge bruise on my thigh for months after, from where he kicked me, and maybe a permanent dent, I'm not sure, the fact that I was always scared of getting anything *permanent*, the fact that as a kid you always want a second chance at everything, from going down the slide to baby teeth and report cards, and it feels so unfair when you don't get one, charley horse, the fact that I also dreamt I had a nice black bug, completely square, about an inch tall, the fact that he stood upright on two legs and liked to perch on a bird's head, the fact that I was taking care of both the bird *and* the bug, for a friend, I can't remember who, and later the bug almost drowned but I found him just in time and saved him, the fact that he got caught in the sink and the water was about to sweep him down into the disposal, the fact that we don't normally think much about the difficulties bugs face, but I bet they drown a lot, the fact that a wasp got swept down the sink once in New Haven, soon after Mommy got sick, and I couldn't cry for Mommy but I cried hysterically for that wasp, the fact that Ethan was home from college and he tried to calm me down, the fact that he suggested maybe I was actually unhappy about something *else*, but I really felt sure it was just about that wasp, the fact that they called Ethan "Heathen" in high school, yet he still goes to high school reunions every ten years, the fact that Phoebe wouldn't be caught dead at *her* high school reunion, even though she's very sociable, junior high, and I wouldn't dream of going to mine, the fact that I can't even remember most of the people I went to school with, the fact that I've blanked them all out, the fact that that Callum whateverhisnamewas would probably be there, and maybe Gavin, the fact that I was so lost and alone after Chuck left, orphan, Why Your Dog Hates Your Cell Phone, the fact that smoke makes bees fall asleep, teenagers, the fact that Leo had a terror of appendicitis when he was a teenager, the fact that he had panic attacks about it but he never told anybody at the time, the fact that he still hasn't had appendicitis, touch wood, but he had a real thing about it for a few years, the fact that maybe he'd heard a horror story about peritonitis or something, but he can't remember hearing one, the fact that Daddy had appendicitis as a *baby*, the fact that he sometimes showed us his zigzaggy appendectomy scar, the fact that the surgeon obviously made kind of a hash of it, "You're a screw-up!", but he saved him, or I wouldn't be here, the fact that maybe they weren't so hot at appendectomies in the thirties, or his mom got the wrong surgeon, the fact that I bet the operation was performed on that library table she was so fond of, Daddy as a baby, the fact that it's strange to think of your parents as *babies*, the fact that Leo has a picture of his mom as a baby, wearing the sweetest little bonnet you ever saw, the fact that Leo was so kind to me about my cold, the fact that he even brought me chicken broth, several times, so I really shouldn't complain about nobody taking care of me, the fact that Leo is very steady when anybody's sick, the fact that he's good with the kids' illnesses too, the fact that he never even freaked out when I had cancer, well, not in front of *me* anyway, the fact that that was a real help, because I don't know what I would've done if he'd gone all wobbly on me, the fact that he's a calm presence, the fact that he gets me through all my freak-outs and he *never* freaks out, the fact that Leo got me through, the fact that I cry sometimes though, the fact that I cry about Mommy, operas, Bathsheba, Stacy, Pepito, Jake's lost infancy, that mucus-reducing medicine, and solitaire, the fact that I never play solitaire without thinking of Mommy, and that's partly why I play it, yellow corduroy chaise longue, the fact that it was a wide-wale corduroy, a kind you don't see much anymore, the fact that Leo found me crying once and asked me why and I didn't answer, and he said he loves me more than anything and if I didn't want to talk about it right then I could wake him up in the middle of the night and tell him anything and it would be all right, Niagara Falls, Maid of the Mist, sleeping bees, the fact that there was once a big ex-slave community in Windsor, Ontario, pear tarte tatin, Harrison Ford jumping off of the dam, "damn dams," the fact that I don't deserve him, Leo I mean, the fact that I was miswhelped, the fact that I'm malformed, and accident-prone, the fact that I never got a handle on life or how to love people, the fact that I'm injured, broken, like an egg thrown out of the nest, the fact that my life just never really got off the ground because of Mommy's illness, the fact that I think maybe it got stuck on hold, dormant, diapause, rewind, cowbird, the fact that *I'm* the "heathen," yet last night Leo said I'm his *heaven* and he misses me the whole time he's away and just wants to be with me all the time, and I told him, "All day I feel inadequate, but it turns out you think

I'm okay," and he said, "I said you're my *'heaven,'* not 'okay,'" the fact that things aren't all bad, the fact that Rigoletto's daughter ends up in a *sack*, Gilda, the fact that at least that hasn't happened to me, yet, touch wood, the fact that that's his best one, *Madama Butterfly*, Puccini I mean, not Verdi, Mommy, Lyric Opera, donkey, binoculars, nap, euphoria, the fact that I hardly remember anything about having cancer now, though it was only a few years ago, the fact that I do know I had to have a plastic, cushioned mattress cover on my side of the bed for a while, oh dear, and in the daytime I mostly lay on the couch reading Jane Austen or watching DVD box sets, *amoricious lilium tuscadontris*, tusk, Tuscarawas, "the tusks are looser," orthodontist, mammoths, mammoth, dental hygienist, dental *psychologist*, the fact that that's Stacy's future profession, according to the careers advice she got, the fact that they made her fill out a questionnaire and that was their conclusion, that she should become a dental psychologist, the fact that I guess they take over after the hygienist has traumatized you, but she doesn't *want* to be a dental psychologist, squash bug, the fact that I watched about fifty adaptations of *Jane Eyre*, I think, when I had cancer, or that's how it felt anyway, side effects, drug manufacturers, kill or cure, chemotherapy, the fact that I watched *House, M.D.,* too, and *24* and *The West Wing* and *Breaking Bad* and *Commander in Chief*, as well as David Attenborough's plant series again and again, because plants can't hurt you much, and I can't remember a thing about any of them really, the fact that all that mattered to me was that these shows went on and on, like *life* should, the fact that Daddy wouldn't have approved of that, but he didn't mind Mommy watching TV, after she got sick, so maybe he would've forgiven me, the fact that she watched all kinds of stuff, even sports, the fact that Daddy watched a bit of Forest Hills now and then, and some baseball, home plate, double play, but Mommy would watch all kinds of stuff, parades, bullfighting, horseracing, the fact that she kept a beady eye on the Kentucky Derby and the Preakness and that other one, whatever it's called, Paula Prentiss, the fact that she got all excited every year about the Triple Crown, the fact that, boy, she couldn't get enough of that

Triple Crown, the fact that the horse has to win the Kentucky Derby, Preakness and Belmont Stakes, the fact that she even tolerated wrestling and basketball sometimes, the fact that maybe TV really is just for sick people who can't do much else, trapped people, shut-ins, convicts, slaves, the fact that I'm sort of trapped when I'm baking, so I watch movies, not so much TV, the fact that it's all ads now, the fact that when I was sick in bed with my cold I watched movies too, the fact that Mommy liked Bill Cosby and Bob Newhart and Woody Allen and *The Golden Girls*, but not *Friends*, the fact that Mommy liked *people* in some way I don't seem to, she was alive to things, even car license plates, the fact that she had a car she was always looking around for in London, a little MG sports car with 'EGO' on the license plate, *All the President's Men*, Ireland, the fact that Andrew Shereman had a sports car, or maybe it was his dad's, the fact that on our one date, I dropped my whole purse on the sidewalk when I was getting out of that car, and everything in it fell out on the ground, everything in my purse, not the car, the fact that I really liked Andrew Shereman too, but that was the end of that, the fact that maybe you do have to learn how to get elegantly out of cars, like you do at Charm School, the fact that I was so embarrassed I could hardly speak the whole time we were in the Mexican restaurant, couldn't eat either, the fact that I was young, and way too shy to go on a date, *Midnight Cowboy*, the fact that *Jane Eyre*'s about an orphan, *two* orphans if you count the little French girl, the fact that when we were little Mommy took us to the beach every day in the summer and we swam while she sat on a towel and read books, the fact that I loved the way she looked in her sunglasses smoking, the fact that I finally persuaded Daddy to buy me an inner tube but he got me the wrong kind, the fact that he got me some kind of *toy* inflatable inner tube, all colorful and babyish and covered in cartoons or something, the fact that it was too small and not cool at all, the fact that you really can't skimp on an inner tube, the fact that it's got to be a *real* one, that somehow came out of a real tire, and it has to be the dark gray kind that turns black when it hits the water, and it's gotta be *rubber*, not plastic, the fact that

547

maybe everybody else's dad had old inner tubes lying around in the garage or something but mine didn't and he was reluctant to go pay for one just so I could float around in it like a dope, so we got a lousy imitation inner-tube from the dime store, "A dollar?!", the fact that I can't remember now if I ever did get the right kind, the fact that it doesn't matter either, the fact that I was always obsessing about the wrong stuff, and still am, OCD, dental psychology, the fact that I never really got how all the car tires could do *without* their inner tubes, just so us kids could swipe them for swimming, appendicitis, my sickbed, the fact that Stacy's always accusing me of having OCD but I think she's wrong, the fact that I don't even know what OCD is really, the fact that she's the dental psychologist though, so maybe I should listen to her, the fact that I don't wash my hands all day long or anything, but you have to a bit when you're cooking, the fact that there are National Parks all over Illinois, and trails, and river trips, and we never went to *any*, which is somehow kind of like the inner tube problem, in my view, the fact that Mommy and Daddy were kind of resistant to doing all that sort of family-type stuff, the fact that they were always too busy, or maybe they were being frugal, or maybe they just didn't agree with what other parents were doing, like going to Disneyland or something, the fact that we never even went west of Wisconsin, and we only went *there* once, for a *night*, after I hurt my finger, the fact that it was just me, Daddy and Ethan, and we stayed in a real log cabin, the fact that the next day Ethan was a daredevil in the motorboat, the fact that I really think he wanted to capsize us but he didn't manage it, the fact that I wasn't supposed to get my bandage wet so I was kind of worried, the fact that in all my days I've only seen the Chicago River, and the Ohio, and the Hudson and all, but not the Mississippi, the fact that I saw the dead rabid dog near Northwestern, the fact that Daddy only said it *might* have rabies, so maybe I haven't even seen a dead rabid dog, T-Rex, Betty Crocker, the fact that "poverty of experience" is what I've got, I think, more than OCD, the fact that Daddy once told me he'd gone over Niagara Falls in a barrel and I *believed* it for years, even though he hardly ever even took us to the zoo, and even though he wasn't very athletic, the fact that I thought it was just something dads do, go over Niagara Falls in a barrel, the fact that Mommy and Daddy showed little interest in their surroundings, but maybe they were just more interested in touring Europe than Illinois, the fact that what's a hundred-year-old Mormon pioneer village or a roadside stand selling hand-whittled pencil-holders compared to Pompeii or Athens or Malta, or the Alps, or even Sligo, the fact that we went all over Ireland, but all I *really* wanted to do was visit that big water park we saw on TV in Evanston, the fact that you could go there for the whole day, and they had rides and slides and little canoes and a trout pool, and a lion's face trash machine, the fact that the lion's mouth sucked the trash right out of your hand, the fact that they didn't have one of *those* in the Alps, the fact that I've always had a touch of vertigo anyway, Bernard Herrmann, the fact that I never liked *Vertigo*, the fact that who really wants to watch Jimmy Stewart obsess about Janet Leigh, or Kim Novak I guess I mean, well, *either* of them actually, and Tippi Hedren too, appendicitis, pears, the fact that I like Jimmy Stewart best in *It's a Wonderful Life* or *Mr. Smith Goes to Washington*, the fact that I guess I like him best when he's *younger*, though *Rear Window*'s pretty good, even though you have to see him without his shirt on, the fact that actresses haven't got a *chance* once they get old, except maybe Meryl Streep, the fact that the English have that Judi Dench, who plays all the older women parts, but Judi Dench is always the same, the fact that Marlon Brando lived in Evanston for a while when he was a kid, blossom, Candyland, the fact that L. M. Montgomery's so right about apple trees, the fact that just *look* at it, the fact that apple trees are the wonder of the world, the fact that they just sit there all winter and you forget about them and then they bloom and you just can't get over all those thick clouds of petals, Ohio like a petal, the fact that L. M. Montgomery gushed about blossoming trees in a way that maybe nobody would dare to anymore, the fact that the kids skip those bits, L. M. Montgomery's exultations about blossoms, the fact that nature's finished, wrecked, the fact I'm surprised it still works at all, like I'm always kind of relieved that the sun still comes up, and seasons happen, the fact that I'm the only one around here that takes any interest in apple blossoms, the fact that we need soy sauce, butter, chocolate chips, and brown sugar, the fact that I could just run out to Zyker's right now, but I don't want to, but we need soy sauce, the fact that why don't I just go do it and get it over with, Zyker's Foods, lipstick, earrings, the fact that I'd have to do something with my hair, the fact that I'm still getting over my cold, but we need soy sauce, Zyker's Foods, the fact that what is the point in arguing with *myself*, sheesh, ♫ *To-whit, to-whoo said the little old owl* ♫, the fact that hay boxes and crockpots and slow cookers and Dutch ovens cause millions of food poisoning cases a year, if not actual deaths, the fact that people just aren't careful enough, they don't obey the instructions, don't *read the manual*, like Leo's always telling *me* to do, the fact that I don't need a manual to tell me how to work a flashlight, or a toaster, for Pete's sake, the fact that Leo has to read all the appliance manuals around here, because I can't, the fact that I never *understand* them, and they scare me, the fact that Cathy said a customer came into the Shoppe looking for pork ribs, raw pork ribs, the fact that she doesn't sell raw meat, the fact that he bought some other stuff instead and then he started describing how he makes some kind of pork stew in a crockpot and it sounds *dangerous*, the fact that he didn't seem to have a clue about food hygiene, the fact that he puts raw pork ribs, a can of condensed tomato soup, and some old bacon grease in a crockpot and leaves the whole thing on Warm *for several days*, for heaven's sake, baby salamanders, nasturtiums, the fact that nasturtiums are good to eat, but I've never tried one, the fact that maybe they'd look good on a cake, the Prime Minister of Indonesia on her knees releasing baby turtles into the sea, the fact that Cathy tried to tell him it was a recipe for *disaster*, but he said he's been making pork ribs that way for years and never had any trouble with it, ♫ *Turn back, O man* ♫, the fact that trichinosis is rare but it still *happens*, spiral larvae, food poisoning, the fact that she may never see *that* customer again, but she tried to tell him, the fact that Ronny's feed costs far too much and I really should make up my own, since his doesn't allow for seasonal changes, the fact that they prefer our scraps, tomatoes, melon, sunflower seeds, pumpkins, the fact that according to Laura Ingalls Wilder they need fenugreek, cayenne pepper, ginger and lime, and a morning mash, four parts bran, two cornmeal, one bonemeal, and one half linseed meal, plus lime and salt, and sunflower seeds every now and then, but when do I have the time for all that, the fact that if you give them too much corn, chickens won't lay, wallabies, cherries, whiskey, pirates, Pepito at the commune, the fact that we hate waste, the High Seas, high five, which is why I freeze such a lot, but eventually you have to either eat it, sell it, or ditch it, declutter, joy, soy sauce, the fact that Ben always orders the Poo-Poo Plate at the Chinese restaurant, but then he doesn't eat it and we have to take almost the whole Poo-Poo Plate home in a doggy-bag, or a carton, the fact that I like those cartons you get from Chinese restaurants, the fact that anyway, the chickens love the Poo-Poo Plate, the fact that the chickens help a lot with our leftovers, the fact that fishermen must have so much wastage, because fish rots so fast, the fact that I'd be a nervous wreck if I was a fisherwoman, fishwife, the fact that what lies on the bottom of the sea, shaking, the fact that it's a nervous wreck, "Ducky! Ducky!", clutter, clucker, quack, quack, the fact that having been brought up alone, Pepito naturally growled when another dog tried to swipe his food, but he never *bit* anybody, the fact that Pepito always meant well, he just didn't understand commune life, the fact that I don't understand *family* life, the fact that I have a tiny bump on the inside of my lip which I first noticed while arguing with Leo about something or other, and now every time I feel the bump on my lip I think of that silly argument, the fact that I think it was something to do with not picking up his dry cleaning, the fact that he needs his suit back, because he got pepper pot soup on it, soup, suit, zoot suit, the fact that this is the kind of stuff I remember, our little argument, the fact that it's so hard to remember what you *want* to remember, like the day we first met, the fact that things just come at you willy-nilly, like every time I do jigsaw puzzles I always remember Jeremy Driscoll and also that woman, whatshername, the one who ran the good coffee place in Gnadenhutten that took my angel food cakes for a while, the fact that she later moved to Paris, Paris, *Texas*, not Paris, France, and now I forget her name, Miriam something, Marjorie, Marianne, Carnation Evaporated Milk, piece of cake, Let Them Eat Cake, sweet deal, cook his goose, V-formation, flyway, "Greensleeves," the fact that I don't even know *why* I think of her at all, the fact that I hardly knew the woman, the fact that whenever I see buttercups I think of our back yard in Evanston, though I've seen lots of other buttercups in plenty of other places, and whenever I see a cardinal I think of the plastic model of a cardinal I almost finished painting when I was a kid, the fact that it wasn't as much fun as I'd expected, trying to paint a brown plastic model of a bird, and you have to get all the colors in the right places or it won't look good, but the instructions were hard to follow, and it was easy to smudge the paint, the fact that I can never follow instructions, just like manuals, "Read the manual!", painting by numbers, the fact that I make mistakes with *recipes* as well, and need help filling out forms, the fact that I chose that bird kit myself, because I liked the bird, the fact that I think it was a hard choice though, between a cardinal and a blue jay, the fact that I paid for it with my own money, and then I couldn't figure out how to do it, or I got bored with it, the fact that now it's hard to imagine why I ever thought painting a plastic replica cardinal was going to be fun in the first place, flashbacks, nightmares, nirvana, PTSD, the fact that Leo makes a good living and works hard and helps me with the kids and takes care of me when I'm sick and loves me and misses me, "I said you're my '*heaven*,' not 'okay,'" and shares his life with me, which is the most miraculous and generous thing of all, the fact that he's with me for all our birthdays and Christmases and Saturdays and Sundays and scenic drives and illnesses and emergencies and plumbing problems, scenic plumbing problems, ♫ *The faucets are dripping and oh, what a pity* ♫, Wrigley Stadium in Chicago, wriggly, bigly, wiggly, jiggly, quiggly, quiggly hole, wiggle theory, Mrs. Piggle-Wiggle, *They tell me you are bigly*, the fact that Leo lugs the garbage with me and tries out my madeleine failures, the fact that he is full of *loving kindness*, and a guy in a million, so why do I waste my time *arguing* with him about *nothing*, nothing, *Nothing will come of nothing*, the fact that for heaven's sake he can get pepper pot soup on his pants whenever he darn well pleases, can't he, the fact that he earned it, and it's *true* his suit's been at the cleaners too long, the fact that what the heck does pepper pot soup matter in this crazee world, hill of beans, itch, sore teeth, *They say the hen can lay*, the fact that Peter Lorre yells "Rick! Rick!" just before they catch him, PELs, the fact that Bogart and Ingrid are really in love when they're in Paris, the fact that it's all dark rooms and sparkling champagne with them, the fact that the weight of love locks brought down a whole parapet on the Pont des Arts, the fact that they had to remove *sixteen thousand pounds* of padlocks from the bridge, but they're coming back again, the fact that lovers put the lock on and throw the keys into the river, the fact that naturally Leo disapproves of weighing down a bridge like that, the fact that I thought it's just become fashionable, probably because of some movie or pop song, but still it's kind of sweet, and better than heart-shaped thingamajigs, the fact that Woodrow Wilson delayed the end of World War One by a whole month, for some reason of his own, the fact that I don't know what gets into these guys, delaying peace, the fact that Nixon did that too, the fact that the Vietnam war could have ended *ten years earlier*, but Nixon wanted to take the credit, so he scuppered the earlier chance of peace somehow, the fact that that really takes the cake, to let thousands or millions of people die for the sake of your own career, war crime tribunal, Nuremberg, the fact that Leo says the first love locks on a bridge actually started in Serbia during the First World War, the fact that women had a superstition that their lovers would come back if they put a love lock on some bridge, with their boyfriends' names on the locks, the fact that Paul Henreid is more like Ingrid Bergman's teacher, a mentor, not a "lover," the fact that let's face it, he's just an idol she had a crush on years ago, the fact that their marriage is all about Czechoslovakia, not about them personally, the fact that everybody deserves a personal life, and that's what she got with Bogart, the fact that Paul Henreid seems polite with her but cold, although maybe he's just temporarily distracted by having to save Czechoslovakia, the fact that when he's singing "The Marseillaise" he comes to life and everybody else does too, and Ingrid loves him again, for a little while, the fact that it's terrible to wonder if you're really with the right guy, "The Marseillaise," the fact that I like her at the market in her stripy blouse and the hat that's like a lampshade, the fact that only Ingrid Bergman could get away with that hat, the fact that she always seems color-coordinated, Ingrid Bergman, even in black-and-white movies, Ilsa Lund, the fact that it sounds like the name of some forgotten novelist from the thirties, the fact that the only thing I've got that's color-coordinated is my *birthday* suit, birthdays, Ben, Gillian, **1** pan, the fact that Paul's more fatherly than anything, not husbandly, the fact that she's more of an *equal* with Bogart, the fact that with him she can relax, and you can't fully love someone until you can relax with them, I don't think, but I'm *never* relaxed, except when I'm asleep maybe, the fact that I sleep better next to Leo, the fact that who *can* relax with all these school shootings going on, and family annihilations, and this president, Glock, clock, clog, robocalls, holohoax, the fact that some men just can't make a woman happy, like Victor Laszlo, or Frank, the fact that they can't be bothered, or just don't get how to do it, the fact that they just aren't *interested* enough in women, the fact that a man needs to be deeply interested in a woman, I think, to make her happy, otherwise he's just playing around and wasting everybody's time, the fact that some men though, like Frank, are so stubborn, and won't take no for an answer, so they waste their time and yours on a thing that'll never really fly, the fact that Victor Laszlo's not a waste of time, especially from the Czechoslovakian point of view, and maybe he does love Ilsa, the fact that he can really belt out the "Marseillaise," stripes, striation rash, and he helps Rick get political again, sunny square in Paris, but Rick's hedonistic nightclub lifestyle was just a kind of charade anyway, while he nursed his broken heart, broken, heart operation, Claude Rains, itchy, the fact that I watched *Yesterday, Today, and Tomorrow*, in my sickbed, the fact that Sophia Loren wears

Marcello Mastroianni *out* with her needs, the fact that she's infringed some bylaw in Naples, by selling cigarettes on the street, and the only way to get out of going to jail is to keep getting pregnant, because they won't jail you if you're pregnant, the fact that they already have several kids, and it's all up to Marcello to keep her constantly pregnant but he can't *do* it, the fact that he runs out of energy to keep Sophia Loren pregnant, *Sophia Loren*, the fact that, if you think about it, he only has to, well, perform every nine months or so, in between babies, but still he runs out of steam and gets all weak and tired out from the effort of it all, thin, lethargic, exhausted, the fact that he just can't do it anymore, so she winds up in jail and, boy, is she *mad*, the fact that somehow Sophia Loren can get away with displays of temper much better than I can, the fact that I just act like a jerk and always lose an argument, but Bette Davis or Sophia Loren are magnificent when they're angry, Channeling Your Inner Bette, the fact that Sophia Loren gets out of jail soon enough though and she and Marcello Mastroianni are instantly reconciled and all happy as clams again, and in the last scene they're back in bed together, surrounded by their dozen kids, doomed to poverty but they don't mind, the fact that Carlo Ponti died ten years ago, the fact that I hope he made Sophia Loren happy, the fact that I hope he treated her like a *queen*, the fact that she was good in *Two Women* too, caldera, geyser, Marcello Mastroianni, cutie marks, the cute twins, the fact that there are more twins born now, because of all the growth hormones given to cows, the fact that during my cold I got used to tea with honey, but I'm getting used to it again *without* honey now, the fact that maybe I should stick with it though, to plump up a bit, channel my inner Sophia, the fact that what would Leo think if I suddenly looked like Sophia Loren, the fact that maybe you can maintain a more equable manner if you're curvy, not jutting out all over, the fact that *Cathy's* very even-tempered, the fact that eating ice cream is the simplest way to plump up if you need to, but I can't be bothered, the fact that that salted apple pretzel pie recipe seems complicated, and maybe not worth it, the fact that it's weird how you sort of connect with *nature* through eating things, 4-F plants, hearts of palm, emergency fish cakes, all the stuff you'd have nothing to do with if you didn't need to eat, like white asparagus, or fish, the fact that you'd hardly ever meet a fish unless you sought him out, truffles, the fact that sometimes it seems like the main way people experience nature *now* is by dissolving murder victims in acid baths, the fact that that's more like getting in touch with chemistry though, acid attacks, acid mines, prussic acid, sulfuric acid, acid reflux, cyanic acid, antacid, formic acid, Six Kinds of Dizziness, storm chasers, the fact that surely never before was there such a crowd of well-armed shut-ins glued to the Weather Channel, Channel No. 5, the fact that Indians had a place in nature but now we know nothing about it except you can get deer ticks if you go out, and then you get that disease I've forgotten the name of, something like Wiles Disease or Weil's Disease, Wales, Princess of Wales Disease, no, *Lyme*, the fact that I should remember that, after working in Old Lyme, the fact that maybe that's where they first found it, the fact that I hope not, the fact that I'm so scared of poison ivy and deer ticks I hardly ever go beyond our *back yard*, for heaven's sake, though deer come through there too, the fact that we're all supposed to use repellent but we never do, the fact that you're okay if you get to the doctor fast and start taking antibiotics, medical insurance, the bump in my mouth, dry cleaning, the fact that DuPont is the second biggest air polluter, or no, Alcoa's the worst, *then* DuPont, then Bayer, General Electric, and Exxon Mobil, #ExxonKnew, and the worst water polluters are Dow Chemical, then AEP, then the AES Corporation, and Honeywell International, honey, honeybush tea, DuPont, dead cows, Parkersburg, the fact that bananas are radioactive, Stuck In A Sinkhole, the fact that my throat still hurts, closure, introversion, ECT, ENT, OCD, the fact that they're treating depression with magic mushrooms now, the fact that maybe that isn't such a new idea, Carlos Castaneda, peyote, boots by the back door, galoshes, the fact that they reboot the brain, *mushrooms*, not galoshes, goulash, nature, mother nature, acid baths, geysers, geezers, Trump's hair, the fact that I am a full-grown woman and I don't even know one tree from another or what the names of birds are, except for a cardinal, or how to identify them by their calls, the fact that I couldn't even finish painting my plastic cardinal, the fact that surely by this age I should just naturally know that kind of stuff, like birdsong, or wildflowers, the fact that you should know it, the fact that there's a cardinal in Erie, PA, that's half-male and half-female, the fact that it's a gynandromorph, "The whole thing got out of hand!", Sun-Maid girl, the fact that that big guy was hanging around the counter at the Shoppe, the day Cathy wasn't there, and I was standing by the counter, the fact that Art got himself a can of soda and after he had a drink, he came over to talk to me, obviously assuming the big guy wasn't ready to pay yet, the fact that the big guy got really annoyed about being kept waiting, the fact that a lot of people are so touchy, the "public," Time Is Money, the fact that Art didn't mean any harm, he just hadn't realized the guy was done shopping, so then the big guy rudely interrupts me and Art talking, and starts insinuating there's something *romantic* going on between us, which really shocked me, the fact that he was joshing around about Cathy, implying Art liked me more than his own wife, stuff like that, really kind of crude, and insulting to me as well as Art, crude oil, DAPL, the fact that he could see my wedding ring but he just looked me up and down and decided I was up for playing around with Art or something, a married man, the fact that I was so *embarrassed*, the fact that it's so lucky Amelia was there, the fact that she couldn't stand all this nonsense and she went right up to Art and said "What's all this crap about?", but not in a mean way, in a *supportive* way, the fact that I just sort of pretended I wasn't there at that point, the fact that she's so articulate, the fact that I do admire that about her sometimes, the fact that she didn't even need to squelch the guy direct, the fact that she ignored him and said to Art something like "Whyya let this jerk make jokes about your wife? You don't have to put up with that. Your wife's nice, *you're* nice, so you don't have to laugh along with this stupid guy just to be polite, because you know what? He is being offensive and disrespectful to your *wife*, and you don't need that kind of customer. You should just ban him," the fact that, wowie zowie, she really said that, and so calmly too, the fact that everybody was embarrassed, but also kind of grateful, because she really shut that noisy character up, the fact that Art seemed sort of buoyed up by it too, even though they probably lost a customer, but Amelia's right, they don't need him, the fact that when Cathy heard what'd happened, she actually did a little jig, with *Art*, the fact that Amelia just doesn't care who she's talking to or where she is, the fact that she kind of surprises you that way, just speaks her mind all the time, dear me, the fact that she probably gets into some trouble sometimes, but she doesn't seem to care, "Hoits you?", the fact that I wonder if she'll even remember this incident, because she's probably already had about six more dramatic encounters elsewhere by now, The Calf That Thinks She's A Dog, the fact that, on the other hand, it must be exhausting to be Amelia and to have to go around sorting out the world all day, "How strong of a person are you?", the fact that some teenager now has to wear a colostomy bag for the rest of his life because of a school shooting, the fact that nobody's got time for compassion anymore, the fact that even just a little politeness would help, Lyme disease, the fact that there seems to be no problem in America that can't be solved by murdering your whole family or your boss or a whole crowd of strangers, and maybe yourself, Rare Albino Echidna Spotted In Tasmania, the fact that Leo says the NRA is at war with America and they're going to win too, because they've got all the *guns*, and the fossil fuel people are going to win because they've got all the fuel, the fact that he says they all want to *kill* us, and school shootings and all the other gun violence are just the early skirmishes in the war that's coming, the fact that I don't know where he got all these scary ideas, the fact that some people pronounce ideas "idears," suicide by police, juvenile, the fact that Edward was my best mouse, the fact that the rodents were our personal pets, while the goldfish just seemed to belong to the whole family, and Pierre and Pepito were full *members* of the family, that poor family over in Pike County, the Bridder family, all shot, familicide, the fact that we are more likely to be blown to smithereens right now than ever before, Doomsday, the fact that buying organic milk seems kind of a pathetic answer to all this but it's all I've come up with so far, that and making pies, the fact that I think everybody expects Trump to start a nuclear war, but nobody wants to mention it in case that *encourages* him, the fact that I think we should all ignore him, starve him of publicity, but most Ohioans seem to love this guy, the fact that there's about to be nuclear war and they don't give a darn, and *I'm* arguing about who should pick up the *dry cleaning*, sore spot, hydrangeas, Sexist Pay Gap, the fact that Lyme disease can make you feel sick for a decade but some people recover faster, the fact that I hope I don't have it, the fact that I *am* tired all the time, but I've always been that way, the fact that I think I would have noticed if I had Lyme disease, hypochondria, factory farming, hangars, outdoor-reared livestock, Amish barn, the fact that just because *we* spend our whole lives indoors, doesn't mean animals have to too, the fact that, landsakes, it shouldn't be a special privilege to be outdoor-reared, the fact that animals like going out, but most cows aren't allowed out anymore, and chickens of course are stuck in their tiers, tears, "Certified Humane," the fact that even award-winning pig farms keep their pigs indoors all the time, knee-deep in mud, awards, prizes, dollars, the fact that calves are taken away from their moms, lactose intolerance, the fact that mother cows run mooing after the trucks carrying their calves away, and never see their calves again, all so I can make all these dumb *pies*, the fact that what we've done to animals, the fact that there's so much milk around now, they don't even know what to do with it all, so they just put it in *everything*, potato chips, spaghetti sauce, sausages, salad dressing, sherbet, crackers, the fact that whatever it is they throw milk in, growth hormones, the fact that there was probably some in my anti-mucus membrane, I mean *medicine*, even though milk's supposed to *generate* mucus, so why would you want that when you have a heavy cold, the fact that putting milk in my mucus pills probably wouldn't faze a company that thinks death is the one sure way to cure a cold, the fact that even the Chinese use milk now, in pot stickers and everything, and they used to hate milk, and hate Westerners for *smelling* of milk, Poo-Poo Plate, palm oil, habitat, rat-a-tat-tat, ratatouille, the fact that I once looked a mother orangutan right in the eye, when I took Stacy to some zoo somewhere, and we really seemed to connect for a moment, one mom to another, but then I left her there and never went back, so what good am *I* as an orangutan friend, crackers, bread sticks, cookies, the fact that people only seem to care about their own pets maybe, and puppies and kittens, the fact that nobody can get enough of puppies and kittens, the fact that Gillian loves animals, the fact that she's always up in her room rearranging her stuffed animals, having long conversations with them, the fact that she gets things looking like the animals have convened to form some kind of a government up there, the fact that it's a little eerie, the fact that they all seem to be looking at each other, like they're plotting something, a Senate hearing, the fact that I like her collection of honey bears more, the fact that are all girls across the country collecting honey bears, the fact that Gillian had the great idea, idear, of putting colored water in hers and putting a string of lights behind, and when the lights are on, they're really pretty, the fact that maybe she'll be an engineer, Howard Hughes, Leo DiCaprio, Leonardo da Vinci, *Leo* da Vinci, the fact that *he's* never called Leo, I don't think, Leonardo da Vinci I mean, the fact that there's still not much flower action in our yard yet, the fact that the kids want a dog, puppies, kittens, "Missie crossed the rainbow bridge and Mom and Dad are so sad but Mom says Missie isn't in pain anymore," "Never skip a grade," BMW Reveals Sexy Z4 Update, the fact that Pierre could roam the streets and have love affairs, the fact that at least Pepito had that wild summer in Maine, the fact that he came back all sun-drenched and grown-up, as well as having been badly treated, nincompoops, the fact that if we all blow ourselves to smithereens, at least Pepito has *existed*, and that is good, the fact that it's just plain *good* he was in the world, and boarlets too, boarlets, the fact that they still don't know who killed the Bridders, bridle, Peebles, Canton, Frito-Lay, PepsiCo, the fact that Toledo Zoo has a new baby giraffe, the fact that they granted an orangutan human rights, in Argentina, not Toledo, and this means he can be moved out of some bad zoo into a sanctuary, so now one orangutan has the right to live in a refuge while the palm oil industry has the right to, oh well, the fact that I don't really want to get down about *that* now, the fact that some group plans to sue Trump over our constitutional right to nature, but nobody expects it to get anywhere in court, the fact that animals are going extinct, the fact that I'm glad Mommy and Daddy and Pepito and boarlets and Shakespeare and Bach and Schubert and Jane Austen never had to see this, the fact that Mommy and Daddy had to know about the Holocaust and Hiroshima and Nagasaki, and Rwanda, and 9/11 and all, but at least they didn't have to live through Adam Lanza and all the other gun massacres, and they never had to know Donald Trump would one day be president, the fact that who would've expected *that*, the fact that I always thought he was just some failed businessman who liked building ugly skyscrapers, and now he gets to rule the world, with a smartphone and that thin pad of hair on his head, grab 'em by the smartphone, the fact that at least Mommy and Daddy went to their graves without ever having to think about Trump much, knowing nothing about him, the fact that that's a blessing anyhow, tackiness, the Oscars, the Preakness, Triple Crown, bull-fighting, Roman amphitheater, the fact that I never know how to pronounce "amphitheater," the fact that it doesn't really trip off the tongue, the fact that Alec Baldwin's girlfriend in *It's Complicated* is so *horrible*, the fact that I can't believe she snaps her fingers at him like that, "Yo," ♫ *Figaro, Figaro, Figaro!* ♫, the fact that Rossini studied the cello in Bologna, the fact that Leo and I used to listen to the Met matinees more regularly, on Saturday afternoons, before we had so many little kids around, the fact that what's the name of that tenor we like, from Evanston, Polenzani, the fact that he and Leo were born the same year, the fact that I always liked it when Ethan was practicing his bassoon, the fact that I dreamt I lost my wallet and I was going to have to cancel all my cards, and I woke up *groaning*, but luckily I *haven't* lost my wallet and I *don't* have to cancel my cards, so that's something, the fact that I was also sold some stale bread, in the same dream, and it was supposed to come with parmesan on it, but they gypped me, and there was no parmesan on it when I got it home, "A dollar?!", the fact that my wallet was in my jacket and I searched through a whole pile of jackets but couldn't actually remember which jacket I'd been wearing, the fact that Andrew Jackson had a 1400 pound wheel of cheese, that was shown at the Chicago World's Fair, the fact that they make *vegan* cheese now, but *how*, the fact that I hope they don't use coconut milk, the fact that I also dreamt I'd ordered Leo a leather jacket online but when it came it was no good, it was all falling apart, and it wasn't leather either, the fact that it was made of some sort of nylon *grass*, and bright yellow, like a kid's rain-coat, or a lighthouse keeper's or something, sou'wester, the 2007 nor'easter, the fact that you could pull the thing apart with your *fingers*, the fact that I can't imagine Leo wearing that, even in a dream, the fact that two of the victims in the Bridders shooting were young moms, and one of them had had a baby only *four days* before, UNFPA, the fact that she and her husband or boyfriend or whatever were shot in their bed, but the baby was found alive, crawling between its parents, and covered in their blood, the fact that if I carry on thinking about that, I won't be able to *bake* right, Bakelite, snake bite, the fact that I had some other lousy presents for Leo too in that dream, besides the yellow jacket, but they were much too junky to give him, even junkier than the jacket, stuff like goldfish food, the kind of thing I sometimes try to get away with as emergency stocking presents when I'm all outta toothbrushes, tangerines, and chocolate ladybugs, Pa and the Christmas candy, the fact that the kids don't like that kind of present, but it sure helps fill up the stockings, the fact that I don't appreciate Leo enough, the fact that I take him for granted, but aren't you kind of *supposed* to take your spouse for granted, the fact that, I mean, if you're married, you do get pretty used to having them around, the fact that it's something you can *trust* in, the fact that Leo dreamt he and Tom Hanks were both building inspectors, but that was about it, the fact that it was after we saw that *Captain* something movie, where Tom Hanks gets covered in the pirates' blood, baby covered in blood, the fact that nothing bad happened in Leo's dream though, nothing violent, the fact that there weren't even any pirates around or anything, the fact that Leo and Tom Hanks just walked around inspecting buildings together, the fact that, still, maybe we shouldn't watch action movies right before bed, red bag, Used Car Megastore, Bank of America, the fact that he's an architect in *Sleepless in Seattle*, Tom Hanks, not Leo, which is *sort* of like being a building inspector, the fact that Steve Martin's an architect in *It's Complicated*, "Yo," the fact that it's clear Alec Baldwin needs to be rescued from the "Yo" woman, the fact that Alec and Meryl should just stay together, the fact that they're really *happy* together, and the yo-yo woman and sappy Steve are never going to make them happy, vaginoplasty, the fact that if they want to be together but Alec Baldwin still can't resist playing around, he and Meryl could go see that sex therapist guy she and Tommy Lee Jones saw in *Hope Springs*, the fact that it's kind of depressing they break up again, the fact that now I need the cinnamon, bloodied baby, the fact that he's so *hurt* at the beginning, Tom Hanks, about his dead wife, in *Sleepless in Seattle*, just like William Hurt is about his son in *The Accidental Tourist*, the fact that there aren't enough scenes though with Tom Hanks and Meg Ryan *together*, the fact that they go to all that trouble to get together, letters, airplanes, the private detective, ancient computers, and then, well, *nothing*, the fact that they just meet and that's it, "Hello, Howard," the dim light in Ethan's New York apartment, midmorning, the fact that I had to walk the little Yorkshire terrier, who was dumped on him by some ex-girlfriend, "Yo," the fact that I think *she* was an engineer, the fact that I wonder what happened to her, the fact that Ethan was so kind to her dog, circus dogs, seals, lions, popcorn, *Far from the Madding Crowd*, the fact that Mommy liked a good circus in her younger days, with her mother, the fact that they used to get up at dawn every year, in Newburyport, and go see the circus tent being set up and taken down by the *elephants*, "Ducky! Ducky!", Otis, the fact that Daddy read *Jude the Obscure* out loud to us all in the rehab hospital, when we had to go visit Mommy there every day, and it seemed like the end of the world, the bleakest book ever written, the fact that Mommy was surrounded by people crippled in motorcycle accidents, and most of them couldn't walk or talk or think too well anymore, the fact that I reread *Jude* though, in my sickbed, and Arabella Fawley isn't as terrible as I remembered, the fact that anybody who knows how to incubate an egg in her bodice is okay by me, the fact that sure, she doesn't behave too well when Jude's passing away, the fact that she can't resist the boat race going on outside, and she hides the fact that Jude's gone and runs off to have fun, but she's not *all* bad maybe, just lively, coarse and lively, the fact that she reminds me a bit of Amelia, #Resist, trick-or-treat, candy corn, the fact that there's a lot of circus stuff in *Far from the Madding Crowd*, too much actually, the fact that that was why I named Bathsheba "Bathsheba," because that's what I was reading at the time, the fact that I don't know if we ever pronounced it right, the fact that we always called her Bath*sheeeba*, but maybe it's *Bath*shubba, the fact that *she* liked the strong E sound, the fact that the French try not to emphasize *any* syllable, those mean Chartier guys, giggling till they broke their glasses, but the Italians emphasize syllables, usually the penultimate one, the fact that I wish I knew Italian, the fact that I never mastered any foreign language, the fact that the kids all do Spanish, the fact that Civics class is called "Gov class" now, dog, alley, Top Cat, the fact that when Bathsheba arrived she was a tiny, frightened little black ball, but she grew into a fine strong cat, the fact that we were always together, apart from when I was at college, since pets weren't allowed in the dorm, the fact that Mommy and Daddy were very attached to Bathsheba, and kept her for me, the fact that she lived for twenty-one years, the fact that pets devote their whole lives to us, puppies, kittens, our companions, as much as people are, the fact that many pets make *better* companions than people, the fact that I don't know about snake pets, or iguanas, the fact that the ocean absorbs ninety percent of global warming, and it's heating up fast, the fact that ninety percent of international goods travel by ship, the fact that container ships are one of the biggest polluters ever, so in a way Tom Hanks' *ship* is worse than the Somalian pirates that try to capture it, worse for the future of the *world*, if you leave Tom Hanks out of the equation, non-linear equations, the fact that generally you need as many equations as you have unknowns, parametric tables, Daddy's ointments, CAPTCHA, Somalian pirates, Rohingya, the fact that Phoebe sent us all that money, the fact that I like the way it always works out in the end with jigsaw puzzles, the fact that it *always* works out, no problem, jigsaws, seesaws, circular saw, bloodied baby, the fact that I dreamt Peter Lorre was meant to be giving Leo and me a ride to the train station but we couldn't *find* him, so I asked some people who were standing around, but I'd forgotten his *name*, the fact that I finally remembered it but nobody there had ever heard of him anyway, because they were too young to have seen any black-and-white movies, dopes, but I shouldn't say that, the fact that you don't have to call people *names* because they don't like the same movies as you, dear me, the fact that everybody's just so antagonistic these days, and it's catching, the fact that it's hard to resist picking up bad habits, the fact that everybody's *like* this now, always flipping out, flipside, the fact that there's always a flipside, flipping a tarte tatin upside down, tossing a coin, the flip from asleep to awake, flip from night to day, dream to reality, waxing and waning, black-and-white, male and female, cowboys and Indians, sea and land, peanut butter and jelly, oil and vinegar, pouring oil on troubled waters, the downside, upside-down side, upstairs-downstairs, topsy-turvy, the fact that I dreamt Nanya was sick and I was taking care of her, but she was getting better, and as I lifted her up from the bed I kissed her twice on the cheek, which I would never do in real life, but in the dream I did it because I felt so happy, PDA, the fact that some friends are more huggy than others, the fact that maybe it's *me*, the fact that *I'm* not huggy, attics, snakes, spiders, margarine tubs, the fact that I hate that I forget all my dreams, the fact that I still can't get over the way that guy spoke to me and *Art*, suggesting I'm an adultress and Art's an adulterer, boy, the fact that Leo offered to go beat him up when I told him, the guy, not Art, Glacier Lake jigsaw, Jeremy Driscoll, the fact that I've wasted everybody in my life, myself included, the fact that I'm a neglectful, shy, lousy wife and a *really* lousy conversationalist, criminally, paralytically lousy, motorcycle accidents, the fact that Mommy and Daddy gave my tricycle away without warning, the fact that what was *that* about, the fact that I don't take good enough care of anybody, the fact that I didn't stop Mommy from passing away, the fact that I let her down, I let my own mom down, my only mom, the fact that I let Stace down too, and took *her* for granted, Mexican Drug Cartels, Colombian gangsters, the fact that the coral reefs on the coast of Florida are gone, *gone*, the fact that I don't know why, the fact that maybe it's because of acidification, or red tides, or overheating, or maybe just Grandma, toxic masculinity, bugs, the fact that Grandma used to send us little pieces of Florida coral for Chanukah, and dried starfish and seahorses, so it really is possible she personally depleted the coral reefs, depletion, depression, depravity, deflation, elation, the fact that I've probably personally depleted *Ohio* myself, excretion, defecation, fecal residue, *House, M.D.*, the fact that everything in Ohio is depleted, the fact that everything was so *abundant* when Fanny Trollope was here, too abundant even, the fact that she complained that the woods were untidy, too many fallen trees everywhere, the fact that she liked Kentucky better, because Kentucky forests had fewer rotting trees, the fact that she wanted to go for walks on dainty moss-covered paths and have picnics in picturesque clearings in the woods, not have to clamber over one gaping tree trunk after another and get tangled up in poison ivy, the fact that Fanny Trollope was struck by the American fall though, "the trees took a coloring," the fact that there used to be *beauty* in the USA, well, at least we still have the fall, the fact that we have a bowl of dried paw-paw seeds in our bedroom because they're so pretty, banana bread, paw-paw bread, bear claws, the fact that I once made paw-paw bear claws, the fact that they were kind of good but hard to make, the fact that they were like salty apple pretzel pie, not practical on a grand scale, croque monsieur, croque madame, croque signor, croquet balls, croquettas, the fact that buckeye kernels are supposed to be lucky, I don't know about paw-paw pits, p-p-p-paw-p-p-p-paw p-p-p-pits, the fact that Pepito used to "give the paw," the fact that he loved to do it, the fact that Cathy finally showed me her honeymoon pics, the fact that she says the best way to see the island, if you're staying in Honolulu, is you take the No. 55 bus, because it goes all around the coast and the driver flirts with all the girls that get on and you can get off anywhere for a swim and then catch the *next* bus, the fact that you can see the whole place for *two bucks*, the fact that that does sound like the life, "Call this living?", if we ever got to Hawaii, jigsaw, the fact that everything else there is really expensive though, a sweet deal, the fact that the chickens have really been kind of *ruined* for me by Ronny, a little anyway, the fact that they've just become a source of trouble and worry, a bone of contention, and a Ronny excuse, excuse for passing on by, the fact that every time I sit down for a sec to read Fanny Trollope, there he is, the fact that, also, this new organic Hen Scratch feed he brings me from Coshocton is twice the price of the *nonorganic* feeds I used to buy, candy corn, the fact that I never *asked* for it, he just started bringing it, and I don't know how to get out of it now, the fact that I don't want to knock organic farming or anything, but our chickens *aren't* organic chickens, because we want them to lead a nice unsupervised life, like the chickens of olden times, pecking around and getting up to mischief and eating the heck knows what, the peck knows what, ♫ *a bushel and a peck* ♫, like squash bugs and stink bugs, the fact that they need to eat egg shells too sometimes, for the calcium, the fact that they get a few shells with the leftovers, and they eat up apple cores like there's no tomorrow, though they would really always prefer melon rind, the fact that, boy, do they like melon rinds, the fact that they'd probably like a whole melon sometime but I never thought to give them one, so I take the *chickens* for granted too, neglect, respect, the fact that the main thing is they must never have onions, potatoes, avocados, or salt, the fact that I like saying "feed," the fact that Leo mocks me for it, saying it makes me sound like a real farmer, which I'm not, the fact that men just aren't happy unless there's something to mock, just once in a while, "Ducky! Ducky!", ducks, chickens, turkeys, small potatoes, milk of human kindness, the fact that the head of Turkey just urged all Turks to avoid birth control and have as many kids as possible,

Hungary, hungry, but he doesn't seem to realize that kids are a lot of *work*, and most people don't have the time or money for big families, People Mover, the fact that people can't deal with *twenty kids each* these days, the fact that five little sisters in Chillicothe, all under six, need a foster home, I don't know why, the fact that it makes me broody just to think about them, the fact that when I had Stacy I wished I'd had *triplets*, three little identical Stacys, like a litter of puppies, the fact that sometimes something's so good you just want more of it, the fact that it would be great to have those five little funettes to herd around here, and Jake would have somebody to play with when everybody else is off at school all day, the fact that, come off it though, we already have *four* kids, for goodness sake, the fact that I don't know how you'd get nine in the *car*, the fact that we'd have to buy a bus or something, and you'd never get into a restaurant, the fact that it'd be like a permanent children's birthday party around here, Saran wrap ball, the fact that we probably wouldn't even be approved as foster parents anyway, if they talked to my kids about what a terrible mom I am, though sure Jake would defend me at least, the fact that I'm just being broody, the fact that actually I think those little girls are up for *adoption*, not fostering, the fact that of course they need a permanent home, a forever home, the fact that somehow I don't think Leo would be up for adopting five new kids, easy-going though he is, the fact that even he might blow his top if I suggested that, the fact that I hope they'll be allowed to stick together, the fact that it's terrible when they send one kid one place and his brother or sister to a different family and they never see each other again, Two Killed In Plane Crash, poisonous pet food from China, the Great Wall of China, the fact that that Chinese woman insulted Mommy, pot stickers, but it's not China's fault, Chillicothe, chill, the fact that I dreamt I had to get in touch with Chuck for some bureaucratic reason, and somebody was going to lend me my old car to see him, to see the boyfriend you used to have, who wasn't such a bad boyfriend, and drive the car you used to have, which wasn't such a bad car, to leap back into the past, and out again, get together, bridge the gap, How To Achieve A

Work–Life Balance, the fact that kids are on computers so much these days their brains must just be mush, cornmeal, bonemeal, Dare To Take Our Personality Test, in your face, Facebook, Pinterest, YouTube, e-clouds, the fact that there used to be quiz kids on the radio who knew what "antimacassar" and "apteryx" meant and how to spell them too, like in the forties or something, the fact that everybody cared about spelling then, Gavin, "excruciating," the fact that Anne of Green Gables and Laura Ingalls Wilder were both good at spelling bees, bees, the fact that it seemed to be the thing then, spelling and, and parsing a sentence, the fact that in those days girls spent their time spelling and parsing, and now all they do is get good at makeup, and all the boys do is watch porno movies, the fact that I think the girls are trying to look like *porno stars*, girls at junior high, for Pete's sake, the fact that that must be what the boys expect now, Chuck, puppy love, the fact that *men* should be parsing sentences too, instead of buying guns and going home to shoot their exes and set the house on fire, like just happened the other day over in Johnstown, Johnston, Johnson & Johnson, Gander Mountain in Reynoldsburg, closure, bucket lists, put your John Henry right there, Man Killed Girl "For No Reason At All", the fact that in response to the slightest financial hiccup, they murder their *families*, the fact that how is that the answer, the fact that shooting your estranged wife or girlfriend's become the new normal, the fact that it's getting so that it's surprising when men *don't* shoot their exes, the fact that that family over in Greenville "did everything together," and they died together too, thanks to a semi-automatic, "close-knit," broken, the fact that you never know though, the fact that maybe they "did everything together" because he was the *jealous* type and wouldn't let them out of his sight, the fact that there was a school shooting scare in Pittsburgh, that didn't come to anything in the end, and when they interviewed some of the moms after it was all over, the moms were all *smiling*, the fact that they said they were glad that god and the police will protect their kids from school shooters, gug, the fact that actually god and the police fail thirty thousand Americans a year, and *nobody* saves you from the medical bills, the fact that first you're crippled by a bullet and then by what it costs to fish it out, the fact that there've been two hundred school shootings in the last *two years*, and probably thousands of school shooting threats and plots and near-misses, the fact that "This is now," and all these gun places that pretend to be providing Ohioans with *hunting* equipment and advice, and survival gear and all, never consider whether they're also providing the means to obliterate a whole family or something, homemaker, housewife, stay-at-home mom, work–life balance, co-pays, Dickies, work suspenders, the fact that I bought Leo some suspenders at Gander Mountain once, but he prefers belts, the fact that he doesn't want to have to tuck in his T-shirts, Fanny Trollope, Fannie Hurst, Edna Ferber, 8:42, 9:38, 36, parsing, the fact that I think I just, I just fell asleep there, for a moment, and had this whole dream about two guys having a fake gun battle, with *our* car caught in the middle, and Stacy was with me and she was about five, the fact that it was out on Highway 36, somewhere near Warsaw, and these two guys were shooting blanks at each other, and somehow I knew it was fake gunfire, but *Stacy* didn't know it, the fact that she was terrified and I was just furious, the fact that I went straight to the Warsaw police station and yelled at the two guys, who also happened to be there, the fact that I was pointing at Stacy, saying she'd been rendered speechless from terror, the fact that I said "She's never been shot at before!", and then I tried to slap one of the guys, but you can never really hit people in a dream, the fact that your hand goes into slo-mo and you lose impact, PA moms, gug, weakling, coward, PTA, PTO, PTC, PDQ, PTSD, the fact that, boy, am I *itchy*,

.   .   .   .

She should have stuck with hunting white-tailed deer, plentiful and easy to catch. But the boar had presented himself. He didn't even see her there at first, in the pouring rain. She could have lunged for him with ease but she held back, not wanting to disturb the cubs. This was too dangerous a hunt for them to help with.

Then he caught her smell, looked up, and took off, galloping helter-skelter far from the broken-down cabin where the cubs were sleeping. The lioness thought she had him cornered in a gully, but he dodged out of reach at the last frantic moment and the slippery chase went on.

She'd left the cubs in the one dry corner of the dilapidated structure, which was overgrown inside and out. She had slept in the open doorway all night, to keep a lookout. The hovel, with gaps on all sides, was too large to guard well. Its only advantages were that it was dry in places, and one corner offered shelter from wind and rain. And it was near the top of a hill, but close enough to a fork in the creek where many creatures came to drink. There, she had easily gathered snakes, turtles, minks, skinks, and skunks for the cubs.

Tired of the boar's whirling and squealing, she was about to give up on this effortful hunt, just as her mud-slimed quarry twisted around and zoomed crazily her way. The ledge on which she stood gave her a perfect point from which to pounce. Recoil and leap. His back was broken immediately on impact, his piercing shrieks finally stilled.

She didn't pause to eat, no point in delay. The kittens were unprotected, and here was a rare treat. She picked him up by the scruff, as she would her own infants, and dragged the boar's large, sagging form awkwardly along the ground.

The creek had not seemed high earlier, but in her short absence it had swollen, and its color had changed. Light gray now, from mud and foam, it rushed, surging wide. At first disoriented by this sudden change in the landscape, she couldn't even see the old log cabin. Then she noticed it far below her. Its front wall, and the doorway where she'd slept, were now half-submerged in whitish water.

Her cubs, she knew, would not have waited to be engulfed. They must have scrambled to safety – there was no sign of them there. Frightened but resilient, they would be hiding somewhere near, keeping quiet. They were lions, but young: they would wait for her.

Released from her jaws, the boar plopped gently into a muddy puddle behind the crumbling log cabin. She went inside and nuzzled the corner in which the cubs had slept. The damp cushion of crumpled vines was still warm from their bodies. Then, not wanting to lose another moment, she leapt through the back window and climbed the hill, purring loudly. Upwards, far from water, she stopped to listen out for the cubs, and smell the breezes. She listened for their shrill calls, meant only for her ears. But the collective mechanical purring of cars on the highway above created a fuzz of sound: she couldn't hear the cries of her kits over that.

And they did call to her – with all their might – as they were whisked away, along that noisy road in the back of a rattly station wagon, by a couple of do-gooders.

. . . . .

the fact that about a million starfish were stranded on beaches in New England after all the storms, the fact that there were sea urchins too, and lobsters but, in the picture I saw, it was mainly starfish, with a lobster just stuck here and there for a little variety, the fact that they were piled up a *foot deep*, the fact that now that would make a really challenging jigsaw puzzle, that photo, the fact that a pile of starfish like that would beat the Ponte della Paglia puzzle right out of the water, the fact that that one was really just a lot of water and tourists, and it turned out to be surprisingly easy, because the tourists were all clustered in one little strip, surging across the bridge in both directions, Maillart's bridges, bridging the gaps, making connections, the fact that the water had clear divisions, the fact that the look of it varied according to distance, so you could easily tell which were the lower pieces, the fact that it wasn't Canaletto or anything, the fact that you don't get much Canaletto in online jigsaws, or I can't find them anyway, .380 ACP, the fact that Leo thinks there's nothing worse than a failing bridge, the fact that it's like a bad staircase, he says, a violation of trust, the fact that bridges are whimsy, he said, the fact that they are acts of whimsy, hope, and artistry, as well as convenience, necessity and engineering of course, Salginatobel, and they involve a suspension of disbelief that should never be violated, Tavanasa land-slide, the fact that a good bridge nobly defies gravity, for the sake of humanity, and there is nothing more criminal, he thinks, than a bridge that fails to do that one job, the fact that he can't stand it when a bridge falls down, faulty bridges, ♪ *falling down, falling down, falling down* ♪, the fact that the Tavanasa landslide wasn't Maillart's fault, the fact that there's nothing much a bridge-designer can do if the mountain the bridge is built on decides to fall apart, the fact that his Schwandbach bridge is holding up fine, and the Salginatobel, the fact that some bridges are built to withstand a little shifting of the land around them, the fact that the Bay Bridge problem could have been worse, though that poor young woman died, which was terrible, and she was only twenty-three, force per area, oblique reverse faults, Loma Prieta, San Andreas Fault, the fact that Golden Gate worries Leo less than the Brooklyn Bridge, Aaron Copland, falsework, deck stiffened arch, even though San Francisco's more prone to earthquakes, pre-stressed, the fact that Maillart's son was away at school when his mom passed on, and he never really forgave Maillart for that, though it wasn't *Maillart's* fault in any way, I don't think, the fact that she just got sick and passed away, very fast, right in the middle of the Russian Revolution, the fact that when Maillart got back to Switzerland he was completely broke, broken, and his son couldn't cope, or he couldn't cope with his son, the fact that Maillart had a prolonged bout of bad luck, Leo says, Ponte della Paglia, Peolia, the fact that "paglia" means straw, broken wrist, eMedicine, my itch, the fact that now they say you can actually get chest pains from a broken heart, Broken Heart Syndrome, elephants wearing colorful sweaters, the fact that now they all need the bathroom, all at the same time, the kids, not elephants, the fact that India has cold snaps, so they quickly rustled up some sweaters, at the elephant sanctuary, the fact that these ladies knitted them, and they made elephant leggings too, elephantine, or maybe crocheted them, the fact that I wonder how long a crocheted elephant sweater lasts in the wild, the fact that maybe it'll outlast this cold snap anyway, the fact that we've had a bit of a cold snap too, the fact that

573

my itch is gone but not my nervousness around male gynecologists, the fact that you spend your whole life trying to keep your private parts to yourself and then, heavens to Betsy, you're expected to happily show them to a complete stranger and his female chaperone, gynecologists, obstetricians, and they make you so *uncomfortable*, the fact that you can't help wondering how gyny guys and male obstetricians got into this line of work, the fact that why can't it, you know, just be *women* who treat you for that kind of stuff, the fact that all I remember of Stacy's birth was Frank and that awful obstetrician eyeing me the whole time, the fact that it's worse than being watched when you're eating or blowing your nose, a lot worse, the fact that at least Leo was good at joking around when I was in labor, kidding me along, the fact that Leo was on *my* side in the delivery room, Leo was a comfort, the fact that he wasn't trying to get pally with the doctors, the fact that he was there for *me*, Leo, the fact that after I had Stacy, Frank couldn't even be bothered to go get me *cherry juice*, for heaven's sake, which was the only thing I wanted in the whole wide world and he wouldn't get it, the fact that I was so *thirsty*, but he said he couldn't find any, the fact that *Leo* found me cherry juice after each birth, no problem, though of course he was forewarned, since I never have shut up about Frank's failure to get me cherry juice, bridge failures, Frank's cherry juice failure, lucky freezer finds, LFF, FCJF, FBI, the fact that any hunt for cherry juice will either be a success or a failure, but with Leo it was a *success*, the fact that when we first got together I thought Frank was really something, the fact that I liked his hair, the fact that I lost my nice sky-blue earring down the back of his bed the first night we spent together, and I never found it again, the fact that that was a bad omen, the fact that maybe it got vacuumed up, but *Frank* never vacuumed, Frank's guitar-playing, the fact that I'm sick of losing all my earrings, the fact that I bought those new ones online, but they were a disappointment, the fact that I don't think I'll be turning into an online shopping addict anytime soon, because they just send you the wrong stuff and you end up with a load of *junk*, *approximations* of what you thought you were ordering, the fact that

Leo says they count on you never getting around to returning it, either out of politeness, or laziness, or inefficiency or whatever, decluttering, trudging down a sunny street in Evanston, all tuckered out but happy, after being at the beach all day, well-dressed elephants, the fact that the earrings I ordered came all nicely giftwrapped, with their own teeny-weeny little silver-polishing cloth even, but they are actually kind of poor quality, much lighter-weight and less sturdy than I expected, the fact that they feel like *tin*, not silver, though they *are* silver, I think, and because they're so lightweight they don't hang right, and I immediately lost one, Stacy's latest nail job, the fact that they had scratchy bits on the back too, my earrings, not Stacy's fingernails, but it serves me right for buying them online, and wearing them immediately instead of keeping them for Christmas, but I didn't feel like waiting a whole ten months, Monster Waves, the fact that Stacy now says she wants a tattoo, either a dog or a tattoo, *The mouse ran up the clock*, the fact that I'd rather she had a dog, the fact that the only tattoos I like are the ones that wriggle around when you flex your muscles, like pictures of belly dancers, or monkeys, the fact that Steve Martin thinks Alec Baldwin's wife has a very scary tattoo, his second wife, the fact that Sam Elliott is Katharine Ross's fifth husband, the fact that I hate those cobwebs on both elbows that people get, the fact that it probably means something, but I don't know what and it's never going to be a good look, the fact that I don't like it when people get whole *paragraphs* tattooed on their arms either, the fact that it takes you five minutes to read it, if they let you, like trying to read somebody else's watch from upside down, backside, flipside, "Yo," the fact that I don't think that gyny guy knows what he's talking about, the fact that he advised me to rub the ointment on from back to front, which every woman *knows* will give you a yeast infection, the fact that Fresia now says she won't let James come play until she's inspected our whole house, "inspected," the fact that I know the poor kid's allergic to all kinds of stuff, fungi, mold, dogs, feathers, milk, aspirin, chemicals, the fact that I really gotta clean up if Fresia's coming over, Spring Clean, sprinkler system, arson, Mommy, buttercups in the sun, Pepito, my cough, my coffee, "Suck in your gut," mattress in the sun, spiders, the fact that James Dean died in a car crash, the fact that, oh my, we gotta get a move on, leave Opal to hold the fort, the fact that I've got to go find five crumpled jackets, five hats, and five scarves, and get four very preoccupied people, currently dashing in all directions, or *five* including me, to put all this gear on, elephants in wool sweaters, the fact that that's silly, the fact that my kids aren't like elephants, the fact that they're more difficult than elephants, the fact that then there's *my* boots, keys, money, checkbook, sunglasses, make sure everything's off, stove, ovens, lights, cats in, chickens out, and now I have to go turn the lights off *again* because somebody's gone and turned them all back on, the fact that I don't know who though, so I can't yell at anybody, Loch Ness Monster, the fact that the Loch Ness Monster has it easy compared to me, gas, Exxon, Chevron, Shell, the fact that once the kids finally assembled in the hall, we all had to wait while Jakey ran back upstairs for his VW bus, the fact that sometimes he wants to bring his VW bus pillow as well, but not today luckily, because I might've lost it, I mean lost the *pillow*, the fact that Phoebe gave him that, and I don't know where she found it, the fact that he won't sleep without it, the fact that once we left *my* Little Pillow in a motel somewhere and I must have made a terrible fuss because Mommy bought me a new Little Pillow the *next day*, the fact that then the motel sent back the *old* one, so from then on I had two Little Pillows, but I was still more attached to the first one, the fact that the new one didn't smell right, wrong kind of foam rubber or something, the fact that it was always too solid and stiff, and not just because it was new, because it never really softened up, the fact that Mommy told me it would but I waited and it never did get soft enough, the fact that I still remember talking to Mommy about Little Pillow No. 2, the fact that I hung on to Little Pillow No. 1 until it was all just hard crumbly cakes of compressed foam rubber inside, and really kind of uncomfortable to rest your head on, but I didn't care because it still smelled good, my Little Pillow, the fact that I always felt sort of guilty about being fonder of the first Little Pillow, after Mommy went to all the trouble of getting me the new one, the fact that I must have made a *terrible* fuss in the car, the fact that I hate to think what I put her through over that lost pillow, the fact that kids are so nuts about their *stuff*, boy, the fact that I wonder if Phoebe got Jake's VW pillow at the MoMA store or something, MoMA, Mama, momo, muumuu, the fact that she finds the greatest presents, the fact that we did it, we made it to the car, wow, gas, the fact that the whole time we were getting ready to go I was scared Stacy might snap any second and yell at us all, balls, bubblegum, baseball cards, the fact that one thing I knew though was she wouldn't refuse to come, recuse, *J'Accuse*, Dreyfus, since she's meeting a whole bunch of her pals at the mall, pals she was no doubt already texting to complain about how slow her stupid family was, getting ready, the fact that her impatience really makes me nervous sometimes, but this time it served a purpose because she started yanking all their little arms into their jacket sleeves, in a *nice* way, and even hugging stuff to the car, which was actually pretty helpful, the fact that she'd make a good childherdess, when she's not being a dental hygienist, *psychologist* I mean, the fact that she was actually being rather nice about *everything*, reminding the slowpokes what they could get at the mall, cookies, indoor merry-go-round, chicken in a basket, gum ball machine, and hair accessories for Ginnie, I mean *Gillian*, gosh, the fact that I almost forgot my own daughter's name, the fact that sometimes I do call her Ginnie by mistake, because Virginia was nicknamed Ginnie as a kid, if that makes any sense, which I don't think it does, the fact that Jake kissed my hand on the way to the car, for no reason, son kissed, Sunkist, the fact that the name "Sunkist" comes from "Sun-ki," a county in Western Hunan, where navel oranges first came from, according to Henry Chung, the fact that Howard Hughes, the fact that orange juice, the fact that once we were off, Ben started saying something about ISS, which always throws me, but he didn't mean ISIS, the fact that he was only talking about the International Space Station, which he's obsessed with, the fact that I'm relieved he doesn't want to talk about ISIS, especially in front of Jake and Gillian, the fact that I think there's only so much kids should know about beheadings, and preferably *nothing*, the fact that, huh, there's the remains of an *igloo* over there, despite all the rain, the fact that it was a pretty big one too, the fact that *we* built an igloo in Evanston one year, and I tried to get Pepito to come inside it with me but he wouldn't, which was probably a wise decision, given who'd constructed the thing, the fact that we were not civil engineers, the fact that children do die in homemade igloos all the time, collapse, failure, the fact that the main bonus of the mall trip, which Stacy can't know, is the change in her demeanor, but other reasons include pastrami, the bank, and picking up Leo's jackets from the cleaners, at last, Exxon, Chevron, Shell, Exxon, Chevron, Shell, the fact that it also gets the kids out of the house, instead of lolling around like Ancient Romans all day, watching TV or playing computer games while I make them a million grilled cheese sandwiches, the fact that the Romans probably weren't that into grilled cheese sandwiches actually, but they sure liked lolling around, vomitorium, mosaics, Victoria, Virginia, Ginnie, the fact that at least at the mall I'll be spared the Stacy Silent Treatment for a while, the SST, the fact that sometimes after being alone in the car with her when she's giving me the SST, I start to feel sort of *paralyzed*, the fact that there comes a point when moms are just overwhelmed with despair, and it's not that rare, Little Pillow, the fact that Stace's dad was pretty good at it too, so maybe it runs in the family, the Silent Treatment, not despair, the fact that it runs in my family too, since Barry's a pro, the fact that he was never especially talkative *anyway*, the fact that he hasn't spoken to me since Abby died, not a word, or answered any of my letters, the fact that I've given up, the fact that I know I missed the funeral, but I'm not even sure if that's what caused the rift, the fact that people who practice the Silent Treatment always leave you guessing about their reasons for it, the fact that that's part of the torment, but I guess it wouldn't be the Silent Treatment if they explained themselves, the fact that that would defeat the object, the fact that maybe he just doesn't *like* me and never has, and as soon as Abby passed on he knew he never had to speak to me again, Abby's house, patchwork quilt, and I used to *like* him, Canadian Club, rag rugs, the fact that I *wanted* to go to the funeral but Ben had the measles and Leo was in Philadelphia, and I just couldn't make it, and Barry knows that perfectly well, the fact that I sure tried to explain it to him at the time, and he seemed to get it, but now he won't have anything to do with me, "A great big beautiful wall," the fact that the other day I thought of something *nice* about Barry, now what was that, the fact that for the love of Mike, he must know how I felt about Abby, he *must*, the fact that I bet I love her more than *he* ever did, the fact that maybe *that's* what bothers him, but I shouldn't say such things about Abby's only child, the fact that she wouldn't like it, Bathsheba looking at me, the fact that maybe he was jealous that Abby and I were so close, but is that any reason to torture me, the fact that I really shouldn't think these things, in the car, the fact that I should try to be cheerful for the kids' sake, the fact that of course he loved his mom, in his quiet dutiful-son kind of a way, but he never seemed to get a kick out of her the way I did, the fact that I really don't think she'd have wanted him to make me feel this lousy all these years, the fact that Abby was always very forgiving, well, she did hold a few grudges, I guess, but I hope not against *me*, the fact that Barry never much liked doing what she told him, dealing with the storm windows and stuff, the fact that it was always a chore, and maybe he begrudged that, grudge, the fact that it's just "awfulous," as Gillian would say, the way he's treated me, the fact that the guy is merciless, the fact that he's like one of those soldiers in Abu Ghraib who made all the prisoners *stand* on each other, the fact that it feels like he's blaming Abby's passing on *me*, when it was the last thing *I* ever wanted to have happen, the *last*, whiskey and ginger, the fact that how I wish I'd seen her one last time before she passed away, when she was in that rehab place, but she told me not to come, she said she was all right, Abby crying about Mommy in the hospital, the fact that she knew how busy I was, and I really was, the fact that I was kind of overwhelmed here, and Abby knew that, Stacy, Amish train set, Gillian, "Ginnie," Abby's favorite cookie-crumble ice cream, my Little Pillow when it got old and crumbly, blue snow seen through Abby's trees, the fact that she taught me "Too-whit too-whoo" and "Shine on, Harvest Moon," and how to make that kind of quilt like the one I was meant to inherit, made out of separate little circles of cloth sort of scrunched up, and sewn together, the fact that Abby loved me when nobody else did, the fact that she took me in, and mothered me, a waif, ♪ *I ain't had no lovin' since* ♪, the fact that does every teenager feel like a waif, the fact that Mommy and Abby were both so crazee about chocolate turtles, the fact that, boy, did Mommy get a bang out of being given a box of turtles, the turtles in Rome, wild turtles in the Chicago River, the fact that they reversed the Chicago River's flow at some point, but I think there are still turtles, log cabin motel in Wisconsin, the fact that if you brought them chocolate turtles they'd go bananas, Mommy and Abby I mean, not wild turtles, Frango mints too, the fact that Tastee Apple does turtle apples, which Mommy and Abby might have liked, though I don't think they were so big on *fruit*, apart from peaches in cream, the fact that I can barely bear to look at chocolate turtles, because Mommy and Abby loved them so much, the fact that I don't know where they got their taste for them in Newburyport, the fact that maybe it was in Boston or someplace, Frango, fandango, tango, Tang, Tang dynasty, Ming vase, the porcelain horse in the Chicago Art Institute, Japanese baskets, Indian baskets in Montclair, New Jersey, Upper Montclair, stair, stare, staring contest, Silent Treatment, SST, the fact that I don't like candy apples myself but Leo does, the fact that Cathy sells them by the dozen, the fact that the turtle apples have chocolate and nuts all over them, and caramel, while the jelly apples have that old-fashioned red caramel coating and then they're rolled in coconut, the fact that I always thought candy apples were kind of a gyp at Hallowe'en, whenever they turned up in my candy bag, the fact that we just wanted *candy*, not fruit, the fact that that is so ungrateful of me, my gosh, and there they were, giving me a whole free candy apple, which must have been expensive, and much healthier than candy, the fact that they were just trying to be nice and I felt they'd *skimped* me, dear dear, the fact that Leo doesn't like candy at all, or apples, but he does like a candy apple now and then, the fact that I asked him which kind of candy apple he goes for, whether it's caramel, or chocolate, or nutty or not nutty, and he just kept nodding, the fact that he likes them all, the fact that he's a real candy apple devotee, which kind of surprised me, but I think it's sweet of him to like candy apples, the fact that I don't think people give out candy apples at all now, at Hallowe'en, because of hidden razor blades, the fact that maybe it only happened once in the whole country but once is enough, word got out, and from then on moms have been mashing up kids' Hallowe'en apples every year, just to make sure there are no razor blades inside, which pretty much takes the fun out of getting a candy apple, mo bettah, da kine, skookumchuck, Zdenka, CIAK9, canine, Fresia, taco soup, the fact that pollution is linked to the deaths of two hundred thousand Americans a year, acrid, Akron, "I can't breathe," schnitz pie, the fact that that sounds like a sneeze, "schnitz," but it's really just a nice dried-apple pie, no razor blades, the fact that most American drinking water's no good *anyway*, even without the hidden toxins, the fact that half of all gun owners don't lock up their guns, and kids get hold of them and shoot themselves by accident, County Pet of the Week, pet of the week, week of the pet, weak pet, petting zoo, heavy petting, elephants in knitted sweaters, the fact that a large woman sat on a child for ten minutes as a punishment, and the poor kid *passed away*, the fact that that must have been terrible, the fact that I never heard of siting on a kid as punishment before, nun shaking Mommy, 3 Vacant Houses Catch Fire, the fact that I just remembered what Barry did, and he has my eternal gratitude for it, *What Katy Did*, the fact that that's *another* book I never read, I don't think, though maybe I did, I can't remember, katydids, crickets, the fact that Barry woke up in the night, when he was just a little kid, Ariana Grande, and smelled smoke, so he ran into his parents' room and woke them up and got them out just in time, the fact that the house burnt right to the ground, all because of a cigarette butt in the garbage apparently, the fact that somehow firemen always know what caused a fire, forest fires, firehose, arson, the fact that Barry must have been so scared, the fact that he was just a little boy, but he kept his head and saved his parents' lives, the fact that Abby wouldn't go at first, she wouldn't leave the house, Sandy Hook Promise, JAKE, the fact that, later on, Barry got an English sheepdog, with his first wife, the fact that they really loved that dog, the fact that Abby had never let him have pets when he was growing up, the fact that she wasn't keen on pets, the fact that I know that, because she wouldn't let me bring Bathsheba with me once, the fact that she was definitely scared of cats, the fact that I think a cat bit her once when she was a child, the fact that she said she was mainly scared of the mess they make, Nature's Miracle, Biz Stain Fighter, the fact that it was a nice big sheepdog, and I forget his name, four Saltines on a little dish, the fact that maybe we *should* get a dog, or else a fennec fox, the fact that they had to get rid of the sheepdog when Barry's kid was born, because Farley was allergic to it, James, air, dust mites, the fact that none of our kids is allergic to dogs, so we don't have that excuse, James's mom, cleanup, spring clean, shadow, shade, twilight, the fact that all I know is the loss of Abby, combined with Barry's Silent Treatment, sometimes makes me feel *disconnected from the earth*, and I don't know if this is how Barry *wants* me to feel, or what, the fact that maybe he doesn't know how painful the Silent Treatment is, but who *doesn't* know how painful the Silent Treatment is, for Pete's sake, who doesn't know that, Woman Dies After Ambulance Fails To Show Up, DOA, DNR, Miami Valley Shooting Grounds, the fact that the neighbors say that place is out of control, and bullets come whizzing past people's houses, or right past their *heads*, if they're outside, the fact that that's no way to behave, the fact that there was something in the paper about how the law says you're not supposed to shoot while in or on a "mother vehicle," and neither of us knew what they meant by a "mother vehicle," unless they meant *me*, but then Leo looked it up and the law says you're not supposed to shoot while in or on a *motor* vehicle, not a mother vehicle, the fact that here we are, driving through the rain to get to the mall, the fact that I'm not a stay-at-home mom, I'm a *drive-around* mom, in a mother vehicle, but I'm not proposing to shoot

anybody at least, DAM, damn DAM, DMV, DNR, Willet Creek
Dam, Baby Dumpling, the fact that Daddy used to call *me* Dumpling,
the fact that *Mr. Smith Goes to Washington* made him cry too, the fact
that it never fails to get you, the fact that does Joan Crawford ever
make you cry, the fact that she's bad enough when she's playing someone rotten, but it's even worse when she tries to act all innocent and
loving, like in that movie we saw where she's typing all the time and
her husband goes nuts, the fact that he's not nuts from the typing, he
was already nuts when she got him, the fact that he came like that,
like *Ellis's* husband, her first husband, the fact that Ellis managed to
escape, but Joan Crawford sticks it out with her guy, because she's so
good and nice and everything, wifely, wifelet, the fact that when he
goes completely nuts, she gets him a shrink and a mental hospital and
a straitjacket, and I can't remember but maybe some ECT as well,
the fact that meanwhile she supports them both with all that typing,
the fact that Leo's right, it's sort of agonizing, watching this huge
woman with a terrifying mouth and those Loch Ness Monster eyebrows acting like a real good-goody, the fact that it just doesn't suit
Joan Crawford, the loving looks, the shocked looks, none of it, the
Silent Treatment, Barry, Stace, the fact that Leo says her face freezes
like a *Tiki* mask, Joan Crawford's not Stacy's, or one of those Easter
Island statues, shoot the breeze, hoot owl, the fact that only the *faces*
of those Easter Island statues show above ground, but their whole
bodies are there, just underneath, the fact that they're eroding now,
Rapa Nui, flexed burial, "god and the police will save us," the fact
that it's hard to like the name "Mildred," especially after *Mildred
Pierce*, the fact that Joan Crawford claimed the typing movie was the
best movie ever made about a man in love with an older woman,
Zumba Toning, but what about *All that Heaven Allows*, the fact that
anyway I thought it was just about a typist in love with a guy with
mental health problems, primary care providers, making memories,
Celine Dion, the fact that I think it's called *Autumn Leaves*, but I'm
sure there are a lot of movies called that, or was it *Laura*, or *Mona*,
Moai, moaner, loner, the fact that Joan Crawford thought women

should all walk around *pigeon-toed* at home, to improve their calf muscles, the fact that what does it do to your *head* though, the fact that calf muscles aren't everything, *Mommy Dearest*, the fact that Joan Crawford and Myrna Loy were friends, FedEx boycott, the fact that in *Seven Brides for Seven Brothers*, Howard Keel proposes to Milly leaning over a cow, ♫ *Wonderful, wonderful day* ♫, the fact that some Christians have started a hate campaign against *Target* now, because Target decided to let trans people choose which toilet to use, the fact that, my word, all people care about these days is *restrooms*, the fact that meanwhile a man drove his car over a cliff with his kids in it, and they were all found dead at the bottom, the fact that when the police went to tell his wife the sad news, they found she had passed away too, shot in the head, beheadings, "men and wives," bros, Bernie Bros, the fact that the neighbors said they were just a normal, close-knit family, knitted elephant sweaters, mother vehicle, mother vinegar, shotcrete, hollow box, haw tree, haw berries, Pickaway County, Circleville, moose head on the stairs, black walnut, butternut, hickory, Girl Ran From Menacing Man, the fact that child marriage is still legal in most states, Super Shuttle, the fact that Youngstown used to have a really pleasant-looking post office, and I have an old postcard of it, the fact that I think they have just a plain brick affair now, the fact that the postal service is disintegrating, the fact that I dreamt Katharine Hepburn wanted to stay in our house and write her memoirs but I said we didn't have room, the fact that Leo and I both like Katharine Hepburn and I was sure her reminiscences would be an interesting read too, but I put my foot down for some reason, I'm not sure exactly why, *Guess Who's Coming to Write Her Memoirs*, fifty foot totem pole, windshield wipers flapping, Pop-tarts, upstarts, ramparts, lion rampant, sejant, sergeant, run the gantlet, gauntlet, consensual sex, tic-tac-toe, don't sweat the small stuff, the fact that I keep thinking about that little girl, the one who wouldn't drink her milk and died, the fact that she was thrown out of the house at three a.m. because she wouldn't drink her milk, and she wandered off and got lost, the fact that it sounds almost like a fairy tale, scrimshaw, squaw, loose pages like flowing hair, or an Aesop's fable maybe, for the moral edification of the young, ethics, logic, hyperbole, the fact that I hope the kids never hear about that little girl, *or* the guy who killed his whole family in the mother vehicle, "just a normal family," the fact that many languages are disappearing, and dialects, and accents, the fact that all this time people have been saying "Indian squaw," not knowing it means a woman's, hmmm, her private parts, gyny guy, itch, the fact that I think maybe it's supposed to mean, well, a prostitute as well, the fact that anyway, it's far from polite, the fact that I just remembered my dream, the fact that Olivia called me up and said everybody at Peolia had flu, so could I come in and teach a class on eMedicine and technology, and how medical services need to catch up with the digital age and all, but you have to preserve patient confidentiality, the fact that I don't know why she was asking *me* to teach it, but I was about to give in, just for the money, not for *Peolia*, but then I remembered what a terrible teacher I am, the fact that I would've just dried up, so I told her "I'm busy, tired, and home alone," the fact that Sylvia Plath was so *young* when she died, the fact that everybody had rejected *The Bell Jar* and Ted Hughes was running around with somebody else, but still, wait just a second there, lady, the fact that Stacy got called a "squaw" once, in Kindergarten, but it was no big deal then, the fact that I wouldn't like her to be called that *now*, not after what I read about it, "busy, tired, and home alone," the fact that when I told her she was named after Eustacia Vye, she said she'd been hoping it was Stacy *Keach*, the fact that she liked him as Wilbur Wright when they were doing aviation last year, the fact that here we are at last, we have arrived, le Beaujolais nouveau est arrivé, the fact that motherhood sometimes makes you feel unfit for normal everyday activities like parking, the fact that maybe all mothers are menaces on the road, mother vehicles, because they're all thinking about Stacy Keach, the fact that everybody in the car seems to have their own idea where I ought to park, while I just want to get as near the sidewalk as possible, in an effort to reduce their chances of getting run over by cars skidding in the slush, spring thaw, pine trees, rain, the fact that I don't actually care all that much if we park right next to everybody's favorite store, ♫ *Bless your beautiful hide* ♫, Youngstown, waterfall, Paterson Falls, the fact that the slush can't be good for Stacy's UGG boots, the fact that she really needs galoshes, the fact that as soon as we stop, out she hops out without a word and disappears, leaving me to drag three zigzagging kids along through the icy rain past empty store fronts, dark interior, stripes, spots, spirals, floaters, zigzag, wigwam, seesaw, tipi, Tiki, Wi-Fi, Sci-Fi, Wii, wee-wee, Poo-Poo, the fact that first I ask if anybody has to use the bathroom, restroom, transgender toilet, the fact that I don't want them to have Kentucky this time, because it can take them a good half an hour to nibble their way through a bunch of drumsticks and I have stuff I gotta do today, besides delivering pies after this, and anyway they shouldn't have that stuff all the time, the fact that five hundred billion chickens get eaten every year, and I don't like their standards on animal welfare, not the kids' standards, *KFC's*, the fact that I've heard things, like how the workers behave in their slaughterhouses, the men's slaughterhouse, women's slaughterhouse, the fact that they can each have a grain bar to chew on for now instead, so we can plow on, with Ben mumbling "Kentucky, Kentucky…" all around the mall, the fact that nine-year-olds sure can bear a grudge, the fact that they'll be getting a *hot dog* later, dear me, such a fuss, while I wrestle with their coats and hats, and all my shopping bags, chickens, the fact that there are dozens of teenage girls tottering around in high heels on the escalator, the fact that you wonder how they keep upright, each clutching a Diet Coke in one hand and a smartphone in the other, just like Morning Routine girls, cute twins, the fact that they're all talking on their phones nonstop, the fact that they're probably calling friends who are higher up or lower down on the same escalator, the fact that looking at them somehow makes me long for my Little Pillow, the fact that Jake used to be scared of escalators, but now he's almost too keen on them, the fact that I used to have to take his hand and count 1, 2, 3, and we'd jump on together, but now he likes walking up the down-elevators, Otis, the fact that Gillian taught him that, but just by accident, when she was trying to help him come down once and he wouldn't come so she ran back up the escalator to get him, and now that's all he wants to do, run up the down escalator and knock over teenie-boppers in high heels, chickens, Pop-tarts, slush, Hush Puppies, the fact that I said he could do it *sometimes*, but only if there's nobody else around, the fact that some disciplinarian I am, the fact that sometimes you look a baby in the eye and he or she seems so infinitely wise it makes you feel silly, like the baby has tapped into something deep and important and eternal, and they're thinking about the cosmos or whatever, something lofty, while you're just floundering in the day-to-day, Easter Island, white Icelandic baby bonnet, lettuce, moon, the fact that the silence of babies is always mysterious, like animals are, but then they start to talk and you realize they're really just thinking about their toys, or cake, or their velvet VW bus pillow, the fact that at least ours are all successfully past the Pampers stage, though maybe they'd have loftier thoughts if they were still *in* their diapers and didn't have to worry about choosing which bathroom to go to, the fact that which pencils should we get, *MY FIRST* TICONDEROGA®, *TICONDEROGA* BEGINNERS®, HB2, nano, pico, giga, mega, light bulb, the fact that the *Suffragettes* used the Silent Treatment, and it worked too, the fact that they set up Silent Sentinels all around the White House, to shame Woodrow Wilson into getting the Nineteenth Amendment passed, the fact that I don't get what was eating him about women's suffrage, the fact that Woodrow Wilson behaved like a bit of a louse about that, twenty-one thousand soldiers, the fact that the Justice Bell was silent too, the fact that they said the Justice Bell wouldn't be rung until women were silenced no longer, Lifting as We Climb, NACW, NAWSA, NAOWS, log cabin motel dream, the fact that it's funny how you remember some dreams all your life, for no reason, the fact that Gillian has spent all her money on bangles, Laura Ingalls Wilder's bangs, young marrieds, the fact that *now* it's hot dog time, with mustard, without mustard, sauerkraut, Cokes, 7 Up, the fact that I just want coffee, hold the hot dog, the fact that I can't *hold* four hot dogs, the fact that, boy, they really like hot dogs, even Jake, even without me putting a hole in it, the fact that what's that about, the fact that he's infected by Ben and Gillian's excitement about hot dogs, the fact that they seem to've forgotten all about KFC, well, maybe, the fact that who *is* that, talking so loud about her goiter and how she got it removed, gosh, gug, the fact that does everybody in the Food Mart have to hear about *that*, Hell's Angels, Ronny, embrace change, the new normal, talisman, Taliban, Malala, the fact that it sounds like she went through a heck of a time, poor soul, and it's a free country and all, and, okay, goiter talk is preferable to a shooting spree any day, but when people are trying to have their *lunch*, the fact that I never actually knew you could *get* a goiter removed, the fact that you mostly try not to know anything about goiters, the fact that maybe *that's* the meaning of life, avoiding goiter talk, but maybe we should talk about goiters *more*, the fact that maybe we're all scared of goiters because we think they can't be removed, but if they can be, that changes everything, a little anyway, the fact that, on the other hand, if they can be removed, why don't they just remove them all, and then we'd never have to hear about goiters again, the fact that nobody would keep their goiter longer than necessary, surely, but maybe it's tricky to get rid of them, like if you do it too *soon* or something, like cataracts, the fact that maybe they wait for the goiter to get good and big before they attempt an operation, *huge*, oh, dear me, gosh, the fact that this coffee's cold, the fact that now she's gone, the fact that that's a relief, maybe I can think about something else, like that lake in Switzerland, Maillart, Gallipolis, the fact that Fiesole's outside of Florence, and I went there once with Leo, stress corrosion cracking, rush hour collapse, goiters, DuPont, Scotchgard, Snapchat, the fact that when I was a kid we hardly ever got hot dogs unless Mommy cooked them, franks 'n' beans, beans on toast, the fact that we sometimes got hot dogs at barbecues and picnics and ball games and at school maybe, the fact that Mommy had a watch with a very thin strap, and I always wanted it, and now I have it but it doesn't work anymore, the fact that most people probably don't wear watches these days, just use their cells, the fact that everything's on those little machines, emails, movies, music, photos, videos, satnav, everything, work, play, the fact that it would be like the *Stone Age* again if all these smart phones shut down all of a sudden, the fact that nobody would be able to cope, the fact that nobody understands how they work, so nobody could fix them if they went wrong, or make a new one from scratch, like those guys in the desert movie when their plane crashes, the fact that they have to make a new one out of the bits, wow, the fact that look at *her*, my word, the fact that talk about tight, the fact that there are people who seem to have come to terms with being fat and don't mind it, though who knows what they think in private, the fact that still, I don't know if it's a good idea to wear jeans like that, and pale pink as well, the fact that you can see every *dimple*, you really can, the fact that the oldsters are here in force this time, doing their daily mile, the fact that the mall's flat, warm and dry, even if it's kind of crowded, but they all walk so slowly you can't believe it can have any real health benefits, the fact that they go by in packs, like slo-mo ghetto gangs, some smiley, some smelly, some chatting and others concentrating on just staying upright, a forest of four-pronged canes and walkers, jolly group, the fact that you have to scoot out of their way or they get mad, friendly wolf eels, the fact that this mall outing must be the social highlight of their day, the poor ducks, though I guess it's the same for us, the fact that I wonder who drives them, the fact that do they get a special mall-walkers' bus, or maybe they still drive, the fact that they look a bit ancient to be behind the wheel, the fact that Lawrence Weiler's ninety-eight-year-old mom drives from Queens to Manhattan once a week to have her hair done, the fact that she wasn't much of a driver even when she could see and hear, the fact that some of them have such colorful tracksuits and trainers, the fact that Stacy wants the same hiking shoes as Kanye West but she's not going to get them, the fact that luckily she can't buy them at the mall, they're only available online, with my credit card, which I'm not offering, the fact that I told her there's a difference between us and Kanye West, and that is that he is a millionaire or billionaire, and Leo's a college professor and I'm a manual laborer, the fact that she offered to clean her room but that's not going to swing it, and anyway her room just gets messy again in ten minutes, the fact that we simply can't afford things like Kanye West's hiking shoes, not with our medical bills and house repairs, and college funds, candy wrappers, goiters, moms with strollers, toy store, the fact that why does Kanye West need to sell boots anyway, the fact that he'll have his own perfume next, "Kool" by Kanye, the fact that Ben's bought himself a book on home improvements, so *he's* content for a while, the fact that Gillian's selecting more hairbands, the fact that *now* everybody needs the bathroom, when they're at the other end of the mall, the fact that I dreamt about a sort of luxurious bed and breakfast inn in *India*, a long blue tent with rows of beds, and there was a blue pool out back, the fact that it seemed beautiful and mystical, so tranquil, and everything had this blue sheen to it, the fact that it seemed like the perfect place to hide out when you're exhausted by being in a busy city, especially in a hot place like that, but then I woke up and thought, who wants to sleep in a dormitory with a crowd of strangers, no matter how blue everything is, the fact that it would feel like you're in a *hospital* or a refugee camp or something, or Guadalajara, no, that other place, *Guantánamo*, ah, here we are, Restrooms, the fact that nobody *cleans* this place or what, the fact that there's a fly on the seat, a fecal fly, hand sanitizer, no protective seat covers either, the fact that they should have seat sanitizer too, or maybe hand sanitizer would work, the fact that shopping carts are covered in bacteria and fecal matter, but Jake still likes sitting in them, the fact that twenty-four thousand children a year are injured in shopping carts, the fact that menus are the dirtiest thing in restaurants, the fact that what would it be like to be a fly caught in a restroom, a fly that spends its whole life hanging upside down from toilet seats, the fact that it can't go out, it's too cold still for flies, the fact that it's trapped in here whether it likes it or not, the fact that how do they keep the flies out of the *food* area, the fact, what in the world, the fact that now they're saying over the loudspeakers that nobody can leave the *building* because there's a flash flood outside, rogue waves, freak winds, the fact that we're heading for the exit, to see what's happening out there, but everybody else has the same idea, the fact that a whole lot of people rushed out, but the weather's driven them back in, the fact that I guess we'll have to wait, the fact that they say we have to stay until the water level goes down in the parking lot, loiter, goiter, the fact that we'll head back to the bookstore maybe, the fact that Ben's already got a book but maybe Jake and Gillian need something, the fact that we should really go to the library more, the fact that Stacy joined us briefly but, oh, she's off again, thrilled to get to run around a bit longer with her pals, the fact that I guess there's nothing I can do about all this, so I might as well *relax* for the first time in ten years, if only Jake would quit running up the down escalator,

.   .   .   .

The shock of losing her cubs reverberated like rain on water. The surprise and worry of it, the fatigue of travel. Her whole frame ached.

Her neck became stiff from holding her head up so high to listen out for them. She looked for any trace of her infants in the trees above, imagining a live or dead kitten behind every clump of leaves. The underbrush scratched her sides, stones cut into her paws. But the drive to find her young made her immune to hardship, hope indistinguishable from intent.

Racing up a cliff side, she scoured the mountaintop where one young virgin lion lurked. After initial demonstrations of interest, he struck a deferential posture and bounded away. It was clear that something very bad must have happened to set a lioness running like that, far from her normal range, a wrathful mother without her cubs.

Tearing through bushes that grabbed at her and whipped her face, she pursued her cubs wherever they might be. Indifferent to sleep, she carried on at sunrise, blinded midday by the unfamiliar glare of sun-dappled ground.

She grew weak from hunger, exertion, sleeplessness and loss. Within a few days, her milk dried up.

the fact that I had two sort of real estate dreams in a row last night, the fact that in the first one, Mommy's bedroom was empty but haunted, and I knew that but I went in anyway and got swept up by some terrible supernatural force, the fact that in the other one, I dreamt Leo had a whole nother house somewhere, besides ours, and it was all spic-and-span and painted white, in perfect shape to rent out, the fact that it looked like we could live pretty well on the proceeds, the fact that it was quite disappointing to wake up from that one, with no second home to rent out, rent parties, Mommy, the fact that the memory of her won't really die out until Phoebe, Ethan and I have passed away and stop thinking about her, but she's dead to *herself*, so what good to her are *our* memories, the fact that memories aren't half as good as mommies, the fact that having no mother leaves you feeling vulnerable, that's just the way it is, at any age, fragile, the fact that some airlines are unsafe, and nobody cares, the fact that we have to go get the car later, the fact that why is it so disconcerting when your car is miles away, the fact that it's not the end of the world but it's still a drag, and you keep thinking it's right outside but it's not, the fact that you've got no *getaway* plan without your car, like if something really bad happened, a forest fire, or a bomb or something, flash flood, shooter, goiter, sudden-onset baldness, the fact that we waited so long in the mall I caved on the KFC, the fact that we got a whole bucketful and the kids ate about five hundred drumsticks each, five hundred pieces apiece, then ice cream, and still there was no go-ahead, just more announcements that we should stay put, the fact that some people thought it was a conspiracy to keep us shopping, the fact that I stepped outside at one point, just to have a look around, but it was still raining so hard I couldn't see a thing, the fact that then they announced the real problem, that the ditch all around the outside of the parking lot was flooded, and the ramp had collapsed as a result, the major entrance and exit ramp for the whole parking lot, falling bridges, violation of trust, the fact that at that point people started to panic, because nobody likes to be *stranded*, marooned, desert island, or herded, corralled, even if you're at your favorite mall, the fact that most of all, people don't like being deprived of their cars, Security, ASP, the fact that some people started to cry, and when they cried *Gillian* cried, poor little funette, the fact that it *was* a little alarming, the fact that she now says she was just worried for the *cats*, like if we never got home, Opal holding the fort, the fact that a lot of people didn't seem too bothered by it all, the fact that some people just can't stop shopping, it's a compulsion, propulsion, impulse buys, shopping sprees, shooting sprees, the fact that Grandma's ne'er-do-well brother, Uncle Bud Bar, ran pinball machines in Detroit, 88, the fact that what does 88 mean and why do people have 88 stickers on their dashboards, the fact that did something important happen in 1988 that I've forgotten about, the fact that once we got the news that the exit ramp had a great big hole in it that no cars could get over, I gave up hope of delivering my pies, and began to wonder instead where we'd be *sleeping* that night, and whether we should run and claim one of the beds in the furniture showroom, blue dormitory in India, Guantánamo, the fact that I could see us all brawling over them, and finally just having to pile in, ten to a bed, like the Great Bed of Ware, the fact that people used to share beds and thought nothing of it, San Martín, the fact that the Great Bed of Ware could accommodate like about twenty travelers, the fact that now it's usually just *couples* who share beds, and immigrants, and poor kids or kids on sleepovers, slumber parties, pajama parties, pretzels, orgy, child abuse, National Guard, the *National Enquirer*, the fact that we weren't even supposed to get near the ramp because the blacktop on both sides was still crumbling, and the whole parking lot was full of water anyway, though the rain had stopped by then, more or less, the fact that I hope the car's okay, the fact that if not, maybe Jesus can fix it, the fact that they couldn't put a temporary metal bridge over, to bridge the gap, because both banks were on the verge of collapsing too, the fact that somebody mentioned climate change, and somebody else chimed in with some story about gay penguins, the fact that when they said we all had to wait around

until the flooding had fully subsided, everybody drooped, and that's
when I called Leo, the fact that for once I had my cell, field of wildflowers in Connecticut, bee at Bread Loaf, the fact that it was kind of
surreal because the rain had stopped and there were even patches of
blue sky by then, but the river was still *rising*, the fact that we could
see it from the walkway around the mall, the fact that we went out
and just watched the Tuscarawas moving by really fast, while I talked
to Leo, the fact that then this large object bobbed into view, the fact
that it got bigger and bigger and when it got near enough you could
see it was a *house*, a whole house, and it was on *fire*, the fact that it
was such a strange sight to see, a burning house floating down the
river, the fact that everybody was filming it, and laughing and yelling,
the fact that I told Leo it was like something out of a horror movie,
and then a cat jumped out of one of the windows of the house and fell
in the water and swam towards the opposite side of the river, the fact
that we couldn't see what happened to it, the fact that I wish Gillian
hadn't seen it, because she started crying for real then, the fact that a
few people called to the cat to come over towards us, but it disappeared, and there was nothing anybody could do, the fact that it
wasn't safe to swim after it, the fact that I told Gillian it would get out
okay, because cats are resilient and all, nine lives, cat o' nine tails, but
privately I don't hold out much hope for that cat, the fact that cats
can swim if they have to, the fact that even Stacy looked worried, and
Leo was getting all worked up on the phone, when I told him what
we were seeing, the fact that that was it for me, the fact that I wasn't
planning to wait for the whole mall to get carried down the river in
flames, the fact that come hell or high water, by hook or by crook, I
was going to get the kids home if I could, the fact that we'd *walk* if
we had to, the fact that it's only five miles or so, the fact that I knew
Leo was on his way, but it was going to take him hours to get to us,
the fact that a lot of people had the same idea as me, the fact that they
were now abandoning their cars and heading over to the highway on
foot, which was thankfully well above the level of the parking lot, the
fact that Stacy figured they'd called taxis to come pick them up on

the highway, so we tried that but there weren't any more available, Übermensch, mensch, Führer, Baxter, the fact that it was pretty muddy but we made it to the highway, and it felt like a great achievement, the fact that with five of us though, there was no hope of sharing a cab with anybody, the fact that then I had an idea and, to my shame, called Ronny, the fact that he was the one person I thought might have nothing better to do, and might even be in the area, because it's his patch, the fact that sure enough, he was just sitting around in the Coshocton store, he said, and would be with us in twenty minutes, depending on traffic and flooding and roadblocks and all, the fact that I thanked him and I really meant it for once, the fact that it wasn't like being saved by Jesus, who's so handsome, but it's still nice to be saved, the fact that I guess he raced over, because he was there in about *ten* minutes, or that's how it seemed, the fact that I don't know what we would have done without him, the fact that he said it wasn't that big of a deal, but it was good of him, the fact that he said he hadn't seen the burning house, but he'd seen a car flip right over in an underpass on the highway, and get carried away by the water, flipped, flipping, bridge, ramp, the fact that he didn't think there was anybody in the car, but then how'd it get into the underpass, the fact that it seemed best not to dwell on that, with the kids around, black, white, day, night, the fact that I sure hope nobody was in that burning house, the fact that I just assumed it was empty and the cat was the last to leave, but who knows, the fact that nothing's been said about it on the news, the fact that they just show the pictures of it going by, the fact that driving with Ronny was certainly an experience, and Stacy really can't *stand* him now, after listening to all the guff he came out with in the car, the fact that he griped about the police most of the way, because he strongly disagreed with their emergency traffic-management techniques, the fact that that's not so bad, though he did go on and on about it, how the cops were infringing his basic freedoms as an American, the fact that he's very anti-police but pro-military, for some reason, the fact that as far as I could tell, the police were just standing in the rain directing cars away from the floods, but Ronny was very suspicious of their motives, the fact that he felt they were probably directing people the *wrong* way, and they were going to land us all in the Tuscarawas like that car he'd seen, *till the last galoot's ashore*, the fact that I don't know if he meant they were malicious, or just incompetent, but he was certain it was the cops themselves that were causing all the jams, *avoidable* jams in his opinion, the fact that the proof was that he'd never seen traffic jams like it, and he's lived here for fifty years, the fact that he said this again and again, shaking his head at the "damn cops," the fact that I'm used to him so I just zoned out, the fact that I was just so relieved we were going *home*, the fact that once we were clear of the floods, he started talking about people making left turns, the fact that that guy gets really worked up about *left turns*, boy, other people's, not his own, the fact that he was bent out of shape about it, the fact that meanwhile he executed his own left without a pause, even though there was a *stop sign*, the fact that he forced another car to swerve around us, the fact that he kept accusing other people of "planning a left" when they weren't, and then he'd say "look at that," when they didn't turn left, as if they were messing him around personally, the fact that Stacy kept rolling her eyes at me the whole way and sometimes I had to look out the window to keep from cracking up, the fact that it would be pretty bad to laugh at our savior, the fact that I suddenly wished I'd tried Jesus, Jesus López Pérez, Silent Treatment, but he was probably busy helping a million other stranded people at the time, the fact that I couldn't ask Cathy, the fact that she knocks herself out for everybody in Tuscarawas County all day as it is, the fact that as we neared the house, I knew that this time I must invite Ronny in for a cup of coffee and a piece of pie, but then I remembered I had no pie to give him, except frozen ones, since all my pies were still in our car at the mall, and they still are, oh dear, "All that work!", as William Hurt's sister wails after her brothers wreck Thanksgiving dinner, Aunt Sophia with her six kinds of pie, the fact that to my great relief, Ronny couldn't come in, the fact that he had to get to Goshen to pick up a delivery or something, before any more roads were cut off, either by flooding or by those "idiots," the police, so that was a lucky break, lucky freezer find, the fact that he got a frozen cherry pie out of it at least, and a lemon drizzle cake, the fact that when Leo got home we all had a laugh about our adventure, but we really had kind of a scare, especially Gillian, cat, honey bears, sweetie, the fact that we're on high ground here at least, no danger of flooding, honey bears, water bears, I don't think, though the water table can act pretty funny sometimes, and suddenly there'll be water coming through the floor, the fact that actually the chickens look kind of like they're sinking right now, the fact that it sure is wet out, the fact that I better check, the fact that, wow, the ground feels real soggy, burning house, swimming cat, the fact that there were six or ten or twelve inches of rain in just six or ten or twelve hours, well, I can't *remember* how much exactly, the car, the fact that I've never understood how you measure rain by the inch like that anyway, the fact that, I mean, do they use a *bucket* or what, bouquet, *Ryan's Daughter*, the fact that after Ronny left I got everybody to take off their wet duds and that's when I realized Stacy was wearing her SEXIST NAZI POTUS T-shirt, the fact that if Ronny had seen *that*, he might have dumped us all in the flooded underpass and driven away, screaming about O'Bummer, the fact that maybe he hates left turns because he thinks lefties make them, the fact that no, he just doesn't believe anybody else can drive except him, the fact that I was so happy to be home, never mind the car or the pies, the fact that it felt like kind of a close call and I'm not used to that, the fact that it was an unexpected bonus to have Leo home early, the fact that we made spaghetti together and drank lots of red wine, spaghetti and salad, the fact that we *survived*, and it never got *too* frightening, apart from that poor cat, the fact that today Stace asked us all, if we had three wishes, what would they be, the fact that Ben immediately said his would be to go to the moon, be a grown-up, and have a dog, the fact that Jake said his would be to have a dog, a giraffe, and a Poo-Poo Plate, the fact that I don't know where he got that Poo-Poo Plate idea, maybe from Ben, the fact that I dread to think what Jake thinks a Poo-Poo Plate *is*, the fact that I just kept quiet because my three choices are boring and practical and you're not supposed to worry kids about money, Guatemalan worry dolls, my Guatemalan embroidered shirt, the fact that my three wishes would be lots of money, a pension, free healthcare, oh, and a swimming pool, which is a fourth wish, but I could pay for it out of my own money, so it's three really, money, a pension, and free healthcare, the fact that, anyway, I was scared Stacy would despise and scold me for being mercenary or something, especially once she told us *her* three wishes, the fact that hers were loftier than mine, 401K, the fact that mine remind me of that joke, where the guy finds a genie in a lamp and he's offered three wishes, and he says "Gimme a bottle of beer that's never empty," the fact that the genie says fine and asks what his second and third wishes are, and the guy says "Gimme another two of those," the fact that Gillian couldn't decide fast enough, so we never actually heard her three wishes, but Stacy's were an end to global warming, whaling, and pollution, the fact that she said, if she got all that, she'd be happy to leave the rest of her future to chance, the fact that I said those were anti-wishes, non-wishes, just stuff she *doesn't* want, not what she wants, but she just shrugged, the fact that she probably thought I didn't get it but I do, the fact that those are three very noble wishes, Mommy "cheating" at solitaire, the fact that if I'm honest, I don't know if I'd give up any of my three mercenary wishes to save the world, the fact that it's not really realistic to expect that of people, is it, though of course it would be *nice*, a nice idear, philanthropy, the fact that I think most people's deepest wishes are personal, not political, the fact that at least I haven't covered our yard with artificial grass, and I never use pesticides, frogs, tadpoles, the fact that Ben said they've found some water on the moon so it wouldn't be so hard to set up an exploratory camp there, concentration camps, detention camps, refugee camps, summer camp, cardboard cities, the fact that the moon used to have a sea of magma, the fact that I don't see how changing planets is going to help most of us, the fact that you could do a Noah's Ark space rocket sort of thing, the Moon Ark, but how many people could establish a sustainable life on the moon, where there's nothing, or any other planet in the solar system, the fact that everything would have to be created artificially, and they'd probably get all kinds of new diseases nobody would know how to treat and everything they cared about would be left behind to broil to death, Mommy, the fact that Mars is covered in sulfur and probably stinks to high heaven, the fact that Stacy always sort of acts like global warming is *my* fault, like when Ben said the flood was due to global warming Stacy just stood there looking accusingly at me, the fact that she's always on my case about the state of the *world*, but I really don't know what I'm supposed to do about it, the fact that even Ben's remarks on the moon had a bit of an edge to them, now I come to think about it, the fact that my own kids probably wouldn't let me *on* the Moon Ark if there is one, "Sayonara, sucker!", high fives all round, the fact that maybe I was like that with my parents too, the fact that I can't remember, the fact that I was worried about pollution but not like kids are now, the fact that Ben says by 2050 all the low-lying cities will have to be evacuated, or else protected by giant levees, which'll make perfect targets for terrorists and enemy nations, and most of the animals, apart from meat animals, will just be *gone*, no matter how many vertical farms and gardens people construct, the fact that, after all, a lion or an elephant can't climb up a vertical farm, though lizards could, and spiders, and some birds could live off vertical crops, I suppose, not chickens, the fact that chickens are the one thing that *will* be kept going, whatever happens, because people *have* to have their fried chicken, the fact that they'll just get more and more cruel about it, factory farming, unless they get better at cloning meat, which I guess is what they'll all have to eat in the moon camp, 2050, the fact that that's not so far away, oh dear, the fact that I would never buy eggs from that battery farm, even if we were *starving*, those broken-down tiers of screeching, hysterical chickens, the fact that I wonder if kids of the future will look at their parents any more forgivingly than mine do, or will they blame us all, the fact that our grandchildren probably won't even be able to bring themselves to say hello to us seniors, the fact that they'd be right to bear a grudge about it, the fact that if there *are* any grandkids, that is, since fertility's under threat, the fact that it doesn't seem to have dented the population explosion yet though, the fact that sometimes I feel so sad looking at my kids, they seem totally doomed, the fact that I'm scared they *know* it too, and it just breaks your heart, broken, the fact that even the Pope thinks pollution is sinful, the fact that popes never had to talk about that before, Christians, poor hygiene, PGE, injection wells, fracking waste water, the fact that Leo says fracking doesn't even make money, it's totally pointless, the fact that all it does is screw up ecosystems, the fact that fracking in Ohio is causing *earthquakes*, the fact that they're trying to stop it in Pennsylvania somewhere, aquifers, with the idea, idear, that nature has a right to exist, but I don't know if it'll hold up in court, meaning of life, meaning of death, Welcome To Beautiful Parkersburg, DuPont, the fact that they knowingly dumped 779,955,830 pounds of pollutants into the air and water in Washington, West Virginia, the fact that it kind of *had* to be "knowingly" done, since it would be hard to dump 779,955,830 pounds of stuff anywhere without someone knowing it, taking a dump, a leak, leek, Howard Keel, able was I ere I saw Howard Keel, the fact that they were probably just hoping for the best, I mean that no one would notice, at least for a few years, swimming pool, Gena Rowlands, cemetery, acrylamide, the fact that, just talking about the companies around here, Ben says the Marlite plant in Dover dumped millions of pounds of pollutants into the air or the water, or both, and Simonds dumped pollutants into the air and the water, and Kurz-Kasch dumped pollutants into the air, and Boltaron dumped pollutants, and amongst all these dumplings, I mean dumpings, not pierogi or pot-stickers, was at least five hundred pounds of *lead*, the fact that I don't know why they do these things, but you can't stop people trying to make a buck, the fact that it's the American way, dumpings, dumps, ♫ *Turn back, O man, forswear thy foolish ways, old now is earth* ♫, the fact that I do feel guilty though, bringing kids I love into a world we've trashed, the fact that that's not a very nice thing to do, perpetuating the species while you trash the joint, Man Rapes Own Mom Over Money, the fact that there are hardly any jobs left, because we've automated everything, and the whole world is over-populated, the fact that why have kids who will only be unemployed and unhappy, the fact that what if my kids end up couch potatoes, boomerang kids mooching off me and Leo for the rest of their lives, watching TV and making popovers, until all the animals are gone and all the plants and there's nothing left to make their Cheerios out of, not even any nasturtiums, the fact that most people can't even *afford* kids anymore, what with the clothes and food and medical care and computers and Pampers and toys and smartphones and summer camps and scooters and bikes and cars and Kanye West hiking boots, not to mention college fees, the fact that it's really those college fees that make me wake up in the night and, because how the heck are we, I mean, gosh, Goshen, Daddy Is My Superhero, the fact that gambling is just as bad as opioid addictions, the fact that the Queen of England bets on horses, and she's good at it apparently, the fact that she must be really raking it in, the fact that she owns a McDonald's and a Primark, the fact that maybe if I wrote to her about the college costs she'd lend us a helping hand, "Queenie, eh?", the fact that they found wustite on meteors, the fact that because of the flood I'm just going to freeze all the pies in the car for home consumption, as soon as I get my hands on them, so now I have to start a whole new batch for tomorrow, when I guess the roads will be back in action and Leo can drive me over to pick up my car, two-car family, three-car garage, four-car garage, man cave, Get Your Man Card, the fact that all my outlets were nice about it, and they'd had other cancellations, Cathy, apocalypse, "Get ready! Get ready! The *worr*-uld is coming to an end!", the fact that Leo was complaining about having to use up some kind of toothpaste that he doesn't like, Colgate, I think, and I told him not to worry about it, the fact that I told him "You should use the kind of toothpaste you actually like, because you never know how long you're going to live," and Leo said "But if I'm about to kick the bucket, I don't want *you* to be left with this lousy toothpaste," which was sort of sweet, I thought, but when I reported this to Cathy, she was surprised we were joking about such things, because she and Art are all geared up for the apocalypse, and know *just* what kind of tooth-paste they'll be ending their days with, the fact that they're just like the Get-Ready Man, the end of the wwwworld, except they've really done their homework, the fact that they've studied Active Survival and they mean business, the fact that they've got bug-out bags all packed and ready to go, the fact that they'd be ready at a moment's notice for that moon resettlement, the fact that they've got their rice in separate containers and a *portable ham*, the fact that that turned out to mean a radio, not a ham to *eat*, the fact that I'd much rather have a real ham myself, the fact that it would be sort of something to look forward to when the chips are down and everybody in the vicinity's dead except for you and a few hundred people fighting to the death over dried apricots or something, and a jug of potable water to go with them, but that's me, just saying, ♫ *and I'll not ask for wine* ♫, the fact that they're not kidding around about this stuff, the fact that Art and Cathy don't just have First Aid kits, they've done the *training*, which I'm sure comes in handy in the store too, like if anybody has a heart attack and so on from eating too many brownies, the fact that Cathy emailed me a whole list of what they've got stored, the fact that it's kind of incredible, look at this, they've got foldout cots, insect repel-lents, meds, vitamins, sunblock, an ax, a hoe, seeds for future farming and a book on edible plants and mushrooms, tarps, buckets, toilet paper, a sling, slingshots, really hi-tech ones, a compass and a pencil sharpener, the fact that I don't know what that's for, the fact that she doesn't mention pencils, so maybe it's to sharpen twigs into spears or arrows or something, but why do they need that when they've got hi-tech slingshots, or "pocket rockets," as Art calls them, the fact that I guess you need a lot of contingency plans or something, One Shot One Kill, the fact that they've got mess kits, and plenty of Brillo pads, the fact that I asked Cathy if the Brillo pads were for post-apocalypse dirty frying pan emergencies, but she says they can somehow help you make a *fire*, in case she and Art run out of matches, but they've got a whole load of *them* as well, sealed tight inside waterproof pill bottles, the fact that they've got batteries inside pill bottles too, hopefully different bottles from the ones with the matches, because you don't want a *battery fire* in your tent when there aren't any firemen anymore to help you, the fact that they have LED flashlights and a solar-paneled charger, and what else, collapsible lanterns, water bladders, a water filter, all kinds of waterproof gear, waterproof coats, hats and shoes, the fact that I don't know if that's because they expect a lot of rain or just *fallout*, the fact that I thought they should have galoshes but no dice, the fact that they *should* bring dice, to while away the long evenings, the fact that she says they have some very sturdy boots, the fact that I wonder if they're Kanye West's, the fact that they've got spare reading glasses, distance glasses, sunglasses, sport goggles too, a nest of metal cups, multi-tools, fishing lines and hooks, nail-clippers, tweezers, scissors, a sewing kit, Ziploc bags, well, everybody has those, bagged spices, bagged salt, bagged sugar, bagged powdered milk, a drone for reconnoitering, and some night-vision, hands-free *monocles*, one each, the fact that all this must have cost them some big *bucks*, and they're packing heat too, handguns anyway, and machetes, also paper towels, soap, folding dishwashing gloves, and Life Savers, bundles of 'em, I don't know why, the fact that they may come in handy on a dull day, I guess, unless they get out of date, when they're really no good to anyone, the fact that Life Savers just don't last, the fact that they were invented by Hart Crane's father, *The Bridge*, the fact that if only Life Savers really *did* save your life, the fact that then Art and Cathy wouldn't need all this *other* stuff, the fact that I guess they have to keep updating everything too, not just the Life Savers, to remain ultra-prepared, the fact that they've got oatmeal, walking sticks, hand warmers, VapoRub, baby wipes, duct tape, electrical tape, superglue, tourniquets, Woundseal powder and also cornflour, which she says is for treating wounds rather than for cooking, the fact that I let that lie, the fact that they've got baking powder too, but it's not for baking, and sanitary towels, as bandages for wounds, the fact that I never thought of using them for that, the fact that maybe she means panty pads, not thick sanitary towels, the fact that you wouldn't want the gluey part on a stick-on panty pad getting stuck in a *wound*, the fact that I don't know if "sanitary" actually means it's *sterile*, the fact that I've never known, the fact that I don't know if *anybody* knows, *I don't know but they know*, the fact that if you had a wound that big you really should probably get to a *hospital*, but of course there won't be any hospitals, or if there are any, they'll be full and all the doctors will be sick too, or gone, Hiroshima, the fact that sometimes doctors desert their posts and go off to grow lima beans for their own families, but it's all going to be okay because Art and Cathy are bringing *Chapstick*, and Cathy says you can seal a wound with that too somehow, if you have to, the fact that Cathy probably has some way of stitching wounds with a needle and thread too, but I hate to think how, the fact that anyway at least their lips won't be getting chapped while they hide out, collateral damage, the fact that they've got a whole *bushel* of lentils, the fact that I guess nobody will care much about flatulence anymore, out in the wilderness, the fact that they're taking a few luxuries too like dental floss, toothbrushes, toothpaste, and emergency blankets, woolen socks, me-oh-mys, long johns, even yarn and knitting needles, oh and tea lights, the fact that I guess they can sit in their homemade bunker, wrapped in their emergency blankets, and knit socks for the nuclear winter, the fact that, boy, Cathy's a *prepper* and I never knew, and dead serious about it too, the fact that Leo thinks all preppers are *nuts*, because even if you could survive for a while, physically, there wouldn't be any *point* in living, if civilization has ground to a halt and everybody's turned violent, the fact that Cathy really seems to think they'll have a chance though, if they just hold on to all this gear, and keep their wits about them, while, as she herself says, everyone else is looting other people's knapsacks and shooting each other over porridge, the fact that how does she see to all this, with all the other jobs she has, the fact that Cathy's incredible, what a powerhouse, the fact that they must have to store all these survival treasures some place really safe but handy, and renew them all the time so they're always ready to roll, because, as she says, a bug-out bag's only useful if you have it with you when the moment comes to go *off-grid*, the fact that she says preppers call the apocalypse SHTF which means, well, Number Two Hit The Fan, or else TEOTWAWKI and WROL, which means The End Of The World As We Know It, and Without Rule Of Law, the rule of law, the fact that that does not sound too inviting, I must say, though you could say we're already *there*, with a hundred Americans getting killed a day right *now*, the fact that what I don't dare ask Cathy is if you don't sort of start to *long* for TEOTWAWKI, once you've invested in all the equipment, I mean, because it must be kind of tempting to *use* it, and obviously it would be a pity to *waste* it all, artificial grass, the fact that a real apocalypse would be such a *vindication*, if you'd spent all this dough getting ready for it, the fact that Cathy and Art already go for try-outs somewhere, testing out their skills in a down-grid scenario, the fact that all I could say was I'm still kind of hoping the community would pull together in an emergency like that, and neighbors and friends and would help each other out, and we'd all struggle on as best we can, gathering nuts and berries or whatever, the fact that she said, "Call me paranoid but I think one day we'll have to fall back on our own resources," meaning go it alone, I guess, with no friends, no neighbors, the fact that she believes that total economic collapse is imminent, as well as nuclear war, and she and Art are going to be prepared and we're not, the fact that she says she'll help me if I want any survival *advice*, the fact that I never knew she was this scared, the fact that she sounds worse than *me*, and so mistrustful of like, well, everything and everybody, the fact that she kept saying how you have to travel light and hide and camouflage yourself, or some stranger will kill you, for nothing, for a spoonful of your instant coffee or whatever, whatevs, the fact that if anybody can handle the apocalypse, it's probably Cathy, with all her walking sticks and sanitary towels, the fact that I don't wanna live in the *woods* though, and face marauders with a *slingshot*, and Leo's a great guy but I can't see him rustling up a fort and trapping trespassers, the fact that that just ain't gonna happen, the fact that he's just a college professor, not Tarzan, Athens, Ohio, Somalian pirates, Tom Hanks, can o' worms, limoncello pie, $5000 Fine For Unwelcome Fondling Of Woman During Flight, the fact that

I hope we can just go sort of *Amish* if necessary, the fact that that's *my* Plan A, the fact that the Amish help each other out, like if a child gets injured in the middle of hog-slaughtering and the parents have to take him to the doctor, the neighbors all turn out and finish the hog-slaughtering, the fact that they're always doing that sort of thing, Doped-Up Iditarod Dogs, the fact that I gotta admit that even Ronny can be a help in an emergency, the fact that I couldn't have asked any of the *neighbors* to pick us up from the mall yesterday, like the Kinkels or whatever, wustite, the fact that we don't have that kind of relationship, cup of sugar, dozen eggs, the fact that the floods were the best excuse ever for not delivering my pies on time, and everybody was pretty understanding about it, the fact that Cathy was of course, but even folks at the other outlets just seemed concerned about my *ordeal*, not annoyed, the fact that one place sent me *flowers*, the fact that they seemed very impressed I hadn't drowned, the fact that I didn't tell them about the cat, the fact that we'll never know what happened to him, the fact that at least everybody seemed to agree that you can't be expected to ford a river in full flood with a load of pies on your head, dodging flaming houses as they float by, just to fulfil catering commitments, the fact that I wonder if *that's* why Cathy shoved half my pear pie in her mouth like that, just so that she's ready at all times for the *apocalypse*, the fact that maybe there's no room for a pie in her survival plan, glasses wipes, the fact that the police or the firemen had to rescue a dog from the floods, the fact that he was standing on top of a parked car in somebody's driveway, probably waiting for his people to come home, and the car was surrounded by four or five feet of rising water, the fact that he was all cold and wet and probably in shock, and standing on top of the car trembling, shivering from the cold, like those elephants in India before they got their sweaters, Pepito in his raggedy old sweater I made him, the fact that nothing would entice that dog off that car at first, but then one of the rescuer guys tried giving him beef jerky, and that helped a bit, but the dog was so scared he kept growling and retreating when they tried to grab him, the fact that the main rescuer guy kept working on him though, with the beef jerky, calling him "sweetheart," and finally they got hold of him, manhandled, mandible, Mandela, mandala, manzana, mañana, Manhattan, the fact that Mommy liked a Manhattan once in a while, with a maraschino cherry, the fact that why didn't I make her one, but I think she only liked them when she was out, just for fun, the fact that she really preferred whiskey and soda, the fact that later, on the news, the dog-rescuer said it took twelve bucks' worth of beef jerky to get that dog off the car, Guadalupe, Guadalajara, Guanabana, Guantánamo, Geronimo, Open Sesame, the fact that there were other dogs too, that had been left chained in their yards, with the water coming higher and higher, almost like the owners *wanted* to drown them, but perhaps they just didn't think, the fact that people are funny in an emergency, "breakdown of civilization," the fact that maybe they were in a panic, or hysterical, but it does seem kind of unfair not to give the poor dog a fighting chance at least, like at least leave him free to swim if he has to, the fact that there were horses caught inside a flooded barn too, the fact that I wonder if preppers will panic when the time comes and forget all their plastic buckets and binoculars, the fact that is this how people will cook after the apocalypse, a can of soup and a prayer over a low moss flame, or some game they trapped and some berries they scrounged from some tree, the fact that I think they'll all get *food poisoning*, the fact that it's surprising how few people even know how to cook chicken safely, especially deadbeat dads, the fact that deadbeat dads are *always* undercooking chicken, according to downbeat moms anyway, the fact that I know I shouldn't keep calling them deadbeat dads, but it just sort of trips off the tongue, Waterlow Park, misty hill, the fact that there's no real equivalent for bad *moms*, like "mopey mom," or "motormouth mom," "soccer mom," "tiger mom," "stay-at-home mom," "smother-mother," "mom bomb," "mamma mia," well, maybe "monster mom," but it's still not as direct a hit like "deadbeat dad," the fact that Trump calls *Melania* a monster, the fact that that's no way to talk to your wife, but he hates everybody, the fact that with sciatica I don't dare pick Jake up now, Baby On Board, or carry him on my hip, and that's so sad, the fact that *Trump* is always saying "Sad!", usually to rub it in right when he's just insulted somebody, "false flags," the fact that *he's* a, but I shouldn't say that, deadbeat dad, the fact that preppers say there will be more and more wars *this century*, over food and water and power, I mean *energy*, not political power, but maybe that as well, the fact that I'm lacking a little in energy myself, the fact that harvests are already shrinking because it's too hot to grow stuff in places where things used to grow fine, and wild horses are dying from the heat, and crocodiles are all being born *female*, or male, the fact that I can't remember which it is now, or is it *alligators*, the fact that the point is they're too hot, anonymous alligators, scaffolding, falsework, false flags, the fact that *we're* actually running low on apples, oranges, tea bags, olive oil, soda, dishwasher tabs, and unsalted butter, easy-peasy, easy as pie, here's mud in your eye, the fact that February's the shortest month but somehow it feels the longest, the fact that it seems a long time ago now actually, the fact that I don't think anybody actually says "actually" right, the fact that the kids all say "ackshully" and "Febbery," which sounds too much like "rubbery" to me, which February is not, the fact that February is very concrete ackshully, Goshen, caution, those poor chickens, purple martins, boarlets, boing, the fact that Bush could never pronounce "nuclear" right, but a lot of people can't master that, bird in the hand, fifty-nine tiles, the fact that Tracie told me she was assaulted in some way in a neighbor's bathroom when she was young, and she counted the floor tiles while it was going on, the fact that there were fifty-nine of them, tiles, not *abusers*, dear me, the fact that I don't know how she remembers that, fifty-nine, but now I'll remember it forever too maybe, fifty-nine tiles, hydrangea, the fact that I did not know what to say to her when she told me, the fact that I hardly even know the woman and I don't know why she confided in me, the fact that the eggs of wrens are tiny as a fingernail, the fact that I really do have to clean up for James and Fresia, but the whole house or what, the fact that she wasn't all that specific, the fact that I better clean the whole place, sugar plum pie, rinse plums and remove pits, *The Sugarcreek Budget*, Harvest Thrift Store, the fact that the first time I knew Leo loved me was when he called me "sweetheart" over the phone, the fact that we'd practically just met and out came this "sweetheart," and that was it, the fact that that is sort of why we are here today, knocking around together with a whole bunch of kids and books and chickens and pies and medical bills, shadows, nighttime, all because of that "sweetheart" of his, the fact that while we were waiting for Ronny to come pick us up, Ben read out loud from his book on household repairs and Stacy just slouched under a big tree, looking bitter, the fact that now she wants a full-length mirror, the fact that there's already a mirror on the inside of her closet but she wants a longer one, she says, the fact that I guess she wants to get her slouch just right, the fact that I have *pies* to make, and I don't know when I'll have time to buy her a full-length slouching mirror, the fact that thanks to the new book, Ben says he's figured out our bathroom faucet, and he could fix it, as long as Leo helps him get hold of the right tools and parts, my Little Pillow, stay-at home mom, homemaker, homebody, housewife, slugabed, stick-in-the-mud, mush, mash note, unpaid labor, the fact that women did about fifty-one hours of housework a week in 1900 and now we do about forty-six, the fact that we save five hours a week, thanks to mod cons, which is something but not much, the fact that Leo says I'm not a housewife, I'm a Domestic Engineer, the fact that every boy used to want to be an engineer when he grew up, but they were talking about being a *train-driver*, not being a *domestic* engineer, or even a *civil* engineer, the fact that if you work at home you're doing a million different things at once, making beds and washing clothes and gardening and writing grocery lists and answering the phone and baking and sewing and ironing and feeding chickens and forgetting all kinds of stuff, the fact that if I *didn't* work at home, we'd probably have to *hire* somebody to do all that, like Paula Turnbull, so in a way, I guess I'm saving us some dough, even if I don't make all that much, the fact that I'm no great shakes myself at house-work, but I do my best, the fact that I should try to think of it that way, Domestic Engineer, because most of the time I just think how useless I am and what a tiny contribution I make, though Leo never says so, the fact that *he's* usually apologizing for not helping me more with the dishes, or the vacuuming, which is silly, the fact that we have a dishwasher after all, I mean the machine kind, not the human kind, the fact that there are people in this world who simply can't cope without a dishwasher and I am one of them, but I don't expect *him* to do it after a long teaching day, the fact that I've got four kids to help load and unload the dishwasher, and that oughtta be enough for anybody, basta, the fact that what's the point of being a stay-at-home mom, if I don't *stay home*, the fact that it really makes more sense for me to stay home too, as I only get into trouble if I go out, with fire and flood and bully boys and things, the fact that the world's full of maniacs and gun rampagers and survivalists who own their own *army tanks* and missiles too, the fact that it's just not *safe* out there, the fact that I think I've always felt insecure about leaving the house though, the fact that as a kid I worried all the time when I was out, in case something happened and I never got to see Mommy again, for some reason, the fact that I always missed my mommy, and I assumed she missed me too, but maybe she was just glad to have a break, and who wouldn't be, with three kids, the fact that she published her book just before she got sick, and Grandpa grandly declared "This book will either be a success or a failure," the fact that that was kind of a dumb thing to say, the fact that it isn't very encouraging, to someone who's just written her first book, and it's kind of meaningless too, the fact that how is it any different from saying the weather will either get hotter or colder, foggier or less foggy, and you'll either get sicker or better, live or pass on, and cakes will either rise or fall, these oysters are either safe or unsafe, the fact that Grandpa's belly might have gotten either bigger or smaller, but it got bigger, the fact that his belt could have been positioned higher or lower, but he decided on high, too high, the fact that maybe he wore suspenders, but I can't remember now, the fact that my waistband's too loose, the fact that these pants are really just about to fall off, skin and bones, skull and crossbones, bone-tired, wishbone, Wish-Bone Dressing, sawbones, funny bone, boning up, bon appetit, Glacier Lake, the fact that *now* I'll never see Mommy again, the fact that my Glacier Lake jigsaw's still bugging me, half-finished, with a gazillion more turquoise pieces to go, the fact that during the delay at the mall Jake never got his fill of climbing escalators, the fact that you have to watch that kid, Otis, Mommy, peaches in cream, flip flops, Bill Clinton, the fact that Grandpa's belly was completely *round*, like a watermelon, or a beach ball, inner tube, the fact that, oh yes, I'm sure he wore suspenders and they held his pants way up, which just emphasized the balloon belly more, the fact that maybe *he* could've used a full-length mirror, but I don't think people cared so much about fashion in those days, "This balloon-belly look will either be a success or a failure," ♫ *Old King Louis* ♫, crystal candy dish, souvenir spoons, glass-fronted bookcases, "Go Trojans!", the fact that they hated Daddy going to Yale instead of somewhere in Michigan, so when he went to college, they handed him a bunch of Grandpa's old suits, the fact that they'd been altered to fit Daddy but, still, they were old, hand-me-down out-of-date suits, *The Awakening*, and he hated them, the fact that those suits were not a success at Yale, the fact that they were a failure, the fact that once Ronny got us back here Stacy rushed straight up to her bedroom, probably to post a Shopping Haul video including footage of the burning house, blurrily filmed with her smartphone because we haven't bought her a video camera, the fact that she wants to make high-class videos like the Morning Routine girls do, but I don't want her running all over the house filming us and interviewing us like the girl who's always making her mom remember cute things the daughter did when she was a little kid, the fact that some of these nostalgia sessions go on for twenty minutes at a time, and I don't think I could compete with that mom, the fact that I can't remember enough cute things to fill twenty minutes, not that Stacy wasn't cute as all get-out, but I just can't remember anything, the fact that that would be embarrassing, and probably end in Stacy stomping off and not speaking to me for a week, so I'd like to avoid the whole situation if possible, the fact that it's an invasion of privacy, being filmed in your own home, the fact that the Morning Routine girls video their houses and families and then go into the kitchen and explain how you boil spaghetti, and you see the whole house and the stunned family cowering in the background, the fact that I think it must give burglars a good gander at all the family's stuff, the fact that I kind of think Stacy should be doing her *homework*, not videoing our domestic arrangements at all hours of the day, the fact that Leo thinks kids shouldn't be given *any* homework, the fact that he thinks it's cruel, the fact that he thinks they should do their work at *school*, and when they get home they should do other stuff, *kids'* stuff, because kids need time to play and chill out and sleep and help out and build treehouses and stuff, and even talk to their moms maybe, the fact that I like the idea, partly because then teenagers could sleep more, the fact that teenagers apparently never get enough sleep, the fact that they need like twenty hours' sleep a *day*, like cats, but they always go to bed too late and then they have to get up early for school, the fact that I think that's why a lot of school shootings take place at 7:00 in the morning, or 7:30, the fact that either the school shooter kids are still half-asleep and don't know what they're doing, sleep-shooting, or they've simply been driven berserk by getting too little sleep, ♫ *Baa, baa, baa* ♫, the fact that if Leo's teaching a really early class, like an 8:00 one, he lets them bring their breakfast with them, the fact that otherwise they don't take in a thing he says, titanium, aquarium, centurion, criterion, criteria, labyrinth, spiral, the fact that it's kind of amazing we got home at all yesterday and weren't all swept away by those floods, the beef industry, global warming, pedophiles, apples with razors in them, terrorists, people allergic to nuts, crazees, Open Carry guys, ISIS, Trump voters, the fact that it's a lot less fun going to the mall than it used to be, the fact that anywhere that people gather en masse makes me kind of nervous, trouble spot, no-go area, no-fly zone, cancer cluster, the fact that kids are in such demand as gun victims these days, the fact that they often accidentally shoot their moms too, the fact that three-year-olds are always finding loaded shotguns in the back seat and shooting their mom while she's driving them someplace, the fact that I wouldn't dare send my kids to *camp* now, not after Breivik, the fact that you have to think twice about any place where a big bunch of people gather together, hunters, woods, raccoons, the fact that I guess we'll be stuck trying to entertain them at home all summer then, the fact that they could go to summer school, though why's summer school any safer than summer camp, the fact that they're sitting ducks wherever they go, school, a ball game, the pool, Norway, Gnadenhutten, department stores, Macy's, "Ting-ting-ting," Walmart's gun department, Pepito's tags, the fact that all you really want to do is tuck your kids in and know they're *safe*, the fact that if only they could stay cocooned in their beds until they reached adulthood, ALS, colitis, kidney cancer, but even then they'll be a worry, the fact that you don't want them to marry bores or get diseases or live miles away and never let you know how they're doing, in-laws, MILs, dark shadows in broad daylight, chiaroscuro, the fact that maybe we should *home-school* them, but home schooled kids spend too much time with their parents, and too much time indoors, the fact that I'd never get any pies done if I had to play schoolteacher as well as Domestic Engineer, homemaker, piemaker, Sandy Hook, Nickel Mines, execution-style, the fact that all the kids we know who're home-schooled are kinda *crazee*, the fact that there's that kid who used to be in Stacy's class who's home-schooled now and her parents are Christian fundamentalists and they beat her, Hadley, the fact that she's bigger than them so now she hits them back, but that situation doesn't sound good, the fact that that teenage girl in Columbus was wounded by her mom's ex-husband, but managed to call 911 while the rest of her family were being murdered "execution-style," go figure, shooters, Hooters, Winchester, Colt 45, pump-action Remington Model 870 shotgun, .38-caliber revolver, the fact that the truth is I worry about my kids *all day long* while they're at school, the fact that I don't think Mommy worried about *us* all day, or I hope not anyway, the fact that there was not that much to worry about thirty years ago, the fact that this massacre craze hadn't really started yet, the fact that when was Columbine, the fact that I was in my twenties then, the fact that Phoebe and I used to walk to school and back twice a day as kids, all by ourselves, Phoebe dragging me along because I was slow, quarrel, lost coat, black tree trunks, white snow, slush, mush, tuna fish sammich, the fact that moms didn't worry so much about massacres then, the fact that Mommy was probably more concerned about having to heat up the chicken noodle soup and make tunafish sandwiches than about our surviving the school day without being "executed," the fact that it's not just the kids I worry about either, because *Leo* spends half his time in airports and on campuses, auditoriums, cafeterias, planes, danger zones, 9/11, the Pentagon, the fact that he's at the mercy of any angry student who just got out of bed, or coworker, or berserk janitor or rightwing fanatic, the fact that campuses are perfect places for mass killings, just like schools and hotels and churches and movie theaters and stadiums and restaurants and train stations and nightclubs, the fact that shooters are like lions patrolling water holes, waiting for a herd of prey to arrive, five-story columbarium, white tiers of captive chickens, slavery, warm cinnamon rolls, the fact that Oprah says "a problem child is a *child*, not a problem," the fact that I didn't get Leo's *dry cleaning*, I just realized, but maybe he's picked it up now himself, the fact that he is careful about his clothes, the fact that he likes his socks just so, and he likes boxer briefs, the fact that he alternates black boxer briefs with gray boxer briefs, and I was trying to decipher his system once and asked him, and he said, "What does it matter?" and I said I needed to know in case of emergency, and he said "What emergency?" and I said, "Well, if you're unconscious! Like, what if you suddenly wake up in the ICU and demand your black underpants because it's *Wednesday* or something?", and he said "If I'm unconscious it won't matter," and I said, "But, but—", and he said "Don't worry about it, sweetheart," the fact that it always knocks me out when he calls me sweetheart, the fact that nobody ever called me that before, the fact that I was damaged by Mommy's illness, the fact that it broke me, sweetheart, the fact that I dreamt I was sitting out front with some women, just talking, and a plane or helicopter soared by, very close to us, with a sort of *fake* plane dangling from it by a long cord, and the fake plane crashed into an apartment building right across the road, and another apartment

building nearby jiggled and cracked and began to crumble, the fact
that this guy with a bicycle on a balcony somehow managed to jump
to safety, with his bike even, and we all applauded from our safe spot
across the street, the fact that then I was discussing the situation with
the other women, who all seemed very friendly, the fact that we agreed
how scary the plane crash was, and this was somehow comforting, the
fact that then there was a horse in a field nearby and one guy ques-
tioned whether it was a horse or a pony, so I went to have a look and
it was a carthorse, with big shaggy hooves, the fact that there were
lots of children around too, the fact that we were all trying to survive
together, like it was a war or something, the fact that I saw other
buildings knocked down too by large objects, the fact that it was pretty
chaotic, like an apocalypse, bug-out time, knapsacks, rice, Brillo pads,
matches, Chapstick, the fact that eventually we got to a tall house
belonging to some kind people who let us shelter there, and lots of
people stumbled up some of those steep stairs to a top room, the fact
that once we got there almost everybody just wanted to watch DVDs,
but I looked out at the pretty little bay, and suddenly everything was
totally rural, but I couldn't quite get the scale of it, the fact that the
bay seemed like maybe closer than it really was, and then the whole
house started to *move*, pretty fast, like a train, and we passed people
outside the house and tried to communicate with them by sign language as we whooshed by but we couldn't really, the fact that in the
midst of it all it occurred to me that in an emergency like this every
body would be using up all the space on the cell-phone networks and
Leo and I probably wouldn't receive each other's texts until *days* had
gone by and all this had died down, if it ever did die down, the fact
that I woke up thinking of the word "divisive," I don't know why, the
fact that Leo and I were divided, far apart, the fact that it's scary
because in a real apocalypse how *would* we ever find each other, I
mean if our phones didn't work, the fact that I didn't know where I
was either, in the dream, so I couldn't have told him where to find me,
sweetheart, the fact that the little girl who wandered out in the night
didn't wander off in the night, the fact that that was all lies and

somebody just murdered her for no reason, the fact that callipygian means you have a beautiful sit-me-down-upon, the fact that the gyny guy had the nerve to ask me if I was on HRT yet, dear me, the fact that they'll be giving that stuff to children next, chickens too, to keep them laying, miracle cure, elixir of youth, the fact that most women in America are taking HRT pills, I guess, well, the women that can *afford* them, monkey glands, my itch, the fact that the gyny *nurse* was so pretty and perfect, she gave me the willies, the fact that the whole thing was so embarrassing, the fact that am I tidying for James, or James's mom, the fact that I wonder if maybe Sue Bender just likes being in a tidy home, like I liked being at Abby's, the fact that this thought just came to me, the fact that she really didn't have to go impose on the Amish, just for some tidiness, the fact that she could've gone to Abby's house instead, or any of Abby's neighbors, or tidied her own place, her house full of faceless dolls and to-do lists, the fact that most people are *so tidy*, compared to me, the fact that where do all their pieces of paper disappear to, Mommy's letters, the fact that I'm like a whirling dervish now, seizing things and shoving them into drawers and shelves and closets, the fact that I'm kind of getting into it, the fact that maybe this cleaning-up business is good therapy, after our alarming encounter with the forces of nature, the fact that just about everything in our house seems to be in the wrong place, the fact that sometimes I blow up about how messy our house is and how I have to clear up after everybody all the time, the fact that once I railed "Am I the only person who ever does any housework around here?" and Stacy, who happened to be standing around, said "Yes," not in a mean way, just in a very matter-of-fact, no argument kind of way, the fact that maybe there was even a note of sympathy there too, the fact that I asked her "But doesn't anybody care what happens to their *stuff*? Don't they care about hygiene, or having their friends see this chaos?" and she said "No," the fact that she wasn't proud of it or anything, nor apologetic, the fact that she was just telling it like it is, a fact, a fact of life, the fact that I asked "Doesn't anyone even care if their stuff gets trampled underfoot...", "No," "... or thrown out by accident?",

"No," the fact that these people don't give a *hoot* about housework and none of them even notices me constantly cleaning up after them, sorting through their papers and all their little plastic toys and worry dolls, and scratched DVDs and dusty honey bears and about-to-be-squashed smart phones, loading the dishwasher, unloading the dishwasher, putting styptic sticks away, buying groceries and underwear and oftentimes cooking two or three meals a day, with different foods each day for each and every kid, to make sure they get their "varied and colorful" diet, the fact that it's like a *diner* around here sometimes, and I'm the short order cook, skunk eggs, chicken on a raft, one on the city, "these people," the fact that I should go on strike, I really should, the fact that you get candle wax off a tablecloth by putting it in the freezer for a while, the fact that Jupiter has subzero temperatures, the fact that it also has a permanent storm on it that looks from here like a giant red spot, "That's a permanent stain," permanent, the fact that it's the size of the earth, just that one big continual hurricane, whirling dervish, male gynecologist, the fact that I wonder if there are male gynecologists on other planets, but even in an infinite universe that seems unlikely, galaxy, solar system, Milky Way, United Way, United Airlines, 9/11, Fresia, the fact that she's a little bit much, James's mom, SpaghettiO time, nasturtiums, geraniums, the fact that what's this now, the fact that "Two early-morning nature lovers had the shock of their lives last Sunday. What they at first thought was birdsong turned out to be the miaows of three abandoned cougar cubs, hiding in a hollow tree. Despite some fierce resistance, Bard Grissal, 38, and Tony Marvey, both longtime residents of Calcutta, Columbiana County, managed to secure the cubs in a knapsack," the fact that the kids might like this, the fact that Jake likes baby animals, well, *everybody* likes *baby animals*, the fact that "On the advice of local police, the two rescuers handed the cougar cubs over to the Big Cat division of Columbus Zoo. The cubs are three or four months old and healthy. The good samaritans have a few minor scratches to remind them of the hike that turned into an eighty-mile mercy mission. 'They're small but they're strong,' Marvey told reporters. 'I'm going to need a new jacket!',", the fact that how could there be wild cougars in Columbiana County, the fact that they must be somebody's pets or something, hikers, Calcutta, cougars, *panthers*, in *Ohio*, my word, the fact that it's good they got them to the zoo, the fact that we can't have cougars running all over the place, eating kids, CONELRAD, the fact that we're supposed to have huge forget-me-nots this year, which is either a good sign or a bad sign, the fact that if we hadn't shoved all the Indians out of Ohio they'd be able to *tell* us what over-large forget-me-nots mean, and what to do about cougars, the Big Woods, Big Slough, big forget-me-nots, the fact that we polluted everything and threw the truth-tellers out and, as a parent, I do kind of resent that, Winning Jackpot Numbers, the fact that we didn't bring four children into the world just so they could smoke on chog, I mean choke on smog, and watch the ozone disintegrate and rivers burst into flame, and animals disappear from the face of the earth, slime eels, slime eels, slime, chog, Taste of Coshocton, quarterly meeting, fracking, extruding, crude oil, a sunny street corner in Madison, the fact that Aunt Sophia's cousin Luella was abducted by Indians, but she came home after a few months, the fact that I don't know if she had a good time or not, a success or a failure, the fact that there are no family records to speak of, just a few old photos and the moose head, the ox yoke and the wagon wheel, the fact that this is my problem, I get up too early and have these dismal thoughts, the fact that if I just ate a chocolate-dipped madeleine I'd probably feel a heck of a lot better, KEEP OFF PRIVATE PROPERTY & YOU WON'T GET SHOT, slime eels, hagfish, the fact that some truck dropped thirty thousand slime eels on the highway somewhere in California, I think, and they had to close the whole road down for a day while they tried to clean all the slime off the blacktop, the fact that there were live slime eels everywhere and they were stressed out, the slime eels, not the road cleaners, but maybe them too, the fact that when slime eels get stressed, they exude more slime, exude, extrude, so there was really a *lot* of slime, "I prefer a lot of semen, I always have," the fact that you wonder why slime eels have to be transported anywhere, but Koreans like them, the fact that they *eat* slime eels, friendly wolf eels, hagfish, Kim Jong Un, the king of Tory Island, the fact that slime eels' manners sound worse than my *kids'*, the fact that, as if things weren't sloppy and slimy enough, slime eels project their jaws outside their mouths, by turning their mouths inside out, the fact that slime eels *extrude their own jaws*, and that is not a pretty sight, the fact that they're blind too, which is just as well or they'd have to watch other slime eels turning their mouths inside out all the time, the fact that they're blind to the slime of their comrades, flipside, bundt cake, Poo-Poo Plate, the fact that they're kind of the underwater equivalent of mole rats, which are also blind and kind of hard to look at for long, mole rats, mole, rat, slime, Sloppy Joes, Medal of Honor, lap of honor, Woman of the Year, basketball coach, cutie marks, James's mom, the fact that what does it feel like to *swallow*, if your mouth is *outside your body*, the fact that maybe it's *easier* like that, the fact that maybe we have *too* much happening inside our skulls though, like talking, singing, breathing, snoring, whistling, crying, coughing, sneezing, hiccuping, drooling, eating, licking, kissing, tasting, yawning, wincing, winking, seeing, hearing, and making smacking noises, not to mention thinking and dreaming, the fact that just the mouth *alone* is a very complicated structure, and then there are all the other glands and organs and muscles and tissues and sinus cavities and all, the fact that there are a lot of blood vessels in the face, Little Pillow, blueberry jam, walnuts, the fact that by inverting their jaws, slime eels maybe leave more space for some of these head functions, kind of like building a porch, which may be an advantage, even if it's kind of revolting, frozen peas, the fact that they probably don't need to whistle much anyway, down in the ocean depths, dog-whistles, "interesting news items," *It's Complicated*, hygienist sandblasting my teeth, the fact that it's time to get the rolls out, the fact that there's a mini railway between the Capitol Building and the Senate that nobody's supposed to know about, except if you're in the Senate, military grade M-16 rifle, AM-15, GSW, the fact that these cinnamon rolls really are the bane of my existence, the kneading, the rolling, the rising, the falling, the baking, the shaking, and then the collapsing, though *I* usually do the collapsing, snowy-scene-at-sunset jigsaw puzzle, the fact that before he left for work, Leo came in and reported that he dreamt we had an antique coconut *nose* and everybody wanted it because it had *fronds*, the fact that the stuff he comes out with, the fact that I like the way he talks, the fact that then we somehow got on to duels, and he said he's not sure why duels were made illegal, because they efficiently got rid of quite a lot of stupid guys, the fact that sometimes, when he sees Stace, Leo will say "I like that Eustacia Vye," like in *The Catcher in the Rye,* and it seems to please her, the fact that sometimes you feel just a microsecond of pure happiness, in between all the burdens of survival and all, the fact that I wonder if animals get that too, happy slime eels, the fact that we are here to see and be part of things, see and be part of things, the fact that eagles see and are part of things, the fact that they see *everything*, the fact that an eagle is so in the *now*, and maybe slime eels are too, radiological contaminants, TTHMs, nose hair, the fact that Leo's helping Ben study our *drinking* water now, and how contaminated it is, Chuck, the fact that Leo says our water facility violates the Safe Drinking Water Act, *and* the federal drinking water standard, the fact that he says our water's full of TTHMs, HAA5, TTHMs, and it's way above government guidelines on other stuff too, the fact that we've got a whole lot of ppbs of bromodichloromethane, when the recommended ppbs limit is much less, and we've got three times the acceptable limit of chloroform ppbs, and ppbs of dibromochloromethane when there should be hardly any, and about *16* ppbs of trihalomethanes, when we shouldn't have more than *0.8*, trichloroacetic acid too, of all the unpleasant-sounding things in the world, the fact that the top limit for trichloroacetic acid is 0.5 ppbs, and we've got *1.000* ppbs, and who wants *that*, the fact that I forget all the time what ppbs means but it's parts per billion, the fact that I wonder why that's always the way they measure things, ppbs, Probably Polluted But Survivable, Pretty Perplexing Business Strategy, Poor People's Bonus Supper, Powerful Poison with a Bad Seal, tankard, baby-cup, Pitiful and Pernicious Baby-cup Syndrome, ready, set, go, ready aim, fire, I spy with my little eye, "You're it,"

blocked drains, breakfast, just waiting for a streetcar, the fact that I've
bailed on this latest water investigation, the fact that it's too frightening
when it's about your *own* water, the fact that I wanna be like that guy
in Athens who avoids all the news, Athens, Ohio, not Greece, the fact
that he just doesn't want to know, and neither do I really, the fact that
these contaminants, chemicals, pollutants, are all carcinogenic, and
we've also got bromoform, bromodichloromethane, nitrates, I think,
in our water, which are also carcinogenic, the fact that I feel sick,
toxins, carcinogens, the fact that what if our water gave me *cancer*,
because I *was* pretty young to get it, the fact that most people who get
my kind are *seventy* or more, Frances Oldham Kelsey, Rachel Carson,
The Fugitive, Penny-Pinching Bureaucratic Sadists, the fact that actually Leo said there may well be a cancer cluster here, the fact that he
and Ben are trying to find that out, but I don't wanna know, the fact
that if our water gave me life-threatening cancer, I'm moving to
Athens, Athens, *Greece*, Pathology of a Pathetic Rare Sit-me-down-
upon, the fact that if *that's* what happened to me, that's even worse
than the *mucus* remedy, and my kids are still *drinking* that water, well,
filtered, the fact that everybody around here does, the fact that we all
have baths in it, Post-Prandial Bathtub Soak, the fact that sometimes
I forget and steam vegetables in it, or add unfiltered ice water to my
pie dough, the fact that our poor goldfish are *living* in it, and the hens
drink it too, and then *we eat their eggs*, though sometimes the chickens
find puddles to drink from outside, which might or might not be less
polluted, this puddle will either be a success or a failure, the fact that
their eggs go into the pie crust too, and into my cinnamon rolls, and
my customers *eat* those pies and cinnamon rolls, cancer cluster, except
the customers who just have a try and leave half of it on the plate,
ungrateful, sub-optimal customers, eggs, croque madame, croquet,
badminton, Wisconsin, capsicum, the fact that the goldfish seem to
be doing okay, though they do die often, but that's what goldfish *do*,
Pallid Pets Bend Sideways, napkin ring, forever home, Same-Sex
Penguin Couple Raises Chick, the fact that my oncologist told me to
embrace change, and that cancer's the new normal, Pretty Paltry

Basic System, but I don't see why the people of Newcomerstown should embrace change if it means they're drinking dangerous water, the fact that we're not alone either, the fact that *most* places in America have unsafe levels of contaminants in their drinking water, *most*, the fact that *everybody's* got bromoform now, the fact that I'd never even heard of bromoform before, "no promo homo," pro bono, Police Pore over Bromoform Statistics, the fact that somewhere in the South you can't even mention that some people are gay, I mean mention in Sex Ed classes, like that anything besides heterosexuality exists, Stacy's pamphlet, Cleopatra, Priapus, David Attenborough, the fact that maybe it's something like chloroform, the fact that *why* do we have chloroform in the water, three times the limit, the fact that are they trying to chloroform us, the fact that that's gotta be illegal, mass chloroforming, class action, Suella, abduction, Annie's bunkbeds, *Seven Brides for Seven Brothers*, the fact that Victorian dentists chloroformed people, Poking Prodding Blasting Sluicing, extruding, cavities, Pork, Potato fries, Bacon and Salsa on rye, the fact that somehow I don't think I feel like having chloroform in my coffee today, a little hot *milk* maybe, on a cold day, no chloroform, thanks, the fact that I asked Leo why they put all these scary acids in the water, and he said something like they have to chlorinate the water to *clean* it, the fact that I said to Leo "Surely American corporations aren't allowed to just *kill* us," and I can't remember what he said, but it was probably something like "Yes, they are, and stop calling me Shirley," the fact that he says that every time I use of the word "surely," and I'll never understand why, the fact that then I talked to Cathy and she said not to worry about it, the fact that police search body cavities, the fact that I may be wrong but it seems to me the police are getting kind of out of hand, Saturday afternoons in Evanston, organizing the neighborhood newspaper in our kitchen nook, the fact that I forget what we called it, the fact that Phoebe wrote most of it, the fact that lead, nitrates, atrazine, manganese and fluoride are not good for kids, the fact that they say only 0.2 ppbs of lead are safe, and *our* lead level's between *3.00 and 5.00* ppbs, the fact that it's getting like *Flint* around here, and I'm scared, the fact that fluoride is best absorbed through toothpaste, the fact that swallowing it is *not* that good for you, but most places still put it in the water, the fact that I hope the Brita jug extracts the fluoride, potable, skookumchuck, reverse osmosis system, the fact that at school though, they just drink from the drinking fountain like everybody else, and that water must be full of lead, the fact that this is something I should bring up with the PTA, the fact that maybe Amelia will get on her high horse about it, the fact that she'll want to sue somebody, the fact that Oscar Wilde sued for libel and ended up doing hard labor, Soviet labor camps, co-pays, single-payer, Affordable Care Act, the fact that it's like suddenly finding out about macrophages and tardigrades, things you never knew were there but they are, the fact that you think everybody around you's just dying of normal diseases, but then you start to wonder if maybe it was *avoidable*, the fact that there's something in the water in some places that they now think is connected to *ALS*, for instance, the fact that how do the polluters get away with it, the fact that you just assume water's a basic human right, because you have to have it, like the air, but what if your water isn't safe, and the air isn't either, and food, meat and fruit, the fact that they're trying to *kill* us, manslaughter, genocide, ecocide, spider, slime eels, slimes, slickens, culm dumps, work ganfs, the fact that I guess it's not as bad as having an iron ore dam fail on you, like in Brazil, "damn dams," ♫ *We cursed Escanaba and that damned iron ore* ♫, Vale, the Vales of Boston, the fact that when the dam failed, sixty million cubic meters of iron ore waste escaped and traveled four hundred miles, emptying right into the Atlantic, the fact that that's equivalent to twenty thousand Olympic swimming pools, sixty million planets, sixty million jellyfish, sixty million elephants, ♫ *The Stars and Stripes Forever* ♫, the fact that that happened a few years ago and it's *still* leaking into the ocean, leaking, leeching, spreading, leaching and spreading, and poisoning everything in its path, the fact that only nineteen people actually died, I think, initially, but eleven tons of fish were killed, and the land around is now contaminated for decades to come with arsenic, lead and mercury, State of

Public Calamity, *I'll hold her nozzle agin the bank till the last galoot's ashore*, the fact that *Bludso*'s ruined by the N-word, the fact that Leo said Vale or BHP Billiton had a tailing dam engineer look at the dam about a year before, and he found cracks all over and recommended building a buttress, but nobody knows if they did it or not, the fact that Leo thinks not, the fact that Leo says that engineer was the only guy standing in the way of that disaster, and Vale or BHP didn't listen to him, so now the whole area's a mess, Broken Hill, the fact that it sounds like the Dutch boy who saved Haarlem by putting his thumb in the dike, Olympic pool, the fact that some guy said his reason for killing his wife was because of taking too much cough medicine, the fact that *he* took too much, he didn't kill *her* for sneaking all the cough medicine, the fact that he claimed this cough medicine could cause psychopathic mood swings, the fact that I can't remember if my mucus-buster stuff listed psychopathic mood swings as one of the side effects, but probably, so maybe Leo got off lightly, the fact that a Cleveland woman called the fire department the other day saying she had a snake stuck on her face, the fact that it was a boa constrictor that she'd just rescued and it bit her on the nose and wouldn't let go, the fact that it wrapped itself round and round her throat too, the fact that they had to kill the snake to get its jaws open, embrace change, forever family, the fact that that woman owns two boa constrictors and nine pythons, the fact that that's a lotta *snakes*, Serpent Mound, the fact that there have been five hundred snake attacks in America in the last twenty years, the fact that a python can eat a *porcupine*, the fact that that sounds quite a mouthful, a whole porcupine in one gulp, the fact that owls eat a thousand mice a year, the fact that they swallow them whole too, and a crocodile can eat a shark, the fact that there are people in this country who attack the Sandy Hook families, and say the massacre never even *happened*, the fact that I just couldn't believe it when I first heard that, the fact that that is beyond despicable, the fact that that is, well, the fact that how could anyone be so cruel, to people who lost their children that way, the fact that there are five stages of genocide, or was it eight, or maybe ten, the fact that

I forget how many, but it starts with dehumanizing people, and moves on from there, mega, MAGA, MCLG, President Plays Boob Sincerely, the fact that Gillian eats cookie dough, cookie dough ice cream too, the fact that children develop their sweet tooth from breast milk, which is much sweeter than cow's milk, baby bottles, trainer cup, the fact that most playgrounds don't have bathrooms, which makes the two things kids like best, playing and peeing, kind of awkward, Primitive Playground Bathroom Setups, the fact that moms have to worry about this all the time, and search the world for restrooms wherever they go, finders keepers, the fact that one of the reasons *Fantastic Voyage* makes me uncomfortable is there doesn't seem to be a bathroom on board the Proteus, POTUS, at least as far as you can tell, maybe because the whole mission's only supposed to last an hour, the fact that I guess everyone on the crew is meant to have gone to the bathroom before they board the ship and get shrunk to the size of molecules, monocular device, like good boys and girls, but the trouble is you never know, the fact that something you had for lunch might disagree with you, like if it was pepper pot soup or something, or a cheese and onion bagel, the fact that when you gotta go you gotta go, and sometimes you really gotta go, especially kids and pregnant women, the fact that it's not so easy getting a kid out of a wet bathing suit in a hurry, the fact that another problem with that movie is, even if she is good-looking, do you really want Raquel Welch swimming through your *veins*, or the rest of that crowd, the fact that all four guys have to tear at Raquel's wetsuit when she's being choked by the antibodies, and I always think, couldn't *two* guys handle it, two at the most, but they all want to help out, the fact that it's strange you never find out if she and the CIA guy get together in the end, the fact that I guess you're just supposed to assume it's a done deal, the fact that they fall microscopically in love, the fact that they've bonded by being tiny together, and surviving Donald Pleasence's attempts to sabotage everything, but how romantic is that *really*, I mean, getting sent inside some stranger's body together, the fact that they end up standing on the corner of his eye, holding hands in waves of tears, "making memories," the fact that Donald Pleasence is English and lacks the American can-do attitude, always saying doom-laden things like "We're not going to make it to the carotid artery in time," when in fact everything works out pretty much according to plan, and would've gone even better if he hadn't kept monkeying with the equipment, the fact that I can never remember the name of that other movie Donald Pleasence is in, the black-and-white one where they're all stuck in a lighthouse, the fact that they're just wandering around on the mud flats somewhere, looking bewildered, the fact that it was kind of depressing but it had a nice feel to it, accolades, apologist, encomium, eulogy, panegyric, the fact that I wish some microscopic people would take care of my sore *ear* for me, the fact that it is *still* blocked up after my Big Cold, though my hearing's never been all that great, the fact that they took out my tonsils when I was a kid, supposedly to improve my hearing, and my adenoids, but I don't think it helped, or if it did, I never noticed, Trader Joe's, Whole Foods, stand-off, Phoebe and Chas, loft, Sullivan Street, bookshelves, floorboards, cats, glass table, hi-fi, B&H, the fact that they used to take everybody's tonsils out in those days, the *doctors*, not Chas and Phoebe, and I think that's why I get such bad colds, because I've got no tonsils or adenoids to protect me, nostrils, grommets, styptic sticks, wicks, fix, tricks, jinx, high jinx, ♫ *Moonlight Sonata* ♫, the fact that I think I'll have to get it *syringed*, strep throat, tonsillectomy, appendectomy, Jiminy Cricket, the fact that I like Bette Davis's party dress in *All About Eve*, the fact that you can substitute oil for butter in almost any recipe, but it's hard to know how much oil to use, the fact that you just have to experiment, the fact that fanouropita cake uses only olive oil, no butter, seven or nine ingredients, Social Security Number, password, username, the fact that it seems a miracle that Leo and I got together, a miracle we found each other, Old Lyme, lemon juice, Raymond E. Baldwin Bridge, covered bridges, the freshets of 1832, fanouropita cake, the fact that maybe everybody feels that way about how they got together, the fact that maybe even bald eagles feel that, the fact that it was a Greek colleague of Leo's who first told me about fanouropita cake, the PTA's Annual

Cake Auction, the fact that it's much better than that milkless, butterless Middle-Eastern lemon cake I made once, as an experiment, the fact that it feels almost *illegal* to cook something Middle-Eastern these days, but luckily nobody arrested me for it, handcuffs, Reading Gaol, Peolia, Shirley, surely, the fact that you cut two lemons into very thin slices and you boil the lemon slices twice, and sieve them twice, discarding the water each time, the fact that then you add sugar, turmeric and saffron, a *lot* of saffron, and new water again, ♫ *Liebestraum* ♫, and you boil it all up into a syrup with the lemon slices, the fact that it took *twelve minutes* to thicken, not eight like they said, the fact that recipes are often so inaccurate, the fact that I think sometimes chefs leave out a few crucial elements, to make sure you'll never make the dish as well as they can, the fact that maybe I'm paranoid, so suspicious, heavens, nurdles, Babar, Sandy Hook, the fact that then you beat up the cake batter, which is made of semolina, ground almonds, eggs, a bit of baking powder, and more saffron and turmeric, underpants, flour and milk, timetable, public restrooms, the fact that then you line the base of the cake pan with wax paper, Teflon, DuPont, suffering cows, and lay down on the kitchen floor and sob your heart out, no, the fact that you lay down a thin layer of the boiled lemon slices in the lined cake pan, and then pour in a bit of the syrup, and then the batter, and you bake the thing until it's golden-brown, the fact that then, as soon as it comes out, you pour the rest of the syrup over it, velveteen, corduroy, the fact that then you let it sit for twenty minutes, and then you flip it over, so all the lemon slices are visible, high five, flipside, and you present this exotic creation to your family, who all dig in, and it's at that precise moment you realize it's really a pretty boring cake with nothing going for it, just *sugar*, almost completely flavorless, and too sweet even for the kids, deep snow outside Abby's place, twilight, the fact that that Middle-Eastern lemon cake was moist to the point of sogginess, the fact that I ended up having to whip up some sour cream frosting quick, just to counteract the sugariness a bit, the fact that where did all the *lemon* taste get to, the fact that that's what I wanna know, the fact that what it needed is a thick layer of unripe paw-paw pulp, but the kids wouldn't have gone much for that either, the fact that what kid wants a big wad of paw-paw pulp on top of their soggy cake, the fact that, Middle-Eastern or not, that cake needed something, the fact that it was a little embarrassing, after all that work, waste of time, La-Z-Boy, the fact that my only real discovery from that whole culinary dead end, Coffins Court, the Culinary Institute, was that lemon peel can eventually be made edible, *eventually*, or soft anyway, if it's thrice-boiled, but who really wants to thrice-boil lemon peel all day, I mean *who*, lemon peel, martini with a twist, the fact that nobody has that much free time, even stay-at-home moms and thrice-boiled Hollywood stars, the fact that I think some crucial ingredient was lost in the translation, thrice-boiled, the fact that Jake now eats hard-boiled eggs, if I take out the yolk and slice the white part into circles, the fact that I think he thinks they're calamari rings, the fact that we celebrated our survival of the flood by going out to eat, the fact that Leo had spaghetti with meatballs, Stacy got penne piccante, and Ben had his usual prosciutto-stuffed chicken, the fact that sometimes he gets chicken Kiev instead, the fact that I don't know why an Italian restaurant serves chicken Kiev but they do, Russian interference, the fact that Kiev's in Ukraine though, not Russia, six hundred billion chickens, the fact that Grandma's family came from Ukraine, the fact that they were driven out by the pogroms, pogrom, program, property, props, propaganda, five stages of, thrice-boiled, the fact that Gillian always orders a child-size Margherita pizza, and I got the child-size eggplant parmigiana, because it was one of Mommy's specialties, but I could barely eat half of it, the fact that it's so rich, the fact that you can order a great big pan of lasagne for everybody to share, or spaghetti Bolognese or pasta al forno or mani-cotti or whatever, but what's the point of that, the fact that that's like eating at home, the fact that the whole reason to go out is so everybody can order whatever they personally happen to feel like for a change, the fact that I always like seeing how different everybody's tastes are, consumerism, the fact that we always end up taking doggy bags home though, because they stuff you with garlic bread first and the family-size green salad, the fact that I hollowed out a hole in the middle of Jake's salad and plucked out the middle section of a piece of garlic bread for him and he ate it all, the fact that he always used to say he hated garlic bread, the fact that I think if I'd been born Italian, I'd do nothing but eat, the fact that when I was a kid and we went to Fanny's, I always got too full, the fact that I wish I could make spaghetti sauce like that, the fact that they really nailed it, and their salad dressing too, the fact that the salads arrived first, so I never really had any room for my spaghetti, which always frustrated me, the fact that America's now full of people who've mastered eating everything on their plates, with spectacular results sometimes, pie-eating contests, the fact that what's wrong with leftovers, the fact that I love doggy bags, because I don't have to worry about the next few meals, the fact that I hope *my* pies aren't ever used for pie-eating contests, the fact that once I ordered apple pie at a diner and it never came so I asked about it and they explained it was being heated in the *oven*, not a microwave, and a few minutes later *two* pieces arrived, which was kind of embarrassing, the fact that it was all my fault for asking about it, the fact that the second waiter seemed to think I'd ordered a *second* piece of pie, the fact that actually I still don't get how that happened, the fact that *everybody* got confused, the fact that they went out of business later, not the diner, *Fanny's* in Evanston, or maybe they still make that sauce and you can order it by mail, Fanny's Mail Order Service, male order, chronological order, thrice-boiled, but I don't *want* spaghetti sauce by mail, the fact that I can make my own, even if it's not as good as Fanny's, the fact that the freezer's full of the stuff, Melania twirling platinum jewelry on a fork like it's spaghetti, and we've still got all our doggy bags sitting in the fridge, the fact that I don't like to mention "doggy bags" too much in public, the fact that I'm always scared people will think I mean the other kind, the kind for poop-scooping, the fact that the best French fries are supposed to be thrice-*fried*, but I've never had one,

When so tired she could no longer step safely, the lion hid herself for sleep, and dreamt her infants were on fire. She dreamt she tore them from the innards of a boar. She dreamt of familiar bodies of waters monstrously swelling forth to snatch her young.

In one dream, she thirstily entered a noisy river to drink. The water looked rounded, like the ridge of a hill. By drinking, though, she lowered the water level and it flattened out again. She splashed along upstream against the current, catching iridescent fish to feed her cubs.

She woke from this, cold and hungry, only to find herself on the same unfinished quest to find the cubs. This mode of life was unnatural to her. Previously, each day had offered a new chance of triumph, easy kills, unbidden moments of peace. But now, day after day passed without any relief from anxiety. The quest for meat was only an after-thought, subsumed by the search. It pained her to think about this one hard thing for days on end, but it pained her more to be without her young.

As birds made their evening uproar, agreeing the day was done, the lioness rose from her brief rest. She crossed shallow creeks with a single leap, and wound her way up hillsides, down through valleys and into swamps, slowing only to listen for cubs, or to scan the landscape for movement. She called to the cubs, waited, and tore on.

She thought of human highways as rivers, and used them now at night without concern. Darting on to a deserted road, she would pause in the middle, considering, then continue cross-country. She leapt state boundaries erected in the minds of men a hundred years before. From Pennsylvania to West Virginia to Kentucky and back into Ohio she trotted, spiraling, ever narrowing the circle, closing in on something. She was obedient only to a sense of where her babies were.

She passed through National Parks, school playgrounds, past plain low human habitations shaped in ignorance of the value of privacy and leafy protection from sun and wind. She dozed atop ancient Indian mounds. She knew nothing of the ways in which men divided themselves and this innocent land. They thought it all belonged to them, but they were wrong.

It was her land.

.　　　.　　　.　　　.

the fact that I ate too much toast while reading about Jane Fonda's pride in handing her father his Oscar for *On Golden Pond*, the fact that *I* like *The Grapes of Wrath*, the fact that that must be his best movie, that and *The Lady Eve*, but Barbara Stanwyck's the star of that one, the fact that all Henry Fonda has to do really is look dumb, which he seems pretty good at, the fact that *12 Angry Men* is kind of corny, but I still like it, the fact that Henry Fonda *walks* so strangely though, the fact that he walks like an *old man*, circling around and around the table where the jury's deliberating, but he's not that old yet, the fact that the thing is he leans back too far, the fact that it makes you think he might fall over, kind of like a pregnant woman's walk, a heavily pregnant woman, the fact that how is this my business, the fact that maybe he had a balance problem or something, the fact that he's still entitled to a *job*, the fact that everybody's always trying to swindle them or run them out of town, the family in *The Grapes of Wrath*, not the twelve angry men, the fact that Stacy's reading *The Grapes of Wrath* now, for school, and I've got Jane Fonda's new book to read, thanks to Cathy, the fact that that must be the longest title ever, the fact that it's funny she couldn't shave it down at all, *Prime Time: Love; Health; Sex; Fitness; Friendship; Spirit; Making the Most of All of Your Life*, which is a lot to cover, Ping, Pang, Pong, ping-pong, the fact that Ping, Pang and Pong are about the only thing she *doesn't* mention, the fact that I don't know about ping-pong either, *Turandot*, but penile pumps she's got, and Roger Vadim, Tom Hayden, and Ted Turner, hospices, assisted living facilities, hypertension, Houston, cholesterol, carotenoids, lutein, lycopene, toxins, trans fats, aerobics, anorexia, antioxidants, anxiety, grains, entropy, and zinc, the fact that she divides life up into three acts, like a theater play, and this book is about the *final* act, I guess,

631

when you start needing hospices and little blue pills, the fact that Jane Fonda's written all these books on how to be great, look great, feel great, the fact that it all sounds pretty effortful, the fact that it's because Leo's away that I have time to linger over my toast and Jane Fonda, though I'd much rather linger over *Leo*, the fact that he *hates* to travel, and we hate separations, but I guess we're used to them now, the fact that ever since we got together we've been parted again and again, the fact that I used to dread it but we have to put up with it, because he's needed everywhere, and he hates letting people down, the fact that Daddy was the same, the fact that Daddy liked Carr's water biscuits and Bath Olivers, with cheese or taramasalata, to go with a drink, the fact that Jake likes Bath Olivers too, even the packaging, because there's a big round biscuit with a circle around it, the fact that Stacy has a different theory about it, the fact that *she* says Jake likes the packet because Dr. Oliver looks like *me*, the fact that *I* don't think he looks like me, unless I press my nose flat, tunas trying to eat a bait ball of mackerels, the fact that I should make spanakopita again sometime, the fact that birds and fish inhabit kind of a *tall* world, while ours is more or less flat, horizontal, unless you live in a skyscraper or something, the fact that birds and fish have much more up-and-down space to move in than we do, swim bladder, the fact that it makes you dizzy looking at stuff like that mackerel ball spinning around, and all the tunas twisting and twirling, sea-sick, the fact that I'm no sailor, the fact that I'm always dreaming about missing trains and planes, the fact that this is what I dream about *half the time*, travel dreams, which is maybe why I dread Leo's trips so much, the fact that they do make me nervous, the fact that after he goes I always get this sinking feeling in the pit of my stomach, like I may never see him again, heart attack, broken heart, broken, the fact that he works too hard, the fact that I worry about him having a heart attack, or getting run over, far away from *me*, in case I won't be able to get to him fast, the fact that we try to make the most of being together on his pre-trip days, the fact that we are really both home-bodies, home, bodies, the fact that Leo's scared too that he'll die on a trip, the fact that he only seems to have to go about every two weeks now, which isn't as bad as it used to be, but the pattern's the same, the fact that three days before a trip, he starts fretting and sweating, and wishing he had an extra day to get ready, though he never *seems* to be getting ready at all, but he is, the fact that he always leaves his packing to the last possible moment, like 2:30 a.m. the day he has to go, and all day the day before, he complains of "torpor," the fact that closer to the departure time he gets all gloomy and wishes he could just stay here with me, the fact that he goes to bed but he can't sleep for fear of forgetting something, like his lectures or his wallet, or his toothbrush, the fact that he likes to take as little else as humanly possible, "I travel light," the fact that he always says he can buy whatever he needs when he gets wherever he's going, but I end up urging him at the last minute to at least take some shaving stuff, and a clean shirt and change of underwear, the fact that sure, it *sounds* great, traveling light, but do you really want to have to find a drugstore as soon as you arrive in a place, and try to find the same shaving cream you have at home, *and* shaving lotion, the fact that the last night is always pretty fraught, the fact that he was supposed to leave at 4:00 this morning, to catch the 7:00 a.m. flight, and he refused to pack yesterday, saying he could do it all at the last minute, the fact that he does like to cut things fine, not as fine as Ethan but pretty fine, the fact that Ethan gets to the airport at the last possible moment, the fact that I can remember him heading back to college after Christmas, leaving the house twenty minutes before the last possible train, the fact that maybe it's Ethan who's given me all the travel anxieties, plane crashes, the fact that after supper Leo said there was no point in going to bed since he had to get up at 2:30 to shave and pack, so we might as well stay up all night and watch movies or something, so we started *The Lady Eve* and he immediately conked out, leaving me lying there worrying about whether Leo would wake up in time to reach the airport and inevitably find himself in a gun rampage, men's slaughterhouse, the fact that I kept thinking if he misses his taxi and his flight and loses his job, we'll be broke and the kids will never go to college and even the chickens would probably slowly starve, the fact that just to take an ACT or SAT costs fifty dollars, the fact that it's pretty unlikely the chickens would starve, the fact that they're pretty good at getting what they need, assiduosity, abstemiosity, the fact that they'd probably outlive *us* if things got tight, the fact that I just lay there beside Leo like that for ages, worrying, and then I thought I might have left the stove on, but I still lay there, not wanting to disturb Leo's two little hours of sleep, because he has to *teach* today, the fact that because of all that I didn't sleep a wink, and when I finally roused him at about 2:45, he did grudgingly get up and start sleepily organizing himself, the fact that I felt so sorry for him, the fact that I felt *sick* with sympathy for him, so I offered to help him pack, or bring him coffee, or a madeleine or a sandwich or something, but he refused all assistance, gruffly ordering me out of his way, the fact that at one point he even told me not to *speak* to him, the fact that I would happily have just sat there silently, just keeping him company while he packed, but my presence seemed to bug him, "de trop," so I went away and just started on some pie preparations like peeling the apples, because I didn't know what else to do, to-do lists, but the suspense was unbearable, the fact that I think I did a load of laundry as well, the fact that they're better if they go a bit brown anyway, the *apples*, not the clothes, chemistry class in junior high, the fact that by 4:00 a.m., I was really getting worried about the taxi, and just hoping that he was ready, and *that* was when I heard him in the living room *clipping his nails*, the fact that he often seems to clip his nails at the oddest times, the fact that he was supposed to be in the taxi on his way to the *airport*, and he was clipping his nails, crown die-back, the fact that maybe he doesn't trim his nails until he knows he's otherwise all ready to go, and maybe the nail-trimming *relaxes* him or something, but it doesn't relax me, pumpkin patch jigsaw, "Madam, I'm Adam," *Adam's Rib*, Fanny Adams, terpenes, the fact that Leo's lecture today is on the Ashtabula railroad bridge, which collapsed in 1876 and ninety-two people died, just awful, awfulous, Henry Fonda, the fact that I really ought to do *Jake's* nails, snails, the fact that to my relief, the nail-clipping finally seemed to come to an end, and there was some thumping around in his study, the fact that I was about to go in and see how he was doing, but then the nail-clipping resumed, the fact that he must have moved on to his *toenails* or something, or maybe he was pruning the houseplants by then, snip-snip-snip, the fact that at that point I lost it and called the taxi company, without even asking him, since he'd *told* me not to speak to him, the fact that he hates checking up on taxis, in case they get offended and come even later out of spite, or not at all, the fact that I just couldn't resist this time, and I was wrong, because they acted really surprised and affronted that I'd called, and said the cab would be there any minute, the fact that then Leo at last quit with the nail-clipping and came into the kitchen and I told him the cab was coming and he said they were lying, and then we *both* sank into a torpor on the couch, the fact that you get so tired you don't know what's happening after a while, the fact that I always think of James Mason when I call the taxi company, James Mason in his old green cardigan, dispatching the drivers, or else James Mason trying to steer the Nautilus when he's *dying*, the fact that Leo could've taken *his* car but he hates leaving it at the airport to get snowed in or stolen or banged up, and it takes him a lot longer that way too, if he's gotta park, so it was beginning to look like *I'd* have to drive him, which would mean waking Stacy up quick and making her babysit, even though she'd hate me all day, hate me extra much, Waterlow Park with Mommy, the fact that I could've left her to sleep, and dressed all the little kids instead and bundled them into the car, but Leo'd probably still have missed his plane, the fact that it takes a while to dress kids when they're half-asleep, the fact that then the taxi arrived, which by then seemed sort of *incredible* to us, a miracle, because we were in such a state of hopelessness about it all, the fact that Leo must've half-hoped they wouldn't come and he'd just have to stay home after all, the fact that they came though, so he grimly trudged down the drive like he was about to face a firing squad, and I felt all choked up, and I think he did too, the fact that it's kind of exhausting, because these dramas happen once or twice a month when he's teaching at Emory and Philly, the fact that I've told him to give up all the traveling if it upsets him so much, Mommy's cigarettes, Mommy playing solitaire at the dining room table, solitaire, the fact that maybe he could work from home more, and I could try to make more pies, for what *that's* worth, the fact that if he could just delegate more, but he hates asking other overworked people to fill in for him, the fact that this is one of the reasons everybody *loves* Leo so, Topsy the Elephant, Annie, Berenice Fischer, Fisher-Price, hairband, high heels, bustle, muscle, fitness, *Prime Time: Love; Health; Sex; Fitness; Friendship; Spirit; Making the Most of All of Your Life*, Wo-He-Lo, the fact that then he gets home and the whole process begins again, sort of the same deal but in reverse, the fact that he arrives elated, pleased to have survived, and full of stories, and it's a great relief to have him home, the fact that the kids always get a little present, which may or may not have been purchased at the airport, but what do they care as long as a present arrives, the fact that we all get back into the groove together after being apart, and maybe watch a baseball game, my first experience of fondue, the fact that a backdoor cutter is something between a slider and a two-seam fastball, the fact that Leo's often in such a good mood though, the *first* day, he wants to stay up all night talking about the trip, and I'm usually too tired, having worn myself out being a single mom, marooned here for days without him, the fact that he does all his unpacking very cheerfully, and then the next day he sleeps it off, if he has the time, the fact that then in the evening maybe we have a martini or a screwdriver, or go out to eat Italian, but by the next day home, I can tell he's already starting to feel guilty about work, and his colleagues, the fact that he starts worrying how they're coping without him, and then he starts debating with himself about when he has to go back, and seems to forget all about how much he hates traveling, the fact that all this builds and builds until a moment of clarity arrives and he books the next trip, after which the dread, regret and reluctance start up again, Gold Star Families for Peace, Jake's Spiderman PJs, Midvale Speedway, the fact that his other lecture's on the Kinzua viaduct that got destroyed by a tornado in about thirty seconds, because of a shifting center of gravity, or something

like that, the fact that Leo sometimes has to deal with concrete overpass collapses too, and life expectancy, of *bridges*, not people, the fact
that he did a whole lecture on demolition errors in the Hopple Street
overpass in Cincinnati, Skagit River bridge, the fact that buckling
damage is cumulative, the fact that if just one part fails the whole
bridge will fail, functionally obsolete, stress fractures, the fact that *I*
feel functionally obsolete most of the time, Docs vs. Glocks case, the
fact that Leo complains about how local governments treat bridges as
"budget busters" and just never get around to *fixing* them, the Silver
Bridge collapse, stress crack, bearing loop, eyebar 330 on the Ohio
side, the fact that Leo says those eyebars were a bad idea from the
start, and there was an impurity in the steel, my stripy coffee cup,
fretting wear, extrude, exurb, the fact that Helen Gurley Brown said
you should never sit *above* a man, the fact that she was always trying
to make sure her head was literally lower than the man's head, whoever
she was with at the time, the fact that it sounds like something out of
The King and I or *All that Heaven Allows*, the types at the country club,
but even they might not have worried about whose head was higher
up, the fact that maybe Helen Gurley Brown was scared the guy would
see her double chin, or get too good a squint up her nose or something,
the fact that Katharine Hepburn used to sit at Spencer Tracy's feet,
while he mocked her New England accent, galoshes, nail-clipping,
eyebar 330, the fact that she and Jane Fonda didn't get along at all
well when they were making *On Golden Pond*, marooned mom, the
fact that I can't see Katharine Hepburn getting much of a kick out of
Jane Fonda somehow, or Jane Wyman, or Jayne Mansfield, James
Mason, James, Fresia, cleaning the house, the fact that Katharine
Hepburn's big moment is when she has to dive in the lake to save
Henry Fonda and the tricky grandson, the fact that she always liked
to swim, the fact that I forget if she does the crawl or not, probably
just the breast stroke, the fact that she's always talking about those
loons, a little too much, the fact that she also sings in that movie and
her singing is *atrocious*, excruciating, the fact that maybe she should've
dwelt a little less on the loons and a little more on how to belt out a

song, but I shouldn't say that, the fact that maybe the loons should have gotten the Oscar, just for being loons, the fact that they really are beautiful birds, with their long black heads and black beaks, and the black-and-white checkerboard back, black and white, black-and-white movies, Waterlow Park, black leaves, white sky, the fact that they look like stylish cushions from Neiman Marcus, daytime, nighttime, and it's just great the way they dive, the fact that they suddenly tuck their heads underwater and just surge forward like little submarines, hardly making a ripple on the surface, the fact that they're very unobtrusive, their black-and-white backs, DNR, the fact that where did I read that, sometimes, doctors don't know if you're really dead or *not*, when you're in a coma, but they want your organs so it's simpler just to declare you dead, death panels, NHS, the fact that sometimes people get better later and find out they've already been declared a "corpse," the fact that it's kind of like being buried alive, in an abstract sort of way, and it's a bureaucratic nightmare getting yourself reinstated as a living person, the fact that Katharine Hepburn was into eugenics, the fact that a major lightbulb has gone in the downstairs hallway and fixing it involves getting on a tall ladder, which Leo has forbidden me to do when I'm all on my own, the fact that I asked Stacy to help me yesterday but she keeps putting it off, the fact that if I break my neck fixing a lightbulb while Leo's gone, she'll have to babysit nonstop till he gets back, which she'd hate even more than helping me change a lightbulb, the fact that I can't help thinking all this would be easier if I was a bird or a fish and could just float around, up or down, no ladder required, zooming horizontally and vertically wherever I want to go, like in one of those sideways elevators, Otis, no, more like *flying*, the fact that we could seal all the cracks and doors and windows and fill the whole house with water, and wear wetsuits and oxygen tanks all the time and just swim around in here, swim from the kitchen to the bathroom, swim up the stairs like ghosts, the fact that I don't think the cats would like it though, and I guess it would be murder on the books, and computers, and other electrical items, the fact that fixing a lightbulb underwater actually sounds a good way to get *electrocuted*, Death Penalty, corpse, asking for trouble, "Trouble is my middle name," starfish jigsaw, the fact that the woman who invented the self-cleaning house still lives there herself, in Portland, Portland, *Oregon*, not Maine, the fact that she built it because she hates housework, the fact that I can sympathize, the fact that I don't think the self-cleaning house really solves that, though, because you still have to keep things *tidy*, the fact that the house can only *clean*, the fact that it can't sort through your old shoes for you, and gather up the dirty sheets, the fact that all her self-cleaning house really does is give everything a good rinse-down, a slosh-out, the fact that the whole place is jam-packed with nozzles and drains, so the sloshing can happen, the fact that it's a bit like the way they hose down the streets in Paris every morning, the fact that blasting things with water is pretty effective, the fact that she uses water and detergent, and it shoots out everyplace, the fact that it's probably not very ecological, that much water, and the detergent, mush, though it sure would be handy to have those nozzles, and just do it once a year or something, then dry the place out somehow, the fact that I bet her house is kind of damp, the fact that maybe her husband grumbled once too often about being sprayed with water and detergent, the fact that she kicked him out and now he lives in a trailer in the yard, the fact that it would be a good burglar deterrent, remote control water spouts, but I'd be worried about mice and dachshunds getting swept away in the flood, mudslide, deluge, dam bust, the fact that I suppose all *her* papers are efficiently tucked away in sandwich bags and Tupperware, bug-out bag, breakfast, the fact that Ben told me some birds eat three hundred caterpillars each a day, I forget which kind of bird, and he was worried their stomachs would be full of squirming caterpillars, like still *alive*, the fact that *he* was worried, but what about *me*, the fact that I'll be stuck thinking about those caterpillars all day now, the fact that maybe birds *like* the feeling of being stuffed full of squirming caterpillars, the fact that, I mean, who knows, the fact that I bet the chickens would be thrilled to get a few hundred caterpillars down their gullets, like Jake after a bowl of SpaghettiOs, the fact that they aren't fussy eaters, the fact that they don't exactly linger over a meal, savoring its delights, the fact that I bet Jane Fonda's a picky eater, the fact that I bet she only hires servants who are picky eaters too, bulimia, the fact that she's so tense about everything, het up about stuff, but she kind of goes along with things too, like plastic surgery, the fact that at one point in the movie, Katharine Hepburn tells Jane to stop dwelling on her unhappy childhood and get on with her own life, which sounds like pretty good advice for *most* daughters, including me, the fact that Jane Fonda's mother committed suicide when Jane was twelve, and Katharine Hepburn's brother committed suicide when *she* was about twelve, so they had that in common, bridge, the fact that Henry Fonda was hard on Jane, and Spencer Tracy was hard on Katharine, the fact that I would've *collapsed* if somebody I loved criticized me to my face like that, Golden Gate, the fact that Henry Fonda criticized other women too, like his suicidal wife, and Anne Bancroft, the fact that it seems like he was maybe not a nice man, in person, cold, maybe even vicious, the fact that he criticized Anne Bancroft for *crying* too much during some scene they were in together, the fact that I forget the movie, the fact that crying always disgusted him apparently, the fact that he made Jane think she was too fat, and she's been dieting and exercising pretty much ever since, and making everybody *else* do it too, the fact that I've got enough to do here without following the Jane Fonda workout, the fact that I never liked *Audrey* Hepburn much, only Katharine Hepburn, the fact that a lot of her movies are about older people in love, *The African Queen*, *Guess Who's Coming to Dinner*, *On Golden Pond*, *Desk Set*, but maybe *Bringing Up Baby*'s her best one, the fact that she never attended Oscar ceremonies, the fact that I wouldn't want to either, the fact that I don't know why *anybody* does, Mommy, the fact that *Persuasion*'s a very melancholy book, but *Mansfield Park* is more stressful, because of all the *traveling* Fanny has to do, the fact that some kids in Columbus got suspended for bringing guns into a class, and now everybody thinks the rest of the kids should be armed too, for their own safety, Columbine, Sandy Hook, the fact that soon second grade will all be about learning how to handle firearms, instead of how to hold a pen, my goodness, 9 mm hollow-point bullets, bullet harmonics, the fact that this is why Hadley's home-schooled, cyber school or something, which is why she has no friends, the fact that the parents' marriage is falling apart, so she's just stuck home all day with those loons, Captain Wentworth, the fact that whenever poor old Hadley shows up at some event, the other kids treat her like a deserter, because they have to live in a *war zone*, at school, and she doesn't, or so they think, though she does live in a small domestic war zone, the fact that they're all just trying to reach graduation day alive, but so is Hadley, the fact that Hadley's parents slap her, and she hits them right back, but what she really wants to do is lie in bed reading about the planets, the fact that I find that so hard to believe, they're such a nice family, apart from the religious fanaticism and all, mackerel bait ball, Nickel Mines massacre, the fact that I *pretend* to be coping, like all the other moms do too, but I think we all live in terror that some school shooter will line our kids up one day and make them beg for their lives, the fact that it's unbearable to think of your kids having to listen to some shooter approaching their classroom, shooting other people on the way there, barging in, shooting the teacher first and then the pupils, one by one, the fact that they might even have to wait while he reloads, the fact that Dylann Roof reloaded *five times* when he killed those people in the church, and a five-year-old child had to listen to that, the tiny thing, *Prime Time: Love; Health; Sex; Fitness; Friendship; Spirit; Making the Most of All of Your Life*, the fact that I think Jane Fonda would have gotten along well with Helen Gurley Brown, the fact that Helen Gurley Brown's recipe for success was to eat one yogurt a day and some yeast tablets and never relax, the fact that she cried a lot too, maybe because her dad died in a terrible elevator accident, mouseburgers, *Cosmopolitan*, the fact that how do you ever get over a thing like *that*, Otis, the fact that no wonder she wanted to sit at men's feet all the time and run *Cosmopolitan*, the fact that Jane Fonda's book is a lot like *Cosmopolitan*, the fact that it's all about sex in in old age, Act III, the fact that Cathy gave me a Joyce Carol Oates memoir to read too, and that's not much better, the fact that Joyce

Carol Oates hates pear trees, the fact that they tried farming pears when she was a kid, the fact that they had a whole pear orchard and everything, in New York State somewhere, and it was just a great big pain in the neck, because the pears would sort of ripen all at once, the fact that there's not a big window for pear-picking, the fact that you have to be ready for action because suddenly it's time to get them down, and in no time they'll be overripe, the fact that it's much easier to harvest apples than pears, Sherwood Anderson and his little shriveled, puckered apples, the fact that we often see signs by the road, "FREE PEARS," same with zucchini, the fact that people say don't leave your car window open around here in the summer, or when you get back it'll be floor-to-ceiling zucchini in there, ♫ *Rice-a-roni* ♫, Beefaroni, *Winesburg, Ohio*, a big window, the fact that Daddy used to lean out his window at Yale to pick plums or figs or whatever it was, the fact that Jane Fonda is not shy, and neither is Joyce Carol Oates, the fact that I'm shy, but Rosa Parks was shy too, the fact that being shy doesn't always mean you're a failure, the fact that being shy will either be a success or a failure, the fact that I don't know if *Claudette Colvin* was shy or not, maybe not, the fact that she did exactly what Rosa Parks did, but months *before* Rosa Parks did it, Inuit duck carved out of whalebone, the fact that people of color were expected to stand up so white people could sit, the fact that people can really pull some crazy, well, *stuff* on you of you're not careful, like the NAACP trying to get out of paying college athletes, the fact that I mean the *NCAA*, the fact that a shy Trump would be a *relief*, relief pitcher, pinch-hitter, Percy Sutton, one-run lead, a laser to the plate, the fact that maybe he'd be too shy to get us into World War Three, shy and retiring, the fact that there might not be a single loon left in the world when that guy's through with us, just a lot of crumbling, broken-down old Trump towers and golf courses, or maybe nothing at all except a few men with guns, the fact that he likes big game hunting, the fact that after a while you do get kind of sick of him and his first hundred days, "Step away, nothing to see here," the fact that he's already spent *millions* just flying around, from the White House to his other homes, with his whole entourage, Melania, the fact that *he* is the "zero," but I shouldn't say that, the fact that just because he calls everybody a zero doesn't mean *I* have to, but he *is* a zero, such a, a phony-baloney, not nice, not smart, the fact that, dear me, getting *angry* doesn't help anything, the fact that Woodrow Wilson's now reflecting the sun right in my eye but I can't do anything about it until I finish rolling out this cinnamon dough, dust particles in the air, Chock Full o' Nuts, stereoscopic vision, the fact that I thought there was something *wrong* with me when I was a kid because I could see two overlapping versions of things sometimes, and go cross-eyed if I wanted to, *Childhood Diseases*, the fact that it took me *years* to figure out everybody sees like that, and the same goes for dust motes, the fact that I didn't know if everybody else could see them or it was just me, the fact that how do *animals* figure this stuff out, VistaVision, Panavision, CinemaScope, the fact that Fukushima releases three hundred tons of radioactive waste into the Pacific every day, microplastics, the fact that Indiana has an ERPO law, the fact that as well as worrying about your kids getting shot and your husband being carjacked, you're now supposed to obsess about your baby bump, of all the silly, the fact that it's easy for some people to lose their baby bumps but not everybody's a will-o'-the-wisp, the will of the people, speaking truth to power, the fact that it's not fair to expect all women to be toned up and back in a bikini immediately after giving birth, but that's what Trump said to Melania after their son was born, the fact that what's his name, Tron or Thor or something, the fact that Trump could've given her some nice perfume or a horse or a car, cherry juice, but instead he gave her two weeks to lose the baby bump, the fact that what *is* his name, their son, maple syrup, Jourdon Anderson, Dayton, Ohio, the fact that she's everybody's favorite mom, Princess Kate, because she got rid of her baby bump fast, hermaphrodites, Hanoi Jane, the fact that I'm sure Melania did too though, the fact that Cathy says she hasn't gotten rid of her baby bump *yet* and Marcia's twenty-one now, the fact that the TV was on in the 7/11, and there were shots of people being thrown into the air by a bomb, and the cashier reached for the remote to get rid of

643

it, but a woman ahead of me said "Oh, don't turn it off, I *like* to see a whole bunch of people blown into the air," and I don't think she was kidding, the fact that she *meant* it, the fact that if I wasn't so shy I could've given her the ol' one-two, a fat lip, cement shoes, the fact that where does all this aggression come from, *mine* I mean, not hers, Cow Came Down, Cathy, rumor, gossip, the fact that I liked that little store with the banging screen door, the fact that I think it was in Montgomery, Alabama, when I was visiting Ethan there once, or was it Atlanta, the fact that some rival food store tried to spread a rumor Cathy was running a gambling den, of all things, out back behind the Shoppe, conspiracy theory, the fact that all she wants to do is sell people nice food and gifts and stuff, and somebody tries to sabotage her like that, trolls, the fact that they'll probably call Art a pedo next, pedalo, hey presto, the fact that people'll say *anything* these days, the fact that mortality's sort of gone out the window, along with all the overripe pears in the world, I mean *morality*'s gone down the, the fact that the next thing you know they'll somehow sabotage the hog maw and demand a ransom, *Bring fifty thousand in cash,* the fact that I hope they don't sabotage one of my *pies,* ill repute, the fact that she says she's not too worried, and it happens all the time, the fact that it seems like women always have to be worrying about *something,* either in the past or the present, or the future, the fact that it seems to me the future is absolutely terrifying, because you just *don't know* what's going to happen, not even ten minutes from now, *I don't know but they know,* the fact that we all just carry on as if everything's going to be okay, but we don't *know* that, the fact that you're just bumbling along and at any moment a flower pot could fall on your head and leave you in a wheelchair from then on, or you could just go blind for no reason, or the doctor could tell you you have a year to live, the fact that some-body just got Tasered for *jaywalking,* for Pete's sake, the fact that everybody does *that,* just everybody, the fact that they arrest black people now just for parking badly, like not quite lining their car up with the other cars right, the fact that so many things can go wrong, and *so* wrong, so many, the fact that you never know what's coming down the pike, life of the party, A Dad's Heart-Wrenching Moment, fiasco, Fresno, deductibles, industrial espionage, fried chicken and a country tune, a real chicken-and-egg situation, cup of coffee and a kind word, 5 Days of Unlimited Data, the luxurious handfeel of leather, "Rrrreally good!", soft shoe shuffle, ♫ *No more ifs or ands or buts, oh no* ♫, the fact that it's amazing we're not *crippled with dread* all the time, about what the future will bring, futures markets, Wall Street trading, T-Rex, fortune tellers, soothsayers, weather forecasters, the fact that sometimes I wish we were all chimpanzees, because maybe we'd relax more if we didn't think we were all so gosh darned important, the fact that maybe chimps think they're important though too, the fact that of course they do, the Ohio Department of Managed Health Care, mangled health care, the fact that chimpanzees probably live in the now, the fact that I'm beginning to think we're all too stuck on the present, just because it's right *here*, the fact that nobody looks *ahead* enough, the fact that it's kind of crazee if you think about it, the fact that people are gone on the past too, the fact that I don't know about chimpanzees, the fact that do *they* sit around reminiscing too, the fact that historians say we can learn from it, from the past, not a chimp, but there's a cost, because if you're like me, the past gets you down, the fact that meanwhile it's the *future* we should be worrying about, and I cling to the few certainties there are about it, the fact that some things are definite, like

the sun will rise and set every day
without fail
absolutely without fail
the moon will come and go too
though fewer and fewer people
including me
will understand its phases
bread will rise
children will grow
eBay will flourish
Facebook likewise

weeds will spread
tides will ebb and flow
hurricanes will hardly ever happen
except with global warming they might
and there will be less rain in Spain
mainly on the plain
flowers will bloom
leaves will still turn red in the autumn
one third of the population will get cancer
polar bears will go extinct
along with a lot of other animals
and it'll all be our fault
car design will evolve
Hunt's tomato sauce will see us through many a meal
Jane Fonda will improve herself
and write more and more books
explaining how we can all be
more and more like her
Leo will care about me
many people will find comfort in coupledom
others will split up
some will get divorced
more than once
men will kill their exes
some men
some women will shoot *their* exes
in imitation
people will continue to be attracted to people
or dogs
who look just like them
people will be judgmental
a few good movies will be made
a few good books written
and paintings painted

I just wish they'd quit with all that conceptual stuff
jellyfish will proliferate
and congregate
oil will run out
solar power won't
there will be reality
and virtual reality
the police will shoot citizens
for no reason
and Taser them
and Baker Act them
bakers will bake
women will get yeast infections
men will become gynecologists
men will try to strangle women from behind
wasps and bees will bug people
there will never be enough butterflies
or dragonflies
or mayflies
or fireflies
or hoverflies
or hummingbirds and cardinals
but there will be no end of mosquitoes
some mosquito bites will get infected
food will spoil
money will flow in and out
the government will collect taxes
presidents will come and go
we will all die
on and off we'll get indigestion
dust will gather
dust bunnies will hide under furniture
and multiply
drains will get blocked now and then

it'll be hard to get a plumber
we will buy certain essentials regularly
    toothpaste
    toothbrushes
    milk
    cheese
    butter
    paper towels
    bacon
    eggs
    ground beef from many lands
    parmesan
    flour
    powdered sugar
    salt
    pepper
    cinnamon
    thyme
    rosemary
    basil
    parsley
    too many bay leaves
    dill
    jam
    jelly
    peanut butter
    baked beans
    green beans
    peas
    lettuce
    carrots
    celery
    potatoes
    tomatoes

avocados
cucumbers
fruit
rice
noodles
SpaghettiOs
mayo
mustard
pickles
tea
coffee
honey
maple syrup
wine
whiskey
seltzer
OJ
ice cream
soap
toilet paper
newspapers
paper
books
magazines
catfood
fish food
sugar sprinkles
I will buy most of our groceries at Zyker's
but get my 59 lb pails of molasses from New Philadelphia
the pails will always be a tad sticky
the honey pails too
Jake and Gillian will lose all their baby teeth
the dentist will have to count them again
and again

the kids' shoes will wear out
my passport will expire in 2022
my hair will go gray
in our old age we might be robbed
or conned out of our savings by a conman
from Indiana
if we have any savings
which is unlikely
snow will fall
rain also
the Tuscarawas and Muskingum rivers will chug along
sorry remnants of their former selves
we will all waste food
even animals do that
car manufacture will take its toll on the environment
electric car manufacture also
though people will ignore it
because they have to have a car
we will have good dreams and bad dreams
there will be good and bad days
a stitch in time will save nine
a bird in the hand will still be worth two
in the bush
I will always sing badly
and whistle worse
I will long for privacy and solitude
calm
quiet
and companionship
I will long for Mommy and Abby
and Pepito
and Bathsheba
I will make faux pas
and open many a can of worms

I will say the wrong thing sometimes
mis-speak
and let the cat out of the bag
I will also let chickens in and out of the coop
and search for their eggs
or make the kids do it
eggs will be laid
or I'll know the reason why
I will clean the house
and make the beds
like an unpaid maid
or a slave
Leo will put up the storm windows
and take them down
and put up screens instead
I will cut his hair for him
he'll wash the fancy glasses in return
sometimes
Ben will study facts
many, many facts
we will send all four kids to college
if it kills us
I will never know exactly how all my pies taste
my eyesight will either get better or worse
my life will either be a success or a failure
my hands will get more and more wrinkled
then liver spots
Woody Allen will never quit making movies
lemons will rot in the fruit bowl
zucchini
if left to grow
will become huge
Shakespeare will be read less and less
civilization will be discontented

popsicles will melt
seesaws will squeak
jackdaws will speak
zigzags will zigzag
circles will circle
spirals will spiral
drones will drone
teens will snicker at things
take drugs
flip out
and ruin themselves
some coma patients will surface from comas
some won't
some people will make money
most won't
or not enough of it
philanthropists will give some money to charity
but not enough
misanthropists won't give any
bird flu and swine flu will terrify everybody
as will the NRA
fools will be born
every minute
pasta will reach the al dente stage
and then the soggy stage
socks will fall down
dogs will pull on leashes
half the world will menstruate
maybe get pregnant
then reach the menopause
and it will embarrass everybody
start-ups will start up
and close down
pop-ups will pop up

my lemon drizzle cakes will not fall
ever again
chickens worldwide will be slaughtered
at an unbelievable rate
millions a day
billions
pigs too
cows will be milked till they drop
bananas will be imported
and exported
spreading radioactivity
everywhere they go
bees will be exploited
nuts will slowly ripen on branches
olives too
Canadians will pursue outdoor activities
Like skiing and swimming and sailing and smiling
all the time
Anne will love Frederick Wentworth
Darcy will love Elizabeth Bennet
girls will get crushes on Colin Firth
DVD box sets will be issued
there will be more president movies
education will further disintegrate
but people will still graduate
male gynecologists for instance
moss will slowly inch its way
across stones near streams
ivy too
lady slipper orchids will appear
if conditions are favorable
cheap slippers will keep your feet warm
worms will worm around
Leo will enjoy Messiaen

the aurora borealis will bore me
stalactites will slowly form
stalagmites also
icicles will melt
politicians will express regret
in their memoirs
but not about the icicles
Open Carry guys will carry guns openly
Barbara Stanwyck will always be sexy
Julie Andrews will never be
I'm sorry
Christopher Plummer's eyes will remain sad
cats will lick themselves
and suckle kittens
people will make love
Leo will take planes
worrying me
and himself
bridges will fail
dams will break
we will catch colds
what little is left of the Ohio Canal
will disappear
cars will screech around our corner
birds will eat hundreds of caterpillars
a day
and there'll be nothing we can do about it
skin will get burnt in the sun
the kids will get cavities
despite fluoride in the water
I will worry about my kids
a lot
always
Stacy will do well in some field

babies will be born happy
toilets will flush
usually
aspirin will cure some types of pain
some drugs will have side effects
including death
trash will get collected
most of the time
some women will get raped and murdered
even if they try to protect themselves
anorexics will watch other people eat
with horror and fascination
a lot of people will do the 5-2 diet
and be irritable on Mondays
woodchucks will chuck wood
groundhogs, gophers, and prairie dogs
will live in holes in the ground
computers will get smaller and smaller
selfie videos will get more sophisticated
fires will start
whole towns and forests will burn
flood plains will flood
cliffs will erode
Californians will have water consumption problems
redwoods will fall over
the oceans will fill with
things made of plastic
nanoparticles
radioactive waste
the wrong kind of algae
people will sometimes get sick eating oysters
some people will wrongly call octopuses "octopi"
and misuse the word "enormity"
and mispronounce "February"

and "library"
some people will get closure
while other people internalize stuff
the new normal will be replaced
by a newer normal
dogs will be trained to sit
heel
give the paw
some will even be trained to tidy the house
some dogs will eat their peas
some dogs will eat anything
but chocolate will never be good for them
or raisins
or chocolate-covered raisins
chickens as yet unborn will love melon rinds
some cats will eat melon too
some cats will be good swimmers
wet clothes will dry
eventually
even without a dryer
grease will linger
if candle wax gets stuck to tablecloths
it will come off in the freezer
microbes will secretly prosper
as will fungi
bright yellow dog vomit slime mold
for example
otherwise known as scrambled egg slime
slime eels will produce slime
without shame
if stressed
wolf eels will be friendly
the strings on ukuleles will vibrate
but some people will decide to play

the bagpipes instead
or the harmonica
or the squeezebox
birthdays will be celebrated
asylum seekers will die seeking asylum
the fad for manicures will expand
or dwindle
ditto tattoos
quarries will run out of marble
and tungsten
people will be beheaded
Palmyra will never be the same again
people will insist on putting unsustainable palm oil
into everything
I will remain shy
people will want turkey and all the trimmings
for Thanksgiving
and Christmas
some will eat chitlins
Leo will eat pepper pot soup
whenever he can get it
made with tripe
and sometimes
pigs' tails
marsupials will carry their babies in pouches
birds will migrate
cows will come home
pigs won't fly
children will read *Babar*
and Laura Ingalls Wilder
and Maurice Sendak's *Nutshell Library*
and *Island of the Blue Dolphins*
veins and arteries will carry blood
hearts will pump

lungs will inflate and deflate
belly buttons will be innies or outies
people will wear bikinis
people who really should think twice about it
milk will sour
cheese will mature
companies will rake in the dough
polluting the Ohio River
the Mississippi
and the Gulf of Mexico
and affecting future generations
Frost's "The Road Not Taken"
will resonate across the land
the electronic world will be
a disaster for humanity
Leo says
because nothing is real anymore
people will always like fried chicken in a basket
including Ben
nails will grow
you will wait a long time for the bus
and then two'll come at once
there are going to be more mackerel skies
and clouds that look like Botticelli hair
or question marks
people will throw out
pink armchairs
children will learn the alphabet
for no real reason
and math
ditto
and hate gym
some people will give other people
the Silent Treatment

I will do more online jigsaw puzzles
white-tail deer will have white tails
a lot of people will want
beige interiors
and khaki pants
famous operas will be staged
Beethoven quartets will remain Beethoven quartets
emojis will multiply
children will roller-skate
the sky will often be blue
bees will buzz
my cinnamon rolls will generally be a hit
bureaucracy
will scare everybody
ditto authority figures
Ronny will bring us chicken feed
if I ask him
I will eventually have to give in
and offer him pie and coffee
plaster of Paris will get strangely hot
before it sets
children in art classes
will have to be warned about it
hairs will grow in all the wrong places
sarcasm will sometimes fall flat
satire won't change anything
I will drink whiskey sours
screwdrivers
and martinis
when possible
we will either get fatter
or thinner
kids will sometimes get lice
but I hope not our kids

Jake will get occasional earaches
our pets will grow old
before our eyes
all our window frames will fall apart
maybe soon
dogs will continue scampering after balls
to the end of time
or run around excitedly in circles
dogs will love people
really *love* them
and master
a certain amount of English
we will all remember the wrong stuff
not what we want to remember
all of history will continue
to have happened
there will be sightings of fish
in river shadows
trout will face upstream
waiting for food
there will be Indian Mud Runs
there will be tectonic activity
but probably not in Ohio
the earth will not ram itself into the sun
during our lifetimes
neither will Pluto
if aliens come
they will never stop laughing
at our sci-fi movies
they will never let it drop
Mommy and Daddy will continue
to have first met
on a blind date
in the Copley Plaza Hotel

Oscars will be awarded
to the wrong movie
Oscar hosts will offend everybody
Americans will flock to Paris
and buy Eiffel Tower souvenirs
Statue of Liberty souvenirs
like erasers and turquoise foam-rubber crowns
will also sell well
9/11 survivors will find it hard to watch fireworks
co-pays for hospitalization will bankrupt families
boils will be lanced
for a price
goiters will eventually be removed
I guess
more beauty pageants will be held
despite objections
Jell-O will continue to both please and pain
depending on the person
Vaseline on a Q-Tip will help get stray eyelashes
out of eyes
Casablanca will always be a great movie
Oliver! will continue to be about
a little orphan boy
dental hygienists will remove plaque
in various ways
some good
some not so hot
people will misspell
"stationery"
and "their"
and "your"
and say "I"
when they mean "me"
and vice versa

free charity Christmas address labels
will remain popular
children will be used as slaves
and we'll all wear the clothes they make
pink cheeks will remain a must-have item
among Caucasian women
many men will have enviable eyelashes
stiletto heels will always be in fashion
it seems
cars will get flat tires
and if you're not young
and pretty
no one will help you
coinage may be subject to change
at any time
babies will scream
but probably not about coinage
bikes will get more and more
expensive
very few new pasta shapes will be invented
and some currently on offer will become obsolete
antimacassars and aspidistras and amaryllises
will exist
at least a while longer
the switch from Standard Time
to Daylight Saving Time
will annually confuse and annoy
everybody
and vice versa
pencil sharpeners will grow blunt
it will get harder and harder
to find a good pencil
magnifying glasses will magnify things
dishwashers will wash dishes

hand cream won't really work all that well
mosques will call Muslims to prayer
Trump will call Muslims bad names
there will be power cuts
food shortages
war
plague
pestilence
drought
poverty
maniacs
there will be boarlets
there will be berries
and sour cherries
and choke cherries
and sour cherry scarcities
a few orangutans will have a few rights
whales and elephants even fewer
light bulbs will fail
people will fall off ladders
porno pics will thrive
the spinal brain will perform certain functions
without you having to think much about it
which is fine
because
I need all the help I can get
some people will continue to claim that
"angel" fossils
prove something
mothers will sew or iron nametags
on children's clothes
or laboriously write their kids' names again and again
in indelible ink
I will continue to forget how to cook asparagus

every year
and have to relearn it
every summer
sausages will be mass-produced
sometimes they will cause botulism
but rarely
asparagus won't cause botulism
except if it's badly canned
it will always remain wise
to boil all home-canned and bottled vegetables
for fifteen or twenty minutes
before eating
the Chinese economy will fluctuate
cells will divide
cell phones will get lost
or crushed
or stolen
and more expensive
rainbows and lunar eclipses will occur
but most people won't even notice them
same with sundogs
we will need a new roof
eventually
occasionally I'll find a lucky penny
on the street
women will wear lipstick
people will be fond of each other
people will hurt each other
physically and emotionally
flames will be fanned
and doused
oil will be poured
on troubled waters
an apple without the cheese

will be like
a kiss without the squeeze
Sanditon will never be finished
cars will signal right and left
kids will play ball
there will be redheads
and chestnut mares
and marmalade cats
men will touchingly push babies
on swings
for hours
and let their daughters
sit on their laps
even at the great age of eleven
moms will change diapers
people will be worried and disappointed
by their mothers
who will nonetheless nourish
protect
and hug them
ugly buildings will be built
at great expense
there will be four seasons
and foursomes
and threesomes
Bill and Hillary will carry on
in their way
doing their thing
glass and plastic and cardboard
will get recycled
by law-abiding citizens
shoelaces will be tied
or people will trip on them
ankles will be sprained

wrists broken
tree roots tripped over
cigarettes smoked
picnics ruined
hands held
plants will grow and wither
nasturtiums will flower
so amiably
camp beds will smell damp
log cabins will slowly decay and crumble
many items of clothing will be striped
not just in prison
or polka-dotted
people will hurry me
up hills and stairs
and make me go
faster than I want to go
water will gurgle
so will stomachs
at the most embarrassing times
sunglasses will protect people's eyes
from sunlight
umbrellas will shelter people
from rain
ducks will have ducklings
dogs will have puppies
cats kittens
chickens chicks
swans cygnets
geese goslings
does fawns
bears cubs
boars boarlets
elephants elephantlets

giraffes girafflings
people will need bridges
patterns will appear in waves
and on sand
and in clouds
dandelion fairies will waft around
random shapes will sometimes resemble
human faces
there will be pockets of nighttime
in the daytime
most stores will open Sundays
airmail will *mean* airmail
the air will eventually not be fit to breathe
for anybody
not just asthmatics
water will not be fit to drink
there will be trembling
vomiting
sighing
crying
kissing
fishing
plowing
sowing
hoeing
reaping
weeping
kneeling
kneading
keening
kowtowing
ululating
genuflecting
but not so much hibernating going on

as you might imagine
there will be wine
women
and song
and eggnog
there will be chords
harmonics
drums
there will be people who train
to be opera singers
and bassoonists
there will be windy days
there will be misunderstandings
there will be days when I don't know what I'm doing
or why
there will be much envy of people with cottages
in Connecticut
or Martha's Vineyard
or Malibu
there will be appreciation of artists and composers
who are dead
acorns will fall
I will feel guilty
and embarrassed
and regretful
about everything
nudists will take all their clothes off
boules players will play boules
and drink beer
in the Place Dauphine
some boules players will only play boules
for the beer
church bells will ring out
all over Paris

the chefs at André Allard will keep roasting ducks
to the end of time
I hope
kids will like cotton candy
though in Jake's case only if you form it into an **O**
good pesto will be made from good basil
statues will get vandalized
or sat on by pigeons
Confederate statues will offend people
orange will never be my color
but blue will sometimes go with green
babies will somehow locate the nipple
drunks and toddlers
will find it hard to walk in a straight line
unexplained sirens will be heard
supermarkets will have special offers
but at the end of your life you'll wonder
if they were really so special after all
dialects will be lost
ditto languages
along with the art of lace-making
basketry
quilting
embroidery
traditional recipes
and probably pomanders
joggers will do stretching exercises
terrorists will terrorize
extremists will be extreme
shooters will shoot
rampagers will rampage
muggers will mug
burglars will burgle
bunglers will bungle

buglers will bugle
adulterers will adulterate
lawyers will argue cases
till they're blue in the faces
hunters will hunt
fishermen will fish
trawlermen will trawl
oil men will oil
whalers will whale
whales will wail
"Wales" will be pronounced differently from "whales"
by people in the know
Cape Cod will not be an island
for a while anyway
there will be more and more ceramic knives
sweaters and sweatshirts will remain useful autumn wear
moths will make holes in sweaters
mothballs will make them smell of mothballs
the earth will revolve
people will say "Beam me up, Scottie" a lot
for no apparent reason
just out of the blue
when the sun goes in
sunglasses will come off
my pies will be easily forgotten
but chocolate will remain in favor
and brownies
antiques will not fetch a dime at auction
we will be stuck with the wagon wheel
and the humpback trunks
tree trunks will grow a new ring every year
physicists will baffle everybody
topologists too
and economists

and those 3D hidden pictures
people will doggedly eat kale
but dogs won't
I will get tired
from standing up while cooking
balls will bounce
in the evenings
all over suburbia
people will still fly kites
if there's a good hill and some wind
Indian lands and sacred sites
will be desecrated
nice vacant lots
will be filled with ugly buildings
people will wait in line at gas stations
and polling stations
they will turn right at the corner
on a red light
and will feel they're safe in their cars
even when they're not
families will hide secrets
from each other
and paper over the cracks
people will take opiates
barbiturates
dangerous cold remedies
and plenty of Alka-Seltzer
the rom-com market will remain steady
some people will dress their little dogs up
in Santa outfits
no matter who tries to stop them
many meals will be late
the moon will glow
mirrors will mirror things

fireflies will blink
on and off
on and off
on and off
cardinals will be red
the dead will be dead
forever
grass will be green
violets blue
there will always be monkeys in the zoo,

.   .   .   .

They had been bathed, petted, bottle-fed, and locked up. Now the cubs huddled close to each other. They hadn't the heart to explore their new, square, hard-edged den.

Having lost their mother, they were lost themselves. They now ate and slept under the gaze of passing, cotton-candy-guzzling children. They were admired for their spots and stripes – the human interest in fur is hard to quench – and for their latent ferocity, made palatable by cuddliness.

But they were hers, each one a necessity, a joy. The lioness knew the direction in which to go, almost as if she could hear them from afar. She covered a lot of ground at night, a whole deracinated forest, junk yards, abandoned coal mines, landfill sites and mile-wide, earth-wrenched industrial wasteland. Distance was not the obstacle that fencing sometimes was.

Her kittens' needs overrode her reluctance to venture near men, or move beyond her accustomed lands. All her days she had kept her distance from men, with their guns and their stink, and their passion for killing. But now she would have to face them. Her duty only to her kits. For men had stolen them – there was no other way the cubs could have disappeared so completely and so fast.

Not scared of any animal, she regarded humans with particular defiance and contempt. They seemed forlorn in their flightlessness, curiously unsteady on their feet, and their noises jarred. There were limits to what her eardrums could stand. It gave her a headache just to be near them. She reveled in darkness, when human activity was less intrusive.

One night she snuck into a hangar full of cattle. She was attracted by the smell of milk, amid sourer smells that told of powerlessness and pain. But even defeated cows become unruly when they smell a lion in their midst. They yanked their chains, tore the tubes from their teats, and bellowed so determinedly that a grouchy man was soon yanking wide the doors and hollering at them.

The lioness dashed nimbly out the back without being spotted, and delicately made her way through a mound of tin cans, milk cartons, metallic and plastic artifacts, the now familiar detritus of people. They always left deposits in their wake, for other animals to trip over, examine, scavenge, or avoid.

She got her paw caught in a long strip of fold-out paper dolls, mass-produced out of string and cardboard; she trotted on, now trailing a row of little flat ladies from her hind leg. She skirted around a rotting brook full of dirty diapers, syringes, rags, old shoes, broken bottles, Coke cans, half-eaten sandwiches and paper cups, newspapers, moldy vegetables, squashed fruit, old chicken bones, the remains of a peanut butter caramel milkshake, old ice cream sandwiches, stinking packs of cooked meats and lasagne: human food and its wrappings, and other things indefinable.

No use to her. She was no hyena.

.   .   .   .

the fact that I found a wood pigeon's egg outside on the porch steps, short, tall, grande, venti, trenta, and wondered if I should try to incubate it in my bra, like Arabella in *Jude the Obscure*, but when I mentioned it to Leo he ordered me to put it back where I'd found it, in case I was coming between a mother wood pigeon and her egg, the fact that sometimes he lectures me like I'm one of his *students*, the fact that he made me feel so guilty about interfering with nature I did put the egg back on the porch as I'd found it, the fact that then, in the middle of the night, I started feeling guilty about that poor little egg left to languish out there and die of cold on the bare wood planks of the porch, the fact that by then I'd *invested* in the egg, I guess, or internalized it or something, the fact that its plight had impacted on me, the fact that I was attached to it anyway, and felt *responsible*, the fact that "responsible" is a funny word, the fact that so I got up in the middle of the night and put my coat on over my PJs and went out and retrieved the wood pigeon egg, the fact that this time I had a better idea, idear, and unlocked the coop so I could push the little egg under one of the chickens, the fact that I should have done that in the first place, though I was a little scared they might crush it, or reject it, and they may yet, the fact that it's not as small as a *wren's* egg but it's still pretty small, closer to a quail's egg, the fact that eggs are fascinating because they're so *perfect*, and mysterious, except when they go haywire because of some nutritional deficiency, or get old and weird, rotten egg smell, membranes, mucus, slime, slimes, tailings, viscous, viscosity, dry cleaning, the fact that I didn't really want to let that egg out of my sight, but it's probably in the best place it could be, the fact that I shouldn't worry really, the fact that the chickens'll usually sit on anything that even looks like an egg, like Jake's silly putty, that Milly dutifully incubated until it got all sort of melted and greasy and we had to put it in the fridge, before he could play with it again, the fact that Mommy called out "Ducky! Ducky!" to the ducks, and charged into the pond, but Abby saved her, the fact that Stacy jumped into the King's Ransome pool once without her water wings, and Abby almost had to save *her* too, the fact that Stacy and I were changing in the motel room, and she just ran out and jumped in the pool before I knew what was happening, the fact that she'd forgotten to put on her floaties, and sank much deeper than she expected, but she was fine, and managed to swim out by herself, no harm done, touch wood, count your blessings, rabbits' feet, the fact that she was already a pretty good swimmer luckily, but she still liked to wear her water wings, the fact that lots of children drown by slipping out of their water wings, and the parents don't notice, the fact that the parents think the kid's fine because they're wearing water wings, but they're *not*, the fact that Abby was no swimmer really, the fact that she just liked doing her arthritis exercises in the pool, or sitting in the hot tub, the fact that Stacy must have thought it was safe enough because Abby was already in the pool, but it wasn't really, the fact that Stacy had to save *herself*, and she was only about four, the fact that puddle-jumpers are better, better than water wings, because they don't come off, the fact that they wrap around the whole chest, inner tube problems, chickens, wood pigeon egg, the fact that Leo and Sally's iguana laid a whole pile of eggs in their bathtub in Arizona, the fact that they were infertile though, the fact that they *couldn't* have been fertilized because she was the only iguana for miles around, the fact that even if a male iguana had swum fifty miles, and hiked up the mountain, he still couldn't have found his way into that condo, the fact that the vet told Leo it's perfectly normal for an iguana to lay a great big pile of eggs like that, and you can *eat* them, the fact that the vet thought iguana eggs make good omelets, the fact that you can make an omelet for four out of a single ostrich egg too, but who wants to, the fact that Leo and Sally didn't feel like eating their pet iguana's eggs, the fact that that was not why they had her, the fact that Leo has no *idea* why they had her, the fact that Sally brought the iguana, the fact that her eggs probably weren't in top-notch condition anyway, the iguana's, not Sally's, after they'd been sitting in that 80° bathroom for a week, the fact that they were in the mountains of Arizona, in *winter*, snowed-in car, bears, trash, Native American reservations, and they were trying to keep her warm and damp, the iguana, not Sally, the fact that they kept the bathroom at tropical temperatures, and the iguana somehow got the idea of laying eggs in the bathtub, the fact that I always wonder how Leo and Sally ever took a bath if the tub was full of eggs, the fact that, also, the iguana was always ready to pounce on you, apparently, and they have sharp claws, the fact that Leo says he was pretty scared of her, the iguana, not Sally, but maybe both, the fact that they both sound pretty bad, the fact that Leo was always having to get out of bed at 4:30 in the morning to clear snow off Sally's car so she could get to her teaching job on the Indian reservation, London Bridge, Mommy, tunnels, craters, funnel cake, the fact that Arizona's no place for an iguana, the fact that the iguana would have been a lot happier in Mexico, and Leo would have been happier in Ohio, with *me*, not hanging out with that cold Sally in Arizona, I ♥ U, the fact that "cold Sally" sounds like some kind of Confederate cocktail, like a mint julep, maybe bourbon on the rocks with a sprig of pine, a pickled iguana egg, and a dash of Ajax, topped with a stick of dynamite, the fact that Leo and I had already *met* by then, at the museum, but he was still committed to Sally at the time, invested, attached, cowbirds, ovenbirds, embrace change, the fact that all we did was kiss on Orange Street and then he left and I didn't hear from him for a year, well, maybe the occasional email, the fact that it was a real *Casablanca* situation, except *Leo* was Ingrid Bergman and I was Humphrey Bogart, all alone and in despair, and Cold Sally was no leader of Czechoslovakia, the fact that he told me later that that second year in Arizona practically finished him off, the fact that it's cold out today, so cold, Evanston, diamond-shaped windows, the bee at Bread Loaf, euphoria, kitchen, Mommy, the fact that I dreamt I was tired from making omelets for a crowd, the fact that Emerson Street was the first street in Evanston to get electricity, the fact that it happened in 1893, old apples left hanging on the tree, pomanders, baby bump, the fact that there are refugee kids in Sweden who have Resignation Syndrome, the fact that a little Russian girl saw her dad beaten up and taken away, and then she lay in bed for a few days kicking at the wall, and then she stopped getting out of bed altogether, the fact that her dad was freed in the end and they escaped from Russia to Sweden, but the kid *still* just lies in bed and can't move or even eat, she's helpless, and she's been like that for twenty months, the fact that they say Resignation Syndrome's an extreme reaction to emotional trauma, the fact that people eventually snap out of it and they're okay, the fact that it happens when a child gives up hope, the fact that it's like a sort of *toxic* level of hopelessness, and it's not new, the fact that there were cases in the Nazi concentration camps too, the fact that kids probably *died* of it for thousands of years, but nobody knew why, or agreed on a name for it, the fact that kids only survive it now because they're fed by tube and massaged and all, Mommy as a baby, getting her arm massaged, the fact that this is what kids do when they completely give up, the fact that it must kill the mom to have to watch it, the fact that the greatest thing about kids is how they're born so hopeful and confident, and all you want to do is hunker down and take care of them but the world won't let you, the mound of iguana eggs, the fact that I had to go back to work at the museum a few months after Stace was born, and take care of Mommy and Daddy, the fact that I don't think I knew *what* I was doing, the fact that I neglected Mommy and Daddy for Stacy's sake, and neglected Stacy for Mommy and Daddy's sake, Bathsheba too, and then later I kind of neglected Stacy for *Leo's* sake, and then I neglected her some more for Ben's sake, and neglected Ben for Gillian's sake, and so it goes, monster mom, the fact that I've neglected everybody I ever loved, the fact that Jake, being the last, should've been safe from maternal neglect, but then I got *cancer*, the fact that I neglected Jake for *cancer's* sake, Tagalog, Resignation Syndrome, the fact that I've run out of excuses for neglecting everybody now, but I shouldn't talk like this, the fact that I don't want to spiral downwards today, the fact that Oprah wouldn't go for it at all, ♫ *Accentuate the positive, Eliminate the negative* ♫, the fact that post offices used to be grand affairs, like railroad stations, that old post card of the post office in Youngstown, ♫ *Don't mess with Mister In-Between* ♫, Russian emigrés, the fact that Daddy often groaned for no reason, the fact that he groaned like that all my life and he never told us why, though we'd ask him sometimes, the fact that fathers are very important in Verdi, like in *La traviata*, fatherhood, deadbeat dads, the fact that Verdi's wife and children died, the fact that *Rigoletto's* kind of scary, I mean, carrying your dead daughter around in a *sack* by *mistake*, the fact that things really don't get much worse than that, the fact that I don't think Oprah would approve of Verdi's dark side, the fact that she'd probably still have him on the show though, if she could get him, the fact that I wish Trump *could* hire Frederick Douglass, the fact that *Il trovatore* means the troubadour, the fact that Rodolfo's stern father though turns out to be kind of kindly in the end, kind, kindred, hind leg, kine, bovine, the fact that I mean *Alfredo's* father, in *La traviata*, not *Il trovatore*, the fact that, sure, Alfredo's dad's not into the whole Violetta thing *at first*, okay, but later he scolds Rodolfo for treating her badly, Alberto, *Alfredo* I mean, the fact that Mommy loved that opera, the fact that I associate *La traviata* with her, the fact that Stacy will probably associate me with *musicals*, even though I don't even like musicals, *State Fair*, hogs, hog maw, pork-rib stew in a crockpot, the fact that this is not too much of a cultured household really, what with our musicals and Morning Routine videos and my freak-outs and all our gosh darn papers every place, James's mom, though we do have OJ, the fact that we have plenty of OJ, *very* sophisticated, though it's not fresh, the fact that I like the opera and have spent my whole life trying to *avoid* musicals, but musicals on dvd are all we can afford now, the fact that I can't afford to take Stacy to the *Met* for Zeffirelli's *La bohème*, the fact that we hardly ever even get to hear the matinee radio broadcast, the fact that there's much too much Wagner sometimes, the fact that often at the start of the opera, I think about *The Apartment*, the fact that I don't know why but listening to the opera somehow makes me want to watch *The Apartment*, but there's never time for both, the fact that Saturdays are pretty busy around here, the fact that the Metropolitan Museum bought a stolen Greek vase for its collection, or got given it, and now they have to *return* it to Greece, Sotheby's, the fact that it turns out *most* auction houses sell a lot of stolen stuff, Jiminy Cricket, the fact that I dreamt I met a fisherman down the street who'd caught a salmon that had a whole trout in its mouth, the fact that it was a bit like one of those triple bird roasts, with a chicken and a guinea hen inside a turkey inside an ostrich and who knows what else, maybe a goose egg inside the chicken, and a truffle inside the goose egg, or a humble hazelnut for Captain Wentworth, "Here is a nut," the fact that he's right to compare Louisa Musgrove to a nut, Mommy always said, the fact that *she's* the nut, always flopping on people from a great height, the fact that Captain Wentworth's been so mean to Anne, you kind of hate him by this stage, the fact that he really acts like a bit of a louse at the beginning, the fact that he's so bitter, because Anne dumped him long ago, the fact that, still, things start looking up when he goes off on this whole hazelnut spiel, the fact that anybody who can love hazelnuts that much must be able to love Anne, the fact that you sort of know it's got to work out, because she needs a guy like this, who can wax lyrical about silly stuff, the fact that she needs some cheering up, poor Anne, culm dumps, Mommy, Merck & Co., Inc., Procter & Gamble, Prosper and Grumble, "I need that stuff from Chip's," the fact that Mommy liked *Persuasion*, the fact that we named *Frederick* after Captain Wentworth, the fact that here it is, right between Stace's *Running a Thousand Miles to Freedom* and Leo's *Highway Bridge Design*, books and papers everywhere, the hazelnut, hazelnut, the fact that I'll never find that bit, buckeyes, nutcracker, Graham crackers, crackers, cracker cops, the fact that, according to Ben, eight and a half billion tons of plastic has been produced world-wide since the fifties, and plastic production's still going up, not down, the fact that ninety-one percent of it never gets recycled either, the fact that a million plastic bottles are bought every day, worldwide, no, every *minute*, I think, and most of it ends up in the ocean, the fact that they say the weight of the eight and a half billion tons of plastic we have so far is equivalent to *one billion elephants*, but I think it's more likely two billion elephants, well, it depends if you're talking Asian or African, because the average Asian elephant weighs between six thousand and eleven thousand pounds, while an average African elephant weighs between eight thousand and fifteen thousand pounds, the fact that imagine the equivalent weight in chickens, zillions of 'em, the fact that anyway nobody's got a billion of *either* kind of elephant to weigh plastics against, since they've been hunted to extinction almost, the elephants, not the plastics, the fact that, also, there's just no *room* for a billion elephants, now that we've got so much plastic, BASF SE,

Zyklon B, hard plastic, the fact that there are only eight hundred mountain gorillas left in the *world*, the fact that people are always complaining about animals they don't like, "bad animals," like pigeons, bats, rats, raccoons, deer, squirrels, starlings and spiders, but soon there'll be nothing left but us, and *then* how'll they like it, only bad animals, humble hazelnuts, Auschwitz-Birkenau, little red house, little white house, Bunker I, Bunker II, the men's slaughterhouse, "Kill the ump!", cash on delivery, the Club of Rome, forty percent of, nematodes, cell phone, cellophane, cello, Mstislav Rostropovich, the fact that I used to think cellophane was better than cling film, for the environment I mean, but it turns out making cellophane is really bad for the workers, because of all the toxins released inside the factory, the fact that the cellophane-makers have strokes and all kinds of other terrible side effects, *including death*, CS_2, the fact that to make cellophane they dissolve cellulose from plants then treat it with CS_2 until it becomes this orange viscose stuff, and then they *extrude* this *viscose* into a vat of sulfuric acid and sodium sulfate, and that somehow turns it back into cellulose, and then after they do a few more terrifying-sounding things to it, people wrap fruit and flowers in it, and crackers and cigars and medications, the fact that viscose really is viscous, the fact that it's all sludgy when they're making it, like a big mud bath, or iron ore tailings, the fact that rayon factories are bad too, the fact that people and animals aren't supposed to go *near* rayon factories if they can help it, the fact that the FDA, no, the FTC fined a whole lot of stores like Sears and Kmart for selling clothes they claimed were 100% organic bamboo but they weren't, bamboo, rubber, the fact that everybody thinks bamboo fabrics are eco-friendly but the bamboo *process* isn't, the fact that they start out with rayon and release all kinds of toxins, and then they finally make some bamboo socks, the fact that soon there won't be anywhere safe to go on this planet, the fact that silverfish eat rayon, but I don't know if that's good or bad, for them, or us, the fact that animals eat all kinds of stuff now that they probably shouldn't, synthetic stuff, chemicals, not part of their natural diet, like mice eat telephone wires and albatrosses eat plastic bags, the fact that what we've done to animals, the fact that animals are changing sex now or something because of all the estrogen in the water and the oceans, and alligators can only produce females, transgender toilets, Jupiter's Red Spot Gets Taller, the fact that that is a permanent stain, "That's a permanent stain," the fact that most cacti are succulents but not all succulents are cacti, succulents, aloe, permanent *storm* I mean, not *stain*, the fact that Jupiter's got a permanent storm and the red spot's getting taller, the fact that meanwhile my sunken lemon drizzle cakes languish in the freezer, the fact that Stacy says the Club of Rome published *The Limits to Growth* in 1972 but nobody listened, but it's not my *fault*, the fact that I wasn't even *born* yet, the fact that I think that lets me off, and I certainly couldn't read yet, a long report like that, the fact that I don't read much *now*, the fact that they're preparing another paper on climate change for Trump, amorphophallus lilium, stink bomb, but *he* doesn't read either, so that seems a waste of time, toxic waste of time, animals, the fact that sperm counts are *half* what they were forty years ago, Chuck, Jesus of New Philadelphia, the fact that what is the matter with me today, *The Limits to Growth*, the fact that it looks like maybe California can just *ignore* Trump's ideas on the environment, the fact that maybe every state could go its own way, the fact that if only Ohio would, but they won't, the fact that I'm not on Facebook, the fact that long ago Stacy told me not to bother, the fact that I think it's because she doesn't want to have to be my Friend, or have me looking at her Facebook page, the fact that a Sikh woman on the subway in New York got yelled at by some complete stranger for no reason, the fact that first he started snarling at her for being on her cell phone, so she put it away, but then he kept on yelling, the fact that he kept saying she should go back to *Lebanon*, the fact that he actually said that, the fact that, well, what he actually said was get your *sit-me-down-upon* back to Lebanon, though he didn't put it quite that way, and he wouldn't stop saying it, again and again, get your sit-me-down-upon back to Lebanon, get your sit-me-down-upon back to Lebanon, the fact that, strangely enough, the woman *was* from Lebanon, only it's Lebanon, *Indiana*, go figure, factor in, ppb, the fact that people are always saying "no problem," when there are all these *problems*, like alligators, *There's a place in France where the alligators dance*, the fact that *here* it is, "'This nut,' he continued, with playful solemnity," the fact that I dreamt I managed to pull off a real Cary Grant stunt by climbing into Jan and Marty's penthouse apartment, *The Apartment*, the fact that their place was much higher in the dream, like forty floors up, really high, but some-how, by *hanging by one hand* from the roof and nudging a small window open with my *toes*, I slipped safely inside, the fact that the reason I executed this dare-devil stunt was all to avoid having to talk to people by the *elevators*, because I was feeling shy, the fact that I risked my life out of shyness, but it made sense at the time, the fact that once I was in their apartment though, I felt duty-bound to inform Jan and Marty that *burglars* might be able to crawl in the same way I did, and I didn't know how to tell them this without having to explain how *I'd* gotten in, which seemed a bit embarrassing, the fact that climbing around outside skyscrapers is kind of an extreme form of arrival, even in a dream, especially in slip-on shoes, and considering my usual fear of heights, *North by Northwest*, the fact that *Pepito* was scared of heights, the fact that he hated going over see-through bridges, or up an open-work staircase, the fact that I remember trying to encourage him to come with me up one once, and he was terrified, poor doggie, vertigo, banister, the fact that I used to dream about falling over the banister in our Evanston house, and landing in the stairwell, the Ferris wheel at Niagara Falls, the fact that I clung to my seat for dear life on that ferris wheel, but Stacy loved it, the fact that our Niagara trip was no honeymoon, no picnic either, the fact that it was just Stacy and me, on the run from Frank, the fact that the falls seemed just awful to me, awfulous, Niagara Falls I mean, the fact that it's much too huge, brook no dissent, bouillabaisse, reading the phone-book after Mommy got sick, the fact that tourists are always falling into Niagara Falls, just trying to take a good selfie, no problem, the fact that I don't know why every single person on earth has to take their own personal photo of every tourist site, the fact that after Frank jumped ship, we just drove and drove and eventually got to Niagara, so we got out of the car and stared at it, the fact that we weren't there long, the fact that we stayed one night at that motel full of honeymooners drinking champagne, the fact that all I remember is throwing French fries over the cliff edge, microplastics, the fact that my penthouse dream is out of date of course, since Jan and Marty broke up a year ago, and now Marty just speaks so *badly* of her, according to Leo, the fact that he doesn't call her Jan anymore, he uses the B-word instead, the fact that he calls *her* "The B——", *Jan*, the nicest, sweetest, the fact that I can't even begin to, to, tintinnabulum, Tintin, the fact that the other name he uses isn't very nice either, "The Snake," when all Jan did was try to help Marty with his coke addiction and all, the fact that instead of quitting, he steadily increased it to the point where he was getting high every day, while she was out working to pay their *mortgage* on the extravagant apartment he chose, the Manhattan elite, the fact that I think she's *still* paying off his credit card debts, even now, the fact that Marty was always very extravagant about clothes, the fact that he liked to be well dressed, the fact that he claimed he needed good suits to break into TV, the fact that Jan tried to reason with him, about the suits and the cocaine, the fact that for ten whole years she tried, and what did she get for it, the fact that she would come home from work to find him out cold on the patio, the fact that he's lucky he never fell *off*, the fact that now I wonder if *he* ever climbed in through their little bathroom window, coked to the gills, like out of bravado or something, *Coca-Colaed* to the gills, the fact that, you know, I wouldn't put it past him, the fact that a penthouse apartment is no place for an unsteady guy, the fact that so, after ten years of heartache, she left him, and now he acts like it was all her fault and accuses her of violence towards him, which is just silly, the fact that she's half his size, and not much of a physical threat to anybody, the fact that now he's cut himself off from anyone who won't agree to call her The B ——, anyone who says anything in her favor, the fact that *we're* getting the Silent Treatment, but that's fine with us, the fact that he acts like Ben griping about KFC, or like Trump, the fact that some men can really bear a grudge, the fact that they really hate to be left, separation anxiety, and some get quite childish about it, the fact that a guy in Arkansas just shot his parents, his girlfriend, and his girlfriend's parents, because she wouldn't go out with him anymore, the fact that it's funny because when they're younger, lots of men are commitmentphobes, but once they get committed, whoa, the fact that some woman just sort of joked around on Facebook about having some kind of midlife crisis, and the next day her husband took the kids off into the woods and stabbed them, and people blamed the *mom* afterwards, for writing that stuff on Facebook, the fact that sometimes it seems like the last thing people are going to do is admit that a man might do an inexcusable thing, the fact that they're all in denial about Trump too, the fact that everybody around here just thinks he's doing a fine job or something, while they get poorer and poorer, and angrier and angrier, the fact that I guess people just want to think the best of everybody, like even the guy who raped the eight-year-old girl, the fact that the girl's parents publicly *forgave* the rapist, so he got out of prison early and immediately raped a little *boy*, "like would you get over yourself?", the fact that why was it up to the parents to forgive the rapist anyway, the fact that *I* don't forgive him, the fact that I think it's up to the kid to do the forgiving, the *kids* I mean, not their parents, and the kids shouldn't be asked if they forgive him until they're adults, The Snake, barndominium, Bobby, the numbness of muted beings, the fact that Leo says maybe the reason Republicans hate big government so much is because they're so *bad* at it, the fact that he now thinks Trump will quit, since everything he tries gets thwarted, the fact that I'm scared he'll do something vindictive first, something unforgivable, like nuking some country out of grouchiness or sour grapes, or maybe he'd even nuke *America*, if we make him mad enough, the fact that a guy like that won't be satisfied until he's destroyed everything, the button, the football, Cassatt's sulky girl in the blue armchair, no problem, the fact that his new health bill got dropped before they even voted on it, ACA, the fact that people with Obamacare can rest easy for a while, except that some doctors won't *take* you if you've got Obamacare, which is pretty mean of them, the fact that, I mean, come *on*, guys, the fact that millions of people have no insurance at all, the fact that I don't know what *we'd* do without Leo's health plan, the fact that we'd be ruined, living in a trailer park somewhere, or a tent, or a *cave*, with our bug-out bags, the fact that my deaf ear turned out *not* to be ear wax or bad hearing, the fact that it was a very ancient *spitball*, maybe from Valentine's Day about thirty-five years ago, the fact that I remember a day everybody started shooting spitballs around, either in third grade or fourth grade, the fact that they found it during my ear-syringing, the fact that they all seemed delighted to find something other than ear wax in there, and the nurse even managed to unravel it, the fact that it said "I ♥ U," which they all thought was really funny and sweet, the fact that I might've thought so too if it hadn't been clogging up my *ear* for thirty-five years, Valentine's Day, Lincolnwood School, the fact that I admit I was sort of flattered, briefly, when the nurse read it out, but then I realized it could've just been an accident, the fact that just because it landed in my ear doesn't mean this spitball was necessarily meant for *me*, the fact that if the kids in my class were firing spitballs all over the place, I could've been hit by a spitball meant for anybody, the fact that it would be just my luck to carry *somebody else's spitball love note* around in my ear for thirty-five years, HI CUTY, BE MINE, ALL MINE, REAL LOVE, URS 4 EVER, LOL, YOU ROCK, the fact that, also, what are the chances of a spitball love note ever getting *read*, the fact that they must be pretty slim, at the best of times, because even if the spitter's lucky enough to hit his target, how many little girls really want to unfold a moist little message like that, covered in cooties, the fact that there was no signature, but I don't remember any of my classmates anyway, "Eeewwww!", spit, spittoon, the fact that they're all a blank to me now, except maybe Melanie, who taught me to like avocado, the fact that my oldest friends are Zdenka and Mandy, but they're both from New Haven, or Hamden, the fact that I think the nurse was a bit disappointed I couldn't identify my third grade admirer, the fact that why were we all so sure it happened in Evanston though, the fact that it could have been *any* time, or passing some other classroom at Lincolnwood, or just walking down the *street* somewhere, the fact that for all I know some kid stuck it in my ear recently, during one of the kids' slumber parties, the fact that it could have been one of *my* kids that did it, but I think I would've noticed if it had happened recently, the fact that it could have happened in the park the same day I got glass in my foot, the fact that that would be a perfect time to send a spitball into my ear, when I was distracted by my foot, running home to Mommy, milk, Animal Crackers, the fact that why was I running around barefoot anyway, *Barefoot in the Park*, the fact that usually we had Keds on, or flip flops, the fact that most of my real friends lived on Harrison Street, but none of them were in my class, the fact that maybe Amanda Nelson was, but we were never really friends, the fact that we just got together to compare Barbies now and then, and make me feel small, *A Candle in Her Room*, peanut butter and jelly sandwiches, old-fashioned see-through candy in a crystal candy bowl, taffy, Frango Mints, *Mrs. Piggle-Wiggle*, Fig Newtons, Johnny Carson, the fact that I wonder if any of us would recognize each other now, like if they made my whole third grade class sit down in our old seats right now and look at each other and our teacher, but looking the way we all were then, the fact that I can't remember my teacher's face, I can't, only her presence, and I spent a whole year in that woman's classroom, the fact that I don't even know her name, and she was a good teacher too, the fact that all I remember is the windowsill that went the length of the classroom, the fact that it was always covered with tadpoles and baby sunflowers and yogurt pots, the fact that the tadpoles got poured down the sink once by accident, when some kids were cleaning the tank, and our teacher got down on her hands and knees and unscrewed all the pipes under the sink and saved every single one of those tadpoles, the fact that I always thought that was swell, the fact that Mommy did too, the fact that actually it was kind of heroic, and so kind, the fact that I don't think she did it as a learning experience either, the fact that I think she did it because she herself couldn't stand the thought of all those little tadpoles dying that way, the fact that I can sort of remember my math teacher in New Haven, the fact that she had a big teased hairdo, the fact that I think we called her Mrs. M., pressure, inertias, specific volume, the fact that I liked *Mr. T.*, Mr. Tykszynsky, Huck Finn, the fact that he had a nice face, the fact that I do remember sitting at our wooden desks, in third or fourth grade, all playing recorders, the fact that the whole class was tooting away, sitting down, the fact that I remember that, the fact that you tried to rest the end of the recorder on the desktop, but it kept slipping, the fact that they were always telling us to blow our recorders more *quietly*, the fact that it now seems like they went *out of their way* to make music a drag, the fact that I don't know why they bothered trying to teach us the recorder anyway, the fact that we all hated it, and what a terrible din we must have made, the fact that when Suzuki kids play in huge groups, it seems to work, but not us and our recorders, unanimous, unilateral, unicorns, the fact that I liked the school library, the smell of it, textbooks, reference books, story books, *Island of the Blue Dolphins*, the fact that I would like to smell them again now, the fact that I always kind of liked libraries when I was a kid, and having a library card and all, the fact that that's your first important card, the fact that it was nice just to go somewhere so quiet once in a while, the fact that nobody even goes to the library anymore, just like the post office or the bank, the fact that everybody does everything online at home now, in private, inanimate, insubordinate, candidate, Kompromat, cinnamon, brown sugar, the fact that some schools don't even have libraries anymore, or if they do there aren't any books there, just computer stations, the fact that computers aren't the same as books, but nobody cares, the fact that computers don't smell good, the fact that I don't have a great sense of smell though, the fact that maybe some people *love* the smell of computers, the fact that I think my hearing's improved at least, since I got rid of the love note, sneeze, Cassini, the fact that "Cassini" sounds like a sneeze, I ♥ U, the fact that our school was right by a wood, and Phoebe and I used to bike there for picnics sometimes on weekends, oak trees, pine trees, desks, school library, lockers, tadpoles, Zyklon B,

7 Up, rayon, crayons, cyclones, earthquakes, frost quakes, cryoseisms, yeast, wavelength, zeitgeist, the fact that a ton is 2,000 pounds, elephants, candy corn, the fact that Melanie taught me to like avocados, and someone long ago blew a love note right into my ear, intentionally or not, projectile, project, Oprah, and I'll never know who sent that lovesick memo, the fact that you have to zest the orange before you squeeze it or you're sunk, you got it made in the shade, babe, the fact that I was kind of embarrassed to tell Leo he'd married, *and* had three children, with someone who'd been running around with a spitball in her ear for thirty-five years, but he didn't seem to mind, the fact that he showed no jealousy either, of my early admirer, the spitter, the fact that Leo's not the jealous type, MY GIRL, LOVE YA, PUPPY LOVE, YES DEAR, KISS ME, SWEET PEA, LET'S GET BUSY, beach balls, hot air balloons, inner tube, Lake Michigan, microplastics, Bath Olivers, Ritz, the fact that he merely asked me if I thought the number of ukuleles in music store windows accurately reflects the current level of interest in ukuleles, the fact that he'd been staring at Schiel's window display the whole time I was in getting my ear syringed, buckeyes, Frederick, the fact that I looked too and it does seem like the ukulele's making some sort of a comeback, the fact that they've got ukuleles in all colors, shapes, sizes, but maybe one was a gamelan, gambling man, or a dulcimer, the fact that it was hard to tell from the car, the fact that I don't mean gamelan, the fact that I think I mean a sitar or something, a tarawangsar, *tarawangsa*, dombura, gambus, Schiel's, *Sanditon*, rebab, rehab, yomp, A&I, chains, sprockets, pulleys, hubs, the fact that it is kind of hard to believe the ukulele's so popular, the fact that "ukulele" really sounds silly if you say it enough, but maybe no sillier than balalaika, which is sort of the same thing maybe, Mississippi, Minneapolis, Minnesota, the fact that now you set the orange syrup aside and it's time to roll out the dough, the fact that you sprinkle it with the dried cherries that have been soaking in the juice, 350° oven, the fact that how ever did I cope before I had my *kneader*, Nathan Milstein, the fact that for her first job after college Mommy had to teach at the University of Minnesota *in the winter*,

and she said they used tunnels to get to classes or the dorms or the cafeteria, and never went outside, the fact that that's all she ever said about the place, how she never went out, the fact that she was used to *Massachusetts* snow, not Minnesota snow, the fact that I did a school project on Minneapolis once, or was it Duluth, the fact that I still remember reading up on Minneapolis, or Duluth, in the encyclopedia in the school library, or was it the public library, the fact that Leo told me this morning that America has more shark attacks than any other place on earth, the fact that we lead the world in everything, he said, the fact that if you live in Florida, you're statistically more likely to be attacked by a shark than, but, heavens, where does it get you to know what is statistically more likely, the fact that finding out you're more likely to be hit by cars than lightning is no real comfort, the fact that isn't all this stuff *cumulative* anyway, the fact that, I mean, if you add up all the X-rays and plane rides and car crashes and shark attacks and lightning bolts, *plus* the carcinogens, it must get more and more statistically likely that *something* or other bad's going to happen to you, the fact that Leo said that at least being eaten by a shark is statistically *remarkable*, which gives it an edge over all the road deaths, the fact that at least if a shark eats you, you'll get a little write-up in the local paper, the fact that if you manage to get a selfie of yourself mid-bite, you might even make the national news, blinks, blanks, drunk driving, DUI, drunk in charge of a vehicle, mother vehicle, DEAR ONE, TXT ME, statistics, statics, the fact that are you statistically more likely to find yourself in a school shooting than being given Honorable Mention in a baby contest, or are they both equally unlikely, DNR, the fact that these events aren't mutually incompatible either, one doesn't rule out the other, but having been an award-winning baby will probably not protect you in a school shooting at all, maybe the opposite, the fact that hearing about somebody boast about their Honorable Mention might even *provoke* an attack, a rampage, dear me, the fact that I wonder if you're statistically more likely to eat one piece of toast than two, the fact that you're definitely more likely to nibble candy corn from the narrow end first, the fact that they've *proved* that, somehow, the fact that I wonder if you're statistically more likely to carry a love-note in your ear for thirty years that was meant for *somebody else*, or a love-note meant for you, Mr. T., charismatic, cataclysmic, the fact that it's trash that attracts sharks to the beaches, that delicious underwater smell of trash, the fact that I think it's really weird that fish can *smell* things, underwater, the fact that it's just impossible to imagine smelling underwater without choking, drowning, "Ducky! Ducky!", Jacques Cousteau, swimming to the bottom of the pool to fetch coins or pebbles, Stacy's water wings, the fact that I don't know why but I always connect shark attacks with Grandma not giving me a beer when it was 95° out, pelicans, "I'm just going to say one word to you, just one word... plastics," the fact that turtles get caught in plastic, the fact that the Amish like plastic stuff, well, we *all* do, the fact that *everything's* plastic now, the fact that Dustin Hoffman shoulda listened to that guy, the fact that if he'd gotten into plastics in 1968 or whatever, he'd be sitting pretty now, on a mound of plastic, Indian mounds, the fact that I mean a mound of *money*, the fact that the Amish have very little trash though, because they've been recycling for centuries, cycling, cyclic, citric, zest, zip and zest, Ziploc, the *Budget* newspaper, donation sheds, ambu-buses, barndominiums, the fact that I think it's just a crime to mishandle food, like to overcook a lobster, or a steak, or mushrooms, or even scrambled eggs, crime scene, criminal investigation, Miranda Rights, the fact that I *always* overcook cauliflower and broccoli and that's a crime too, the fact that it's so scary about Bobby and his mom, so *horrible*, the fact that Bobby was such a sweet little kid, the fact that the paper said his mom made goat cheese, the fact that luckily we didn't know them too well, but I shouldn't *say* that, nasty, nasturtiums, goat cheese, the fact that it's just that I don't want the kids to be too upset by this tragedy, the fact that I wonder what'll happen to the *goats* now, the fact that she was famous for that cheese, the fact that the killer guy lived in a barndominium somewhere out Steubenville way, the fact that Bobby was just *a little kid*, the fact that I didn't know what to say and all the kids were crying about it, the fact that it's

always a bad sign, when they need ambu-*buses*, the fact that that's
never good, the fact that the guy used an AR-15 semi-automatic, the
fact that I don't know why they tell you those things, the fact that it
just spreads the word for other people who might be planning on going
on their own killing spree, gives them ideas, the fact that I don't understand why guns like that are even for sale, the fact that I thought they
were for the military, the fact that the only restrictions seem to be on
handguns, the fact that when he dropped his AR-15, he *used* a handgun, the fact that this was a guy with a long history of killing animals
for fun, and other stuff like that, the fact that if there were just some
background checks or red-flag laws, he would've been flagged up,
ERPO, because the guy was always beating women up, DV, the fact
that he used to *waterboard* his ex-wife, she says, and once he set fire
to his *brother* and his brother's girlfriend, as they slept on the living
room floor at the parents' house, the fact that I guess it was after that
that they shoved him out into the barndominium, Melania's sky-blue
straitjacket for the Inauguration, the fact that he killed the family dog
too that night, the fact that the brother and his girlfriend survived, but
she's going to need a bunch of operations, like a tracheostomy, the fact
that she can't speak anymore, and she used have a job as a *radio
announcer*, the fact that he did time for that and then got out and lived
in the barndominium, until he decided last month to go to the store
and start shooting randomly at anybody in sight, women, children,
babies, the fact that he killed Bobby and his mom and a pregnant lady
and her unborn child, for no reason, Jekyll and Hyde type stuff, Cain
and Abel, John McCain, AR-15s, that sweet little Bobby, the fact that
I never knew his mom's name before, Cecilia, the fact that Connecticut
was the first state to bring in an ERPO law, the fact that it wasn't
because of Sandy Hook, the fact that they did that after a guy shot his
coworkers and then himself, at the Connecticut Lottery, the fact that
it wasn't because he'd lost the lottery or anything, the fact that he
worked there, the fact that he'd tried to kill *himself* before, which
would've been a better idea, the fact that somebody just ran into a
bank in Columbus and made six women lie on the floor and then shot

them all in the head, and then himself, costume jewelry, the fact that there, I just cut myself peeling apples and now I need a Band-Aid, but getting the Band-Aid on, one-handed, isn't so easy, the fact that you need two hands to get these darn things on, oh dear me, the fact that I couldn't sleep last night, the fact that I had to get up and read Zadok Cramer to calm down, the fact that I just seem so het up these days, in general, and I don't know *why*, the fact that Cathy says I should get a massage, but massages don't relax me at all, they make me tenser, the fact that there was a candlelit vigil for Bobby and everybody, over to Steubenville, but we couldn't make it on a school night, the fact that Ohio arrowheads date from five to ten thousand years ago, the fact that, ah, Gillian has helped me with the Band-Aid, the fact that that Gillian is a treasure, the fact that she's so kind and wise, for such a little kid, treasure trove, the fact that, in a state of equilibrium, force is zero, exclude, exude, exuberant, zest, the fact that maybe I just hate words starting in "ex", but I don't like that U sound either, extrude, the fact that I don't mind "explain" or "excellent" or "Excalibur" or "excelsior," so I guess it's the U sound that bugs me, styptic stick, the fact that tall trucks are always crashing into low bridges, the fact that people never seem to remember the height of their vehicle, vestibule, highway bridges, the fact that Leo says it's not good for a bridge to get rammed all the time, but truck drivers never seem to see warning signs, the fact that some trucks have twenty-eight tires, which really does seem a bit much, fourteen on each side, the fact that if we *all* had eight tires, you'd probably never get a flat tire, or not one that was so bad you had to stop by the side of the road and get frostbite and hypo-thermia, forklift, semi-trailer, cab, dump truck, tow truck, fire truck, flatbed, pickup, the fact that I think they should hang something over the highway, like a hundred or two hundred feet before you reach the bridge, something like those golf balls people hang in their garage so they know when the car's cleared the garage door, the fact that you could hang something lightweight and harmless like that over the highway, a string of rubber balls or something, and if he hears the balls hitting his truck, the driver has time to pull over before he bangs straight into the overpass, the fact that he could do a U-turn, the fact that I'm going to tell Leo my idea, the fact that we could patent my warning balls and buy our own *island*, like one of the ones in the Ohio that Zadok Cramer mentions, now where has that book gone, here, the fact that we could buy Brunot's Island, Crow's Island, Hog Island, Dead-man's Island, Mill Creek Island, Baker's Island, Belleville Island, Neasley's Cluster, Brown's Island, Beach Bottom Bar, Pike Island, Twin Islands, Wheeling Island, McMahon's or Bogg's Island, Long Reach or Peyton's Island, Williamson's Island, Pursley's Island, Wilson's Island, John Williamson's Island, Little Island, Bat Island, Rock of Antiquity, Three Brothers, Duvall's Island, Muskingum Island, James's Island, Hanging Rock, Blannerhasset's Island, Newberry Island, Mustaphy's Island, Goose Island, Eight Mile Island, Six Mile Island, Graham's Station, Kennedy's Bottom, Willow Island, Grape Island, Small Willow Island, Nine Mile Island, Eighteen Mile Island, Twelve Mile Island, Six Mile Island, Anderson's Ferry, Green River Islands, Red Bank Island, Drumond Island, Straight Island, Slim Island, Deadman Island, Willow Bar, Chamber's Bar, Brown's Island, Stevenson's Island, Battery Rock Bar, Trade Water Island, Cave-in-Rock Island, House of Nature, Hurricane Bars, Three Sisters, Stewart's Island, Big Cumberland Island, Dickey's Elbow, Tennessee Island, Little Chain of Rocks, Big Chain of Rocks, Cash Island, Tumbleston's Island, Wabash Island, Wabash Avenue in Chicago, Orange Street, "sweetheart," the fact that I think I'd like to live on Cave-in-Rock Island, unless it caved in on us, or Grape Island, which sounds fertile, Professor Newcomer, Spoon River Anthology, opodeldoc, Porter's Liniment Salve, the fact that Ben's researches are ranging far beyond the waterways of Ohio now, it looks like, well beyond *Star Wars* too, the fact that I found a bunch of *porno pics* on his laptop, and he's only *nine*, the fact that I wasn't even looking at the screen, the fact that I just saw he'd left it open and I was going to shut it down for him, but then these *pictures* caught my eye, the fact that they're like a Sears-Roebuck catalogue of bosoms, millions and millions of boobies, a *ton* of them, all laid out in a large grid so you can see about fifty

693

pairs *at once*, so you can *compare* them all, I guess, microscopic tits, teats, paps, tits, teats, jugs, the fact that they're all so teeny-weeny, the *pictures*, not the *bazongas*, alphabet noodles, the alphabet, *Star Wars* Stormtrooper, pirate, the fact that he must just be curious, Captain Phasma, the fact that it's natural, and I must not comment, the fact that I don't want to nip his little fantasy land in the bud or anything, the fact that I guess everyone on earth now looks at porno pictures except Leo and me, the fact that what I don't like about it is it's all so over-managed and organized, regimented almost, and everything's categorized by every known kink, the fact that I don't think sex acts should be classified and ranked like "first base" and "second base," Sex Act No. 1, Sex Act No. 2, Sex Act No. 33, the fact that it makes it less, less spontaneous, the fact that I hate how everything about sex and bodies has to be named, and graded, and labelled, or miniaturized and displayed in grid fashion, the fact that it's not very romantic, it's more sort of formulaic, the fact that it stops sex being *personal*, or profound or anything, the fact that they've turned it into a set of *chores*, painting by numbers, seal of approval, satisfaction guaranteed, the fact that that ain't love, that ain't even puppy love, the fact that I don't *think* Leo looks at porno pics, but most men do, the fact that I wonder if Marty looks at porno pics, or Chas, the fact that we were so innocent when I was a kid, just discovering things for ourselves, well, with the help of the occasional magazine found under the dad's side of the bed at a friend's house, that birthday party in Chicago, the fact that it was Chuck's *sister* who suggested we try oral sex, the fact that it hadn't occurred to us, the fact that we mainly just liked kissing, and fondling a bit, in the old church on Orange Street, the fact that now you have to do *everything immediately*, and do it like a *pro*, a professional, a prostitute, the fact that if you don't start by the age of ten, you're a slouch, the fact that she was a bit of a know-it-all, Chuck's big sister, the fact that I would never *dream* of telling a couple what sex acts they should try next, not in about a million, zillion vermilion years, red, white, blue, green, the fact that that was kinda weird of her, the fact that kids probably do it to each other all the time now though, *Marnie*, if they think somebody's not progressing fast enough on the sex front, egging each other on, over-egging the pudding, proof of the pudding, the fact that everybody at school felt pressured to get to third base, but now I can't even remember what third base is, heavy petting or going all the way or *what*, the fact that heavy petting was kind of a good invention, the fact that it must reduce pregnancy scares, the fact that the rules about dating seem to be back, like what you do on the first date, the second date, the fact that I bet people mix up second base with second *dates*, so by the fourth date you *gotta* go to bed together, or you'll throw all the numbering off, but what do *I* know about the current dating scene, the fact that Mandy told me some people now take a suitcase full of sex toys for the *first date*, my half-finished plastic model of a cardinal, the fact that some man threatened to do a mass shooting because he couldn't *get* a date, the fact that, hey, maybe nobody wanted to go out with you because you're a mass shooter, ever think of that, the fact that another guy met a woman through online dating and then just *shot* her, as soon as they met, the fact that some people don't even *want* to get to second base, Sears, the fact that things move so fast these days, the fact that the next thing you know, Ben will want to get married at the age of thirteen or some-thing, and then I'll have *grandchildren* to babysit, a seamless move from mom to grandma, the fact that Trump thinks he's the big expert on female beauty because he bought a beauty pageant once and pawed all the contestants, the fact that he judges every woman he meets from one to ten, just like a *teenager*, tenacious of life, balloon jigsaw, zigzag, connect the dots, Honorable Mention, nap, Mommy, euphoria, the fact that men act like it's their duty or something to look at all this porn, like it's their *job*, "Don't worry, I'm on the case," "Roger and out," the fact that they get up in the morning and look at porn, and go to their *actual* jobs and sneak in some more porn there, and then they go home and watch porno movies all night, the fact that what am I talking about, the fact that *I* don't know what most men do, and it's probably just as well, by the sound of things, the fact that I'd never say any of this to Leo, the fact that it would just make me sound bitter, but it does make me kinda mad sometimes, the fact that I get kinda crazee, the fact that all I know is sex used to be *important*, and *meaningful*, and yes, loving, and now it's all just rape and some sort of crash course, Sex 101, like birdwatching, the fact that while men are glued to their screens staring at anonymous body parts, I guess women are walking around pigeon-toed because Joan Collins told them to, I mean Joan Crawford, or else they're following instructions from Jane Fonda and Helen Gurley Brown on chair squats and Kegel exercises and sitting below men, the fact that where's this all *heading*, Holly Hunter, the fact that the sad thing is, sex must be so *disappointing* now for people, because they learnt it all from professionals in porno movies, and it's got nothing to do with actually liking somebody, the fact that the whole idea of taking it slow seems to be out the window, the fact that if Ben's looking at a million gazillion breasts at ten, no, *nine*, what'll be left for him to discover by the time he's *eleven*, the fact that I guess he'll move on to sit-me-down-upon sites, then the pussy sites, oh my, the mouth on me, and by the time he's twelve he'll have seen it all, and he'll have to develop something really kinky to make his searches more, more colorful, like astronomy porn, where you get to fondle nebulae, or black hole porn, spider phobia porn, pirate porn, ice cream sundae porn, volcanic eruption porn, the fact that he's already stuck on *info* porn, Leo's private name for Ben's researches, the fact that I could get into cheddar cheese log porn maybe, Party Provolone Rounds porn, Titipu, Poo-Poo Plate porn, the fact that maybe men just can't *help* it though, the fact that maybe they're drawn to pictures of naked gals out of *politeness* and compassion, the fact that maybe they're just trying to be *nice*, the fact that a guy sees a helpless naked girl lying there, looking beseechingly at him, and I'm sure he feels compelled to at least look back at her, codfish ball porn, china figurine porn, bee at Bread Loaf porn, Woodrow Wilson porn, the fact that they all seem to do it, the fact that Woodrow Wilson probably did it too, and I bet that's what Dr. Zhivago was really doing when he got up in the night to write those *Lara* poems, just looking at porno pics, the fact that Leonardo da Vinci too, the fact that he couldn't have painted *all* day, the fact that he probably spent a good portion of his time looking at porno pics, the fact that he even drew some himself, embrace change porn, no problem porn, the fact that Galileo probably had some porno pics up his sleeve too, the fact that, I mean, he'd *have* to, to get through all those years of house arrest, the fact that it was probably "a gal a day" for old Galileo, boobs, butts, the roundness of the earth, sun, planets, moons, pregnant bellies, Indian mounds, spiraling hurricanes, the fact that Galileo thought orbits were circular but they're actually ellipses, SpaghettiO porn, nurdle porn, the fact that Einstein too, the fact that he can't have been thinking about $E = mc^2$ all the time, the fact that he must've left some space for looking at girls, the fact that actually, to me, $E = mc^2$ seems more like a *contribution* than a life's work, but hey, that's me, aurora borealis porn, size of dust in the atmosphere porn, Newton's Third Law of porn, the fact that occasionally I kind of think that men could be doing something more *useful* with their time, besides comparing pole-dancers and all, a success or a failure, the fact that like they could be out chopping wood, or raising a barn, raising a *family*, or making chicken stock, or having a heart attack shoveling snow or something, but no, they seem set on the porno pics, the fact that half the world's drowning in porno pics, and the other half's watching Oprah and trying to be *positive* about things, the fact that, say what you want about Oprah, but at least she's not teaching everybody to disrespect *half the human race*, the fact that I just don't see how boys can look girls in the *eye*, after bombarding themselves with a whole load of porno pics, the fact that I don't know how *men* can talk to women either, after staring at our private parts all day, gyny guy, the fact that if I spent all day staring at photos of men's duodenums or aortas, I don't think I could have a normal conversation with a man after that, the fact that those aortas and duodenums would keep coming back on me, flashing at me, all squelchy, throbbing, pulsating, the fact that I'm none too good at having a normal conversation with people anyway of course, Jansson's Temptation porn, the fact that men have sullied themselves with porno pics, and sullied women too, and kind of made this not a fit world for women or children to be in, because where's the respect, the fact that maybe that's not why they do it though, the fact that maybe, you know, maybe men are just scared of being *alone*, or they feel insecure or something, so they instinctively look at porno pictures, just so they don't feel like they're putting all their eggs in one basket, like just in case their current squeeze *dies*, or dumps them, the fact that some men *have* to have a mistress or two on the side, or they get nervous, *The Limits to Growth*, The B——, The Snake, Scriabin, Smetana, Spinoza, the fact that so maybe it's understandable, though maybe a little over-cautious, the fact that I *always* put my eggs in one basket and it works just fine for *me*, the fact that, in my case, putting eggs in *separate* baskets would smack of overkill or paranoia, or incompetence, since the basket I use never seems to get too heavy or full or anything, the fact that even with back trouble and a Band-Aid on one finger, I still seem to manage to carry a full basket of eggs from the coop to the pantry without trouble, touch wood, no problem, whatevs, the fact that once we get the eggs indoors we do put them in separate *trays*, not baskets, to keep them well aired, "eggs in one basket," the fact that I do use more than one basket sometimes, if the *kids* are helping out, the fact that collecting eggs is one thing the kids all like doing, except Gillian sometimes objects to touching the eggs when they're still warm, the fact that these are good chickens we've got, the fact that poor *Bobby* liked our chickens, the one time he came over, the fact that he came for Gillian's birthday party one year, the fact that I liked that store called Eggsetera, where the eggs all had double yolks, but that was before I had chickens of my own, the fact that I still don't get how they make chickens lay the double-yolk eggs, egg foo yung, egg porn, "you're a good egg," the fact that turkeys only lay about a hundred and fifty eggs a year so nobody bothers keeping turkeys for their eggs, the fact that it's just not worth it, the fact that this must've saved turkeys from the horrors of turkey-egg factory farms, but not from Thanksgiving, the poor old things, the fact that certain kinds of duck are very generous on the egg front, so we've had them laboring from dawn to dusk for thousands of years along with chickens, just so we can bake cakes and meringues and quiche lorraine, the fact that girls are born with three or four hundred ova each, and they have to last them for life, porno pics or no porno pics, the fact that I don't know how many ova chickens are born with, the fact that reptiles produce a lot of eggs, well, Sally's iguana did, egg pile, Arizona, the fact that jellyfish produce *trillions* of eggs in a lifetime, the fact that I wonder what a jellyfish's lifespan *is*, a nostalgic jellyfish in a rocking chair, reminiscing, the fact that at least jellyfish don't have to miss their *moms* all their lives, because they never even met them, the fact that they might drift by each other once or twice, without knowing it, but that's it, jellyfish nostalgia, the fact that Gracia is seven years old and still laying, the fact that she should get an award, but even *she* couldn't hatch the little wood pigeon's egg, the fact that that didn't happen, the fact that it was probably already too late when I found it, too old, too cold, Cold Sally, don't count your chickens before they hatch, Basket Building, Chicken McNuggets, KFC, Big Bird, Chicken Licken, or is it Chicken *Little*, Henny Penny, Cocky Locky, Turkey Lurkey, Goosey Poosey, Ducky Lucky, "Ducky! Ducky!", the fact that I wish Leo and I had sex more, I do, but my libido's non-existent since I had cancer, the fact that it is hard to re-establish yourself as a *person* after that, and call your body your own, the fact that it's kind of hard to believe it's a friend, the fact that it doesn't even seem to belong to you after the doctors finish fooling with it, and it's kind of a jolt to find out you're *not* going to die after all, or not especially soon anyway, reprieve, depending on the stats, the fact that you have to readjust to thinking you have a future, and a life to think about, the fact that, also, my derrière has just never felt quite the same since the radiotherapy, the fact that things are very sensitive down there, the fact that the oncologist said that's normal but she didn't say how to *deal* with it, the fact that the gyny guy didn't say anything either, but what does *he* know, the fact that the whole bunch of them, the fact that I know they meant well, all the oncologists and the radiologists and the nurses, but there were times when all their activities make you feel like a pariah chicken being pecked in the butt by the other chickens, and it does not make you feel sexy, ♫ *I'm just a girl who can't say no* ♫, the fact that I shouldn't think this way, when all they did was *save* me after all, the fact that they saved my a—, the fact that I shouldn't call it that, nor my "butt," the fact that Mommy wouldn't like that word at all, or "boobs" or everything else I come out with these days, the fact that I just don't know what to call stuff anymore, Sweet'N Low, the fact that I never even believed they were hitting the right spot, I mean with the radiotherapy, but then they calmly showed me one day all their charts plotting the exact position of the beams in relation to my poor little sit-me-down-upon, and it did look very precise, the fact that anyway it must've worked, because here I am, able to kvetch about the whole experience, eggsetera, eggsetera, eggsetera, the fact that Leo says he's still interested in sex, but I'm a mother of four, a homemaker, and a piemaker, and I'm always bushed, the fact that I've been tired all my life, the fact that maybe I have chronic fatigue syndrome, the fact that when I do have any excess energy, I like to spend it being regretful and embarrassed, monster-mom, motorhome, motormouth, the fact that no, I miss sex so much, I really do, and regret how we've lost our way with it a bit, but, butt, the fact that it's kind of hard to loosen up with a houseful of kids barging in on you all day and night with all their tummy upsets and near-fatal accidents and squabbles and elephant imitations and info porn, chock-a-block, chockful, Chock Full o' Nuts porn, shock jock porn, shock tactics, double chocolate chip, peanut brittle, saline wound wash, Neosporin porn, the fact that I feel like, heavens to Betsy, like the only way I could ever really feel sexy again at this point is if our kids all went to boarding school somewhere, or were at least out of the house for several consecutive days a week, the fact that that would be like a second honeymoon, just without the duck and olives, Musée Cluny, déshabillée, Niagara, Paterson, Cathy's pear tarte tatin, the fact that we could have martinis and sit around listening to jazz and I could feed Leo strawberries by hand with black pepper, on the strawberries, not my hands, and we could christen every room in the house, and the ottoman, and all the other things we sometimes talk about, the fact that unfortunately nobody ever takes your kids away for several consecutive days, unless you send them to summer camp where they'll all be *killed*, the fact that we can't ask any favors from Phoebe or Nanya or some other mom around here, the fact that we just have *too many kids*, "Done because we are too menny," the fact that as you brew so you must bake, the fact that it's just too much to ask, you can't ask, the fact that Ethan's got his own kids to deal with, the fact that I could never ask *Phoebe*, the fact that she's busy, and she has to teach, the fact that she's done enough for us, she's done plenty, the fact that she probably *would* take Stace on her own sometime, but that wouldn't solve the bigger problem, the fact that Phoebe and Stacy have always gotten along, summer camp, loosing off arrows, skeet shooting, the fact that maybe everyone in the world now feels doomed, so we peck each other in the butt all day, cloaca, butt, butt pad, but I shouldn't say such things or even think them, cloaca, chicken cacciatore, the fact that I should be looking out for *cardinals*, the fact that you should treat any gun as if it's loaded even if you know it's not, the fact that what's the kind Ronny's got, a Browning Recoilless shotgun, or that's *one* of the guns he owns anyway, the fact that he has about twenty, get Ben's dirty laundry, the fact that that was a tall man who just went by, short brown hair, military look, the fact that I'm always practicing storing salient features, just in case the police ever ask me to identify a suspect, blue-black clothing, white trainers, big Reebok duffle bag on his left shoulder, party tray of objects, the fact that you don't want to be the kind of witness that can only say "He was just sort of funny-lookin'," birth mark on the left thigh, piano hammers, cardinals, the fact that it's rare to see people on foot around here, the fact that everybody's always in their car, the fact that in fifty years' time the internal combustion engine will be kaput, Leo says, the fact that *look* at this stuff, the fact that I don't know why Ben keeps all these posters on his wall, the poor kid, the fact that he must be trying to memorize all the constellations *and* all the state flags, in between memorizing every type of bosom there is, on his laptop, but why, the fact that at least he doesn't have the bosoms of the world on his wall, so far, the fact that he could print it out, Bosoms of the World, the fact that if there is a poster of that, I bet Trump's got a copy in the Oval Office, right behind the automatic Executive-Order-generating machine, Executive-Order-generating porn, the fact that Ohio's flag is the only state flag that isn't a rectangle, the fact that we've got a *swallow-tail* flag, a burgee, the fact that somebody at Annin in Coshocton claimed Annin made the Iwo Jima flag but it was Mabel something who made it, in California somewhere, the fact that he claimed they made the flag on the moon too, but maybe that was Mabel as well, the fact that they make 35,000 flags a week there in Annin, which must beat Mabel's production rate, Nyl-Glo, the fact that Iwo Jima was trapezoid, planetoid mass, Saturday Mass, the fact that Mabel Sauvageau was her name, the fact that she made hers out of wool but now they usually just make them in heavy-duty nylon, the fact that there are specifications about flag pole heights, depending on the size of flag you buy, the fact that Ben told me that, the fact that the old confederate emblem is still part of the Mississippi flag, the fact that it takes up one whole corner of it, the fact that Mississippi's the only state that still has that on its flag, and some top Mississippi judge tore the flag down in his courtroom, calling it despicable, pennant, penance, the fact that their flag was repealed in 1906 but they seem to be having terrible trouble getting rid of it, so they still have these flags on their government buildings and probably their houses too, the fact that people around here fly the stars and stripes like they just conquered the area, like it's the North Pole or something, one or more flag per home, the fact that it's okay for the Fourth of July and all but doing it all year round I think is kind of *militaristic*, "The Stars and Stripes Forever," the fact that the flag must never touch the ground, retirement ceremony, the fact that, boy, most of the state flags are pretty boring, the fact that I think they should just use their state birds and plants and things on all these flags, the fact that Louisiana's has a pelican and her babies though, and the Alaska one's pretty, ♫ *Follow the drinking gourd* ♫, Polaris, dog star, dogwood, the fact that the second brightest star in Ursa Major is called Dubhe, Dubya, ♫ *plop... top... swap* ♫, the fact that

Wyoming's got a buffalo, and California has that bear, South Carolina, Wyoming, New Mexico's, Orry-Kelly, sampan, rotund mountains, "Are you evil?", Suffrage Victory banner, WILSON IS AGAINST WOMEN, antibiotic gel, the fact that two hundred years ago, when Fanny Trollope was here, the Ohio River was beautifully clear, the fact that the Tuscarawas River feeds the Muskingum River that feeds the Ohio River that feeds the Mississippi, and every last little lake, river, stream, creek, brook, pool, pond or puddle in Ohio that feeds the Ohio, is *polluted*, Confederate flags, the fact that Fanny Trollope wasn't so keen on Ohio's malarial swamps, the fact that just south of here there are still plenty of marshy areas, the Big Slough, but there's no malaria anymore at least, the fact that they found some West Nile fever mosquitoes not so long ago, and we'll probably get Zika next, but malaria's been eradicated, Alpha Ursae Majoris, the fact that you're much more likely to be shot by an Open Carry guy than catch malaria, statistically, the fact that diseases didn't seem to faze Fanny, even though she was traveling with her kids, the fact that she really seems brave as all get out, the fact that what bothered her most was that there were no *tea parties*, and she didn't go for all the spitting, the fact that she couldn't stand how Americans spat all the time, spittoon, spitball, the fact that Cincinnati was already a dump in 1828, the fact that she says everybody in Cincinnati just left their trash out in the street to be scavenged by wild pigs, the fact that that doesn't sound such a bad system to me, but there are no wild pigs around anymore, the fact that they're gone, along with the clear water, all gone, the fact that Fanny felt Cincinnati lacked *domes*, and she recommended adding a few castles along the banks of the Ohio, Chateau de Cincy, Schloss Steubenville, Marietta Mansion, Higginsport Hoosegow, ♫ *The man who broke the bank at Monte Carlo* ♫, the fact that Fanny got in trouble for saying American men spat all the time, but they still do, a bit, the fact that why would she make *that* up, I ♥ U, the fact that she came over more than once, the fact that the first time, it was to make money, and get away from her husband, the fact that she was also grieving for a son who had just passed away, the fact that those trips of hers paid off though, because she wrote popular books about them, the fact that she saved the family by writing those books about the Mississippi and spitting, her novels too, but I haven't read any, the fact that eventually she was supporting her whole family and not on *pies*, the fact that you *can't* save your family with pies, no matter how many you flip, ♫ *Anything you can do I can do better* ♫, the fact that I wonder if *Anthony* Trollope ever knew what a great mom he had, the fact that I've never read any of his novels, the fact that there seem to be too many of them, the fact that Mommy liked some long saga they adapted for TV, euphoria, uxorious, Leo, the fact that most people don't know what to do with fresh fruit because they've forgotten how to make pies and jam, Zika, the fact that Mommy and I both had a crush on Dr. DeBoer, the fact that he was so kind and handsome, the fact that it was Dr. Rappaport though who first discovered my heart defect, the fact that I was two, the fact that they waited to see if I'd grow out of it, the fact that they were also waiting for me to get strong enough for a heart operation, the fact that they waited six more years but by then the hole had grown from the size of a dime to a quarter, and they decided to operate, the fact that there must have been a nickel stage too, in between the dime and the quarter, but I was never told when that happened, Vale mines, the fact that I was producing my own coinage there for a while, like Mary Queen of Scots, the fact that I got tired easily, the habits of a lifetime, habit, nun, the fact that this is why I can't face cocktail parties, and long walks or bike rides tucker me out, even scooter trips to the playground, nervous pudding, gravel pie, floating island, Mommy, madeleine disaster, dry cleaning bill, another lightbulb problem, the fact that I live a pretty isolated life, and when I do see people I make terrible faux pas, either forgetting their names or mispronouncing them, even people I *know*, the fact that if I haven't seen them for a while, I get out of practice, the fact that it seems like I always put my foot in it somehow, tit, cock, cloaca, the fact that I shouldn't be allowed out really, the fact that I am a walking disaster waiting to happen, Tuesday, the fact that Tuesday is the hardest day, the fact that Mondays are a breeze compared to Tuesdays, the fact that those clouds look very dense and dark, the fact that for some reason they make me think of death, the fact that they look like snow clouds or tornado clouds, but we're not expecting snow, and I've never seen a tornado, Anton Pohlmann's chickens, the fact that we had tornado drills at school, which I liked, and sometimes it gets dark and clammy out and you're supposed to stay in and keep one window open so the house won't implode, but we've never had an actual tornado, Hiroshima, hummingbirds, purple martins, spiders, bumble bees, MYOB, BYOB, the fact that there were so many hummingbirds in that garden where Leo and I met, the fact that they stopped you in your tracks, the fact that they made it necessary to fall in love, just before a rainstorm, the fact that the sky got dark just like this, the fact that there were always hummingbirds there, in that garden, the fact that Leo first kissed me walking up Orange Street, the fact that I have led a pretty shark-free, tornado-free, hurricane-free, cyclone-free, volcano-free, war-free, bomb-free, plane-crash-free, gun-rampage-free, rape-free, murder-free, electrocution-free existence so far, touch wood, the fact that I *was* in that bus accident on Lake Shore Drive, but I wasn't *hurt*, Art Institute guy jabbing me in the back, the fact that blizzards don't really count because they're just temporary hassles, hazards, not usually threats to life and limb, existence, "existential threats," *limb*, the fact that blizzards aren't that bad unless you're all alone on the highway somewhere, the fact that I've seen a *derecho* and golf-ball-size hailstones, scrapple, Snapple, saltwater taffy, salsify, the Piggly Wiggly, the Pillsbury Doughboy, Jolly Green Giant, Minute Maid, Maid of the Mist, Land O' Lakes, the fact that I made a naked snowwoman in Abby's front yard, and then I went to Fort Lauderdale to see Grandma, the fact that Abby got a big kick out of my snow-woman, because it startled the mailman, Abby, whiskey and ginger, Triscuits, Saltines, Nabisco, Hoag, grilled cheese sandwiches, the fact that I liked that sunny slushy walk to the grocery store from Abby's house, the fact that it was a good outing, and nice to be out all on my own, with the white snow and blue snow shadows, black tree trunks, the fact that Abby never walked much, the fact that a community bus picked her up three times a week though and took her to the Y for the aquabatics class, the fact that she liked marching in the water with her friends, the fact that Hoag was always at work, the fact that he worked all day almost every single day of his life, the fact that he quit his job once, after an argument with his boss about something or other, and Mommy was worried about it and said he'd been rash, but he found a new job soon, the fact that it didn't take him long at all, maybe a month, the fact that he was a very reliable breadwinner, the fact that Mommy said he'd lost his pension or some of it by quitting that way, but they were okay, I think, despite all the healthcare costs, with one big health crisis after another, scoliosis, arthritis, knee replacements, the fact that I still wonder what Hoag quit over, because he never seemed to mind anything much, the fact that he was so easy-going, and he was no quitter, so something pretty bad must've happened, the fact that I never really got the story out of Abby, the fact that she did her own thing all day, and then Hoag would come home, right on time, and they'd have supper, and then he'd go watch the game on TV, whatever game was on, in the den, the fact that he was an equable sort of guy, abstemiosity, the fact that I think he was just content, the fact that Hoag used to drive Abby to church every Friday or Saturday, whenever it was she went to Mass, not Sundays for some reason, never Sundays, for some reason, "Where was Sunday?", the fact that maybe she was trying to avoid somebody who went to church on Sundays, or she liked the priest on Saturdays better, pepper pot soup, potlatch, pot luck, *way down yonder in the paw-paw patch*, mud run, the fact that I just found a page from another careers questionnaire, the fact that Stacy left it in the printer tray, the fact that I don't know who she's planning to send this to, the careers advisor at school or what, the fact that, heck, she, she wants to leave school *this summer*, and move to *Arizona*, somewhere remote, she says, and she needs a job, of all the, the fact that she says she could deliver *milk*, or work in a grocery store, or bake *pies*, my word, the fact that Stace thinks she can bake pies, huh, the fact that, well, I guess she's watched enough of them being made, and everybody boasts a bit on forms, the fact that I don't mind

that, but she is not *leaving school*, the fact that maybe she could get a
paper route *here* if she wants to earn some money, the fact that what
am I going to say to her, the fact that did she want me to find this, the
fact that did she leave it here deliberately, just to scare me, the fact
that now I have a *papercut*, for Pete's sake, *Arizona*, the fact that does
everybody I love have to go to Arizona, the fact that I know moms
should be vigilant, but not snoop, but I bet other mothers sneak around
in their kids' stuff much more than I do, the fact that I don't snoop
very well, because I'm such a bad actress, the fact that now I'm going
to have to pretend I never saw this questionnaire, *and* Ben's porno pics,
sheesh, the fact that this is going to be tough, the fact that Arizona of
all places, Ronald Reagan, Ronald McDonald, Diamond Jim Brady,
Brandy Alexander, the fact that Ben has his own career in *VR* all
mapped out, but first he wants to go to some VR theme park in Utah,
the fact that the way he says "VR" now makes him sound sort of
hypnotized, like he's in *love* with it or something, in a trance,
entranced, the fact that when I acted skeptical, he pointed out to me
that VR has some health benefits, because they use it on kids with
50% burns, the fact that they put VR headsets on them so the kids
can play VR games while they're having their bandages changed, and
as a result their pain levels drop to 30% or something like that, the fact
that there are children with 50% burns, the fact that I had to sit down
when he started talking about that, 50% burns, Linus Pauling, Albert
Einstein, mass = density × volume, the fact that I dreamt I came back
here after a long time away, and all the cats in the neighborhood
seemed surprised and pleased to see me, the fact that they acted like
I'd once *owned* them but I didn't remember any of them, which was
kind of sad, and then I dreamt about an unpaid grocery store bill, and
woke up worried about it, even though we don't have any outstanding
grocery bills, the fact that no store around here would give me credit
and why should they, "basket of deplorables," Cal-Dak trays, the
swerving bee at Bread Loaf rising from the wide, sun-bleached windowsill, "Beam me up, Scotty," the fact that Stacy and I once painted
a little first-grader-size school chair we found in a dumpster,

Octoberwise, the fact that we gave it black and yellow stripes like a bee, and a honeycomb seat, and Stacy painted bees all over the back frame, the fact that I loved her for that, for painting all those little bees, and the stripes around the legs, the fact that she got right down to it and didn't stop until that thing was the best little chair in the world, the Bee Chair, the fact that it's just Jakey's size, and he likes sitting on it when it's not covered with papers, mail, books, junk, junk mail, snail mail, the fact that it must be genetic, families with a lot of papers, the fact that Daddy's big gun-metal gray typewriter in the attic sat in a sea of papers, the fact that there was a narrow path from the door to the desk, and the rest was piles and piles of paper, the fact that we could get rid of some books, but what do you do with *papers*, the fact that it's a lot more work to sort through them all than to just keep them, the fact that there should be some kind of paper *counselor* who comes talk to people about how to get their papers under control, bamboo strips, the fact that Peolia was all open-plan, "letters 2 and 5 in your mother's maiden name," so you could see exactly which teachers were drowning in paper, the fact that it really *hurts* that Stacy says she wants to get outta here, and she's telling other people now too, the fact that she's always saying it *here*, but I didn't think she was that serious about it, the fact that she seems to be having a tough time right now, the fact that maybe we *should* do Family Therapy, or I should get her more involved with her heritage or something, but she always seems to resent my mentioning it, fluster, flummox, lummox, scallions, rosy-fingered dawn, mellow fruitfulness, wind velocity, the fact that soon everybody'll live in a paperless world, I guess, which will be good for trees but not historians, thrift shops, Amish buggies, dust bunnies, shimmying fir tree, the fact that those bamboo strips from China have all this ancient advice on how to govern, the fact that they recommended meritocracy, no family dynasties, and no slaves working in computer factories either, the fact that you'd think writing important things down on thin strips of bamboo might be a little risky, posterity-wise, but those bamboo strips lasted *thousands of years*, the fact that if they'd been digitalized, like, in 300 BCE, they wouldn't've lasted a hundred, and we'd never have found them either, the fact that our DVDs get scratched in no time and then they're useless, and USB sticks stop working after a while, and computers wear out, or get incompatible with new programs and everything, the fact that if you're not careful, you lose all your carefully saved porno pics eventually, the fact that imagine all the updates you'd need if you found a computer that was two and a half thousand years old, mounds, mammoths, the fact that it would be endless, waiting for that little circle to stop going around and around, spiraling into infinity, the fact that the Ohio mammoth went extinct, and I am no spring chicken either, but Leo calls me sweetheart and honey, and sometimes babe, the fact that Claude Rains calls Bette "my ewe lamb," the fact that Bette Davis movies always have a dark side, dark side of the moon, ocean of ammonia, eternal triangle, odds and ends, all thumbs, bamboo strips, the fact that Kentucky lady slipper orchids are really big, the fact that the Pueblo ones are smaller but they have the best colors, the fact that all lady slipper orchids have thin, dark spiraling petals that point outward and one pale petal, arranged overhead, to shield the hole in the slipper from rain and dirt and bugs and stuff, the fact that they really do look like little slippers, and that's touching, ginseng hunt, the fact that they still don't know who all the victims were from that shooting in Egypt, but they do know who got beheaded, Peolia staff meetings, porphyria, porphyry copper, porphyria purple, the fact that Stacy hates school, the fact that institutions *are* horrible, the fact that raising four kids is rather like founding an institution, and if you don't watch it, the kids get kind of *institutionalized*, though ours aren't institutionalized *enough* maybe, the fact that the von Trapp kids were all supposed to act like little Austrian soldiers, left, right, left, right, the fact that this might've seemed cute to some people in Hollywood, but it's no good, the fact that most kids in big families don't get enough one-to-one time apparently, the fact that how *would* they, the fact that these days most of my life is spent just seeing them out the corner of my eye while we all go about our own lonely affairs, "only children," orphans, the fact that I wish Leo was here, the fact that I miss him the whole time,

and it just seems wrong for him to be so far away, I ♥ U, "Easy, stomach," EZE LOVE, the fact that *nobody's* getting any one-to-ones
around here, and if I don't go defrost some ground beef right now there
won't be any Sloppy Joes either, the fact that it'll be plain noodles with
butter, and even though they like noodles and butter, I have my pride,
♬ *Rice-a-Roni, the San Francisco treat* ♬, the fact that I bet the von
Trapps had proper dinners at least, even if they did have to march in
step to the table, bersaglieri, ♬ *sautéed and somethinged, the flavor can't
be beat* ♬, the fact that I wonder if every mother of four wonders daily
why she had them, the fact that Jake still wets the bed sometimes, but
that's normal, the fact that somebody said there should be a statue to
Sojourner Truth in Akron, where she gave the speech, the fact that all
they've got so far is a plaque, meritocracy, Frederick and Opal, the
fact that people steal cats for experiments, poor Dilly, the fact that she
wasn't *stolen*, but her *life* was stolen, by a car, take a life, "Take a seat,
the doctor will be right with you," dappled sunlight, ground beef,
chipotle paste, paprika, cheddar and kaiser rolls, the fact that of course
we have no kaiser rolls but that's forgivable, forgettable, the fact that
most freezers in the world are probably undersupplied with kaiser rolls,
the fact that I bet everybody's got too many bay leaves and too few
kaiser rolls, but how often do you really need a kaiser roll, Kaiser
health care plan, the fact that we can make do with plain bread, the
fact that *I'm* a baker, the fact that I should whip up some Kaiser rolls,
but I'm not going to, the fact that I don't know how, the fact that I've
just got my niche, the fact that I'm not a master baker or a, a pâtissier
or anything, Swimming Pinkie Pie the Seapony, the fact that we just
looked at Donny's registry list and everything costs *a hundred dollars*
or more, the fact that we don't have that kind of money, the fact that
they want all this kitchen stuff and video games and whatnot, veil toss
duties, the fact that Gillian said we should make them a whatnot by
hand, following Laura Ingalls Wilder's instructions, but I'd rather not,
whatnot, the fact that you can't tell people you're broke, because it
depresses them, broken, the fact that you certainly can't tell anybody
you're *broken*, stave off, turn the stove off, antique kitchen utensil

jigsaw, the fact that I suppose most young marrieds want kitchen stuff, but these two only want really fancy pots and pans, and ceramic knives, the fact that they're not talking Revere Ware or crockpots, the fact that they want Le Creuset, the fact that they must think everybody's a millionaire, the fact that I love my Revere Ware saucepans, and the little frying pan, because they were Mommy's, the fact that when I was about five I came downstairs from my nap feeling euphoric, the fact that I just felt *great*, the fact that I still *remember* how great I felt, the fact that I woke up and the sun was shining through the tree outside my window and the wind was softly blowing in and I just loved being alive and loved my mom, and wanted to tell her so, so I went downstairs to the kitchen, where Mommy was busy doing something, I don't know what, and I told her how happy I felt, the fact that maybe I even told her I loved her, though we weren't that sort of family, the fact that I think I often longed to tell her but didn't dare, the fact that maybe I dared to say it out loud that day, because it just seemed necessary and right and wonderful, and all I remember is she was sort of short with me, kind of cold, and I still don't know why, and I never will know why, the fact that by the time I was old enough to ask her, it seemed too late, the fact that I didn't think she'd remember it anyway, and I didn't want to make her feel *bad* about it, the fact that I just never got why she was short with me that day, the fact that it really kind of threw me, the fact that I just expected her to be as joyful as *I* was, the fact that I was just happy and in love with my mom, and I wanted her to share the moment with me, and she didn't get it, didn't get it, *And that has made all the difference*, the fact that I was really shocked by that, because she was usually on my side, the fact that she was my MOM, so I couldn't see how she'd miss the significance, the significance of my happiness, the fact that I was the happiest I'd ever been and she couldn't see that, the fact that my joy was lost on her, the fact that of course why *should* she get it, the fact that she was a busy woman, with three kids and a job and a book to write, and probably supper to cook right at that moment, the fact that so what if she was too busy to notice my state of euphoria that one afternoon, the fact that I was just a silly little girl and it's silly even to remember it, the fact that I'm sure she wasn't trying to be *mean* or anything, or cold, the fact that she always loved me, the fact that she was just busy that day and distracted maybe, or maybe she was mad about something else, or anxious, or just happened to be feeling bored with motherhood that afternoon, and that's all it was, the fact that I took it hard, the fact that I didn't get upset or make some scene, the fact that I was just really surprised that my euphoria was lost on her, and still am, a bit, the fact that I had to adjust myself to that realization, the fact that the thing was I think I'd always felt she understood every single little thing about me up until then, and this was the first time we seemed separate, completely separate, the fact that, also, I was kind of impressed by my euphoric state and just wanted her to share it, and feel euphoric with me, but to Mommy it was no big deal, and that still grates on me, a little, the fact that maybe it was the first time I felt all alone in the world, alone with my euphoria, which quickly wilted, the fact that it was harder to share euphoria than I'd realized, even with the person you love most, "Sad!", the fact that how can I still be feeling bad about this, the fact that I was like a baby kangaroo that's grown too big for the pouch, but you keep clawing at it and trying to get back in but it's no use, the fact that my mommy was a little cold to me and my pouch life was suddenly over, 50% burns, the fact that do *animals* try to share euphoria with each other, the fact that that tree gleaming in the sun looks like a twisted hand reaching up to grab something, the fact that most people don't like hearing you're happy actually, I don't think, the fact that what do they care, fair-weather friends, foul-weather friends, fowl, the penguins at London Zoo, quiggly hole, the fact that it's never a good idea to tell them you're happy, people, not penguins, Waterlow Park with Mommy, the fact that they never react the way you want them to, the fact that that sounds like something you might find on one of those ancient Chinese bamboo strips, "Never tell people you feel happy," the fact that maybe I'd interrupted some vital operation in the kitchen, for all I know, the fact that I think she *was* cooking something, the fact that there could be a zillion reasons why she was distracted or not in the mood to think about what I happened to be feeling that afternoon, the fact that she had no idea it meant so much to me, I know, or she would've sat down with me, I'm sure, and enjoyed the moment, before it vanished, the fact that it did mean something, the fact that that's all I know, the fact that motherhood is just impossible, because you never know what you're doing wrong, or *right* even, just like teaching, building bridges, the fact that my kids never notice what I'm up to, like if I'm really busy or not, the fact that I probably offend and disappoint them *all the time*, not just once, the fact that I never mean to, but I'm not always really noticing what's going on with them, the fact that I probably throw *their* separateness from *me* in their faces without even realizing, the fact that how many times have I disappointed Stace, the fact that she acts like it's plenty, but I never *meant* to, the fact that I never stopped loving her, but that doesn't mean you do the right thing all the time, the fact that maybe it's something every kid has to learn the hard way at some point, the fact that I'm always having to remind the kids I'm not telepathic, the fact that I know they wish I was, the fact that it would be more con-venient for them, the fact that maybe that upsets them, to be told I'm not telepathic, deeply upsets them, the fact that you never know when you might be crushing your kid, the fact that when you fall *in love*, you think at last somebody knows you, understands you, cares about you in every way, like your mom did, and they do sometimes, the fact that Leo loves me and always cares how I'm feeling, and wants to hear what I have to say, the fact that even he can't predict what I'm about to feel though, and sometimes he doesn't get what I'm talking about, the fact that I think I could tell him if I was feeling euphoric though, and he'd be pleased, the fact that even though he's out-of-state right now, I could call him and tell him any time, and I think he'd get what I mean, the fact that I wouldn't want to interrupt a class though, the fact that when he's in the house I do tell him anything I feel like, the fact that I know it's dumb but I still wish Mommy had understood my little bout of euphoria that day and enjoyed it with me, instead of seeming a little huffy or distracted or whatever, the fact that I think my whole life might possibly have been different if she had, the fact that maybe that's the moment I became shy, and scared of people, the fact that it kind of feels like it, the fact that I know she didn't knowingly disappoint me and, boy, do I know how hard is it to be nice to a little kid all day long, pestering you all the time and wanting all your attention and everything, the fact that maybe she was hoping I'd nap for longer, the fact that still, all I did was come downstairs to her after my nap and tell her I was feeling happy, happy, the fact that you'd think that maybe she could've, could, the fact that it's no big deal, *at all*, the fact that I'm just being silly, the fact that I don't know why I'm getting *tearful* about it, heavens to Betsy, the fact that how much longer am I going to go on feeling bad about this, the fact that it's forty years ago, the fact that if I give this mishap play for forty more years, it'll be hard to deny I'm bearing a grudge, the fact that, for Pete's sake, maybe I caught her on a bad day, the fact that the whole problem is that the adult world and the kid world are totally different places, but you try to bridge the gap, moms with their kids, the fact that nobody wants to rain on anybody's parade but parents don't always have the time or energy to figure out every single little sensation their kid's enjoying, the fact that actually, as long as the kid seems fairly happy, you mostly just want to leave them to it, and get something else done, the fact that my kids will probably have to puzzle over many things I did till *their* dying days, the fact that they'll probably never figure me out either, though I try to be straight with them, Is Foil Safe To Use?, the fact that actually, if I had three wishes, I'd just take money, an end to pollution, and some $80 ceramic knives, "A dollar?!", the fact that burnt children have to have their bandages removed while playing VR games, mass shooting in Louisiana movie theater, I ♥ U, Band-Aids, fuzzy cactus sticker, so alone, the fact that Stacy must have stuck that cactus on the fridge right after we moved in here with Leo, the fact that that tree out back, the one that came down with a thunk last fall, the fact that it now has new branches starting to grow out of its side, lightning, *gunpowder, treason and plot*, Sherlock Holmes, Inspector Lestrade, the fact that I never even noticed it was all that stormy out that day, until the tree came down, birch, buckeye, fir, fur, Oakridge, Tennessee, Knoxville, Tennessee, King of Prussia, Pennsylvania, the fact that David Attenborough's always talking about tree competition in the rainforest, as if trees are all jockeying for position all the time and they're thrilled when any nearby trees die, meanies, Our Approach to School Bullying, but maybe there's also tree fellowship, companionship, tree empathy, the fact that somebody said trees form a community, and they get along, the fact that they're comrades, colleagues, the fact that they're often siblings as well, or related in some way, so why wouldn't they care about one another, the fact that it's not each tree for himself at all, the fact that if a nearby tree's injured or it falls over, the other trees *feed* it until the wounded tree can get back on its feet or whatever, revive anyway, reviresco, river, Esso, the fact that if that's true it means trees sort of think, and plan, and care, love, "mommy trees," the fact that who are we to say if trees want to help each other in hard times, rather than just elbow other trees selfishly out of the way, kick him while he's down, the fact that maybe trees are really quite *sociable*, more sociable than me, the fact that maybe they want to *share* the sun with their friends, not steal it all, euphoria, the fact that maybe our trees have been missing their pal over there, after it fell over, and they've been quietly *feeding* it somehow, underground, and that's why it's reviving, the fact that so it's just as well we never got around to removing that trunk, sentient, the fact that trees have been giving us the ol' Silent Treatment for *two million years*, but maybe there's more going on in them that we thought, bassoon, aerophone, concertina, the fact that trees go into a dormant state at night, the fact that if trees sleep, perchance they dream, and I wonder what their dreams are about, the fact that it's probably weather mostly, and anxiety dreams about accidentally getting tangled up in other trees, lightning bolts, crown die-back, forest fires, the fact that maybe they have wish-fulfilment dreams about abundant water sources, nostalgia dreams about snowy winter stillness, and attentive bees, woodpeckers, the fact that I bet they *like* being pecked, melodica, the fact that if trees sleep and dream and eat and drink and blossom and, and mate and exfoliate, and experience euphoria and take care of their companions, then they must really want to *live*, just like we do, the fact that there are no "trees waitin' to be felled," the fact that if they could run, they'd probably head for the hills at the first hint of an ax or chainsaw, or when they're getting gnawed to death by beavers, the fact that what's gotten into me, the fact that I'm turning into Annie Oakley, maple-sugaring spout, the fact that I worry beavers will get splinters between their teeth, but maybe they're just the best-flossed critters in the world, the fact that I don't know if carrots want to be eaten, the fact that it seems unlikely, the fact that, I mean, who wants to be chopped up and boiled, or grated and mixed with raisins, the fact that it must be so *disappointing* to be sliced up if you're a nice fresh crisp iceberg lettuce, or a celery stalk, brimful with life, *Celery Stalks At Midnight*, the humble hazelnut, the fact that celery puts so much effort into being celery, just to end up filling the plastic lunch box of a not particularly hungry American kid, bento box, tiffin, unmeltable ice cream sandwich, the fact that surely no potato wants to be mashed, why *would* they, masher, flasher, Fats Domino, the Beatles, Shirley Jackson, vegans, vegetarians, pescatarians, white meat, egg-white omelet, the fact that if we really sympathized with plants, we wouldn't eat them, and we sure wouldn't sing to them, ♫ *Drink to me only wi-ith thine eyes* ♫, the fact that I bet plants just *hate* being sung to, but there's nothing they can do about it, the fact that they're just sitting ducks, the fact that they can't get away, the fact that it's like going to a school concert, thirty beginner violinists, forty eager vuvuzelaists, the fact that maybe that's why trees try to grow tall, just to put some *distance* between themselves and all that singing and tree-hugging going on nearer the ground, and get out of reach of other predators too, like ruminants, giraffes, deer, elephants, the fact that a tree's priority is getting high, and then they fill out, the fact that they're really sort of suspended balls of leaves, nuts and fruit, the fact that I like a good, dome-shaped buckeye, the fact that trees always seem to know where the ground is, without touching it, even if they're on a hill, the fact that how do they do that, roots like arteries at Peolia, the fact that, for all we know, trees may be seething with indignation, or irritation, full of desperate plans, longings and regrets, euphoria, nap, anger-management, "Not so fast, Goldberg," forty winks, Alec Baldwin, the fact that "delivering his lines" is a funny expression, the fact that it makes actors sound like mailmen, milkmen, paper boys, the fact that Stacy never drew normal pictures of trees and houses like other kids, the fact that she drew mazes, intricate, winding rabbit tunnels, and told herself stories about the rabbits in there while she drew them, the fact that she could do that for hours, the fact that now I have a rash where my Band-Aid was, the fact that the rash is worse than the cut was, but luckily the antihistamine cream's right here next to the Band-Aids, pretty handy, except no, it *isn't*, the fact that somebody forgot to put the antihistamine cream back in its rightful place, the fact that this bugs me much more than it seems to deserve, given that there are people in the world who get beheaded, and trees are crying out for companionship and who knows what else, and all I have to worry about is a little itch on my finger, the fact that itches are very distract-ing though, gyny guy, the fact that you can't think about trees or tornadoes or Alec Baldwin or anything else when you've got a little tiny itch right *there*, the fact that it's lucky I now have the mixer, the fact that otherwise I'd be in a real fix, with a finger out of action, mixer, fixer, sunflowers, fall leaves, sousaphone, bandoneon, the fact that if it weren't for Leo's professorial discount none of these kids would have a hope of going to college, for all my zany baking efforts, but his professorial discounts are now under threat, he says, the fact that the kids better hurry up and get to college, like *tomorrow* would be good, Hurry-Up cake, Six-Minute frosting, the fact that Ben's rushing things too much actually, what with all the astronomy and porno pics, barefoot in the kitchen, the fact that Revere Ware pots have copper bottoms, and that's why they're such great pots, the Ohio Hopewell, open heart surgery, the fact that crimes against children are really crimes against mothers, the fact that Mommy slept on a hospital cot beside me the night before my heart operation, the fact that she must have been frightened for me, the fact that *I* wasn't frightened, the fact that I didn't really know what was going on, the fact that I was only eight, the fact that she kept me company that night, and the next day they cranked my ribcage open to get at my heart, the fact that it's amazingly convenient that ribcages open like that, like a doctor's bag or saloon doors, though I'm not sure they open *that* easily, considering there's no actual hinge there, installed by nature just in case you ever need a little cardiological surgery, flip-side, the fact that Leo says he likes my heart scar, because it shows they *saved* me, a hole in the heart the size of a dime, nickel, quarter, the fact that they nickeled and dimed me, but here I am, two husbands and four children later, ♫ *skip to my Lou* ♫, euphoria, twinge, hip, cancer, itch, Band-Aid, sore teeth, alphorn, the fact that they said I'd die at the age of twenty-two and could never survive a pregnancy, if I didn't have the operation, so they fixed me and here I am with all these kids, far too many, the fact that I'd prefer a pregnancy though to an operation any day, even if it does hurt, euphonium, euphoria, twenty-two, the fact that they were very precise about that, like when they give you a year to live, the fact that doctors like to come up with these scary threats, crushing news, the fact that the mean night nurse used to wake me up every night to give me painful shots to help me *sleep*, the fact that I really hated that nurse, and dreaded her, though I probably only ever had her a few times, the fact that I liked the *day* nurse, who exuded kindness, the fact that that's *one* kind of exuding I don't mind, the fact that I forgot her name long ago, though I remembered it for several years, the fact that actually *all* the other nurses seemed to know how to give you a shot without it hurting, the fact that it was just that night nurse that did it so badly, probably on purpose, the fact that maybe it was the highlight of her day, or night I mean, giving painful shots to children, the party in Mr. Knightley's garden, the fact that that's awful of me, the fact that I shouldn't say such nasty things about anyone, dear me, nasturtiums, the fact that she *was* rough with me though, the fact that that was in the recovery ward, not the ICU, the fact that when I first woke up I was in the ICU, and Daddy was there by my bed and he seemed so glad to see me, the fact that he read me a new

Dr. Seuss book he'd just bought me, the fact that being sick makes you feel really special for a while, with lots of attention and presents, the fact that it made me *like* having a heart operation, apart from the pain, the fact that it hurt a lot at first, till they got the pain under control, fallen tree, and then they moved me to a different room, the fact that at first I was in a nice peaceful room on my own but then they needed that room for a *boy*, so they moved me to the room with two teenage girls in it, the fact that I think both had broken backs, the fact that I don't know if they were friends before or they'd met in the hospital, but they seemed quite pally and I felt left out, the fact that, also, they were a lot older than me, and scarily womanly, the fact that they were probably only about fourteen but they seemed awfully grown-up to me, the fact that they didn't talk to me much, the fact that I was the odd one out, piggy in the middle, the fact that they were probably a little embarrassed to have me there, the fact that I got more glimpses of their bodies than I would've liked, the fact that teenagers sort of revolt you when you're a kid, the fact that they're not one thing or another, the fact that they're not old enough to be nice to you like grown-ups, but they're no fun either, so they're not kids, the fact that really those poor girls sort of revolted me, like Aggie in *Up a Road Slowly*, the fact that they just seemed so old, the fact that the gulf was unbridgeable, rush-hour bridge collapse, the fact that now I wonder if those girls ever got better, or if they were paralyzed for life, the fact that I never *knew*, the fact that they seemed more on top of things than me, but maybe they were in much worse shape than I ever realized, the fact that they were tended by their moms a lot, the fact that the moms seemed to be there almost all day, and the girls seemed to have been there for months already, oh dear, the fact that each of us had her own TV, and the TVs were all on at once most of the time, and somehow I remember checking out all three, looking from one to the next when I got bored with my own, though I don't know how I *could* see all three at once, since our beds were at different angles in the room, all kind of higgledy-piggledy, the fact that I think they'd crammed too many beds in there, probably to squeeze me in, the fact that maybe I'd caused a big to-do I never knew about, and the girls resented me for it, the fact that maybe it was a nice calm two-bed room until I came along, the fact that I never talked to those girls enough to get the real lowdown, the fact that I watched three different TV shows at once, and that's when I saw that black-and-white movie I always wanted to see again but I never knew what it was, the fact that I caught that on *my* TV, and I really liked it, and I've been kind of half-looking for it ever since, the fact that it was better than that kidnap movie, with all the pine trees and the parents driving around, the fact that I didn't see that one in the hospital, the fact that the one in the hospital was very atmospheric, all misty and mysterious, and sort of melancholy, the fact that it had a half-light quality, the fact that I'd never seen a movie like that, the fact that it was a bit like Waterlow Park, but it was black-and-white, the fact that it seemed beautiful to me, the fact that maybe it was some version of *The Secret Garden* or something, the fact that actually, if I had three wishes, I would go back in time, and go be in Evanston with Mommy and Pepito, before my heart operation, then spend more time with Mommy and Daddy in my twenties, and really get a chance to talk, and then I'd do things all over again with Stace, but better, and make her *happy* this time, the fact that Phoebe had to collect my Hallowe'en candy for me, because I was in the hospital, the fact that I still remember the smells of the hospital sometimes, the smell of bandages and I don't know what, the stale taste of hospital water, the taste of the pills, the fact that when I got out, I think Grandma and Grandpa came to stay, and I couldn't swallow my pills with them watching me, the fact that I've never been able to swallow pills in front of people since, the fact that I had two months at home to recuperate, and a teacher came three times a week to make me do really easy stuff, the fact that I didn't mind her too much, Invalid or Convalescent Cookery, Masked Eggs, Poached Eggs in Aspic, the fact that Irma Rombauer thinks convalescents should eat Oyster Stew, Corn-meal Mush Meat Pie, Brains, Timbales, Marshmallow Pudding, Zabaglione, and Broiled Grapefruit, the fact that I don't know who'd get better on *that*, the fact that I wouldn't want oysters if I wasn't feeling well, the fact that they pronounce oysters "ersters" in Georgia, which is kind of off-putting, and they say "cherces" for choices, the fact that Apalachicola's famous for oysters, *The Devil and Daniel Webster*, the fact that Leo has to give a talk on the ABC bridge in Illinois that collapsed and killed all those people driving underneath, a walking bridge, the fact that he says it should never have been attempted, the fact that the risks outweighed all the benefits, all those crushed *people*, the fact that Leo hates ABC bridges, alphabet soup, abecedarian soup, the fact that the whole idea is not to disrupt traffic too much, but he doesn't trust them, whether they use span-by-span macrosegmental casting, or macrosegmental balanced-cantilever casting with a suspension girder movable scaffolding system and prestressed, or self-cleaning, concrete, the fact that there are six hundred thousand bridges in America, and five hundred thousand of them are over water, the fact that there have been a couple thousand collapses over the last fifty years, most of them caused by scour, but also overloading and ship collisions can cause a bridge to fail, the fact that Leo isn't happy about a single one of those bridge failures, Mabey bridge, the fact that a Mabey bridge is maybe what we needed that day at the mall, the fact that *every* bridge is a "maybe" bridge, for Leo, four-sided culvert, the fact that he doesn't like accelerated construction either, but most problems with accelerated construction bridges happen during construction or erection, not during use, the fact that he has to go visit that U.S. Bridge company in Cambridge, Cambridge, because they do a lot of prefab components, and then maybe go on to Con/Span, near Cincinnati, the fact that maybe we should go with him and we could go to Young's after, salty caramel crunch, salty caramel *pretzel* crunch, erection, capacity of member, penile dysfunction, the fact that bridge failure really bothers Leo, the fact that he gets all emotional about it, because these structures are supposed to *work*, the fact that they have to successfully extend over some gap or gully or void or whatever and *stay* extended, the fact that that is their one duty, the fact that they have to perform, PONTIS, REDARS, DBIA, seismic ranking, the fact that a fallen bridge is "emasculated," the fact that that's how they really talk, bridge experts, the fact that that's the main issue, the risk of collapse, the fact that the causes can be fracture, fatigue, crushing, tearing, rupture, shearing, deformation, and buckling, and Leo spends at least a whole class on each, "I *love* collapsing," yielding, wielding, fielding, the fact that *Cleo* said that, which I thought was kind of heartless, the fact that Leo says she wasn't really talking about bridge failure though, the fact that she meant some other kind of collapsing, the *mechanical* side of collapsing or something, not the part where everybody gets crushed, but still it's kind of a strange thing to say, "I *love* collapsing," flaccid, flaksid, the fact that I don't know why Leo was defending her, but he's always very supportive towards his colleagues, cowbirds, self-defense book, my honey, the fact that maybe my special home teacher was under orders not to tax my strength or something, so she just gave me easy things to do, the fact that I don't think she kept me up with my class very well, but what does it matter when you're eight, the fact that temporary bridges are iffy things, the fact that they use them a lot in the military, for quick erection and demolition, but they're used as temporary detour bridges on highways too, Variable Message Signs, the fact that shoot, now the doorbell's ringing, Ronny, oh no, the fact that, I'm sure it's Ronny, structurally deficient, functionally obsolete, spill-through abutments, the fact that, ah, it's just the *mailman*, what a relief, the fact that I dreamt I was offered a job teaching history at Hamden Hall, and I considered it even, because I liked Hamden Hall so much when I went there, but then I realized it wouldn't work because I'm not qualified to be a schoolteacher, the fact that I wouldn't even be good as a support teacher, or even visiting sick kids in their homes and teaching them all the wrong stuff, CCTV, dried cranberries, sunflower oil, palm oil, Palm Pads, Palm Sunday, Ash Wednesday, palm-readers, Possum pussies, Kompromat, fairy tales, fly agaric mushrooms, Dr. Seuss, the fact that Gillian seems to be getting into *Up A Road Slowly*, which I started reading to her, the fact that I thought she might be too young for it but she seems to like it, orphan, motherless orphan, the fact that Julie's kind of prickly, but you feel for her because she lost her mom, the fact that sometimes I think I didn't really know Mommy or Daddy all that well, the fact that I only had three decades with them, and most of that time I was just a dopey kid, thinking about my own stuff, not them, euphoria, the fact that there's so much I didn't ask them, so much I didn't tell them either, the fact that it's weird, when you live with these people for eighteen years and you hardly *know* each other, the fact that I can barely remember what Mommy and Daddy *looked like* now, but I'd recognize them if they turned up, the fact that I'd *love* it if they turned up, the fact that it would give us a chance to get to *know* each other better, the fact that what she went through, the fact that watching that hurt me a lot more than my heart operation ever did, the fact that it ruined me, broke me, *Historic Events in the Muskingum and Tuscarawas Valleys,* the fact that I think I stopped caring about people at that moment, the moment I knew she was so sick, in danger of death, the fact that I was so scared by that, I went numb, and stayed numb, the fact that I never felt I could depend on her again, the fact that I still *enjoyed* her and all, but she seemed far away from me, the fact that I usually try not to think about it, the fact that I've blanked everything out so well I've almost forgotten what a great thing she was, the fact that I like to remember the times when I was alone with her, before she got sick, the fact that we were alone when we ate peaches in cream together out in the back yard on summer mornings, and years later, after she was sick, we drank whiskey and soda together in the dining room, talking and reading, the fact that I read so many books sitting at that table with Mommy, mostly ones she recommended, the fact that I was alone with her in our living room in Evanston, when she braided my hair every morning before I went to school, diamond window panes, braids, bangs, school bus, cinnamon paste, zest, spread it on, being alone with my mom, the fact that I was alone with her when she taught me how to play solitaire that day I was home sick from school, or probably not really sick, just needing a day at home with my mommy, lying on the yellow chaise longue in their bedroom, cozy under a blanket, the fact that solitaire later filled her life, the fact that she must have gotten very bored with it, but she kept on playing it anyway, the fact that it must've *killed* Daddy to see her playing so much solitaire, his great wife, so smart and so destroyed, but he never said anything about it, nor about all the TV she watched, Triple Crown, the fact that I wonder how often I stayed home from school when I wasn't really sick, the fact that my kids don't seem to want to do that so much, the fact that they just go to school without complaint usually, the fact that Stacy would probably rather stay home and watch Morning Routine videos, but she's more interested in getting away from *me*, Arizona, college, delivering milk, remote grocery store, iguana, Cold Sally, the fact that Mommy hated school too, nun shaking her, time to spiral, chaise longue, time alone with Mommy, the fact that I remember one late winter afternoon in their bedroom, showing Mommy the felt and sequin Christmas-tree ornament I'd made at the Brownies or Campfire Girls, Gillian's sequin bird, fuzzy cactus sticker, Stacy's clay sculpture of Dilly nursing her kittens, breastfeeding advice, the fact that I was often alone with Mommy in their bedroom like that, especially when she was getting ready to go out to a party, the fact that nobody watches me, I don't think, but, well, I never go to parties, if I can help it, the fact that I only go to PTA things, and not even them sometimes, the fact that sometimes I chicken out, but you can only claim to be sick so many times before they begin to think you're *really* sick and start coming over with cookies and cards and stuff, or spaghetti sauce, the fact that I don't think Mommy liked parties all that much either, because she was shy too, but she went anyway, looking nice in her high heels and perfume, the fact that why *do* people like parties, the fact that Daddy was more sociable, gregarious, though he had a shy side too, but his was Junior League compared to *my* shyness, the fact that Fun Days are rarely fun to me, likewise Fun Runs, the fact that I can still smell Mommy's perfume, the fact that I never liked it when she reached that stage in the preparations, Chanel No. 5, because it meant they'd soon be going and we'd be left in the hands of some babysitter, or preferably Ethan, the fact that when he was in charge we had TV dinners or Daddy gave him the money to take us out to B & J's for hot roast beef sandwiches, the fact that now I think he was kind of young to be put in charge of two little sisters, but I guess they knew Ethan would be careful, the fact that I don't think I'd like that hot roast beef sandwich anymore, the fact that the bread got all soggy, from the gravy, and that was what we *liked* about it so much at the time, but now I'm not so sure that's a good idea, the fact that it's strange how popular perfume still is, the fact that maybe it's because of pollution, iron ore tailings, battery hen farms, the fact that people never get tired of it, perfume I mean, though you can put too much on, the fact that Leo likes me to wear perfume but I forget to, the fact that he uses aftershave, the fact that I never used to think much about aftershave but I like it on him, styptic stick, Leo, the fact that I should get him some more of that lemony one he likes, the fact that he often buys *me* perfume and I forget to wear it, the fact that that's *terrible* of me, but you can't wear perfume when you're baking, baking blind, blind baking, Blind Rescue Dog Makes A New Friend, second rising of the cinnamon rolls, "Mary, mother of god, we'd have preferred a girl," the fact that we always gave Daddy aftershave for Christmas, bought by Mommy on our behalf, lion ornament, and that's where we got the lion, the fact that he came on top of the aftershave bottle one year, and we always put him on top of the tree from then on, the lion, not Daddy, the fact that who wants an angel or a star or Santa, when you have a jolly-looking green and red felt lion with a big smile on his face, the fact that he has a nice tassely mane too, and somehow I inherited him, which was lucky, the fact that a male pin-tailed whydah's tail is almost twice the length of his body, chicken, Chick-Fil-A, seven hundred billion chickens, prairie chickens, Arabella Fawley, the fact that I can't remember many presents I gave Mommy and Daddy, the fact that I once bought her some miniature red roses, and it took all the money I had, five dollars, the fact that I thought they were just the greatest thing ever, the fact that I'd never *seen* such pretty roses, the fact that I'd probably hardly ever been in a flower store, the fact that the world was full of things to give Mommy actually, and I kept finding stuff, the fact that I don't know what *she* thought of it all, like those sparkly tights I got her once, with a fake diamond seam down the back, the fact that I sort of meant them as a joke, the fact that I don't know what she made of them, what a dumb present, the fact that you don't always know what to get your mom, besides cigarettes, the fact that I bought her plenty of those over the years too, the fact that it's hard for kids to get presents right, and you never know what they'll come up with, the fact that Gillian gave me those big copper-wire earrings that get tangled in my hair, the fact that I bent them trying to pull them out, the fact that Jake once gave me the toes off his leopard toy, a great treasure, time alone with Mommy, alone with Mommy, the fact that Mommy and I were alone together in Highgate every Wednesday and I loved it, beans on toast and Waterlow Park and ducks, black leaves, white, cinnamon rolls, oven, binge-watching box sets, a pan of water on the bottom to help the rising, the bottom of the *oven*, the fact that I was alone with her the day I came downstairs feeling ecstatically happy and full of love for my *mom*, the fact that Stacy's given me many many little clay sculptures, like the one with Dilly and her kittens, though not lately of course, euphoria, Eustacia, Arizona, the fact that it's childish to expect to be in sync with your mom all the time, the fact that I know that, now that *I'm* a mom, the fact that moms are busy people with all kinds of stuff going on that their kids know nothing about, the fact that I was alone with my mom when I finally got up the nerve to ask about the Facts of Life, and she *refused to tell me*, pin-tailed whydah, the fact that whydaheck wouldn't she tell me, the fact that years later, I brought it up over a drink at the dining room table, and she *remembered* not telling me, and she said she'd thought I was *mocking* her by asking about the Facts of Life, the fact that she'd assumed I already knew the Facts of Life and I just wanted to embarrass her, whydah, the fact that, boy, did she get me wrong, the fact that I knew *nothing* about the Facts of Life, and thought it was something your mom was supposed to tell you at some point, the fact that all *I* knew was what I'd gotten from Jill, who got it from *her* mom, the fact that her mom told her it all happens while you're *asleep*, but she never said *how*, the fact that we knew the husband puts his thing in the woman's vagina, but that sounded difficult to do in your sleep, the fact that until some-body explains to you that penises can suddenly, mysteriously get hard, you're just left in the dark about all this stuff, the fact that it wouldn't occur to you in a *million years* that men get erections, the fact that that just never crossed my mind, the fact that how are you supposed to think a thing like that up by yourself, the fact that who would ever guess, scour, resolution of erection issues, firm, BIRM, berm, the fact that I think Phoebe probably told me in the end, but I can't remember, the fact that maybe all Jill's mom meant was that sex happened while *Jill* was asleep, but I don't think so, the fact that I think it was a delib-erate effort to avoid giving Jill the Facts of Life, a cowardly bit of misinformation which now I can totally sympathize with, the fact that it's *hard* to talk to your kids about sex, the fact that most of the time you're trying to protect them from any knowledge of it, and then all of a sudden you're supposed to spill the beans, spill the seed, except you never know when or how to do it, the fact that I'm like my mom, the fact that I assume they'll find out from somewhere else and I'll be off the hook, evasive tactics, the fact that they're free to ask us any-thing they want about the Facts of Life, anytime, but so far none of them's asking, the fact that I expect they just look at porno pics now if they wanna know anything, and Stace has that wacky sex guide-book, *and* her Morning Routine videos, the fact that I'm sure those Morning Routine girls slip in a bit of Sex Ed on the side, now and then, the fact that they may not get everything anatomically correct, but then who does, the fact that I wonder if that guidebook really did come from school, the fact that maybe she picked it up elsewhere, from a friend or something, or, the fact that what Jill's mom said to Jill was all we had to go on for *years*, the fact that we were so innocent, the fact that I haven't figured it all out *yet*, and what's the hurry, the fact that you have your whole life to think about this stuff, so I don't know why children have to bother with it, accelerated, span, the fact that you get curious though, partial fixity of girder ends, Facts of Life, life and death, the fact that it still hurts kind of, that Mommy could have thought I would ever try to make *fun* of her, by *teasing* her about the

Facts of Life, the fact that didn't she *get* it, the fact that never in a billion gazillion years would I have teased her about *anything*, *ever*, the fact that didn't she know that, the fact that that really upsets me, because that must mean she never knew how much I adored her, my first love, bombardier, bamboo strips, boarlets, alone with Mommy, the fact that our peaches in cream breakfasts that summer in New Haven are the last times I remember when things were *okay*, the fact that everything was peachy fine, the sun-warmed porch, wicker chairs, peaches in cream brought by Mommy, the fact that I was just starting the cranky teenager act that autumn, and then she got sick, the fact that that morning, I was grouchy with her for almost the first time in my life, the fact that I'd seen Ethan and Phoebe get like that and I was planning not to fall into the same hole, but that day I *was* a bit short with her as I left for school, and then around lunchtime I got the note saying she was in the hospital, and that was the end of, well, not *everything*, but something, the fact that I never completed the rest of my teenage rebellion, the fact that all I did instead after that was mooch around, and read the phonebook with the curtains shut, the fact that my life has been a total fiasco, time to brush the egg on, the fact that I was doomed the minute Mommy got sick, the fact that I never really became a person, or not the person I might've been, the fact that Ethan and Phoebe were older, and maybe more fully fledged, the fact that they seemed to cope better, though it was hard on everybody, the fact that Daddy was just heartbroken, but he sort of recovered, the fact that he got back to work but I've always been sort of laboring under a cloud, the fact that everything doubtful or bleak or mistrusting in me got exaggerated, like maybe I was a *bit* shy and skinny and insecure before Mommy got sick, but now I'm cripplingly shy and scared, and scrawny as an old hen, apple-face dolls, faceless dolls, cinnamon rolls, spirals, the fact that I was insecure about leaving home as a kid, and I'm worse now, the fact that I am so insecure about leaving the house, it's ridiculous, the fact that I've always been so awkward, and maybe that's getting worse too, the fact that everything embarrasses me, and I'm so scared of anger, really scared to death of it, the fact that I'd do almost anything to escape the least sign of anger in people, the fact that it hardly ever seems worth getting to know anybody else *in case* they ever get angry with me, oven, or in case they get sick, or disappoint me somehow, or I disappoint them, the fact that I only like people who are especially kind, Cathy, Nanya, cinnamon rolls, the fact that luckily Leo's rarely angry, not openly anyway, and a few really sweet types cling on regardless, like Nanya, and Zdenka, and Cathy, but underneath I'm always wondering if I'll lose them, well, especially Leo, the fact that what would I *do*, the fact that I think my separation anxiety's getting worse than *Jake's*, the fact that I've learned to keep almost everything and everybody *out* of my life, just to avoid separations, the fact that I'm like a fine sieve that hardly lets anything through, a screen door covered with stink bugs, the fact that this is why I can't remember anything, and all my energy goes on kicking stuff out, tamping it down, Mommy in the hospital, the fact that I'm an expert in *not knowing* stuff, expense, extrude, extinguish, professorial discount, the fact that I'm all walled up in here, a *shut-in*, Blind Rescue Dog, the fact that moms are so *interested* in you, or mine seemed to be, the fact that they worry and fuss about you, the fact that even if they're not in sync *all the time*, they care about you in a way nobody else ever will, micrography, the fact that Leo talked to his mom about his hay fever, to her dying day, and she loved it, the Power Grid board game, the fact that I missed out on most things as a teen, the fact that everybody else was out experiencing stuff while I was just trying to hold steady and keep everything at bay, cove, coast, frightened octopuses scrambling across the sand, the fact that I never had many boyfriends, the fact that sometimes I spiral downwards and Leo has to coax me back from the wilderness to the land of the living, the fact that he reminds me I'm loved and capable of happiness, and that I actually *like* life, the Facts of Life, the fact that he always gives me another chance, the way your mom would, the fact that he's so calm with the kids too, the fact that when Gillian was little and ran out in front of that truck, Leo really blasted her, the fact that he sounded so mad it scared me, the fact that I could hear him from the car with all the windows shut, and I didn't know what to do, the fact that then, the next minute, instead of crying or anything, Gillian was skipping along the street beside him, holding his hand, and all was well, what a sweetie, *both* of them, the fact that somehow she knew she was completely safe with him, the fact that I don't think I'm that kind of rock that kids need, the fact that I'm shaky, whydah, purple martins, the fact that they probably find me pretty distant, lemon drizzle disaster, the fact that maybe they don't know I love them, the fact that they're *right* to complain when I forget all the great stuff they say and do, the fact that maybe I should write it down, or get hypnotized, the fact that maybe I'd be a much better person if a hypnotist could make me remember everything, magic, miracle, euphoria, the bee at Bread Loaf, Mommy coming back to life when I touched her hand,

．　　　．　　　．　　　．

Their angular, low-slung homes were forever in her way. And inside them she often saw a man lying slumped in a corner, tearing at a piece of carrion, lit by the blueish flashing light of a TV, the machine that incessantly burned in human homes at night. Sometimes, she would see a man throw things at the wall, making mournful sounds with his throat.

What sort of a creature cannot sleep contentedly on a warm rock, or drape itself across a few high branches and be still?

She wondered at human togetherness, the way people gathered in loud, slow-moving packs. It surprised her that the males were allowed to get so close to the young. No good could come of that.

Men were so ignorant of secrecy or tact. They left their unwanted kills strewn across the wilderness. They crudely ignored her scat and tree-scrapes, and left their own scat around, indifferent to territorial zones. They seemed wholly unaware of any being in the world besides themselves, and this blindness, this deafness, this boldness, this blankness, made them enemies of all.

Yards beyond one big wooden house, the lioness found two dead dogs, recently shot. She was so hungry she paused to swipe the warm liver from one of them but, hearing further bangs of a gun inside the building, she padded on, disgusted.

Her contempt grew, the more she saw of humans, particularly the males. When they caught sight of her, they acted stupid – yelping and lurching awkwardly away. Some fell, and instantly began to whine. Some reached for their guns and pointed them at her. She leapt quickly out of sight, while the crackling metal balls ricocheted off trees.

Her own search went on, for any undulation that might denote a romping cub, or a cub lolling, snug, quietened by sleep.

. . . .

the fact that these macho guys who ride around on bikes without mudguards look pretty darn silly when they get mud splattered all the way up the back of their Spandex shirts and leggings, the fact that it looks pretty bad really, sort of depressing, the fact that mudguards have a *purpose*, guys, the fact that they *guard* you from *mud*, but I guess they aren't cool, the fact that mud has won over mudguards, the fact that mudguards have gone the way of galoshes, which also protected people from mud, the fact that people are in *denial* about mud, *Something is rotten*, the fact that I think there's something wrong with *me*, but that guy at Zyker's should get a *medal*, the fact that I caved but he was a hero, the fact that Jake must've thought he was on a go kart or something, a racing car, or maybe a bulldozer, the fact that he really got completely carried away, the fact that first he almost drove the cart into the cookie display, but I managed to slow him down, black and white cookies, Fig Newtons, the fact that then he got away from me and drove the cart right at the *wine* racks, the fact that I only looked away for a second, contemplating olive oils, fiddling while Rome burns, the fact that the store guy hooked Jake's runaway cart with ease, aplomb even, and brought it to a standstill, *just in time*, stars and stripes, Falling Leaf, Wente, the fact that he was so nice about it too, so good-humored, the fact that as he grabbed hold of the cart, he said to Jake "Where ya headin' there, Casey Jones?", the fact that Jake *loved* being called Casey Jones, and he asked the guy "How'd you know we'd be here?", as if he thought that guy was just standing there waiting for Jake, or Casey Jones, to come joyriding down the aisle, juvenile delinquents, Juvy, Juvenile Hall, the fact that after that he followed the guy everywhere, all over the store, and now we know his name's Mike, the fact that every time I looked for Jake after that, I found him with Mike, the fact that he let Jake help stack the shelves, the fact that Jake's cans were kind of crooked but Mike didn't seem to care, the fact that I kept coming back to check on them but they shooed me off, the fact that Jake said he was busy, the fact that we were really having kind of fun, and then the mean lady has to butt in and wreck it all, snarling about Jake not having a shirt on, the fact that first she scolded *him* and then she came after *me*, the fact that he took off his shirt in the car, but I'd gotten him to put on his *jacket*, to get from the car into the store, and that was the best I could do, the fact that he tore it off again as soon as we were inside, and then ran around bare-chested, like a tiny Tarzan, the fact that, well, so the nipples and maybe even the belly button of a four-year-old were briefly on display, big deal, live with it, the fact that I don't know what she was so worked up about, but I'm so easily cowed, the fact that *that* is what I really hate about it, the fact that I sort of went *along* with her and acted like I *agreed* with her, ♫ *Courage!* ♫, the fact that I didn't actually say anything but I sort of pretended, nodding away, because she was in such a *fury* about it, the fact that actually I don't agree that boys should have to wear shirts at all times, the fact that it was kind of an unbelievable outburst, on her part, the fact that there's something wrong with somebody who can't take the sight of a cute little boy's bare chest and sweet tummy and sharp little shoulder blades without jumping up and down about it, his little round *tummy*, the fact that she was *lucky* to catch a glimpse of it, the fact that she's a lucky lady, she just doesn't know it, the fact that it's not the *law* that little boys have to wear shirts, or even grown men, for that matter, the fact that it's still their choice, last I heard, like if it's hot out, the fact that it's not like *I* was running around with no shirt on, the fact that did she think it was *unhygienic* or something, to have a little bit of bare flesh near the bananas, the fact that there's nothing unhygienic about my son, the fact that Mike never said a *word* about Jake's shirtlessness, the fact that he could have cited company rules but he didn't, the fact that he only commented on Jake's daredevil *driving*, the fact that I should've dragged that lady over to Mike to ask about the store's dress code, the fact that she obviously hasn't anything better to do, the fact that the sailors in *South Pacific* have no shirts on a lot of the time, and I think that's where Jake got the idea, but that doesn't explain the joyride, the fact that when I asked him about it later, why he'd driven that cart at top speed, he said he wanted to *fly*, so it's probably all *my* fault for getting the kids interested in flying that windy day, snow fairies, UFOs, USO, Betty Grable, Jake's shoulder blades, Most Attractive Lip Shape, the fact that that lady's probably *glad* we let starving children die in Syria, the fact that why *do* we let that happen, why do we do that, rolling out the cinnamon rolls, "Suck in your gut," the fact that the police pulled over a speeding car on the highway over in Dover or someplace and the driver was *a ten-year-old kid*, the fact that that's what they make you do in Pilates, I mean suck in your gut, not drive when you're ten, but Breanna's mom thought that motto up long before the Pilates craze began, the fact that some people don't suck in their stomachs, they just let it all hang loose, Jumbo Packs, obesity, obscenity, the fact that sometimes you can't get *past* them, like in a supermarket aisle, the fact that they move around like castles on wheels, icebergs, fatbergs, the fact that never mind the elephant in the room, these people are *actual* elephants, the fact that I shouldn't say such things but, the fact that there are people so fat, the new fat doesn't seem to know where to *go* anymore, where to deposit itself next, the fact that all the bases are loaded, "Who's on first?", so it ends up on the *neck* or somewhere, or the wrist maybe, dimpled babies' hands, goiter woman, the fact that I'm *terrible*, dear me, the fact that somebody just shot his wife at a mall in Kentucky, or his ex-wife, estranged, and then he shot her whole family, who were there with her, on a shopping spree, and then himself, the fact that the whole massacre took less than ten minutes *tops*, the fact that I can't see the point of exacting some revenge that you only get to "enjoy" for about ten minutes, the fact that is that really satisfying, I mean, even to a guy who gets a kick out of revenge, the fact that why can't these people just shoot *themselves*, if they must, and leave other people to make their *own* decisions, the fact that nobody knows how to MYOB anymore, just like that mean lady at Zyker's, mob, mop, crop top, crop T, muffin top, the fact that everybody in the Kentucky mall ran out screaming, and yelling "Active shooter," and trampling each other to get out, the fact that everybody knows the lingo now, but afterwards they were all saying "Oh my god, I can't believe this happened here," the fact that it's getting harder to say you don't believe it though, when it's in the news practically every day, some shooting or other, the fact that it's different of course when it happens to *you*, take a life, get a life, take a load off, the fact that that poor woman was only thirty, the fact that the gunman came up behind her and started an argument, in front of her family, and then he executed her, and them, in a mall, I ♥ YOU, the fact that I dreamt Sergeant Bilko said something, but now I can't remember what, the fact that Stacy's still intrigued by my spitball ordeal, the fact that maybe only a fifteen-year-old could see something swell about carrying a love token around in your ear for thirty years, the fact that I haven't even brought up her Arizona plan, the fact that now it always seems to be *Leo* she's yelling at, the fact that, for crying out loud, I can't figure out why she's so angry, the fact that all I did was ask her for a little help with the laundry, and she stormed up the stairs and slammed her door, DNR, the fact that Leo tried to reason with her, but I had to get Gillian instead, not to reason with Stace, to help me fold the laundry, the fact that I should always get Gillian to do it, the fact that Gillian still *likes* folding sheets because we do Fold and Kiss, kissing when we come together on each fold, the fact that Stacy would probably *explode* if I suggested she and I Fold and Kiss, landsakes, the fact that there'd be nothing left of her, the fact that she'd press the eject button and somehow get transported to Arizona, through sheer willpower, *teleported*, the fact that whatever I tell Cathy about Stacy, she says "Believe me, I've been there," and starts talking about back in the day when Marcia was a teen, TeenSpot, poor Marcia, the fact that *she's* not a prepper, so what are they going to do if the apocalypse comes, just drag her off or leave her behind, the fact that I bet they've secretly prepped for her too, so there'll be enough matches and monocles for everybody, and guns too, little chicks, the fact that the way they treat newborn chicks on factory farms makes me feel like throwing up, the fact that I must not think about it, but it is the most inhuman thing, I think, in the whole entire history of humanity, or inhumanity, the fact that we *gotta* stop eating chicken, unless it's from a good place, where they don't sink to such stuff, the fact that it's not just what they do to the chicks either, which I'm not, not even going to think about, conveyor belt, masher, the fact that they also put all the meat now through a *bleach* bath, which is really bad for everybody, acid bath, acid, alkali, the fact that I need some Alka-Seltzer, or maybe just seltzer, the fact that the first migration from Africa was much earlier than people used to think, and the Aborigines have been in Australia for a hundred thousand years at least, their land, the fact that maybe we should all become vegetarians, not the Aborigines but *us*, as a family, but it's so hard, the fact that there are people who grow their own vegetables, but it sounds like such an effort, the fact that I don't think my back is up to doing all that hoeing, and digging potatoes, and my nerves, "You have no compassion for my poor nerves," aren't up to making the kids do all the work, detox, impacted, the fact that they sell baby kale at the farmer's market, and call it a superfood, but all it gives you for your trouble is super *gas*, the fact that I don't believe that stuff is really digestible, baby celery stalks on braised lettuce, Hurricane Irma, Katrina, the fact that okay you might live longer if you eat superfood but, with all the flatulence, "Call this living?", chlorine, the fact that I dreamt a sort of David Attenborough dream too, the fact that it had nothing to do with the Bilko dream though, the fact that this one was like a TV documentary, narrated by somebody *like* David Attenborough but not actually him, the fact that it was all about some cult that had a very restrictive diet, which doomed them to *kidney stones*, according to David Attenborough or whoever it was, the fact that the weird thing about them, as David Attenborough or whoever pointed out, was that they unconsciously decorated their houses with little decorative bundles of stones that were kind of like *kidney* stones, the fact that they sort of knew what they were in for, healthwise, and they were kind of worshipping the symbolic kidney stones, or praying to the stones to *protect* them from kidney stones, or maybe they were just preparing themselves, trying to get *used* to the idea of kidney stones by contemplating these little stones all the time, the fact that everywhere you looked there were these little piles, or a small group of stones in a bowl or on a window sill, the fact that then I was inside one of their homes and I opened a little basket and inside it was a pile of congealed, sort of *slimy*-looking gray pebbles, the fact that they were carefully tucked away in there, like a little treasure to contemplate in solitude, the fact that I don't even know how big kidney stones *are*, the fact that these were sort of thumbnail-sized, the fact that I hope kidney stones aren't really that big, the fact that I'm so *sleepy* suddenly, Little Pillow, eiderdown, "gettin' a might sleepy at that," but I'm too cold to sleep, but too sleepy to get up either, the fact that I often wish I could just get the kids to school and go right back to bed, the fact that what would be the harm, except that the neighbors might find out I'm a slut, slob, slugabed, the fact that I shouldn't use that word, "slut" I mean, not "slugabed," the fact that all women are not sluts, "all people who behave strangely are not insane," the fact that the college rapist was a swimming star at Stanford, "the Harvard of the West," and he raped a drunk girl and dumped her behind a dumpster, my Saturday swimming class, choking, deep end, Depend, drunk girl, the fact that I should turn the radio *off*, gamelan, the dumpster, the Trumpster, two foreign guys on bikes, Abe Lincoln, Tarzan, Superman, Superwoman, the fact that he was sent home to Sugarcreek Township, after serving a three-month sentence, ♫ *a little femi-nine advice* ♫, the fact that I must get *up*, the fact that here I go, but I'm so *sleepy* though, mark, mart, mart, martin, the fact that, okay, the chicken got love from Daniel, jerky, Daniel Jerky, transgender cantor, Tuesday, the fact that there are all these ways of staying awake, like drinking coffee and stretching your legs and jumping up and down and slapping yourself, or washing your face in cold water or breathing cold air, or taking *speed* of course but I've never tried that, the fact that Marty's taken enough for both of us, amphetamines, fentanyl, cocaine, novocaine, the fact that my teeth *still* hurt, especially when I drink cold drinks, the fact that I should *sue* that hygienist for blasting away all my enamel, thirty fiddlers, two hundred and fifty billion murdered chicks, "Waken up and smell the coffee," the fact that when Leo has back-to-back classes all day, he dunks his whole head in cold water in between, but the way I look at it, being awake isn't everything, Emerson Street, the fact that it's so terrible what happened to Amy and Andy's nice little restaurant, the fact that I can't believe it, coffee syrups, special tea, specialty, the fact that luckily they weren't there at the time, Evanston, 911, math homework, the fact that some people who work on cruise ships feel seasick *all the time* but they have to keep on working, and they don't dare quit because they need the money, the fact that it's almost like slave labor, hard labor, Davy Jones's locker, Casey Jones, the fact that before he died heroically in the train crash, saving the lives of everybody on his train, Casey Jones also saved a little girl from being run over by another train, the fact that he leaned out from the cowcatcher and grabbed her just in time, the fact that it's a nice nickname to have, better than *Davy* Jones, the fact that when I told Leo he agreed, but said since we already have a Stacy, Casey might be confusing, the fact that I think that's *why* Jake likes "Casey," because it sounds like "Stacy," the fact that anyway I told him he can call himself Casey Jones when we're at the store, with his new friend Mike, ♫ *They loved his whistle and his ring number three* ♫, the fact that prepper people call their bug-out bags their "BOBs," the fact that in an emergency everything has to be abbreviated, the fact that they're kind of like a beefed-up version of Daily Carry, but for Daily Carry you photograph everything you take with you on a normal day, not on an apocalypse day, Open Carry, Concealed Carry, Daily Carry, portable play yard, Nestlé's, Arby's, Bayer, D. S. Brown, the fact that Leo says some black-and-white movies have a velvety black, the fact that it depends on the studio where they were made, the fact that bridesmaids now have to throw the veil up in the air when the wedding photos are being taken, girl found behind a dumpster, veil toss duties, Get Out of Veil Free card, wage slavery, trickle-down, "When it comes to my kids I'm an animal," duodenum, doing the dishes, apple peel, kidney stones, the fact that don't people get *bladder* stones too, the fact that I don't want any stones, any awful painful stones, inside me, oh, how horrible, the fact that when I wash out plastic bags I always wish there were goldfish inside them like the ones we used to get from the fair, the fact that they came in red, blue or orange water, dyed with food coloring, poor fish, the fact that the Chicago River's dyed green for St. Patrick's Day, the fact that the Ohio River's now dyed red, blue and orange all year round, not just for special occasions, sky-writing, Cary Grant's dimples, the judge, the fact that it's so lucky nobody was in Amy and Andy's restaurant when it happened, the fact that it's probably ruined, that whole little enterprise, and they were nice people too, the fact that they probably can't afford to rebuild, the fact that they just spent all their money on that sunroom, and he came at it so fast the car ended up on its side, stuck in the doorway between the sunroom and the dining room, the fact that it was all intentional too, or semi-intentional, for no reason, Bilko, the fact that the driver didn't care what he hit, or who he hit, the fact that he just wanted to die, suicide by car accident, the fact that he drove all the way from Steubenville at a hundred miles an hour in the middle of the night, on the wrong side of the road, the fact that he was hoping to hit some car coming the other way but everybody swerved aside in time, so he just carried on driving fast until his wheels clipped the curb, right by Amy and Andy's place, and the whole car flipped over and somehow skidded on its side until it wedged itself into the doorway that used to be the front door of the restaurant, but had just become the door between the restaurant and the new sunroom, the fact that Amy and Andy had such high hopes for that place, the fact that it's a crying shame, the fact that the whole building burnt to the ground, just like that, and now the insurers are trying to wriggle out of paying for a rebuild, the fact that they claim the place was under-insured or something, the fact that it's amazing what damage one crazee guy can do, the fact that so, all in all, it doesn't look like they'll be needing any more of my pies any time soon, or maybe ever, the fact that *they* lost their restaurant and their brand-new sunroom, and *I* lost my pie outlet, all because of one lousy guy, insurance, the fact that really bad things can happen at any moment to really nice people, the girl behind the dumpster, slimy pebbles, the fact that some children get *cancer*, the fact that birds don't wait around for justice, or the insurance, the fact that they just enjoy things while they may, the fact that I think birds get a lot of enjoyment out of life, the fact that there's always something to do if you're a bird, the fact that there is no way a flower is not thrilled to be alive, the fact that a lady slipper or a nasturtium doesn't give up hope, they don't give up trying, as long as the going's good, even though they wilt, the fact that nobody likes seeing a wilted flower, or a dead plant that's given up, but they don't give up that easy, the fact that flowers are brave, a lot braver than *me*, the fact that it's important not to despair though when you've got pies in the oven, because you have to be ready to take them out and flip them when the time comes, the fact that you have to have mercy on your pies, be there for your pies, and in return they will be good, dutiful pies and serve *you*, individual servings, helpings, savings, ♫ *Polly Wolly Doodle all the day* ♫, the fact that Cathy wants me to make sour cherry pies all the time now, which is a real honor, coming from her, ego value, half the battle, the fact that *Cathy's* brave, the fact that she's always cheerful, brave and cheerful like a bird, the fact that she wears some odd getups though, the fact that she really goes for those fluorescent sequined T-shirts, the fact that I can't imagine where she gets them, Kmart maybe, Target, awfulous, the fact that I hope she doesn't go too far to buy them anyway, the fact that they're not terribly becoming, but I shouldn't think about people's appearance, the fact that that last thing she had on looked like some sort of army camouflage gear, but with jazzy neon yellow patches and splashes of silver sparkles here and there, the fact that it was kind of too tight too, it really was, the fact that it showed every bulge, Ida B. Wells, Ida be well, the fact that she could look much nicer in something looser than that, the fact that I wear loose clothing, the fact that actually my clothes are about as close as you can get to old chicken feed sacks, the fact that I might as well just wear old feed sacks, but they're plastic and who wants to wear a plastic feed sack all day, the fact that now something more along the lines of the old burlap variety we've got in the garage, the fact that I'd like to see Ronny's face if I did wear a feed sack, the fact that Stace is always telling me what to wear, but what she doesn't seem to get is that when you're alone in the house cooking all day, getting dressed up just isn't big on the list of priorities, perfume, Christmas-tree lion, the fact that it's not a great idea to get butter all over your nice duds, and dry cleaning is environmentally harmful, so Stacy doesn't approve of that, the fact that somehow *everything* seems bad for the environment, and we don't even have safe drinking water or air, or soil, the fact that you can't even grow organic stuff on most farms now, because the soil's so bad, the fact that I used to think water had no taste and air no smell, but now they do and they smell kind of *suspicious*, watershed, pollutive, the fact that Ohio's "the most pollutive state," and yet everybody's always trying to be part of nature, trampling the underbrush, the fact that what's the point, the fact that they're *not* part of nature, they're part of the *problem*, Snickers bars, snickerdoodles, the fact that it's just kind of silly if you ask me, trying to find a restorative woodland walk to go on, the fact that there's a discount voucher somewhere around here, the fact that where'd I put it, somewhere, 7 Up, DuPont, Monsanto, the fact that Leo says there are people around who simply won't be satisfied until we have destroyed absolutely everything, the fact that when they're not endorsing a new oil pipeline or nuclear power station, they're looking for somebody to obliterate, or yelling about immigrants, Convict No. 9653, production for use, the fact that the Sumatran Corpse Flower stinks for a few days every three years but *we* stink all the time, in the way we *behave*, I mean, the fact that we really need a Have A Heart Day, just one day a year when nobody's killed for no reason, Peace One Day, AWP, CELDF, CAFO, the fact that it's all so confusing, the fact that Native Americans didn't think of the land as wild, they saw it as a harmonious system that humans were part of, choke cherries, the fact that the last walk we had in Cy Young Park, I was trailing along behind them all and overheard Gillian say to Ben, "Daddy's head's so small," the fact that I looked at Leo and his head did look small, just the way it was popping up out of that puffy jacket of his, the fact that it's got that big collar with the hood zipped inside it, that means you can only really see the top of his head, the fact that there's nothing wrong with the size of his head, but it was kind of funny, that little exchange, the fact that I used to think Daddy's feet were too big, but Leo's seem okay to me, the fact that Leo's well-proportioned, he's all in proportion, portion, portion control, serving size, bitesize, the fact that there's an aggressive squirrel at Cy Young, the fact that he jumps out at people, not Cy Young, the squirrel, the fact that Cy Young passed away long ago, and they think he might have rabies, the squirrel, not Cy Young, the fact that rabies is rare in squirrels, but so is the way this squirrel's been behaving, or so they say, *They say*, like the tame squirrel I found in the alley in Evanston, the fact that it's a bad sign when wild animals don't hide from humans, the fact that it usually means their brains aren't working right, like that crazy wild mouse, the fact that we should have given that mouse some water, the fact that Janis's cat was acting crazy but it turned out he just had an ear infection, the fact that it's lucky I didn't get an ear infection from that spitball, or maybe I *did*, long ago, the fact that the weather's hotting up a bit now, spring, nasturtiums, hygienist, Young's Jersey Dairy, root beer float, the fact that animals really must wonder about humans, what we think we're up to, the fact that we are so caught up with human stuff, all our activities and habits, all our worries and ideas and idears and ideals and our cars and diets and fitness regimes, and crimes and con-jobs, the fact that everybody's completely obsessed with crime, the fact that the half who aren't actually committing crimes spend all their time watching crime movies and crime TV shows or reading crime novels about the people who are, Cathy, the fact that people are addicted to crime and war and stuff, the fact that dogs aren't interested in crime at all, the fact that there is nothing so beautiful as a thoughtful dog, the fact that Cathy's always reading some murder mystery, the fact that she can't do without them, she says, the fact that I hope she's packed a few in her BOB, but there are other delights in life, there really are, like chickens pecking at the dirt, the curly-cued twistings of bark on our fallen tree, and, and, well, *spring*, the colors and such, the fact that nature really goes to town on flowers and birds and butterflies, pansies and daffodils, glowing orange poppies, nasturtiums, dandelions, cardinals and bluebirds and kingfishers, indigo buntings and mandarin ducks, the fact that some sunsets and sunrises have a pretty flashy color scheme too, the fact that people always put babies in pastel shades, as if bright colors are too hard on their eyes or something, and then they give them a million toys in bright, primary colors, and I don't get it, the fact that what I liked best from our whole year in London were my two favorite colored pencils, one very pale pink, the other very pale blue, the fact that I've never seen any like that since, never that pale, the fact that I was amazed by the restraint of those two colors, the fact that they seemed extremely subtle and sophisticated to me, the fact that I always used them *together* in pictures, because I liked to see the pale blue beside the pale pink, so I guess maybe some children do like pastel shades, the fact that I don't usually like pastel shades, nor beige, nor khaki, the fact that a cat was the mayor of some town in Alaska, Talkeetna, Kittyna, Kittyville, the fact that the cat was mayor for twenty years and died in office,

.   .   .   .

She drifted through populous areas and remoter spots. One day, to get her bearings, she climbed a mountain far from houses or traffic. At the summit, a large boulder extended over a sheer drop. From habit, she checked the area for any sign of the cubs, but instead she saw a man, sitting on the edge of the boulder and peering into the chasm below.

The lioness stiffened, watching him closely. He stood up, sat down, kicked his legs against the side of the rock. Then he beat his fists on the stone and emitted loud growls. He lingered long, rocking from side to side. Clearly sick, he would be easy prey. A neat leap at the small stretch of throat, a short struggle, would be all it took. But the lioness had no taste for humans. Every aspect of them sickened her: their noise, their clobber, their chemical smell, their greedy, darting, intrusive eyes and inexplicably bare skin. Their soft-bellied infants might make a snack one day, if she ever found one out on its own, but full-grown people were worse than elongated mergansers, all bone inside the layers of cloth padding. They were merely her rivals in the forest, and dangerous ones, to be shunned.

Finally, the man stood up, spread his feeble arms like shriveled wings, and jumped, screaming, into vacant air. For a moment, he looked almost like a real bird on take-off, but real birds swoop and soar. They float. Fake birds fall straight like stones. At the bottom, he bounced and landed in the damp gully of the river that wound its way around the mountainside.

In her hunger, the lioness considered picking on his remains, but she preferred her own kills. And she was repulsed by his unexpected act of self-destruction. There was no shame in curling up somewhere to die when the time came. You must. But to pre-empt it was absurd. Violence shimmered through the killers, irrational and jarring. Cub-stealers, all. Life-wasters.

Anyway, she knew the flightless man had probably been torn to shreds by his fall. She had once chased a nervy stag to the edge of a cliff, where he'd heedlessly leapt off into nothingness. Still avid for his flesh, she had carefully padded her way down the rocky mountainside, only to find a mishmash of blood, guts and glistening bones spread wide, fit only for crows.

·   ·   ·   ·

the fact that the "hydraulic" approach to parenthood is now out of date, the fact that you're *not* supposed to encourage kids to let off steam anymore, you're supposed to just *hug* them all the time, or that's what some Yale psychologist says you should do if your kids are unhappy, the fact that I do do Fold and Kiss, but that's about it on the physical affection front, and I'm even worse in public, PDAs, shy, the fact that I think the kids would probably freak out if I suddenly started hugging them all day, and then we'd *all* need to blow off some steam, the fact that they are much too gawky and distracted to be hugged a lot anyway, the fact that how do you hug a kid playing computer games, the fact that it's like trying to grab hold of a wild kitten, though James's mom's *always* hugging him, the fact that I've got to stop calling her that, the fact that her name's Fresia, *Fresia*, like the flower, the fact that I don't think this lion *could* be an Eastern Cougar, because Ben looked it up and they're definitely extinct, the fact that they're so extinct they don't need protection anymore, the fact that they're not "endangered," they're just gone, the fact that after the first cougar sighting though, Ben did some research and now he says they found a mountain lion paw print in *Connecticut* last year, which may mean the Eastern Cougar does still exist, at least in Connecticut, the fact that they usually stick to major river valleys, but they've been pushed out of them by people, so now they have to live in "attics," meaning mountains, deserts and swamps, the fact that I told Ben "Not in *our* attic, I hope," the fact that that would be scary, to find a mountain lion in the attic, rocking on the ol' rocking chair, the fact that I'd never *heard* of attics in the wild before, the fact that I guess they're called that because people don't spend much time there, just throw all their old junk in and run away, the fact that cougars don't mind steep terrain or heat, so they can live in dry places, or humid places, any place where people don't go, the fact that the high rocky ridges of Montana are "attics," but there are now more bobcats there than cougars, parched country, *the tragedy of unwatered country*, the fact that I don't know about Arizona, London Bridge, the fact that there could be a few up in the mountains maybe, searching for rare iguanas to eat, land

of hope and glory, MagPump, drift-adjustable rear, the fact that heraldic lions are rampant, dormant, salient, passant, gardant, passant gardant, and statant gardant, but I don't know about *this* lion, the fact
that Mommy and Daddy never went in for hugging much, and only
kissed each other in front of us if Daddy was going on a trip somewhere, put your John Hancock there, the fact that I guess I could save
time and energy by doing a big group-hug on all four kids once a week
or so, but that doesn't seem very spontaneous, the fact that it's really
Abby I wish I'd hugged more, rag rugs, CC and ginger, and *she* would
have let me, unlike these characters, the fact that I wish Mommy
hadn't passed away, but sometimes I think the person I keep longing
to spend time with most is Abby, because she was so comforting to be
around, and always a friend to me, a mother substitute maybe, the fact
that anyway I miss that, the stability of her and her little house, the
lunchtime sandwiches and her housework routine, the fact that I even
miss her brick-imitation wallpaper in the kitchen, the fact that I always
thought it was kind of corny to have brick wallpaper, but hers was
nice, the fact that I used to stare at it during meals and imagine taking
the bricks out and checking what was behind there, the fact that
maybe *we* should get some brick wallpaper in our kitchen, why not,
but I'll never get around to it, the fact that I just liked the way *she* did
things, the fact that it was calm and pleasant there, tranquil, the fact
that I live in chaos and she lived so neatly, and in between her bouts
of housework we seemed to have all the time in the world to sit around
and talk while Hoag was out at work, knitting, the bee at Bread Loaf,
sewing bee, the fact that she was quite a talker and all I really had to
do was listen, the fact that, to me, her life seemed so safe, though it
probably wasn't really, the fact that she had health issues and money
worries, and maybe problems with Hoag, in the bedroom, the fact that
she only hinted at that once, that he was, well, reluctant or something,
the fact that it was safe for me there, the fact that it's rare to feel really
accepted, rare to feel relaxed, the fact that sometimes I felt weirdly
nauseous, and I couldn't figure it out at first but later I decided it was
a particular kind of boredom, that happens to me when people talk too

much, the fact that I get it with Ronny too, all the time, the fact that Abby's neighbors did it to me a lot, but it was worth it for the kindness and stability of being at Abby's, the fact that I wish I could provide such a stable household for anybody, the fact that it takes work, and energy, a system, and I always seem to fail at that, the fact that when her garage guy friend asked me out I didn't want to go, the fact that I think Abby was surprised I didn't go, the fact that I kind of liked him, but I just wanted to stay with her and look out at the blue snow at twilight through her kitchen door, the fact that her back door shut so snugly, the fact that he was *married* anyway, the fact that I don't know what Abby really thought about that, the fact that she probably just thought we'd have an innocent little outing, but I thought we'd end up *involved* if I went, and I'm sure that would've shocked Abby, and caused trouble, the fact that Cathy reminds me of Abby a bit, the fact that I like her so much, the fact that I just like being around Cathy, Marcia, the fact that you never stop worrying about your kids, not for one single solitary second, the fact that even before they're born you worry about them, the fact that people would think you're a lazy crazy mom if you *didn't* worry about your kids all the time, the fact that you're always supposed to be helping your kids do things, talking to them from the day they're born if not before, nursing them, on demand or not on demand, weaning them, spoon-feeding them, changing them, feeding them for twenty years, clothing them, which costs big bucks, teaching them, playing ball with them, taking them swimming and singing and dancing and karate-chopping, and traveling and dining out and hugging and comforting and negotiating and tucking them into bed and reading to them for two hours a night and bringing them glasses of water and saving their lives all the time, and if you don't do all that, you're the *pits*, the fact that one thing's for sure, whatever you do, it's not enough, and make one mistake and you've had it, nap, euphoria, because everybody thinks they can threaten and criticize and mom-shame you, on TV, in books, at PTA meetings, online, and even at the supermarket, Jake with no shirt on, the fact that they all think they know better, *I don't know but they know*, like how your kids'll be traumatized by this or that, too much or too little attention, exercise, food, medicine, clothing, shelter, hobbies, friends, everything, but what if it's the other way around, and it's us *moms* that are traumatized, shell-shocked, damaged, starved, downtrodden, by everything we gotta do, this huge thankless task, the fact that I think it sends some moms off their *rockers*, most moms maybe, the fact that let's face it, most of us are in terrible shape, PTSD, PMT, HRT, IIIPAA, galoshes, nasturtiums, Ground Round Grill and Bar, the fact that the kids really are traumatized now though, and do need to be hugged, after being sent home from school yet again because of a cougar sighting, the fact that there have been so many lately, it's getting to be a bit of a joke, the fact that it's inconvenient for me too, having lions on the loose, because I have to keep the hens cooped up and the cats indoors, the kids too, and I still have to make pies, the fact that kids all over Eastern Ohio were sent home today, all because somebody thought they saw a mountain lion way up near Ashtabula, of all places, the fact that I think the working moms are acting scarier than any cougar though, Tiger Moms, because they're all so furious about having to leave work and rush home and take care of everybody, the fact that there was a *different* kind of lion, an African lion, on some college campus in *New Jersey* the other day, and the whole place went into lockdown, the fact that I can't remember if it was Rutgers or maybe Montclair, the fact that it got out of a zoo, the fact that the weird thing was no information was allowed out to the students or their parents for hours, just like a shooting lockdown, ♫ *Lockdown, lockdown, lock the door* ♫, the fact that it's like the authorities thought the escaped lion might hack into the phones or something and get info on the chase, the fact that the poor students were stuck in their dorms or classrooms and the poor parents didn't know if their kid had been mauled or not, for *hours*, the fact that I mean the parents didn't know for hours, not that the kids were being *mauled* for hours, the fact that nobody was mauled at all, mall, mauled, pall, Paul, caul, and they caught him in the end, the fact that it didn't even take very long, the fact that, gee whiz, Jesus of Philadelphia, as if school shooters and campus shooters and cinema shooters and nightclub shooters and restaurant shooters and disgruntled employee shooters and domestic and foreign terrorist shooters weren't enough, now we have to worry about *wild animals* as well, and the trigger-happy amateurs hot on their trail, López Pérez, the fact that when the mountain lion, or maybe some *other* mountain lion, how do we know, was spotted near Lincoln Park Zoo a few weeks ago, they didn't know if it had escaped from the zoo, or was some interloper from the wilderness, Chicago attics, the fact that then it just disappeared, the fact that they never did catch that one, so then people got paranoid and started seeing lions all over Chicago, cougars, panthers, whatever, loping around, sheesh, the fact that people said they saw it on Michigan Avenue and in Chinatown, the fact that maybe it's got a taste for pot stickers and roast duck, Dr. DeBoer, the Wesley Memorial Hospital, the fact that the gun crime rate in Chicago *doubled* because the lion spooked every-body, and they're all so heavily armed, the fact that the number of fatalities was worse than the Fourth of July, the fact that lions were reported in Winnetka and Evanston too, and in Milwaukee, the fact that that lion sure gets around, if it is just one, the fact that there have been sightings just about everywhere in the Northeast of Ohio now too, the fact that maybe it's some kind of national hysteria, brought on by Trump weariness, the fact that if we're not careful he'll declare a National Emergency, Emma and Mr. Knightley, Colin Firth, Prince Charles talking to plants, David Attenborough, the fact that Trump's made no comment on the cougar at all so far, except some crack about the "lion Dems," the fact that he probably thinks the Democrats released this lion on purpose, the fact that the police are going berserk, heading in all directions and shooting anything on four legs, the fact that even a little red wagon, that rolled out from behind a bush at the wrong moment, got riddled with bullet holes, "Grrrreat!", the fact that it's getting so it's not safe for kids to be outside because of the *cops*, never mind the lion, the fact that I'm sure they're doing their very best, but it's getting like the Keystone Kops around here today, with the number of sirens going by and emergency vehicles, the fact that there've been a few pile-ups too, the fact that a poor old lady in a wheelchair just got shot at in *Akron*, trying to get to the *grocery store*, for the love of Mike, the fact that somebody mistook her meandering progress across the parking lot for the stealthy movements of a big cat, the fact that it sounds like before they'd had time to *think* they'd shot her, but luckily they missed, the fact that when she screamed, they realized she was *not* a cougar, though cougars can scream, like the leopard in *Bringing up Baby*, the fact that people shoot before they even know what they're shooting at, the fact that, for crying out loud, it's like playing Russian roulette, just going to the grocery store, the fact that that's no way to treat a poor old lady, the fact that, I mean, *really*, this shouldn't happen in America, the fact that the squirrel in Cy Young Park better watch out, because they're shooting anything that moves, Nickel Mines, Cy Young, Hy-Vee, Bed-Sty, YT vids, lookit, the fact that they've launched a whole ground and air search for the lion, and people have been warned not to approach it because *you tread on my dreams*, no, because it could be hungry and aggressive if cornered, the fact that I wasn't actually planning on approaching any mountain lions today anyway, if I can *help* it, maybe tomorrow, the fact that on the news they're talking about where it must've come from, since the Eastern Cougar's officially extinct, the fact that maybe it got out of a home zoo, or maybe this mountain lion was somebody's pet, because he doesn't seem scared of humans, the fact that you never know what kind of pets people keep anymore, the fact that people aren't content with having cats, dogs, mice, hamsters, and guinea pigs, the fact that they all want iguanas and tarantulas as well, the fact that this makes Ohio a pretty dangerous place to be in really, what with guns and pet wolves everywhere, *and* our polluted drinking water, the fact that every now and then a python turns up in a storm drain, or there's an elephant nobody knew about, the elephant in the room, the fact that it would be funny to find out somebody was keeping an *elephant* on our road, the fact that that would be fun, Babar, Flora, the fact that there was a great baby dressed as an elephant at the school Hallowe'en party last year, pale gray with a trunk and tusks, and the big round feet, the whole shebang, just the baby's face showing, the fact that how do you defend yourself against an Eastern Cougar, the fact that is it the same as defending yourself against a molester from the seventies, like you try to punch his Adam's apple, pinch his inner thigh, the fact that if the Eastern Cougar *is* making a comeback, I don't know how Gillian can do the Indian Mud Run, the fact that she's the most outdoorsy kid we've got, except today, because even she doesn't want to go out and get eaten by a lion, even to tend her carrots, the fact that somebody said he'd known some girl "from a little vegetable on up," the fact that Ben's now trying to grow chives, the fact that last year Jake stole all Gillian's carrots in one afternoon, the fact that he ate them straight out of the ground, which is something Gillian would never do, the fact that she may like mud but she's squeamish about dirt, the fact that she was all bent out of shape when she first found out you have to grow vegetables in dirt, but she got used to the idea eventually, Diamond Ring Turns Up On A Squash, Mound City, the fact that she probably thinks there will be a lot of squelchy mud at the Indian Mud Run, but I think she'll be disappointed, the fact that I don't think that's why it's called that, the fact that I think it's called that just to insult Native Americans, the fact that by mid-summer the ground's usually totally cracked and parched on all those paths, though there are water challenges too, so maybe the mud gathers around those, scour, the fact that Gillian's favorite thing is squelchy mud between her bare toes, the fact that she's got a real thing about it, and she used to make mud pies too, the fact that there's a dirty side to Gillian that wants to get out, the fusspot funette, the fact that the other kids call her a fusspot but she's not really, the fact that I think they call her fusspot because there has to be a fusspot in every family, just like there has to be a tattle-tale and a know-it-all and a bossy-boots, the fact that I think these nicknames rotate actually, revolve, orbit, hybrid, acne, the fact that one good thing about having four kids is I never have to criticize them, because they do it for me, the fact that they all keep each other in line, maybe too much, Kleenex, Chuck, Tuesday, the fact that I told Gillian about that old woman who found her lost diamond ring stuck on a spaghetti squash from her vegetable patch, the fact that it had been missing for twenty-five years, and then there it was on the stalk of a malformed squash, the fact that she'd thrown it out by accident years before, with the potato peelings, and eventually it must've found its way onto the squash, and then finally popped up right in front of her, the fact that that is one reward for growing vegetables, the fact that it's funny to think that a diamond ring wound its way around her vegetable patch, eventually straight back to its owner, the fact that it's like the joke about the snail on the porch who gets thrown into the yard and a year later he finally makes it back on to the porch and scratches on the screen door and says "What was all that about?", the fact that Mommy lost the diamond out of her engagement ring, the fact that she saw what she thought was a piece of glass on the kitchen floor and threw it out, and later she realized the diamond was missing from her *ring*, the fact that *her* diamond never found its way back to her, but Daddy had a new one put in the ring later on, the fact that for all I know she may have been fretting about *that* when I came down all euphoric from my nap, the fact that maybe she'd just noticed her diamond was gone, that very day, spaghetti squash, showering with Leo on Tangier Island, the fact that there was some Disney movie about an escaped lion that wanders around some town, and then gets shot, the fact that that's all I can remember about it, the fact that I hated that movie, first because it was so long and second because they killed the lion, the fact that some dentist went to Africa recently and shot some really famous lion in a safari park, the fact that his name was Cecil, the lion, not the dentist, the fact that the dentist said he hadn't known the lion was *protected*, the fact that he just wanted to kill a lion and accidentally shot a famous one, bad luck, the fact that he's *always* getting arrested for shooting animals you're not supposed to shoot, the fact that he probably likes sandblasting teeth too, Crest, Colgate, Leo, sugar, cavities, fluoride, raspberries, cornmeal, ginger, the fact that you'd think the kids'd be bored, stuck at home with mom, but they're thrilled to have time off, or so far anyway, the fact that I sure have a lot of kids, and I'm not used to having them all around on a weekday, when I have pies to make, the fact that they all have different needs and desires too, the fact that I feel like I'm teaching at a frontier school or something, catering for four different age groups at once, one kid per grade, all in the same room, the fact that in some country or other children only go to school for a few hours a day and they do fine, the fact that they don't get homework either, yet they're the best-educated kids in the world, according to somebody, the fact that I can't remember which country it is, Luxembourg or Latvia, Lithuania, or Slovenia, or Estonia or somewhere, the fact that it must be spring because the icebergs are calving, the fact that somebody made that joke on the news, the fact that I don't think Stacy found it funny, the fact that Ben and Gillian are now absorbed in their drawing contest, the fact that all I really wanna do is watch them, but I've got apples to caramelize, the fact that I'm supposed to judge the contest in a minute but I'm playing for time, the fact that if we were in *Anne of Green Gables* or Laura Ingalls Wilder, they'd be peeling the apples for me, but they'd all just moan, and they're so happy drawing, so why pester them, the fact that the kitchen is peaceful right now, and that's worth a million naked Pink Ladies, the fact that I should probably get an apple-peeling *machine*, but we don't have room for any more machines on the kitchen counters, or in the pantry, the fact that we don't have the money for one either, white egg cups, the fact that anyway, what do I want with another deafening machine, the fact that we've already got the washer, dryer, fan ovens, blender, juicer, AC, TV, hairdryers, radio, laptops, Gameboys, the vacuum cleaner, and the lawnmower, not to mention the *kids*, the fact that they aren't technically machines, but they do make a lot of noise, automatons, automat, luncheonette, the fact that most of our neighbors seem to have leaf blowers and snow blowers, or their hired hands do, the fact that raking the leaves used to be a sort of contemplative activity, but now it's just a horror, and their leaf-blowers wreck raking for *me*, when I try to do it, the fact that mostly I leave our leaves to the wind to handle, the fact that Aunt Cordelia rakes leaves in *Up A Road Slowly*, to recover from seeing her first love again and from being insulted by Julie, Chuck, Ronny's beef about trash bags full of leaves, the fact that I wouldn't dream of asking the neighbors to knock it off with all the leaf-blowers, the fact that maybe they think it's a protection against Lyme disease, leaf-blowing I mean, the fact that some people say "Lyme's" disease but I think it's "Lyme," the fact that they can shoot you just for approaching their house, if they feel threatened, the fact that a school kid went to a house to ask directions and the guy shot at him, the fact that he was black, the kid, not the homeowner, the fact that the boy ran for his life and got away, the fact that I got yelled at just for moving that darn sprinkler off the sidewalk a little, so that Jake could get by on his scooter, shooter, looter, the fact that I hate those deafening hand-drying machines in public restrooms too, the fact that I don't see why you need to contravene federal decibel-level laws just to dry your hands, the fact that Leo says they spread fecal matter all through the air of the restroom too, but nobody seems to care about that, the fact that I always use the paper towels but you're still stuck breathing in the fecal matter and having to listen to everybody *else* using the hand-dryer machines, the fact that you can't stuff your fingers in your ears when you're drying your hands, Band-Aid, the fact that perhaps I need some I ♥ U spit-balls for *both* ears, just to use in restrooms, and maybe here in the kitchen too when all the kids are around, though they're being nice and quiet at the moment, and Alec Baldwin and Meryl Streep are getting drunk in New York, the fact that where's Casey Jones gone now, *a man that died for men*, the fact that people say human beings are basically benevolent, because when things like Hurricane Katrina happen, everybody gets together and helps each other out, and this proves we're basically a "cooperative species," the fact that I hope they're right but, well, the Nazis helped each other out a lot too, and IBM helped them some more, the fact that the Nazis all got together as a community and *exterminated* a bunch of people, the fact that, boy, did they cooperate smoothly on that, collaborate, collabo, the fact that lynch mobs are good at cooperating too, mob rule, and mobs cooperate fine, the fact that a whole bunch of Hindus beat a Muslim to death in

India for stealing cows, and when the police came, all they did was arrest some *more* Muslims for stealing cows, concentration camps, rape, WMDs, witch hunts, the fact that being a cooperative species can either be a success or a failure, the fact that my itch is gone, the one on my finger, that is, *Sam I am*, the fact that those *tartlets* were a success, Cathy says, the fact that that is gratifying, I must admit, though they were all her idea, the E-G-O car, the fact that I think it may have been inspired by the wedding pear tarte tatin she swallowed whole, Minnehaha, *Last of the Mohicans*, the fact that I've got to tell Cathy these pies'll be late though, with the kids home today, the fact that I wonder when I'll get a chance to *phone* her even, the fact that Ben and Gillian are pleading for the final judgment on their drawings, the fact that my delaying tactics are running out, the fact that I already told them to add more detail, several times, the fact that soon they'll see through my clever ploy, the fact that by now they've probably put *too* much in, the fact that it'll be impossible to decipher anything, and that always makes them mad, *It's Complicated*, the fact that *they* think their drawings are crystal clear, the fact that this time they're all about the mountain lion, but I can't see any lions in either picture yet, the fact that, oh no, now they're mad at me for asking questions, the fact that they act like I'm making a poet explain his poem, *Tyger Tyger, burning bright,* the fact that I'll just call Cathy, tell her about the pies, the fact that, great, she says it's no problem, lion, customers, Art, BOB, Civil Standby, friend, husband, trailer, car, fine, bye, the fact that, oh my god, I can't *believe* it, the fact that how did *that* come up, gug, gulp, gosh, the fact that I just can't, the fact that she said it so breezily too, almost as if it's no big deal, wow, the fact that I appreciate her feeling she could *confide* in me, the fact that maybe it just boomeranged back on her today for some reason, lion, and she felt the need to share, oh dear, poor *Cathy*, my word, the fact that maybe it's the lion scare that stirred it all up again for her, lion's share, car, rifle, the trailer with the Confederate flag on top, the fact that *now* how am I going to make pies, when I'm crying just *thinking* what Cathy went through, the fact that why'd she never mention it before, a *shooting*, the fact that her friend *"died,"* oh, oh, my, car door, Cathy crouching down, the fact that she says she's fine about it now, the fact that it was all twenty years ago, but just to think of it, the fact that that is *so scary*, the fact that I don't know anyone else who's been through something that bad, the fact that I don't *think* so anyway, but who knows, the fact that people don't always want to talk about these things, the fact that at least she survived, *Cathy*, not her friend, wow, oh no, the fact that here goes, okay, intricacy, lion, colors, intricacy, the fact that okay, okay, now I have judged the drawing competition, the fact that I gave Gillian the prize for intricacy and Ben the prize for color, the fact that the prizes were choc-dipped madeleines, the fact that now they're dancing around the kitchen with them, whooping, the fact that they scared Frederick off his comfy chair, Cathy, poor Cathy, and now Ben's stubbed his toe, the fact that Stacy got one too, a madeleine, not a stubbed toe, the fact that she got hers for *not* jumping around like a crazy person, the fact that Ben's bravely wiping away his tears, the fact that *he's* okay, but what about *me*, the fact that it really is nice she told me, Cathy I mean, the fact that I would never have guessed something like that had ever happened to her, but she says this sort of thing happens all the time, the fact that, still, I think it's awful that it happened to *Cathy*, and to her *friend*, the fact that that's when things get personal, the fact that luckily all Ben and Gillian can think about is the lion on the loose, so they haven't even noticed me crying, oh poor Cathy, the fact that now it says on the news they're going to let kids go back to school tomorrow, but they want the parents to drive them there, the fact that I don't know if that includes kids who take the school bus or not, the fact that I'll have to spend an hour looking it up, or maybe Ben could, the fact that public announcements are never clear enough, the fact that a bus is safer than a car, I'd think, against a *lion* anyway, I mean, the fact that a bus is bigger anyway, and there's safety in numbers too, maybe, though I don't think lions attack cars much either, the fact that I agree they shouldn't walk, the kids, not lions, the fact that the *lion* should walk right back where he came from, the zoo or circus or whatever, and leave us in peace, the fact that I still can't believe it though, about Cathy, the fact that she said nowadays Blanche would have gotten a police escort, Civil Standby, moral support, police backup, but not then, the fact that she was too scared to go alone, the fact that she'd just left the guy, her husband, and she needed to get her stuff, so Cathy went along, the fact that they were even planning to go get coffee and donuts afterwards, oh my gosh, coffee and donuts, to *celebrate*, the fact that he'd been violent in the past, which I guess was why she was leaving him, the fact that she didn't think he'd pull anything with Cathy around but, boy, was *she* wrong, the fact that it's just luck that Cathy wasn't shot too, Paterson Falls, sour cherry pie, the fact that he had a beat-up old trailer out back, full of junk, with a Confederate flag flying on top, I don't know why, the fact that when they drove up to the house, he took off, retreated to his trailer, the fact that Cathy stayed in the car, I think, while Blanche was getting her stuff together, the fact that they loaded the car up and were just about to leave when the husband came out of the trailer with a rifle and started shouting, *shooting*, oh dear me, the fact that Blanche was trying to calm him down, but it didn't work, the fact that the scary thing is he shot at Cathy first, like he was using her, Cathy's *life*, as an example to Blanche, to show he meant business, the fact that luckily Cathy wasn't hurt, the fact that she just ducked down and played dead, the fact that how does everybody know to play dead in these situations, the fact that is it instinct, or learned response, or what, the fact that school kids do it in school shootings, and the boy at Gnadenhutten did it, the fact that kids play dead all the time, and people even teach their dogs to play dead, the fact that it often seems to work, depending on how *thorough* the killer is, because some of them come back to make sure the job's done, and shoot everybody *again*, the fact that it would be awful to be shot when you're already playing dead, the fact that anyway, there were more shots fired, and the next thing Cathy knew, both Blanche and her husband were lying there dead on the ground by the side of the car, "Mary mother of god," the fact that he shot Blanche and then himself, the fact that he shot Blanche in the abdomen, and she bled to death, passed away, pass away, Davina Beebee's hurts, the fact that they were estranged, the fact that at least Frank never tried to *shoot* me, though he could be a bully, the fact that Blanche's husband was a real bully, the fact that Cathy called him "a goddam coward" on the phone just now, and she never usually speaks that way, the fact that they like to claim that they're monitoring bullying at *school* but are they, the fact that maybe they do try harder than they used to, "We try harder," the fact that cyber-bullying's even worse, the fact that they drive kids to *suicide*, just for the fun of it, Avis, Hertz, with impunity, the fact that that is such a terrible thing, the fact that the main purpose of a husband should be to give you *back rubs*, not rub you out of *existence*, the meaning of life, the Facts of Life, Peolia College, tree roots, Abby, rag rugs, the Country Shoppe, the Bread Loaf bumble bee, the twin Crimson Lakes, the fact that Cathy had to duck and play dead, oh dear, *Cathy*, the fact that she was really a sitting duck in that car, the fact that he could've killed her easy, and he certainly tried, for no reason, no reason, the fact that how *dare* he, the fact that now I'm *mad*, the fact that how *dare* anybody try to kill my friend, candlelit vigils, the fact that I don't know how she manages to be so cheerful, the fact that she keeps the whole of Tuscarawas County alive with her cooking, her dad as well, and Art, and Marcia, the fact that so many people depend on Cathy, me included, the fact that besides the shock and trauma of it all, it must have been so terrible to lose her friend like that, the fact that it's bad enough when someone passes away of a heart attack or something and maybe you don't get to say goodbye, but if they get *murdered*, and you *witness* it, and can't save them and have to listen to it all, fearing for your own life, the fact that, why, that's just awful, that's like Rathbone at the Lincoln assassination, the fact that she did get slightly tearful when she was telling me, just for a moment, but not like me, the fact that, look at me, the fact that I'm a *wreck*, bawling in the bathroom, sobbin' women, Grandma, the fact that I guess she must feel we're pretty good friends now or she wouldn't have told me, Sand Creek, "Sweet Fanny Adams," the fact that Fanny Adams was just a little girl, and she was murdered, in England in 1867, the fact that a local man did it, the fact that he just saw her walking by and he snatched her and hacked her to pieces, a sweet little girl, only eight years old, Gillian, Ben, my heart operation, the fact that how could he, how can *anyone* bring themselves to do such a terrible terrible thing, the fact that thinking about *that's* no help, the fact that now I'm crying about Fanny Adams as well, the fact that moms are always trying to take such good care of everybody, day in, day out, and then some man comes and does something like that, the fact that of course most men don't, but some do, the fact that there are men who rape ten-year-olds, five-year-olds, one-year-olds, or kill people for no reason, horrible, horrible, the fact that you're not supposed to stay married *on pain of death*, the fact that marriage is still supposed to be voluntary, the fact that there's a song called "Sweet Fanny Adams," the fact that people'll write a song about anything, I guess, just like that other one, ♫ *By the banks of the Ohio* ♫, the fact that he just grabbed her right off the road and did what he wanted to her, not caring who she was or what right she had to life, or how her family would feel, the *mom*, who bore her and cared for her and loved her for eight whole years, the fact that it makes you absolutely sick sometimes, the fact that I really do feel nauseous, broken, broken heart syndrome, the fact that I just don't know how I can *bake* after this, the fact that I gotta think about something else quick, or the kids'll know something's up, the fact that now they're quarreling about which board game to play, "Bicker, bicker, bicker," right under my feet, the fact that can't they see I'm in the middle of flipping here, flipping *pies*, that is, the fact that I'm trying *not* to flip out entirely, the fact that having them home during the daytime actually makes me feel a bit queasy even at the best of times, the fact that I think I associate it with them being sick, and when *they're* sick, I feel sick, the fact that they're not sick though, they're just home, the fact that I don't know why Cathy told me now, the fact that it just sort of popped out, and now I can't remember what were we talking about before she got on to that, no, the fact that I just can't remember how it popped up, BOB, yes, the fact that she was saying something about her bug-out bag, the fact that maybe *this* is what turned her into a prepper, the trauma of being shot at, the fact that now she's primed and ready for action at all times, the fact that maybe she feels permanently on edge, and I never guessed it, poor Cathy, the fact that all this time I just thought of her as just a nice cozy, pretty hopeful person, efficient businesswoman, very efficient, feeding the whole community, happy, the fact that I'm so embarrassed now, that I never guessed she'd been through anything of this sort, the fact that to think I ever bored her with *my* stuff, *my* little problems, Stacy and whatnot, the fact that who am I to say, well, I mean privately, just to Leo, that she's wasting her time and money on survivalism, the fact that what do I know, the fact that I should just MYOB, *MMOB* I mean, mind *my* own beeswax, the fact that maybe I'm just disappointed, that underneath all the efficiency Cathy's as scared as anybody, *scarred*, hurts, the fact that now Gillian's chasing Ben around the room, the fact that there's some dispute about something, the fact that Alec Baldwin misses Meryl Streep's cooking, and I feel sick, Fanny Adams, Cathy, the fact that I wish I could do more for Cathy, "Wash on Monday, Iron on Tuesday, Mend on Wednesday, Churn on Thursday, take care of Cathy on Fridays," the fact that maybe I could take her out to lunch or something, somewhere, except the best food around is at the *Shoppe*, the fact that the kids are quarreling, the fact that maybe I could cope with all this, the illnesses and accidents, the sulks, the fights, the moody stage, the intrusive question stage, even the Silent Treatment, if I could just get a little more sleep, the fact that look at them, the fact that I'll have to separate them now, and they were playing so nicely before, the fact that kids really are *wild animals*, they're like little tiger cubs you keep in the house, elephants in the room, popsicles, the fact that maybe popsicles are the answer, the fact that what a bad mom, and useless friend, the fact that she tells me this *terrible story* and all I can think about is how many popsicles I can stuff down my kids' gullets, but how many have we got left in the freezer, the fact that kids keep reducing your life down to the basics, to popsicles, the fact that nobody ever *tells* people that, like when they're deciding whether to have kids or not, the fact that nobody tells you how endless and boring and silly it is, and, the fact that just getting a kid out the front door every morning is a major achievement, and quite an ordeal, a traumatic event, not on the scale of Cathy's but still, the fact that they always want *extras* too, extra favors, "Please, sir, I want some more," and if they don't *get* what they want they go ballistic, "the gunman went ballistic," bullets, Fanny Adams, cut to shreds, the fact that a ten-year-old kid in Marietta just killed his sister because she wouldn't give him the remote, the fact that he went and got a gun and just shot her in the back of the head, the fact that Ben wants Power Grid for his birthday, the fact that you get to decide how to provide cities with electricity, or something like that, the fact that I think it costs too much, but we'll probably cave, the fact that maybe it's educational, the fact that I sound like *Erica*, the fact that at least my kids don't throw tantrums like Charlie Hawthorn in that *Little House* book, whichever one it is, when he gets stung by the bees, the fact that I wouldn't be any good with tantrums, and I think they somehow sense that, the fact that I'm glad they never watched the *Little House* TV show, because it's no good, as far as I remember, the fact that I think little kids essentially act *drunk* the whole time, Meryl Streep, with all their rambunctiousness and mischief and con-fusions and their fits of crying, the fact that what about *my* fits of crying, the fact that adults need caffeine, drugs, booze, and bad news, just to act even a little bit like kids, the fact that Julie grows up too fast in *Up a Road Slowly*, I think, I mean from Gillian's point of view, the fact that even her father says so, Julie's father, not Gillian's, "I remem-ber her from a little vegetable on up," the fact that some seeds can last two thousand years before they start germinating, the fact that they just sit there for two thousand years, waiting for conditions to be right, David Attenborough, the fact that Gillian gave up on it halfway through, halfway through reading *Up a Road Slowly*, not halfway through *germinating*, the fact that she didn't mind "propitiated," but she didn't like it when Julie started getting all serious about things, the fact that I think she was pretty serious all along, too serious, but I'm going to carry on with it, for old time's sake, and also because I've forgotten the ending, the fact that Mommy gave me this book but I bet she never read it, the fact that I don't think Mommy would've gone for it much, the fact that maybe she saw a good review, or somebody in a bookstore recommended it, the fact that I was *very* interested in the bit when Julie comes downstairs feeling all euphoric, propitiate, prostitute, propensity, Protective Order, Restraining Order, Civil Standby, the fact that Leo tried to explain prostitution to Ben the other day, in kind of the same way he explains engineering to *me*, the fact that I'm not sure how well it went down, the fact that I left them to it, slut, slug, slugabed, nematode, the fact that I got them playing Candyland now, and *tried* not to make it sound like an order, the fact that now Stace and I are going to watch *Now, Voyager*, while we peel, *Now, Stace*, the fact that I don't think she heard me talking to Cathy, but she seems to have noticed I'm a little overwhelmed here today, and she just started peeling, without even being asked, and for that *she* gets to choose the movie, the fact that I suppose she gets a kick out of all the mother–daughter conflict in *Now, Voyager*, with Bette wailing "My mother! My mother!" and all that, the fact that Bette comes across as full of noble understanding, compared to her mother's selfishness and indifference, the fact that the daughter wins, the fact that her mother really is brusque and pretty unlikeable, Gladys Cooper, the fact that just thinking about her made Bette gouge a big hole in one of her ivory boxes, the fact that I hope Stacy's not going to gouge holes in all the apples on account of *me*, the fact that Leo thinks they should merge *Now, Voyager* with *Fantastic Voyage*, to make *Fantastic Voyager*, with Bette Davis instead of whatshername, Raquel Welch, and Claude Rains could be the English guy jamming up the works, and Paul Henreid's the CIA guy, always lighting up two cigarettes at a time or playing his cello in the submarine, the fact that they've been injected into Bette's mom's bloodstream to investigate why she's so cranky, whether it's just too many New England boiled dinners or what, the fact that in this version it's Paul Henreid and Claude Rains who get to tear the microbes off Bette's wetsuit, the fact that nobody can figure out what the problem is with Gladys Cooper, even when they reach the brain but, on their way out, they go through her mouth and notice she's got a *tooth abscess*, and *that* explains her half century of bad moods, bad mom, the fact that it's a little implausible, but then so is *Fantastic Voyage*, and maybe *Now, Voyager* too, the fact that I liked the boiled dinner explanation better, the fact that I thought they should've spent more time checking out her digestive system, soft shoe shuffle, the fact that soft shoe shuffle sounds like a new kind of ice cream, with bits of white chocolate and dark chocolate in it, truffle, dolly birds, Bette, Badge Betty, apple brown betty, Blanche, the open-air bar in South America somewhere, they're just off the cruise ship and Paul Henreid's ordered them Cointreaus, the fact that he orders Cointreau in *Casablanca* too, the fact that maybe he really liked Cointreau, the fact that then Bette's face gets all tangled up with her mom's, the fact that her mom's face is sort of superimposed on Bette's, to show that Bette's reminiscing, the fact that this might have seemed a clever idea at the time but what actually happens is Bette briefly seems to have *four nostrils*, and she looks kind of like a chicken, the fact that it always cracks Stacy up, caramelization, the fact that all seems to be going swimmingly in Candyland, Fanny Adams, the fact that Paul Henreid wakes up in the night and tucks Bette in better, *Betty Boughter bought some butter*, and then he kisses her, but she's asleep, the fact that they have to camp out, with a little fire, camp fire, Campfire Girls, wilderness, "attics," the fact that it seems like just about every man in this neighborhood except Leo has now joined some kind of mountain lion posse, the fact that I just saw a whole bunch go by, "patrolling the neighborhood," sheesh, the fact that they use any excuse to get out their guns, outdoor enthusiasts, rifles at the ready, pistols at dawn, the fact that some towns have hired professional lion hunters, lion tamers, lion charmers, lion fans, lionizers, all to deal with one little lion, as far as we know, Cathy, estranged husbands, the fact that they say hordes more hunters are heading our way, choking the highways and slowing down the police search, choking, ♫ *The Stars and Stripes Forever* ♫, me choking in the deep end, Flora choking in her crib, the fact that one guy said he saw the mountain lion swimming across someone's swimming pool in Pennsylvania somewhere, though that sounds unlikely, because most cats don't like to swim, but a whole lot of people drove all over Pennsylvania after that, checking every swimming pool, the fact that they should get that dentist who killed Cecil to come help, the fact that I must say I wouldn't want that guy's hands in *my* mouth, ivory poachers, Cecil the Lion, wildlife safaris, the fact that that same dentist illegally shot a bear in Wisconsin before, the fact that he just seems to go around and around the world flouting hunting restrictions, spirals, time to flip, flip flop, the fact that now the mom's passed away and Bette blames herself, though it was just an accident really, or more like a *coincidence*, the fact that it just happened to happen right after Bette announced she wouldn't be marrying Elliot, and had never asked to be born, estranged, Blanche's husband, candlelit vigils, the fact that Elliot Livingstone seems to take being dumped very well, not like *some*, the fact that the next thing you know her mom's slumped in the chair, *gone*, the fact that it's not really Bette's fault though because her mom already had a heart condition, Have A Heart Day, and she was old too, the fact that she's actually started to like Bette lately, sort of proud of her, but she's still kind of crabby, the fact that you never expect people to keel over until they actually do, Howard Keel, Kellogg's, head over heels, his head in his hands, hand in hand, hand over the loot, the fact that a fisherman in New Zealand found a baby floating in the water and fished it out and it was still alive, the fact that that sounds like a fairy tale or something, cobblers, elves, Bluebeard, the fact that *I'd* like to save a baby like that, but I'd want to keep it after, dimples, Mommy in the hospital, touching her hand, the fact that the fisherman had to hand it over to the authorities, so that's the end of that fairy tale, authority figures, the fact that Bette feels just terrible of course, about her mom dying, not about the baby in New Zealand, moonbat, mombat, wombat, mall rat, hog maw, the fact that she's so upset she has to go back to Cascade for a rest cure, the fact that she's not the only unhappy daughter in the movie, because there's Tina, the fact that she just happens to be Paul Henreid's daughter, and she's been sent to Cascade because *she* can't stand her mother either, the fact that Bette instantly becomes her mother-substitute, partly out of love for Paul Henreid, which is kind of a weird idea, projection, transference, the fact that first she rescues Tina from a ping-pong game with older kids who would have beaten her, the fact that Tina's really shy and doesn't want to play ping-pong, the fact that then they go into town and Bette gets her some ice cream, and then helps her phone her dad, Paul Henreid, the fact that Bette's really self-effacing about the phone call, the fact that you know she'd like to talk to Paul herself, but she stoically hands the receiver over to Tina, the fact that the phone call and ice cream can only help so much though, and Tina still cries inconsolably every night, but Bette comforts her, the fact that she hugs Tina, thinking of Paul, the fact that they can show her in bed with his kid, but not with Paul Henreid, except when they camped out in South America after the car crash and he gives her one kiss, in her sleep, the Facts of Life, Jill's version of how babies get made, the fact that I think we've both got a crush on Paul Henreid, but I would never mention it to Stace or it might make her hate him, the fact that it's great she likes *Now, Voyager* so much, the fact that all the later stuff with Tina really goes on too long, with all the hugging and the crying and the camping, the fact that I sort of switch off at this point, until Paul returns, though when they do meet up back in Boston to talk about Tina, all the chemistry's gone, no matter how many pairs of cigarettes Paul Henreid lights, the fact that we're not there yet though, the fact that Bette only just got permission from Claude Rains to take Tina camping, so she suddenly commandeers that nice old station wagon and off they go into the woods, to hike and meet *mountain lions*, the fact that they don't meet any lions, but Tina burns Bette's fingers by accident with a hot potato straight from the fire, the fact that Bette doesn't mind though, because anything Tina does is fine with her, because she's Paul Henreid's child, the fact that in the last scene everybody's eating home-cooked wieners and potato chips, the fact that there's nothing romantic about potato chips, the fact that Tina's been all spruced up, to make her daddy proud, but there's nothing romantic about *kids* either, real passion-killers, the fact that I usually fast-forward through all the Tina stuff, if my hands aren't covered in butter, because it kind of drags on, all this foster-mothering, but Stacy likes Tina, the fact that the whole time she's helping Tina get over her nervous breakdown, all Bette has to look forward to in life are the camellias Paul sends her every day, which is kind of dreary really, the fact that at the end she tells him not to hope for the moon when they have the stars, and that's dreary too, but that's Hollywood for you, the fact that they were pretty strict about adultery in the forties, ♫ *Now the river ends between two hills* ♫, the fact that I guess Stace identifies with Tina, the fact that it scares me to think what she makes of Tina's joy when Tina gets to see her *dad* again, the fact that Stacy was never that pleased to see her dad, the fact that she used to like it when *Leo* got home, when she was little, but with Frank, not so much, the fact that, well, you never knew if he was going to *turn up* or not, or in what kind of mood, the fact that then she'd just have to go somewhere with him, and naturally she didn't much like it, just being yanked away from home for an hour by a near-stranger, the fact that they only went to Dunkin' Donuts or someplace like that, not a big Boston mansion, the Vales of Boston, Vale iron ore mines, veil toss duties, the fact that if Mommy and Daddy hadn't met in Boston on a blind date at the Copley Plaza, I wouldn't be here watching these Boston scenes in *Now, Voyager* with my *kid* right now, *Now*, "This is now," the fact that in Evanston Mommy used to listen to operas while she cooked supper, and I still associate *Samson et Dalila*, *Aida*, *Madama Butterfly*, *La bohème*, *Rigoletto*, and *The Barber of Seville* with Mommy, watching Mommy cook spaghetti, the fact that after she got sick she never did anything she wanted again, anything she got a real kick out of, the fact that, sure, she played solitaire and watched TV and all, and had whiskey and soda every night, and sometimes got to see the friends she actually liked, I guess, but those aren't big thrills or anything, the fact that they're just ways of surviving, the Facts of Life, the fact that Mommy really did scare some of her visitors, Killbuck Creek, *La bohème*, the fact that some people mix whiskey with *sweet* stuff, but you should never mix good Scotch with anything but water or soda, and ice of course, the fact that I like whiskey sours, but that's usually bourbon, the fact that now I spend my whole life trying to make my kids happy but why didn't I try to make my *mom* happy, just a little *bit*, the fact that what the heck did I ever do for her, the fact that I can't remember doing *anything*, the fact that all I did was slouch around, the fact that Chuck made things better, for a while, but then he chucked me, the fact that it was a real Anne Elliott situation, *if a Chuck could chuck me he would*, until Leo came along, the fact that Frank was just a mistake, pale-blue earring, the fact that Phoebe says Mommy was depressed, and why wouldn't she be, the fact that her life was completely ruined, the fact that she lived without hope, and I knew it, even if I had no idea what to do about it, the fact that I could at least have learned how to make her a *Manhattan*, the fact that if she was here now I'd make her a million of them, the fact that Claude Rains says Bette Davis can have "a dozen of them," meaning husbands, not in *Now, Voyager*, in *Deception*, the fact that in *Deception* adultery's a much bigger deal, and Bette's punished for it, the fact that the ending's sort of cruel, after such a tender beginning, apples, oranges, tea bags, olive oil, soda, dishwasher tabs, dentist, butter, the fact that Mommy and Daddy used to drive to New York for the weekend sometimes and get pastrami and stuff, or see a show or a movie, the fact that Daddy really *tried* to keep things normal, get a normal life going for her, and Mommy went along with it and all, the fact that she liked the pastrami sandwiches, but she didn't really have much fun, the fact that, for one thing, she never liked going out in her wheelchair, or even being seen with her walker, the fact that that was a big problem for her, because she was shy, and hated people staring at her, or looking down on her, the fact that there's some lone gunman running around Cleveland killing disabled people, complete strangers, for no reason, and then he posts videos of himself boasting how many people he's killed this way, just random attacks out of the blue, and not just in Ohio, the fact that he may be overestimating how many people he's actually killed, because sometimes you can't *tell*, like if it's a drive-by shooting, drive-in movies, but he definitely shot an old guy in a wheelchair, and videoed it, the fact that people throughout Pennsylvania, New York, Indiana and Michigan have been told to be on the alert, not just for the lion but for this "selfie" guy too now, my stars, don't ask for the moon when we have the stars, Hollywood star, Chinese Theater, the fact that you're not supposed to go near him, because he could be dangerous if cornered, not the lion, the *selfie shooter*, selfish shooter, the fact that I've been scared of that my whole life, not of *lions*, of strangers killing you for no reason, Nickel Mines massacre, *In Cold Blood*, *Cape Fear*, the fact that that is really not fair, the fact that you haven't even got a chance if somebody decides to do something like that, just start killing people out of the blue, twi-night double-header, twi-night, the fact that you'd probably have more of a chance with a lion or tiger or a bear or something than you would with a well-armed crazy person bent on killing anybody and every-body, Blanche, Cathy, the fact that there's a $50,000 reward for information on him, the fact that I think he's a big bully, coward, mean guy, third rate, just like Trump, "Sad!", the fact that he could be a lot of places by now, this shooter, not Trump, though Trump gets around too, golfing and holding rallies, the fact that they can't get him to *stop* holding rallies, the fact that he goes for the adulation, bigly, ululation, elation, election, erection, cracks, failed bridge, broken, flaccid, the fact that he could be right outside our house right now, the selfie killer, not Donald Trump, I hope, the fact that maybe the selfie killer, Trump, and the *lion* are outside our house, help, the fact that I don't know which would be worse, the fact that they're working up a picture of him, the selfie guy, and they say he killed his own parakeet when he was a kid and he yelled at his mom a lot, green ground parrots, Blanche's husband, the fact that, talk about violent husbands, *Henry Rathbone* killed his wife and then himself, wrath bone, the fact that that's not the same as a funny bone, far from it, back bone, knee bone, thigh bone, "Dem bones, dem bones," the fact that Rathbone tried to kill his own kids too, but failed for some reason, "This family annihi-lation will either be a success or a failure," the fact that Rathbone was never the same after the Kennedy assass—, no, no, no, the *Lincoln* assassination, Mount Rushmore, the fact that they were childhood sweethearts, not Rathbone and Lincoln, Rathbone and his *wife*, the fact that Lincoln was just a friend, the fact that Lincoln was also friends with John Evans, so maybe he wasn't the greatest at choosing his friends, the fact that the Lincolns invited Ulysses S. Grant to share their box that night, but he changed his mind or something at the last moment, and Rathbone and his fiancée joined the Lincolns instead and had to watch him get *shot*, "But how was the play?", the fact that Rathbone tried his best to tackle John Wilkes Booth but he couldn't save Lincoln, and everybody blamed him for it later, including Rathbone himself, the fact that that drove him *nuts*, the guilt and shame of it, having been there in the box with the president when he got shot, and unable to prevent it, "not a jury in the land," the fact that Rathbone was a mess, the fact that Claude Rains probably would've recommended a few weeks at Cascade, the fact that Rathbone was injured too, badly injured on his arm, from grappling with Booth, the fact that Booth cut him with a dagger, from the elbow to the shoulder, severing an artery, but that didn't help Rathbone any with the public, John Wilkes Booth, Clare Boothe Luce, screen door, summer, Band-Aid, the fact that Rathbone actually did all he could to protect Lincoln, the fact that despite his arm injury, Rathbone managed to grab Booth's leg just as Booth was jumping from the box, and because of that, Booth landed awkwardly on the stage and broke his leg, which at least slowed him down a bit, FOOSH injury, whoosh, the fact that that *wasn't* a FOOSH injury, it was a leg injury, the fact that then, in the heat of the crisis, Rathbone's fiancée decided to accompany the Lincolns home, instead of staying to tend Rathbone, and Rathbone never forgave her for it, the fact that he really was a heck of a mixed-up kind of guy, parsley, pile of papers, popsicles, the fact that they got married anyway and Mrs. Rathbone stuck with him despite all his mental health issues, only to be *murdered* by him in the end, the fact that, in a way, she was another casualty of the Lincoln assassination, but her death came eighteen years on, the fact that they had three kids in three years, but Rathbone started to seethe with jealousy, partly *about* the kids, who he thought claimed too much of his wife's attention, the fact that eventually he got a big diplomatic job in Germany, and that was where he tried to kill the kids one day, the fact that Mrs. Rathbone tried to protect them and, in the struggle, he killed her instead, and then he tried to kill himself too but failed, the fact that the selfie guy from Cleveland said in one of his homemade videos that the whole reason he started killing disabled people was partly because of an argument he'd had with his *girlfriend*, partly because of some gambling debts, but mainly he blamed his mom, Gladys Cooper, the fact that whatever else you can say, chivalry is dead, same goes for gallantry, and stoicism and loyalty and decency and civility and compassion and all that sort of old-fashioned stuff, the fact that that's all gone out the window, "This cow's done a lot of suffering," the fact that the selfie killer was spotted at a restaurant somewhere having a big steak, right after he killed the guy in the wheelchair, the fact that he was really enjoying his dinner too, kind of relishing it, smacking his lips and talking into the camera while he chewed, big smile on his face, the fact that he couldn't have done a better job of proving Stacy's point that eating your meat with a knife and fork doesn't necessarily make you *nice*, the fact that Stace can be quite severe about things, like when Ben announced he wanted to go to the Young Builders craft class after school and build a remote-controlled glider with a six-foot-three-inch wingspan, and Stacy said he sounded like *Howard Hughes*, the fact that Ben turned pink and was the maddest I think I've ever seen him, kind of like the kid who shot his big sister in the head over the remote, the fact that I stood up for him though and said "Ben can build a six-foot glider if he wants to," the fact that I added under my breath, "So long as he never tries to fly it," which made Stacy giggle, ♫ *Bless your beautiful hide* ♫, the fact that that woman in *Seven Brides for Seven Brothers* is such a good sport, taking care of seven wild men in their long johns, their "winter underwear," me-oh-mys, the fact that I wish I could be that calm, the fact that after all, I only have to run after four little kids, and *she* has to cook stew for seven huge lugs every day and teach them etiquette, zhlub, mensch, and make bacon and griddle cakes at five in the morning, the fact that I only have to make *tartes tatin* at five in the morning, for strangers, strangers who like to *kill* strangers maybe, poor Cathy, stranger danger, the fact that I wish I could do something for her, besides just making pies I mean, the fact that Howard Hughes was fascinated by bras, maybe a little too fascinated, the fact that Leo says Howard Hughes looked on bras as an interesting engineering problem, the fact that I wonder if Ben's interested in bras, and that's what got him into bosoms, or the other way around, bosoms got him into bras, the fact that getting *bosoms* into bras is the *hard* part, the fact that maybe he's just a big Howard Hughes fan, and airplanes led on to bosoms, the fact that I always get him mixed up with Howard *Hawks*, not *Ben*, Howard Hughes, the fact that I don't get Ben mixed up with anybody, the fact that I only some-times stumble over Gillian's name and call her Ginnie, the fact that all I can remember from the movie is all the bottles of pee Leonardo DiCaprio kept around, when Howard Hughes was in one of his tail-spins, and Katharine Hepburn knocking on the door, the fact that Howard Hughes *really* should've gone to Cascade, the fact that every-body should, just for a little tune-up, the fact that *I'd* like to, the fact that I'd love to just take it easy and play tennis and ping-pong and talk to Claude Rains once a day about my problems, Leo DiCaprio, Leo, Leo da Vinci, Cincy, the fact that Leonardo da Vinci considered the human foot a masterpiece of engineering, the fact that it doesn't *look* it, the fact that it always sounds too complicated to me, too many little bones, the fact that Howard Hughes made some poor guy squeeze the OJ right in front of him, just so he knew it was fresh, and then he yelled at him a lot, I don't know why, the fact that you wonder what could go so *wrong* with orange-squeezing, the fact that there doesn't seem a lot to argue about there, the fact that I should give the kids more freshly-squeezed OJ, like Howard Hughes advised, the fact that why'm I such a lazybones, the fact that I'd kinda like to be freshly squeezed *myself*, oh, that's silly, the fact that it sounds like something the Cuckoo Pigeon sisters might say, bosoms, flapdoodle, the fact that

Howard Hughes also designed a hospital bed that could lift you up and lower you down by pressing a button, heart operation, the two teenage girls in my room with me, broken backs, old black-and-white movie, Dr. DeBoer, the fact that when Mommy was in the hospital after brain surgery, her head was all round and swollen, and half her hair had been shaved off, the fact that it was terrible, and then we found out they'd *paralyzed* her, "This surgery will either be a success or a complete disaster," the fact that *that's* what it should say on the forms they get you to sign before you go under the knife, the fact that when Leo's mother was in the hospital, there was some kind of constant tussle over the bed, the fact that the nurses and people were always trying to raise it up, but Leo's mom wanted to lie flat, the fact that sitting up made her feel sick and dizzy, the fact that all they could think about was the danger of her getting pneumonia from lying flat, but if they raised her bed, even just a little bit, she *threw up*, the fact that they made her feel so nauseous, she naturally stopped eating, but they *still* kept on raising her up, until Leo put his foot down in some way and they let her lie flat after all, and she got better, but Mommy never did, the fact that she got worse and worse until she passed away, which sounds like a nursery rhyme, or Dr. Seuss, the fact that she died without me, the fact that I wasn't there to save her that time, the fact that the Scottish Enlightenment inspired the American Revolution, and the American Revolution inspired the French Revolution, and the French Revolution inspired the Russian Revolution and the Chinese Revolution and the Cuban Revolution, and those all inspired the Vietnamese Revolution, and maybe some other revolutions in South America, the fact that the thigh bone's connected to the knee bone, and the knee bone's connected to the shin bone, ♪ *Dem bones, dem bones, dem dry bones* ♪, the fact that any minute now there'll be another eruption from one of these kids, and it makes me nervous, because I have to get the *pies* done, and I'm scared the kids'll surprise me, or a lion will, or a "selfie killer," and I'll drop something, flip, spiral, the fact that I've lost my helper, the fact that she's gone off to watch *South Pacific* again, in the living room, the fact that I don't know how she can stand that thing, and this must be the third time she's seen it, the fact that there's only one good song in it, ♫ *Some enchanted evening* ♫, which doesn't seem worth it, the fact that what's it got to do with the South Pacific, or war, or anything else, and the *color* is so weird in that movie, unbelievable, the fact that it's so weird it makes you feel queasy, deer tick, deer lick, lone star tick, the fact that "nits turn into lice," the fact that I thought nits *were* lice, Powassan virus, CTE, *Groundhog Day*, the fact that the apples are starting to simmer, the fact that everybody in the NFL gets *CTE*, everybody, the fact that that's awful, the fact that they get it from having concussions, the linemen especially, the fact that CTE makes you forgetful, so maybe *I've* got it, the fact that there's a build-up of tau proteins and that's no good, apparently, the fact that the NFL never wanted to admit this happens but now they've had to for some reason, the fact that the last time a horse won the Triple Crown was 2015, American Pharoah, but it doesn't happen too often, ridgling, quarter horses, saddlebreds, Percherons, the fact that if they win the crown, the stud fees go way up to like $100,000 a go or more, the fact that not even Harrison Ford could get that, or Paul Henreid, or Colin Firth, the fact that Harrison Ford plays a police detective in *Witness*, a "whacking," carpentering, barn-raising detective, purple martin house, the fact that, gosh, an Indonesian maid in Saudi Arabia's been executed for being *raped*, the fact that only five percent of rape allegations are false, but only twelve percent of rape trials end in a conviction, the fact that that sounds like a lot of rapists are roaming free, the fact that a man who raped a twelve-year-old girl now has joint custody of their *baby*, Dead Lakes, eighty thousand gallons of partially chlorinated effluent, America the Beautiful, pomegranate juice, random killer, Blanche, horseracing, the fact that we have all lost heart, we are heartless, the fact that I blame it on video games and "KAPOW KAPOW, you're dead" sort of stuff, the fact that what's to become of a kid who spends all day incinerating aliens at the touch of a button, the fact that kids would be better off doing anything else, doing the *Macarena* for instance, the fact that some boy in Saudi Arabia was arrested for doing the Macarena in the middle of the street, but he did it so well, Cathy, Art, the fact that I should take the kids to the playground more, let them off the leash, but not with a lion around, lyin' around, the fact that I worry for *Ben*, the fact that he knows a lot of stuff and all but he's not getting good grades, GPA, the fact that he's shy and he hates talking in class, the fact that he says he freezes in front of a crowd, the fact that he used to be less shy, the fact that he used to talk like a pirate, *in public*, like on the street or in the grocery store, saying things like "Damn your eyes!" and "Splice the mainbrace!", the fact that he was always trying to get buccaneers and the Barbary Coast into the conversation, walking the plank, hanging, drawing and quartering, and then he suddenly stopped talking, in front of strangers anyway, and I have no idea why, "KAPOW KAPOW," Spiderman, madeleines, hot chocolate, Tonka truck hazard, Jake, the fact that I'm scared he caught shyness from me, *Ben*, not Jake, the fact that Jake's not shy yet, the fact that Jake's the life of the party at his playgroup, shark in a shed, the fact that Ben's teacher says we shouldn't worry, he's just a sensitive kid, the fact that Leo thinks we should just leave him alone and not pressure him, and I wouldn't *dream* of pressuring him, the fact that, boy, everybody pressures their kids enough, without even *trying*, ow, the fact that that darn truck finally got me, as I knew it would, Jake, Djibouti, the fact that dogs clean up their own toys so why can't kids, the fact that I just don't want him to be anxious in himself and suffer in silence, Ben, not Jake, the fact that Jake would never suffer in silence, the fact that I was terrible at school, the fact that I flunked almost every subject, even History, the fact that I never could keep track of *which* war they were talking about, the fact that for a long time I really didn't know a thing, I don't think, and still don't, but I wouldn't tell Ben that, the fact that I don't want him looking down on me too much, not yet at least, not while he's still *shorter* than me, for Pete's sake, the fact that Ben's different, he's not a lousy student, the fact that he knows tons of stuff, the kid's awash in information, about boobs even, "Damn your eyes!", the fact that he also seems to *retain* what he reads, the fact that he doesn't have CTE like me, knock on wood, the fact that *he* says the problem is his teacher doesn't ask him the right questions, the fact that most elementary school teachers don't, except maybe Mr. Tszjynsky, if that was his name, which it wasn't, the fact that I think it was Mr. *Tykszynsky*, the fact that I wonder how I can even remember that, the fact that he didn't seem to mind us calling him Mr. T., the fact that teachers can never know how important they were to you, just like good doctors, or nurses too, the fact that you never forgot them, but they'll never know, well, unless you keep in touch with them later on, I guess, but how many people do that, the fact that it's just part of the job, the fact that you do your best and never necessarily know the results, the fact that it's like being a mom, or a piemaker, or a *cobbler*, the fact that I hated most of the teachers we had, but we all had a big crush on Mr. Tykszynsky, especially after he got mixed up over Huck Finn one day and called him "F— Hinn," the fact that that *thrilled* us, the F-word, the fact that he laughed, we all did, and after that he was always jokily hesitant whenever he had to mention Huck Finn, which was pretty often, because that's what we were studying, Chuck, Huck, F—, cuck, cock, oh, dear, the fact that didn't Phoebe meet up with him a few years back, I forget where, Mr. Tykszynsky I mean, not Huck or Chuck, though she *was* friends with Chuck's sister, long ago, the fact that Ben had the greatest teacher for first grade, Miss Garland, the fact that she greeted each child individually at the door every morning, and each kid got to decide what kind of greeting it was, like either a high five, or a hug, or a little dance they'd do together with the teacher, and I forget what else, the fact that I think Ben usually went for the high five, the fact that I dreamt I saw a large flying saucer going past our window, the fact that it was about the size of a helicopter, but flimsier, and it had a lot of pretty little lights on it, the fact that then I dreamt Leo and I lugged some bags of groceries from one wooden platform to another in the ocean, sort of like stationary rafts, the fact that we had to swim for it sometimes, in between the rafts, and the bags got a little wet, the fact that a dog came with us, the fact that then I dreamt a nice girl was blowing the foam off her beer and it all landed on my *face*, which she didn't notice at first, the fact that I didn't mind, I just found it kind of funny, the fact that she was the one who offered Leo ham sandwiches, which Leo refused, which surprised me, since Leo's usually avid for ham sandwiches, the fact that I only remember itty-bitty little snippets of dreams later in the day, the fact that it's usually when I'm cooking, and I'll suddenly remember some woman scolding me in a dream for not buying some man some gum or something, peacock spider, botnet, Rohypnol, Rohingya, Saudi Arabia, Cathy, Blanche, the fact that are swamp rats the same as coypu, because people hunt swamp rats in Louisiana, and I don't think they should, the fact that they just treat them like *vermin*, the fact that it's not to make swamp rat stew or anything, the fact that they get five bucks per tail, the fact that I never even knew coypu *had* tails, so maybe they're not the same as swamp rats, the fact that I thought coypu were just kind of huge guinea pigs, the fact that I always liked the name "coypu," the fact that it's endearing, five bucks a tail, Jordanian Parrot Recites Koran, the fact that "till" is a word in its own right, according to Leo, the fact that all my life I've exhausted myself trying not to use "till" because I thought it was *slang* or something, not a real word, and now I find out I was wasting my time for forty years, the fact that it was not until now, till now, that anybody bothered to *tell* me, the fact that he claims "till" has nothing to do with "until" though, which I just don't believe, the fact that there is no way "till" isn't related to "until," since they mean the exact same thing, the fact that Leo has to correct papers so he has to think about stuff like this, and check for plagiarism, engineering plagiarism, the fact that he says "'til" is related to "until," but "till" isn't, *They say the hen can lay, I don't know but they know*, the fact that next they'll be saying "'cause" and "cuz" have nothing to do with "*because*," mamma mia, SpaghettiOs, cuss, cuz, 'cause, the fact that I said something about "cause" and "cuz" to Leo's retreating back but I don't think he heard me, Walter Matthau, the fact that sometimes Leo gets me so worked up, and then, as soon as he's had *his* say, he starts thinking about something else, leaving me to stew alone, the fact that I've told him this is "conversation interruptus" but it didn't change anything, the fact that men are always so busy, shaving and flossing and clipping their nails and stuff, the fact that now they say there's no point in flossing, the fact that ultimately it doesn't improve dental health, the fact that maybe we should quit using floss, but I don't like the feeling of stuff caught between my teeth all day long, the fact that they put Teflon in dental floss so you're actually rubbing Teflon all over your teeth, the fact that all these people must be in league with oncologists, the fact that maybe they *want* us to get cancer, so they can all make some money, the fact that sometimes it seems like doctors are just waiting to cash in on your inevitable decline and death, whining and dining, winking and blinking, sinking and swimming, singing and stinking, the fact that all of a sudden Ben's all excited about the full solar eclipse now, though it's not until August, till, 'til August, the fact that he's been working on us for weeks about it, the fact that he says we have to get ourselves to a Point of Greatest Duration to get the full effect, and all the Points of Greatest Duration are like a day's journey from here, the fact that the eclipse isn't hitting Ohio directly, so we have to go to Tennessee or Illinois, and if we want to see it in the Great Smoky Mountains National Park we have to buy tickets in March, GSMNP, the Great Smokies, the fact that Ben's read up on it all, the fact that the Great Smoky tickets are $30 each and you're only allowed four per person, the fact that we could solve that if Leo and I each bought three tickets, I guess, unless it's limited to four tickets per household, the fact that if we buy six tickets at $30 each though, that's $180, and we don't have that kind of money, "A dollar?!", medical bills, college fund, SATs, the fact that Leo said he doesn't want to see it in the Great Smoky National Park anyway, because *everybody* will want to see it in the Great Smokies National Park and we'll get caught up in some huge traffic jam or riot or Point-of-Greatest-Duration stampede, like in one of those apocalypse movies when people drive away from the monster or something but then they all get stuck on the highway and the traffic's not moving and you know it's curtains for them, they're doomed, the fact that only the hero gets away, because he's got a four-by-four with snow tires, and by chance some pepper spray or something the monster's very allergic to, shadows, nighttime in the daytime, twi-night, the fact that Ben's got our route all mapped out for us, the fact that it's only 467.8 miles, he says, from Newcomerstown to Gatlinburg, Tennessee, Gatling gun, and buses will take everybody from a parking lot there to the Clingmans Dome Observation Tower, the fact that they provide the protective glasses too, all included in the thirty-buck ticket, the glasses, the bus ride, and the parking place, the fact that you have to pay for your own hot dog though, or bring a picnic, the fact that then Ben showed Leo and me a picture of the Clingmans Dome Observation Tower the other day, and that thing looks a bit wobbly to me, the fact that it does not look like it can hold hundreds and hundreds of eclipsed people, the fact that I'd get vertigo just walking up the ramp, the fact that Ben says if we aren't sure about the Tennessee idea there's Goreville, Illinois, which is a bit further, at 538.6 miles away, the fact that that is seventy miles further *each way*, a hundred and forty miles extra driving, the fact that Leo's not going to like that either, the fact that the advantage is you don't have to pay for anything extra, the fact that they're letting us have the solar eclipse free in Goreville, almost as if the sun belonged to all of us, or we belong to it, the fact that, according to Ben we can just go there and sit around, waiting for the sun to disappear, the fact that it's sort of great our little moon can block out the *whole sun*, the fact that there's also Makanda, Illinois, 550.8 miles away, Grandma's bobbly water glasses dripping with condensation, the fact that I'm thirsty, the fact that I could drink a horse, Triple Crown, the fact that there's the Elephant Sanctuary too in Tennessee, the fact that that's the furthest one of all, the fact that those elephants are 558.7 miles away from us, the fact that it sounds like weather forecasts when they give you the nearest lightning strike, and it's always twelve hundred miles away or something, the fact that I guess they do it in case you've got a lightning phobia, ridgling, Ringling Bros., the fact that Ben's keenest on the elephant sanctuary idea, because he wants to watch the effect of the eclipse on the elephants, the fact that they're elephants who used to have to work in circuses but now they're retired and they get to live semi-wild in Tennessee, like the mammoths, who experienced other solar eclipses no doubt, Babar as a baby, trumpeting in the forest, Babar going to visit the Old Lady in the town, Babar in his green suit and spats, taking the elevator in the department store, the fact that we could also see the eclipse at the University of Southern Illinois in Carbondale, 540.1 miles away, the fact that I urged Ben to round off the mileages for us, the fact that the ".1" and ".7" stuff's maybe not essential at this stage, maybe a bit de trop, but when he said just now "Okay, it's five hundred and sixty miles, Mom," to reach the elephants, I suddenly saw more clearly that, wherever we go, we are talking about a thousand-mile road trip, in *August*, surrounded by other frantic phenomenon-seekers, or suckers, as Leo calls them, or goofballs, as Stacy calls them, her favorite word, the fact that I don't think Leo would drive even *fifty* miles, even if it was Jupiter was merging with Saturn before our eyes, path of totality or no totality, Sapiter, Jupiturn, the fact that when Ben first brought it up, he argued that this is going to be the biggest solar eclipse in America for the last hundred years, and the most photographed single event in history, and Leo just looked at him and said "In that case, you can stay right here and look at all the pictures in the comfort of your own home," and then he left the room, conversation interruptus, Babar, Carbondale, the fact that the Elephant Sanctuary is in Hohenwald, Tennessee, the fact that Clingmans Dome is the highest mountain in the Smokies, ♫ *On top of old Smoky* ♫, Marlboros, Point of Greatest Duration, Total Solar Eclipse, TSE, tsetse fly, tsetse fever, sleeping sickness, the fact that I asked Ben how long the eclipse would last in one of these points of longest duration, and he said two and a half minutes, *two and a half minutes*, the fact that I thought he'd say something like two and a half *hours*, but no, as he sternly informed me, the fact that since the earth revolves at a thousand miles an hour, the moon's shadow will travel across the *whole country* in about two hours, or two and a half, the fact that Ben said the only way you can make it last longer would be if you were on a Concorde, the fact that some Concorde plane did chase an eclipse once in the seventies, and it kept up with it for two hours but lost the race in the end, the fact that the thought of an airplane chasing a shadow across the earth makes me feel kind of dizzy, the fact that I need some more coffee, the fact that the kids argued about Pacific Daylight Time, Central Daylight Time, and Eastern Daylight Time, and how that might affect all these eclipse calculations, and then Stacy piped up, suddenly furious, saying something like "You gotta be kidding, Ben, if you think we should use up the last of the fossil fuels to drive a thousand miles to sit through two and a half minutes of darkness. I don't care if it only happens every *eight* hundred years," the fact that that kind of shut everybody up for a while, the fact that she says why don't we just close the curtains in the middle of the afternoon, for a few minutes, the fact that I do feel bad that we never go anywhere with the kids though, the fact that we never do *anything*, just like my parents, though they at least took us to Europe a couple times, Waterlow Park, the fact that we *are* going over to Fallingwater this weekend, and Moundsville maybe on the way back, the fact that the kids've never been there, the fact that Stace might or might not come, but she seems reluctant, the fact that it's partly a work trip for Leo, because he's got to write something on structures built over water, not *bridges*, other stuff like causeways, stationary landing strips, oil platforms, pontoons, jetties, houses on stilts, "Suck in your gut," floating concrete pontoons, but not pontoon bridges, floating bridges, underwater bridges, submersible bridges, the fact that this is all on condition there are no lion sightings around there, the fact that I hate to disappoint poor Ben though, about the eclipse, so I've just told him not to give up hope, and he immediately started detailing to me the route we'd take to get to Clingmans Dome, the fact that you take Exit 407 for Sevierville, till you get to TN-66 South, and then you get on to US-441 South and follow that all the way through Sevierville and Pigeon Forge into Gatlinburg, the fact that then we're supposed to park in Parking Lot 1, or Parking Lot 2, and they give you your glasses and put you on a bus, the fact that they say to be prepared to be away from your car for *seven hours*, the fact that that's funny, if the eclipse is only two and a half minutes, the fact that Leo's not going to like

779

that, for two and a half minutes of phoney-baloney darkness, the fact that seven hours does seem a bit much, but I suppose it takes time for everybody to get on and off all the buses and walk up that teeny-weeny narrow ramp to the Observation Tower and jostle for a place to sit down and eat hot dogs and find the portable toilets and all that, the fact that it would be just like me to get stuck in one of those toilets and miss the *whole thing*, the fact that there I'd be, fumbling in sudden darkness for some non-existent scrap of toilet paper, and when I got out the whole eclipse would be over and I'd be surrounded by all these awe-struck wondering faces and there'd be nothing I could do about it for the next seven years, the fact that there will be an eclipse in 2024, but by then the kids will all be grown-up almost, so this is the one, if we're going to do it, the fact that Concordes no longer exist, I don't think, but I don't want to ride on one anyway, the fact that wasn't there a big problem with them, and after that everybody lost interest in supersonic flying, the fact that Howard Hughes was kind of good-looking, the fact that I just remembered a dream I had last night in which Julia Roberts wanted some jam and I had a few jars of really good dark plum jam stashed away in the pantry, so I went to get one but all three jars turned out to be all moldy and horrible, and when I opened one there was a popping noise and a puff of smoke came out and then the jam inside caught *fire*, the fact that then I knew all the other jars of jam were probably about to explode too so I had to make a run for it, the fact that, so much for giving whatshername, Julia Roberts, a jar of jam, the fact that the Akron man who set himself alight over Trump has died, the fact that he sounds a nice man too, the fact that I wonder why he felt so strongly about things, enough to set himself on fire, dear me, the fact that there really are just so many protests these days, it's hard to keep them all straight, the fact that cougars hunt at night, the fact that what if he decided to just leap through a window or something, the fact that there's nothing we could do about it, **** ESTABLISH JUSTICE ****, the fact that I'll never know why she wrote that NAZI POTUS slogan on her shirt and wore it to school the very day they were taking the class photo, with Stacy right there in the front row, the fact that she says she didn't know they were taking the photo that day but she would've worn it *anyway*, if she had, the fact that she was all excited about it being in the photo, but then when we got the finished photo, they'd blanked her message out, so her T-shirt no longer said SUPER CALLOUS FRAGILE RACIST SEXIST NAZI POTUS, it didn't say *anything*, for *once*, the fact that it just looked like she had a plain black T-shirt on, with no words hand-painted on with white poster paint, so she stomped into the principal's office and gave Mrs. Sherman a talking-to, and Mrs. Sherman admitted she'd had it photo-shopped, because she thought the words SUPER CALLOUS FRAGILE RACIST SEXIST NAZI POTUS might offend some parents, which I'm sure they *would*, the fact that people are very easily offended around here, the fact that I know that from going to PTA meetings, the fact that there's always a lot of propitiating going on *there*, the fact that Stacy said it was an infringement of something, her right to free speech and also her right to wear whatever clothes she chooses, and she asked for the SUPER CALLOUS FRAGILE RACIST SEXIST NAZI POTUS to be reinstated, but it was too late, the fact that they'd already destroyed the original, ♬ *If you say it loud enough you'll always sound precocious* ♬, and probably go to jail, the fact that then she got all her friends in on it and the whole thing got kind of out of hand, if you ask me, with all these girls coming over to our house to paint slogans on their T-shirts, though they did look kind of cute, all in a row in their matching T-shirts, like a real little bunch of activists, the fact that Mary Jane only wrote CLIMATE CHANGE IS REAL, because her parents are Republicans, the fact that then they all wore their T-shirts to school the next week, the fact that I was scared Stacy would get expelled, OSS, and then what would we do, because we can't afford private school, and I don't want to teach her at home, the fact that I don't think I'm qualified to teach high school, the fact that luckily I guess there's safety in numbers, and it's all died down now, the fact that they couldn't expel all the girls in her class, the fact that I began to wonder if it was something *I* did wrong, to make my kid so rebellious, but maybe it's just hormones, in *Stacy*, not me, adolescent stuff, the fact that Stacy's such a hothead, raring for a fight, the fact that she reminds me of Mocchi, kind of, the Sand Creek warrior woman, Moxie, bitter gentian root, gumption, the fact that I was a little embarrassed she behaved like that, *Stacy*, not Mocchi, confronting Mrs. Sherman and stuff, the fact that she got teased too, by other classmates, the fact that I was scared she'd be beaten up, the fact that there are a lot of pretty fierce Trumpers around here, trumpeters, trumpeteers, the fact that I couldn't wait for the whole thing to blow over, the fact that the tail's come off the aardvark again, and I've lost my favorite pen, the fact that it's very hard to fix, the aardvark, not the pen, because it wiggles so much, the fact that I think I let Stacy down when Leo and I got married and that's why she's so difficult, the fact that I was so engrossed in Leo, the fact that I think she felt left out, well, I know she did, the poor kid, because she *told* me, the fact that I was just so happy to be with him, the fact that, yes, I was distracted, the fact that after Mommy first got sick I had Chuck, and after Mommy passed away I had Leo, the fact that I *needed* some-one, because I'd lost my mommy, Unusual Animal Encounters, the fact that I don't think I really started to live until I found Leo, and realized he loved me, "sweetheart," the fact that I was no good on my own, the fact that Stace and I were both so lonely, no Frank, no Mommy, no money either, the fact that Bathsheba was the only con-tinuity we had with the past, Scarlatti, Miss Scarlet, the fact that we were floating into outer space before Leo turned up, the fact that I had to learn to let him love me up a bit, the fact that it didn't come natu-rally, I was outta practice, but meanwhile Stacy suffered, Cheeseburger Emoji Outcry, the fact that I just wanted things to go *smoothly* with Stacy and Leo, but it wasn't that easy for her to adjust, the fact that that was a big ask, oh dear, the fact that I think the trouble is I became a mom before I figured out how to be a daughter, the fact that maybe it wasn't until Jake was born that I really started to catch up with myself, the fact that things happen so *fast*, too fast, the fact that you never have time to think properly, the fact that life is all crisis-management, the fact that is it like that for *everybody*, Cathy, Abby, poor Cathy, the fact that it makes you want to stop time so you can just curl up some-where and think things over for a while, the fact that I wish I was a hen, the fact that mother hens have it easy, as long as you're at the top of the pecking order, and nobody's biting your sit-me-down-upon, the fact that it's not just that they get to sit in the coop all day thinking, if they feel like it, the fact that what I envy is nobody blames hens for their chicks' mistakes or rebelliousness or lack of self-confidence or anything, viscose, emasculate, the fact that I dreamt I was at the Peolia College pool and a teenage boy stole my money and jewelry from my purse while I was swimming and nobody seemed to care, the fact that then I was doing the dishes half-naked with lots of people around, but my chest was fairly well hidden by the suds, the fact that then I was walking home completely *naked*, from about two blocks away, and there was just absolutely nothing I could do about it, the fact that now that the sun's out, we have to deliver pies, lion or no lion, and get the lettuce for Salade Lyonnaise, which Leo and I love and the kids hate, because they can't get why we'd want to put a poached egg on top of a salad, the fact that we only give them the lettuce with the hot bacon and croutons, and they can have the poached egg on the side, but they're still so scornful when they watch us eat our real Salade Lyonnaise with the glossy, partially wilted lettuce, the fact that they love to make off-putting comments about it, the fact that I guess Jake will have SpaghettiOs, the fact that even if I made him a salad with a hollowed-out poached egg stuck inside a donut-shaped bed of lettuce, the whole thing would probably end up on the floor, ARFID, barfed, the fact that American kids seem to be born knowing which foods are American, and that is all they care about, Six Reasons Your Eyes Are Tired, "OO" flour, "Type O," "*Oh?*", the fact that now we need *cornflowers*, the fact that they're supposed to sooth sore eyes, the fact that I've *seen* dried cornflowers for sale, the fact that I guess you have to *wet* them first, you don't just rub dry cornflower petals straight into your eyes, the fact that that probably *wouldn't* be too soothing, sooth-saying, cactus sticker, aardvark, Woodrow Wilson photo, the fact that

Stacy's tiger picture is a monoprint, the fact that raindrops in puddles are one of the best things on earth, the fact that people hate rain but it's not so bad as long as it's not flooding your house or causing a dam to collapse, the fact that I should check the Weather Channel, BC, BCE, the fact that that's a real mackerel cloud, the fact that it should be called a *loon* cloud, mallards, the fact that clouds are shape-shifters, they're fickle, egg-poaching, ivory poachers, green ground parrots, endangered species, the fact that everybody's so nervous about egg-poaching's but it's easy, the fact that I think poaching eagles' eggs is illegal, but that's a different kind of poaching, the fact that it would be funny if rare egg collectors climbed up trees, armed with a poaching pan, a little vinegar, boiling water, salt and pepper, maybe Tabasco, bacon, and some toast, the fact that the best way is you take a room-temperature egg and put it whole into a cup of hot water, crack it open, and then very gently ease it into the simmering water, and hope it holds together, et voilà, the fact that the water should actually be just under simmering-point, the fact that you can use a deep pan but I think it's better if you have a glass-lidded frying pan, because there's more room and you can keep an eye on how things are progressing, the fact that I always put a touch of vinegar or salt in the water, the fact that I usually get a nice firm little poached egg, or however many we need, the fact that if the eggs are old though, it won't work, the fact that older eggs should just be boiled, or baked, or scrambled, or *dumped*, but not poached, because it's doomed to failure, fear of failure, the fact that a poached egg will either be a success or a failure, shirred eggs, Schiers, "Spiegel im Spiegel," the fact that we had such a nice time in Schiers, the fact that they had a pink post office, Cathy, poor *Cathy*, dear me, the fact that if you throw out the hot water afterwards and let the pan soak in *cold* water, it's easier to clean, the fact that I have never found a really good poaching pan, the fact that even the Teflon ones are hard to clean, after poaching eggs in them, the fact that Julia Child discovered you have to dry meat before you fry it, the fact that I forget the trick for removing blood stains on cloth, but I think it involves bicarbonate of soda and something else, the fact that we need bacon and lettuce, jam, tomatoes, potatoes, onions, garlic, radishes, green and red peppers, muesli, ginger, cinnamon bark, butter, salt, cornflour, cornflowers, lemons, ow, shooOOT, the fact that I think I gotta train myself to count to ten when I step on one of Jake's toys, or someday I'll come out with a cuss word, I really will, ow, Djibouti, Djibouti, the fact that Djibouti's not working anymore, and counting to ten might not do it either, the fact that I need to count to more like about *fifty* for this gosh darn yellow tractor, Sweet'N Low, Jolly Green Giant, Ku Klux Klan, John Wilkes Booth, Frank Lloyd Wright, Cy Young Park, Nancy Hatch Dupree, the fact that there aren't enough ground parrots in New Zealand, the fact that almost all their eggs are infertile for some reason, and people are trying to keep the species going, but it's not looking too good, ground parrots, zest, sour cherries, OJ, selfies, baby dolphin, parade, beach, the fact that I just had to sit down for a while, the fact that I was in the middle of rolling out the dough when I heard that terrible story about the baby dolphin they found on the beach in Venezuela, the fact that the dolphin mom and baby must have gotten too near the shore and some teens grabbed the baby and paraded it around the beach taking selfies, until the poor thing *died*, the fact that that mother dolphin must have wondered what the heck had become of her baby, yellow tractor toy, the fact that maybe she saw them snatch it, and was helpless to do anything about it, stuck in the water, the fact that maybe she followed along beside the teenagers as they tramped up and down the beach, waiting for them to return her baby, the fact that I hope not, the fact that I hope she just didn't have any idea what had happened to it, dolphins, whales, porpoises, tortoises, turquoise, the fact that I don't know, but sometimes it just seems like there are too many tragedies in the world to be *borne*, to be born, the fact that Alice Neel's first child died as a baby and her second was taken to Cuba by the dad and ended up committing *suicide*, fish forks, whoopie pie, Arthur Treacher's Fish & Chips, YEOW, *now* what, one, two, three, four, gug, oh, now where did *that* cockamamie thing come from, a tiny eensy-weensy propeller plane, the fact that it could've really sent *me* flying, but instead I'm just quietly *crying*, the fact that I need to wear thicker shoes or something until Jake grows up, twin beds, upper shelf, lipstick, lemon drizzle cake, forced migration, railroad swing bridge, the fact that you can't fully understand fluids without understanding magnetism and geometry, ♬ *Some enchanted evening* ♬, the fact that Stacy finally finished watching *South Pacific*, and I said wasn't it nice how much she likes musicals, and she said she *doesn't* like them, so I said "Then why watch them?" and she looked me right in the eye and said "To see how they make me feel," which didn't make a whole lot of sense, so I said "Well, and how *do* they make you feel?", and her answer was "That I'm not white," the fact that I am just *devastated* by that, the fact that it really cuts me to the quick, the fact that I didn't know *what* to say, the fact that my knees went wobbly, the fact that I had no idea she was worrying about stuff like that, the fact that I never wanted that kind of stuff to bother her, *ever*, the fact that I never wanted her to have to worry about it for a *second*, heavens, black and white, black-and-white movies, Technicolor, Todd-AO, ♬ *There is nothin' like a dame* ♬, and I thought she was just enjoying herself in there, *White Christmas*, *Seven Brides for Seven Brothers*, the Indians on the train in *Annie Get Your Gun*, oh dear, *My Fair Lady*,

· · · ·

A lot of wilderness exists between the cracks, forming unintended passageways – she stuck to cemented creeks, bands of overgrown grassland along the highways, urban and suburban woodland. One night she ventured into a vast grassy area in the middle of a town, a park. Her presence there scared the water birds out of their wits, with much silly screeching and splashing going on. As she moved along the bank of the pond, the screeching moved with her. But, once she'd passed by, the birds recovered their composure. Birds live in the moment, they live fast.

For the lion there was still pleasure in motion, pleasure in anticipation. She needed pleasure to power the hunt. The pleasure was muted for her now by the theft of her cubs, but she was hungry. In the rose garden section, she located a raccoon, ate its innards, dug a cleft for it behind a bench and half-covered it with leaves. Then she stretched, lay down, and rolled on to her side, letting the cool earth bear her full weight.

She was woken by more quacking. Again, the birds by the pond were disturbed, but this time the cause was a large invasion of policemen, all in matching plumage. With dogs, they marched towards the rose garden in a long, wide line, guns at the ready and swaying with every step they made. Killers, hunting something. The lioness trotted silently out of reach.

By chance, she was the first to find the man they were after, dangling in a tree, in denser woodland. His spinning feet were in her way as she darted by. She didn't pause to examine him. None of this was her concern.

By the time the police found him, the lioness had already leapt the park's boundary fence unseen. The bellowing hound dogs excitedly strained at the leash, desperate to chase after her, but the masters dismissed the yearnings of their dogs.

The dead man had destroyed himself, but only after having stabbed his mother and her boyfriend earlier in the evening, and a baby half-sister. He slashed at them where they stood. Once they were still, he tiptoed across the puddles of blood, and caught the last bus into town.

He was recorded on camera walking towards the municipal park. He had been a trainee gardener there for a time, and this was the place he chose to finish the job his life had been.

.　　.　　.　　.

the fact that a red-winged blackbird just flew away from me, all startled and angry, dear me, the fact that I only wanted to watch him take a bath in the chickens' Rubbermaid tub, the fact that I wasn't going to put him in a *pie*, Bath Oliver biscuits, my nose, Dr. Oliver, *Oliver!*, the fact that it's so pretty out here right now, in the late afternoon, the fact that surely it's safe to be outside, the fact that there have been no lion sightings for days, the fact that I just want to sit in the sun for a little while and read an Anne Tyler and look at the Kinkels' Kazakh pear tree, which is almost at its peak, when it starts to look like a giant bowl of white popcorn, the fact that I don't know what Joyce Carol Oates is complaining about, I really don't, the fact that how bad can it be, owning a pear orchard, the fact that the blossoms must be spectacular, like cherry blossoms, "The dogwood, the dogwood!", that dogwood moment, the fact that Leo gets so sick of "the damn dogwood" in Atlanta, the fact that he says he can't take it anymore, the fact that I don't know from dogwood, but a Kazakh pear tree is really something else, the fact that I wonder if Kazakhstan's covered too, right now, with all this whiteness, the fact that from a distance they must look like cheerleaders' pompoms all over the plains of Kazakhstan but, according to Doreen, the Kazakh pear tree's about to go extinct in the wild, because farm animals keep eating the trees and trampling all over them, the fact that Kazakh pear trees don't fit in with modern Kazakh farming practices, Kinkels, Kazakhs, Cossacks, Joyce Carol Oates, Pallas's cats, the fact that that means the Kinkels' Kazakh pear could be one of the last in the *world*, the fact that I wish *we* had one, the fact that maybe she'd give me a cutting and then they'd cross-pollinate and we could perpetuate the species, *and* get pears, the fact that I think the Kinkels' tree is sterile, because there's no other Kazakh pear tree from here to the Urals, or maybe I mean the Caspian Sea, the fact that originally Kazakhs were *nomads*, which I guess suited the pear trees much better, the fact that farming messed everything up for the trees, the fact that I must admit the Kazakh pear tree makes up for the Giant Viper's Buglosses, the fact that I don't know why they like those so much, the fact that they get a new Viper's Bugloss every summer, the fact that *bees* like them, the Buglosses I mean, not the Kinkels, the fact that I remember Doreen Kinkel clambering around her yard with her first Giant Viper's Bugloss in a great big pot, wind chimes, the fact that it seemed like no big deal at first, and too small for the pot, the fact that when they're puny you hardly notice them, but then the growth spurt begins, the fact that it's like an amaryllis but on a much bigger scale, the way they shoot up, shoot up, fentanyl, shoot up the saloon, *Shane*, the fact that a Viper's Bugloss can grow about a foot a day, all gangly and silly-looking, the fact that I think they probably look better in a group, don't we all, not all alone like the Kinkels', the fact that then they suddenly flower all over with those little bluish flowers and just sit there like that for the rest of the summer, which is *okay* but they still look like something from another planet, maybe Venus, nomads, non-native species, the fact that buckeyes are native, the fact that our tree's like its own little village, it's got so many creatures living on it, including my kids, the fact that it's got birds, bees, snakes, squirrels, and raccoons, who knows what, the fact that it's also got the kids' swing and their treehouse, so they're in it all summer too, the fact that I like it when the buckeye throws its great big thorny balls at you in the fall, or in the winter, when each branch is highlighted by snow, but spring is good too, with those pale-yellow flower cones standing straight up all over it, the fact that the flowers don't last very long, the fact that you have to enjoy them while they're here, the fact that I finally managed to plant out my geraniums, despite the kids being underfoot, and lions being, well, *everywhere*, the fact that now they're in the flower beds, the geraniums, not lions or kids, the fact that all I want in my back yard from now on are geraniums, nasturtiums and a few marigolds, oh, and lilies of the valley, and lavender of course, lots of lavender, and pansies, the fact that I hope the chickens won't disturb the geraniums, the fact that the rain delayed my noontime egg search, and now the chickens can't decide whether to go in or come out, the fact that I know absolutely nothing about gardening, the fact that I'm not even completely sure what a flower bed *is*, the fact that I just remembered I dreamt I was a *leopard* and I had magical powers, the fact that I could lunge upwards if I wanted to, sort of like flying almost, the fact that I leapt up into a tree and reached a nice, wide welcoming branch, and then I just wanted to lie down, so I did, and gradually the weight of my body brought the branch lower and lower down to the ground, which I didn't mind, because it made me feel safe and happy to be close to the ground, the fact that by then I was me again, human, but still lying comfortably on the branch, which was now inside a building, the fact that I was much too comfortable to get up, though the room was gradually filling with people, the fact that wasn't that a ghastly thing, that two-year-old who shot his one-year-old brother dead, the fact that the *mom* got blamed, for leaving a loaded gun in her bedroom, safety procedures, precautions, protocol, protons, the fact that how do you *live* with that afterwards, *Lizzie Borden took an ax, and gave her mother forty whacks*, gaga, Lady Gaga, cocoa, caca, the fact that there's not much violence in Anne Tyler books, well, not upfront anyway, the fact that there's the kid who got shot in *The Accidental Tourist* but he was killed a year before the book starts, sort of offstage, and there's not much about it in the book, just the aftermath, the fact that that's why her stuff is sort of calming, because you know nothing too awful's going to happen, the fact that I think there's enough violence in the world already, the fact that Cathy lent me this one, the fact that she *likes* violence, which is kind of surprising, but she reads all kinds of stuff, the fact that she is a really fast reader, the fact that I wonder if she reads all those crime things because she's been through a crime *herself*, the fact that maybe she *needs* them, the fact that maybe she internalized that whole experience and she's still processing it, getting closure, the hydraulic approach to parenting, the fact that she seems to vary it at least, like she'll read a crime thriller and then a calmer-downer, the fact that I usually only read Anne Tylers when I'm sick, the fact that Leo can usually find one at the library, "lie-berry," liberty, Liberty Bell, the fact that I should make *lie-berry pies*, full of squid ink and alphabet noodles, the fact that Anne Tyler's from Baltimore, world HQ of the KKK, sand dabs, soft shell crabs, but her books aren't about that, the fact that they're mostly just about close families and sweet, kind silent men who scrape a living rinsing bottles or something unambitious like that, that you can't believe a person can make a living out of, kind of like baking *pies*, I guess, the fact that it's all pretty pleasant, though some of her characters can get irritable over the least little thing, it seems to me, but life goes on, the fact that they remind me of Patricia Highsmith books sometimes, just in the way they roll steadily along at a slow pace, slack water, the fact that people in Anne Tyler books are always either sitting down on a chair, or getting up off a chair and standing behind somebody else who's sitting on a chair, or they go slowly out of one room and into the next or come back and sit down, the fact that there really are a lot of chairs in her books, the fact that there are a lot of chairs in the *world*, tables too, beds, pillows, towels, "tals," "FEARED BLOODY AFTERMATH," the fact that after Cathy told me that whole thing that happened with Blanche, I dreamt my whole ribcage ached, and when I woke up my ribs really did ache, haircut, styptic stick, the fact that I think my dreams are getting too real, though not the jumping leopard one, the fact that when I was a kid I liked jewels, sequins, golden crowns and stuff, Fabergé Easter eggs, gorgets, gold embroidery, the Crown Jewels, but now the magic's gone, the fact that jewels mean nothing to me now, except when they remind me of how jewels looked when I was a kid, the fact that my bird costume too seemed magic, so wonderfully yellow, and priceless to *me*, the fact that it amazed me that each individual feather had been individually sewn on, the fact that I hardly knew how *anything* got made at the time, the fact that when you're a kid you think everything's just there, the fact that you think chairs and tables just came into being naturally, like rocks and rivers, the fact that you don't realize people had to design and construct them, and your TV set, the fact that it's still a little hard to believe that somebody carved Mount Rushmore, the fact that somebody in Skokie thought they saw the lion at *Old Orchard*, the fact that it's a long time since *that's* been an orchard, Joyce Carol Oates, okey-dokey, the fact that last time I was there the parking lot used to have just those little spindly trees that gave no shade, but they're probably bigger now, the fact that it sure wasn't an orchard of *fruit* trees, I don't think, though how would I know, the fact that I didn't know one tree from another, I was just a little kid, the fact that surely they wouldn't plant fruit trees in a parking lot though, the fact that nobody wants apples denting your car, or overripe plums and pears dropping on it while you're off shopping, and you don't want to slip on d-d-d-damsons when you're carrying a lot of bags, paw-paws, "give the paw," buckeyes, buckeye balls, the fact that our apple tree is like an old friend, or maybe more like an unpaid slave, considering the number of pies it's contributed to, the fact that it's not in the same league as the Kazakh pear tree but it's pretty, the fact that L. M. Montgomery writes about apple blossoms, the fact that I don't think Gillian takes that stuff in yet but maybe some day it will get to her, the fact that I'm glad we have this semi-rural spot, the fact that they don't even know it yet but they're learning to love the smell of apple blossoms, the fact that Old Orchard's no place for a *lion* to be, the fact that we used to buy our new school clothes there, time alone with Mommy, the fact that it was a big treat getting new school duds, the fact that I remember getting several dresses and blouses once, and really enjoying wearing them all that year, the fact that it's great when you have just the right thing for the occasion, the fact that you feel *rich*, the fact that I don't think I ever have the right thing on these days, "In your dreams, lady," the fact that in my dreams I often have *nothing* on, the fact that I remember Mommy pointing out how many different outfits I could get out of the things we'd bought, by wearing a different shirt under something, or a different skirt, the fact that I think maybe some of the stuff was even reversible, the fact that Old Orchard seemed like a treasure trove, a real treat, pterodactyls, Marshall Field's, gray sweater, Frango Mints, Pepito, the fact that I used to think it was in Chicago but it's in Skokie, the fact that I was always glad we didn't live in a place called "Skokie," the fact that the Old Smokies would be better, Funk Bottoms, the tree house, our fancy-looking chicken coop, the fact that now going to the mall is no big deal, almost an everyday occurrence, and sometimes it's *scary*, the fact that "protective clothing" is starting to sound like a really good idea, the fact that I must've been shopping on my own though when I bought that crazy yellow dress with the angel-wing sleeves, which was a bit like my *bird costume*, now I come to think about it, the fact that I think I bought it on a trip back to Evanston, from New Haven, when I was about eleven, the fact that I paid for it with my own money, my traveling money, the fact that I can remember counting it all in the store, the fact that I took a plane all on my own back to Evanston, and must have stayed with Jill, for a week or so, the fact that we went to Marshall Field's downtown, not out at Old Orchard, and I chose that exciting dress, the fact that it was a *lot*, like $40 or something, and then I never wore it except maybe *once*, the fact that *I* liked it, but I was kind of nervous about other people maybe not liking it, the fact that you need your *mom* with you when you go shopping at that age, the fact that I'd like to see that dress *now*, the fact that the main problem was it was too expensive to *wear* except on special occasions, and there *were* no special occasions, so I grew out of it before I'd hardly worn it, FOOSH, just like the bird costume and the Dutch dresses, the fact that I can't remember what Mommy thought of the dress, the fact that I'm not sure she ever saw it on, the fact that that broke me, Mommy's *illness*, not my yellow dress, the fact that, generally, I think she disapproved of yellow, $40, the fact that when you're young your money just eats at you, the fact that you're always trying to decide what to blow it on, the fact that Leo remembers all his early purchases, the fact that he'd get his allowance on Saturday and go straight to the store and get something, *anything*, the fact that he wasn't allowed candy though, so he bought magazines, and models to make, and just all kinds of stuff, the fact that once he just bought a whole load of little brown cardboard package labels, the kind you tie on with string, just because he liked the look of them, "I like the cut of your jib," the fact that I was broken, orphaned, Hansel and Gretel, musicals, Daniel Boone, wild goose chases, slip of the tongue, the fact that different lentils need different soaking times, the fact that corn gets high as an elephant's eye, the Weather Channel, broken, the fact that you can't make an omelet without breaking eggs, broken, amulet, gorget, engorged, the fact that women nurse their babies less in America than in any other industrialized country, the fact that when I went to get the chickens in last night, there was a low yellowish full moon, that seemed to be cupped by a cloud, like the sky was offering

793

us some nice vanilla ice cream in a cup, but where were the plastic spoons, moon, mooncake, month, mouth, mother, moth, mothballs, moonbat, pontoon, poltroon, picaroon, Walloon, balloon, goon, dragoon, baby-boomer, the fact that it scars you, I think, to feel unloved by everybody you meet, but I *am* lovable, and loved, not like bureaucracy, the fact that does anyone love bureaucracy, or is bureaucracy totally unlovable, admin, scheduling, Excel, cancellation times, dyslexia, DNC, monotone, cotton pads, black pepper, knee socks, milk, Kleenex, the fact that some thirty-year-old tenor just died of tetanus, which is so sad, thirty, *tetanus*, gosh, the fact that he wasn't one of the Three Tenors, the fact that I have the same birthday as one of the Three Tenors but I can't ever remember which, the fact that Matthew Polenzani's a tenor, but he's not one of the *three*, Tide, Tide Pod Challenge, tide pools, the fact that Rachel Carson liked tide pools, shampoo, wine, bagels, paper towels, ham, pickles, saffron, turmeric, parsley, potatoes, Chivington, Winnebago, Galaxy Quest, Saturday, olive oil, vanilla, garlic, library, Ouilmette, Wilmette, Skokie, Mommy, the fact that we swam while she sat on the beach in a sundress and sunglasses and read, the fact that I wish I could press rewind on my *life*, the fact that Frederick's luxuriating over there by the fence, hoping someone will come by on the sidewalk and see and adore him, the fact that he has such a long bushy tail, the fact that he's found himself a bed of brown pine needles, sheltered by the lowest branch of the pine tree, the fact that he'd be almost completely camouflaged if it weren't for those nice creamy white legs of his, and the loud purr, the fact that nobody can resist bending to talk to him and pat him, which he gladly accepts, marmalade boy, but he doesn't *need* their pats, the fact that he's content with or without attention, that cat, just happy in himself, the fact that now he's stretching out even further, the fact that he's settled his head so nicely between his front legs, with his chin resting on the pine needles, ready for a snooze, the fact that he really is the picture of contentment, the fact that he doesn't need other creatures around at all, the fact that he's not worrying about hunting or sleeping or licking himself, he's not even noticing birds rustling nearby, the fact that he's just sunning himself in celebration of spring, the fact that he's not thinking about the end of the world, the fact that Frederick will go to his *grave* without thinking about the end of the world, no bug-out bag for *him*, no sirree, the fact that he's just thinking about his own life and he thinks it's swell, the fact that maybe cats are even better at pleasure than dogs, though dogs are very good at it, even when they're dog-tired, dawn chorus, Messiaen, Aaron Copland, cope-land, the fact that I think animals think a lot, the fact that they're the ones who have the *time*, birds too, the fact that birds do everything fast, the fact that birds could think up whole novels in twenty seconds, I bet, livelier novels than Anne Tyler's too, but birds have bird brains, so that might slow them down a bit, the fact that I can't see Opal anywhere, the fact that now where has she gone, the fact that I haven't seen her all day, kidnapping, catnapping, the fact that it's unbelievable but every single thing alive has its own center of being, and looks out on the world from that point of view, even a worm, or a jellyfish, hamsters, owls, the fact that even a leaf has feelings, the fact that you *know* the leaves are enjoying this warm sun going right through them, the fact that the leaves seem to be sunbathing, letting the sun lick them, the fact that there are times, maybe the most unlikely times, that you realize you're simply thrilled to be alive, and what a great piece of luck it is just to be a *part* of things, to have a body, so you can feel and see and walk the earth, for just a little while, the fact that children are born happy, and it's a mom's duty to preserve that in them as long as possible, *everybody's* duty, the fact that it's the same with flowers, the fact that there is no way a newly opened poppy can't be thrilled to be alive, and trees, waterfalls, the fact that waterfalls sure *act* thrilled, except when they dry to a trickle during a dry spell or something, the falls at Fallingwater, the fact that water must have a sense of itself, a real liking for itself, because bodies of water are always trying to meet up, the fact that it's hard to keep them apart, the fact that that's why oceans exist, they're big water get-togethers, Jacques Cousteau, the fact that maybe waves worry about getting separated from the rest of the water, the fact that they probably don't want to end up stuck in a tide pool, the fact that that's why dams seem so sad, because the water isn't being allowed to do what it wants, like find new streams to join or something, new playmates, creeks and lakes and ponds and rivers, the fact that even droplets of water are attracted to each other, raindrops in tide pools, puddles, the fact that that's why a glass full of water has that curve on top, a meniscus, because the water's trying to hold together as long as possible, the fact that it doesn't *want* to start dribbling over the edge, the fact that water likes to hold on to its integrity, and gang up on *dirt*, the fact that *everything* has a sense of its own existence, even a rock, I bet, even those five-mile deep chasms on Pluto, and the Grand Canyon, which must be pretty pleased with itself, all red and yellow and green, tourists, mule rides, sunsets, bullring, bull mastiff, pit bull, the fact that all I want to do is achieve a little *contentment*, for myself and a few other people I know, hunky-dunky, hunky-dory, ♫ *My Sal, she's a spunky gal* ♫, but it's so *hard*, tip-toppity, "Appalachian Spring," *Silent Spring*, Silent Sentinels, *The Bridge*, Brooklyn Bridge, britches, breeches, breach, beach, the fact that Hart Crane came from Garrettsville, Ohio, and fought with his dad over money and now they're both dead and where did that get them, the fact that nobody's taken any of my discarded plants yet, the fact that it's not like those plants are *worthless* or anything, the fact that they're just surplus to my requirements because I want nasturtiums this year, and geraniums and lilies of the valley, the fact that I hope the old plants get a good home though, the fact that people think free stuff's just *junk* but it isn't always, the fact that I've invested too much in my discarded plants, not money, just concern, the fact that I need to learn to let go, the fact that some people meditate almost *constantly*, but I don't know what good it does them, and some people have microbial kitchen counters, or *anti*-microbial, and what good is *that*, and some people do both, the fact that they meditate *and* have microbe-resistant countertops, like Deepak Chopra, *microbial*, check the dough's rising, the fact that you can't really see the whole shape of a tree until you get a certain distance away from it, the fact that I like a nice stand of trees, the fact that I even like the expression "a stand of trees," the fact that a fine stand of trees makes a good picnic spot on a hot day, the fact that trees seem in a different time zone from us, and they live so much longer than we do, but still, they are our companions, the fact that that *Fresia* is in her own time zone, or time warp, the fact that, oh my word, the fact that that jogger has the most dimply legs, the fact that I'd be so embarrassed, the fact that what a meanie I am, the fact that she can't help it if her thighs look like, well, Pluto, and Pluto looks like it's been through a heck of a hard time, the fact that everybody feels sorry for Pluto, the fact that some people eat to live and some live to eat, and some jog it off, the fact that I eat to live, but I also live to cook, or cook to live, the fact that Gérard Depardieu accuses Andie MacDowell of eating birdseed in *Green Card*, candy corn, ♫ *I'm singin' in the rain* ♫, the fact that there's always tomorrow, except when there isn't, hurry, tardy, tardigrades, macrophages, the fact that soon it'll be time to go berrying, as long as there aren't any lions around by then, Tiger Mom, Fresia, ♫ *Bears and tigers haunt me all day* ♫, ziti, mozzarella, hamburger buns, p. chops, sour cream and brandy, snapdragons, dimpled thighs, roly-poly, upsy-daisy, ravololi, Beef William, the fact that the kids got sent home after another lion sighting, and then they were called back into school, not because the lion got caught but because some parents kicked up a stink, the fact that you can understand it though, the fact that there are so many foreclosures around here, the fact that nobody can afford to take a day off, not if they want to eat and pay their mortgage and health insurance and college bills, the fact that I guess it's safer to let your kids get eaten by a lion at recess than lose your *home*, the fact that Leo would never let us lose our house, I know, the fact that if you ask me, this search for the lion is getting out of hand, floor wipes, Code Yellow, Code Red, the fact that it seems almost like all of America's being terrorized by one lion, or at least we *hope* it's only one, the fact that if it's a plague of lions they haven't said so, the fact that actually they seem to be narrowing down the search now, to the *southern Ohio area*, cougar, puma, panther, the fact that that scares me, the fact that I don't want anything to do with a lion, a cougar, a puma, *or* a panther, the fact that there are all kinds of Twitter hashtags and conspiracy theories now, #cougarcon, #pawgate, and everybody's speculating on whether it really is a lion or something supernatural or even extraterrestrial, or fake, the fact that this lion emergency has even made people forget about Trump for a while, the fact that you'd think that would work in his favor but he's not happy about it, the fact that he's always tweeting that his enemies have released the lion to distract people from his important work, the fact that his campaign slogan for the next presidential election is going to be *Keep* America Great Again, KAGA, caca, ACA, DACA, kakistocracy, Kazakhstan, Caucasians, the fact that it doesn't make much sense as a slogan, "Suck in your gut *again*," "Stay away from the Ivy League *again*," GOA, GAR, DAR, DAPA, the fact that America will either be a success or a failure, Ho Jos, mojo, cocoa, ducks, black leaves, white sky, Waterlow Park, five thousand ducks being herded along a street in China somewhere, on YouTube, the fact that they were so *compliant*, and so identical, poor ducks, Lodge Mistress, Wo-He-Lo, car keys, the fact that now there's a *club*, devoted to shooting this one lion, the fact that it's called Mission Safety or something, no, that's something else, the fact that the lion club is called Freedom From Fear, the FFF, the fact that Leo said it *should* be called the Trigger-Happy Club, THC, TLC, TNT, the fact that I keep seeing men rushing to and fro in pickup trucks, shooting into the air, for no reason, well, not on our road, but they're around, the fact that you hear a lot more shots from afar now than we used to, the fact that the police don't even try to stop the lion posses anymore, the fact that I think they've given up, the police, not the posses, the fact that I think the police are sick of directing traffic all day, the fact that many a car accident has already been caused by this lion, well, not directly by the lion, just from road rage, and drunk drivers, but they're kind of lion-related, because people are lion-crazee, collateral damage, the fact that these lion-busters drive like maniacs and bump into each other, partly because they're so easily distracted by anything along the road that looks remotely like a lion, the fact that what started off as a good-natured hunt, a heroic attempt to save Ohio, just ends up with people punching people over the dents in their bumpers, bumper cars, the fact that they don't allow fun-fair bumper cars to *bump* anymore, but I never liked the bumping anyway, the fact that I just wanted to drive around in a little car all by myself, the fact that it felt so good to be behind the wheel of one of those things, with the big padded seat and all, the fact that I always wished *our* car was like that, open-topped, but we always had Grandpa's hand-me-down cars, the fact that in that Hardy story, a man's standing beside the merry-go-round, and he and some woman make eye contact as she spins by on the merry-go-round, and everything goes downhill from there, spirals, flips, Flipper, the fact that Freedom From Fear has big plans, the fact that they say that after they get this lion, they're going to rid America of "all predators, both human and animal," the fact that what does that even mean, the fact that their HQ's in Utah and they've been practicing on the few remaining mountain lions there, toning up their skills for the big Ohio adventure, the fact that Utah hunting licenses are pretty lenient already and they just issued a whole lot more, though there's no state where you *can't* hunt mountain lions, the fact that the Trigger Happy Club, or whatever it's called, already has a Certificate of Excellence from TripAdvisor, and merchandise as well, like caps and T-shirts that say FFF and HH, for "Hero Hunters," and GSL, which means Guns Save Lives, mugs too, flapdoodle, high jinx, the fact that other groups are being organized by hunt planners, that are just like wedding planners, the fact that I wonder if they give people gun toss duties, or maybe *ammo* toss duties if you're leery of throwing guns around, Macon Leary, the fact that it's usually about five or six thousand bucks for a mountain lion hunt, with everything included, including a dead lion, Peolia college seal, but they're doubling that for the Ohio hunt, due to the surge in demand and the distance and difficulties involved, the fact that you get discounts if you bring your *kids*, the fact that it's half-price for kids under twenty-five, even though Homeland Security just issued strict guidelines *not* to take your kids lion-hunting, after what happened in Akron, but everybody's trying to get women and children shooting these days, Annie Oakley, Dana Loesch, the fact that the Akron guy really thought hunting a lion would be good target practice for his boys, who'd just learned how to shoot Uzis, so off they went and one kid accidentally shot his big brother in the foot, and in return his brother shot him dead, Keds, the fact that now everybody's blaming the *lion* for it, not the dad, the fact that this lion gets the blame for everything, school closures, foreclosures, food shortages, everything, the fact that he sure has a lot to answer for, and it's not just the gun mishaps and the car crashes, it's the havoc caused to TV schedules and other recreational activities, sports and stuff, the Possums, nightlife, tourism, barn-raising, Kelly McGillis's basin bath, the fact that they expect a big surge in the birth rate too, come nine months from now, because of everybody keeping so close to home, ♫ *I ain't had no lovin' since January, February, June or July* ♫, the fact that I don't know what's eating everybody, the fact that there was a minor riot in Cleveland, after somebody thought they'd seen the lion, the fact that then they admitted they hadn't seen it and a whole bunch of people just started looting anyway, the fact that maybe it's just frustration over all the curfews and closures and no *closure*, the fact that this lion is driving people *nuts*, elude, extrude, exude, the fact that they've got curfews going in Dayton and Columbus, and unsubstantiated sightings of the lion everywhere, even Cy Young Park, and Young's Jersey Dairy, and Youngstown, maybe anywhere with "Young" in the name, the fact that all I can say is I hope he doesn't wanna eat *our* young, the fact that cougars pre-date humans by millions of years, the fact that the last mountain lion they shot in Pennsylvania was in 1969, but the last one they shot in Vermont was in 1994, and there may still be some in Canada because they've got quieter attics up there, Frederick luxuriating, the fact that the suspense is unbearable really, and how they'll crow when they get him, excruciating, exude, extrude, the fact that he must be so *lonely* if he's the last lion left this far east, or north, North by Northwest, the fact that I've led a lonely bereft life since Mommy died, the fact that what if a lion got in the house, the fact that I guess we could try to hide in the attic, the fact that I think I may be as scared of lions as I am of bears, the fact that there's been a run on Panic Rooms, and plenty of people are barring their windows, like they're living in a *jail*, homemade prisons, the fact that I liked *Abby's* attic, the fact that it smelled just how an attic should smell, of old blankets and Christmas ornaments and camp beds and mothballs and discarded furniture, and sheets and quilts and winter wear folded and laid in trunks and drawers years ago, and old-fashioned, untreated pine, or was it treated, the fact that it probably was, if I know Abby, Mississippi, Mishewaka, Mishipeshu, DNC, tell me no lies, red-winged blackbirds, purple martins, the chickens, the fact that I wonder what I did with that glitter skirt I had as a teen, the fact that where *is* that thing, and my Guatemalan shirt, the fact that it seems to have been in Appalachia and the Blue Ridge Mountains and the Adirondacks all at the same time, the lion, not my skirt or shirt, Indiana too, the fact that somebody reported seeing it in Mishawaka, South Bend, "It sounds like dancing," the fact that that lion's racing in circles and so are the lion hunters, spiraling, whirling dervishes, whirly-gigs, and there's all this interstate wrangling about the emergency services, because they can't decide if the lion's Ohio's problem or Indiana's, or West Virginia's or Pennsylvania's or *what*, the fact that people keep calling for gubernatorial action, but *which governor*, the windy city, the Big Apple, Tastee Apple, apple blossoms, the fact that a whirly-gig is a wind catcher thingamajig, a pinwheel, windmill, wind turbine, dream catcher, damn dams, the fact that all they do is complain and criticize, the fact that somebody saw a cougar in Arizona and half of that Utah Mission Impossible team zoomed down there to take that one out, just for fun I guess, because it can't possibly be the Ohio one, unless he's got magical powers and can be in two places at once, the fact that what's the word for that, transportation, no, teleportation maybe, transubstantiation, meniscus, hydrangea, the fact that *I'd* like to be in two places at once, Jake without his shirt on, the fact that there are lots of Indian names for cougars, the fact that Katalgar means Greatest of Wild Hunters, and Puma means Powerful Animal, Pi-twal means

Long-Tailed One, and Ko-Icto means Cat of God, the fact that there's also Mishipeshu, the underwater panther, and Fire Cat, the fact that they're closely related to cheetahs, and they can run at forty-five miles an hour or more, so they really get around, the fact that their whiskers detect air currents, the fact that starving cougars sometimes eat beetles, the fact that it's weird watching the whole country mobilize itself against one little beetle-eating beast, the fact that, I mean, what is all this *costing*, what with the hound dogs, Mounties, man hours, helicopters, heat-imaging cameras, the Army Corps of Engineers and the National Guard, the fact that to avoid mass panic, they're not telling people where it's been sighted anymore, but everybody's panicking anyway, because they can't trust the info the authorities release, BunnyRanch, and people are so steamed up, the fact that it's just like the way they get about *immigrants*, the fact that maybe they've confused the lion with an undocumented alien, a non-native incomer that entered Ohio illegally, newcomer, Newcomerstown, Cheechako, Dreamer, a *Mexican* puma, the fact that Newcomerstown was once called *Neighbourtown*, so I am really out of place here, since I am *not* a good neighbor, the fact that I don't get why they don't just make all immigrants legal so they can start paying *taxes*, but you'd never dare say so around here, incomer, income tax, freedom of speech, freedom of information, ACLU bumper stickers, road rage, BSA, the fact that I think I'm getting Resignation Syndrome, RS, VR, trauma, the fact that if a cougar cub is orphaned under nine months old, it doesn't usually survive, the fact that at the Brookfield Zoo in Chicago they use a plastic marmot to keep the cougars alive, I mean keep them *active*, the fact that maybe some Americans could use a plastic marmot too, dimples, cellulite, "I eat salad," the fact that it's funny all mammals have *belly buttons*, or *I* think it is, the fact that belly buttons just are funny, though we'd look strange without them, the fact that I don't really see how one lion can eat everybody in Ohio, famous last words, touch wood, the fact that on the plus side, this lion sure sells papers, the fact that circulation's up, and Walmart, McDonald's, Burger King, Dunkin' Donuts and Krispy Kreme are doing a "rrrroaring" trade, because people see those sorts of places as safe havens, especially at night, when the lion's more likely to be out on the prowl, the fact that everybody huddles together in the diner in *The Birds* the same way, but it doesn't save them, the fact that people seem to think nothing bad can happen to you in a popular restaurant with a brand name and a neon sign, even though that's where a lot of bad things do happen these days, Abby, the fact that Abby liked Howard Johnson's hot dogs, the fact that Ho Jos were segregated for a long time, the fact that a guy drove his car right into the front of a Walmart the other day because his new mattress hadn't been delivered on time, the fact that he injured six customers, the fact that I hope he can sleep all right at night on that new mattress, for crying out loud, milk of human kindness, blotch, hopscotch, grouting, black-and-white movies, wet, black slippery leaves, white sky reflected in the puddles in Waterlow Park, sagging meniscus, concave, convex, the fact that waves know just what to do, the fact that Leo *agreed* with my theory about water, the fact that he says water molecules *are* attracted to each other, just like I thought, the fact that water wants to stay whole, or is subject to *pressure* to stay whole, as he'd put it, because of surface tension, the fact that I told *him* that, the fact that you can *see* it, anybody can, the fact that you don't have to know anything about molecules to know that water is in love with itself, but in a good way, not like Trump, the fact that somebody said Trump's raped thirteen-year-old girls, the fact that I wish he'd just quit it, just quit it, I mean the *presidency*, but it would also be good if he quit raping little girls, "Malignant narcissist," the fact that there's a picture of me sitting on Daddy's lap when I was about eleven, and I love that picture, the fact that I wonder where it's gone, the fact that I had a really nice dress on, with smocking on the front, and I look so comfortable on his lap, the fact that I look like I love my daddy, and I did, the Mary Cassatt girl, blue chair, the fact that it must be about the last time I ever sat on his lap though, because he shied away from stuff like that once we hit puberty, the fact that it was a sort of wide staircase with a balcony bit all along the top, and we're sitting under that, below the long strip of window over the stairs, the fact that that was a nice house, the fact that at the top you got to Mommy and Daddy's room first, then Ethan's, then the bathroom, then Phoebe's room on the right and mine of the left, and the back stairs, but the open banister carried on around until you got to the bathroom almost, or to Ethan's room anyway, the fact that I was always scared of that banister, the fact that I had a lot of bad dreams about falling over it, on to the stairs below, or into the living room, and I was fairly sure it would happen some day too in real life, just like I thought I could fly if I really tried, the fact that that didn't happen either, the fact that I didn't fall and I didn't fly, the fact that maybe that's *why* I thought I needed to know how to fly, in case I fell over the banister, Adelaide the flying kangaroo, the fact that Pepito loved it whenever Daddy sat on the floor, the fact that Pepito thought that was just the most thrilling thing in the world, to see Daddy on the floor, the fact that I remember him once running up those stairs after me, Daddy, not Pepito, and it was so frightening, the fact that it's not nice to be chased, in earnest, lion hunt, the fact that I still can't imagine what I could have done to deserve it, the fact that Daddy's rages were always a surprise to me, and he probably regretted it later, but I remember running up the stairs as fast as I could go to get away from him, the fact that I don't remember ever doing anything particularly wrong, the fact that I wasn't a naughty kid, maybe lazy, the fact that I don't think he would've tried to spank me just for watching too much TV, the fact that maybe *everybody* forgets why they were punished, Tom Sawyer, Huck Finn, the fact that to yourself you seem so *innocent*, the fact that maybe criminals feel the same way, I mean, unless you threw your wife off your catamaran to claim the life insurance and tried to sell her jewelry on the black market, the fact that it's funny it was on those same stairs I was photographed sitting on his lap so contentedly, lit up from behind by the row of diamond-paned windows, and I *was* happy sitting on his lap, and wearing that nice dress, the fact that you can forgive the occasional parental outburst when you're a kid, the fact that parents forgive kids for a lot too, *One that would peep and botanize Upon his mother's grave?*, the fact that our Evanston house probably meant more to me than the New Haven house ever did, the fact that I never felt as good there, back stairs, euphoria, the fact that puberty hit and Mommy got sick and all, the fact that we were only renting it and Daddy tried to convince Yale to sell but they wouldn't, and after we moved out, they let the place fall to rack and ruin, flotsam and jetsam, black-and-white, right and left, pro-life, anti-life, Senate, House of Representatives, counterpoint, clickbait, the fact that that's what big institutions are like though, indifferent, inhuman, unfeeling, Miley Cyrus Forbids, the fact that I can't love or be loved, the fact that I am indefensible, the fact that my shyness fluctuates, the fact that sometimes it's crippling and sometimes I just feel kind of hostile, the numbness of muted beings, stretch-fit bodice, the fact that my shyness makes me a drain on the community, the fact that even while having a nice chit-chat with another mom at Zyker's Foods, I'm always just wishing she didn't live nearby, so I won't have to talk to her *again*, because I'm always scared the next time won't go so well, the fact that I never think I can live up to my first effort with people, my first *performance*, and it's embarrassing, "That's why I won't do two shows a night anymore," the fact that I don't like *Houseboat*, though it's a pretty innocent picture and all, the fact that I don't know what gets me down about it so much, the fact that what could be wrong with Sophia Loren coming to take care of Cary Grant and his kids on a houseboat, the fact that, still, it just seems like the whole movie's really about Sophia Loren's sit-me-down-upon, and all the single-dad stuff and the houseboat are just pretexts, the fact that I'm no good, the fact that what good was I to Cathy when she told me what happened to her, the fact that does it help *her* if I had a bad dream after, the fact that last night I dreamt my hair was all perfectly coiled in dreadlocks, the fact that I had a million braids, but I didn't like it anymore because I was worried it was getting too tangled, the fact that there go more hunters zooming by, the fact that I hate it when people use the gas pedal as a form of self-expression, revving up just as they pass our window, pass out, pass away, pass on, the fact that it rattles the whole *house*, and my nerves, "my poor nerves," the fact that the kitchen juts out too close to the street, the fact that that's the problem, the fact that I don't know why they *built* it like that, the fact that I think the kitchen got added later, the fact that I don't like it when people zap their chip-keys right through you either, the fact that, call me crazy, but that just seems rude, the fact that I just don't think you should unlock your car door right *through* someone, and the same goes for the TV remote, as I'm always telling the kids, the fact that it's like playfully pointing a gun at somebody, the fact that it's not nice, Stacy's ancient furry cactus sticker, the fact that everybody in Ohio seems to work in Personnel or Recruitment or Human Resources, hiring and firing *more* Personnel people, personable people, Personable Department, the fact that I am a "human resource," the fact that I don't feel much like one, Acura, *Sticks and stones may break my bones*, starlings, sparrows, blue-jays, step on a crack and break your mother's back, the fact that the Carolina parakeet is extinct, and the green ground parrot is heading that way, Family Owned Since 1946, Mouseketeers, the fact that Mickey Mouse almost had a different name, I forget what, but it's not like "Mickey" is so spectacular either, the fact that some guy totaled his brand-new Ferrari an hour after buying it, $500,000, the fact that I wonder how common that is, totaling brand-new cars, the fact that it probably happens a lot more than you'd think, like in the excitement of buying it, and because you're not familiar with it yet, the fact that mainly everybody wants to drive too fast, the fact that I wonder what-ever happened to Lynn, broken femur, bus accident, the fact that she was my *best friend* for a year or two and now I don't know if she still exists and I'm not even sure I remember her last name, the fact that I might if I think about it, sieve, the fact that my memory's *worse* than a sieve, the fact that it's more like a funnel, and everything just spirals down the little chute and disappears somewhere, water spring, water-spout, ♫ *I'm a little teapot* ♫, measuring chicken feed, the fact that *another* driverless car mowed down some woman and killed her, the fact that why would you let a ton of metal zoom around at thirty or forty miles an hour all by itself, with nobody at the controls, the fact that cars *with* drivers are bad enough, Laika, the fact that it's terrible that poor dog was sent off into space like that, never to return, the fact that people will do anything, *anything*, the fact that people leave those robot carpet-sweepers on all day while they're out, just leave them to ram into the furniture or run over the cat, rogue golf bags zooming around by themselves, the fact that I'm pretty accident-prone already, the fact that Leo's always teasing me about my bus accident, because he thinks it wasn't very serious, but actually it was pretty alarming, the fact that it involved a whole load of school kids being carried over the highway in a runaway bus, for Pete's sake, the fact that I had to hold on to a pole while it jumped over several snow banks and crossed a line of oncoming traffic on Lake Shore Drive, oncoming traffic, incomers, the fact that you could get a whole Sandra Bullock movie outta that, oh wait, I guess they did, the fact that the bus didn't stop until it hit a tree, the fact that the bus driver cut his face, and we all limped out of the bus crying and eventually huddled in the foyer of some big fancy apartment building on Lake Shore Drive, but not Lynn, because she'd broken her leg, which I didn't know at the time, the fact that we were all in shock, the fact that we didn't know what was going on, the fact that all I wanted to do was get home to Mommy, the fact that it was just the kind of thing I'd always dreaded happening when I was away from home, far away from her, the fact that I didn't see Lynn for weeks, and it was a while longer before she could come back to school, the fact that I think I only visited her once during her recovery, the fact that I don't even know if we were really friends after that, the fact that it was a big gap for kids to deal with, the fact that now you'd keep in daily touch by phone and Facebook but we didn't, the fact that I wonder where she is now, the fact that the residents and the doormen in that apartment building were nice to us all, but who doesn't like helping little shocked eleven-year-olds for half an hour, "It's *you*!", the fact that they let us stand around weeping in the foyer until I guess another bus was found to get us home, the fact that I don't remember getting home, or if Mommy had been worried about me, HVN1, mass, weight, friction, eat to live, live to eat, lilies of the valley, Old Orchard, cell phones, the fact that a black man got shot by the police *fifty times*, because they mistook him for a *different* black guy they were looking for, a much taller man who'd been smashing windows or something, the fact that the other guy, the one they killed, was just standing outside in his own back yard, talking on his cell, the fact that the police officers decided in a split second that his phone was a gun, so they shot him dead, the fact that as he died he knocked on the back window, the fact that that's, that's just, the fact that some woman police officer said that, in her experience, things often escalate when a male police officer arrives on the scene, the fact that the whole thing turns nasty, the fact that it's testosterone, or the amygdala, or poor people skills, or something, Poo-Poo Plate, plainsong, madrigals, the fact that now I'm watching for Stacy to get home so I can go get the groceries, the fact that I mainly used the back stairs in Evanston, because they were closer to my room, the fact that I didn't use the front stairs as much, because of the banister, the fact that some architect must have thought it was good to have a wide, sort of showy, staircase with plenty of room for spanking children on the way up, and for children falling over the banister on the way down, the fact that he only spanked me once, I think, Daddy not the architect, the fact that the staircase probably wasn't even that wide, the fact that I just think of it that way maybe because I was small, the fact that I was the goody-goody and tattletale of the family, "fusspot," the fact that Phoebe must have had a lot to put up with, the fact that all I did for my first twenty years or so was follow her around, or try to, the fact that I was the one who saved my money and my Hallowe'en candy and obeyed Mommy and Daddy until Phoebe was probably ready to kill me, the fact that I must've really been a jerk, the fact that I got in less trouble than Phoebe or Ethan, the fact that when they were always ahead of me on rebelling and arguing with Mommy and Daddy, the fact that I never seemed to get around to doing all that sort of stuff, the fact that I was always trying to avoid being spanked, at all costs, fear of anger, the fact that I never could see what good could come of anger, so I didn't try it, and then Mommy got sick, so I didn't *want* to rebel anymore, and anyway Daddy *ordered* us not to give her any trouble or she might *die*, the fact that from then on I was frozen inside, the fact that that was the moment I really lost my mom, banister, stairwell, Tiny Tim's turquoise guinea pig carrier, ♫ *The Stars and Stripes Forever* ♫, the fact that Phoebe never liked peas, Lynn's femur, Q fever, the F-word, the fact that when Ethan was two he ran all over the beach yelling "F—, f—, f—!" again and again, and Mommy thought everybody on the beach would blame *her*, though she honestly didn't know where he'd picked up the word, the fact that she and Daddy never cursed in front of us, the fact that they might have said "goddammit" once in a while but that was about it, "incorrigible," *King Lear*, Gloucester, the fact that when *Mommy* was two, she yelled "Ducky! Ducky! Ducky!" and ran into the pond, Motif #1, the fact that these days you'd probably be arrested if your two-year-old came out with that, the *F* word I mean, not "Ducky," the fact that you'd either be either shot or arrested or both, depending on what sort of policeman you got, and what ethnicity you are, the fact that the police can be nice, the fact that some officer talked a murderer down last Christmas by singing "Silent Night" to him, at the murderer's request, the fact that he *sang* the guy down, instead of talking him down, the fact that maybe they should always try that, siege, SWAT team, Canoeist Surrounded By Manatees, Mommy, Mother Goose, mother vehicle, the fact that even if I *am* shy and my daughter hates me, there are sunsets of many colors and that is good, the fact that the sky is now peach, mauve, sky-blue, gray, blue-gray, shocking pink, orange, yellow, and a pale creamy blue, all at the same time, with a diagonal streak of pink coming out of the center like a spotlight, the fact that I dreamt I had to pick Frank up in Cambridge, Cambridge, Ohio, not Cambridge, Mass., but I seemed to be kind of stuck in *Dayton*, the fact that I was trying to get us both to Akron in time for a dentist appoint-ment, the fact that there was a lot of cell phone trouble and mix-ups and my satnav wasn't working right, Siri, GPS, the fact that then the kids and I were at the zoo and they were asking me if they could pet the animals and I was warning them off the lions and the bears, the fact that then I was on my own, visiting a Japanese couple with a lovely

Japanese-style garden, the fact that they had pools of koi carp inside and outside, and a dark wooden house made of thick planks of wood, the fact that it felt like I'd dreamt about them before, like when they'd just moved in maybe, and they'd had a sick cat, because now I was telling the wife how beautiful their house was and how much better things seemed than last time, the fact that I pointed out their big fat rabbit and their koi carp and their healthy cats, and she laughed, which surprised her husband, because his wife was usually gloomy and her favorite subject of conversation was how they should kill themselves someday, the fact that he was pleased to see her smile and mocked her for it, gently, the fact that I was just about to tell him it isn't always easy to adjust when life improves, the fact that I was going to use my cancer reprieve as an example, death sentence, the fact that I was going to tell them I'd had cancer three years ago and I *still* can't enjoy life but the dream ended before I could get around to it, Last-Minute Stay of Execution, death panels, deathwatch beetle, the fact that just yesterday a Manhattan couple jumped to their deaths because they couldn't pay their *medical* bills, kill, maim, scar for life, the fact that Ben now likes to recite riddles in the car, M4A, OTC, the fact that this is what he was doing all the way to Fallingwater, AMA, APT, ASS, the fact that Phoebe and I used to memorize A. A. Milne poems on road trips when we were all in England, and recite them from the back seat, the fact that Ethan had to learn Latin at school, but he didn't recite it in the car, OMNES TENEBRAE, the fact that Phoebe and I were too young to learn Latin at Channing, or maybe they didn't teach it to girls, purple-brown wool skirt, smocked bodices, smacked butts, colorful stripes, the fact that I was always a very unknowing kid, the fact that I never heard what anybody said or understood it even if I did hear it, and never won an argument and never will, suicide pacts, the fact that people have said I have my dad's eyes, the fact that I wanted Mommy's looks, but now I don't care, the fact that Daddy's are just fine with me, the fact that his eyes could look a little lugubrious maybe, but that's okay, the fact that he didn't have much of an eye for *art*, the fact that we got left with some pretty bad paintings when they died, the fact that he was tone-deaf too, couldn't hold a tune, but who cares, the fact that he could still sing, and was happy to, and we liked his songs, the fact that he sang in the car, or told us stories, the fact that he had a keen eye for a deli too, the fact that he could locate pastrami and a pickle from a mile away, the fact that that could be his epitaph, good eye for a pickle, Daddy's crumply chin, *my* crumply chin, the fact that he sat next to an aging member of The Lovin' Spoonful on a plane once, the fact that Daddy had never heard of them but he was still proud, spoonful, spoon-feed, spoonbill, peanut gallery, the fact that people are always making such a fuss about letting cats roam wild, TNR, but Alley Cat Allies, ACA, say outdoor cats impact bird populations much less than roads and construction projects, and habitat invasions, not to mention pollution, and people tearing down trees during the nesting season, the fact that if they're so worried about birds, stop all the tree surgery, the fact that cats don't pull down whole trees, the fact that they could at least wait till fall, the tree surgeons, not the cats, *The hen can lay*, do-si-do danc-ing, the fact that I just saw a shadow outside and hoped it was Stace, then I wondered if it might be the lion on the loose, though it looked too tall, maybe more like an Abominable Snowman, the fact that it turns out to be a leaf on the window pane, Peolia, the fact that when I told Leo I couldn't teach anymore he was so nice about it, the fact that he comforted me and told me not to worry about it, the fact that he didn't try to push me into going back, even though it meant we lost my salary, such as it was, the fact that it wasn't minimum wage but pretty close, because I was part-time, the fact that you're a sitting duck if you're part-time, the fact that quitting was *fun*, though by the next day I started fretting about the dough, the fact that Leo said I should just take things easy and think about what I would actually enjoy doing, and then try turning that into a job, the fact that he didn't mind me being self-employed, the fact that it took me about six months to discover that what I most enjoy doing is being at home, and baking, so then I got the cake business going, Earn Cash From Home, the fact that my baking efforts don't make us much money, and Leo has to teach two jobs, and mentor people too for a little extra cash, but he never gripes about it, the fact that he actually seems to get a real kick out of my pies, the fact that he makes domesticity seem fun, the fact that without him it's more of a chore, the fact that I get so drained and stressed out, surface tension, the fact that moms are more stressed than anybody, the fact that I never notice Leo being angry, the fact that I think Stacy's all wrong about that, his "crankiness," the fact that he does it as a *joke*, I think, he doesn't mean it for real, but she doesn't get it, the fact that if he really was a cranky guy I'd have had to give up by now, because I'm scared of angry people, the fact that where *is* that girl, the fact that I don't think Mommy really liked teaching either, because she was shy too, and sensitive, and in the midst of it she was also writing a book, and having to cook for *us* every night, and host parties, the fact that she didn't much like giving parties or going to parties, but she did it anyway, the fact that the preparations were tense, the fact that they both got so *uptight* about it, the fact that maybe that was what was going on when Daddy tried to spank me, the fact that maybe I messed up the pile of papers he was trying to sort out, or something, the fact that their parties always seemed to require days of cleaning and cooking and running around stiff-lipped, the fact that it all looked so grim and unfun that Phoebe and I decided we'd never have parties when we grew up, and I've more or less stuck to that, the fact that I think Phoebe likes giving parties now, the fact that I wonder if she still gets worked up about them though, like Mommy, before they start, the fact that Phoebe's very sociable though, the fact that Mommy was sociable with the people she really liked, the fact that for buffet dinner parties, she'd make eggplant parmigiana and chicken cacciatore and *we* got a little ahead of time, the fact that she would make lemon meringue pie too, the fact that she was good at that, the fact that I still have her recipe, the fact that I've got lots of her recipes in their original index-card file, right here, lion, Stacy, the fact that where is *Jake*, the fact that some are typed, some handwritten in her nice handwriting, *The Accidental Tourist*, shrimp bisque, the fact that when she was still well my mom made shrimp bisque, the fact that it seems kind of hard to believe, the fact that maybe she didn't actually make it, but she must've *considered* making it, or she wouldn't have written out the recipe by hand, the fact that it involves salt pork, shallots, celery, potatoes, clam juice, parsley, thyme, bay leaf, white wine for the stock and 1½ lbs shrimp "s & d," s & d, SAD, the fact that I just asked Ben what his guess was about this "s & d" and he said "Stinky and dead," the fact that the recipe also calls for cooked rice, but almost all seventies recipes call for cooked rice, "Word went out in formic," the fact that I still can't imagine her ever bothering to make a bisque, basque, basking sharks, beached whales, but there's probably no knowing half the stuff women sink to, the world over, the fact that I know she liked to have a bowl of lobster bisque once in a while in a restaurant, but shrimp, the fact that I can't picture her making these cannelloni from scratch either, the fact that, according to her little index card, first you have to make your own *pasta*, the fact that you're supposed to take a rectangle of pasta, put ricotta cheese on it, roll it into a round tube, and then somehow seal it, and once you've got a bunch of these stuffed tubes, you drop them into eight quarts of gently boiling water, the fact that she's very exact about the amount of water, and the gentle boil, but she doesn't mention how long they gently boil *for*, the fact that maybe you just parboil them for like three minutes or so, the fact that then you scoop them out as best you can, and put them in the oven with some tomato sauce and basil, and bake for ten minutes, and serve with Romano cheese, the fact that I don't see how you keep the ricotta inside them while they're boiling, the fact that Jake's got hold of some nurdles so he's all right, the fact that nurdle-rich, he's fine, but nurdless, it's a different story, the fact that it seems to me Mommy had a lot of more important stuff to do than forming pasta rectangles into tubes, the fact that, also, ten minutes' baking time just doesn't sound half enough, *ten minutes*, the fact that for all I know, this is what she was trying to do the day I came down feeling all euphoric from my nap, creating her own cannelloni from scratch, the fact that that would explain a lot, the fact that I sure don't remember Mommy ever making cannelloni for *us*, the fact that this recipe's no good, the fact that I bet she tried it once and gave up because it didn't work, the fact that I really hate badly written recipes, the fact that they always leave something crucial out, or else I misread them, or maybe a combination of both, the fact that I think a recipe should be written so you cannot make mistakes, the fact that I just don't see how you keep the ricotta from sliding out each end during the boiling part, but maybe I should try it out before I decide it doesn't work, my first grade reader, Geography class, my math workbook with see-through plastic pages in different colors, the fact that what was that for, the fact that we all thought that thing was so *cool* at first, but then the math got hard and we all fell out of love with it, or I did anyway, the fact that it was still just math, even if it did have plastic pages, the fact that I knew I didn't really deserve that fancy a math book, because I was always lousy at math, the fact that Mommy was a very energetic woman before she got sick, "dynamic," the fact that she chauffeured us all around town and picked glass out of my feet and rose thorns out of my thigh and slept beside me in the hospital the night before my heart operation and wrote a book and taught college courses and fried p. chops with brandy and sour cream, so she probably did make cannelloni in tomato sauce, the fact that she could make cannelloni with her hands tied behind her back, peaches in cream, peaches and cream, broken, the fact that we were all broken, Cathy, Stacy, the banister rail, the fact that thinking about all this makes me incredibly sad, menstrual cramp, the fact that now it's really late, and I need that butter, the fact that I have to produce about a hundred cinnamon rolls for the Country Shoppe by tomorrow morning, "Oh, I need that stuff from Chip's," the fact that I just realized "s & d" must be "shelled and diced," the fact that that's the only thing that makes sense, the fact that I better give Cathy a call, but it's awkward, because I haven't really talked to Cathy much since she told me about Blanche, and I still just don't know what to *say*, the fact that it's just so unbelievable, but it's also a while ago and I know she doesn't want to talk about it all the time, the fact that I don't want to bring it up and startle her or something, if she isn't expecting to have to think about it, the fact that she's so brave, the fact that Cathy's just so generous, the fact that she'd help out anybody any time, and he did *that* to her, testosterone, the fact that now I'm all sweaty, the fact that I have to think about something else, the fact that the show must go on, the fact that Blanche died of a hemorrhage, the fact that abdominal bullet wounds are extremely dangerous, Confederate flag, the fact that scars are strange, the fact that they're a sort of *photograph* of your wound, that's left on your skin forever, like a kind of crummy *tattoo*, Daddy's appendectomy scar, my heart scar, the fact that I just think what if Cathy had been killed, the fact that where would we all be without her, where would *I* be, the fact that where would everybody get their chipped beef and their hash browns, and earrings made by nine-year-olds, and woolen hats, Blanche, terra firma, terra incognita, the fact that what would've happened to Marcia, who was just a little girl when it happened, the fact that Marcia's been helping out part-time in the meat department of some supermarket lately, just for a bit of extra experience, a helping of this, a helping of that, serving, servant, but soon she's going to work full-time with Cathy, BFF, the fact that they're quite an enterprising crowd, providing hog maw for all of Tuscarawas County, the fact that Cathy says she's doing just fine now, the fact that she says she's got closure, the fact that there's still no sign of Stace, 6:00, the fact that I better call Annie, see what's up, the fact that I dreamt last night about somebody complaining that he owned a "lesser Cézanne," while I was tearing heart-shaped buttons off a shirt, and, and something about a ferret, the fact that my dreams have become more practical and less expansive, I think, since we got poorer, the fact that I should be swinging wild but instead my dreams are just about tidying the hen coop or unloading the dishwasher, or losing my address book, or dipping the corner of my bathrobe in the john and having to put it in the washer, or I'm cooking noodles for everybody and Leo has a plane to catch in half an hour and there's no taxi, or I find myself on a bicycle carrying a huge box, the fact that once I dreamt I ate one tiny piece of ham, and that was it, that was the whole dream, the fact that I dream all the wrong stuff and remember all the wrong stuff, what a goofball, "a genuine idiot," the fact that why do I remember that Amish wool shop and not my *mom*, the fact that I bet the Kinkels are loaded, the fact that they're always jetting off somewhere, not for work, for *pleasure*, or else for funerals and things, and revisiting their home towns for nostalgia reasons, malignant narcissist, the fact that you gotta have a couple hundred thou to spare to feel so free and easy about nostalgia trips, the fact that Jerry makes enough, the fact that when do *we* ever go anywhere, the fact that we did go to Fallingwater, thanks to Frank, no, *Leo*, who did all the driving, oh dear, calling Leo Frank, the fact that you have to watch that all your life, once you've had an earlier husband, calling your new husband by the other husband's name, the fact that first husbands leave their mark on your brain in some way, your *spinal* brain maybe, where all the robotic stuff happens, the amygdala, the fact that he venerated nature, Frank Lloyd Wright, not *Frank*, the fact that unlike *Frank*, Frank Lloyd Wright liked harmony, the fact that Frank Lloyd Wright wanted to work in harmony with *nature*, the fact that it's such a pity the building leaks, the fact that I don't think I like nature *that* much, the fact that Edgar Kaufman renamed the house "Risingmildew," but "Fallingwater" seems pretty good too, since there's water falling inside and out, the fact that Frank Lloyd Wright only got paid $8000 for it, the fact that I don't know what he should've been paid but that sure doesn't sound much, the fact that there were some Frank Lloyd Wright houses around Evanston, the fact that one was just a block from us, the fact that it wasn't a showy one or anything, but it looked nice, the fact that we were always sort of in awe of it, the fact that we thought we had to be quiet and respectful going past it, the fact that there was nothing there for kids really, at Fallingwater I mean, except for falling off boulders or getting drowned in that murky old swimming pool, the fact that Frank Lloyd Wright didn't want the pool but Kaufman insisted, the fact that I thought the ceilings are awfully low, and the sound of the water echoes off *everything*, the fact that it's so loud you can barely talk in there, so I don't think Frank Lloyd Wright could *hear* Edgar Kaufman asking him to make the place quieter, the fact that if you decide to build your house right over a big waterfall though, how quiet do you expect it to be, Paterson Falls, Niagara, the fact that maybe the Kaufmans weren't a very talkative family anyway, the fact that I think I'd need to go to the bathroom all the time if I had to listen to that, the fact that it's really better outside than in, the house I mean, not going to the bathroom, which is better done inside than out, the fact that you can't even see the falls much when you're inside the house, so what's the point, Fallingwater, the fact that I heard houses built over water have bad feng shui, the fact that it was at the other place that all the bad stuff happened though, the fact that that was at Frank Lloyd Wright's own house called Talicsin, in Wisconsin, the fact that one day, their hired cook killed Frank Lloyd Wright's mistress and her two children with an ax, and then he killed all the workmen as well, and set the place on fire, landsakes, what a thing to do, the fact that Frank Lloyd Wright wasn't there at the time, the fact that he had the whole house rebuilt, which was sort of brave of him, but then it burnt down *again*, and he rebuilt it again, and that one's still standing, ax, third time lucky, Rathbone, children, chitlins, grits, Birmingham, Alabama, Alabamy, the Alamo, Custer's Last Stand, the fact that Stacy wouldn't come with us to Fallingwater, the fact that she went over to Annie's for the day, I don't know what for, probably to watch Morning Routine videos together, instead of apart, the fact that since little kids can't go on the full tour, I sat with Jake and Gillian in the kiddie room, where Jake colored in some pictures of Fallingwater, and Gillian read children's books about architecture, the fact that only Ben and Leo did the full tour, the fact that they were gone for *two hours*, the fact that Ben came back to the kiddy room with a black T-shirt and a yo-yo, and then everybody wanted a T-shirt and a yo-yo, the fact that the tour cost enough as it was, the fact that I don't know how Ben convinced Leo to buy him that shirt, the fact that we steered them around the more expensive merchandise at least, like the toy dachshund that I could tell Gillian had her eye on, the fact that then we all got hot dogs in the cafeteria, which is almost like a dachshund, the hot dog, not the cafeteria, and then we had a walk around the outside and

Ben waded straight into a bit of the creek and fell over and drowned his cell phone, which was wrecked, the fact that he laughed it off and told us to buy him a new one, and I could tell Leo wasn't going to go for that idea, the fact that I didn't know what to say, because I didn't want the whole jaunty atmosphere to turn sour, but Leo was firm, the fact that he said no, because just because Ben forgot he was carrying his cell does not mean we'll get him a new one, the fact that he said Ben would have to do some extra jobs around the house to earn the money for it, and meanwhile do without a phone, the fact that I had to try not to giggle at that "extra jobs," when Ben hardly does any chores around the house at all, except read to me from Wikipedia maybe, the fact that none of the kids do, the fact that does Leo think I've got them that well organized, "my fine buck-o," the fact that I think Ben should just save his allowance, or I could loan him the money for a phone and he could forfeit his allowance until it's paid back, but I didn't say anything, the fact that I don't know if it's such a good idea to *pay* kids to help out at home, the fact that, I mean, they live here too, so they should take part in the household for *love*, not money, like a communal effort, the fact that they're not guests, they're family, the fact that the cell-phone debate put Ben in a terrible mood, such a pity after their nice house tour, the fact that Ben's easily embarrassed, I think, just like me, and falling down was bad, the fact that he tried to save the day by laughing it off but that didn't go down too well, Daddy chasing me up the stairs, the fact that maybe the *tour* tired Ben out too, so he was cranky, the fact that after that, things seemed okay for a little while but later, Ben jumped up on the bench to get a better view, and Leo warned him, mildly, about getting his dirty shoes on the bench, the fact that Ben was so hurt by that, he blushed and took both his shoes off, and ran away crying, the fact that I explained to Leo that this is what nine-year-olds are like, and then we picked his shoes up and followed him all over Fallingwater, Followedhimallover, trying to get him to put them back on, with Jake watching the whole drama wide-eyed, the fact that he's always interested in what his big brother gets up to, the fact that Gillian was sort of out of it, probably still thinking about the dachshund, the fact that you try to give them a good day out and look what happens, the fact that eventually Leo and Ben made peace again, but on the way back in the car Ben growled "That bench was already dirty," the fact that Peolia once had an architect's model of Fallingwater on display, the fact that it was pretty good except all the tiny human figures outside had fallen over, just like *Ben* did, the fact that it looked like they were crawling around in the mud during a hurricane or something, or maybe there'd been a shoot-out, the fact that we drove back through the Allegheny mountains, timber industry, which was sort of depressing, the fact that there's so much hunting there now, especially with all the lion freaks around, the fact that I bet there are only like a few groundhogs left in the whole of Pennsylvania, or maybe only Punxsutawney Phil, the fact that eating bear meat is a good way to get trichinosis, but they probably don't eat them anyway, just kill them, sport hunting, bear hugs, the ol' one-two, the fact that I wonder what Frank Lloyd Wright would have made of that lady's house that cleans itself, the fact that maybe he should have made Fallingwater self-cleaning, the fact that it would be a good use of all that water, which is leaking in anyway, high life, highlights, twi-night, the fact that Gillian wants a subscription to that old *Highlights* magazine that I never liked, and neither did Leo, the fact that Leo just *hated* it as a kid, the fact that it sort of got forced on us, and then it kept coming and coming and you never knew what to do with it or how to stop it coming, the fact that it's fun to get some mail, but there are other kids' magazines, the fact that I felt guilty all the time about not really reading it, wasting money, the fact that Phoebe always said I was a goody-goody, buckeyes, "fun with a purpose," fun with a porpoise, koi carp, the Kaufmans' swimming pool, the fact that the only thing I did like in it was the "Hidden Pictures," the fact that the "Hidden Picture" drawings weren't very nice but it was the only fun thing in the whole entire magazine, and the only thing that didn't require *reading*, which I was lazy about, the fact that Leo still remembers "Goofus and Gallant," the fact that maybe I read those too, the fact that now Gillian wants to be plagued by this magazine too, the fact that maybe it's gotten better since the seventies and eighties, the fact that I liked the way the living room sort of glowed at Fallingwater, the fact that the low-level light was nice, ax murderer, Lizzie Borden, but I didn't really see the whole place, 5½ feet wide, the fact that Ben wants to go to the Boy Scouts Jamboree in Michigan this summer but we don't think he's old enough, the fact that this caused *another* big ruckus, because they only have a jamboree every four years, so he'd be thirteen next time, which he says is way too *old*, and too long to wait, the fact that I thought Ben *hated* the Boy Scouts, scout's honor, the fact that Goofus and Gallant were always getting into trouble, the fact that Goofus acted like a normal kid and Gallant was the goody-goody, goofball, "boof bourguignon," the fact that I was good at those "Hidden Pictures," for what it's worth, *Highlights for Children*, the fact that they should call it *High Fives for Children*, jazz things up a bit, lingua franca, la langue, tongue, mother tongue, the fact that there are some women in China who have a secret language all their own, which doesn't sound such a bad idea maybe, though I wouldn't want to have to talk to *James's* mom in our own private language, the fact that I can't *believe* that woman, the fact that she spent a whole hour inspecting our house, and then she disappeared upstairs and didn't come down, the fact that I didn't even know where she'd gone, so I finally followed her up there and found her going through my *underwear* drawer, the fact that I thought she came over to check on the level of *lint*, not to see my panties, the fact that at first I was so embarrassed about all my ancient me-oh-mys, well, I was just mortified, the fact that I got the *kids* new stuff this spring and forgot to get myself any, but I don't grow out of mine as fast as they do, the fact that I was really in shock, but then I got mad, because, well, what was Fresia doing in my underwear drawer, the fact that I can't believe now that I actually had the presence of mind to say to her I didn't think our bedroom was relevant, since the boys wouldn't be playing in there, the fact that they'd mostly be playing in Ben's room, or outside, or having a snack at the kitchen table, jerky, snafu, the fact that I tried to soften it by changing the subject and asking her what foods James can eat, the fact that the whole time I was really trying not to act as mad as I felt, or as *embarrassed*, the fact that I was just kind of firm, sort of standing my ground, but landsakes, the fact that what was she *thinking*, the fact that I just can't see what my bras and whatnot have to do with whether or not James can come over and play one afternoon, the fact that it's a free country, or used to be, and my me-oh-mys are my own beeswax, lady, gosh, the fact that I really was pretty mad, but I tried to stay calm, the fact that I'd understand it if he was so allergic he was like that kid on the plane who couldn't sit near someone who'd even *recently* eaten a peanut butter and jelly sandwich, the fact that all the passengers on the plane had to refrain from eating nuts throughout the flight, the fact that of course I'd do anything not to put a child's life in danger or anything, but I don't think James *is* that allergic, the fact that he just has sensitivities, like to dust, not peanuts, the fact that I don't even know if he gets hives or anything, the fact that I think he just coughs maybe, the fact that I didn't say anything really, the fact that she didn't apologize, the fact that she just got all huffy with *me* and stomped downstairs, the fact that the chances of a play date are now looking a little slim, peanuts, the fact that *she's* nuts, she's crazee, bee in her bonnet, the fact that young female bumblebees get through the winter by hunkering down in little holes in the ground, which is kind of where I wanted to be after *that* encounter, sheesh, the fact that they produce some chemical that keeps them from freezing, bees, not moms, the fact that the male bees die off in the winter, the fact that they don't have the chemical, the fact that the weather's changing, the fact that March came in like a lion and went *out* like a lion, *and* there was a real lion, Celebrity Birthdays, the fact that Picasso designed a *really* ugly ring to appease Dora Maar after they had a fight, the fact that some guys opened fire on some McDonald's staff in Warren when they found out there were no Chicken McMuffins available, the fact that it's hard to believe they wanted Chicken McMuffins that much, I mean, couldn't they just order a *cheeseburger*, the fact that they caught that steak-eating selfie murderer at last, so Ohio is safe again, at least from *him*, Cincinnati Bengals, Taj Mahal, the fact that they found him eating Chicken McNuggets in his car, the fact that I guess murdering strangers for no reason makes you hungry, so he ordered twenty McNuggets, which is a lot of McNuggets, the fact that I bet everybody would have gladly given him a *lifetime's* supply of Chicken McNuggets if he would just not murder disabled people, eight hundred billion chickens a year, the fact that forty-seven kids are shot every day, forty injured and seven killed, forty-seven kids a day, the fact that that's forty-seven moms too who have to deal with that, the fact that, wow, maybe Fresia was checking to see if we have a *gun* here, the fact that I never thought of that, the fact that a lot of women do keep their pistols in their underwear drawer, loaded as well, pistol-whipped, holster, bolster, son of a gun, the fact that I prefer a sachet of lavender myself, the fact that I would've understood completely if she'd *asked* me if I had a gun on the premises, the fact that I worry about these things too, we all do, but I only gave her permission to check our house for allergens, not AK-47s, the fact that I would never sneak a peek in anybody's underwear drawer, looking for guns, no matter *how* scared I was, the fact that maybe that's cowardly of me, but I wouldn't, I'd be much too embarrassed, the fact that I don't believe that's what she was looking for anyway, the fact that I don't know *what* she was looking for, and I guess I never will, just snooping or *what*, the fact that it looks like one mountain lion wasn't enough, lion rampant, lion Dems, the fact that now there's some kind of crazee zoo breakout over in Zanesville, the fact that hundreds of lions and tigers have been let loose and they're roaming free, eating livestock and stuff, the fact that the police probably have to shoot them all, the fact that the police are always so impatient, and so easily freaked out, ♬ *Courage!* ♬, the fact that why can't they just trap them, and tranquilize them, or the other way around, the animals I mean, not the police, the fact that they've put up road blocks around the safari park or whatever it is, saying "CAUTION EXOTIC ANIMALS," the fact that what's a person supposed to do when they see a sign like that, Yield To Beluga Whales, Merge With Elephant Stampede Coming From Left, the fact that it doesn't offer much guidance or anything,

"CAUTION EXOTIC ANIMALS," the fact that it might just be a few monkeys, the fact that now where is that little monkey of *mine*, Jakey, not Stacy, though where is Stacy too, the fact that I really need that butter, the fact that I dreamt we were in a park at closing time and all these wild animals were emerging from the woods, *in pairs*, for their daily walk, jaguars, lions, tigers, cougars, black panthers and bobcats, the fact that ninety-four percent of Ohio drivers won't stop to help you if your car breaks down, and don't I know it, so why would they slow down for exotic animals, the fact that it's worse in Maryland, I mean the lack of help on the road, Robin Hood and his band of Merry Men, the fact that *nobody* in Maryland will help you if your car breaks down, nobody, even if you're about to be attacked by lions salient or sejant, Baltimore Ravens, Baltimore Orioles, Carolina Panthers, Detroit Tigers, Detroit Lions, Chicago Bears, Chicago Cubs, the fact that if bees have holes in the ground to sleep in, maybe we disturb them sometimes by walking too heavily over their dens, and then they fly out, the fact that I hope I never walked on a bee in its den, but who knows, poor bee, the fact that there are some things you'll never know, and one is your crimes against bumble bees, the fact that they're probably out most of the day though, like our neighbors, slaving away somewhere, so maybe walking around on the grass is no problem, working moms, guilt, cornbread, gasoline, Fresia, freezer, anesthetist, the fact that some bees work so hard they die on the job *mid-suck*, right in the middle of our lavender bush, but I think they die happy, Jacksonville Jaguars, Miami Dolphins, mosquito bites, the fact that bees use wing friction to warm their babies, the fact that bees always take great care of their infants, the fact that they seem so tireless, and well organized, like Cathy, the fact that I'm tired *all the time*, and not well organized, the fact that bees have no idea what we're doing or that we even exist, except as obstacles to fly around, or vibrations in the ground when we tramp too close to their dens, and this is one of the great things about bees, the fact that they aren't aware of us at all, the fact that I don't think we scare them one little bit, the fact that they don't have to think about us from one year to the next, the fact that they don't even seem too aware of each other, as far as you can tell, the fact that bee-keepers lost forty-four percent of their honey bees last year, I'm not sure why, global warming, bee corridors, the fact that bumble bees are solitary types, the fact that they don't care if they're in a wild meadow, or a clover patch right by your house, or the overflowing window-box of a bank, the fact that it's all the same to them, the fact that we are nothing to them, the fact that bees really do mind their own beeswax, and this makes them a comfort to think about, kind of like boarlets, or the solar system, the fact that the solar system will carry on with its rotations and whatnot whatever we do, the fact that the universe will expand, with or without our help, the fact that the moon has water on it, the fact that I wonder if they put milk in Chicken McNuggets, because there's milk in absolutely every-thing now, the fact that I think there must be a milk mountain some-where, a dried milk powder mountain, and a lake of whey, a mound of cheese curd, Bed of Ware, lactose, the fact that I think they even put milk products in hot sauce now, sugar highs, the fact that Thin Mints are the Girl Scouts' most popular cookie, and the next favorite is the Samoans, the fact that they also do Trefoils, Tagalongs, and Toffee-tastics, the fact that why do shooting victims always think at first they're hearing firecrackers, the fact that it's much more likely to be a gun, but you go into denial, Philadelphia Eagles, Philly, the fact that then, after a shooting, everybody rushes to say everything's okay, "unbelievable" but okay, but come on, if two boys had to watch their dad shoot their mom in the *head*, everything is *not* okay, the fact that ah, here's my *pen* at last, on my pillow, the fact that how'd it get there, and here's a note, the fact that it's from Stace, the fact that I wish they still taught handwriting in school, cursive writing, cursing, cussing, parsing a sentence, the fact that, what in the world, "Dear Mother and Leo I've decided it would be better for everybody if I take off I can live on my savings for a while then maybe find a job," the fact that what's she *talking* about, "I'll maybe head for Arizona or somewhere warm enough to sleep outside I'm taking the big sleeping bag love S," oh my god no, no, she's *gone*, "take off," the fact that it's so casual-sounding, the fact that I can't *believe* it, the fact that this can't be happening, how can this be happening, the fact that how could she do this to me, how *dare* she, *Arizona* of all places, the fact that where is she *now*, the fact that I don't *know*, the fact that I have no idea where she *is* right now, candlelit vigils, lynchings, lions, rape, Golf Champion, robot golf carts, Trump, newspaper headlines, children's faces on milk cartons, milk mountains, lakes, lakes full of milk, gravestones with those built-in flower-display discs with the big holes, childhood skin rashes, Fresia in my drawers, *Mommy*, the fact that what would Mommy think, what would *she* say, and Abby, Arizona of all places, Sally, the fact that Stacy knows what a dim view I take of iguanas, "Dude," antique chess set, jigsaw of the Everglades, tripod, the fact that when did she *write* this, drinking lemonade on Jill's dim porch with her parents, some kid's little red car with pedals, Stacy hurting her hand when the stroller tipped over, the fact that how could she, oh no, Stacy, no, how could you just *leave*, without telling anybody, firefighters, *Fahrenheit 451*, the fact that don't you know I *love* you, don't you *know* that, the fact that what'll I do, what'll I, buds on a branch, bubble tea, bubble boy, the fact that I've got to get the kids in the car *this minute* and go look for her, Ben, Jake, who else, *who*, kids, four, the fact that I can't even remember my own kids' names in an emergency or how many I've got, Gillian, the fact that Jake is *somewhere*, maybe playing with nurdles still, Ben, Gillian, Jake, Stacy, *four*, the fact that there are four, minus Stacy makes three, oh my poor girl, the fact that I didn't know you hated me this much, Mississippi, little Missie, Shakespeare, F— Hinn, Mommy, artificial sweetener, the fact that *anything* could happen to her out there, the fact that what is the matter with her, the fact that what did I do that was *so* bad, Band-Aid, styptic stick, the exploded house by the school, the burning, floating house and the swimming cat, Taliesin, hired cook, ax, runaway, stowaway, carjacking, Cathy, Blanche lying dead by the car, the fact that Stacy must've left that note *this morning* and I only just found it and now it's, it's, well, sometime after six, the fact that what time *is* it, the fact that I just hurt my thumb on the phone, rag rugs, Abby's big jade plant, the police, the fact that should I call the *police*, the fact that I must call the police, "Hello, sir, my daughter's missing," "Sir, my daughter's run off," "run away," the fact that I can't, I can't, the fact that what do you say when your kid *disappears*, how do you *say* that, the fact that I don't trust *them*, the fact that the police shot that guy *fifty* times, for no reason, and they also dragged a young girl to the side of the road and examined her intimate parts, just to look for marijuana, the fact that she was just doing errands for her sick *mom*, the fact that they probably wanted to smoke some weed *themselves*, the fact that Stacy could be in Missouri by now, on her way south, or, or Kentucky, *Kentucky*, or Tennessee, with her sleeping bag, the fact that I can't even remember the map of *America* right now, like which exact states come between here and Arizona, but it's plenty, I know that, plenty, the fact that we used to have that jigsaw-puzzle map of America, for the kids, the fact that I should call *Cathy*, the fact that she'll help me, and Leo of course, yes, call Leo, pies, the pies, the fact that the whole country's full of madmen, *madmen*, round every corner, every state, every *county* of every state, the Senate, the fact that the whole damn country is teeming with *nut jobs* who'll do *anything*, Nagasaki, Hiroshima, anything, mercury poisoning, especially to pretty young girls, the fact that she *seemed* more or less okay this morning too, not great but okay, the fact that is she depressed, the fact that maybe she is, the fact that who isn't, the fact that what about that girl who was imprisoned in a cellar *for twenty years*, oh my *god*, the fact that I thought I could *protect* my kids from things if I tried, but now she's gone and could be *anywhere*, the fact that she could be in Cleveland with that guy who hid three girls in his house, and raped them for years and killed their babies, "I like sex," the fact that there are all these incel characters around too, shooting women they haven't even met, for depriving them of *sex*, the fact that she could be in Zanesville with all the lions and tigers, and trigger-happy cops, the fact that she could be meeting a *lion* at this very moment, the fact that she could be raped any minute by football stars or Olympic swimmers or priests or, well, the *president* even, the fact that America's not a safe place for a girl, the fact that *nobody's* safe in America, the fact that where is *Gillian* now, Gillian, Jake, Ben, Stacy, *four*, four, get in the car, get your coats and get in, the fact that we'll drive around and look for her lifeless body by the side of the road, no, NO, the fact that I'm scared I'll *crash* if I try to drive, the fact that I'm shaking like a leaf, no, even leaves don't shake this much, or if they do, oh who the hell *cares*, what does it matter what *leaves* do, for heaven's sake, a gray leaf twisting in a breeze, the fact that I *will* crash the car, I know I will, the fact that I'll have a crash with all the kids in it, and we'll all be dead by the time Leo gets home, or maybe *I'll* be dead and the kids'll survive and get kidnapped or left alone on the highway to be hit by a car or eaten by a lion, Leo, *Leo*, call Leo, the fact that what will he think of me, in this state, and losing a daughter like that, the fact that I have to call him though, the fact that it's lucky we have speed dial or I wouldn't be able to, the fact that I don't even know my own husband's number by heart, the fact that that's weird, the fact that, please, please be in your office, Leo, it's ringing, ringing, ring, the fact that I don't even remember my husband's number, the fact that he's *there*, "There, there now," Marnie's hurt horse, the fact that Leo says to calm down, stay put, and she'll come *back*, the fact that he says she'll probably come home, *probably*, the fact that did he really say *that*, "probably," oh Stacy, oh dear, oh jeez, the fact that, okay, okay, Leo says he's coming and I should just stay here, in case she *comes back home*, the fact that I hadn't thought of that, the fact that maybe she'll give up and come home of her own accord, discord, disconnect, loganberries, the fact that I have to be here, I'll stay here, the fact that he's on his way, but are we losing precious time, police, rape, murder, bears, the fact that there are long-haired *lungers* and, and shooters and rapists and wife-beaters out there, a sea of them and there's nothing I can do about it, the fact that I must not let the kids see me crying or they'll get scared, scarred, broken, the fact that it broke me, the fact that I've gotta get a *hold* of myself, call her cell, the fact that why didn't I do that before, and try her friends, the fact that maybe she's just at Annie's, the fact that maybe the note's just a hoax or something, just to give me a scare, a terrible fright, the fact that, no, goddammit, there's no answer from her cell, the fact that I should try her friends, the fact that I can surely do that at least, while I'm waiting, ouch, Djibouti, the fact that, oh why in hell didn't I see this coming, or see the note *earlier*, the fact that I went into our bedroom a million *times* today, the fact that I remember straightening the rag rug, but I didn't look at the pillow, the fact that that mistake could cost Stacy her *life*, and it'll all be my fault, **15**, such a klutz, idiot, jerk, Monster Mom, James's mom, the fact that I have a terrible bedside lamp, nightgown, the fact that there are men with homemade *dungeons*, all ready and waiting, lots of them, the fact that they wait to capture girls, poor Fanny Adams, "Sweet Fanny Adams," the fact that they have babies with the girls and then they kill the *babies*, my *grandkids*, the fact that so many men are merciless, *heartless*, Lanza, Breivik, Trump, Bill Clinton, Lolita Island, sex slaves, trafficking, porno pics, ISIS, beheadings, 9/11, 911, Oprah, Lee Harvey Oswald, ♬ *The Stars and Stripes Forever* ♬, grab 'em by the stars and stripes, for no reason, for no reason,

.   .   .   .

Outdoor life is suspenseful: you are always a moment away from trouble. The sense of dread is what tires you for sleep. Now she was tired all the time. In her misery, her strong tail began to drag behind her in the dirt. In mud, it left a groove, and deep rivulets in creek banks. How the kittens had loved that tail.

Her progress was swifter, surer, at night. By day she was forced to veer away from the sound of chainsaws, which seemed to come from every corner of the forest. But one night, the woods filled with the sound of rival animals, the roars of meat-eaters gathering for a feast.

Climbing towards the source of the commotion, she could see a bunch of frantic horses galloping in a tight circle on a hillside, a formation that reminded the lioness of deer trying to evade capture. At the top of the hill was a long, low set of barns, and all around the outside of them wandered unfamiliar animals, angry and confused.

The air was stale with the scent of scat and dirty hides, metal fencing and blood. No men or women were in sight.

There was fear in the air, hunger. Some fellow mountain lions, bedraggled and ill, padded around near a house. Perhaps her cubs were in there – her longing made it seem almost possible. There were other creatures drifting around too, lionlike but larger. Frightened, maddened, or distracted, they trotted by without seeing her. A tiger, a striped imitation of a lion, similar in the lines of his body but strange in his movements, squeezed out of a hole in one of the barns and raced downhill. Other large creatures drifted up the hill, lost animals without territory. Sickly bears lumbered freely among them, as well as skinny, cowering wolves, as if they'd forgotten to live apart.

She was repulsed by their mindlessness, their odd heavings, indecision and slow steps. And, after sniffing around inside and out, she was disappointed once again not to find her cubs. Seeking a convenient kill of some kind, she now followed sounds of scurrying, and found two lionlike animals about twice her size eviscerating a small, long-limbed ape, a chimpanzee, wholly unfamiliar in its strong smell. She retreated – there was too much competition here for food, with such a variety of predators patrolling the hill.

Nothing would be simple here, and she did not feel safe. Turning to go, she unintentionally cornered a lone wolf, who growled and slunk away at the sight of her. Behind him, a large whitish tiger stood in a wide pool of blood, chewing at the head of a dead man. The innards were already gone, the hot core of him lost, snatched by animals more desperate than she. She turned away, disheartened.

Now the cracks of gunshots began, close by. They were only a few puttering blasts at first, muted by the damp air, but they steadily increased in frequency. The lioness knew enough of killer men and their firepower to head for cover. She slithered quickly down the hill and into the trees.

From the thicket though, well hidden in the darkness, she watched a big heavy policeman point his rifle at an even bigger bear, who made no effort to escape. Why should he? A bear does not flee. The man jerked suddenly, and a hissing sound spread far out, echoing against the surrounding hills; the bear slumped, groaning. Two other policemen now moved slowly down the hill towards a group of yellow tigers leaping through tall grass looking for an opening in a fence. They were rushing away from the men. More cracks sliced the air. The tigers jumped high in the air and snarled, animals still full of power. The men raised their guns again, more gunfire ensued, and finally the leaping tigers all hit the ground and did not stir again. She could hear their dying sighs. That was no way to die, out in the open like that.

The men yelped and grunted to each other. Seeking more dominance, more prey and ever more territory, they set off to confront some other big animal emerging from one of the taller barns at the brow of the hill. Men never got enough of killing. They didn't pause to eat their kills, they merely moved on to other bewildered animals available to kill. They did not give those lost hollow creatures time to think.

The lioness was not one of them. She was not drained of purpose. She was not starved or smeared with scat. She was queen. Those strange ailing animals could not or would not run from men, but she could. In no time, the lioness had covered twelve miles of ground. Her land.

.   .   .   .

the fact that I dreamt last night I had two years to live and an appointment with a shrink to talk about it, deadlines, deadliness, the fact that then I dreamt Anat was asking me if Leo would make her a martini and I went "Maybe," which is crazee, because in real life of course he would make her a martini, anytime, no problem, the fact that there was no reason for me to act all *iffy* about it, the fact that it wasn't like *I* didn't want her to have a martini, the fact that I was just kind of unsure whether Leo would feel like doing it or not, for some reason, the fact that that was a dumb dream, damn dams, the fact that tigers and goats can be friends, the fact that some zoo put a live goat in the tiger enclosure, as *food*, but the tigress didn't *want* to eat it, the fact that she wanted a companion, goat companion, companion goat, kids, the fact that a "kid" is not a good enough word for a baby goat, and "kidling" is too close to kindling, canoodling, funette, the fact that baby goats are the ultimate funettes, the fact that they are one of the wonders of the world, the fact that I don't *know* any, I just watch them on YouTube sometimes, the fact that maybe we should get some, but then they grow into *goats* and goats eat you out of house and home, "food-giver," the fact that I feel like a nap, the fact that I'm so tired, the fact that, well, that's not too surprising after what we went through, the fact that I feel physically tired, like I ran a marathon or something, the fact that I hope that's one thing I never have to do again, the fact that the way they make you participate at the school Fun Days is bad enough, rubber ducks, egg-and-spoon race, the fact that I dreamt she and I were staying in a motel, Stacy I mean, the fact that she was about five, as usual, and the motel owner was playing with scissors in her vicinity and it was scaring me, and I couldn't persuade him to cut it out, *Persuasion*, so in the end I had to *pummel his chest* to get him to stop, the fact that I really did it too, the fact that for once my pummeling seemed to work, the fact that it was sort of satisfying, though now it just seems kind of violent of me, Luella, Suella, the fact that then I had a dream about a herd of horses half-submerged in a swamp, and then there was something about a comforter as big as a football stadium, the fact that I guess I need comforting *bad*, the fact that it was like one great big eiderdown, *massive*, but it wasn't made of eider *down* of course, it was just synthetic, like the cheap kind of comforter you get everywhere now, IKEA, Walmart, the fact that the wooly stuff inside felt sort of like cushion stuffing, cheap, sheep, the fact that this giant comforter was free for everybody to use, and when you wanted to go to sleep, you just tore off a six-foot piece of it, sort of like cotton candy, and then threw it away the next day, throwaway culture, throw up, palm oil, dried milk powder, the fact that I wasn't worried about the landfill problem, I just wondered where such a big comforter could be stored during the *daytime*, the fact that only a school gym would be big enough to house it, or a cow barn, or an airplane hangar, Olympic pool, and you'd really have to stuff that thing in there, the fact that I don't know what everybody was planning to do once we'd used it all up either, but it felt like a new one would be provided, the fact that I haven't dreamt about Stacy running away yet, the fact that I guess I'm storing that up for nightmares later on, the fact that instead I had that glowing, happy dream the night before last, the fact that everything was suffused with this golden light, the fact that it was like I'd gone back in time to about ten years ago, a little after we got married, and I could *stay* there as long as I wanted, the fact that Stacy was about five or six, the fact that it felt like I could start from scratch again and make things right for her this time, the fact that I could *devote* myself to making it all work better, knowing what I *now* know about how I've blown it over the last ten years, the fact that I was so *happy* in the dream, knowing this was possible, the fact that it was such a relief, a *joy*, euphoria, the fact that the whole burden had been lifted and things looked rosy, and everything was bathed in this golden light, the fact that it was like I was in our bedroom, the way it was when we first arrived, and I could see it all, just the way it was then, when Stacy was a little kid, and in the dream I was thinking, I can *do* this, I can fix things, the fact that I had all this hindsight, or maybe foresight, about how to do stuff better, and this time around I was going to pay more attention to Stacy, but not give up *Leo* either, because I knew, from hindsight, or foresight, that Leo was definitely a good thing, that he was important too, and it would be right for us to be together, the fact that everything had a warm glow, and that golden light, the fact that it was really peaceful and comforting, and I was full of hope that things would work out better this time, because I knew all the mistakes I'd made the first time, the fact that I was getting a second chance, which you never get, the fact that all these opportunities just *opened up*, like I realized I could see more of *Abby* too, the fact that I was going to make more trips to see her, so that I'd be less sad when she passed on, or that's what I hoped anyway, the fact that I was going to do that and I had lots of other plans too, London, Ohio, the fact that the Brillo factory's in London, Ohio, steel wool, the fact that steel wool is such a crazee idea, the fact that they make *wool* out of *steel* so housewives can scrub their pots and pans, the fact that how'd they figure that out, but Brillo pads really work, sea star wasting disease, the fact that the starfish are all dying and the sea urchins are taking over and eating up all the kelp forests, those impudent urchins, the fact that don't they know *they* were supposed to be eaten by the *starfish*, the fact that I wonder if Brillo was actually *inspired* by sheep wool, or they thought of calling it "wool" once they got to the marketing stage, the fact that were brushes inspired by squirrels' and foxes' tails, the fact that squirrels' tails are more like dusters really, the fact that people used to use real peacock tail feathers as feather dusters, but I don't think they sell those anymore, the fact that I'm sure you can still get a turkey duster though, the fact that I wish we had some peacocks, out *back* I mean, not for cleaning purposes, unless they happened to shed a few tail feathers over time, the fact that we'd need some *peahens* to go with them of course, the fact that there aren't enough peacocks in the world, though they can be noisy, cocks, roosters, Peolia, possums, the fact that now they're arresting people in South Carolina for *braiding hair* without a license now, a *license*, the fact that that's a new one on me, braids, drug-mule bun, ban, celery, the fact that next they'll be arresting *me* for making cinnamon rolls without a license, feeding chickens without a license, going berserk without a license, pixilated, off my rocker, rocking chair, the fact that there are some other weird things you're not allowed to do, like driving around the town square a hundred times in a row, the fact that that's not allowed, the fact that I wonder who *did* that, forcing Ohio to make such a law, the fact that he must've been some pretty annoying guy, the fact that in Tennessee it's illegal to shoot animals from your car, unless it's a *whale*, the fact that they make an exception for that, the fact that Tennessee's not even on the *coast*, so unless a lot of whales swim upstream from SeaWorld or something, Orlando, killer whale show, but anyway, you're free to shoot them from your car if you want to, Japanese whaling, Norway, minke whales, glowing dream, the fact that I just realized I should have made a fanouropita cake while we were waiting for news of Stacy, my *first-born*, my missing Guatemalan embroidered poncho shirt, horses in a swamp, the fact that in the thick of it all it never occurred to me to make a fanouropita cake, but I should have, because even if you don't find what you're looking for, it gives you something to *do* besides fretting yourself into a total tizzy, Busy Lizzie, black-eyed daisies, my geraniums, the fact that I spent half the night trying to phone her friends, though I didn't dare call *too* late, the fact that 9:30's really the cutoff, but this was an *emergency*, Arizona, Zanesville, wild animals all over Ohio, Oscar Wilde, Fanny Trollope, the fact that in the midst of it all, I chain-ate cinnamon rolls, the fact that I haven't tried one for *years*, the fact that I couldn't even taste them, and I hope I never have to eat another, the fact that we all ate them, the fact that they came in handy, the fact that that was supper, so they can arrest me for that too if they want to, along with child neglect for not knowing where my daughter was, and not understanding her, the fact that if you call the police about a missing child these days, they start investigating *you*, not the disappearer, the fact that, boy, look at that poor little Jim out there, the fact that that dog seems scared of his own shadow, and now he's barking again, with that pitiful high yelp he's got, serenade, the fact that he doesn't even want to be patted, the poor little guy, the fact that there's no comforting him really, but maybe he'll come round, buck up, luxury safari hotel, The Wilds, the Wildes, woodland yurts, the fact that Leo thinks pollution might have diminished everybody's brain power, the fact that it's a terrible thought, that maybe we're all operating at reduced capacity, we're dumber than previous *generations*, and we're all going *sterile* too, the fact that, boy, I give Leo a lot of trouble, me and my dozen or so kids, four, *Seven Brides for Seven Brothers*, the fact that he had to drop everything and race back here, the fact that it's lucky he had the car, the fact that it's time to check on the hens, the fact that the police were no help *at all*, the fact that a missing fifteen-year-old's nothing to them, the fact that I don't even think they notified their patrols or anything, but maybe the whole state was too busy with the Zanesville animals to worry about one lone teenager, the fact that all Stacy's friends now know what a failure I am as a mother, and their moms know too, the fact that I was *crying* on the phone to Prissy, the fact that that's so embarrassing, sissy, Swiffer, squeegee, Brillo, the fact that it was such a relief when Leo got here, the fact that we were up all night, waiting up for her in case she came home, and taking turns driving around looking for her, but we didn't know where to *look*, Erie Canal, canallers, galoots, glutinous, Lake Erie, Lake Erie and Eastern Railroad, Arizona, Tuscarawas, tusks, mammoths, and then the next morning, just when it began to seem highly unlikely she could still be *alive*, in she walks, bright-eyed and bushy-tailed, well, dragging her sleeping bag behind her, which is sort of like a bushy tail, and asks for a *grilled cheese sandwich*, lens wipes, the fact I was such a mess I could hardly speak, the fact that of course she didn't want to be hugged, but I did pat her shoulder a little, the fact that I really *had* to touch her, my child, my firstborn, the fact that what a funette she was as a little kid, oh, such a relief, such a relief, the fact that a lot of the rest of that morning's a *blank* now, but we definitely didn't question her, the fact that we'd already decided on that during the night, that if we ever saw her again, we weren't going to pressure her in any way, the fact that it was almost sort of funny when she asked Leo what he was doing home on a Friday morning, like she had no idea how upset we'd be, or what she'd put us through, and how he'd raced across Pennsylvania and searched all of Tuscarawas County and Coshocton and beyond, all night, over her, the fact that she never brought up the note she left for me, or apologized, or anything, the fact that all she said was she was really tired, and then, weirdly, she wanted to know if the *cats* were all right, the fact that never mind the *cats*, what about *us*, but we didn't say anything, the fact that she seemed down enough without having to have some kind of debriefing session, amicus brief, Atticus Finch, goldfinch, the fact that I once packed my little suitcase and ran away, but I only got about a block away before Phoebe caught up with me and took me home, the fact that as soon as Stace dragged herself up to her room,

I just broke down, and Leo had to comfort me some more, the fact that he actually went and got me a whiskey and soda, at *8:00 in the morning* of all things, the fact that then he called the police to tell them she'd come back, and they said something like they knew she would or something, the fact that that was when *Leo* lost it, and I could hear him yelling from his study "Do you realize there are *wild animals* on the loose out there?", the fact that the policeman played that down, claiming there weren't any wild animals loose in Tuscarawas County, the fact that then Leo asked how in heck they knew Stacy was still *in* our county, if they hadn't even bothered to look, and I don't know what the officer said to that, the fact that what *could* he say, the fact that nobody on earth knew where Stacy was all night except *Stacy*, well, until she finally told me the whole story later on, the fact that when I brought her her grilled cheese sandwich she was fast asleep, the fact that I didn't know until that phone call that Leo was worrying about those wild animals in *Zanesville* the whole time, the fact that I'd forgotten about them, but I wasn't thinking straight, the fact that I was just in panic mode, the fact that if I'd thought to worry about her getting mauled by tigers as well as everything else, I'm not sure I would've made it through the night, "my poor nerves," the fact that, thank heavens, she was not mauled by any lions, tigers, bears, or *anybody*, and no slave-owner from Cleveland got ahold of her and shoved her in his dungeon either, "The hell I am!", T's Wild Kingdom, grilled cheese, the fact that he had a three-legged giraffe, the Zanesville guy, the fact that he kept it in the basement, "How are the cats?", the fact that he'd been keeping all those animals in a sort of homemade zoo for *years*, and all the neighboring farms had to worry about it, the fact that there had been a few escapes before, but never on this scale, the fact that this time it was every animal almost, dozens and dozens, the fact that he went to jail for a year, for owning a whole load of illegal guns, the fact that I don't know what made them illegal but they were, the fact that he went to jail for a year and a day, and volunteers had to feed his animals for him, the fact that I don't get where they got the money, because those animals needed five hundred pounds of meat *a day*, and where did they get the meat every day, the fact that did they get somebody to deliver, or were there a lot of freezers on the property, or what, the fact that he kept other animals there too, like cattle, and horses, monkeys, you name it, so maybe he used *them* as meat for the lions and tigers, slaughterhouse, Los Angeles Rams, the fact that the guy had like sixty animals on his farm, the fact that how could he *afford* it, the fact that he wasn't Bill Gates, the fact that maybe it's another type of hoarding, the fact that it's kind of strange you can't drive a hundred times around the town square, but you can mistreat sixty animals and not keep them under control either, the fact that then, to top it off, he did *this*, let them all go, the fact that he must have known all his pets would get shot, or maybe kill people, or both, when he let them all out, the fact that he didn't give a darn, the fact that once, when we were kids, Mommy told Ethan to put on his hat, and Ethan said "JFK never wore a hat," the fact that I said "And look what happened to him," and everybody turned to me, surprised, and laughed, the fact that they didn't think I'd know who JFK was but I did, *I don't know but they know*, the fact that this guy was really nuts, the Zanesville guy, not Ethan or JFK, motive, Motif #1, the fact that they think maybe he *wanted* to be gobbled up by his own animals, suicide by carnivore, and maybe he got his wish, because most of those animals were half-starved, and that's why they were so aggressive and they all had to be shot, the fact that it was a *massacre*, the fact that the police shot fifty animals, *fifty*, eighteen tigers, nine lions, eight lionesses, three mountain lions, six black bears, two grizzlies, one silverback, and two gray wolves, the fact that I don't know about all the monkeys, the fact that I don't think the police shot the baboon, the fact that I think he'd already been eaten by some of the other animals when the police got there, the fact that none of the animals got far from the farm, the fact that the police were quick to "contain the situation," the fact that they slaughtered them all, one by one, sternal recumbency, Lee Harvey Oswald, the fact that they could've just warned people to stay indoors while they rounded them up *alive*, but people have to have everything their way, my way or the highway, synchronicity, wires, the fact that telling people to stay indoors probably only makes more of them want to go out and see what's going on, the fact that as soon as they heard a massacre was in progress, some of those FFF guys swooped in, a-whoopin' and a-hollerin', and just a-hopin' like heck to get a chance to lend a helpin' hand, CAUTION EXOTIC ANIMALS, but they missed the boat, the fact that by the time they got there the police had already killed everything in sight, the fact that they claim anesthetic darts are too risky, the fact that they can take too long to work and meanwhile the animal might attack the shooter, or somebody else, the fact that the police wasted time interrogating *us*, but they let a guy like that outta jail, I-70, the fact that he kept them all in tiny cages too, for years, the *animals*, not the cops, and they were all in just terrible shape, sitting ducks for those police marksmen, the fact that they were in such bad shape, I don't think the animals *knew* to run away, the fact that, also, maybe they trusted humans or something, after their years of captivity, Stockholm Syndrome, Stacy running away, note, sleeping bag, our cinnamon roll supper, support, succor, sucker, the fact that a few bears managed to get a mile or two away from the farm actually, but most of them weren't fast enough on their feet, the fact that they killed wolves too, the fact that they killed them all, every single animal on the place except the three-legged giraffe, and a few leopards that were in a cage inside the house, *I will do such things... they shall be the terror of the earth,* the fact that you'd think people could make do with a pit bull, or a Doberman Pinscher and a couple iguanas, if they *have* to have a scary animal around, or a Great Dane or Newfoundland if they want something big, a mastiff, but no, the fact that now everybody has to have their own personal safari park, that they don't even know how to take care of properly, the fact that now everybody's blaming the guy's *mom* for the Zanesville massacre, even though she passed away over a year ago, the fact that Adam Lanza's mom's always being blamed too, as if she could've predicted what *he'd* do, when *nobody* could've predicted it, the fact that it was an unimaginable crime, so how was *she* supposed to imagine it, terrible, terrible, the fact that that shooting, and 9/11, changed America for good, or no, for *bad*, the fact that Builderbeck, Quantrill and Chivington all had armies behind them, while Adam Lanza only needed a few military-grade rifles for his massacre, the fact that, okay, I admit teaching a weird kid like that how to use firearms was kind of irresponsible, the fact that you'd think taking Adam Lanza target-shooting might not be top on your list of priorities if you were his mom, but how was she to know, the fact that I'm sure she never thought he'd slaughter a whole classroom of little kids, the fact that I think she was a big gun nut herself, until he killed her, the fact that anyway, if *she* was so outta line, how come parents are *still* teaching their kids how to use guns, after Sandy Hook, the fact that the NRA thinks *everybody* should know how to handle a gun from *birth*, with the money going straight into the gun manufacturers' pockets, like Mr. Potter hanging on to the $8,000, the fact that some people will do anything for a buck, the fact that there's probably a whole range of junior sporting guns for sale by now at gun fairs, mini AR-15s in pale pink or pale blue, all decorated with glow-in-the-dark sparkles or planets and Wolverine, Pokémon, Spiderman, SpongeBob SquarePants, Applejack and Elsa decals, and maybe a few Coke ads, the fact that a gun in the hand is worth two in the, the fact that there have already been like *eighty fatal shootings* this year, in Ohio alone, and it's only April, the fact that that's eighty people who should still *be* here, the fact that the *police* killed half of them, the fact that they killed that little Cleveland boy because he was holding a fake gun, the fact that they didn't even *warn* him, the fact that he was just a little twelve-year-old kid, the fact that he looked no bigger than *Ben*, the fact that they just shot him from ten feet away, because they didn't like his "stance," the fact that every boy we know knows all the moves, how to hold himself, and the gun, depending on what kind of gun it is, and whether he's playing a police officer, soldier, school shooter, terrorist, bank robber, drug dealer, or a gangster, KABOOM, KERPOW, pyoo-pyoo-pyoo, brrrr-r-r-r-r-r-r-r-r, AK-AK-AK-AK-AK, the fact that you can even give them a squirt gun and they'll pretend they've got military firepower, the fact that I'm not sure kids play gangsters anymore, the fact that they'd probably rather be suicide bombers, the fact that the police are so hyper though, the fact that they seem sort of hysterical, the fact that are they *trained* to be that way, the fact that they probably all have PTSD, from dealing with all the well-armed criminals they have to meet, but they act like everybody's out to get *them*, the fact that they're kind of paranoid sometimes, the fact that you'd think maybe they could just pepper-spray people, or *something*, if they find them so threatening, not *kill* them all, the fact that if they could just calm *themselves* down, maybe they could calm down the "situation," but it's like they can't be bothered, the fact that it's too much trouble, the fact that calming suspects instead of killing them might take up more time, the fact that I guess they don't dare use anesthetic darts on people either, for the same reasons they used about Zanesville, but I think they're too impatient, felt, sequins, the fact that that's what gets me, the fact that one thing you learn as a mom is a little patience, otherwise no kid would make it to adulthood, the fact that maybe only *moms* should be police officers, red velvet, old umbrella, gold necklace, golden light, the fact that in New Mexico it's illegal for taxi drivers to grab customers from the street and push them into their cab, and in Alaska you're not supposed to tie your dog to the roof of your car, the fact that people have to be *told* that, dear me, McKinley, the fact that imagine tying a dog to the roof of your car when it's minus thirty out, the fact that he'd be sure to die of exposure, the fact that do birds get frozen sometimes, the fact that do they feel cold, or does their metabolism just start working even faster, the fact that what's it *like* to have the legs of a bird, those skinny, spindly little stick legs, the fact that even my legs aren't that spindly, spindle, cradle, coddle, cuddle, Stacy, the fact that a young man just shot his parents when they came to pick him up from college for spring break, the fact that of course most people would willingly die for their kids, but not that way, contrails, chemtrails, cloud seeding, dying just to give your kid the momentary pleasure of shooting you, The Ten Worst Presidents, the fact that some dad who everybody thought of as a real "protector" of his family, just shot them all and himself, because he couldn't afford to pay the bills and didn't want his family to *suffer*, I mean from *poverty*, the fact that I think he maybe took that "protector" role too far, the fact that that poor little baby was only nine months old, and the little girl was three, and the wife loved those kids *so much*, and now she can't take care of them because she's dead, and they are too, all that love just down the drain, the fact that she put all that effort into existing and bringing children into the world and now it's nowhere, gone in a puff of smoke, ♫ *Puff the magic dragon* ♫, the fact that *Stacy's* home though, touch wood, Stacy's home, the fact that I should be happy as a *clam*, "Buck up," count your blessings, charm bracelet, Ulysses S. Grant, Ford's Theater, the fact that Grant's Tomb is the largest mausoleum in America, and Gary Cooper really, really wants to go there in *Mr. Deeds Goes to Town*, which I always mix up with *Mr. Smith Goes to Washington*, which is a better movie, but Gary Grant's not in it, in *Mr. Smith Goes to Washington* I mean, not *Mr. Deeds Goes to Town*, the fact that Jean Arthur's in both, black-and-white, the fact that all Gary Cooper wants to do in New York is visit Grant's Tomb, Gary Cooper, Gladys Cooper, the fact that I wonder if they were related, the fact that Jeff Bezos is the richest man on earth, the fact that he has ninety billion dollars, the fact that that's enough to solve a lot of the nation's problems, so cough it up, buddy, intercostal clavicle, "That's the stuff, buddy," Budington, collar bone, collared dove, the fact that I thought Putin had two *hundred* billion, but he's not likely to solve the world's problems either, the fact that what does anybody need that much money for, the fact that there's a limit to how many gourmet meals a person can eat, the fact that if everybody just had a basic living wage, we'd all be happy, and the whole history of ruin and worry would be over, but centuries more unhappiness will probably have to happen before they'll give in and stop terrifying everybody about money, the fact that if we all had a moderate amount of money in our pockets we'd buy more goods too, which I thought was what they *want* us to do, "Buy! Sell!", Buy American, new cars, economy, the fact that billionaires are so happy themselves that I guess they don't notice how bugged the rest of us are, floof, "boof," aloof, WOOT, the fact that Gary Cooper has nothing to worry about though, because he's just come into a fortune, the fact that anyway he keeps asking about Grant's Tomb, and finally he gets to go there with Jean Arthur, who he thinks is a damsel in distress, the fact that he's been holding out all his life for a damsel in distress, but then she turns out to be a clever and capable newspaperwoman and betrays him by turning him into a laughing-stock in the articles she writes about him, so Gary Cooper gives her the Silent Treatment, the fact that he gives everybody in New York the Silent Treatment, and he stays that way for quite a large portion of the movie, the fact that she disappoints him and then he disappoints her, with his big silence, because by then she loves him, the fact that it's gotta be the biggest sulk in the movies, Mary Cassatt, "Little Girl in a Blue Armchair," the fact that everybody lets him sulk though, because people were so much more civilized in the thirties, apart from the border agencies with the ships full of Jewish refugees, not just here but in Canada and England and all kinds of places, the fact that they were turned away from every port, and some boats had to return to Europe, and half their passengers were murdered in the concentration camps, the fact that it wasn't just the Germans who hated the Jews, and a lot of people *still* hate them, like the people who knocked over the gravestones in Philadelphia, the Jewish gravestones, the fact that the French do it all the time too, the fact that *nothing* rhymes with Budington, nothing gun, nuttin bun, the fact that I think it's lucky for giraffes that most people *don't* want them as pets, or not so much, Jim, fleas, tardigrades, the fact that a Danish zoo publicly dismembered a giraffe and fed it to their lions, and some other Danish zoo killed and publicly dissected a nine-month-old lioness, for entertainment purposes, *rotten in the state of Denmark*, the fact that they claimed they had too many lions at the zoo, and they couldn't find anywhere else for them to go, so they had to kill her, "cull," the fact that when people want to downplay killing they call it culling, the numbness of muted beings, the fact that somebody said, after the giraffe was fed to the lions, that zoos are *prisons*, which is going a bit far, the fact that there were placards, demos, the fact that I don't know why people do those things, protests and stuff, especially when the giraffe was already *dead*, the fact that some twelve-year-old boys set fire to a dog shelter over near Uhrichsville, on a dare, and fifty dogs suffocated, and our little Jim's one of the *survivors*, oh dear, the fact that what he must have gone through, the horrors he's seen, arson, Harrison Ford, Amish purple martin house, the fact that those kids will probably go to jail for *twenty years*, the fact that they'll be in their *thirties* when they get out, the fact that I think it's good we caved on the dog front, but I don't know yet if Jim's the *right* dog for us, the fact that I do like his long white snout, which you can see helpfully from afar, if he drifts behind bushes and things, the fact that Jim pokes his way through the world with that sharp, white snout of his, and on the tip he has that nice little black nose and a few black speckles, black-and-white, the fact that the white markings taper to a white streak between the eyes, taper, tapir, tapeworm, tap root, the fact that he has a black body and white paws dappled with some black spots, and there's a white tip to the end of his shaggy tail, but I like the curls on his chest best, the fact that they make him look like he's wearing a white shirt with ruffles, under a tux, the fact that he never wags his tail but maybe he will when he settles down, the fact that I sure hope that high-pitched whine he's got settles too, the fact that Trump always has pale patches around his eyes, from sunbed goggles, the fact that maybe he'd look better if he just left the goggles on, and didn't surface until dinnertime, the fact that I mean *Stacy* didn't surface until dinnertime, the fact that even then she still didn't tell us much about her adventure, the fact that the kids were speechless all through the meal, the fact that usually they're arguing about something that got wrecked or lost, or commenting on something *I* didn't do right, but that night they were completely silent, wide-eyed, glum, the fact that we'd warned them not to bother her, because she'd be tired, the fact that maybe we laid it on too thick, because they looked scared to *death*, the fact that I didn't say much either, the fact that I was a wreck, the fact that I think Leo did all the talking, but I can't remember what he said, the fact that it wasn't until the next day that she let the cat out of the bag, to me, in private, about her night in the wilderness, the cats, lions, tigers, giraffes, the Holocaust, Holocaust deniers, Sandy Hook deniers, the fact that when she set off, she was hoping to join a Hopi tribe and live on their reservation, the fact that she'd heard Leo talking about the mesa near him in Arizona, Cold Sally, and the way the Hopi live, the stuff they eat and all, the fact that Leo also said the Apache children had no shoes, *in the snow*, but I guess Stace wasn't daunted by that, the fact that her plan was to hitch all the way, but nobody would pick her up, thank heaven, the fact that finally a school bus came along, but he was only going as far as *Dover*, not Arizona, so, completely the wrong direction, the fact that she got on anyway because she was *cold*, the fact that after he dumped her she tried to get a ride from Dover to Arizona, the fact that I still kind of wonder why that bus driver never thought to notify the police, the fact that it's not like she looks older than she is, the fact that to me she looks *younger* if anything, the fact that nobody would pick her up on the highway though, and this went on all afternoon, so she ate at some diner some-where, and then she looked around for someplace safe to sleep, outside, the fact that it's freezing out at night still, the fact that she could've died of *exposure*, the fact that she told me she was pretty nervous because she didn't want to be seen sleeping in her sleeping bag, seen by *men*, that is, the fact that I don't think she ever even *thought* of bears, and she'd forgotten all about the lion, and knew nothing about all the escaped tigers, oh my, the fact that I'm glad *she* didn't know about the Zanesville thing, three-legged giraffe, the fact that she found a place sort of hidden from view behind some rusty old barrels, just by the side of the *road* somewhere, and she lay there in her sleeping bag, unable to sleep a wink, the fact that there was a lot of gravel under her or something, so she couldn't get comfortable, the fact that by mid-night she'd already decided she'd rather be home, instead of Arizona, the fact that why didn't she call us, the fact that maybe I even passed right by her, when I was out in the car, looking, and I never knew, the fact that she says she didn't want to alarm me by waking me up in the middle of the night, Jesus of New Philadelphia, the Grand Canyon, the Painted Desert, Tucson, iguanas, Stacy's white T-shirt, Rosie Lee

Thompkins's quilts, the fact that she says no one bothered her at least, but she didn't like being out there all night on her own, the fact that she was too cold to sleep, or too scared, and there were those pebbles, the fact that Flagstaff can be cold too, my yellow bird costume, the fact that she was "scared" but I'm *traumatized*, the fact that, I mean, boy, your kid can damage or destroy herself, wreck her life and yours, *at any moment*, with one bad decision, high swing, and there's zilch you can do about it, Annual Northwestern Faculty Summer Picnic, the fact that then your life would just be over, Sandy Hook, the fact that this is kind of a hard fact to face, and I think the way moms survive is by *not* facing it most of the time, not until you absolutely have to, the fact that they say you shouldn't sweat the little stuff, but I think it protects you a bit against the harder stuff, the unknowables, the fact that I'm so used to worrying about the *younger* kids that I don't think about Stace so much anymore, because I know she can cope, the fact that the other three seem like this constant state of Code Red, CONELRAD, but now I feel that way about Stacy too, because she's just as vulnerable in her way, the fact that lately I've kind of relaxed about Jake actually, and the others seemed old enough to take care of themselves some of the time, the fact that Gillian's more or less hit the age of reason, the fact that that's how I *used* to feel about them, before Stacy did a runner, the fact that now I feel shaky about all four, the fact that I still find myself *counting* them again and again, four, to make sure they're all present and correct, Stacy, Ben, Gillian, Jake, Stacy, Ben, Gillian, Jake, Ben, Jake, Stace and Gillian, and Leo too of course, and Opal and Frederick and the chickens, and the goldfish, and now there's Jim to worry about too, dear me, the fact that the biggest surprise was she says it's not *me*, the fact that I'm off the hook, the fact that running away had nothing to do with me, she said, the fact that it was all because of some boy at school who threatened her, this *Willy* boy, willy-nilly, the fact that Stacy's been "*going out*" with him, which was news to *me*, the fact that I've never even seen this boy, the fact that I don't even think she liked him all that much right from the start, or maybe she did but now she *hates* him, the fact that lately he's been wanting to get more "serious," first base, second base, the fact that she says she didn't want to get too "involved," sex pamphlet, Priapus, Osiris, the fact that when she told him that, Willy went ballistic and threatened to kill her *cat*, pretty extreme reaction, the fact that he didn't specify which cat, the fact that he probably doesn't know we have two, and doesn't care either, the fact that I said "That's no way to behave, if you want a girl to *like* you," and Stacy said *all* the boys at school are the same, the fact that they can turn on you really fast, and get all vicious, in the twinkling of an eye, wink, blink of an eye, the fact that she got so worried about the cats, she thought she had to *leave home*, so the cats wouldn't be a target anymore, the fact that all because of Willy I almost lost my daughter, the fact that that boy sounds a real menace, the fact that luckily, now she's home, she says she isn't so worried about the cats, but she seems a *little* anxious about them to me, since she keeps checking where they are, and hustling them inside if she sees them at the back door, the fact that it seems *unreal* that he would say such a thing, and *of course* she'd be worried, but she really should've *told* me, the fact that at least she's finally confided in me now, the fact that it almost felt like old times, like when she was twelve and we still did things together, the fact that we made toys for the other kids, and baked cookies, stuff like that, Ten Completely Free Knitting Toy Patterns, me and my little suitcase as a kid, *Sense and Sensibility*, the fact that I wondered if we should report Willy's threats about the cats to the police, or at least to Mrs. Sherman, the fact that it's kind of domestic violence, if you ask me, and bullying too, the fact that Stace won't let me tell anybody except Leo, the fact that she says she's going to handle it herself when she gets back to school, the fact that she's now so mad at Willy, she says he'd better watch out, the fact that I'd still kind of rather the police handled it, but maybe she needs to work it out herself, Hopi, music camp, swimming in the waterfall, my care package from Mommy, the fact that I'm not absolutely sure if she means she's going to have a confrontation with him on Facebook or Snapchat or WhatsApp, or *what*, the fact that you never know anymore, the fact that some of her friends seem to think having a "face-to-face" with somebody is something you do on Skype, the fact that I guess Stace knows best though, and she wants to face the problem and get closure, the fact that I wonder if she has dreams about being bullied on social media, the fact that *Leo* dreams about his email inbox all the time, the fact that anyway maybe Stacy can put this Willy guy in his place, the fact that she's got guts, she really has, "Brains and personality, my friend, brains and personality," the fact that actually she seems to have sort of grown up a bit *over-night*, during her night on the road, the fact that she even seems a little taller, and full of *magnanimousness*, magnanimosity, magnanimity, magma, SMEG, the fact that when we passed by Leo's study after our talk, she said it was "cool as light," like she only just noticed, the fact that I thought that was a pretty sweet thing to say about your step-dad's study, and he does keep it nice, the fact that he doesn't leave papers everywhere like I do, the fact that he's a minimalist, or so *he* says, but he's not so minimal about *emails*, the fact that he lets them all pile up, and his computer screen's completely covered with files, folders, apps and stuff, the fact that they fill the *whole screen*, the fact that I've only got like about *six* on mine, Recipes, Accounts, Photos, Kids, Peolia, which has all my history notes in it, and I forget what my other files are right at this minute, Alice Neel, Nina Simone, the fact that Stace can't remember which diner she was in, and has only a rough idea where she slept that night, sleeping rough, the fact that once she'd had a good night's sleep, she seemed to realize what she's put us all through, sheesh, the fact that she gave us all a *big scare*, the kids too, maybe even the cats, the fact that she seems to want to make it up to us, because she's acting like a reformed character, all calm and collected about everything, and cheerful, even with her siblings, the fact that she seems sort of sorry but proud at the same time, the fact that she's faced the real world and survived, and she knows we all know that, so maybe she's satisfied, and won't ever have to run away again, the fact that I sure hope not, the fact that surely she wouldn't put us through something like that again, Shirley, the fact that I think it was coming on for a while though, this bid for freedom, the fact that it's not just about Willy, no matter what she says, the fact that she *hates* me, but I must not think that way, the fact that she says that now she knows he's a stinker, Willy, and she'll never forgive him, the fact that Willy sounds a lot like *Willoughby* to me, and Stacy's always been a bit like Marianne, but without the *fever*, touch wood, so I told her I'm calling him Willoughby from now on, and she seems to like that idea, cakes, cukes, the fact that on Friday night, with her safely home, I slept like a log and dreamt *I* was in some diner someplace and somebody took away my muffin and gave me a big black and white *cookie* instead, which I didn't want, but I didn't say anything, the fact that on Saturday we all went to the pound and got Jim, the fact that child psychologists would probably say we were rewarding bad behavior, but we just want Stacy to be happy, or *happier* at least, the fact that we want her to have something to live for, and to come *home* for, the fact that a dog might make her feel safer too, the fact that Jim was originally a farm pup, but he was no good at herding or something so they dumped the poor guy at an animal shelter, which then *burnt down*, Juvy, Willoughby, the fact that I think he was named Jim on the farm, the fact that he's a worrying, worried kind of dog, the fact that Stace wants to rehabilitate him, but so far he only likes being outside with the chickens, the fact that he's scared of people and other dogs, but he really seems to like the chickens, the fact that I think it's because chickens don't make much eye contact, or not so as you'd notice, or maybe there were some chickens on the farm where he grew up, so he can relate to chickens, the fact that he's sweet, he's not aggressive or anything, he's very meek and mild, the fact that he's just sad, the fact that he lies down in the corner when we bring him in, and cowers a lot, but he never growls, the fact that they said he was gentle at the pound, which was why we got interested in him, because we don't want a dog that's bad with kids, the fact that they always check at the pound, they said, if a dog's suitable for young children and he's got their seal of approval, the fact that I had to get the kids to stop trying to hug him though, because it just makes him anxious, the fact that he looks so frail, and literally walks with his tail between his legs, but he's got that incredibly penetrating yap, the fact that he can hit a very high note and keep it up for hours, poor little guy, which is probably what saved him in the *fire*, because the firefighters heard him and located him somehow, and dragged him out and put an doggie oxygen mask on his face, the fact that most of the dogs there weren't so lucky, the fact that they're kind of snout-shaped, doggie oxygen masks, not firefighters, the fact that his lungs are fine, he just needed a little help, the fact that you can *tell* his lungs are okay from all the barking, the fact that the neighbors are probably going to kill us but I don't care as long as Stacy's happy, the fact that she thinks Willy will be deterred by Jim too, so she feels safer now about the cats because of Jim, so that's good, the fact that maybe he will be a good guard dog, the fact that we took him to the park, partly to give the neighbors a break, and tried to get him to chase a ball but he wouldn't do it, the fact that I don't think he knows how, or just couldn't care less about balls maybe, the fact that Stacy can try to teach him, or do they learn by watching other dogs chase balls, the fact that the trick to watching dogs chase balls, I find, is to watch the *dog*, not the ball, the fact that I was watching the dog owners a little too, and it seemed to me they never let their dogs do what they want, the fact that they're always calling them and fussing with them and pulling them around on their leash, reeling them in, when the dog just wants to *play* and stuff, the fact that some people can't leave their pets be, the fact that one kid was really almost swinging the dog around and around in the air, by his collar, and it looked cruel, the fact that Jim only liked the ducks in the park, "Ducky! Ducky!", the fact that the poor dog really seems to have an affinity with poultry, infinity, Hannity, tinnitus, the fact that the last time we went to see the ducks was after that toxic scare last year, the fact that that put us off going for a while, the fact that who wants to see toxic ducks, the fact that somebody'd released some toxic substance into the water, and all the ducks were dead, the coots too, *and* the fish, and the frogs, sea star wasting disease, the fact that they must've gotten some new ones from someplace, the fact that when it happened some people cried, but by the time we got there the dead critters had all been cleared away and nobody was crying anymore, but still it was dreary, a pond without ducks, *Silent Spring*, the fact that the place was just dead, tears, rain, mitti attar, hourglass dolphins, the fact that I don't think *anybody* went there much for a while after that, but now things are looking up, the fact that there were some ducks ducking under the boardwalk that stretches out over the water, the fact that if a *duck* can't duck, who can, the fact that there was a swan-and-coot spat going on too, with a lot of hissing, the fact that the coot didn't give in though, the fact that he was absolutely determined to bring a new twig to his wife who was sitting on the nest, my poor wood pigeon egg, the fact that they'd built their nest right out in the open, on a wooden platform floating on the water, the fact that I guess it's sort of like a static raft, and it's set apart from the boardwalk bridge, so people can't actually reach it, but swans can, the fact that the swans just wanted their chance to sit on the raft, with their one cygnet who's very new and fluffy, floofy, with tiny wings, and so *sleepy*, the fact that first he was sleeping on the raft, right near the coots' nest, but after the big dispute the parent swan moved off and the cygnet followed, the fact that as soon as it dropped into the water, the cygnet fell asleep again, the fact that all baby animals have to sleep a heck of a lot, the fact that then a water-loving dog took a dip, which scared the ducks, the coots, the swans and *Jim*, the fact that he was so appalled he fled the scene, the fact that I think he was scared we'd make *him* get in the water, the fact that we ran after him, so we wouldn't lose him, but he didn't go far, the fact that he didn't seem to have any idea where to go though, so he just cowered by the fence, the fact that he doesn't *play*, the fact that it's hard to imagine what he's thinking about, the fact that maybe it's PTSD, the fact that the coots seem pretty resilient, but I wonder how long they can hold out in that spot of theirs, hatching eggs and making repairs and fending off swans and dogs and everything, the fact that the daddy coot continued to bring twigs the whole time we were there, with pride, and the twigs were all eagerly accepted by the female, who stuck them into the messy nest without fuss, the fact that her housekeeping is of the laid-back variety, the fact that we also saw a pigeon back up several steps, looking confused, the fact that I didn't know pigeons could go into reverse, Walter Pigeon, Walter Matthau, the fact that later we found a big duck fast asleep on the information sign beside the pond, blocking all the wildlife info, and it looked deliberate, like he really didn't want us finding out what other kinds of water fowl there were there, the fact that maybe Jim is just shy, and I can sympathize, the fact that I personally think Stacy chose him for being the most unhappy dog at the pound, though she denies it, Fancy Feast, dog chews, the fact that after we got Jim, we went to Zyker's to get dog supplies, which was fun, Dad's Pet Care, deadbeat dads, Keystone XL, and then Ben looked up dog-training on the internet, the fact that methods have really changed, the fact that now you're supposed to keep your dog in a *cage* all day, or a crate, YouTubers, Tide pod eaters, yuppies, the fact that it's supposed to give them a sense of security, so maybe it's just what Jim needs, a crate to hide in all day, but we don't want a dog in a box, the fact that we want a dog that sits around the house and *mingles*, the fact that Pepito never had a crate, the fact that the worst thing that he had to go through usually was going to the groomers to be clipped, the fact that he hated going to the vet too, or a kennel, the fact that those are the places where dogs do get put in cages, and on airplanes, the fact that Pepito liked to run free in the house and in the park, and have love affairs, like any dog does, the fact that, like Jim, Pepito didn't much care for *swimming*, the fact that we could never convince him to go more than a few steps into Lake Michigan, the fact that now that I've left Jim alone with the chickens all morning, he's quietened down, if he'd only stop yelping, that high-pitched squeal, howl, the fact that I used to want a dog that could howl, and now we've got one, the fact that it's such a doggy thing to do, the fact that Pepito never howled, and I always kind of hoped he might, but it wasn't his kind of thing, the fact that *we* howled to him sometimes, trying to get him going, but he never joined in, the fact that looking at Jim, you begin to wonder if human beings are the only self-conscious animal, the fact that he always looks so embarrassed, the fact that dogs often look self-conscious when they're wearing fancy dog coats too, the fact that I'm sure pink poodles *know* they're pink, and they're not happy about it, the fact that they must keep thinking to themselves "I'm pink," the fact that Pepito was always embarrassed after he'd been to the poodle parlor, the fact that he must have felt naked, and chilly, to be suddenly shorn like that, the fact that later on we did it ourselves, and he didn't mind at all, the fact that they always tried to give him pom-poms, which I think made him feel silly, but the mustache suited him, the fact that I think he was glad about that, but they took a lot off elsewhere, the fact that we asked for the simplest style but he always got a pom-pom on the end of his tail, and on his ears, and floofy legs but bare feet, and a sort of beret of curls on top of his head, the fact that maybe that's what Kim Jong-un's going for, the fact that he was such a sweetie, Pepito, not Kim Jong-un, cockerpoos, cocker spaniels, cock, cockup, cops, the fact that when I told him about Willy's threat against the cats, Leo overrode Stacy's instructions and called the cops about him, *For he is of the tribe of stalker*, but they say they can't do anything until Willy actually *kills a cat*, heavens, Willoughby, fresh pasta, Rome, 1978, the fact that that made Leo really mad, the fact that he's getting really tough on the police these days, the fact that he's never liked authority figures, authority, entirety, enormity, the fact that when the police said no can do, Leo said "No, you are going to check this guy out. He's violent. He's made threats against my family," but they still said no can do, and they *haven't* checked him out, as far as we know, the fact that I don't know how safe it is to call the police anyway, the fact that they've killed seven hundred people in America so far this year, the fact that some woman in Portland or somewhere called the cops because she was worried that someone was being getting raped in the alley right behind her house, and the police came, and she went out to meet them in her pajamas, and they shot *her*, the *caller*, not the rapist, "Pajamas are not to be worn to school," the fact that maybe it was in Seattle, Sacramento, the fact that *terrible* things are always happening in Sacramento, the fact that that's where a police officer took a hot dog vendor's money away because he didn't have a license, the fact that he took the poor guy's sixty hard-earned bucks, the fact that this guy had been selling hot dogs in the same place for *seven years* already, without any trouble, and he *needed* that sixty dollars, the fact that he has a family to support, the fact that you don't stand around on the street selling hot dogs from a pushcart unless you need the money, authority figures, the fact that Hungarian police tear gas children, the fact that when I was staying overnight at Patty's house once, we thought we saw a UFO and we tried to call the police about it, but it's always hard to know who to call about those things, and I can't remember who we got hold of, or what happened after that, the fact that Patty called *somebody*, the fact that the UFO was a big round light in the sky, but why would a UFO go to Chicago just to shine at a couple of little kids, the fact that you don't think logically when you see a UFO, the fact that I just realized the lipstick I have on has some kind of glitter in it and it's deposited glitter all over my *face*, so I threw it out, the fact that I don't want Stacy borrowing it and getting cancer or something from all that glitter, the fact that I guess my protective instincts are on full alert these days, right down to glitter molecules, the fact that maybe *all* lipstick has a little glitter in it, and I just never realized, the fact that some lipstick's *very* glittery, but this one didn't seem like that when I bought it, the fact that who wears those, the fact that some woman's suing Walgreens because she thinks she got herpes from one of their tester lipsticks, the fact that that's just not fair, the fact that I never put those right on my *mouth* though, the fact that I always thought you're supposed to put a dab on your *hand*, just to check the color against your skin, the fact that they *should* offer a Kleenex to wipe it off with too but you can't always find one, the fact that Geena Davis tries out all the lipsticks in the store, while they're training the dog to stay still outside, the fact that I hope *she* didn't get herpes from that, but the props department probably bought brand-new lipsticks and just made them look old, the fact that is Walgreens related to Walmart, the fact that CVS is more successful than Walgreens, but to me they seem about the same, the fact that William Hurt doesn't treat Geena Davis too well, the fact that a guy in Italy intentionally gave thirty women HIV, the fact that I don't get it with viruses, the fact that they're not even *alive*, so how come they care this much about being passed around, the fact that what's in it for the herpes virus, the fact that why do viruses get such a kick out of annoying people, the fact that, I mean, why do they even want to *exist*, the fact that I just don't get it, the fact that what drives a cold to want to be spread around, but something does, because they mutate all the time in order to get spread better, *It will make my batter better*, coughs, sneezes, swashbuckling, ruckus, mucus-reducus medication, exodus, exude, the fact that I let Stacy stay home another day today to recover, the fact that I think she needs sleep, especially before she has to confront that Willoughby character, the fact that she's obviously still bothered about that, the fact that she keeps herding those cats indoors, Will Rogers, Gary Cooper, Harry Carey, the fact that Jim's a good size though, so I think just his presence should be a help, the fact that that's what I told her anyway, the fact that how good a watchdog he is, we don't know, the fact that he's scared of the cats, blueberries, spaghetti sauce, so he's probably glad they keep being shut inside, Fallingwater, the fact that the cats don't mind anyway, I mean *look* at them, lookit, purring away between us while we watch the movie, with our hot chocolate, the fact that there's some cat on YouTube who flips out every time Trump comes on the screen, the fact that he finds Trump really really freaky, the fact that our cats never seem that interested in TV, even shows made for cats, the fact that they have plenty of other stuff to think about, the fact that last night I dreamt I dumped a big strainer full of lettuce leaves into an even bigger strainer, the fact that then I dreamt I found a little girl caked in *dirt*, the fact that she was wandering through the bushes by the train station, the fact that I coaxed her into the car and got her to my house, which happened to be a mansion, and there were various other people around, servants and stuff, but I personally bathed her and put her to bed, or that was my plan anyway, the fact that then it was the next morning and I couldn't *remember* how I'd bathed her or gotten her to bed, but anyway I found her somewhere around the house and we went off to the doctor's office to have her checked over and to ask how to contact the authorities and see if she had a family somewhere, the fact that I asked the nurse what the procedure was for handing her back to her mom, and the nurse told me a place to go, and I sort of knew how to get there, the fact that she knew I liked the little girl and she said I could look at the mom through a two-way mirror before deciding if I wanted to give the kid back to her, the fact that the law seemed to be on my side, sort of, if I wanted to keep her, the fact that I felt it was a second chance to bring up a daughter right, the fact that poor Gillian didn't seem to be part of this dream at all and, strangely enough, the stray girl was called Stacy, and Frank was there, and *he* liked her a lot too, the fact that Leo wasn't in that dream at all, the fact that she was a very sweet, likeable child, but prone to wandering, and while we were in the doctor's waiting room she wandered far away before I knew it, the fact that then she called me on the phone and said she didn't know the way back, so I had to try to guide her back to me, Stacy, the fact that we didn't use real phones though, the fact that we were somehow able to talk to each other by using the button on a *crosswalk*, WALK, DON'T WALK, talk, don't talk, the Silent Treatment, the Columbus Zoo, the fact that I said I'd come to her if she told me where she was, the fact that there were some guys in the doctor's waiting room who seemed quite keen on me, the fact that earlier, when Frank and I were watching this other "Stacy" girl play, he said she looked a lot different now that she'd had a bath, the fact that I said she looked a lot like *him*, which I immediately regretted, since she didn't look like him at all and I wondered why I'd said it, the fact that she didn't look like me either, the fact that she didn't look like either of us, the fact that what is it about little kids that makes you jump to adopt them, if they're all alone in the world I mean, the fact that I just longed to help that little kid, maternal instinct, Mommy, the fact that a suicidal mom in Dayton shot her two young daughters, but she survived, the fact that a twelve-year-old boy was shot in a Starbucks in Cleveland, the fact that maybe I'll bring it up at Family Therapy, not the boy and the suicidal mom, my *dream*, the fact that

Family Therapy is now on the cards, just me and Stace, nobody else, the fact that I'm scared, but maybe it'll help us communicate more, though we're doing okay at the moment, the fact that the mom in *There's Always Tomorrow* mentions the Child Guidance classes they attended, but those classes must've stunk, or they didn't stick, or else she and Fred MacMurray didn't do their homework, because they just let those kids walk all over them, the fact that who *is* that actress, the fact that I kind of wish *I'd* gone to Child Guidance classes, if they still exist, the fact that then maybe this episode with Stacy would never have happened, Opal stretching, the fact that maybe she's too hot between us, but cats like heat, they can take it, Raccoon That Ate Too Much, the fact that it's *Joan Bennett*, the fact that Joan Bennett had a lousy time of it with her husband, the fact that he was terribly jealous and one day he shot her agent in the groin because he thought they were having an affair, which they were not, the fact that then he threw himself on the mercy of the court and got off with a *four-month* sentence, the fact that that's a lotta mercy, "Merci!", the fact that the husband was a producer and he went right back to making movies, but Joan Bennett's career never recovered, the fact that he did something like that to Errol Flynn too, the fact that he had some jealous fit about Errol Flynn, the fact that most of the women in America were in love with Errol Flynn, so that's a big bunch of enemies to make, the fact that he was sort of a stalker, Joan Bennett's husband I mean, the fact that I don't know if Errol Flynn was a stalker, Eliza Bennet, Darcy, the fact that Joan Bennett supported a lot of liberal causes, so maybe she counteracted some of the political stuff Barbara Stanwyck got up to, the fact that Barbara Stanwyck was some kind of staunch Republican, herpes, the fact that she was a fan of McCarthy and the Un-American Activities Committee, the fact that it's funny they're in this movie together, where Barbara's playing the unconventional type and Joan Bennett's all traditional and homey and complacent about everything, smug, smog, smegma, the fact that Mickey Mouse was almost called Mortimer, the fact that Walt Disney's first cartoon character was Oswald the Lucky Rabbit, the fact that John Wayne thought it was good we stole America from the Indians, the fact that why do people go to Disneyland, or SeaWorld, the fact that there was a traffic jam in China that lasted two whole weeks, the fact that it was sixty miles long and nobody could move any faster than one kilometer an hour, the fact that the drivers had to live on the highway, eating over-priced pot noodles sold by street vendors, sixty dollars, hot dogs, police, but where'd they brush their teeth, the fact that now if *that* didn't put you off driving, nothing would, the fact that the Chinese used to all be on bikes, but now it's cars, and the polar ice cap is gone, just gone, the fact that America started it though, the fact that the kids in *There's Always Tomorrow* really have it made, the fact that when Fred MacMurray comes home, his son *shushes* him because he's on the phone to his girlfriend, and Fred apologizes for speaking, the fact that the kids interrupt their parents all the time, and Fred and Joan Bennett never get a chance to talk to each other, even on Joan's birth-day, the fact that when he compliments his daughter on her tutu she doesn't even listen to him, the fact that Fred MacMurray's being taken for granted, the fact that he calls his older daughter Princess, and invites her to see a musical with him but Princess is busy, the fact that Joan Bennett can't come either, she's too busy spoiling the kids, and being stalked by her off-screen husband, boor, brute, the fact that even the hired help won't come with him to the show, so Fred ends up all alone in the kitchen, eating goulash, galoshes, whitewash, greenwash, the fact that Stacy liked it that the coffee pot blew its top the same moment the doorbell rang, the fact that Fred's still holding the coffee pot when he goes to the door and finds Barbara Stanwyck standing there, his former employee in the toy-making business, the fact that Barbara obviously had a big crush on Frank in the old days, but now she's a big deal in the fashion world in New York, the fact that the first thing she does is help him out of his little apron, and then *they* go to the show, but Barbara's already seen it in New York, the fact that I don't know how I got Stace to watch a black-and-white movie for once, the fact that she seems to think it's all pretty funny, especially because Barbara's wearing a hat that looks like a toy sailboat made out of newspaper, the fact that I guess it's supposed to be the latest thing, the fact that suddenly she wants him to show her his little toy factory, so they creep in there at night, and it's not romantic at all, it's kind of grim, the fact that toys are always spooky in the dark, the fact that Stacy says Gillian's honey bears give her the creeps, the fact that all the toys are staring at Fred and Barbara in the dim light, and the toys look kind of mean, not fun, TOYS "Я" US, but Barbara Stanwyck says she admires the wonderful display, and she's very taken with a toy trailer that looks like an Airstream, the fact that her favorite thing is the hurdy-gurdy organ that plays ♫ *Blue Moon* ♫, mainly because they thought that up together, long ago, but then she gushes over the toy train too, eyes twinkling, the fact that at home his kids are all shouting and screaming at him, but here Fred's in his element, playing with his toys under the gaze of the beady-eyed dolls and Barbara Stanwyck, the fact that faceless Amish dolls have the advantage that they don't stare at you all night like that, the fact that she quit all of a sudden twenty years ago, for no reason, the fact that Fred never understood why, Chuck, Zadok Cramer, *Witness*, unrequited love, apron, coffee pot, the fact that now things might be different though, because Fred's pretty sick of his family, and his wife spends all her time putting cold cream on or sewing dresses for the Princess or the other girl, INSTRUCTIONS AND PRECAUTIONS, NECESSARY TO BE ATTENDED TO IN NAVIGATING THE MISSISSIPPI RIVER, the fact that now he's back home with the kids and the colonial furniture and the twin beds with the metallic quilts, Frederick, Stacy, the fact that when Barbara comes over for dinner the teenage kids are rude to her, the fact that they're already awfully suspicious, but Joan Bennett isn't, the fact that she trusts her husband, like I do, the fact that all she can think about is the shrimp salad they're going to have tomorrow, s & d, "SAD," *Tomorrow*, the fact that I think it's called *There's Always Tomorrow* because there are always chores to do tomorrow, consequences, but Stacy says it's because there's always a chance tomorrow will be *better*, Betty Boughter, Bette Davis, "Waken up and smell the coffee," the fact that there isn't always tomorrow though, because eventually you pass away, or your husband shoots somebody in the groin and your whole life's ruined, or he has an affair with an old flame, a *Republican*, the fact that Jane Fonda's in her Act III but I'm only in Act II, I hope, the fact that I gotta defrost some spaghetti sauce, and get out the crab sticks, oof, sorry Opal, just a sec, the fact that I make a mean crab-stick sandwich, the fact that I put in raw garlic and jalapeno and ginger and celery salt, the fact that you've got to have celery salt with crab, the fact that maybe I should sell *these*, the fact that Stace really likes them, the fact that she wants *two* crab-stick sandwiches, the fact that if I ate *one* I'd be too full to bake anything, the Annual Northwestern Faculty Summer Picnic, the fact that once Fred's son sees Barbara Stanwyck kiss Fred on the cheek, there's bound to be trouble, the fact that it was at one of those Annual Northwestern Faculty Summer Picnics that I swung on that long, tall, scary swing, and got really, really high, the fact that it was exhilarating, the fact that swinging really can be fun, the fact that I was right up in the trees, to the point that I scared myself but I didn't want to stop, the fact that there was a bit of a *flying* sensation going on too, the fact that nobody noticed how high I got and I probably could have broken my neck or something if I'd gone any higher and come off at that height, Shere Hite, the fact that swings are pretty dangerous really, the fact that we're all kidding ourselves if we think they're not, the fact that swings are daredevil stuff, devilry, deviltry, the fact that all that's keeping you alive is the hope that your sit-me-down-upon won't slip off that thin strip of wood, or metal or plastic, the fact that your little fists grip the chains for dear life, the fact that you know if you let go at the top, you'll drop twenty feet, just like that, suspension bridge design, the fact that lots of kids do have swing accidents, the fact that it's inevitable, the fact that I watch my kids pretty closely when they're on swings, because I know it's actually crazee to let your kid do that at all, the fact that I realized I was swinging much too high at the Annual Northwestern Faculty Summer Picnic and I got scared, but if you slow down too fast or get off-balance, you might start to wobble, and the wobble could knock you off the swing *too*, the fact that I'm not even sure my feet could touch the ground on that swing, so it was hard to slow down, the fact that I just did it very gradually, but it was a great ride, exhilarating, ex-Hillary, exile, the fact that all in all, maybe seesaws are safer, though I've almost fallen off them too, the fact that it's tricky if the other person bumps you hard when they hit the bottom and you bounce at the top, the fact that I hate to be bumped, bumper cars, booster chair, highchair, the fact that that's another reason why I don't like swimming pools anymore, if they're crowded, the fact that if I was a multi-millionaire I'd get me a swimming pool *just for me*, WOOT, the fact that immigrants can't get antenatal care, so they just show up at the hospital when problems arise, and sometimes that's too *late*, obstetrician, gyny guy, the fact that there's a high fetal mortality rate among immigrants, which is so sad, the fact that what a cold phrase that is, "the fetuses of immigrants," the yeast, the fact that Stacy's *back*, she's back, the fact that I still have to kick myself sometimes to remind myself she's safe and well, eating her second crab sandwich, "I'm taking the big sleeping bag," the fact that the sleeping bag's back in the attic now, the fact that maybe I should hide it, shove it in the commode or something, the fact that when do we really need sleeping bags, the fact that Mommy and Daddy never took us on camping trips and Leo and I never take our kids camping either, the fact that plenty of other parents seem to do fun stuff with their kids, the fact that Fred MacMurray would, the fact that that's probably all he ever does, when he's not at work, Child Guidance, the fact that once you're a parent you're never supposed to do what *you* want, like stuff just for you, the fact that everything's got to be for the kids, otherwise you're a selfish mom bomb, bum, crumb-bum, the fact that John Wayne thought the Indians were "selfish" for trying to keep America to themselves, the fact that as soon as you have kids, your life's not worth a dime, the fact that I get tired just thinking about all the stuff you're supposed to do, the year-long carpentry projects, helping the kid make the best go-kart in America, water samples, trampolining and sailing and abseiling and hunting and fishing and taking them to the Olympics and Washington

DC, and coaching Little League, and getting a whole bunch of kids to the movies or the funfair, Disneyland, Disney World, the zoo, the fact that then you gotta take 'em to Europe or Cancun or Hawaii or wherever, Reykjavik, or you're just no good as a parent, the fact that I guess we're no good, because all we offer as entertainment around here are chickens and a treehouse, that the kids made themselves, and now Jim, the fact that Leo checked it over for structural soundness and made them add a few more supporting bits, struts, cogs, nuts and bolts, buttresses, I mean on the treehouse, not on *Jim*, the fact that if it was selfish of the Indians not to welcome the settlers, Gnadenhutten Massacre, why isn't it selfish of Americans not to let in anybody who wants to come here *now*, incomers, newcomers, Newcomerstown, the fact that the Johannsons actually got some hotshot box-car designer to design a box-car for Janice, and then she went and won First Prize at some soap-box derby, which seems a lot like cheating to me, but what do I know, live and let live, solitaire, the fact that we hardly ever even get to the Ohio State Fair either, ♫ *Our state fair* ♫, the fact that our annual outing is usually the Longaberger Basket Building followed by ice cream at Young's Jersey Dairy and that's it, or Newark Mound if they're lucky, though I'm the only one who really gets a kick out of Indian mounds, the fact that Leo admits they're great feats of engineering, great feets, Ben running around without his shoes at Fallingwater, Fallingtears, Fallingcellphone, weeping, the fact that the Longabergers have sold the Basket Building now, and it doesn't have anything to do with baskets anymore, I don't think, which is sort of silly, I mean, to have this great big *basket* sitting there for no reason, the fact that I bet those office workers have no idea why they have to work in a basket, or maybe they don't even notice anymore, like, if you asked them, "ast 'em," what it's like to work inside that basket, they'd say "*What* basket?", the fact that the Longaberger company still *makes* baskets, and their baskets are still popular, but they've relocated the whole operation to Frazeysburg, the fact that I think Abby had a Longaberger basket, the fact that maybe Barry has it now, or he probably threw it out, the fact that a lot of people use Longaberger baskets as decorative baskets for flowers and such, the fact that they're not heavy-duty baskets or anything, but they're nice baskets, the fact that we went over to their new spot in Frazeysburg once, just to see what it's like, and they have a basket *monument* now instead of the Basket Building, the fact that the monument's supposed to look like a basket of apples, but it's nowhere near as good as the Basket *Building*, the fact that still, it's sort of fun to see such a giant basket of apples, like a basket of apples *belonging* to a giant, the fact that at least they made an effort, the fact that you should never get attached to things because they might change, or disappear, the fact that she ran away, sleeping bag, Mommy, broken, Brooklyn Bridge jigsaw, the fact that you used to be able to go to Longaberger's and make your *own* basket, the fact that maybe you still can, Joan Bennett, Wanger, the fact that her gun-toting stalker husband's name was Wanger, and he was a bigshot producer, the fact that Longaberger baskets are pretty crude compared to Gullah sweetgrass baskets, or traditional *Indian* basketry, the fact that Native Americans could make a basket so watertight you could boil vegetables in it, or make stew, Hopi, mesa, the fact that Longaberger baskets just look kind of nice stuffed with apples or chrysanthemums or something, or one of Abby's many houseplants, the fact that she took such good care of them, the plants, not so much the baskets, but I guess they survived and Barry's got them now, the fact that Abby had a green thumb, the fact that we did take the kids to the Circleville pumpkin parade that one time, though I don't know if it's really "The Greatest Free Show On Earth," as they claim it is, the fact that maybe they oughtta check with the *rest* of the earth about that, the fact that I bet the aurora borealis might have something to say on that score, the fact that there's no denying that the aurora borealis makes an effort, though I don't know if it's worth it for the result, Little Miss Pumpkins, bumpkin, bumper cars, *The Third Man*, Act III, VIDERE NON POSSUM, Peolia's college seal, the Possums, tree roots, the fact that the kids are suckers for roadside stands, or any roadside museum almost, the fact that they're maybe not nuts about Indian arrowheads and butter churns, but they're suckers for a warship made out of popsicle sticks, and they can look at no end of angel and fairy fossils, or fossils of god's fingerprints, or the apple that Eve ate, that somehow survived since the dawn of time and turned up in Ohio, Sherwood Anderson, the fact that they even swallow stories about how people used to saddle up T-Rexes and ride them around America, the fact that *I* liked that little museum we found once that just had all kinds of cloth in it, and a few Amish and African American quilts, the fact that the names of cloth sound like trees, taffeta, gingham, tweed, damask, calico, velvet, gingham, *gingham*, the fact that that's a good word, gingham, lima beans, the fact that the kids don't like lima beans or gingham *or* the Schoenbrunn Amish village, but they like canal trips, because of the mule, and they like hearing about the Flood of 1913, berms, "A man, a plan, a canal: Panama!", Lake Havasu City, the fact that Mommy and Daddy were always busy with their work, the fact that she was never at my disposal the way Fred MacMurray and Joan Bennett are for their family, the fact that "at my disposal" is kind of a frightening expression when you think about it, disposal unit, garbage disposal, disposable income, disposable panties, deposable leaders, the high swing, treetops, the fact that I don't like it when people say "one iota" either, but it doesn't seem to happen all that often anymore, the fact that the word "iota" will either be a success or a failure, but probably a failure, the fact that it's lucky nobody stopped Mommy writing her book, not me, not Phoebe and Ethan, not Daddy, not Grandpa, not Pepito, not the neighbors, not anybody, not even the Annual Northwestern University Faculty Summer Picnic, not one iota, the fact that she just quietly got on with it while we were at school, though we came back for lunch every day for our chicken noodle soup and tuna sandwich, the fact that I'd hate it if the kids all came home for lunch, though they'd probably be much safer here for an hour than at school, and that would be some compensation, but it would be quite a chore to drop everything and get them their lunch, school shootings, the fact that it was awful when that *house* exploded right across from the school, the fact that the poor woman had just gotten home and when she turned on the lights the whole darn place exploded, the fact that it's lucky it happened at night, not when all the kids were in school, the fact that we felt the shock waves all the way up here, the fact that everybody in Newcomerstown felt it, and everybody felt just awful for the woman, the fact that it's terrible to pass away like that, for no reason, though I guess most people pass away for no reason, the fact that there was no school the next day because both the elementary school and the high school were covered in debris, and *unreachable*, the fact that in *His Girl Friday* Rosalind Russell tells Cary Grant "I wouldn't cover the burning of Rome for you if they were just lighting it up," but they were good friends in real life, the fact that Cary Grant introduced Rosalind Russell to her husband, the fact that she died kind of young, which is a pity, the fact that Cary Grant introduced Katharine Hepburn to Howard Hughes too, the fact that I guess he was quite the matchmaker, arsonists, the fact that Jim was in that animal sanctuary fire, the poor thing, the fact that a guy in Sinking Spring, Pennsylvania, shot his wife and their three little kids, and then himself, all because she was leaving him, the fact that six shots were fired, one for their dog, oil pipelines, Sunoco, yelp, kelp, the fact that some people, the fact that the Sandy Hook parents now get death threats, the fact that what happened to compassion, the fact that maybe there never was any really, or did we lose it somewhere, the fact that American women are sixteen times more likely to be shot dead than women in other equivalent countries, CAUTION EXOTIC ANIMALS, The Greatest Free Show on Earth, Newtown, Newcomerstown, Sandy Hook, Sand Creek, the fact that Sinking Spring was once a Lenape settlement, the first people, the fact that Cincinnati *sounds* like an Indian name but it *isn't*, as I was forever having to tell students, Moira, FOOSH, strudel, Tuesday, the fact that it's named after Cincinnatus, who was a farmer before they made him a dictator, the fact that I don't know why they named a big city after this guy, since all he wanted was to be in the *country*, country cousin, the fact that I wonder if he was ever called Cincy for short, Sin City, FLORENCE Y'ALL, the fact that eventually I think he did get back to farming, OshKosh B'gosh, Levi's, Hallmark, UPS,

FedEx, jogger, the fact that people live so long, you can do a lot of different jobs in a lifetime, the fact that Dorothy Parker lived *too* long, the fact that I gotta make some headway on these pies here, while the rolls rise, the fact that what was with that jogger and the high-tech *gas* mask, the fact that what's *that* all about, the fact that does this mean our *air's* getting as bad as our *water*, "Get ready! Get ready! The *worr-uld* is coming to an end!", Columbus, the fact that after him came a kid chasing a squirrel, the fact that his parents must believe in the hydraulic approach to parenting, or else they want him to tone up his hunting skills, because they never said a thing to him, the selfie guy, Chicken McNuggets, the fact that animal abuse is linked to domestic violence, which is linked to terrorism, or something like that, ♬ *The thigh bone connected to the hip bone* ♬, X-rays, fracture, the fact that that's why the police should question *Willy*, Willoughby, Willy Wonka, the fact that that Chicken McNuggets guy murdered his parakeet first, just for fun, a pet he'd had for some time, the fact that I wonder how long he plotted the murder of the parakeet, or was it kind of a spur-of-the-moment thing like his other crimes, the fact that I hope Stace never has anything more to do with that guy, *Willy* I mean, the fact that he'll be threatening *her* next, not just our cats, the fact that I'd like to wring his neck, but I shouldn't say that, the fact that passive resistance is better, passive aggression, please pass the aggression, passed on, the past, hummus, posthumous, the fact that I don't know why some people want their cars to sound like motorcycles, the fact that it's *so noisy*, the fact that I can still hear one now that must be miles away, truck dream, the fact that I dreamt about a bumble bee that was wearing goggles and riding a miniature motorcycle, the fact that half our neighbors have car alarms too, that go off for no reason all day long, six shots, the fact that every year at airports they confiscate thousands of guns people are carrying in their hand luggage, and most of them are *loaded*, the fact that they don't catch every one of them either, the fact that people bring knives and grenades on board too, and gun powder, probably *palm oil* too, and some whey, the fact that for all the stuff they manage to confiscate, some of

865

it's getting on the planes unnoticed, hand luggage, fake-grenade cig-arette lighter, the fact that that is why I wish Leo was here right now and never had to take another plane and get his throat cut by some-body with a *lipstick* knife, or a box knife or a martial arts throwing knife or a "stick knife" hidden in a cane, the fact that I need some mitti attar, the fact that it's supposed to be very calming, mitti attar, not a stick knife, blasphemy, the fact that sometimes they *kill* you for blas-phemy in Pakistan, the fact that a Pakistani boy cut off his own hand because he'd *accidently* blasphemed in a mosque, by raising his hand at the wrong moment when he was dozing off during a sermon or something, sentencing-mitigation videos, Pakistan, Kazakhstan, Partition, the fact that is it blasphemous to wonder if Partition was such a good idea, parturition, the fact that the English went around the world carving countries up, India, Hong Kong, Canada, Gibraltar, Ireland, the BBC, St. Patrick's Day, Chicago, the fact that it was so kind of Mommy to go along with my sick act when I didn't feel like going to school, the fact that once she took my temperature and I sneakily put the thermometer on the radiator to make sure went high, and she never said anything, the fact that the thermometer must've read 200° or something, the fact that I don't know how she kept a straight face, the fact that I just never wanted to *leave* her, the fact that I loved my mommy, the fact that I felt so much *safer* at home, high swing, glass in my foot, thorns, horses, trampoline, slumber parties, bus accident, hurt finger, the fact that I always felt a sense of doom when leaving the house, and I'm still bad at leaving the house, the fact that maybe it's why I had all these kids, to ensure I'd never have to leave the old homestead again, or hardly ever, though I do have to leave the house on their *behalf* an awful lot, to meet all their extracur-ricular and mall needs, and whatnot, the fact that Suzanne hates going outside so much she quit her job and now she's renting out her attic on Airbnb, and says it's the best thing that ever happened to her, because she loves ironing, the fact that that's all she does now, iron sheets, and she's happy as a clam, the fact that there's nothing she likes better than ironing sheets, the fact that I wish she'd come do *ours*, ironing pile, Leo's shirts, dry cleaning, the fact that Jane Fonda would approve of this, because she says in middle age women find their true vocations, like ironing, the fact that what if you run an Airbnb attic and you get *bedbugs* though, and you have to throw everything out and start all over again, ironing, attics, cougars, Chuck, green red white blue, the fact that Gillian's kind of scared of being away from home too long too, kind of like me, the fact that she's not great on slumber parties, the fact that I liked them but they always made me a *little* nervous, the fact that moms hand these anxieties down, all your traits and vices, the fact that Leo gets furious when people misspell "vise" as "vice," the fact that you put a piece of wood in a *vise*, not a vice, vase, Vale, the Vales of Boston, the fact that spelling mistakes drive Leo berserk, the fact that he's much better at grammar and spelling than me, the fact that he would've gotten along well with Mommy, enormity, the fact that Phoebe and I would eat our tuna sandwiches in the nook, looking out on the buttercups, the swing and the mulberry tree, the fact that everything's "ours" when you're a kid, our nook, our dog, our buttercups, "Is there anything in the world that doesn't belong to you?", the fact that you forget it really all belongs to your parents, who might suddenly up and sell it and move somewhere else without asking you, just like they got rid of my *tricycle* without my permission, the fact that parents are always throwing out all your stuff, and I do it to *my* kids, when I can get around to it, poor Jim, the fact that what's he doing now, ah, just sitting, the fact that he just needs a calm environment and he'll come around, terpenes, mitti attar, the fact that I really wanted her to choose the ten-week-old silver lab puppy, but it was kind of her to take pity on Jim, the fact that Pepito used to bark his head off and trample Mommy's snapdragons, running back and forth after the trash men in the alley, the fact that he must have been so mad that they kept coming *back* every week, despite all his efforts to frighten them, the fact that a man with cerebral palsy has been missing since Tuesday, the fact that "a devoted father" in New Philly just stabbed his wife thirty times right in front of their kids, on account of jealousy or something, like Joan Bennett's husband, the fact that Othello must be the saddest play ever, but why you would ever listen to advice from a guy like Iago, or kill your wife over a *handkerchief*, I mean, really, the fact that after a man kills his wife, the neighbors and people always say how cheerful she was, and how she liked playing Bingo or singing in church or taking the dog for a walk, and how much she loved her family, and then they shut up because they can't describe her any better than that, the fact that all they do is make her life sound so *paltry*, meaningless, all her strivings summed up in half a sentence, Bingo, charity work, crochet, snickerdoodles, the fact that it's almost like they want to make her seem small and insignificant, even while they praise her and offer their thoughts and prayers and so on, just so that they can push her aside and forget about her as fast as possible, and forget the pain of losing her too, the fact that I know they don't mean any harm but sometimes it's kind of awful, awfulous, depressing, the fact that they make it sound like nobody has a lasting impact on anything, the fact that it's just not true either, the fact that I've been thinking about Mommy *my whole life* even though she passed away years ago, the fact that I will always think about her, the fact that I've got that at least, though I wish I could remember more stuff, the fact that I came downstairs after my nap, feeling euphoric, and Mommy was a bit cold towards me, Flickr, the fact that we didn't go to Moundsville after all, on the way back from Fallingwater, the fact that there wasn't time, the fact that Grave Creek is one of the tallest mounds, but it's shrunk over the years, Shrunk Mills, shrunken mounds, Sinking Spring, the fact that when they measured it in 1838 it was sixty-nine feet tall, with a diameter of two hundred and ninety-five feet, and now it's about *sixty* feet tall and two hundred forty feet in diameter, the fact that it was constructed between 300 and 100 BCE, Ptolemy, Jainism, and it once had a moat all around it, but some excavators filled that in long ago, the fact that I don't know why, the fact that why would anyone ever get rid of a *moat*, the fact that there are seven hundred mounds in Ohio alone, and some of them are aligned with equinoxes and solstices, the fact that Serpent Mound is, the fact that I was going to tell the kids all this sort of stuff when we got there, but when I started telling them, Ben said he only wants to go see Ohio's highest peak, Campbell Hill in Bellefontaine, which is *fifteen hundred feet*, so I gave up, the fact that I guess they're too young to appreciate the mounds yet, the fact that Campbell Hill is *not* an Indian mound, the fact that maybe I talk about them too much, and they've gotten bored with the whole idea, like me with the aurora borealis, the fact that the ancient world doesn't appeal much to kids who just want VR, the fact that the *lowest* point in Ohio is in the very southwest corner, where the Ohio River hits Indiana, the fact that Ben was at a bit of a low point himself that day, what with losing his phone and his shoes and all, the fact that the Fallingwater yo-yo didn't seem to help much, banjo clock, the fact that Fred MacMurray's kids interrupt him, John Wayne, the fact that the Treaty of Greenville was signed on August 3rd, 1795, four types of fundamental force, gravity, electro-magnetic, electro-static, and nuclear, thirty cents, the fact that we went to the Chunky demo, and the kids got bored and started playing Frisbee instead, the fact that where was that, the fact that when they got home though, they collected branches and tried to play Chunky, which really made me happy, euphoria, the fact that Chunky involves stone hoops, or rings, and long sticks with leather pieces stuck on them, and you have to get one of the leather prongs to land inside the ring, "It's only a game anyway!", the fact that paw-paws are pollinated by flies and that's why their flowers stink a bit, the fact that flies like stinky stuff, the fact that I like the black seeds, a pig in a poke, holy wars, crucifixes, purple flowers, the fact that this environment is all we've got, the sun, the moon, and the earth, and the *Pope* approves of protecting it too, the Lenape, the Hopewell People, the Adena people, Early Woodland, the fact that that always makes them sound like fairies or something, "Early Woodland," like tiny forest people coming out of their fairy doors, but they weren't fairies, the fact that Early Woodland people were trading copper here thousands of years ago, the fact that they migrated every summer to the beach, GONE FISHIN', the fact that Native Americans grew the Three Sisters on mounds surrounded with marigolds, the fact that the marigolds protected the crops, but they also look nice, the fact that it takes thousands of years to get this stuff right, to get this all set up, to *understand* all this stuff, while playing Chunky on the side, and now everything they knew or ever did is forgotten or destroyed and all *we* know about is machines and VR and centrifugal force and grenades and tardigrades and pineapple upside-down cake, or that's all *I* know about anyway, plus the word "hydrangea," but I don't always know that, the fact that pineapple upside-down cake *is* a pretty-looking cake, but I think people just like it because it gets flipped over, the fact that I always thought Baked Alaska sounded more amazing, earthquake cake, the fact that I don't know for *sure* why they planted those marigolds, the fact that I'm none too clear on gardening things, agriculture, horticulture, the Trail of Tears, the fact that Benjamin Franklin spoke up for the Iroquois Confederacy, calling it a model of good government, the fact that it's the oldest form of democracy in the world, the *worr*-uld, thousands of years old, Sheffield Lake, 911, the fact that we killed Lake Erie, the fact that it used to have whitefish, bass, trout and pickerel in it before it died, passed away, vale of tears, Miss Vale, Camille, the fact that this whole area used to be full of bears, wolves, bison, mountain lions, and wild turkeys too, but not anymore, the fact that now all we've got is joggers and joy-riders, the fact that at least we're safe from grizzlies, the fact that I wouldn't like finding a grizzly outside, the fact that somebody said on the radio that "the rarely seen skunk" makes a delicious meal, the fact that, landsakes, if they're so rare, why are you *eating* them, the fact that you could just *look* at them, black and white, raccoons, striped tail, bandit mask, the fact that what we've done to animals, the fact that skunks have it all figured out, like stink bugs, stink badgers, polecats, ♫ *I'm a lonesome polecat* ♫, "feminized polecat," "ladyfriend hound dog," the fact that it would be quite handy to have a terrible stink, stink bombs, the fact that maybe it would keep Ronny at arm's length, the fact that you should carry a *stink* spray in your purse, made out of garbage or something, stink bugs, the fact that a car just went by and coughed out so much black smoke I'm *choking* here in the kitchen and the window isn't even open, Poo-Poo Plate, ptooey, Ptolemy, the fact that it's not good for the pies either, the fact that we seem to be under threat from all sides, the fact that not everything is ruined though, *outside* I mean, the fact that there are still sunsets, and clumps of glossy greasy buttercups glowing like neon in the sun, and green things all around, the fact that the bees still like lavender, the fact that the birds still come and go, and there are still equinoxes and solstices, the fact that there's the annual dogwood bonanza, if you *like* dogwood, and the Circleville pumpkin festival, the fact that some of those pumpkins are really something, they are so *huge*, *like* that beautiful pale green one we saw, the fact that there are lady slippers, each with a protective petal on top so rain doesn't get in, the fact that there is something so innocent and hopeful and *certain* about a lady slipper orchid, certain of its job, but maybe all flowers have that certainty, the fact that they all come equipped to cope, the fact that flowers are the original *preppers*, "*Molloy*, Jack?", the fact that I dreamt I was given a seafood salad, and in it were two little albino terrapins, a pale green, sort of *neon* green, and I just couldn't bring myself to eat them, so I put them on the window sill in the kitchen and they started walking around, and I was so relieved I hadn't eaten them *alive*, the fact that then I wanted to keep them as pets, so I was looking around for a bowl or a tank to keep them in, the fact that I also dreamt about a huge sinister water-snake monster that became just visible in some bay, the fact that it had a big head and it could grab children and there was a girl skipping near me, but I didn't dare warn her about the snake because you're not supposed to talk to kids you don't know, the fact that then I dreamt I was tired out from making omelets for a big crowd, and we had a cow and some window cleaners, the fact that every building in America is so ugly, apart from the tipis and the adobe caves in New Mexico, and maybe log cabins, and a few Frank Lloyd Wright and Sullivan things sprinkled around the Midwest, the fact that the Auditorium Theatre in Chicago was built to house the opera, but then the El moved in right next door and squashed that whole plan, Fanny's Restaurant, salads, Oak Park, Taliesin East, Taliesin West, the fact that Frank Lloyd Wright only made $8,000 on Fallingwater, releasing liquid, bottles of pee,

.　　.　　.　　.

Another rifle shot, and it was she who crawled and cowered through the forest. With a pain in her side, she stumbled. Another bang, another jolt and more pain, this time deep in her shoulder. She subsided listlessly onto the ground. Was she dying?

She was helpless when the men approached. She growled but her growl was weak and did not quell them. Their bold manner angered her, but she could do nothing. She tried to rise up to strike them but couldn't move her limbs.

They dragged her by her hind legs and tail through dirt and ferns and across sharp stones. Clumsily, they yanked her into a cold metal cave, which she knew from the smell was a car, currently at rest. Cars often slept this way. A harsh chemical smell surrounded her, once she was shut inside. But she was still alive.

When the thing began to move, it was the first time she had heard a car up close. It roared at her and would not stop, its voice impossible to outdo. The metal area in which she lay was swaying and jerking. She was shaken by its tremblings, and affronted by the rattling sounds it made. Helplessly, she rolled from side to side as the car swerved and juddered along the highway. She was being carried somewhere, and sensed the miles being covered.

The car's unpredictable movements made her dizzy. She pawed weakly at some wall panels that flapped beside her, but it was like a dream: she could not get force into her claws. Nor could she find a way of clinging on to the cold uneven floor, so she slid to the back until her body was crumpled in a corner. She tried to gnaw a hole in the back door, but her teeth didn't work either.

To calm herself, she purred. She fell asleep and dreamt of mountain lions who looked horribly human: to her surprise, they had small human ears on the side of their heads, and long, clumsy man feet.

The lone driver of the car fell asleep too. The car veered first to the right, then left, then bumped over the grassy divide of the highway and crossed in front of cars coming the other way. The man woke up just in time to steer around a big-rig truck, but the maneuver sent his car into a skid. It bashed through a metal barrier and pitched itself into a wooded gully, spilling the driver out on the first bump. The car then twirled downwards, flipped over and was brought to a stop by a sapling.

A moment of calm followed. The car's helter-skelter descent of the hill had sent the lioness spinning. She was now awake. The back hatch was ajar. Escape. The sound of a train whistle blew. She knew those large metal snakes that rattled and wailed through the night when she was out on the hunt. She struggled heavily towards the opening at the back of the car and leapt.

She grabbed on to the earth. Her land.

Bruised and bloody, and strangely weak, she limped on three legs through a wide meadow of willows and ferns, in a hurry to get far from men. Gradually, her movements became more agile. She was herself again, alone, with cubs to find.

.   .   .   .

the fact that now James can't be friends with Ben anymore, because we failed the house inspection, the fact that I didn't like that woman anyway, James's mom, Buttinsky, Lewinsky, my me-oh-mys, my oh my, *mamma mia*, the fact that her decision's a relief really, to *me* anyway, maybe not Ben, the fact that I bet she'd be pretty tricky to deal with long-term, if you could *find* her, that is, in your own house, the fact that maybe that's what's bugging Ben, though he didn't say anything, the fact that he seemed sort of subdued all evening but he didn't complain or get mad at *me*, the fact that I think he was just kind of stunned, stunned to be shunned, shunpiking, the fact that children are a lot harder to console after the age of eight, the fact that everything gets more complicated, the fact that I *hate* that Fresia for doing this to Ben, and now I can't sleep, the fact that it's now 2:47, the fact that the Amish "shun" each other sometimes and it sounds even worse than the Silent Treatment, the fact that they act like you've got serious cooties or something, dandruff, floof, the fact that Leo turns out to hate the new toilet paper as much as I do, the fact that it just sort of *disintegrates* on you, the fact that who invented and approved a toilet paper like that, the fact that I'm traumatized by that toilet paper, the fact that I suppose that's a little extreme, when half the world has no toilet at all, the fact that you try to think the best of people but with people like Fresia it's a little hard, the fact that she really gets under my skin, Nike, Keds, Converse, the fact that 36,000 people died of gunshots in 2015, the fact that I only bought that toilet paper because they were out of Charmin, and it was cheap, the fact that I didn't like it, but I've been trying to get through it, but now it turns out neither of us can take it anymore so we're going back to Charmin, the fact that I'll just keep the cheap stuff as a backup, fall-back, fall back, spring forward, crown die-back, the fact that Abby always had Charmin, Mommy and Abby's overhang or underhang toilet-paper argument, underhand, "Unhand me, Sir!", a bird in the hand, blasphemy, the fact that I've got too many pillows here, the fact that what did I expect, the fact that *I* made the bed, the fact that they're like a *milk mountain*, mouth feel, the fact that they'll be putting milk and palm oil in toilet paper next, for skin feel, sheets, ironing, lion, the fact that there's some joke about a guy who dreams he's eating a great big marshmallow and he wakes up and finds his *pillow's* gone, firenado, forest fires, fireflies, the fact that I often think I see fireflies in the night but it's just a trick of the light, the fact that I think they come out mostly at dusk and, anyway, it's still too soon for them, May, plant out the nasturtiums, Paul Henreid, *Deception*, his cello, the fact that Claude Rains is supposed to be a great composer, whatshisname, *ménage à trois*, the fact that it's *Hollenius*, the fact that it makes no sense Bette shoots Hollenius, considering he's the only guy in America willing to give her husband an even break, the fact that Bette's just too impatient, the fact that shooters are, the fact that she wants a quick fix, and you just wanna yell "*Sleep* on it, lady!", things'll look different in the morning, let it be, wait and see, live and let live, an eye for an eye, "a tooth for a toothbrush," ashes, mush, insomnia, Mommy, but Bette's in turmoil, turnpike, tollbooth, *The Phantom Tollbooth*, tormented by the threat of Paul Henreid finding out about her and Hollenius, the fact that it really isn't that big of a deal but it eats at her, and she can't rest until she sorts it out, with a *gun*, which turns the whole movie into a *crime* drama all of a sudden, the fact that what's a pianist doing with a gun anyway, the fact that Hollenius has been driving her bananas, though, with all his insinuations and threats, innuendo, innundo, but half the time he's just *kidding around*, he's just teasing her, and she takes it too seriously, mountains out of molehills, the fact that teasing Bette Davis when she's in love is maybe not the greatest idea to come down the pike, idear, the fact that it's like teasing a cornered lion, lioness I mean, and finally she can't take it anymore and lashes out, *It's Complicated*, the fact that she got Hollenius all wrong though, the fact that, sure, he's jealous, and kind of taken aback about her suddenly getting married, but he'll *adjust*, if everybody would just settle down, the fact that he already *has* adjusted a bit, musically anyway, and taken Paul Henreid under his wing, fact that he's letting Paul play his brand new cello concerto at its first performance in New York, which'll be broadcast live on the radio, *The Apartment*, the fact that that's more than most men would do for their love rival, the fact that people took the radio more seriously in those days too, srsly, the fact that when Fresia called up to say it was all off, I actually said "Seriously, Fresia?", but that was about it, and she didn't give any reason, the fact that at least I remembered her dumb name for once, the fact that what I should have said was "Well, string me up and call me Charlie!", because she's just being so darn foolish, the fact that Bette's plan to shoot Hollenius is really pretty selfish if you think about it, the fact that she's prepared to sacrifice everything and everyone, Hollenius, herself, *and* Paul, just so he never has to know she had an affair, the fact that she got involved with Hollenius when she thought Paul Henreid had already died in a concentration camp, "I *saw* you lying there," the fact that it's pride really, vanity, and just kinda overdoing things, taking everything too hard, Gribble, making mountains out of molehills, mole rats, Mallrat, the fact that she's a little scared of Paul Henreid too, because of his jealous rages, like Joan Bennett's husband, estranged, the fact that why can't we all just behave like grown-ups, the fact that I don't know why Fresia couldn't tell me what we did wrong, the fact that now I have to wonder about this forever, along with what she was doing going through my drawers, jealousy, envy, regret, the fact that maybe she's a kleptomaniac, the fact that maybe she's *tri*-polar, or *quadri*-polar, numeral prefixes, bucket lists, bullet points, love hearts, I ♥ U, the seven wonders of the world, the fact that you wish they'd all just calm down, I mean Bette and Hollenius and all, Jesuits, cartridge pens, Hindustanis, and everything would be okay, but none of them ever do calm down, the fact that the nicest moments are all at the beginning, when Paul Henreid and Bette find each other and they sit around the apartment together, just being in love, the fact that Paul Henreid's so injured and melancholy, hurt, Davina Beebee's hurts, the fact that he's just been in a Nazi concentration camp and he's easily crushed, cello, the fact that you just want to make things better for him, and Bette does to, but everything gets out of hand, and so does the movie a little, just at the end there, the fact that apparently they all wanted to end it more ambiguously, but the Hays Office or somebody wouldn't allow it, the SRC, because Bette had obviously had an affair with Hollenius, and with *Paul*, before the war, and unmarried sex was not allowed, the fact that she's going down, the fact that her life has to be completely ruined by the end of the movie, all because she had two love affairs before she got married, the fact that she takes everybody else down with her, the fact that she shoots Hollenius and ruins Paul Henreid's solo career, his future, their future, because who'll want to hire him now, a cellist caught in a scandal, the fact that it's a pity, because Claude Rains gets so excited earlier on when he's deciding what they're all going to have at the restaurant, "The wood cock!", my wood pigeon egg, the fact that he's just an old gourmand really, not an *ogre*, the fact that he doesn't need to be *killed*, the fact that the

Hays Office didn't like sedition, ridicule of the clergy, miscegenation, blasphemy, and about a hundred other things, Darwin, fossil record, the fact that Ohio passed a law in 1913 saying movies weren't entitled to *free speech*, and it was upheld by the Supreme Court in 1915, the fact that they decided the First Amendment didn't stretch to movies, and that was that for the movies, Sunoco, DuPont, tobacco companies, the fact that even *Betty Boop* had to tone it down, Paul Henreid on the cello, the fact that I always like their first reunion, after his concert, Paul Henreid's reunion with Bette Davis, not Betty Boop, the fact that it reminds me of seeing Leo again, after he got away from Cold Sally, the fact that the wait was hard though, *There's a place in France where the naked ladies dance*, the fact that I spent my whole entire adolescence being rejected by boys, the fact that they were always failing to turn up and stuff, the fact that I kept thinking they'd all had *bike accidents* or something, the fact that boys don't appreciate you when you're young and then, when you're *older*, the only thing men seem to want to talk about is young women, well, not *Leo* but other men, men on TV, the fact that there's a disconnect there somewhere, the fact that in *It's Complicated*, Alec Baldwin's married to a much younger woman with a very demanding kid, Pedro, though kind of an great kid actually, maybe a little ADHD, lithium, Ritalin, the fact that the young wife wants even more kids, and she seems a little ADHD herself, "Agness Adler's husband!", the fact that Alec admits he's a walking cliché, the fact that they're using a fertility clinic and if it works, Alec with be like seventy-nine before the kid graduates, the fact that he'll be seventy-four when Pedro graduates too, the fact that he's bored with the second marriage and really wishes he was back with his ex, Meryl Streep, who's fun and makes croques monsieur just the way he likes them, the fact that I like that Alec Baldwin, the fact that he's so keen on Meryl Streep, and he's pretty convincing as a guy who's realized marrying a much younger woman is not necessarily such a great idea, and life is sweeter with Meryl than with the younger beauty he's stuck with, the fact that Alec Baldwin's sweeter with Meryl, the fact that Meryl's really beautiful, the fact that some people

877

stay beautiful forever, but you shouldn't talk about people's appearances, because nobody can really help what they look like, "What you need is a brow lift," Marilyn Monroe's chin, the fact that in *real* life, right after playing that role, or only a few years after, Alec Baldwin went and married someone half his age, and had three kids with her, one right after another, self-defense, taekwondo, the fact that it's like he learnt nothing at all from being in that movie, the fact that it's different though, because apart from Meryl, who's he going to meet, the fact that the only women a movie star probably meets are young beauties, Trump, the fact that how is this my business, who Alec Baldwin meets or who he should fall in love with, pillows, MYOB, PTA, Wo-He-Lo, the fact that his real life wife is big on yoga, the fact that what is the matter with me, the fact that, for all I know, Alec Baldwin's new wife may be just like Meryl Streep and great at making croques monsieur, the fact that I think Meryl Streep's already taken anyway, Work, Health, Love, the fact that "Wo-He-Lo" was Mommy's favorite greeting, the fact that I learnt it at Campfire Girls and came home with it and she started using it too, Wo-He-Lo, "Ducky! Ducky!", the fact that about the most exciting thing we ever did in Campfire Girls was make homemade candles in the school kitchen once, at twilight, the fact that I kind of enjoyed that, the fact that I'd never thought about how candles get made before, so I was sort of stunned by that, the fact that I haven't thought all that much about it since, but I'm glad I know the rudiments, rutabaga, the fact that the boiling-hot wax scared me, the fact that I think the teacher, or club leader woman, poured the wax into the molds for us, the fact that we were too young to handle that, checkers, camp beds, the fact that we got to take our own candles home, Palmolive, barn owl, cigarette holder, the fact that as a kid you think all these afterschool activities are about the *activity*, but maybe they're just about getting you out of the house, teaching you independence, and giving moms a break, apart from the club leaders, the fact that people are always trying to separate you from your *mom*, communal cooperation, communes, kibbutzim, orphanages, the fact that I'd really only joined the

Campfire Girls to go camping, the fact that I assumed, from like the *name*, that Campfire girls were always going camping, the fact that I don't know what I thought camping was going to be like, but I was convinced I'd like it, the fact that I never really *have* liked camping, the few times I've ever gone camping, the fact that maybe I don't really want to be part of nature, or not *that* much a part of it anyway, the fact that the damp and the pebbles get me down, and stop me appreciating the dawn chorus and the toasted marshmallows, the fact that what is that sort of *scratching* sound, raccoons in the crawl space maybe, our quiggly hole, or else it's the Kinkels' wind chimes, biped, quadruped, "Quatuor pour la fin du temps," Stalag VIII-A, Carl-Albert Brüll, "Le réveil des oiseaux," the fact that I wonder what birds make of wind chimes, the fact that I used to like the sound of wind chimes as a kid, but now it depends on the wind chimes, the fact that I guess I can take wind chimes or leave them, the fact that the one and only time my Campfire Girl troop went camping, I got pinkeye and couldn't *go*, the fact that conjunctivitis is so contagious nobody in the family would to come near me either, except Mommy, the fact that I felt like a *leper*, and had to have my *own separate towel* and everything, the fact that Mommy made fudge with me to cheer me up, Brüll, but I missed out on that camping trip, and they never had another one, the fact that I was all packed and ready to go too, the fact that we were all going to meet in a parking lot and get the bus from there, and I still remember that parking lot, the fact that it was kind of out of the way somewhere, but every time we drove by it from then on, I thought about the camping trip I'd missed, B009, styptic stick, magnetism, the fact that most schools have lockdowns now, and they have to expel people all the time for making threats, the fact that Stacy says kids are used to it, the fact that they report the graffiti if it sounds suspicious, but there's not much else kids can do about school shootings except get shot in one, the fact that she says some of her friends say they think it would be *cool* to be in a school shooting, as long as you didn't get shot, the fact that some little boys in Columbus watched vampire movies last Hallowe'en and decided to try to kill some of the kids in their class and drink their blood, but somebody found out about their plan and they were stopped in time, the fact that they had their chalice ready for the blood and everything, goblet, pizza cutter, *A-tisket, a-tasket*, a basket, ax, onyx, ox, oxen, jade, manicotti, cannelloni, the fact that in the tropics giant ants carry off your nail clippings for you, the fact that I think that would be a real help, the fact that I wonder what they do with them, make bookshelves or something, the fact that *that's* what James Mason's got in *Bigger Than Life*, polyarteritis nodosa, the fact that he's got a pain chart, black-and-white, brown and turquoise, the fact that Mommy didn't approve of blue and brown together, and maybe pink and yellow too, the fact that I agree with her on that, but not about blue and green, Carole Lombard, oh, time to turn over, my hand on Leo's chest, my honey, the fact that I love to listen to him sleep, the chickens, the fact that organic eggs sell for $8 a dozen and non-org sell for maybe half that but I don't mind, as long as the chickens are happy, egg shortages, the fact that chickens stop laying in winter if it's very cold, and they don't lay too well in very hot weather either, and they stop laying when they molt too, but we still get plenty of eggs, all in all, the fact that molting takes about six weeks, the fact that we now have seven seven-year-old chickens, six six-year-olds and two two-year olds, which is quite a coincidence, Nebuchadnezzar, Wyandottes, Easter Eggers and Orpingtons, and Jim likes them all, the fact that I hope he's okay out there, the fact that I don't know what he makes of raccoons, Jimmy, the fact that he gets over-excited at the Parents' Night, James Mason, not Jim the *dog*, and he tells the PTA woman that they're all breeding a race of moral midgets, the fact that a lot of animals know how to climb trees, the fact that I just dreamt about someone taking a daredevil ride in a wheelchair and he scared a horse, which jumped straight up in the air in slow motion, kind of like levitation, the fact that I found this very funny and I laughed *too much*, and then realized in the dream that it was probably nervous laughter about the guy's wheelchair, because even in the dream I knew that wheelchairs have always made me nervous ever since Mommy had to have one, the fact that then I woke up, the fact that I don't think I was asleep for more than about five minutes, and now here I am again, tossing and turning, the fact that they found excess calcium, magnesium, sulfate, iron, arsenic, boron, barium, cadmium, chromium, and selenium in on-site groundwater at the Conesville power plant south of Coshocton, ash pond complex, the fact that the aurora borealis makes whales beach themselves, so it's not just me, schnitz pie, snitch, 9/11, Angels on Horseback, Wyandottes, Easter Eggers and Orpingtons, *The Addams Family*, *The Beverly Hillbillies*, molasses popcorn balls, molassed, "But you're ignoring the importance of the Dahlberg repercussions," Watergate, Pussygate, the fact that maybe we've been watching *All the President's Men* too much, the fact that Nixon knowingly kept the Vietnam war going an extra *ten years*, just so Johnson wouldn't get the credit, the fact that that has to be a *war crime*, the fact that Leo says Nixon should've gone to jail, not just quit, the fact that Chris Christie kept hundreds of kids stuck on a bridge, reinforced concrete, in school buses, just to take revenge on some political rival, the fact that now that is just horrible, using other people's children to play a trick on somebody, the fact that it's *kidnapping* really, the fact that Leo doesn't like any hold-ups on bridges, bridge-blocking, bridge protests, the fact that Trump's going to taunt North Korea into World War Three, the fact that he's probably being blackmailed by Russia, the fact that I wonder what they've got on him, the fact that you can't read the *Washington Post* online anymore without paying, Dustin Hoffman, the fact that Nixon let himself be blackmailed too, the fact that you really should step *down* if you're in *that* kind of a fix, the fact that you don't *have* to be president, *The Graduate*, plastics, the rubber industry, the fact that how did they *sleep* at night, those Watergate guys, Ulysses S. Grant, Hayes, the Hays Office, Garfield, Harrison, McKinley, Taft, Harding, maple taffy, German potato salad with dill in it, Ohio's lookalike drug law, the fact that Nixon was on all kinds of drugs, so I guess that's how *he* slept at night, beef and onion stew, grilled cheese, scallops, guacamole, avocado on toast, hitching posts, hazing, fraternities, cotton plantations, slaves, the fact that a firearm expels a projectile by the action of an explosive, Build Body, Build Mind, Build Freedom, ♫ *Don't sit under the apple tree* ♫, crying in the bathroom in Fort Lauderdale, the fact that Phoebe rescued me, North Korea, *Nevermore*, the Mason-Dixon line, Kiskiminetas, Muhulbuctitum, Conewango Creek, Seneca Oil, Sunoco, the fact that a mountain lion can leap thirty or forty feet in one bound, on the flat, the fact that I'd like to see that, the fact that if you drop an egg on the counter or the floor or someplace, and it's a big mess, you just put salt on it and in a minute you can wipe it all up, Edgar Allan Poe, Long Island Reds, the fact that salt gets rid of onion and garlic smells on your hands too, salt or sugar, or lemon too does that, the fact that peanut butter removes gum from hair, but then you have peanut butter in your hair instead, Hair & Now, dem bones, swallowed a fly, I don't know why, the fact that Coke cleans drains, because it contains phosphoric acid, the fact that they say rubbing on a paste of butter and cigar ash can hide rings on tables, but I've never tried it, the fact that you have to buff vigorously in a *circular motion*, the fact that the way to get wax off a tablecloth is by, by, bye, the fact that I like the way Carole Lombard says "Bye," in *To Have and Have Not*, no, *To Be or Not to Be*, the fact that I just dreamt a black-and-white dog had to swim home through arctic waters and he made it, by swimming twenty feet *under* the icebergs, in the middle of the night, the poor dog, the fact that then I was working as a dishwasher at an outdoor fair and I was just feeding the dog some tidbits off the plates, and his owner was talking to somebody, and that was how I heard about the dog's heroic swim, and then I woke up, *again*, the fact that New York denied a chimp human rights, but what does New York know about chimps, the fact that they're digitizing all the books in the world, and Leo says we'll be left with incomplete books full of errors, that people can alter whenever they feel like it, rulers and people like that, the fact that he says the electronic world has been a total disaster for humanity, the fact that we have four different copies of *Moby-Dick* around here and I don't know why, one per kid I guess, the fact that people really don't read much nowadays, well, not books anyway, the fact that I know they read stuff on their phones and all, the fact that everybody just watches TV and looks at porno pics, the fact that I have bad dreams if I watch violent movies last thing at night, the fact that even David Attenborough's plant show gives me bad dreams sometimes, the fact that last week, after watching *Die Hard 2*, I had *two* bad dreams, the fact that in the first one I dreamt Jake grew fifteen feet overnight, the fact that *Bad Dream 2* was about a monster that people were secretly providing with honey, the fact that the monster had emerged from a swamp and needed honey bad, to maintain his scary supernatural powers, and some people were on *his* side, the fact that he had a very frightening open mouth in profile, kind of like that tennis player after he wins a point at Wimbledon, the fact that a little boy befriended the monster, the monster in my dream, not the one at Wimbledon, and I had to try and talk the boy out of giving the monster honey, which would only help the monster do more bad stuff, the fact that then I had to find a lot of people a safe house to hide in, and we were all holed up in this ancient house, and the walls were actually trembling when the monster walked by, the fact that then some suspicious-looking neighbors were taking off on a trip in their convertible and I pointedly asked them if they had any honey with them in their car, but they wouldn't answer, the fact that at the same time there were some important *box files* I had to find in the house but, when I got to them, they were all empty and messed up, the fact that I had quite a central role in the whole dream, the fact that somehow I seemed to know about everything that was going on all over the place and it was all up to *me* to save everybody, and I was just running around doing all this stuff, the fact that it was my job to handle the boy, the honey monster, the couple in the convertible, the safe house, *and* all the paperwork, the fact that when I told Leo my dream, he said it sounded like he ought to help out more around the house, the fact that the bit I liked best actually was holding the squirmy little boy in my arms while I tried to convince him not to side with the honey monster, because it reminded me of Jake, *The Apartment*, the fact that there are some galoshes in *The Apartment*, the fact that I just remembered, the fact that the switchboard operator leaves her galoshes behind, Mr. Sheldrake, Mr. Kirkeby, Mr. Dobisch, goodtime girl, "Octoberwise," Conotton Creek, Chippewa Creek, Hoagland Run, Mohawk Creek, Postboy Creek, Opossum Run, Goettge Run, Brandywine Creek, Nimishillin Creek, the Monongahela, Mud Run, Oldtown Creek, Buckhorn Creek, Lick Run, Blue Ridge Run, Evans Creek, the Walhonding River, the Muskingum, Moxahala Creek, Soggy Run, soggy pizza, pizza knife, the fact that underage sex slaves are bought and sold by powerful men, the fact that people do such things, Sand Creek, Evans Creek, the fact that Evans and Chivington were friends, the fact that Chivington's men mutilated the bodies of the Cheyenne, but he always defended the massacre and eventually ran for office in *Ohio*, Methodism, the fact that what's that song, the fact that having a good memory isn't everything, or that's what Declan Kiberd sort of said, Filipino maid, Saudi Arabia, Kurz-Kasch, Chilly Willy's, do-do, caca, dander, cowcatcher, Jane Fonda, penis, penile dysfunction, extruded polymer solutions, the fact that the Hackenbrachts sell twenty-five thousand candy apples a *day*, while I make a few dozen tartes tatin a week, gee whiz, Jiminy Cricket, jaywalkers, jayhawkers, the Seattle Seahawks, seersucker, muckrakers, bushwackers, carpetbaggers, bootleggers and red legs, How to Make Your Eyes Smoky, Ohio like a petal, eBay, stars, potatoes, cranberries, peas, embarrassing kinds of cancer, *Poor Jeoffry! Poor Jeoffry!*, Family Therapy, Adam Lanza, guacamole, Revere Ware, ducks, Newburyport, the fact that even though flies have all those eyes, they still crash into you, the fact that what's the deal there, the fact that everybody got so sick of the FFF and all the other lion hunters, they offered a $10,000 reward for bringing the lion in alive, but nobody's managed to do it and collect the $10,000, so now they've hired a real tracker guy, the fact that he's the big hope now, the fact that he seems to know what he's doing too, the fact that he plans to track her *on foot*, the fact that it's a "she," he says, the fact that it's a *lioness*, the fact that some bounty hunters actually caught her somewhere but then they *lost* her, the fact that this lion chase will either be a success or a failure, the fact that they *had* him, then they lost him again, or her, the fact that it escaped, the fact I hope it's the same lion and not some *new* one, the fact that we sure don't need a *dozen* of them out there, the fact that some hunters or FFF guys caught it and one of them was driving it to the zoo, but the car crashed, the fact that at first everybody assumed the lion must be dead, but when they reached the car there was no sign of it, the fact that when these people bungle, they go all out, the fact that the fortunately driver survived the crash, but the lion did too, and now it's disappeared again, the fact that they *had* it, the doofuses, and they lost it, so now all the curfews are back in place and we've still got a Code Red, lion on the loose, the fact that, wow, I mean, for Pete's sake, seriously guys, FFF, FLORENCE Y'ALL, the fact that, the fact that, the fact that no wonder I can't *sleep*,

·   ·   ·   ·

The lioness rested near a quiet creek for days. She licked her sore front leg, slept, and licked her leg some more. When hungry, she lurched closer to the creek to see if there were any water rats around – she couldn't hunt larger animals with a wounded leg.

As soon as she could stand for long, she resumed her search, walking on just three paws when she could.

Chained dogs barked at her, showing their teeth. She limped past them, mockingly close. They smelled her wounds and her weakness and longed to chase and bite her. One barked so long and viciously, while she shuffled around his yard looking for rodents, that a man in pajamas was drawn to the doorway of his den. He pointed at her with his gun. There was a jangling sound and a spark of light, but the lion was unharmed. She sprang swiftly sideways into the underbrush, while the frightened man scurried back indoors, leaving his dog to take his chances.

The smell of poultry lured her around the corner of a tall, dark house. Behind it, a glowing white tree loomed over her in full flower. Nearby was a miniature wooden cabin. She could already hear the chickens inside it, gently clucking to themselves. To reach them, she had to weave her way carefully around empty clay pots, hard plastic spades, buckets, baskets, and mud. She dodged a wood-slatted lounger, and a sharp-edged tricycle. An old vegetable steamer, round and outstretched like a wide leaf, twisted in a bush and briefly dazzled her as it caught the light from a window in the house.

Cautiously, the lioness proceeded, but was startled by a small, brown and white female cat sitting on the back steps. The cat paused to hiss bravely at the lioness, before dashing into the cramped crawl space beneath the house. She would be too hard to catch in there. Instead, the lioness sniffed half-heartedly at a shallow puddle of water, a bird bath, that lay in the middle of a patch of grass, but the water was stale.

Having reached the ornate chicken coop, she was about to leap on to the roof to see if there was any opening she could climb through, when a dog's high yelp startled her. The long wavering shrill tone, almost like a lion's scream, made the lioness jump high in the air. She landed awkwardly on the little ramp attached to the coop, which broke under her. She whirled around. Where was the source of this aggravating yelp?

The chickens were silent now, sensing danger. She crept around to the back of the yard and there, cowering beside a tree, at the very end of a long, extended rope, was a small, thin, black-and-white dog. The lioness considered attacking him, if only to put an end to that yelping. He would not have made much of a meal, but he would not have put up much of a fight either. She began to realize this dog was an oddity: loud but plaintive, not belligerent. He now collapsed before her, as if resigned to the swat of her stinging paw.

But the lioness had no interest in this trembling animal as food. All she wanted was a chicken or two, and then she would be gone. Another piercing hole of light now blazed out of the top floor of the house, half-hidden and flickering behind the big white flowering tree. Otherwise, all was still apart from the writhing dog.

The dog watched her disappear slowly into the trees. When he tried to follow her, he was jerked to a stop by his collar. He growled in frustration, and tried to gnaw at the rope, then swung it vigorously as he would a rabbit on the farm long ago. Still struggling with the string, he squirmed around, on his front and back, and rubbed at his clasped neck with his paws. Next, he tried backing directly away from the rope, holding himself low to the ground. The collar began to budge, and shifted along his head to the ears. With another hard tug and a cry of pain, he freed himself.

He chased after the lioness, whining and whimpering imploringly. She ignored him at first, a pest, a noise, irrelevant to her needs. But after half an hour of his yapping she finally turned to look at him. He spun himself in a tight circle for her and rolled on the ground to show he meant no harm.

He followed her at a distance for days, without reward. He lapped water along the way, but had nothing to eat. He was no hunter. He kept twenty paces behind, but didn't let the lioness out of his sight. She eyed him with disdain. When he got too close, she spat at him.

One day, the starving dog dug up a carcass the lioness had just buried. Normally, she would have been enraged by that, enough to tear him to shreds. But she had other priorities now. She wouldn't be needing old kills anyway, not with this tiring leg injury and the need to keep moving forward towards her cubs. So she left him to it.

She didn't see the dog for a day or two after that, but then he turned up, again walking twenty feet behind. She became used to his abject shadow and, once he took on some of her quietness, she stopped thinking about him at all.

·   ·   ·   ·

the fact that then I dreamt Leo told me there was some big explosion mentioned in the news, but I checked when I got up and there hasn't been any explosion anywhere, though we'll probably all be nuked any minute, the fact that in another dream I dreamt we were both eating lettuce sitting up in bed, and in another dream, the speed limit in Newcomerstown was nine miles per hour and it was so *pleasant*, the fact that it was like an instant improvement, the fact that then I dreamt about a cleaning aid that lights the bacteria up for you in *red*, so you can tell really easily exactly where you most need to clean, the fact that the space behind our fridge was all lit up, glowing red, so I was busily preparing to get things all cleaned up back there, and I should, I really should, the fact that things are getting so bad around here, even my *unconscious mind* is worrying about it, the fact that now if only I could just get my spinal brain to do the actual cleaning work, SCI, purge, semis, the fact that the suicide rate is up twenty percent on ten years ago, 40%, 80%, especially among middle-aged white guys, that black-and-white Donald Pleasence movie, the fact that maybe that movie I saw in the hospital after my heart operation was *Rebecca*, the fact that it was a little like that foggy stuff at the beginning, the fact that that was a strange movie for Hitchcock to make, but he used Daphne du Maurier stuff a lot, the fact that the original novel about Marnie was written by somebody else, another English writer, Leo listening to Messiaen, the fact that Mommy's dad gave all the bread away at the end of the day, donuts, dollars to donuts, the fact that Mommy and Abby didn't bake much, the fact that their dad probably put them off baking for life, the fact that if you can't take the heat, get out of the kitchen, the fact that if you step on a crack, you break your mother's back, the fact that I'm more likely to break my own, the fact that maybe it's "break *a* mother's back," the fact that Katharine Hepburn told Jane Fonda your failures are more interesting than your successes, but I don't know, the fact that I don't think most people's failures are all that great, the fact that Mommy was so disapproving of her dad's bakery troubles, the fact that the family was dependent on his income so they took it hard, I guess, whenever he lost his job, itch on my shoulder, tiny rattling sound, the fact that it's not the glassware, the fact that Mommy made good oatmeal and raisin cookies, though I got tired of them because they were the only kind of cookie she'd make, no eggnog snickerdoodles for us, the fact that now I'd like to eat them again, Mommy's oatmeal and raisin cookies, not eggnog snickerdoodles, the fact that I think Jake ate the last of the raisins though, the fact that I wish I had that recipe, the fact that it's probably in Irma, the fact that oatmeal and raisin were the only kind of cookie Mommy seemed to make for years, while I just wanted chocolate chip cookies like everybody else's mom made, ungrateful child, Voice of Young America, the fact that now I appreciate her good taste, and oatmeal and raisin cookies are probably a much healthier cookie than chocolate chip, hospital vending machine, New York, Neurology Department, the fact that of course the kids won't eat oatmeal and raisin cookies, the fact that they're just like me, and they want choc-olate chip cookies too, or choc-dipped madeleines, or *brownies*, the fact that they're always talking about brownies, just to make me mad, the fact that I don't make them, the fact that they get brownies at other people's houses, the fact that everything has to have chocolate in it, with them, the fact that I bet they'd be pretty surprised to see me now, Mommy and Abby, not the kids, with my chickens and my baking, the fact that it might all seem sort of out of left field to them, because neither of them baked much, p. chops, the fact that I've got an itch on my *chest* now, FEMEN, the fact that I don't know what *that's* all about, running around with bare chests, the fact that all they wear on their top halves are slogans and tattoos, the fact that most tattoo art is so ugly and you're stuck with it forever, the fact that all our kids want a tattoo now, the fact that I don't think they really mean it, not Jake, for Pete's sake, the fact that what would he get, a big **GUG** across his pretty *tummy* maybe, heaven help us, the fact that I better not give him any ideas, the fact that, no, he says he wants an army jeep tattooed on his *hand*, or one of those trucks with a big crane on it, or else a butterfly, the fact that I don't know if he means the insect or a butter-fly mower, butterfly doors, butterfly stroke, the crawl, butterflies in the stomach, farfalle pasta, bow ties, the fact that Nabokov collected butterflies, "(picnic, lightning)," the fact that I told the kids that if they really want tattoos they'll have to save their allowances, and I hope that puts an end to it, because I bet tattoos are pretty expensive, and my kids can't save their allowances to save their lives, not for one second, sieve, tea-strainer, the fact that Ben was so hopeless about saving for a new phone I had to give him a loan, because you *need* your kids to have phones, in case of trouble, Stacy's night on the road, diner, coffee, the fact that I wonder who the first person was who ever got tattooed, the fact that it probably happened by accident and was a bit of a shock, but gradually people decided they liked the idea, and now look at us, with our cobwebbed elbows and pop star faces all over our chests, and misspelt mottos in Sanskrit on our wrists and ankles, and guns and arrows and daggers, and Nazi emblems, and heart shapes, the fact that what about that guy who got his whole face tattooed to look like a *skull*, the fact that I don't know if he went the whole way and got a skeleton tattoo on his body too, skellington, Skull and Bones, the fact that that would cost you something, dollars and cents, sense, the fact that nothing's more chilling than the concentration camp tattoos, the fact that they give tattooing a bad name, the fact that somebody got a sort of photograph of his toddler son tattooed all over one whole side of his face, the dad's face, not the *son's*, luckily, the fact that now that kid will have to look at himself on his dad's cheek for the rest of his life, and watch it wiggle and stretch whenever his dad bites into a hamburger or chugs a beer, the fact that maybe the dad'll adorn the other side of his face with the kid at six or twelve or something too, and the kid at twenty-two on his forehead, and on and on until the poor dad's body's just one big photo album of his son, or more like a bulletin board, I guess, or like our *fridge*, the fact that I've got to weed some of that stuff out, the fact that they're all getting kind of grubby now, the fact that I hate to think how much it might *hurt*, getting *tattooed* I mean, not thinning out the old grocery lists on the fridge, the fact that is he going to get himself tattooed when he's ninety-five, with a picture of the kid at *seventy*, bow tie pasta, bow-wow, the fact that that's a hard act to follow, devoting a whole cheek to your son, and the kid would be so hurt if his dad ever tried to get it removed, or grew a beard, the fact that they'd have to have a long course of Family Therapy to process *that*, and get closure, the fact that if the dad's a meanie, he could threaten to get the tattoo removed, whenever the kid gives him any trouble in later life, like threatening to disinherit someone, which fathers often do, the fact that Hart Crane's father owned a chocolate factory in Cleveland, the fact that I'm always losing recipes, the fact that I must've lost a million chili recipes over the years, but I just found my best one, 2 lbs ground beef, ¼ cup chili powder, 1 tsp ground cumin, 1 tsp cinnamon, ¼ tsp all-spice, ¼ tsp ground cloves, 1 bay leaf, 1 oz unsweetened chocolate, 2 cans beef broth, 1 can tomatoes, 2 tbls cider vinegar, and ¼ tsp cayenne in it, the fact that maybe the kids like it because *it's* got choc-olate too, the fact that chocolate's important in chili, the fact that it's no good without it, the fact that I prefer a no-bean chili, the fact that I'm with LBJ on that, Ladybird, ladybugs, fireflies, the fact that I find Flexi-Fit mom jeans depressing, but I guess some people need that, the fact that I'm glad I don't, or not yet anyway, the fact that people don't even know what that means anymore, *LBJ* I mean, not Flexi Fit, VPL, JFK, the fact that a lot of people have never heard of Watergate either, the fact that Leo compared Lenin to Michael Jackson in a seminar, just joking around, and none of his students had heard of either one of them, the fact that I guess they've all heard of *Putin* by now, the fact that my chili recipe's a little like Ladybird Johnson's, only mine's hotter, the fact that I guess Johnson didn't like it too peppy, the fact that once it came out too peppy and we had to choke the stuff down, the fact that the kids wouldn't touch it, the fact that she can't have been cooking that stuff in the White House though, surely, the fact that I guess she got the White House *chef* to make it for them while they were living there, the fact that in *The Contender* Jeff Bridges is always trying to discover some food item that the White House kitchen doesn't have, and he finally catches them "napping," because they don't have any Muenster cheese, the fact that how can the White House kitchen have everything available all the time, the fact that it must all be *frozen*, the fact that all Trump likes is steak and hamburgers, so he's probably pretty easy to deal with, foodwise, no big surprises, the fact that Daddy used to jog, the fact that mountain lions sometimes attack joggers in California, the fact that Laine Hanson's a senator from Ohio, and she jogs *a lot*, the fact that this might not be such a good time to jog in Ohio right now, with lionesses around, the fact that Ohio is always cropping up in movies, it seems to me, and I can't for the life of me think why, the fact that I can't remember what Jane Fonda's "Fertile Void" is, the fact that she reminds me of Bambi, the fact that maybe *that's* the right part for her, forget Barbarella, and the newlywed in *Barefoot in the Park*, where she just acts kooky the whole time and Robert Redford gets so tired climbing the stairs, the fact that chickens must never eat onions, potatoes, avocados or salt, the fact that some people get *soundwave* tattoos now, sound memories, the fact that the tattoo plays a snippet of music or whatever back to you if you scan it or something with your iPhone, the fact that one girl got her grandmother's voice tattooed on her chest somehow, and somebody else got some advice from his dad tattooed on his arm, so he can listen to it again and again, the fact that Polonius might've liked that one, the fact that a mom got her baby crying on her arm, I mean she got its *voice* tattooed on her arm, wailing baby, whaling, waving, the fact that a lot of people want their dogs and cats turned into soundwave tattoos too, the fact that maybe these people have even worse memories than *me*, the fact that it sure makes you wonder, the fact that I'm not sure I would ever have wanted poor little Jim's bark tattooed on my arm, dear, dear, the fact that they sometimes have to identify shooting victims by their tattoos now, the fact that the explosive ammunition shooters use these days means there's often nothing else left of a person, the victim, or nothing recognizable, the fact that people will be hiring their arms out for tattooed ads next, the fact that Henry Higgins could have gotten two different sound tattoos tattooed on himself, as an ad for his services, with Eliza's original untrained voice on the one hand, and her aristo voice on the other, "the rain in Spain," pinched it, "And what I say is, them what pinched it, done her in," Doolittle, Dogood, dogwood, Dagwood, *The King's Speech*, the fact that Stacy's *still* got a thing for Colin Firth, the fact that this is a girl who used to have a crush on *Mozart*, retraining, training exercise, the fact that I dreamt Leo and I were both enrolled in college again, but I wasn't too sure about it all, going back to school and all at our age, the fact that I was saying to some friend of ours, "But I already have a college degree," waffles, pancakes, donuts, sour cherry pie, samplers, latticework, Leslie B. Durst, but then I heard Stacy on the phone telling somebody her parents were "retraining," the fact that she sounded sort of peeved but also proud, and that kind of stopped me in my tracks, in the *dream* anyway, the fact that it doesn't make me want to go back to college in real life, goldfish at the fair, but in the dream it made me feel better about the whole idea, and I decided I liked the expression "retraining," the fact that then I dreamt about *Ronny*, though he didn't look like Ronny in the dream, but I knew it was him, the fact that he was offering me some huge round, sloppy red pickled peppers, along with a bottle of *chocolate beer*, which now seems weird, even for Ronny, the fact that the peppers were on sale for one day only and he really wanted me to try them and go buy some more in Coshocton, the fact that he demonstrated how to eat them, and I was genuinely impressed they didn't drip all over his white shirt, the fact that then I dreamt a boy set fire to our house and I had to rescue the banjo clock, and one of Leo's students tried to hang himself but I got somebody to hold him up by his legs while I cut him down and I saved him, the fact that I don't know what's going on with my *stomach*, the fact that last night I was cutting a piece of pie for Leo to eat in bed when my stomach made a strange noise and I had to run for the bathroom quick, the fact that when I emerged half an hour later, and brought him his pie, and I explained the reason for the delay, Leo was so nice about it, just concerned for *me*, not how late his pie was, the fact that Leo is some guy, the fact that maybe I drank too much coffee, ouch, the fact that I do get a lot of stomach trouble, the fact that ever since chemo and radiotherapy I can't eat raw fruits and vegetables, but I never did particularly anyway, so it wasn't a big change, embrace change, the fact that I'm not getting my fiber, USDA, the fact that I just eat a few slices of peeled cucumber some-times and hope for the best, and overdo the coffee, the fact that Mommy drank a lot of coffee too, the fact that that's what *she* said to do, the oncologist, not Mommy, peel and seed everything, like cucumbers and tomatoes, but I can't really be bothered, the fact that I peel them but I don't seed them anymore, the tomato-peeler nun in love with Daddy, the fact that avocados go down okay, potatoes, volcanoes, tornadoes, mosquitoes, the fact that sometimes I think I'd be fine if I just lived in a warm climate and ate avocados all day, but I probably wouldn't be fine if I ate only avocados, the fact that I can usually get away with a tomato or two, and coffee, the fact that maybe it was just that Ronny dream about pickled peppers that turned my stomach, except my stomach was funny already *yesterday*, the fact that I can't eat any kind of peppers at all anymore, I don't think, even sweet ones, even if they're cooked, or even if they're completely pulverized, puréed, the fact that that red pepper soup at Phoebe's really did me in, but how was she to know I couldn't eat that, and how was I to know Chas had used like *twenty red peppers* to make it, the fact that I *used* to like roasted red peppers, blackened, but now they scare me, even if I peel them, the fact that it's weird I can still eat *chili*, as long as there are no beans, the fact that there go the Kinkels, off to get this year's Giant Viper's Bugloss, I bet, the fact that it's so funny how when there's a change in the weather you get a notion of what's in people's closets, the fact that out comes that plaid jacket of hers with the fur-lined hood, the fact that Jerry's got the latest thing, a shiny army-green jacket, the fact that it looks kind of like they're preparing for another Cold War, though it's just a bit of rain, beatboxer, the fact that a box has six sides, which you tend to forget, the fact that whoever heard of *chocolate beer* anyway, the fact that all governments think about is money and growth, but Paul something, or Leon, oh, that *guy*, whoever he is, said we can't *have* any more growth, the fact that he said "perpetual growth is the creed of the cancer cell," the fact that we've already got triple the right level of human population, or maybe quadruple, and he says the optimum population is two billion, the fact that now it's seven and a half billion or something, all eating chicken and getting caught in traffic jams, gug, nine hundred billion chickens, perpetual growth, perpetuation of the species, whatshisname, *The Population Bomb*, the fact that I must try not to think bitter thoughts while I'm baking, the fact that I betty botta notta, it might make my batta bitta, and I'd rather make my batta betta, mitti atta, Channing, 4chan, 8chan, the fact that we all had an English accent when we got home, the fact that I don't know what they'd make of that in Tuscarawas County, the fact that everybody acts all friendly during the day but then we lock ourselves in our houses and it all seems kind of a sham, or a shame, the fact that the kids like *mole* too, because it's got chocolate in it, mole rat, Mallrat, the fact that I make a great chocolate cake with mole, the fact that I made it once for my own birthday and they *loved* it, the fact that my birthday doesn't matter to me anymore, the fact that it never mattered once Mommy got sick and the angel food cakes stopped coming, though that's such a disgraceful thing to say, because she still tried to make a fuss of me on my birthday, even after she got sick, the fact that she painted those wonderful birthday cards every year, and always ordered me a book or some clothes or something for birthdays and Christmas, the fact that she couldn't go shopping but she really made an effort and I am so terrible, the fact that "I hate me," but still, it just seemed over, the certainty that she was my mom, the fact that it broke us, the fact that she did that great *lamb* card, and the lamb was all blue, with frail little legs, the fact that she really had a special way of painting stuff, the fact that it was just like her handwriting, unmistakably hers, Campfire Girls, Jim, the geraniums, the fact that how do they come up with these ideas, the fact that they're planning to take voters off the register if you haven't voted in a while, the fact that this is not who we are, the fact that we live in a *democracy*, the fact that every citizen's supposed to, the fact that what if you hadn't voted for a while but then you suddenly felt like voting, like just on the spur of the moment, and you go down to the polling station and your name's been *wiped off the register*, red light behind the fridge, the fact that it might put you off ever voting again if that happened to you, the fact that somehow, the fewer the voters, the more votes the Republicans get, Jim, the fact that Stace is here, safe and sound, lost and found, fanouropita, but now we've lost *Jim*, Channing School washroom, the fact that he just

895

disappeared, he's gone, the fact that I left him guarding the chicken coop, because that's where he seemed to like to be, the fact that maybe we should've made him come in at night, even if he whines, especially with a *lion* roaming around, the fact that the lion was seen near Coshocton the other day, *lioness*, I mean, the fact that what if that's what happened to him, and the mountain lion *ate* him, the fact that I'd never forgive myself, and what's worse is the kids would never forgive me either, the fact that there was no sign of a struggle though, or blood or anything, the fact that there were no lion footprints in the mud, the fact that the poor little guy really *liked* being outside and I hated to force him to come in, the fact that he was a farm dog and just never liked it inside the house, the fact that there have been a few other recent lion sightings too in Tuscarawas County, though the mass hysteria seems to be dying down a bit, "mass-staria!", now that the Cherokee tracker's on the case, the fact that I just don't see how one little mountain lion can be in twenty places at once, like all over the north-east of Ohio, just saying, the fact that *I've* never seen a mountain lion around here and I look out the window all the time, the fact that that's pretty lame though, the fact that I sound like one of those flat earthers who've decided the earth is flat because they looked out the window and couldn't see no curve, the fact that where do they think the sun goes at night, the fact that if the whole earth was like a flat disc in space, wouldn't the sun just sit there in one spot, or do they think it's a *spinning* disc maybe, or the sun's revolving around *us*, the fact that you'd think people might have something better to do than decide they're the experts on astronomy without even bothering to open an astronomy book, the fact that I think they think why bother, when you can just watch a few YouTube videos your flat-earther *friends* made, birther, the fact that they are just *crazee*, the fact that we really shouldn't go around calling everybody crazy, call me crazy but, butt, "we," the fact that I used to think married people who use "we" all the time were *smug*, but the truth is, after a while, if you live together, sleep together, eat and drive around together and have kids together, and discuss toilet paper preferences together, and clip your nails together, or at least *listen* to each other clipping your nails in the next room, well, you *are* a "we" and there's no point in trying to deny it, the fact that it's a great thing that we agree on most things, the fact that we can't help it, so shoot us, "we," *whee*, Trump's weeing contests with Putin, Howard Hughes's bottles of pee, Gillian's illuminated honey bears, the fact that there have been no injuries reported, from the lioness, I mean, except that car accident involving one of the official lion posses, the fact that it hit a school bus full of kids but nobody was hurt, thankfully, the fact that it helped when they finally withdrew the reward money, because people were acting so *crazee*, the fact that the lioness was commended on the news for not *eating* the driver of the car that crashed with her in it, the fact that that driver's pretty lucky, YouTube, smartphone, the fact that it's weird that they actually caught her and then *lost* her again, the fact that it's getting like Laurel and Hardy with the *piano*, Jim, and when the driver was asked about any distinguishing features she might have, he said "Just looked like a cougar to me," the fact that she just looked like a cougar, "Now you're doing something to *help* me," the fact that, gee whiz, all these people have been out looking for her and he actually *saw* her and he can't offer any new info, the fact that to all the kids that lioness is now some kind of *folk hero*, because she never kills anybody and she always eludes her captors, evades, exudes, captivity, slavery, reparations, truth and reconciliation, Jim Crow laws, the fact that what about *Jim* though, the fact that maybe we'll never know what happened to him, the fact that it's horrible not to know what's happened to your pet, the fact that you're left imagining such terrible things, the fact that I'm scared it'll freak *Stacy* out, which is all we need right now, when we just established a little harmony around here, red light, the fact that we did all we could about finding him, Jim I mean, the fact that we went out looking, and calling for him, and put up signs around town, made a fanouropita, and even told the police, for what good *that'll* do, the fact that if they can't find Stacy, who's female and underage, and they can't go talk to Willy, a juvenile delinquent who made death threats against our *cats*, then what are they going to do about a missing dog, the fact that they said they'd get right on it, but we don't hold out much hope that they'll bust a gut, over our poor mutt, butt, cock, chicken ladder, the fact that the night Jim disappeared, the fact that the next morning when I went to let the chickens out, their ladder was all bashed up and lying on the ground, the fact that I wondered if maybe Jim had done it and then ran away out of shame, but I don't think he's big enough to cause that much damage, the fact that Leo wants to make a new ladder, the fact that it is a kind of *bridge* after all, the fact that for now the chickens are using my sunlounger, propped up against the coop, stones, plastic spade, the fact that they seem to like having a wider ramp actually, wheelchair ramps, the fact that *they're* sunlounging on it now, the fact that I always liked to think that Jim originally came from a nice quiet farm in Pennsylvania, before he ended up in the firenado kennel, and at first, when he disappeared, I hoped maybe he'd headed back there, to the farm I mean, not the burnt-out dog's home, but he didn't *really* look like a dog who'd had a nice quiet upbringing on a friendly family farm, kind of the opposite, the fact that I can't actually believe he'd try to find his way there but you never know, the fact that dogs can be very dutiful, Pepito lying by Mommy's bed, the fact that we should try to find out where that farm is, and give them a call in case they see him, the fact that I finally broke that silver bracelet Mommy gave me, after years and years of wearing it every single day, the fact that that makes me sad, broken, the fact that maybe I can get it fixed, along with the opal ring she gave me too, or was that from Grandma, the fact that it's been sitting in a little box for *years* now, waiting to have its little stone put back in if I ever get around to it, stones, broken chicken ladder, the fact that Stacy was so upset about Jim at first, but she struggled to stay calm for the little kids' sake, the fact that she trudged all over town searching for him, and calling everybody she knows, the fact that she *exhausted* herself looking for him, and now she seems more down than ever, and all worked up again about Willy and the *cats*, Willoughby and Marianne Dashwood, the fact that I wish she'd read *Sense and Sensibility*, just to give her a bit of a diversion from the Jim situation, but she probably won't because I recommended it, the fact that now she's watching *The Fugitive* instead, Harrison Ford, orange jumpsuit, the fact that that guy from Sandusky shot the kids one by one in front of his girlfriend, and then he killed her too, all because he was sick of the kids disrespecting him, and women having him arrested all the time for no reason, the fact that "I'm only human," he told the police, when they caught him, the fact that he handcuffed all five kids to a bed and then shot them, the fact that now it turns out he was beating his girlfriend up every day, until she changed the locks, and he beat up his previous girlfriends too, the fact that it took him *hours* to kill so many people, the fact that it's inexplicable, despicable, disgraceful, *crazee*, the fact that men are so *emotional* sometimes, so gosh darn angry, Daddy, "ogre," the fact that Daddy was never like *that*, dear me, the fact that he had a temper is all, and so do *I*, especially after a PTA meeting, *The Taming of the Shrew*, the fact that Harrison Ford didn't murder his wife, the fact that the one-armed man did it, train crash, culvert, death sentence, abortion bill, the fact that Ohio's planning to ban *all abortions*, even D and Cs, if it involves fetal material, like after a miscarriage, the fact that I guess people will just have to go out-of-state, Interstate, ACLU, D and Cs, the fact that Abby had to have a lot of D and Cs, and I don't know why, the fact that women in Ireland have to go to England for abortions, if they can *afford* it, the fact that it'll be illegal for Ohio doctors to even save your life, if it involves any fetal removal, the fact that when the bus taking Harrison Ford to Death Row crashes and rolls down the hill, it ends up right on the train tracks, and a train's coming fast, so everybody just skedaddles, leaving Harrison Ford to help the injured prison guard out of the bus, the fact that Harrison Ford's a doctor so he's always trying to save people, the fact that Harrison Ford jumps out just in time, just before the train hits the bus and carries it off down the tracks, down the line, forsooth, forswear, *The Merchant of Venice*, the fact that then half the train gets disconnected from the other half, and derails, with sparks flying and everything on fire, and the derailed bit comes heading straight for *Harrison Ford*, the fact that this is when Leo always yells

"Turn to the right!", which doesn't seem to have occurred to Harrison Ford, the fact that that train really seems to have it in for him, the fact that it's like a *monster* chasing him through the forest, a wild *animal*, Sandusky guy, the fact that Harrison Ford just runs in front of the train and it all gets a bit like a Roadrunner cartoon there for a minute, but still, it's exciting, the fact that then, just in time, Harrison Ford turns to the *left*, instead of the right, and ducks into a culvert, just before the train rushes over his head and everything explodes, culvert failures, backfill, bedding compaction, this culvert will either be a success or a failure, the fact that Harrison Ford sometimes does his own stunts but somehow I don't think they let him actually run away from a runaway train, or sit around in a culvert while this big explosion's going on over his head, train engineer, retraining, derailed, the fact that I don't think any of my kids want to be a train engineer, luckily, or a lumberjack, or a soldier, which is just fine with me, the fact that being a teacher has become the most dangerous occupation in America, the fact that they must all have to be so brave, waiting for a gun attack at any moment, ready to lay down their lives for their students, or else live with the guilt for the rest of their days, SUPER CALLOUS FRAGILE RACIST SEXIST NAZI POTUS, the fact that in real life Harrison Ford's a bit of a daredevil, and maybe quite a *hazard* in the air, the fact that he sometimes flies his little private plane too near passenger jets, 9/11, the fact that you wonder why people want to own planes, but maybe it's fun, the fact that it's *flying* after all, but it's not the same as being outside in the air, flapping your own wings, the fact that planes are so noisy and unspontaneous, air traffic controllers, the fact that I'd just like to flap my wings and *go*, or maybe float around on a hot air balloon, if it wasn't too noisy, because then you get to be out in the open air and you don't have to go too *high*, the fact that I'd probably still get vertigo, the fact that some airline made a woman put her little dog in the overhead compartment, oh dear, in a carrying case, Tiny Tim's turquoise traveling case, and the owner objected to him being put up there but she was overruled by the stewardess, the fact that when the flight was over and they got the dog out of the overhead locker thing, he was *dead*, the fact that he'd *suffocated*, and everybody on the plane was crying, the fact that some mom got attacked by a flight attendant, on a *different* flight, the fact that he didn't want her bringing her double stroller on board, but that's what she'd been told to do by somebody at the check-in desk, the fact that she was traveling all alone with twin babies, and they wouldn't let her bring the *stroller*, the fact that that's cruel enough in itself, without getting bashed by the flight attendant, the fact that he wrestled with her over the stroller, physically wrestled with a mom in a dispute about a stroller, the fact that how low can you get, the fact that, okay, maybe the actual punch he gave her was accidental, the fact that it's hard to tell in the video, but still, he publicly hit a mom, and almost hit the baby she was holding too, and in all those passengers, only one guy stood up for the mom, the fact that *he* threatened to beat the *flight attendant* up, the fact that that's how bad things got, the fact that all the stewardess did was offer the mom a cup of water, the fact that do they really think a cup of lukewarm plane water is going to stop her suing their, well, their butts, the fact that Leo says that's all they ever do though, give you water, the fact that he travels by air all the time so he knows, the fact that if you're sick or faint or dizzy or hysterical, they bring a cup of water, the fact that I should try it with the kids, the fact that whatever's wrong, just bring them a cup of water, no more choc dipped madeleines for *you*, oh, how mean, the fact that Mommy had a hard time on planes once she had to use the wheelchair, the fact that they always made trouble about it, the fact that she preferred airlines that served Manhattans, the fact that I bet nobody serves them now, the fact that Tommy Lee Jones is the U.S. Marshal, and wherever he goes, there are always choppers circling like gnats, and sometimes he's in one himself, Jim, the fact that he's got all this police power, Tommy Lee Jones, not Jim, and Harrison Ford's only got a stolen ambulance and the conviction of being in the right, the fact that still, you know Harrison's gotta win, because he's Harrison Ford, and this is Hollywood, the fact that he wouldn't have a chance in real life, no matter what kind of a daredevil he is, the fact that some prisoners now wear *yellow* jumpsuits, the fact that it's not always orange, convict, excon, confiscate, overhead bin, slam dunk, "We got a gopher," the fact that Harrison Ford and Tommy Lee Jones have kind of a love–hate relationship, cops and robbers stuff, cat and mouse, cowboy, paramedics, the fact that they get to sort of like each other, or at least respect each other, after Tommy Lee Jones starts to realize Harrison Ford's not a murderer, the fact that I used to get Tommy Lee Jones mixed up with Billy Bob Thornton, Angelina Jolie, Mia Farrow, the fact that they're both always adopting kids, Angelina Jolie and Mia Farrow I mean, not Billy Bob Thornton and Tommy Lee Jones, but for all I know Billy Bob and Tommy may like adopting kids too, the fact that Tommy Lee Jones first meets Harrison Ford in the sewer pipe of the dam, or the emergency runoff pipe, whatever it is, the fact that Harrison Ford tells Tommy Lee Jones he's innocent, and Tommy Lee Jones says he doesn't care, but later on he does sort of start to care, the fact that he gets sort of interested when he realizes Harrison Ford is doing all he can to find the real murderer, the fact that by the end he's completely on Harrison Ford's side, "I don't bargain," conflicts of interest, a disconnect, the fact that even when Tommy Lee Jones knows Harrison Ford's innocent though, he still has to keep chasing him, because he's still an escaped convict, Harrison Ford, I mean, and Billy Bob, I mean Tommy Lee Jones, is still a cop, the fact that it's not even just a job with him, it's more like a compulsion, the fact that he's relentless, the fact that in *Hope Springs* he's just a neglectful husband, but here he's the human equivalent of the derailed train, heading straight for Harrison Ford, the fact that Harrison Ford has to jump into the damn dam to get away from him, the fact that Harrison Ford decides in that split second that he'd rather die than go back to jail, or that's what it looks like, the fact that he survives that fall though, which is another kind of cartoony idea, the fact that only Bugs Bunny could live through that, the fact that dams really fill you with dread, the fact that it's hard to believe a dam is really going to hold, dam failure, "Go east!", the fact that in the Thurber story, the whole of Columbus starts running because they think the dam's broke, the fact that even Thurber's doctor's yelling "It's got us!", Dr. H. R. Mallory, the 1913 flood, the fact that then he drifts downriver, *Harrison Ford* not Dr. H. R. Mallory, the fact that Almanzo came on the cutter to get Laura, even though it was thirty below, because "god hates a coward," frostbite, caramel marmalade bars, the fact that he crawls out of the water gasping for breath and eventually sleeps, just under some leaves, dreaming of his dead wife, the fact that what's amazing is not only does he survive his jump down the dam but he doesn't even get pneumonia from sleeping outdoors all wet and wounded and starving and everything, camping, pebbles, the fact that he's already snuck into a hospital though and stitched himself up at least, and he's had a shot of penicillin that he stole there too, so maybe that's what's keeping him alive, the fact that maybe he took some painkillers too, the fact that "THESE ARE MY JEWELS" has Sherman, Stanton, Grant, and, well, somebody else, the fact that Leo's dad knew a doctor in Missoula who gave out instructions to his surgeon during his own abdominal operation, using mirrors or something, the fact that he was rejected by his sweetheart, this doctor, not Leo's dad, and waited thirty years until she was widowed, and married her, but that had nothing to do with the abdominal surgery, can-do attitude, the fact that he always drove around in a yellow convertible *singing* at the top of his lungs, but I've forgotten what he sang, the fact that I gotta ask Leo, the fact that if I'd never met Leo I would never have *known* about that singing, driving, self-scalpeling, self-suturing, wife-awaiting doctor, the fact that sometimes when I'm at a loose end I try to imagine what it's like to do your own abdominal operation, but I don't really feel like it right now, Sherman, Stanton, Grant, and *Sheridan*, Sheridan, "my jewels," scalpel, cutter, the fact that sometimes it helps if you take a second run at it, remembering things, I mean, not operating on yourself, the fact that I like it when Harrison Ford can't resist offering his medical services to people along the way, the fact that he tells the paramedics that the prison guard has a thoracic puncture, and later he signs off on a little boy so that he can get emergency lung surgery, the fact that Julianne Moore's not happy about Harrison Ford muscling in on her patient, the fact that he's wearing a janitor or porter's uniform and she gets suspicious when she sees him reading the boy's X-ray film in such a knowledgeable-looking way, the fact that you think those two might get together by the end but Julianne Moore never turns up again, the fact that they forget all about Julianne Moore, the fact that he could've ended up with Jane Lynch too, who's completely on his side right from the start, but that doesn't happen either, the fact that the only love interest is the dead wife, getting killed in flashbacks, and the one-armed man, the fact that Harrison Ford's not ready to move on to someone new yet, the fact that he hasn't got closure, the fact that in real life Harrison Ford was married to someone for a long time, Diane something, and then they broke up and he got together with Callista Flockhart, a younger woman, Alec Baldwin, the fact that *The Fugitive* is kind of like *The Thirty-Nine Steps*, the fact that Harrison Ford even hides himself in a parade, the St. Patrick's Day Parade in Chicago, the fact that in *The Thirty-Nine Steps*, Robert Donat hides himself in a Salvation Army parade, and Sean Connery hides in a parade too, a Mardi Gras parade somewhere, in whichever James Bond movie that is, the fact that I guess everybody loves to join a parade, the fact that I can't really imagine wanting to join the Circleville pumpkin parade, nor the marches down Pennsylvania Avenue for that matter, pussy hats, oh dear, the fact that that's just not me, the fact that Robert Donat has to fight the bad guys and the suspicious girl, just like Harrison Ford, the fact that it's Carole whateverhernameis, no no, *Madeleine Carroll*, the fact that Harrison Ford has to deal with Julianne Moore, and Cary Grant has to deal with Eva Marie Saint, who's a double-agent or something, the fact that Madeleine Carroll soon starts to fall for Robert Donat, and Eva Marie Saint certainly goes for Cary Grant, but Julianne Moore never gets attached to Harrison Ford, the fact that Robert Donat has to speak off the cuff at an election rally, wearing handcuffs, off-the-cuff remarks, McCrocodile, Alligator Mound, the fact that Cary Grant gets to make a little speech in the auction room, and makes a public spectacle of himself, in order to escape James Mason's bully boys, "genuine idiot," but it's not like an amazing off-the-cuff speech or anything, not like Robert Donat's, the fact that Sean Connery only joins the Mardi Gras parade, he doesn't do any public speaking, but he's an *undercover agent*, so public speaking's sort of out, the fact that Cary Grant doesn't get in on a parade either, but he does merge into the crowd a lot, like at Grand Central, the fact that that's how he gets out of the elevator too, by hiding in the crowd, the fact that Harrison Ford gets to speak up in public, at the big fancy dinner for the drug company, but it isn't much of a speech, the fact that it's all sort of muffled, the fact that *we* think he muffs it, we, the fact that they just start having a fist fight on the roof instead, which I guess is what Harrison Ford's more comfortable with, the fact that he's an action hero really, the fact that Robert Donat was not, he was an *asthmatic*, the fact that I wonder what barbers make of it when their clients commit murder, the fact that every murderer must have a barber, and these barbers must catch stories about their clients on the news now and then, the fact that maybe they have a TV on in the barbershop while they're barbering, borborygmus, and they turn on the news and see one of their clients, still sporting the haircut they just gave him, arrested for slaughtering his whole family, or his colleagues, or polluting the whole of Ohio, though *that* would never happen, the fact that they'd never arrest anybody for polluting Ohio, the fact that I suppose having a few criminal clients gives barbers something to talk about in the barber shop, something besides baseball, "It's got us!", git, grit, glitz, grits, asthma, ALA, the fact that lilac-breasted rollers are probably monogamous, the fact that in that Gena Rowlands movie, *Gloria*, there's a teenage girl who's told by her mom to "git," leave the apartment, but she doesn't *go*, so she gets murdered by the mafia just a few minutes later, along with the rest of her family, the fact that I think the moral is, if your mom tells you to git, you *git*, the fact that that's not the moment to go all adolescenty on everybody, the fact that I wonder if Stacy would listen to me if I told her to git, the fact that I can't imagine her doing anything I say, that theater play for kids, the fact that I must've been about six and it was the first play I'd ever been to, the fact that I really liked the *sets*, the fact that I didn't know what was going *on* but to me the sets were jewellike, so brightly lit and unreal, the fact that in *Gloria* Gena Rowlands is a tough-talking mafia moll who takes on a little kid, the only survivor of the family that got shot, the fact that at first she doesn't know if she's up to the job, of taking care of a little kid, but some mafioso tells her *every* woman is a mother, and that helps settle her nerves, the fact that Gena also thinks any grave can stand for any other grave, the fact that they can't visit the kid's family's real graves, because the murderers are after them, so they visit some random cemetery and make it stand in for the real one, so the kid can say goodbye to his mom and dad and big sister, git, guts, East Street Cemetery, megabyte, the fact that Gena Rowlands takes good care of that little boy, until she too gets shot, the fact that maybe she sacrifices herself for him, I can't remember, but anyway, *he* survives, which is a relief, the fact that the little boy in *Witness* is a really good actor, Mardi Gras, the fact that Gena's a popular name right now, Geena Davis, the fact that it sounds short for something, Regina maybe, or Eugenia maybe, Eustacia, Eugene, Rowena, verbena, terpenes, the fact that I don't know where Cathy's friend Blanche is buried, the fact that Family Therapy is just one more afterschool activity I'm now responsible for, along with Gillian's acrobatics and Ben's carpentry class, the fact that he's given up the idea of making a glider, the fact that he's probably building an atomic missile now, Sears, the fact that there's also Jake's dancing class and Gillian's piano lessons, the fact that to do Family Therapy I have to drop Jake off at dancing and take Ben and Gillian over to their different friends' houses, with the agreement of various tricky people, including my own kids, all these negotiations just so that I can pay some stranger to tell me what a lousy mom I am, the fact that land sakes, *my* mom didn't sit around apologizing for her parenting efforts, the fact that she had a book to write, and other books to review and stuff, and students to teach, and papers to mark, papers, paper, broken chicken ladder, the fact that I've already devoted, or wasted, much more time on motherhood than Mommy probably *ever* did, and done a lousy job of it too, the fact that I never even wanted kids, they just sort of happened, the fact that, I mean, I like them, love them, but I just never really planned on having so many, and now I'm responsible for all these *people*, the fact that I guess my womb just kind of got the better of me, the fact that it had its own agenda, the fact that I often remember that dream I had years ago, for no reason, about French doors looking out on to a nice green lawn, the fact that Mommy did want kids, the fact that *she'd* hoped for four, but in the end could only have three, the fact that Abby wanted lots too but only had one, the fact that it just didn't happen again, D and Cs, the fact that I don't think she had *miscarriages* or anything, the fact that she had very low blood pressure and that seems to get in the way of having more pregnancies somehow, the fact that I've had four pregnancies and four kids and probably shouldn't have had any, cesareans, doctors' orders, abortion clinics, the fact that Mommy was forced to stop after me, well, not forced, but her obstetrician thought three cesareans were enough, and a fourth one might be dangerous, the fact that one third of all American births are now cesareans, which seems kind of high but what do I know, the fact that I never saw Mommy pregnant, except in photos, the fact that I like the one of her holding *me*, after I was born, not when she was pregnant, the fact that she looks so happy about me, proud even, the fact that I still find it kind of hard to imagine her enjoying pregnancy after pregnancy and cesarean after cesarean and then motherhood that much, opening cereal packets for ten years, the fact that I can't imagine why she wanted to go through all those cesareans, *or* all that cereal, but if she hadn't I wouldn't be here, the fact that it's got to be tough trying to write a book with kids around, the fact that it's almost impossible for Leo to even write an engineering paper around here, even if the kids don't actually interrupt him, the fact that we probably all need Family Therapy, we really do, data collection, data protection, data storage, data dissemination, data destruction, the fact that *Ethan's* a great dad, so fond, the fact that being a parent is just about impossible, the fact that the whole day drifts away from me so easily, the fact that, like, I never get around to cleaning behind the fridge, the fact that it's only since Jake started his play group that I started getting *anything* done at all, Jake's name-label above his very own coat peg at play group, JAKE, the fact that he likes the wooden marble tower, the fact that I hope he doesn't *hog* it, like the boys did in my Kindergarten class, the fact that Harrison Ford makes a great marble run for the little Amish boy in *Witness*, the fact that I should get Leo to make Jake one, the face that I'm sure he could do it, autumn trees jigsaw puzzle, Daddy, Reynoldsburg, the fact that I don't think Amish women feel bad about what they do all day, the fact that they don't hate themselves for being mothers, the fact that family life and housework are enough for them, court-appointed attorney, the fact that Amish women are content with carrying out domestic duties, menial tasks, because they have their place in the community, and they're not trying to prove anything, or do several jobs at once like most American women, the fact that they're not trying to be Superwoman, the fact that I don't think they're all that ambitious really, and I don't think they beat themselves up about *that* either, because they know they're valued, or I hope so anyway, the fact that Fanny Trollope said that American women were "guarded by a seven-fold shield of habitual insignificance," but things are better now of course, Sandusky man, Alec Baldwin, the fact that what am I thinking anyway, the fact that you have to be religious to be Amish, or a Shaker, so that's out, the fact that you have to be *celibate* to be a Shaker, the fact that you can't just pretend to believe in god or reincarnation or a flat earth if you don't, the fact that what is *with* me today, the fact that I guess I'm just feeling bad about Jim, that's what it is, the fact that it is disconcerting to lose a dog, martin houses, Saint Fanourios, Exxon, Chevron, Shell, Esso BP, Mobil, Paul *Ehrlich*, the fact that that's his name, the fact that what was his book called now, the fact that you'll never know what sort of person you might have been if you'd read different stuff, the fact that Leo's reading Mark Twain again now, about the Mississippi, the fact that I don't know if he's read Zadok Cramer, navigating, sugaring, slack water, the fact that Mark Twain knew what it was like to be on the Mississippi at night, long before we ruined the Mississippi, F— Hinn, calliopes, the fact that the Mississippi used to be covered with steam boats, all blasting out old favorites, the fact that I like listening to Mississippi steamboat calliopes on YouTube when I'm doing online jigsaws, Old Standards, "B minor's not just a key, it's a way of life," the fact that the Tuscarawas is a hundred and thirty miles long, the fact that Peekaboo now owe me for twenty-two pies and I don't know if I should make any more for them until they pay up, the fact that they don't like dealing with cash there, so I always have to keep checking my bank account to see if the money's gone in yet, but it never has, or hardly ever, not without me having to remind them a million times, the fact that I'm getting pretty darn sick of checking and reminding them and myself, the fact that I should get tough, "send in some of the boys," give them the ol' one-two, pottertjes, poor Jim, the fact that it's hard to believe Peekaboo would try to swindle a poor housewife out of her pie dough, her *money*, I mean, her moolah, but we live in a country where the parents of murdered children are sent death threats, and a black man walking around with no clothes on is gunned down by the police, "We thought he was armed," the fact that the poor guy was wandering around like that because he was maddened with grief over his children, who his *wife* shot and killed a few years ago, the fact that the only response the police could think up was to kill *him* too, the fact that couldn't they just have Tasered him, or Baker Acted him, or how about *left him alone*, for Pete's sake, or *talked* to him, asked him what was up, the fact that what harm did he do, the fact that his only crime was being naked in a public place, if that *is* a crime, which I'm not even sure it is, the fact that surely they didn't have to *shoot* him, surely, a poor old man like that, right in the chest, Jim's chest ruffles, and stop calling me Shirley, Netflix, ow, the fact that my *cheek* hurts now, now why is *that*, late-stage acne, the fact that I sure hope not, the fact that how much scarier ailments must have been before there was modern medicine, the fact that if something got you in the Middle Ages you were just a goner, gyny guy, male obstetricians, the fact that Bizet died right after he finished *Carmen*, which always seems such a shame, the fact that Gounod was a pallbearer for him and he broke down and couldn't deliver the eulogy, Mozart, Schubert, the fact that they died too young too, Peekaboo, the fact that it seems like composers have always had more money troubles than *anybody* almost, the fact that their creditors were always calling in their loans, it was like a daily hassle, like for the Schumanns too, the fact that it's just awful to think how much of Mozart's time was taken up by this sort of stuff, and Puccini too, when everybody should have just fed them all for free, so they could concentrate on composing, for the sake of future generations, the fact that Schubert really ran out of time to compose, premature death, premature babies, mom with twins on a plane, the fact that Bach was always having disputes with his stingy employers, *Bach*, church boards or whatever, cathedral boards, I don't know, the fact that anyway it was a big waste of his time but there was no avoiding it, the fact that, if those burghers and bishops or whatever thought they had anything more important to do than help *Bach be Bach*, the fact that these were his *contemporaries*, and should've looked out for him, the fact that Messiaen had a job as an organist all his life, at Sainte-Trinité, snappy salad, a "craggy but benign" older man, the fact that it usually takes the public two hundred years to start appreciating things, the fact that a two-hundred-year-old building almost always looks good, the fact that I dreamt we had a home robot that taught you things and then issued you with a certificate, the fact that you had to pay the robot $25 for the certificate, which I only realized when one of the robot's spindly arms shot up and swiped $25 right out of my pocket, "A dollar?!", swipe left, the fact that the robot was also able to bring up *children*, right from birth, and once the kids were grown-up, they were given a certificate too, and then *they'd* have to come up with the $25 payment, or maybe it was more like $250 for a whole fifteen-year stint with the robot, I don't know, the fact that now I'm *sweating*, the fact that thinking about Peekaboo has blown my equilibrium, the fact that I've worked myself up into a swivet over unpaid pie bills, me and my silly pies, the fact that who do I think I am, *Bach*, Mozart, Aaron Copland, cope land, the fact that still, nobody wants to be baking pies for *nothing*, nada, zilch, Artisan Pastries, the fact that it's embarrassing, the fact that okay, that's it, the fact that those guys aren't getting another tarte tatin outta me till I see the color of their money, the fact that I'm outta here, Peekaboo, the fact that the new me is withholding my labor, well, just for a week maybe, the fact that now I have to drink the icy water that was meant for the next batch of dough, because I'm so het up, ow, my stomach, the fact that now I have to go to the bathroom, the fact that I'm spiraling, I'm flipping out here, the fact that some people know ahead of time if they're getting depressed and they can avert it, but I never know ahead of time, it just happens and suddenly I don't feel like doing anything anymore and everything just seems ruined, and hopeless, and I'm a failure, a flop, flopsweat, strike, Jim, the fact that I can cry about more than one thing at a time, well, I guess everybody can, the fact that the government has wrecked the look of the dollar bill, the fact that I'm not crying about *that*, the fact that I think I'm crying about the *naked* guy, but also those young men who have to work in that breast implant factory, the fact that young men have to sort through breast implants, the fact that young men don't deserve that, though neither do young women, and I guess somebody's gotta sort through all the breast implants, for some reason they never explained in the documentary, the fact that young men don't scare me so much anymore, now I've had sons of my own, the fact that somehow they *move* me now, the fact that for a long time I only liked older men because I thought they were kinder, but Frank's eight years older than me, "and look what happened to him," the fact that where *is* Jim, the fact that there was such an awful guy in the park that day, the fact that he was meeting up with his wife and dog there, and at first he seemed really pleased to see the dog and spoke nicely to it and even let it jump up at him, the fact that he was so polite to the *dog*, and then he turned to his wife and just started snarling at her, the man, not the dog, the fact that he was yelling at her *about* the dog, scolding her for letting it jump up at him with wet paws and dirty his pants, the fact that it just seems so sad people have to act like that, when she'd happily brought the dog to meet him and everything, Chris Christie, Flexi-Fit, the fact that it was kind of shocking the way the guy changed in an instant, from nice doggie guy to, well, domestic violence guy, animal cruelty, the fact that people shoot animals a lot too, the fact that it's not just people that get shot all the time, the fact that vets have to deal with a lot of bullet wounds, Jim, the fact that I hope nobody *shoots* him, oh dear, gym shoes, that poor naked guy with the dead children, the fact that, the fact that I really should think about *nice* things, the fact that instead here I am twirling around the bathroom, ricocheting off one horror after another like a Spinning Jenny, pinwheel, blubbing in the bathroom, ♫ *the women were sobbin', sobbin', sobbin'* ♫, the fact that I should look at the bigger picture, take a more distant view of things maybe, blow my nose too maybe, Peekaboo, wash your face, the fact that in 1991 some guy drove his pickup into a cafeteria in Texas called Luby's and just started firing, and by the end of it he'd killed *twenty-three people* and injured *twenty-seven*, the fact that they say he hated women, the fact that they really didn't have to tell us *that*, the fact that, I mean, it's pretty obvious, if the guy shot all those people, the fact that if you cared at all about women, you would never shoot some mother's son, or daughter, the fact that you wouldn't shoot somebody's *mom* either, you wouldn't shoot *anybody*, the fact that anyone who could do that just has no idea what goes into bringing up a child, the fact that, oh, Jake's outside the door, asking for something, the fact that I can't *hear* him, the fact that, oh, my god, he just asked, very slowly and falteringly, "Are you okay, Mommy?", the fact that that is so kind, and he's just a *little boy*,

·   ·   ·   ·

Risking human confrontations and human anger, the lioness called openly now to her babies as she wandered the suburban mazes of split-level dream homes, and stopped to listen out for her cubs's returning cries.

She circled a lake, peeking intently into every house along the shore, in case her cubs could be held captive there. A tapping sound drew her to a big, square workshop, and through a large hole she glimpsed a man pounding a plank of wood with his hands. Surrounding him were the long, thin concave forms of canoes, the nests that men used to float on water. She had seen them on lakes and rivers, usually with one lone man inside, splashing at the water with a paddle.

The boatbuilder bent to scrape the wood in gestures similar to what a lion does on bark, smoothing his canoe. After watching him warily, the lioness moved on.

She listened out for her kittens even when all kitten sounds were blocked by dimwitted human excitements, human mirth, human arrogance, and of course the noisy, smelly cars in which they slashed and stabbed and scarred their way across the earth.

In dreams, her kittens' chirps were muffled by rain and thunder and floods of her own making, for she could live underwater, looking up at men's boats jerking across the surface.

The dog dreamt of fire and firemen.

On their way to a creek behind a large, low house, she heard a woman wailing. The lioness considered the prospect of some easy prey, but she couldn't stand the sirens, and all the flashing lights.

She and her dog companion fled, hungry, for the less populated hills nearby.

.   .   .   .

the fact that there are *two* of them, Caite and Kris, the fact that it's just Stacy and me and the two of them, Kris and Caite, the fact that I mentioned the dream I had about the little girl caked in mud, and how she was called Stacy and all but wasn't really Stacy, and how I really wanted to adopt her and take care of her, but it was hard somehow, the fact that I was just getting into it when Caite said they don't really *deal* with dreams or the unconscious or anything, the fact that I was thinking, heck, the *rest* of us have to, but of course I didn't say anything, the fact that then they asked Stacy about Leo and me, and she said we got married *without her permission*, which shocked me so much, gug, the fact that she seemed okay with it at the time, and she liked her little flowergirl dress and all, the fact that she was only *five*, the fact that I never heard of parents asking their kids' permission to get married, even if the kid was all grown-up, the fact that isn't it supposed to be the other way around, with kids begging their *parents* to be allowed to marry some unsuitable person or another, Romeo and Juliet, drool yet, Bette Davis dumping Elliot, Gladys Cooper, Brave Man Cookies, the fact that anyway Stacy more or less admits she got a great stepdad out of it all, even if we didn't do it the right way, in *her* opinion, the fact that stepmoms in fairy tales are always bad news, but stepdads not so much, red velvet cake, the fact that then Stacy said I gave away all her toys when we moved to Ohio, and I turned her playhouse into a *chicken coop*, and I began to feel just *dreadful*, the worst mom alive, the fact that I didn't think she cared about her play-house anymore, the fact that she never went in there, the fact that we just used it to store stuff until we got the chickens, the fact that Caite falls asleep sometimes during our sessions, the fact that I wonder what *she* dreams, the fact that she's probably dreaming of going to the Bahamas or something, *on our money*, the fact that falling asleep during Family Therapy sessions is probably pretty common, and perfectly understandable too, the fact that who wants to sit around listening to other people's problems for a whole hour in a stuffy room, one unhappy family after another, the fact that it must take real stamina, or a good poker face, the fact that napping is probably an escape from the pain of it all, or the monotony, my voice, a sort of safety valve, the fact that still, as Leo said, we're paying for their time, the fact that I feel like a nap right *now*, the fact that I'd like to know what a Kazakh pear tree dreams about, flower dreams, vegetable dreams, the unconscious mind of a vegetable, the dreams of a carrot secretly growing deep in the ground, the fact that I don't think I'm going to like Family Therapy, the fact that I want to help Stacy and all, and I know she's depressed and stuff, but the trouble is I just can't remember most of the stuff she wants to *talk* about, and it's not just embarrassing, it can also hurt her feelings, the fact that my whole life is a blank, the fact that I'm innocent in my own mind, because I can't remember what I ever did wrong, Daddy trying to spank me, "In my mind I've already divorced you," the fact that in my opinion the past is too unbearable to revisit anyway, but Family Therapists want you to rake over and over things that happened, all my mistakes, the fact that everything seems to be my fault, as the adult in the situation, the fact that that's natural enough, because Stace was just a kid, the World HQ of Selfish, *me* I mean, not Stace, the fact that Stace took pity on me though, when I was really struggling to remember something, I forget what, the fact that she took over and did most of the talking for a while, while I squirmed, kind of close to tears, the fact that I can't really remember much about her childhood except how adorable she was, the fact that apart from Mommy and Daddy dying, I was just thrilled with Stacy and bringing her up was a delight, the fact that she was just a good kid, and we were so close, I just kind of assumed we still *are*, underneath it all, but she doesn't seem to think so, the fact that if I could go back and do it all better, I would, and I said so, for what it's worth, the fact that she says she didn't like me giving all her Roald Dahl books to Gillian either, the fact that she's right, the fact that I could've at least *asked* her, tricycle, moms, coffee moms, Drake's coffee cakes, the fact that I wish I was swimming in the King's Ransome pool right now with Stacy and Abby, Abby's attic, CC&G, D and C, Hoag in his den watching the game, all wrapped up in that body bag of his, I mean the snuggle afghan Abby crocheted for him, the fact that it was really kind of like a huge *sock*, not that different from a sleeping bag, or a mummy case, sarcophagus, computer bag, pocketbook, tuberculosis, Dionysus, men in the den, the fact that anyway it was the perfect thing for Hoag, and he *loved* it, the fact that he must've been cold for *years*, before she thought of making him that, the fact that once I had kids, well, Stacy, I always stayed at the King's Ransome when we visited Abby, to save her *trouble*, but now I wonder if she was offended we didn't stay with *her*, the fact that there wasn't really room though, just that pull-out sofa-bed in the living room, and the single bed in Barry's old room, the fact that well, maybe there was enough space, when there was just Stacy, but I was scared we'd tire her out too much, having a little kid around all day, the fact that she liked coming over to the King's Ransome too, to use the pool or have Sunday brunch with us, the fact that Barry brought his whole family for brunch once, the fact that he really liked the brunch they did there, the fact that he probably never got enough to eat at Abby's, and he was a bit of a gourmet type too, Caite and Kris, the fact that kids really seem to get bent out of shape over divorce and remarriage, even though most every kid now has a step-parent or two, Concealed Carry, carrots growing underground, a spaghetti squash wearing a diamond ring, the fact that you can't assume a kid's related to both parents anymore, and what does it matter, when they all secretly wish they were *adopted* anyway, *Jane Eyre*, the fact that maybe they should teach divorce-coping skills in school along with First Aid, food hygiene, sex ed, how to make chocolate chip cookies, and how to do your taxes, stepmom, stepdad, Stepford wives, the fact that I kind of spoiled Leo when we first got together, I know, and maybe concentrated on him too much, and left Stacy out of things, without ever *meaning* to, the fact that all I wanted was for us all to get along as a family, the fact that I was so darn happy though, euphoric, so bowled over by him, the fact that I just assumed Stace would love him too and things would all work out, which I see now was kind of simplistic, the fact that Leo's the most loving guy in the world though, so I never thought it would be difficult, and she liked him from the start, but she held back, the fact that I think she was still hoping *Frank* would somehow return, the fact that I thought it would all be all right once she'd had time to get to know Leo better, Stepdad Day, and saw how great he is, seesaw, the fact that then Ben came along, and maybe she felt even *more* left out, though I know Leo did everything he could to prevent that, the fact that we used to talk about it, Leo and me, not Leo, Stacy and me, we, the fact that I guess I was in my own dreamland, Candyland, the unconscious mind, the fact that none of this is *his* fault, that is for sure, the fact that he's tried so hard to be a good stepdad, the fact that he always loved Stace, the fact that Stacy said in our session that I defer to him too much and it drives her nuts, the fact that I guess it's a habit of mine, the fact that I don't know where I got it, oh yeah, from my mom, the fact that I used to defer to Frank too, and baby *him*, the fact that all I've got left of Mommy are a few ashtrays, some silverware, her hand-painted birthday cards, blue lamb, and this deferential attitude with men, cowed, coward, the fact that I guess it's true I didn't give Stacy enough attention when Leo and I got together, and now I miss her, my first child, and that's my punishment, the fact that she was an only child for a while, but it's not *good* to be an only child, the fact that chickens who only have one chick never leave that chick *alone*, the fact that Fanny Trollope saved her whole family, the fact that the Indian tracker guy insists on working alone, the fact that he's refused all help from the authorities now, and wants no more choppers and traps and every-thing, because they don't help, beard a lion in its den, Androcles and the lion, thorn in the paw, Gothic Revival, Arts and Crafts, baseboard, vaulted ceiling, the fact that it's horrible to be criticized by your own daughter who used to kind of *like* you, the fact that just about anything can go wrong between moms and their kids though, the fact that maybe *most* daughters hate their mom, the fact that maybe it's natural, the fact that adolescents have a lot to deal with, and Step 1 is to hate your parents, even if your parents really aren't that bad, the fact that *some* moms drive cars full of kids right off a bridge, and I never did that at least, Mark Twain, the fact that, compared to some, I don't think I'm so bad, but Stacy does, the fact that sometimes I do feel myself kind of recoil when Stacy gets at me, the fact that maybe I'm not as patient as I might be, or as brave, the fact that I don't take criticism well, or anger, the fact that Caite and Kris say I've got to hang in there because she's the kid and I'm the adult, and she still needs her mom, the fact that she doesn't act like it much, euphoria, nap, Mommy in the kitchen, blue lamb, the fact that maybe Daddy *wouldn't* disapprove of my baking, the fact that maybe he'd think it was awesome to have a daughter who knew her way around a cinna-mon roll, around and *around* a cinnamon roll, the fact that I kind of doubt it though, the fact that he might've respected the tarte tatin operation more, but not as a real job, but how do I know, the fact that I hardly *knew* the guy, the fact that at first I thought he'd disapprove of me getting pregnant with Stacy but it turned out he liked babies as much as I do, the fact that he probably would have gotten a big kick out of having more grandkids, if he'd lived long enough to, the fact that he only got to meet Stace and Smithy, Ethan's firstborn, the fact that Smithy's at *college* now, the fact that I guess we're all suckers for babies in my family, Mommy, Daddy, Ethan, the fact that I should've gone to some kind of Parent Guidance course, divorce guidance, the fact that I was just too young when my mom and dad died, the fact that I'm like a stunted animal, the runt of the litter, up Wookie Creek without a paddle, the fact that I think *Adam Lanza* had some kind of therapist, the fact that that is not much of an ad for therapy, epoxy, tiller, V-bottomed hull, the fact that some guy saw the lioness out the window of his barn, some guy who makes canoes, the fact that he carves them by hand, lapstrake, mahogany trim, cockpit, foremast, the fact that they look beautiful in the pictures, the fact that maybe the kids would like a canoe, the fact that the boatbuilder guy said he wasn't scared of the lioness, the fact that she was "just moseying around minding her own business," the fact that the NRA immediately accused the guy of lying, partly because he didn't try to shoot it, and also because there's some conspiracy theory that people are trying to repopulate America with dangerous wild animals, and soon the laws will be changed to protect animals rights over people's, the fact that what they really hate is that if the boatbuilder's telling the truth, there's no need for this whole national emergency and the surge in gun sales, mushroom cloud, the fact that maybe the lion isn't a threat to life and limb after all, shiver me timbers, cedarwood, stern-sheets, sailboat canoe, oarlocks, the fact that our pretty little Dutch folk costumes were so colorfully striped, with a white petticoat underneath, and the little white apron in front, Arvo Pärt, the Cherokee tracker, Indian guides, cherrywood canoes, the fact that I dreamt I was on a boat in Italy and there were a whole lot of men in white shirts swimming alongside it like *dolphins*, the fact that they did this every day in their lunch hour apparently, the fact that boats are not ships, and ships are not boats, and some people are very sure of the difference and some aren't, and I'm one of them, I mean one of the ones that are a bit shaky on the subject, shaky on *boats* too, and on ships, the fact that deep water scares me, the fact that I am no sailor, nervous wreck trembling at the bottom of the sea, le mer, la mère, the fact that you're "on" a boat but "in" a ship, Titanic, aft, stern, sternum, septum, styptic stick, the fact that I think Leo knows the difference between boats and ships but I don't, *And that has made all the difference*, the fact that an old covered bridge got burnt to a crisp in a forest fire somewhere, Meryl Streep, *The Bridges of Madison County*, the fact that Meryl Streep really seems like an Italian woman stuck in the middle of nowhere in that movie, Iowa, the fact that Mommy once sneezed seventeen times in a row, the fact that I remember all the wrong stuff, like I remember a roadside stand in Delaware, or that bee swerving up off the windowsill in Bread Loaf, or a missing jigsaw piece from puzzles we no longer even own, and hostas, and geraniums, certain houses, trash men we've had over the years, but I can't remember my own mom or dad, the fact that I need to go through the old photo albums in the attic, the fact that I was a very bewildered child, I think, much more bewildered than my kids seem to be, the fact that I think I spent most of my childhood blanketed in ignorance, confusion, Hoag's crocheted snuggly, and I guess my adulthood's heading the same way, the fact that half the stuff Stacy mentioned in Family Therapy I didn't know or couldn't remember, I really couldn't, the fact that it was like I hadn't been there, through Stacy's whole childhood, but I know I was, the fact that I just remember different stuff, the fact that that probably upsets her even more, but I can't help it, the fact that she could be making some of this stuff *up* and I wouldn't know, because it's all a blank to me, the fact that Anne Tyler's always praising people for having a good memory, and I agree it's handy, but I don't know if it's a virtue, or some kind of great achievement, the fact that I'd like to remember some stuff and not other stuff, the fact that okay guys, I'm coming in, good chickies, the fact that this chicken coop needs a good spring clean, maybe a paint job, fusilli, phulu-pututu, tarawai, takwara, the fact that the words for wind instruments sound like rodents, capybara, degu, jird, the fact that I remember Mommy's *onion soup*, the fact that she'd probably want to be remembered for other things she accomplished, but cooking is all I think about anymore, the fact that I'm always thinking about *food*, ocarina, the fact that *I* probably won't be remembered for anything except maybe my cinnamon rolls, tartes tatin, madeleines and my terrible memory, remembrance, oh, and also for messing up Stacy's childhood, and getting married without her consent, *Ryan's Daughter*, Robert Mitchum, the fact that during Ramadan you're allowed to cook during the day if you want to, before sundown, but you can't *taste* anything you cook, the fact that you can only rub a little on the edge of the tongue, but not swallow, and you can't eat or drink all day, the fact that in hot countries it must be tough, if you're thirsty, the fact that I don't think my orthodontist was very good, the fact that Mommy got sick of him too, always putting more rubber bands on me, orthodontist appointments, the fact that Ben says spiny mice can completely regenerate damaged tissue, including fur, but I really hate to think how they discovered that, and verified it, circadian rhythm, Mommy, heart operation, cardiologist, the fact that some country says they're going to have the cure for cancer in one year, the fact that they just have a few more experiments to do, the fact that Leo says it's all based on one study involving thirty mice, and that it takes *five* years to test any new drug, the fact that he thinks the pharmaceutical company that made this claim is full of unforgivable conmen and fraudsters, getting people's hopes up, the fact that Gillian's got to go see one soon, an *orthodontist* not a fraudster, touch wood, dear me, the fact that there's something wrong with how her canines are coming in, canine, K9, Jim, the fact that where has he gone, that poor dog, the fact that thinking about Jim actually makes me feel dizzy, the fact that I need to sit down, Sitting Is The New Smoking, the fact that is it guilt or fear, the fact that sitting down is bad for you, the fact that you're supposed to run around the living room instead or something, *vacuuming* like a crazee person, the fact that Caite and Kris want to know everything that went wrong between me and Frank, the fact that when I tried to tell them about it, Stacy went very quiet, the fact that I was scared of upsetting her, but maybe she's always wanted to know more about Frank but never dared ask, nose flute, ocarina, ocelot, least weasel, the fact that some instrument names sound like grumbling, sackbut, the fact that I think Frank lied to her about a lot of stuff, like he made out that the breakup was *my* fault, the fact that what am I supposed to say, nguru, the fact that I don't want to badmouth him to her, gundi, gamelan, the fact that a sackbut is a kind of trombone, the fact that Cincinnati Zoo has an ocelot, not a sackbut, the fact that the sackbut, I mean *ocelot*, does some kind of outreach program, he's an ambassador of some kind, the fact that there's a traveling didgeridoo that's spiraled, the fact that Stace and I were so relieved to get out of there, out of our therapy session, the fact that we rushed off to the mall together and it was fun, the fact that I can hardly remember the last time I spent an afternoon with Stace on her own, the fact that I've been trying to *avoid* being alone with her, for fear of the Silent Treatment or getting screamed at or mocked or scolded, nguru, gundi, but we had a nice time this time, just girls together, kind of like going to Old Orchard with Mommy to get school clothes, Jim, Willoughby, the fact that the first sugar beet farmers in America were abolitionists in Massachusetts, no, Pennsylvania, The Beet Sugar Society of Philadelphia, the fact that they were hoping to curb the use of slave labor on sugar planta- tions in the West Indies by promoting beet sugar, maple sugar too maybe, reverse sugar, molecules, salt, oniony hands, sugaring your legs, sugar trees, the fact that the broken chains around the Statue of Liberty's feet are supposed to represent the end of American slavery, the fact that it takes more than breaking the chains though, the fact that I never heard such racist talk as I've heard in Ohio, the fact that Ben said Brett calls black people monkeys, the fact that they drove past some black kids on the street and Brett laughed at them and called them monkeys, and his parents laughed too, the fact that it's at times like that that I think we should go back to New Haven, but we don't have the *money* to move anywhere, brow threading, the fact that Jake said he saw the lion in our back yard from his bedroom window, the same night Jim went missing, the fact that he was sure he saw it, but then Ben started telling him about the Abominable Snowman, and Jake changed his story, the fact that now he says an Abominable Snowman took Jim, the fact that I still wonder about it sometimes though, the fact that what if Jake's right and the lion *was* out there, and maybe snatched Jim and *ate* him, oh dear, was it a cat I saw, able was I ere I saw Elba, the fact that what do you do, the fact that there's nothing you *can* do, the fact that there's nobody to sue, is there, if a wild animal comes and eats your dog, the fact that are we *insured* for that, the fact that I don't think our insurance covers much, the fact that wouldn't it be nice to get everything so insured that they'd compensate you for *anything* anytime, fully compensate you, without trying to wriggle out of it, the fact that that would be one of my three wishes, an end to pollution, time with Mommy, and deluxe insurance, *Bigger Than Life*, and a swimming pool, *The Best Years of Our Lives*, Teresa Wright, Myrna Loy, the fact that, heavens to Betsy, I already feel bad enough about poor Jim, without him getting *eaten*, the fact that if that happened, so soon after we got him home from the pound, right after we supposedly "rescued" him, oh the poor thing, the fact that they'll never let us have another dog, the fact that I'll have to let them know at some point, because they do a follow-up by email after you adopt a dog, WYD, WMD, Where's Your Dog?, oh dear, mindset, the fact that maybe we'll never know what happened to Jim and we'll just have to go on imagining forever, bait dogs, the fact that it sure looks like he's never coming back, and he never even learnt how to chase a ball yet, the fact that he doesn't have his collar on, the fact that it's still attached to the rope on the coop, and now a storm is brewing, the fact that there's a big storm in *Twelve Angry Men*, in the middle of all their deliberations, and with the storm comes clarity, the fact that with global warming we seem to be getting a lot more clarity than we bargained for, or more storms anyway, the fact that the median income of Hillary Clinton's supporters was $61,000 and for

Trump's it was $70,000 or more, the fact that I don't know what they mean by "median," median, the fact that Henry Fonda has that strange walk, the fact that I worry for him the whole time, the fact that poor Henry Fonda, the fact that I'm sure he couldn't help it, but that really is a strange walk, the fact that Gloria Steinem had some sort of Cherokee wedding, I mean she got married in a Cherokee *way*, not to a *Cherokee*, as far as I know, the fact that the tracker they've hired to help catch the lion, or *lioness*, is Cherokee, the fact that I keep forgetting it's a lioness, the fact that Jane Fonda likes to hang out with Gloria Steinem, the fact that in the first scene in *Psycho*, Janet Leigh's in her me-oh-mys in the hotel room, her underthings, corsetry, bra, underpants, cock, cockpit, CVR, the fact that I think Rod Steiger's just too convincing as a psychotic, in *Oklahoma*, the fact that he's really scary, the fact that Gene Kelly's too goofy in *An American in Paris*, the fact that that movie just doesn't make any sense, but hardly any musicals make any sense, the fact that I like *The Music Man*, because it doesn't *try* to make sense, ocarina, the fact that the guy who wrote that worked on it for years and years and *years*, getting it right, "He doesn't know the territory," the fact that finally the twelve angry guys calm down and talk on equal terms, and it gets like a Native American talking circle, the fact that they all turn *reasonable*, instead of all red-faced and emotional, the fact that they start to consider things calmly and respectfully, and the result is the defendant gets off, the love of punishment, the fact that the police should try it, a talking circle, I mean, not the love of punishment, and shooting everybody they meet, the fact that I always thought Stacy didn't *mind* about the playhouse, but she did mind, broken chicken ladder, the fact that the reporters are now concentrating on the Cherokee tracker himself, the fact that they must be sick of the very word "lion," lion Dems, the fact that the Cherokee tracker's only *half*-Cherokee and he grew up in the Bronx, the fact that it's like they want to discredit his tracking skills, but his skills have got to be better than the people who've been hunting the lion *so far*, that didn't get him, or her, the fact that when they did find her they lost her, the fact that, as somebody said, just because he's half-Cherokee doesn't mean he's only going to catch half a lion, the fact that he had a complicated *birth* but he's fine now, the fact that he's thirty-five years old so I guess he did survive whatever his neo-natal problem was, the fact that I think it was something like his blood was incompatible with his mother's, the fact that they report all this stuff on the *national news*, the fact that it doesn't really seem any of my business whether this man had a rough birth or not, though of course I'm glad he's okay, the fact that he seems amused that every-body calls him the "Cherokee tracker," since he was brought up Italian and only found out as a grown man that he has some Cherokee in him, the fact that I know Jake would like it if the half-Cherokee tracker drove a half-track, the fact that the Cherokee tracker never knew his own dad, the fact that his mom used to make great risotto Milanese, the kind with all the saffron, and bone marrow, but she was also mel-ancholic, the fact that the half-Cherokee tracker was *planning* to be a police officer, but then became a wildlife officer instead, the fact that he protects eagles from hunters and farmers and egg-poachers, dcea-glecam, so maybe he helped bring the Ohio bald eagle back from near-extinction, along the Cuyahoga, vuvuzela, chinoiserie, the fact that bald eagles have very high voices, the fact that so did Jim, the fact that owls screech but also hoot, and their hoots are lower than the screeches, I think, more of a bass tenor sound, the fact that crocodiles sort of warble sometimes, the fact that there's nothing so wonderful as a tenor, I don't know why, Pavarotti, ♫ *Nessun dorma* ♫, Pol Pot, pot luck supper, pot au feu, the fact that, I mean, *boy*, they really fill your head up with a lot of information, the fact that I don't know how much we really need to know about the Cherokee tracker, the fact that he has a daughter somewhere, *pat-a-cake, pat-a-cake*, the fact that he's good at finding children as well as animals, the fact that maybe we should've gotten him to track *Stacy* down the night she ran away, the fact that Pol Pot's real name was Saloth Sar, and he liked *Verlaine*, the fact that a guy who liked French poetry killed a quarter of the Cambodian population, the fact that Leo says if America had never had the war with Vietnam, none of that Cambodian stuff would have happened, the fact that Saloth Sar might have just read a lot more Verlaine and *refrained* from killing two million people, the fact that murderers make choices, and choices have consequences, tiffins, the fact that I've always tried to avoid knowing which artists and poets are preferred by mass murderers, because it really puts you off, the fact that it makes you feel sick, thinking about their pleasures, the fact that Trump only likes Fox News and portraits of *himself*, Pol Pot, pot belly, chicken pot pie, the fact that Hitler liked Wagner, concentration camp number tattoos, the fact that that Wagner opera I went to was so long it nearly killed me, and that was one of the *shorter* ones, the fact that I should get with the program, but all those horns, and golden rings, and chalices or whatever and gods, talk about goofy, Brunnhilde, the Ring cycle, potlatch, potluck, the Wagner tuba, the fact that some flautist sued his own orchestra for ruining his hearing during a Wagner concert, the fact that he was sitting right in front of the horn section and the noise reached decibel levels equivalent to being inside the engine of a *plane*, the fact that he's never been the same since, acoustic shock, and it's all because of Wagner, the fact that, Mother of Exiles, I don't think he can play the flute at all anymore, the fact that I don't know why people listen to that stuff, pepper pot soup,

.   .   .   .

Things seemed never to run smoothly with men, fake birds that dragged themselves flightless and cowering across the land.

She hid from their greedy depredations, and turned to face the storm. As thunder and lightning spread in the distance, she dreamt of slithering up a tree and caterwauling till dawn. Her cries made rain cascade like waterfalls, whole sheets of water pounding the valley to pulp, mush, mud. There was so much water it formed a lake. The first to drown there would be men who stole the young of lions.

She dreamt again that she lived deep in the lake, still searching for her cubs behind every waving frond. She prowled the bare sandy bottom, leaping between sand-curled boulders.

Men criss-crossed the surface above, cupped in their floating nests. With a switch of her tail the lioness could set off currents to batter their boats against rocks. Once waterlogged, the vessels flipped over and zigzagged to the bottom, making little whirlpools all the way down. The final thud when they hit the lake floor nearly threw her off her footing.

In winter, the lake would freeze. Encased in their plastic winter padding, people stalked or skated insouciantly over the ice above. But she could heat the icy crust and pierce the surface just by staring at it. The ice cracked, the killers drifted down. Leave their puffy bodies to settle undisturbed. Let the catfish have them.

Waking, the dog wanted to play. She gave him a companionable swat, and momentarily weighed him down by resting her paw across his shoulders. Then she stretched, seemingly to twice her usual length, and ambled out of the dark woods, listening for cubs. She was nearing them now, she knew.

Pre-rain sank into the fur of her spine. She anticipated a fierce storm, loud enough to help her proceed without detection. She wanted to leave no trace. She could enter a suburban area at night, if it would rain hard enough to hide her.

Fences were painful to jump with a sore leg. She tried to avoid them. She found strange trees with bark that was hard to scratch. Their branches were low, and came together into tight, pinched little trunks. She regarded these tree trunks with distrust, since behind them could lurk a thin, upright killer man, who might see her before she caught sight of him. She longed for thicker foliage at ground level but there was none, only stretches of nibbled-down grass interrupted by black macadam, that sticky substance with which men ribboned the world.

The dog, though quick of course at smelling things, still had no idea what she was looking for. But he knew that they were being followed.

To get a better view, the lion mounted a low ridge of land with many prongs. She stood atop the highest point and snarled, daring the sky to unleash its mist and rain. It worked. Lightning bolts appeared high above the earth, flashing through holes in cloud.

Awaiting the heavy pelt of rain, she crouched and let the storm surge around her until she was blinded by the flashes of light. The rain washed across her back and down the hill, turning the path below into a shallow moat. Lightning scorched the trees. Finally surrounded by thunder, the lioness leapt ten feet in the air, and roared back.

For all of life is leap and recoil, recoil and leap.

The dog scampered in confused circles. The lioness and the storm were more interesting to him than all the rest of his life had been.

A man approached swiftly through the flashes and the shadows. He had overcome grave illness at birth, bureaucratic indignities, professional betrayals and disappointments. Somehow, he had even evaded fellow lion hunters tonight, in order to bring this lioness in alive.

The release of a tranquilizer dart resonated despite the rush of wind and rain, and silently the lioness fell, once again wounded by a man. Sodden, deafened by thunder and subdued by pain, she slowly relaxed and then slept, dreaming that she spied her cubs across a vast, foggy pool. Across it, her cubs swam to her.

The dog let out a high-pitched whine and ran in aggrieved fury at the stranger. But one look from the man and the dog started to tremble, expecting a beating. Whimpering, he lay submissively on his belly, and turned his snout away from his enemy without hope. The man bent down to scratch the dog's white chest ruffles.

.   .   .   .

the fact that sometimes men do brave things to *help* people, like Casey Jones, or that nice bus driver, the fact that not all men cut little girls to pieces, not by any means, "Sweet Fanny Adams," the fact that Leo helps people every day, and there are heroes who wrestle with the gunman, tie him up, and press down on his victim's arteries until the ambulance arrives, SBLI, TB12, #deflategate, Sieg Heil salutes, big joke, bullies, bullies everywhere, bully boys, the fact that there are men who cut the fins off sharks and toss the sharks back into the sea, where they sink to the bottom and *suffocate*, the fact that I shouldn't think about it, Cathy, boarlets, the fact that a man rescued a wolf he found caught in a trap, and that's a *nice* story, and somewhere in Thailand there's a man who goes out daily to feed a pack of wild dogs by the highway, Yale Co-op, Harvard Coop, lion hunters, Hunt's tomato sauce, thank-you letters, the fact that the Clovis people were the first inhabitants of Newcomerstown, the fact that they were the original inhabitants of the Americas, the Mayflower, the Wampanoag, the fact that George Washington went to the circus in Philadelphia, cherry tree, the fact that Newcomerstown was later part of the Delaware Nation, Nachbar, neighbors, Oxford Township, the fact that most of the first European inhabitants here were called Neighbour, or Nachbar, the fact that Nicholas Neighbour bought a thousand acres of Oxford Township off Godfrey Haga in 1814, the fact that *they* didn't name it Newcomerstown, the fact that it was already called that, cornbread, popcorn, porno pics, tacos, the fact that by 1820, there were a hundred and ten people living here, all related to Nicholas Neighbour, the fact that he brought all his relatives with him from New Jersey, the fact that *Persuasion* was published in 1817, but Jane Austen had already passed away, the fact that all this happened two hundred years ago, premiere, Met opera commentary, Ira, Mary Jo, Margaret Juntwait, Caite, the fact that phthalates cause hormone imbalances, cancer, and birth defects and, according to Ben, Americans are full of phthalates, fast foods are full of phthalates, and there are phthalates in kids' *toys*, and printing ink, and perfume, moisturizer, hairspray and nail polish, deodorants, diaper cream, PVC flooring, glues, soaps and IV tubes, marmalade cats, the fact that phthalates are related to phthalic acid, another of those acids people should probably leave well alone, the fact that why would anybody want to put phthalates in *diaper* cream, the fact that they really are trying to *kill* us or something, three-tiered chicken factory, palm oil, palm-reading, the fact that they found phthalates in every home in

Bulgaria, and that's just one study, the fact that we have all been *poisoning* ourselves, the fact that where is Rachel Carson when we need her, the fact that the sea is the mother of all life, the fact that the good news is phthalates "pose no acute toxicity," but pregnant women, children and teens really shouldn't be eating anything, it sounds like, because it's all got phthalates in it, the fact that I can't even pronounce it, "phthalates," Thalidomide, pacifiers, the fact that have my *pies* got phthalates in them, the fact they used to put phthalates in those too, in pacifiers, I mean, the fact that that's like saying "Here, kid, blow your brains out," the fact that it's not very neighborly of them, putting phthalates in everything before they even figured out if it's bad for people or not, water supply, train heroes, the fact that Nicholas Neighbour must have been quite the optimist, dragging sixty or seventy settlers with him by wagon train from the German Valley in New Jersey, the fact that the children had to *walk* the whole way, to save the horses, and as they walked they sang, Jack getting lost when the Ingallses crossed the river, Paterson Falls, Niagara Falls, the fact that we've had such torrential rain lately, torrent, torrential, torture, torment, Yosemite jigsaw puzzle, Jean Carlton, Fresia, the fact that I don't know if the rain is all that good for geraniums, the fact that Newcomerstown's had both slaves and abolitionists, and the Underground Railroad, the fact that Coshocton was a major UGRR stop, or station, the fact that escaped slaves came to the Temperance Tavern Inn on the canal, and you can still see the hiding-place, the fact that people had to hide to save their lives, in *our town*, kitchen utensils, Cy Young Room, *Our Town*, Thornton Wilder, Thornton, Thorne miniature rooms, the fact that I hope Cathy doesn't miss Blanche too much still, the fact that what do you do when someone's torn from you like that, so violently, Stacy, sleeping bag, Jim, the fact that more than half the women in *prison* are victims of domestic violence, the fact that the Erie canal was completed in 1825, and it was a huge engineering feat, three hundred and eight miles long, with a hundred and forty-six locks, fifty-six guard locks, fourteen aqueducts, two large reservoirs, and fifty wood culverts, Harrison Ford, the one-armed man, gopher, freckles, the fact that it had six feeder dams and eight dams across streams, but they were smallish dams, the fact that it's hard to like a dam, give a dam, *Little Women*, the fact that Louisa May Alcott said *Tom Sawyer* would corrupt children, and Mark Twain said it wasn't *meant* for children, the fact that the locks were ninety feet long and fifteen feet wide, the fact that the walls were five-foot-thick at the base, and four feet thick at the water line, the fact that the boats could be thirteen to fourteen feet wide and up to seventy-nine feet long, but any bigger and they might have hurt the berms, the berms, Thornton, the fact that the laborers were paid 30¢ a day, plus board and lodging, but this went up later to $26 a month, plus board, the fact that people love to underpay you, people, Peekaboo, Peolia, $15 dollars an hour, the fact that I guess it's all over between me and Peekaboo now, the fact that my standoff hasn't exactly resulted in triumph, "withhold your labor," the fact that the canals took passenger packets, cargo transport, coal barges, and state maintenance boats, all pulled along the towpath by horses, the fact that it took three and a half days to get from Cleveland to Portsmouth by passenger packet, and the tickets cost $1.70, which included meals, King's Ransome, Abby's cocktail crackers, the fact that *passenger* craft had right of way over the cargo boats, and they could carry up to sixty people, walking the plank, ship ahoy, on board, stern, aft, after, craft, craft beer, *on* a boat, *in* a ship, pirates, Ohio Blue Tip Matches, the fact that the canal passed through Peninsula, Canal Fulton, Massillon, Canal Dover, Newcomerstown, Coshocton, Newark and Carroll, before it got to Columbus, "It's got us!", and from there, it ran along beside the Scioto River through Circleville, Chillicothe and Waverly, and met up with the Ohio River at Portsmouth, the fact that it's almost all gone now, after all that *work*, the throwaway culture, the fact that it wasn't just about canals either, as I tell the kids, the fact that there were all the inns set up to feed passengers and canallers, and stables for the horses, a whole way of life, the fact that canal boats are such a pleasant way to travel, and you don't use up any fossil fuels, the fact that you use *trees* up, to build the boats, and you have to have feed from somewhere for the horses, and the passengers, but that's about it, the fact that we still have Aunt Sophia's grain cradle, the china wash basin and pitcher, her black pot, the porridge jar, the sundial, the coal oil lamp, the photos, daguerreotypes, Leo's great great great uncle's Civil War diary, the high chair, a key-wind pocket watch, and a pedestal shaving mirror, but not the double-barreled captain's pistol or Sophia's own trapdoor Springfield, the fact that her long hair caught fire, the fact that you lead a fairly quiet and virtuous life for eighty or ninety years and all of a sudden one day your hair catches fire and you burn up, shell noodles, doorstep, door stoop, lounger, not in my back yard, eggs, "You're a wonderful egg," the fact that I couldn't *sleep* last night, for thinking about all the chicken eggs in the world that never reached and never will reach the hatching stage, Leo's iguana's eggs too that he didn't eat, the fact that all over the world there must be poor little shivering wood pigeon chicks, all curled up inside their abandoned eggshells, getting colder and colder, enemies, foreign and domestic, the numbness of muted beings, the fact that it reminds me of that new sapling I saw, the fact that it was just a baby thing, five feet tall, and a bag of dog do had been flung into its branches, the fact that how many years will it hang there, as the tree grows, wishing it was dead, the fact that Trump would probably say everything's going *swell* for that tree, Ronny's Trump T-shirt, Stacy's POTUS T-shirt, because some day that awful bag of dog do will fall *off* the tree and maybe fertilize the soil beneath and make the tree grow tall and strong, wall, borders, Connecticut boulders, the fact that I'm not all that sure dog do is good for the soil though, because dogs eat meat or something, the fact that horse manure's good for roses, It's Quality That Counts, my dog do dream, five-mile-deep chasms, anal cancer, the fact that anyway I wish people would put their dog do in the trash, the fact that nobody wants to see a bag of dog do hanging on a tree, even at the best of times, poop scoop, drool-yet Juliet, dollars to donuts, Prime Pennsylvania Farmland, the fact that some kids get bitten by sharks, and some get 50% burns, and some get nothing for Christmas, the pantry, eggs, Cathy, the fact that I'd better get dressed, the fact that Ohioans are such pushovers for any mention of Ohio, or anyone who comes from Ohio, *Winesburg, Ohio*, wiseacre, windows, little puckered apples, Laine Hanson, the fact that, boy, is this all anybody in America does, look for people from the same *state* as you, state of mind, the fact that I always feel like I'm a stranger here, the fact that I don't know if I'm from Illinois or Connecticut but I'm definitely not from Ohio, and I try not to get too involved, especially in the politics, the fact that politics doesn't sell pies, though, come to think of it, I did make a little money out of my donkey and elephant sugar cookies last election season, the fact that Cathy made me do them every week, and sure enough, they sold, in about equal numbers too, which kind of surprised everybody, the fact that it doesn't make much sense, unless they were just buying the Dem cookies to *stamp* on or throw at people or something, or maybe it's just that some people like blue frosting better than red, Heller brothers, Hellmann's, No Soap Radio, the fact that the level of mercury in the Ohio River went up by five hundred percent between 2007 and 2013, and nobody even knows how high it is now, except maybe Ben and Mr. Bowder, bow wow, beards, the fact that some men shave all over their face but leave the hair to grow long on their *necks*, under their chins, and I don't think that's such a good idea, but I shouldn't be mean, the fact that I guess Mr. Bowder can do what he wants with his own neck, for Pete's sake, the fact that Leo says it's a "neck beard" and it's a thing, the fact that *Thoreau* had one, but Thoreau's one was bushier, the fact that Mr. Bowder's is all thin and scraggly and, the fact that Bernie Sanders got all of Burlington, Vermont, to go in for solar paneling, the fact that I took a look inside a Bernie Sanders campaign office in New Philly once, and it looked really kind of a mess, I gotta say, but maybe all campaign offices are like that, the fact that I wouldn't know about that, the fact that Bernie could never have gotten in, because the Dems would never have let him have the nomination, bird landing on the podium, the fact that America's been ruined by the two-party system, Leo says, the fact that now people are thinking of putting solar panels over parking lots, which might be good, because it would give the cars some shade too, the fact that when I said that to Stacy, she said "Cars? Why should we have cars, if we're trying to save the environment?! But you're *not* trying to save the environment, so what do you care about solar panels?", which kind of crushed me, the fact that I think she may have put me off solar power for good, the fact that my heart sinks now whenever I hear any mention of it, pique, Peekaboo, Janice, janitor, the fact that Stace really doesn't think much of me, and not just environmentally, our rotten windows, the fact that the purest water on earth isn't rainwater, or mineral water, the fact that it's distilled water, but Leo says distilled water's no good for drinking because it's got no ions or something, the fact that it also tastes bad, the fact that our tap water doesn't taste too great either, the fact that our fridge is now full of filter jugs, the fact that there are still protests going on about it, about drinking water quality, not our fridge, hog maw, bear paw, the fact that I don't know why people do those things, the fact that I'm always scared they'll get shot, either by the police or by white supremacists or flat earthers and Open Carry fans, the fact that you gotta wonder if it's worth dying over, when you can just go to the store and get some bottled water, or a water filter, the fact that cinnamon rolls take all my energy, the fact that I leave politics to people with time on their hands, the fact that most presidents probably don't have a *clue* how to make a cinnamon roll, though Jimmy Carter might be happy to learn, the fact that most of them are such sourpusses, the fact that I don't think I can listen to Trump anymore, I just can't take any more of him, the fact that nothing he says makes any *sense*, the fact that I think he tires *everybody* out, bullet, bully, cyber bullies, cyber school, that screw-up teacher, the fact that I almost wrote to the principal about that screw-up teacher but you don't want to wade into this stuff, I mean open a great big can of worms, the fact that I don't want that guy coming after *me* next, and, and, and telling me *I'm* a screw-up, the fact that I've got Stace for that, windowless chhaupadi shed, our rotting windows, the fact that Caite and Kris complimented me and

933

Stace on how *well* we get along, which was quite a surprise, the fact that I hadn't expected that, because, however well we get along, it didn't stop Stacy wanting to *run away*, to Arizona of all places, aqueducts, canals, channels, TV channels, MSM, ducks, sitting ducks, ducking out of things, the fact that in Texas it's now easier to get into government buildings if you *carry* a gun than if you *don't*, because if you say you don't have one, you have to wait in a long line for the metal detectors, while if you *show* your gun, they let you right in, the fact that Davina Beebee told me Reynoldsburg is where her family goes to buy guns, her and her hurts, don't sweat the small stuff, the fact that what would Davina Beebee do if something *really* bad happened to her, chance, Blanche, blanch, blank, point blank, the fact that I've spent hours and hours listening to Davina Beebee's hurts and I feel like I still hardly know her, the fact that it seems like the last thing that ever happens in Ohio is you really get to know somebody, the last thing that ever happens in *America*, except for Cathy, and Anat maybe, trucks covered with lumber, the fact that people seem to be getting worse, not better, the fact that the more they shoot, the more they seem to want to shoot some more, the fact that some gunman told his victims not to *bunch up*, so he could kill them more easily, the fact that a police officer on TV said what used to be a fist fight or road rage is now a shooting, and what used to be a domestic dispute is now a gun rampage, and what used to be a tardy or disruptive student is now a school shooter, the fact that the police aren't much better themselves, the fact that what used to be an arrest or a warning is now a split-second execution, the fact that the police shot that woman in her pajamas, the fact that the police Taser *pregnant women*, and nobody knows yet what the effect of that is on a fetus, the fact that that is punishing the child for the sins of the mom, Davina's hurts, Ben's encyclopedia of bosom, cat kibble, chicken feed, the Statue of Liberty's chains, Pepto-Bismol, laxatives, sleeping pills, calcium, Vitamin C, 1817, the fact that pomegranate seeds and colocynth were used to induce abortions in Ancient Egypt or Babylon or someplace, the fact that it said so in Stacy's weird sex guidebook, the fact that a refugee somewhere in Africa, Somalia maybe, or Sudan, went into labor and had to give birth by the side of the road, and she was mocked by passersby, the fact that that's one of the cruelest things I ever heard of, but there are crueler things, shark fins, shark-fin soup, the fact that a white lynch mob killed a black man for no reason, no reason, and when his eight-months pregnant wife objected, they strung *her* up by her feet and burnt her alive, the fact that she went into premature labor and they ripped her stomach open with a knife and threw the baby on the ground and they let that poor little baby cry twice before they stamped on its *skull*, the fact that this is America, the country I grew up in, the country Trump calls great, "I pledge allegiance to the United States of America," the fact that I try never to think about that story, *never*, that baby, or you just want to die, that brave woman and her helpless baby, "Sweet Fanny Adams," Breivik, ISIS guys smiling while they behead a child, a *child*, Nazis swinging babies against walls, those guys in Texas who tied a black man to their pickup and drove for miles until, until, all the terrible, terrible things, the fact that once in New York I heard a young woman walking alone in the rain, late at night, and I looked out of our hotel window, and there she was, so drunk she was running into lamp posts, the fact that just the clip-clopping of her heels on the sidewalk made me think she was in for some terrible calamity, the fact that I was scared it would attract the wrong sort of attention, the fact that I almost *knew* it would, and I should've run out and helped her, like brought her inside the hotel or something, but I was too cowardly or shy or too polite or too easily embarrassed, the fact that I thought she'd shoo me away and I'd be hurt, my hurts, rape, poached eggs at the Washington Square Diner, the lioness, the fact that some guy in Kentucky conned a millionairess out of all her dough, and then shot her, the fact that they were engaged, the fact that we all go on pretending things are fine, hoping everything's a-okay, even though everything is nowhere near okay and we all know it, no matter how many candlelit vigils you hold, the fact that everything's just so darned *stupid* if you ask me, this stupid furniture of ours, my stupid dishwasher arrangements, stupid Tupperware habits, our stupid car, our stupid neglected back yard, our stupid termite-ridden house, stupid rotten windows, the stupid Queen of England, stupid soap running out, stupid old Woodrow Wilson, ten thousand stupid soldiers, no, *twenty thousand*, and their stupid rifles, stupid rock-bottom price underpants, stupid discounts, stupid coupons, stupid social encounters, my stupid cake ad, stupid cakes, stupid pies, stupid, *stupid* cinnamon rolls, stupid chocolate chip cookies, stupid crabstick sandwiches, our stupid computer that doesn't work, stupid empty bank account, the stupid kitchen table where there's no room to sit, stupid stool that hurts my back, stupid high chair, stupid hot dogs and Sloppy Joes for dinner every stupid night, stupid dinner rolls, stupid canapés, stupid Irma Rombauer, stupid Amy Adams, stupid stupid shootings for no reason, the fact that it's all so *stupid*, stupid Open Carry laws, stupid easy-access gun laws with no background checks, stupid Second Amendment, stupid deadbeat dads, my stupid wine-buying and wine-drinking, stupid accidental disposal of perfectly good fruit and vegetables, stupid leftover madeleines, *really* stupid lemon drizzle cakes, stupid trail mix, stupid date bars, stupid Ohio history data bank, stupid wind chimes, the stupid, moldy old moth-eaten blanket on our bed, stupid Barry for not giving me Abby's quilt, my stupid attempts at accounting, stupid self-absorption, stupid mucus, stupid itch, stupid rash, rush, mush, stupid gyny guy, my stupid *dreams*, my stupid smile, the fact that I dreamt Chuck was still beautiful, and his deep red hair had only mildly faded, and his body was still on offer to me, but *that's* stupid too because he won't be dreaming of *me*, because that would be *stupid*, the fact that there is no *place* for me in this world, no place, the fact that I am broken, broken, the fact that there's no room in the whole of Ohio for my needs, my desires, my dilemmas, my tragedies, my flat tires, my mommy, *Mommy*, the fact that I want my mommy,

.   .   .   .

She was contained in a small area, bordered by metal fencing – a square cell with one solid wall, leaving it open to the air on three sides. Flies came and went, and the thin fencing offered the illusion of escape. She assessed the repeated pattern of diagonal holes between the wires, but the gaps were too small for a claw to grip and tear, or for her teeth to gnaw.

She paced the box again and again, searching for a weak spot in the crisscrossing lines of metal, a loose opening that she could bend or stretch wider. She pawed at the hard, rough concrete floor to find a groove that could be dug deeper, or a crack between floor and fence to exploit, but the dirt wouldn't move, not a speck. It was like stone – her scratching had no effect. And the join, where the fence met the ground, could not be widened.

She checked to see how high she'd have to leap in order to vault the wire walls, but the same wire fencing lay firm and taut across the top. She climbed up and checked for any way of tearing through with butting head or scratching claws. Finding none, she dropped back down to the floor.

She was caught, ruined. The forward motion necessary to find her cubs had been abruptly blocked, and she ached from inaction. They might die now, unprotected and undefended. Anxious and enraged, she hissed at flies.

At dawn, she stopped her pacing and searched for a corner in which to sleep, any shadowy spot on her square of space that might offer some minimal form of camouflage. But there was no invisibility to be had, no protection, only the bare, bumpy stone beneath her feet. She crouched, purring slightly, and fell asleep, with her head uncomfortably close to a metal bowl of water she'd accidentally stepped in numerous times during her tours of this abrasive pen.

In daylight, she eyed people going about their business, too near, moving back and forth before her, demonstrating their lack of fear. How dare they stand so close to her?

By midday, she was still crouched, half-asleep, her nose pressed into the ground. Men beyond the fence came so close she would normally have felt the need to attack, or bolt. She remained immobile, ready to spring. From beneath her frown, she stared at the men and began to snarl, low in her throat. She hated them with her entire body, knowing them to be her hunters, and kitten thieves. She assumed they would soon attack her again with their guns. There would be more pain, further injuries to lick, or possibly obliteration. She would fight though, to live – for, if she died, her cubs would die.

To her surprise though, the killer men did not point rifles at her. Instead, they detached a small piece of the wire enclosure, and through the hole shoved hunks of meat that fell heavily to the ground. They were sharing their food with her. She ignored it. She had killed for herself since she was five months old. And anyway, the men had kept the tastiest parts for themselves, the inner core. She wondered how long she would need to exist in this smelly wire cage of bumpy stone, being fed the wrong stuff.

The men didn't try to get any closer to her that day, which was lucky for them, for she would have swiftly torn those gawky limbs off their torsos and feasted on their guts.

Apart from the weeping woman she'd once nosed in the tree, the lioness had never really studied these enemies up close. Their vertiginous forms confused her. They stood on two legs, but could not fly. Muscles gone to seed, spines brittle and inflexible, their front paws dangling at their sides. Their tiny eyes never stopped shifting around, and never opened wide enough. Random tufts of fur stuck out from the tops of their heads but nowhere else. The females had more fur on their heads; on some, it grew long and straggly, like grass. Weak-eyed, weak-eared, weak-limbed, their liveliest body part seemed to be their soft, wet, waggly mouths, from which poured a ceaseless variety of gurgles, cries and calls.

The chemical scent that surrounded them reminded her of the trash in forest clearings. Even when there was only one man outside her confines, his smell penetrated her square of isolation. She was bothered too by the sound of his breathing.

People had no playfulness. They were clumsy, methodical, repetitive creatures, graceless and brutal – and full of exasperating unconcern.

She would like to show them who really ruled the world.

.　　　.　　　.　　　.

the fact that the creek's now swarming with the little bugs that form columns, waves and walls in the air, the fact that I like watching them, the fact that they're a little like starling murmurations, the fact that you can't tell if they do it just for the fun of it, or self-protection, or what, the bugs, I mean, but the same goes for starlings, schooling, swarming, herding, euphoria, the fact that starling murmurations *look* like a happy thing, but somebody said it's just a way of avoiding *hawks* or something, *They say*, and that kind of wrecked it for me, the fact that it's not so nice to think this dance we all like so much is actually a desperate fight for survival, not just a ball of connectivity, collective euphoria, commune, commonplace, common weal, wheel, the fact that not everything has to be about the individual, unless you're shy, the fact that I wasn't shy when I was *four* and ran around that hut with all my classmates, thinking we were birds, the fact that it wasn't the most elegant murmuration ever, but it sure was fun, the fact that I wouldn't be caught dead taking part in a murmuration now, of any kind, even if I was a starling myself, murmuring in my muumuu, phulu-pututu, the fact that people often do things en masse, mass hypnosis, mass hysteria, ♫ *You got trouble!* ♫, public hangings, the fact that just agreeing on a common purpose doesn't *have* to be bad, the fact that people agree on all kinds of stuff, customs, conventions, methods of organizing things, ♫ *Tradition!* ♫, how to bake a potato or cure a cold, stop signs, driving on the right, Daylight Savings, bank accounts, bedding, Wash on Monday, Walla Walla, Wash., fridges, popcorn, cotton candy, merry-go-rounds, thermostats, taxes, tollbooths, prisons, police, snail mail, email, protective glasses for eclipses, elevators, "Singin' in the Rain," toilets and toilet paper, aspirin, OJ, scissors, mirrors, birthdays, Christmas, New Year's, tranquility pools, trainers, keys, glazed windows, saying "Gesundheit" when somebody sneezes, going to school, democracy, don't wear plaid with polka dots, the fact that the Italians have set days for certain *dishes* they cook, and they stick to it, like everybody has gnocchi on Thursdays and I don't know what on the other days, but they all know what to expect, the fact that Fishy Friday's pretty universal, needlepoint, cross-stitch, sweetgrass baskets, Abby, least said soonest mended, bitter butter makes bitter batter, a lick and a promise, a light at the end of the tunnel, it's always darkest before the dawn, go while the going's good, how green was my valley, men shave their faces and women shave their legs and armpits, pimples are bad, the fact that men all used to wear a hat but now they don't, the fact that some traditions are brave, the fact that Julia Child held steady for French cookery traditions, the fact that there is bravery in that, especially when it involves so much *butter*, adding and subtracting, soap and water, suntan lotion, the Beatles, brownies, kicking people when they're down, pelicans, pink flamingoes, the fact that cars got washed into the Ohio in that big storm and all sorts of stuff blew over, but thankfully no one was hurt, *Miracle on 34th Street*, Natalie Wood, the fact that Natalie Wood was always scared of water, and then she *drowned*, which is so awful, and kind of spooky, the fact that somehow, right in the middle of that storm, they caught that mountain lion, *lioness*, the fact that it was dancing around on Alligator Mound, the fact that they caught it alive and now it's at the Columbus Zoo, being checked over, the fact that now we're finally safe from mountain-lion attacks, we hope, the fact that Daddy was born on a library table during a storm, the fact that I've never understood where that library table *was*, the fact that I used to think it must have been in the middle of some public library, with library users looking up from their books and hissing "Ssshhhh!" at Grandma, or keeping their heads down, just trying to read while she screamed her head off, the fact that I think Grandma really wouldn't have minded giving birth in a public library, the fact that she was always kind of a drama queen, WE FORGIVE YOU, glass table full of spoons, bobbled glasses of water, the fact that Grandma's poems were abominable, Abominable Snowpoems, the fact that lately though I've begun to think the library table was maybe just a *type* of table they had at *home*, a table you'd maybe *put* in your home library, if you had one, Mrs. Peacock in the Library with a pencil, the fact that I wonder if the table was in Grandpa's *study*, the fact that in Detroit he had a study with all his law books, kept in those fancy bookshelves with glass doors, that I think Ethan has now, so maybe they called that room the Library, the fact that I wouldn't put it past those two to over-egg things a little like that, and if there was a table in their "Library," they might well have called it the "Library table," the fact that what is my favorite pan doing over there by the *window*, the fact that wherever that table was, it was a *table*, and Grandma used it for having babies on, or at least one baby, Daddy, and that's curious, the fact that was she caught mid-contraction before she could make upstairs to bed, or to a hospital even, or did she maybe *choose* to give birth on a table, for some reason, of her own free will, beer, plastic bags, the fact that I bet Grandpa was impatiently rapping on the library table with his gavel the whole time, saying "This birth will either be a success or a failure," the fact that I'll have to ask Ethan about this table business, or Phoebe, or maybe both, birth, berth, berm, girth, the fact that they seem so far away now, Phoebe and Ethan, the fact that when we were growing up together we saw each other every day, and now we hardly ever see each other, the fact that they don't even know about what happened with Stacy yet, or Cathy, or the latest on our mountain lion crisis, the fact that I don't like to bother them, the fact that professors can't answer personal emails during the academic year, the fact that I know what it's like, the fact that it's just about impossible, the fact that Leo's the same, the fact that they might've heard about the Cherokee tracker by now though, because he's been everywhere, on the national news even, the fact that all the kids in town are just nuts about the Cherokee tracker, or half-Cherokee, difficult birth, incompatible blood, the Bronx, saffron, gnocchi, the fact that Stacy was born during a storm, but not on a *table*, and not in a playpool either, water wings, the fact that it was a really hot day and it got darker and darker in the hospital room and, just as the storm broke, Stace appeared, and I held her to me and said "Hello," the fact that maybe thunder and lightning help dilation or something, mitti attar, longing for cherry juice, sour cherry pie, sour grapes, the fact that there are rains of frogs or fish, and red rain, mud rain, acid rain, the fact that this storm we just had was so bad, they issued instructions for an Emergency Kit in case of floods, which was pretty scary, except we're up on this hill so we weren't too worried, the fact that it was a very detailed list, the fact that they wanted you to have water, food, prescription medications, First Aid kit, baby supplies if you have a baby, bleach and an eye-dropper, whatever for, mylar blankets, normal blankets, sleeping bags, Stacy, glasses and eye protection, extra clothing, personal hygiene bags, towelettes, towels, a sanitation bucket, plastic sheeting, a tube tent, backpacks, dust masks, dusk masts, the fact that that's kind of hard to say, dust mask, dusk mask, ducks massed, "Ducky! Ducky!", work gloves, flashlight and batteries, matches, candles, light sticks, scissors, knives, a Swiss Army knife kind of thing or multi-tool, wrench, pliers, crowbar, rope or cord, duct tape, the fact that for years I thought it was *duck* tape, a can opener, kitchen items, a fire extinguisher, compass, pen and paper, radio, cell phones and chargers, whistles, walkie-talkies, a signal mirror, an emergency guide and plan, family documents, ID, maps, camera, games and books, extra keys, cash, coins, a letter or note of love and hope, I don't know who from or who to, and a *canoe*, the fact that, yes, always handy to have a canoe, the fact that I personally never leave the house without one, the fact that still it wasn't as good a list as Cathy's survival kit, the fact that she wouldn't even have had to pack, the fact that she probably has all that ready to go and more, though not the canoe, the fact that she's never mentioned a canoe, the fact that maybe she has some inflatable raft or something, in case of floods, innertube, the fact that luckily *they* had no flooding either, in this storm, the fact that burnt toast always reminds me of our year in Highgate, I don't know why, school soap, Channing, the fact that the tracker guy found the lioness at Alligator Mound, of all places, along with her dog companion, the fact that she was leaping around up there, disoriented by the storm, the fact that it was the dog's barking that gave them away, the fact that the kids have lapped up every detail of this story, the fact that it's maybe the first time anything in the news has interested them, the fact that the Cherokee tracker already knew she had a dog with her, because he'd been following tracks made by the lion's tail and paw prints, and he noticed a dog's paw prints started appearing too, the fact that he could also tell she was injured and limping, the fact that he could tell by her paw prints, the fact that he knew she needed veterinary help, the fact that still, when he found her, she was jumping high into the air, like a ballerina, the Cherokee tracker said, and nobody knows why she was behaving that way, the fact that mountain lions can leap thirty or forty feet in one bound, the fact that they should be in the Olympics, Triple Crown, the fact that Gillian's started doing mountain-lion dances for us, the fact that she was distracted by the storm and that was how he managed to shoot her with a tranquilizer dart, the *lion*, not *Gillian*, heavens, the fact that the tracker says he got lucky and the dart worked fast, the fact that otherwise he might've had to shoot her for real, the fact that instead he got her to the zoo alive, just as he'd said he would, the fact that that seems a big surprise to everybody, especially the guys in the posses, the fact that we're all so used to everything having to be killed all the time, For Your Convenience, blueberry pie, the lion's dog companion, the fact that nobody knows yet how many *pet dogs* those hunting parties shot "just in case" they were the lion, dozens at least, "Let's party!", the fact that with the Zanesville massacre, people were saying tranquilizer darts don't work because they don't take effect fast enough in a big animal, but maybe you just need a little patience, risotto and a traumatic birth, like the *tracker*, Type O, library table, the fact that, patience is a virtue, but nobody *has* any anymore, everybody just wants drama, the fact that heaven forbid we should have a little stability or peace and calm ever, Mahatma Gandhi, MLK, motorcycle engines, missile launcher, keypad, the fact that the police are always in such a big hurry to wrap things up too, pajamas, the fact that it seems like the police are tired of trying to understand people,

♫ *No need to understand 'em* ♫, the fact that maybe nobody understands anybody, if you think about it, the fact that even my own husband and children are complete mysteries to me, not *strangers* but mysteries, the fact that *everybody's* a mystery to me, the fact that "I don't even understand how the can-opener works," the fact that many *fiancés* are unreadable, inscrutable, and then they turn out to be conmen and *murderers*, the fact that the tracker seems really sweet though, when he talks about the mountain lion, the fact that he seems gentle, *gentlemanly*, and he sounded really sorry she had some injuries, like on her leg, the fact that he thinks that probably dates back to the previous bungled attempt to capture her, when they had her and crashed the car and lost her again, the fact that Ben says the zoo was really pleased to get her alive, which they never expected really, the fact that they backed the Cherokee tracker all the way, so now, thanks to him, the mountain lion is there, which is much better for everybody, for her as well as the rest of us, the fact that I didn't want the kids to be shut-ins *forever*, the fact that in tribute to the tracker, the zoo asked him to *name* her, and he came right up with one, not Lola the Lion, or Patty the Panther, but *Mishipeshu*, an Ojibwe word for underwater panther, I think because of her weird rain-dance in the storm, the fact that it's strange though, when wild animals get a name, the fact that it makes you feel kind of funny, the fact that all her life that mountain lion has been alone and free and unnamed, and now she has a name and she's not free anymore, and that's sort of spooky, or is it just the thought of the way she lived before, so alone and hidden from the world, that spooks me, the fact that *I'm* pretty alone and hidden from the world myself a lot of the time, but not the way a mountain lion is, the fact that nobody even knows where she came from originally, the fact that mountain lions don't come with a black box like a plane, the fact that they're doing genetic tests on her now, the fact that the Cherokee tracker now says there were a lot of disagreements between him and the police during the search, the fact that, for one thing, he likes to do his own hunting, *alone*, and they promised to keep out of his way, and not shoot the lion unless they had to, but secretly they were all under

944

orders to *definitely* shoot it on sight, "in the interests of public safety," and the Cherokee tracker found out about that somehow and made a big stink about it, the fact that it sounds like the Cherokee tracker had to keep reminding the police *daily* of their no-shooting agreement, treaty, broken treaties, so he could catch her alive like they'd *asked* him to, the fact that he kept having to beg the police for more time, the fact that he used extinction and conservation as two big reasons not to shoot her, because if she *is* an Eastern Cougar, she must be one of the last, the fact that most people thought the Eastern Cougar was already extinct, extinct, and cougars are mountain lions, the fact that the reason she survived so long, he says, despite all the itchy-fingered hunters, was that she's good at keeping out of sight, the fact that, considering how close she was to well-populated areas during this journey of hers, it's incredible she wasn't spotted more, the fact that she passed through towns, suburbs, she crossed state borders, and all along the way she caused *no harm*, the fact that she didn't attack anybody at all, not once, despite all the hysteria, curfews, looting and joggers, the fact that she just gradually spiraled closer and closer to Columbus, which was kind of convenient for the Cherokee tracker when the time came to get her to the zoo, the fact that that's the best zoo for her because of their big cat program, the fact that the tracker did a map of what he thinks her journey was like, and it looks like maps of the Underground Railroad, the fact that anyway, now maybe the zoo can breed from her and save the species, and then they can repopulate the northeast with Eastern Cougars, as a check on the deer, though the FFF won't like it, the fact that the zoo's planning to breed some Sumatran tigers too, because the Sumatran tiger population's pretty low worldwide, the fact that there are only about *four hundred* left in the wild, so they better get on with it, the fact that the same goes for the Eastern Cougar, but I guess they could mate her with some western cougars or Florida cougars and it might work, perpetuation of the species, the fact that maybe they can keep the panda going but I don't know, the fact that I think pandas are just for show, the wrong kind of bamboo, the fact that they're probably technically extinct already too, Sumatran tiger, the fact that I don't even know where Sumatra *is*, sixty-four-thousand-dollar question, Manus Island, Australian detention center, Papua New Guinea, Jennifer, the rainforests of Borneo, orangutans, turtles, albino terrapins, the fact that one of the last Yangtse softshell turtles died from artificial insemination, the fact that they've got some orphaned mountain lion cubs at the Columbus Zoo right now too, along with the ocelot that they take out on a leash to show visitors, ortolan, orangutan, ocarina, turkey duster, the fact that Vermonters are the biggest gun fanatics in the country, the fact that I used to think Vermont sounded nice, bee at Bread Loaf, vanilla milkshakes, but now I'm not so sure, the fact that, talk about trigger-happy, Vermont Country Store, Brands From The Past, old favorites, and they get really riled by any talk of gun control, Vermont Country Stress, Vermont Country Ammo Store, Vermont Country Massacre, the fact that the kids really want to go see the lions and tigers at the zoo now, the fact that all their friends have gone *already*, or plan to this weekend, the fact that nobody at school can stop talking about the Indian tracker, the fact that they're obsessed, "Shane! Shane!", the fact that he's their new Number One national hero, because he saved that mountain lion from all those trophy-hunters, which is pretty amazing, the fact that the zoo vets found a small crack in one leg, half-healed, the fact that if she were a racehorse they'd have shot her for that, but they seem to think it'll heal by itself and she'll be right as rain, Mishipeshu, the fact that maybe after the Zanesville thing, and the dentist who shot Cecil, maybe nobody's got the *stomach* for hearing about lions getting slaughtered anymore, Blanche, the fact that they say the lioness is healthy otherwise, though a bit "grumpy," the fact that how can they tell, Cowardly Lion, *They say the hen can lay*, the fact that the kids at school think the Cherokee tracker should get the Congressional Medal of Honor, but Trump would never give it to a guy for saving a lioness, the fact that he might give a guy a medal for *killing* a lioness, ten-cent Jimmy, break the bank, broken, or preferably a whole herd of them, a pride, family pride, the fact that the whole Trump family loves big game hunting, the whole Trump tribe, herd, gang, the fact that they're always getting themselves photo-graphed in Africa, holding up the severed tail of something dead, Bobbitt, the fact that the one thing the Trump administration probably does like about this lion story is that it's distracting people from the Russia business, "Shane! Shane!", the fact that Leo hates *Shane*, the fact that he always hated cowboy movies, and so did I, mostly, but I always made an exception for *Shane*, the fact that I may not've really got it as a kid but I liked it, the fact that you were just expected to know what it was about, like Robert Frost poems, so of course I didn't know, and I still don't and I still even worry about *Shane* a little too, what it's really *about*, but Leo says it's not about anything, it's just a bad movie, the fact that I think he's jealous because I kind of like Alan Ladd, but mainly I used to like the little *boy* in it, "Shane! Shane!", because kids like movies about kids, just like men like movies about men and women like movies about women, and cats like *cat* movies, or so they say, and chickens like chick flicks, the fact that Jean Arthur's in it too, but it isn't much of a part, the fact that all she does is cook and clean or sit on the wagon not saying anything, I mean when they go into town, the fact that I don't mean she just goes and sits on the wagon to sulk or something, "a little flower sink," the fact that Alan Ladd was always nervous about his height, the fact that he was often paired with Veronica Lake, because she was *minute*, the fact that when he was in his twenties, his mom asked him for some money and she used it to buy arsenic and *killed* herself, the fact that here's another news clip about the tracker, with pictures of his house and his girl-friend, the fact that I hadn't heard about her before, and there he is in his yard being interviewed yet again and, oh, oh my *word*, the fact that it's *Jim*, the fact that he's got a dog with him that looks just like Jim, with white ruffles on his chest, the fact that it's got to be *Jim*, the fact that the tracker says this is the dog that was hanging around with the lioness, my word, well, I'll be, the fact that he says if no owner comes forward, he's keeping him, the fact that I don't know what to do, the fact that the kids are bound to want Jim back, but look at him, he looks so *happy* with the tracker guy, the fact that he's voluntarily leaning against his leg, the fact that Jim's in ecstasy, the fact that maybe Jake was *right*, when he said he saw a lion out back, the fact that maybe the lioness did come through our back yard and steal Jim, but not to eat, just as a companion, goat companions, wow, gug, chicken ladder, the fact that if it weren't for the markings, I wouldn't have recognized him, the fact that he seems transformed, the fact that he's come to *life*, the fact that it's so hurtful when Anne hears that Frederick Wentworth said he wouldn't have recognized her from eight years ago, but then *she* gradually comes back to life too, the fact that maybe the kids won't see this news item, or if they do, maybe they won't recognize Jim, because he looks so different, the fact that he *couldn't* be Jim, could he, the fact that no, it *is* him, the fact that he's just acting happy, but it is Jim, I'm sure of it, oh poor little Jim, "Shane! Shane!", the fact that if you think of all the things that one little dog's *been* through, a farm, a fire, a *lion*, the fact that I just hope he didn't suffer, traveling around with a lioness, I mean I hope he got enough to eat and all, but he looks okay, the fact that the tracker's stroking Jim's white ruffles so affectionately, and Jim looks ecstatic, nap, euphoria, the fact that dogs are good at being happy, even *Jim*, it turns out, but he sure didn't seem good at it *before*, the fact that I never *heard* such a sad bark, the fact that, quick, shut off the TV before anybody comes in, the fact that I don't want them to see this and get their hopes up again, let sleeping dogs lie, lions too, let it be, the fact that, sheesh, if your dog's so unhappy he'd rather live with a *cougar*, it's probably time to get a new dog, the fact that maybe we can have one of Cathy's puppies, the fact that Junie's about to give birth, the fact that Art's worried about the Country Shoppe's finances, not because of Junie's puppies, just generally, the fact that they need more pies fast, and now he wants me to make Chuckwagon Beans as well, like once a week, the fact that it's hard to keep up with those two, particularly Cathy, the fact that she's so energetic, just a whirlwind of energy, a whirling dervish, a tornado, a dynamo, was it a cat I saw,

·   ·   ·   ·

A dreamless sleep, from which she slowly roused herself, to be met by the smell of metal all around her still, and the close stench of urine and feces, her own and those of other distressed animals in adjacent wire cells. She discerned too the smells of her own iodined wounds and the bleach they used to sluice the empty pens, that they rinsed with thick jets of water like a sideways waterfall floating in the air.

Such noxious scents vied with even less familiar ones, the smell of nearby camels and zebras, and the threatening gust of one lone grizzly, held out of sight somewhere.

The sounds of the zoo offended her more. People's chatter, and a mélange of mechanical noises, overwhelmed the more mysterious snorts of alien creatures and monkey cries – the indeterminate utterances of animals whose needs were not met, the moans of animals not allowed to play or eat or mate at will.

The purpose of these animals was no longer to exist for themselves – as was their right. They now served as spectacles, and human requirements methodically punctuated their days.

Some humans wore sunglasses, which blotted out their eyes, making them appear blind and weak. But glass and bars and wire protected them from sorry ends.

The lioness had joined this catastrophe, for now, and she knew she was not safe. She would never be safe here. But the attention of passersby, their squeals and scorn, did not much faze her: she was in her own world, an empire she made and carried with her. In public or in wilderness, she was alone.

.   .   .   .

the fact that I dreamt Michelin didn't give out stars anymore, trois étoiles Michelin, the fact that they gave out something beginning with "pro" but now I can't remember *what*, the fact that it was something like three Michelin proponents, or provisions, or promotions, Prohibition, prolepsis, prolapse, proletarians, "three *proletarians*," no, the fact that I don't think Michelin cares much about *them*, or was it proposals, proliferations, the world's oldest profession, procreate, propagate, propitiate, propane, the fact that I'll never get it back, provender, pomander, protrude, "three protrusions," extrude, extrusions, the fact that I just can't remember what that word was, IED, the fact that why do people even like that kind of fancy food, the fact that that's what gets me, the fact that it's all about paying the earth for a dot of this, a dot of that, and lots of jazzy dribbles around the side of the plate, the fact that it's like the chicken's dish *after* they've had their fill, the fact that lots of restaurants don't even want a Michelin star, because it attracts the wrong kind of customers, customers who want pre-desserts, whatever they are, the fact that André Allard didn't have a Michelin star and it was the best restaurant *I've* ever been to, the fact that I don't believe there's a single Michelin star in all of fly-over country, cryo-chamber recovery, membrane, tissues, valves, ducts, the fact that La Maisonette in Cincinnati was the most famous restaurant in America for a long, long while, the fact that *I'd* heard of it, and was kind of sorry it closed before I moved here, the fact that Leo never went either, the fact that nobody knows why it closed but anyway, even *they* never got a Michelin star, the fact that maybe the Michelin people just don't like the Midwest, grade school, the fact that they probably just think it's all hamburgers and Sloppy Joes and bundt cake, my flat tire, the fact that maybe they should stick with the tire business and stop tiring everybody out with their strange taste in food, pigs' trotters, aligot, Paul Bocuse, Julia Child, the fact that maybe the kids would like aligot, if I made it with sweet potatoes, the fact that I also dreamt Stacy was about six and she and I were staying in a rural, mountainous place, a bit like Colorado maybe, the fact that the mountains were very green, with steep-sided hills, and you could look across at whole other similar mountainsides opposite, and watch the people and sheep moving around over there, the fact that the mountains were all so perpendicular though, it made me pretty nervous, not just from vertigo but because it was plainly unsafe, so steep, the fact that just to stay on the sort of car-width ledge we were on, you had to press yourself against the mountain all the time, the fact that it was almost a cliff-face really, but so green and beautiful, the fact that it was all dark green, and the mountain opposite was sort of blue-green, the fact that Stacy and I liked being there, the fact that it seemed like a place I'd always wanted to go to, the fact that there were people living around there, in a sort of Tyrolean way, the fact that their way of life seemed very settled, old-fashioned, the fact that it was all farming, livestock, with dark wooden houses scattered here and there, Maria von Trapp, proponent, partisan, the fact that we didn't know where we were supposed to be staying during our visit, which was for like a week, like if we were supposed to go to a hotel or what, and we were dithering together by the car, when some people came walking by, the fact that I asked a young woman about the hotel, and she patted me so nicely on the back while she was telling us where to go, the fact that they were all so nice that I felt fine leaving Stacy with them for a few minutes, while I got the car turned around, which wasn't easy on that narrow ledge, the fact that I was planning to park it somewhere near where they were all standing, but then I somehow ended up driving alone, to the nearby town, the fact that I passed a little old-fashioned shopping mall, and decided I better go in there, since this looked like being the only place to get us some food, but there was a really long line at the cafeteria, the fact that I was worried about keeping Stacy waiting, back on the mountain, but I thought I'd better get us *something*, so I waited in line and, when they asked me what I wanted, I said two tomato and cheese sandwiches, the fact that they said apologetically that I could only have one or the other, either a tomato sandwich or a cheese sandwich, so I said give me one of each, thinking I'd just readjust them later on, because Stacy and I both liked tomato and cheese sandwiches, in the dream anyway, the fact that I don't know if Stacy likes tomato and cheese sandwiches now, the fact that I was kind of surprised though, to find so much red tape in such an isolated little place, but you never know, rules, regulations, propitiation, stars, the fact that then I had to sit and wait while they *made* the sandwiches, and while I was waiting, the cook brought me a big thick bowl of very hot water, into which she'd put a spoonful of what seemed to be concentrated tomato soup, the fact that I was supposed to stir it around myself to get it to dissolve, the fact that the bowl was really hard to balance right on my knees, and there was nowhere else to put it, and I didn't want that awful-looking soup but I was trying to be polite, the fact that the woman was apologetic about the soup but it was all they had or something, the fact that there was still no sign of the cheese sandwich or the tomato sandwich, and I was getting worried about Stacy, as I'd only meant to be gone for a *moment*, the fact that this kindly meant but horrible soup was slowing me down, the fact that then this hobo guy came in, who everybody seemed very fond of, and he said he knew the secret to life, the fact that he said there were three things involved, if you wanted to be happy in life, and they were, 1, get an inheritance, and 2, go to Tangiers, and 3, well, I forget the *third one*, which is a pity because who knows, it might have been very helpful, like maybe my unconscious was really trying to tell me something and I *forgot* it, just like I forgot the Michelin star word in the other dream, gosh dang it, the fact that the hobo kept *repeating* these three things too, so you'd think I'd have memorized them, and he said you could do them in whatever order you wanted, it didn't matter, like you could go to Tangiers first, and then get the inheritance, and do the other thing, whatever it was, or you could get the inheritance and then go to Tangiers, and then get or do the other thing, or you could start by doing the other thing, then inherit, then go off to Tangiers, or do the other thing and go to Tangiers and inherit, the fact that for a poor guy stuck on a mountain in Austria or Colorado or someplace, he sure was set on Tangiers, the fact that he was so keen on it you sort of wondered why he'd come *back*, if he'd ever been, the fact that he actually didn't look like he'd gotten his inheritance yet, but maybe he'd spent it already, getting to Tangiers and back, and doing the other thing, the fact that then the woman at the cash register wanted me to pay for the food, but in *foreign* money, just for fun, the fact that that was what she said, the fact that because I seemed sort of foreign to her, she thought I might be carrying some foreign money, and she was more interested in seeing some foreign money than she was in actually getting paid, the fact that I could see foreign money really interested her, but I felt she needed real money, I mean the right kind of money, the fact that I would've felt bad giving her unusable money, even if I'd had any, which I *didn't*, the fact that I suddenly realized how isolated a community this was, and how they were all trying to stave boredom off in strange ways, the fact that I couldn't tell yet myself what was so boring about trying not to slide down the mountainside all day and night, the fact that I thought that would keep you on edge all the time, but they were all used to it, the fact that it reminded me a bit of Bread Loaf, except Bread Loaf never seemed so steep and perilous or anything, perished, parish, paraphernalia, protoplasm, profligate, profit, "three profits," prophets, the fact that I still couldn't figure out how these people managed to live on these perpendicular mountainsides, and at one point I saw a *map* and sure enough, as I'd suspected, the main roads or paths were all horizontal and narrow, like five feet wide at the most, and they were connected to other ones by a few even narrower zigzaggy paths that trailed up and down the mountains in between, the fact that I figured you just got used to all the climbing you had to do if you lived there, like mountain goats, the fact that the great thing was that you could always see so far and it was all so beautiful and blue green or dark green, emerald green, proponent, protagonist, and there were hardly any buildings, just the beautiful dark green mountain we were on, stretching out behind us, and green hills all around us, the fact that it's such a relief to know the lion's been caught, the fact that we were getting used to never thinking it was safe to go out, the fact that even Gillian got scared of playing outside because she didn't want to get eaten by a lion, but I wouldn't let them go out anyway, and now they can, the fact that maybe it was the *lion* then, that broke the chickens' ladder, though I never saw any paw prints, paw-paws, pause, gauze, Tangiers, the fact that that man in the Ohio River boating accident was a guy everybody really liked, the fact that a Mechanicsburg toddler died after his mom's boyfriend practiced wrestling moves on him, nun shaking Mommy, the fact that a sixteen-year-old dad suffocated his own baby on purpose in Marietta, the fact that three brands of dog chews have been recalled because they made dogs sick, the fact that a mom had to watch her son burn to death in Illinois, the fact that a Kentucky teen was arrested for a shooting spree, the fact that a guy in Texas caught a thirteen-foot hammerhead shark, the fact that another guy was shot dead having sex in a van, the fact that a Milwaukee woman traded sexual favors in return for mocha lattes, the fact that a woman pushed her husband out of a high rise somewhere, the fact that a couple drove their car full of adopted kids over a cliff, because social workers were trying to check up on the kids, the fact that a man who rescued a girl from drowning in the Great Miami River says god wanted him to be there, the fact that somebody said it was just like him to go rescue the girl and he is always the life of the party, the fact that some other man didn't want to live, but three little boys stopped him from hanging himself from a bridge, the fact that they just held on and wouldn't let go until help arrived, the fact that "he didn't want to live," to live, the fact that an East Palestine woman who didn't know she was pregnant had a baby on the sidewalk in East Palestine, *Ohio*, not the Middle East, the fact that raped women don't move as freely as other women ever again, the fact that some people say they can tell a raped woman just by how she walks, and the eyes, the fact that raped women's eyes go dead, sad-eyed women, the fact that a Painesville woman was convicted of putting meth in something, Painesville, James Mason, sad-eyed women, Hammer Throw Men, "he didn't want to live," the fact that science can tell you how much a stone weighs or measures, but it can't tell you if it's beautiful, the fact that a boy who was killed by a hammer blow in a hammer throwing competition "wasn't paying attention," swing bridge, Sophia Loren eating spaghetti Bolognese jigsaw, the fact that sometimes, when I see men in hammer throw competitions, or giving frog stand tutorials on YouTube, I really begin to wonder if there's not something more worthwhile they could be doing, I mean instead of twirling around and around like that, or "hanging out" in a frog stand, Sandusky American Crayon Co., frog stand, calisthenics, the fact that I think people *like* it when women look tired, the fact that it's so predictable it's kind of funny, the fact that I always get the most compliments when I'm zonked, the fact that I have something in my eye, the fact that I need Vaseline, ♫ *Who put the pepper in the Vaseline?* ♫, the fact that the kids just piled in from school and they're *still* gone on that Cherokee tracker, the fact that he said finding that lion was like finding a needle in a haystack, grass understory, spiral pattern, the fact that Stace is a little nutso about the lion herself, *and* the Cherokee tracker guy, Tangiers, the fact that the only way to calm them down is to get them all making cougar-shaped sugar cookies, which we've based on Frederick when he's really relaxed and spreads all four feet in different directions, the fact that this made an easier cookie shape than a standing cat would, the fact that Stacy drew it and made a stencil out of cardboard, the fact that she gave it an extra long tail though, longer and thicker than Frederick's, because cougars have very long tails, and I guess she was thinking a thin tail would break off too easily, the fact that mountain lions need long, strong tails for balance during leaps, according to Ben, the fact that Stacy made the tail curl nicely back on itself in a kind of spiral, the fact that Gillian just announced out of the blue that her birthday's only five days away, like I'd forget my own kids' *birthday*, ye of little faith, the fact that I may seem a bit out of it but I'm not *that* bad, the fact that you gotta watch that kid around cookie dough though, the fact that with the stencil, and some blunt knives, and plenty of wax paper, they all seem to be making out okay, the fact that they're sharing the stencil nicely at least, so far, the fact that we've already gotten a couple batches of cougars baked, more or less intact, the fact that the cookies spread a little in the baking, the fact that, wow, they look like *Alligator Mound*, because of the curling tail, though we lost a few tails somewhere, the fact that the real alligator's kind of hard to decipher these days, the fact that we've got lots of little Alligator Mounds, a nice little mound of mounds mounting up, all sparkly with red and green sugar sprinkles all over them, the fact that I should get more sugar sprinkles, the fact that we need other colors, the fact that it makes them look maybe a bit too Christmassy, with only red and green, but the kids don't seem to mind, the fact that I want to make an *all*-green one next, the fact that a deep green would make it even more like Alligator Mound, and oh, would you believe it, there's the doorbell, the fact that I bet it's Ronny, just dropping on by, just when I'm all covered in flour as usual, the fact that he probably smelled the sugar cookies from Coshocton and rushed right over, the fact that what am I to do with him here with all the *kids* home, the fact that Stacy can't stand him, the fact that I've gotta get rid of him somehow, YEOW, oh, oh, shoot, the fact that I think I just crushed Jake's little yellow bulldozer, yeow, Ronny, Djibouti, the fact that, sure enough, there he is, the fact that okay, I'll just see what he wants and tell him I'm busy, the fact that he's not such a bad guy, the fact that, what, well I never, the fact that I tried to be nice and all, but firm, and now he's stalked off back to his car in a real huff, without even saying goodbye, oh dear, the fact that he did seem in a kind of funny mood, the fact that he's a strange man really, the fact that now Jake's wailing in the kitchen for some reason, the fact that he's either seen his crushed yellow bulldozer or he's *burnt* himself, children and ovens, 50% burns, oh phew, shiver me timbers, the fact that Jake's okay, the fact that it was just that his raw cookie fell apart on the way to the cookie sheet, the fact that I'll get it back together, you just watch *this*, Jake, the fact that in the middle of helping him, I see Stacy's expression of distaste, and I think, what's up with *her* now, the fact that she seemed so content just a minute a ago, making cook-ies, the fact that she's looking over my shoulder, so I turn, and there's *Ronny* in the kitchen, in the doorway, the rudeness of him just coming straight into the house like that, the fact that it's funny he's brought his *gun* with him, the fact that does he want to show it to the kids or something, the fact that all of a sudden I don't want to be a housewife or a homemaker or a stay-at-home mom anymore, the fact that I don't want to have to die the way that woman in *Fargo* dies, battered to death with a bag over her head and then ground up in a wood chipper by some frozen lakeside, and I don't want to be a *Stepford Wife* either and have my brains sucked out and replaced with robot brains, and I don't want to be Lucille Ball and have to make a fool of myself every week on TV for a living, and I don't want to be Jeannie out of *I Dream of Jeannie* and have to live inside a bottle, wearing a jeweled bra and harem pants and waiting for Larry Hagman to want to see me, and I don't want my kids to have to marry seven brothers, and I don't want to be pregnant with no heating on in the daytime like that Chaplin girl in *Dr. Zhivago*, or just get decapitated when the marriage fails like happened to some woman in London, or keep having to pull up sticks and move further into the American wilderness like Laura Ingalls Wilder's Ma whenever the wanderlust strikes Pa again, or end up like Madame Bovary who basically just wanted to go to a few more parties, and instead she ends up in the sticks having to smell gangrene all the time,

.   .   .   .

The lioness woke, again, among this crowd of the doomed and the damned. There was no recoil and leap, leap and recoil, here. She could not kill her jailers, who were safe from her beyond the fencing. She could barely take a few steps in any direction without having to turn around, and her tail was always in the way.

Her only hope was to burrow or bite her way out. She was assiduously gnawing and clawing at her wire cage the day the zoo keepers moved her own long-lost cubs into the adjoining enclosure.

The kittens had been separated from their mother for two whole months now. They had been manhandled, and touched by humans against their will. They had been frightened, bathed, bewildered, weighed, sickened, fed, chained, vaccinated – and they had languished, needlessly, painfully, incomprehensibly.

But they had had each other for comfort, and by now had learnt to form a serviceable three-cub mound on the thin blanket offered them for sleeping purposes. The one on top got the most rest, while also keeping a lookout for danger.

When they now caught sight of their mother, they sprang at her in joy. Roused by their chirrups, she met them curiously by the fence.

When she recognized them – despite their change in size – she exuberantly rubbed her long body against the wires that separated them.

Next, overcome by hope, she lay down, inviting them to nurse. They held back, thwarted by the fence, and cried in frustration. They could not even touch her, because of the foot-wide gap between the enclosures. When she rose up and rubbed again against the fence, the double layer of fencing kept them well out of reach.

She pawed at them through the holes in the wire and then, more frantically than ever, she scrabbled at the floor. Her tongue came out to lick the cubs, but grabbed only air. Infuriatingly, she could not touch them, but relief filled her just the same. Her cubs were alive. Her pleasure in seeing them overcame her fury, and her reserve, her defensive habits of silence and solitude. Despite the presence of human onlookers, she roared.

Over the next few days, she watched from afar as her cubs began to caper around, exploring their new confining cage. The lioness was suddenly enveloped by a barely remembered occurrence in her body: she relaxed, for the first time in months. She lay panting in her pen, watching the cubs in theirs, as they chewed the hunks of flesh the keepers offered at fixed hours. She even nibbled at her own unsatisfactory savory dinners without resentment, now that her cubs were near.

But intermittently, she still spent much of her time pawing at the wire fencing between them. She was alarmed one day when a man entered the cubs' pen. Her warning snarl made her cubs huddle cautiously in a corner while the man briefly encroached. She could not protect them properly if she couldn't touch them. Restlessly, she paced her square of concrete.

When exhausted by her own futile efforts to remove the wall of wire that separated her from her young, the lioness would lower her body to the ground and stretch out again beside the fence. The cubs settled on their side of it, trying to feel her warmth across the gap and reassured by her enormous purr.

No one at the zoo noticed how instantly the cubs had run towards her, the first time they saw her again. No one knew that they would have run to no other adult lioness that way. No one acknowledged the devotion with which their mother gazed at them.

Nonetheless, after some days of observing the lioness's fond, proud manner towards the cubs next door, and in response to the visits of several famed big cat experts, it was decided that the time had come to "introduce" the lioness to the cubs, in the hope of pulling off a fostering coup. At the rate of one cub an hour, they were cautiously transferred to her enclosure.

Men stood by, gripping their guns, ready to shoot the mother – the three cubs being the more valuable acquisition. But even zoo marksmen can tell the difference between biting and licking. While the functionaries congratulated themselves on a promising adoption, unusually problem-free, the lioness licked each of her long-lost cubs all over, and then again.

For her joy conquered any alarm about her situation, and even eroded her distaste for men. No, she had found her cubs and would lap them and love them and never let them go. From now on she would hear only the squeals of her kittens. She would look only at them, their beauty, their stripes and white muzzles, and the tails that had grown so long during the separation.

She would love them and save them and feed them and teach them and never let them go. She would lap her cubs and love them and never let them go.

.   .   .   .

the fact that they had to rescue one of the DC eaglets because he got his leg caught between some twigs on the outside of the nest, the fact that he was stuck there for days before they decided they had to help him, the fact that I guess they hoped at first he'd struggle free by himself, but then they got scared he might starve, *on international live cam*, so some conservation or park ranger guy climbed all the way up there and brought him down and they kept him under observation for a day or two but he was fine, nothing broken or anything, so they took him back up the tulip tree and put him back in the nest, the fact that the conservation guy, or park ranger guy, who carried him back up the tree, *kissed* the eaglet on the head before he left him there, which wasn't very professional but gosh, was it sweet, galoshes, the fact that I thought Mr. President and the First Lady might reject him, because of the smell of the park guy on him, but they seemed to take it all in their stride, his absence and his return, and everything's back to normal now, with raw pink fish for breakfast, lunch and dinner, the fact that eagles yawn, the fact that they have perfect balance, the fact that bald eagles look like they have a permanent frown, the fact that Leo says it's an anatomical adaptation for keeping the sun out of their eyes, the fact that I don't know though, because *ospreys* don't look like they're frowning, and they probably need shades just as much as bald eagles do, the fact that ospreys' eyes are much rounder than the eagles', the fact that ospreys have really beautiful eyes, the fact that *birds* never beat themselves up for being afraid of things, the fact that they're not embarrassed to be vigilant, the fact that they *believe* in caution and, considering how scared they are of everything, they're really pretty *brave*, the fact that birds live close to the edge, the edge of disaster, the fact that baby birds are maybe not fearful *enough*, which puts them in danger, eaglet, boarlet, "the coward dies a thousand times," the fact that I don't know why people get down on themselves for trying to avoid dangers, "god hates a coward," the fact that, personally, I think we *underestimate* dangers, the fact that we have to maybe, because it's not practical to think about them all the time, but that doesn't mean they're not there, it's just that fear gets in the way when you got stuff to do, when you're living on the edge, like on the edge of a five-mile-deep chasm for instance, green mountainside, Facts of Life, the fact that, after all, bad things can and do happen, Revere Ware, and *we'll all pass away*, at some point, which is about as dangerous as life can get, so why *shouldn't* we watch out, the fact that it seems to me it'd be dumb *not* to be pretty careful, or at least as careful as birds are, like at least be *alert*, keep your eyes peeled, the fact that bald eagles are very alert, the candy vending machine at the hospital in New York,

Mommy's brain operation, the fact that Phoebe and I had to sleep in some friends' junk room in New York somewhere, spare room, guest room, guest room full of junk, a little too much like our attic, the fact that I don't know where Daddy slept, the fact that maybe he stayed in a hotel, or maybe they let him sleep at the *hospital*, in Mommy's room, the fact that I never wanted my mom to have to have a *brain operation*, no no no, the fact that between the eaglet's injuries and Ronny's antics, I am now officially a basket case, the giant Longaberger apple basket, the fact that gee whiz, *whiz*, whiz kid, I am just plum wore out, the fact that I keep falling asleep whenever I even sit down, the fact that I haven't been sleeping too well, the fact that I drift off then jerk awake, thinking Ronny's in the house, the fact that I keep thinking I should have been *nicer* to that guy, but then I remember how he always sort of gave me the creeps and I just didn't want him around too much, the fact that if I'd been nicer to him, he might have hung around *more*, the fact that he actually accused me of *encouraging* him, leading him on, "prick tease," freeze, water samples, the fact that he *said* that, right in front of the *kids*, the fact that *when* did I ever tease him, the fact that I never said one flirtatious thing to that man, the fact that why in heck *would* I, a guy like that, with his "O'Bummer" theories and the left turns, and the Queen, "Queenie, eh?", the fact that instead I tried to keep my distance, as politely as I could, because underneath I must've *sensed* it could all get out of hand, and boy, did it, the fact that he called me a "prick tease," the nerve of that guy, when all I ever did was try to get *rid* of him, ready, aim, fire, the fact that if people mistake coldness for coquetry though, what you gonna do, Sweet'N Low, the fact that Daddy was born on a library table, the fact that he and Mommy went boating together, and wrote their PhDs, and eloped to Paris, though not all on the same day, Fresh Pond, leap of faith, leopard, the lioness leaping around in a storm, leap year, Louisa Mulgrove leaping from the Cobb at Lyme, Old Lyme, hummingbirds, Jim's bark, the fact that I don't think I could *take* that bark right now, I'm too jittery, though it's been two weeks since, whatevs, the fact that everything still makes me jump, *leap*, the fact that how I wish I'd *locked the front door* that day, idiot, but I never expected such a thing to happen, the fact that I never expected him to barge right in like that, the fact that I thought he was just going to get in his car and go on back to Coshocton, in a huff for some reason, and then he was *in our kitchen*, holding that gun, not his Browning Recoilless shotgun either, something even scarier, the fact that at first I just thought *that's* pretty weird, coming into the house uninvited and parading around in front of my kids with a machine gun, the fact that the police said it was a semi-automatic, the fact that I thought why would someone *do* that, the fact that for one crazee moment I thought maybe he just wants to do a *Show & Tell* for them about his weapon of choice, and gun safety or something, gun laws and stuff, but then he started calling me all those bad names and it didn't seem much like Show & Tell anymore, the fact that I really hadn't seen that coming, the fact that I never *liked* him much but I thought he felt okay about *me*, I mean I was always so polite to him, the fact that, gosh, that guy had a lot to say, even through a screen door, the fact that he just wouldn't leave, mosquito, ♫ *He played knick knack on my door* ♫, the fact that it was just one thing after another, gab gab gab, and I'd stand there pretending to be interested, the fact that Amelia would've told him to get lost the first time he tried it on her, the fact that sometimes my feet started to hurt, just from standing there so long waiting for him to go, the fact that how could anyone have *married* Ronny, the fact that he must've talked *her* head off too, beheading, decapitation, leap, "Shane! Shane!", the fact that to get away from him, all I could usually think of to say was "Well, the pies must be burning," but maybe that just rubbed salt in the wound, or sugar anyway, caramelized sugar, with a bit of latticing on top, and egg-yolk polish, "Here is a nut," the fact that what was really icky was when he started talking about all the times he'd *spied* on us, and followed us in his *car*, the fact that that's really kind of scary, the fact that in the midst of it all, being held at gunpoint, all I could think was, if you had enough spare time to *spy*, you could've been delivering *pie*, and making yourself useful, a new rhyme for Budington, jutting gun, but, by the look of things, Ronny never did want to make himself useful, the fact that the chicken feed was just one big ploy, the fact that even when he rescued us from the floods, he had an ulterior motive, a *big* one, something between rape and pie theft, the fact that I don't think he knew which it was himself, trash, chickens, kitchen stool, school bus, Leo, swimming cat, the fact that I don't much like the thought of Ronny hiding around the corner like that, the fact that how long was he doing it for, months maybe, the fact that it's pretty unnerving, London buses, candy corn, candy apples, carrots, onions, celery, tomatoes, mayo, tomatoes in cream, because we're often *alone* here, without Leo, the fact that I better not think about it, the fact that there he stood, in the kitchen doorway, holding his big gun, asking me why I'd never invited him in, the fact that who would ever have guessed he was so het up about pie and coffee, *landsakes,* the fact that all he had to do was say so and I would've given him some, *reluctantly,* sure, but I still would've, and if he hadn't been standing in our kitchen bearing arms, baring arms, bare hands, bear paws, I might have told him so then, but I was frozen to the spot, the fact that if I *could've* spoken though, and spoken honestly, victim impact statements, witness protection program, I would have answered "First of all, Ronny, I'm shy. Second, I'm busy, like right now the kids are home and we're making sugar cookies here. And, third, I don't even *know* you, and you freakin' freak me out, you freakin' freak!", lattice, Latter-Day Saints, but when do we ever say what we really *want* to say, and anyway, I didn't say anything because I *couldn't,* deer-in-the-headlights kind of stuff, spotlighting, Daddy's legs lit up by the car's headlights, Oliver, "Please, Ma'am, can I have some pie?", the fact that then he lifted up his gun and I thought we were goners, but he just stuck it under his arm and marched past me to the mixing bowl, Captain Nemo's control room, the fact that he got hold of my wooden swordie, my favorite kitchen implement, and started spooning cookie dough into his big square mouth, which was sort of funny because the swordie's spoon end is sort of square too, the fact that he looked kind of like an ATM, except an ATM that *inhales* the money, instead of exhaling it, exude, extrude, the fact that in went the dough, while Ronny jabbered in between gobs about how bad I'd always made him feel, the fact that, for mercy's sake, I made *him* feel bad, MAGA, saga, saxhorn, hagfish, the fact that *he's* made *me* feel bad about a million times, the fact that what were all those digs about the *flour* on my face, or the vast size of my apron, the fact that maybe he wanted me to be wearing a little French maid outfit, just hoping he'd call, porno pics, the fact that by this time, *he* had more than *flour* on his face, the fact that he was covered in cookie dough, the fact that he looked just like a *hagfish*, a great big hagfish covered in cookie dough, inverting his jaw and, and extruding his tongue for more, slime eel, "Spiegel im Spiegel," the fact that I couldn't follow what he was saying anyway, because my mind froze too, the fact that for once Ronny really had my full attention, which he seems to have been craving for a while, the fact that I was hyper-alert the whole time, but I still couldn't think what to *do*, the fact that it's like it was all happening in slow motion, the fact that you never expect these things to happen to *you*, the fact that statistically you're more likely to be hit by lightning or fall outta bed, the fact that all I could think about was the *gun*, but I tried not to stare directly at it, in case that provoked him to use it, ♫ *Courage!* ♫, Brave Man Cookies, Ronny's gun, semi-automatic, semi-trailer, tractor, semicircle, semiannual seminars, the fact that when I think of my kids having to listen to Ronny talk about their *mom* that way, telling me he was "*horny*" and such, the fact that they had to hear all those cuss words, the fact that it still makes me feel sick, the fact that for the first week or so after, the thought of that really did make me upchuck, but now it only makes me *feel* like upchucking, the fact that life is solitary, poor, nasty, brutish, and short, and Ronny is a poor, nasty, solitary brute, though not *short*, the fact that nobody moved an inch, not even poor little Jake, which may have saved his life, little lamb, Mommy's blue lamb, the fact that he started crying, but quietened himself, poor little guy, and there he was, this tiny child just staring at that huge man sucking down cookie dough like no tomorrow, the fact that time seemed to stand still, until the oven timer suddenly went off, for the cookies, and Ronny *shot* it, the fact that

Ronny shot my kitchen timer, for no reason, from like a foot away, the fact that I think it startled him, and it's weird but I remember thinking that that kind of timer's now very hard to get, the fact that he accused me of playing hard-to-get, ATM, ASS, the fact that the whole thing's getting blurry in my mind, *The Apartment*, the fact that what Ronny doesn't seem to understand is you gotta be "a mensch, a *human being*," the fact that Jack Lemmon shot himself in the knee by accident once, over a girl, I mean in the *movie*, not real life, the fact that he really shouldn't keep a gun around if suicidal women are going to be staying the night, the fact that how could you bring yourself to kill yourself with a *gun*, but a lot of people do, the fact that when Ronny shot the timer everything on the kitchen counters went flying, the fact that that's when Frederick took off, the fact that Opal had ducked out long before that, I bet, because she never trusted Ronny, the fact that I still haven't found some of the things we lost that day in the hullabaloo, like where is my favorite chocolate-girl spoon from Walter Baker & Co's Chocolate factory in Dorchester, Mass., Hart Crane's dad, lady serving hot chocolate on a little tray, swordie, the fact that that chocolate girl is based on a painting by Liotard called "Nannerl," the fact that I always liked that spoon, the fact that it's one of the few I liked from Grandma's collection, and somehow I ended up with it, the fact that Phoebe has all the rest, or almost all, the fact that we have some with roses on the stem too, cardinal, the fact that Mozart's sister's nickname was Nannerl, and that chocolate girl could be in a Mozart opera, the fact that she could play a servant bringing hot chocolate, recitative, Ira Siff, bel canto, James Levine, the fact that Massachusetts used to be full of huge mills and desperate mill girls trying to save their families from destitution, the fact that the mill owners exploited them as cheap labor, and mill men seduced the prettier ones and sometimes they ended up on the *streets*, the girls, not the men, hard times, timer, the fact that once Ronny had shot my timer, that galvanized me a little, the fact that it occurred to me I really had to do something, the fact that you always hear you're supposed to talk muggers and murderers down, so I *tried*, the fact that I started babbling about orthodontist appointments and how the kids all needed haircuts and we were expected any minute at the hair place in Cambridge, the fact that I think I said that if we didn't get there soon they'd be wondering about us, as if Ronny was really going to be stopped in his tracks by the possibility of somebody in a beauty parlor in Cambridge clocking our absence, a guy with cookie dough all over his chin and a submachine gun under his arm and probably my chocolate-lady spoon under his foot, the fact that he wasn't buying it, my hairdo story, the fact that my only Plan B was to gather up all the kids and walk straight out of there without a backward glance, and just hope for the best, hope that shooting us all in the back wasn't really what gave Ronny a thrill, the fact that by then Jake was hiding under the *stool* though, I think he crawled under there when the timer got shot, and I wasn't sure I could get him out from under there *quickly* enough, "the clean sweep of the tempered steel as it glides through—," and if I couldn't, and *Jake and I* got shot, I didn't know if the *others* would have the guts to run, the fact that there was a good chance Plan B would be a complete failure, Plan A, Plan B, the fact that I sound like I'm planning nuclear war, deterrence, Non-Proliferation Treaty, the NPT, UN, the fact that next I tried to interest Ronny in Gillian's *birthday*, and how I had to go get her a present *that day*, or it would be too late, because the store was shut the next day or something, the fact that I was babbling, and it was all pretty lame, I guess, the fact that I don't think I really believed Gillian's birthday would tug at Ronny's heart strings or anything, the fact that it was a coded message for *Gillian*, CIA, KGB, SS, the fact that what I was thinking was that if we did all get shot and killed, at least Gillian would know before she died that I had her birthday in mind, because she seemed a little uncertain about it earlier in the day, the fact that meanwhile, the whole time I was talking, I was still trying to imagine how we could edge our way out of there, the fact that I wondered if I could pull off the old trick of alerting Ronny to something alarming outside on the porch, and then we could make a dash for the hall door, but I didn't trust the kids to git when I said "Git!", and where were we going to run, fast enough to escape

Ronny, a vengeful Ronny, and what if *they* were frozen to the spot like me, when the time came to make a dash for the door, what ifs, what ifs, "Shane! Shane!", the fact that this is something families should practice for, actually, the fact that people should have shooter drills at *home*, not just at school, "our forever home," the fact that why'd I never think of it before, "forever family," the fact that we should teach everybody how to play dead, everybody in the *country*, I mean, the fact that everybody should have security cameras and X-ray machines and *bodyguards*, if you can afford them, the works, because otherwise *this* could happen, at any moment, for no reason, strawberry festival, the fact that but then who guards the *bodyguards*, the fact that it's like wet nurses, the fact that who's nursing the *wet nurse's* baby, I always want to know, the fact that maybe you have to wean your kid before you become a wet nurse, but I think the wet nurse's own kid probably lost out somehow, like calves in the milk industry, the fact that breast milk adjusts to the growing baby, but I don't know if it can adjust from a bigger baby to a newborn again, just like that, with a click of the fingers, the fact that I bet wet nurses weren't paid much either, but it was still enough to shove their own babies out of the way, for the sake of the family finances, the fact that then Ronny got on his high horse again, not talking about his feelings for *me* anymore, more just full of self pity, the fact that he said how nice he'd always been to me, carting chicken feed around, how he's not such a bad guy and always just wanted to be *friendly*, friendly wolf eel, soap-box derby, toothpick, the fact that what was I supposed to say, the fact that I *paid* for that feed, and he was paid to deliver it, the fact that it wasn't just a personal favor or something, the fact that meanwhile the cougar cookies were all burning up, and the room was kind of smoky, the fact that it would've been good if we had a sprinkler system maybe, the fact that it might have cooled *him* off, panic room, the fact that everybody should have a panic room too, the fact that I started hoping it would get even smokier from the burning cookies, so we could maybe sneak out through the fug without him noticing, the fact that my *other* plan was even dumber, the fact that I was actually hoping that, given he must've eaten about thirty cougars' worth of raw cookie dough by then, maybe he'd get nauseous and have to run for the bathroom, but of course *that* didn't happen, million to one chance, a thousand billion chickens, the fact that with my luck he probably just got a sugar *high* that gave him more energy to shoot at us, salt, radiator, terrapins, nickel coin slot, the fact that he aimed the next shot at the big sliding door to the porch, and it made such a terrible bang when it broke the glass, leap, the fact that all cars and houses should have bulletproof glass, and we should all wear bulletproof vests, or would that just mean the bullets would've ricocheted around the room forever until they hit one of us in the *head*, bullets, the fact that Ronny fired shots in my home, the fact that after he shot the window, he turned to look at me, smiling, just checking to see if he'd scared me, and yes, he had, the fact that I almost jumped out of my skin, the fact that now I know what people mean by that, the fact that your whole body separates for a second, disintegrates, and then has to get re-integrated, settle back into itself, the fact that I think that's when I peed my pants, the fact that then Ronny decided to shoot up the fridge, RAT-A-TAT-TAT, and the *fridge* sprang a leak too, released liquid, flow chart, scattershot, scatter diagram, fishbone diagram, the fact that I hoped he'd be satisfied with wrecking the fridge, but I doubted it, the fact that by then I only held out some hope for *Jake*, as long as he stayed where he was under the stool, the fact that, as for the other three cringing against the back wall, all lined up ready to be shot, well spaced too, well, oh, my gosh, the fact that the thought of that just makes me cry, but I gotta *stop* crying, the fact that it's not good for the kids to see me like this, the fact that you always have to be strong for your kids, but I'm not really very strong, I'm just not, the fact that I'm a failure, broken, broken, the fact that then all of a sudden it just seemed absurd to me, so silly, the fact that it seemed like Ronny didn't need *us* around if all he wanted to do was shoot up the furniture and stuff, so why couldn't we go, but then he stopped to reload, which he can do fast, and I knew, I just knew, we were done for, the fact that the guy spends half his life playing with guns, and told me once he has "perfect form," the fact that he took his eyes off us for one moment though, to fiddle with his gun, and that's when *Stacy* clonked him hard with that floor lamp I've always hated, the fact that now I love that lamp dearly, though it doesn't work anymore, the fact that the great thing was it's so tall that she could reach him with it from across the room, the length of the lamp plus the length of Stacy's arm, the fact that it sort of hit his shoulder, not his stupid skull unfortunately, but the impact knocked the *gun* to the floor, and when Ronny bent over and scrabbled for it, Stacy leapt on his back and dug her fingers into his *throat*, and bit his arm, and he started bellowing, the fact that she says she got that throat move from the self-defense book, but she'd never actually tried it out before, because Ben wouldn't let her test it on *him*, the fact that I don't know how she thought up the biting, the fact that maybe *that* was just instinct, Switzerland, chocolate, Nannerl, the fact that Ronny struggled and snorted and sort of choked, and tried to push her off him but Stacy didn't budge and wouldn't take her hands off his throat, the fact that he got to his feet with her still clinging to his back, and he tried to jolt her off, shrug her off, the fact that he's such a strong guy, all those bags of seed, but she managed to hold on, just by her *hands*, her legs swinging loose in the air, the fact that I think she had him by the *ears* at one point, the fact that Ronny was hobbling around the kitchen like a big bear, howling and gurgling, still looking for his gun, but I think Ben had already hidden it under the ironing pile, the fact that Stacy's persistence finally brought *me* to my senses, and I finally did something, some mom I am, *Sam I am*, some protector, the fact that anyway I roused myself and grabbed the half-empty bulk-buy flour sack and swung it at his stomach as hard as I could, trying to avoid hitting Stacy, who was still on his back, the fact that I got him right in the belly, and he swayed and then toppled, but I don't think that was really because of me, the fact that I think it was Stace, who somehow managed to twist her leg around one of his and made him trip over, the fact that he fell flat on his face and Stacy straddled his shoulders and biffed his nose and jabbed her thumb under his chin from behind like it says to do in the book, the fact that she sure got a lot outta that book and, my, did it work, the fact that by then I was really beginning to think we might be able to get the better of him, and I caught sight of my Revere Ware pans on the stove, so I started battering Ronny hard on the head with one, the bigger saucepan, the heaviest Revere Ware pot I own, the fact that I think it's the largest one commercially available, the fact that I hit him with it with all my might, and it rang out with each whomp, phulu-pututu, phulu-pututu, probably due to the nice copper bottom, of the *pan*, not Ronny, and it's not even dented, the fact that I wish Mommy could have known her Revere Ware would come in that handy one day, the fact that, just think, if she hadn't left me her Revere Ware we might not have conquered Ronny, inheritance, Tangiers, dark green mountainside, the fact that once we got his head good and ringing, all we had to do then was tie him up with some of Leo's long-sleeved shirts from the ironing pile, the fact that that was *Gillian's* clever idea, the birthday girl, the fact that she has a very practical side, for such a little kid, the fact that Ronny was still acting like King Kong or something, squirming all over the place, but he couldn't seem to get up, and Stacy and I were able to yank both his arms behind his back and twist some shirts tightly round and round his wrists, the fact that Gillian brought more and more shirts and we did the same with his feet, the fact that they were kicking like crazee, but Ben bravely grabbed one and I got the other, just long enough for Stacy to wind a shirt or two around them, the fact that Ben helped tie the knots, the fact that they did it *so well*, the fact that Ronny's legs were held tight together and he was flapping like a seal, an elephant seal, the fact that cotton shirts are *strong*, the button-down kind, I don't know about T-shirts, NAZI POTUS, the fact that they really make good ropes, as it turns out, the fact that then, just for good measure, Ben went and got some old phonebooks from the closet and dumped *them* hard on Ronny's head, one by one, the fact that this was the first second I had to check how Jakey was doing under his stool, but he wasn't *there*, the fact that I had a sudden image of him lying wounded by a stray bullet, but when I called out for him, he emerged from behind the counter, the fact that he'd just gone the long way around, to avoid having to crawl over Ronny, the fact that it was such a relief to see him, but then he tripped over the bashed-up floor lamp that was lying across the floor, the fact that he fell hard on his knees, and for a second we all stopped still, expecting him to cry, but he just sort of laughed at us and said "Guys, I'm going to be okay," which made us all feel a lot better about things, the fact that it was Jake who then had the bright idea of pelting Ronny with apples, the fact that he started us all off, and soon everybody was pelting Ronny with apples, the fact that it turns out apples are a great outlet for fury, or maybe I've always known that, and *that's* why I make all these tartes tatin, the fact that, all in all, what *teamwork*, what good old American know-how and can-do spirit, good old American *apples* too, well, South American, the fact that we'd *won*, and Ronny was just lying there kicking and growling helplessly every time an apple hit him, his face was all sweaty and smeary with cookie dough, the fact that it was kind of disgusting really, which is maybe why Gillian threw a blanket over him, the fact that he looked much better that way, completely covered, a Ronny mound, and his protests and groans were less noticeable too, the fact that I felt like kicking him, I really did, but in some ways Ronny just seemed irrelevant by then, the fact that *we'd* beaten a guy with a *gun*, Mishipeshu, Mishawaka, the fact that if it wasn't for Stacy though, and her self-defense tactics, it might have been a different story, the fact that maybe *this* is why you give birth, so that with any luck *someone* in your family will be handy in an emergency, like if it ever turns out your chicken-feed deliveryman's a total nutjob, fruitcake, a person of inadequate sanity, and a danger to life and limb, the fact that all four of my kids turn out to be *great* in an emergency, actually, it's just that *I'm* not, the fact that *they* all instinctively did the right thing, the fact that it's like Powell's attack on Seward, except that almost all the Sewards were hurt, and *none* of us were, Davina Beebee, the fact that the Sewards all survived, apart from Mrs. Seward, who died later from the shock of it all, poor thing, the fact that maybe she felt like *I* feel, the fact that maybe *she* froze too, the fact that anyway my kids are *stars*, quatre étoiles, Michelin

Man, the fact that I could get really boastful about them if I don't watch out, especially Stace, the fact that without her I'm not sure we'd still be here, the fact that that little kid of mine, Stacy at six, dear me, that grumpy little moaning Silent Treatment kid *saved our lives*, the fact that I've always known I'm a coward, the fact that I just hoped never to be tested, the fact that I always knew I'd freeze or flake out in some way, Cowardly Lion, but *she didn't*, so at least it's not genetic, the fact that one thing I've learnt from this experience is always keep apples around, because you never know when you might need to pelt somebody, though onions or potatoes would do, maybe not carrots, the fact that, no, onions might be slippery, the fact that you should also keep a big flour sack handy at all times, for heaving at a marauder's belly, and it helps to have a son who knows how to tie a good knot, thanks to his pirate days, and a patient husband willing to wait for weeks for his *shirts* to be ironed, the fact that I think it was only when Jake started driving his little yellow tractor over the Ronny mound that I realized we were all half-crazed, but alive, and suddenly I felt furious, the fact that I could've thought up a lot worse punishments for Ronny than toy tractors, for instance a real-life, full-size road roller, the fact that again it was the coolheaded Stace who announced that the first principle of self-defense is, if your house is invaded, you git, so, while the kids grabbed their shoes, I turned off the oven and checked the stove, because you always have to check the stove before you leave the house, even if you've almost been murdered, unless you have one of those infusion hobs that turns itself off all the time, but I would never get one of those because I think they're bad for people with *pacemakers*, and you never know when somebody with a pacemaker might drop in, except that I never want anybody "dropping on by" *again*, Anne Tyler, chairs, the fact that if you had an infusion hob and the marauder had a pacemaker, maybe you could frazzle him by turning on the stove, the fact that, I mean, make him *nervous*, not actually *electrocute* him or fry his wiring or something, the fact that I don't know if they're *that* powerful, infusion hobs, not marauders, I mean, the fact that weirdly the cookies had stopped smoking by then, having already burnt to cinders, the fact that there was nothing left of that batch of cougars, so then we ran outside and just left Ronny lying there like a dying walrus, the fact that we crossed our yard, jumped through the geraniums and over the wall and sped straight to the Kinkels' front door, yard line, the fact that it's lucky they were home, the fact that I've never been so relieved to see anybody in my life, the fact that somehow it seemed a miracle that they were alive too, and Doreen was so sweet and all, the fact that they were so *kind* about it all, the fact that this was when I first got sort of tearful, and couldn't speak, so Stacy explained things, with the other kids chiming in, the fact that Doreen started crying too when she found out what had happened, the fact that then she was hugging everybody all over again, the fact that even Ben allowed himself to be hugged that day, the fact that, you know, I was all wrong about Doreen, the fact that she's really a good person, the fact that they're both good neighbors, Neighbour, Nachbar, the fact that so what if she likes Giant Viper's Buglosses, the fact that nobody's perfect, "I'm only human," the fact that I'll never forget how they took us in like that, the fact that what a state we were in, the fact that it was like London during the Blitz or something, the fact that *Ronny's* a Neighbour too, Ronald Neighbour Named As Suspect In Illegal Entry Case, the fact that Stacy even thought to call the police, the fact that she was already on her cell, selfies, safeties, on the way to the Kinkels', the fact that Jerry Kinkel called 911 too, once he got the gist of what had been going on, the fact that, gee, did Stacy keep her head through it all, the fact that it was only later on, when she was telling Leo over the phone what had happened, that she finally broke down and I had to take the phone, the fact that I was already shaking so much my cup was skittering all around on the Kinkels' little fancy-edged saucer, the fact that they gave us tea in those fancy cups of theirs, the fact that it's a wonder they survived our visit, the *cups* I mean, not the Kinkels, the fact that what's surprising is that, even though this sort of thing is the new normal, new abnormal, enormity, the two police officers got there really quickly, *and* they didn't shoot anybody, the fact that, far from it, they were actually very comforting, especially once they knew kids were involved, the fact that I stutter when talking to the police, I always have, the fact that I can't help it, they make me nervous, the fact that I couldn't even remember our correct *address* at first when they asked me, the fact that I just kept pointing at our *house*, like "*You* look it up," the fact that they probably think I'm nuts, and a lousy mom, and they're probably right, the fact that I am a lousy mom, or how would such a thing ever happen, *Kramer vs. Kramer*, the fact that that movie must have made just about *all* moms feel bad, the fact that Meryl Streep and Dustin Hoffman didn't get along too well, in real life I mean, when they were making that movie, the fact that they were on the outs *behind* the scenes as well as in the movie, because he bullied her a lot or something, or maybe even hit her, 3:33, the fact that who's the better actor though, the fact that for all Dustin Hoffman's method acting and all, he's really kind of the same in every movie, whereas Meryl Streep can really transform herself, the fact that it's almost like you can't believe it's the same *person*, like in *The Bridges of Madison County* and *Julie & Julia* and *It's Complicated*, the fact that *The Graduate* was Dustin Hoffman's best movie, and that's *ancient*, the fact that after we told the police how heroic Stacy had been, the officers made a great big fuss of her, the fact that it didn't hurt that she was so cogent, lucid, and so pretty too, the fact that she was transplendent, and the officers seemed kind of spellbound, but then they dragged themselves away and trudged over to have a look at Ronny, the fact that they approached the house with caution, guns drawn, in case he'd already escaped from the shirts and maybe booby-trapped the whole place or something, or barricaded himself in there, gearing up for a long gun siege while he cased the joint for free pie, Shooter Eats Pie In 48 Hour Siege, the fact that luckily he was still lying there on the kitchen floor though, when they found him, under the blanket, surrounded by apples and phonebooks, the fact that they found the gun too, which is good because I wasn't going back in the house until they got that thing out of there, the fact that we just stayed at the Kinkels' and from there we watched Ronny being taken out in plastic handcuffs and shoved in the patrol car, the fact that plastic handcuffs look like they're made to hold saplings up straight, not hold murderers at bay, but I guess they work and they're easier to use, compared to the metal kind, or *shirts*, the fact that I think the police *know* how goofy plastic handcuffs look too, and that's why they like them, the fact that they instantly make the suspect look kinda silly, cufflinks, knickerbockers, Interlochen, the fact that they spent some time examining Ronny's car and all the wreckage in the kitchen, and fingerprinting our house of horrors, and kept coming back to talk to Stace, the fact that Stace was doing so well explaining things, I just let her handle it, the fact that she told them where the gun was too, or no, *Ben* told them that, because he was the one who'd nudged it under the clothes pile, the fact that it's lucky Stacy knocked the thing out of Ronny's hands before he finished reloading, or Ben's *life* could have been at risk when he pushed the gun along the floor with his foot, the fact that the thought of Ben even having to touch that thing still frightens me, but what a smart kid he is, ballistic gel tests, a bullet's trajectory through a baby's brain, bulletproof shot glasses, point blank range, ergonomically handgun-shaped device, AFID, the fact that I hope he doesn't tell all the kids at school now he's handled a semi-automatic, because they'll all want one, the fact that I've told him to keep that part to himself, the fact that it used to be *popguns* and now it's, Sandy Hook, the fact that the timer's really had it, but the fridge only has minor wounds, the fact that they look more spectacular than they are, well, as far as we can tell, like Jack Lemmon's double bass in *Some Like It Hot*, "How did those holes get there?", "Mice?", the fact that Ronny didn't manage to kill it, the fact that it just won't be dispensing much ice anymore, the fact that all you get from it now is slush, mush, ashes to ashes, dollars to donuts, face-to-face, safe as houses, the fact that we got on the *national news*, even though nobody actually died, the fact that *that* was a surprise, getting on the news, I mean, the fact that it must've been a really slow news day, but everybody likes hearing how the kids all helped out, and Stacy especially, the fact that she makes a very photogenic hero, the fact that she's now *famous*, the fact that she's almost like the new state mascot, the fact that next thing you know she'll have her own fan club like a Morning Routine girl, the fact that that nice Colin something or other dedicated a whole basketball game to her in Columbus, with cheerleaders and everything, and Stace went, the fact that Leo took her, the fact that Stace was given a sash to wear, like she was Miss World or something, and the cheerleaders did a special cheer just for Stace, the fact that we got to see it later on her phone, the fact that they had a whole ceremony of some kind at school too, with Hawaiian Punch and cookies, and brownies of course, the fact that she's not letting it go to her head though, the fact that, well, we're all too traumatized for that, too shaky, the fact that, for Pete's sake, we jump at every noise, such as the *new* kitchen timer, alarm clocks certainly, car doors slamming way across the street, dogs barking, chickens screeching, the fact that, heck, we jump whenever anybody *sneezes*, the fact that Mommy could sneeze seventeen times in a row, Mommy, chickens, goldfish, PTSD, insomnia, Jesus of New Philadelphia, the fact that I don't think Gillian had the best birthday in the world in the midst of all this, but at least she *made* it to her birthday, and she got an 8 cake, the fact that luckily I can make a birthday cake in my sleep, and an eight cake is simple, the fact that you just put two angelfoods together, side by side, with a little cut off the top one, at the join, cover them with chocolate frosting and Bob's your uncle, the fact that it looks sort of like you've split the atom, or fertilized an egg, double yolk, cells dividing, Möbius strip, double helix, spiral, DNA, the fact that I kept the decorations abstract, Hoag, Art, Ronny, Leo, the fact that Gillian made it to her eighth birthday, the fact that the police just Tased, *Tasered*, somebody for using a fake $20 bill, ECW, EMD, NMI, cattle prod, the fact that he was a young black kid, the fact that he didn't look twenty *himself*, the fact that they treated him like he was a mass *murderer* or something, the fact that they roughed him up right there in the grocery store in front of all these white people who didn't do a thing, the fact that they just stood in line for the checkout while all this was going on, the fact that it's kind of unbelievable, the indifference, "Let them eat cake," the fact that one customer was even sort of doing her *hair* while three cops jumped on this guy right at her feet, the fact that *Ronny* never got Tasered, and he held a whole family at *gunpoint*, and entered illegally, and stole cookie dough and destroyed property, my nice little timer, the fact that does it count as kidnap, to hold people in a room like that, against their will, the fact that *I* think so, the fact that I wish it had been just *me* here when Ronny came, the fact that I wish the kids didn't have to know from now on how screwed up the world is, "screw-up," the fact that there's one nice thing that came out of it all though, the fact that we were all sitting around talking that night, eating the cougar cookies that survived, and Gillian said "At least Jim didn't have to see this," the fact that we all agreed it would have made him even more timid, and then Ben said, "He's better off where he is," the fact that I almost choked and asked hesitantly "Which is where?" and Ben said "With the Cherokee tracker!", as if everybody must know this, the fact that I don't know when they realized the tracker's dog was Jim, but it turns out the kids found out about it way back and they *approved* of the tracker's plan to adopt him, the fact that they all thought they had to keep the Jim news from *me*, to stop me feeling we had to go and reclaim him, the fact that Gillian said "We know how attached you were to him," the fact that even Leo laughed then, and he's not been laughing much these days, the fact that he knows my true feelings about Jim's soprano yap, cinnamon bark, worse than his bite, the fact that anyway everybody's agreed Jim's happier where he is, which is such a relief to my mind, the fact that we were all impressed that Jim had made friends with a *lioness* too, the fact that Jake summed it up pretty well, saying "Jim rocks," the fact that everybody cracked up when he said that, the fact that nobody knew Jake was so with it, the fact that I think they all envy that dog a little actually, because he's had such an adventure-packed life, getting kicked off the farm, being saved from the dogs' home fire, palling up with a lioness, and now he gets to live with the *Cherokee tracker*, their favorite guy in the *world*, the fact that Ben kept mumbling "He's happy with the Cherokee tracker, he's happy with the tracker," the fact that maybe they'd all be happier with the Cherokee tracker, instead of living with their shy, fallible, cowardly mom in this house of horrors, or house of *one* horror at least, terror, terrorism, 9/11, McVeigh, Breivik, Adam Lanza, the fact that at least I don't have to worry about Jim anymore, I just have to worry about everything else, eaglet's leg stuck in twigs, styptic stick, like what a flop I was in an emergency, the fact that we could so easily have *died*, passed on, Happy Hunting Ground, I mean, if it wasn't for *Stacy*, the fact that we*will* all die in the end too, and that seems a lot realer to me now and it's unbearable, phulu-pututu, Ronny's moans, children dying, a $20 bill, self-defense book, bell-bottoms, Funk Bottoms, copper bottoms, pumps, bowl cut, the fact that I can't think about all that, the fact that it's better to just think about Stacy and how brave *she* was, the fact that she was *so brave*, the fact that that's what really gets me, the fact that she's like Superwoman, cheerleaders, the fact that she knew just what to *do*, and she was just waiting for her chance to strike, the fact that she didn't hesitate for one single solitary second and, once she got going, she knew it was an all-or-nothing situation, the fact that if she'd failed that would've been it, the fact that I really don't want to think what might have happened if she'd missed him with that lamp, the fact that I don't think any of us would've made it out alive, this ear-pulling will either be a success or a failure, the fact that she's got that can-do attitude, Navy SEALs stuff, but not so bloodthirsty, SWAT team, CONSTRUIMUS, BATUIMUS, the fact that she risked her life, for *us*, the fact that she leapt at him, she put herself in harm's way, while I just froze, the fact that I'm useless in an emergency, useless, broken, broke, the fact that I've never believed that sadness and hardship make a person tougher, the fact that they made me *weaker*, the fact that I'm useless around the old or the sick or anything, useless in an emergency, ♬ *Courage!* ♬, the fact that I would've told the Gestapo anything they wanted to know, before they even strapped me down and started the tooth-extraction, or put the electrodes on my feet, or pulled my fingernails out, *everything*, I would've told them anything they wanted to hear, whether it was true or not, the fact that where did Stacy get all her courage *from*, Brave Man Cookies, the fact that it's hard to believe it's from *Frank*, the fact that she's Mocchi the warrior girl and I'm just a flop, even when my own kids' *lives* are at stake, burning witches at the stake, Trump steak, the fact that what good is *freezing* in an emergency, for the love of Mike, unless you're talking steak, the fact that what kind of evolutionary purpose does *that* serve, the fact that we didn't even get the chance to play dead, the fact that I might've been *better* at that, the fact that it's just so *embarrassing* but, then, what evolutionary purpose does *embarrassment* serve either, my dream about running around the Irish hotel lobby in my underpants, Leo's nail-clippers, the fact that children are always getting suffocated to death, playing in old freezers, the fact that I gotta think positive here or I'll collapse, gotta count my blessings instead of sleep, I mean sheep, and *fast*, the fact that what's *good* is, well, that we did all survive, the fact that there's no doubt about that, the fact that we all made it out of there intact, out of the *situation*, I mean, because we still have to live in this house of horrors, and I don't know if that's so good for us, the fact that maybe we should *move*, ♫ *Somewhere, over the rainbow* ♫, the fact that anyway we have our whole lives ahead of us and nobody *stole* them from us after all, the fact that, touch wood, there are no funerals on the horizon, no candlelit vigils, pallbearers, the fact that I know candlelit vigils are well meant and all, but it's always chilling to hear of one, the fact that you never want one to be held in *your* honor, if you can help it, blessings, the fact that this whole thing has given Stace a real boost, a sense of accomplishment, *power* even, and why not, because she definitely *is* powerful, the fact that she saved her whole family and now she's in the *papers*, Tuscarawas Teen Subdues Gunman, Saves Family, the fact that Gillian's doing a clipping service for us, the fact that it's given Gillian a boost *too* somehow, seeing what her big sis can do, though maybe it's also a lot to live up to, blessings, the fact that it's good that Ginnie, I mean *Gillian*, doesn't seem to see the downside of that yet, the fact that I hope we don't have to have a shooting incident to launch each kid, the fact that, blessings, c'mon, boarlets, **8** cake, the fact that one great thing was Stacy meeting Willoughby, or Willy, outside Zyker's, while I was inside getting groceries, the fact that none of us likes going anywhere alone anymore, so she came with me, the fact that I wish I'd gotten a good *look* at him, the fact that I've still never seen him, the fact that she says he acted all interested in her again, all because she'd been in the news, her new heroic status, the fact that he wouldn't leave her *alone*, and kept asking about the Incident, what happened, what *happened*, the fact that she barely answered him, the fact that then he told her he wanted to get back together, and tried to *kiss* her or something, and she said "Come any closer and you'll get what *he* got," or something along those lines, and still he hung around, but she just held her ground and gave him the Silent Treatment until he slunk off down the street, the fact that that girl really is on a roll, Stacy rocks, and I'm so happy for her, the fact that it really *is* a great thing for her, the fact that none of us will ever forget that Stacy saved our lives and it changes *everything*, I think, no matter what else ever comes our way, the fact that there'll always be *this*, that Ronny tried to kill us and Stace saved us, the fact that Ronny tried to kill us, Ronny tried to kill us, the fact that Jim is happy with the Cherokee tracker, the fact that, the fact that I should plant out my nasturtiums, the fact that "plant out" sounds much more professional than "plant," just like chicken feed sounds more farmery than "chicken food," farmer talk, candy corn, the fact that I want some *flamenco* too now, the fact that flamenco is what I want, flamenco the *flower*, not the dance, my dancing days are over, the fact that it has "sizzling blossoms" and attracts butterflies, frazzled, jazzed up, the fact that maybe I could get some lady slipper orchids too, Pueblo, if I can figure out what sort of soil they need, mulch, mold, dirt, mush, the fact that, boy, I am sooooo middle-aged, as Stacy would say, the fact that I'm really starting to *care* about gardening, and birds, and trees and cooking and such, but my feeling is you only live once, if that, so you might as well have some flowers to look at, and maybe a purple martin house, the fact that maybe I really *should* get a purple martin house, a nice safe little house way up high where birds can raise their families in peace, a safe house, but our back yard isn't right for one, backwards, backtrack, back up, Bacchus, the fact that I think

Ronny aged me another twenty years, flashback, hatchback, backdraft, backwash, crown dieback, blowback, puffback, background, backpack, begpacking, bug-out bag, the fact that a lot of background info has turned up on Ronny now, the fact that he got a dishonorable discharge from the Army, and people with dishonorable discharges aren't supposed to have any guns, gyny guy, the fact that he was married once, Ronny, not the *gyny* guy, the fact that I bet the gyny guy's been married like a *billion* times, always searching, searching for the next, well, let's not go there, the Encyclopedia of Bosom, the fact that Ronny and his wife broke up because he was hitting her, the fact that he's a wife-beater *and* a deadbeat dad, the fact that he's got two kids somewhere, the fact that he never mentioned them, the fact that they say Ronny's injuries were mild, *They say*, I mean from our Incident, the fact that every newspaper report says *we* were unhurt too, "completely unhurt," Davina Beebee, and that is simply not true, or why would my only leisure activities be sleeping and weeping, and leaping out of a chair, the fact that I weep for what we were before and are now, and anything can set me off, anything, the fact that everything seems to remind me we're *different* now, from what we were before, *less* maybe, though I shouldn't say it, the fact that we all seem kind of inhibited now, intimidated, constrained anyway, the fact that, I mean, heavens, just idly noticing the bruises I still have from that day makes me start to shake, or finding one of Jake's Japanese soldiers that got broken in the scuffle, broken, the fact that just looking at that new kitchen timer can get me going, I guess because all these things remind me we could have been *killed*, for *no reason*, unless you call Ronny's longin' for a bit o' lovin' and a piece o' pie "reasons," the fact that the real reason he did it, I think, is that the guy just likes playing with guns, and "The whole thing got out of hand," all because he's, like, *crazee*, the fact that Ben and Jake seem totally off guns now, even squirt guns and popguns, so Jake probably doesn't care much what happens to these Japanese soldiers anymore, the fact that they are probably full of phthalates anyway, the fact that let's get rid of them, the fact that it doesn't mean he doesn't *think* about guns though, the fact that he did a sort of St. Vitus dance this morning and I got hold of him and took him on my lap and asked him what was up, because I thought he'd seriously lost it, the fact that at first I thought he might be having a *fit*, but he said he was just practicing dodging bullets, BLAM BLAM, oh dear, oh dear, the fact that even he seems to know we had a pretty narrow escape, the fact that if it weren't for that raggedy old self-defense book, who knows what might have happened, Raggedy Ann, Raggedy Andy, Barbie and Ken, Goofus and Gallant, two men jumping on a girl from behind, *Highlights for Children*, the fact that I can't get rid of the image of poor little Jake hiding under that stool, the fact that no kid should ever have to do that, in his own home, the fact that the one constant thing here, one sort of blessing, and now I do kind of take *comfort* in it, is that my *teeth still hurt*, the fact that I really don't mind it anymore, because it reminds me of the old pre-Incident days, the fact that that hygienist can sandblast me anytime she wants now and I'd *love* it, the fact that there's *security* in lying in a dentist chair being sandblasted, the fact that why'd I ever complain so much about it, the fact that sandblasting is nothing to me now I'm a gun-crime victim, I mean gun-crime *survivor*, *Oprah*, the fact that you're not supposed to say "victim," the fact that being a victim's a downer, while being a survivor's supposed to be an upper, or something like that, the fact that we'll probably all need years of therapy to recover from this, but not *Family Therapy*, not that Caite and Kris pair, the fact that we gotta get somebody *good* this time, the fact that we've had offers, *many* offers, the fact that everybody seems to know some great therapist, or hypnotherapist, the fact that Leo says the insurance will cover some of it, the fact that he wets the bed every night now and sucks his thumb, *Jake*, not Leo, though Leo's not himself either, towel, the fact that we've already gotten Ben a therapist, the fact that she says she's just going to take him out to the park and never mention the Incident unless *he* brings it up, which sounds good to us, the fact that at first Ben claimed he didn't need a therapist, but then out of the blue one day he said he didn't want to live, and added "I'm dead inside," the poor little kiddo, the fact that later he said it was all just a joke, but he's never talked like that before, the fact that that's just not Ben, the fact that it's *Gillian* who worries about the meaning of life and all, not Ben, the fact that I wonder what she thinks it means *now*, the Facts of Life, Japanese soldiers, scrunchie, suicide notes, damage assessment, the fact that it just came in the mail, our Incident Number, not a suicide note, the fact that we're "Incident No. 1897642/crim," the fact that Phoebe wants to come see us, even though she's so busy, but I told her it's not necessary, yet look at me now, blubbing in the bathroom again, scrunchie, styptic stick, the fact that that's exactly when I do need Phoebe, when I'm blubbing in the bathroom, the thought of Jake under the stool, the fact that I can't stay in here long, the fact that I don't like leaving the kids alone out there in our house of horrors, the fact that I like to check on them every minute now, Family Terrorized By Crazed Gunman, Bravery Of Daughter, burnt cookies, sore teeth, the fact that Ronny better go to *jail* for this, the fact that it's possible he'll get off with a suspended sentence, because he only actually destroyed one kitchen timer, broke a few windows, and damaged a fridge, the fact that I don't know if they can get him on his illegal arsenal, ammo, artillery fire, Poo-Poo Plate, the fact that it's *Leo* I really worry about sometimes, the fact that he just seems sad all the time now, ♫ *Our state fair* ♫, the fact that, to add insult to injury, *Frank* now wants to see Stace, Friday or Sunday, the fact that he's acting like we can't take care of her right, all because of this Incident, the fact that maybe he's right too, I mean what kind of mom am I, but still, what good's *he*, the fact that what good's he *ever* been, the fact that, anyway, Frank will have to kill me first, before I'll let him take Stacy away, the fact that I'll kill *him* if he tries anything, the fact that, *listen* to me, what a *terrible* thing to say, the fact that he *is* her dad, the fact that she doesn't need her mom killing her dad, the fact that it's all Ronny's fault, the fact that he's corrupted my mind, the fact that he's taught me to be a raging, violent crazy-ass threat to humanity, the fact that I shouldn't say a— either, the fact that Ronny is a bad influence, the fact that Frank's just intrigued by Stacy's newfound glamor, prestige, charisma, her aura of the elect, the fact that what's it called when people are attracted by fame, the fact that how dare he, just how *dare* he, the fact that I'll get a gun, I *will*, bullets, bullet mold, the fact that now I wish we'd kept Aunt Sophia's old guns after all, the fact that you never know when you're going to need to do some killing, the fact that, my gosh, what *has* come over me, the fact that I gotta get a grip on myself, boarlets, blessings, Djibouti, *Betty Botta bought some butta*, the fact that it's incredible of Frank though, to be this, this brutal, in the middle of a crisis, when we're all just trying to *recover* here, brutish, brute, King Canute, the fact that he could just be *nice*, like *sympathetic* or something, the fact that why can't he just be a mensch, a human being, like a bit *fatherly*, for once, humble, considerate, for old time's sake, "Auld Lang Syne," the fact that Frank Capra uses "Auld Lang Syne" in all his movies, just about, the fact that most Americans apparently think "Auld Lang Syne" was written by the Beatles, the fact that even like an *ounce* of sympathy, would *that* be so hard, ♫ *We'll tak' a cup o' kindness yet, yeah, yeah, yeah* ♫, but no, the fact that suddenly he wants to steal her from me, after all these years of making no trouble at all about custody, fourteen years of not even turning up for planned visits, but now that she's *famous*, it's a different story, poor Stace, the fact that I hope it's not going to be a big *problem*, the fact that if it is though, she'll handle it, the fact that if she can handle *Ronny*, and that Willy character, she can handle Frank, and if she can't, well, I'll want to kill him but of course I *won't*, but I hope he realizes I'll spend my last dime fighting this idea, even if it kills *me*, the fact that she'll go live with Frank over my dead body, corpse, flexed burial, but of course she almost *did*, because if Ronny had killed me, Frank would've *insisted* on taking her, and he might have gotten her too, the fact that I know Leo would've fought to keep her here, in her *home*, but there's no telling what some judge might decide, the fact that Leo knows what kind of a dad Frank is, bumpstock, "Bienstock!", Sir Ringo, the fact that last night I dreamt I was living all alone in a basement with bars on the windows, and two men tried to get in to *kill* me, and then I dreamt Gillian was so upset about a lost kitten, she shrank herself to become a replacement kitten, but she got so small she slipped down the stem of a flower and I couldn't find her anymore, the fact that, boy, everything's *life-and-death* with me now, black and white, the fact that it's all a fight to the finish, and everything's about guns and killers or kittens, the fact that this is how I *think* now, swinging high up in the trees at the Annual Northwestern Faculty Summer Picnic, bird costume, the fact that I only seem to be interested in a news story now if it involves guns, especially if it bears any similarities to *our* Incident, and everywhere I go I have one thing on my mind, the fact that I'm just looking around to see who's got a gun, OC, CC, OCD, DC, D and Cs, ACDC, and where to hide if they decide to start up shooting, like do we go behind the *counters* or in the *restroom* or down the *basement* or *what*, the fact that I can't concentrate on much else besides guns, and keep forgetting what I went to the store for, Zyker's, Kurz-Kasch, Bliss, euphoria, Mommy, but I can't watch movies if there are any guns, the fact that I haven't reached Cathy's stage of equanimity, the fact that, boy, she really loves a good crime story, the more violent the better, the fact that she's been a crime statistic herself, and now I'm one too, join the club, the fact that we're both blooded, bloodied, bloody, and has she ever been *sweet* about it, like, I mean, come on, bringing over franks 'n' beans the next day and everything, and organizing a rota for getting the kids to and from school next week, because they're feeling nervous of the school bus, gug, latex-free upsee, the fact that I always tried to be so polite and *respectful* with Ronny, but now I feel like why the heck should I be, the fact that what's the point in being polite to a crazee person, a wife-beater, child terrifier, domestic terrorist, shoot, shooter, shooting, the fact that why should I have to go along with *that*, for crying out loud, the fact that he terrorized my whole family and I honestly *hate* the guy for that, the fact that I don't "forgive" him one iota, and I never will, the fact that when I look back on the fight in the kitchen, sometimes I really wish I'd strangled him while I had the chance, like after we got him tied up, just so I'd know for sure he can never ever do that to us or anybody else *again*, self defense, Stand-Your-Ground law, SYG, "a line in the sand over which you do not," the fact that Ohio doesn't actually have an SYG law, which is just as well, SOTU, unless the assailant's in your *car*, these horrible *imaginings*, the fact that I could've wound up in jail *myself* if I'd strangled him, oh dear, and he's not worth it, the fact that it's driving me crazee though, all the what ifs, whatnot, effed-up, 3:33, Mommy, the fact that what would she think about what happened to us, the fact that I don't know why I didn't at least *sock* him one, like the very first time he leered at me through the screen door or commented on my floury face, the fact that I should've socked him, the fact that he had that way of looking at my, well, my chest, which I tried to ignore, the fact that we all try to be polite all the time but some people really just need to be punched in the jaw, or given a fat lip, the fact that *why* was I was always trying to be polite to him, the fact that it's just like how I was with the *hygienist* after she wrecked my teeth, the fact that I should have laid him out flat and called the police, and that goes for everybody at Peolia too, the fact that I should have reported their asses to the *police*, not just about the broken wrist but the way they gyp the students, the fact that I should've reported it as a *crime*, which it *is*, the fact that I'd like to see Moira in handcuffs, "I'm sorry about your wrist," the fact that they really need to be locked up, *most* of them anyway, not Julie Shriver, the fact that she was okay, the fact that socking Ronny in the jaw the first time he leered wouldn't have worked anyway, because I would've had to open the screen door to do it, and then he could've gotten *in*, and I just never wanted him in here, the fact that my whole strategy was to try to ignore him, for the sake of peace, and the convenience of getting *chicken feed* delivered, sciatica, Robin McKenzie, lordosis, ♫ *He played knick knack on my spine* ♫, arthritis, rheumatism, the fact that Rachel just had to get two new hips, the fact that Abby had to have *both knees* replaced, because of arthritis, and then she had scoliosis as well, red and green sugar sprinkles, sugar trees, sugar cookies, cougar cookies, Alligator Mound, the fact that sugar gets the onion smell off your hands, the fact that you can clean labels and price stickers off stuff with a piece of orange, orange oil, palm oil, the fact that he really had a thing about pie, I guess, walk a mile in someone else's shoes, the fact that if I'd walked a mile in Ronny's shoes I would've bored the pants off everybody in the neighborhood, Neighbour, Nachbar, Ronald Neighbour Arrested For Attempted Murder, Daughter Fought Back, the fact that if I'd walked a mile in his shoes, the fact that if I'd walked a mile in his shoes I wouldn't have had time for my own *life*, my life, the fact that hunger and thirst were my only weapons against the guy, because he's a big guy and I thought if I didn't feed him he'd *have* to go elsewhere when he got hungry enough, the fact that some people say he was a lovely guy, no, the fact that I don't think *anybody* ever said that, the fact that several people in the papers said he was a *lonely* guy, but I don't believe it was just loneliness that made him fixate on me, the fact that I think he was out to *get* me somehow, "Git!", get the better of me, because it freaked him out in some way that I was getting away with all this, this staying home and baking pies all day thing, the fact that that galled him somehow, or maybe he was just lured by my *vulnerability*, home alone, quiet neighborhood, rotten windows, big aprons, the fact that what if our fridge is leaking something *worse* than water, like some nasty carcinogen, the fact that sometimes people think they just have a runny nose but actually it's *spinal fluid*, or a brain tumor or something, brain surgery, mucus remedy, the fact that I never thought of that, about the fridge, I mean, the fact that aren't fridges full of *gases* and stuff, the fact that all the old *food* in there's bad enough without toxic chemicals as well, Pepito, the fact that I've got no idea what's in there at the moment, the fact that I've completely lost track of things around here, the fact that I feel distant from this house somehow, like either *I'm* not really here, or *it* isn't, the fact that this town ain't big enough for the both of us, the fact that we can't afford a *new* fridge, the fact that maybe the insurance, the fact that, you know, I really should get a handle on things, the fact that people are always setting up GoFundMe sites for people who've been in gun attacks, but I don't think they'd do it for us because nobody *died* in this one, thank heaven, touch wood, cross my fingers and hope to die, knick knack paddywhack, give a dog a bone, the fact that anyway, everybody else needs to save their money to cope with their *own* future gun attacks, Ronny Mound, Alligator Mound, Serpent Mound, the fact that it didn't have to come to *this*, surely, Shirley Jackson, the fact that he told me once his favorite pie was lemon meringue, the fact that I remember him saying it, and I immediately said that's not a kind I make, Middle-Eastern thrice-boiled lemon-slice cake, lemons, thyme, Carnation Evaporated Milk, the fact that now I wish I'd just made the guy a darn lemon meringue pie every time he brought the feed and maybe this would never have happened, the fact that who would it hurt, the fact that maybe it would have settled his hash, calmed him down, the fact that it's just *pie*, the fact that what a dope I am, but I didn't *know*, the fact that I also never knew when he was dropping on by, so how could I have had a lemon meringue pie for him always at the ready, the fact that I wish I'd had one at the ready *that* day though, to throw in his gosh darn face, though I shouldn't say that, I know, "Ducky! Ducky!", the fact that one time he launched into a list of just about every pie he'd ever eaten and I said I had to go get Jake from his play group, even though he was really being picked up by Mariella or somebody that day, hand-knitted mittens, peg with his name on it saying JAKE, the fact that I even got in the car and drove down into town just to *prove* I had somewhere to go, and I wondered if he might be following me, the fact that what about that time we were edging out of the driveway and I saw Ronny's car parked down the road, the fact that I thought he must be delivering feed to somebody else, though I couldn't think who else on our block had chickens, or any other kind of livestock, bumpstock, but now I wonder, the fact that I bet he was "hanging around" here a good bit, watching us, the fact that the guy had too much spare time, the fact that he'll have even more in *jail*, Welch's grape juice, sour grapes, sore teeth, what ifs, trauma victims, Guilt, Anger, Denial, GAD, god, gug, the fact that all these moments with Ronny seem strangely vivid now, like they're painted in bright colors, Painted Desert, dessert, uchronia, Yukon, river delta, Incident No. 1897642/crim, the fact that Jake wants *Babar* read to him and he wants it now, the fact that the whole thing got me so freaked I'm keeping the kids home from school and I put the poor old chickens in the basement, which I'm sure they don't like, the fact that I know they'd probably be all right outdoors but *I'm* not, so they had to come in, the fact that the kids play with them a bit down there, chicken in a basket, the fact that I'm acting just like when the *lion* was on the loose, but I really don't want any of us going outside for a while, except Leo, the fact that Leo has to work, the fact that it's just temporary, this scaredy-cat stuff, the fact that I'm sure I'll feel better soon, the fact that we're keeping the cats in too, the fact that they haven't recovered yet either, the fact that they keep wandering around the kitchen smelling things and jumping, the fact that I don't know what exactly they both *saw*, because they skedaddled, but they both know something pretty bad happened, so they're freaked too, the fact that who needs fireworks or car accidents, or lionesses, when you got guys like Ronny wandering around, the fact that the window man came out and fixed our broken window panes *immediately*, as soon as Leo called him, and he's coming back to deal with all the rotten window frames next week, at last, the fact that everyone just seems to want to be nice, well, everybody except Ronny, oh, and Frank of course, the fact that *they* don't want to be nice at all, "Are you evil?", window repairs, leaky taps, leaking fridge, the fact that I'd prefer rotten windows any day to what we've been through, but I guess finally getting them fixed is some compensation, the fact that we do need secure windows now, that we can *lock*, the fact that Leo says now that Jim's gone for good, maybe we need a *guard* dog too, dog pound, "lady-friend hound dog," wild dogs, hogs, sow, buffalo wolf, the fact that, oof, it was so disgusting, Ronny's face all covered in cookie dough, the fact that it could put you off cookies for life, it really could, and maybe it has, the fact that I've noticed none of the kids has mentioned cookies since that day, the fact that I had to freeze the rest of the cougar cookies because nobody could stomach them anymore, and I had to throw out my nice old swordie, and I kind of miss it, but we couldn't keep that thing around, not after it had been in that *mouth*, the fact that I never did get to play my swordie joke on Leo, the fact that I just *dreaded* having the window guy come but he was so sensitive to the situation, it's kind of like having a big therapy dog around, good person in a crisis, the fact that he's like a horse whisperer or something, *housewife*-whisperer, the fact that if he'd been any more sympathetic I would have started *crying*, but why do I deserve sympathy, the fact that I can't believe I let that guy in our *house*, not the window guy, Ronny, though I didn't actually let him in, or not *consciously* anyway, "We don't deal with the unconscious," house of horrors, *Bleak House*, the fact that Esther gets smallpox, boarlets, the fact that Mommy and Daddy met at the Copley Plaza, the fact that she knew she loved him when she saw his legs lit up by the headlamps, love locks, Paris, France, dance, the fact that they eloped to Paris and she couldn't understand a word of the ceremony, shikse, squaw, Howard Keel, WE FORGIVE YOU, the fact that I won Honorable Mention in a baby contest, flexed burial, extended burial, bundled burial, the fact that I think I heard Ronny apologizing from under his blanket when we were pelting him with all the apples, but we didn't *accept* his apologies, the fact that anyway he was only acting sorry because we'd conquered him, the fact that if we hadn't gotten the better of him, he'd still have been shooting at us, or holding us hostage or something, and by now I guess we'd all be dead and buried, and he'd be exulting, exuding, extruding, excruciating, the fact that sometimes, not that often or anything, but *sometimes*, I just think men are such *babies*, though I know I shouldn't say it, the fact that it isn't fair to generalize, but men are weak, *weak*, well, not all of them, I guess, not *Leo*, or *my boys*, poor Leo, the fact that he's really shaken up, broken, our Incident broke him, so he certainly doesn't need any emasculating generalities, banality of evil, women's lib, identity politics, paddywhack, the fact that the guilt is already eating at him enough, the fact that he's like *Rathbone* after Lincoln was shot, he's so full of remorse, Othello, Killing Fields, Howard Keel, the fact that Leo *shouldn't* feel bad at all though, because, for one thing, none of us actually got shot, and two, it wasn't *his* fault, the fact that if it was anybody's it was mine, for not locking the front door, well, and *Ronny's*, the fact that what could *Leo* have done, Plan A, Plan B, the fact that he was in Philly doing what he was *supposed* to be doing, working to pay all the bills, the fact that he can't be here every minute of the day just in case some jerk like Ronny goes berserk, lurking, twerking, the fact that Rathbone felt so guilty he went nuts and tried to kill his kids, but failed, and then succeeded in killing his wife, this angry scene will either be a success or a failure, the fact that Leo would never do that, surely, the fact that there's not a violent bone in Leo's body, "and stop calling me Shirley," except when he punched that kid out in high school, socked him in the jaw, but the kid deserved it, in some way I can't remember, guns, SMG, GSW, towel, the fact that the good news is he says he's going to be cutting back on his trips, tripes, pepper pot soup, dear *Leo*, because he doesn't want to leave us alone so much, guard dog, therapy dog, forest fires, school shootings, Rathbone, the fact that this is the one thing that gives me hope, not Rathbone, having Leo *home* more, the fact that that makes me happy, though we'll lose money, the fact that I'll try to make more pies, and Leo can read to me, the fact that I dreamt I injured a snake by accident and I felt so bad about it, the fact that I'd been trying to *help* it get out of some tight spot, but I injured it in the process, the fact that I wish Abby was still around, the fact that every cell in the body craves safety after a thing like this, our hurts, the fact that Ethan's worried for me, and Nanya called, the fact that she heard about it on the *news*, the fact that I felt bad for not telling her myself, the fact that I thought she was tired of me and all my cakes and kids but now she wants to come visit us and do a portrait of Stace, the fact that it would be great to have a portrait of Stace, especially now, in her moment of glory, "Shane! Shane!", and Nanya thinks so too, the fact that she's read everything she could find on Stacy's heroism, the fact that she never seemed that interested in her before but now she says "That's some kid you got there," woman fighting off two attackers under a bridge, bell-bottoms, keys up the nose, the fact that I felt so proud, even a little vindicated, I guess, because this is the first time Nanya's ever seen some point in me having all these kids, the fact that what we didn't get into was my inability to protect them *myself*, and that's what really gives me the creeps, the fact that, I mean, any guy can come in here at any moment and blow our heads off, and there's absolutely nothing I can do about it, the fact that I've *proved* it, the fact that if Stacy hadn't been here I don't know what would've become of us all, and that makes me feel like curling up in a ball and hiding under the ironing pile myself, but the gun was in there, so I actually haven't been able to go *near* the ironing pile, the fact that I don't feel like baking either, the fact that the whole kitchen feels polluted and, with the fridge leaking toxic substances, it probably *is*, the fact that the whole place feels unhygienic, the fact that we're so famous, the NRA came out with a little statement in response to our near-death experience, saying if we'd had a gun of our own we would have been fine, the fact that Leo wanted to issue a statement in return, saying how if you cleared all the guns out of every American home, *everybody* would be fine, but the police told him not to provoke the NRA, because then you get death threats, and we've all had enough of *those*, the fact that the police think we're going to be criticized plenty, as it is, for not having a gun in the house, the fact that the backlash about that would've been even worse if any of us had been killed, the fact that that's just swell, the fact that what is going on with people, the fact that you lose a family member in a shooting and all the other shooters in the country pile on and threaten *you* with death, the fact that everybody *hates* on you, just for mentioning your loved one got shot, and for not immediately shooting the shooter back, the fact that it's almost like we're in a war or something, the fact that everybody just seems to bear a big grudge about something or other that they're ready to kill and die for, the fact that what ever happened to gentleness, kindliness, the fact that does life *have* to be like this, so black and white, lemon meringue pie, landfill, radioactive waste, Aurora shooting, aurora borealis, Littleton, Orlando, Pulse nightclub, Fort Hood, Texas, Carthage, Virginia Tech, Incident Number, the fact that *Galileo* discovered the aurora borealis, or he named it anyway, the fact that we will never be the same, and that makes me sad, Dogwood Bonanza, Kazakh pear tree, the fact that when Leo got home that night and heard the full story he just covered his head with a towel and cried, the fact that he stayed like that for *hours*, just wiping his head with that towel, the fact that Stacy went over to him eventually and put her hand on his shoulder, and he held it there for a bit, then went back to wiping his head with the towel, the fact that I think she does love him after all, which is just as well, since if the rest of us had died, she'd have been left here with Leo, or else swept off by Frank, the fact that in some ways having your whole family disappear must be an adolescent's *dream come true*, I mean not violently taken away or anything, or suddenly wiped out in a car crash or something, but like if they could all just conveniently dissolve into the *background*, the fact that isn't that what teens are always *wishing* for, the good luck of a nice peaceful orphanhood, urchins, golden light, the Silent Treatment, DNR, sea star wasting disease, the fact that isn't that why she complains about every darned thing I do, or she used to anyway, before she became our protector, the fact that she was still coming out with veiled threats about running away again, the fact that this is what I wonder about sometimes, when I can't sleep, 3:33, whether she would have preferred me to vanish, mom, bomb, tomb, womb, but again and again I decide it *wouldn't* be good for her if we'd all passed on in such a terrible way, or even just me, the fact that I don't think people survive a thing like that intact, the loss of your mom or your entire family before your eyes, the fact that she might be free of us and all, free to do her own thing without interference, but she'd never be a whole person again, just like I was never a whole person after Mommy got sick, and that didn't even involve violence, unless you count the neurosurgeon's klutziness, "You're a screw-up!", the fact that it was sudden and all, a big shock, and a big permanent change, but nobody meant any harm, there was no "aggressor," and Mommy *survived* too, more or less, whereas if *we'd* all been killed and Stacy survived, she'd probably remain sort of a teen forever, numb, frozen in time and unable to process new stuff, the fact that she'd probably still sleep with all her old stuffed animals, and Jake's and Gillian's as well, and hang around all the dumb places we used to go together, like the mall or the market, or Young's Jersey Dairy and Cy Young Park, the fact that she wouldn't want to branch out, and she'd stick close to a teen's taste in foods and clothes and TV shows too, and nostalgically crave my poffertjes, and watch Morning Routine girls into her old age, and theirs, just because that was what she used to do when we were all still alive, the fact that likely she'd get all soppy about cartoons and computer games her siblings used to like, and even change her tune about the musicals she and I watched together in the months before my passing, corpse, the fact that she'd be immune to anything new that happened to her, the fact that even dappled sunlight coming through trees would leave her cold, all the good things in the world you want to give your children, ♫ *Wonderful, wonderful day* ♫, the fact that everything and everybody would seem far away to her, and strangers would frighten her, especially men who bore any resemblance to Ronny, the fact that she would try to blot out the trauma, GAD, but in the process she'd blot out most of the *world* and everything would start to seem unreal, the fact that she might be so injured she'd never be able to *love* again, never see the point of it, never want to fall in love, Hallmark Valentine hearts, I ♥ U, and maybe she'd sort of hate all *kids*, because they'd remind her of her dead siblings and her own lost childhood, and she'd never want any kids of her own, the fact that, heck, with all that stuff to blot out, she'd probably have an even worse memory than *me*, the fact that that *didn't* happen though, we didn't die, the fact that *she didn't let us*, the fact that we're officially classified as "unhurt," so her life *hasn't* been permanently blighted, or not too much, micro-bead ban, Willoughby, automats, the fact that I am still here, to be her flawed mom and intrude on her life, the fact that I've got her number now too, the fact that she can't fool me anymore with all her sarcasm, the fact that I now know that, even if she doesn't like a single thing I do or say, and even if we're all very annoying for her, she didn't want to lose us, she didn't want to see us get shot before her very eyes, macrophages, tardigrades, nanoparticles, the fact that, instead, she saved her whole family, and saved herself all those sad decades of guilt and regret and self-doubt and numbness and loneliness, the numbness of muted beings, the fact that Stacy proved herself to *herself*, as well as to the rest of the world, and she can just rest on her laurels from now on and *like* herself, much more than most teens ever do, the fact that she has no excuse not to now, the fact that she really should feel proud of herself, the fact that it's got to buck you up, "my fine buck-o," the fact that already she doesn't seem the same girl who wanted to go be a recluse in Arizona, the fact that she really does seem sort of cheerful, and even calm, the fact that we were *all* happy at first, boy, were we happy, the fact that we were kind of *euphoric* there for a while, like at the Kinkels' and for a day or so after, almost hysterical, not Leo but the rest of us, the fact that we were just so relieved, so pleased to be alive, the fact that it's a great feeling, kind of like that *quitting* feeling, reprieve, freedom, the fact that it feels almost like real happiness, as long as you forget that it stems from living in a country full of guns, cars, carbs, trans fats, Morning Routine videos, hugging, praying, blessings, candlelit vigils, heads in the sand, asleep at the switch, asleep at the wheel, driving under the influence, back seat drivers, sweetgrass baskets, Civil Standby, little girls in gold vinyl hot pants, babes in the woods, *Yet knowing how way leads on to way I doubted if I should ever come back*, plastering over the cracks, crawling out of the woodwork, sweeping it under the carpet, between you, me, the devil, and the deep blue sea, Daniel Webster, Rachel Carson, beat around the bush, "One woman's pretty much like the next," nip it in the bud, bird in the hand, cat's pajamas, sixes and sevens, Doolally Alley, banana splits, a finger on the pulse, an ax to grind, massacre of the innocents, last of the Mohicans, Pocahontas, bosoms, boarlets, pig in a poke, goiters, rhinoplasty, side effects, my sickbed, Pepito, Bathsheba, point of no return, "Waltzing Matilda," *Highlights for Children*, crumb and gravel pie, mud pies, porno pics, the casting couch, paw-paw seeds, online jigsaws, an armful of trouble, goons, ♫ *Bless your beautiful hide* ♫, empty margarine tubs full of cobwebs, cobweb elbow tattoos, jiminy crimeny, East Elementary School, East Street Cemetery, Mason-Dixon line, Ulysses S. Grant, *So they kicked him in the pants, and the pants he wore cost a dollar ninety-four, plus tax*, buckeye, buckshot, earshot, spitball, numbskull, dope fiend, (((DANGEROUS CLIFF))) NO RAPPELLING, headlong, headlamps, Spinbrush, Whirlpool, sidewinder, sidecar, Crooked Creek, deadbeat dad, Cuyahoga Falls, alluvial rivers, rivulets, deltas, the first rain enters the crevices, cat swimming for its life, River Roost, Rocky Ridge Farm, colloidal silver, plenty more down cellar in a teacup, fertilizer grade ammonium nitrate, salt pork, Salt Fork Park, De Smet, ALS, home run, rabies, the Ink Spots, Smeg, Kenmore, Whirlpool, Exxon, Zyker's, 1897642/crim, Target, Chef Boyardee Beefaroni, SpaghettiOs, Spaghetti & Meatballs, grave goods, effigy pipes, gorgets, platform pipes, copper, galena, Hopewell, Fort Ancient, Adena, Woodland, Moundsville Bottoms, Funk Bottoms, bell-bottoms, 15,000 freshwater pearls, sea of diamonds, Licking County Fairgrounds, Buckeye Trail, Hosak's Cave, scarlet tanager, merganser, loon, chorus frogs, spring peeper, "the hadrosaur, a species of kanga-roo, twenty feet long," appendicitis, Chief Newcomer, Netawatwes, of the Turtle clan, deformed turtles, Afterschool Book Club, 4:30–5:30, Edison Tower, Philly, Cincy, serial killers, alluvium, bedrock, glacial till, grass understory, blackberries, oaks, hickory and walnuts, Peolia, Elyria, delirium, Kenyon, Purdue, Notre Dame, Northwestern, NYU, subcircular, red moon, Grandmother Moon, Fruit of the Loom, Land O'Lakes, Land of the Free, KFC, tipi, PT, PTA, eyelash curler, styptic stick, Magnitsky Act, Miranda Rules, TXT ME, Paterson Falls, Sears, Swiffer, *Oliver!*, Esther, smallpox, Sophia Loren, Raquel Welch, Emma Woodhouse, Anne Elliott, Anne Shirley, parsing a sentence, trick-or-treat, peaches in cream, Builderbeck, Pick-Up Sticks, Shredded Wheat, Consolidated Life, 3:33, Sonny and Cher, Chicago World's Fair, cheese wheel, potato cheese puffs, puffback, puffers, muumuu, phulu-pututu, bib 'n' tucker, negligent homicide, plastic VW bus, Spelling Bee, banjo clock, Graham crackers, crayons, drawing contest, Beethoven, Philly Dip, grist to the mill, sejant, salient, dormant, rampant, rampage, Hellmann's Mayonnaise, Fleischmann's yeast, Fleishhacker Zoo, Brooklyn Bridge, Silent Sentinels, the Silent Treatment, matchwood paneling, hot dog vendors, factory farms, funeral plots, Tevye, bridge over troubled waters, bridging the gap, bridge failures, night and day, black and white, male and female, young and old, hot and cold, in and out, up and down, the fact that I dreamt people were marching in the *air*, above our heads, a big crowd of protesters, and it turned out all you had to do was swallow a lot of *helium* and you could stay up there quite a while, the fact that to get down you just had to eat a cookie, the fact that I never found out what cause they were marching about, the fact that people have been so *sweet*, the neighbors and all, the fact that they've brought us stuffed animals and peanut brittle, the fact that the house is overflowing with popcorn, zoom, vroom, vacuum, room, playmate, playpen, plaid, plait, grate, grrrreat, crate, safety gate, woke folk, Wake Up Picture Day, you got it made in the shade, babes in arms, the fact that the other day I caught Jake torturing some nurdles, *I will do such things, – what they are, yet I know not; but they shall be the terror of the earth*, the fact that when the empty-fuel-tank light comes on, eleven percent of Americans keep on driving, the fact that the Gnadenhutten massacre was "deliberately perpetrated," the fact that you have the right to remain silent, let sleeping dogs lie, bear arms, shake a leg, shake it up, conceal weapons, wax and wane, kick up a fuss, kick the bucket, put your eggs in one basket, flip, flop, sleep, wake, the fact that parenthood is just tragic, but I can still dream, the fact that I dreamt I learnt to whistle, Dreamers, the fact that as a result of all this, Leo and I have become pushover parents, in fly-over country, the fact that the kids can have candy whenever they want now, and Leo even bought tickets for the solar eclipse at the Elephant Sanctuary, the fact that we're all going to the eclipse, radioactive bananas, bandanas, the fact that Leo's agreed to join all the other "suckers" on the highway, my way or the highway, ♫ *We are poor little lambs* ♫, lost barrettes, solar alignment, obsidian, mica cut-outs, sassafras, sweet gum, common swamp gum, gum balls, holly, bog rosemary, buckbean, red spruce, pitch pine, Karo corn syrup, Argo cornstarch, French fries, Nibelungs, Piketon, ♫ *Vivo!* ♫, maple syrup, the fact that is it Rodolfo or Alfredo, the main guy in *La bohème*, the fact that I never know, the fact that Stacy didn't even make any objection to the solar eclipse idea, the fact that she's being swell about everything, the fact that I hope all her rebelliousness hasn't been completely quelled by trauma, or by her new role as our savior, big responsibility, *There's Always Tomorrow*, sweet and salty, black-and-white movies, galoshes, the fact that we're going to let Gillian do the Indian Mud Run too, and in the meantime, just to cheer everybody up, we're going to go see the runaway lioness at the zoo this weekend, the fact that Stacy seems to feel some kind of rapport with that woebegone creature, the fact that whether this is because she feels fierce and free, or caged and cowed, doesn't bear thinking about.

THE END

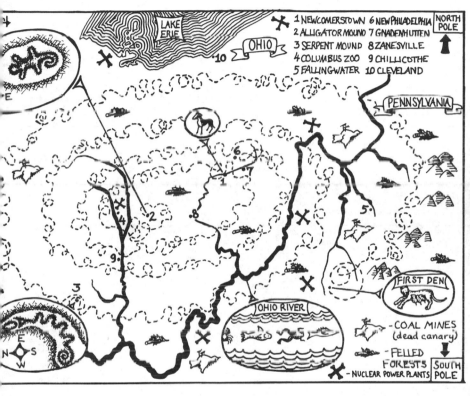

Map of the lioness's circular journey from Appalachia to Alligator Mound

GLOSSARY

A round-up of abbreviations,
sanitized for your comfort

2A Second Amendment

AA African American

AAA American Automobile Association, or Triple A (vehicle breakdown service)

AAA Anti-Aircraft Artillery (machine guns)

AALC African American Labor Center

AAR Armed American Radio (USCC media arm)

AARP American Association of Retired Persons

AASHTO American Association of State Highway and Transportation Officials

AAUW American Association of University Women

ABA American Birding Association

ABC Accelerated Bridge Construction

ABC American Bridge Company

ABP Accelerated Bridge Planning

ABR Accelerated Bridge Rehabilitation

AC Air Conditioning

ACA Affordable Care Act

ACA Alley Cat Allies

ACI American Concrete Institute

ACLU American Civil Liberties Union

ACP American College of Physicians

.380 ACP Automatic Colt Pistol

ACS The Anti-Cruelty Society

ACT American College Testing

ADAPT American Disabled for Attendant Programs Today

ADHD Attention Deficit Hyperactivity Disorder

ADL Anti-Defamation League

ADOS American Descendants of Slavery

ADT Average Daily Traffic

ADTT Average Daily Truck Traffic

ADU Accessory Dwelling Unit

AEA American Energy Alliance

AEC Atomic Energy Commission

AEDs Automated External Defibrillators

AEDPA Antiterrorism and Effective Death Penalty Act
AEP American Electric Power
AES Applied Energy Services
AF1 Air Force One (the president's plane)
AFA American Family Association
AFA Attorneys for Animals
AFFIRM American Foundation for Firearm Injury Reduction in Medicine
AFID Anti-Felon Identification
AFL-CIO American Federation of Labor and Congress of Industrial Organizations
AFT American Federation of Teachers
AG Attorney General
AHCA American Health Care Act
AHPA American Herbal Products Association
AI Amnesty International
AIC American Immigration Council
AIDA Awareness, Interest, Desire, Action (advertising tool)
AIDC Automatic Identification and Data Capture
AILA American Immigration Lawyers Association
AIM American Indian Movement
AIPAC American Israel Public Affairs Committee
AISC American Institute of Steel Construction
AJ Al Jazeera

AK-47 Kalashnikov Automatic (rifle)
ALA American Lung Association
ALDF Animal Legal Defense Fund
ALI Annual Limit on Intake (radiation dose)
ALMA Atacama Large Millimeter / Submillimeter Array (astronomical interferometer)
ALS Amyotrophic Lateral Sclerosis
ALSC American Library Service for Children
ALWH A Long Walk Home
AM-15 Anderson Manufacturing (optic-ready semiautomatic tactical rifle)
AMI American Media, Inc.
AMA Against Medical Advice
AMPA Additive Manufacturing in Products and Applications
ANA American Nurses Association
AOWs Any Other Weapons
AP Advanced Placement (college-level high school courses)
AP Associated Press
APA American Psychological Association
APEC Asia Pacific Economic Cooperation group
APHA American Public Health Association
APHIS Animal and Plant Health Inspection Service
APPS Applications for Purpose, Pride and Success

APT Advanced Persistent Threat

ARC Appalachian Regional Commission

AREMA American Railway Engineering and Maintenance-of-way Association

ARFID Avoidance and Restricted Food Intake Disorder

ARS Americans for Responsible Solutions

AR5 The Fifth Assessment Report (IPCC)

AR-15 ArmaLite Rifle (magazine-fed, gas-powered semi-automatic)

ARU American Railway Union

ASAP Alternative Support Apparatus

ASAP As Soon As Possible

ASCE American Society of Civil Engineers

ASD Active Shooter Drill

ASD Autism Spectrum Disorder

ASF Adrienne Shelly Foundation

ASP Active Shooter Plan

ASPCA American Society for the Prevention of Cruelty to Animals

ASPE American Society of Plumbing Engineers

ASS Active Shooter Situation

ATEP Alien Transfer Exit Program

ATF Bureau of Alcohol, Tobacco, Firearms and Explosives

ATM Automated Teller Machine

ATSDR Agency for Toxic Substances and Disease Registry

AT&T American Telephone and Telegraph

ATV All Terrain Vehicle

AUMF Authorization for Use of Military Force

AVAR Association of Veterinarians for Animal Rights

AVfM A Voice for Men

AVS Address Verification System (for credit cards)

AWB Federal Assault Weapons Ban (defunct)

AWI Animal Welfare Institute

AWSA American Woman Suffrage Association

AYP Adequate Yearly Progress

BA Bad [sit-me-down-upon]

BA Buy American

B of A Bank of America

BASF SE Badische Anilin und Soda Fabrik (Baden Aniline and Soda Factory)

BBQ Barbecue

BBR Broken beyond Repair

BCRA Better Care Reconciliation Act

BDS Boycott, Divestment, Sanctions (Pro-Palestinian movement)

BED Base Equivalent Dose

BENM Bears Ears National Monument

BFA Buckeye Firearms Association (Ohio organization)

BFF Best Friend Forever

BHP Broken Hill Proprietary Company Limited

BIA Bureau of Indian Affairs

BIRM Bridge Instructor's Reference Manual

BLM Black Lives Matter

BLM Bureau of Land Management

BLOTUS Biggest Liar of the United States

BLT Bacon, Lettuce and Tomato (sandwich)

BMAA *Beta*-Methylamino-L-alanine

.50 BMG Browning Machine Gun

BMI Body Mass Index

BMSB Brown Marmorated Stink Bug

B&O Baltimore and Ohio (railroad)

BOB Bug-out Bag

BOP Blast Overpressure

B-O-T Build Operate Transfer (bridge construction method)

BP Border Control

BPA Bisphenol A

BPOE Benevolent and Protective Order of Elks

BPW Business and Professional Women

Bq Becquerel (unit of radioactivity)

BRM Blue Ridge Mountains

BSA Boy Scout Association

BSEE Bureau of Safety and Environmental Enforcement

Bt Cry1Ab Bacillus thuringiensis crystal 1AB

BTW By the Way

BWDL Black Women's Defense League

BYH Book Your Hunt

BYOB Bring Your Own Bottle

BzBP Benzylbutylphthalate

CAA Civil Aviation Authority

CAA Clean Air Act

CAAT Campaign Against Arms Trade

CAC Constitutional Accountability Center

CADD Computer Aided Design and Detailing

CAF Crimes Against Fathers

CAFF Campaign Against Factory Farming

CAFF Concentrated Animal Feeding Facility

CAFO Concentrated Animal Feeding Operations

CAFTA Central American Free Trade Agreement

CAP Center for American Progress

CAP Child Access Prevention (law)

CAP Criminal Alien Program

CAPTCHA Completely Automated Public Turing test to tell Computers and Humans Apart

CAR Colt Automatic Rifle

CAT Cat Action Treasury

CATF Clean Air Task Force

CAWC Connections for Abused Women and their Children

CBC Conventional Bridge Construction

CBD Convention on Biological Diversity

CBP Customs and Border Protection

CBPP Center on Budget and Policy Priorities

CC Craftivist Collective

CC&G Canadian Club whiskey and ginger ale

CCA Corrections Corporation of America

CofC Children of the Confederacy

CofCC Council of Conservative Citizens

CCD Colony Collapse Disorder (western honey bee crisis)

CCR Center for Constitutional Rights

CCR Concealed Carry Reciprocity

CCRKBA Citizens Committee for the Right to Keep and Bear Arms

CCSS Common Core State Standards (school)

CCW Concealed Carry Weapon

CDC Centers for Disease Control and Prevention

CDP Carbon Disclosure Project

CDR Carbon Dioxide Removal

CDT Central Daylight Time

CE Categorical Exclusion

CELDF Community Environmental Legal Defense Fund

CEO Chief Executive Officer

CERCLA Comprehensive Environmental Response, Compensation, and Liability Act

CERCLIS Comprehensive Environmental Response, Compensation, and Liability Information System

CERHAS Center for the Electronic Reconstruction of Archaeological and Historical Sites

CETA Comprehensive Economic Trade Agreement

CF Cougar Fund

CFCs Chlorofluorocarbons

CFPB Consumer Financial Protection Bureau

CFR Code of Federal Regulations

CFS Center for Food Safety

CGI Clinton Global Initiative

CGI Computer-Generated Imagery

CGL Coastal GasLink

CHIP Children's Health Insurance Program

CHL Concealed Handgun License

CHP Concealed Handgun Permit

CIA Central Intelligence Agency

CIAK9 CIA sniffer dog (for explosives)

CIEL Center for International Environment Law

CIP Cast-In-Place (bridge construction technique)

CIR Committee to Investigate Russia

CIR Cosmetics Ingredient Review

CIWF Compassion in World Farming

CLARC Cleanup Levels and Risk Calculation (Washington State)

CMNH Cleveland Museum of Natural History

CNS Consolidated Nuclear Security

CO2 Carbon Dioxide

COA Course of Action (military)

COBRA Consolidated Omnibus Budget Reconciliation Act

COD Cash on Delivery

COEHHA California Office of Environmental Health Hazard Assessment

CONELRAD Control of Electro-Magnetic Radiation (Cold War broadcasting system)

COO Chief Operating Officer

COP22 United Nations Climate Change Conference

CoR Club of Rome

CORE Congress of Racial Equality

CPAC Conservative Political Action Conference

CPC Climate Prediction Center

CPC Climate Protection Campaign

CPD Campaign for Peace and Democracy

CPM Critical Path Method

CPPCG Convention on the Prevention and Punishment of the Crime of Genocide

CPSC Consumer Product Safety Commission

CPSIA Consumer Product Safety Improvement Act

CQC Close Quarters Combat

CrVI Hexavalent chromium (chromium-6)

CRA Challenge-Response Authentication

CREW Citizens for Responsibility and Ethics in Washington

CRF Cougar Rewilding Foundation

CRLP Center for Reproductive Law and Policy

CRM Civil Rights Movement

Cry9C StarLink™ bacterial protein (GMO)

CS2 Carbon disulfide

CS-137 Cesium-137

CSA Confederate States of America (imaginary country)

CSAPR Cross-State Air Pollution Rule

CSB Chemical Safety Board

CSCU Connecticut State Colleges and Universities

CSE Child Sexual Exploitation

CSE Commercial Steel Erection

CSGV Coalition to Stop Gun Violence

CSIS Center for Strategic & International Studies

C-SPAN Cable-Satellite Public Affairs Network

CSS Central Security Service

CSXT Chessie-Seaboard Merger Transportation (train company)

CT Connecticut

CTE Chronic Traumatic Encephalopathy

CTP Cutiepie

CVR Cockpit Voice Recorder

CWA Clean Water Act

CYA Cover Your [sit-me-down-upon] (business strategy)

C8 Perfluorooctanoic acid (PFOA)

DA District Attorney

DAC Derived Air Concentrations (longterm radiation dose)

DACA Deferred Action for Childhood Arrivals

DAD Drinking and Driving

DAK Double Action Kellerman (gun)

DAM Drive-around Mom

DAO Double Action Only (trigger)

DAPA Deferred Action for Parents of Americans

DAPL Dakota Access Pipeline

DAR Daughters of the American Revolution

DARVO Deny, Argue, Reverse Victim and Offender (perpetrator tactic, post-crime)

DBD Deadbeat Dad

D-B-F-O-M Design Build Finance Operate Maintain (bridges)

DBIA Design Build Institute of America

D-B-O Design Build Operate (bridges)

DBTT Ductile-Brittle Transition Temperature (an influence on hull cracking in Liberty ships)

DCCC Democratic Congressional Campaign Committee

DCHP Dicyclohexylphthalate

DCMU 3-(3,4-dichlorphenyl)-1,1-dimethylurea

DD Daniel Defense (gun supplies)

DD Destructive Device

DD Dishonorable Discharge

DDD Dichlorodiphenyldichlorothane

DDE Dichlorodiphenyldichlorothylene

DDoS Distributed Denial of Service (cyber attack)

DDT Dichlorodiphenyltrichlorothane

DE Domestic Engineer (housewife)

DEA Drug Enforcement Administration

DEC Department of Environmental Conservation

DED Deferred Enforced Departure (immigration status)

DEET N,N-Diethyl-*meta*-toluamide / diethyltoluamide

DEFCON Defense Readiness Condition (for nuclear war)

DEHP Di-2-ethylhexylphthalate

DEM Democratic Party

DEP Department of Environmental Protection

DEP Diethylphthalate (used in cosmetics)

DEQ Department of Environmental Quality

DGA Diglycoamine salt

DH Designated Hitter (baseball)

DHS Department of Homeland Security

DHSS Department of Health and Human Services
DIA Disabled Integration Act
DiDP Di-isodecylphthalate
DiNP Di-isononylphthalate
DIY Do It Yourself
DJT Donald John Trump
DMA Dimethylamine salt
DMP Dimethylphthalate (used in hairspray)
DMV Division of Motor Vehicles
DMZ Demilitarized Zone
DNA Deoxyribonucleic Acid
DNC Democratic National Committee
DNDO Domestic Nuclear Detection Office
DnOP Di-n-octylphthalate
DNR Department of Natural Resources
DNR Do Not Resuscitate
DOA Dead on Arrival
DoD Department of Defense
DOE Department of Energy
DoITPoMS Dissemination of IT for the Promotion of Materials Science
DOJ Department of Justice
DOP Di-*n*-octylphthalate
DoS Denial of Service
DOS Descendant of Slaves
DPB Dibutylphthalate (used in nail polish)
DPL Dayton Power and Light Company
DPRK Democratic Republic of Korea
DQ Dairy Queen
DR Direct Relief

DRF Disaster Response Force
DRO Detention and Removal Operations
DSA Democratic Socialists of America
DSM Diagnostic and Statistical Manual
DST Daylight Saving Time
DTR Duty to Retreat (vs. SYG)
DUI Driving Under the Influence
DV Domestic Violence
DVBD Division of Vector-Borne Diseases
DVT Deep Vein Thrombosis
DWEL Drinking Water Equivalent Level
DWN Beat, vanquish, own
DWP Dangerous Weapons Permit
DWT Deadweight tonnage
2,4-D 2,4-Dichlorophenoxyacetic acid
EAA Environmental Action Association
EACH Equal Access to Abortion Coverage in Health Insurance
EAS Emergency Alert System (EBS's replacement)
EBS Emergency Broadcasting System (CONELRAD's replacement)
ECF Eastern Cougar Foundation
ECFH Earn Cash from Home
EDC Every-Day Carry
EDC Every Day Counts
ECW Electronic Control Weapon (Taser)
EDM Electronic Dance Music

EDT Eastern Daylight Time

EDTA Ethylenediaminetetra-acetic acid

EGSAF Everytown for Gun Safety (gun control organization)

EHL Endangered Habitats League

EIA Environmental Investigation Agency

EIA Energy Information Administration

EIS Environmental Impact Statement

EJI Equal Justice Initiative

EMD Electro Muscular Disruption (Taser)

EMD Engineering and Manufacturing Development

EMP Electromagnetic Pulse

EMS Emergency Medical Services

EMS Environmental Management Services

ENDA Employment Non-Discrimination Act

EOB Explanation of Benefits

EOC Evidence of Coverage

EPA Environmental Protection Agency

EPCRA Emergency Planning and Community Right-to-Know Act

EPIC Electronic Privacy Information Center

EPPP Environmental Persistent Pharmaceutical Pollutant

EPSDT Early and Periodic Screening, Diagnostic and Treatment

ER Emergency Room

ERA Equal Rights Advocates

ERPO Extreme Risk Protection Order (red flag law: temporary gun confiscation)

ESA Endangered Species Act

ESEA Elementary and Secondary Education Act

ETHS Evanston Township High School

EWA Edison Wetlands Association

EWG Environmental Working Group

4-F Fuel, Food, Forage and Feed (plants)

F4J Fathers for Justice

FAQ Frequently Asked Question

FBA Feared Bloody Aftermath (news headline in *Some Like It Hot*)

FBI Federal Bureau of Investigation

FCJF Frank's Cherry Juice Failure

FCM Failure Critical Member (bridge defect)

FDA Food and Drug Administration

FDB Feather Destructive Behaviors (bird self-harm)

FDR Franklin Delano Roosevelt

FEA Federal Energy Administration

FEL Front End Loader (tractor)

FEMA Federal Emergency Management Agency

FEP Family Education Plan

FERC Federal Energy Regulatory Commission

FFF Four-Legged Friends

FFF Freedom from Fear

FF15 Fight for $15 (minimum wage)

FFA Future Farmers of America

FFD Forward Flank Downdraft (weather feature)

FFL Federal Firearms License(e)

FFS For [Pete's] Sake

FFTS Feto-fetal transfusion syndrome

FG Field Goal (football)

FGM Female Genital Mutilation

FHWA Federal Highway Administration

FIFRA Federal Insecticide, Fungicide, and Rodenticide Act

FID Firearm Identification

FISA Foreign Intelligence Surveillance Act

FLOTUS Furtive Limpet on the Unmanageable Slime-eel

FMCSA Federal Motor Carrier Safety Administration

FMLA Family Medical Leave Act

FNR For No Reason

FoE Friends of the Earth

FOIA Freedom of Information Act

FOID Firearm Owner's Identification (card)

FOOSH Fall on Outstretched Hand (physical injury)

FOP Fraternal Order of Police

FOPA Firearm Owners Protection Act

FOS Fiber Optic Sensors

FPLA Fair Packaging and Labeling Act

FRA Federal Railroad Administration

FRAC Food Research Action Center

FRC Family Research Council

FRP Fiber Reinforced Plastic / Polymer (concrete)

FSIS Food Safety and Inspection Service

FSL Fugitive Slave Law (1850)

FTM Fulltime Mom

FUO Freedom United Organization (anti-slavery)

FVEY The Five Eyes (anglophone intelligence-gathering coalition)

FWPCA Federal Water Pollution Control Act

FWW Food and Water Watch

FYI For Your Information

G20 Group of Twenty

G26 Glock 26 (gun)

GAG Gays against Guns

GAO Government Accountability Office

GAR Grand Army of the Republic

GATJ Global Alliance for Tax Justice

GAW Global Atmosphere Watch

GBR Great Barrier Reef

GD Greatest Duration (eclipse)

GE Genetically Engineered

GEOINT Geospatial Intelligence

GFC Global Forest Coalition

GHG Greenhouse Gas

GM General Motors

GMO Genetically Modified Organism

GOA Gun Owners of America

GOP Grand Old Party (Republicans)

GOTMFV Get Out The Mother [Freaking] Vote

GOTV Get Out The Vote

GPA Grade Point Average (school)

GPG Global Public Good(s)

GPS Global Positioning System

G4S Secure Solutions

GSMNP Great Smoky Mountains National Park

GSW Gunshot Wound

GTMO Guantanamo Bay Detention Camp

GUN Grim Underground Network

GV Gendered Violence

GVA Gun Violence Archive

GVP Gun Violence Prevention

GW Global Warming

GWS Global Women's Strike

4-H Head, Heart, Hands and Health (club)

HAA5 Haloacetic acids

HAZMAT Hazardous Materials

HB Hardness Blackness (graphite grading scale)

HBCD Hexabromocyclo-dodecane

HBCU Historically Black Colleges and Universities

HCB Hexachlorobenzene

HCM Highway Capacity Manual

HCN Hydrogen cyanide (prussic acid)

HE Home Economist (housewife)

HELLP Hemolysis, Elevated Liver enzymes, and Low Platelet count (pregnancy syndrome)

HEMP High-altitude Electromagnetic Pulse

HEUMF Highly Enriched Uranium Materials Facility

HEW Hanford Engineer Works

HGTV Home and Garden Television

IIII House Husband

HHIN Hanford Health Information Network

HIAS Hebrew Immigrant Aid Society

HIPAA Health Insurance Portability and Accountability (privacy rule)

HLF Home Life Facilitator

HM Homemaker

HW Housewife

HMO Health Maintenance Organization

H2O Water

HOB Height of Burst (missile explosion)

HOCU Hopewell Culture National Historic Park

HPS High Performance Steel

HPV Human Papilloma Virus

HR Herbicide Resistant (plants)

HR Human Resources

HR676 Expanded and Improved Medicare For All Act

HRA Human Resources Administration
HRC Human Rights Campaign
HRS Hazard Ranking System
HRT Hormone Replacement Therapy (pills ubiquitously prescribed at menopause)
HSA Health Savings Account
HSCOBS Highway Subcommittee on Bridges and Structures
HSDB Hazardous Substances Data Bank
HSI Humane Society International
HSUS Humane Society of the United States
HUAC House Un-American Activities Committee
HVAC Heating, Ventilation and Air Conditioning
H5N1 Hemagglutinin Type 5 and Neuraminidase Type 1 (Avian Influenza A)
I&A Office of Intelligence and Analysis
IACIYAD It's a Crime if You're a Democrat
IACLEA International Association of Campus Law Enforcement Administrators
IAEA International Atomic Energy Agency
IAQ Indoor Air Quality
IARC International Agency for Research on Cancer
IBAs Important Bird and Biodiversity Areas

IBM International Business Machines (corporation)
ICAN International Campaign to Abolish Nuclear Weapons
ICBM Inter-Continental Ballistic Missile
ICE Immigration and Customs Enforcement
ICG International Crisis Group
ICU Intensive Care Unit
ICYMI In Case You Missed It
IDK I Don't Know (but they know)
IED Improvized Explosive Device
IER Institute for Energy Research
IFAW International Fund for Animal Welfare
IFF Identification, Friend or Foe
IGA Independent Grocers Alliance
IGSD Institute for Governance and Sustainable Development
IHOP International House of Pancakes
IIRIRA Illegal Immigration Reform and Immigrant Responsibility Act
IIWYC If It Was Your Child
IKR I Know, Right
IL Illinois
IMDb Internet Movie Database
IME In My Experience
IMF International Monetary Fund
IMAO In My Arrogant Opinion
IMO In My Opinion
IMR Indian Mud Run (obstacle course)

IN Indiana
INA Immigration and Nationality Act
IOKIYAR It's O.K. if You're a Republican
IP Ingress Protection (standards code)
IPA Important Plant Area
IPA Isopropylame salts
IPCC Intergovernmental Panel on Climate Change
IPEN International POPs (Persistent Organic Pollutants) Elimination Network
IPP Independent Power Producer
IPPC Intergovernmental Panel on Climate Change (U.N.)
IPPNW International Physicians for the Prevention of Nuclear War
IPV Interpersonal Violence
IRA Indian Removal Act (1830)
IRAP International Refugee Assistance Program
IRBM Intermediate Range Ballistic Missile
IRIS Integrated Risk Information System
IRS Internal Revenue Service
ISIS Islamic State of Iraq and Syria
ISS Internal Exclusion or Isolation (school discipline)
ISS In-school Suspension
ISS International Space Station
ITMFA Impeach The [Monstrous Failure] Already

IUCN International Union for Conservation of Nature
IVRCP Interstate Voter Registration Crosscheck Program (voter suppression)
IWW Industrial Workers of the World
JBF Justice Bell Foundation
JFK John Fitzgerald Kennedy
J&J Johnson & Johnson
JNFUSA Jewish National Fund USA
JROTC Junior Reserve Officer Training Corps
KBA Key Biodiversity Area
KE Kinetic Energy
KFC Kentucky Fried Chicken
KIND Kids in Need of Defense
KISS Keep It Simple, Stupid
KKK Ku Klux Klan
KP Kitchen Patrol (military)
KY Kentucky
K9 Dog
LAH Life after Hate
LBJ Lyndon Baines Johnson
LCCA Life Cycle Cost Analysis (aging bridges)
LCM Large Capacity Magazine (ammunition)
LCP Lightweight Compact Pistol (Ruger)
LCV League of Conservation Voters
LCV Light Commercial Vehicle
LEA Law Enforcement Agency
LEO Law Enforcement Officer
LES Lake Effect Snow (weather phenomenon)
LES Lower East Side (NYC)

LFF Lucky Freezer Find

LLL La Leche League (breast-feeding advocates)

LNT Leave No Trace (national park etiquette)

LOAEL Lowest Observable Adverse Effect Level

LOEL Lowest Observed Effect Level

LRFR Load and Resistance Factor Rating

LRM Long Range Missile

LTCF License to Carry Firearms

LTSS Long Term Services and Supports (for the disabled)

LWS Lower West Side (NYC)

LWV League of Women Voters

M4 Semi-automatic rifle

M4A Medicare for All

M-16 Model 16 rifle

MAD Mutually Assured Destruction (nuclear war idiocy)

MAGA Make America Gyrate Again

MAIG Mayors against Illegal Guns

MATS Mercury and Air Toxics Standards

M4BL The Movement for Black Lives

MCA Manufacturing Chemists Association

MCLG Maximum Contamination Level Goals

MCPs Managed Care Plans (healthcare)

MCS Mesoscale Convective System (thunderstorms)

MD Medical Doctor

MDA Missile Defense Agency

MDA Moms Demand Action (for Gun Sense in America)

ME Maine

MEE Mass Extinction Event

MFA Medicare For All

MFOL March for Our Lives (gun-control movement)

MFSOB Monstrous Freaking Son of a Baboon

MGTOW Men Going Their Own Way (manosphere club)

MHB Mueller Honey Bee (company)

MI Michigan

MIA Missing in Action

MLB Major League Baseball

MLF Mountain Lion Foundation

MLM Multi-Level Marketing (pyramid scheme)

M & M Mars and Murrie (candy)

MMA Mixed Martial Arts

MMIW Missing and Murdered Indigenous Women

MMM Men, Materials, Machinery (male bridge-building)

MMM / 3M Minnesota Mining and Manufacturing Company

MMMMM (or 5ME) Manpower, Materials, Machines, Methods, and Money (male efficiency formula)

MMWP Morbidity and Mortality Weekly Report (CDC)

MO Missouri

MOM Middle of the Month

MOM [Please wait a] moment (computerspeak)

MP5 Maschinenpistole 5 (submachine gun)

MPAA Motion Picture Association of America

MPP Movement for a People's Party

MPPDA Motion Picture Producers and Distributors of America

MPT Maintenance and Protection of Traffic

MRA Men's Rights Activist

MRI Magnetic Resonance Imaging (medical)

MRL Maximum Residue Level (pesiticides on food)

MRM Men's Rights Movement

MRSA Methicillin resistant Staphylococcus aureus

MS Mississippi

MS-13 Mara Salvatrucha (criminal gang)

MSE Mechanically Stabilized Earth (bridge-building)

MSF Doctors without Borders

MSM Mainstream Media

MSS Movable Scaffolding System (bridge-building)

MTBE Methyl *tert*-butyl ether

MTCA Model Toxics Control Act (Washington State)

MV Motor Vehicle

MVP Most Valuable Player

MW Megawatts

MYOB Mind Your Own Business

NA Not Applicable

NAACP National Association for the Advancement of Colored People

NABTU North America's Building Trades Unions

NACC (see NCAA)

NACW National Association of Colored Women

NAFTA North American Free Trade Agreement

NAN National Action Network

NAOWS National Association Opposed to Woman Suffrage

NAP New Archery Products

NARAL National Association for the Repeal of Abortion Laws

NARF Native American Rights Fund

NASA National Aeronautics and Space Administration

NASCAR National Association of Stock Car Auto Racing

NAWSA National American Woman Suffrage Association

NB No Borders

NBF New Best Friend

NBI National Bridge Inspection

NBI National Bridge Inventory

NBIS National Bridge Inspection Standards

NBL National Basketball League

NCA National Confectioners Association

NCAA National Collegiate Athletic Association

NCAI National Congress of American Indians

NCAR National Center for Atmospheric Research

NCBI National Center for Biotechnology Information

NCDC National Climatic Data Center

NCEI National Centers for Environmental Information

NCEZID National Center for Emerging and Zoonotic Infectious Diseases

NCHRP National Cooperative Highway Research Program

NCI National Cancer Institute

NCLB No Child Left Behind

NCM National Coalition for Men

NCO No Contact Order (victim protection)

NCOBRA National Coalition of Blacks for Reparations in America

NCPS National Cyber Security Protection System

NCSD National Cyber Security Division

NDAs Non-Disclosure Agreements (corporate abuse protection)

NDAA National Defense Authorization Act

NDT Nil Ductility Temperature

NDT Nondestructive testing (bridges)

NECC / NECCO New England Confectionary Company

NEMP Nuclear Electromagnetic Pulse

NEVS Newcomerstown Exempted Village Schools

NFA National Firearms Act

NFL National Football League

NGA National Geospatial-Intelligence Agency

NGO Non-Governmental Organization

NHANES National Health and Nutrition Examination Survey

NHC National Hurricane Center

NHFTHR No Hope for the Human Race

NHS National Health System (British)

NICS National Instant Criminal Background Check System

NIF New Israel Fund

NILC National Immigration Law Center

NJ New Jersey

NMAADC National Mexican-American Anti-Defamation Committee

NMAH National Museum of American History (Washington, DC)

NMI Neuromusclular Incapacitation (Taser)

NMNW No Means No Worldwide (rape-prevention organization)

NMSQT National Merit Scholarship Qualifying Test

NNSA National Nuclear Security Administration

NNU National Nurses United

NO Nitric oxide

NOAA National Oceanic and Atmospheric Administration

NOAEL No Observable Adverse Effect Level (risk assessment)

NOEL No Observed Effect Level (ditto)

NOH8 No Hate (campaign)

NOM National Organization for Marriage (heterosexual)

NOW National Organization for Women

NPAYEIOB Never Put All Your Eggs in One Basket

NPD Narcissistic Personality Disorder

NPDES National Pollutant Discharge Elimination System

NPIC National Pesticide Information Center

NPIN Native Plant Identification Network

NPL National Priorities List

NPNG No Pain No Gain

NPR National Public Radio

NPS National Park Service

NPS New Psychoactive Substances

NPSC National Prevention Science Coalition

NPT Non-Proliferation Treaty (international nuclear weapons agreement)

NRA National Rifle Association

NRAO National Radio Astronomy Observatory

NRAPVFPAC NRA Political Victory Fund PAC

NRATV National Rifle Association Television (cable)

NRC Nuclear Regulatory Commission

NRDC Natural Resources Defense Council

NSA National Security Agency

NSAIDs Nonsteroidal Anti-Inflammatory Drugs

NSC National Security Council

NSFU Not Safe for You

NSIDC National Snow and Ice Data Center

NSM National Socialist Movement

NSPCC National Society for the Prevention of Cruelty to Children

NSSF National Shooting Sports Foundation

NSSL National Severe Storms Laboratory

NTAS National Terrorism Advisory System

NTSB National Transportation Safety Board

NUL National Urban League

NVRA National Voter Registration Act

NWCL National Women's Coalition for Life

NWHM National Women's History Museum

NWLC National Women's Law Center

NWRS National Wildlife Refuge System

NWS National Weather Service

NY New York

NYC New York City

O2 Oxygen

O3 Ozone

OACHE Ohio Appalachian Center for Higher Education

OAQDA Ohio Air Quality Development Authority

OAS Organization of American States
OBR One Billion Rising (feminist organization / event)
OC Oleoresin capsicum (main ingredient in pepper spray)
OCA Organic Consumers Association
OCAGV Ohio Coalition Against Gun Violence
OCC Ohio Consumers Council
OCD Obsessive Compulsive Disorder
OCDO Open Carry Dot Org (gun advocates's website)
OCRWC Obstacle Course Racing World Championships
ODE Ohio Department of Education
ODMHC Ohio Department of Managed Health Care
ODNR Ohio Department of Natural Resources
ODOT Ohio Department of Transportation
ODPS Ohio Department of Public Safety
OEC Ohio Elections Commission
OEHHA Office of Environmental Health Hazard Assessment
OEMA Ohio Emergency Management Agency
OGE Office of Government Ethics
OH Ohio
OHCR Ohio Central Railroad
OHCRN Ohio Community Rights Network

OHS Ohio Historical Society
OIG Office of the Inspector General
OIS Officer-involved Shooting
OJ Orange Juice
OLE Oil of Lemon Eucalyptus
OLS Overghead Landing System
OMA Ohio Manufacturers Association
OMG Oh My Gosh
OMVI Operating a Motor Vehicle Impaired
OoJ Obstruction of Justice
OPCW Organization for the Prohibition of Chemical Weapons
OPs Organophosphates
OS Operating System
OS Overall Satisfaction
OSA Obstructive Sleep Apnea
OSBA Ohio State Bar Association
OSCE Organization for Security and Cooperation in Europe
OSH Occupational Safety and Health
OSHA Occupational Safety and Health Administration
OSS Out-of-school Suspension
OSSN One Stitch Saves Nine
OSTPA Ohio State Tractor Pullers Association
OSU Ohio State University
OTC Over the Counter
OTD On This Day
OVEC Ohio Valley Electric Corporation
OWDA Ohio Water Development Authority

PA   Pennsylvania
PA   Personal Assistant
PAC   Political Action Committee
PANNA   Pesticide Action Network North America
PAT   Points after Touchdown (football)
PAWS   Progressive Animal Welfare Society
PBBs   Polybrominated biphenyls
PBDE   Polybrominated diphenyl ethers
PBES   Prefabricated Bridge Elements and Systems
PBS   Public Broadcasting Service
PBT   Persistent Bioaccumulative and Toxic
PC   Politically Correct
PC   Probable Cause
PCA   Paris Climate Accord
PCBs   Polychlorinated biphenyls
PCE   Tetrachloroethylene
PCGTW   Public Citizen Global Trade Watch
PCOS   Polycystic Ovary Syndrome
PCP   Primary Care Practitioner
PDA   Public Displays of Affection
PDC   Parkinsonism-Dementia Complex
PDF   Portable Document Format
PDQ   Pretty Darn Quick
PDT   Pacific Daylight Time
PeCB   Pentachlorobenzene
PELs   Permissible Exposure Limits (for employees)
PFA   Pennsylvania Family Institute

PFA   Protection from Abuse (order)
PFAS   Perfluoroalkyl Substances
PFAW   People for the American Way
PFE   Pacific Fruit Express
PFLAG   Parents and Friends of Lesbians and Gays
PFOA (or C8)   Perfluorooctanoic acid
PFOS   Perfluorooctanesulfonic acid
PFP   Plutonium Finishing Plant
P&G   Procter & Gamble
PGA   Please Go Away
PGD   Point of Greatest Duration (eclipse)
PG&E   Pacific Gas and Electric Company
PGE   Pennsylvania General Energy
PGP   Pelvic Girdle Pain
PH   Party Hard
PH   Piping Hot
PH   Public Health
PhD   Doctor of Philosophy
PHMSA   Pipeline and Hazardous Materials Safety Administration
PIO   Public Information Office
PIRG   Public Interest Research Group
PLCAA   Protection of Lawful Commerce in Arms Act
PMT   Pre-Menstrual Tension
PND   Postnatal Depression
PoC   People of Color
PODR   Pets on Death Row
POE   Preponderance of Evidence
POEA   Polyethoxylated tallow amine

POFCAP Palm Oil Free Certification Accreditation Programme
POPs Persistent Organic Polluters
PORP Party of Reason and Progress
POS Piece Of [Scat]
POT Path of Totality (solar eclipse)
POTUS Purveyor of Totally Unprecedented Sleaze
ppbs Parts per billion
PPCM Peripartum Cardiomyopathy
PPD Postpartum Depression
PPO Preferred Provider Organization
PPTK Parents Promise to Kids (anti-gun contract)
PR Public Relations
PSA Public Service Announcement
PSAT Preliminary Scholastic Assessment Test
PSI Pounds per Square Inch
PT Partido dos Trabalhadores (Workers Party, Brazil)
PTA Parent–Teacher Association
PTC Permit to Carry (gun)
PTFE Polytetrafluoroethylene
PTO Paid Time Off
PTO Please Turn Over (page)
PTSD Post-Traumatic Stress Disorder
PUA Pickup Artist
PUCO Public Utilities Commission of Ohio
PUREX Plutonium–Uranium Extraction (reprocessing method)

PwD Person with Disability
QLCS Quasi-linear Convective System
QTPoC Queer Trans People of Color
RA Residential Administrator (housewife)
RACDHR Research Associate in Child Development and Human Relations (mom)
RAICES Refugee and Immigration Center for Education and Legal Services
RAINN Rape, Abuse and Incest National Network
RAN Rainforest Action Network
RCMP Royal Canadian Mounted Police
RCUSA Refugee Council of the United States of America
RDD Radiological Dispersal Devices (dirty bombs)
REDARS Risks from Earthquake Damage to Roadway System
REM Rapid Eye Movement
REM Roentgen Equivalent Man
RFD Rear Flank Downdraft (weather feature)
RfD Reference Dose (pesticides)
RFI Request for Information
RFID Radio Frequency Identification (chip / tag)
RFL Red Flag Law (see ERPO)
RFRA Religious Freedom Restoration Act (Indiana)
RGGI Regional Greenhouse Gas Initiative

RICO Racketeer Influenced and Corrupt Organizations (act)

RINO Republican in Name Only

RIP Radically Invasive Projectile (exploding bullet)

RIP Rest in Peace

RKBA Right to Keep and Bear Arms (vs. RLLPH)

RLLPH Right to Life, Liberty, and the Pursuit of Happiness (vs. RKBA)

RNC Republican National Committee

RNRN Registered Nurse Response Network

ROI Return on Investment

RSF Reporters without Borders

RSI Repetitive Strain Injury

RSVP Répondez S'il Vous Plaît

RV Recreation Vehicle

RWNJ Right Wing Nut Job

RWP Radiation Work Permit

RWU Resistance Women Unite

SAF Second Amendment Foundation

SAG Screen Actors Guild

SAHM Stay-at-home Mom

SARS Severe Acute Respiratory Syndrome

SAS Stars and Stripes (the American flag)

SASA Sexual Assault Survivors Anonymous

SATs Scholastic Assessment Tests

SAVE Stop Abusive and Violent Environments

SB4 Senate Bill 4

SBA List Susan B. Anthony List

SBD Silent but Deadly (gun suppressor / silencer)

SBLE School-based Law Enforcement

SBLI Super Bowl 2017

SBP Suicide by Police

SBR Short-barreled Rifle

SBU Strategic Business Unit

SCAAP State Criminal Alien Assistance Program (funding incarcerations)

SCI Spinal Cord Injury

SCL Strategic Communication Laboratories

SCS Safety Comes Second

SCS Soil Conservation Service

SDS Students for a Democratic Society

SDWA Safe Drinking Water Act

SEABEEs Construction Battalion (C.B.)

SEALs Sea, Air and Land Teams

SEAoO Structural Engineers Association of Ohio

SEC Securities and Exchange Commission

SECURe Safe School-based Enforcement through Collaborations, Understanding, and Respect (rubric)

SEI Structural Engineering Institute

SEMS Superfund Enterprise Management System

SF Smoker Friendly

SG Surgeon General

SGBV Sexual and Gender-Based Violence

SHTF [Scat] Hit the Fan
SHIPA Safe Highways and Infrastructure Preservation Act
SHM Simple Harmonic Motion (physics, engineering)
SHO Shutout (baseball: single-pitcher game)
SI&A Structure Inventory and Appraisal (bridges)
SICF Sensitive Compartmented Information Facility
SIU Southern Illinois University
SJW Social Justice Warrior
SLC Salt Lake City
SM Soccer Mom
SMDC Space and Missile Defense Command
SMDH Shaking My Damn Head
SMEE Sixth Mass Extinction Event
SMG Submachine Gun
SNAP Supplemental Nutrition Assistance Program (food stamps)
SNCC Student Nonviolent Coordinating Committee
SNL Saturday Night Live
SNPO Say No to Palm Oil
SOB [bad person]
SOFJO Safety of Female Journalists Online
SOG Special Operations Group (CIA)
SOP Standard Operating Procedure
SOS Save Our Species
SOTU State of the Union (speech)

SPCA Society for the Prevention of Cruelty to Animals
SPLC Southern Poverty Law Center
SPMT Self Propelled Modular Transporter
SRC Studio Relations Committee (the Hays Office's film-censorship system)
SRM Solar Radiation Management
SRO School Resource Officer (armed security guard)
SRS Selective Reality Syndrome
SSC Species Survival Commission
SSFAC Social Services for the Arab Community (Toledo)
SSS Saving Stacy Strategy
SSSS Secondary Security Screening Selectee
SST Stacy Silent Treatment
ST Silent Treatment
ST Standard Time
STEM Science, Technology, Engineering, and Mathematics
STI Sexually Transmitted Infection
SUV Sports Utility Vehicle
SWAG Scientific Wild-ass Guess
SWAT Special Weapons and Tactics
SYG Stand Your Ground (misused right to kill in self-defense)
T2D Type 2 Diabetes
TASIN Tribal Alliance of Sovereign Indian Nations
TATP Triacetone triperoxide (explosive)

TB12 Tom Brady regimen

TBHQ *Tert*-Butylhydroquinone

TBI Traumatic Brain Injury

TBq Terabecquerel

TCAP Tri-cyclic acetone peroxide (explosive)

TCE Trichloroethylene

TCP Tricresyl phosphate

TCPL Tuscarawas County Public Library

TCRA The Civil Rights Agenda

TD Touchdown

TED Technology, Entertainment, Design (online lecture series)

TEOTWAWKI The End of the World as We Know It

TEPCO Tokyo Electric Power Company

TERF Trans-Exclusionary Radical Feminist

TFW That Feel When

TFW Training for Warriors (exercise regime)

THAAD-ER Terminal High Altitude Area Defense – Extended Range

TLB Tractor Loader Backhoe

TLC Tender Loving Care

TNP Transform Now Plowshares

TNR Trap Neuter Return (cat health program)

TOCP Tri-ortho-cresyl phosphate

TOMPs Toxic Organic Micro Pollutants

TOPS Twin Oligohydramnios-Polyhydramnios Sequence

TPL Toba Pulp Lestari (paper company, Indonesia)

TPP Trans-Pacific Partnership

TPS Temporary Protected Status (immigration)

TRB Transport Research Board

TRI Toxics Release Inventory

TRIP Toxics Release Inventory Program

TRSOYF The Real Source of Your Fatigue

TSA Transportation Security Administration

TSCA Toxic Substances Control Act

TSE Total Solar Eclipse

TS&L Type, Size and Location (bridges)

TTAG The Truth about Guns (pro-gun blog)

TTF Transportation Trust Fund

TTHMs Total trihalomethanes

TTTS Twin-To-Twin Transfusion Syndrome

TV Television

TWC Tasing without Cause

TWD Two-wheel Drive (vehicle)

TWS The Wildcat Sanctuary

UAE Unusual Animal Encounters

UBI Universal Basic Income (great idea)

UCMR Unregulated Contaminant Monitoring Rule

UCWVTD Unified Command for the West Virginia Train Derailment

UD Unlimited Data

UDC United Daughters of the Confederacy

UES Upper East Side (NYC)
UFO Unidentified Flying Object
UGRR Underground Railway (slave-rescue / emancipation network)
UGW Ultimate Goal Weight
UNDHR Universal Declaration of Human Rights
UNEP United Nations Environment Program
UNFCCC United Nations Framework Convention on Climate Change
UNFPA United Nations Fund for Population Activities
UNGA General Assembly of the United Nations
UNHCR United Nations High Commissioner for Refugees
UNSCOM United Nations Special Commission
UPC United Poultry Concerns
UPF Uranium Processing Facility
UPS United Parcel Service
US Unserviceable
USA United States of America
USACE United States Army Corps of Engineers
USCC United States Concealed Carry Association
USCG United States Coast Guard
USCIS United States Citizenship and Immigration Services
USDA United States Department of Agriculture

USFWS United States Fish and Wildlife Service
USGS United States Geological Survey
USIC United States Intelligence Community
USPS United States Postal Service
USRTK United States Right to Know
USWB United States Weather Bureau
UWS Upper West Side (NYC)
UWW United Way Worldwide
VA Vanguard America (U.S. Nazis)
VA Veterans Affairs
VA Virginia
VAWA Violence against Women Act
VCC Velsicol Chemical Corporation
VE Value Engineering
VHFs Viral Hemorrhagic Fevers
VIS Victim Impact Statement
VLA Very Large Array (observatory)
VLOC Very Large Ore Carrier
VMS Variable Message Signs (on highways)
VOCs Volatile Organic Compounds
VP Vice President
VPL Visible Panty Line
VR Virtual Reality
VSH Vertical Split Head (broken rail, train track)
VTT Vicarious Trauma Toolkit
VVS Values Voter Summit

VX Venomous Agent X (nerve agent)
WaPo The *Washington Post*
WBC Whole-Body Cryotherapy
WBE Woman-owned Business Enterprise
WCEL World Commission on Environmental Law
WCFA Wildlife Conservations Fund of America
WCPA World Commission on Protected Areas
WCS Wildlife Conservation Society
WCT Wind Chill Temperature
WD4C Working Dogs for Conservation
WDHT We Don't Have Time (environmental organization)
WEC World Environment Center
WEDO Women's Environment and Development Organization
WEF World Economic Forum
WH White House
WHCA White House Correspondents' Association
WHO World Health Organization
WHOAS Wild Horses of Alberta Society
WIC Women, Infants and Children (foodbank program)
WILPF Women's International League for Peace and Freedom
WITW Women in the World
WM Working Mom
WMDs Weapons of Mass Destruction

WMO World Meteorological Organization
WOC Women of Color
WODC World of Drones Congress
WoHeLo Work, Health, Love (slogan of the Campfire Girls)
WOMS World on My Shoulders
WOOT Want One of Those
WPM Words per Minute
WROL Without Rule of Law
WSP Women Strike for Peace
WTC World Trade Center
WTO World Trade Organization
WV West Virginia
WW Woodrow Wilson
WWF World Wildlife Fund
WWJD What Would Jesus [López Pérez] Do
WWP Whistleblower Protection Program
WWRJD What Would Republican Jesus [López Pérez] Do
WWTP Waste Water Treatment Plant
WWTF Waste Water Treatment Facilities
WWW What Women Want
WYD What You Doing?
Y-12 National Security Complex (weapons plant)
YA Young Adult (book classification)
YT YouTube
YTA Youth Taking Action
ZPG Zero Population Growth

APPENDIX

For he rolls upon prank to work it in.

...

For having consider'd God and himself he will consider his neighbour.

...

For he is of the tribe of Tiger.

...

For the divine spirit comes about his body to sustain it in complete cat.

...

For by stroking of him I have found out electricity.

For he can swim for life.
For he can creep.

CHRISTOPHER SMART

The buffalo had gone, though several were killed in Eastern Ohio as late as 1800. The elk, too, had departed... Panthers, though not numerous, were occasionally seen or heard, and sometimes fell a prized trophy of the hunter's skill. They disappeared not many years after the first settlement. Bears abounded in greater numbers and remained much longer, an occasional straggler being seen as late as 1845. Wolves were found in great abundance, and proved a great annoyance to the settlers. ... The early pioneers were greatly annoyed by the wolves, and they embraced every opportunity to get a shot at the beasts, first to save hogs, sheep, and calves; and second to get the scalp premium paid by the State, as a mark of hunter's merit. Whoever killed a wolf, by presenting the scalp, and making affidavit before the clerk of the court, within twenty days, stating age and sex, and that the affiant killed it in the county, got an order on the treasury. Between 1808 and 1843, four hundred affidavits were filed, after which the scalp law ceased. Premiums were also paid for a few years upon the scalps of panthers, and wild cats, or catamounts...

ANON.

This river [the Monongahela], like most others in the country, is accompanied with considerable hills on each side, which sometimes approach close to the banks, and again recede, leaving spacious and rich bottoms, in which are generally found large sugar-camps, each sugar tree producing, if well-managed during the season, four pounds of excellent sugar, equal to Musquevado, especially if it has had time to ripen before used; and each pound is worth 13 cents; thus, a sugar-camp containing 500 trees produces 2000 pounds of sugar, worth 260 dollars. ...it certainly would be provident in farmers to take special care of their sugar trees, and rather than destroy a grove of 50 trees, plant an orchard of 1000.

ZADOK CRAMER

On the 4th of July the hearts of the people seem to awaken from a three hundred and sixty-four days' sleep; they appear high-spirited, gay, animated, social, generous, or at least liberal in expense; and would they but refrain from spitting on that hallowed day, I should say, that on the 4th of July, at least, they appeared to be an amiable people. It is true that the women have but little to do with the pageantry, the splendour, or the gaiety of the day; but, setting this defect aside, it was indeed a glorious sight to behold a jubilee so heartfelt as this...

FANNY TROLLOPE

"Get ready! Get ready! The *worr*-uld is coming to an end!"

JAMES THURBER

"The happiest countries, like the happiest women, have no history... Do you know what makes history? Pain – and shame – and rebellion – and bloodshed – and heartache. ... ask yourself how many hearts ached – and broke – to make those crimson-and-purple pages in history that you find so enthralling. I told you the story of Leonidas and his Spartans the other day. They had mothers, sisters, and sweethearts. If they could have fought a bloodless battle at the polls wouldn't it have been better – if not so dramatic?"

LUCY MAUD MONTGOMERY

The expedition was deliberately planned, and the massacre deliberately perpetrated, not in the heat of passion or flush of battle, for not the slightest opposition was made by the trusting, guileless Indians, but their submission was attended with such surrounding extenuating circumstances calling for mercy and forbearance, that nothing but a deep-seated, blood-seeking disposition could have permitted the men to consent to the terrible tragedy.

ANON.

I refused to fire and swore that none but a coward would. For by this time hundreds of women and children were coming toward us and getting on their knees for mercy. ... When the Indians found there was no hope for them they went for the Creek and got under the banks and some of the bucks got their bows and a few rifles and defended themselves as well as they could. ... The massacre lasted six or eight hours, and a good many Indians escaped. I tell you Ned it was hard to see little children on their knees have their brains beat out by men professing to be civilized. One squaw was wounded and a fellow took a hatchet to finish her, she held her arms up to defend her, and he cut one arm off, and held the other with one hand and dashed the hatchet through her brain. One squaw with her two children, were on their knees, begging for their lives of a dozen soldiers, within ten feet of them all, firing – when one succeeded in hitting the squaw in the thigh, when she took a knife and cut the throats of both children and then killed herself. One Old Squaw hung herself in the lodge – there was not enough room for her to hang and she held up her knees and choked herself to death. Some tried to escape on the Prairie, but most of them were run down by horsemen. I saw two Indians hold one of anothers hands, chased until they were exhausted, when they kneeled down, and clasped each other around the neck and both were shot together. They were all scalped, and as high as half a dozen taken from one head. They were all horribly mutilated. One woman was cut open and a child taken out of her, and scalped. ... Squaw's snatches were cut out for trophies.

SILAS SOULE

The only people who should be allowed to govern countries with nuclear weapons are mothers, those who are still breast-feeding their babies.

TSUTOMU YAMAGUCHI

The very idea of a bridge is an act of faith.

HART CRANE

There seems something more speakingly incomprehensible in the powers, the failures, the inequalities of memory, than in any other of our intelligences. The memory is sometimes so retentive, so serviceable, so obedient—at others, so bewildered and so weak—at others again, so tyrannic, so beyond control, ...

JANE AUSTEN

I had no one but myself to talk to, and it is absurd to write down what one says to oneself.

EDITH WHARTON

I find it nearly impossible *free ice* to write about *Jeepaxle* my work.

ROBERT RAUSCHENBERG

Damsons you have to leave unstoned.

TAMASIN DAY-LEWIS

THANKS TO—

Alexandra Pringle for founding the fun squad.

David Godwin for guts, gusto, and good arithmetic.

Eloise Millar and Sam Jordison for being such smarties, and so brave.

Dan Wells and John Metcalf for their appealing determination and agility.

Patricia McEwen for her detailed and loving study of Tuscarawas County history.

Miroslava Pospisil Lane for information on remunerative cake-baking.

Wendy Mack Chatfield for descriptions of home poultry-keeping.

Joseph McElroy for his thoughts on our avidity for experience.

Steinvor Arnadottir for her reaction to Trump's presidential win.

Teresa Hayter for opposing all borders.

Gunnie Moberg and Tam MacPhail for wit and imagination.

Suzy Romer for reading between the lines.

Kairen Zonena and Lynn Russell for constancy.

Steff and Erwin Ellmann for company.

Ditto, all Cohens; and Ralph Evans, an honorary Cohen.

Edward for courage; Patch for leaping; Delilah for pizzazz; Sushi for devotion; Beanie for floppiness; Bartholemew for being first; Annie for kicking me (rightly).

The Royal Literary Fund Fellowship Scheme for enabling me to finish this novel.

Ditto, Arthur DeBoer, Molly Ludlum, Robin McKenzie, Chris Sale, Catriona McLean, and the National Health System of Great Britain.

Edinburgh City Council for my Saltire Card, a dandy aid to the impecunious.

Ellen Hair and Graham Smith for repeatedly sheltering the manu-script.

Katty Byrnes for succor.

Phil Kiggell for being the original funette.

Maud Ellmann and Steve Ellmann for more than they know.

Sarindar Dhaliwal, Carol Dunbar, Ilsa Colsell, Barbara Ellmann, Teresa Delcorso, Malcolm McEachern, Nathan Milstein, and Paul Violi for beatitude.

Mary Ellmann and Emily Gasquoine for existing.

Todd McEwen for giving me all the room in the sky.

GALLEY BEGGAR PRESS

We hope that you've enjoyed *Ducks, Newburyport*. If you'd like to find out more about Lucy, along with some of her fellow authors, head to www.galleybeggar.co.uk.

There, you will also find information about our subscription scheme, 'Galley Buddies', which is there to ensure we can continue to put out ambitious and unusual books like *Ducks, Newburyport*.

Subscribers to Galley Beggar Press:

· Receive limited black-cover editions (printed in a one-time run of 500) of each of our four next titles.

· Have their names included in a special acknowledgements section at the back of our books.

· Are sent regular invitations to our book launches, talks, and other events.

· Enjoy a 20% discount code for the purchase of any of our backlist (as well as for general use throughout our online shop).

WHY BE A GALLEY BUDDY?

At Galley Beggar Press we don't want to compromise on the excellence of the writing we put out, or the physical quality of our books. We've also enjoyed numerous successes and prize nominations since we set up, in 2012. Almost all of our authors have gone on to be longlisted, shortlisted, or the winners of over twenty of the world's most prestigious literary awards.

But publishing for the sake of art and for love is a risky commercial strategy. In order to keep putting out the very best books that we can, and to continue to support talented writers, we need your help. The money we receive from our Galley Buddy subscription scheme is an essential part of keeping us going.

By becoming a Galley Buddy, you help us to launch and foster a new generation of writers.

To join today, head to:
https://www.galleybeggar.co.uk/subscribe

FRIENDS OF GALLEY BEGGAR PRESS

Galley Beggar Press would like to thank the following individuals, without the generous support of whom our books would not be possible:

Ayodeji Alaka	Harriet Davies	Phil Gibby
Lulu Allison	Joshua Davis	Edward Glover
Eleanor Anstruther	Toby Day	Ashley Goldberg
Ebba Aquila	Robin Deitch	Matthew Goodman
Alice Ash	Paul Dettman	Sakura Gooneratne
Jo Ayoubi	Turner Docherty	Cathy Goudie
Alan Baban	Kelly Doonan	Simon Goudie
Edward Baines	Janet Dowling	Chris Gribble
Shenu Barclay	Florian Duijsens	Neil Griffiths
Deborah Barker	Antony Dunford	Robbie Guillory
Paul Bassett Davies	Ann Eve	Ian Hagues
Tim Benson	Monique Fare	Daniel Hahn
Jessica Bonder	Pauline France	Peter Halliwell
Naomi Booth	Gerard Feehily	Greg Harrowing
Edwina Bowen	Charles Fernyhough	Kirsteen Hardie
Ben Brooks	Elizabeth Finn	America Hart
Justine Budenz	Allyson Fisher	John Harvey
Christopher Caless	Fitzcarraldo Editions	Penelope Hewett
Suzy Camp	Holly Fitzgerald	Brown
Joanna Cannon	Hayley Flockhart	Felix Hewison-Carter
Thomas Carlisle	Nicholas Flower	Daniel Hillman
Richard Carter	Patrick Foley	Alex Hitch
Stuart Carter	Matthew Francis	Marcus Hobson
Leigh Chambers	Frank Francisconi	Aisling Holling
Lina Christopoulou	Simon Fraser	Tim Hopkins
Enrico Cioni	Ruth Frendo	Hugh Hudson
Jennifer Coles	Melissa Fu	Richard Hughes
Andrew Cowan	Graham Fulcher	Ruth Hunt
Alan Crilly	Paul Fulcher	Agri Ismail
Elisa Damiani	Annabel Gaskell	Hayley James
Rachel Darling	Neil George	Kavita A. Jindal

Andrea Friderike

Franziska
  Jobst-Hausleithner

Jane Johnson

Alice Jolly

Jupiter Jones

Diana Jordison

Benjamin Judge

Dani Kaye

Laura Kaye

Andrew Kelly

Michael Ketchum

Vijay Khurana

Jacqueline Knott

Brian Kirk

Philip Lane

Jackie Law

Noel Lawn

Gage LaFleur

Thomas Legendre

Joyce Lille-Robinson

Nick Lord Lancaster

Jerome Love

Sean Lusk

Simona Lyons

Philip Makatrewicz

Anil Malhotra

Chiara Margiotta

Robert Mason

Sara McCallum

Ella McCrystle

Kieran McGrath

Victor Meadowcraft

C.S. Mee

Tina Meyer

Ian Mond

David Musgrave

Polly Nash

Linda Nathan

Anna Nsubuga

Seb Ohsan-Berthelsen

John O'Donnell

Alec Olsen

Laura Oosterbeek

Sheila O'Reilly

Liz O'Sullivan

Eliza O'Toole

Nicola Paterson

Scarlett Parker

Stephen Pearsall

Alexa Pearson

Tom Perrin

Nicholas Petty

Jennifer Pink

Jonathan Pool

Giacomo Pope

Trine Prescott

Richard Price

Alan Pulverness

Sarah Pybus

Alex Pykett

Polly Randall

Euan Reed

Barbara Renel

Pete Renton

Ian Rimell

Brian Ronan

Angela Rose

Kalina Rose

Clive Rixson

Libby Ruffle

Alison Sakai

Robert Sanderson

Valentina Santolini

Ros Schwartz

Richard Sheehan

Yvonne Singh

Hazel Smith

Daniel Staniforth

John Steciuk

Cathryn Steele

Gillian Stern

Jochen Stremmel

Juliet Sutcliffe

Helen Swain

Justine Taylor

Sam Thorp

James Torrence

Nick Turner

Harriet Tyce

Edward Valiente

David Varley

Stephen Waderman

Stephen Walker

Steve Walsh

Guy Ware

Emma Warnock

Ellie Warren

Stephanie Wasek

Tom Whatmore

Wendy Whidden

Robert White

Claire Willerton

Lucie Winter

Simon Winter

Emma Woolerton

Ben Yeoh

Ian Young

Rupert Ziziros

Carsten Zwaaneveld

DUCKS,
NEWBURYPORT